998

Y0-EHE-677

BY ANDRÉ GIDE

Non-Fiction

THE JOURNALS OF ANDRÉ GIDE
Volume I, 1889–1913
Volume II, 1914–1927
Volume III, 1928–1939
Volume IV, 1939–1949

IMAGINARY INTERVIEWS

THE FRUITS OF THE EARTH
(*Les Nourritures terrestres & Les Nouvelles Nourritures*)

MADELEINE
(*Et nunc manet in te*)

SO BE IT, OR THE CHIPS ARE DOWN
(*Ainsi soit-il, ou Les Jeux sont faits*)

Fiction and Theater

THE COUNTERFEITERS
(with *Journal of "The Counterfeiters"*)

THE IMMORALIST

LAFCADIO'S ADVENTURES

STRAIT IS THE GATE

TWO LEGENDS
(*Œdipus & Theseus*)

TWO SYMPHONIES
(*Isabelle & The Pastoral Symphony*)

THE SCHOOL FOR WIVES, ROBERT, and GENEVIÈVE

MY THEATER
(*Saul, Bathsheba, Philoctetes,*
King Candaules, Persephone,
& the essay *"The Evolution of the Theater"*)

These are Borzoi Books
published in New York by Alfred A. Knopf

THE *André Gide* READER

THE ANDRÉ GIDE READER

Paul Guillaume

, 1869-1951 G453

EDITED BY

David Littlejohn, 1924-

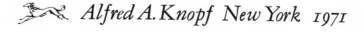 *Alfred A. Knopf New York 1971*

PROPERTY OF
HIGH POINT PUBLIC LIBRARY
HIGH POINT, NORTH CAROLINA

This is a Borzoi Book published by Alfred A. Knopf, Inc.

Copyright © 1971 by Alfred A. Knopf, Inc.
All rights reserved under International and Pan-American Copyright Conventions.
Published in the United States by Alfred A. Knopf, Inc., New York.
Distributed by Random House, Inc., New York.
Library of Congress Catalog Card Number: 72–111251
ISBN: 0–394–41531–0

Acknowledgment is gratefully extended to the following publishers
of the existing translations on which this edition's revisions
and adaptations are based:

ALFRED A. KNOPF, INC.:
TRAVELS IN THE CONGO, *translated by Dorothy Bussy.*
Copyright 1929, renewed 1957 by Alfred A. Knopf, Inc.
THE FRUITS OF THE EARTH, *translated by Dorothy Bussy.*
Copyright 1949 by Alfred A. Knopf, Inc.
RETURN FROM THE U.S.S.R., *translated by Dorothy Bussy.*
Copyright 1937, renewed 1965 by Alfred A. Knopf, Inc.
THE JOURNALS OF ANDRÉ GIDE, *Volumes I–IV, translated by Justin O'Brien.*
Copyright 1947, 1948, 1949, 1951 by Alfred A. Knopf, Inc.
IMAGINARY INTERVIEWS, *translated by Malcolm Cowley.*
Copyright 1944 by Jacques Schiffrin.
MADELEINE: ET NUNC MANET IN TE, *translated by Justin O'Brien.*
Copyright 1952 by Alfred A. Knopf, Inc.
SO BE IT, OR THE CHIPS ARE DOWN, *translated by Justin O'Brien.*
Copyright © 1959 by Alfred A. Knopf, Inc.
IF IT DIE . . . , *translated by Dorothy Bussy.*
Copyright 1935, renewed 1963 by Random House, Inc.
STRAIT IS THE GATE, *translated by Dorothy Bussy.*
Copyright 1924, renewed 1952 by Alfred A. Knopf, Inc.
LAFCADIO'S ADVENTURES, *translated by Dorothy Bussy.*
Copyright 1925, renewed 1953 by Alfred A. Knopf, Inc.
THE CORRESPONDENCE BETWEEN PAUL CLAUDEL AND ANDRÉ GIDE,
translated by John Russell. Copyright 1952 by Pantheon Books, Inc.
"The Pastoral Symphony," from TWO SYMPHONIES, *translated by Dorothy Bussy.*
Copyright 1931, renewed 1959 by Alfred A. Knopf, Inc.
DOSTOEVSKY, *published 1925 by Alfred A. Knopf, Inc.*
THE COUNTERFEITERS, *translated by Dorothy Bussy.*
Copyright 1927, renewed 1955 by Alfred A. Knopf, Inc.

PHILOSOPHICAL LIBRARY, INC.:
AUTUMN LEAVES, *reprinted by permission of Philosophical Library, Inc.*
Copyright 1950 by Philosophical Library, Inc.

THE WORLD PUBLISHING COMPANY:
PRETEXTS: REFLECTIONS ON LITERATURE AND MORALITY.
Translation Copyright © 1959 by Meridian Books, Inc. Used by permission.

BANTAM BOOKS INC.:
"The Return of the Prodigal Son," translated by Wallace Fowlie in FRENCH STORIES,
edited and translated by Wallace Fowlie. Copyright © 1960 by Bantam Books Inc.

Manufactured in the United States of America
First Edition

179805

for Sheila, Victoria, and Gregory

It is my hope in this book—which combines certain of the qualities of a biography, of an autobiography, and of a "Selected Works"—to come as close as one can in a thousand pages to *presenting* the notoriously fluid, diverse, and "unseizable" man who is its subject; presenting him as fully and as honestly as possible.

For this a biography would not serve, even if all the materials needed for a biography were yet available, as they are not. One of the inherent defects of literary biographies is that they are rarely able to convey to the unconvinced reader what it was that made their subjects worth writing about in the first place—which is to say, the quality and importance of their works. Detaching the "life" of a writer from his "works," one is rarely able to do justice to either. The works, one presumes, were what made the life matter (to us), and by taking them out of the story one runs the risk of reducing the life of an artist—which can be a noble thing to read of—to a mere collection of anecdotes about a celebrity.

Nor would Gide's own "autobiography" quite serve my purpose, extensive and outspoken as it is. The most autobiographical of all major modern authors, Gide filled notebook after notebook with journals, reminiscences, and self-analyses, and selections from these make up more than half of this book. I think that his *Journal* is the most important thing Gide ever wrote, and that it would be presumptuous for me to attempt to tell his story (most of his story) better than he has told it himself. But no one is able to tell the whole truth about himself. Gide's own autobiographical efforts were often dedicated to arranging the image he wanted posterity to receive. I have tried, in seven introductory essays, to correct the imbalances and fill in the gaps.

A simple "Selected Writings" would be inadequate as well, although that is in effect what this volume is: writings selected, let us say, with a difference, with a particular purpose in view. I have tried to include Gide's most important, most successful, most readable works of fiction—all of *L'Immoraliste,* all of *La Symphonie pastorale,* Alissa's Journal from *La Porte étroite (Strait Is the Gate),* Lafcadio's story from *Les Caves du*

Vatican. Les Nourritures terrestres (The Fruits of the Earth) and *Les Faux-Monnayeurs (The Counterfeiters)*, which are presented here in selections, should probably be read complete as well, but there are limits to a book such as this; perhaps the selections here will serve as an enticement to read the rest. I have tried to include a large, readable, and representative selection of the great *Journal* and its adjuncts (the travel diaries, the memoirs, the *Journal intime*), both because of their own unique savor and as a major contribution toward my endeavor to present simultaneously the man *and* his works. The essays on Nietzsche, Dostoevsky, Montaigne, and Goethe tell us at least as much of Gide as they do of their subjects. *Le Retour de l'Enfant prodigue (The Return of the Prodigal Son)*, the exchange of letters with Paul Claudel, the speeches and letters on communism were all included at least as much for their biographical interest as for their separate and substantive content. But then the same may be said of *L'Immoraliste,* of virtually everything here.

The exclusions—Gide's name is affixed to over a hundred separate books, I have no idea how many million words—are clearly a reflection of my own taste; I do not pretend to be giving equal time to his best and his worst. The André Gide who emerges from this volume will be, ultimately, my own André Gide. All the same, I do not think it a false or a falsified image of the man. If I omit *Corydon,* it is simply because I think it badly written. It is certainly not a matter of reticence. The story of Gide's private life is told here, if anything, more frankly and completely than in his own published writings. I exclude most of the early symbolic tales because I find them of little importance in the developing shape of Gide's life, *and* of little interest to the general reader. An exception is the selection from *Le Voyage d'Urien,* which will at once afford the reader a pungent sampling of this early style and tell him something about the strange state of Gide's imagination at twenty-three.

As the selections in this book may be explained by its special intention to present as thoroughly as possible the whole of André Gide, both his life and his works, so too may its particular structure. To begin with, I divided his life into seven periods—somewhat arbitrarily, of course, but I think there is a certain dramatic logic to the division. The first, that of his childhood and youth, concludes as he sets sail on his emancipating voyage to North Africa in 1893. The second covers his early travels, *Les Nourritures terrestres,* and the first years of his marriage; it ends with the publication of *L'Immoraliste* in 1902, a vital psychological "watershed," as we shall see. The works of the third period, *La Porte étroite* and *Le Retour de l'Enfant prodigue,* provide a kind of counterbalance to those of the second, and Gide's moods and attitudes undergo a similar change. This period is marked by the founding of the *N.R.F.* (*La Nouvelle Revue Française*), and ends on the brink of war. The fourth period I have made essentially coterminous with World War I, but it is also a distinct stage in Gide's career and a time of severe dislocations in his private life. The fifth, the decade of the twenties, is the period of Gide's greatest fame and influence. I have tried, in my introductory essay to this section, to describe both the nature of that fame and Gide's response to it. The dividing line between the fifth and sixth periods is more than usually arbitrary: I wanted to reserve the Communist, or "social conscience" materials, which begin most earnestly late in 1931, for the latter; and yet conclude the former with the first usable journal reference (from early 1932) to Gide's *Œuvres complètes,* a kind of crowning symbol for his decade of fame: so I compromised by drawing the line early in January 1932. Madeleine Gide's death in April 1938, then, provides a natural break between the period of social activism and what Gide liked to call his "posthumous years": 1938–1951.

Each of these seven period-chapters begins with a biographical introduction in which, as I say, I have tried to fill in the most important missing details, and to correct whatever major imbalances or distortions remain in Gide's own accounts. For these, I have made use of all the existing published records, particularly correspondences, memoirs, and the one definitive (although partial) biography attempted so far. There follow directly, in chronological sequence, the relevant passages from Gide's own diaries or memoirs. The selections from *Amyntas* and the Congo journey, as well as the passages relating to his marriage (from the *Journal intime*) and to his romantic escapades of 1939 (from *Carnets d'Egypte*), were all published separately from the *Journal* itself; they have here been reinserted in proper chronological place. Then, after biography and autobiography, come the selected works: letters, essays, and fictional works written during the period, printed here in the order of their composition. (An exception is the 1902 "Normandy and Bas-Languedoc" essay, which I preface to the first chapter as a kind of legendary genealogy.)

All of the texts included in this volume have been either translated directly from, or checked against, the standard current edition of Gide's works in French, that of the "Bibliothèque de la Pléiade" of the Librairie Gallimard (Paris, 1951, 1954, 1958). In the case of works not included in the Pléiade series (the fourth volume, of Gide's critical works, had not yet appeared as of this writing), the text used was that of the most recent book publication.

The degree to which the English translations may be called original varies from selection to selection.

In the case of works untranslated before (the essays on Nietzsche and Montaigne, the selections from *Littérature engagée* and the Egyptian Notebooks), the English version is my own.

In two cases—*L'Immoraliste* and *La Symphonie pastorale*—I chose to undertake entirely fresh translations. The reasons for this were my particular admiration for these works, my decision to include the complete texts, and my dissatisfaction with the original English versions.

In every other case, the text printed here may be considered my revision, sometimes slight, sometimes thorough, of a previous translation. In general, the changes I have made in the earlier translations of Gide's fictional and lyrical work will be found to be more frequent and more radical than those I have made in the translations of his non-fiction. The nuances in works of the imagination strike me as far more crucial than those of journal-entries or critical essays. Moreover, I found myself far less frequently in disagreement with the interpretations or the style of Justin O'Brien, the late master of American Gidians, and the first translator of the *Journal,* than with Gide's other translators—although I should like to pay special tribute here to the sympathetic translations of *Amyntas* by Viliers David, and of the Gide–Claudel letters by John Russell.

The specific earlier translations on which my versions are based are those of:

Dorothy Bussy: *Si le grain ne meurt (If It Die), Les Nourritures terrestres (The Fruits of the Earth), La Porte étroite (Strait Is the Gate), Les Caves du Vatican (Lafcadio's Adventures), Voyage au Congo, Les Faux-Monnayeurs (The Counterfeiters), Les Nouvelles Nourritures (The New Fruits), Retour de l'U.R.S.S. (Return from the U.S.S.R.)*

Justin O'Brien: *The Journals,* including *Numquid et tu, Journal intime; Madeleine (Et nunc manet in te); Ainsi soit-il (So Be It)*

Malcolm Cowley: *Interviews imaginaires,* including "An Introduction to Goethe's Dramatic Work"

Wallace Fowlie: *Le Retour de l'Enfant prodigue (The Return of the Prodigal Son)*

Wade Baskin: *Le Voyage d'Urien*

Louise Varèse: *Dostoevsky*

Elsie Pell: "The Radiance of Paul Valéry," "Justice or Charity"
Angelo P. Bertocci: "Letter to M. Edouard Ducoté"
Jeffrey J. Carre: "Normandy and Bas-Languedoc," "Marcel Proust," "La
    Nouvelle Revue Française"
Viliers David: *Amyntas*
John Russell: The Gide–Claudel Letters

I should like to thank Mr. William A. Koshland and Mr. Herbert Weinstock of Alfred A. Knopf, Inc., for patiently bearing with me in a project I first proposed in January 1965, and once dreamed of having completed in 1967. I should like to apologize to my wife and children for the hundreds of evenings and weekends I borrowed from them and gave to André Gide over these last five years, with a promise that they shall be repaid. I am happy to acknowledge my debts to Albert J. Guerard, who first introduced me to André Gide; to Joel Kurtzman, for many hours spent in library stacks on my behalf; to the pioneer English translators of Gide referred to above, and to the whole world of Gide scholars and critics, on whose work so much of this volume depends; and to the various copyright holders of the works included here, whose rights and whose generosity are specifically recorded elsewhere.

Berkeley, California   D. L.

CONTENTS

SIX   *1932–1938*

SEVEN   *1938–1951*

THE *André Gide* READER

INTRODUCTION

I

André Gide is a very difficult author to place. The role he is usually assigned is that of one of the shaping spirits and intellectual leaders of "Modernism" or "The Modern Tradition"—a tradition generally assumed to have begun in the third quarter of the nineteenth century, and to have ended not long ago. The editors of a recent anthology of the basic texts of this tradition turned to Gide five times, for citations on a variety of subjects. But they also began by asserting that "the age of Yeats, Joyce, Eliot, and Lawrence, of Proust, Valéry, and Gide, of Mann, Rilke, and Kafka, has already passed into history." [1]

Unlike some of the others on that list, however, Gide is often regarded as no *more* than an important piece of the past—a very influential thinker, intellectual hero, and man of letters during a discrete and now concluded period of time in Western Europe, particularly in France. Even among his apologists and defenders, there seems to be a readiness to conclude that his day is done; that he did indeed help to create our intellectual, moral, and artistic world, the freer, more highly charged air we breathe today; but that now—thanks in part to him—we can take the things he fought for, the things he so agonized over as a matter of course; in a word, that we can do without him.

The first count Gide has against him, in 1969, is that of his "success." The essential part of his message—a many-sided message of emancipation, of the battle against restrictions, obstructions, traditions—has been accepted and assimilated, and it composes an integral (and hence anonymous) element of the contemporary mentality. The sensual exaltation of the *Nourritures,* so new and so useful in 1897, has by now lost much of its power to shock, its disturbing and scandalous quality. In the same way, the long warfare waged on the invert's behalf; the critique of a moralizing and mutilating religion; the campaign against colonialism; the war against political totalitarianisms of every sort—if these issues have unfortunately lost none of their urgency today, they have become too much "common property" for us to identify any of them explicitly with Gide. Even his own victories abandon him.

(Claude Martin, "Gide dépassé par sa victoire,"
in *Le Monde,* November 22, 1969.)

Jean-Paul Sartre made a similar point, somewhat more tactfully, in an essay written shortly after Gide's death in 1951. He paid handsome tribute to Gide's pioneering, his trail-blazing: because Gide went so far, and cleared the ground so well, Sartre implies, *we* are able to go much farther than he did. "He allows us to avoid the traps into which he has fallen . . . Starting from there"—from the point at which Gide ended—"men of today are capable of becoming new truths." [2]

Such judgments seem to suggest that Gide's "place" is fixed somewhere in intellectual or literary history like Henri Bergson's or William Dean Howells's; that however important he may be judged to have been, he is no longer a living force.

This is not true. He is still a living force to me, as vital as any other author, alive or dead. This may seem scant evidence, but it is, ultimately, the only evidence I know of that one can offer in support of an author's vitality. The durability and liveliness, the simple worth of an author is not a thing to be measured by sales figures and polls and questionnaires—although this is precisely what the French press tried to do on the occasion of Gide's centennial in 1969. Most of the French students questioned found Gide an unreadable bore: *"Maintenant on cherche autre chose"*—Today we're looking for other things. Young French novelists who were polled replied No, they did not count Gide among their influences. "His work is no longer a vital literary or intellectual influence, as it was throughout the greater part of his literary career; and he is as yet nowhere near acquiring major classic status, if he is to acquire it at all." [3]

But does that matter? In the middle of a round-table discussion on the ups and downs of Gide's reputation (particularly among students in French lycées, as if theirs was to be the last word), a British critic rose to protest. "This whole question of popularity, of success and decline annoys me, and I begin to ask myself this: Is it possible for a man to have been a mentor, an intellectual guide (a *maître à penser*), from whom thousands of human beings have been able to draw priceless individual lessons—and then suddenly to *stop* being able to serve as an intellectual guide? Surely every real *maître à penser* retains his function forever. After all, Montaigne and Socrates were dead long before Gide—and *they* are still living forces among us, even if they never came up against the same problems of 'engagement' that we have to cope with. The problem of faith, for example, begins all over again for each generation. Why, I would turn to my Gide just as I would turn to my Bible or Pascal." [4]

My position is close to that of this speaker. Gide did have, between 1920 and 1940, an extraordinary notoriety in France (some of which reached other countries), a "place" utterly unlike that he holds today. It is important to take the measure of this place, to understand the reasons for it, as best one can, and the reasons Gide holds it no longer. But it is also important to realize that even at the time Gide was far more widely read and discussed than he is today, even at the moment of his greatest public reputation, his most widespread apparent influence, his real effect was still no more than a summation of individual effects, repeated over and over; of profound and private meetings between André Gide and one other person. And these meetings are still taking place.

II

The matter of Gide's historical importance, his closed and finished value as a shaper and innovator, is not one I want to go into here. His moral effect on a generation of Frenchmen (and, by extension, others) was regarded as immense. He was denounced as the devil and praised as *"le contemporain capital";* serious international surveys on his "influence" were undertaken. Such a thing is of course impossible to measure, but the attitudes and actions of a great many young Europeans of the generation between the wars do seem to have been markedly affected by the writings and the life of André Gide. His literary influence has been called "perhaps the most widespread in France since Baudelaire," [5] and has been acknowledged by many of the great French writers of the last fifty years. To Kevin O'Neill he is, not the greatest, but the *most important* writer of his age—"an age whose literature he did more to form than anyone else." [6]

In England, and particularly in America, we are accustomed to classifying our literary figures as either novelists, poets, or playwrights, and then judging them accordingly. A few "essayists" are sometimes included, a few historians or biographers, letter-writers, polemicists, and philosophers. But we clearly regard these as only marginally "literary." Such an approach does not, unfortunately, do much justice to Gide. We are now out of the discernible, tangible field of his "influence," so we turn to the visible legacy: to his books. The poems and plays seem of no great importance, so we look first at the novels. (Most of the French students interviewed knew Gide through one or another of four novels, usually because they had been assigned in school, and *Les Nourritures terrestres.*)

I could make, I think, a strong case for *L'Immoraliste.* I find it lucid, compelling, passionate yet contained, an intense and autonomous work of art. Although *Les Faux-Monnayeurs* is now read in schools more as a technical adventure than as fiction to be experienced, it too is charged with meaning. Its emotional construction is like that of a whirlpool or web, and many parts of it still have considerable power. Advocates could be found for *La Porte étroite,* and the more popular *Symphonie pastorale. Les Nourritures terrestres,* although perhaps of primarily historical interest today—it was the key literary weapon in Gide's "emancipation" campaign of the 20's and 30's—still manages, for all its archaic, exotic lyricism, to detonate or unleash deep-lying forces in many readers. Students of French literature, lovers of the French language will find other of his fictions to admire, like the classical, the almost musical *Retour de l'Enfant prodigue*—works whose qualities may well elude the English reader. The lesser works of fiction will probably be savored only by the "Gidean," the person who already knows a good deal about Gide's life and work, and can see all parts of them in relation to the whole. But this is a designation a great many people have been seduced into making their own.

Others of his advocates, putting aside the novels, would prefer to make their case for Gide on the basis of his *Journal* and the various autobiographical writings that surround it. The *Journal* is, I think, one of the greatest written works of the century, perhaps the richest life record we possess. But in thus responding to and favoring the *Journal,* one is probably confessing to an admiration for the life and person of André Gide in excess of what one feels for his works. "Perhaps Gide's most important work," wrote Jean Hytier, "[is] André Gide himself; for some writers, the creation of their eternal countenance, or at least of their countenance *sub specie æternitatis,* constitutes their decisive work . . ." [7] And Albert Guerard reminds us that "the personal history, the actual curve of this one man's life, has troubled or comforted many, and for better or worse been 'exemplary.'" [8]

Still it is not enough, or at least not very clear, to say that what attracts one to, what matters most about André Gide is not the "works" but the "man." For one thing, they are inseparable; for another, the man is a creature of extraordinary complexity. The works alone, the hundred-plus titles—novels, plays, essays, stories, treatises, memoirs, journals—can be read separately and judged on their own merits. You may choose to accept or discard them, to take them into your heart or find them freakish and trivial, to judge them timeless and universal or the dated coterie fantasies of an early-modern Parisian. But by the time you had half-finished them, you would already be so deeply immersed in the life—or at least in Gide's written version of it—that you would find it impossible to ignore, impossible to distinguish where literary judgment ended and moral judgment began.

Nor is this, as I say, the only source of confusion. One may agree with Jean Hytier's proposition—that Gide's most important creation was André Gide; that his greatest work was his life. But which life?

For there is the *life,* recorded in his own and others' memoirs, the living, instant-by-instant, day-by-day facts of itches and ailments and self-abuse and sleepless nights, of ecstasy and ennui, of vast literary reading, often in foreign or little-known authors; of bugs and boys and piano practice, compulsive traveling and movie-going and night wandering, editorial chores, the writing of many books, long chats with friends, discomfort at parties, a love of flowers and Chopin and Racine and the sun, shifting moods, ruses, poses, a prickly, insatiable curiosity; of his actual relations with mother, wife, daughter, colleagues, boyfriends, with a thousand close acquaintances over eighty-two years. This is "life" as most of us understand it—sloppy, confused, mean and generous by turns, in Gide's case homosexual, famous, literary, French, high-strung, mother- and duty-haunted: the life most biographers would try to recover and reassemble.

But there is also what one might call the "Life" with a capital L: what Gide made, or tried to make, of all these scattered, quotidian materials. For he was driven by an absolute compulsion to make of his days, his talents and opportunities something visibly shaped, something artful, measurable, valuable, and if possible enduring; to render a billion billion accidents and occasions into something "exemplary," something almost legendary. Even the unexplained, unreflected events he tried to elevate into decisions and turns almost fictionally symbolic, as if he were really a mythical being created by someone else. Throughout his life, he is constantly assessing and reassessing his attributes, actions, and plans, and then trying to proceed according to his latest summing-up; so that at any moment his life-to-then would have the shape and integrity of a designed and conscious work. His writing, of course, is an integral part of this venture, and it acquires thereby a "mortal" or "fatal" quality it would never possess outside the context of this particular life, this extraordinary effort at what Hytier calls the "aesthetics of personality."

Most of Gide's friends and critics have recognized and acknowledged his unusual project—to shape a Life the way one shapes a work of art. Some have thought it an admirable goal; others have regarded it as unnatural, inhuman, devious, self-seeking. It is remarkable how many make use of the aesthetic image of a "curve" or a "line": "the actual curve of this one man's life . . ." (Guerard); "the romantic concern to lead a life that composes itself like a painting" (Delay). "You are one of those whose life has the value of a parable, and who achieve completely a curve of which others merely sketch the beginning" (Claudel). "His fidelity was to . . . the deliberate and always renewed effort to shape his life and work" (Vino Rossi). "Until now the line of your life has stayed absolutely pure . . ." (Martin du Gard).[9]

Gide admitted this design himself very early in his career.

> A man's life is his image. At the hour of death we shall be reflected in the past, and, leaning over the mirror of our acts, our souls will recognize *what we are* . . .
>
> Rather than recounting his life as he has lived it [the artist] must live his life as he will recount it. In other words, the portrait of him formed by his life must identify itself with the ideal portrait he desires. And, in still simpler terms, he must be as he wishes to be.
>
> (*Journal,* January 3, 1892)

Jean Delay attributes this particular journal entry to the influence of Oscar Wilde, whom Gide had just met at the time. (The older writer, by whom the twenty-two-year-old Gide was enormously impressed, had frequently announced his own intention to make his life his major work of art.) But Gide was to betray throughout his life a pressing concern for the "image" he would leave behind.

> Were I to disappear today, I should leave an image of myself from which even my guardian angel could not recognize me.
>
> "An incomplete, inexact, caricatured, grimacing image is now all that will endure of me."
>
> Will it be possible, later on, to make out my real features under such a heap of calumnies? [10]

He speaks of his old age as "the last act of the comedy," and professes to be annoyed at his recovery (at seventy-nine) from an illness he had intended to be his last. "I even feel a sort of aesthetic disapproval of this postscript, which does not fit in with the ensemble, but remains outside as an appendix, as something extra" (*Journal,* September 7, 1948).

There are two distinct phases to Gide's image-making, his building of a Life. The first is relatively active and unreflective; the second is a re-

flection on, a retouching, a turning into literature of the actions of the
first. Marcel Proust led a life of somewhat the same pattern; but in Gide's
case, unlike Proust's, the aesthetic, shaping consciousness seems to have
been almost as busy during the active years as during the reflective.

To some degree, the very decisions Gide made during the first part
of his life, the steps he took, even the things that just happened to him
have an uncannily tendentious or episodic quality, quite apart from his
subsequent rationalizations of them, his incorporation of them into the
evolving legend of his life. Writing, later on, about his smallpox, his unexpected visit to the rue de Lecat, his marriage, his first trip to North
Africa, his illness and recovery there, his encounter on the sand dunes outside of Sousse, his rewriting his name on the hotel blackboard at Blida,
his trip to the Congo, his wife's death, he *does* describe each event as
something portentous, almost mythical—even though they are all, to
some degree, occurrences drawn from the simple, unreflective, unstructured life of everyday. But even those he did not choose—Wilde's accidental crossing of his path in Algeria in 1895 is an example—seem like
the necessary coincidences of an exemplary career, contrived and inserted
by some heavenly author "to point a moral and adorn a tale." His life
assumes a legendary, fictional, five-act pattern even before his subsequent
redrawing of the curve. An intensely pagan episode follows an intensely
puritan one, a stage of Communist faith comes after the *Numquid et tu*
crisis of near-religious conversion. The decision to go to the Congo in
1926—a kind of conscious descent into "the Heart of Darkness"—has
about it a terrible, willed fatality. And the last act is almost perversely
serene. Gide's fictional work fits an evolving, algebraic pattern so neatly
that most critics are spellbound by it, and can talk of nothing else: but
then so does his life.

This granted, it must be acknowledged that Gide improved on events
in various ways. One method was to reduce, for his written version, what
must have originally been a great tangle of superimposed motives to a
single, conscious one that fits neatly into the shape he wants: he wrote
Saül, he tells us, to counteract the effect of *Nourritures,* and *La Porte
étroite* as an ironic corrective to *L'Immoraliste.* Another is to exaggerate
cause and effect sequence with almost medieval simplicity: his artistic
conscience, his inability to take sides derives from his having a mother
from the damp Catholic North and a father from the warm Protestant
South. He was obsessed by the formulaic image of his career, forever trying to interpret his life as something neater, more shapely, more reasoned
than any man's life ever is—as a Poussin or Cézanne will reduce a land-

scape to, will *see* it in the terms of, his own French-classical imagination. Thus—especially in the older, reflective third of his life, reviewing over and over his past works and deeds—Gide tries to explain his life as something elegantly designed, to see the whole as composing a kind of beautifully worked-out Racinean drama. These self-objectifying formulas so much clearer than real life, these "over-systematic errors of self-analysis" (Germaine Brée) Gide came eventually to believe*—came to see himself, as I say, almost as a creature out of mythology, like his own Prometheus or Theseus.

This may help to explain his fourteenth-century manner of interpreting events from his own private life in terms of fate, or of allegorical qualities, or of cosmic or supernatural forces.

> Till that day, I had been wandering at random; suddenly I had discovered a new star, by which my life was to be guided . . . I kept hidden away in the depths of my heart the secret of my destiny.

> I was led by a fatality . . . It was the marriage of heaven with my insatiable hell. . . . it has lately occurred to me that a very important actor—the devil—may have had a considerable part to play in this drama . . . (*Si le grain ne meurt*)

> I no longer felt as though I had willed it [the Congo journey] . . . but that I had had it imposed upon me by a sort of ineluctable fatality, *like all the important events of my life* [my italics]. (*Voyage au Congo,* July 21, 1926)

Gide's other means of improving on reality may seem more commonplace. He will omit certain events, highlight others, "interpret" all with the after-the-fact freedom of an artist, and slant everything in the direction of a particular theme—again, like a painter before a landscape. Jean Delay and Jean Schlumberger have analyzed with meticulous thoroughness the operation of these principles in *Si le grain ne meurt* and *Et nunc manet in te* respectively—although to them it seems more a self-disguising, self-serving effort at cosmetic surgery on Gide's part than any noble aesthetic undertaking. If the contours of the *Journal* seem closer to the "truth," this is simply because it is a mosaic of ten thousand individual contrivances and distortions, and not the single-minded and coherent carving of *one* significant form.

---

* Not that he was ever entirely taken in. "Perhaps Jacques Raverat is right when he tells me . . . that often my account [*Si le grain ne meurt*], in an effort to be clear, simplifies my acts a bit too much, or at least my motives . . ." (*Journal,* October 5, 1920).

By all of which I do not mean that Gide was not *trying* to tell the truth about himself; no literary figure since Montaigne has tried with such integrity and persistence. Rather that he seemed to know (as all artists know) that no truth that matters is likely to lie in the crude, uninterpreted world of everyday facts we call objective reality. (As he confessed on more than one occasion, he was not even sure he believed in the reality of the everyday world.) His most eloquent individual efforts at interpreting and giving meaning to the facts of his life, elevating them into truth, therefore, are the things we call fiction. In fact, so closely do the events of his novels and stories follow the events of his life that some critics would deny him the right to the title of novelist. But surely the importance of *L'Immoral-iste, La Porte étroite, La Symphonie pastorale,* and *Les Faux-Monnayeurs* depends not on their close correspondence to real biographical materials, but on the new shape and meaning Gide has given to those materials.

The means he chose for this undertaking, this making of a life, was for the most part the written word. He had, according to many accounts, an incomparably seductive effect in person,* and hundreds of people seem to have fallen under his spell—so much so that Claude Martin wonders whether a great deal of the falling off in Gide's reputation since his death may not be due to the simple fact that the man himself, the extraordinary personality whose living presence impressed and disturbed so many people, is no longer around. But others who knew him were unimpressed, or antipathetic; some were even disgusted. For all his fabled charm, Gide

---

* Gide, when he was before you, managed to erase the whole world around him. The people who surrounded him became no more than a kind of painted backdrop. It became impossible to look at or listen to anything but him. Some people have seen in this something diabolic. Perhaps it was—if one is willing to admit that it was not for nothing that Lucifer had been one of the archangels, that there had remained to him something of the radiance of his primal nature.

When Gaston Gallimard and Jacques Rivière first brought us together in 1920, I was simply dazzled. In that glow I felt not only a personality imposing itself on me, but a power of receptiveness the like of which I had never encountered, even in the finest individuals I had met. When once you had won Gide's love or admiration, as soon as you appeared before him, announced or unannounced, he was immediately overjoyed. There was not one of his features that did not express his joy, his satisfaction, almost a sort of drunkenness of the heart all the more lively in that the least familiarity never mingled with the sympathy he showed, with his devotion—a devotion that was, all the same, utterly without limit.

(Marcel Jouhandeau, in *Le Monde,* November 22, 1969)

How aware I am now of the nobility of that face, shivering with emotion and intelligence, of the fine tenderness of his smile, of the music of his voice, of his attention, of warmth and kindness of the look with which he embraces me! For his eyes never leave mine once. He is visibly reaching out for reciprocity, accord; he offers a free, even exchange, he seeks an alliance. I am overwhelmed by his sympathy.

(Roger Martin du Gard, *Notes sur André Gide,* pp. 15–16)

was obviously wise not to depend on the memories of others for the image of himself he wanted to leave.

So the Life he had to make was to be primarily a thing of books. The important events of his life that did not serve as pretexts for literature were often "literary" in their very essence—the foundation and guiding of *La Nouvelle Revue Française,* the epistolary battle with Paul Claudel, the campaigns against colonialist oppression and anti-homosexual prejudice. The grand exception was his attempt to serve the cause of communism in the 1930's—which, he realized, necessitated his abandonment of literature. Perhaps it was this, as much as his specific disillusionment with Soviet practice, that led him to regard his attempt to serve as a serious mistake, a denial of his own nature, and to tell the world so—in another book.

> In 1889, at the age of twenty, André Gide set out to write his *"œuvres complètes."* He began thinking in terms of his complete works, cultivating his life in view of a future biography, transforming everything into a long, varied, and continuous statement about himself and his reactions to the world about him. In May of that year, he remarked that "my whole life's work is grouping itself, is falling into place with such unity that I cannot doubt that I will see it accomplished." Even then Gide did not consider any single one of his future works (including *Les Cahiers d'André Walter,* the *"summa"* of his youth) as an end in itself, dissociated from the whole. Rather, he imagined each work as an aesthetically independent unit that would interact with others in the context of the future *"œuvres complètes,"* where the progression and succession, the implicit readjustment of form and content from one work to the next would be more meaningful and significant than the beauty and perfection of any one alone. Four years later, in a letter to Marcel Drouin, Gide declared that he saw his complete works as a shelf of books, each one appearing, as the years went by, not one after another, but in the spaces reserved for those to come, now before, now after those already in print.
>
> (Vino Rossi, *André Gide, The Evolution of an Aesthetic,* p. v)

This is true enough; but it may lead one to think that Gide regarded this *œuvre* as an end in itself. And in fact there are many who have accused him of precisely this fault. Many of Gide's critics, including some of the most perceptive and sympathetic, have regarded his faith in and dedication to literature, to the written word, as excessive and somehow inhuman. All that writing, all that reading; that everlasting reference to the literary world: "For him," wrote Germaine Brée, "life was subsidiary to literature." And much of Gide's career would seem to bear out such a judgment. In 1918, his wife, despairing of her husband's fidelity or affection, burned all his letters to her.

> I thought I would die . . . But you must understand what those letters were. From my earliest youth—even then my life was dominated by this, my one and only love—I had been writing to her. I had not spent a single day at any distance from her without writing. These letters were the treasure of my life, the best part of me: beyond a doubt, the best part of my work. Every time I happened to reopen those packets, I trembled with joy and pride. The purest thing in my existence, the purest part of my heart was contained in them. Never had I written anything more lofty, more warm, more filled with the sap of life, than those interminable letters, written from one day to the next, reflecting minutely not only all my thoughts, all my work, but also that immeasurably precious love which had never ceased to serve as my guiding light. It was the private diary of my life, it was my life itself in its finest, most irreplaceable aspect! I used to think on it with a certain confidence in the hours when I lost faith in myself, and I often said to myself, *"You,* yes, you may die: but even if you leave nothing behind but these letters, there is in them such a richness of sensibility, of reflection, a life so profound and at the same time so pure, so flawless that you are sure to survive, sure to arouse in all the adolescents of future years that fraternal tremor of recognition which is the mark of the true poet's work. Whatever you become, whatever you do, your guarantee of immortality is there."
>
>   (Jean Schlumberger, *Madeleine et André Gide,* pp. 191–92.
>   Roger Martin du Gard's account of Gide's remarks to him)

To anyone but another writer, this may seem a perversely literary response to a very human crisis. It often seems, in fact, that Gide regarded "real life" as nothing more than a pretext for prose record—as if it did not count, somehow, until turned into words:

> Not for one minute of his day, not for one minute of his sleepless night is his mind ever at rest, does his brain ever stop churning out materials for his books . . . A *man of letters* from morning to night. Even in his pleasures, even in his amours . . . The most fleeting impression is instantly captured, translated into the Gidean

style, condensed into a formula marked with his seal, ready to *serve*. The sole end of his life is the enrichment of his work . . .
(Roger Martin du Gard, *Notes sur André Gide,* pp. 81–82)

But this, I think, is to exaggerate and to miss the mark. What I have called the "Life," the monument that Gide felt driven to compose, did take, for the most part, the form of books. But the sense of obligation, the concept of a Life to be made, an *"œuvre à faire"* in the largest possible sense, is antecedent to any merely literary ambition.

III

This is perhaps the time to inquire into the origins of this peculiar and demanding impulse. It begins, I think, with a conviction of stark, unsupported independence—that one's life will have no shape or meaning *except* that one gives it himself; and with a sense of election, of one's special and precious difference.

From the latter derives Gide's will to lead an exceptional, an exemplary life. And the exemplary value of that life, as Sartre and others have pointed out, comes from the fact that many of us share the former conviction: that we live alone in a godless, morally unstructured universe, and yet feel compelled for some reason to lead a worthy, creative, morally responsible life, with no reference to or dependence on otherwordly support. Gide tried very hard to do this, and he kept a written record of his effort, a record that now stands—taken for all in all—as both the proof and the product of his endeavor.

> Gide cherishes, in all cases, one single wish: that of presenting (as he says of Goethe) an exemplary image "of what man can attain on his own, without any recourse to Grace." . . . He has never for a moment stopped believing that the only life we have is the one we lead on this earth—and that it is quite sufficient. . . . that human will, demanding of man the fullest self-realization, has no need of waiting for "heavenly aid" to give meaning to this life; that our destiny is not that of being enlightened, pardoned, and saved from without; that each man carries his own redemption in himself.[11]

Many will flatly disagree with Gide's premise. On the strength of an assured faith in some religious or political world view, they will insist that our lives are *already* endowed with meaning and purpose, and that all does not rest on our own unaided efforts. Others will feel no compulsion to give their lives shape or meaning one way or another, and be content (or constrained) just to live. But even among those who may share Gide's sense of existential solitude and a residual, personal moral obligation, few will share his faith in literature, in the sure and certain value of the well-written phrase.

André Gide, that defiant resister of creeds, had several fixed faiths, not all of them popular today—a faith in the priceless value of the (superior) individual; a faith in his ability to achieve happiness on earth ("Radiant midsummer days [July 19, 1940] on which I constantly repeat to myself that it is up to man to make it beautiful, this miserable earth on which we are all devouring one another"); an optimist's faith in human progress. But perhaps least tenable of all today was his absolute faith in good writing.

> It is difficult for me to believe that the wisest, sanest, most sensible idea is not also the one that, projected into prose, yields the most harmonious and beautiful lines (*Journal*, 1928).

> The elegance and harmony of a felicitous structure are not then mere aesthetic satisfactions . . . What is hoped for goes far beyond that: it is the assurance that, when all has been put in question, the shape and structure of his sentence will remain as the measure and safeguard of its value . . . to write well [for Gide] is to give truth the greatest possible chance to be told, to give oneself the greatest possible chance of telling the truth . . .[12]

Thus understood, Gide's 15-volume *œuvre* is something more than just literature, and his Life is an experiment in something more fundamental than "the aesthetics of personality." They are both (they are both the same, to a large degree) the evidence, the instrument, and the end result of Gide's attempt to give shape and meaning, at once moral and aesthetic ["But what are morals, in your view?" "An appendage of aesthetics"], to the material he found on his hands—a human life.

He did a good deal of summing up in his later years. One is obliged, in his moral universe, to play one's own judge as well as one's own lawgiver. He would, he decided on second thought, have done a good many things differently; but by and large, he thought he had done well. In the perhaps over-resonant last words of his Theseus,

> If I compare my destiny with that of Oedipus, I am content: I have fulfilled it. Behind me I leave the city of Athens. It has been dearer to me than even my wife and my son. I have built my city. My thoughts can now live on there after me for all time. It is with a willing heart, and all alone, that I draw near to death. I have enjoyed

the good things of the earth. It pleases me to think that after me, and because of me, men will recognize themselves as being happier, better, and more free. I have done my work for the good of future humanity. I have lived.

And in his own words:

. . . as for the game I was playing, I have won it . . . I have said more or less what I had to say . . .

It is in [our]selves, in [our]selves alone, that [we] must seek and find recourse. And should a little pride enter into this, is it not legitimate? and the austere and noble feeling of duty worthily accomplished, of the restoration in oneself of human potentiality?

(*Ainsi soit-il*)

I V

One may come to understand, perhaps even to accept the validity of the terms on which, the means by which, Gide simultaneously lived his life and created his *Life*. But the only real test is to read the record he has left, and decide for yourself if the effort was worthwhile, the game honorably played, the example of this supposedly exemplary life of any use to you.

To go beyond this I hardly dare. To make first-person plural assertions of Gide's effects on "us" would be presumptuous. But to make first-person singular declarations of his effects on me would be needless confessionalism, and probably tell more about me than about André Gide. (Great numbers of the people won over to Gide have done precisely that. His own suave, ingratiating, intimate confessions seem to elicit counter-confessions from his disciples—which is probably just what he wanted. "An extraordinary, an insatiable need to be loved: I believe this is what dominated my life and drove me to write; an almost mystical need, moreover, for I consented to its not being satisfied during my lifetime" [*Journal*, September 3, 1948]. "I think that what above all drove me to write was an urgent need of sympathetic understanding . . ." [*Ainsi soit-il*].)

Many good men have despised André Gide, for one reason or another, or seen nothing of value in his work. Few writers in history have been so violently and persistently attacked—but then few writers have laid themselves so open to attack. Some of the abuse directed against him is merely stupid, based on misreadings or the acceptance of calumnies. Some is born of malice or spite. Much is simply partisan, the response of Catholics and Communists (advocates of the two great orthodoxies of our day) defending themselves against this enemy of all orthodoxy. Much of the criticism comes from those who knew Gide personally, and is directed against his private or social behavior. This is certainly their right; but we who come after can know Gide only through the composed and recorded legacy of his works.

There, one may in good faith find much to criticize: egotism, excess of private moral scruple, shrill and unbalanced defenses of homosexuality (and of André Gide generally), shrill and unbalanced attacks on the Catholic Church (and his enemies generally); a lack of creative (or historical, or sociological) imagination, an incomprehension of politics and power. The very defining characteristics that make him André Gide and not Everyman will prove a barrier to some. *Au fond,* I would describe him as a classicist, a duty-and-work-oriented aesthete and moralist, a rational realist with a special sense of election, demanding sensual urges, and an inextinguishable nostalgia for otherworldly faith. These qualities define, circumscribe, and in some measure limit him, and these limits may prevent his example from being of any use to some readers.

I do not think these qualities place his example out of reach: but others may. I find him, through his written record, a very real man, full of cranky prejudices, and of queer, sometimes mean and annoying ways. But I also see in him the supreme example in modern literature of moral vigilance, of lucid and indefatigable self-surveillance; of one who, as it has been said of Montaigne, "deliberately practiced a vocation of honesty"; not so much a good man as one trying to be good, to be better, to be more honest, more humble, to see and tell more of the truth—and all the while knowing that we are watching, and inviting us to watch.

He is very much a creature of traditional Western civilization; one of its last great representatives. Many of the qualities I have noted as possible limitations in the character of André Gide are rather those of the tradition to which he belongs. For all his humanist faith in rational man, he seems to have been ready, in the difficult years during and after World War II, to admit that his values and his tradition were probably passing away.

> Everything to which we still devote our thoughts may disappear, sink into the past, have no significance for the men of tomorrow but that of the archaic. Other problems, undreamed of yesterday, may disturb those to come, who will not even understand what reason we had for existing.
>
> (*Journal,* April 10, 1943)

I can imagine a time coming when aristocratic art will give way to a *common* well-being; when the individual will lose its *raison d'être* and will be ashamed of itself. . . . Humanity is waking up from its deep mythological sleep, and venturing forth into reality. All these children's playthings are going to be relegated among the obsolete, the worn-out things. People to come will no longer even be able to understand how we could have been amused by them for so many centuries.

                                        (*Journal,* April 19, 1943)

What will remain of all this? Oh, I am not speaking of what I have just written, which could be effaced with one stroke of the pen, but of all that is being written today, in France and elsewhere. What will remain of our culture, of France itself, of what we have lived for? . . . Let's make up our minds that everything is destined to disappear.

                           (*Ainsi soit-il;* the second-to-last entry
                           before Gide's death)

Western writers in their declining years have written such things for centuries—and they are always partly right, since the values of any age are always in the process of being supplanted. But Gide's forebodings may be coming true in a more radical way, and he may soon (he may now) be able to arouse the attention and admiration of only like-minded, anti-modern spirits in search of a momentary respite, a cultural escape from this alien and difficult time. Whether or not this is true, reading and re-reading his works has been for me a vital moral and intellectual adventure, the effect of which has been so intimate and so radical that I can no longer even judge them outside of the perspective they have established. There are individual works and passages which I have found singularly affecting. But the *whole* has revealed to me the rhythm and arc of an extraordinary life, something organic, awesome, compelling, and humane. Reading Gide's life has communicated a greater urgency, a greater ambitiousness, a greater sense of responsibility and validity to my own; and his example, for all its faults, its archaisms, its idiosyncrasies, has incorporated itself, for better or worse, into my private conscience.

 1869–1893

INTRODUCTION

The place to begin a study of André Gide's early life is clearly *Si le grain ne meurt,** the memoir of his first twenty-five years that he wrote between 1916 and 1919. It is a handsome, carefully crafted, very readable memoir, and, moreover, one notoriously frank. But it was written to a purpose, at a time of great internal and external crisis, and shaped by both admitted and unconscious imperatives. The book itself was a major event in Gide's life. The very gestures of writing and then of publishing it were two of the most important acts he ever committed; they helped determine in an essential way the character and image of André Gide for the next thirty years.

But because it is an act as well as a document, *Si le grain ne meurt* is *only* a place to begin. One of its first and wisest readers, Roger Martin du Gard, thought it "quite timid, really, full of evasions, camouflage, refusals." "I have read 300 pages," he wrote to Gide, "and I still don't really know you." [1] It has taken Jean Delay, Gide's most recent biographer, some 1,250 pages to fill in the gaps of just these twenty-five years. And although he protested that he had tried to tell all ("and as indiscreetly as possible"), Gide concluded by agreeing with his critics and biographers:

> This is the fatal defect of my story, as indeed of all memoirs; one describes the most apparent; but the things that matter most, the things that have no contours, elude one's grasp.

> There is a certain fraudulence in this kind of tale: the most futile and the most meaningless events, all the things that can be put into words perpetually usurp the place of all the rest.

> Memoirs are never more than half-sincere, however great one's concern for the truth: things are always more complicated than words can express. [2]

What we do have is an attempt, as far as it goes quite an honest

---

* In English, *If It Die* . . . ("Except a grain of wheat fall into the ground and die, it abideth alone; but if it die, it bringeth forth much fruit." John 12:24.)

attempt, by a well-known, very self-conscious writer to discover what it was that *made* him the man he was now: to study the first shoots of the creature he had become, and then to trace them up, from that now-dead "grain of wheat" to fixed maturity. For a number of reasons, his primary concern was that of tracing the evolution of his sexual nature, in explaining as best he could his very pertinent sexual distinction. In this respect, *Si le grain ne meurt* remains uniquely explicit among the testaments of men of comparable distinction.

But this sexual bias—it is evident from the very opening page—is one of the reasons we are forced to supplement Gide's written recollections. Another is the residual inhibition he professed to feel before the image of his wife. Although she was never to read the book, and although they were estranged, or at least severely disaffected at the time he wrote it, it was very clearly written with her in mind. A third is Gide's innate and remarkable tendency to shape and reshape the events of his own life, to turn life into legend; it is nowhere more evident than in this artful, retrospective rendering of his first twenty-five years. A fourth is the simple human fact that there are certain things about himself that even the wisest, most lucid, most outspoken of self-analysts can never know, or never bring himself to say.

What, then, is distorted, or missing? In this book, as in others, Gide has been accused of a willful *noircissement,* of darkening his own moral character and surroundings for dramatic or psychological reasons. At one point he appears to acknowledge the fault: "It seems to me," he writes, "that I have painted too darkly the shadows in which my childhood lingered on." [3] The selection of incidents, their shaping and shading—the smashing of sand-castles, the biting of cousins—do seem arranged to emphasize the perverse, as though the author has to reconstruct a five- or ten-year-old self worthy of whatever shame or guilt he was feeling at fifty. He is particularly hard on the boy in the matter of the nervous ailments that kept him out of school (and wrapped in his mother's care) from his eleventh to his sixteenth year. Directly or indirectly, Gide seems to be accusing his young self of conscious malingering, of affecting ills he did not feel in order to gain what he wanted—the first of thousands of Gide's dilemmas of "sincerity." "In the nervous complaint that followed my smallpox, I leave it to the neurologists to disentangle what was real and what was assumed." [4]

One neurologist, Dr. Jean Delay, has risen admirably to that challenge (in *La Jeunesse d'André Gide*) and in general cleared the boy Gide of the man's suspicions. To him there is no question of the authenticity of the boy's nervous disorders, and it may be useful to keep in mind something of Delay's clinical sketch of Gide's basic temperament while reading the pages ahead. He sees Gide as one born a *nerveux faible,* high-strung, emotionally over-responsive, capricious, uncertain, edgy, prickly, ridden with anxieties, forever at the mercy of his tingling nerves. From this, the sudden headaches, spasms, and fatigues, the shiverings and sweats, the nightmares and the sleepless nights, the bursts into tears, the terrors, the blushes, the paralyzing timidity: from this also, one may venture, the ecstasies, the keen responsiveness of his skin to changes in temperature and pressure, a source all his life of both voluptuous pleasure and excruciating pain; the extraordinary, super-scrupulous attention to self; the deep shudders of sympathy *and* disgust, the hatred of confinement *and* the need for support, for affection; perhaps even the elemental and essential inconstancy, the constitutional inability to sit down and stay still, to will and to act, that he was to transform into a vital philosophy of non-engagement. From this, added to general physical weakness, a deep sense of insecurity, of inferiority before those not so afflicted—at least until he had evened the balance by other means. From this, in fact, much more, if one cares to venture further into psychoanalytical speculation: but let us stop here.

In any case, Dr. Delay sees the migraines and spasms of Gide's adolescence as at worst "unconscious subterfuges," the escapes and stratagems of an insecure and nervous organism desperate for relief—"emotional disorders translated into organic manifestations"—by means of which the weakling not only obtains physical relief, but also frees himself from guilt, and gains a crucial excess of sentimental power over his protectors and oppressors. "From that moment on he was no longer a nasty little boy who had to be reformed, but a sick little boy who had to be taken care of." [5] In this case, the chief protector and oppressor was his mother, Juliette Rondeaux Gide; and this anxious, sickly, high-strung little boy, Parisian, strictly Protestant, an only child, began the very year his father died to spin about him a warm, smothering cocoon of maternal dependence. The story of that dependence, and of his efforts to break out of it, is perhaps the one most notable omission from *Si le grain ne meurt.*

From the day her husband died, Mme Paul Gide transferred all her care and dedication to her son André. "And I suddenly found myself completely enwrapped [*tout enveloppé*] in her love; from that moment on it was to confine itself [*se renfermait*] to me alone." [6] There is, I think, in Gide's choice of phrases a very conscious ambiguity, a hint of something like the female straitjacket of Strindberg's *The Father.* There

were no brothers or sisters to divide her concern. His "nerves" spared
him most of the rigors of classmates and competition, and assured him of
her constant attention. He did not spend *one single day* away from her
from the day his father died (he was eleven) until he was past twenty.
At twenty-three, he still seemed to his friends very much the Mama's
boy, the *petit garçon.*

Outside of a passing reference to the "frequent insubordination and
continual arguments" of his childhood, Gide makes, until the very end of
his memoirs, no reference to the extraordinary mother–son conflict that
was a natural product of this abnormally intense and prolonged dependence. When he finally breaks the filial silence, it is to raise, after more
than twenty years, a real *cri de cœur:*

> She had a way of loving me that sometimes made me hate her, and
> touched my nerves on the raw. Imagine . . . if you can, the effect
> of being constantly watched and spied on, incessantly and harass-
> ingly advised as to your acts, your thoughts, your expenses, as to
> what you ought to wear or what you ought to read . . .[7]

Mme Gide was the most rigid of puritan mothers, driven by ideals
of duty, austerity, chastity, work, selfless submission, and *"qu'en dira-t-
on":* what people will say. For André she was an indispensable support
and an insupportable frustration: he yielded to, even demanded her solicitude, and at the same time hated it, and longed to be free. To assert his
independence—even his selfhood, his manhood—meant to risk the loss
of her love and protection, a risk he was not prepared to take. And yet,
the gestures of emancipation grew more and more bold.

In the summer of 1889 Mme Gide allowed her son to make a walking tour of Brittany almost on his own; she followed along behind him
and met him only every other day. In October she seems to have acceded
to his plans for a literary career. In the spring of 1890 he is in Paris, she
in Normandy; already he is expressing some exasperation with her
"twenty-four question marks" per letter. He spends the whole month of
June that year in a mountain retreat, alone for the first time: he writes his
mother almost daily, it is true, but these very letters bear witness to a
growing independence and impiety; and at the same time he is writing a
semi-autobiographical novel, in which the first event is the death of the
hero's mother, which we may interpret as we will. And finally, in the
spring of 1892, he writes his mother a series of letters from Munich—a
three-months trip, this time, on his own, which is not even mentioned in

Si le grain ne meurt—of an insolence and self-assertion unheard of before.

And yet, the revolt against *maman* and the world she represents is still far from complete at the end of this period. He is still blushing by her side at the provocative gestures of a Gypsy dancer in Seville, Easter 1893. And despite his declaration to the contrary in *Si le grain ne meurt,* he wrote to his mother, just ten days before he left for North Africa— the grand symbolic gesture of *départ* I have chosen as the terminal point of this chapter—and asked her to send him, among other things, "a thin cloth-bound copy of the Bible." [8]

Paralleling the young André Gide's movement *away* from his mother and her world—the movement that climaxes with her death, in 1895, at the end of Book II—other counter-impulses of attraction may be traced in this short memoir of his youth: one, the road to an artist's career; two, the road to Biskra, or better, to the North Africa of 1893 and 1895 and all that it symbolizes of pagan self-assertion (this is Gide's central thread in the narrative, the line of sexual self-analysis); and three, the road back to Cuverville, to Madeleine and marriage. This last provides a thread, a thematic line second in importance in Gide's design only to the line of sexual analysis. It too concludes, or at least reaches its peak, at the end of Book II; and it represents, as we shall see, a power of stasis and stability opposite and equal in force to all three impulses of rebellion combined.

There are those who see Gide's actual daily life as a sordid, sick affair—a matter of no honorable account *except* as transformed into literature. I think this is an excessive judgment, the result perhaps of looking too closely and seeing too little. But there is no question of the essential, defining position that literature, his own writing and others', held in his life—so much so that he himself was at times brought to see them as one and the same: ". . . what others call a literary career and what I would call my life." [9]

Although charting "The Growth of a Poet's Mind" was not Gide's primary aim in *Si le grain ne meurt* (as it was in Wordsworth's *Prelude* or Goethe's *Dichtung und Wärheit*), he does say a great deal about it, and says it very well. Much of this I have cut in the selections that follow —his intoxicating discoveries of new authors, year by year, his scenes of Parisian literary life circa 1890—but one can still follow the progress of the budding man of letters, from his father's first readings-aloud through the Tuesday *soirées* at Mallarmé's and the publication of his own first novel at twenty-one. Along this path, too, however, he has left a few notable holes.

First, one might not suspect from *Si le grain ne meurt* how much Gide's very choice and pursuit of a literary career was itself an act of revolt against, a declaration of independence from his mother's world. After passing his *baccalauréat* examination in October 1889, he determinedly and very consciously set out to be a writer: he vowed to finish his first book by the time he was twenty-one, and proceeded to rearrange his life in order to do it. His days and nights were now passed in almost exclusively literary milieux; he saw in, and to some degree learned from Mallarmé the ideal of an absolute, religious dedication to art. When his mother, in 1892, presumed to advise him how to write, he exploded:

> . . . I beg you, for once and for all to understand that *I,* I alone, I above all am the father and protector of my work, which I must and shall bring to maturity—and that, in the last analysis, it depends on *no* one but me.[10]

If he could write, in 1893, that "here [in Paris] I am a profoundly different man," it was primarily because he had already become so completely a man of letters.

He does, secondly, make one reference in his memoir to the cathartic or therapeutic effect that writing had on him, apropos of his first novel, *Les Cahiers d'André Walter:* "I seemed to have got rid of the anxiety I had painted by the very act of painting it." [11] Later on, he was to understand and describe with uncanny precision and self-awareness the curative mechanism of his own imagination, the function his writing served in helping to preserve an emotional equilibrium. For the most part, his works before the turn of the century have a queer, excessively "literary" or period flavor—exotic little parables acted out by disembodied voices talking philosophy, or sharing ecstatic moments in vague dream landscapes—a literature that distinctly evokes the time, the time of Mallarmé, Maeterlinck, and Huysmans. But they were remarkably useful to Gide as stages in a kind of auto-psychoanalysis, freeing him from many of his own conflicts and frustrations, developing his own more natural voice and style, strengthening him for more adult games to come; so too are they remarkably useful to the biographer today, who knows how to read the autobiographical revelations beneath the foggy fictions—revelations at times considerably more explicit and profound than those of his non-fictional autobiography. This is especially true of *André Walter,* a windy, clumsy young man's work for which Gide soon grew embarrassed, which has always been more valuable as a work of therapy or a source of unconscious revelations than as a work of art.

The most inexplicably missing acknowledgment of a literary influence in the memoir, as Jean Delay points out, is the one due to Goethe, for it was very specifically upon the image of Goethe's career that the young Gide was trying to model his own. The Arabian Nights and the Bible, Amiel and Rousseau, the seventeenth-century French classics first at school and then, during his pious period, privately; Barrès, Baudelaire, the French symbolists and the German idealists; Balzac and Hugo, Schopenhauer, Flaubert, and Stendhal—it is difficult to do justice to all of the writers who helped so omnivorous a young reader (for some long periods he was devouring a book a day) to find his own voice and figure. But it was the discovery of Goethe that revealed to Gide the life he wanted to lead. It was at eighteen, he claimed, reading the second part of *Faust,* that he first learned of and accepted the artist's vocation. For the four years after 1892 he was reading his German master daily as a kind of pagan Bible, treasuring what he saw as an appeal to Promethean liberation, to pantheistic affirmation of *this*-worldly joys, to classical equilibrium in place of Christian inner combat. He was particularly gripped by *biographies* of Goethe, since it was the shape of life, or life-style, that he wanted to imitate even more than the works. Gide was later to "discover himself" in Nietzsche, Dostoevsky, and Montaigne; but none of them is more important in his development than this crucial first choice of a model. *This* was the kind of career, of reputation, of influence he wanted to have—and it is remarkable how nearly he succeeded, considering the differences of the two men, their two nations, their two centuries. His distraught mother, begging her brother-in-law for advice on what to *do* about poor André scarcely six weeks before her death, was not entirely out of her mind in blaming all of her son's moral defection on "this Goethe!"

Gide admits, in the introductory *apologia* to Part II of his memoir, that he had been on "the road to Biskra" for some time before October 1893. In one respect, his whole narrative seems to have been carefully designed to lead toward that symbolic encounter on the sand dunes outside of Sousse, the moment of self-discovery that Gide thought so all-important. The games under the table, the suspension from school, the passions for

various schoolfellows, the erotic appeal of statues, his terror of prostitutes, the insistence on puritan repression, growing frustration, and culpable carnal ignorance: "I lived until the age of twenty-three completely
virgin and utterly depraved; crazed to such a point that eventually I came
to look everywhere for some bit of flesh on which to press my lips"
(*Journal,* March 1893)—all these selected materials *do* give to his recollections a kind of efficient, inescapable logic, a downhill course of ever-
increasing velocity. The dramatic and rhetorical shapeliness of the climax is further enhanced by the sharp split between Book I and Book II;
by the striking rhetorical pause, a sort of moral catching of breath and
gathering of forces, at the start of Book II; and by a number of little
"hints forward" scattered throughout Book I: "I shall soon be obliged to
tell . . . Could I possibly have understood . . . ?"

But another means of emphasizing this striking pattern of impulse-
to-climax is that of omitting or blurring certain episodes, episodes that
might have altered the descending slope or diminished the final impact.
Crucial as the actual journey to Africa surely was, Gide was better
"primed" for it than one might suspect, less the timid, frustrated boy that
he makes himself out to be; in fact, he was a long way along the road to
moral emancipation before his ship ever left Marseilles. The revolt
against *maman;* the influence of Goethe; the independent morality (if
not independence of morality) implicit in his choice of a literary life—
these have already been mentioned. And from his books, letters, and
journals of 1891–1893, one can reconstruct a growing image of the im-
moralist-to-be.

In late 1891, he appended an explicit defense of artistic amoralism
to his *Traité du Narcisse,* a defense that frankly shocked his cousin Madeleine; she began at once to pray all the harder for André's soul. About
the same time he had his first encounter with Oscar Wilde, a man of
unquestionable importance in André Gide's finding of his destiny. The
encounter is not even mentioned in *Si le grain ne meurt*—though it was
to be repeated at least ten times in eighteen days. The pages of his journal
for the period of their meetings were torn out, but in the next surviving
entries (December 29) he is praying God to free him from turmoil and
tortuous ways; five days later he is quoting Oscar Wilde, whom he then
continued to quote and paraphrase through his journals, *Les Nourritures terrestres,* and *L'Immoraliste.* Wilde's immoralism was ultimately
far more a matter of style and self-defending camouflage than Gide's; but
there can be no doubt of the essential role it played in leading his young
French friend to discover a more substantial (and more influential) im-

moralism of his own. "Wilde is religiously contriving to kill what remains of my soul," he wrote in December to his friend Valéry.[12] He does
handsome justice to the pathetic, brilliant, enigmatic Irishman in an *In
Memoriam* essay of 1908; but to omit him from Part I of *Si le grain ne
meurt* was one of Gide's most serious distortions.

The journals and letters of the next two years bear vivid evidence of
the combined effect of Goethe and Wilde, and of Gide's own emerging
"new self." By March of 1893 he has come to regard virginity as "depraved"; at the end of April he is still praying to God, but this time for
the strength to live fully and freely, unburdened by any Christian sense of
sin. He is now ashamed of his long history of resistance, *willing* himself
to break chains, to turn toward happiness and the sun. His ghastly portrait of the Journey to the Frozen Sea in *Voyage d'Urien* (completed at
the end of 1892) is, at least in part, a symbolic description of the moral
scurvy to which, he now felt, the cold self-denying puritan lies prey. He
begins to see himself in the Goethe of the *Roman Elegies,* in the doomed
Oscar Alving of Ibsen's *Ghosts,* longing for escape from the dark northern shadows, toward the south, the sun, the "joy of life." He now professes himself "pagan"; "the religious question bores me." [13]

These few corrective additions made, we can rejoin the narrative and
accept Gide's own eloquent description of his feelings on setting sail
across the Mediterranean.

Almost everything remains to be said, though, in the matter of his relations during this period with his cousin Madeleine Rondeaux, whom he
was to marry in 1895. He tells of their childhood summers at La Roque,
of the "mystical bond" he felt to be formed one December afternoon in
1882 (he was thirteen, she fifteen), and the period of tender affection
and religious fervor that followed. Suddenly he announces a resolution
he had taken "to marry my cousin as soon as possible." [14] An engagement
is somehow secretly blessed at her father's deathbed in 1890. He writes a
book, intended to serve as declaration of love; she rejects it, breaks off
correspondence; he resolves to wait.

The essential problem in interpreting any of Gide's public writings
concerning his wife, from the first Journal entries to the posthumous
Madeleine (*Et nunc manet in te*), is the extraordinary degree to which
he created an ideal, saintly, fictional image, the image of a woman sad,
pure, pious, and resigned, out of a more or less normal Protestant bour-
geoise. Her own surviving journals and letters, plus the collected testi-

mony of her friends, make it clear that Gide's "Emmanuèle" has only a limited correspondence to the real Madeleine Rondeaux Gide. And yet, for Gide, it was the idealized image that mattered, that he needed: it was this he married, this he held to, this that kept him from ever touching or even seeing the real woman he was asking to play this difficult, dehumanized role.* The making of the myth of Emmanuèle is surely one of the most striking instances of Gide's rendering of life into legend, his tendency to give a fictional, even an epic density and shape to the small materials of every day. One need only note the hushed elevation of tone with which he relates the great "epiphany" of the rue de Lecat—"as important in my life as are revolutions in the history of empires" [15]—or their mystical engagement eight years later on. It is doubtful that Madeleine Rondeaux shared the emotions he describes, or would have subscribed to his interpretations of them, on either of these occasions.

So the "truth" of the affair is in part irrelevant, because Gide was himself motivated by something else, something in his eyes higher; but still, it ought to be known. The details of the December afternoon and of the succeeding mystical fervor, the pure brother-and-sister love that inspired his adolescence, are told accurately enough (on the testimony of their letters), and are quite touching. André may well have proposed marriage soon after his uncle's death, but the "deathbed consecration" tableau seems touched by a bit of retrospective poetic license. Moreover, not only his cousin, but the whole close-knit Gide–Rondeaux family were adamantly opposed to the idea even before the revelations of *André Walter* put them on their guard. André, at the time (of course he was only to get worse), was regarded as a capricious, eccentric, impractical boy, of no profession, utterly unfit for marriage—especially to his older and poorer cousin, already so wounded by her mother's adultery and flight.

So he threw himself into his novel, a novel that made all the more explicit his unfitness for marriage. As Madeleine read it, she saw herself transformed into an ideal figure, snow-white, impossibly pure, unattainable. She saw her dear cousin André revealed as one riven by sensual torments, torn between the ascetic aspirations and solitary lusts—and yet horrified by the idea of sexual possession, by the very specter of adult

---

* He does appear to have realized, finally, what he had done: "I believe that, late in life, I came to understand her much better; but at the strongest point of my love, how very much I was mistaken about her! For the whole effort of my love was bent less on bringing *us* close together than on bringing her close to that ideal figure I had invented . . . I do not think Dante acted differently with Beatrice" (*Et nunc manet in te*).

female sexuality. She was perhaps no better prepared than we are to
interpret exactly such lines as these; but they are the sort to give one
pause, occurring in what was intended as a proposal of marriage:

> In order not to disturb her purity, I shall abstain from all caresses—
> so as not to trouble her soul—even from the most chaste, the inter-
> lacing of hands. . . . for fear that from these she will want more,
> that I shall be unable to give her . . .

> Moreover, I do not desire you; your flesh only troubles me, and
> carnal possessions horrify me . . .

> A monkey came skipping toward her; he lifted up her mantle, set-
> ting the fringes swinging. And I was afraid to look: I wanted to
> avert my eyes, but I looked in spite of myself. Under her dress, there
> was nothing; it was black, black as a hole; I sobbed in
> despair . . .[16]

Moreover, he had quoted exactly from their intimate conversations.
"André," she wrote to her journal, "you had no right to write those
things!"[17] Could he really have expected her to be won by such means,
have been so ignorant of her feelings as he pretends? In any case, she
rejected his proposal, stopped answering his letters, and confided her
grief and confusion to her journal:

> There are two Andrés—the old one, the new one . . . He has
> changed so much in a year.   (February 7, 1891)

> Is it really love, this feeling I have for André? No—in all sincerity
> before myself I must say it. Love, it seems to me, implies *desire*—
> something burning, something passionate which does not exist, nei-
> ther in him nor in me.   (February 21, 1891)

> Sympathy in all things, the somewhat protective friendship of an
> older sister—esteem for his efforts, his ambitions—the affection of
> all my heart—but affection pure of all disturbance, of all desire for
> change . . .

> Oh, André, we must separate, faced with the implacable logic of this
> alternative: either to sustain a mad dream which is bound to make
> both of us unhappy, or to change nothing in our present situation
> and have against us the reprobation of our families, the censure of
> the world—even of our own hearts—the difficulties ahead, the

sickness of my conscience.—we must separate . . . I weep with
all my heart . . . My God, deliver me from myself—deliver us
from one another.—We must separate.   (June 12, 1891)[18]

In 1889 she had been frightened by André's incorrigible egotism;
in 1891 she was wounded by the tactlessness and cruelty of *André
Walter.* She saw clearly the moral revolution implicit in his *Narcisse,*
and wrote in June 1892, "Your sinful pride terrifies me." "My God," she
prayed, "give André faith, increase his faith, and let him learn from you
to be gentle and humble of heart." She mocked the meanness and pretensions of *Les Poésies d'André Walter*—with each successive book, the
portraits of "Emmanuèle" were becoming less flattering; of *Le Voyage
d'Urien* she was later to ask, "How *could* you have written certain pages,
you who have led a life so pure, so intact . . . ?"[19] She was missing very
little in these books, missing very little of what she could only regard as
the moral degeneration of her beloved "brother"—who persisted all the
while in his offer of marriage. On October 14, 1892, he wrote her a long,
eloquent, insistent appeal, begging her to conquer her scruples, assuring
her that separation would only doom them both to unhappiness, that
neither could ever marry anyone else. That failing, he wrote again:

> Let us stay brother and sister, then, Madeleine, if this will comfort
> you . . . It is possible, after all, that I have been deluding myself;
> what I feel for you is so peaceful, so pure, so profound that it may
> well be fraternal . . . The fraternity, the affection of our earlier
> days was so dear to me that I hoped for nothing better in my life;
> and it was, more than anything else, the fear that you would take
> this away from me, stop talking to me, stop writing to me, that
> drove me to push to such an extreme a feeling so calm . . .
> I feel more sad than I have ever felt before; I must have a little
> sympathy if I am to have the courage to go on. *Maman* is gone, as
> one day she will be gone for good, and I feel so utterly alone. I beg
> you, write me one word; I promise to be good if I answer you.
> Please, please tell me what it is that you want. Then, while we wait,
> let us go on calling ourselves brother and sister, and I shall torment
> you no longer, Madeleine; and you will no longer be afraid of me,
> and I shall call you sister, as in the old days, my poor dear Made-
> leine.[20]

By this time André's mother, terribly worried by his increasing independence, was beginning to come round. She hinted as much to her

niece, who wrote back, respectfully, honestly, but very realistically: she loved André with all her heart; she herself was frightened of any prospect but that of the tranquil, the predictable, the passive; and in the prospect of marriage to André, in particular, she frankly saw nothing but grief.

But by 1893, André had other prospects than marriage on his mind. His thoughts were now of Goethe and the southern sun, and his family's five-year-long resistance to the "unthinkable" marriage began to melt under the growing flame of his pagan ardors.

NORMANDY AND BAS-LANGUEDOC

1902

There are lands that are more beautiful and I think I should have preferred them. But it is of these that I was born. Had I been able, I should have had myself born in Brittany—in Locmariaquer the pious, or near Brest, in Camaret or Morgat—but we do not choose our parents. And even this desire I inherited, I think, with the Norman and Catholic blood of my mother's family, the Protestant, Languedocian blood of my father. Between Normandy and the South I would not nor could I choose, and I feel myself all the more French because I am not descended of a single corner of France, because I cannot think and feel especially as a Norman or a Southerner, as a Catholic or a Protestant, but as a Frenchman; and because, born in Paris, I understand alike the *langue d'Oc* and the *langue d'Oïl,* the thick Norman jargon and the singsong speech of the South, because I have a taste for wine and a taste for cider, a love for deep woods and *garrigue,* for the whiteness of the apple blossom and the white flowering almond.

And in these pages, too, I make no choice; not to speak of both regions would be ingratitude to one, and since you urge me to speak, allow me to speak of both.

I

From the edge of the Norman woods I evoke a burning rock—an air all perfumed, eddying with sun, and rolling commingled the scent of thyme, lavender, and the shrill cry of the cicadas. I evoke at my feet, for the rock is steep, in the narrow, receding valley, a mill, washerwomen, water all the cooler for being the more desired. A little farther on I evoke the rock once again, but now less steep and milder, enclosures, gardens, then roofs, a happy little town—Uzès. It is there that my father was born, and there that I came as a very young child.

We came from Nîmes by carriage; we crossed the Gardon at the Saint-Nicholas bridge. In the month of May its banks are covered with asphodels like the banks of the Anapos, where dwell the gods of Greece. The Pont du Gard is very near . . .

Later I came to know Arles, Avignon, Vaucluse . . . A land almost Latin, gravely smiling, of lucid poetry and handsome severity. No softness here. The city is born of the rock and retains its warm tones. In the hardness of the rock, the antique soul is set; inscribed in the hard, living flesh of the race, it makes the beauty of the women, the flash of their laughter, the gravity of their walk, the severity of their eyes; it makes the pride of the men, the somewhat easy assurance of those who, having once declared themselves in times past, have now only to repeat themselves effortlessly, and no longer find anything particularly new to seek; I hear this soul again in the micaceous cry of the cicadas, I breathe it with the aromatic herbs, I see it in the sharp foliage of the holm oaks, in the slender boughs of the olive . . .

From the edge of the flaming *garrigue,* I evoke a thick grass ever damp with rains, boughs down-bent, deep shaded paths; I evoke a wood into which they plunge—but others have already sung of the verdant land of Calvados. There, no buzz of cicadas; all is softness and abundance; one never spies the naked rock under the green. There dwell other gods, other men; the gods are beautiful, I believe; the men are ugly. The race, fattened with material comfort and yet thinking of nothing but how to increase it, has deformed itself. Incapable of song, of music, it spends its finest idle hours on nothing but drink. Love of gain, here, is the only thing that overcomes sloth. The indolent man lets slip from his hands the most precious, the rarest of all his goods . . .

But perhaps the qualities of the Norman race, less evident than those of the Southerners, receive added strength in those who inherit them from the heavier flesh that wraps them round, and gain in gravity and depth what they lose in brilliance and surface.

Everything changes with the region of Caux; there vast fields replace the meadows; the men are better, more sober workers, and the women less misshapen. And on this fifteenth of July, as I write this, near Etretat, now sitting, now walking under the full noonday sun, never has this country appeared more beautiful to me. There are still a few flax in bloom. They are cutting the colza; the rye has been mowed. In the last few days the wheat has turned blond. The harvest gives promise of being superb. Here and there, in spots, everywhere, great poppies mark the ground with red.

II

The few places of which I speak are no more all of Normandy and all of the South, than the South and Normandy are all of France.

I think sadly that if some chance brought them together, the Norman peasant as I know him, the Southerner as I know him—not only would they not love each other, they could not even understand each other. Yet both are Frenchmen.

In the eyes of a German, an Italian, a Russian, what represents "a French city"? I do not know. I do not have sufficient perspective to understand. I see a Brittany, a Normandy, a Pays Basque, a Lorraine, and of their sum I make my France. In Savoy I know that I am in France; and I know that a little farther on I am no longer there. I know it and I want to feel it. But will a mere annexation make a region French? No, no more than a wretched treaty would suffice to make a German province of Alsace-Lorraine, as Germany has fully realized. In order for a country's sense of unity to be formed and strengthened, it is necessary that the different elements that compose it mingle, cross, and blend. The doctrine of *enracinement,* too rigorously applied, would run the risk, by protecting and accentuating the heterogeneity of the diverse French elements, of making them misunderstand one another forever, of forming Bretons, Normans, Lorrainers, Basques, who would be more Breton, Norman, Lorrainer, and Basque . . . than French. Nothing is more private, more particular than the provincial spirit; nothing more general than the French genius. It is a good thing that Frenchmen, like Hugo, are born *"d'un sang breton et lorrain à la fois"* ("of Breton and Lorrainer blood together"); bearing in themselves at the same time the most dissimilar riches of France, they organize them and force them into unity.

It should be added that there are wastelands more barren than those of Brittany; pasturelands greener than those of Normandy; rocks that burn more fiercely than those of the countryside about Arles; beaches more sea-green than ours of the Channel, bluer than those of our South Coast—but France has *all that at once.* And the French genius is, for that very reason, not all heaths, nor all farmlands, nor all forests, nor all shade, nor all light—but it organizes and holds in harmonious equilibrium the diverse elements proposed. It is this that makes France the most classic of countries; just as such diverse elements—Ionian, Dorian, Bœotian, and Attic—formed the classic land of Greece.

from

SI LE GRAIN

NE MEURT

(*If It Die*), *Part I*

I was born on November 22, 1869. My parents at that time lived on the rue de Médicis, in an apartment on the fourth or fifth floor which they left a few years later and of which I have kept no recollection. I do remember the balcony, though; or rather what one could see from the balcony—the bird's-eye view of the square with its fountain and pool; or rather, to be still more exact, I remember the paper dragons cut out by my father, which we used to launch into the air from this balcony; I remember the wind carrying them off, over the fountain in the square below, as far as the Luxembourg Gardens, where they used sometimes to catch in the top branches of the horse-chestnut trees.

I can still see too a biggish table—the dining-room table, no doubt—covered with a cloth that reached nearly to the ground; I used to crawl underneath it with the concierge's son, a little boy my own age, who sometimes came to play with me.

"What are you up to under there?" my nurse would call out.

"Nothing; we're playing."

And then we would make a great noise with our toys, which we had taken with us for the sake of appearances. In reality, we amused ourselves otherwise: alongside each other but not with each other, we had what I afterwards learned are called "bad habits."

Which of us two taught them to the other? And where did the first one learn them? I have no idea. Surely a child may sometimes invent them for himself. Personally, I cannot say whether someone taught me such pleasures, or how I discovered them; but as far back as my memory goes, there they are.

I realize, moreover, the harm that I am doing myself by relating this and other things that will follow; I foresee the use that will be made of them against me. But the whole object of my story is to be truthful. Let us say that I am writing it for a penance.

At that age of innocence, when one would like to believe that the soul is all sweetness, light, and purity, I can remember nothing in mine that was not ugly, dark, and deceitful.

I used to be taken for my outings to the Luxembourg, but I refused to play with the other children; I kept sulkily apart with my nurse and watched their games. Once they were making rows of pretty sand-pies with their pails . . . All of a sudden, when my nurse was looking the other way, I dashed up and trampled on all the pies. . . .

The other incident I want to relate is still odder, for which reason, no doubt, I am less ashamed of it. My mother often told me the story later on, so that her recital kept it fresh in my memory.

It happened at Uzès, where we used to go once a year to visit my father's mother and other relations—among them my De Flaux cousins, who owned an old house and garden in the heart of the town. It was in the De Flaux house that it happened. My cousin was very beautiful, and she knew it. Her deep black hair, which she wore pulled back under a head-band, set off the perfection of her cameo-like profile (I have seen a photo-graph of her since then) and the dazzling whiteness of her skin. I remem-ber the dazzling whiteness of her skin very well—and I remember it especially well because the day I was taken to see her she was wearing a low-necked dress.

"Go and give your cousin a kiss," said my mother, as I came into the drawing-room. (I couldn't have been much more than four years old—five, perhaps.) I went obediently up; my cousin pulled me toward her to kiss me, uncovering her bare shoulder; but at the sight of her white skin, some sort of madness overcame me, and instead of putting my lips to the cheek she offered me, I was fascinated by that dazzling shoulder, and gave it a great bite with my teeth. My cousin screamed with pain, I screamed with horror. She began to bleed and I to spit with disgust. I was speedily carried off and I believe they were all so astounded that they forgot to punish me.

I have found a photograph of myself taken at that time; it shows me half hidden in my mother's skirts, rigged out in a ridiculous little checked dress, with a sickly, mean-tempered face and a crooked look in my eyes.

The other amusements of my early childhood—card games, transfers, blocks—were all solitary. I had not a single friend . . . Yes, now, I do recall one; but alas, he was no playmate. When Marie took me to the Luxembourg Gardens, I used to meet a child there of about my own age, a delicate, gentle, quiet creature, whose pallid face was half hidden by a pair of giant spectacles, the glasses of which were so dark that one could see nothing behind them. I no longer remember his name; perhaps I never knew it. We used to call him Mouton because of his little white woolly coat.

"Mouton, why do you wear spectacles?"

"I have bad eyes."

"Let me see them."

Then he lifted the frightful glasses, and the sight of his poor, blinking, weak eyes made my heart ache.

We never played together; I cannot remember that we did anything but walk about hand in hand without saying a word.

This first friendship of mine lasted only a short time. Mouton soon stopped coming. Oh, how empty the Luxembourg seemed to me then! . . . But my real despair began when I realized that Mouton was going blind. Marie had met the little boy's nurse in the street and she told my mother what she had learned; she spoke in a low voice so that I should not hear; but I caught these words: "He can't find the way to his mouth!" An absurd remark, assuredly, for of course there is no need to see in order to find the way to one's mouth, and I realized this at once; but nevertheless it filled me with dismay. I ran away to cry in my room, and for several days I practiced keeping my eyes shut for a long time and going about without opening them, so as to try to make myself realize what Mouton must be going through.

My father's time was taken up preparing his lectures at the Faculty of Law, and there was very little left for me. He spent most of the day shut up in a vast and rather dark study, into which I was allowed only when he expressly invited me. It is only by means of an old photograph that I can recall his face today, my father with his square-cut beard and rather long, curly black hair; without this picture I should have had no memory but that of his extreme gentleness. My mother told me later that his colleagues had nicknamed him *Vir probus;* and I learned from one of them that they often had recourse to his advice.

My veneration for my father was slightly mixed with fear, a fear enhanced by the solemnity of his room. I entered it as I would a church; the bookcase rose out of the gloom like a tabernacle; a thick carpet of a dark rich color stifled the sound of my footsteps. There was a reading-desk near one of the two windows; in the middle of the room, an enormous table covered with books and papers. My father would go and fetch some big volume, some *Common Law of Burgundy* or Normandy, and open the heavy folio on the arm of an easy chair, so that the two of us could trace from page to page the persevering labors of a gnawing bookworm. Consulting some ancient text, the learned jurist had admired these tiny clandestine galleries and had said to himself, "Ah! this will amuse my little boy." And it did amuse me very much, not least because of the amusement he seemed to take in it himself.

But my recollection of the study is especially bound up with his reading aloud . . . my father read aloud to me scenes from Molière, passages of the *Odyssey, La Farce de Pathelin,* the adventures of Sinbad or Ali Baba, and some of the harlequinades of the Italian Comedy that are to be found in Maurice Sand's *Masques;* in this book there were pictures for me to admire too of Harlequin, Columbine, Punchinello, and Pierrot, after I had listened to them discoursing in my father's voice.

The success of these readings was such and my father's confidence in me so great that one day he ventured on the first part of the Book of Job. This was an experiment at which my mother wished to be present; and so it took place not in the library, like the other readings, but in a small drawing-room which was more particularly in my mother's domain. I would not swear of course that I understood at once the full beauty of the sacred text. But the reading certainly made the deepest impression on me, not only because of the solemnity of the story, but because of the gravity of my father's voice and my mother's expression, as, in order alternately to signify or to shield her pious absorption, she sat with her eyes closed, and opened them only to cast on me a questioning glance, full of love and hope.

Sometimes on fine summer evenings, when we had not supped too late, and when my father was not too busy, he used to say: "Would my little friend like to come for a walk?"

He never called me anything but his "little friend."

"You'll be sensible, won't you?" said my mother. "Don't be too late."

I liked going out with my father; and as he rarely had much time to spend with me, the few things we did together had an unfamiliar, solemn, and rather mysterious air about them which delighted me.

Playing as we went at some game of rhymes or riddles, we would walk up the rue de Tournon and then either cross the Luxembourg Gardens or follow the part of the boulevard Saint-Michel that skirts them, until we reached the second garden near the Observatory. In those days the property that faces the School of Pharmacy had not yet been built over; the school itself in fact did not exist. Instead of the six-storied houses that stand there now, there were nothing but temporary wooden booths, where old clothes were put out for sale, and secondhand velocipedes were rented and sold. The asphalt—or perhaps macadam—space which borders the second Luxembourg was used as a track by the devotees of this sport; perched up aloft on those weird, paradoxical machines which were the ancestors of the bicycle, they circled swiftly past us and disappeared into the darkness. We admired their boldness and their elegance. One could scarcely make out the framework and the minute back wheel on which the equilibrium of this aerial apparatus depended. The slender front wheel swayed to and fro; the man who rode it seemed some fantastic creature of a dream world.

As the night fell, it intensified the lights of a *café-concert* a little farther on, whose music attracted us. We could not see the gas globes themselves, only the strangely illuminated horse-chestnut trees above the fence. We drew near. The planks were not so well joined as to prevent one from getting a peep here and there between two of them, by putting one eye up against the crack: I could just make out, over the dark, swarming mass of the audience, the enchantment of the stage, on which some music-hall star was warbling her absurdities.

Sometimes we still had time to walk back through the big Luxembourg Gardens. Soon a roll on the drums announced that the gardens were closing. The last strollers reluctantly turned toward the exits, with the park-keepers close at their heels, and behind them the broad garden walks, now left deserted, filled slowly up with mystery. On those evenings I went to bed intoxicated with darkness, sleep, and strangeness.

My parents had taken to passing the summer holidays in Calvados at La Roque-Baignard, a country place which had come into my mother's possession at the death of my grandmother Rondeaux. The Christmas holidays we spent at Rouen with my mother's relations, and the Easter ones at Uzès with my paternal grandmother.

Nothing could be more different than these two families, nothing more different than the two provinces of France which combine their contradictory influences in me. I have often persuaded myself that I was driven into the field of art because by no other means could I have reconciled these discordant elements, which would otherwise have remained in a state of perpetual warfare, or at any rate of antagonism. . . .

The vague, indefinable belief that something else exists alongside the acknowledged, everyday reality inhabited me for a number of years; and I am not sure that even today I could not find some remnants of it left. It had nothing in common with tales of fairies, ghouls, or witches; nor even with Hoffman's or Andersen's stories, which I had not yet read at the time. No, I think it was more a kind of clumsy need to give life more thickness, more substance—a need that religion was better able to satisfy later on; and also a sort of propensity to imagine secrets. After my father's death, for instance, big boy as I was, I went so far as to imagine that he was not really dead; or at any rate—how can I express this kind of apprehension? —that he was dead only to our visible, diurnal life, but that at night, when I was asleep, he used to come secretly and visit my mother. In the daytime, my suspicions wavered, but at night, just before going to sleep, I felt them grow more vivid and more certain. I did not try to unravel the mystery; I felt I should put an abrupt stop to anything I might try to discover. No doubt I was still too young, and my mother was too much in the habit of saying about too many things, "You will understand it when you are older"—but on certain nights, as I dropped off to sleep, I truly had the feeling that I was making way, giving up my place. . . .

For a long time Juliette Rondeaux had disdained the most brilliant matches in Rouen society, when one day people were surprised to hear that she had accepted a penniless young professor of law, from the depths of the Midi; who would never have dared to ask her hand if he had not been encouraged by good Pastor Roberty; fully aware of my mother's views, it was he who first introduced the pair. . . .

I can imagine my mother's bewilderment when for the first time she left her comfortable surroundings in the rue de Crosne to accompany my father to Uzès. The century's progress seemed to have forgotten this little town, situated off the beaten track and unaware of the surrounding world. The railway only went as far as Nîmes, or at most to Remoulins; from there one had to drag out the rest of the way in a rattling old wagon. It was considerably longer to go by Nîmes, but the road was much more beautiful. It crossed the Gardon by Saint-Nicholas's bridge: suddenly one entered Palestine, Judæa. The harsh *garrigue* was bedecked with tufts of white and purple cistus and scented with lavender. A dry, exhilarating air blew overhead, which cleared the road but covered everything round with dust. Enormous grasshoppers leaped up as our carriage passed, suddenly spreading their blue, red, or gray membranes up in the air, gay butterflies

for a single moment; but falling down a few feet farther on, their brightness dulled, indistinguishable from the stones and scrub among which
they lay.

Asphodels grew on the banks of the Gardon; and in the river bed
itself, which was almost everywhere dry, the flora was semitropical. . . .
Here I must leave the rattletrap for a moment; there are memories I
must snatch in passing, or I shall not know where else to place them. As I
have already said, I fit them less easily into time than into space; for instance, I cannot say what year it was that Anna came to visit us at Uzès,
which my mother was no doubt delighted to show her; but what I do
remember very clearly is the excursion we made with her one day from
Saint-Nicholas's bridge to some village not far from the Gardon, where
the carriage was to pick us up.

In the sunken, narrow parts of the valley, at the foot of the cliffs
burning with the reverberated heat of the sun, the vegetation was so luxuriant that it was difficult to make one's way through. Anna kept marveling
at all the new species of plant life, kept recognizing one or another she had
never before seen growing wild—I was going to say "at liberty"—those
triumphant daturas, for example, sometimes called "trumpets of Jericho,"
which, with the oleanders, have remained so deeply engraved on my
memory for their splendor and strangeness. We made our way cautiously
on account of snakes, and saw several, though most harmless ones, which
glided out of our way. My father found in everything something to amuse
him and to linger over. My mother, very conscious of the time, tried in
vain to hurry us on. Night already began to fall when we came out from
between the high banks of the river. The village was still a long way off,
and the angelic sound of its bells reached us only faintly; the road that led
to it was nothing but a poorly marked path, weaving uncertainly through
the brush. . . . The reader may wonder whether I am not adding all this
today, after the event; but no; the sound of that Angelus is still in my ears;
I can still see the delightful path, the rosy sunset, and the invading darkness marching up behind us from the bed of the Gardon. At first I was
amused by the long shadows we cast; then everything vanished in the gray
of twilight, and I felt my mother's anxiety growing upon me too. But my
father and Anna, intent on the beauty of the hour, still ambled, regardless
of time. I remember they were repeating poetry; my mother thought "it
was not the moment" and cried: "Paul, you can recite that when we get
home."

———

My grandfather Gide died some time before I came into the world; but my mother had known him, for I was not born till six years after her marriage. She described him to me as a typical Huguenot, single-minded and austere, very tall, very strong and angular, inflexible, scrupulous to excess, and with a confidence in God which he pushed to sublime extremes. Formerly president of the Uzès tribunal, at the time she knew him his days were taken up almost entirely by good works and by the moral and religious instruction of his Sunday-school pupils.

Besides Paul, my father, and my Uncle Charles, Tancrède Gide had had several children who had died in infancy, one from a fall on the head, another from sunstroke, yet another from a neglected cold—neglected apparently for the same reason that he neglected his own health. When he fell ill, which seldom happened, he refused to have recourse to anything but prayer; he considered the intervention of the doctor intrusive, not to say impious, and died without allowing one to be sent for.

Some people may wonder that these impractical and almost antediluvian forms of humanity should have survived so long; but the whole small town of Uzès was in itself a survival, and extravagances like my grandfather's were certainly not conspicuous in a place where everything else was in keeping, where everything accounted for them, explained them, encouraged them and even made them appear natural; and what is more, I think that almost identical conditions would have been found over the whole region of the Cévennes, still barely recovered from the cruel religious dissensions by which it had been so long and so severely tormented. A strange adventure of my own, which I must relate here, though it belonged to my eighteenth (?) year, convinces me that I am right.

I had started from Uzès one morning in answer to an invitation from my cousin, Guillaume Granier, a pastor in the neighborhood of Anduze. I spent the day with him. Before letting me go, he had preached to me, prayed with me and for me, and blessed me or at least prayed God to bless me. . . . But this has nothing to do with my story. The train was to take me back to Uzès for dinner; but I was reading *Le Cousin Pons.* Of all Balzac's many masterpieces, it may well be my favorite; at any rate it is the one I have reread most often. Now it was on that very day that I discovered it. I was in ecstasy, beside myself, oblivious of the world. . . .

The approach of night at last interrupted my reading. After an oath at my carriage for not being lighted, I noticed that it was stopped; the railway people, thinking it was empty, had shunted it on to a siding.

"Didn't you know you had to change?" they asked. "They certainly announced it loud enough. Ah, no doubt you were asleep. Well, you may as well go back to sleep; there is no train from here now till tomorrow morning."

The prospect of spending the night in a dark railway carriage was singularly lacking in charm; and besides, I had not had my dinner. The station was a long way from the village, and I felt less attracted by the inn than by the adventure; besides, I had no more than a few sous in my pockets. I started walking along the road, in no particular direction, and decided to knock at a fairly large *mas,* or farmhouse, which looked clean and inviting. A woman opened the door and I told her that I had lost my way, that the fact of having no money did not prevent me from having an appetite, and that perhaps they would be good enough to give me something to eat and drink; and then I would go back to my railway carriage and wait patiently till morning.

The table was already laid, but the woman who had opened the door at once set another place. Her husband was away; her old father, who was sitting by the fire (for the room where they sat served as kitchen as well), remained bending over the hearth without speaking; his silence, which seemed disapproving, made me feel uncomfortable. All of a sudden I noticed a big Bible on a kind of wall-shelf, and realizing I was in a Protestant household, I mentioned the name of the person I had been visiting. The old man sat up at once; he knew my cousin, the pastor; he even remembered my grandfather very well. I realized from the way he spoke of him how much unselfishness and kindliness may lie under the roughest exterior—and this applied to my grandfather as much as to the old peasant. My grandfather must have resembled him, I thought, in his look of extreme robustness, his vibrant if not melodious voice, and his straightforward though scarcely endearing glance.

In the meantime the children came in from work—a grown-up daughter and three sons; more delicately built than their grandfather; good-looking, but with faces already grave, and even a touch of sternness on their brows. Their mother placed the steaming soup on the table and stopped me in the middle of a sentence with a quiet motion of her hand, while the old man said grace.

It was during supper that he spoke of my grandfather; his language was at once precise and laden with images; I am sorry I did not note down some of his phrases. "Can this be really nothing but a family of peasants?" I kept saying to myself. "How elegant they are, how vivacious, how dignified, compared with our thick, stolid Normandy farmers!" At the end of supper, I got up to go; but my hosts would not hear of it. The mother had already gone off to make arrangements: the eldest son would sleep with one of his brothers; I should have his room and his bed, which she spread with clean coarse sheets smelling deliciously of lavender. With them, they said, it was early to bed and early to rise; but I was welcome to sit up and read, if I wished to.

"But," said the old man, "you will allow us to follow our usual custom—which will not astonish you, as you are Monsieur Tancrède's grandson."

Then he fetched down the big Bible I had noticed and put it on the table, which had been cleared. His daughter and grandchildren sat down again on either side of him at the table in an attitude of devotion that came naturally to them. The grandfather opened the Holy Book and read a chapter of the Gospels, and then a psalm, in a solemn voice; after which they all, the old man excepted, knelt down in front of their chairs. He, I saw, remained standing, with his eyes shut and his hands laid on the closed book. He uttered a short prayer of thanksgiving, very dignified, very simple, without petitions, in which, I remember, he thanked God for having led me to his door, and in such a tone that my whole heart joined in his words. To close, he said the Lord's Prayer; then there was a moment's silence, after which each of the children rose. It was all so noble and so calm, and the kiss of peace he put on the forehead of each so sublime, that I too went up with the others, and, in my turn, offered my forehead.

Those of my grandfather's generation still kept alive the memory of the persecutions that had hammered down their ancestors, or at any rate a certain tradition of resistance. A tremendous internal stiffness had resulted from the attempt to bend them. Each one of them clearly heard Christ's words addressed to him and to the whole little tormented flock: "Ye are the salt of the earth: but if the salt have lost his savour wherewith shall it be salted?" . . .

And it must be acknowledged that the Protestant service in the little chapel of Uzès still kept a particularly salty flavor in the days of my childhood. Yes, it fell to my lot to see the last representatives of that generation of men who addressed God as *"Tu,"* attending divine service with their great felt hats on their heads, hats which they kept on through the whole pious ceremony, only raising them each time the pastor pronounced the name of God, only taking them off for the recitation of the Lord's Prayer . . . A stranger would have been shocked at what looked like irreverence, if he had not known that these old Huguenots kept their heads covered thus in memory of the open-air services, held under a burning sky in the secret recesses of the *garrigue,* at a time when to worship God according to their faith meant to run the risk, if one was captured, of capital punishment.

. . . I was passionately fond of the country round Uzès, of the valley of the Fontaine d'Eure, and above all of the *garrigue.* In the first years, our maid Marie came with me on my walks. I used to drag her up "Mont Sarbonnet," a little limestone mound just outside the town, where I had great fun looking for caterpillars. The hawk-moth caterpillar, which looks like an untwisted turban and has a kind of horn on its hinder part, was to be found on the great milky-juiced euphorbias; and there were other caterpillars of the swallowtail variety, which lived on the fennel in the shadow of the pines, and which, if one teased them, reared up from the backs of their necks a kind of forked trunk with a strong smell and an astonishing color. If you followed the road that goes round the Sarbonnet, you reached the green meadows watered by the Fontaine d'Eure. The wettest of these meadows were enameled in springtime with the graceful white narcissus known as "the poet's narcissus" and called by the people of those parts the *courbadonne.* The inhabitants of Uzès never dreamed of picking them, and would not even turn out of their way to look at them; so that there was always an extraordinary profusion of them in these solitary meadows; the air was perfumed with their scent for a long way round; some of them stooped their faces over the water, as in the legend I had been taught, and those I would not pick; others grew half-hidden in the thick grass; but as a rule each flower, erect on its stalk, shone like a star against the dark background of the grass. Marie, like the good Swiss girl she was, loved flowers; we used to carry them home in armfuls.

The Fontaine d'Eure is that constant river the Romans captured and brought as far as Nîmes by the famous aqueduct of the Pont du Gard. The valley through which it winds, half-hidden by alders, closes in as it approaches Uzès. O little town of Uzès! if you were in Umbria, how the tourists would rush down from Paris to see you! Uzès lies on the edge of a rock, whose steep slopes are partly covered with the thick woods of the Duchy gardens; the big trees that grow at the bottom shelter the river crayfish in their tangled roots. From the terraces of the promenade or public gardens, one can look across the tall nettle trees of the Duchy and see facing one, on the other side, a still steeper and more rugged rock, riddled with caves, arches, needles, and escarpments, like those one sees in sea-shore cliffs; then, above them, the harsh, hoarse *garrigue,* laid waste by the sun.

Marie, who was constantly complaining of her corns, showed very little enthusiasm for the rugged paths of the *garrigue;* but the time came when my mother let me go out by myself and then I could climb the rocks to my heart's content.

After walking for some time along the edge of the rock, where it was worn smooth by footsteps, and climbing down the steps that had been cut in its face, you crossed the river at the *Fon di biau* (I do not know whether I have spelled this name correctly; in Mistral's language it means *Oxen fount*). It was a fine sight to see the washerwomen slowly planting their bare feet on the steps, as they came home from work in the evening, walking arrow straight, their gait ennobled by the load of white linen which they bore, antique fashion, on their heads. And as *Fontaine d'Eure* was the name of the river itself, I cannot be quite sure that the words *fon di biau* actually designated a fountain: I remember a water-mill, which was also a farm, shaded by immense plane trees; between the stream and the mill-race lay a sort of little island in which the farmyard poultry ran and scratched about. I used to go and dream or read at the extreme point of this little island; perched on the trunk of an old willow and hidden by its branches, I watched the adventurous games of the ducks and was deafened deliciously by the purring of the mill, the clatter of the water in the wheel, the myriad whispers and chatter of the river, while from farther away, where the washerwomen were washing, came the rhythmic slapping of their bats.

But much more often, I would cut the *Fon di biau* and run straight for the *garrigue,* already drawn to it by that strange love of the inhuman and the arid which for so long made me prefer the desert to the oasis. The great dry, perfumed gusts of wind, the blinding reverberation of the sun on the bare rock, were as intoxicating as wine. And how much I enjoyed climbing the rocks; hunting for the praying mantis (the people there call it the *prega-Diou*), whose conglutinated little packets of eggs were such a puzzle to me when I found them hanging on some little twig or blade of grass; or lifting up the stones to discover the horrible scorpions, centipedes, and millipedes that crawled underneath them.

. . . at that time I was not in the least inclined to be skeptical, and besides was utterly ignorant of, even incurious about the works of the flesh.

At the Musée du Luxembourg, it is true, where Marie sometimes took me (I imagine my parents had taken me there for the first time themselves, with the desire of cultivating my taste for lines and colors), I cared much less for the historical paintings, despite the great pains Marie took to explain them (or perhaps because of that), than for pictures of nudes—to the great scandal of Marie, who proceeded to inform my mother of the fact; and I was still more attracted by statues. The sight of Idrac's *Mercury* (if I am not mistaken) threw me into a stupor of admiration, out of which Marie had the greatest difficulty in arousing me. But it was not images such as these that induced sensual pleasure, any more than pleasure evoked such images. Between the one and the other there existed no connection. Sexual excitement was caused by quite different things: most often by a profusion of colors or of unusually shrill sweet sounds; or sometimes by the idea of some urgent and important act which I was supposed to perform, which was expected of me, but which I did not perform, and instead of performing only imagined; or by the closely related idea of destruction, which took the shape of spoiling some favorite toy: beyond that, there was no real desire, no attempt at contact. And anyone who finds this surprising can know very little about the matter: without examples and without object, what would become of sensual pleasure? In a random sort of way, it can order up from the realm of daydreams extravagant wastes of life, silly luxuries, absurd prodigalities. . . . But to demonstrate to what lengths a child's instincts may go astray, I will mention in particular two of my sources of physical enjoyment: one was furnished me very innocently by George Sand in her charming story *Gribouille*. Gribouille throws himself into the water one day when it is raining very hard, not to avoid the rain, as his wicked brothers try to make him think, but to avoid his brothers, who are laughing at him. Once in the river, he struggles for some time and tries to swim; then he lets himself go; and as soon as he lets himself go, he floats; then he feels himself becoming tiny, light, odd, vegetable; leaves sprout out of him all over his body; and soon the river is able to set gently down on its bank the slender, graceful sprig of oak which our friend Gribouille has become. Absurd, isn't it? But that is my very reason for telling it; I say what is true and not what I think may redound to my credit. No doubt "the grandmother of Nohant" had not the slightest intention of writing anything demoralizing; but I bear witness that no schoolboy was ever troubled by any page of *Aphrodite* so much as I— ignorant little boy that I was—by the vegetable metamorphosis of Gribouille.

There was also, in a stupid little play of Madame de Ségur's called

Les Diners de Mademoiselle Justine, a passage in which the servants take advantage of their masters' absence to have themselves a feast; they ransack all the cupboards; they gorge themselves with food; then suddenly, as Justine is stooping to lift a pile of plates out of the cupboard, the coachman steals up behind her and puts his arms round her waist; Justine is ticklish and drops the pile. Crash! All of the crockery is smashed to pieces. This disaster made me swoon with delight. . . .

. . . I seem to see already the dawning of a shameful taste for indecency, stupidity, and the worst vulgarity. No, I am not too severe on myself. I shall soon show that there were elements in my character which, unperceived as yet, would eventually incline me to virtue. In the meantime my mind was still desperately shut up. In vain I search the past for some glimmer of promise in the obtuse lad I then was. Outside me, inside me, nothing but dark shadows. . . .

My parents had sent me, as I have said, to the Ecole Alsacienne. I was eight years old. I was not put into the tenth class, in which the smallest children were taught their rudiments by Monsieur Grisier, but into the one above, under Monsieur Vedel, a worthy round little man from the South of France, upon whose brow rose an unexpectedly romantic crest of black hair, contrasting strangely with the colorless placidity of the rest of his person. A few weeks, or a few days, before the incident I am going to relate, my father had taken me to be introduced to the principal. As the term had already begun and I was a latecomer, the boys whispered, as they stood aside to let us pass through the playground, "A new boy! A new boy!" while I clung nervously to my father's side. Then I took my place among the others, though, for reasons I shall soon be obliged to tell, I was to see them for only a short time. On that particular day, Monsieur Vedel was teaching his class that there are sometimes several words in a language to denote the same object and that then they are called synonyms. And he gave us an example: the word *coudrier* and the word *noisetier,* both of which mean *nut tree.* Then, in order to vary and enliven the lesson a little, he passed, as was customary, from teaching to questioning, and asked the new boy Gide to repeat what he had just said. . . .

I did not answer. I did not know how to answer. But Monsieur Vedel was kind; with all the patience of a good teacher, he repeated his definition and gave the same example; but when he asked me again to repeat after him the synonym for *coudrier,* again I held my tongue. Then, for form's sake, he grew a little angry and asked me to go outside into the

playground and repeat twenty times running that *coudrier* was the synonym of *noisetier;* then to come back and say it to him.

My stupidity had sent the whole class into hysterics. If I had wanted
to make a name for myself, it would have been very easy, when Monsieur
Vedel called me back after my penance and asked me for the third time
the synonym of *coudrier,* to have answered "cauliflower" or "pumpkin."
But no; I was not looking for celebrity and I disliked being laughed at; I
was simply stupid. Perhaps I had taken it into my head to be obstinate?
No, not even that; I really think I did not understand what was wanted of
me, what I was expected to do.

As penances were not customary in this school, Monsieur Vedel had
to content himself with giving me a "zero for conduct." The punishment,
however, was none the less rigorous for being purely moral. But it had not
the smallest effect on me. Every week regularly I had my zero for "behavior and conduct," or for "order and cleanliness"; sometimes both. It was a
dead certainty. Needless to add, I was among the lowest in the class. I
repeat, I was still asleep; I was exactly like someone who had not yet been
born.

A little later I was sent away from school for quite different reasons,
which I must now pluck up the courage to tell.

It was clearly understood that I was only to be sent away from school
temporarily. Monsieur Brunig, the head of the lower school, gave me
three months to get cured of "the bad habits" Monsieur Vedel had discovered—easily enough, for I took no great pains to hide them, not having
grasped how reprehensible they were; for I was still living (if one can call
it living) in the half-awakened state of imbecility I have described.

My parents had had a dinner-party the evening before; I had stuffed
my pockets with the sweetmeats that had been left over from dessert; and
that morning, while Monsieur Vedel was exerting himself at his desk, I
sat on my bench, enjoying alternately my pleasure and my pralines.

Suddenly I heard myself summoned.

"Gide! You look very red! Come here and speak to me a minute."

My face became redder still, as I went up the four steps to the desk
and my schoolmates tittered.

I did not attempt to deny it. At the first question Monsieur Vedel put
me in a whisper, as he bent down toward me, I nodded my acquiescence;
then I went back to my seat more dead than alive. Nevertheless it did not
occur to me to think that this interrogation would have any consequences;

before putting his question, had not Monsieur Vedel promised to say nothing about it?

Which did not prevent my father's receiving a letter that very evening from the vice-principal, asking him not to send me back to school for three months.

The Ecole Alsacienne had a reputation for good conduct and high morals; it was their specialty. Monsieur Brunig's decision on this occasion therefore was not in the least surprising. My mother told me later, however, that my father had been furious at his letter and at the abruptness of the punishment. He concealed his anger from me of course, though he showed me his distress. After serious consultations with my mother, it was decided to take me to the doctor's.

My parents' doctor at that time was no less a person than Dr. Brouardel, who shortly after acquired considerable celebrity as an expert in legal medicine. I think my mother did not expect much more from this consultation than a moral effect and perhaps a little good advice into the bargain. After she had talked with Brouardel a few minutes alone, he called me into his consulting room as my mother was coming out.

"I know all about it, my boy," he said, putting on a gruff voice, "and there's no need to examine or question you today. But if your mother finds it necessary to bring you here again, that is, if you don't learn to behave, well then—" (and here his voice became truly terrible) *"those* are the instruments we should have to use; the instruments with which one operates on little boys like you!" And he stared at me, rolling his eyes under darkly knit brows, as he pointed out a panoply of Tuareg spearheads hanging on the wall behind his chair.

The invention was too obvious for me to take his threat seriously. But my mother's obvious anxiety, together with her admonishments, and my father's silent chagrin at last penetrated my torpor, which had already been considerably shaken by my dismissal from school. My mother extracted promises from me; she and Anna went to great lengths to provide me with distractions. The Great Universal Exhibition was on the point of opening and we often used to walk as far as the board fence around the grounds to watch the preparations. . . .

Three months later, I took my place again on the school benches; I was cured—at any rate as much as one ever is. But not long after, an attack of measles left me in tolerably weak health, and my parents decided to remove me from school again until the following year; I should then be able to start from the beginning once more, in the same class of which I had missed so much the year before. They carried me off to La Roque without waiting for the vacation to begin.

When in 1900 I was induced to sell La Roque, I stifled my regrets in a fit of bravado and confidence in the future, shored up by a pointless and rather theoretical hatred of the past (futurism, it would be called nowadays). In reality, my regrets were much less poignant at the time than they afterwards became. Not that the place owes any of its beauty to memory; when, having traveled somewhat more, I had the occasion to see it again in later years, I was better able to appreciate the enveloping charm of that little valley, which in those days of swelling hopes and excessive desires impressed me chiefly with its narrowness.

And skies too little over trees too big,

as Jammes says in one of the *Elégies* which he wrote there.

It is this valley and our house that I have described in *L'Immoraliste*. That countryside furnished me, though, with more than just the scenic background for the book; throughout its pages I have endeavored to trace a deeper resemblance.

It may have been after the vacation that followed my suspension from school that my cousin Albert Démarest, who was twenty years older than I, first began to take notice of me. What can he have seen in me to attract his sympathy? I don't know; but no doubt I was all the more grateful for his attention because I felt how little I deserved it. And I immediately set about trying to deserve it a little more. Sympathy may awaken many dormant qualities; I have often convinced myself that the worst scoundrels must be those who received neither kindness nor affection in their youth. It is no doubt strange that my parents' encouragement did not suffice; but the fact is I very soon became more sensitive to Albert's approval or disapproval than to theirs.

I distinctly remember one autumn evening when he took me aside after dinner, in a corner of my father's study, while my parents were playing bezique with my Aunt Démarest and Anna. He began by saying in a low voice that he could not see that I had any interest in life beyond myself; that that was the mark of an egoist; and that I gave him every impression of being one.

There was nothing of the censor about Albert. He seemed an open-minded, whimsical creature, full of humor and gaiety; there was nothing hostile in his reproof; on the contrary, I felt that if it was sharp, that was because he liked me; that was what drove it home. No one had ever spoken to me in that way before; Albert's words, without a doubt, sank into me more deeply than he ever suspected, or than I myself realized till later. What I generally like least in a friend is indulgence; Albert was not indulgent. If need be, he could provide one with arms against oneself. And though I was not exactly aware of it, that was what I was looking·for.

The winter was severe and long that year. My mother had the bright idea of making me learn to skate. Jules and Julien Jardinier, the sons of a colleague of my father's (the younger was one of my classmates), were learning with me; it was a race to see who would learn first, and we were soon quite at home on the ice. I was passionately fond of this sport, which we used to practice first on the pool in the Luxembourg Gardens, and then on the pond of Villebon in the Meudon woods or on the great Versailles canal. The snow fell so abundantly, and there was so much ice on top of it that I remember being able to start from the rue de Tournon and go all the way to the Ecole Alsacienne—which was in the rue d'Assas, that is at the other end of the Luxembourg—without once taking off my skates; and nothing could have been more agreeable (and more strange) than to glide thus silently down the paths of the big garden between two high banks of snow. There has never been another winter like it since.

There was one boy for whom I had conceived an absolute passion. He was a Russian. I must look up his name some day in the school records. I wonder what became of him! He was of delicate health, extraordinarily pale; he had rather long, very blond hair and very blue eyes; his voice was musical, and his slight accent gave it a singing quality. A kind of poetry emanated from his whole person; it came, I think, from the fact that he felt weak and wanted someone to love him. The other boys had little use for him, and he rarely took part in their games; as for me, one glance from him made me feel ashamed of playing with the others; I remember certain recess periods in which I suddenly caught his eye and then and there left the game to join him. The others made fun of me for it. I longed for someone to attack him, so that I might fly to his defense. During the drawing lessons, when we were allowed to talk a little in a whisper, we sat beside each other; he told me that his father was a very famous man, a great scholar; I did not dare question him about his mother or ask him how he came to be in Paris. One fine day he stopped coming to school and no one was able to tell me whether he had fallen ill or had gone back to Russia; some kind of shyness or shame prevented me from asking the teachers, who might perhaps have given me news of him; and I shut away in my secret heart one of the first and deepest griefs of my life.

. . . At the mid-Lenten holiday every year, the Gymnase Pascaud used to give a ball for its clients' children—a costume ball. As soon as I saw my mother was going to let me go, as soon as I began to look forward to this party, the idea of having to go in costume put me in an absolute state. I try to explain to myself today the reason for this delirium. Is it possible that one can find such ecstasy in the mere prospect of disguise, of depersonalization? At that age, already? No: the pleasure consisted rather in being dressed in bright colors, in being brilliant, in being quaint, in pretending to be something other than oneself. . . . My joy was suddenly and terribly chilled, however, when I heard Madame Jardinier declare that as for Julien, he should go as a pastry-cook.

"The important thing for the children," she explained to my mother (and my mother at once agreed), "is that they should dress up, isn't it? It matters very little what as."

From that moment I knew what was in store for me; for the two ladies, after consulting a catalogue from *La Belle Jardinière,* discovered that the pastry-cook's costume—which was at the very bottom of the list that was headed by "the little marquis," and went on decrescendo to the "cuirassier," "Punch," the "Zouave," and the *"lazzarone"*—the pastry-cook's, I repeat, cost "next to nothing."

With my calico apron, my calico sleeves, and my square calico cap, I looked more like a pocket-handkerchief than anything else. I looked so glum, in fact, that *maman* kindly allowed me to take one of the kitchen saucepans—a real copper saucepan—and slipped a wooden spoon into my belt, with the idea that these accessories might enliven the insipidity of my prosaic costume. And finally, she filled the pocket of my apron with *croquignoles,* "so that you can offer them to the children."

As soon as I entered the ballroom, I saw at a glance that there were at least a score of "little pastry-cooks"—in fact a regular school of them. The saucepan was too big and got terribly in my way; and to complete my confusion, I suddenly fell in love—yes, positively in love!—with a small boy a little older than myself, who has left me a dazzling recollection of his slimness, his grace, and his volubility.

He was dressed as an imp or a clown, that is, his slender, graceful figure was perfectly molded in black tights covered with steel spangles. As people crowded round to look at him, he leaped and capered and spun a thousand turns, as if success and pleasure had gone to his head; he looked like a sylph; I could not take my eyes off him. I longed to make him look at me, and at the same time I feared he might, because of my ridiculous costume; I felt ugly and wretched. He stopped to take breath between two pirouettes, went up to a lady who must have been his mother, and asked her for a handkerchief, with which he proceeded to mop his forehead—for he was dripping with perspiration—after having first undone the black band with which his two little kid's horns were fastened to his forehead. I went up to him and awkwardly offered him some of my biscuits. He said, "Thank you," took one carelessly, and at once turned on his heel. I left the ball soon after with a broken heart, and when I got home, I had such a fit of despair that my mother promised to let me go the next year as a "Neapolitan *lazzarone.*" Yes, I thought, that costume would suit me, at least; perhaps the little clown would think so too . . . So I went to the next ball as a *"lazzarone"*—but the little clown was not there.

We had spent part of September in the neighborhood of Nîmes, in a place belonging to my Uncle Charles Gide's father-in-law. (My uncle had recently married.) From this place my father returned with an ailment which was attributed to eating figs. In reality it was intestinal tuberculosis, and my mother, I think, was aware of it; but tuberculosis in those days was an illness which people hoped to cure by ignoring. The disease, however, had no doubt already advanced too far for my father to have had any chance of getting over it. He passed away quietly on October 28 that year (1880).

I have no recollection of seeing him dead: but I remember seeing him in bed, the bed he was never to leave, a few days before the end. A big book lay on the sheet before him; it was open but lay face downwards, so that I could only see its brown leather back. My father must have just laid it down there the minute I came in. My mother told me afterwards it was a Plato.

I was at Vedel's. Someone—I cannot remember who—came to fetch me—Anna perhaps. On the way home the news was broken to me. But my grief did not burst out till I saw my mother dressed in deep mourning. She was not crying; she controlled herself in my presence; but I felt she had been crying a great deal. I sobbed in her arms. She was afraid the nervous shock might be too strong for me and tried to get me to take a little tea. I was sitting on her lap; she held the cup and gave me a spoonful at a time, and I remember that she said, as she forced herself to smile: "Come now! Let's see whether this one won't get there safely!"

And I suddenly felt myself completely enwrapped in her love; from that moment on it was to confine itself to me alone.

As for the loss I had suffered, how was I to comprehend it? I would speak of grief if I could, but unfortunately what I was most aware of was a certain prestige my bereavement gave me in my schoolfellows' eyes. Imagine! Each of them wrote to me, just as each of his colleagues had written to my father when he was decorated! Then I learned that my cousins were going to come! My mother had decided I was not to attend the funeral; while my uncles and aunts followed the hearse with *maman*, Emmanuèle and Suzanne* were to stay at home and keep me company. The happiness of seeing them almost, perhaps entirely, got the better of my grief. The time has come for me to speak of them.

Emmanuèle was two years older than I, Suzanne just a bit older; Louise† came soon after. As for Edouard and Georges, who were called the "boys" in one word, as if to dispose of them both as shortly as possible, they still seemed to us at that time practically negligible—barely out of their cradles. Emmanuèle was too quiet for my taste. As soon as our games became "rough" or even noisy, she would have no more to do with them. She went off by herself with a book—like a deserter, we thought; and after that no appeal succeeded in reaching her; the outside world ceased to exist for her; she lost the notion of where she was to such an extent that she would sometimes fall off her chair. She never quarreled; it was so natural for her to give up her turn or her place or her share, and always with such a smiling grace, that one wondered whether she did not do it more because she wanted to than because she thought it right, and whether to have acted otherwise would not have cost her the greater effort.

My uncle and aunt lived with their five children on the rue de Lecat. It was one of those dreary provincial streets without shops or any kind of animation, without character or charm; before reaching the quay (more

* Actually Madeleine (later Mme André Gide) and Jeanne.
† Actually Valentine.

dreary still), it ran past the Hôtel-Dieu where Flaubert's parents had lived, and where his brother Achille had practiced as a doctor, like his father before him.

My uncle's house was as commonplace and gloomy as the street. I shall say more of it later on. I saw my cousins, if not more often, at least more willingly, in the rue de Crosne—and more willingly still in the country, where I used to spend a few weeks with them every summer, either when they came to La Roque or when we went to Cuverville, my uncle's country place. At those times we did our lessons together, played together, formed our tastes and our characters together; our lives were interwoven, our plans and wishes all interfused; and when, at the end of each day, our parents separated us to take us off to bed, I used to think in my childish way, "That's all very well now, because unfortunately we are still small; but the time will come when we shall never be separated, even at night."

The garden at Cuverville where I am writing this has changed very little. The circular space surrounded by clipped yews, where we played in our sandpile, is still there; not far off, in the "flower-walk," is the place where our little gardens were laid out; in the shadow of a silver-lime tree is the exercise ground, where Emmanuèle was so timid and Suzanne, on the contrary, so daring; then comes the shady part of the garden—the "dark walk," where my uncle on certain fine evenings used to escape after dinner; on other evenings he would read aloud to us from some interminable novel of Walter Scott's.

The great cedar in front of the house had grown enormous; we used to spend hours perched in its branches; each one of us had fixed up a room of his own there, and we paid each other visits; sometimes, from high up in the branches, we fished with hooks or slip-knots; Suzanne and I used to climb up to the tiptop and call out to the people of the lower regions: "The sea! We can see the sea!" And indeed, when the weather was clear, one could catch a glimpse of the narrow silver line it made fifteen kilometers away.

No, nothing of all this has changed, and I can still easily recognize in the depths of my being the little child I then was. But we are not concerned now to go so far back; when Emmanuèle and Suzanne came to stay with me in Paris at the time of my father's death, the games of early childhood were already beginning to yield to other amusements.

My mother let herself be persuaded by her family to spend the first period of her mourning at Rouen. She did not have the heart to leave me at Monsieur Vedel's; and this was how I started on that irregular and unsystematic mode of life, that constantly interrupted education which I came to find only too much to my taste.

I doubt whether books, music, or painting ever afforded me pleasures as constant or as keen in later life as the play of living matter provided me with in those early days. I had succeeded in getting Suzanne to share my passion for entomology; at any rate she would follow me on my hunting expeditions, and was not too much disgusted at turning up bits of dung and carrion in our search for dung-beetles, burying-beetles, and devil's coach-horses. It seems reasonable to believe that my family ended by having some respect for my zeal, for, child as I then was, it was to me that the great insect collection of the late Félix-Archimède Pouchet, a first cousin of my grandmother's, was handed over. The old scientist, an obstinate theoretician, had had his hour of celebrity when he sustained the venture-some theory of *heterogenesis,* or spontaneous generation, in opposition to Pasteur. Moreover, it is not everyone who can boast a cousin called Archimède. How I wish I had known him! I shall mention later on my relations with his son Georges, who was professor at the Natural History Museum.

This gift of twenty-four cork-lined boxes full of beetles, all classified, arranged, and labeled—certainly it was flattering to have been considered worthy of it; but I cannot remember that it gave me any very enormous pleasure. My own poor little collection seemed humiliated alongside this treasure; and how much more precious to *me* was each of the insects I had captured and pinned down myself. It was not collecting I enjoyed—it was hunting.

I dreamed of those happy corners of France, haunts of the capricorn and the stag-beetle—the biggest of all our European coleoptera—though not to be found at La Roque. But I did discover a colony of rhinoceros beetles (*oryctes nasicornes*) at the foot of an ancient heap of sawdust alongside the sawmill at Val-Richer. These handsome insects of varnished mahogany are almost as big as stag-beetles and carry between their eyes the turned-up horn to which they owe their name. I was wild with joy when I saw them for the first time.

By digging into the sawdust, one found their larvæ as well—enormous white maggots, like *turcs* or cockchafer grubs. One found, too, strange chains or packets of soft, whitish eggs as big as damson plums, all sticking together; I was greatly captivated by these at first; it was impossible to break these eggs, which had, properly speaking, no real shell; it was even rather difficult to tear open their soft parchment-like skin, but when one did—wonder of wonders!—out slipped a slender grass-snake!

I brought back a quantity of *oryctes* larvæ with me to La Roque and kept them in a box full of sawdust; but they always died before reaching the chrysalis stage: the reason, I think, being that they need to burrow deep into the earth before they can effect their metamorphosis.

The following winter my mother took me south to Montpellier—it is really astonishing that such a piecemeal education should have had any good results at all. . . .

My class there, and indeed the whole school, was divided into two factions: there was the Catholic party and the Protestant party. When I had first gone to the Ecole Alsacienne, I had learned that I was a Protestant; at the very first recess, the boys had crowded round me and asked: "You, then: what are you? Catholic or Protestant?"

Hearing these queer words for the first time, I was perfectly dumbfounded—for my parents had taken good care not to let me know that the faith of all French people might not be the same as mine, and the *entente* that reigned between my relations in Rouen blinded me to their differences of religious belief. So I replied that I had not the least idea what they were talking about. An obliging schoolfellow took it upon himself to explain: "Catholics are people who believe in the Holy Virgin."

Upon which I exclaimed that in that case I must certainly be a Protestant. By some miracle there were no Jews among us, but a little whippersnapper, who had not spoken before, suddenly announced:

"*My* father is an atheist." This was said with such a superior air that the rest of us were left perplexed.

I memorized the word to ask my mother what it meant.

"What does *atheist* mean?" I asked.

"It means a horrid, foolish man."

This failing to satisfy me, I questioned her again; I insisted; at last *maman* grew tired of it, and cut short my insistence, as she often did, with a "There's no need for you to understand that just yet" or "You will understand all that later on." (She had a wide choice of such answers, all of which drove me wild.)

Does it seem curious that little tykes of ten or twelve should already be concerning themselves with such matters? I think not. It reveals nothing, after all, but that innate need of all Frenchmen, of whatever age or class of society, to take sides, to belong to a party.

A little later, driving one day in the Bois de Boulogne with Lionel de R. and Octave Join-Lambert, a cousin of mine, in whose parents' carriage we were riding, I got hauled over the coals by the other two boys. They had asked me whether I was a royalist or a republican and I had answered: "Why, a republican, of course," not understanding then how one could be anything else, since we were living in a republic. Lionel and Octave had thereupon pounced on me and pummeled me with all their might. As soon as I got home, I asked all naïvely: "Wasn't that the right thing to say?"

"My boy," said my mother, after pausing to reflect a moment, "when you are asked what you are in future, say that you are for proper constitutional representation. Will you remember?"

She made me repeat these astonishing words.

"But . . . what does it mean?"

"Why, that's just it, my darling—the others won't understand any more than you do, and then they'll leave you alone."

At Montpellier, the question of belief was not important; but as the Catholic aristocracy sent their children to Jesuit schools, the only boys left for the lycée were Protestants (nearly all of whom were on very close terms), and little plebeians, who were often highly unpleasant and very obviously filled with feelings of hatred for us.

The Ecole Alsacienne had improved on the ordinary lycée regime; but some of their improvements, excellent as they were, turned out to my disadvantage. I had been taught to recite poetry more or less decently, which was also my own natural inclination; but at the lycée (at any rate at the Montpellier lycée), the custom was to recite verse or prose alike as fast as possible in one flat monotone, which robbed the text not only of all attractiveness, but also of all meaning, so that nothing was left of it to explain why one had been at such pains to learn it. Nothing more frightful or more grotesque can be imagined; however well one knew the text, it was impossible to recognize a word of it; one could not even be sure one was hearing French. When my turn came to recite (I wish I could remember what), I felt at once that, even with the best will in the world, I should never be able to force myself into their dreadful manner; it really went too much against the grain. So I recited as I should have recited at home.

At the first line there was general stupefaction—the kind of stupefaction that is created by a real scandal; then this gave way to an immense roar of general laughter. From one end of the ascending rows of desks to the other, from top to bottom of the room, the whole class rocked with laughter; every boy laughed as he seldom has a chance to laugh at school; it was no longer mere mockery; so hearty and so irresistible was it, that Monsieur Nadaud himself joined in; at any rate, he smiled, and his smile seemed to give permission for a laughter more uncontrolled than ever. The teacher's smile assured my condemnation; I do not know how I had the constancy to persevere to the end of my piece, which—thank God!—I knew by heart. Then to my astonishment and to the utter amazement of the class, after the laughter had finally subsided, we heard the very calm, even august, voice of Monsieur Nadaud, announcing: "Gide, ten." (This was the highest mark possible.) "That makes you laugh, gentlemen? Well, let me tell you, that is how you ought all to be reciting."

I was finished. This compliment, by setting me apart from my companions, had the certain result of setting them all against me. Fellow pupils do not easily forgive sudden favors, and if Monsieur Nadaud had deliberately wished to crush me, he could not have found a better way. Was it not enough that they should think me affected and my recitation ridiculous? The finishing stroke came when they learned that I was taking private lessons with Monsieur Nadaud. . . .

This recitation of mine with its stupid success, and the reputation it gave me of being a *poseur,* unchained the hostility of my classmates; the boys who had at first been my friends dropped me; the others grew bolder when they saw that I had no one to back me. I was jeered at, beaten, hunted. The torture began as soon as school was out; no, not immediately, for my former friends would still not have allowed me to be bullied under their very eyes—but round the first turning of the street. How I dreaded the end of school! As soon as I was outside, I slipped off and ran. Fortunately we did not live far off; but my enemies lay in wait along the route; then, for fear of ambushes, I contrived immense detours; as soon as the others realized this, they changed their silent, hidden trap into a running chase; there might still have been some fun in it, except that I felt that what moved them was not so much love of sport as hatred of me— wretched game that I was. The worst was the son of a carnival operator, a boy called Lopez, or Tropez, or Gomez, a great athletic brute, who was considerably older than any of us and who prided himself on always being at the bottom of the class. I can see him now—his horrid expression, his hair plastered down on his forehead, glistening with pomade, his blood-colored necktie; it was he who led the gang, and *he* really wanted my head. Some days I got home in a pitiable state, my clothes torn, full of mud, my nose bleeding, my teeth chattering, haggard. My poor mother was at her wits' end. Then at last I fell seriously ill and my torture came to an end.

The doctor was sent for. I had smallpox. I was saved!

I was well cared for; the malady followed its normal course, and I should soon have been on my feet again. But as my convalescence advanced and the moment drew near when I should have to get back in harness, I felt overwhelmed with anguish, an unspeakable, frightful horror made out of the recollection of my torments. I saw the ferocious Gomez in my dreams; I fled panting from his pack; I felt again the abominable sensation on my cheek of the dead cat which he had picked up one day from the gutter and rubbed against my face while the others held my arms; I used to wake up in a sweat, but only to confront the same terror all over again as I thought of what Dr. Leenhardt had said to my mother— that in a few days I should be well enough to go back to the lycée; and I felt my heart fail within me. But what I am saying is not intended as an excuse for what follows. In the nervous complaint that followed my smallpox, I leave it to the neurologists to disentangle what was real and what was assumed.

This, I think, is how it began. The first day I was allowed to get up, I felt a kind of dizziness which made me totter on my legs, as was only natural after three weeks in bed. If this dizziness were a little worse, thought I to myself, can you imagine what would happen? Yes, of course: I should feel my head fall backwards; my knees would give way (I was in the little passageway that led from my room to my mother's) and I should suddenly fall backwards onto the floor. "Ha!" said I to myself, "suppose I were to imitate what I imagine!" And in the very act of imagining it I could feel what a relief, what a respite it would be to yield to this suggestion of my nerves. One glance behind me to make sure of a place where the fall would not hurt too much and . . .

I heard a cry from the next room. It was Marie; she came running. I knew my mother was out; some remnant of shame or of pity had prevented me from doing it in front of her, but I counted on her being told all about it. After this trial run, at first astonished and then encouraged by my success, I grew bolder, cleverer, and more decidedly inspired; I risked a few other movements; sometimes I invented jerky, abrupt ones; sometimes, on the contrary, they were long drawn out and rhythmically repeated in a kind of dance. I became extremely expert at these dances, and my repertory was soon fairly varied; one consisted in just jumping up and

down in the same spot; for another, I had need of the little space between
the window and my bed; I sprang onto the bed, standing up, at every
return journey—three jumps in all and I made it exactly; sometimes I
kept this up for an hour on end. There was another I performed in bed
with the covers thrown off, consisting of a series of high kicks done in
cadence like those of a Japanese juggler.

Many times since I have been ashamed of myself for this, wondering
how I had the heart to carry on this farce under my mother's eyes. But I
must confess that today that self-reproach seems to me less grounded.
These movements of mine, though perhaps conscious, were very nearly
involuntary. That is to say that at most I might have held them back a
little. But performing them gave me the greatest relief. Ah! how often in
later days, when suffering from my nerves, have I regretted that I was no
longer of an age when an *entrechat* or two . . .

At the first signs of this curious malady, Dr. Leenhardt, who was sent for,
was able to reassure my mother. "Nerves," said he; "nothing but nerves."
But as I went on jigging and prancing all the same, he thought it best to
call in two fellow practitioners to his assistance. The consultation took
place (I cannot remember how or why)* in a room in the Hôtel Nevet.
There were three doctors: Leenhardt, Theulon, and Boissier; the last-
named was the doctor of Lamalou-les-Bains, where it was proposed to send
me. My mother was present but said nothing.

I was a little anxious at the turn my little game had taken. These old
gentlemen (two of them were white-bearded) turned me about in every
direction, sounded me with stethoscopes, and then talked to each other in
whispers. Were they going to see through me? Would one of them—the
severe-looking one, Monsieur Theulon—say: "A good spanking, Madame, that's all this boy wants" . . . ?

No; and the more they examined me, the more convinced they
seemed that my case was genuine. After all, could I be supposed to know
more about myself than these learned gentlemen? It was no doubt *I* who
was deceived . . . in thinking that I was deceiving them.

The consultation is over.

I begin to dress. Theulon is bending down in a fatherly way to help
me; Boissier stops him directly; I see a glance, a wink, pass between him
and Theulon. I am warned. An evil eye, fixed on me, is watching me, and

* On reflection this consultation must, I think, have taken place between my two visits to
Lamalou-les-Bains, which explains how we came to be at the hotel. [A. G.]

intends to keep on watching me while I think myself unobserved, to spy on the movement of my fingers as I rebutton my coat. "If that old boy comes with me to Lamalou, I shall have to look out," I thought to myself, and with apparent innocence, I flung him in a few extra contortions, as my fingers fumbled with the buttonholes.

One person who refused to take my illness seriously was my Uncle Charles, and as I did not know then that he took nobody's illnesses seriously, I was vexed. I was extremely vexed, and determined to overcome his indifference by playing my trump cards. Oh, what a dreadful scene to remember! How much I should like to skip over it, if only I had not resolved to omit nothing!

I am in the anteroom of the Charles Gides' apartment, rue Salle l'Evêque; my uncle has just left his library and I know he will soon be coming back; I slip under a side table, and when I hear him return, wait a few moments first to see whether he is going to notice me of his own accord, for the antechamber is large and my uncle is walking slowly; but he is holding a newspaper and reading as he walks; in another second he will have gone out of the room . . . I move slightly, utter a groan; he stops, lifts his eyeglasses, and, over the top of his newspaper: "Hello!" he says, "What are you doing there?"

Wriggling, writhing, contorted, I sobbed out in a voice I took to be irresistibly pathetic: "Oh! I'm in such pain!"

But I was immediately aware of my fiasco. My uncle put his eyeglasses back onto his nose and his nose back into his paper and went on to his library, the door of which he shut behind him with the utmost unconcern. Oh, the shame! There was nothing for me to do but to get up, dust off my clothes, and start detesting my uncle—which I did with all my heart.

When, after ten months of lying fallow, I was brought back to Paris by my mother and sent to the Ecole Alsacienne once more, I had completely lost the habit of work. I had not been there two weeks before I added headaches to my repertory of nervous troubles, as being more discreet and hence easier to manage in class. As these headaches left me completely from the time I was twenty, and even earlier, I judged them for some time with great severity and accused them of being, if not altogether feigned, at any rate greatly exaggerated. But now that they have begun again, I recognize them, at forty-six, as being exactly what they were like when I was thirteen, and I admit they may very well have discouraged my efforts to work. In truth, I was not lazy; and I applauded wholeheartedly when I heard my Uncle Emile say: "André will always love work."

But he was the same one who called me "André the irregular." The fact is, I found great difficulty in tying myself down; even at that age, my steady hard work was done in short bouts, by repeating over and over an effort I could not prolong. I was often overcome by sudden fits of fatigue, mental fatigue, interruptions of the current, so to speak, which persisted even after the migraines had left me, or, to be more accurate, succeeded the migraines and lasted for days, weeks, months at a time. Independently of all this, I contracted an unspeakable distaste for everything we did in class, for the class itself, for the whole system of lectures and examinations and competitions, even for the recesses; nor could I endure sitting still at my desk, the tedium, the tastelessness, the stagnation of it all. That my headaches arrived very conveniently I have no doubt; but it is impossible for me to say how much I feigned them.

Brouardel, who had originally been our doctor, was now so celebrated that my mother hesitated to call him in, being hindered, I suppose, by the same kind of scruples which I have certainly inherited from her and which paralyze me too in my dealings with people of importance. There was no need to have any such fear regarding Monsieur Lizart, who succeeded him as our family doctor; one could rest assured that he, at any rate, would never be seized by celebrity, for there was nothing in him to catch hold of. A good-natured creature, blond and foolish, with a gentle voice, a kind look, a limp bearing: apparently harmless too—but nothing is more dangerous than a fool. How can I ever forgive him the medicines and treatment he prescribed? The minute I felt (or pretended to feel) my "nerves," he ordered bromides; as soon as I slept badly, chloral. And this for a child's brain, a brain scarcely formed. All my later weaknesses of will or memory I blame on him. If one could take action against the dead, I would sue him. I remember, with rage I remember, that for weeks together there was half a glass of a solution of chloral (the bottle of little crystals was put entirely at my disposal, and I could measure out any dose I fancied)—of chloral, I repeat, placed by my bedside each night, in case of insomnia; that for weeks, for months on end, whenever I sat down to table, I found beside my plate a bottle of "Sirop Laroze—the peel of bitter oranges and bromide of potassium," which I sipped in little gulps. At every meal, I had to take one, two, and then three spoonfuls (not teaspoons but tablespoons) of this mixture, and then start over, in a rhythmical series of threes; and this treatment went on, went on indefinitely, nor was there any reason it should ever stop, until it left the poor naïve patient—such as I was—completely stupefied. Especially as the syrup tasted very good! To this day I cannot understand how I ever managed to recover.

Decidedly the devil was on the watch for me; I was quite surrounded by darkness, inside and out, with no sign of any rift through which a ray of light might one day reach me. It was then that occurred the angelic intervention I am about to describe; and the devil had to fight to keep his hold. The event may seem infinitely slight in itself; but it was as important in my life as are revolutions in the history of empires—the first scene of a drama which is not yet played out.

It must have been a little before the New Year. We were once again at Rouen; not only because it was Christmas vacation, but also because, after a month's trial, I had again left the Ecole Alsacienne. My mother resigned herself to treating me as an invalid, and gave in to the prospect of my learning nothing except by some fluke. Once again, and for a long time, my education was to be interrupted.

I was eating very little, and sleeping badly. My Aunt Lucile was all kindness and attention; in the morning, Adèle or Victor came to light the fire in my room; I used to while away the time in my big bed long after I woke, lazily listening to the great logs as they hissed and spurted their harmless sparks against the firescreen, sinking with a delicious feeling of torpor into the comfort that pervaded the house from top to bottom. I see myself sitting between my mother and aunt in the big, pleasant, stately dining-room, its four corners adorned with white statues of the four seasons; there they stood, decently lascivious after the style of the Restoration, each statue in its niche, on a pedestal that doubled as a sideboard (and in winter was provided with a hot-plate).

Séraphine used to prepare me special little dishes, but I stared at them without appetite.

"You see, my dear," said my mother to my aunt, "all the saints in heaven won't get him to eat."

"Juliette," my aunt would suggest, "do you think he might fancy oysters?"

Then *maman:* "No, no, you're much too kind . . . Well, perhaps, one might try oysters."

Let me clearly certify that I was by no means *trying* to make things difficult. I had no craving for anything. I went to table like one being led to torture. It was with the greatest difficulty that I swallowed two or three bites; in vain my mother begged, scolded, and threatened, and nearly every meal ended in tears. But this is not what I wanted to talk about. . . .

I had met my cousins again at Rouen. I have said how my tastes as a child had drawn me more especially to Suzanne and Louise; but even this is not quite accurate; no doubt I played more with them, but this was because they liked playing with me; I preferred Emmanuèle, and more and more as she grew older. I was growing older too, but it was not the same thing; however serious I tried to be when I was with her, I felt I was still a child; I felt that she was one no longer. The sweetness of her expression had now a tinge of sadness in it which drew and held me all the more because I could not fathom it. And I did not actually know that Emmanuèle was sad; for she never spoke of herself, and her sadness was of a sort that no other child could have guessed at. Already I lived with my cousin in a conscious community of tastes and thoughts which I strove with all my heart to make closer and more perfect. This amused her, I think; for instance, when we dined together at the rue de Crosne, she would make a game of depriving me of the desserts I liked best, by refusing them herself; for she knew very well that I would not touch any dish until she had helped herself first. Does all this sound childish? Alas! There is nothing childish in what follows.

The secrets of a soul are as a rule discovered only very slowly; but this was not the way I was to discover the secret grief that had so precociously matured my dear friend. It was the total and abrupt revelation of an unsuspected world to which my eyes were suddenly opened, like the eyes of the man born blind after the Saviour had touched them.

I had left my cousins toward nightfall to go back to the rue de Crosne, where I thought my mother was expecting me; but I had found the house empty. I hesitated a little and then determined to return to the rue de Lecat; this seemed to me an especially good idea because I knew that no one was expecting me there. I have already denounced my childish mania for filling up any unfamiliar space and time with all sorts of mysterious happenings. I was extremely preoccupied with what went on behind my back, and sometimes felt that if only I could turn round quick enough I should see . . . heaven knows what!

I went then at an unlikely hour to the rue de Lecat, hopeful of surprising. That evening my taste for the clandestine was gratified.

On the very threshold I scented something unusual. Contrary to custom, the porte-cochère was open, so that I did not have to ring. I was slipping in stealthily, when Alice, a detestable female, a servant of my aunt's, suddenly appeared from behind the hall door, where she was apparently lying in wait, and in her most disagreeable voice asked: "You, is it? What are you doing here at this time of day?"

I was evidently not the one she was expecting.

But I made my way in without replying.

My Uncle Emile's office was on the ground floor; it was a dreary little room smelling of cigars where he used to shut himself up half the day, and where, I think, he was much more occupied with his worries than with his business; he used to come out from it looking careworn and aged. He had certainly aged a good deal lately; I don't know whether I should have noticed it by myself, but after I overheard my mother saying to Aunt Lucile one day: "Poor Emile! How he has changed!" I was immediately struck by the painful knitting of his brows and the anxious and sometimes harassed expression of his eyes. My uncle was not at Rouen that day.

The stairway was unlighted, and I went up noiselessly. The children's rooms were at the top of the house; below them, my aunt's room and my uncle's; and on the second floor the living-room and dining-room, which I passed quickly. I meant to make a dash past the third floor too, but the door of my aunt's room was wide open; the room was brightly lighted and the light shone out onto the landing. I only gave one rapid glance and caught sight of my aunt stretched languidly on a sofa; Suzanne and Louise were bending over her and fanning her, and I think giving her salts to smell. I did not see Emmanuèle, or rather, a sort of instinct told me she could not be there. For fear of being seen and stopped, I ran quickly past.

Her sisters' room, which I had first to go through, was dark, or, at any rate, there was nothing to guide me but a dim half-light from the two windows, the curtains of which had not yet been drawn. I reached my cousin's door and knocked gently; as there was no answer, I was going to knock again, when the door yielded, for it had not been closed. In this room it was darker still; the bed was at the farther end; I did not see Emmanuèle by it at first, for she was kneeling. I was going away, thinking the room empty, when she called me: "Why did you come? You should not have come back."

She had not risen. I did not realize at first that she was unhappy. It was when I felt her tears on my cheek that my eyes were suddenly opened.

I have no desire to speak here of the details of her anguish, nor to recount the abominable secret that was its cause; moreover, at that time I was able to understand very little of it. Today I can think of nothing more cruel, for a young girl who is still all purity, love, and tenderness, than to have to judge and condemn her own mother's conduct; and what intensified her torment was that she was obliged to keep to herself, and hide from a father she so venerated, this secret she had discovered by some unhappy chance, and which was now crushing her—a secret which was the talk of the town, which the servants laughed over, and which took advantage of her two sisters' innocence and unconcern. No, of all this I should understand nothing till much later; but I felt that in this little creature, already so dear to me, there dwelt a great, an intolerable distress, a grief that not all my love and all my life would be enough to cure. What more can I say? . . . Till that day, I had been wandering at random; suddenly I had discovered a new star, by which my life was to be guided.

To all appearances nothing was changed. I shall return, as before, to the story of the small events that occupied me; the only change was this: they no longer occupied me completely. I kept hidden away in the depths of my heart the secret of my destiny. Had that destiny been less contradicted, less frustrated, I should not now be writing these memoirs.

. . . It seems to me that I have painted too darkly the shadows in which my childhood lingered on; or rather, that I have failed to speak of two flashes of light, two strange jolts which shook me momentarily out of my torpor. Had I recounted them earlier, in their proper chronological place, it would no doubt have been easier to understand the panic that overcame me that autumn evening in the rue de Lecat when I came into contact with the invisible reality.

The first carries me back far into the past; I wish I could state the exact year, but all I know is that my father was still alive. We were at table; Anna was lunching with us. My parents were sad because they had heard that morning of the death of a child of four, the son of some cousins called Widmer; I had not heard the news, but I gathered it from a word or two my mother said to Nana. I had only seen little Emile Widmer two or three times, and had no particular feeling for him; but I no sooner understood he was dead than an ocean of grief suddenly rolled over my heart. *Maman* took me onto her lap and tried to quiet my sobs; she told me that we must all die; that little Emile had gone to heaven, where there were no more tears or suffering—in short, all the most consoling things a mother's tenderness can think of; nothing was of any use: for it was not exactly the death of my little cousin that I was crying for, but something I could not understand, an indefinable anguish or terror; it was not surprising that I could not explain to my mother, for I am incapable of explaining it any better today. . . .

The second of these tremors was still more peculiar: it was a few years later, a little after my father's death; that is to say, I must have been about eleven. The scene again took place at table, at a morning meal, but this time my mother and I were alone. I had been at school that morning. What had happened? Perhaps nothing. . . . Then why did I suddenly break down, and, sobbing convulsively, fall into *maman's* arms; why did I feel again that indefinable anguish, *exactly* the same as at my little cousin's death? It was as though the special sluice-gate of some unknown, unbounded, interior sea had suddenly been opened and an overwhelming flood poured into my heart. I was not so much unhappy as terrified; but how was I to explain this to my mother, who, through my sobs, could distinguish nothing but these bewildered, despairing words, repeated over and over: "I'm not like other people! I'm not like other people!"

As I have often to speak of my mother, I had hoped that my recollections of her as we went along would give a sufficiently good picture of her, but I fear I have quite inadequately shown what a creature of good will she was (I use this expression in the fullest gospel sense). She was always striving after something good, after something better, and was never content to rest in a state of self-satisfaction. It was not enough for her to be modest; she was continually trying to diminish her imperfections or the imperfections she discovered in others, to correct herself or others, to improve herself. During my father's lifetime, all this had been subordinated to, had been grounded in a great love. Her love for me, no doubt, was scarcely less, but all the submission she had formerly shown my father, she now demanded from me. The conflicts that arose therefrom helped to convince me that I was like no one but my father; the deepest-rooted ancestral resemblances do not show themselves till late in life.

In the meantime, my mother, who was very eager to cultivate herself and me, and full of respect for music, painting, and, generally speaking, for everything that was beyond her, did what she could to enlighten my taste and judgment, and her own. If we went to see an exhibition of paintings—and we never missed one of those *Le Temps* was kind enough to recommend—we always took with us a copy of the paper in which the review had appeared, and read the critic's appreciation on the spot, for fear of admiring the wrong thing or of not admiring at all. As for concerts, the narrowness and timid monotony of the programs of the day left little scope for error; there was nothing to do but to listen, to approve, and to applaud.

Maman took me to the Pasdeloup concerts nearly every Sunday. A little later we bought a season ticket for the Conservatoire concerts, and for two years running we attended them every other Sunday. Some of these concerts made a profound impression on me, and even the music I was not old enough to understand (it was in '79 that *maman* began taking me to them) helped no less to fashion my sensibility. I admired everything, almost indiscriminately, as is right at that age, almost without preference, from an urgent need to admire: the Symphony in C Minor and the "Scotch" Symphony, Mozart's concertos, the whole series of which Ritter (or Risler) played at the Pasdeloup on consecutive Sundays, and Félicien David's *Désert,* which I heard several times, for Pasdeloup and the public had a particular liking for this amiable work, though nowadays it would no doubt be considered old-fashioned and slight; I was charmed with it at the time, just as I was charmed with an Oriental landscape of Tournemine's I had seen when I first went to the Luxembourg with Marie, and which I thought the most beautiful picture in the world; there was a background of crimson and orange sunset sky, reflected in still waters, a herd of elephants or camels stretching out their long necks or trunks to drink, and in the far distance a mosque pointing its long minarets up to the sky.

The following year, I went less often to concerts and more often to plays —the Odéon and the Théâtre-Français; and especially to the Opéra-Comique, where I heard almost the whole of the old-fashioned repertory they were good enough to perform in those days—Grétry, Boieldieu, Hérold; their melodious grace filled me with joy. (I expect it would fill me with deadly boredom today.) No, I have nothing to say against any of these charming composers; it is musical drama—the theater in general that I dislike. Perhaps because I had too much of it in my youth? It all seems so predictable, so conventional, so tiresome and dated. If by some accident I still venture into a theater, unless I have a friend at my side who holds me there, I have the greatest difficulty in waiting till the first intermission, so that I can at least slip away more or less decently. It took the Vieux Colombier a short while ago, with all Copeau's art and fervor, to reconcile me somewhat to the pleasures of the stage. But enough comments: back to my memories.

. . . In the summer of '84, my cousins did not visit us either, or came for only a very short time, so that as I was alone at La Roque I spent a great deal more time with Lionel.* Not content with meeting openly on Sundays, the day on which it was arranged for me to have tea at Blanc-mesnil, we made regular lovers' trysts, to which we hastened furtively with beating hearts and trembling thoughts. We agreed to have a hiding place, which we could use as a post office for our notes; in order to settle the times and places of our meetings, we exchanged odd, mysterious letters in cipher, which could only be read with the help of a key or a grille. The letter was put in a closed box hidden in the moss at the foot of an old apple tree, in a meadow on the edge of the wood midway between our two houses. No doubt there was "a bit of ostentation," as La Fontaine says—although no hypocrisy—in the exaggeration of our feelings for each other; after we had sworn eternal loyalty, I think we would have gone through fire and water to get to each other. Lionel persuaded me that such a solemn pact necessitated a pledge; he broke a cluster of clematis in two, gave me one half and kept the other himself, swearing to wear it as a talisman. I put my half in a little embroidered sachet which I hung round my neck like a scapular and wore next to my heart until my First Communion.

Passionate as our friendship was, there was not the slightest tinge of sensuality in it. Lionel, in the first place, was powerfully ugly; and no doubt I already felt that fundamental incapacity for mixing the spirit with the senses, which is, I believe, somewhat singular with me, and which was soon to become one of the cardinal repulsions of my life. On his side, Lionel, worthy grandson of Guizot, affected the sentiments of one of Cor-neille's heroes. One day when I was going away, I went up to give him a fraternal embrace, but he pushed me away. "No," he said solemnly. "Men never kiss." . . .

On Sunday mornings, Madame de R. read prayers in the living-room, which parents, children, and servants attended. By Lionel's orders, I sat next to him; and during prayers, when we were on our knees, he took my hand and held it tightly in his, as though he were offering our friendship to God.

---

* Actually François de Witt; "Blancmesnil" is Val-Richer, his family's estate near La Roque.

. . . At the beginning of the fall semester that year (1884), I had indeed made another attempt at the Ecole Alsacienne, and had hung on there for a few months; but once again I found myself continually impeded by the most troublesome headaches, and was obliged to revert to the former system—the system, that is, of desultory, indulgent education, with as little pressure applied as possible. Monsieur Richard* was the perfect man for this, being himself of a somewhat desultory disposition. How often a long walk took the place of our lesson. If the sun was shining, it evaporated all our zeal, and "It's a sin to stay up in such fine weather!" we would cry. At first, we merely loitered through the streets, observing, discussing, discoursing; but the following year our walks had an object. For some reason or other, Monsieur Richard again took it into his head to move; the rooms he had were decidedly not to his liking; he had to find something better. . . . So, as much for amusement's sake as anything else, we went round to all the notice boards and visited everything that was marked "To Let."

What countless stairs we climbed, in luxurious apartment houses, in wretched old tenements! Our favorite time for hunting was the morning. It often happened that we came upon the inmates before they had left their lairs, when they were only just out of bed. These voyages of discovery were more instructive to me than the reading of many novels. Our hunting-ground lay round about the Lycée Condorcet and the Gare Saint-Lazare, and in the district known as Europe. I leave to the imagination what kind of game it was we sometimes started. It amused Monsieur Richard too; he took care to go first for decency's sake and sometimes he would turn round and call out suddenly: "Don't come in!" But I had time, nevertheless, to see a good deal, and I came away from some of these domiciliary visits absolutely flabbergasted. For a nature other than mine, this indirect initiation might have offered considerable dangers; but the amusement I took in it never troubled me in the least, and excited nothing but my mind; more than that: it planted in me a kind of disgust for what I had spied of debauchery, against which my instinct was in secret revolt. Some particularly scandalous episode may finally have enlightened Monsieur Richard as to the unsuitability of these visits, for he called an abrupt halt—unless he simply ended by finding a lodging to his taste. In any case, our search came to an end.

---

* Actually Henry Bauer.

There were two other boarders at the Richards' table; one a little older than I, the other one or two years younger. Adrien Giffard, the elder . . . attended lectures at the Lycée Lakanal, and Bernard Tissaudier at the Condorcet. Now it happened that one evening as my mother was reading one of the articles in *Le Temps,* she uttered an exclamation: "I hope," said she, in a questioning tone, "that your friend Tissaudier doesn't go through the Passage du Havre, when he comes out of the lycée?" (Let me say for the sake of the uninformed that this passage is within a few steps of the lycée.)

As I had never inquired into my friend Tissaudier's itinerary, the question remained unanswered.

"You ought to tell him to avoid it," *maman* went on.

Maman's voice was grave, and she wrinkled her brow like the captain of a boat I once saw during a rough crossing between Le Havre and Honfleur.

"Why?"

"Because I see in the paper that the wrong sort of people congregate there."

She said no more, but I was left troubled by these enigmatic words. I understood more or less what she meant by "the wrong sort of people," but as my imagination was unchecked by any notion of laws or customs, I immediately saw the Passage du Havre (I had never been down it) as a place of lechery and abomination, a Gehenna, a battlefield where all decency lay slaughtered. Notwithstanding my excursions through the apartments of *cocottes,* I had remained, for the age of fifteen, astonishingly ignorant of the surroundings of debauchery; nothing I imagined had any foundation in reality; my fanciful pictures were woven of the indecent, the charming, and the horrible alike—especially the horrible, because of the instinctive disgust of which I have just spoken; for instance, I had a vision of my poor Tissaudier being orgiastically torn to pieces by hetairæ. And as I sat thinking of all this at Monsieur Richard's, looking at the big, kindly boy, with his plump rosy cheeks and his calm cheerful simple ways, my heart tied up in knots. We were alone in the room, Adrien Giffard, he, and I, doing our homework. At last I could keep it back no longer, and in a voice choking with emotion, "Bernard," I asked, "when you leave the lycée, you don't go down the Passage du Havre, do you?"

He answered at first neither "yes" nor "no," but replied to my question by another, which was perfectly natural, given my unexpected question. "Why do you ask that?" he said, opening his eyes wide.

Suddenly I felt myself overwhelmed by something enormous, something religious, something frightening—the same feeling that had come upon me at the time of little Emile's death and on the day I had felt myself isolated, set apart. Shaken by sobs, I threw myself on my knees before my schoolmate. "Bernard!" I cried. "Oh, I beg you, don't go there, don't!"

My voice, my vehemence, my tears were those of a madman. Adrien drew back his chair, his eyes starting out of his head. But Bernard Tissaudier, who had been brought up in a puritan family like my own, did not for a moment misunderstand the nature of my emotion.

"Do you suppose then," he said very naturally, and in the tone of voice best suited to calm me, "that I don't know all about the profession?"

I swear those were his very words.

. . . One evening, contrary to my custom, which was to run without stopping from the rue du Bac to my aunt's house, making it a point of pride to get there before the tram, into which I had first seen my mother—one evening, then—a fine spring evening—as my mother had spent the afternoon at her sister's, I started earlier than usual and was walking slowly in order to enjoy the first warm weather of the season. I had almost reached my destination when I noticed the curious appearance of some women in the street; they were not wearing hats and were walking vaguely up and down, as if they were undecided where to go, and just at the very place where I should have to pass. The word *profession* which Tissaudier had used stuck in my memory; I hesitated for a split second: should I not step off the sidewalk to avoid going too near them? But there is something in my nature that nearly always wins out over fear—namely, the fear of being a coward; so I kept on going. All at once, right in front of me, another of these women, whom I had not noticed at first, or who had sprung out from behind a door, came up and stared me full in the face, as she stood barring my way. I had to make an abrupt detour, half-breaking into a tottering run. She had been singing to begin with, but now she left off. "There's no need to be so frightened, my pretty boy!" she exclaimed in a voice at once scolding, mocking, coaxing, and playful.

A wave of blood rushed to my face. I was as affected as if I had escaped with my life.

Many years later, these questing creatures still inspired me with as much terror as vitriol-throwers. My puritan education encouraged to excess a natural reserve in which I could see no harm. I had an absolute lack of curiosity with regard to the opposite sex; if I could have discovered the whole mystery of womankind with a single gesture, it was a gesture I should not have made; I indulged myself in the flattering thought that my disgust was rather disapproval, and that my aversion was the result of virtue. I lived withdrawn and constrained, and made an ideal out of resistance; if I ever gave way, it was to my early vice; I paid no attention whatever to any outside provocation. At that age, moreover, and on those questions, how generously one deceives oneself. On the days when it occurs to me to believe in the devil, as I think of my saintly repulsions, my noble shudderings, I seem to hear the Adversary laughing and rubbing his hands in the shadows. But how could I have foreseen what snares—? but this is not the place to speak of them . . .

. . . At that time I had a passionate predilection for poetry; poetry, I considered, was the flower and fulfillment of life. It took me a long time to recognize—I think it is better not to recognize it too early—the greater excellence of fine prose, and its greater rarity. I confused, as is natural at that age, art with poetry; I abandoned my soul to the alternation of the rhymes and their enforced recurrence; I reveled in feeling them spread out to their full amplitude within me, like the rhythmic beating of two wings which gradually set one flying. . . . And yet the most thrilling discovery I made in my father's glassed-in bookcase, I think, was the poems of Heinrich Heine (I am speaking of the French translation). No doubt the absence of rhyme and meter lent them an added though deceitful allure; for what appealed to me in these poems, besides the charm of their emotion, was a quality that I persuaded myself I should soon be able to imitate.

I can see myself, in this springtime of my sixteenth year, stretched out on the carpet Etruscan-style at the foot of the little opened bookcase; trembling to discover, to feel the riches of spring in my heart awakening and responding to the call of Heinrich Heine. But how can one describe the experience of reading a book? —This is the fatal defect of my story, as indeed of all memoirs; one describes the most apparent; but the things that matter most, the things that have no contours, elude one's grasp. So far I have enjoyed lingering over all these slender facts. But now we are at the time when I was beginning to come to life.

The extreme interest I took in everything from this time forward arose chiefly from the fact that Emmanuèle was everywhere my companion. I never learned anything that I did not want to teach her at once, and my joy was never perfect unless she shared it. In the books I read, I used to write her initials in the margin alongside any sentence that seemed to merit our admiration, our wonder, or our love. Life had no value for me without her, and I dreamed that she would always be with me, as she was on those summer mornings at La Roque when we used to roam the woods together. We left while the house was still sleeping. The grass was heavy with dew; the air was fresh and cool; the rose of dawn had long since faded from the sky, but the slanting sunbeams smiled on us, newborn and enchanting. We went along together hand in hand, or, where the path was too narrow, I a few paces ahead. We stepped lightfooted and silent, for fear of startling god or game, rabbit or squirrel or roe-deer, who frolicked and bathed unafraid at this innocent hour, recreating, as they do every morning, their Garden of Eden before man is awake and the day begins to grow drowsy. Pure and dazzling light, in the hour of death, may the memory of you dispel all darkness! How often in the heat of noon has my soul found refreshment in your dews. . . .

When we were apart, we wrote to each other. A regular correspondence had sprung up between us. . . . A little while ago, I thought I would reread my letters, but their tone is unbearable and I find myself odious in them. I try to persuade myself today that it is only the simpleminded who can be naturally natural. As for me, I had to disengage my line from among a multitude of curves; and even so, I was not as yet conscious of the intricacy of the tangle through which I had to find my way. I felt my pen run up against something and stop, but against what I could not say; and as I was still too clumsy to untie the knots, I simply cut them.

It was about this time that I began to discover the Greeks, who have had such a decisive influence on my mind. Leconte de Lisle's translations had just finished coming out. There was a great deal of talk about them, and my Aunt Lucile (I think) gave them to me. Their sharp edges, their unfamiliar sheen, their exotic sonorities were the very things to enchant me; one was even grateful for their roughness and that slight surface difficulty which kept off the profane, by requiring from the reader an increase of attention and sympathy. Through them I beheld Olympus, and man's suffering, and the smiling severity of the gods; I began to learn mythology; fervently I caught and pressed Beauty to my heart.

. . . I began to read the Bible more thoroughly than I had ever done before. I read the Bible eagerly, greedily, but methodically too. I began at the beginning and read on, but starting in several places at once. Every evening, as I sat with my mother in her room, I read one or more chapters of the historical books, one or more chapters of the poetical, one or more of the prophets. In this way, I soon knew the Scriptures from end to end; then I began again to reread them in parts, more steadily, but still with appetite unquenched. I immersed myself in the text of the Old Covenant with pious veneration, but the emotion I drew from it was no doubt not of a character purely religious, just as that which I drew from the *Iliad* and the *Oresteia* was not purely literary. Or rather art and religion were devoutly wedded within me, and I tasted my most perfect ecstasy there where they most melted into one.

But the Gospels . . . Ah! At last I found the reason, the occupation, the inexhaustible spring of love. The feeling they aroused at once clarified and strengthened the feeling I had for Emmanuèle; the former was no different from the latter; it seemed merely to deepen it and give it its true place in my heart. I fed upon the Bible as a whole only in the evenings; but in the mornings I turned more intimately to the Gospels; and I turned to them again and again in the course of the day. I carried a New Testament in my pocket; it never left me; I took it out every moment, and not only when I was alone, but even when I was in the presence of the very people most likely to ridicule me, and from whose ridicule I had most to fear: in the streetcar, for instance, like a priest reading his breviary, and during recess at the Pension Keller, or later, at the Ecole Alsacienne, offering to God my confusion and my blushes when my schoolfellows jeered. The ceremony of my First Communion made very little difference in my habits; the Eucharist neither brought me any fresh ecstasy nor even perceptibly increased that which I already felt. I was shocked, on the contrary, by the kind of pomp and circumstance with which people enjoyed celebrating the day, and which almost profaned it in my eyes. But as there had certainly been no apathy before the day, so there was no relapse of fervor after it; on the contrary, after my Communion, my fervor continued to increase, and reached its highest point in the following year.

For months on end now, I kept myself in a kind of seraphic state— the state, I suppose, attained by holiness. It was summertime. I had almost entirely given up going to classes, having been allowed as an extraordinary favor to attend only those which I found really profitable, that is to say very few. I drew up a timetable and then followed it strictly, for its very rigor was a source of the greatest satisfaction to me, and keeping to it exactly a source of considerable pride. I rose at dawn and plunged into a tub of icy water which I had taken care to fill the night before; then, before beginning my work, I read a few verses of the Scriptures, or rather I reread those I had marked the evening before as the proper food for the day's meditation; then I prayed. My prayer was like a perceptible motion of the soul toward a deeper penetration into God; and from hour to hour I renewed that motion; such were the breaks in my studies, and I never changed the subject of them without offering it up first to God. Out of self-mortification, I slept on a board; in the middle of the night, I got up again, and again knelt down, not so much for mortification as out of the impatience of my joy. I felt then that I had attained the very summit of happiness.

What more can I add? . . . Ah! would that I could wear out the ardor of this radiant recollection! There is a certain fraudulence in this kind of tale: the most futile and the most meaningless events, all the things that can be put into words perpetually usurp the place of all the rest. What ever can I tell of it here? All that then filled my heart to bursting can be put into three words; it is stupid of me to try to inflate them, to draw them out. A heart too encumbered with radiance, too careless of the shadows that this same radiance was casting on the other side of my flesh. Perhaps, in imitation of the love of God, my love for my cousin was too easily content with absence. The most marked traits of a character are formed and accentuated before one is even aware it has happened. But could I possibly have understood so early the significance of what was taking shape inside me? . . .

. . . My whole heart was taken up by a book—the idea of a book—which entirely absorbed me to the neglect of everything else. This was *André Walter,* which I had already begun to write, and into which I poured all my questionings, all my internal debates, all my troubles and perplexities—and, above all, my love, which was the very pivot of the book and around which I made all the rest gravitate.

This book rose up before me, blocking my view so completely that I could not imagine how I should ever get past it. I could not bring myself to think of it as my first book, but saw it as my *only* book, and could imagine nothing beyond it. I felt that it would consume me utterly, that after it lay death, madness, some kind of dreadful void toward which I was pushing my hero along with me. And soon I could no longer have said which of us was leading the other; for if there was in him nothing that I had not first experienced myself, nothing, so to speak, that I had not tried out first on my own person; on the contrary it was often I who drove my double before me and rashly followed after; it was in *his* madness that I was preparing to sink.

It was really not till a year later that I was able to harness myself to this book; but I got into the habit of keeping a diary, from a desire to give some form to my vague internal agitation; and many pages of this diary were copied straight into the *Cahiers.* The state of constant preoccupation in which I then lived had one serious drawback: all my attentive faculties were absorbed by introspection; I wrote, and wished to write, nothing that was not intimate; I disdained the outside world, and considered "events" as impertinent intruders. Today, when there is perhaps nothing that I admire more than a well-constructed story, I am filled with irritation as I reread those pages; but at that time, far from understanding that art can only live in the particular, I insisted that it should be removed from all contingencies; and as I considered any definition of outline to be contingent, I aspired only after the quintessential.

Since sitting for Albert (he had just finished my portrait) I had become very much taken up with my personal appearance; my concern for appearing exactly as I felt myself to be, as I wanted myself to be—namely, an artist—was so great that it prevented me from having any existence of my own and turned me into what is called a *poseur.* Looking into the mirror of a little bureau at which I worked (it had come to us from Anna, and my mother had had it put into my room), I used to gaze unwearyingly at my own features, study them, train them like an actor, try to catch on my lips and in my eyes the expression of all the passions I longed to feel. Above all things, I wished to make myself loved; I gave my soul in exchange. In those days, I could not write—I had almost said *think*—or so I fancied, apart from that little mirror; in order to become aware of my emotions, of my thoughts even, I must first, I fancied, read them in my eyes. Like Narcissus, I hung over my own image, and all the sentences I wrote at that time remain to this day somewhat deflected by that unnatural attitude.

. . . What a pianist Monsieur de la Nux might have made of me, if only I had gone to him earlier! But my mother shared the prevalent opinion that in the first stages all teachers are equally good. From the very first lesson, Marc de la Nux set out to reform everything I had learned. I was under the impression that I had no musical memory, or very little; I could never learn anything by heart except by repeating it over and over again, constantly referring to the text, lost the minute I took my eyes off it. De la Nux set to work so well that in a few weeks I was able to play several of Bach's fugues without once having to open the book; and I remember my astonishment when I discovered that the one I thought I was playing in C sharp was really written in D flat. His teaching gave everything life and clarity, made everything answer to the demands of harmonic necessity, subtly decomposed and recomposed it all: at last I understood. It must have been with something of the same transport, I imagine, that the Apostles felt the Holy Ghost descend upon them. Until then, it seemed to me, I had done nothing but repeat without understanding them the sounds of some divine language, which now I had suddenly become capable of speaking. Every note now had its own significance, became a word. With what enthusiasm I practiced! I was filled with such zeal that the most discouraging exercises became my favorites. One day, after my lesson, when I had made way for the next pupil, I waited on the landing outside to listen to him; the door was shut, but I could still hear. The boy who had taken my place was probably no older than I, and he was playing the same piece I was studying then—Schumann's great Fantasia—playing it with a vigor, a brilliancy, a certainty which were still far beyond me; and I sat on the stairs a long while, sobbing with jealousy.

Monsieur de la Nux seemed to take the greatest pleasure in teaching me, and his lessons often lasted long after the allotted hour. I did not hear till much later of the proposal he had made to my mother: he had tried to persuade her that it would be worth while my sacrificing the rest of my education (of which, according to him, I had had quite enough) for my music; he begged her to confide me entirely to his direction. My mother had hesitated, had had recourse to Albert's advice, and finally had taken upon herself to refuse, thinking there was something better for me to do in life than interpret other people's works; and she begged Monsieur de la Nux not to mention his proposal to me (it was, I should add, entirely disinterested), so as not to arouse vain hopes and ambitions. It was not till years after that I learned all this from Albert, when it was too late to go back on the decision.

In the course of the four years that I studied under Monsieur de la Nux, a great intimacy grew up between us. Even after he had stopped giving me lessons (to my great regret, I heard him one day declare that he had taught me to do without him, and all my protests could not persuade him to go on with lessons he judged useless from then on), I still continued to visit him diligently. I held him in a kind of veneration, the same respectful, slightly fearful affection which I had a little later for Mallarmé and which I never felt for any but those two. Both the one and the other were in my eyes the personification of saintliness in one of its rarest forms. I looked up to them in the pure ingenuousness of my need for someone to revere.

. . . Monsieur L., whose lectures I had attended at the Lycée Henri IV, agreed to guide me through the labyrinth of metaphysics and to help correct my assignments. He was a small man, short and set—in his mind, that is to say, for his legs were long and thin; his thin, dead voice was enough to chill the most promising thought; but even before he began to express the thought he had seized upon, one felt that he had stripped it of all its bloom and all its branches, and that only in the form of a bare concept could it find any place in a mind as barren as his. His teaching was the quintessence of dullness. It gave me the same feeling of disillusionment I had experienced before with Monsieur Couve's religious instructions. Was *this* the exalted science I had hoped would be the illumination of my life —the summit of all knowledge from which I was to contemplate the universe? . . . I consoled myself with Schopenhauer. I plunged into his *World as Will and Idea* with indescribable rapture, read it from end to end and reread it with such intense application of mind that for many months no outside appeal was able to distract me. Later on, I studied under other masters I have come to prefer greatly to him—Spinoza, Descartes, Leibnitz, and finally Nietzsche; I think, in fact, that I freed myself from that first influence rather quickly; but it is to Schopenhauer, and to him alone, that I owe my initiation into philosophy.

I failed the second part of my *baccalauréat* in July, but managed to scrape through the second time around, in October. That, I considered, brought the first part of my education to an end. I had no desire to push on to the *licence,* or to study law, or to go in for any more examinations, and I resolved to launch out at once on my own career. My mother, nevertheless, extracted a promise from me to go on working with Monsieur Dietz for another year. It made no difference: from that moment I felt strangely free, with no burdens, no material concerns—at that age, indeed, I had very little conception of what it would be like to have to earn one's living.

Free? No, not quite: for I was bound both by my love and by the project for a book of which I have spoken, and which I regarded as the most imperious of duties.

Another resolution I had taken was to marry my cousin as soon as possible. My book seemed to me at times nothing but a long declaration, a profession of love; I meant it to be so noble, so pathetic, so peremptory, that when it was published our parents would no longer be able to object to our marriage, nor Emmanuèle to refuse me her hand. Meanwhile, my uncle, her father, had just died from a stroke; she and I had watched over him together, our heads bowed, our hands joined over his last moments. In this bereavement, it seems to me, our engagement was blessed.

But though the needs of my soul were so urgent, I knew very well that my book was not yet ripe, that I was not yet capable of writing it; and so it was without too much impatience that I looked forward to some further months of study, exercises, preparation—and especially to more reading (I used to devour a book a day). A short journey in between, so my mother thought, would be a profitable way of spending the vacation; I thought so too; but we were less in accord when it came to deciding where I should go. *Maman* voted for Switzerland; she agreed to let me travel without her, but not entirely by myself. When she suggested my joining a party of tourists belonging to the Alpine Club, I flatly declared that the very look of such a mob would drive me crazy, and moreover that I had taken a violent dislike to Switzerland; it was to Brittany I wanted to go, with a bag on my back and no companions at all. . . . My mother yielded at last; but she was determined, at least, to follow me. It was agreed we should meet at different halting-places every two or three days. . . .

As I was walking along the coast, going by short stages from Quiberon to Quimper, I came one evening to a little village called, I think, Le Pouldu. It consisted of no more than four houses, two of which were inns; the more modest of the two struck me as the more charming, and I went in, for I was very thirsty. A servant-girl showed me into a whitewashed room, and left me sitting in front of a glass of cider. A large number of canvases and canvas stretchers lined up along the floor with their faces to the wall were all the more conspicuous because of the scarcity of furniture and the absence of wallpaper. . . . No sooner was I alone, than I ran up to the pictures, turned them round one after the other, and stared at them with increasing amazement; they looked to me like nothing more than childish daubs, but their colors were so bright, so individual, so full of joy that I no longer dreamed of continuing my walk. I wanted to see what

kind of artists were capable of producing such amusing freaks; I abandoned my original plan of reaching Pont-Aven that evening, engaged a
room, and inquired what time dinner was.

"Do you wish to dine by yourself or in the same room as the other
gentlemen?" asked the maidservant.

"The other gentlemen" were the authors of those canvases; there
were three of them, and they soon turned up with their easels and paint-
boxes. Needless to say I had asked to be served along with them—that is,
if they had no objection. They soon made it very obvious that they were
not in the least put out by my presence, by ignoring it altogether.
All three were barefooted, in magnificent disarray, and with trumpeting
voices. During the whole of dinner, I sat gasping with excitement, drinking in their words, racked with the desire to speak to them, to tell them
who I was, to find out who they were and to tell the tall one with bright
eyes that the tune he was singing at the top of his voice and in which the
others joined in chorus, was not Massenet, as he thought, but Bizet . . .

I met one of them later on at Mallarmé's—it was Gauguin . . .

In the spring, I felt that the moment had come; but in order to write my
book, I had to have solitude. . . . I discovered, at Menthon near Annecy
and almost on the banks of the lake, a charming cottage, surrounded with
orchards, the owner of which agreed to rent me two rooms by the month.
I arranged the larger one as a study, and as I felt it impossible to do without music, sent to Annecy for a piano. I took my meals in a kind of summer restaurant on the shore of the lake, where, owing to the earliness of
the season, I was the only guest for a whole month. Monsieur Taine lived
near by. I had just discovered his *Philosophie de l'Art,* his *Intelligence,*
and his *Littérature anglaise;* but I refrained from going to see him, partly
from shyness, and partly for fear of being distracted from my work. In the
complete solitude in which I lived, I succeeded in raising my fervor to
white heat and in maintaining myself in the state of lyrical transport in
which I considered it fitting to write.

When I reopen my *Cahiers d'André Walter* today, their ejaculatory
tone exasperates me. . . . And yet at the time I wrote it, I thought this
book one of the most important in the world, and the crisis I was depicting one of universal and momentous interest; how could I have realized in
those days that the problem was uniquely my own? My puritan upbringing had taught me to make a monster out of the demands of the flesh; how
could I have realized at the time that my own nature shrank from the most

generally admitted solution, the solution my puritanism censured as wrong? And yet, as I was obliged to acknowledge, the state of chastity was an insidious and precarious one; as every other relief was denied me, I fell back into the vice of my early childhood, and was smitten anew with despair every time I fell. With a great deal of love, music, metaphysics, and poetry, this was the subject of my book. . . .

Its success was nil. But my character is such that I took pleasure in my very disappointment. At the bottom of every failure there lies a moral—in each mistake there is a voice saying "That'll teach you!" to the man who will listen. And I heard it. I instantly gave up wishing for a triumph that had slipped from my grasp. Or, at any rate, I began to wish for it in a different form. I convinced myself that the importance of applause lies in its quality and not in its quantity. . . .

I had had an embarrassing number of copies of my first book printed; for the future, I would print only just enough—even a bit less than enough. From now on I was going to pick my readers carefully: encouraged by Albert, I intended to do without publicity; I intended . . . But I think I was motivated above all by amusement and curiosity; for my case *was* unusual: I intended to run a risk that no one had ever run before. I had enough to live on, thank heaven, and could thumb my nose at the idea of profit; if my work is worth anything, I said to myself, it will last; I can wait.

One evening, shortly after the publication of the *Cahiers,* I was trying to wipe off the gross, greasy compliments of Adolphe Retté, when suddenly I felt irresistibly impelled to cut them short (for in all I do there is a great deal more instinct than deliberation—I cannot act in any other way) and I got up and left. This happened in the Café Vachette, or the Café de la Source, where I had gone with Louis.*

"If that's the way you accept compliments," said Louis when we next met, "you aren't going to get very many."

And yet I like compliments; but clumsy ones exasperate me; if I am not flattered in the right place, I go all prickly; and rather than be stupidly praised, I prefer not be praised at all. . . .

Directly after the publication of my *Cahiers,* I entered upon the most confused period of my life, a *selva oscura* from which I only succeeded in escaping when I left for Africa with Paul Laurens. A period of dissipation

* Pierre Louis. He was later to spell his name *Louÿs.*

and distraction . . . I should be only too glad to leap over it altogether, were it not that the contrast of its darkness helps to illuminate what follows; just as I find, in the state of moral tension I maintained in order to elaborate my *Cahiers,* some explanation and some excuse for my dissipation. The simplest statement I make immediately arouses in me a desire to assert and maintain the contrary; so it may easily be imagined what sort of reaction the exaggeration of such a book was likely to provoke. I seemed to have got rid of the anxiety I had painted by the very act of painting it; for a considerable time afterwards, my thoughts refused to let themselves be taken up by anything but trivialities, or to be guided by anything but the most profane and absurd vanities.

I had not been able to learn what Emmanuèle thought of my book; all that she let me know was that she rejected the offer that followed it. I declared that I would not consider her refusal as definite, that I was willing to wait, that nothing would make me give her up. Nevertheless I ceased for a while writing her letters which she had ceased to answer. That silence, that unemployment of the heart left me feeling like a ship abandoned and adrift, but friendship came to fill the time and the place left empty by love.

. . . as I meditate over those bygone days, I think how much I should have benefited from the friendship of a naturalist. Had I come across one at that time, my taste for natural science was so keen that I should have thrown over literature and hastened to follow him. Or if I had met a musician . . . In the circle about Mallarmé, into which I was soon introduced by Pierre Louÿs, they all prided themselves on being lovers of music, Louÿs first of all; but it seemed to me that what Mallarmé and his whole circle really looked for in music was still literature. Wagner was their god. They wreathed him with explanations and commentaries. Louÿs had a way of insisting that I marvel at this or that exclamation or interjection which left me with a loathing of all "expressive" music. I fell back all the more passionately upon what I called "pure" music—that is to say, music that does not pretend to signify anything; and, in my protest against Wagnerian polyphony, I came to prefer—I still prefer—a quartet to an orchestra, a sonata to a symphony. But I was already excessively occupied with music; my style oozed with music . . . No, the friend I needed was someone who would have taught me to be interested in other people, and have drawn me out of myself—perhaps a novelist. But in those days, I had no eyes but for the soul, no taste but for poetry. . . .

I really think that if it had not been for Pierre Louis, I should have continued living in solitude like a savage; not that I had no desire to go into literary society and find friends there, but that an invincible shyness held me back, and the fear which still often paralyzes me of boring or being in the way of the people I feel most naturally drawn to. . . .

At Mallarmé's the habitués were more especially poets; or sometimes painters (I am thinking of Gauguin and Whistler). I have described elsewhere that little room in the rue de Rome, a living-room and dining-room combined; our age has grown too noisy for us to imagine easily nowadays the calm and almost religious atmosphere of the place. There is no doubt that Mallarmé prepared his conversation beforehand; often it was not very different from the most carefully written of his "divagations"; but he spoke with so much art, and in a tone so undogmatic, that it seemed he had just that minute invented each new idea he proposed, ideas he was not so much asserting as, it seemed, submitting to your judgment, interrogatively almost, with his index finger raised—as much as to say: "Mightn't one also say . . . ?" or, "Perhaps . . ." and ending up almost every sentence with a "Don't you think?" No doubt it was on this account that he had so much hold on certain people's minds.

He often interrupted his "divagation" with an anecdote or a *bon mot,* always perfectly told, wrought with all of his anxious concern for elegance and preciosity, which made him so deliberately set his art apart from life.

Occasionally, when there were not too many people gathered round the little table, Madame Mallarmé would linger on at her needlework, with her daughter beside her. But the thick tobacco-smoke soon put them to flight; for in the middle of the round table at which we sat was placed an enormous jar of tobacco, into which we all dipped, each one rolling his own cigarettes; Mallarmé himself smoked without stopping, but preferred a little clay pipe. At about eleven o'clock, Geneviève Mallarmé would come back with glasses of grog; for there was no servant in that very simple household, and the Master himself went to answer the door whenever the bell rang.

from

THE JOURNAL

1889–1893

1889   *Autumn*

With Pierre.* We climb to the sixth floor of a house in rue Monsieur-le-
Prince, looking for a place where our group can meet. Up there we find a
huge room seeming even larger because of the lack of furniture. To the
left of the door the ceiling slopes downward as in a mansard. Near the
floor, a trapdoor opens into an attic extending the whole length of the
house under the tiles. In the opposite wall a window, just waist-high, provides a view over the roofs of the Medical School, over the Latin Quarter,
of an expanse of gray houses as far as the eye can see, the Seine and Notre-
Dame in the setting sun, and, in the far distance, Montmartre barely visible in the evening mist.

And together we dream of the impecunious student's life in such a
room, with no more fortune than what one's own free writing could earn.
At one's feet, just across the writing-desk, all Paris. To take refuge there
with the dream of one's masterpiece, and not come out until it is finished.

Rastignac's cry as he looks down on the city from the heights of Père
Lachaise: "And now . . . you've met your match!" †

1890   *January*

My pride is constantly being irritated by a thousand minute slights. I suffer
absurdly from the fact that everybody does not already know what I hope
some day to be, what I shall be; that people cannot foretell the work to
come just from the look in my eyes.

November 10

I am still clumsy; I should learn to be clumsy only when I wish to be. *I
must learn to keep silent.* Merely from having talked to Albert yesterday
about my plans for this book, my will to see it through was weakened. I
must learn to take myself seriously; and not to hold onto any smug opin-

---

* Pierre Louÿs.
† Last words of Balzac's *Père Goriot.*

ion of myself. To have more mobile eyes and a less mobile face. To keep a straight face when I make a joke. Not to applaud every joke made by others. Not to show the same colorless geniality toward everyone. To know how to disconcert at the right moment by keeping a poker face. And especially never to praise two people in the same way, but rather to keep toward each individual a distinct manner from which I would never deviate without intending to.

End of November

The day when I set out once more to write really sincere notes in this notebook, I shall have to undertake such a disentangling in my cluttered brain that, to stir up all that dust, I am waiting for a series of vast empty hours, a long cold, a convalescence, during which my constantly reawakened curiosities will lie at rest; during which my only care will be to rediscover myself.

For the last two months I have not enjoyed a single moment of monologue. I am not even egotistical any longer. I am not even . . . anything any longer. Lost, from the day when I began my book. . . .

1891   *June 4*

Right now I am in the same intellectual state I was in before writing *André Walter:* the same inextricable emotional complexity, the same systems of vibrations that I noted in January '90. I am led to the conclusion that this is perhaps the state of mind which will always precede a new creative effort for me, and always come after a long rest.

June 10

One should want *only one thing* and want it constantly. Then one is *sure* of getting it. But I desire everything and consequently get nothing. . . .

I must stop puffing up my pride (in this notebook) just for the sake of doing as Stendhal did. The spirit of imitation; watch out for it. There is no point in doing something simply because another has done it. It is the moral ideal of great men that one should retain, isolating it from the contingent facts of their lives—rather than imitating just the little facts.

Dare to be yourself. I must underline that in my head too.

Don't ever do anything through affectation or to make people like you or through imitation or for the pleasure of contradicting.

No compromise (either ethical or artistic). Perhaps it is very dangerous for me to see other people; I always have too great a desire to please them; perhaps I need solitude. I might as well admit it frankly: my solitary and sullen childhood made me what I am. Perhaps it would be better to exaggerate that aspect. Perhaps I would find great strength in doing so. (But there should not be any "perhaps" in matters of conduct. There's no use creating question marks. Answer everything in advance. What a ridiculous undertaking! What madness!)

I read in Taine (*Littérature anglaise*) his description of the celebrations and customs of the Renaissance. Perhaps that was real beauty; utterly physical. Some time ago all that luxurious display would have left me cold. I am reading it at the right moment, when it can most effectively intoxicate me. My mind is becoming voluptuously impious and pagan. I must stress that tendency. I can see the readings I should indulge in: Stendhal, the *Encyclopédie,* Swift, Condillac . . . to dry up my heart (*sear* is a better word; everything is mildewed in my heart). Then the vigorous writers and especially the most virile: Aristophanes, Shakespeare, Rabelais . . . these are the ones I must read. . . . And don't worry about the rest. There is enough possibility of tears in my soul to irrigate thirty books.

June 25

I have seen Louis again. Good Lord! Are we going to make up?

He tore up my letter in front of me! Why? It was perfectly sincere. Three times already we have had long explanations; we have already gone through that painful experience; we are incapable of "hitting it off"; therefore intimacy is impossible. Why begin again, then? I could remain his friend; why does he want to be mine, when I don't even admire him any longer, and when these animated and paradoxical discussions only tire and bore me. . . . Oh, how they bore me!

July 22

Yesterday saw Bruges and Ostend. Such boredom, such a lugubrious fatigue strikes me as soon as I am in a new town that I can think of nothing but the desire to get away again at once. I dragged myself through the streets with a real anguish. Even when these things are worthy of admiration, the idea of seeing them alone appalls me. It seems to me that I am taking from Em. a bit of that delight that we ought to enjoy together. I sleep every afternoon, so that at least I can dream a little. Or else I read. The "landscape," instead of distracting me from myself, always desperately takes on the color of my own lamentable soul.

At Ostend the sky and the waves were gray; dire desperations rained down on the sea. I wanted to lose myself in some sensual emotion and, while watching the downpour, I ate ice cream. I had a fever. My nose was bleeding all day long.

July 23

I saw Bruges again with Mother. I nestled in her affection to ward off the cold.

October 8

More than a month of blanks. Talking of myself bores me. A diary is useful during conscious, intentional, and painful moral evolutions. Then you want to know where you stand. But anything I should say now would be mere repetitions on the same theme—myself. A private journal is interesting especially when it records the awakening of ideas; or the awakening of the senses, at puberty; or else when you feel yourself to be dying.

There is no longer any drama taking place inside me; there is now nothing but a lot of stirred-up ideas. There is no point in writing myself down.

This terrifies me: to think that the present, which we are living this very day, will become the mirror in which we shall recognize ourselves later; and that by what we have been we shall know what we are. And each time I make a decision I am anxious to know if it is the right one.

Uzès, December 29

O Lord, I come back to Thee because I believe that all is vanity except the knowledge of Thee. Guide me in Thy paths of light. I have followed tortuous ways and have thought to enrich myself with false goods. O Lord, have pity on me: the only real good is the good Thou givest. I wanted to enrich myself and I impoverished myself. After all that turmoil I am poorer than ever. I remember my former days and my prayers. O Lord, lead me as before in Thy paths of light. O Lord, keep me from evil. May my soul again be proud; my soul was becoming an ordinary soul. Oh, may those early struggles and my prayers not be in vain. . . .

December 31

When one has begun to write, the hardest thing is to be sincere. Essential to mull over that idea and to define artistic sincerity. Meanwhile, I hit upon this: the word must never precede the idea. Or else: the word must always be necessitated by the idea. It must be irresistible and inevitable; and the same is true of the sentence, of the whole work. And for the artist's whole life, since his whole vocation must be irresistible. He must be incapable of not writing (I should prefer him to resist himself in the beginning, and to suffer from the resistance).

The fear of not being sincere has been tormenting me for several months and has kept me from writing. Oh, to be utterly and perfectly sincere. . . .

1892   *January 3*

Shall I always torment myself thus, and will my mind never, O Lord, come to rest in any certainty? Like an invalid turning over in his bed in search of sleep, I am restless from morning till night; even at night my anxiety awakens me.

I am anxious to know what I shall be; I do not even know what I want to be, but I do know that I must choose. I should like to progress on safe, sure roads that lead only to the point where I have decided to go. But I don't know; I don't know what I ought to want. I feel a thousand possibilities in me, but I cannot resign myself to want to be only one of them. And every moment, at every word I write, at each gesture I make, I am terrified at the thought that this is one more ineradicable feature of my face, of my person becoming fixed: a hesitant, impersonal face, sketchy, uncertain, because I have not been capable of choosing and tracing its contours with confidence.

O Lord, permit me to want only one thing and to want it constantly.

January 11

I am torn by this dilemma: to be moral, or to be sincere.

Morality consists in substituting for the natural creature (the old Adam) a fictitious being that you prefer. But then you are no longer sincere. The old Adam is the sincere man.

January 20

Two things provoke each other in me and yet I don't mind: the endless boredom I inspire in myself and my endless love for the pure idea.

———

I had begun again to work over my mediocre poems of last September. But that bores me. Today I have discovered such rich domains of study that any joy in producing is canceled by the wild joy of learning. It is a mad lust. Oh, to know. . . .

Easter Sunday

To know . . . to know what?

Still more philology; very little so far. Read some of Goethe's poems; the *Prometheus;* read *La Faustin;* some Banville; *Adolphe.*

I feel that in a very short while I shall hurl myself again into a frantic mysticism.

Munich, May 12

If I do not write any longer in this diary, if I shudder at the thought of letters to write, it is because I have no more personal emotions. In fact, I have no emotions except those I want to have, or those of other people. On my good days, and they are becoming frequent again, I enjoy an intellectual and nervous exaltation, a powerful vibration of my whole being, that can be converted, as if at will, into joy or sorrow, without either one being more pleasant than the other. I am like a well-tuned harp that sings, according to the poet's whim, a gay scherzo or a melancholy andante.

This mental and emotional mood seems to me excellent for writing. I am myself *ad libitum;* doesn't this amount to saying that I can take on the emotions of my characters? The important thing is being capable of emotions, but to experience only *one's own* would be a sorry limitation.

In any event, egoism is hateful. I am less and less interested in myself and more and more in my work and my thoughts.

I always see, almost simultaneously, the two sides of each idea, and emotion is always polarized in me. But even though I understand the two poles, I also am keenly aware, between them, of the point beyond which the understanding cannot extend—the understanding of a mind which takes the strictly personal view, which can see only one side of truth, which chooses once and for all *one* of the two poles.

. . . when I am with two friends and they disagree, I remain on edge between them, not knowing what to say, not daring to take sides with one or the other, accepting every affirmation and rejecting every negation.

                                             Montpellier, March

I lived until the age of twenty-three completely virgin and utterly depraved; crazed to such a point that eventually I came to look everywhere for some bit of flesh on which to press my lips.

March 17

I like life and prefer sleep, not because of its emptiness, but because of its dreams.

Spain

Bullfights.

    To kill someone because he is angry is all right; but to anger someone in order to kill him is absolutely criminal.

Paris, end of April

Do not read any more books by ascetics. Find one's exaltation elsewhere; admire that difficult joy of equilibrium, of the fullness of life. Let each thing yield all the life it has in it. It is a duty to make oneself happy.

And now my prayer (for it still is a prayer): O my Lord, let this moral code, so narrow, so strict, break, and let me live, oh, fully; and give me the strength to do so, oh, without fear, and without always thinking that I am about to sin!

    It now takes as great an effort to let myself go as it used to take to resist.

    That ethic of privation had so thoroughly established itself as my natural rule of conduct that the other is now very painful and difficult for me. I have to drive myself to pleasure. It is painful for me to be happy.

An easy ethic? . . . Certainly not! it has not been easy, the rule that has until now guided and sustained me, and finally depraved me. But I know that when I begin to taste those things, the things I had forbidden myself as too beautiful, it will not be as a sinner, secretly, with a bitter foretaste of repentance; no, rather without remorse, with vigor and joyously.

    To come out of the dream at last, and live a full and powerful life.

May 5

Really there would be some joy in feeling robust and *normal*. I am waiting.

May 28

What I like in the work of art is that it is calm; no one has longed for rest more than we have, nor has loved unrest more.

June 3

My constant question (and it has become an unhealthy obsession): Could anyone love me?

La Roque, July 14

The cultivation of my emotions was a bad thing; the Stendhalian upbringing is unfortunate and dangerous. I have lost the habit of lofty thought; this is a *most regrettable* thing. I live in a facile manner, and this must not go on. Everything in life must be intentional, the will constantly taut like a muscle.

Yet I do not regret having changed my method for this one year; but one must always come back to oneself. No, I do not regret it; I know that everything can be turned to advantage, provided one keeps reminding himself of it. *And I have lived much. But it is certainly time to pull myself together.*

August. Honfleur

Before leaving I reread all of my journal; I did so with inexpressible disgust. I find nothing in it but pride; pride even in the manner of expressing myself. Always some form of pretentiousness, claiming either to be profound or to be witty. My pretensions to metaphysics are absurd; that constant analysis of one's thoughts, that lack of action, those rules of conduct are the most tiresome, insipid, and almost incomprehensible things in the world when one has grown out of them. I could never get back into certain of those moods—which all the same I know to have been sincere. To me this is all over, a closed book, an emotion that has cooled off forever.

Reacting against all this, I have come to a desire not to bother with myself at all; not to worry, when I want to do something, whether I am doing good or ill, but simply to do it, come what may. I no longer want strange or complicated things at all; I don't even *understand* complicated things any more. I want to be normal and strong, simply so that I shall not have to think of such things any more.

The desire to "write well" the pages of this journal deprives them of all worth, even that of sincerity. They no longer have any significance, since they were never written well enough to have any literary value. In short, all of them take for granted a future fame or celebrity that will render them interesting. And that is utterly base. Only a few pious, pure pages satisfy me now. What pleases me most in my former self are the moments of prayer.

I came very close to tearing it all up; at least I suppressed many pages.*

La Roque

All my efforts this year have been directed toward this one difficult task: to free myself at length from everything useless and restrictive with which an inherited religion had surrounded me to limit my nature; but to do this without repudiating anything that could still educate and strengthen me.

It is natural for the Christian soul always to imagine battles within itself. After a short time one never can understand just why. . . . For, after all, the conquered enemy is always a part of oneself, and this makes for useless wear and tear. I spent my whole youth in opposing two parts of myself, which perhaps wanted nothing more than to come to terms. Through love of strife, I imagined struggles and divided my nature.

Yport, at The Laurens'

I wrote last year, in Munich (this is a torn-out page that I have just found): "There are not so many important things. One could make his happiness out of very little; and enjoy at the same time all the pride that comes from depriving himself of the rest. The rest—all the other things! When I have tried them all, and realized their vanity, I shall retire into study. Soon, in a short while; but first I want to exhaust their bitter taste, so that later on no desire for them will come to disturb my quiet hours."

It is now more than a year since I wrote those sentences; and since then, the things I then scorned have only appeared to me the more attractive and more beautiful, the closer I approached them. And it is for them that, seduced, I now set off on my travels.

* Since then I have burned the first journal almost entirely (1902). [A. G.]

Montpellier, October 10

Christianity consoles, above all; but there are naturally happy souls who do not need consolation. Consequently Christianity begins by making such souls unhappy, for otherwise it would have no power over them.

[Undated]

Oh, if only my thought could simplify itself! . . . I sit here, sometimes all morning, *unable* to do anything, tormented by the desire to do everything. The yearning to educate myself is the most frightening temptation for me. I have twenty books before me, every one of them begun. You will laugh when I tell you that I cannot read a single one of them simply because I want so much to read them all. I read three lines and think of everything else . . . (in an hour I shall have to go and see Paul and Pierre; good Lord, I almost forgot Etienne, and he might have been hurt; on the way I ought to buy some cuffs; and Laure is expecting me to take her some flowers . . .). Oh, my time! my time will be frittered away like this until death! If only I could live on some foreign shore where the moment I stepped outdoors, I could enjoy the sun, the wind, the infinite horizon of the sea! . . . Perhaps I ought to go out. My head is tired; a short walk will cure me. . . . But I had promised myself to spend an hour at the piano. . . .

Ah, a knock on the door! Someone is coming to see me. Good Lord! . . . (Saved; this is at least an hour lost!) Happy, I cried out, are those whose every hour is filled in advance, who are obliged to go *somewhere.* Oh for a pair of blinders!

 1893–1902

On at least three occasions in his life, Gide's inner contradictions reached a point of such perplexity that he was effectively paralyzed until he was able to contrive the ritual gesture, the exorcising, untangling act that permitted him to *passer outre,* as he put it, to rise above himself, to reach a new equilibrium (or a more workable unbalance), to shed the old skin and move on. In each case, the liberating act was the writing of a book— as one might expect from a man so profoundly dependent on written words: *Les Cahiers d'André Walter* in 1890, *L'Immoraliste* in 1901, and *Si le grain ne meurt* in 1919. Each of these books represents the closest he could come to a total statement, a total expression of himself at the time he wrote it. Each has about it the mark of necessity—the mark Gide was referring to when he wrote (apropos of *L'Immoraliste*) "I no longer esteem any books but those the author has just managed to survive." [1]

An author may, in time, write himself out of his problems; after which his writing will lack that mark of necessity, that desperate fullness —Conrad after 1911 (or 1904), Faulkner after 1939. Now, the vaunted "serenity" of Gide's last decades, and the creative drought that accompanied it, may in part be the result of such a successful literary psychotherapy. But, although he may have come to terms with it, learned to live with it more or less easily, I do not think that Gide ever completely resolved his state of inner contradiction—the state, after all, on which his unique moral contribution depends. The writing of the *Cahiers,* or *L'Immoraliste,* or *Si le grain* did not make him what one could ever call a well-balanced or well-adjusted or "normal" man (for which we may be grateful); but it did allow him to untie the *particular* knot in which his contradictions had bound and immobilized him at a particular time, so that he was free to breathe and move again. After each of these emancipations he was a different man—a wiser, more lucid, more useful man (I speak generally: there are lapses, retrogressions, the effects of age and fame).

The magnificence of *L'Immoraliste* derives in great part from the way Gide was able to make it contain, with so little pressure for either one side or another, all the rich, vital, lacerating contradictions of what is probably the most important decade of his life. Thanks to his writing of *L'Immoraliste,* André Gide was freed after 1902 to work in a wider field, to begin to assume his proper public dimensions: but he was never again to write, because he was never again to *need* to write, a work of such harrowing intensity.

For a while, at the start of this period, Gide thought that all the knots of contradiction had been cut. The problem, as he saw it, was simply one of puritan repression; the solution, then, was obviously to shed that repression by means of a determined cultivation of the senses and sensual appetites. This is the Gide of Sousse, of Biskra and Algiers (and Como and Florence and Syracuse), tasting as if for the first time the fruits of the earth, singing the joys of sherbet and sunlight and clear water and the open road.

It is remarkable how persistently the image of this Gide—the determined and doctrinaire hedonist, the proselytizing sensualist, the Immoralist—has monopolized public attention. In fact, it corresponds to a period in his life of less than two years, from 1893 to 1895. Setting sail for North Africa with Paul Laurens, he was consciously trying to break with his puritan heritage and youth, and embarking (he hoped) on a sensualist adventure. Yielding to his sexual urges—and more specifically, to his homosexual urges—first in November 1893, and then decisively in January 1895, he took these moments of corrective excess, this ecstasy of anti-puritan reaction (intensified by illness*) as signs of his "true nature," and began to act, write, think, and preach accordingly.

In some respects, the "self" of 1893–1895, so rhapsodically expressed in *Les Nourritures terrestres,* was "true"; certain of its characteristics were radical and constitutional, and were to remain in force for the rest of his life. But there is far more to Gide, even in this brief period of his life, than the singer of *Nourritures terrestres.* Although it was begun in the full fervor of his sensualist conviction, by the time it was published in 1897, he had already outgrown it. Oh, the book was honest enough, and its appeal was seductive—more seductive, as it turned out, than Gide could ever have dreamed. But neither the problem, nor its

---

* "And then, in that very place, I had the good fortune to fall ill, very seriously it is true, but of an illness that did not kill me—one, on the contrary, that merely weakened me for a while; and the clearest result of it was to give me a taste for the preciousness of life. It would seem that, for the absorption of sensations, a feeble, febrile organism is more porous, transparent, sensitive, more perfectly receptive. Despite my illness, if not because of it, I was all receptiveness, all joy." (from *Amyntas;* November 29, 1903)

answer—as he very soon came to realize—was as simple as he had imagined in 1893.

The time between his twenty-fourth and his thirty-third years is probably
the best-known period of Gide's life, for two reasons: first, because of the
notoriously frank confession, in Part II of *Si le grain ne meurt,* of an
event that took place at its start—the confession toward which all the
selected detail, all the reticences and rhetoric of his memoir may be seen
to have been tending, like the pattern of iron filings about a magnet; and
secondly, because of the durability of *Les Nourritures terrestres,* the renewed need for its message felt by certain members of each generation.

   The confession I refer to is included in the pages ahead, as well as
what I hope is a fair sampling, not hopelessly dimmed by translation, of
the *Nourritures.* Here ends the Road to Biskra. Along with certain travel
notes from the *Journal* in the same ecstatic manner, and the exultant
tribute to Nietzsche, this should provide adequate textual witness of
Gide's brief moment of hedonist rebellion.

   But despite his own insistence on the climactic nature of November
1893, despite the ringing siren-call of *Les Nourritures,* despite the persisting popular image, it is not this aspect of his life during the decade, the
rebellious anti-puritan aspect, that I regard as most important. It was no
more than a temporary, untenable thesis in an ascending dialectic. Less
than three months after his confrontation with, his yielding to his "true
self" (the strangled *"Oui"* in the ear of Oscar Wilde), he was back at his
mother's side; within five months he was engaged, within nine months
married to the woman who in many ways was to take his mother's place.
By the time *Les Nourritures,* the fruit of his anti-bourgeois rebellion, was
published, he was mayor and chatelain of La Roque-Baignard. He had
not discovered, as it turned out, his "true self" in North Africa: it dwelt,
in effect, somewhere between Normandy and the desert, and the really
important story of this period is that of his attempt to come to terms with
that greater discovery, to accept the fact that he was to find his moral
value in *inquiétude,* in the tension *between* the two poles; to write himself into a new equilibrium. Clearly some more subtle synthesis, some
more mature and more complex ideal had to emerge, something larger
than mere repression or mere rebellion. His own upbringing had left too
thick a puritan residue, too strong a moralist's sense of duty, too deeply
ingrained a nostalgia for the higher and better—without which qualities

he would be worthless—for him ever to persevere long in the paths of
self-abandon. The very man who was now shedding the restrictive shell
of commandments had nevertheless been *made* by their restriction, had
been shaped and given his value by it: as he himself realized, before he
ever left the continent:

> All my efforts this year have been directed toward this one difficult
> task: to free myself at length from everything useless and restrictive
> with which an inherited religion has surrounded me to limit my
> nature; *but to do this without repudiating anything that could still
> educate and strengthen me.*
>
> (*Journal,* September 1893. My italics)

Total hedonist rebellion was for him, ultimately, impossible, morally
and psychologically; half the value of his work depends on that impossibility.

When one asks what is missing from the life-records of this period, the
answer seems to be a great deal. There is total silence in the published
Journal for the years 1897–1901, and very little that is personally revealing from the two years preceding. This strikes me as reasonable
enough, on two grounds. The first years of a marriage are likely to be a
time of difficult and uncertain readjustment for anyone, as he struggles to
adapt his own ego and activity to another's; to a conscientious spouse, the
keeping of a journal at such a time may appear an act of hostile self-
assertion. In Gide's case, as we shall see, the struggle was exceptionally
intense, and his return to the keeping of a private journal in 1902 may
be looked on as a kind of surrender. A second explanation may simply be
that he had found, in the writing of *L'Immoraliste,* an alternative that
permitted him to tell more, and tell it to greater personal benefit, than
would ever have been possible in a non-fictional account. Henri Troyat
has explained a similar gap in Tolstoy's diary, during the years he was
writing his two major novels, in this way:

> Absorbed in the fate of his heroes, Tolstoy became less concerned
> with himself. By distributing his contradictory emotions among a
> cast of imaginary characters, he forged his own unity and thereby
> his balance. Significantly, as soon as he began work on the book,
> toward the end of 1863, the entries in his diary became shorter and
> less frequent. He no longer had either the time or the inclination to

analyze himself. . . . In 1865, he closed the notebook in which he had made a habit of relating his life and did not reopen it for thirteen years.*

It is the very intensity of the contained pain and contradiction within *L'Immoraliste,* duplicated nowhere else in Gide's writings, which leads me to consider the first six years of his marriage as the most important period of his life: the period of greatest and most fruitful complication, of the maximum psychological density. In a way, Gide has "told us more" of the period 1895–1902 than of any other: if only we knew how to read it. This short novel, which I have reprinted complete, is his expression of the intolerable tension between self and other, between freedom and order, between North Africa and Normandy, which was only now approaching the surface of consciousness. It is wrong, of course, to read *L'Immoraliste* as a literal account of the story of André and Madeleine Gide. But it is not wrong to see in its sickness and strain, its willed ecstasy and willed agony, its dramatic irresolution within aesthetic wholeness and satisfaction, the story of the first six years—otherwise so sparsely recorded—of André Gide's married life.

Despite all the distractions of his travels, Gide never ceased to keep clearly in view the image of his literary career. "I believe that all of this is preparing me, whether I will or no" (he was writing shortly after his meeting with Wilde and his young friend Douglas) "for the things I am going to write." [2] During his *Wanderjahr*-and-a-half, he was both passively collecting impressions and actively taking stock, and by May 1894 he had already conceived much of the distinct nature of his future role as a writer, in a manner far more detailed than the simple Goethean commitment of 1893. In a remarkable letter to his brother-in-law-to-be of May 10, 1894—a letter that recalls one of Keats's to his brother—he is already laying claim to some of the particularities of his maturity: an incessant and productive "state of dialogue," a readiness to understand *all* positions in a quarrel; an anxiety to force others to act, but to act *freely,* and in their own way:

> I have reached that happy state in which one no longer has any personal faith . . . what one might call the *state of dialogue;* it comes from a penetration, an ever-increasing and ever-deepening comprehension of the beliefs and values of others; from the possibility of being moved in turn just as much by one person's as by another's—and sincerely, passionately;—ultimately, from a com-

* Henri Troyat, *Tolstoy* (New York, 1967), p. 273.

plete disinterest in one's personal opinion. . . . I felt more and
more that the best thing in me was this unknown resonance, this
ability to sympathize, which recalls that of the chameleon
—presuming that he can will himself to turn green by the
simple fact of *thinking* about leaves . . . From that time on, I
began to consider that, for the writer . . . all that mattered was to
bring light to every point; it was his duty to expose lucidly, coldly,
and passionately the diverse forms of *life,* and his conclusions
should be nothing but questions directed at the reader: what I want
is to force him into a corner and make him *answer.* But again, and
more strongly all the time, I have this conviction that if a *moral act*
is to have any *value* it must be made of free choice; I believe, with
Fichte, that the moral life begins with a *personal decision* and that
to accept the decisions of another is a state of death or of non-life:
and so I keep myself from trying to force on people my *own ideas*
(and from that point on, why bother having any?), seeing in this a
jesuitical usurpation on the ideas of other people . . .[3]

And at the same time, when Gide was seeing more clearly his distinct and special role, he was very pointedly *rejecting* the kind of writer,
or *littérateur,* he had been, as well as the precious and inbred Parisian
literary milieux in which he had lived. He did this, symbolically, by
means of a satire, a kind of super-logical caricature of the urbane, cerebral life entitled *Paludes* (*Marshlands*).* "It seems to me now that my
youth is over . . . I feel myself ripe for more serious and stronger
works."[4]

Gide charted the last stages in the "Road to Biskra" with exceptional
fullness and detail because they represented for him the climax, the central issue, in some respects the whole *raison d'être* of his memoir. If his
manner of rendering does seem, as in Part I, excessively dramatic
or "legendary," it must be admitted that such things as the first

* To English-speaking readers, the hero and his world may recall T. S. Eliot's J. Alfred
Prufrock.

> *Mais toi, le plus débile des êtres,*
> *Que peut-tu faire? Que veux-tu faire?*   (*Paludes*)

> . . . And how should I presume?
> . . . And how should I begin?   ("Prufrock")

The similarity may not be entirely accidental, in that both authors were touched by the
influence of the cynical ironist Jules Laforgue.

crossing of the Mediterranean; the fortuitous juxtaposition of circumstances at Sousse (geography, occasion, independence, and illness, with
all that illness implied of both weakened resistance and heightened susceptibility); and particularly the unlooked-for encounter with Wilde
and Douglas at Blida—that such things have about them an extraordinary sense of the fated and symbolic. His life did "happen," sometimes,
in a legendary way.

So complete are his accounts of these adventures, in fact, that they
provide almost all the materials one needs for a psychological analysis of
his character and behavior at the time. I might only add, as a reminder,
that between the time he sailed with Paul Laurens on October 18, 1893,
and the time he returned to France on April 14, 1895, he had been
(with the exception of two very short visits home in August and December 1894) a free traveler for a total of nineteen months. During those
months, André Gide discovered that an unquenchable, almost pathological *Wanderlust* was to be an essential trait of his character; by the time
the nineteen months were over he probably knew that he would never
overcome it. He was scarcely out of Africa before he was aching to be
back; his second trip there, in January 1895, was clearly a matter of
involuntary attraction, however much he may have tried to rationalize or
to justify it. He *had* to go back; as he was to have to go again and again.
The second trip, moreover, was of a quality quite unlike the first, and not
only because of Oscar Wilde. "Africa" now was a matter less of free,
lyrical, unpremeditated abandon than of something willed, determined,
and hard. "That stage of my life is finished and past—the lyrical stage:
my mistake is in wanting to bring it back to life, artificially." [5] The bed-
rock of this experimental "descent into hell" can perhaps be located during his last two months in Algeria, when he was alone and burning
fiercely. His extraordinary letters of that early spring betray a greater
degree of rebellion and independence than he had ever shown before,
and, at times, a sensual self-abandon near to madness. His mother was
appalled.

The road away from his mother and the road back to Madeleine—
which turned out to be on one and the same circular track—provide the
theme of the last pages of *Si le grain ne meurt*. But the road as written is
considerably smoother and more direct than the road as lived (in fact, he
says nothing at all of the progress of his proposal of marriage between
its rejection in '91 and its acceptance in '95), and one can trace a great
number of obstacles and detours through his and the family's letters.

First, one may note some additional instances of his mother's lingering dominance. The reader of *Si le grain ne meurt* who is surprised, to say the least, to read of *maman*'s dropping in in the midst of André's heterosexual experiments should know that André had written asking her to come two weeks before. (What really impelled her were second-hand accounts of his illness; André later did try to cancel his invitation by wire, after Meriem's visits began. But he *had* asked her first.) It is the opinion of Jean Delay, Gide's psycho-biographer, second, that her remonstrances, her tears, her very inhibiting presence at his side for six weeks in Africa at this crucial time may have been a major determinant of his future sexual orientation. Third, in January of '95, on the eve of his second and perhaps decisive trip to Africa, he wrote again, this time begging his mother (and Madeleine) to accompany him. By the next morning he seems to have abandoned the plea; ten days later, he is professing that he knew in advance they would refuse. But Dr. Delay sees this letter as one, last, desperate cry in the night of the "old André," a reaching toward the past and security, a plea for help to the representatives of what he was, knowing all too well what he is going to become if he returns to Africa alone. And fourth, one should keep in mind that even in the early months of 1895, at the time of fullest revolt, he was still writing to his mother almost daily, professing his love at the same time he was describing, in incredible detail, both the corruptness around him and the rebellion within.

These accounts alone would have been enough to frighten the poor woman; but beyond that, André's correspondence with her during the last two years of her life took on an increasing tone of personal hostility. The biblical citation he quotes in his *Journal* of 1895—"Woman, what have I to do with thee?"—assumes in this light a special and private meaning. From Geneva in June, from La Brévine in October, in answer to her daily letters of advice and injunction, he is insisting that she stop interfering in his life, that she leave him alone. And in March, from Biskra, in the course of a quarrel, he issues a series of insolent declarations of independence:

> . . . a life is *not* necessarily the better for being the more reasonable. If I were to lead my life according to your "counsels," it would be a constant lie against my own ideas. Nothing irritates me more than this need you have to interfere with the actions of others; it may end up making them more "sensible," but it makes them lose all their value, lose all their "originality," because they come from *you* instead of the other person.

. . . you had better convince yourself, resign yourself, make up
your mind in advance *not* to try to suppress from my existence
every peculiarity that happens to push through, like some native
weed (and I call them "peculiarities" to please you: to me they
don't seem so at all, but entirely *natural* things), and I have nothing but horror for the perpetual feeling you are trying to impress on
me—that I am not acting like everyone else . . .
Can you not understand that there is such a thing as *useful* madness? . . .

   Letters like these last four of yours (which unfortunately no
longer surprise me very much, coming from you) make me see ahead
a veritable conjugal hell if I *do* marry, because of the role of "coun-
selor" and "experienced person" you would never be able to give off
playing . . . Many of the best things in my life I have gained only
by an obstinate resistance to the invasions of your will. Should I
have children, I fear they would be very badly brought up, very
weakly disciplined, out of the horror that the excesses of *your* system have given me for any education "which has no other purpose
but to suppress." [6]

"Mme Gide," writes Dr. Delay, "dumbfounded by this correspondence
from Biskra, realized from that time that the hour had come for her to
hand over her powers to her niece, for no doubt Madeleine would be able
to 'save' André, by exercising over him a moral and Christian influence." [7]
   What had happened, all this while, to André's plans for marriage?
For a time, he seems to have tried to sustain the dream that his two
illusions were compatible. He invited his cousin to join him in Algeria,
or in some other foreign place—the clearest sign of self-delusion, of the
fact that he had closed off one half of his mind from the other.
Madeleine, of course, resisted, and shared his mother's increasing fears
for André's moral welfare. André, on his part, seemed to lose interest in
the idea of marriage as his adventures accelerated, which only served to
increase his mother's anxiety and, eventually, to bring her round. When
the crisis came, in the spring of '95, Madeleine was ready, for all her
fears ("I am not afraid of death, but I am afraid of marriage" [8]), to do
her Christian duty by her dying, desperate aunt and her "dear brother"
André.
   What brought André to agree to marry, so soon after the fullness of
revolt? A life's affection for Madeleine, filial respect certainly played a

very large part: but one may also see in his acquiescence a certain deep-rooted longing for security and normalcy returning in force; and perhaps also the exhausted return of a Prodigal Son, who had looked into the abyss of himself, and returned not at all certain he liked what he saw.* "This very freedom, which, during my mother's lifetime, I had so craved, now stunned me like a wind from the open; it suffocated, perhaps even frightened me. I felt dazed, like a prisoner unexpectedly set free, like a kite whose string has been suddenly cut, like a boat broken loose from its moorings, like a drifting wreck, at the mercy of wind and tide." [9]

Of the forty-three-year-long marriage that succeeded, thousands of words have been written, some of the most perceptive and persuasive of them —as well as some of the most unconvincing and blind—by André Gide. His most extended and intimate reflections on the subject will be found in the essay *Et nunc manet in te* (it is subtitled *Madeleine* in English; see pages 941–949), which was published after his death. In the same book were printed for the first time many of the pages from his journal referring to their conjugal griefs, which are here returned to their proper place. (The impartial student may also wish to consult *Madeleine et André Gide* [1956], an angry defense of Mme Gide by Jean Schlumberger, an old friend of both the Gides, against what he regards as her husband's cruelly deforming portrait.) So intricate are the emotions involved in this union, so much of it rests in a decent silence, that no single quotation from anyone's letter or journal can possibly be telling the whole story. There is bound to be another quotation somewhere else, no less private and sincere, that contradicts it. But two texts, one a letter of Madeleine's written at the time of their most grievous separation, the other a reflection from Gide's journal written after her death, may cast some light on the tortuous journey ahead.

> André dear,
> You are mistaken. I have no doubts of your affection. And even if I had, I should have nothing to complain of. My portion has been a handsome one: I have had the best of your soul, the tenderness of

* Oscar Wilde had been sentenced to two years of hard labor for his "corrupting of youth" on May 25, six days before the death of Mme Gide. Jean Delay proposes that the reception of this dreadful news may have contributed to Gide's impetuous retreat into the sanctity and apparent security of marriage—if not, in fact, to a ghastly realization on his mother's part, and possibly even to her heart attack.

your childhood and your youth. And I know that, living or dead, I shall have the soul of your last years.

I have always understood, moreover, your need to move from place to place, your need for freedom. How many times in your fits of nervous anguish—the price you pay for your genius—have these words been on the tip of my tongue: "But my dear, leave, go, you are free, there is no door on the cage, nothing is keeping you here." (I did not say it, for fear of wounding you by giving in so easily to your absence.)

What pains me—and you know it without my saying so—is the road down which you are traveling, and which is going to lead you and others to perdition. Again, please believe that I am not saying this with any feeling of condemnation. I pity you as much as I love you . . .

(June 1918)[10]

If I had listened to my own advice (I mean: the man I once was, listening to the one I am today), I should have gone around the world four times . . . and I should never have married. As I write these words, I shudder as at an act of impiety. This is because I have remained through it all very much in love with what most re-strained me, and I cannot swear that it was not that very restraint that got the best out of me.

·(*Journal,* September 9, 1940)

What can one add, then, to fill the gap of those first six years? Gide's literary career, first, was progressing; he was sharpening its contours and extending its reach. During this period, he was writing book reviews and literary essays with some regularity (including the one on Nietzsche re-printed here), which he collected in two published volumes; engaging in literary quarrels on behalf of friends, like Francis Jammes, or against foes, like Maurice Barrès—the "Normandy and Bas-Languedoc" essay in the last chapter is in part aimed at him. He published "Leaves from the Wayside" (travel notes from his honeymoon trip to Italy and North Africa), and wrote important essays *In Memoriam* of Stéphane Mallarmé, who died in 1898, and Oscar Wilde, who died in 1901 —Gide had seen Wilde several times during his last years of exile in France. In a series of narrative or dramatic fables, Gide used the lives of legendary characters—Prometheus, Philoctetes, Saul, King Candaules— to develop and express, explicitly or indirectly, the tenets of his maturing philosophy. He was invited to lecture "On Influence in Literature" at Brussels and "On the Limits of Art" in Paris. And of course, he was writing *L'Immoraliste.*

Domestically, the tranquil and agreeable routine of life on the Gides' Normandy estates began to establish itself during these years, as both their own letters and those of their frequent house-guests attest. "I now begin an indefatigable repose, at the side of the most tranquil of wives." [11] For four summers they divided their time at home between two of their late Grandfather Rondeaux's Norman estates: "his" at La Roque (the La Morinière of *L'Immoraliste*) and "hers" at Cuverville (the Fongueusemare of *La Porte étroite*). In 1900 he sold the former, a moated, ivy-covered, partly-sixteenth-century château surrounded by six hundred acres of farms and woodland, where Francis Jammes insisted he awoke in a haunted tower room, during a visit in 1898, to find an owl in his slipper.

The other estate, Cuverville, was to be Gide's retreat and his wife's home for the rest of their lives. Life at this comfortable country house has been described somewhere in print by virtually every one of their many literary house-guests over the years; perhaps the best formal portrait of it is this by Justin O'Brien, with its lovely inset sketch by Roger Martin du Gard.

> The long three-story house with its fourteen master bedrooms dates from the eighteenth century, of which it has the typical mansard roof and small-paned windows. The pale yellow, white-shuttered dwelling is ornamented solely by the precision of its proportions and its central pediment, bright against the slate roof. It stands in a seventeen-acre park surrounded by over three hundred acres of farmlands. In front of the stone steps extends a vast lawn shaded by a giant cedar planted one hundred years ago by the grandfather. On the left runs an avenue of tall beeches. Behind the house, protected by a thick curtain of trees, a flower-garden basks in the sun, its winding paths outlined by espalier fruit trees. As is customary in such houses, the common rooms extend from front to back, receiving light from windows at both ends; both facades command a broad view of the wild, monotonous landscape of the Caux region, intersected by beech groves for shelter against the Channel winds. . . .
>
> The interior of the large dwelling possesses the same charm as the sober exterior. On the right of the entrance hall, one enters a white-paneled drawing-room with windows at both ends. Its ma-

hogany furniture and petit-point armchairs harmonize with the gay
draperies and honey-colored parquet floor. On the left of the hall
opens the dining-room, with its three wicker armchairs by the wood
fire, each sheltering a majestic Siamese cat. Meals are served with an
Anglo-Saxon simplicity at a round table by one of the windows.
Near the table a door leads to Mme Gide's domain: the pantry,
milk-room, storeroom, and vast kitchen with its gleaming coppers.
"There Mme Gide spends hours at her daily tasks in a stifling odor
of kerosene, wax, and turpentine. For the religion of polish
reigns at Cuverville. Everything that can be rubbed shines like a
mirror," writes Roger Martin du Gard; and, faithful to the technique of his *World of the Thibaults,* he gives a striking example:
"The staircase is a model of its kind: according to an unalterable
rite at least fifty years old, every morning patient servants with
wool cloths tirelessly caress all its surfaces, all its flat spaces, all its
reliefs—from the red tiles of the steps and their oak borders to the
least projections of the iron balustrade. As an alluvium of several
generations, a thick layer of hardened wax, transparent like a
topaz-colored varnish, makes the whole staircase look as if carved
out of some precious, polished, indefinable material, a block of dark
amber." [12]

There in Normandy Gide wrote his books, took his naps, worked in
his garden, practiced the piano for hours; he went for long country walks
or carriage rides to the sea with his guests, then diverted them with readings aloud or after-dinner games. When the Gides were alone, by all
accounts, life was of course quieter, but no less genial—at least not until
André's nerves began to tighten and he was driven out onto the roads
once more. To Jammes, shortly after finishing *L'Immoraliste,* he wrote
from Cuverville, "Here we swim, we plunge, we disappear in the calm; I
am learning to think green—I am learning not to think at all. I am a
thousand leagues away from my last book, ten thousand from the next
. . . Happy? I think we are . . . enormously." [13]

But Gide was rarely content anywhere for very long. In fact, he and
his wife were only at home in Normandy a short fraction of each year.
Gide was forever being drawn back to Paris (where he had kept his
mother's apartment) by his literary activities, however much he professed to despise the capital. They saw the Exposition of 1900, Sarah
Bernhardt in *Hamlet.* There were cures to be taken at spas in France,
Switzerland, Austria. Even more potently, more irresistibly was he drawn

back to the South, to the scenes of his sensual rebirth. It was from these
returns, these reunions with his "natural self" of 1893 and '95 that *L'Im-moraliste* began to grow. Its seed is to be found in the fact that for these
six years, on five progressively less happy expeditions, he took his wife
along—each time under the pretense of improving her failing health;
for she was ill, or at least weak, most of this time. There is no question
here, I think, but that Gide—like his hero Michel—was self-deluded;
my only question is as to how *conscious* the delusion was, how much one
half of his mind knew what the other half was doing.

Both in the *Journal* (the references to Donatello) and, more explic-itly, in *Et nunc manet in te,* Gide reveals that his homosexual tastes were
not held in abeyance during these trips with his wife. Unlike his poor
Michel, he knew quite well what his various urges implied. By 1900, he
has become a "prowler by night"; in 1901 he will leave Madeleine alone
for twelve days in Biskra, writing a series of anguished letters begging
him to come back, while he goes off across the desert with Athman and
Henri Ghéon; and by 1902 he is openly writing in his *Journal* of "little
Emile" and "little Bernard." And yet he could keep pretending, despite
the sandstorms and sea storms, despite her loneliness and fatigue and the
illnesses that only worsened from place to place, that he was making
each of these trips for Madeleine's sake. He can write to his friends of his
love for Athman, of his love for the very *inhumanity* of the desert ("I
am obsessed with soon going back *there,* and some nights it keeps me
from sleeping"[14]); while, from that very desert, his wife writes to her
aunt, "Here I feel myself too far from, too separated from the only na-ture that my eyes have ever known and loved before now." [15] Paul
Valéry politely wonders whether he is not making her travel more than
is good for her. "Each new move," Gide admits, "still wears her out so
much that I fear *all* this moving about may be serving no good—good
for what?—why above all for making her better." [16] After describing
their ghastly return voyage from Africa by way of Spain in 1899, during
which Madeleine fell so ill that he thought she might be dying of ty-phoid, he writes, "We can bear no more of this atrocious exile; why ever
did we impose it on ourselves?" [17]—and one wonders whether or not he
knew the answer.

These, then, are some of the human materials of which *L'Immoral-iste* was made. Reading the story in the light of them, one may begin to
appreciate what an an arduous effort of self-understanding it represents;
and to understand why the man on the other side of it is not the same
man as the André Gide we have seen up to now.

from

SI LE GRAIN

NE MEURT

(*If It Die*), *Part II*

The facts, the motions of my heart and mind which I am now obliged to relate, I wish to present in the same light in which they first appeared to me, undistorted by the judgment that I myself came to make of them later on. All the more so in that this judgment has changed more than once: I tend to look back on my life by turns indulgently and severely, depending on the brightness or cloudiness of my interior sky. And finally, although it has lately occurred to me that a very important actor—the devil—may have had a considerable part to play in this drama, I shall nonetheless relate it without acknowledging an intervention I did not come to recognize until long after the events occurred. Down what detours I was led to a state of the blindest happiness—that is the story I propose to tell. At that season, in my twentieth year, I was beginning to convince myself that nothing could happen to me that was not fortunate. I held onto that confidence, in fact, until just a few months ago—and I regard the event that suddenly led me to lose it as one of the most important events of my life.*
Yet even after this blow I recovered myself, so imperious is my sense of joy, so potent is my interior certitude that the event most unhappy on first view is the very one most suited to instruct us on closer consideration; that there is some profit to be drawn from the worst, that all evil is good for something, and that if more often than not we fail to recognize good fortune, it is because it appears to us in another guise than the one we were expecting. But clearly I am anticipating; and I shall be ruining my whole story if I lead the reader to believe that I had already attained a state of joy which at that time I should scarcely have thought possible; which, in point of fact, I should scarcely have dared to think permitted. When I grew wiser, later on, better advised, all this of course seemed very simple; I was able to smile, then, at the extraordinary torments that tiny difficulties had caused me; I was able to call by their proper name those impulses, at that time still vague, which had so frightened me because of my utter inability to make out their nature or shape. At that time I still had everything to discover; I was forced to invent both the torment and the cure, and I can-

* See page 500.

not say which of the two I thought the more monstrous. My puritan upbringing had so formed me, had taught me to attach such importance to
certain things, that I simply could not conceive that the questions which
agitated me were not of passionate interest to the whole human race, and
to each separate man privately. I was like Prometheus, wonderstruck to
learn that man can live without his eagle, without letting it devour him.
What is more, without knowing it, I loved my eagle; but I was beginning
to come to terms with him. Yes, my problem stayed the same; but as I
advanced further into life, I no longer considered it quite so terrible, I no
longer regarded it from quite so acute an angle. —What problem? I
should be hard put to define it in a few words. But to start, was it not
already a significant thing that such a problem existed? Reduced to its
simplest terms, this is what it was:

In the name of what God, what ideal, do you forbid me to live according to my nature? And this nature of mine—where would it lead me
if I *were* to follow it? Until that point in my life, I had accepted the
teaching of Christ, or at any rate a certain puritan ethic that I had been
told was the teaching of Christ. In forcing myself to submit to it, I had
done nothing but create the most profound disorder of my entire being. I
refused to live licentiously, and the demands of my flesh were unable to
win the assent of my spirit. Had those demands been more commonplace,
I doubt that my difficulties would have been any less. For it made no
difference *what* my appetites happened to crave, so long as I thought it
my duty to refuse them everything. But eventually I came to wonder
whether even God could require such constraints; whether it was not impious to be so constantly resisting, whether it was not in fact to be resisting
Him; whether, in this battle that divided me in two, it was reasonable to
consider my "other self" always in the wrong. It dawned on me at last that
this discordant dualism might be resolved into harmony. And then I saw
at once that such a harmony was to be my sovereign goal from that moment on, and the search to achieve it my actual *raison d'être.* When, in
October of '93, I embarked for Algeria, it was not so much toward a new
land that my impulse was urging me as toward *this,* this golden fleece. I
had determined to leave home in any case; but for a long time I had hesitated whether or not to accept my cousin Georges Pouchet's invitation to
accompany him on a scientific expedition to Iceland. And I was still hesitating when Paul Laurens won a traveling fellowship in some competition
or other which obliged him to spend a year in exile. He chose me as his
companion, and my fate was decided. And so we set forth, my friend and

I: it was not with a more profound enthusiasm that the chosen youth of Greece set off with Jason in the *Argo*. . . .

 . . . After the publication of the *Cahiers,* my cousin's refusal of my marriage proposal, though it had not exactly discouraged me, had at any rate obliged me to postpone my hopes; moreover, as I have already said, my love was still quasi-mystical; the very idea of adulterating it with anything carnal I regarded as repulsive. This folly may have been due to some trick of the devil's; but I had no way of knowing that at the time. In any case, I had made up my mind to dissociate pleasure and love; I even thought this divorce to be something desirable, believed that pleasure would be purer and love more complete if the heart and the flesh had nothing to do with one another. Yes, Paul and I were resolved when we started . . . And if anyone were to ask me how Paul, who had been brought up, morally no doubt, but in a Catholic and not a puritan family, had managed to keep his virginity till he was past twenty-three, living as he did in an artistic milieu, and with the constant provocation of art students and models—I should answer that it is my story I am telling and not his, and that, besides, such cases are much more frequent than one supposes; for people generally dislike having it known. Timidity, shame, distaste, pride, ill-judged sentimentality, nervous fright caused by an unfortunate experience (this was Paul's case I believe), all these things may stop one on the verge. Then follow doubt, disquiet, romanticism, and melancholy. Now we were tired of all that, we were determined to be quit of it all. But our predominant feeling was one of horror for anything peculiar, odd, morbid, or abnormal. And in the conversations we had before starting, we urged each other, I remember, to pursue an ideal of equilibrium, plenitude, and health. It was I believe, indeed, my first aspiration toward what is now known as "classicism"; how contrary this was to the Christian ideal I had been brought up on, I can never stress strongly enough; and I realized this so immediately and so thoroughly that I decided not to take my Bible away with me. This may perhaps seem a trifle, but it was of the highest importance: up till that time not a day had gone by without my going to the Holy Book both for moral sustenance and for counsel. But it was just because this sustenance seemed to have become indispensable, that I felt the need of cutting the cord. I did not bid farewell to Christ without a sort of anguish, a rending of my heart; so that I wonder today whether I ever really left him.

We stayed a few days at Toulon with the Latils, friends of Paul's family. I caught cold and was beginning to feel unwell even before we left

France, though I said nothing about it. I should not have mentioned this if the question of health had not been so important in my life, particularly beginning with the time of this journey. I had always been delicate; two years in a row the army medical board had pronounced me unfit, and the third time it had definitely rejected me; "tuberculosis," read my medical release from army service, and I don't know whether I had been more delighted at getting off or frightened by the reason given. Besides, I knew that my father had already . . . In short, the kind of treacherous cold I caught at Toulon alarmed me so much that I hesitated whether I should not let Paul sail alone, and join him myself a little later. Then I abandoned myself to my fate, which is almost always the wisest thing to do. Besides which I thought the warmth of Algeria would set me back on my feet, and that no climate could be better for me. . . .

We had a fairly calm crossing from Marseilles to Tunis. In our cabin the air was stifling, and the first night I perspired so profusely that the sheets stuck to me; I spent the second night on deck . . . Great flashes of sheet lightning throbbed in the distance, in the direction of Africa. Africa! I repeated the mysterious word over and over again; I blew it up into something gigantic with terrors, with alluring horrors, with hopes and expectations; and throughout the hot night I stared transfixed toward the promised land, sultry, oppressing, streaked by lightning.

Oh, I know that there is nothing very extraordinary about a journey to Tunis; no; but the extraordinary thing was *our* going there. In truth, the coconut palms of the South Sea islands would amaze me no more today —and tomorrow, alas, even less—than the first camels I ever saw, from the deck of our boat. On a tongue of low land that encircled the narrow channel we had entered, they were silhouetted against the sky like a classroom display. I had of course expected to see camels at Tunis, but I had never imagined them quite so strange; and then, when our ship drew up alongside the quay, what a shoal of golden fish it sent splashing, flying up out of the water! And the crowd straight out of the Arabian Nights, which came bustling round to seize our luggage! We were at that point in life when everything new is intoxicating and enchanting: we could savor at once both our thirst and the quenching of it. We found everything astonishing, beyond all our expectations. With what innocence did we fall into all the vendors' traps! But how lovely were the materials of our haïks and burnouses; how delicious we thought the coffee the shopman offered us, and how generous of him to offer it! On the very first day, as soon as we made our appearance in the bazaar, a little guide of about fourteen took possession of us and escorted us into the shops (we should have been indignant if anyone had suggested that he was paid a commission); then, as he talked French fairly well, and moreover was charming, we made an appointment with him for the next day at our hotel. He was called Ceci and came from the island of Djerba, which is said to be the isle of the Lotus-eaters. I remember our anxiety when he did not turn up at the appointed hour. And a few days later, when he came into my room (we had left the hotel and taken a little apartment of three rooms in the rue Al Djezira) carrying the things we had just bought, I remember my mixed and troubled feelings when he half undressed in order to show me how to drape myself in a haïk. . . .

We were to sleep at Zaghouan, and all day long we watched the mountain in front of us slowly drawing nearer, growing more pink with each passing hour. And gradually we found ourselves falling in love with that vast monotonous landscape, with its iridescent emptiness, its silence. But the wind! . . . If it stopped blowing, the heat was overpowering; if it rose, one was paralyzed with cold. It blew swiftly and steadily, as water flows in a river; it pierced one's blankets, one's clothes, one's very flesh; I felt chilled to the bone. I had not entirely recovered from my indisposition at Toulon, and fatigue had made it worse; but I would not give in. I felt it too hard not to do whatever Paul did, and I went with him everywhere; but I expect that had it not been for me he would have done still more, and that he held back out of friendship and tact when he saw my resistance beginning to weaken. I was constantly having to take precautions, constantly worrying that I was inadequately, or too warmly, covered. In those circumstances, it was madness to launch off across the desert. But I would not give up the idea, and besides, I fell a victim to that lure of the South, to that mirage which deludes us into thinking it mild.

Zaghouan, however, with its pleasant orchards, its running waters, nicely sheltered in a fold of the mountains, would have offered a great many advantages, and I should no doubt soon have recovered my health —if I could have brought myself to stop there. But how was I not to imagine that, just a little farther on . . .

For most of the second day, our road was nothing more than a half-obliterated track; immediately after leaving the mountains, it plunged into a region even more arid than that of the day before. Toward the middle of the day we came to a great hollowed-out rock swarming with a kingdom of bees, whose sides were streaming with honey—or at least so our guide told us. We reached the model farm of Enfida in the evening and spent the night there. On the third day we arrived at Kairouan.

The holy city rises suddenly and unannounced straight out of the desert; its immediate surroundings are wild, ferocious; not a trace of vegetation except nopals—those extraordinary plants like green rackets, covered with poisonous prickles, whose thickets are said to be the haunt of cobras. Near the town gate, at the foot of the ramparts, a magician was making one of those terrible serpents dance to the sound of his flute. All the houses of the town had just been whitewashed, as though in honor of our arrival. I prefer those white walls, with their shadows and strange reflections, to any but the clay walls of the southern oases. I was glad to recall that Gautier despised them.

We had letters of introduction to the principal personages of the town, and rather imprudently made use of them, for it greatly curtailed our liberty. We went to dinner at the caliph's to meet some officers; it was all very splendid and gay; after dinner, I was set down to a wretched piano and had to rack my brains for music for the guests to dance to . . . Why do I tell all this? Oh, simply to put off telling what must follow: I know it isn't interesting.

We spent the whole of next day at Kairouan. There was a gathering of Aïssaouas in a little mosque, which surpassed in frenzy, in strangeness, in beauty, in nobility, in horror, anything I have ever seen since; in my six other journeys to Algeria, I have never met with anything approaching it.

We started off again. I was feeling more and more ill every day. Every day, the wind grew colder; it blew incessantly. When we arrived at Sousse after another day's travel in the desert, I was breathing with such difficulty, and beginning to feel so uncomfortable, that Paul went to look for a doctor. I could see very clearly that he thought my condition serious. He prescribed some kind of revulsive, I cannot recall which, to relieve the congestion of my lungs, and promised to come again next day.

Needless to say there could be no further question of our continuing our tour. But Biskra seemed not a bad place to spend the winter, once we had given up the idea of reaching it by the longest and most adventurous route. If we returned to Tunis, the train would take us there prosaically but practically, in two days. In the meantime, I had first of all to rest, for I was not yet fit to travel.

I ought now, I suppose, to describe my state of mind when I heard the doctor's verdict, and say to what extent I felt alarmed. I cannot remember that I was very much concerned; either because at that time I was not really much afraid of death, or because my idea of death was not in the least urgent and precise, or because my state of mindless exhaustion precluded any strong reaction whatever. Moreover, I have no great love for the elegiac strain. I gave myself up to fate therefore, without feeling much regret except for having involved Paul in my breakdown; for he would not hear of leaving me alone and continuing his journey without me; so that the first result of my illness, and I might almost say its reward, was to give me the opportunity of measuring the inestimable value of his friendship.

We stayed at Sousse only six days. But against the background of those monotonous days, that dreary wait, there stands out a little episode which was to have a considerable effect on my life. If it is indecent to relate it, it would be still more dishonest to pass it over.

At certain hours of the day, Paul left me to go and paint; but I was not so miserable as to be unable sometimes to go and join him. For that matter, during the whole time I was ill, I did not stay in my bed, or even my room, for a single day. I never went out without taking a coat and a shawl with me: as soon as I got outside, some boy would appear and offer to carry them. The one who accompanied me on that particular day was a brown-skinned Arab boy, quite young, whom I had already noticed on previous days among the troop of little rascals who loitered in the neighborhood of the hotel. He wore a chechia on his head like the others, and a coat of coarse linen and baggy Tunisian trousers directly over his skin— trousers that made his bare legs look even slenderer than they were. He seemed more reserved or more timid than his companions, so that as a rule they got to me before he did; but that day, I don't know how, I got out without any of the gang seeing me, and suddenly it was he who had joined me at the corner of the hotel.

The hotel was situated on the outskirts of town, and the terrain thereabout was of sand. It was sad to see the olive trees, so handsome in the adjacent fields, half submerged here by the drifting dunes. A little farther on one was astonished to come upon a stream—a meager water-course, springing out of the sand just in time to reflect a little bit of sky before reaching the sea. A gathering of Negro laundresses squatting beside this trickle of fresh water was the subject Paul had chosen to paint. I had promised to meet him there, but, although I was exhausted from walking through the sand, I let myself be led up into the sandhills by Ali (that was the name of my young guide); we soon reached a kind of funnel or crater, the rim of which was just high enough to command the surrounding country and give a view of anyone coming. As soon as we got there, Ali threw my coat and shawl down on the sloping sand; he flung himself down too, and stretched on his back, with his arms outspread, he looked at me and began to laugh. I was not such a simpleton as to misunderstand his invitation; but all the same, I did not answer it at once. I sat down, not far from him, but not too near either, and in my turn looked steadily at him and waited, extremely curious as to what he would do next.

I waited! I am amazed today at my fortitude. . . . But was it really curiosity that held me back? I am not sure. The secret motive of our acts— I mean of the most decisive ones—escapes us; and not only in memory but at the very moment we commit them. Was I still hesitating on the threshold of what is called sin? No; I would have been much too disappointed if the adventure had concluded with the triumph of my virtue— which I already loathed and despised. No; it was really curiosity that made me wait . . . And I watched his laughter slowly fade away, his lips close down again over his white teeth, and an expression of sadness and chagrin darken his charming features.

"Well, then; *adieu,*" he said.

But I seized the hand he held out to me and tumbled him onto the ground. In a moment he was laughing again. The complicated knots of the strings that he used for a belt did not detain him long; he drew a little dagger from his pocket and severed the tangle with one cut. The garment fell, he flung away his coat, and stood up naked as a god. Then he raised his slight arms for a moment to the sky, and dropped laughing against me. Though his body may have been burning, it felt as refreshing to my hands as shade. How beautiful the sand was! In the lovely splendor of that evening light, my joy was wrapped in the setting sun's rays. . . .

In the meantime it was getting late. I had to join Paul. No doubt my countenance bore traces of my delirium, and I think he guessed something; but as he did not question me (perhaps out of discretion), I dared tell him nothing. . . .

. . . Incapable of work, of any prolonged concentration, I dragged miserably through the day, finding no distraction, no joy except in watching the boys at play on our terrace, or in the public garden, when the weather allowed me to go down to it; for the rainy season had begun. And it was not with any one of them in particular that I fell in love, but with their youth, indiscriminately. The sight of their health sustained me, and I had no wish for any company but theirs. Perhaps I found in their naïve gestures, their childish talk a mute counsel to give myself more freely to life. Under the combined influence of climate and illness, I felt my austerity begin to melt, my brows to unknit. At last I realized how much pride lay concealed in my resistance to what I no longer called temptation, now that I had stopped arming myself against it. "More obstinacy than fidelity," Signoret once wrote of me; I prided myself, it is true, on being faithful; but thenceforth I placed all my obstinacy in clinging to the resolution Paul and I had made—the decision to "renormalize" ourselves. Illness did not weaken my determination. And I should like to have it understood how much sheer resolution entered into what I am about to relate; if I am to be accused of giving way to my natural inclinations, let it be understood that they were the inclinations of the mind and not of the body. My natural propensity, which I was at last forced to recognize (but to which I did not yet think it possible to assent), was only fortified by resistance; I merely strengthened it by my struggles; in despair of ever conquering it, I thought I might be able to beguile and transform it. Out of sympathy for Paul, I even went so far as to invent imaginary desires; that is to say, I adopted his, and each of us encouraged the other. A winter resort like Biskra offers particular facilities in this respect; a troop of women live there who make a business of their bodies . . .

Paul came back one day very much excited; on his way home from a walk he had met the troop of Ouled Naïl going to bathe at Fontaine-Chaude. One of them, whom he described to me as particularly charming, had managed to escape from the group at a sign from him; an appointment had been made. And as I was not yet in sufficiently good health to go to her, it was agreed that she was to come to us. . . .

Of all that evening, there is one moment of which I have kept the most thrilling recollection: I see Meriem, still hesitating, outlined on the edges of the night; she recognizes Paul and smiles, but before coming in, she steps back, and leaning over the balustrade of the terrace behind her, waves her haïk in the dark—a signal to dismiss the maidservant who had accompanied her to the foot of our staircase.

. . . She was wrapped in a double haïk which she let fall at the door. I cannot remember her dress, for she soon shed it; but she kept the bracelets on her wrists and ankles. I do not remember either whether or not Paul took her first to his room, a separate little pavilion at the other end of the terrace; yes, I think she did not come to me till dawn; but I can remember Athman's lowered eyes the next morning as he passed in front of the Cardinal's bed, and his amused, prudish, comical "Good morning, Meriem!"

Meriem was amber-skinned, firm-fleshed; her figure was round but still almost childish, for she was barely sixteen. I can only compare her to a bacchante—the one on the Gaeta vase, for instance—because of her bracelets too, rattling like the castanets of a Cretan priestess, bracelets which she was continually shaking. I remember having seen her dance in one of the cafés of the rue Sainte, where Paul had taken me one evening. Her cousin En Barka was dancing there too. They danced in the antique fashion of the Ouled, the head straight and erect, the torso motionless, the hands agile, the whole body shaken by the rhythmic beating of the feet. How much I liked that "Mahometan music," with its steady, obstinate, incessant flow; it went to my head, quickly stupefied me like some narcotic drug, left my brain drowsily and voluptuously benumbed. On a platform beside the clarinet-player sat an old Negro, clacking his metal castanets, and little Mohammed, lost in a lyrical ecstasy, thumping on his tambourine. How beautiful he was! Half naked under his rags, black and slender as a demon, open-mouthed and wild-eyed . . . Paul had bent toward me that evening (does he remember it, I wonder?) and whispered in my ear: "Do you suppose he doesn't excite me more than Meriem?"

He had said it in jest, meaning no harm, he who was attracted only by women; but what need had he to say it to me, of all people? I said nothing; but that avowal has haunted me ever since; I had taken it as mine; or rather it was already mine even before Paul had spoken; and if that night I was valiant with Meriem, it was because I shut my eyes and imagined I was holding Mohammed in my arms.

After that night I experienced an extraordinary sensation of calm and well-being. And I am not speaking only of that feeling of repose which sometimes follows sexual pleasure; it is certain that Meriem had then and there done me more good than all the doctor's revulsives. I should hardly dare recommend this treatment; but my case was so much a matter of nerves that it is not surprising my lungs were relieved by so radical a diversion, and that a kind of equilibrium was re-established.

Meriem returned; she returned for Paul; she was to return for me, and the appointment was already made, when we suddenly received a telegram from my mother, announcing her arrival. A few days before Meriem's first visit, I had had a hemorrhage; I had not attached much importance to it myself, but it had greatly alarmed Paul. He had told his parents about it, and they had thought it their duty to warn my mother. . . .

I was of course glad to see her, and to show her the country; but the telegram brought consternation nonetheless: our life together was begin-ing to be so well organized; the re-education of our instincts, which we had only just started—were we going to have to interrupt it? I vowed we should not, that my mother's presence should change nothing in our habits; and that to begin with, Meriem's visit should not be canceled. . . .

My mother arrived, then, one evening, in company with our old Marie, who had never made so long a journey. The rooms they were to occupy—the only vacant ones in the hotel—were on the other side of the courtyard and opened straight onto our terrace. If I remember rightly, it was that very evening that we were expecting Meriem; she arrived almost directly after my mother and Marie had retired to their rooms; and at first everything went off without a hitch. But in the early morning . . .

A remnant of shame—or rather of respect for my mother's feelings —had made me lock my door. So it was to Paul's room that Meriem went straightaway. The little pavilion he occupied was so situated that one had to cross the terrace from one end to the other in order to reach it. In the early morning, when Meriem knocked at my window as she passed, I rose hastily and waved her good-bye. She stepped furtively away and melted into the reddening sky, like a ghost that fades at the first crowing of the cock; but just at that moment, that is to say, before she had quite vanished, I saw the shutters of my mother's room open and my mother lean out of her window. Her glance followed Meriem's flight for a moment; then the window closed. The catastrophe was upon us.

It was obvious that this woman had come from Paul's room. It was certain that my mother had seen her, had understood. . . . What could I do but wait? I waited.

My mother had her breakfast in her room. Paul went out. Then my mother came and sat down beside me. I cannot remember her words ex-actly. I do remember that I had the cruelty to say, with a great effort, both because I did not want her blame to fall on Paul alone, and also because I intended to safeguard the future: "But you know, she doesn't come only for Paul. She's coming back."

I remember her tears. I think, in fact, that she said nothing, that she found nothing to say to me and could only cry; but her tears softened and saddened my heart more than any reproaches could have done. She wept and wept; I felt she was inconsolably, infinitely sad. So that if I had the face to tell her that Meriem was coming back, to share with her my resolu-tion, I had not the courage afterwards to keep my word, and the only other experiment I made at Biskra was outside our hotel, with En Barka, in her own room. Paul was with me, and for him as well as for me that fresh attempt was a miserable failure. En Barka was much too beautiful (and, I should add, a good deal older than Meriem); her very beauty froze me; I felt a kind of admiration for her, but not the smallest trace of desire. I came to her as a worshipper without an offering. The case of Pygmalion was reversed, for it was the woman who became a statue in my arms; or rather, it was I who seemed made of marble. Caresses, provocations, nothing availed; I was mute, and left her without having been able to give her anything but money.

In the meantime, spring was touching the oasis. An indistinct sense of delight began to stir under the palm trees. I was feeling better. One morning I ventured to take a much longer walk than usual; the country, for all its monotony, held an inexhaustible attraction for me; I felt that, like it, I had begun to revive; that I was alive, in fact, for the first time, that I had left the Valley of the Shadow of Death and been born into real life. Yes, I was entering upon a new existence with open arms and a free spirit. A light azure haze made the foreground appear distant, dematerialized every object. I myself, freed of all weight, walked slowly on, like Rinaldo in the garden of Armida, quivering all over, dazzled and amazed with a wonder beyond words. I heard, I saw, I breathed as I had never done before; and as the sounds, perfumes, and colors blended into a stream that flooded my empty heart, I felt it dissolve in passionate gratitude.

"Take me, take me body and soul," I cried, sobbing out my worship to some unknown Apollo; "I am yours; I obey you; you have won. Turn everything within me into light, yes, into light and air. Until this day I have struggled against you in vain. But now I know you. Your will be done: I resist no longer; I resign myself to you. Take me."

And so, my face flooded with tears, I entered a new, enchanting universe full of laughter and strangeness. . . .

. . . I went to Geneva to consult Dr. Andreæ, a latter-day Tronchin, great friend of the Charles Gides, and not only one of the cleverest of men, but one of the best and wisest as well; I owe him my salvation. He very soon persuaded me that there was nothing wrong with me but my nerves, and that a cure of hydrotherapy at Champel to begin with, and a winter in the mountains afterwards, would do me more good than all the precautions and medications in the world.

I brought back with me, on my return to France, the secret of a man returned to life, and felt at first the same sort of abominable anguish that Lazarus must have known after he escaped from the tomb. Nothing that had concerned me before seemed now to have any importance. How had I been able to breathe the stifling atmosphere of the salons and coteries, where a dusty scent of death was stirred up by all their agitation? And no doubt I suffered too in my self-conceit at seeing that the ordinary course of events had been so little disturbed by my absence, and that now everybody went about his business as if I had never come back. My secret took up so much room in my heart that I was astonished to find that I myself took up so little in the eyes of the world. . . .

One will readily imagine that with such feelings as I have described I was longing to go away again. But it was still too early to take up my winter quarters in the little village in the Jura that Dr. Andreæ had recommended. (I followed his instructions to the letter, and with the greatest success.) In the meantime, therefore, I settled at Neuchâtel. . . .

For months I had let my thoughts unravel and go to pieces; now at last I got them back under control, rejoicing to feel them still so active, and full of gratitude to this peaceful land for helping me to collect and concentrate them once again. It is impossible to imagine anything less sublime, less Swiss, more temperate, more human than the quiet shores of this lake, where the ghost of Rousseau still wanders. There are no haughty peaks in the neighborhood to humble or dwarf the efforts of man, or to distract the eyes from the intimate delights of the foreground. Venerable trees droop their low branches down to the water, and sometimes the line of shore wavers among reeds and rushes.

I spent one of the happiest times I can remember at Neuchâtel; I had recovered hope in life; it seemed to me now strangely richer and fuller than my pusillanimous childhood had first imagined. I felt it waiting for me; I counted on it; but I was in no hurry. That uneasy demon, bred of curiosity and desire, did not yet torment me, that demon who, since then . . . In the quiet garden paths, along the banks of the lake, on the roads and in the precincts of the autumn-laden woods outside the town, I wandered, as no doubt I should do today—but at peace.

According to Andreæ's advice, I spent the winter at La Brévine—a little village near the Swiss frontier on the iciest summit of the Jura. . . .

———

I stayed at La Brévine about three months without having any dealings with anyone; not that I was in an unsociable mood, but I found the inhabitants of the region the most inhospitable and unfriendly I have ever met. Armed with Dr. Andreæ's letters of introduction, I called upon the doctor and the pastor of the village, but received not the smallest encouragement to return and see them again, and still less to accompany them, as I had hoped, on their rounds among the sick and the poor. One must have lived in that part of the world to understand the passages of Rousseau's *Confessions* and *Rêveries,* in which he speaks of his stay at Val Travers. Ill-will, spiteful talk, scowling looks, mocks and jeers—no, he invented none of it; I met with them all myself, even to the stones thrown at the stranger by the pack of village children. And one can imagine how his Armenian costume must have aroused their xenophobia! The mistake, the madness began when he saw this hostility as some sort of plot.

Every day, notwithstanding the hideousness of the country, I forced myself to take long walks. Is it unfair to say "hideousness"? Perhaps; but I had taken a loathing to Switzerland; not perhaps to the Switzerland of the high plateaus, but to that belt of forest-land, where the fir trees seem to have infested the whole of nature with a kind of morose and Calvinistic stiffness. In reality, I longed for Biskra; a great nostalgia for that vast, featureless land and its people in their white burnouses had pursued Paul and me all through Italy; the memory of its songs and dances and perfumes, of its children too, and of the idyllic intercourse into which such a voluptuous charm had already insidiously crept. Here there was nothing to distract me from my work, and in spite of my exasperation with Switzerland, I managed to stick to it long enough to finish *Paludes;* with the *idée fixe* of leaving for Algeria as soon as it was done.

It was not till January that I set out, after a short stay at Montpellier with the Charles Gides. . . .

Blida, to which in the springtime I returned to find all loveliness and perfumes, I now thought dreary and unattractive. I roamed up and down the town looking for a lodging, without finding anything to suit me. I longed for Biskra. I had no taste for anything. My despondency was all the greater because I was carrying it about with me in a place where my imagination had proposed wonders and delights; but it still lay under the gloomy spell of winter, and I with it. The lowering sky weighed heavy on my thoughts; the wind and the rain quenched every spark of fire in my heart; I tried to work, but I felt uninspired; I dragged about in unspeakable boredom. My disgust for the weather was mixed with disgust for myself; I hated and despised myself; I wanted to harm myself somehow; I looked for a way to provoke my torpor to some desperate act.

Three days passed in this way.

I was on the point of leaving, and the bus, with my bag and trunk, had already gone. I can see myself standing in the hall of the hotel, waiting for my bill; my eye falls by chance on a slate on which the names of the hotel guests are written; I begin to read them mechanically. First my own, then the names of various strangers; suddenly my heart leaps: the two last names on the list are those of Oscar Wilde and Lord Alfred Douglas. . . .

I had seen a great deal of Wilde in Paris; I had met him in Florence; I have related all of this at length in another book,* as well as what follows; but not with all the details I wish to add here. . . .

Wilde, up till that day, had observed in my regard the most absolute reserve. I knew nothing of his tendencies except from hearsay; but in the literary circles we both frequented in Paris, people were beginning to talk a great deal. . . .

[Some days later, at Algiers]
One evening, immediately after Douglas had left for Blida, Wilde asked me to go with him to a Moorish café where there was music to be heard. I agreed, and called for him after dinner at his hotel. The café was not very far off, but as Wilde had some difficulty in walking, we took a carriage which dropped us in rue Montpensier, at the fourth terrace of the boulevard Gambetta, where Wilde told the coachman to wait for us. A guide, who had got up beside the coachman, now escorted us through a labyrinth of small streets inaccessible to carriages, until we came to the steep alley in which the café was situated. . . . As we walked, Wilde expounded in a low voice his theory of guides, and how important it was to choose the vilest, who was invariably the best. If the man at Blida had not been able to show us anything interesting, it was because he didn't feel ugly enough. Ours that evening was a terror.

There was nothing to show that it was a café; its door was like all the other doors; it stood ajar, and there was no need to knock. Wilde was a

* *Oscar Wilde: In Memoriam* (Paris, 1910).

habitué of the place, which I have described in *Amyntas,* for I often went back to it afterwards. A few old Arabs were sitting cross-legged on mats and smoking kief; they made no movement when we took our places among them. And at first I did not see what there was in this café that could attract Wilde; but soon I was able to make out a young *caouadji* standing in the shadow near the hearth; he was busy preparing us two cups of mint tea over the embers—a drink Wilde preferred to coffee. Lulled by the strange torpor of the place, I was just sinking into a state of semi-somnolence, when in the half-open doorway, there appeared a marvelous youth. He stood there for a time, leaning with his raised elbow against the door jamb, and outlined on the dark background of the night. He seemed uncertain whether to enter or not, and I was beginning to be afraid he would go; but then he smiled at a signal made him by Wilde, and came up and sat down opposite us on a stool a little lower than the raised area covered with mats where we were sitting, legs crossed in Arab fashion. He took a reed flute out of his Tunisian waistcoat, which he began to play exquisitely. Wilde told me a little later that he was called Mohammed and that "he was Bosy's"; he had hesitated at first at the door because he had not seen Lord Alfred. His large black eyes had the languorous look of hashish-smokers; he had an olive complexion; I admired his long fingers on the flute, the slimness of his boyish figure, the slender grace of his bare legs coming from under his loose white drawers, one of them bent back and resting on the knee of the other. The *caouadji* came to sit beside him and accompanied him on a kind of *darbouka.* The song of the flute flowed on through an extraordinary silence, like a limpid, steady stream, and you forgot the time, the place, who you were, all the cares of this world. We sat thus, without stirring, for what seemed to me an infinite time; but I would have sat on for longer still, if Wilde had not suddenly taken me by the arm and broken the spell.

"Come," he said.

We went out. We took a few steps in the alley, followed by the hideous guide, and I was beginning to think that our evening was to come to an end there, when at the first turning, Wilde came to a standstill, dropped his huge hand onto my shoulder, and bending down—for he was much taller than I—said in a whisper: *"Dear,* would you like the little musician?"

How dark the alley was! I thought my heart would fail me; what a great summoning up of courage it took to answer—"Yes"; and in what a strangled voice!

Wilde immediately turned to the guide, who had come up to us, and slipped into his ear a few words which I did not hear. The man left us, and we went on to the place where the carriage was waiting.

We were no sooner seated in it, than Wilde burst out laughing—a resounding laugh, not so much of pleasure as of triumph, an interminable, uncontrollable, insolent laugh; and the more he saw me disconcerted by his laughter, the more he laughed. I should say that if Wilde had begun to disclose the secrets of his life to me, he knew nothing as yet of mine; I had taken care that nothing, in my words or my actions, should give him reason to suspect a thing. The proposition he had just made me was a bold one; what amused him so much was that it was accepted at once; he was relishing this like a child, like a devil. The great pleasure of the debauchee is to debauch others. No doubt, since my adventure at Sousse, there was not much left for the Adversary to do to complete his victory over me; but Wilde did not know that, nor that I had already been conquered—or, if you prefer (for is it proper to speak of defeat when one carries one's head so high?), that I had already, in my imagination, in my thoughts, triumphed over all my scruples. To tell the truth, *I* did not know it; it was only, I think, as I answered "Yes," that I suddenly became aware of it myself. . . .

Every time since then that I have sought after pleasure, it is the memory of that night I have pursued. After my adventure at Sousse, I had relapsed wretchedly again into my solitary vice. If I had now and then snatched some sensual joy in passing, it had been as if furtively; there had been one delicious evening, I grant, in a boat on the lake of Como, with a young boatman (just before going to La Brévine), when my ecstasy was enveloped by the moonlight, the misty magic of the lake, the moist perfumes melting from its shores. And then nothing; nothing but a frightful desert, full of cries without answers, transports without object, anxieties, struggles, exhausting dreams, imaginary exaltations, abominable relapses. At La Roque, two summers before, I had been afraid of going mad; I spent nearly the whole time I was there shut up in my room, where I ought to have been working, where I tried in vain to *force* myself to work (I was writing *Le Voyage d'Urien*), obsessed, haunted, hoping perhaps to find some release in excess itself, hoping to come through it out into the fresh air on the other side, to wear out my demon (I now recognize his scheme), and all the while wearing out nothing but myself, pouring myself out maniacally to the point of utter exhaustion, to the verge of imbecility, of madness.

Ah! what a hell I went through! And without a friend I could speak to, without a word of advice; because I had believed all compromise impossible, because I had begun by refusing to surrender anything, I sank, I went under. . . . But what need is there to recall those lugubrious days? Does their memory explain that night's ecstasy? My attempt with Meriem, my effort toward "renormalization" was never repeated because it had not been in consonance with my nature; but now I had found my norm. Nothing constrained, nothing precipitate, nothing doubtful here; there is no taste of ashes in the memory I have kept. My joy was unbounded, and I cannot imagine it more full, even if love had been mingled. But how should there have been any question of love? How should I have allowed mere lust to dispose of my heart? My pleasure was neither clouded by scruple nor attended by remorse. But if not love, what name then am I to give the rapture I felt as I clasped in my naked arms that perfect little body, so wild, so ardent, so lascivious and dark? . . .

My mother was beginning to worry a great deal about the letters I was writing her, and as she could not believe that the exaltation they breathed was possible without some definite object, she imagined me entangled in some love affair, some liaison; she did not yet dare speak of it openly, but she filled her letters with allusions which made very clear the kind of phantoms she feared. She implored me to come back, to "break it off."

The truth, if she could have known it, would have frightened her still more; for it is easier to break ties than to escape from oneself. And to do so, in fact, one must first of all wish to; at the very moment I was beginning to discover myself—on the point of discovering in myself the tables of a new law—I was hardly likely to want to escape. For emancipation from the rule was not enough; I now insisted on legitimating my delirium, and rationalizing my madness. . . .

Yielding at last to my mother's objurgations, I went to spend a fortnight with her in Paris before she left for La Roque, where I was to join her in July, and where I was to see her again only as she lay dying. In those last days of our life in common (those we spent in Paris, I mean), the tension between us was relaxed and we enjoyed a truce; it is some consolation to me to remember them, when I consider the arguments and battles which, it must be admitted, formed the most obvious part of our relationship. I use the word "truce" here, in fact, because no lasting peace between us was possible; the reciprocal concessions which allowed us a little respite could only have been temporary, and were based on a silent agreement to misunderstand one another. But even beyond that, I did not regard my mother as actually wrong. She was playing her proper role, I thought, even when she was most tormenting me; to tell the truth, I could not conceive of any mother properly conscious of her duty who would not insist on her son's submission; but as I also thought it perfectly natural the son should refuse to submit, and as this too seemed to me perfectly just, I was astonished when I sometimes came across an example of perfect accord between parents and children—like that between Paul Laurens and his mother.

Is it not Pascal who says that we never love people for themselves, but only for their qualities? I think that it might have been said of my mother that the qualities she loved were never those possessed by the people singled out by, weighed down by her affection; but those she wished to see them acquire. At any rate, that is how I try to explain to myself her unremitting efforts to "work" on other people, and on me in particular, which irritated me so violently that I am not at all sure my exasperation did not end by spoiling all the love I had for her. She had a way of loving me that sometimes made me hate her and touched my nerves on the raw. Imagine, you whom I shock, imagine, if you can, the effect of being constantly watched and spied upon, incessantly and harassingly advised as to your acts, your thoughts, your expenses, as to what you ought to wear or what you ought to read, as to the title of a book. . . . She disliked, for instance, that of *Les Nourritures terrestres,* and as long as there was still time to change it, she unwearyingly returned to the charge. . . .

But, as I have said, that fortnight which we spent together after a long separation was spoiled by no clouds. I certainly brought a great deal of good will to it on my part, as if some presentiment had warned us both that these were the last days we should pass together; for *maman,* on her side, showed herself more conciliatory than I had ever known her. The joy of finding me less degenerate and destroyed than she had imagined from my letters no doubt also disarmed her; she seemed to me all that a mother should be, and I was happy to be her son.

I now began to wish for the resumption of our life in common, which I had ceased to think possible, and planned to spend the whole summer with her at La Roque. She was to go there first to open the house and it was not impossible that Emmanuèle might come and join us. For, as if to seal our more perfect understanding, *maman* had at last confessed to me that she wished for nothing so much as to see me marry my cousin, whom she had long looked upon as her daughter-in-law. Perhaps too she felt her strength failing and was afraid of leaving me alone.

I was at Saint-Nom-la-Bretèche, staying with my friend E.R.* until it should be time for me to join her, when a telegram from our old maid Marie suddenly summoned me. My mother had had an attack. I hurried off. When I next saw her, she was lying in bed in the big room which I had used as my study the past summers; it was the room she preferred when she stayed at La Roque for a few days without opening the whole house. I am almost sure that she recognized me; but she seemed to have no clear idea of the time or the place or of herself or of the people about her; for she showed neither surprise at my arrival, nor pleasure at seeing me. Her face was not much changed, but her eyes were vague and her features so expressionless that it seemed as though the body they still inhabited no longer belonged to her, that she had ceased to control it. And this was so strange that I felt more amazement than pity. She was in a half-sitting position, propped up on pillows; her arms were outside the bedclothes, and she was trying to write in a large open account-book. Even then her restless need to intervene, to advise, to persuade, was still wearing her out; she seemed the prey of some gnawing internal agitation, and the pencil she held in her hand ran over the blank sheet of paper, but without making any mark; and the uselessness of this supreme effort was inexpressibly pathetic. I tried to speak to her, but my voice no longer reached her; and when she tried to speak herself, I could not make out the words. I took away the paper in the hope that she might rest, but her hand continued to write on the bedsheets. At last she dropped off and her features gradually relaxed; her hands stopped twitching . . . And suddenly, as I looked at the poor hands I had just seen laboring so desperately, I imagined them at the piano, and the thought that they too had tried in their unskillful way to express a little poetry, music, and beauty, filled me with a great wave of respect and admiration, and, falling on my knees at the foot of the bed, I buried my face in the covers to stifle my sobs.

It is not my personal sorrows that draw tears from me; however grief-stricken my heart, my eyes remain dry. There is always one part of me which hangs back, which looks mockingly at the other and says: "Come! Come! You're not so unhappy as all that!" On the other hand, I have a great abundance of tears to shed over other people's griefs, which I often feel more keenly than my own; but I have even more for any manifestation of beauty, nobility, abnegation, devotion, gratitude, or courage, and

* Eugène Rouart.

sometimes for a very ingenuous, very pure, very childlike expression of feeling. . . . So that at the time it was not my sense of loss that upset me so greatly (and to be quite sincere, I am obliged to confess that my loss afflicted me very little; or perhaps I should say the sight of my mother's suffering afflicted me, but not very much the idea of her leaving me). No, it was not so much grief that made me cry as admiration for that heart that had never allowed anything vile to touch it, that beat only for others, that bound itself constantly to its duty, not so much out of devotion as out of natural inclination, and with a humility so great that my mother might have said, like Malherbe—but how much more sincerely—"I have always held my service so contemptible an offering, that to whatever altar I bring it, it is always with a heart ashamed and a trembling hand." And above all I admired her for her life, which had been one continual effort to draw a little nearer to whatever she thought lovable or worthy of being loved.

I was alone in the big room, alone with her, watching the solemn approach of death, and feeling re-echo in my own heart the restless beatings of her own, which refused to give up. How it still fought on! I had been the witness of other deaths, but none of them appeared so pathetic as this one; either because they had seemed to put a more conclusive and natural end to a life, or simply because I had looked at them less fixedly. It was certain that *maman* would not recover consciousness, so I felt no need to summon my aunts; I was jealous of watching over her by myself. Marie and I assisted her in her last moments, and when at last her heart ceased to beat, I felt my whole being sink into a great abyss of love, sorrow, and freedom.

It was then that I experienced the singular propensity of my mind to let itself be dazzled by the Sublime. I spent the first weeks of my bereavement, I remember, in a sort of moral intoxication which led me to commit the most ill-considered acts; all they had to do was seem noble in order to win at once the approval of my mind and my heart. I began by distributing as souvenirs to distant relations, some of whom had scarcely known my mother, the trifling jewels and *objets* which had been hers, and which for that reason I especially prized. Out of exaltation or love or some strange thirst for privation, I would have given away my whole fortune at the very moment I was inheriting it; I would have given myself away too; the feeling of my inward wealth filled me to overflowing, inspired me with a sort of drunken abnegation. The very idea of keeping anything back for myself would have seemed to me shameful, and I listened to nothing that did not help me to admire myself. The very freedom, which, during my mother's lifetime, I had so craved, now stunned me like a wind from the open; it suffocated, perhaps even frightened me. I felt dazed, like a prisoner unexpectedly set free, like a kite whose string has been suddenly cut, like a boat broken loose from its moorings, like a drifting wreck, at the mercy of wind and tide.

There was nothing to attach myself to now but my love for my cousin; my determination to marry her was the only light left me by which to guide my life. I loved her, certainly; that was the only thing I was sure of; and indeed I felt I loved her more than I loved myself. When I asked for her hand, I was considering her more than myself; and above all I was hypnotized by the vision of an infinitely widening horizon toward which I wanted to lead her along with me, despite the fact that I knew the road to be full of perils; for I refused to believe perils existed which my fervor could not overcome in time; all prudence I would have thought cowardly—and cowardly the very notion of danger.

Our sincerest acts are also the least premeditated; the explanation one looks for after the event is in vain. I was led by a fatality; perhaps also by the secret desire to set my nature at defiance; for in loving Emmanuèle, was it not virtue itself I loved? It was the marriage of heaven with my insatiable hell; but at the actual moment, my hell was in abeyance; the tears of my mourning had extinguished all its fires; I was as if dazzled by a clear blue sky, and the things I refused to see had ceased to exist for me. I believed that I could give her my whole self, and did so without any reservation whatever. Shortly afterwards, we became engaged.

. . . I thought of Cuverville and La Roque and of my grief at not being there. I thought that at that same hour the members of my family were looking likewise at the beautiful edges of the woods and were slowly returning home. The lamp is already on their table, the tea, the books of others. . . .

. . . Every autumn I read Dickens, Turgenev, or Eliot, but especially Dickens, whom I like to read more than anyone else at the end of the day, on my return from a long walk in the woods; then in slippers beside the fire while drinking tea and always in that same big green armchair at La Roque.

And the sound of the dinner bell; and the shadow cast by my mother, seated reading at the big table. . . . Is all that over?

Every year at this time a refrain of all my old devotions and ardors is reawakened; I become a good, quiet boy once again.

I am unwilling to understand a rule of conduct which does not permit and does not teach the greatest, the finest, and the freest use and development of all our powers.

O Lord, I must hide this from everyone else; but there are minutes, hours even, when everything in the world strikes me as without order and lost, when every harmony that my mind has invented disintegrates, when the very thought of the pursuit of a higher order annoys me, when the sight of poverty upsets me, when my old prayers and my old pious melancholy rise again into my heart, when the passive, self-denying virtue of the humble man once again seems to me the most beautiful.

——————

Take upon oneself as much humanity as possible. There is the right formula.

1895   [*Algiers*]

There, among the heavy, shapeless pillars of the dimly lighted room, the women dance, large women, not so much beautiful as strange, and excessively adorned. They move slowly. The voluptuousness they are offering is a grave one, strong and secret as death. Near the café, over a common courtyard filled with moonlight or with night, each leaves her door half open.

Their beds are low. You go down as into a tomb. Arab dreamers look on at the undulating dance, led by a music as constant as the noise of a rolling wave. The boy brings coffee in very small cups from which one feels that one is drinking oblivion.

Of all the Moorish cafés, I chose the darkest, the most distant. What is it that attracted me? Nothing; the darkness; a supple form that moved about; a song;—and not being seen from outside; the sense of the clandestine.

I enter without a sound; I sit down quickly, and, so as not to disturb anything, I pretend to read; I shall see . . .

But no; nothing—an old Arab is sleeping in a corner; another is singing in a very low voice; under a bench a dog is chewing a bone; and the serving-boy, near the hearth, stirs the ashes to uncover a few embers to heat my bitter coffee.—The time that flows by here is not measured in hours; but so perfect is everyone's idleness that boredom is impossible.

[*from* THE JOURNAL]

1895   *December 16*

Race through the corridors that join the Uffizi to the Palazzo Pitti; the wonderful Palatine Gallery. The head of the young man on the left in Giorgione's *Concert* is made of a marvelous substance. All the tones are

* Although written in 1899, and published in 1906, the recollection seems to be of the early part of this year.

melted and fused to form a new, unknown color at any given spot on the canvas—and all so closely linked together that you could not take anything away or add a single touch. Your eyes follow the forehead, the temple, the soft approach to the hair, without finding any trace of a joining; it all seems a melted enamel that had been poured, still liquid, onto the canvas.

In front of this painting you think of nothing else, and that is characteristic of a masterpiece: to be exclusive; to make any other form of beauty seem inferior.

December 26

This morning at the Museum of Santa Maria dei Fiori and at the National Museum. Looked especially at Donatello, whom I admire above all. At this exhibition of his work, originals or casts, you feel such an extraordinary and such a victorious struggle against the antique tradition. . . . Amazing preference for the male body and odd understanding of the forms of the child. That little *Amor,* one foot half-raised over a snake that the other is crushing—the short legs still weighed down, deformed by the badly tied breeches, which are falling down and half uncovering him, the belt remaining around his waist—as if for an ornamental complication; the awkward and charming gesture of his little arms in the air.

The ornamented nudity of his *David;* the flavor of the flesh; the disappearance of the muscles between the bone structure and the total expression; emaciation, greenness—the set purpose, etc. Return to it as to a subject of study.

December 28

After dinner I joined Roberto Gatteschi at the Arena, where we were to find D'Annunzio. The latter arrives around ten o'clock, and an hour later we leave the circus with Orvieto, who introduces me to his friend. Together we go to the Gambrinus; D'Annunzio indulges greedily in little vanilla ices served in small cardboard boxes. He sits beside me and talks gracefully and charmingly without, it seems to me, paying any special attention to the role he is playing. He is short; from a distance his face would seem ordinary or already familiar, so devoid is he of any exterior sign of literature or genius. He wears a little pointed pale blond beard and talks with a clearly articulated voice, somewhat cold, but supple and almost caressing. His eyes are rather cold; he is perhaps rather cruel, but perhaps it is simply the appearance of his delicate sensuality that makes him seem so. He is wearing a black derby quite unaffectedly.

He asks questions about French writers; talks of Mauclair, Régnier, Paul Adam—and as I say to him laughingly: "But you have read everything!" "Everything," he replies gracefully. "I believe one has to have read everything." "We read everything," he continues, "in the constantly renewed hope of finally finding the masterpiece that we are all awaiting so eagerly." He does not much like Maeterlinck, whose language strikes him as too simple. Ibsen displeases him by "his lack of beauty." "What do you expect?" he says as if to excuse himself. "I am a Latin."

He is preparing a modern drama of classical form and observing the "three unities." . . . With Herelle, last summer, he followed the coast of Greece in a yacht and "read Sophocles under the ruined gates of Mycenæ." . . .

. . . And when I express my amazement that his great erudition allows him so sustained and so perfect a literary production—or that his work as a writer leaves him the time to read so much: "Oh," he says, "I have my own method for reading lots of books quickly. I am a terrible worker; nine or ten months of the year, without stopping, I work twelve hours a day. I have already produced about twenty books."

Moreoever, he says this without boasting at all, in fact quite charmingly. In this way we talk on through the evening without difficulty.

December 30

After lunch we return to the Bargello. Wonderful *David* of Donatello! Small bronze body! ornamented nudity; Oriental grace; shadow of the hat over the eyes, in which the source of his glance is lost and becomes immaterial. Smile on the lips; softness of the cheeks.

His small delicate body, with its rather frail and affected grace—hardness of the bronze—the figured armor-plate on the legs covering only the calf, from which the thigh seems to rise all the more tender by contrast.

The very strangeness of that immodest accouterment and the taut nervousness of the little arms, which hold either the stone or the saber. I should like to be able to call him up before me at will. For a long time I observed—trying to memorize, to retain within me those charming lines, that fold of the abdomen, immediately under the ribs hollowed out when he breathes, and even that leanness of the muscle joining the top of the breast to the right shoulder—and that somewhat broken fold at the top of the thigh—and that extraordinary flatness of the loins immediately above the sacrum. . . .

What can I say of the bust of Niccolò da Uzzano? When I look at it,

I prefer it even to the *David.* He has more life in him now than when he was alive, and his lips are worth all his words. These two works are the most beautiful, and immediately after them: the little bronze *Amor* and the *Zuccone* of the Campanile, of which, alas, one can see only the bust here. Verrocchio's *David* is admirable too.

December 31

. . . Return along the shores of the Arno—setting sun; water losing itself in golden sands; in the far distance, some fishermen; the smoke rising from the roofs, at first gray, becomes gilded when the sun touches it. That radiance lasts for a long time; the roofs near San Miniato, the white walls of the villas now the color of unripe apricots; the cypresses around them seem all the darker. The fall of the Arno has as it were some pearly glints of an extremely pale green and, lower down, of that same color with a tint of orange.

The fishermen in the distance are carrying their bow-nets and returning to their boats. . . . The wonder of these lengthening days. . . .

Obsessions of the Orient, of the desert, of its ardor and its emptiness, of the shade of the palm gardens, of the loose white garments—obsessions in which my senses stampede, my nerves become exasperated, and which, at the beginning of each night, make me think sleep impossible.

Em. somewhat tired. Bad overcast weather. I go out a bit toward evening and shadow a couple of fellows who intrigue me. In *Valentin Knox** I shall speak at length of that mania for following people.

In the evening we play parlor games. Em., too ill to take part, went to bed right after dinner. And all evening long I suffer because of not having remained with her and think, each time that someone opens the door or shouts too loudly, that the noise is going to wake her up and make her migraine worse. At the end of the evening, around midnight, an almost irresistible sadness takes hold of me because of the lack of seriousness of all this and because Em. is not with me. I should have liked to be able to leave, and never did I so long to be able to return to her side. I thought also, amid the laughter, of our New Year's Eve vigil two years ago at Biskra, Paul's and mine, so calm and so solemn. I wondered how I had reached so definite a decision not to indulge in any personal melancholy, and if my decision was really so sure as all that. Instead of these dances and shouts at the approach of the New Year, which we want to be espe-

* A book Gide planned but never wrote.

cially impressive, I longed rather for common prayers or some religious service, or merely for some serious vigil. Horror of everything that is not serious—I have always had it. What was Em. thinking of, all alone, during this time? . . .

1896   *Rome*

This afternoon visited the horrible enormity of St. Peter's. I see Rome through Stendhal, despite myself. I have found the secret of my boredom in Rome: I do not find myself interesting here.

Syracuse

. . . Rather thick, the water here seems most extraordinarily blue. Great azure fish are swimming in it; one would like to throw in a ring. . . . I think of the swimming pools of Gafsa, those pools of warm water where huge blind fish, supposedly left by the great Tanit, brush against the swimmers; one can see blue snakes wriggling over the tiles on the bottom.

Latomie; closed gardens; caves; orchards in a deep quarry; delicate trickling of the fountain of Venus; lianas. This is where prisoners were locked up, in these abandoned quarries. The thick air, heavy and moist, was horribly charged with the scent of orange blossoms. We bit into not quite ripe lemons; the first unbearably acid taste gradually disappeared, leaving only an unbelievably delicate perfume in the mouth. This is a scene of rape, of murder, of abominable passion, one of those subterranean gardens of which Arabian tales speak, in which Aladdin seeks fruits that are precious stones, where the Calender's cousin shuts himself up with his beloved sister, where the wife of the King of the Islands goes at night to find the wounded black slave whom her enchantments keep from dying.

Greek theater seen at night at the hour when the moon rises. Above it is the avenue of tombs which leads to fields of asphodels. I have never seen anything more silent.

February–March

In the autumn, three years ago, our arrival in Tunis was marvelous. Although already considerably spoiled by the wide boulevards cutting through it, it was still a classic and beautiful city, harmoniously uniform, whose whitewashed houses seemed to light up from within at night like alabaster lamps.

. . . In the evening all the white was mauve and the sky was the color of a tea rose; in the morning the white became pink against a pale purple sky. But after the winter rains the walls have turned green, for mosses cover them, and the rim of the terraces looks like that of a basket of flowers.

I missed the white, serious, classic Tunis of that autumn. . . .

I also sought in vain that dark café where no one came but tall Negroes from the Sudan. Some of them had their big toes cut as a sign of slavery. Most of them wore, stuck in their turban, a little sprig of white flowers, of fragrant jasmine, which intoxicates them; it falls along the cheek like a romantic curl of hair and gives their face an expression of voluptuous languor.

They love the odor of flowers so much that sometimes, unable to smell them as strongly as they would like, they insert the crushed petals into their nostrils. In that café one of them would sing, another would tell stories, and tame doves would fly about and perch on their shoulders.

. . . I like the desert enormously. The first year I feared it somewhat because of its wind and sand; moreover, having no destination, I didn't know when to stop and tired myself quickly. I preferred the shady paths under the palms, the gardens of Ouardi, the villages. But last year I went for long, long walks. I had no other aim than to lose sight of the oasis. I walked; I walked until I felt infinitely alone in the plain. Then I began to look about me. The sands had velvety patches in the shadows on the slope of their hillocks, where insects' footprints could be seen; colocynths were wilting, tiger-beetles were running over the sand; there were marvelous rustlings in each breath of wind and, because of the intense silence, the most delicate sound could be heard. At times an eagle would fly up from the direction of the big dune. The monotonous expanse seemed to me each day to contain a more apparent diversity.

Touggourt, April 9

Because of the extraordinary drought, all the livestock died this year, and meat has become so scarce that people are reduced to eating camel.

On the way out of town you can see, under a little roof of dried palms, one of those enormous animals cut in pieces, a mass of purple flesh, which is covered with flies the minute one stops driving them off. The flies in these districts are as numerous as the posterity of Abraham. They lay their eggs on abandoned carcasses of sheep, horses, or camels left to rot in the sun; their larvae fed freely there, then, after their transformation, fly to the towns in swarms, in hordes. You swallow them, you breathe them, you are tickled, driven crazy, beclouded with them; the walls vibrate with them, the butchers' and grocers' stands are crawling with them. At Touggourt, the merchants have little palm whisks and try to drive them over to their neighbors. At Kairouan, there are so many that the best thing is to pay no attention to them. The merchants drive them away only when a customer asks to see the merchandise. Our carriage, when we arrived, was enveloped in a cloud of them. At the hotel the plates and glasses were protected from them by metal covers that were taken off, or raised rather, only to eat or drink.

M'Reyer, April 11

Amazing salt lakes bordered with mirages. From the top of a sandy hill, after the immense expanse of the desert, one thinks: "Look! the sea!" A vast blue sea dotted with small boats and islands, a sea that you fancy to be deep and that refreshes your soul. You approach, you touch the edge, and that blue suddenly disappears, for it was merely a reflection of the sky on a white salty crust, which burns your feet and hurts your eyes, splendidly dazzling. Fragile, it gives way under your steps, for it is nothing but the thin surface of a sea of moving mud in which caravans are swallowed up.

Biskra

The sounds of the Negro drum draw us in. Negro music. How often I heard it last year! How often I got up from my work just to listen! No tones, just rhythm; no melodic instrument, nothing but long drums, tom-toms, and castanets. . . . *"Florentes ferulas et grandia lilia quassans,"* * castanets that in their hands make almost the sound of a downpour. In a trio they execute real compositions; uneven rhythm oddly cut by synco-pated notes, which drives you mad and sets your skin to twitching. They play at funeral ceremonies, at gay fêtes, and religious affairs: I have seen them in cemeteries feed the frenzy of the professional mourners; in a Kairouan mosque exacerbate the mystic rapture of the Aïssaouas. I have seen them beat out the rhythm for the stick dance and the sacred dances in the little mosque of Sidi-Maleck. . . .

Negro music! How many times, far from Africa, I have thought I heard you and suddenly the whole South was recreated around the sound. In Rome for instance, via Gregoriana, when the heavy wagons, going

* "Shaking flowering branches and tall lilies." (Virgil: *Bucolics*, X, 25)

down in the very early morning, used to wake me. Their dull bounces on the paving blocks would fool me a moment in my half-sleep, and then leave me desolate for a long time afterward.

We heard it this morning, the Negro music, but it was not for an ordinary celebration. They were playing in the inner courtyard of a private house, and the men at the entrance wanted at first to keep us out; then some Arabs recognized me and let us go in. I was amazed at first by the large number of Jewish women gathered there, all very beautiful and richly dressed. The courtyard was full; there barely remained place enough in the middle for the dance. The dust and heat were stifling. A great ray of sunlight fell from the upper opening; clusters of children were leaning down from it, as from a balcony.

The staircase rising to the roof-terrace was also covered with people, all attentive, as we too immediately became; what they were watching was terrible. In the center of the courtyard, a large copper basin full of water. Three women got up, three Arab women; they took off their outer garment for the dance, undid their hair in front of the basin, then, bending forward, spread it on the water. The music, already very loud, swelled. Letting their wet hair fall over their shoulders, they danced a while; it was a savage, frantic dance involving the whole body. If you have not seen it, nothing could give an idea of it. An old Negress presided, who kept jumping around the basin and, holding a stick in one hand, occasionally struck the rim. We were later told, as we were beginning to understand, that all the women who danced on this day (and sometimes, so numerous are they, on these two days) were, whether Jewesses or Arabs, possessed by the demon. Each one in turn paid to have her right to dance, and the old Negress with the stick was a famous sorceress who knew the exorcisms and was able to make the demons pass from the bodies of the women into the water, which was frequently renewed. As soon as it was impure, it was thrown into the street. . . .

The dance became animated; the women, haggard, wild-eyed, seeking to lose consciousness of their flesh or, better, to lose all feeling, were reaching the crisis in which, their bodies escaping all control of the mind, the exorcism can operate effectively. After that instant, exhaustion, sweating, dying; in the prostration that follows the crisis, they were going to find the calm of deliverance.

Just now they are kneeling before the basin; their hands clutching the rim, and their bodies beating from right to left, from front to back, swiftly, like a furious pendulum; their hair whips the water, then spatters their shoulders; with each jerk of their loins they utter a low cry like that of woodsmen chopping; then suddenly tumble backward as if in an epileptic fit, frothing at the mouth, their hands twisted.

The evil spirit has left them. Now the sorceress takes them, lays them out, dries them, rubs them, stretches them, and, just as in a treatment for hysteria, seizing them by the wrists and half raising them up, presses with her foot or her knee on their abdomens.

More than sixty took part today, we are told. The first ones were still twisting about when others rushed forward. One was short and humpbacked, wearing a yellow and green gandourah, unforgettable; her hair, black as ink, covered her completely.

Some Jewesses danced too. They sprang in disorder like delirious little spinning tops. They made only one leap and fell back immediately, dazed. Others held out longer. . . . Their madness communicated itself to us; we fled, unable to stand it any longer.

[1896–1901]

That strange weakness of the mind which constantly makes us doubt that future happiness can equal past happiness is often our only source of suffering. We attach ourselves to the outward show of our mourning as if it were fitting to prove our sorrow to others. We look for souvenirs and ruins, we would like to relive the past and yearn to extend our joys long after they are exhausted.

I detest all melancholy and fail to understand why confidence in the beauty of the future should not prevail over adoration of the past.

Do we not resemble those people of the seashore who every evening weep over the sun that has set in the sea and cry for a long time before the ocean, facing the west—even after the renewed sun has already risen behind them?

. . . "No conditions are more contrary than living according to nature and living according to grace" (Bossuet: *Panégyrique de sainte Thérèse*). So much the worse!

"The self is hateful," you say. Not mine. I should have admired it in someone else: should I be harder to please simply because it is mine? On what worse "self" might I not have fallen? (To begin with, I am alive, and that is magnificent.)

I pity you if you feel something hateful in yourself. I hate only such sorry ethics. If I like my self, do not think for a moment that I like yours any the less, or that I do so because of any greater or lesser happiness.

But you are alive too, I believe, and *that* is magnificent.

The gods, if they existed, would see our endless struggle as the play of children on beaches, amusing themselves with the relative advances of the waves. One is coming; oh, progress! It rises; it overruns and submerges everything; it leaves a froth and withdraws; another follows and rises a bit higher—oh, progress! Why, it's a tide! The tide recedes; the next day it wins over a few more inches of beach—oh, progress! just think how far it will go tomorrow! But the day after tomorrow the equinox has passed and the sea goes down—but it never stops working, moving, slowly gnawing away at the land.

Time and space are a stage that innumerable truths have set up, with the aid of our minds, and upon those boards we play like willing, convinced, devoted, sensuous marionettes. I don't see anything in this to be upset about; on the contrary, I enjoy, I prefer this understanding of my role; and, after all, even if everything motivates that role, each one of us invents his own.

Social question? Yes indeed. But the moral question is antecedent.

Man is more interesting than men. God made *him,* not them, in His image. Each one is more precious than all.

I am amazed that Protestantism, while rejecting the hierarchies of the Church, did not at the same time reject the oppressive institutions of Saint Paul, the dogmatism of his epistles, in order to derive from the Gospels alone. We shall soon come, I believe, to isolating the words of Christ in order to let them appear more emancipatory than they had hitherto seemed. Less buried, they will appear more dramatically, finally negating the institution of the family (and that will serve as authority for suppressing it), taking man himself out of his environment to lead an *individual* career, and teaching us by his example and his voice to have no possessions on the earth, and no place to lay one's head. Ah, my whole soul longs for the coming of that "nomadic state" in which man, without hearth or home, will no longer affix and limit his duty and affection to such objects —nor his happiness either.

No matter how much I read and reread the Gospels, I do not find a single word of Christ that strengthens, or even authorizes, the family and marriage. On the other hand, I find words that negate them: It is "because of the hardness of your hearts . . ." says Christ, speaking of the old educative laws of Moses on divorce, which imply also those on marriage. The recruiting of each disciple is a carrying off from his family; out of filial respect one of them wants, before following Jesus, to bury his father: "Let the dead bury their dead," the Master says to him. "Who is my mother? and who are my brethren?" he replies when someone tells him that his mother and brothers have come to see him, and, indicating all those who are listening to him, he adds: "Behold my mother and my brethren!"

"Woman," he says to his mother, who continues to love him with a special love—"Woman, what have I to do with thee?" Then later, from the cross, as if fearful of having saddened her, and as if to show her that widespread and constantly available affection for one's neighbor is to replace localized affection: "Woman, behold thy son!" he says to Mary, pointing to John; and to John, as he points to Mary: "Behold thy mother!" Some would see in this the beauties of adoption. I have no objection to that, for adoption, too, ruins the family. Others would see the tearful union of two griefs; I still have no objection. But then let me see in it also the possibility of immediate consolation, suggested by Him who said: "Let the dead bury their dead"; grief suppressed, made impossible by a perpetual chain of adoptions.

Finally, did not Christ affirm more than once that whoever did not leave everything to follow him would not enter the kingdom of heaven? And indeed it must be understood that one cannot follow Christ without abandoning everything one has. Will it be said that the family is not a part of "everything one has," when the same One has also said: "I am come to set a man at variance against his father, and the daughter against her mother," etc. . . . For "he that loveth father or mother more than me is not worthy of me. . . . I came not to send peace, but a sword." And elsewhere: "And every one that hath forsaken houses or brethren, or sisters, or father, or mother, or wife, or children, or lands, for my name's sake, shall receive an hundredfold." Endless broadening of the object of love, as soon as the family is denied.

Meditation II (*outline*)

The value of ill health.
   (See Pascal: *Prayer for the Proper Use of Ill Health.*)

Ill health a source of unrest.

Nothing to be expected from "satisfied people."

Great invalids: prophets, Mohammed, Saint Paul, Saint John (does M. Jules Soury think that today he can diminish the divine importance of Christ's words by making him out to be tubercular and subject to hysteria?), Rousseau, Nietzsche, Dostoevsky, Flaubert, etc. . . . sick heroes: Hamlet, Orestes, etc. . . .

The need for ill health that antiquity felt.

System of compensations (hardly understood at all). Homer's blindness; story of Orpheus (save for another place); he sang only out of pain and suffering; possessing the *reality* of his love, he was silent. Whence his songs *seemed* sad; because they are the expression of desire and not of possession. In *reality* they are not sad, but simply recount the *absence* of . . . (too subtle; must be elucidated).

The vast sickly unrest of ancient heroes: Prometheus, Orestes, Ajax, Phædra, Pentheus, Oedipus (Oedipus deserves a place by himself, in my meditation on the theater: antipodal to Macbeth).

Apropos of Homer, recall the blinding of nightingales, a much more satisfactory explanation than the system of compensations. Eyes closed to the real world. The blind nightingale sings better, not from regret, but from enthusiasm.

Ill health offers man a new restlessness that he is obliged to legitimize. Whence the value of Rousseau, as well as of Nietzsche. Without his poor health, Rousseau would merely have been a boring orator in the manner of Cicero.

The illusion we enjoy as to the health of great men: see Molière, Racine, etc. . . . The writer who has said the best things on this subject is precisely the one who is generally cited as a model of the *healthy* man of letters: Goethe. See *Faust* (admirable dialogue with Chiron). He recognized incontrovertibly the advantage in, etc. . . . see his *Torquato Tasso,* etc. . . .

The famous question as to why Sparta had no great men must come up at this point. The perfection of the race prevented the glorification of the individual. But it also allowed them to create the masculine canon;* and the Doric order. By suppressing the puny, you suppress the rare variety—a well-known fact in botany or at least in *floriculture:* the most beautiful flowers often being produced by apparently sickly plants.

* The classical modular standard for sculpture and architecture, based on the proportions of an idealized male figure.

Sorrento, Villa Arlotta; at Vollmoeller's

Impossible to describe the vividness, the somber magnificence, the order, the rhythmic beauty, the softness of this garden-orchard. . . . I went in under the shade of the orange trees, half weeping, half laughing, fully drunk; through the dense branches one could hardly see the sky. It had rained; the sky was still gray; it seemed that the light came entirely from the profusion of oranges. Their weight bent the branches. The lemon trees, frailer, more gracefully shaped, had at once less ostentation and greater elegance. At times protective mats strung above them created a shelter for them which was almost dark. On the ground, among the trunks whose number, modest height, and oily, polished look reminded me of the rich pillars in the Córdoba mosque, a thick, unbroken carpet of wood-sorrel of a paler green than grass, more on the bluish side, more subtle, more fragile. And on the paths of hard black earth, straight, regular, narrow, where the shade, the warmth, the humidity had allowed mosses to creep, one would have liked to walk barefoot.

The garden ended in a terrace, or a cliff rather, dropping straight into the sea. On the extreme edge, the orange grove yielded to holm oaks and pines. A much wider path followed the brink, but in such a way that a fringe of trees rose between the walk and the sea. At intervals, where the rock jutted out, the bold terrace offered a circular bench, a table, a charming spot to rest. On one of these marble benches the diligent gardener had placed some oranges for our pleasure. They were of four kinds: to the largest, almost tasteless, sweet as watermelons, I much preferred the egg-shaped ones with a thick skin; they had an ethereal taste such as I fancy Oriental oranges to have; but I especially delighted in the very small tangerines, hard as small red apples, with an orangey-green skin of delicate texture that looks like glove leather. I can't say how many we ate, nor yet, alas, with what rapture. . . . They satisfied at once both hunger and thirst. From the bench on which we were seated talking, we threw the skins over the railing, where they fell straight into the sea some hundred yards below.

. . . it was not merely a question of music: the mere sound of a stringed instrument, or of a flute, or of a voice was enough to dominate my thought immediately. Likewise a gesture, a ray of sunlight on the ground, a smile from a human being or from palpitating nature (more readily, alas, than art) now made my heart swoon completely. So that all the slow preparation, the admirable effort of refinement that, through my ancestors, a whole race had put forth to produce me, broke its bonds at that point and ended in a re-establishment of savagery—just as you see natural plants reappearing in the ruins of patiently erected palaces.

That shade—I felt it at once through my whole body. My bare feet were suddenly touching a cooler earth. The air, now less burning, entered my lungs like a wine. My eyelids found acute pleasure in its caress.

Very few people really love life; the horror of any change is a proof of that. The thing they least like to change, with their lodging, is their thought. Wife, friends, all that comes afterwards; but lodging and thought involve too great an effort. There you have squatted and there you stay. You furnish the surroundings to your taste, make everything resemble you as closely as possible, avoid anything that might contradict you. It is a mirror, a prepared approbation. In this environment you no longer live; you take root. Very few, I assure you, really love life.

Listen to people talk. Who listens to anyone else? Those who contradict? Not at all. You listen only to those who repeat your own thoughts. The more it is expressed as you yourself would have expressed it, the more willingly you listen. The trick of the great journalists lies in making the imbecile who reads them say: "That's exactly what I was thinking!" We want to be flattered, not rubbed the wrong way. Oh, how slow is the passage of time! What long efforts to move from one place to another! And how we rest between struggles! At the slightest rise in the path, we sit down.

1902   *January 8*

Why do I limit *L'Immoraliste* to three hundred copies? . . . To hide from myself as much as possible the bad sale. If twelve hundred were printed, its sale would seem to me four times worse; I should suffer four times as much.

Besides, everyone ought to risk a new adventure. I alone can risk this one; everything inclines me toward it; it amuses me; its results will educate me the more because they are unforeseen; and that is really all that matters.

January 18

(. . . last night, about to meet Emile X., I felt myself trembling so, so full of anguish, that I had to go into a café and drink two glasses of whiskey. . . . I could go no farther.)

Emile X. used to work in his father's tailoring shop. But for the last two months the fact that they are working on half-time leaves him free almost every day. And every day he spends his whole afternoon at the pool. He gets there at one and stays until seven. Is that why he is as beautiful as a Greek statue? He swims remarkably well; and nothing so much as swimming, I think, imposes a rhythm, a harmony on the muscles, so hardens and lengthens them. Naked, he is perfectly at ease; he only seems awkward when he is dressed. I hardly recognized him in his workman's clothes. Most likely he also owes to his habitual nakedness the dull and even luster of his flesh. Everywhere his skin is blond and downy; on the hollows of his sacrum, exactly on the spot where ancient statuary puts the little tuft on fauns, the slight down becomes darker. And indeed yesterday afternoon, in the Praxiteles pose, his shoulder leaning against the wall of the pool, planted there so naturally like the Apollo Saurochtonus, with his slightly snub-nosed and mocking face, he looked like a latter-day faun.

    He is fifteen; one sister and one brother; all that remains of eleven children.

January 21

Every morning I go to the Louvre, and I am completely lost every Monday, when it's closed.

Saturday, February 8

At old Papa La Pérouse's.* His joy to see me again. He reproaches me sadly for not having come sooner. . . . He comes out onto the stairway with me, awkwardly holds my hand tightly clasped in his, then suddenly, not able to resist any longer, makes me go back up three steps and falls sobbing into my arms.

It is very adroit to persuade yourself that what bores you educates you.

---

* Actually Marc de la Nux, Gide's old piano teacher.

There's a lot of foolishness in this. And that's what seems to me abominable. Racine is good enough to do without this showing off. Sardou isn't. The habit of playing mediocre dramatists makes the actor see his contribution as too important. He therefore uses the same artifice in presenting Racine's pure gold as in duping us with Sardou's tin-plate.

During the first two acts I was sobbing; I didn't think I could see it through, so great was my emotion. I thought I was admiring Sarah; but I was especially admiring Racine; and there was no mistake about it in the following acts. I couldn't see it through, in fact, but this time because of my annoyance. As long as she remained in the *mezza-voce* of the first two acts, I was aware only of Racine. But with the beginning of the third there was no room for anything but Sarah. At the fourth I left. "Plastically," she was marvelous. And just as she is, despite all her shortcomings, she remains unique, incomparable. What she should have had is a Sardou with the qualities of a Racine; and an intelligent public that would not applaud her when she is at her worst.

Cuverville, March 23

The weather continues to be rainy, cold, morose. But I am much better and, once again, feel well disposed to work.

Study of Schubert's Fantasia in C and Impromptus. I am reading Renan's *Souvenirs* and Stendhal's.

Since we have been here—that is, since the 2nd of March—without even excepting the two days in Paris, I have got up at six o'clock at the latest; almost every day I am at work at five-thirty; and sometimes even at five o'clock. The day, according to the weather, is spent, somewhat at random, on gardening, reading, and piano-practice. The garden takes (and especially took in the beginning) an enormous amount of time. The drawing-room not being ready yet, Em. remains in the dining-room and I in my study; a fire is lighted in these two rooms, and the big stove heats the rest of the house. Then dinner comes; in the evening we bring our lamps together.

March 25

Hellebores, lilies, and tiger-lilies have come from Holland. From seven in the morning until six in the evening I work in the garden without stopping.

That some day a young man of my age and my *worth* should be moved as he reads me and *remade,* as I still am at thirty on reading Stendhal's *Souvenirs d'égotisme;* I have no other ambition. At least so it seems to me as I read them.

Pierre Laurens's summary of *L'Immoraliste:* "I am ill; too bad for me. I am cured; too bad for her!"

from

LE VOYAGE D'URIEN

1893

VII

For the seventh time the ship stopped. That island, where we disembarked full of hope, and which we were to leave only long afterwards, our hearts broken with a grandiose horror, was for many the end of the voyage. Those of us who continued onward, leaving behind us so many dead companions and hopes, were never again to find the splendid dawns which had awakened us until then. But sailing aimlessly under a sullen sky, we longed for the city—so beautiful despite all its sensuality—the royal city, the palaces of Haïatalnefus with their terraces, terraces that frightened us when we walked on them because their sheer beauty made them unsafe. Terraces! Merciful Bactrian terraces bathed in the morning sun! Hanging gardens, gardens with a view of the sea! Palaces we no longer saw, but still longed for! How we would have loved you, anywhere else but on that island!

The winds had ceased completely. But we were apprehensive, because of a certain splendor that made the air vibrate along the shores, and only four disembarked at first. From the *Orion* we saw them climb a knoll covered with olive trees, then return. The island was wide and beautiful, they said; from the knoll one could see plateaus, high, smoking mountains and, along the shore that curved inward, the last houses of a city. Since nothing that they had seen justified our first fears, all of us, including the sailors, disembarked and made our way toward the town.

The first inhabitants that we encountered were women drawing water beside a fountain; they came up to us as soon as they saw us. They were dressed in sumptuous garments which weighed heavily upon them and fell in straight folds; their hair was arranged in the shape of a diadem, giving them a priestly air. They offered their lips to be kissed and their eyes glittered with vicious promises. But when we refused them, these women, whom we had not recognized at first, were horrified; seeing that we were foreigners, ignorant of the customs of the island, they half-opened their purple cloaks and revealed their rose-painted breasts. When we still rejected them, they were astonished; then, taking our hands, they led us toward the town.

Through the streets there wandered none but admirable creatures. Early in their childhood those not perfectly beautiful, feeling the weight of reprobation, went into seclusion. Not all, however: for some of the most horrible and most deformed ones were pampered and used to satisfy abnormal desires. We saw no men, however—only boys with the faces of women and women with the faces of boys; the men, sensing the approach of new disturbances, had fled toward certain plateaus on the island which they alone inhabited. Since the death of Camaralzaman, the men had all left the town. Maddened by the desire for men, the forsaken women, like those whom we had met, would sometimes venture into the countryside; thinking that perhaps some men from the plateaus might come down, they disguised themselves in order to seduce them. We did not learn this at first, but only afterwards, when the queen, having led us into the palace, came to tell us that she was holding us prisoners.

Enticing captivity, more perfidious than harsh jails. These women desired our caresses and kept us imprisoned in order that they might satisfy their desires.

From the first day the sailors were lost; then one by one the others fell; but there remained twelve of us who would not give in.

The queen became enamored of us; she had us bathe in warm pools and perfumed us with mirbane; she reclothed us in splendid cloaks; but avoiding her caresses, we longed only for our departure. She thought boredom would overcome our resistance, and long days elapsed. We waited; but over the monotonous ocean moved not a single gust; the air was as blue as the sea; and we did not know what had become of the ship.

From noon until evening we slept in small rooms with glassed doors that opened out on a wide stairway leading down to the sea. When the rays of the evening sun struck the panes, we would go outside. Then the air was calmer; it arose from the sea like a scented coolness; we would stay a while, enraptured, breathing it in before descending; at this evening hour the sun was falling into the sea; oblique rays on the marble steps infused them with the scarlet transparency of a fever. Slowly then, all twelve of us, majestic, symmetrical, solemn because of our sumptuous attire, walked down toward the sun, down to the last step, where a light breeze sprayed our robes with foam.

At other times or on other days we would sit, all twelve of us, on a raised throne, each like a king, facing the sea, watching the tides rise and fall; we were hoping that perhaps on the waves would appear a sail or in the sky a cloud swollen by a propitious wind. Restrained by our nobility, we made no gestures and remained silent; but when in the evening our fallen hope departed with the light, then, like a wail of despair, a great sob welled up in our breasts. . . .

Stately gardens with tiered terraces descended from the palace to the sea. Seawater flowed in through marble canals, and the trees hung low overhead; strong creepers and lianas looped from one side to the other, forming swaying bridges and swings. At the mouth of the canals they floated in a dense web that resisted the sharpest blades; farther along, the water in the canals was always calm. We moved through the canals in boats, and we saw fish swimming in mysterious shadows; but we dared not bathe there because of stinging crabs and cruel lobsters.

On the shore just below the town was a grotto to which we were taken by the queen. The boat entered through a narrow opening that vanished from sight soon after we passed through it; the light, traveling through the blue water under the rocks, took on the color of the waves, whose motion reflected on the walls, and mingled pale flames into the light. The boat circled between two basaltic colonnades; the air and the diaphanous water intermingled until we could not distinguish one from the other; everything was shrouded in an azure luminescence. We saw the columns descend, and from the sand, algæ, and rocks at their base the indeterminate light seemed to flow. Above our heads played the shadow of the boat. In the depths of the cave the sand fanned out into a beach lashed by little waves. We would have liked to swim in that ocean fairyland, but we dared not bathe for fear of crabs and lampreys.

In this manner the queen entertained us; though we continued to resist, our hearts filled with song at the sight of the marvels with which she had hoped to seduce us. At night, at sea, in the boat, watching the stars and constellations wholly unlike those that appear in our skies, we sang:

"Queen! Queen of chimerical islands, queen with necklaces of coral, you whom we would have loved if you had come at dawn, queen of our despair, beautiful Haïatalnefus, oh let us depart!" . . .

Our deliverance came about in a most tragic manner. Appearing and spreading throughout the town, but mildly at first, was the horrible and lamentable plague that later ravaged the whole island, leaving it as forlorn as an immense desert. It was already interfering with the festivities.

. . . In the morning the fresh juices that we drank on the terraces, the fruits, and the glasses of cold water after walks in the sunshine; and in the evening, worn out by the excitement of the long day, in the perfumed gardens that led down to the sea, citron ices under the trees; all this—and the baths still much too warm, and idle musings near the women's insidious garments—all this would soon have led us into that languor that

comes before the plague, if the fear of excessive suffering had not preju-
diced us against so many pleasures. Hence we resisted smiles, nocturnal
entreaties, the desire for thirst-quenching fruits, shadows in the gardens,
music; we even stopped singing for fear of growing faint; but in the
morning before sunrise we walked down to the beach, immersed our
naked limbs in the wholesome water, and drank in new strength and comfort from the sea and the air.

From hidden sewers, from wash-houses, there arose in the evening a
pestilential exhalation, a product of the filth left there by the careless
townspeople; and these paludal vapors carried deadly germs. The sailors
and the women felt them in their troubled flesh; it began with a nascent
uneasiness; they rinsed out their mouths with balms, and the heavy scent
of aromatic oils blended with their hot breath.

That evening even the dances and the music fell sick. Never had the
winds blown so warmly; the waves sang, and each soul was driven mad by
its body. Bodies, beautiful as marble statues, glistened in the shadows; they
sought out each other for embraces, but their splendid desire was not
sated; their fever was only intensified by their lust; each added the other's
burning to his own. Their kisses were bites; wherever their hands touched,
they bled.

All night long they exhausted their fever in these false embraces, but
morning washed them in a bath of dawn; then they went toward the
fountains to cleanse their plague-tainted tunics. There, new festivities
began; light-headed, they laughed from weariness, and bursts of gaiety
echoed through their empty heads. The water from the bath-house had
been defiled. With big poles they stirred up the slime at the bottom;
clouds of mud arose; bubbles arose and burst; leaning over the edges, they
breathed in the pestilential smells, but without alarm; they laughed because they were already sick. Again they put on their damp tunics and,
chilled, drew comfort from the illusion that their bodies had been revital-
ized. But in the evening their fever underwent a radical change; they
ceased laughing; they were overcome by torpor, and each of them flung
himself on the grass-covered lawn and thought of nothing but himself. . . .

On the island were flowers whose bruised corollas discharged a scent
like that from a glacial mint. From these plants, which grew in the sands,
they gathered flowering branches; they chewed the petals all day long,
then placed them on their hot eyelids. A delightful freshness moistened
their dry eyes. This soothing sensation slipped through their cheeks, then
penetrated their brains and filled them with torpid dreams. They dozed

like Hindu fakirs. As soon as they stopped chewing, the freshness they had been drawing changed to a burning, as happens with sweet-smelling spices or herbs with a peppery flavor. Thirsty, they drank from metal goblets water tinged with tart gooseberry juice. They stopped chewing only to drink.

When their tunics slipped and bared their chests, one could see under their arms, near their breasts, a purplish bruised spot where the malady had begun; sometimes their bodies were completely covered with violet drops of sweat. All twelve of us remained silent, too solemn even to cry, and watched our companions die.

Oh! the terrible part was the arrival of the men; they came down from all the plateaus hoping to find women still robust, women whose lust would make it possible for the men to infect them with the sickness. They came running, hideous, livid; but when they saw the women so pale and understood why, they were seized by a desperate terror and ran through the town screaming. Some women still desired them; and as the certainty of death restored them to a sinister valiance, the men and women embraced furiously. They sucked in all the joy they could with a thirst, a rage, a sort of frenzy that struck us dumb with terror; it seemed that they were trying in that way to suppress the hour of remorse. And other women sobbed because they had arrived too late.

A light wind began to rise, and forced the heavy smoke from the volcanoes back toward the town, drenching them with gray ashes. Exhausted, they had disentangled themselves to go and vomit. Now they were rolling confusedly on the grass, and their entrails were making hideous attempts to escape. And so they died, crumpled, twisted, hideous, already decomposed; and silence fell upon the town.

Then clouds appeared; a cold rain toward morning finished glazing their souls, and covered them with a muddy shroud of water mixed with ashes.

And we thought of great sails, of departure; but having hoped in vain for so long, under circumstances so monotonous, now that nothing prevented us from departing, we felt so tired, so upset, so concerned over the solemnity of our tasks, so exhausted by everything, that for twelve more days we remained on the great island, sitting on the beach and facing the sea, speechless, pensive, aware of the uncertainty and superfluity of our wills.

What really made us leave was the unbearable stench of the corpses. . . .

VOYAGE ON A FROZEN SEA

. . . Each climate has its rigors, each land its diseases. In the warm
isles we had seen the plague; near the marshlands, lingering illness. Now
an illness was springing up from the very absence of sensual delights. The
salted meats, the lack of fresh fruits, the assiduous resistance in which we
took such great pride; the joy of living wretchedly in unkind lands, and
the strong attraction the outside world held for our enraptured souls
gradually eroded our strength; and while our souls had then longed, serene, to set off for magnificent conquests, scurvy was beginning to afflict
all of us and we remained dejected on the deck of the ship, trembling for
fear that we would die before finishing our tasks. Oh, chosen tasks! Most
precious tasks! For four days we remained in that condition, not far from
the land of our expectation; we saw its icy peaks plunging into the melting frozen sea; and I believe that our voyage would indeed have come to
an end at that point had it not been for the exquisite liquor that Eric had
taken from the Eskimos' hut.

Our blood had become too thin; it was escaping from all over our
bodies; it oozed from our gums, from our nostrils, from our eyelids, from
under our nails; it seemed at times to be nothing more than a stagnant
humor and almost to cease circulating; with the slightest movement it
gushed out as from a tilted cup; under the skin, in the tenderest areas, it
formed livid spots; our heads swam and we were overcome by a feeling of
nausea; our necks ached; because our teeth were loose and shook in their
sockets, we could not eat dry sea biscuit; cooked in water it formed a thick
pap in which our teeth stuck and remained. Grains of rice tore the skin
from our gums; about all we could do was drink. And, lying listlessly on
the deck all day long, we dreamed of ripe fruits with fresh, tasty meat, of
fruits from the isles we had once known, from the evil isles. But even then
I think we would have refused to taste them. We rejoiced because Paride
was no longer with us and did not share our suffering. But the hemostatic
liquor brought an end to our sickness.

It was the evening of the last day; the sun that marked the season's
end had disappeared into the earth, leaving behind for a long time a cre-
puscular glow. The sun set without agony, without purple on the clouds;
it had disappeared slowly, though its refracted rays still reached us. But it
was already beginning to become very cold; the sea around us had frozen
once more, imprisoning the ship. The ice thickened by the hour and constantly threatened to crush the ship, which offered us only the flimsiest
protection; so we resolved to leave it. But I want to state clearly that our

decision resulted neither from despair nor from timorous prudence but rather from a maniacal urge, for we could still break the ice, flee from the winter, and follow the course of the sun; but that would have taken us backwards. And so, preferring the hardest shores, provided that they were new, we moved toward the night, our day having come to an end. We knew that happiness is not simply escape from sadness; we were going, proud and strong, beyond the worst sorrows to find the purest joy.

We had fashioned a sled from parts of the ship. After hitching the big reindeer to the sled, we began to load it with wood, axes, and ropes. The last rays were disappearing as we set out toward the pole. On the deck of the ship was one spot, hidden by piles of rope, which we never went near. Oh sad adieu to the day, when, before leaving the ship, I walked the full length of the deck! Behind the rolls of cordage, when I untied them to take them along, alas, what did I see?

Paride!

We had sought for him in vain; I supposed that he, too weak to stir and too sick to reply, had hidden there like a dog who looks for some corner to die in. But was this really Paride?

He was hairless, beardless; his teeth lay white on the deck around him, where he had spat them out. His skin was mottled like a faded piece of cloth, violet and pearl; nothing more pitiful to see. His eyes had lost their eyelids, and at first I could not tell whether he was looking at us or not, for he could no longer smile. His huge, swollen, tumescent, spongy gums had retracted and split his lips, and now bulged outward like some large fruit in his mouth; I could see one last white tooth protruding from the middle. He wanted to hold out his hand; his bones were too fragile and they broke. I wanted to grasp his hand; it fell apart in mine, leaving blood and rotted flesh between my fingers. I think that he saw tears in my eyes, for he seemed to understand then that it was he I was crying for; and I think that he had still cherished some hope concerning his condition, but my tears of pity dissolved it, and he suddenly uttered a raucous cry meant for a sob; and with the hand that I had not crushed, in a gesture of despair, tragic and truly hopeless, he seized the one tooth and his swollen lips, ironically and as if in jest, and suddenly tore out a great strip of his face and fell back dead.

That evening, as a sign of mourning and farewell, we burned the ship. Night was approaching majestically, moving in slowly. The flames leaped up in triumph, the sea was aflame; the great masts and beams burned and then, the vessel consumed, the purple flames sank once again. Leaving the irreparable past, we set out for the polar sea.

Silence of night on the snow—of the night. Solitude, and you, calm relief of death. Vast timeless plain; the sun's last rays have withdrawn. All shapes are frozen; the cold now rules on the calm plain, cold and stillness. Stillness. And serenity. O rapture, pure rapture of our souls! Nothing stirs in the air, but a fixed, frozen radiance hovers in the air about the sea full of glistening icebergs. All is pale nocturnal blue—should I say, of the Moon? The Moon . . .

from

LES NOURRITURES

TERRESTRES

(The Fruits of the Earth)
1897

*Here are the fruits by which
we were nourished on the earth.*
The Koran, II, 23

. . . when you have read me, Nathaniel, throw this book away—and go out: leave. May it have given you the desire to go away—to go away from wherever you may be, from your town, from your family, from your room, from your thoughts. Do not take my book with you. If I had been Menalque, I should have led you by your right hand, but your left would not have known it, and soon—as soon as we were far from any town—I should have let go the hand I held and told you to forget me.

May my book teach you to care more for yourself than for it—and then more for all the rest than for yourself.

FIRST BOOK: I

There is profit in desires, and profit in the satisfaction of desires—for so they are increased. For I tell you truly, Nathaniel, each of my desires has enriched me more than the possession, the always deceitful possession of the very object of that desire.

Many are the delectable things, Nathaniel, for which I have worn myself out with love. Their splendor came from this: my own endless ardor for them. I never allowed myself to tire. All fervor was for me exhausting, a loving exhaustion—loving and delicious.

A heretic among heretics, I was always drawn to the most devious opinions, the farthest sidepaths of thought, the wildest detours. Nothing interested me in a mind but what made it different from the others. I went so far as to forbid myself sympathy, which seemed to me the mere recognition of a common emotion.

No, not sympathy, Nathaniel—but love.

Act without *judging* whether the action is right or wrong. Love without caring whether what you love is good or bad.

Nathaniel, I will teach you fervor.

A harrowing life, Nathaniel, not a quiet one. Let me have no rest but the sleep of death. I am afraid that every desire, every energy I have not satisfied during my life may survive to torment me. I hope that, after I have expressed on this earth all that I had in me to express—I *hope* to die satisfied and utterly *hopeless.*

No, not sympathy, Nathaniel, but love. You understand, do you not, that they are not the same thing? It was the fear of losing love that made me sometimes sympathize with sorrows, troubles, sufferings that otherwise I could hardly have borne. Leave to each one the management of his own life.

Nathaniel, I will teach you fervor.

Our acts attach themselves to us as its glow does to phosphorus. They consume us, it is true, but they are the source of our splendor.

And if our souls have been of any worth, it is because they have burned more ardently than others.

I have seen you, great fields, washed in the whiteness of dawn; blue lakes, I have bathed in your waters—and each caress of the laughing breeze has made me smile in return: this is what I shall never tire of telling you, Nathaniel. I will teach you fervor.

Menalque is dangerous; beware of him; wise men condemn him, but children are not afraid of him. He teaches them to love something besides their own family; teaches them to leave it, slowly; he makes their hearts sick with longing for fruit that is wild and sour, with curiosity for strange loves . . .

. . . ASSUME AS MUCH HUMANITY AS POSSIBLE—let this be your motto.

Indeed I hope that I have known all the passions and all the vices; at any rate I have been partial to them. All my being is passionately drawn to all creeds; and on certain evenings I was so mad that I almost believed in my soul, so near I felt it to escaping from my body.

And our life will have been set before us like that glass full of ice water, that moist glass which a sick man holds in his feverish hands, which he longs to drink, and which he drinks at one draft, knowing that he ought to wait, but unable to remove the delicious glass from his lips, so cool is the water, so hotly does his fever long for it.

I I

. . . Sometimes I said to myself that sensual pleasure would put an end to my trouble, and I tried to liberate my mind by exhausting my flesh. Then I would sleep again for hour after hour, like small children who feel drowsy with the heat and are put to bed at noon in the stir of a busy household.

Then, called back from some great distance, I would wake up in a sweat, with fast-beating heart and still-sleeping brain. The light that crept in from below through the cracks of the closed shutters and cast green reflections of the lawn on the white ceiling—that evening light was my one solace; it was soft and charming, delicious as the glimmer that filters through leaves and water and trembles on the threshold of dim grottoes, long after one has accustomed oneself to their enveloping gloom.

The household noises reached me vaguely. Slowly I came back to life. I washed in warm water and went languidly down to the plain, as far as the garden bench, where I waited for the evening to draw in, doing nothing. To speak, to listen, to write—for all this I was perpetually too tired.

I I I

Nathaniel, I will speak to you of waiting. I have seen the plains in summer waiting, longing for a little rain. The dust on the roads had become so light that a breath raised it. It was not even longing—it was apprehension. The earth had cracked from the drought, as though better to welcome the coming water. The scent of the wild heath-flowers had become almost

unbearable, and the world lay gasping in the heat of the sun. Every afternoon we went to rest below the terrace, where we could be sheltered a bit
from the extraordinary fierceness of the day. It was that time of year when
the cone-bearing trees are laden with pollen and gently wave their
branches in order to scatter their fertilizing dust abroad. Storm clouds had
piled themselves in the sky, and all nature was waiting. The moment was
too oppressively solemn; all the birds had fallen silent. From the earth
rose a breath so hot that all life seemed to be swooning; the pollen from
the conifers floated from their branches like a golden smoke. Then it
rained.

I have seen the sky shiver as it waited for the dawn. One by one the
stars faded. The fields were flooded with dew; from the air, nothing but
icy caresses. It seemed to me for some time that the indistinct life all
around me was lingering, reluctant to awake, and my own head too was
heavy, lethargic, filled with torpor. I climbed to the outskirts of the wood;
I sat down; all the animals, assured of the return of day, resumed their
labors and their joys, and the mystery of life began once more to rustle in
the fretwork of the leaves.—Then the day dawned.

I have seen still other dawns. I have seen men waiting for the night.

You must make a bonfire in your heart, Nathaniel, of all your books.

It is not enough for me to *read* that the sand on the seashore is soft; I
want my bare feet to feel it. I have no use for knowledge that has not been
preceded by sensation.

I have never seen anything sweetly beautiful in this world without
desiring to touch it at once in all tenderness. O loving beauty of the earth,
what is marvelous is the efflorescence of your skin. Landscapes into which
my desire plunges, open lands that my longing explores! Alley of papyrus,
closing over the water; reeds bending down to the river; glades opening
out in the forest; visions of the plain through an embrasure of branches,
visions of unbounded promise! I have walked in narrow passages through
the rocks and the plants. I have seen springtimes unfold.

From that day onward, every moment of my life brought me the savor of
its freshness as an absolutely ineffable gift, so that I lived in an almost
perpetual state of passionate wonder. I became intoxicated almost at once,
and enjoyed marching about in a kind of daze.

Certainly I have wanted to kiss all the laughter I have seen on lips; I have wanted to drink all the blood in red cheeks, the tears in eyes; to bite into the pulp of all the fruits hanging down toward me from branches. At every inn a hunger greeted me; at every spring a thirst was waiting—a different thirst for every one; and I wanted other words to express my other desires

> of walking, where a path lay open;
> of resting, where the shade invited;
> of swimming, where the waters were deep;
> of loving or sleeping in every bed that offered.

I have boldly laid my hands on each thing and believed I had a right to every object of my desires. (And besides, what we want, Nathaniel, is not so much possession as love.) Ah! wherever I go, may each thing turn iridescent, wonderful; may all beauty be clothed and colored with my love!

SECOND BOOK

Food!

I am waiting for you, food!
My hunger will not rest with halfway measures;
Nothing but full satisfaction will silence it;
No moralities can put an end to it,
Self-denial has never fed anything but my soul.

Satisfactions! I seek you.
You are beautiful as summer dawns.

Springs, more sweet in the evening, more delicious at noon; icy waters of early morning; breezes blowing from the sea; bays crowded with masts; the beat of warm tides on the shores. . . .

Oh, if there still are roads that lead toward the plains, hot gusts of noon, and country drinks, and at night the hollowed haystack;

if there are roads toward the East, the wake of ships through beloved seas, the gardens at Mosul, the dances at Touggourt, songs of shepherd lads in Helvetia;

if any roads lead northward, fairs at Nizhnii, sledges scattering the snow, and frozen lakes; then certainly, Nathaniel, we need never fear our desires will grow stale.

Here are boats come to our harbors bringing ripe fruit from unknown shores. Quick! Unload them of their freight, so that at last we may taste it.

Food!
I am waiting for you, food!
Satisfactions, I seek you;
You are as beautiful as summer laughter.
I know that not one of my desires
But has its own answer ready.
Each one of my hungers awaits its reward.
Food!
I am counting on you, food!
Throughout all the universe of space I seek you,
Satisfactions of all my desires!

*   *   *

The most beautiful thing I have known on earth,
My Nathaniel, is my hunger.
It has always been faithful
To everything that has always been waiting for it.
Is it wine that intoxicates the nightingale?
Or milk the eagle? Or juniper berries the thrush?

The eagle is drunk with its flight. The nightingale is intoxicated with summer nights. The plain trembles with heat. Nathaniel, let every emotion be capable of becoming an intoxication for you. If what you eat fails to make you drunk, it is because you were not hungry enough.

Every perfect action is accompanied by pleasure. This is how you know that you ought to perform it. I have no use for people who pride themselves on taking pains with their work. If their work was painful, they would better have done something else. The delight one takes in one's work is the sign of its rightness, and the sincerity of my pleasure, Nathaniel, is the most important of my guides.

I know the daily capacity of my body for pleasure, and how much of it my mind can bear. And then my sleep will begin. Heaven and earth are no longer worth anything to me after that.

* * *

I have often enjoyed justifying my acts to myself by a doctrine, even by a complete system of ordered thought; but at other times I could not help suspecting that I was merely providing a shelter for my sensuality.

* * *

. . . I exhausted myself when I was young by tracing the results of my actions as far as I could, and I was never sure of not sinning save by not acting.

Then I wrote: "I owed the health of my body only to the irremediable poisoning of my soul." Then I no longer understood what I had meant by the words.

Nathaniel, I no longer believe in sin.

* * *

Nathaniel, never stay with what is like you. Never *stay* anywhere, Nathaniel. When your surroundings have taken on your likeness, or you yourself have begun to resemble your surroundings, they have ceased to profit you. You must leave them. Nothing is more dangerous for you than *your own* family, *your own* room, *your own* past. Take from each thing nothing but what it teaches you; and let the pleasure that streams from it drain it dry.

THIRD BOOK

The Adriatic (3 a.m.)

O earth, so excessively old and so young, if you knew, if you only knew the bittersweet taste, the delicious taste of man's brief life!

Rome, Monte Pincio

I was sitting in this garden; I did not see the sun, but the air was shining with such an effusion of light that it seemed as if the blueness of the sky had turned liquid and was raining. Yes, really, there were ripples and eddies of light; on the moss there were sparkles like drops; truly, it seemed as though a river of light were flowing down this broad garden path, and that golden spray had been left on the tips of the branches by this rushing stream of sunshine.

Amalfi (night)

One waits at night
for one knows not yet what love.

Soft bodies close-wedded under the branches.
Soft touch of my fingers on his pearly skin.
Soft feet I watched treading silently on the sand.

Tunis

Amid all this blue, there is only just enough white for a sail, only just enough green for its shadow in the water.

Night. Rings glitter in the dark.

Moonlight, where one wanders. Thoughts different from the thoughts of day.

Sinister light of the moon in the desert. Demons prowl in the cemeteries. Bare feet on blue tiles.

Malta

In Seville, near the Giralda, there is an old courtyard in a mosque; orange trees grow in part of it, symmetrically planted; the rest of the court is paved; on very sunny days there is only a tiny streak of shade to be found in it; it is a square court, surrounded with walls; it is extremely beautiful; I can't explain why.

On board

How many nights, O round windowpane of my cabin, closed porthole— how many nights, lying in my berth, have I looked toward you and thought: there, when that eye begins to whiten, it will be dawn; then I shall get up and shake off my sickness; and dawn will wash the sea, and we shall land on the unknown shore. But dawn came without calming the sea; the land was still far off, and on the moving face of the waters my mind still swayed.

Sickness of the waves, which all my flesh remembers. Can I fasten a thought to that vacillating maintop? I asked. Waves, am I to see nothing but spindrift blown in the evening wind? I cast my love upon the waters —my thoughts on the barren plain of waves. My love dives into the waves, forever passing, every one the same. They pass on, and the eye knows them no more. Formless, ever-restless sea! Far from man, your waves are silent; nothing opposes their fluidity; but then no one can hear their silence; even the frailest skiff shatters them, and their noise makes us think that a great storm has come up. The great waves advance and suc-ceed one another in silence. They follow one after another, and each in turn lifts the same drop of water and barely moves it from its place. Only their form moves on; the water is lent them, and leaves them, and accom-panies them never. Form never dwells in the same being for more than a few seconds; it passes on through each one, then leaves it. O my soul, never let yourself cling to any single thought! Cast each of your thoughts to the sea-winds and let them carry it away. You will never be able to carry it up to heaven yourself.

Moving, moving waters, it was you who made my thoughts so un-steady! You can build nothing upon a wave; it gives beneath the slightest weight.

Will sweet haven come at last, after all this wearisome drifting, these tossings to and fro? Where my soul can at last come to rest on some solid pier, beside a turning beacon, looking at the sea?

FOURTH BOOK

"Tell us the story of your life, Menalque," said Alcide.

And Menalque replied: "At eighteen years of age, when I had fin-ished my first schooling, with a mind weary of work, an empty heart sick of its own emptiness, a body exasperated by constraint, I took to the road, with no end in view but simply to wear down my vagabond fever. I expe-rienced all the things you know so well—the springtime, the smell of the earth, the flowering of wild grasses in the fields, the morning mists on the rivers, the haze of evening on the prairies. I passed through towns, but would let myself stop nowhere. Happy, thought I, the man who is at-tached to nothing on earth and who carries his fervor unremittingly with him through all the ceaseless mobility of life. I hated homes and families and all the places where a man thinks to find rest; and lasting affections, and the fidelities of love, and attachment to ideas—all that compromises justice; I held that each new thing that comes along should find us wholly at its service, uncommitted, *disponible.*

"Books had taught me that every 'liberty' is provisional, and never really anything more than the freedom to choose this slavery or that, this or that object of devotion—as the thistle seed flies hither and thither, seeking a fertile soil in which to fix its roots—and can flower only when motionless. But as I had learned at school that men are never led by reason, and that to each argument may be opposed a contrary which needs only to be found, I set about looking for it, sometimes, in the course of my long journeyings.

"I lived in a perpetual, delectable expectation of the future—whatever it might be. I taught myself that, like questions before their attendant answers, the thirst that arises for every pleasure should come as short a time as possible before its fulfillment. My happiness came from this—that each spring revealed to me a new thirst, and that, in the waterless desert, where thirst is unappeasable, I preferred the fierceness of my fever under the excitement of the sun. In the evenings there were wonderful oases, all the cooler for having been so longed for during the day. On the sandy plain that lay stretched in the sun, that lay as though struck down by a vast and overpowering sleep, I have still felt, so great was the heat, I have still felt a pulsing life that could not sleep, even in the very vibration of the air—I have felt it tremble and faint in the curve of the horizon, and grow big with love at my feet.

"Every day, and from hour to hour, I wanted nothing but to be more and more simply absorbed into nature. I possessed the precious gift of not being too greatly encumbered by myself. Remembrance of the past had only just enough power over me to give the necessary unity to my life; it was like the mysterious thread that bound Theseus to his past love but did not prevent him from pushing on to newer prospects. Even so, that thread had to be broken. . . . Ah, wonderful palingenesis! Often in my morning walks I have had the delicious sensation of a new self, a fresh delicacy of perception. 'The poet's gift,' I cried, 'is the gift of perpetual discovery'; and I welcomed whatever came. My soul was the inn standing open at the crossroads; anyone who wanted could enter. I made myself ductile, amiable, at the disposition of each one of my senses, attentive, a listener without a single thought of himself, a captor of every passing emotion, and so little capable of reaction that, rather than protest against anything, I preferred to think ill of nothing. . . .

"In the evening, in little obscure villages I used to watch the households that had been dispersed during the day come together again in the evening. The father returning tired from this work, the children from their

school. For a moment the house door would open on a glimpse of welcoming light, of warmth and of laughter, and then shut again for the
night. No vagabond thing could enter now, no blast of the shivering wind
outside.—Families, I hate you! closed circles round the hearth; doors fast
shut; jealous guardians of happiness. —Sometimes, invisible in the night,
I stood for a long time leaning against a windowpane, watching the
simple comings and goings of a household. The father was there beside
the lamp; the mother sat sewing; the grandfather's chair stood empty; a
boy was doing his lessons beside his father—and my heart swelled with
the desire to lead him away with me on the open road.

"The next day I saw him again, coming out of school; the day after, I
spoke to him; four days later he left everything to follow me. I opened his
eyes to the glory of the plains; he understood that they were waiting just
for him. And so I taught his soul to become more vagabond, to become
joyful—and at last to free itself even from me, to come to know its own
solitude.

"Alone, I tasted the violent pleasure of pride. I liked to rise before
dawn; I called up the sun to shine on the stubble-fields; the lark sang my
fancies; the dew was my morning lotion. . . .

"My soul was in a state of lyrical ecstasy, which my solitude enhanced and which wore me down as evening came. I sustained myself by
pride, but at times like this I longed for Hilaire, who had shared and
moderated the over-wildness of my moods the year before.

"Toward evening I used to talk to him; he was a poet himself; he
had an ear for harmonies. . . . He too was devoured by a thirst for adventure; his strength had made him bold. No other glory will ever equal
it, I am sure, that adolescence of our hearts! We breathed in everything
with rapture, we tried in vain to exhaust our desires; every thought was
intense and passionate; every touch was incredibly, poignantly sharp. We
wore out our splendid youth in the expectation of a fairer future, and the
road that led to it never seemed interminable enough; we marched along
with great strides, chewing those hedgerow flowers that fill the mouth
with a taste of honey and an exquisite bitterness. . . .

"Some people accused me of egotism; I accused them of stupidity. I insisted that I loved no one in particular—man or woman—but rather
friendship itself, or affection, or love. I refused to deprive another of what
I gave to one, and would only *lend* myself. No more did *I* wish to monop-

olize the body or heart of anyone else. A nomad in love, as in nature, I
settled nowhere. Any preference seemed to me unjust; wishing to remain
everyone's, I would give myself to no one. . . .

". . . When I had realized my fortune, I began by outfitting a ship and
went to sea with three friends, a crew of sailors, and four cabin boys. I fell
in love with the least beautiful of the four; I relished his sweet caresses,
but even more my contemplation of the ocean waves. I anchored at sunset
in magic harbors and left again before dawn, after spending the whole
night, sometimes, searching for love. In Venice I found a courtesan, unbelievably beautiful; three nights long I loved her, for she was so beautiful
that by her side I forgot the delights of my other loves. It was to her I sold
or gave my boat.

"I lived for some months in a palace on Lake Como. There I gathered round me a number of the sweetest musicians and a few beautiful
women who could talk discreetly and well; in the evenings we would
converse while the musicians wove their spells; then we would go down to
the shore by a flight of marble steps, the last of which dipped into the
waters of the lake; wandering boats bore us away and we lulled our loves
asleep to the quiet rhythm of the oars. Drowsily we returned home; the
boat started awake at the shock of landing, and Idoine, hanging on my
arm, silently mounted the stairs.

"The year after that, I spent some time in the Vendée in an immense park not far from the coast. Three poets sang the welcome I offered
them in my house; they sang too the garden pools with their fishes and
plants, the avenues of poplars, the solitary oaks, the clumps of beeches,
and the noble disposition of the park. When the autumn came, I had the
finest trees cut down and took pleasure in laying waste my domain. No
words can describe the appearance of the park as I strolled with my many
guests, wandering down the paths I had let the weeds take over. From one
end of the avenues to the other, one could hear the blows of the woodcut-
ter's axe. The women's dresses were caught by the branches that lay across
the roads. A splendid autumn spread over the fallen trees. So magnificently did it lie upon them that for a long time I could think of nothing
else—and I recognized this as a sign that I was growing old.

"Since then I have lived in a chalet in the high Alps; in a white
palace in Malta, near the perfumed wood of Città Vecchia, where the
lemons have the sharp sweetness of oranges; in a traveling chaise in Dal-

matia; and at the present moment, in this garden on a Florentine hill, across from Fiesole, where I have assembled you this evening.

"You cannot say that I owe my happiness entirely to circumstances; evidently they were propitious, but I did not use them. Do not think that my happiness has been made with the help of riches; my heart, freed from all earthly ties, has always been poor, and I shall die easily. My happiness is made of fervor. I have adored, passionately, not things themselves, but by *means* of things—all things, indiscriminately."

FIFTH BOOK: I

Rainy countryside of Normandy, domesticated land . . .

"We shall possess each other next spring," you said, "under certain branches I know of; I know exactly the spot, covered over, soft with moss, and what time of day it will be, and just how mild the air; and the bird that sang there last year will be singing there again." But spring came late that year; the air, much too cold, proposed a different sort of joy.

The summer was warm and languorous—but you were counting on a woman who did not come. And you said: "Autumn in any case will make up for these disappointments, and bring me some consolation. She will not come, I suppose—but in any case the great woods will turn red. There will be days still warm enough for me to go and sit beside the pond, where last year the leaves fell so thickly. I will wait there for the coming of evening. . . . On other evenings I will go to the edge of the wood, where the last rays of daylight will linger." But autumn was rainy that year; the woods decayed with only the slightest change of color, and it was impossible to sit beside the flooded pond.

That year I was constantly occupied on the land. I took part in the harvest and plowing. I could see the autumn coming on. The season was incomparably warm, although rainy. Toward the end of September a terrific gale, which did not cease blowing for twelve hours, withered the trees, but only on one side. A little later the leaves that had been sheltered from the wind turned gold. I was living so far from the world of men that this seemed to me as important a thing to speak of as any other event.

* * *

There are days and then there are other days. There are mornings and evenings.

There are mornings when one gets up before daybreak, full of torpor. O gray autumn mornings, when the soul wakes up unrefreshed, so weary, after such a burning, wakeful night that it longs to sleep again, to sample the taste of death. Tomorrow I leave this shivering country; the grass is covered with frost. Like a dog that has hidden its morsels of bread and bone in the earth for the time when it shall be hungry, I know where to look for my little stores of pleasures. I know a breath of warm air at the deep turning of a brook; a golden lime-tree, not yet stripped, over the gate that leads into the woods; a smile and caress for the little boy from the smithy on his way to school; farther on, the smell from a great pile of fallen leaves; a woman I can smile at; a kiss for her little child near the cottage; the sound of the blacksmith's hammers, which travels so far on an autumn morning. . . . And is that all?—Oh, to fall asleep! It is too little—and I am too weary of hoping. . . .

*   *   *

Horrible departures in the half-light before dawn. Shivering of body and soul: vertigo. We look round to see what else we can take away with us.

"What is it you like so much about departures, Menalque?"

"The foretaste of death."

No truly, it is not so much to see something new as to leave behind everything that is not indispensable. Oh, how many things, Nathaniel, could we still have done without! Souls that are never sufficiently bared to leave enough room in them for love—love, expectation, and hope, our only real possessions.

Ah, all those places where one might have settled so easily, where happiness would have flourished! Toiling farms, inestimable labor of the fields, fatigue; immense serenity of sleep. . . .

Away! and let there be no stopping unless it be—no matter where! . . .

II

Inns

I have known the heady wine of inns; it leaves an aftertaste of violets and brings on the thick, drugged noonday sleep. I have known that evening drunkenness in which the whole world seems to rock under the weight of one's own potent thoughts.

Nathaniel, I will speak to you of drunkenness.

Nathaniel, often the simplest gratification was enough to intoxicate me, so drunk was I beforehand with desires. And what I looked for on the road first of all was not so much shelter—as hunger.

Intoxications—the drunkenness of fasting, after one has walked from early dawn, when hunger has turned from appetite into dizziness. Drunkenness of thirst, when one has walked until evening.

The most frugal repast became for me then as extravagant as a debauchee's feast, and I drank in lyrically the intense sensation of my life. At those times the voluptuous pleasure my senses brought me turned every object that touched them into a kind of palpable happiness.

I have known the kind of drunkenness that distorts one's thoughts ever so slightly. I remember a day when one thought drew out of another like the tubes of a telescope; the last but one always seemed the slenderest, and then out of it would come one that was more finely drawn still. I remember a day when they became so round that I could truly do nothing but let them all roll away. I remember a day when they were so elastic that each of them in turn took the shape of all the others, and vice versa. And sometimes two of them ran parallel and seemed about to run on in that way to all eternity.

I have known the drunkenness that makes you think yourself better, greater, more respectable, more virtuous, richer than you are.

Autumns

It was plowing-time in the plains. The furrows smoked in the evening, and the tired horses moved at a slower pace. Every evening intoxicated me as if I were breathing the smell of the earth for the first time. I used to like going to sit on a bank at the edge of the wood, among the dead leaves, listening to the plowmen's songs, watching the exhausted sun sink to sleep in the distance of the plains.

Season of mists; rainy land of Normandy. . . .

Walks

Simply *to be* became an enormous delight for me. I wanted to experience every form of life—that of fishes, of plants. Among all the joys of the senses, it was those of touch I envied most.

Autumn, a solitary tree on the plain, surrounded by a gentle shower;

its leaves had turned and were falling; its roots, I thought, were drinking in enough water from the soaking soil to satisfy them for a very long time.

At that age my bare feet enjoyed touching the wet earth, splashing in puddles, feeling the coolness or warmth of the mud. I know why I was so fond of water and especially of wet things: because water gives us more immediately than air the different sensations of varying temperature. I loved the wet breath of autumn. . . . O rainy land of Normandy.

I I I

Ah, if the seasons were only trustworthy! . . . If I were but resting near the barn, deep in the warm hay . . . instead of setting out, a vagabond, to conquer the arid desert by the sheer force of fervor! . . . I should listen to the songs of the reapers; I should watch the harvest, tranquil, reassured, and see its inestimable riches coming home on the overloaded wagons—like the waiting answers to my questioning desires. I should no longer go to search for their satisfactions in the plains; I should stay here and gorge upon them at my leisure.

There is a time for laughter—and a time for having laughed.

There is a time for laughter, yes—and then for the memory of having laughed.

Indeed, Nathaniel, it was I, I myself, and no one else, who watched the stirring of that same grass—that grass which has now faded for the sake of the scented hay, as all things fade that are cut down—it was that very grass I watched, alive, green and golden, waving in the evening breeze. Ah! if the time could but return when we lay on the grassy lawns and sheltered our love in the deep green of the fields.

Wild animals passed on their way under the leaves; each of their tracks was an avenue; and when I stooped down and looked at the earth close to, I saw, from leaf to leaf and flower to flower, a moving host of insects.

I used to know how damp the soil was by the vividness of the green and by the kinds of flowers that grew in it; one meadow was starred with daisies; but those we preferred, those that sheltered our love, were all white with umbels, some light and feathery, others, like the great cow-parsnip, opaque and wide-outspread. Toward evening they seemed to float in the deeper, darker grass like gleaming medusas, free, detached from their stalks, uplifted by the rising mist.

SIXTH BOOK

Commandments of God, you have wounded my soul.
Commandments of God, are there ten of you or twenty?
How much narrower can you pull in your limits?
Will you go on teaching that there are more, always more forbidden things?
Does the thirst for all that I have found beautiful on earth condemn me to still further punishments?
Commandments of God, you have made my soul sick,
You have set walls around the only waters that could quench my thirst. . . .

*   *   *

Nathaniel, I will inflame your lips with a new thirst, and then I will put to them cups full of a cooling drink. I have drunk; I know the springs where lips can quench their thirst.

Nathaniel, I will speak to you of springs:

There are springs that gush forth from rocks;
There are some that one sees well up from under glaciers;
There are some so blue that they look deeper than they are.
(At Syracuse, this is why the Cyane is so wonderful.
Sky-blue spring; sheltered basin; water blossoming into papyrus; we bent over the boat's side; azure fish were swimming over a ground that looked made of sapphires.

From the Nymphæa at Zaghouan spring forth the waters that cooled ancient Carthage.

At Vaucluse the water comes out of the earth as abundantly as if it had been flowing for a long time; it is already almost a river, and one can trace its course back underground; it flows through caverns and becomes imbued with darkness. The torchlights flicker and grow dim; then there is a place so dark that you think: No, impossible to go up any farther.)

There are ferruginous springs that give a gorgeous coloring to the rocks.

There are sulphurous springs whose green, warm waters at first look poisonous; but, Nathaniel, when you bathe in them, your skin becomes so exquisitely soft that it feels more delicious than ever to the touch.

There are springs from which mists rise in the evening—mists that float round them all night, and in the morning slowly dissipate.

Little, very simple springs that dwindle away to nothing among reeds and moss.

Springs where washerwomen come to wash their clothes and which turn mill-wheels.

Inexhaustible supply, the up-welling of waters! Beneath the springs, abundance of waters, hidden reservoirs, unsealed wells. The hardest rock will be riven. The mountainside will be clothed with shrubs; wastelands will rejoice and all the bitterness of the desert will break into flower.

More springs gush from the earth than we have thirsts with which to drink them.

Waters ceaselessly renewed; celestial vapors which fall and fall again.

If you run short of water in the plains, let the plains come to drink at the mountains—or let the subterranean channels carry the water of the hills to the plains. The prodigious irrigations of Granada. —Reservoirs; water-temples. —Indeed, there are extraordinary beauties in springs—and extraordinary delights in bathing in them. Pools! Pools! we step out of you purified.

> As the sun bathes in the light of dawn,
> As the moon bathes in the dews of night.
> So in your running moisture
> We shall wash our weary limbs.

There are extraordinary beauties in springs; and in waters that filter underground. They come up as clear as if they had been coursing through crystal; there is extraordinary delight in drinking them; they are as pale as air, as colorless as if they did not exist, and as tasteless; one becomes aware of them only by their excess of coolness, and that is the secret of their virtue. Can you understand, Nathaniel, that one can long to drink of them?

> The greatest joys of my senses
> Have been the thirsts I have quenched.

Now, Nathaniel, you shall hear

THE LAY

of My Quenched Thirsts

For we have stretched our lips toward brimming cups
More eagerly than toward kisses;
Brimming cups, so soon emptied.

The greatest joys of my senses
Have been the thirsts I have quenched. . . .

*   *   *

There are drinks that are prepared
With the juice of squeezed oranges,
    Or lemons, or limes—
Drinks that refresh, because they taste
    Both sweet and sour at once.

I have drunk out of glasses so thin
That your mouth was afraid of breaking them
Before your teeth even touched them;
And drinks seem to taste better in them
Because there is almost nothing to separate them from your lips.
I have drunk out of elastic goblets
Which you squeezed between your two hands
To make the wine rise to your lips.

I have drunk thick syrups out of coarse inn glasses
After days spent walking in the sun;
And sometimes after the icy water of a cistern
I have better enjoyed the evening shade.
I have drunk water that had been kept in skins
And that smelled of tarred goat-hide.

I have drunk water as I lay stretched on the banks
Of streams where I wanted to bathe,
While my two bare arms plunged into the running water
Until they touched the bottom, where one sees white pebbles stir-
    ring . . .
And the coolness entered in through my shoulders too.

The shepherds drank water out of their hands;
I taught them to suck it up through straws.

There were days when I walked in the blazing sun
During the hottest hours of the summer day
In search of a fiercer thirst to quench.

And do you remember, my friend, one night during that frightful journey when we got up, perspiring, to drink icy water out of an earthenware jar?

Cisterns, hidden wells, to which the women go down. Waters that have never seen the light, and taste of darkness. Waters that are bubbling with air.

Waters abnormally transparent, which I should have preferred blue, or, better, green, so that they would have seemed icier—with a slight taste of anise.

The greatest joys of my senses
Have been the thirsts that I have quenched.

* * *

Sleeps

Five o'clock.—Waking bathed in perspiration; beating heart; shivering; a light brain; the flesh ready for any call—flesh porous, too deliciously open to invasion from the outside. A low sun; yellow lawns; eyes that open at the close of day. O luscious wine of evening thoughts! Unfurling of evening flowers. Now to bathe one's forehead in warm water; to go out. . . . Espaliers; walled gardens in the sun. The road; cattle returning from their pastures; sunset—why bother to look? Sense of wonder already filled.

Now to go in. Begin work again beside the lamp.

* * *

At Lecco, on Lake Como, the grapes were ripe. I climbed to the top of an enormous hill where ancient castles were crumbling. The smell of the grapes was so sweet that it nearly made me sick; it penetrated like a taste to the back of my nostrils, so that there was no particular revelation when I ate them later on—but I was so thirsty and so hungry that a few bunches were enough to make me drunk.

SEVEN TH BOOK

Biskra

There were women waiting on the doorsteps; behind them a narrow stair-case mounted steeply. They sat there on their doorsteps, grave, painted like idols, crowned with diadems of coins. At night the street became ani-mated. Lamps were burning at the top of the staircases, and in each niche of light made by the well of the staircase sat a woman; their faces were in the shadow beneath the gleaming gold of their diadems; and each woman seemed to be waiting for me, waiting for me in particular; in order to go upstairs, you added a gold coin to the diadem; as the courtesan passed, she put out the lamps; you went into her small room, drank coffee out of little cups, and then fornicated on a kind of low divan.

Oumach

Then there was that oasis set in the rock and sand; we reached it at noon, and in such blazing heat that the village seemed too exhausted to notice us. The palm trees did not bend; old men sat gossiping in the doorways; the grown men had fallen asleep; children were chattering at school; the women were nowhere to be seen.

Streets of that earth-built village, pink by day and violet at sunset; deserted at noon, you will come to life in the evening; then the cafés will fill up, the children come out of school, the old men still sit gossiping on their thresholds, the last rays of the sun fall asleep, and the women go up to their rooftops and, unveiled, like flowers, talk endlessly of the tedium of their existence.

Touggourt

Arabs encamped in the marketplace; fires are lighted—their smoke barely visible in the evening.

Caravans! Caravans arriving in the evening; caravans gone before morning; horribly wearied caravans, drunk on mirages, now at last given up to despair! Caravans! Would that I too might leave with you.

Some were going east to fetch sandalwood and pearls, honey cakes from Baghdad, ivories, embroideries.

Some were going south to fetch amber and musk, gold dust and ostrich feathers.

Some were going west; they started in the evening and were lost to sight in the sun's last dazzling ray.

I saw the harassed caravans coming back; the camels knelt down in the marketplace and were at last freed from their burdens—bundles done up in coarse canvas; one had no idea what was inside them. Other camels were carrying women hidden in a sort of palanquin. Others carried the material for the tents which were set up for the night. Oh, the splendor, the immensity of fatigue in the incommensurable desert!—Fires are lighted in the marketplace for the evening rest.

* * *

Oh, how often, rising at daybreak, with eyes turned toward the crimson east, streaming with more rays than a celestial corona—how often, at the edge of the oasis, where the last palm trees dwindle away and life no longer triumphs over the desert—how often, as though irresistibly drawn toward that fountain of light, already too dazzling for human eyes to bear, have I yearned for that vast light-flooded, heat-scorched plain! . . . What transport of ecstasy, what violence of love will ever be ardent enough to vanquish the ardor of the desert?

Harsh land; unsmiling, ungentle land; land of passion and of fervor; land beloved of the prophets—ah! sorrow-stricken desert, desert of glory, I have loved you passionately.

EIGHT BOOK

Our acts attach themselves to us as its glow does to phosphorus. They consume us, it is true, but they are the source of our splendor. . . .

In vain, now that I am at rest, I try to count my riches. I have none. . . .

It was reported that I was doing penance —but what have I to do with repentance?
SAADI

Yes, it is true—my youth was spent in darkness;
It is that which I repent.
That salt of the earth was not to my taste,
Nor that of the great salt seas.
I thought that *I* was the salt of the earth,
And I was afraid of losing my savor.
The salt of the sea does not lose its savor; but my lips have already grown too old to taste it. Ah, why did I not breathe the sea air when my soul was greedy for it? What wine will now suffice to make me drunk?

O Nathaniel, satisfy your joy while it can still gladden your soul—and your desire of love while your lips are still sweet to kiss, while your embrace is still joyous.

For afterwards you will think, you will say: The fruits were there; their weight bowed down the tired branches; my mouth was there, and full of desire; but my mouth remained closed, and my hands could not reach out because they were clasped together in prayer; and both my soul and body suffer now from a hopeless thirst. The hour is past, hopelessly past. . . .

(Pleasure knocked at my door; desire answered in my heart; I stayed on my knees, and would not open.)

Sleeplessness

Longings. Longings; fever; past and gone hours of youth. . . . A burning thirst for all you call Sin.

A dog was howling forlornly at the moon.
A cat was wailing like a baby.
The town was at last going to taste a little calm, before waking next morning with all its hopes revived.

I remember those bygone hours; my bare feet on the tiles; I leaned my head on the wet iron of the balcony railing; in the moonlight, the glow of my flesh like a marvelous fruit ripe for picking. Longings; how you have withered us, blighted us. . . . Overripe fruit! we bit into you only when our thirst had become agonizing and we could no longer bear its burning. Rotten fruit! you filled our mouths with a poisonous sickliness, you have profoundly troubled my soul.—Happy the man who tastes you while he is young, while your flesh is still firm, and who sucks your love-perfumed milk, without delaying, so that he may run on his way refreshed—on that same road where we shall at last bring to an end all our wearisome journeys.

(It is true that I have done all I could to arrest the cruel wasting of my soul; but it was only by the wasting of my senses that I was able to distract it from its God; it was devoted to him night and day; it ingeniously invented difficult prayers; it ate itself out with fervor.)

From what tomb have I escaped this morning? (The seabirds are bathing, stretching their wings.) And the image of life for me, O Nathaniel, is a fruit full of savor on lips filled with desire.

There were nights when it was impossible to sleep.

There were long watches—watches through the night, oftentimes, for what? . . . I do not know.—I on my bed, trying in vain to sleep, my limbs aching with fatigue, as if twisted by love. And sometimes I sought, beyond the pleasure of the flesh, as it were another, further, more secret pleasure.

. . . My thirst increased from hour to hour in proportion as I drank. At last it became so vehement that I could have wept with desire.

. . . My senses were worn through to transparency, and when in the morning I went down to the town, I was penetrated by the blue of the sky.

My teeth horribly set on edge by biting the skin of my lips—their tips as it were worn away. And my temples fallen in as though by some kind of internal suction.—The smell of a field of flowering onions: another whiff, and I would have vomited.

Sleeplessness

. . . And in the night a voice was heard weeping and wailing. "Ah!" it wept, "this is the fruit of those tainted, those poisonous flowers: lovely. From now on I shall drag along the highroads the vague ennui of my desire. Your sheltering rooms stifle me, I am sick of your beds . . ."

Ah! thought I, all humanity tosses wearily between thirst for sleep and thirst for pleasure. After the fearful tension, the fierce concentration, and then the flagging of the flesh; one's only thought is for sleep. Ah, sleep! Oh, if only we were not wakened into life again by a fresh onslaught of desire!

And all humanity tosses like the sick man who keeps turning in his bed in the hope of easing his pain.

O agonizing desire! How many wakeful nights I have spent, caught up in some dream that took the place of sleep! Oh, if there are evening mists, the sounds of a flute under palm trees, white garments in the darkness of the paths, soft shade near the burning light—I will go! . . .

The moon is hidden now; the garden below me is a pool of green. . . .
A sob; close-pressed lips; overwhelming convictions; anguish of thought.
What am I to say? *Things that are true.* . . .

ENVOI

And now, Nathaniel, throw away my book. Free yourself from it. Leave
me. Leave me; now you are in my way; you hamper me; the love that I
have exaggerated on your behalf takes up too much of my time. I am tired
of pretending that I can educate anyone. When have I said that I wanted
you to be like me? It is because you differ from me that I love you; the
only thing I love in you is what differs from me. Educate! Whom should I
educate but myself? Nathaniel, shall I tell you? I have been educating
myself interminably. And I have not done yet. I esteem myself only for
what I might still do.

Nathaniel, throw away my book; do not let it satisfy you. Do not
think *your* truth can be found by anyone else; let nothing shame you more
than that. If I found your food for you, you would have no appetite for it;
if I made your bed, you would not be able to sleep in it.

Throw away my book; say to yourself that it is *only one* of the thousand possible postures toward life. Look for your own. Do not do what
someone else could do as well as you. Do not say, do not write, what
someone else could say, could write, as well as you. Care for nothing in
yourself but what you feel exists nowhere else, and out of yourself create,
impatiently or patiently, my Nathaniel, the most irreplaceable of beings.

LETTER

TO ANGELE: XII

(on Nietzsche)

1898

Dear Angèle,*

You will receive by the same post two thick books of Nietzsche's. You will probably not read them: but I want you to have them all the same. It's my little Christmas present.

I should have preferred, it is true, to send you dates from deepest Algeria, as I have done so happily in the past. But alas! I am still stuck in Paris, and if I let myself think too much about it, the approach of a new year will make me sad. Not to be able to write you of palm trees and sand! There I understand myself, better than among philosophers . . . But I am far away from all that, and here is Nietzsche, dear friend; if I am serious, forgive me.

Thanks are due to M. Henri Albert, who has finally given us *our* Nietzsche, and in a very good translation. We have been waiting for it so long! Impatience has already forced us to fight through the original—we who read foreigners so badly!

And perhaps it was all to the good that this translation did take so long to appear: for thanks to this cruel delay, the influence of Nietzsche among us has preceded the appearance of his work, so that now this latter falls on cultivated ground; otherwise it would have run the risk of not "taking," not finding a hold. Now it no longer surprises, it confirms; what it shows us above all is his splendid and enrapturing vigor.

But we had reached the point where his writings themselves were almost dispensable. For one could nearly say that Nietzsche's *influence* counts for more than his work—or even that his work is exclusively "influential."

Still, and despite all, the work *is* important, because people are beginning to distort that influence. To understand Nietzsche correctly, one must give oneself to him, and the only ones who can do this properly are

* "Angèle" was a fictional correspondent to whom Gide addressed a series of informal literary essays.

those whose brains have been made ready for him long in advance by a
sort of innate Protestantism or Jansenism, who are more terrified of skepticism than of anything else; or in whom skepticism, as a new form of
belief which sheds both love and hatred, retains all the fervor of faith.—
This is why such ingenious and supple minds as that of M. de Wyzewa fall
into error: few studies of Nietzsche (and I speak only of the most noteworthy) betray Nietzsche as much as his.* He wants to make a pessimist
of him; but Nietzsche is before all else a believer. He is unable to see in
Nietzsche's work anything but destruction and ruin; they are there—but it
is they, thank heaven, that allow us to build! The only real destroyers are
those who discourage or diminish our belief in life . . . :

> I want the proudest, the most ardent, the most affirmative of men; I
> want the world, and I want it AS IT IS, and I want it again, I want it
> eternally, and I cry insatiably, "Encore!"—and not only for myself,
> but for the whole play, the whole spectacle; and not only for the
> whole spectacle, but ultimately for myself, because I *need* the spec-
> tacle—because it makes *me* necessary—because I am necessary for
> it—and because I make it necessary.

Yes, Nietzsche destroys; he undermines; but not as a man discouraged—as one enraged. It is done nobly, gloriously, superhumanly, like a
young conqueror ripping up worn-out things. He takes the fervor that he
puts into this task, and passes it on to other men for the business of re-
building. The horror of repose, of comfort, of everything that proposes to
man's life a diminution, a deadening, a sleep, *this* is what impels him to
crack down the vaults and ramparts. "No one produces anything except
those teeming with antagonisms," he says. "One can only stay young on
the condition that his soul never relax, never aspire toward rest." He
undermines the crumbling constructions and, I grant, creates nothing new
out of them himself—but he does something more: he creates workers.
He demolishes in order to demand more out of them; he drives them to
the wall.

The wondrous thing is that he fills them at the same time with a
sense of life, of joyful life, that he laughs with them in the midst of the
ashes, that he sows new seed in the ruins with all his might and main. He
is never more flushed with life than when he is about his work of tearing
down tiresome, melancholy things. Then each page is saturated with creative energy; new, indistinct ideas swarm about. He looks ahead, catches a

* Wyzewa. *Revue bleue*, November 7, 1891; *Ecrivains Etrangers* (Perrin), February 1896.

glimpse of the future, calls out to us—and laughs. An admirable work, this? No—but a *preface* to admirable works. Nietzsche a destroyer? Nonsense. He builds—he builds, I tell you! He builds, with fire and sword.

I would like to be able to praise more highly Lichtenberger's little book on Nietzsche. If not in Nietzsche himself, dear Angèle, it is there that I would advise you to read. Yet I would do so more willingly if a certain diffidence of spirit had not made the author treat his subject almost too conscientiously. Yes, to write well of Nietzsche one needs more of the passions, less of the schoolroom; above all more passion, and consequently less timorousness, less fear. In the last chapter, by way of conclusion, he weighs up the whole of Nietzsche, tries to find wherein he is good, wherein bad, and so on. He ponders, draws limits, sets up guard-rails. Nietzsche, after all, drags so many appalling things behind him! So much does timidity dominate this book that I would rather see Nietzsche banished completely, than see admitted only the "reassuring" portions of his work. They are parts of a whole. Moderation only suppresses him. And I realize that Nietzsche may frighten one; but ideas that shock no one at first can hardly be reforming.

All this would be insufficient to make me criticize this little book; my complaint against it is a more specific one. Certain of our friends, Christians it is true, have found it possible to depict Nietzsche, in contradiction of his true nature, as "a man inordinately sad." This is, you will admit, truly perverse—for a man who sought for joy to the point of madness, glorifying it through all his sufferings, a martyr in the full sense of the word—for him to appear in the eyes of certain people as "a man inordinately sad"! But Christians are uncomfortable about admitting joy in any other form; unable to diminish it, they deny it.

"A profoundly sad life-work," M. de Wyzewa says as well, and others will be saying it for a long time still. Clearly, it was time for this translation to appear!

These two books* allow us to know Nietzsche as well as the whole Collected Works together—Collected Works of a remarkable monotony. Twelve volumes; from one to the next, not the slightest new idea; only the tone changes, becoming more lyrical, more bitter, more wild with rage.

From the very first book (*The Birth of Tragedy,* one of the finest), Nietzsche affirms and displays himself exactly as he will continue to be: all his future writings are there in embryo. From that time on, he is pos-

* *Beyond Good and Evil* and *Thus Spake Zarathustra.*

sessed by a fervor that will touch every part of his being, that will reduce to ashes, vitrify anything that cannot stand so much heat.

The work of philosophers is inevitably monotonous: there can be no surprises in it, since it is a studied deduction from the self. And from the time the deduction is made, every contradiction must be regarded as an error. "The mind builds its house," says Emerson, "and then the house shuts up the mind." It is a closed system; the very solidity of the surrounding walls is what gives it its force. One never loses sight of them—or only by delusion. You think you have found a way out of the system, think the philosopher is mistaken? "Mistaken! How could *I* be mistaken?" Who here is deceiving whom? A philosopher never deceives anyone but other people. (But then no one ever deceives anyone but other people.)

And Nietzsche himself is imprisoned. This passionate, creative man struggles within his own system, which entangles him from all sides like a snare; he knows it, he roars out that he knows it; but he does not escape. He is a lion caught in a squirrel-cage. What could be more dramatic—the anti-rationalist who wants to "prove"? So his means are those of others; so what? Though an artist, he does not create; he "proves"; he proves passionately. He denies reason, and then uses it. He denies it with the fervor of a martyr. From one end to the other, his work is nothing but a polemic —twelve volumes of polemic. Open it anywhere, read no matter what; from one page to the next, it is all the same. The fervor simply renews itself and the sickness feeds it more; there is never a breath of calm. He exhales his anger, his burning passion, with never a pause. Was it here, then, that Protestantism had to end? I think so—and that is why I admire him: his is the greatest possible liberation.

I am myself too much a Protestant, and for that reason I admire Nietzsche too much to dare speak in my own name. I would rather leave it to M. Fouille, who wrote, in 1895, in the *Revue des Deux Mondes:**

> Protestantism, after having been more reactionary than Catholicism itself, took it into its head to combat the immobility of Catholicism with the idea of "free examination." Once this was discovered, the Protestants had won the battle—but also lost it. They had found the death-sentence for their adversaries; for, against a religion self-imprisoned, fixed to its past like a statue on a pedestal, they offered a religion liberated, progressive, open to everything that free scientific research could bring to it. But their own death-sentence as well: for

* "A Study of Auguste Comte," August 1, 1895.

having put no limit to this "free examination," they created thereby a limitless religion, hence one undefined, hence one indefinable; a religion which would not know, the day when free examination brought atheism up before it, whether atheism was a part of itself or not; a religion destined to vanish in the indefinite circle of "philosophism" which it had opened. All free thought, all "philosophism," all intellectual anarchy were contained in Protestantism from the moment it ceased to be only a more radical Catholicism.

Certainly, this brings us no rest: nothing is more opposed to rest. And nothing is more opposed to these masterful words of Bossuet, in his pastoral letters:

> We have never condemned our predecessors; we leave the faith of our Churches just as we find it. . . . It is the will of God that the truth should come to us from shepherd to shepherd and from hand to hand, without the slightest visible innovation. It is thus that we recognize what has always been believed, and consequently what must always be believed. It is, so to speak, in this "always" that the force of truth and of promise appears, and we should lose it all the first time an interruption should occur in a single place.

But Nietzsche was not looking for rest. He was to write again:

> Nothing has become more alien to us than this ancient, Christian desideratum for "peace of soul." There is nothing we envy less than this bovine morality, the thick, gross happiness of a good conscience.

And elsewhere:

> The most beautiful life, for a hero, is to ripen for a warrior's death.

I hope I have clarified the argument for you somewhat by these quotations, and made you to understand why to certain people Nietzsche appears, and will continue to appear, "an inordinately gloomy man." It would be more clumsy than correct for me to say to you that it is not "happiness" he is looking for; since it is precisely "what one is looking for" that we call "happiness." But it is always difficult to go on calling "happiness" something we wouldn't want ourselves. So much the worse. *I,* my dear, will vote for the happiness of Nietzsche.

How many things I still have to tell you about him! But time is pressing; I am writing hastily, almost at random. Forgive me: I will return to all this again. How could one avoid it? I moved into Nietzsche despite myself; I was expecting him before I knew him, before I ever heard of his name. A sort of seductive fatality led me to the places he had been, in Switzerland, in Italy; made me choose to spend my winter there precisely at Sils-Maria in the upper Engadine Valley, where I later learned that he had eased his dying years. And then step by step, while I was reading him, he seemed to arouse my *own* thoughts.

We all owe to Nietzsche the thanks of grown-up men; without him, generations might have been wasted in insinuating timidly what he has affirmed with hardiness, with mastery, even with madness. Speaking more personally, we were in danger of encumbering all our works with the shapeless weight of unspoken thoughts—thoughts which now have been spoken. It is *from this point* that creation must take place, that the work of art is possible. It is this that leads me to esteem the whole corpus of Nietzsche's work, on a higher level, as a Preface—what one might call "A Prologemena to any Future Dramaturgy." Nietzsche knows this, he demonstrates it constantly. It seems, anachronistically, that all of his work could be subsumed in that of a Shakespeare, a Beethoven, a Michelangelo. Nietzsche is infused into all of them. One could even put it more simply: every great creator, every great affirmer of Life is of necessity a Nietzschean.

> See then what naïveté there is in saying that man should be this or that. Reality displays before us an intoxicating abundance of types, a multiplicity of forms, an exuberance, an unheard-of profusion . . .

Nietzsche, acting in the same manner as a literary creator of human types, is *intoxicated* by the contemplation of the human potential. But whereas other creators escaped from the madness of their genius by the constant purgation of artistic creation, by the fictionalizing of their passions, Nietzsche, a prisoner in his own philosopher's cage, in his Protestant heritage, was driven mad by it.

I said that I was waiting for Nietzsche long before I knew of him: this is because Nietzscheism began long before Nietzsche. Nietzscheism is at once a manifestation of that superabundance of life which expresses itself in all the greatest artists and a tendency which, depending on the century, has been christened "Jansenism" or "Protestantism," and which now we call Nietzscheism—because Nietzsche has dared to draw out to their final conclusion the ideas that were whispered or hidden in the earlier formulations.

If I had more time, I might amuse myself in describing for you Nietzscheism before Nietzsche. I could surround his image with easily chosen quotations from every side. But that would be too long for today; and what one would need to quote above all would be certain passages from Beethoven's final works. I shall come back to this. Let me only, in passing, show you this passage from Dostoevsky. There is no one who has *helped* Nietzsche more than Dostoevsky. I quote, then proceed; if you do not understand, let me know; I will explain it in my next letter. The passage is found near the end of *The Possessed:*

The one who is talking (Kirilov) is half-mad. He *must* commit suicide in fifteen minutes. The man who is listening to him hopes to benefit from his suicide; it is a matter of attributing to Kirilov a crime that he, the listener, has committed. Kirilov, before killing himself, *must* sign a statement declaring himself guilty. At the precise instant when we enter, the conversation between the two has gone off course; Kirilov is hesitating, is no longer capable of anything, not even of suicide; he is in danger of regaining his reason; all will be lost for Pierre, the listener, if he cannot bring Kirilov back to the *state* of a suicide. (So true is it that every unconscious pathological state can propose new actions to an individual, actions which his reason will then soon set to work to accept, to support, to systematize.) The whole of a philosophy, of a suddenly improvised morality must appear to motivate this single act—an act which, reciprocally, motivates the philosophy. Here is what, driven by Pierre, Kirilov finally says— Superman for one instant; one instant only, if you please, but just long enough to kill himself:

> "Ah, at last you've understood!" Kirilov shouted ecstatically. "So it must be quite understandable if even you can see it! Now, if this thought* can be proved to everybody, it will bring salvation for all. And who is to prove it but me? I don't understand why an atheist who is certain that God doesn't exist doesn't kill himself right away. To recognize that there's no God without recognizing at the same time that you yourself have become God makes no sense, for if it did, you'd have to kill yourself. On the other hand, if you do realize that you have become God yourself you are the king and don't have to kill yourself but can live in the greatest glory. Only one—the first one to realize it—must kill himself. And who else will begin and thereby prove it? So I'll kill myself to begin and to prove. Still, I'm a reluctant god—I'm unhappy because I must prove my free will. Up to now, man has been poor and unhappy because he has been afraid

---

* "If God exists, then the whole will is His and I can do nothing. If He doesn't exist, then all will is mine and I must exercise my own will, my free will."

to exercise his free will on the crucial point and has only exercised it in marginal matters, like a schoolboy. I'm terribly unhappy because I'm terribly afraid. Fear is the curse of man. But I shall establish my free will. It is my duty to make myself believe that I do not believe in God. I'll be the first and last, and that will open the door. And I'll save them. That alone can save people, and the next generation will be transformed physically. Because the more I've thought about it, the more I've become convinced that, with his present physical make-up, man can never manage without the old God. For three years I've searched for the attribute of my divinity and I've found it—my free will! This is all I have at my disposal to show my independence and the terrifying new freedom I have gained. Because this freedom is terrifying all right, I'm killing myself to demonstrate my independence and my new, terrifying freedom." *

Kirilov kills himself; Pierre "becomes tsar." Nietzsche goes down into madness; his Superman lives today!

I realize that Dostoevsky put these words into the mouth of an insane man; but perhaps a certain insanity is *necessary* in order to say certain things for the first time;—perhaps Nietzsche realized this. The important thing is that these things were said; for now we no longer need be insane in order to think them.

But when "reasonable" men come to say, "He is sick," and the orthodox, "His final madness condemns his system," I protest and say that they are the same men who cried to Christ on the cross, "If you are the Christ, then save yourself." There is a serious misunderstanding here. I no longer want to know what is cause, what effect. I prefer to say that Nietzsche "drove *himself* insane." And in order to write such pages, perhaps he *willed* himself to sickness:† it is one form of devotion. The books of Lombroso upset only fools. Nietzsche's reason, at the very beginning of his life, proposed to him a tragic game; the stake was to be reason itself. He plays against himself, loses his reason—but wins the game. He won *because* he was insane.

Nietzsche wanted to *know*—to the point of madness. His clairvoyance became more and more sharp; cruel; deliberate. The clearer he saw, the more he preached unconsciousness. Nietzsche wanted joy at any price.

* From *The Possessed* by Dostoevsky, translated by Andrew R. McAndrew, copyright © 1962 by Andrew R. McAndrew. Reprinted by arrangement with The New American Library, Inc., New York.
† "Better? I don't want to be! My mind is all-powerful! If I were 'healthy' I would be as abject as the rest." (*Faust,* Apostrophe to Chiron) [A. G.].

With all the force of his reason he drove himself into insanity, as if toward a refuge. May his overdriven genius there find its rest. Last year I read, in the *Débats* I think, a short article that spoke of Nietzsche. He was depicted there living with his sister, distracted, careless, not at all sad. "He chats with me," his sister wrote, "and takes an interest in everything around him, just as if he were sane—except that he no longer knows that he is Nietzsche. Sometimes, looking at him, I cannot keep back my tears; then he says, 'Why are you crying! Are we not happy?'"

Au revoir, my dear friend! May God grant you happiness—in reasonable proportions!

Paris, December 10, 1898

L'IMMORALISTE

(The Immoralist)

1902

I will praise Thee; for I am
fearfully and wonderfully made.
Psalms 139:14

PREFACE

I offer this book for what it is worth. It is a fruit filled with bitter ashes. It is like those colocynths of the desert which grow in barren, burning places; you come to them parched with thirst and are left with a burning all the more fierce. Yet on the golden sands they are not without beauty.

Had I offered my hero as an example, it is clear that I would have succeeded quite badly. The few readers willing to interest themselves in Michel's adventures did so only in order to reproach him with all the force of their own goodness. It was not for nothing that I bedecked Marceline with so many virtues; my readers found it unforgivable that Michel should prefer himself to her.

Had I intended this book to be an indictment of Michel, though, I should scarcely have succeeded much better; my indignant readers were scarcely grateful to me for their indignation. It was as though this indignation at my hero was felt in *spite* of me, and spilled over onto me from Michel. In fact, the two of us were very nearly mistaken for one another.

But I no more intended this book as an indictment than as an apology, and have taken care to pass no judgment. The public today no longer forgives the author who, after describing an action, will declare himself neither for nor against it. They want him to take sides, in fact, while the drama is still in progress, to come out clearly in favor of either Alceste or Philinte, of Hamlet or Ophelia, of Faust or Marguerite—of Adam or Jehovah. I do not claim, of course, that neutrality (I was about to say "indecision") is the sure sign of a great mind; but I do believe that many great minds have been very loath to . . . draw conclusions; and that to state a problem clearly is not to presume it solved in advance.

I use the word "problem" here reluctantly. To tell the truth, there are no problems in art—no problems that are not adequately solved by the work of art itself.

If by "problem," though, one means "drama," then let me say that the one recounted in this book, although played in the very soul of my hero, is nonetheless too general to remain circumscribed by his private adventure. I do not pretend to have invented this "problem"; it existed long before my book. Whether Michel triumphs or succumbs, the "problem" will continue to exist, and the author takes for granted neither triumph nor defeat.

Certain distinguished minds have refused to see in this drama anything but the account of a bizarre clinical case, and in its hero anything but a sick man. But if they have failed to recognize that certain ideas of general interest and great urgency may nonetheless inhabit it, the fault lies neither in the ideas nor in the drama, but in the author: by which I mean, in his clumsiness, even though he has put into this book all his passion, all his tears, and all his care. But the real interest of a book and the interest taken in it by a passing public are two very different things. One may, I think, without too much self-conceit, prefer to risk offering substantial matter to an audience of shallow first-nighters—rather than to satiate a public greedy for trifles, at the risk of having *no* audience tomorrow.

Beyond this, I have tried to prove nothing; I have only tried to paint my picture well and set it in the proper light.

*   *   *   *   *

To Monsieur D.R., Prime Minister

Sidi b. M., July 30, 189–

Yes, you were right, my dear brother: Michel has spoken to us. Here is the story he told. You asked for it; I promised to let you have it. But now that the time has come to send it, I find myself still holding back. The more I reread it, the more dreadful it appears. What will you think of our friend? For that matter, what do I think of him myself? . . . Are we simply to condemn him, to deny the possibility of converting such manifestly cruel faculties into good? —But I fear that not a few people today would boldly admit seeing their own likeness in this account. Shall we be able to devise some way of using all this intelligence, all this force? Or must we outlaw them altogether?

In what way can Michel serve society? I must confess I have no idea. . . . He must have some occupation. The high position you have so deservedly won, the power that you hold—will they permit you to find him one? Do hurry. Michel is a devoted man, still: but he will soon be devoted to nothing but himself.

I am writing to you beneath a perfectly blue sky. For the twelve days that Denis, Daniel, and I have been here, there has not been a single cloud; never for a moment has the sun lost its intensity. Michel says that the sky has been like this for two months.

I am neither sad nor in good spirits. The air here fills one with a sort of vague exaltation and induces a state which seems as far away from gaiety as it is from grief; perhaps it is happiness.

We are staying with Michel. We don't want to leave him—you will understand why when you have read these pages. So it is here in his house that we wait for your answer. Please don't put it off.

You know how close the friendship was that bound Michel to Denis, to Daniel, to me: it was strong even in our school days, but it grew stronger every year. The four of us established a kind of pact: to the least appeal from any one the three others would reply. So when I received Michel's mysterious cry of alarm, I immediately informed Daniel and Denis; the three of us left everything and set out.

We had not seen Michel for three years. He had married, and had left with his wife on a trip. At the time of his last stop in Paris, Denis was in Greece, Daniel in Russia; I, as you know, was busy looking after our sick father. We did not go without news of him, however; but the account given us by Silas and Will, who did manage to see him, was surprising, to say the least. He was apparently no longer the learned little puritan of his earlier days, whose very earnestness made him so clumsy, whose clear, simple gaze could so often put a stop to our own idle chatter. He was . . . but why should I reveal in advance what his own story will tell?

So I am sending the story to you exactly as the three of us heard it. Michel told it on his terrace, where we were stretched out beside him in the shadows and the starlight. At the end of his tale we saw day break over the plain—the plain that Michel's house overlooks, as it overlooks the nearby village. In the heat, shorn of all its crops, this plain looks like the desert.

Michel's house, though barren and strange-looking, is delightful. One would freeze here in the winter, for there is no glass in the windows —or rather there are no windows at all, only huge holes in the walls. But now the weather is so fine that we sleep outdoors on mats.

Let me add that we had a good journey out. We arrived here in the evening, worn out from the heat, intoxicated with the novelty, having stopped only briefly at Algiers and then at Constantine. From Constantine we took a second train to Sidi b. M., where a small carriage was waiting for us. The road comes to an end some way from the village, which is perched on the top of a rock, like certain little hill-towns in Umbria. We climbed up on foot; two mules had taken our luggage. When you come by the road, Michel's house is the first in the village. It is surrounded by the low walls of a garden—or rather a sort of orchard, in which grow three stunted pomegranate trees and a superb oleander. A little Kabyle boy was there, but he ran away as we approached, scrambling over the wall without so much as a hello.

Michel welcomed us with no indication of pleasure. He acted very simply, and seemed afraid of any outward demonstration of feeling. But on the threshold he stopped and in a strange, grave manner, embraced each one of us.

Until nightfall we barely exchanged a dozen words. An almost excessively frugal dinner was laid for us in a *salon* so sumptuously decorated that we were astonished—but this was to be explained by Michel's story. Then he served us coffee, which he made a point of preparing himself; afterwards we went up to the terrace, where the view stretched away into infinity, and the three of us, like Job's comforters, sat down and waited, admiring the sudden decline of the day over the burning plain.

When it was night, Michel said:

FIRST PART

I

My dear friends, I knew you were faithful. You ran at my call just as I should have run at yours. And yet it has been three years since you saw me last. I pray that your friendship, which has endured this absence so well, will bear up no worse under the story I am going to tell you. For it was only so that I might see you and have you listen to me that I called out to you so suddenly and asked you to travel all this way. I ask no other help; just listen and let me talk.

For I have reached a point in my life where I can go no further. It is not a matter of fatigue. I simply no longer understand. I need . . . I need to talk, I tell you. Oh, to know how to free oneself is nothing; the burdensome thing is to know what to *do* with one's freedom. Bear with me if I speak of myself. I am going to tell you my life, simply, without modesty, without pride, more simply than if I were talking to myself. Hear me.

The last time we saw each other, I remember, was in the neighborhood of Angers, in the little country church where I was married. There were very few people at my wedding, and the presence of such real friends as you made that commonplace ceremony very touching. Others, at least, seemed to be moved, and that was enough to move me. After we left the church, you joined us at my bride's house for a short meal, a sober meal, without shouting or laughter. Then she and I drove away in a hired car, according to the custom by which we always associate the idea of a wedding with the image of people waving good-bye.

I knew my wife very little; without being too distressed about the fact, I appreciated that she knew me no better. I had married her without love, largely in order to please a dying father, who was anxious about leaving me alone. I loved my father dearly; I was so concerned with his suffering that I thought of nothing else that whole melancholy time but how to make his last moments easier; and so I pledged my life before I even knew what life was. Our engagement was sealed at the bedside of the dying man: there were no smiles, there was no laughter; but there was, in the great peace it brought to my father, a certain austere joy. If, as I said, I did not love my fiancée, at any rate I had never loved another woman either. That seemed enough in my eyes to guarantee our happiness. Completely unaware yet of what I was, I thought I was giving her the whole of myself. She was an orphan too, and had lived with her two brothers. Her name was Marceline. She was barely twenty. I was four years older.

I have said that I did not love her—at least I felt for her nothing of what is generally called love; but I did love her, if one can use that word to mean tenderness, a sort of pity, and a considerably high esteem. She was a Catholic, I a Protestant . . . but so little a Protestant, I thought! The priest accepted me; I accepted the priest; it all went off without a hitch.

My father was what is called an "atheist"—at least I think he was, for a sort of unconquerable shyness (which I sincerely believe he shared) had always made it impossible for me to talk to him about his beliefs. The severe Huguenot teachings of my mother had slowly faded from my mind, along with her own dear image—I lost her, you know, when I was quite young. I had no idea then, though, how much one is governed by those first moral lessons, nor what a lasting imprint they leave on the mind. In impressing moral principles, strict, rigid moral principles at such an early age, my mother had left me with a certain taste for austerity; when she was gone, I applied them to my studies. I was fifteen when I lost her. My father took me in hand, lavished all of his attention and his passion on my care and my education. I already knew Latin and Greek well; under him I quickly learned Hebrew, Sanskrit, and finally Persian and Arabic. When I was about twenty, I had already been so intensely crammed that he went so far as to make me his collaborator. It amused him to claim me as his intellectual peer, and he was anxious to put me to the test. The *Essay on Phrygian Cults* which appeared under his name was in reality entirely my own work—he scarcely even bothered to read it over. Nothing he had written ever brought him so much praise. He was delighted. For my part, I was confounded by the success of such a ruse. But from then on my reputation was made. The most learned savants treated me as their colleague. I can only smile now at all the honors that were paid me. . . .

And so I reached the age of twenty-five, having looked at nothing but ruins and books, knowing nothing of life; whatever fervor I had, I dedicated to my work. I loved a few friends (you were among them); but it was actually not the friends I loved so much as the *idea* of friendship. It was my craving for *noblesse,* for high-mindedness that made my devotion to them so great; I cherished every trace of fine feeling in myself. Beyond that, I knew as little of my friends as I knew of myself. The idea that I might have lived a different existence—that *anyone* could have lived differently—never for an instant crossed my mind.

My father and I were satisfied with simple things; we spent so little between us that I reached the age of twenty-five without knowing that we were rich. Without giving it much thought, I had always imagined that we had just enough to live on. And so ingrained were the habits of economy I had acquired from my father that I felt almost uncomfortable when I learned that we possessed a great deal more. I was so heedless of such matters, however, that it was not until after my father's death (I was his sole heir) that I made a reasonable assessment of my fortune. I was able to do this at the time the marriage settlements were being made—when I also learned, by the same chance, that Marceline had brought me virtually nothing.

I was also unaware of something else, perhaps even more important —that I had very delicate health. But how could I have known it when it had never really been tested? Oh, I had colds from time to time, but I had never bothered much about them. I had been protected by the extraordinarily calm life I had led; but weakened by it at the same time. Marceline, on the contrary, seemed the picture of health. That she was indeed stronger than I is what we were very soon to learn.

We spent our wedding night in my apartment in Paris, where two rooms had been readied for us. We stayed in Paris just long enough to do some indispensable shopping, then took the train to Marseilles and embarked at once for Tunis.

So many urgent things to be done, so many recent events following one another in dizzying succession, the unavoidable agitation of my wed-

ding coming so soon after the more genuine emotion of my bereavement
—all this had left me exhausted. It was not until we were on the boat that
I realized just how tired I was. Until then, each day's occupation, while
adding to my growing fatigue, had also kept me from thinking about it.
The enforced leisure on board ship at last gave me opportunity for reflection—the first, so it seemed, I had ever had.

It was also the first time I had ever consented to forego my work for
any length of time. Until then, I had never allowed myself anything but
relatively short vacations. A trip to Spain with my father shortly after my
mother's death had lasted, it is true, over a month; another to Germany,
six weeks; there were others, too—but these were all research trips. My
father was never to be distracted for a moment from his meticulous inves-
tigations, and when I was not accompanying him, I was reading. And yet
we had scarcely left Marseilles when scattered memories of Granada and
Seville came back to me—of a purer sky, of franker shadows, of festivals
and laughter and songs. That, I thought—that is what we are going to
find. I went upon deck, and watched Marseilles disappear in the distance.

Then, suddenly, it occurred to me that I was neglecting Marceline.

She was sitting on deck forward. I moved near where she was, and
for the first time really looked at her.

Marceline was very pretty. You know; you have seen her. I was cross
with myself for not having noticed it sooner. I had known her too well to
see her with fresh eyes; our families had been friends for ages; I had
watched her grow up. I was used to her grace—but now that very grace
seemed to me so grand that for the first time I was astonished.

She wore a simple black straw hat with a long flowing veil. She was
fair, but did not look delicate. Her skirt and matching jacket were made of
a Scotch plaid we had chosen together. I had not wanted my mourning to
cast its shadow over her.

She felt me looking at her and turned toward me. Until then I had
shown her only the conventional attentions. In place of love, I made do as
best I could with a kind of frigid gallantry, which, I could see well
enough, somewhat bothered her. Did Marceline feel at that moment that I
was looking at her differently for the first time? She in her turn looked
directly at me, and then smiled very tenderly. I sat down beside her without speaking. Until that instant I had lived only for myself, or at any rate
according to my own tastes. I had married without imagining that my wife
would be anything other than a comrade, without once perceiving clearly
that my own life might be changed by our union. At last I had come to
understand that the monologue was over.

We were alone on the deck. She lifted her face toward me; I pressed it gently against my chest. She raised her eyes; I kissed her on the eyelids —and suddenly, under cover of my kiss, I felt possessed by a strange new pity, which filled me so violently that I could not hold back my tears.

"Why, what is it, my dear?" Marceline asked.

And so we began to talk. I was delighted by the charm of her words. I had picked up, somewhere or another, certain ideas about the silliness of women. But that evening, next to Marceline, it was I who seemed stupid and gauche.

So the woman to whom I had joined my life had a real and individual life of her own! I woke up several times in the night, struck by the importance of that idea. Each time, I sat up in my berth and looked at Marceline—my wife—asleep in the berth below.

The next morning the sky was splendid, the sea very nearly calm. A few leisurely conversations reduced our diffidence still further. Our marriage was truly beginning. On the morning of the last day of October, we landed at Tunis.

My intention had been to stay there only a few days. Let me tell you how foolish I was: here, in a country unlike any place I had ever seen, I was attracted by nothing except Carthage and a few Roman ruins—Timgad, which Octave had told me about, the mosaics of Sousse, and above all the amphitheater of El Djem, to which I proposed we should hasten at once. That meant going first to Sousse, and then catching the mail-coach from there. I had decided in advance that nothing between here and there could be worthy of my attention.

But Tunis surprised me. At the touch of new sensations, certain parts of me awoke—certain dormant faculties which, having never been used before, had kept all their mysterious freshness. I was more astonished, more bewildered, than amused; but what pleased me most of all was Marceline's delight.

In the meantime, my fatigue was growing greater every day; but I thought that it would be shameful to give in. I had a cough and a strange feeling of discomfort in the upper part of my chest. We're heading south, I thought: the heat will put me back on my feet.

The Sfax stagecoach leaves Sousse in the evening at eight o'clock; it passes through El Djem at one o'clock in the morning. We had booked seats in the enclosed rear compartment. I had expected it to be some rickety old wagon, but on the contrary, we found ourselves quite comfortably seated. What I had not expected was the cold! Out of some childish confidence in the warmth of the southern sky, the two of us—both lightly dressed—had neglected to bring along anything but a single shawl. As soon as we were out of Sousse and the shelter of its hills, the wind began to blow. It leaped across the plain in great bounds, howling, whistling, coming in through each crack in the doors: there was no way of escaping it. We both arrived paralyzed with cold; I was worn out as well from the jolting of the carriage, and from my horrible cough, which shook me even worse. What a night!—When we got to El Djem, there was no inn; nothing but a frightful native *bordj*. What to do? The coach was going on. The village was asleep; the lugubrious mass of the ruins lowered dimly through the dark immensity of the night; dogs were howling. We went into a room whose walls and floor were made of mud, where two wretched beds had been prepared. Marceline was shivering with cold, but here at least we were out of the wind.

The next day was dismal. We were surprised on going out to see a sky of unbroken gray. The wind was still blowing, though less impetuously than the night before. The stagecoach was not to come by again until evening. . . . I tell you, it was a dismal day. It took a few minutes to go over the amphitheater, and I found it a disappointment; I thought it actually ugly under that dreary sky. Perhaps my fatigue aided and increased the sense of tedium. Toward the middle of the day, finding myself with nothing to do, I went back to the amphitheater and looked about in vain for inscriptions on the stones. Marceline found a place sheltered from the wind, and sat reading an English book which she had fortunately thought to bring along. I went and sat beside her.

"What a miserable day!" I said. "You must be so bored."

"No, not particularly. I have my book."

"Why on earth did we come to such a place? You're not too cold, I hope."

"Not too. Are you? Oh, you are! You're so pale!"

"No, no . . ."

That night the wind turned violent again. . . . At last the coach arrived; we set off.

At the very first jolts I felt broken, worn. Marceline, who was very tired, had gone to sleep almost at once on my shoulder. My coughing is going to wake her up, I thought, and gently, very gently, I freed myself and rested her head against the side of the carriage. In the meantime I had stopped coughing; no, now I was spitting. This was something new: I was bringing it up without the least effort; it came in little jerks, at regular intervals. The sensation was so odd that at first it almost amused me, but I was soon nauseated by the unidentifiable taste it left in my mouth. I could no longer use my handkerchief, my fingers were already covered: should I wake Marceline? . . . Fortunately I remembered a large silk foulard she had tucked into her belt. I slipped it out quietly. The spitting, which I could no longer keep back, came more and more freely, and gave me the most extraordinary relief. This is the end of my cold, I thought. Then suddenly I felt terribly weak; everything began to spin round, and I thought I was going to faint. Should I wake her up? . . . No, no, for shame! (I have retained, I think, from my puritanical childhood a hatred of any surrender to physical weakness; I immediately regard it as cowardice.) I got hold of myself, made a desperate effort, and finally conquered my dizziness . . . I felt as if I were at sea again, and the noise of the wheels turned into the sound of the waves . . . but I was no longer spitting.

Then I rolled off into a kind of sleep.

When I came out of it, dawn was already filling the sky. Marceline was still asleep. We were almost at Sousse. The foulard that I held in my hand was dark-colored, so that at first I saw nothing; but when I took out my handkerchief, I stared at it in helpless amazement: it was soaked with blood.

My first thought was to hide the blood from Marceline. But how?—I was covered with it; I saw it everywhere now, especially on my fingers . . . —I might have had a nose-bleed . . . that's it; if she asks me, I shall say my nose has been bleeding.

Marceline was still sleeping. The coach arrived. She had to get down first, and saw nothing. Two rooms had been reserved for us. I was able to dart into mine and wash away every trace of the blood. Marceline had seen nothing.

I was feeling very weak, however, and ordered some tea for us both. And as she was pouring it, a bit pale herself, but smiling and very calm, a kind of irritation came over me that she had not the sense to see anything different. I knew I was being unjust, of course, and said to myself that if she saw nothing it was only because I had hidden it so well. It made no difference, nothing could stop it: the irritation grew in me like an instinctive response, overcame my sense of judgment . . . until finally it was too strong for me. I could no longer hold it back, and I said, with mock casualness, as though it had just occurred to me: "I spat blood last night."

She made no sound, no cry; she simply turned much paler, wavered, tried to hold herself, and fell heavily to the floor.

I sprang to her in a kind of fury: "Marceline! Marceline!"—Good heavens, what had I done? Wasn't it enough for *me* to be ill?—But as I said, I was terribly weak. I was on the point of fainting myself. I managed to open the door and call out, and someone came running.

I had in my suitcase, I recalled, a letter of introduction to an officer in the town, and on the strength of that I sent the man for the regimental doctor.

Meanwhile Marceline had come to, and was now alongside the bed where I lay trembling with fever. The army doctor arrived and examined us both. There was nothing wrong with Marceline, he declared, and she had no ill effects from her fall. *I* was seriously ill. But he did not want to give a definite opinion yet; he promised to return before evening.

When he came back, he smiled and talked to me and prescribed various remedies. I could tell that he had given me up for lost.

Would you believe that I was not shocked in the least? I was tired, tired of it all; I simply gave up. "After all, what had life to offer me?" I thought. "I have done my work dutifully, resolutely, passionately up to the end. As for the rest . . . what does it matter?" I thought my stoicism, in fact, rather handsome. What really pained me was the ugliness of my surroundings. "This room is ghastly," I thought, and I looked around. Suddenly it occurred to me that my wife, Marceline, was in an identical room next door; I could hear her talking. The doctor had not left; he was talking to her, carefully keeping his voice low. A little time passed; I must have slept . . .

When I woke up, Marceline was there. I could see that she had been crying. I was not so much in love with life that I could feel any pity for myself; but the ugliness of the place was a torture. My eyes rested on her almost voluptuously.

At the moment she was writing, seated next to my bed. She's very pretty, I thought. I watched her seal several letters. Then she stood up, came up to the bed, and tenderly took my hand. "How do you feel now?" she asked.

I smiled, and said sadly, "Shall I get better?"

"Of course you shall!" she answered at once, with so passionate a conviction that I was almost convinced myself. I felt suddenly a vague intimation of all that life could mean, of Marceline's own love—a confused vision of such pathetic beauty that tears leaped to my eyes and I wept long and helplessly without trying or wanting to stop.

With what prodigious, loving efforts did she manage to get me away from Sousse, surrounding and supporting me with her delicate attentions, protecting me, watching over me . . . from Sousse to Tunis, then from Tunis to Constantine: she was wonderful. It was at Biskra that I was to get well. Her confidence was perfect; never for an instant did she waver in her zeal. She took care of everything, arranged for our tickets, reserved our rooms. It was beyond her power, unfortunately, to render the journey itself any less atrocious. Several times I thought I should have to stop for the end. I sweated like a dying man, I gasped for breath, I lost consciousness for moments on end. At the end of the third day, I arrived at Biskra more dead than alive.

I I

Why speak of those first days? What is there left of them now? Their frightful memory has no tongue. I no longer knew who I was, where I was. The only image I have retained is that of Marceline, my wife, my life, bending over my bed of agony. I know that it was only her love, her passionate care that saved me.

Finally one day, like a shipwrecked sailor who catches sight of land, I felt something like a gleam of life returning; I was able to smile at Marceline.—But why do I tell you all this? What matters is that Death had touched me with his wing, as the saying goes. What matters is that I began to think it a very astonishing thing to be alive, and to look on every day as an unhoped-for blessing. Before that, it seemed to me, I had not even *understood* that I was alive. I was about to make the thrilling discovery of life.

The day came when I was able to get up. I was utterly enchanted by our home. It was almost nothing but a terrace—but such a splendid terrace! My room and Marceline's opened onto it; it extended out over the roof-tops. When you climbed to the highest part, you could see palm trees over the houses, and over the palm trees, the desert. On the opposite side, the terrace overlooked the public gardens and was shaded by the branches of the nearest cassias; on the fourth side it overlooked our courtyard—a small, formal courtyard, planted with six formal palm trees—and came to a stop at the staircase that led down into this court. My room was spacious and airy, the walls were whitewashed and bare. A little door led to Marceline's room; a large door with glass panes opened onto the terrace.

There the hourless days slipped by. How many times, here in my solitude, have I lived over those long, slow days! . . . Marceline sits beside me. She is reading, or sewing, or writing. I am doing nothing. I am looking at her. Oh, Marceline! . . . I look; I see the sun; I see the shade;

I watch the line of shadow move; I have so little to think of that I stare at it. I am still very weak. I breathe badly. The least effort wears me out, even reading. Besides, what should I read? Simply to exist is work enough for me.

One morning Marceline came in laughing. "I have brought you a friend," she said, and I saw come in behind her a little dark-skinned Arab boy. His name was Bachir, and he had large silent eyes that looked at me. I was a bit disconcerted, and the uneasiness was enough to exhaust me. I said nothing, simply looked cross. The child was taken aback by the coldness of my welcome, and turned back to Marceline; with a graceful, coaxing, cat-like movement he nestled up against her, took her hand and kissed it with a gesture that uncovered his bare arms. I noticed that he had nothing on under his thin, white gandourah and patched burnous.

"Come, sit down there," said Marceline, who had noticed my embarrassment. "You may play, but do it quietly."

The little fellow sat down on the floor, took a knife and a piece of djerid wood out of the hood of his burnous, and began to whittle. I think he was trying to make a whistle.

After a little while I no longer felt uncomfortable in his presence. I looked at him; he seemed to have forgotten where he was. He was barefooted; his little ankles and wrists were delicate, charming. He handled his crude knife with amusing dexterity. . . . Was I really going to be interested in all this? . . . His hair was shaved in the Arab fashion; he wore a battered chechia, with a hole where the tassel should have been. His gandourah had slipped down and uncovered a delicate little shoulder. I felt the urge to touch it, and bent down; he turned to me and smiled. I signaled to him to hand me his whistle, which I took and pretended to admire greatly.—Now it is time for him to go. Marceline gives him a little cake, I give him a penny.

The next day I was bored for the first time; I was waiting—for what? I felt restless and inert. At last I could hold back no longer: "Bachir isn't coming, then, this morning?"

"If you like, I'll go fetch him."

She left me and went downstairs. After a very short time she came back alone. Whatever had this illness done to me? When I saw her come back without Bachir I felt sad enough to cry.

"It was too late," she said. "The children had already left school, and heaven knows where they are now. Some of them are really charming, you know. I think they all know me by sight now."

"Well in any case, do try to get him to come tomorrow."

Bachir came back the next day. He sat down as he had two days before, took out his knife, and tried to carve a piece of wood so hard that he ended by jabbing the dull blade into his thumb. I shuddered with horror, but he laughed and showed me the glistening cut, watching the blood run down his hand with amusement. He showed his shining white teeth when he laughed. He licked his cut complacently; his tongue was pink, like a cat's. Ah, how well he looked! That was what I had fallen in love with—his health. The health of that little body was a beautiful thing.

The next day he brought some marbles. He wanted to make me play. Marceline was not in, or she would have stopped me. I hesitated, and looked at Bachir; the little fellow took my arm, put the marbles in my hand—forced me. Stooping down left me quite out of breath, but I tried to play all the same. After a while I simply had to give up. I was drenched with sweat. I pushed the marbles aside and dropped into an armchair. Bachir looked at me, somewhat worried: "Are you sick?" he asked sweetly; the timbre of his voice was exquisite. At that moment Marceline returned.

"Take him away," I said. "I am tired this morning."

A few hours later I began to spit blood again. I was walking laboriously up and down the terrace. Marceline was busy in her room and fortunately saw nothing. Greatly winded, I had taken a deeper breath than usual, when suddenly it came, filling my mouth. But it was no longer bright, clear blood as on the first occasion; it was a frightful great clot which I spat onto the ground with disgust.

I took a few tottering steps. I was horribly upset, and shaking badly. I was frightened; I was angry. Until then I had thought that my recovery was progressing step by step, and that all I had to do was wait. Now this brutal accident had set me back. My first hemorrhage—and this was the strange thing—had not affected me nearly so much; as I now recalled it, it had left me almost calm. Why then was I so frightened, so terrified this time? Sadly for me, it was because I had begun to love life.

I walked back, bent over, found the clot of blood and, with a piece of straw, picked it up and put it on my handkerchief. I looked at it. It was hideous blood, almost black, sticky and vile . . . I thought of Bachir's bright beautiful red blood. . . . And suddenly I was seized with a desire, with a desperate craving, something more furious and imperious than I had ever felt before—to live. I want to live. I want to live. I clenched my teeth, my fists, concentrated my entire being in one wild, distracted, desperate effort toward existence.

I had received a letter from T. the day before; in answer to Marceline's anxious questions, it was full of medical advice. T. had even enclosed with his letter one or two popular medical pamphlets and a book of a more technical nature, which for that reason seemed to me all the more serious. I had read the letter carelessly and the literature not at all. In the first place, the pamphlets reminded me of the little moral tracts which had plagued me as a child, which did nothing to dispose me in their favor; in the second, I regarded all "good advice" as a nuisance; and finally, I did not see what "Advice to Tubercular Patients" or "How to Cure Tuberculosis" had to do with my case. *I* did not think I was tubercular. I readily attributed my first hemorrhage to some different cause—or rather, to tell the truth, I did not attribute it to anything. I wouldn't let myself think about it, I hardly thought of it at all, and considered myself, if not altogether cured, at least very nearly so. . . . Now I read the letter; I devoured the book, the pamphlets. Suddenly, with terrifying clarity, it became evident that I had not been treating myself properly. Until then I had let myself live passively, trusting to the vaguest of hopes; suddenly my life seemed to be attacked, horribly attacked at its very center. The enemies, numerous and active, were living inside me. I could hear them, spy on them, feel them moving. I should never vanquish them without a struggle . . . I added, half-aloud, as if to convince myself more fully, "It is all a matter of will." I put myself in a state of war.

As evening fell, I organized my strategy. For some time to come, my recovery was to be my one and only concern. My duty was my health. I must, from now on, consider as good, as *right* everything that contributed to my cure, and forget, push out of my mind everything that did not. Before dinner that evening, I had made up a set of resolutions concerning my breathing, exercise, and diet.

We used to take our meals in a little summer-house surrounded by the terrace on all sides. We were alone, quiet, far from everything, and the intimacy of our meals was delightful. An old Negro would bring us more-or-less edible food from a nearby hotel. Marceline superintended the menus, ordering one dish, rejecting another. . . . Not having much appetite as a rule, I did not mind particularly when the dishes were a failure or the meals insufficient. Marceline, who was a small eater herself, did not know, did not realize that I was not getting enough to eat. To eat a great deal was the first of my new resolutions. I intended to put it into practice that very evening—but I could not. We were brought some sort of inedible stew, and then an absurdly overdone roast.

My irritation was so great that I poured it out on Marceline, bursting into a flood of intemperate words. I blamed her for it all; to listen to me, you would have thought her personally responsible for the poor quality of the food. I had vowed to adopt a new diet, and this slight delay in beginning it suddenly took on the gravest importance. I forgot all the preceding days; one spoiled meal ruined everything. I was obstinate. Marceline had to go down into town to buy a can or jar of anything she could find.

She soon returned with a little jar of potted meat which I devoured almost completely, as though to prove to both of us how much I needed more food.

That same evening we settled on this plan: meals were to be much better and more frequent, one every three hours, beginning at six-thirty in the morning. We would keep an abundant provision of canned food of every sort to supplement the mediocre dishes from the hotel.

I could not sleep that night, so intoxicated was I by the vision of my future virtues. I had, I think, a bit of a fever. There was a bottle of mineral water beside my bed; I drank a glass, two glasses; the third time I gulped it straight out of the bottle and finished it off without stopping. I examined my willpower over and over, like a schoolboy going over his lessons. I summoned up all my hostility, and directed it against everything. I must fight against *everything*. My salvation depended on me alone.

At last I saw the night grow pale; the day had dawned. My night of vigil before the battle was over.

The next day was Sunday. I must admit that until then I had paid very little attention to Marceline's beliefs. Either from indifference or from tact, I decided they were no business of mine—and besides, I do not attach much importance to such things. That morning Marceline went to Mass. When she came back, I learned that she had been praying for me. I looked straight at her, and then said as gently as I could: "You mustn't pray for me, Marceline."

"Why not?" she asked, a little troubled.

"I don't want any favors."

"You reject the help of God?"

"He would have a right to my gratitude afterwards. It would entail obligations. I don't like obligations."

We might have seemed to be joking, but both of us were completely aware of the importance of our words.

"You will not get well all by yourself, my poor dear," she sighed.

"Then so much the worse." But seeing how unhappy she looked, I added less brutally, "You will help me."

III

I shall be speaking for some time about my body. I am going to speak so much about it that you may begin to wonder whether I have forgotten completely everything but the physical. For the purposes of my story, the concentration is intentional; but out there it was a fact. I simply had not the strength to keep up a double life. The soul, the mind, all that side of things, I told myself, I will worry about later—when I get better.

I was still far from being well. The slightest thing would put me into a sweat or give me a cold; I had, as Rousseau says, *"la courte haleine,"* the short breath; and sometimes a bit of fever. Many days I was oppressed by a dreadful feeling of lassitude, and remained prostrate in an armchair from early morning on, indifferent to everything, totally self-centered, doing nothing but trying to breathe correctly. I breathed laboriously, methodically, carefully; my exhalations came in two short jerks, which, even with the greatest effort of will, I could never completely control. For a long time afterwards I had to concentrate very carefully to keep from doing this.

But what upset me most was my pathetic sensitivity to every change of climate. When I think back on it today, I wonder whether I was not affected by some general nervous disorder, in addition to my illness. I know no other way to explain a whole series of phenomena which now seem to me to have been unconnected with my tubercular state. I was always either too hot or too cold; I covered myself with a ridiculous number of clothes, and only stopped shivering when I began to perspire; the moment I took anything off, I began to shiver as soon as I stopped perspiring. Certain parts of my body seemed to freeze, to become (even when I was sweating) as cold as marble to the touch; nothing I could do would warm them up. I was so sensitive to cold that a little water spilled on my foot while I was washing was enough to give me a cold. And I was just as sensitive to heat . . . I retained this sensitivity; in fact I still have it. Today, though, it is a source of the most exquisite sensual pleasure. I believe that any keen sensibility can be the occasion of either delight or discomfort, depending on whether the organism is robust or feeble. So many things that once distressed me have become utterly delightful.

I do not know how I had managed to sleep until then with the windows shut. On the advice of T., I now tried to keep them open at night; a little at first, but soon I was pushing them open all the way. Soon it became a habit, a need so great that the minute a window was shut again I began to suffocate. Later on, what a joy it was to feel the night wind blow in on me, to lie bathed in the light of the moon. . . .

I would like very much to be done with the story of these first stammerings after health. As it turned out, in fact, thanks to constant attention, pure air, better food, it wasn't long before I began to improve. All this time I had not left the terrace, as I feared I would run out of breath on the stairs; but toward the end of January I at last went down and ventured into the garden.

Marceline came with me, carrying a shawl. It was three o'clock in the afternoon. The wind, which can be violent in this region (and which I had found especially unpleasant the three days before), had dropped to a breeze. The air was soft and charming.

A very wide path ran down the center of the public gardens, shaded by two rows of that species of very tall mimosa which the Tunisians call cassia. Benches in the shadow of the trees. A canalized river, by which I mean one deeper than it is wide, and very nearly straight, runs alongside the path; other, smaller canals divide up the river's water and lead it across the garden to the plants. The thick, heavy-looking water is the same color as the earth, the color of a pink or gray clay. Scarcely any foreigners, only a few Arabs; they walk about, and as they move out of the sunlight, their long white cloaks take on the color of the shade.

A marked shudder came over me as I stepped into that strange shadow; I wrapped my shawl tighter around me. But it was not an uncomfortable feeling—quite the reverse. . . . We sat down on a bench. Marceline was silent. Some Arabs passed by; then came a flock of children. Marceline knew some of them; she waved to them and they came up to us. She told me their names; there were questions, answers, smiles, pouts, little jokes. It all rather irritated me, and I felt my discomfort returning. I was weary and perspiring. But what disconcerted me, I must confess, was not the children; it was Marceline. Yes, however slightly it may have been, I felt myself constrained by her presence. If I had arisen and left, she would have followed; if I had taken off my shawl, she would have asked to carry it; then if I had put it on again, she would have said, "Are you cold?" And as for talking to the children, I would not have dared to in front of her. I saw that she had her favorites; in spite of myself—but deliberately, as if I had no alternative—I myself favored the others. "Let's go in," I said at last; and I privately resolved to come back to the garden alone.

The next day, she had to go out about ten o'clock, and I seized my advantage. Little Bachir, who rarely failed to come by in the morning, carried my shawl. I felt alert and light-hearted. We were almost alone on the center path. I walked along slowly, sitting down for a moment, then going on. Bachir followed, chattering away, as faithful and obedient as a dog. I came to that stretch of the canal where the washerwomen come down to do their laundry. There was a flat stone in the middle of the stream, and on it lay a little girl, leaning over the water; she was dabbling in the stream, throwing and catching little twigs. She had dipped her bare feet in the water; they were still slightly wet, and the wet skin seemed darker than the rest. Bachir went up and spoke to her; she turned around and smiled at me, then answered him in Arabic. "She is my sister," he said. Then he explained that his mother was coming to wash some clothes, and that his little sister was waiting for her. Her name was Rhadra, which means "green" in Arabic. All this he told me in a voice as charming, as clear, as childlike as the emotion with which I heard it.

"She wants you to give her two sous," he added.

I gave her ten and was about to walk on, when the mother, the washerwoman, arrived. She was a magnificent, heavily built woman, with a broad forehead tattooed in blue; she carried a basket of washing on her head, and looked like an ancient Greek caryatid—she had draped herself simply, like a statue, in a single width of dark blue cloth which caught itself at her girdle and then fell in straight folds to her feet. When she saw Bachir, she called him harshly by name. He made some angry reply; the little girl joined in, and the three of them carried on a most spirited argument. At last Bachir seemed defeated, and he explained to me that his mother wanted him that morning. He handed me my shawl sadly, and I was obliged to go on by myself.

I had not gone twenty paces when the weight of my shawl began to seem unbearable. I collapsed, all in a sweat, on the first bench that I found. I hoped that another child might happen along who could relieve me of the burden. The one who soon appeared (and who offered to carry it of his own accord) was a big boy about fourteen years old, as black as a Sudanese and not in the least shy. His name was Ashour. I should have called him handsome had he not been blind in one eye. He liked to talk: he told me where the river came from; he told me that, after running through the public garden, it flowed on to the oasis and crossed it to the other side. As I listened to him, I forgot my fatigue. Although I still thought Bachir charming, I had come to know him too well by then, and I welcomed the change. I even promised myself to come down to the garden alone another day, and to wait on a bench for another such fortunate encounter. . . .

After stopping to rest a few minutes more, Ashour and I arrived at my door. I would have liked to invite him in, but I hadn't the courage because I didn't know what Marceline might think.

I found her in the dining-room, busying herself over a tiny little boy, so frail and sickly-looking that my first feeling was more of disgust than of pity. Marceline said, rather timidly, "The poor thing is ill."

"It's not contagious, I hope. What's the matter with him?"

"I don't know yet exactly. He says he feels ill all over. He speaks French very badly; when Bachir comes tomorrow, I'll ask him to interpret. . . . I'm making him take a little tea."

Then, as if to excuse her action, and because I stood there without saying anything, "I've known him for a long time," she added. "I didn't dare bring him in before; I was afraid it might tire you, or displease you."

"Why, whatever for?" I exclaimed. "Bring in all the children you like, if it amuses you!" And I realized, with some irritation for not having done so, that I might perfectly well have brought up Ashour.

And yet, as I thought this, I looked at my wife; she was so maternal, so caressing. Her tenderness was so touching that the little creature soon went off quite revived. —I told Marceline of my walk and tactfully explained to her why I preferred to go out alone.

At that time I still awoke frequently and suddenly in the night, to find myself either freezing or soaking with sweat. That night, though, was a very good one; I scarcely woke up at all. The next morning I was ready to go out at nine o'clock. It was a fine day. I felt well rested, not at all weak, happy—or rather, pleased, amused. The air was calm and warm, but I took my shawl all the same, to serve as a pretext for getting to know whatever child I would have carry it for me.

As I said, the garden was just below our terrace, so I was there in no time at all. I was in raptures as I walked into its shade. The cassias, whose blossoms come out quite early (even before the leaves), gave off a marvelous scent—unless that faint, strange perfume, which seemed to penetrate me through several senses at once, which I felt lifting me up, came simply from the air itself. I was breathing more easily, too, and walking more lightly; yet I sat down at the first bench on the path, feeling not so much tired as giddy, exalted.

I looked around. The shadows were light, mobile; they did not fall on the ground, but seemed barely to rest on it. Oh, marvelous light! I listened. What was I hearing? Nothing; everything; every sound enchanted me. I remember a particular shrub, whose bark looked from a distance of such a strange consistency that I felt compelled to get up and go feel it. I virtually caressed it; it was ecstasy. I remember . . . Had the time finally come, that morning, for me to be born?

I forgot that I was alone, and sat on, expecting nothing, waiting for no one, forgetting the time. It seemed to me that until that day I had effectively given up feeling in order to think; so now I was astonished to find that my sensations had become as strong as my thoughts.

I say "It *seemed* to me," for now, from the depths of my earliest childhood, there reawoke a thousand gleams from a thousand forgotten sensations. This new awareness I had gained of my sensual self made it possible for me to recognize them, though with a certain uneasiness. Yes, my senses, awake at last, were able to rediscover a whole history, to recompose a whole past of their own. They were alive: alive! They had never ceased to live, really; what I discovered was that even during those barren years of study, they had been leading their own secret, wily lives.

I met no one that day, but I didn't mind; I took out of my pocket a little Homer which I had not opened since Marseilles, reread three lines from the *Odyssey,* and learned them by heart; then, finding in their rhythm all the nourishment I needed, I dwelled on them for a while with leisurely delight, then shut the book and sat still, trembling, more alive than I had ever thought it possible to be, my mind benumbed with happiness. . . .

I V

Marceline, meanwhile, was delighted to see my health returning at last, and for a few days she had been telling me of the marvelous orchards of the oasis. She loved taking walks in the open air. My illness left her time for long promenades, and she returned from them simply glowing. Until then, she had not said much about them because she dared not tempt me to follow her, and was afraid of depressing me with an account of pleasures I could not share. But now that I was better, she began to count on the appeal of such exercise to complete my recovery. As I had, in fact, begun to feel my old taste for walking and observing coming back, the very next morning we set out together.

She led the way along a road so curious that I have never seen its like anywhere. It meanders indolently between two fairly high mud walls; the shapes of the gardens behind these walls bend in and out, and direct its course at their pleasure. The road winds about, changes direction without warning: from the first sharp bend at the entrance, you are completely lost, you no longer know where you have come from or where you are going. The river keeps to the road faithfully, running alongside one of the walls. The walls are made out of the same earth as the road, as the whole oasis, in fact, a pinkish or soft gray clay which is darkened a bit by the water, cracked by the burning sun, hardened by the heat, but then softened again by the first sudden shower, so that bare feet leave their imprint in the plastic ground.

Above the walls, the palm trees. Turtledoves flew about them as we approached. Marceline looked at me.

My discomfort and fatigue had disappeared. I walked along in a sort of ecstasy, a speechless delight, an elation of the senses and the flesh. At that moment a light breeze came up; all the palm leaves waved, and we could see the tallest trees bending with the wind. Then the whole air was still, and I heard distinctly, behind the wall, the song of a flute. We found a breach in the wall and went in.

It was a place full of light and shade, tranquil, as if sheltered from time. It was full of silences and rustlings—the soft noise of the flowing stream that waters the palms, slipping from tree to tree, the soft cooing of the doves, the song of the flute that a boy was playing. He was watching a herd of goats, and sitting, almost naked, on the trunk of a fallen palm. Our coming did not trouble him; he did not run away; only stopped his playing for a second, and then went on.

I noticed, during this brief silence, that another flute was answering him in the distance. We went on a little way, then: "There's no point in going any farther," said Marceline. "These orchards are all alike. They become a little larger at the other end of the oasis, that's all." She spread the shawl on the ground. "Sit down and rest."

How long did we stay there? I have no idea; what thought had I for time? Marceline was near me. I lay down and rested my head on her knees. The song of the flute flowed on, stopped from time to time, went on again; the sound of the water . . . now the soft bleating of a goat. I closed my eyes. I felt Marceline's cool hand resting on my forehead. I felt the hot sun, softly filtered through the palms. I thought of nothing; why should I think? I *felt* extraordinarily . . .

And from time to time there was another noise; I opened my eyes. A gentle breeze was blowing in the palm trees. It stirred only the highest branches, but did not come low enough to reach us.

The next morning I returned to the same garden with Marceline; that evening, I went back alone. The goatherd who played the flute was there. I went up to him, talked to him. He was called Lassif. He was only twelve years old, and a good-looking boy. He told me the names of his goats, and that the little canals were called *séghias*. Not all of them run every day, he explained. The water is parceled out carefully and stingily, just enough to satisfy the thirst of each tree, but no more. At the foot of each palm tree a small cup has been hollowed out to hold just enough moisture to water the tree. An ingenious system of locks (which the boy demonstrated for me) controls the water and directs it to wherever it is most needed.

The next day I met one of Lassif's brothers. He was a little older and not quite so attractive; his name was Lachmi. He climbed to the top of a palm tree with the help of a sort of ladder made of the stumps of old chopped off branches left in the trunk; then slipped cleverly back down, revealing a golden nakedness beneath his rippling cloak. From the top of the tree (the upper portion had been pruned away) he brought down a little earthen gourd: it had been hung near the fresh cut in order to collect the palm sap, from which is made a sweet wine the Arabs are extremely fond of. At Lachmi's invitation I tasted it, but did not care for its flat, bitter, syrupy taste.

The following days I went farther: I saw other gardens, other goatherds, other goats. As Marceline had said, all these gardens were alike; and yet each one was different.

Sometimes Marceline still came with me; but more often, as soon as we reached the orchards, I would leave her, persuading her that I was tired, that I wanted to sit down, that she must not wait for me, as she needed more exercise; so that she would finish the walk without me. As for me, I stayed behind with the children. Soon I knew a great number of them. I had long conversations with them. I learned their games, and taught them new ones, lost all my spare change pitching pennies. Some of them used to come with me on my walks (each day I went farther); they would show me some new way home, take charge of my coat and my shawl when I happened to bring them both along. Before leaving the children I used to hand around some pennies. Sometimes they would follow me to my door, playing all the way; sometimes they even came inside.

Then Marceline, on her part, invited others. She brought boys from the school, whom she helped with their work. As soon as school was out, these good, gentle little boys would come up. Those that I brought were different, but the two groups made friends over their games. We took care always to have on hand a store of syrups and sweetmeats. Soon other boys came on their own, even when we hadn't invited them. I remember every one. I can see them still. . . .

Toward the end of January, the weather suddenly changed for the worse; a cold wind began to blow, and my health immediately began to suffer. The great open space that separates the oasis from the town once again became impassable for me, and I was obliged to content myself with the public garden. Then it began to rain—an icy rain, which covered the mountains on the far northern horizon with snow.

I spent those gloomy days beside the fire, cast down, fighting bitterly against the illness which was once again winning out in that vile weather. Dismal, dismal days. I could not read, I could not work. The smallest effort brought on the most tiresome perspiration. Simply trying to fix my attention wore me out. The minute I stopped taking great pains to breathe properly, I began to suffocate.

The children were my only possible distraction during those melancholy days. When it was raining, only the old regulars came by. Their clothes were soaked; they sat in a circle around the fire. A long time would pass without anything being said. I was too worn out, too unwell to do anything but look at them; but the mere presence of their fine health did me good. Those whom Marceline petted, though, were weak and sickly, and much too well behaved. I found myself becoming irritated at them (and at her), and ended by pushing them away. To tell the truth, I was afraid of them.

One morning I had a curious revelation into my own character. Moktir, the only one of my wife's protégés who did *not* irritate me (perhaps because he was handsome), was alone with me in my room. Until then, I had thought him at best tolerably attractive, but now I found myself fascinated by the brilliant, somber look in his eyes. By a kind of unexplainable curiosity I was driven to watch what he was doing. I was standing in front of the fire, my elbows on the mantel, apparently absorbed in a book; but I could see all of his actions behind my back reflected in the mirror. Moktir had no idea that he was being watched; he thought I was buried in my book. I saw him go noiselessly up to a table where Marceline had left a little pair of scissors beside her sewing; he snatched the scissors furtively, and in a flash they were hidden inside the folds of his burnous. My heart beat violently for a moment; but all my power of reason could not rouse me to feel the least bit indignant. Even worse—for

I could not manage to fool myself—the *real* feeling that filled me as I watched him was one of pure and simple joy.

When I had allowed Moktir more than enough time to rob me, I turned around and spoke to him as if nothing had happened. Marceline was very fond of the boy; but I do not believe it was the fear of hurting her that made me, next time I saw her, conjure up some fiction to explain the loss of the scissors rather than accuse Moktir. From that day on, Moktir became my favorite.

V

Our stay at Biskra was not to continue much longer. Once the February rains were over, the heat blazed down again with a vengeance. After several miserable days spent under the downpour, I woke up one morning to find the skies once again a brilliant blue. As soon as I was up, I ran to the highest part of the terrace. The sky was clear from one horizon to the other. Mists were rising under the heat of the sun, which was already fierce; the whole oasis was steaming; you could hear the overflowing *oued* rumbling in the distance. The air was so pure, so delicious that I felt better almost at once. Marceline joined me. We both wanted to go out, but that day the mud kept us inside.

A few days later we went back to Lassif's orchard. The stems of the plants looked heavy, softened and swollen with water. At that time I was not familiar with the long hibernation of the African earth; buried in sleep for many days, it was now waking from its long winter's nap, drunk with water, bursting with fresh sap. It rang with the laughter of spring madness, which found an echo, a redoubled echo, in my heart. Ashour and Moktir accompanied us at first. I still enjoyed their slight friendship, which cost me only half a franc a day. But they soon grew tiresome. I was no longer either so weak that I needed the example of their health or so amused as I once had been by their play; it no longer seemed to feed my need for joy, and I turned the elation of my mind and my senses back to Marceline. She was so overjoyed by this that I realized how sad she must have been all along. I begged her pardon like a child for having left her alone so often, excused my strange, shifty moods on the grounds of my illness, swore that until then I had been too weak to love her properly, but that from that day on my love would grow stronger with my health. I was speaking the truth. But no doubt I was still very weak, for it was not till more than a month had passed that I felt any desire for Marceline.

Meanwhile it was getting hotter every day. There was nothing to keep us at Biskra—except that charm which was later to call me back. Our decision to leave was made suddenly. In three hours our things were packed. The train left next morning at dawn.

I remember that last night well. The moon was almost full; its light poured into my room through the wide-open window. I think Marceline was asleep. I had gone to bed, but could not sleep. I felt as if I were burning with a kind of beneficent fever, the fever of life itself. . . . I got up, splashed my hands and face with water, then pushed open the glass doors and went out.

It was already late; not a sound; not a breath; the very air seemed asleep. From a distance one could just barely hear the Arab dogs, which howl all through the night like jackals. In front of me lay our little courtyard. The opposite garden wall cast over it a slanting band of shadow. The tall, straight palm trees, bereft of color and life, seemed struck forever motionless . . . but some palpitation of life can still be found in sleep; there nothing seemed to sleep; everything seemed dead. I was terrified by the calm. And all at once there arose in me again the sense of the tragedy of my life. It rose up as if to protest, to assert itself, to wail aloud against the silence. It was so violent, so impetuous, so nearly agonizing that, if I had been able to howl like an animal, I would have cried out into the night. I took hold of my hand—my left hand with my right, I remember. I wanted to lift it to my head, and I did. Why? To assure myself that I was alive, and to feel the wonder of it. I touched my forehead, my eyelids. A shudder passed over me. A day will come, I thought, a day will come when I shall not even have the strength to carry to my lips the very water I most thirst for. . . . I went back in, but I did not lie down again at once; I wanted to fix that night, to engrave its memory on my mind, to hold it fast. Undecided what to do, I picked up a book that was lying on my table and opened it at random; it was the Bible. By bending over into the moonlight, I was able to read. I read these words, words of Christ to Peter; words that I was never to forget: "When thou was young, thou girdedst thyself and walkedst whither thou wouldest: but when thou shalt be old, thou shalt stretch forth thy hands . . ." Thou shalt stretch forth thy hands . . .

We left the next morning at dawn.

V I

I shall not speak of all the stages of the journey. Some of them have left only a confused impression; my health, some days better, some days worse, still wavered in a cold wind, was still troubled by the shadow of a cloud; and the state of my nerves was the cause of frequent difficulties; but at least my lungs were improving. Each relapse was shorter and less severe; the attacks were just as sharp, but my body was better armed against them.

From Tunis we went to Malta, from there to Syracuse. I found myself back on the classical ground whose language and past I knew so well. Since the beginning of my illness, I had lived without question or rule, simply applying myself to the business of living like an animal or a child. Now that I was less absorbed by my ailments, my life became more conscious and defined. I had thought that, after my long struggle with death, I would find myself reborn exactly the same as I had been before, and be able to tie up at once the present and the past. In the distracting novelty of a strange country I had been able to delude myself into thinking that this had happened. But not there, not at Syracuse; though I still found it hard to believe, everything there impressed on me the fact that I was changed.

When, at Syracuse and then later on, I tried to take up my studies again, to plunge once more into my minute examination of the past, I discovered that something had, if not killed, at least modified my taste for historical research; this "something" was my new feeling for the present. The history of past ages had now taken on for me the immobility, the terrifying fixity of those nocturnal shadows in the courtyard at Biskra, the immobility of death. In the past, it had been that very fixity that I enjoyed; it allowed me to work with such precision. All the facts of history appeared to me like objects in a museum, or rather like plants in a herbarium; plants neatly dried and preserved so that one forgets they were once alive and full of juice growing out under the sun. But now, if I was to take any pleasure in history at all, I had to imagine it in the present tense. The great political events of the past, therefore, came to affect me less than certain poets and men of action, for whom I began to feel a reawakened emotion. At Syracuse I reread Theocritus, and dreamed that his goatherds with the beautiful names were the same ones I had loved at Biskra.

All my past education, recollected at every step I took, now became an encumbrance, a hindrance to my joy. I could not see a Greek theater, a temple, without immediately reconstructing it in my mind. Each ruin conjured up for me the ancient festivals it represented, and I was miserable to think that they were dead. I had an absolute horror of death.

I ended by avoiding all ruins; to the noblest monuments of the past I came to prefer those sunken gardens they call the Latomies, where the lemons have the sharp sweetness of oranges; or the banks of the Cyane, which still flows among the papyrus reeds as blue as it was the day it wept for Proserpine.

I ended by despising the very erudition of which I had once been so proud; the studies which had once been my whole life now seemed to have no more than an accidental and conventional relationship to me. I found out that I was something different from them, that I had—thank God!—a separate existence of my own. Insofar as I was an "expert," a specialist, I thought myself a fool; insofar as I was a man, did I know anything at all about myself? I had only just been born—it would have been impossible for me to know yet *what* I had been born. That was what I had to find out.

There is nothing more tragic, for someone who has been expecting to die, than a long drawn-out convalescence. After the wing of Death has touched you, things that once seemed so important no longer do; other things take their place, things you had thought unimportant, or had not even known existed. The great mass of acquired knowledge begins to peel off the mind like old layers of paint, laying bare in some places the very skin, the authentic self that lay hidden beneath.

From then on, my duty would be to uncover him, that authentic self, "the old Adam," the man the Gospels pronounced dead, the man whom everything around me—books, teachers, relations—and I myself had begun by trying to suppress. He was already coming into view, somewhat defaced and hard to uncover thanks to all those superfluous overlays; but my discovery of him would be all the more valiant and useful for the additional effort. From then on I came to despise that secondary, artificial self which education had painted on top of the original. It was time to scrape off that mask.

I compared myself to a palimpsest, and tasted the joy of the scholar who discovers on a single page, underneath a recent hand, a more ancient and infinitely more precious text. What did it say, that occult text? In order to read it, was it not first of all necessary to *erase* the more recent one?

I was no longer, moreover, the sickly, studious creature so well served by my early morality, with all its rigidity and restrictions. This was more than a convalescence; it was an increase, a recrudescence of life, the influx of a richer, warmer blood which was bound to reach my thoughts, to touch them one by one, to penetrate them all, to stir and color the most remote, secret, and delicate fibers of my being. For one grows accustomed either to strength or to weakness; each creature forms itself out of the powers it possesses; but if these should *increase,* if they should enable one to do *more,* then . . .

I did not think all this at the time, and my description may give the wrong impression. To tell the truth, I did not think at all; I never questioned myself. I let myself be guided by a generous fate. I was afraid that if I were to stop and to investigate it too soon, I might disturb the mystery of my slow transformation. I must allow time for the hidden lines to reappear, not attempt to rewrite them myself. So while I did not let my brain go entirely neglected, at least I let it lie fallow, and gave myself up to the pure sensual enjoyment of myself, of outside things, of all existence, which seemed to me divine. We had left Syracuse, and as I ran along the steep road that connects Taormina and Mola, I remember shouting out loud, "A new self! A new self!" as if my calling would awaken him.

My only effort—a constant effort at that time—was to identify, condemn, and suppress systematically everything which I believed to have resulted from my past education and early moral beliefs. Out of deliberate disdain for my learning, out of scorn for the tastes of a scholar, I refused to visit Agrigento; a few days later, on the road to Naples, I drove right on past the beautiful temple of Paestum, where the spirit of Greece still breathes—and where I was to go two years later to offer prayers to whatever god would listen.

"My only effort," did I say? Could I possibly be interested in myself *except* as a perfectible being? Never had my will been more exalted than it was then, reaching for that unknown and vaguely imagined perfection; I dedicated every ounce of will I possessed to the task of strengthening and bronzing my body. We left the coast near Salerno and went up to Ravello. There the sharper air, the attraction of the rocks with their little nooks, their surprises, the unplumbed depth of the valleys all contributed to my strength and my joy, and helped to sustain my high spirits.

Near to the sky, not far from the shore, Ravello stands on a sharp cliff facing the flat and distant coast of Paestum. In the days of Norman rule, it was a city of some importance; today it is not more than a narrow village where we were, I think, the only outsiders. We were lodged in an ancient religious establishment which had been turned into a hotel. It was situated at the very edge of the rock, and its terraces and gardens seemed to hang suspended over the sky. Looking out over the vine-covered wall, at first we could see nothing but the sea; only after going right up to the edge did we discover the steep cultivated slope that connects Ravello with the shore by paths that seem more like staircases. Above Ravello, the mountain continues. First olive trees, enormous carob trees, with cyclamen growing in their shade; higher up, chestnut trees in great numbers, a fresher air, northern plants; and down below, lemon trees near to the sea. These last are set out in small plots because of the steep slope of the ground, plots that are like little gardens, and nearly all alike; a narrow path goes down the middle from one end to the other. You enter them silently, like a thief, and then dream beneath the green shade. The foliage is thick, heavy; not a single direct ray of sunlight gets through. The lemons hang perfumed, like drops of opaque wax; they are white and greenish in the shade, within reach of the hand, of the thirst; they are sweet and sharp and refreshing.

The shade beneath them was so dense that I did not dare linger in it after my walk, for exercise still made me perspire. And yet the steps did not wear me out. I practiced climbing them without opening my mouth, and took longer and longer between my rests. "I will go so far without giving in," I used to say to myself, and then find my pride rewarded with a glow of satisfaction when the goal was reached. Then I would take a few long, deep breaths, and it seemed to me that I could feel the air fill my lungs all the more efficaciously for my patience. I turned all my old persistence now to the care of my body; I was making progress.

Sometimes I was astonished that my health came back so quickly. I began to think that I had exaggerated the gravity of my condition at the start, to doubt that I had really been so very sick, to laugh at my blood-spitting, to regret that my recovery had not been more arduous.

In my ignorance of my real physical needs, I had treated myself very stupidly at first. I now made a patient study of them, and came to regard my ingenious exercise of prudence and care as a kind of game. What I still suffered from most was my morbid sensitiveness to the slightest change in temperature. Now that my lungs were cured, I attributed that hyperæsthesia to the nervous debility left me by my illness: I vowed to overcome it. I envied the beautiful, brown, sun-burned skin which I could see beneath the open shirts of peasants working in the fields, and longed for a skin as tanned as theirs. One morning I took off my clothes and looked at myself: the sight of my thin arms, my stooped shoulders (which I could not pull back no matter how hard I tried), but above all the whiteness—or rather the absolute colorlessness—of my skin, shamed me to tears. I dressed quickly and, instead of going down to Amalfi as I usually did, I headed toward some mossy, grass-covered rocks, a place far from roads and houses where I knew no one could see me. When I got there, I undressed slowly.

The air was quite sharp, but the sun was burning. I exposed my whole body to its fire. I sat down, lay down, turned over. I felt the hard ground beneath me; I was touched gently by the moving grass. Although I was well sheltered from the wind, I shivered and thrilled at every breath. Soon a delicious burning enveloped me, and my whole being surged into my skin.

We stayed two weeks at Ravello; every morning I returned to those rocks and went on with my cure. Soon I found that all the extra clothing I had been wearing had become superfluous and annoying. My skin had recovered its normal resilience, my constant perspiration had stopped; my own natural warmth was enough.

One of the last mornings at Ravello (we were in the middle of April), I ventured still further. In one of the winding channels in the rocks that I have mentioned, a spring of clear water fell in a little cascade. It was not, to be sure, a very abundant spring, but the waterfall had hollowed out a deeper basin at its foot where the water lingered, exquisitely pure. I had been there three times already and leaned over it each time, stretched out along its bank, thirsty and charged with desire. For a long time I had gazed at the bottom of polished rock, where not a stain, not a weed was to be seen, and where the sun shot its dancing and iridescent rays. On the fourth day, I came up to the spring with my mind already made up: the water was purer and clearer than ever, and I plunged straight in without a thought. At once I was chilled to the bone; I climbed back out, and stretched myself on the grass beneath the sun. Wild, fragrant mint was growing nearby; I picked some leaves, crushed them in my hands, and rubbed my whole wet, burning body with them. I looked at myself for a long time: no longer with shame, but with joy. No, I was not yet robust; but I could be, I could be: harmonious, sensual, almost beautiful.

VII

And so in place of all activity, all my work, I contented myself with physical exercise, which certainly implied some change in my moral sense; but I soon began to regard it as a mere training, a means to an end, and no longer satisfying in itself.

Let me tell you, though, of something else I did, which may seem ridiculous to you; but its very childishness will make clear the tormenting urge I felt to reveal by some outward sign the change that had taken place in my innermost self. At Amalfi I had my beard cut off. Until that day I had kept my beard and moustache full and my hair cut very short. It had never occurred to me that I might have worn them differently. And suddenly, the first day I stripped to sunbathe on the rock, my beard made me uncomfortable; it was like a last piece of clothing which I could not take off. I felt as if it were false. It was carefully trimmed, square, not in a point; then and there it struck me as ridiculous and very unpleasant. When I got back to my hotel room, I looked at myself in the mirror and was displeased with what I saw; I looked like what up till then I had always been—an archæologist, a bookworm. Immediately after lunch, I went down to Amalfi with my mind made up. The town is very small; I could find nothing better than a vulgar little barber shop in the piazza. It was market day, the place was full, I had to wait an interminable time; but nothing—not the suspicious-looking razors, nor the dirty yellow shaving-brush, nor the smell, nor the barber's chatter could put me off. I felt my beard fall beneath his scissors, and it was like taking off a mask. But even so, when I looked at myself after he was done, the emotion that filled me, however hard I tried to repress it, was not joy—but fear. I do not criticize this feeling; I simply recount it. I thought myself good-looking enough . . . but no, what frightened me was the feeling that now the world could see my naked thoughts; and all of a sudden they struck me as something . . . formidable.

On the other hand, I started to let my hair grow.

These two gestures were all that my new and still unemployed self found to perform. I expected it to give birth to actions that would astonish me—but later, later, I told myself, when the new self is more fully formed. Forced to play this waiting game, I maintained, like Descartes, a "provisional" mode of action. This way I was able to delude Marceline. The new look in my eyes, the new expression of my features—especially on the day when I first appeared without my beard—these things might, it is true, have aroused her suspicions; but she loved me too much already to see me honestly; and then I did all I could to reassure her. The important thing was that she should not interfere with my own *renaissance;* to keep it from her eyes, I would have to play a part from now on.

For that matter, the man Marceline loved, the man she had married was not my "new self" at all. I told myself this over and over, as a reminder to keep him hidden. In that way I presented her with an image of myself—an image which, by the very fact of its being constant and faithful to the past, became every day more and more false.

For the time being, therefore, my relationship with Marceline remained the same—if anything growing more intense from day to day as my love each day grew stronger. My dissimulation (if I may use this word for the need I felt to preserve my thoughts from her judgment), my very dissimulation increased that love. What I mean is that this game forced me to think about her all the time. At first, perhaps, this necessity for deception cost me a little effort; but I came quickly to understand that the things we think of as the worst offenses (lying, to mention only one) are difficult to commit only so long as one has never committed them; but they all become—and very quickly—easy, pleasant, and agreeable the third or fourth time around, and are soon quite the natural thing. Once the initial disgust is overcome, one takes genuine pleasure in the act. So it was, at least, with this masquerade of mine. I even prolonged it, as sport for my undiscovered faculties. And every day I moved farther into my richer, fuller life, advancing toward a happiness of greater ripeness and savor.

V I I I

The road from Ravello to Sorrento is so beautiful that I had no desire, that morning, to see anything more beautiful on earth. The rugged rocks warmed in the sun, the fullness, the limpidity of the sweet-smelling air, all this filled me with a heavenly *joie de vivre,* with such contentment that there seemed no room inside me for anything but dancing delight. Memories and regrets, hopes and desires, the future and the past were all silent; I was conscious of nothing in life but what the passing moment brought and then carried away. "Oh, the joys of the body!" I cried out. "Health, at last, health; to feel my muscles so sure, so easy . . ."

I had started early in that morning, ahead of Marceline, for her calmer pleasure would have tempered my own, and her gentle pace would have forced me to a walk. She was to join me by carriage at Positano, where we were to have lunch.

I was nearing Positano when the noise of wheels, which made up the bass accompaniment to a wild kind of singing, forced me to turn around abruptly. At first, I could see nothing because of a bend in the road which at that place runs along the edge of a cliff. Then suddenly a carriage leaped into view, driven at a frantic pace; it was Marceline's. The driver was singing as loud as he could, standing on top of his seat, making wild gestures, and beating ferociously his poor, terrified horse. Why, the brute! I thought. He passed in front of me so quickly that I had only just time to get out of his way; I shouted, but he would not stop. . . . I ran after him, but the carriage was going too fast. I was terrified at the thought that Marceline might suddenly leap out of the carriage; but no less terrified at

the thought that she might stay in it; one jump of the horse could have
thrown her into the sea. . . . All of a sudden the horse fell down. Marceline climbed out and started to run, but I was already beside her. As soon
as the driver saw me, he broke out in horrible oaths. I was furious with the
man; at his first word of abuse, I rushed at him and threw him brutally to
the ground. I rolled on the ground with him, but kept the advantage; he
seemed dazed by the fall; when I saw that he was trying to bite me, I hit
him in the face with my fist, which stunned him even more. But still I
would not let go of him, and kept my knee pressed against his chest while
I tried to pinion his arms. I looked at his hideous face, which my fist had
made still uglier; he spat, slobbered, bled, swore—my Lord, what a horrible creature! Really, it would have been fair to strangle him—and I
might very well have done it . . . at least I felt fully capable of doing it.
I really think it was only the idea of the police that prevented me.

I managed, with some difficulty, to get the madman securely tied,
and then flung him into the carriage like a sack.

Ah, what looks, what kisses Marceline and I exchanged when it was
over. The danger had not really been great; but I had been forced to show
my strength—and that in order to protect her. At that moment I felt I
could have given my life for her—and given it with absolute joy. . . .
The horse had got to its feet. We left the drunkard at the bottom of the
carriage, got up onto the driver's seat ourselves, and, guiding the horse as
best we could, managed to get first to Positano and then to Sorrento.

It was on that night that I first possessed Marceline.

Have you understood, really, how new I was to the things of love—
or must I tell you once more? It was to its novelty, I suspect, that our
wedding night owed its charm. . . . For it seems to me, when I think of
it today, that that first night was the *only* one, really—the anticipation, the
surprise added so much to the sheer delight of sensual pleasure. One single
night, after all, is more than enough to express the very greatest love; and
what is more my memory persists in refusing to recall any other. A single,
momentary laugh in the night, and our souls were compounded. . . .
But I believe there comes a point in love, a unique moment which the
soul tries later on to surpass, but in vain. I believe that the effort it makes
to recapture its old happiness can grind down the soul; that nothing im-
pedes happiness so much as the memory of happiness past. And how well
I remember that night. . . .

Our hotel was outside the town, surrounded by gardens and orchards.
A very large balcony opened out from our room, and the branches of the
trees brushed against it. The dawn-light poured in freely through wide-

open shutters. I sat up in bed quietly, and bent tenderly over Marceline. She was asleep; she seemed to be smiling in her sleep. Now that I was stronger, she seemed to me more delicate, her very gracefulness became fragility. A tumult of thoughts came whirling about my brain: she was telling the truth, I realized, when she said that I was all she had. "What do *I* do to make her happy? All day, every day, virtually, I abandon her. She depends on me for everything, and what do I do? I neglect her . . . oh, my poor, poor Marceline!" Tears filled my eyes. In vain I sought to excuse myself by reason of my former weakness; what business had I now with such constant attentions, with such egoism? Was I not now the stronger of the two?

The smile had left her cheeks. The early daylight, which had touched everything else with gold, suddenly revealed her to me as pale and sad. Perhaps the approach of morning helped to foster my anxiety. "Will it be my turn next, Marceline, to take care of you, to worry over you, one day?" Inside, I was crying; I felt myself shudder; transfixed with love, with pity, with tenderness, I placed softly between her closed eyes the most gentle, the most loving, the most pious of kisses.

I X

The few days we spent at Sorrento were smiling days, days of great calm. Had I ever before enjoyed such repose, such happiness? And should I ever enjoy them again? . . . I was constantly with Marceline; less concerned with myself, I could concern myself more with her, and now found as much pleasure in talking to her as I had formerly found in being silent.

At first I was astonished to find that she looked on our wandering life, with which (I insisted) I was perfectly contented, as only a temporary state. But its idleness soon became apparent to me, and I agreed that it should only continue a short time. My newly recovered health left me with hours and hours of leisure, and that very leisure, in the end, gave rise to a new desire for work. I began to speak seriously of going home; from the joy this evoked in Marceline, I realized that she had been dreaming of it for a long time.

Meanwhile, I had returned my attention to some of my old historical studies, but I found that they no longer held their old attraction. As I have said, since my illness I had come to consider abstract and neutral knowledge of the past as mere vanity. I had formerly dedicated myself to philological research, setting out to demonstrate, for example, the influence of the Goths on the corruption of the Latin language; I neglected completely

—because I did not understand them—the figures of Theodoric, Cassiodorus, and Amalasontha with their magnificent passions, to concentrate
all my enthusiasm on mere documents, the signs and residue of their
lives. But now those same signs—indeed, the whole study of philology—
were nothing more for me than a means of penetrating deeper into the
savage grandeur and nobility that I only now recognized in their lives. I
resolved to concentrate more thoroughly on their period, to limit myself
for a time to the last episode of the Gothic empire, and to make good use
of our coming stay at Ravenna, the scene of its dying years.

I must confess, though, that what attracted me most in the period was
the figure of the young king Athalaric. I pictured to myself this fifteen-
year-old boy, secretly excited by the Goths, turning in revolt against his
own mother Amalasontha, kicking over his Latin upbringing and pushing
aside his own culture, like a headstrong young stallion that throws off a
troublesome harness. Preferring the company of the uncivilized Goths to
that of Cassiodorus, too old and too wise, he plunged for a few years into a
life of violent and unbridled pleasures with rude companions of his own
age, and died at eighteen, rotten and gorged with debauchery. In this tragic
impulse toward a wilder, more natural state, I recognized something of my
own "crisis," as Marceline used to call it in jest. I tried to get my mind, at
least, to direct itself to the question, as I could no longer interest my body
in it; and I told myself over and over that there was a lesson for me in the
ghastly death of Athalaric.

So we stopped to spend a fortnight at Ravenna, then glanced quickly
at Rome and Florence; but we skipped Venice and Verona altogether, cut
short our travels, and made no more stops until we arrived at Paris. I
found an altogether new pleasure in talking to Marceline about the future.
We were still a little uncertain as to how we should spend the summer; we
were both tired of traveling, and I wanted absolute quiet for my work.
Then we thought of a piece of property I owned between Lisieux and Pont-
l'Eveque, in the greenest part of Normandy—it had formerly belonged to
my mother, and I had spent several summers with her there in my childhood; but I had never gone back since her death. My father had left it in
charge of a bailiff, an old man by that time, who collected the rents and
sent them to us regularly. I had retained memories, enchanting memories
of a large and very pleasant house standing in a garden watered by running streams. It was called La Morinière. I thought it would be a good
place to live.

I talked about spending the next winter in Rome—working this time, not simply sight-seeing . . . but that plan was soon overturned. Among the many letters which had been waiting so long for us in Naples was one that informed me, to my total surprise, that a chair having fallen vacant at the Collège de France, my name had already been mentioned several times in regard to the appointment. It was only a substitute post, but one that would leave me therefore with a considerable amount of freedom in the future. The friend who told me all this informed me of the few easy steps to take if I was interested—and urged me very strongly to accept. I hesitated at first, seeing in it nothing more than a form of slavery; but then I considered that it might be interesting to put forward my ideas on Cassiodorus in a course of lectures. . . . The pleasure it would give Marceline finally turned the scale, and once the decision was made, I saw only its advantages.

My father had maintained several connections in the learned world of Rome and Florence, men with whom I myself had been in correspondence. They made it possible for me to conduct all the research I wanted, at Ravenna and elsewhere. I thought of nothing but my work. Marceline strove to help me in a thousand charming ways, with a thousand kind attentions.

Our happiness, during those last days of our travels, was so equable, so tranquil, that there is nothing for me to say about it. Man's finest works always grow out of his misery; how can you tell a story of happiness? Only what leads up to it can be told—or what destroys it. And now I have told you everything that led up to it.

SECOND PART

I

We arrived at La Morinière at the beginning of July, having stopped in Paris just long enough to do our shopping and pay a very few visits.

La Morinière is situated, as I have said, between Lisieux and Pont-l'Eveque, the darkest, wettest countryside I know. The rolling ground divides into endless little ups and downs, narrow valleys and gently rounded hills, until it reaches the wide Vallée d'Auge, where it suddenly levels out into a large plain stretching all the way to the sea. There is no horizon; a few dark groves full of mystery; a few planted fields: but mostly meadowland, softly sloping pastures where the thick grass is mown twice a year, where numerous apple trees join their shadows together when the sun is low, where the flocks and herds graze freely. There is water in every hollow—pool or pond or stream. The sound of running water is constantly in the ear.

Oh, how well I remember the house! its blue roofs, its walls of brick and stone, its moat, the reflections in the sleeping waters. . . . It was an old house which would easily have lodged a dozen persons; Marceline, three servants, and I, who occasionally lent them a helping hand, found it all we could do to animate just one wing. Our old caretaker, who was named Bocage, had already prepared a few rooms as best he could. The old furniture was awakened from its twenty years' sleep. Everything had stayed just as my memory had pictured it—the paneling not too dilapidated, the rooms comfortable, easy to live in. For our welcome, Bocage had filled with flowers all the vases he could find, and had had the great court and the nearest pathways in the park weeded and raked. As we approached, the house was touched by the last of the sun's rays, and from the valley before it there had arisen a hovering, motionless mist through which the river appeared and disappeared. We were not yet quite up to the house when I suddenly recognized the scent of the grass. And when I heard anew the sharp cries of the swallows darting round the house, my whole past suddenly rose up, as if it had been waiting for me; and now, recognizing me, hearing me approach, wanted to close over me again.

After a few days, the house was made more or less comfortable. I might have settled down to work, but I held off. I was still listening to my past, as it recalled itself to my memory in meticulous detail. Next my attention was seized by another emotion, one totally unexpected: just a week after our arrival, Marceline told me that she was going to have a child.

From then on I felt that I owed her greater care than ever, that she had a right to greater tenderness. In any case, during the first weeks that followed her revelation, there was scarcely a minute of the day that I did not spend in her company. We used to go and sit near the wood, on a bench where my mother and I had sat in the old days; there each moment brought a richer pleasure than the last, each hour flew weightlessly, insensibly away. If no distinct memory stands out from that period of my life, it is not, believe me, because I have lost the vivid sense of what it was; but rather because everything in it mingled and melted together into one uniform state of well-being on which everything else rested, in which evening joined to morning without a break, and day passed into day without surprise.

I gradually set to work again, my mind tranquil, alert, sure of its strength, looking calmly and confidently, unfeverishly into the future. My will seemed to be softened, as if it were listening to the counsels of that temperate land.

I had no doubt that the example of that particular country, where everything was ripening toward the harvest, toward a useful fruition, would have the most excellent influence on me. I saw in my mind's eye the peaceful future promised by the great oxen and fat cows that grazed in those opulent meadows, and stared at them in admiration. The apple trees, set out in rows on the sunny slopes of the hills, portended a magnificent harvest for the summer. I could already imagine the rich burden of fruit that was soon going to bend down their branches. From that well-ordered abundance, that joyful subjection, that smiling cultivation, there had grown a harmony—a harmony no longer fortuitous but intended; a rhythm, a beauty at once natural and human, in which one could no longer tell which to admire more—the fecund explosion of untrammeled nature or the wise effort of man to keep it under control: so blended were the two in the most perfect accord. What good would be the effort, I thought, without the powerful savagery it controls? And the savagery, that wild spurt of overflowing sap—what good would *it* be without the intelligent effort that banks it, guides it gently, transforms it into rich, luxurious fruit? And I let myself drift into a dream of lands where all force should be so regulated, all expenditure so compensated, all exchanges so strict, that the slightest waste would be noticed at once. Then, applying my dream to life, I constructed for myself an ethical ideal—a scientific scheme for the perfect utilization of oneself by means of intelligent restraint.

What had become of my turbulence of just a few weeks before? Where had it buried itself, where was it hiding? It seemed never to have existed, so calm was I now. Everything had been covered by the rising tide of my love. . . .

Meanwhile old Bocage was growing overzealous around us; he gave directions, he superintended, he advised; his need to appear indispensable was tiresome in the extreme. In order not to hurt his feelings, I had to go over his accounts and listen for hours on end to his interminable explanations. Even that was not enough: I had to accompany him on his walks about the grounds. His sententious platitudes, his everlasting speeches, his evident self-satisfaction, the display he always made of his integrity left me exasperated after a very short time. He was becoming more and more persistent, and I searched for any means I could find to win back my liberty. Then there occurred an unexpected event which was to give a totally different character to our relationship. One evening Bocage informed me that he was expecting his son Charles the next day.

I said "Oh," rather indifferently, not having greatly concerned myself until then with whether or not Bocage had any children; then, seeing that my indifference offended him and that he expected from me some show of interest and surprise, I inquired, "Where is he now, then?"

"At a model farm near Alençon," Bocage answered.

"He must be about . . . ah . . ." I went on, pretending to calculate the age of this son (of whose existence until that moment I had been totally unaware), and speaking slowly enough that he might have time to interrupt me.

"Past seventeen," Bocage put in. "He was not much more than four when Madame your mother passed away. Ah! He's a big lad now; he'll soon know more than his dad. . . ." And once Bocage had started there was no stopping him, no matter how openly I let my boredom show.

I had forgotten all about this, when Charles, freshly arrived, came by the next evening to pay his respects to Marceline and me. He was a handsome, strapping fellow, so exuberantly healthy, so supple, so well made, that not even the frightful town-clothes he had put on in our honor could make him look too foolish; his blushes added very little to the fine natural ruddiness of his cheeks. His eyes were so bright, so innocent, so childlike, that he looked no more than fifteen. He expressed himself clearly, without embarrassment, and, unlike his father, did not speak when he had nothing to say. I don't know what we talked about that first evening. I was so busy looking at him that I found nothing to say, and let Marceline do all the talking. But the next day, for the first time, I did not wait for old Bocage to come and fetch me in order to go down to the farm, where I knew they were setting to work.

The job at hand was that of repairing a leaking pond, a pond as big as a lake. The leak had been located and had to be cemented. For the repairs to be made, the pond had first to be drained, something that had not been done for fifteen years. It was full of carp and tench, some of them huge, that had never come up from the bottom of the pond. I wanted to transfer some of these fish to the moat and give some to the workmen; so that the pleasure of a fishing-party had been added to the day's work, and as a consequence there was extraordinary animation about the farm. Some children from the neighborhood had come, and ran about among the workers. Marceline herself was to join us later on.

The water level had already been going down for some time when I arrived. Every now and then a great shudder suddenly rippled the surface, and the brown backs of the agitated fish came into sight. The children, paddling in the puddles round the edges, caught gleaming handfuls of small fry, which they threw into pails of fresh water. The water of the pond, muddy to begin with, was stirred up by the thrashing fish, and became thicker and more opaque as the draining went on. The numbers of fish exceeded all expectation; four farmhands were pulling them out by just plunging their hands in anywhere. I was sorry that Marceline had planned to come down later, and had just decided to run back to get her when a shout went up announcing the first eels. But none of the men could succeed in catching them; they slipped between their fingers. Charles, who up till then had been standing beside his father on the bank, could restrain himself no longer; he quickly took off his shoes and socks, threw down his jacket and his vest, and then, rolling up his trousers and his shirt-sleeves as far as he could, waded resolutely into the mud. I immediately did the same.

"Hey, Charles!" I shouted, "a good thing you came back yesterday, wasn't it?"

He was already too busy with his fishing to answer, but he looked at me with a laugh. Soon I had to call out to him to come and help me trap a fat eel; we joined hands to grab hold of it . . . after that one, another. Our faces were all spattered with mud; sometimes the ooze gave way suddenly beneath us, and we sank in it up to our hips; we were soon completely soaked. In the fury of the sport, we exchanged only a few shouts, a few words; at the end of the day, though, I realized that I was calling him "*tu*," without quite knowing when I had begun it. We had learned more about each other from working together that way than we could have from the longest conversation. Marceline still had not come—in fact, she never did come. But already I had given up regretting her absence. She might, I thought, have got a bit in the way of our fun.

From the next day on, I went down each morning to the farm to look for Charles. We would set off together for the woods.

I knew almost nothing about my own estate, but my ignorance had never troubled me in the least. So I was astonished to find how much Charles knew about it and the way it was divided up into farms. He told me—I had only the vaguest notion of it before—that I had six tenant farmers; that I might have made from sixteen to eighteen thousand francs a year from my rents; and that if at very best I earned about half that amount, it was because almost everything was swallowed up by repairs of every sort and by fees paid out to middlemen. His way of smiling as he looked over the crops soon made me suspect that the management of the estate was perhaps not quite so excellent as I first had thought (and as Bocage had led me to believe). I pressed Charles further on the subject, and the same practical intelligence that had so exasperated me in Bocage amused me in the boy. We kept up our walks day after day; the property covered many acres, and when we had peered inquisitively into every corner of it, we began again, more methodically. Charles never tried to hide from me his irritation at the sight of certain badly kept fields, certain pieces of land that were overgrown with gorse, thistles, and deep-rooted weeds. He brought me to share his hatred for fallow land, to share his dream of agricultural reforms.

"But," I said to him at first, "even if the grounds are badly kept, who suffers? The farmer himself, is it not? His rent stays the same no matter what his profits are."

Charles was a little annoyed. "You know nothing about it," he ventured to say—of course I smiled at once. "You think only of the income, and refuse to realize that the capital is deteriorating. Your land is slowly losing its value by being badly cultivated."

"If the land were to bring in more money by being better cared for, I very much doubt the farmers would neglect it. I know these men: they're too mercenary to pass up a chance for more profit."

"You forget the cost of the extra labor," countered Charles. "These fields are sometimes a long way from the farms. Keeping them up would bring in no additional profit, or virtually none; but at least they wouldn't be spoiled. . . ."

And so the conversation went on. Sometimes, as we rode about surveying the fields, we seemed to be going over and over the same things for a whole hour. But I was listening, and little by little I was learning.

"After all," I said one day impatiently, "all this is your father's business."

Charles blushed slightly. "My father is old," he said; "he has enough to do as it is, looking after the carpentry, seeing to the upkeep of the buildings, collecting the rents. It's not his job to make reforms."

"And what reforms would *you* make?" I asked. But at that he became evasive, pretended to know nothing about it; only by insisting was I able to force him to reveal his scheme.

What he advised me to do, in the end, was to take back from the tenants all the lands they left uncultivated. "If the farmers leave a part of their fields lying fallow, it's proof that they have more than they need to pay the rent. If they insist on keeping it all, then you are justified in raising their rents. . . . They're all lazy around here," he added.

Of the six farms that I found to be mine, the one I most enjoyed visiting was situated on a hill overlooking La Morinière; it was called La Valterie. The farmer who rented it was a pleasant enough fellow, and I enjoyed talking with him. Nearer La Morinière a piece called "the home farm" was let on a sharecropping system that left Bocage, in my absence, owner of half the cattle. Now that my distrust had been aroused, I began to suspect the honest Bocage, if not of cheating me, at least of allowing several other people to do so. One stable and one cow-shed on this farm had been, it is true, reserved for me; but it soon became clear that this fiction had merely been invented so that the farmer might feed his cows and horses with my oats and my hay. Until then I had listened indulgently to all the highly improbable accounts Bocage had given me from time to time on the deaths and diseases and malformations of my livestock. I swallowed them all. It had not then occurred to me that it was enough for one of the farmer's cows to fall ill for it to become one of my cows, or that when one of my cows was doing especially well, it just might become one of his. But a few imprudent remarks from Charles, coupled with a few observations of my own, and I began to be enlightened; and my mind, once set on the alert, ran rapidly on ahead.

Marceline, at my warning, went over the accounts minutely, but could not uncover the least error; Bocage's honesty was well protected. What was to be done? For the time being, nothing: let him be. But from then on, inwardly vexed, I kept my eye on the livestock, without letting him know what I was about.

I had four horses and ten cows—quite enough to plague me severely. One of my horses was still called "the colt," although he was more than three years old; he was just now being broken in. I was beginning to take an interest in him, when one fine day I was informed that he was absolutely intractable; that it would never be possible to do anything with him; that the best thing I could do would be to get rid of him. And, just in case I had had any intention of doubting the information, the horse had been made to smash in the front of a small cart, and to bloody up his hocks in doing it.

It was all I could do that day to keep my temper; what held me back was Bocage's own embarrassment. After all, I thought, this is really more a case of weakness than of ill-will; the workmen are the ones to blame; what they need is a firm hand, but he's past keeping them in line.

I went out into the yard to see the colt. One of the men, who had been beating him, began to stroke him as soon as he heard me coming; I pretended to have seen nothing. I did not know much about horses, but that colt had seemed to me a handsome animal; a half-breed, light bay in color and remarkably trim, even elegant in his proportions, with a very bright eye, the mane and tail nearly blond. I made sure that he was not injured, demanded that his cuts be properly dressed, and then left without saying another word.

As soon as I saw Charles that evening, I tried to find out what he thought of the colt.

"I think he's perfectly gentle," he said, "but they don't know how to manage him; they'll drive him wild."

"How would *you* manage him?"

"Would monsieur let me have him for a week? I'll answer for him."

"What will you do?"

"You'll see."

The next day, Charles led the colt down to a corner of the field shaded by a superb walnut tree and bordered by the river; Marceline and I went along. It is one of my most vivid recollections. With a rope a few yards long, Charles had tied the colt to a stake driven firmly into the ground. The high-strung, mettlesome animal had objected violently, it appears, for some time; but by then, tired and quiet, he was going round his circle more peaceably. The surprising spring of his trot was delightful to watch, as engaging as a dance. Charles stood at the center of the circle and skipped over the rope at each turn with a sudden jump, exciting or calming the horse with his voice. He held a long whip in his hand, but I did not see him use it. Because of his youthfulness and delight, everything in his manner, his gestures, gave to his work the beautiful and fervent aspect of pleasure. Suddenly—I have no idea how—he mounted the animal. It had slackened its pace, then stopped; he had stroked it for a moment; then in a flash I saw him astride, so sure of himself, barely holding onto the mane at all, laughing, leaning forward, still stroking the horse gently. The colt had resisted for an instant, ever so slightly; then it recommenced its even, equable trot, so handsome, so easy, that I envied Charles and told him so.

"A few more days' training and the saddle won't even tickle him. In two weeks, madame herself won't be afraid to mount him. He'll be as gentle as a lamb."

He was right. A few days later, the horse allowed itself to be stroked, harnessed, led without a sign of resistance; and Marceline could indeed have ridden it if her condition had not forbidden it.

"You should try him yourself, monsieur," said Charles. I should never have done so on my own; but Charles offered to saddle another of the farm horses for himself, and the pleasure of accompanying him proved irresistible.

How grateful I was to my mother for having let me take riding-lessons when I was a little boy! The memory of those lessons, so far away in the past, stood me in good stead. The sensation of being on horseback was not overly strange; after the first few minutes, I lost all fear and was completely at my ease. Charles's horse was heavier, not purebred, but a decent-looking mount all the same. What really mattered was his style—he rode excellently. We got in the habit of going out for a bit each day. Preferring to leave in the early morning, we rode through grass still bright with dew to the edge of the woods; we were soaked by drops from the hazel trees, whose branches we had shaken riding through. All at once the horizon opened up, and there in front of us lay the wide valley of the Auge; far in the distance, very dimly, the sea. We stopped there a moment without dismounting; the rising sun began to color the mists; then it parted them; then dispersed them. We set off at a brisk trot; lingered a while at the farm, where the day's work was just beginning, to relish the proud pleasure of being up before (and up above) the farmhands; then left them abruptly. I returned to La Morinière just as Marceline was getting up.

I used to come in drunk with the open air, dazed with speed, my limbs almost numb with sensual exhaustion, my spirit filled with health, appetite, freshness. Marceline approved, even encouraged this fancy. She said she liked the smell of wet leaves that I brought to her bedside; she used to linger on in bed waiting for me to return and come up, still dressed in my riding clothes. And she listened while I told her of our ride, described the awakening fields, the starting up of a new day's work. . . . She took as much delight, it seemed, in feeling *me* live as in living herself. —Soon, though, I was to take unfair advantage of that delight of hers, as I had of others. Our rides grew longer, Charles's and mine, and sometimes I did not come back till nearly noon.

I did all I could, however, to keep the late afternoons and evenings free for the preparation of my course. I was making progress—in fact I was quite satisfied. I was even beginning to consider the possibility of publishing the lectures later in book form. By a sort of natural reaction, the more regular and orderly my own life became, and the more pleasure I took in regulating and ordering everything around me, the more I found myself smitten by the rude ethics of my Goths. So much so that in the end I strove throughout my course to exalt and defend *non*-culture, with a boldness for which I was afterwards taken sufficiently to task: but at the same time I was racking my brains to control, if not to suppress, everything about me or within me that could even suggest it. You cannot know to what incredible lengths I pushed that clever scheme . . . or that insanity.

Two of my tenants whose leases expired at Christmas came to see me with a request for renewal; it was simply a matter of extending the lease-agreement, as had always been done. Strengthened by Charles's assurances, and encouraged by our daily conversations, I awaited the farmers with resolution. When they arrived, they started right in by demanding that their rents be lowered, comfortable in the conviction that tenants are hard to replace. You can imagine their surprise when I read them the new agreement that I had drawn up myself, in which I not only refused to lower the rents, but also withdrew from their farms certain pieces of land which I insisted they were not using. At first they pretended to take it as a joke—surely I was joking! Whatever could I want with these fields? They were worth nothing; if they were not used, it was because they were useless. . . . Then, realizing that I was serious, they turned stubborn; so did I. They decided to frighten me by threatening to leave; it was the word I had been waiting for:

"All right, then; go if you like! I won't keep you," I said. I took the contract and tore it into pieces in front of them.

So there I was, with more than two hundred acres on my hands. I had already planned for some time to assign the management of it to Bocage, thinking that in that way I should be giving it indirectly to Charles. I also intended to look after it myself, to a considerable degree. But to tell the truth I had given the matter very little thought: I was simply tempted by the risk involved. The tenants would not be moving out before Christmas; by that time we should have a good idea how to handle it. I told Charles what I had done; he could not hide his glee, and that annoyed me: it made me feel, more than ever, that he was much too young. Already we were pressed for time—we had reached the season when the first harvests left the fields clear for early plowing. It was the established custom for the outgoing tenant to work alongside his successor. The former gives up his land piece by piece as soon as he has harvested his crop. I had expected the two farmers I had dismissed to try to get even with me somehow, but instead they played a game of perfect amiability (I only later learned how much this masquerade was to their advantage). I took advantage of their "generosity," by running up to the land every morning and evening, the land which was soon to be mine.

Autumn was beginning; we had to hire extra workmen to hurry the plow-ing and sowing. We bought harrows, rollers, plows. I surveyed the whole operation from horseback, directing the work, taking considerable pleas-ure in ordering people about and using my authority.

Meanwhile, in the neighboring meadows, the apples were being gathered. They dropped from the trees and rolled in the thick grass, more abundant than they had ever been before. We had not nearly enough workmen; more had to be brought from the nearby villages, hired for the week. Sometimes Charles and I helped them out, just for the fun of it. Some of the men beat the branches with sticks to bring down the late fruit; those that fell of themselves were gathered in separate piles. Over-ripe apples lay bruised and crushed in the high grass, and it was impossible to walk without stepping on them. The smell that rose from the meadow was bitter and sweetish, and it mingled with the fresh, heavy smell of the plowed earth.

The autumn rolled on. The mornings of those last fine days were the freshest, the most transparent of all. There were times when the wet atmosphere painted all distances blue, made them look more distant still, turned a short walk into a day's journey; the whole countryside seemed to grow. On other days, the abnormal transparency of the air brought all the horizons closer—you could have reached them all with a single stroke of the wing. Which of these two moods filled me with a greater languor, I cannot say. My own work was almost finished—or so I told myself, as an encouragement to distraction. The hours I no longer spent at the farm I gave to Marceline. Together we went out into the garden; we walked slowly, she languidly hanging on my arm. We would sit together on a bench looking out over the valley gradually filling with the evening light. She had a tender way of leaning against my shoulder; and so we would sit there until dark, feeling the day melt away inside us, without a gesture, without a word. . . .

Already our love had learned to wrap itself in silence. Marceline's love had become by that time something stronger than words could tell, so strong that it could become at times an agony for me. As a breath of wind sometimes ripples the most placid water, so the slightest emotion was now written clearly on her face. She was listening to a new life trembling mys-teriously inside her; she was like a deep, pure pond. I leaned over the edge and looked deep, deep down; but as far down as I could see, I saw nothing but love. Ah, if that *was* still happiness, I am sure that I tried from that time on to hold onto it, as you try in vain to hold the water that runs through your cupped hands. But already I could feel, next to my happiness, something else; something that was not happiness, something indeed that colored my love, but as autumn colors the leaves.

And so autumn moved on. Each morning the grass was wetter; now it no longer dried at all on the shady side of the forest's edge; at the first streak of dawn it was white. The ducks beat their wings in the waters of the moat, thrashed about wildly; some days you could see them rise up together, quacking loudly, and make a great raucous circuit about La Morinière. Then one morning they were not to be seen; Bocage had locked them up. Charles told me that they were shut up this way every autumn, at the time for flying south. And a few days later the weather broke. One evening, all at once, there came a great wind, a breath from the sea, strong, steady, bringing the north and the rain, carrying off the migratory birds. Marceline's condition, the problems of settling into a new apartment, the preparations for my lectures—these things would have called us back to town soon enough. The bad weather, starting so early, chased us away.

In November, it is true, I was to be drawn back by the work on the farm. I was greatly vexed to learn Bocage's plans for the winter; his intention was, he told me, to send Charles back to the model farm; he insisted that the boy still had a good deal to learn. I talked to him a long time, used all the arguments I could think of, but could not make him budge. At the very most he might allow Charles to shorten his studies by a few days so as to return just a bit earlier. Bocage did not hesitate to let me know that the running of the two new farms would be a matter of no small effort; but he had his eye on two trustworthy peasants, he told me, whom he intended to employ—partly as farmers, partly as tenants, partly as simple hired men. The whole scheme was too extraordinary in those parts for him to expect much good to come from it, but if that was what I wanted . . . This conversation took place toward the end of October. By early November, we were settled in Paris.

I I

We moved into an apartment which one of Marceline's brothers had found for us, on the rue S., near Passy, which we had been able to inspect during our last stopover in Paris. It was a good deal larger than the one my father had left me, and Marceline was somewhat concerned—on account not only of the increased rent, but also all the other expenses it was surely going to entail. I countered all her fears by insisting that I had an

absolute horror of anything less permanent. I even forced myself to believe that, and deliberately exaggerated my response. Of course, the various costs of setting up house were going to exceed our income for *that*
year; but our fortune, which was already handsome, was sure to grow still
larger. For that I was counting on my lectures, on the publication of my
book, and even (with what madness!) on the revenues from my new
farms. So I gave in to every expense, and at each new bill, simply told
myself that I was tying myself down all the more firmly. In that way, I
could assert, I was helping to suppress any wandering urge that I might
feel (or fear that I might feel) welling up inside.

Our first few days were taken up with shopping and other such
chores from morning to night. And although her brother kindly offered to
take on as much of the work as he could, it was not long before Marceline
felt herself thoroughly exhausted. Then, once we were settled, instead of
resting as she should have, she felt obliged to receive a regular procession
of callers. We had been away from our Parisian friends and relations almost continually since we were married, so now they came in droves. Marceline had grown unaccustomed to society; she did not know how to cut a
visit short, and dared not shut her doors altogether. When I came home in
the evening, I found her exhausted. I knew that the cause of her fatigue
was perfectly natural, and so I was not overly worried; but still I tried to
think up ways of lessening it, and so I often received visits in her stead (a
thing I enjoy very little), and sometimes paid them myself (a thing I
enjoy even less).

I have never been a brilliant conversationalist; the frivolity and the
wit of *salons* were things of no great pleasure to me. Still, I had in the old
days frequented a few—but such a long time ago! What had happened to
me since then? In the company of other people, I felt dull, gloomy, un-
wanted, at once bored and boring. . . . by a singular stroke of ill-luck,
not one of *you* was in Paris at the time, nor were you likely to return
soon—you whom I consider my only true friends. Would I have been able
to speak more honestly to you? Would you have understood me, perhaps,
better than I understood myself? All those things that were growing inside me, all the things I am telling you about today—what did I know of
them then? The future seemed to be absolutely sure; never had I believed
it more under my control.

And even if I had been more perceptive, what possible defense
against myself was I likely to find in Hubert, Didier, Maurice, so many
others—you know them as well as I do, you know what they are worth.
They—why, they could *never* understand me: that much I discovered

very quickly. From our first conversations, I found myself forced to play a role, to imitate the man they still thought I was, at the risk of seeming a fraud. To make things easier, I acted as if I still had the thoughts and the tastes they had assigned to me. One cannot both be sincere and seem so.

I was rather more willing to renew contact with my professional acquaintance, the archæologists and philologists, but I found about as much pleasure (and *not* as much excitement) in chatting with them as in leafing through a good unabridged dictionary. I had hoped, at first, to find a somewhat more immediate comprehension of life in a few poets and novelists I knew; but if they had ever had such a comprehension, I must confess they certainly did not show it then. It seemed to me that most of them did not live at all; it was enough for them to appear to be alive, and they were not far from regarding "life" as a troublesome hindrance to their writing. And I couldn't blame them—I may well have been making the same mistake. . . . For that matter, what did I mean by "living"? That was precisely what I wanted someone to explain. Oh, they all talked so cleverly of this event and that in their lives—but never of what lay behind the events.

As for the few philosophers whose business it should have been to explain all that to me, I had long known what to expect of them: mathematicians or neo-Kantians, they kept themselves as far away as possible from the tediousness of reality, and concerned themselves with it no more than the algebraist worries about the existence of his X's and Y's.

Each time I came back home to Marceline, I made no effort to conceal how tiresome I found these encounters. "They are all alike," I complained. "When I talk to one of them, I feel as if I were talking to the whole lot."

"But, my dear," said Marceline, "you cannot expect each one to be different from all the rest."

"The more alike they are to one another, the more different they are from me. Not one of them has ever been clever enough to be ill," I went on more dejectedly. "They are alive—they *look* as if they were alive, at any rate, and yet at the same time as if they were absolutely unaware of it. I, for that matter, since I have been in their company, *I* have stopped living. Today, for example—and it is only one day out of so many—what have I done? I had to leave you about nine o'clock; I barely had time to read a few pages before I went out—the only worthwhile moment of the day. Your brother was waiting for me at the notary's, and after our business there he simply refused to leave me alone. I had to go to see the upholsterer with him; he was a terrible nuisance at the cabinet-maker's;

and I only got rid of him at Gaston's. I had lunch in the neighborhood with Philippe, then met Louis, who was waiting for me at a café to go with him to Théodore's absurd lecture, which was idiotic, and for which of course I complimented him on the way out. He invited me for Sunday, and to get out of that I had to go with him to Arthur's; Arthur drags me along to see some exhibition of watercolors; I leave cards with Albertine and Julie. . . . I come back thoroughly exhausted to find you just as tired as I am, having been visited by Adeline, Marthe, Jeanne, Sophie. . . . And now, in the evening, when I look back on all this running about, my day seems so empty, so wasted that I desperately want to steal it back and start it all over again, hour by hour; it is all so depressing that I could cry."

And yet I should not have been able to say what I meant by "living," nor whether the real root of my problem, the secret of my troubles, was not, quite simply, that I had acquired a taste for a more spacious, airy life, one less hemmed in, less concerned about other people. No, I thought: my secret was much more mysterious than that; it was the secret of someone just restored to life. For I was an outsider in the company of ordinary people, like a man who had arisen from the dead. At first I felt simply out of place, miserable and confused. But soon a new and different emotion replaced that confusion. I had felt not the least shred of pride, as I told you, at the publication of those studies that had won me so much praise. But what was I to call this new feeling, then, if not pride? It may have been pride; but at least there was no trace of vanity mixed with it. It was simply the first time I had been aware of my own real worth. What separated me from others, what distinguished me from them—*that* was what mattered. What no one else had said, what only I *could* say: that was to be my message.

My lectures began soon after that. Inspired by the subject, I poured all my newborn passion into my first lecture. In describing the later Latin civilization, I compared artistic culture to a kind of secretion: first it wells up inside a people; they come to flower, it bursts out—at first a sign of overfullness, superabundance of health; but then it stiffens and hardens, makes impossible the free and perfect contact of the mind with nature, hides under the persisting appearance of life the real retreat from life within, becomes a mere sheath in which the cramped spirit languishes, begins to waste away, and then dies. Finally, driving my thought to its logical conclusion, I said that culture, the child of life, ended by killing it.

The historians in the audience criticized my tendency, as they called it, to overready generalization. Others took issue with my method. Those who complimented me were the ones who understood me least of all.

It was on my way out of this first lecture that I saw Menalque again for the first time. I was never one of his closer friends, and shortly before my marriage, he had left for one of those distant expeditions of his which used to take him away from us for so long—sometimes for more than a year. In the old days, I hadn't cared for him very much; he had struck me as terribly proud, and had taken no notice of my existence. So I was astonished to see him at my first lecture. His very insolence, which had formerly put me off, now appealed to me, and I was all the more charmed by his smile since I knew it to be so rare. He had recently been involved in an absurd, shameful scandal about a lawsuit, which had given the newspapers a convenient occasion to drag him through the mud. Those whom he had wounded by his disdainful superiority seized hold of that pretext to obtain revenge. What irritated them most was that he seemed utterly unaffected.

"One must allow other people to be right," he used to say when he was insulted. "It consoles them for being nothing else." But "good society" was indignant, and all the people who, as they say, "had any respect for themselves" thought it their duty to turn their backs on him, and so repay him his contempt. For me that was only added encouragement; I felt impelled to him by some mysterious attraction, and went up and embraced him warmly in front of everyone. When they saw to whom I was talking, the last intruders withdrew; I was left alone with Menalque.

After the irritating criticisms and inept compliments I had been receiving, his few words on the subject of my lecture came as a genuine relief. "You are burning up the gods you used to adore," he said. "Good. It is a little late in the day, but no matter: the flame is all the higher for it, all the better fed. I'm not yet altogether sure, though, that I understand you completely; but you interest me. As a rule, I don't enjoy talking with people, but I should like to talk to you. Come and dine with me this evening."

"My dear Menalque," I replied, "you seem to forget that I am married."

"Yes," he answered, "quite true. The cordial frankness with which you dared to greet me led me to believe that you might be free."

I was afraid I had offended him, and even more afraid of appearing a weakling; so I said that I would join him after dinner.

Since he was always on his way to somewhere else, Menalque put up at a hotel whenever he stopped in Paris. On that occasion he had had several connecting rooms fitted up for him as a private apartment. He had his own servants, took his meals apart, lived by himself. The commonplace ugliness of the walls and furnishings had offended his eye, so he had had them covered with some expensive fabrics he had brought back from his last trip to Nepal. He wanted to wear them out, he said, before offering them to a museum. I had been in such a hurry to rejoin him that I found him still at table when I entered, and excused myself for interrupting his meal.

"But I have no intention of letting it be interrupted," he said, "and I depend on you to let me finish it in peace. If you had come to dine, I should have poured you a glass of Shiraz—the wine that Hafiz sang—but now it is too late; one must never drink it after eating. But you will have some liqueur, will you not?"

I accepted, thinking that he would take some too; but when I saw that only one glass was brought in, I expressed my surprise.

"You must excuse me," he said. "I hardly ever drink it."

"Are you afraid of getting drunk?"

"Oh!" he replied, "on the contrary! But I consider sobriety a more powerful intoxication; it allows me to keep my lucidity."

"So you pour it for others . . ."

He smiled. "I cannot expect everyone to have my virtues. It's quite enough if I find them to have my vices . . ."

"You smoke, at least?"

"No, not any more. It's an impersonal, negative sort of drunkenness, too easy to attain. What I look for in intoxication is an enhancement of life, not a diminution. But enough of that. Do you know where I have just come from? From Biskra. I knew that you had just been there, and I decided it might be amusing to retrace your steps. Whatever could this blind scholar, this bookworm, have found to do at Biskra? It is not my custom to be discreet, except with confidences; with things that I find out on my own, I must admit that my curiosity knows no bounds. So I looked about, poked around, asked questions wherever I could. My indiscretion was well rewarded, for it has made me wish to meet you again; and now, instead of the methodical savant I had always considered you before, I know that you are . . . well, that's for you to tell me, is it not?"

I felt myself blushing. "So what did you find out about me, Menalque?"

"Do you really want to know? Ah, but there's no need to be alarmed. You know your friends and mine well enough to realize that there's no one *I* could talk to about you. You saw how well they understood your lecture!"

"But I've seen nothing yet to indicate that I can talk to you any more than I can to them," I said with some impatience. "Come, now. What is it you learned about me?"

"First, that you had been sick."

"But there's nothing in that to . . ."

"Oh, yes! That in itself is very important. Then I was told that you liked to go out alone, without a book (that's where I began to wonder), or, when you were not alone, that you preferred the company of children to that of your wife. . . . Don't blush like that, or I won't tell you the rest."

"You can talk without looking at me."

"One of the children—his name was Moktir, if I remember correctly (I have rarely met a child so handsome, and never one so clever, a little cheat, a little thief) appeared to know a great deal about you. I enticed him, bought his confidence—not an easy thing to do, as you know, and I still think he was lying when he said that he wasn't. Tell me whether what he told me about you is true."

In the meantime, Menalque had got up and taken a little box out of a drawer.

"Are these scissors yours?" he asked, opening the box and handing me a shapeless, rusty, blunted, twisted thing—a thing I had little difficulty in recognizing, for all its transformation, as the little pair of scissors that Moktir had stolen.

"Yes, they are; they were my wife's scissors."

"He insists he took them from you while your back was turned, one day when you were alone with him in a room. But the interesting thing is that, according to him, at the very moment he was hiding them in his burnous, he realized that you were watching him in a mirror, and caught the reflection of your eyes spying on him. You saw the theft, and you said nothing! Moktir was nonplussed by your silence. . . . So was I."

"So am I—at what you have just told me! Do you mean to say he knew I had caught him?"

"But that isn't what matters. You were trying to finesse him; but a child can always beat us at that game. You thought you had him trapped, and it was he who trapped you. . . . But still, that isn't what matters. Explain to me why you were silent."

"I wish someone could explain it to me."

Some time passed before either of us spoke. Menalque, who was pacing up and down the room, lit a cigarette absentmindedly and then immediately threw it away.

"The fact is, my dear Michel," he went on, "that you seem to lack a particular 'sense,' as people call it."

"The 'moral sense,' perhaps?" I said, forcing myself to smile.

"Oh, no! Simply the sense of property."

"You don't seem to have much of it yourself."

"I have so little of it that, as you see, nothing in this place is mine; not even—or rather, especially not—the bed I sleep in. The idea of rest, of repose horrifies me. Possessions simply encourage it; the minute you feel yourself secure, you fall asleep. I enjoy life so much that I insist on being awake while I live it. And so, in the midst of all my wealth, I maintain the sensation of precariousness, by means of which I aggravate, or at least intensify, my life. I cannot honestly say that I like danger, but I *do* like life to be full of risks; I want it to demand of me at every moment all my courage, my happiness, my health . . ."

"Then what do you blame me for?" I interrupted.

"Oh good heavens, my dear Michel; you haven't understood me at all. The one time that I was foolish enough to try to make a profession of my faith! . . . If I pay no attention to the approval or disapproval of others, Michel, it is certainly not so that I may come and approve or disapprove in my turn. Such words mean almost nothing to me. I spoke too much of myself just now; I presumed that you would understand me, and let myself be carried away . . . all that I wanted to say is that, for a person who has no sense of property, you seem to own a great deal. That could be a problem."

"I must say it never occurred to me that I owned so much."

"Well, if you don't think so, then perhaps you don't. . . . But you are just beginning a course of lectures, are you not? And you have an estate in Normandy? And you have just moved into an apartment, a rather luxurious apartment in Passy? You are married; and, I understand, expecting a child?"

"Well!" I said impatiently. "All this simply proves that I have succeeded in making my life more 'dangerous' (to use your word) than yours."

"Yes, simply," Menalque repeated ironically; then, turning abruptly, he held out his hand:

"Well, good-bye. That will do for now; I don't think there is anything to be gained by more conversation this evening. But I shall be seeing you soon."

It was some time before I saw him again.

New concerns, fresh problems occupied my time. An Italian scholar brought to my notice some new documents he had discovered relating to my course, which I had to examine in great detail. The sense that my first lecture had been misunderstood drove me to try to find a different and more persuasive angle of approach for those to come. This led me to proclaim as doctrine what I had put forward at the start as nothing more than an ingenious hypothesis. How many assertions, I wonder, owe their force to the same accidental cause—that when they were proposed quietly, as mere hints or suggestions, no one understood them? In my own case, I admit I cannot distinguish how much my natural tendency to self-assertion may have been adulterated by mere obstinacy and defiance. The new things I had to say seemed to me all the more urgent, in that it was not easy to say them or (above all) to make them understood.

But how pale mere words became when I compared them with deeds. Was not Menalque's life, nay, his slightest gesture a thousand times more eloquent than my lectures? Ah, how well I came to understand that the teaching of the great philosophers of antiquity, which was almost entirely moral teaching, was a matter of examples as much as words—of examples even *more* than words.

The next time I saw Menalque it was at my own house, nearly three weeks after our first meeting. It was toward the end of a very crowded party. Marceline and I had elected to hold a sort of "open house" every Thursday evening; this made it easier for us to keep our doors shut for the rest of the week. So every Thursday those who called themselves our friends used to come to see us; the size of our rooms allowed us to entertain a great many guests, and the gathering usually lasted till quite late at night. I think that what attracted them most were Marceline's exquisite charm and the pleasure they found in talking with one another. For my own part, after the very first of these parties, I found I had nothing more to say (and nothing new to hear), and could scarcely disguise my own boredom. I would wander from the smoking-room to the *salon,* from the antechamber to the library, caught now and then by someone's remark, paying attention to very little, looking about more or less at random.

Antoine, Etienne, and Godefroi were discussing the last vote in the Chamber as they lolled on my wife's elegant armchairs. Hubert and Louis were carelessly leafing through some fine etchings from my father's collection, wrinkling and creasing them as they did. In the smoking-room, Mathias, the better to listen to Léonard, had put his lighted cigar down on a rosewood table. A glass of curaçao had been spilled on the carpet. Albert was stretched out impudently on a divan, dirtying the upholstery with a pair of muddy boots. The very air one breathed was filled with dust, dust made from the horrible wear and tear of *things*. . . . I was seized by a furious urge to grab all my guests and push them out the door. Furniture, fabrics, prints—at the first stain they lost all their value for me; things stained were things touched by disease, as if marked for death. I wanted to protect them all, lock them all up somewhere for myself alone. How lucky Menalque is, I thought, to own nothing! The reason I suffer is that I always want to preserve things. After all, what does all this matter to me? . . .

In a small, more dimly lighted *salon,* partitioned off by transparent glass doors, Marceline was receiving a few of her more intimate friends. She was half reclining on a pile of cushions, and looked so frightfully pale and tired that I was suddenly alarmed, and vowed that this reception should be the last. It was already late. I was about to take my watch out of my waistcoat pocket when I felt Moktir's little gold scissors.

"Why did he steal them, the little wretch, if he was only going to spoil them, to ruin them straightaway?" As I was musing, someone tapped me on the shoulder. I turned about quickly; it was Menalque.

Almost alone of the company, he was in evening dress. He had just arrived. He asked me to present him to my wife, something I should certainly not have done of my own accord. Menalque was distinguished-looking, almost handsome: he had a face like a pirate's, slashed by an enormous drooping moustache, already turned gray; his eyes burned with a cold flame that betrayed courage and decision more than goodness. Marceline disliked him, I could tell, from the minute he stood before her. After they had exchanged a few polite commonplaces, I took him off to the smoking-room.

I had heard that very morning of his new mission for the Colonial Office. Certain newspapers had taken the occasion to recall his adventurous career; they seemed to forget their own base insults of a few weeks before, and now could find no words grand enough to sing his praises. Each tried to outdo the other in exaggerating the service rendered to the nation, to the whole of humanity by the exotic discoveries of his latest explorations—as if he had undertaken the whole trip solely for humanitarian ends. They celebrated his self-denial, his devotion, his intrepidity, as if such vapid newspaper praises were to be his compensation.

I began to congratulate him, but he interrupted me at the first words.

"What's this? Not you too, my dear Michel! But at least you didn't begin by insulting me," he said. "Do leave such nonsense to the papers. They seem to be astonished nowadays to find that a man of unpopular tastes can still be the possessor of a few virtues. I must say I don't know how to use these distinctions and reservations they all insist on making about me; I exist only as a totality. My only claim is to be natural, and my only criterion of duty is the pleasure I am likely to feel."

"That may lead you far," I said.

"I certainly hope so," Menalque replied. "Ah, if only all these people around us could convince themselves of that! But most of them think that unless they restrain themselves, hold themselves back, they will be worth nothing; they can no longer take any pleasure in their genuine selves. The one person each of them is most determined not to resemble is himself. Each one adopts a model, a patron saint, and then imitates him. They don't even choose their own models—they let somebody else do it for them. I believe there are other things than this to be read in man. But people simply don't dare; they don't dare turn the page and look beyond. 'The laws of imitation'; ha! Laws of fear, if you ask me. They are afraid of finding themselves alone, and so they don't bother finding themselves at all. I despise such moral agoraphobia: it's the basest form of cowardice. Why, one *has* to be alone to invent, to create anything—ah, but who of these people wants to invent anything? What we feel to be different, distinctive in ourselves—why, that is precisely our rarest possession, what gives us whatever value we have: and that is what they are all trying to suppress. They are simply imitating—and all the while they insist that they 'love life'!"

I let Menalque talk on; he was saying precisely what I had said to Marceline the month before. I should have agreed with everything he said. Why was it, then, that I interrupted him, out of what detestable cowardice, with the very question, word for word, that Marceline had used to interrupt me?

"But my dear Menalque, you cannot expect each one of them to be different from all the others . . ."

Menalque fell silent at once, looked at me peculiarly, and then, as Eusèbe came up at that very moment to bid me good-night, he turned his back unceremoniously and went off to talk about some trifle with Hector.

As soon as I had said it, I realized how stupid my remark must have seemed; but I was especially sorry to think that Menalque might have understood it to imply that I had taken his words personally, as if they were directed against myself. It was late; my guests were leaving.

When the *salon* was almost empty, Menalque came back to me. "I can't leave you like this," he said. "Doubtless I misunderstood what you said. Let me at least hope so. . . ."

"No," I answered, "you did not misunderstand me. But it was a senseless thing to say, and I had no sooner said it than I winced at my stupidity—especially because I was afraid it would enlist me in your eyes among the very people you were attacking. I assure you they are as odious to me as they are to you. I hate people of principle."

"Yes," Menalque replied, laughing, "they are the most detestable thing in the world. It is impossible to expect any sort of sincerity from them; for they never do anything except what their principles have decreed they should do; or if they do otherwise, they are sure they have sinned. At the mere suspicion that you might be one of them, my words froze on my lips. Not until then did I realize how ardent my affection for you was, so immediate and so poignant was my grief. I hoped I was mistaken—not in my affection, of course, but in the conclusion I had drawn."

"You were mistaken; your suspicion was false."

"Of course it was," he said, suddenly taking my hand. "Listen: I am to leave the country soon, but I should like to see you again first. My journey this time will be longer and more dangerous than the others—I don't know when I shall be back. I leave in two weeks; no one here knows that my departure date is so near; I am telling you this in confidence. I shall start at daybreak. The night before a departure is always one of unbearable agony for me. Prove to me that you are not a man of principle; may I count on your being good enough to spend that last night with me?"

"But we shall see each other before then," I said, a bit surprised.

"No. For the next two weeks I shall not be able to see anyone; I shall not even be in Paris. Tomorrow I leave for Budapest; in six days I must be in Rome. I have friends here and there I want to see once more before leaving Europe. One is waiting for me in Madrid . . ."

"Very well then; I shall spend your vigil-night with you."

"And we will drink Shiraz."

A few days after that *soirée,* Marceline began to feel less well. She was often very tired, as I have said; but she never complained, and as I attributed her fatigue to her condition, I thought it quite a natural thing and never worried much about it. A rather foolish (or at least uninformed) old doctor had, at the start, reassured us more than was wise. But certain new symptoms, accompanied by fever, persuaded me to call in Dr. Tr., who was considered at the time the best obstetrician in Paris. He was amazed that I had not called him in sooner, and prescribed a strict regime which, he said, she should have begun some time before. By an imprudent excess of courage, Marceline had been overexerting herself all that while. She was not to get up until the baby was due, toward the end of January. Marceline was doubtless a bit anxious, and more uncomfortable than she would admit, for she consented very meekly to the doctor's most wearisome orders. She rebelled for a moment, however, when Dr. Tr. prescribed quinine in such heavy doses that she knew it might endanger the child. For three days, she obstinately refused to take it; then, as her fever increased, she was obliged to give in to that too. But this time it was with deep sadness, as if she were mournfully giving up all hope of the future. The firm resolve which had sustained her up till then seemed to have snapped, to have yielded to a kind of religious resignation, and her condition grew suddenly worse in the days that followed.

I tended her with greater care than ever, and did my best to reassure her, using Dr. Tr.'s own words—that he could see nothing very serious in her case. But her fears were so violent that they ended by alarming me too. Ah, how much, how dangerously did all our happiness depend upon hope —and the hope of such an uncertain future! At first I had no taste for anything but the past; one day, I thought, I might be able to feel the present, the sudden, intoxicating savor of the moment as it flies. But thoughts of the future disenchant the present hour—more, even, than the obstinate reality of the present can disenchant the past. And ever since our night at Sorrento my whole love, my whole life had been fixed on the future.

In the meantime, the evening came that I had promised to Menalque, and despite my reluctance to abandon Marceline for a whole winter's night, I did my best to convince her of the solemnity of the occasion and the gravity of my promise. Marceline was a little better that evening, but I was nervous even so; I arranged for a nurse to take my place at her side. But as soon as I was out in the street, my anxiety got the better of me; I shook it off, I fought against it, I was annoyed at myself for not being able to master it more readily. In this way I brought myself little by little to a state of hypertension, of the most extraordinary excitement, very different from, and at the same time very like, the painful anxiety from which it grew—but even closer to happiness. It was late, and I walked along quickly; the snow began to fall in thick flakes; I was glad to be breathing, at last, a keener air, to be struggling against the cold. With the wind, the night, the snow against me, I was happy; I rejoiced in my strength.

Menalque heard me coming and came out on the landing; he had been too impatient to wait easily, and looked pale, exasperated. He helped me off with my coat, and forced me to change my wet boots for some Persian slippers. He had left some sweets on a little round table by the fire. There were two lamps, but most of the light in the room came from the fire on the hearth. Menalque asked at once after Marceline's health; for the sake of simplicity, I told him that she was very well.

"You're expecting your child soon?" he went on.

"In a month."

Menalque bent down toward the fire as if he wanted to hide his face. He was silent. He said nothing for such a long time that I began to feel uneasy, for I could think of nothing to say either. I got up, took a few steps, then went up to him and put my hand on his shoulder.

Then, as if he had just gone on thinking aloud: "One must choose," he murmured. "The important thing is to know what one wants."

"What? Don't you want to go?" I asked, not knowing quite how to take his remark.

"It appears so."

"Are you hesitating, then?"

"What's the use? You have a wife and child; stay here. . . . Out of a thousand forms of life, each of us can know but one. It is madness to envy another man's happiness; we wouldn't know what to do with it. Happiness doesn't come ready-made; it has to be made to measure. —I am going away tomorrow; I know; I have tried to cut out *my* happiness to fit me . . . but as for you—oh, keep the placid happiness of your hearth and home. . . ."

"I cut *my* happiness to my own size, too," I answered with some emotion, "but I've outgrown it. It pinches now, it's too small. There are times I think it's strangling me. . . ."

"Bah! You'll get used to it!" said Menalque. Then he stood up squarely in front of me and looked deep into my eyes. I found nothing to say, and so he smiled a little sadly.

"We think we own things; in reality they own us," he said. "Pour yourself a glass of Shiraz, my dear Michel. You won't taste it very often. And eat some of those rose-colored candies; the Persians always have them with it. For this evening I shall drink with you, forget that I am leaving tomorrow, and talk as if the night were long. . . . Do you know why poetry and philosophy are such dead letters nowadays? Because they have separated themselves from life. In Greece, life itself was idealized, so that the artist's life was already a poem, a work of art; the philosopher's life the incarnation of his philosophy. In that way, philosophy and poetry were intermingled with life; they did not simply run their separate ways. Poetry was fed by philosophy, philosophy found expression in poetry— the result was both admirable and persuasive. Today beauty is no longer active, action has no desire to be beautiful; and wisdom operates in a sphere apart."

"But you are living *your* wisdom," I said. "Why don't you write your memoirs? Or if not that," I added, seeing him smile, "at least the memories of your travels?"

"Because I do not want to remember," he replied. "By doing that I might stop the future from arriving and encourage the past to trespass on the present. It is only out of a total obliteration of my yesterdays that I can create the novelty of each today. To have *been* happy has never been enough for me. I do not believe in dead things. I see no difference between being no more and never having been at all."

His thinking was so far ahead of mine that I ended by growing vexed; I should have liked to back up, to make him stop; but I tried in vain to contradict him. I was more annoyed at myself, in any case, than I was at Menalque; so I said nothing.

He paced up and down the room like a lion in a cage, sometimes stopping to bend over the fire; he would be silent for a long time, then break out suddenly: "If only our second-rate minds knew how to *preserve* our memories, to embalm them exactly! But they keep so badly. The most delicate shrivel up, the most sensual grow rotten, the most delicious become in the end the most dangerous. We end up repenting the things that delighted us most."

Again a long silence. Then he went on: "Regrets, remorse, repentance—these are simply the joys of the past seen from the point of view of one looking back. I don't like looking back, and I leave my past far behind me, as the bird leaves his shade to fly away. Oh, Michel! every possible pleasure is waiting for us; but every one wants to be the *only* one, to find the bed empty, to find us waiting like widowers whose last loves are dead.

Oh, Michel, Michel, every pleasure is like that manna of the desert which rots slowly from day to day; like the waters from the Fountain of Ameles, which, as Plato says, no one could ever hold in any vase. . . . Let each moment carry away all that it brought with it."

Menalque went on talking a good deal longer; I cannot tell you all that he said. But many of his words are still imprinted on my mind, and the ones I would like most to forget are the most deeply graven. Not that they taught me much that I didn't know—but they suddenly laid bare my own thoughts, thoughts I had shrouded with so many veils that I had almost been able to think them smothered for good.

And so the watch-night passed away.

The next morning, after I had seen Menalque off on his train, as I was making my way alone back to Marceline, I felt miserably sad, and full of hate for his cynical joy. I tried to convince myself that it was a sham, to force myself to reject it. I was angry at myself for having been able to think of nothing to counter it with. I could have slapped myself for having said certain things that might lead him to suspect my own happiness and my own love. And I found myself clinging desperately to my own questionable happiness, to my *"calme bonheur,"* as Menalque had called it. I could not, unfortunately, keep it clear of anxiety; but I pretended that love such as mine fed on anxiety. I looked to the future and saw a little child smiling at me; yes, for him I would strengthen my moral character, build it up anew. . . . Yes: I strode on with a confident step.

. . . When I walked into the first room that morning, I was struck by the strange state of disarray. The nurse came out to meet me and told me, very carefully, that my wife had been seized in the night by horrible pains and discomfort, although she did not think it could possibly be time for her delivery. Marceline felt very ill, and asked her to send for the doctor; he had arrived posthaste in the night, and had not yet left the patient. Seeing me turn pale, I suppose, the nurse next tried to reassure me, said that things were going much better now, that . . . I tore into Marceline's room.

The room was darkened, and at first I could make out nothing but the doctor, who signaled me to be quiet. Then I saw in the dark a figure I did not know. Anxiously, noiselessly, I drew near to the bed. Marceline's eyes were closed. She was so terribly pale that at first I thought she was dead. But then, without opening her eyes, she turned her head toward me. In a dark corner of the room the unknown figure was arranging, hiding various objects. I saw gleaming instruments, cotton wool; I saw, I thought

I saw, a cloth stained with blood. . . . I felt myself tottering. I almost fell in the doctor's direction; he held me up. I understood. I was afraid to understand. . . .

"The baby?" I asked anxiously.

He shrugged his shoulders sadly. I no longer knew what I was doing; I threw myself sobbing against the bed. There was my future. The ground had suddenly given way beneath my feet. There was nothing now before me but an empty hole, and I had stumbled into it headlong.

At this point my memories are all jumbled together in darkness. Marceline seemed at first to recover rather quickly. The Christmas holidays allowed me a little respite, and I was able to spend almost every hour of the day by her side. I would read or write in her room, or read aloud to her quietly. Each time I went out I brought her flowers. I remembered the tender care with which she had nursed me when I was ill, and I surrounded her with so much love that sometimes she smiled, as if it made her happy. We exchanged not a word about the pathetic accident that had murdered our hopes. . . .

Then phlebitis broke out; and when that began to subside, a sudden blood clot left her hovering between life and death. It is night: I see myself leaning over her, feeling her heart stop, then start again, and my own heart stops and starts with it. Oh, how many nights I watched over her that way, my eyes staring at her fixedly, hoping to insinuate some of my life into her by the sheer force of love. I no longer even dreamed much of happiness—my single, melancholy pleasure was to see her smile from time to time.

It was time for my course to begin again. Where was I going to find the strength to write my lectures—let alone deliver them? . . . Here my memories are lost. I have no idea how the next weeks went by, except for one small incident I should like to recount to you.

It is morning, shortly after the blood clot had been discovered; I am sitting with Marceline. She seems to be a little better, but she has been ordered, nonetheless, to keep absolutely still; she is not even to move her arms. I hold a glass for her, help her to drink; when she has finished, and while I am still bending over her, she begs me in a voice made all the weaker by her confusion to open a little box which she indicates by a glance. The box, a sort of casket, is there on her table; I open it; it is full of ribbons, bits of cloth, little ornaments of no value—what is it she wants? I

bring the box to her bedside, lift out each object in turn. Is it this? That?
. . . No; no; not yet; I could feel her growing a bit nervous. "Ah, Marceline! It's this little rosary you want!" She makes an effort to smile.

"Are you afraid that I won't take good enough care of you?"

"Oh, my dear," she whispers. And I remember our conversation at Biskra, her timid reproaches when she heard me reject what she calls "the help of God."

I reminded her, rather curtly, "I was cured without any help."

"I prayed so much for you," she replies. She says this tenderly, sadly; I feel in her eyes something anxious and imploring . . . I take the rosary and slip it into her frail hand which rests on the sheet at her side. In return, she gives me a look full of tears and love—but it is a look to which I cannot reply. I wait another minute, still embarrassed, not knowing what to do. Finally I can bear it no longer. "Adieu"; I leave the room, with a feeling of hostility, as if I had been ordered out.

In the meantime the horrible clot had brought on serious disorders. Her heart had managed to push it down, but it then settled in the lungs; it wore them down, brought on congestion, obstructed her breathing, left her gasping and wheezing. I thought I should never see her well again. Disease had entered into Marceline, never again to leave; it had marked her, stained her. She was to be, from then on, something spoiled.

III

The weather began to turn mild. As soon as my lectures were over, I moved Marceline to La Morinière, on her doctor's assurance that all immediate danger was past and that, to complete her cure, nothing could be more useful than a change of air. I myself was in great need of rest. The nights I had spent awake taking care of her (almost entirely by myself), the prolonged anxiety, and especially a sort of physical sympathy which had made me feel the terrifying spasms in my own heart at the time of her attack—all this had left me as exhausted as if I myself had been ill.

I should have preferred to take Marceline to the mountains, but she displayed the strongest desire to go back to Normandy, insisting that no climate could be better for her, and reminding me of my own obligations regarding the two farms which I had somewhat rashly taken in charge. She persuaded me that since I had assumed the responsibility for them, I owed it to myself to see them prosper. No sooner had we arrived, in fact, than she urged me to go at once and have a look at the estate. . . . I suspect that her friendly insistence was in large part a matter of self-denial inspired by the fear that I would feel obliged to stay at her side (for she still required frequent assistance), and thus constrained in my own freedom. . . . But Marceline *was* getting better; the blood had returned to her cheeks, and I felt that her smile was no longer so sad, which relieved me more than anything else. I could leave her without apprehension.

So I went back to visit the farms. The first hay was being made. The air was perfumed and heavy with pollen, and at first went to my head like some intoxicating drink. I felt that, since the year before, I had not breathed at all, or had breathed nothing but dust, so suavely and sweetly did that fresh atmosphere penetrate my being. I sat, as if drunk, on a high embankment, and looked out over all of La Morinière: I could see its blue roofs, the still waters of its moat; all around it the fields, some newly mown, others full of grass; farther on, the bend of the creek; farther still, the woods where I had gone riding the previous autumn. For a few minutes, I had been listening to the sound of someone approaching; now the sound came closer: it was the hay-makers on their way back from the fields, each with a pitchfork or a rake on his shoulders. I recognized almost all of them. The sight reminded me sadly that I was not simply lingering in their midst as some sort of enchanted wanderer, but that I was present as their master. I went up to them, smiled and spoke with them, inquired after each of them at some length. Bocage had already given me a report that morning on the state of the crops; in fact, the whole time we were away he had kept me regularly informed by letter of all that went on on the farms. They were not doing so badly—much better, in fact, than Bocage had led me at first to expect. But they had been waiting for me to make some important decisions, and for a few days I ran things as best I could—not that I enjoyed it much, but I could use it to put together the pieces of my disintegrated life.

As soon as Marceline was well enough to receive them, a few friends came to stay with us. They were affectionate, quiet people, and Marceline enjoyed their company; but as soon as they were there with her, I was able to leave the house all the more willingly. I preferred the company of the farm people; it seemed to me that I had more to learn from them than from our guests—not that I ever questioned them much . . . No. I scarcely know how to express the pleasure that I felt when I was with them. I seemed to feel things *through* them; and while I knew exactly what our house-guests were going to say before they had even opened their mouths, the mere sight of these poor rascals was for me a constant marvel.

At first they appeared to be as condescending in their answers as I tried *not* to be in my questions; but they soon became more tolerant of my presence. Each day I found myself in closer contact with them. Now I was not content with merely following them at their work; I wanted to see them at their games as well. Their clumsy thoughts were of no real interest to me, but I sat with them at their meals, listened to their jokes, fondly watched their pleasures. I felt a kind of sympathy, like that I had felt when my heart sputtered and stopped along with Marceline's; an immediate echo *in me* of each alien sensation; not vague, but sharp and precise. I felt my arms ache with the mower's stiffness, I was worn with his fatigue; the mouthful of cider that he drank quenched my thirst—I felt it as it slipped down his throat. One day one of the men cut his thumb badly while sharpening his scythe; I felt cut to the bone by his pain.

So I came to feel that I was not only learning the countryside through the power of sight, but also coming to *feel* it through some new sense of touch, which my strange power of sympathy had rendered wonderfully powerful.

It was now a nuisance for me to have Bocage around. When he came, I had to play the master, which I no longer had any inclination to do. Oh, I still gave orders—I had to—I still directed workmen, after a fashion. But I no longer went on horseback, for fear of rising too high above them. But for all the precautions I took to accustom them to my presence and prevent them from feeling uncomfortable when I was there, in *their* presence I still found myself filled with an evil curiosity. The existence of each one of them remained a mystery to me. I felt that they were always keeping hidden one part of their lives. What did they do when I was not there? I refused to believe that they had no better ways of amusing themselves than the ones they let me see. And so I credited each one of them with a secret which I then obstinately drove myself to discover. I went prowling about, I followed them, spied upon them. I particularly fastened onto the roughest, most primitive sorts, as if I expected to find some guiding light shining from their darkness.

One fellow in particular attracted me: he was fairly good-looking, tall, not at all stupid, but guided entirely by instinct. He did nothing except on the spur of the moment, gave way to every passing impulse, whatever it might be. He was not from our region, and had been hired through some fluke. An excellent worker for two days, dead drunk on the third. One night I went furtively down to the barn to watch him: he lay sprawling in a heavy, drunken sleep. I stood there staring at him, a long, long time. . . . Then one fine day he left, just as he had come. How I wish I knew what roads he took. . . . That very evening I learned that Bocage had sent him away.

I was furious with Bocage and sent for him. "It seems you have dismissed Pierre," I began. "Will you kindly tell me why?"

He was a little taken aback by my anger, although I was trying my best to control it.

"But . . . monsieur would not wish to keep a dirty drunkard on his staff—a fool who would ruin all the best workers. . . ."

"The men I choose to keep are my business, not yours."

"A bum, a good-for-nothing! No one even knew where he came from; people don't like that very much around here . . . if he set fire to the barn one night, monsieur, you would perhaps not be so pleased."

"I tell you that's my affair; the farm is mine, I presume? I intend to manage it as I please. In the future, you will be so good as to share with me your reasons before you dismiss anyone else."

Bocage, as I have said, had known me since I was a child. However wounding my tone may have been, he was too fond of me to be seriously offended. In fact, he probably did not even take me very seriously. The Normandy peasant, as a rule, refuses to believe anything for which he cannot fathom the motive, that is to say anything not prompted by monetary interest. Bocage simply considered this quarrel of mine as some mad whim.

However, I did not want to break off the interview on a note of reproof; feeling that I had been too sharp, I cast about for something else to say. "Isn't your son Charles due to come back soon?" I decided to ask after a moment's silence.

"Why, I thought monsieur had forgotten all about him; you seemed to trouble your head about him so little," said Bocage, still rather hurt.

"Me, forget him? Why Bocage, how could I do that, after all that we did together last year? I'm counting on him a good deal, in fact, to help me with the farms. . . ."

"You're very good, sir. Charles should be home in about a week."

"Well, I'm pleased to hear it, Bocage," and I sent him away.

Bocage was very nearly right: I had of course not forgotten Charles, but I really was very little concerned about him any more. How can I explain it?—after so ardent, so impetuous a friendship, to feel nothing more at the mention of his name than a peevish lack of interest? The fact is that my occupations and my tastes were no longer those of the year before. My two farms, I must admit, did not interest me nearly so much now as the people who worked on them. If I wanted to spend my time in their company, Charles would simply be in the way. He was much too reasonable, too respectable. So despite the vivid emotions his memory aroused, I looked forward with some apprehension to his return.

He came back. Oh, how right I was to have been apprehensive—and how right Menalque had been to insist on eradicating all memories! I saw enter the room, in the place of Charles, a ridiculous young "gentleman" in a bowler hat. Good heavens, how he was changed! Embarrassed, constrained though I was, I tried nonetheless to respond not too frigidly to the joy he displayed at seeing me again. But even his joy was disagreeable to me; it was awkward, and I thought it insincere. I had received him in the *salon,* and as it was late and somewhat dark, I could not make out his face clearly; but when the lamp was brought in, I saw with disgust that he had let his side-whiskers grow.

The conversation that first evening was rather dreary. After that, knowing that he would be down on the farms almost continually, I kept to the house for nearly a week, and fell back on my studies and the company of my guests. As soon as I did begin to go out again, I found myself absorbed by a totally novel occupation.

Woodcutters had invaded the woods. Every year a part of the timber was sold; the woods of the estate were divided into twelve equal lots which were cut in rotation, and so every year furnished a quantity of twelve-year-old growth which could be chopped up for firewood, along with a few short trees that had obviously reached their full growth.

This work was done in the winter, and the woodcutters were obliged by contract to have the ground cleared before spring. But the negligence of old Heurtevent, the timber-merchant in charge of the operation, was such that sometimes spring came upon the copses while the cut wood was still lying on the ground. Then fresh, delicate shoots could be seen pushing themselves up through the dead branches, and when the woodsmen finally came to clear the ground, it was only at the expense of many of the young saplings.

That year the carelessness of old Heurtevent exceeded even our usual expectations. In the absence of any higher bidder, I had been obliged to let him have the wood at a very low price. Once he was sure of making a profit, he took very little pains to dispose of the timber, which, after all, had cost him so little. From week to week he put off the work with various excuses—lack of workmen, the bad weather, sick horse, taxes, work he had to do elsewhere—heaven knows what; with the result that by the middle of summer nothing had yet been removed.

Such a thing would have irritated me immensely the year before; but by that time I scarcely cared at all. I was not blind to the damage that Heurtevent was causing me. But those devastated woods were beautiful, and I roamed through them with pleasure, tracking and watching the game, startling the snakes, and some days sitting by the hour on one of the fallen trunks which seemed to be still alive, with green shoots springing from its wounds.

Then suddenly, a week or so into August, Heurtevent decided to send in his men. Six of them came at once, with orders to finish the work in ten days. The portion of the woods that had been cut bordered on La Valterie; I agreed to let the woodcutters have their meals brought from the farm, to help expedite the work. The man chosen for this task was a young joker called Bute who had just come back to us from his military service totally corrupted—in spirit, that is; physically, he was still in admirable shape. He was one of the group of farmhands I most enjoyed talking to. This new chore of his, bringing food to the woodsmen, allowed me to see him without going down to the farm—for it was at just about that time that I started going out again myself. And for several days I hardly left the woods at all, returning to La Morinière only for my meals—and often showing up late for those. I pretended I had to keep watch over the work, but in fact I was only watching the workmen.

Sometimes two of Heurtevent's sons joined the band of six work-men. One was about twenty, the other fifteen; both were lanky, wiry, hard-featured youths. They had a foreign look about them, and I later learned that their mother was in fact Spanish. I was surprised at first that she should have wandered as far north as Normandy; but Heurtevent, it seems, had been a regular vagabond in his youth, and had married her in Spain. He was considerably looked down on for that in the neighborhood.

It was raining, I recall, the first time I met the younger of his sons; he was sitting alone on a very high cart, on top of a great pile of cut wood. And there, lying flat on his back among the branches, he was singing, or rather bawling out, a sort of wild song such as I had never heard in that country. The cart-horses knew the road, and moved along without any need for a hand on the reins. I cannot tell you the effect that song had on me, for I had never heard its like except in Africa. . . . The boy was enraptured, wild—he looked drunk; he did not even glance at me as I passed. It was not until the next day that I learned he was one of Heurtevent's sons. It was in order to see him—or at least in hope of seeing him—that I lingered for so many hours in the copse. The cut wood would soon be all cleared. The young Heurtevents came only three times. They seemed proud, and I could not get a word out of them.

Bute, on the other hand, loved to talk. I soon gave him to understand that with me he could say anything he liked. From then on, no one in the countryside was safe: he left off all reserve, and simply stripped people to the skin. I found myself hanging avidly on to his words, to his scandalous secrets. They far surpassed my expectations; but at the same time they left me discontented. Was that *really* what was rumbling beneath the surface —or was it not perhaps just one more hypocrisy? Not that it really mattered: I cross-examined Bute as I had the rude chronicles of the Goths. Dark fumes rose from the abyss as he talked, fumes that I inhaled uneasily and fearfully, fumes that went straight to my head. The first thing I learned from him was that Heurtevent was sleeping with his daughter. I was afraid that if I displayed the slightest disapproval, he might break off his revelations; so I smiled instead, impelled by curiosity.

"And the mother? She says nothing about it?"

"The mother! She has been dead a full twelve years . . . he used to beat her."

"How many are there in the family?"

"Five children. You have seen the oldest boy and the youngest. There is another of sixteen, who's not very strong. He wants to become a priest. And then the oldest girl has already had two children by the father."

And little by little I learned a great deal more, stories that transformed the Heurtevent household into a steaming, pungent place about which my imagination would circle round and around, try as I might to distract it, like a fly around a piece of meat. One night the eldest son had tried to rape a young servant girl; and as she was struggling, the father intervened—to help his son; and held her down with his enormous hands. All the while the second son went delicately on with his prayers on the floor above, and the youngest boy amused himself by looking on. As far as the rape itself was concerned, it cannot have been overly difficult, I imagine, for Bute went on to tell me that the same servant girl, having apparently acquired a taste for the game, tried to seduce the little priest a few days later.

"Tried? You mean she hasn't succeeded?" I asked.

"He's still holding out; but he's become a bit shaky."

"Didn't you say there was another daughter?"

"Yes—who takes as much of it as she can get, and all for nothing too. When she *really* needs it, she wouldn't mind paying herself. Mustn't bed her down at the old man's house, though; he'd smash you down. You can do what you want *en famille,* he says, but the house rules don't hold for strangers. Remember Pierre, that farmhand you had fired? Well, he doesn't go around bragging about it, but he left there one night with a nasty crack on the head. Since then she takes off for the woods for her fun and games."

"Have you had a go yourself?" I asked, giving him a encouraging look.

He looked down, for the sake of form, and said chuckling, "Oh, a few times." Then, raising his eyes quickly, he added, "So has old Bocage's boy."

"What boy is that?"

"Alcide. The one who stays at the farm. Don't you know him, then, monsieur?"

I was absolutely flabbergasted to learn that Bocage had another son.

"Of course it's true that last year he was still at his uncle's," Bute went on, "but it's very odd that monsieur hasn't yet come across him in the woods; he poaches in them almost every night."

Bute had said these last words in a lower voice; he looked at me closely, and I realized that it was essential for me to smile.

Then, apparently satisfied, he went on: "Good Lord, monsieur, surely you knew that people were poaching here? The woods are so big, after all—it can't possibly do any harm."

I clearly must not have looked displeased, because Bute soon grew even bolder; inspired (it seems to me today) by the pleasant thought of doing Bocage an ill turn, he showed me certain hollows in the ground where Alcide had set his traps, and then pointed out a place in the hedge where I could be almost certain of catching him. The hedge, which marked a property line, ran along the top of a slope; there was a narrow opening in it through which Alcide usually passed about six o'clock. It was at this spot that Bute and I, both vastly amused by the whole sport, strung a copper wire, which we then very neatly concealed. Then Bute made me swear not to give him away, and departed, not wanting to be implicated. I lay down on the other side of the bank and waited.

Three evenings I waited in vain. I was beginning to think that Bute had tricked me. Then finally, on the fourth night, I heard someone approaching, stepping very lightly. My heart was pounding, and all of a sudden I learned the terrifying thrill of the poacher. . . . The snare was so well set that Alcide walked straight into it. I watched him as he suddenly fell flat on his face, his ankle caught in the wire. He tried to save himself, fell down again, began to struggle like a trapped rabbit. But I grabbed him at once. He was a nasty little scamp with green eyes and colorless hair and a mean-looking, weasely expression. He kicked at me; then, as he could not move, tried to bite me; and when that failed, began to spit out the most extraordinary torrent of abuse I have ever heard. At last I could contain myself no longer, and I burst out laughing.

He stopped abruptly, looked at me, and said in a lower tone: "You dirty brute! You've crippled me."

"Show me where."

He pulled his sock down over his wooden-soled shoe and showed me his ankle, where a faint pink mark was just barely visible. "That's nothing," I said.

He smiled slightly, then said, crafty, defiant, "I'm going to tell my father that *you're* the one who's setting traps."

"Why good heavens, it's one of your own!"

"Ha. You never set that one yourself—that's for sure."

"Why do you say that?"

"You wouldn't know how. All right, show me how you did it."

"You teach me."

That evening I came in very late for dinner, and as no one had known where I was, Marceline had been worried. What I did not let her know was that I had been setting snares—six of them—and that far from scolding Alcide, I had given him ten sous.

The next day, when I went with him to look at our snares, I had the droll experience of finding two rabbits caught in my own traps. Naturally I let him keep them. As the hunting season had not yet opened, I wondered what he did with this illegal game, since it was impossible to show it openly without arousing suspicion. But Alcide refused to tell me. Finally I learned, through Bute again, that it was Heurtevent who bought it from him, with his youngest son working as middleman between Alcide and himself. Good heavens, I thought; was there no end to the secrets of this savage family? I set about my poaching with a vengeance, in the hopes of uncovering them all!

I met Alcide each evening; we caught great numbers of rabbits; one time even a roe-deer, which still showed faint signs of life. I cannot recall without horror the delectation that Alcide took in finishing it off. We put the deer away in a safe place, where young Heurtevent could come and get it during the night.

From that time on I no longer cared so much for going out during the daytime, when the emptied woods offered me none of these temptations. I even tried to work—dreary, thankless work, pointless work (for I had resigned my temporary post at the Collège as soon as my course was finished), from which I would let myself be distracted by the least song, the least sound coming in from the country; in each passing cry I heard a private appeal. How many times have I leaped from my reading and run to the window to see—nothing; nothing at all. How many times have I hurried outside . . . the only attention I was capable of paying was that of my five busy senses.

But when night came on—and it came quickly in that season—then our hour had arrived. It was an hour whose beauty I had never suspected before, and I slipped outside as a thief would slip in. I had accustomed my eyes to see in the dark, like an owl's. The grass was taller, more easily stirred, the trees were denser, and I marveled at it all. The darkness dug great holes in solid things, stretched out all dimensions, made the ground look far away, and gave to every surface the aspect of depth. The smoothest path became dangerous. Creatures of night could be felt awakening on every side.

"Where does your father think you are now?"

"In the stable looking after the cows."

Alcide slept in the stable, I knew, right next to the pigeons and the hens. As he was locked in at night, he used to get out through a hole in the roof. His clothes still reeked with the warm odor of fowl. . . .

Then as soon as the trapped game had been collected, he would disappear abruptly in the dark, as if down a trapdoor, without a wave of his hand, without even an *"A demain."* I knew that before returning to the farm (where the dogs recognized him and made no noise) he would meet young Heurtevent somewhere and hand over his plunder. But where? Try as I might, I was never able to find out; threats, tricks, bribes—all were to no avail: the Heurtevents would not allow themselves to be discovered. I don't know which of the two revealed my folly more triumphantly—that endless pursuit of an insignificant mystery which constantly eluded me, or my having invented the mystery in the first place, driven by my own curiosity. But what did Alcide do when he left me? Did he really sleep at the farm? Or did he only make the farmer think so? Oh, it was a waste of time for me to make myself his "partner in crime," to compromise myself that way; I merely succeeded in diminishing his respect without increasing his confidence—and it both infuriated and distressed me. . . .

After he had disappeared, I felt myself terribly alone; and I went back across the fields through the dew-drenched grass, intoxicated with the night, with this wild, anarchic life, sopping wet, muddy, covered with leaves. I guided my steps by the one light shining in the distance from the sleeping house, which led me on like a peaceful beacon: the lamp from Marceline's bedroom, for I had convinced her that I should never be able to sleep without going out first thus into the night. It was true: I had grown to hate my bed. I would rather have slept in the barn.

Game was plentiful that year. Rabbits, hares, pheasants came one after another. Seeing that everything was going so well, Bute decided to honor us with his company after the first three nights.

On the sixth night of our adventures, we found only two of the twelve snares we had set; someone had raided the woods during the day. Bute asked me for five francs to buy some copper wire; ordinary steel wire was no good, he told me.

The next morning I had the pleasure of seeing my ten snares at Bocage's, and I was obliged to compliment him on his zeal. The most annoying thing was that the year before I had promised ten sous for each snare that was brought in; so I was forced to give Bocage five francs. In the meantime, with *his* five francs, Bute had bought some more copper wire. Four days later, the same story: ten fresh snares were brought in; another five francs to Bute; another five francs to Bocage. And as I congratulated him,

"Oh, I'm not the one to be congratulated, monsieur. It's Alcide."

"What!" Too much astonishment can give us away. I kept myself under control.

"Yes," Bocage continued. "Ah, monsieur, what do you expect? I'm an old man, I have so much to do on the farm. The lad runs about the woods for me; he knows them well. Oh, he's a sly one—he knows better than I do where to look for traps."

"I can well believe it, Bocage."

"So out of the ten sous monsieur gives me, I let him have five for each trap he brings in."

"Oh, he certainly deserves it. Heavens, yes—twenty snares in five days! He's done his work well. The poachers are in for it now, eh? I'll bet we hear nothing from them for a while."

"Oh no, monsieur; the more you take, the more you find. Game is fetching a very high price this year, and for the few sous that it costs them . . ."

I had been so completely hoaxed that I was half-ready to suspect Bocage of having been in on the game. What incensed me most about the whole affair was not Alcide's three-way profiteering; it was the thought of his having taken me for such a dupe. And then what did they do with the money, Bute and he? I had no idea—I should never understand anything about creatures like them. They would always lie; they would go on deceiving me just for the sake of deceiving. That evening I gave Bute ten francs instead of five, but I warned him it would be the last time. If the snares were taken again, it was just too bad.

The next morning I saw Bocage coming, looking very upset—which immediately made me feel even more so. What had happened? Bocage told me that Bute had been out all night, and had not come back to the farm till dawn, drunk as a Pole. At the first words Bocage spoke to him, he had called him filthy names, then leaped at him and struck him. . . .

"And so I've come to ask, monsieur," said Bocage, "whether I have your permission" (he stressed the word somewhat), "your *permission* to let him go."

"I'll think about it, Bocage. Of course I'm very sorry that he was so disrespectful to you. I shall see . . . leave me alone to think about it, and come back and see me in two hours."

Bocage went out.

To keep Bute would be to insult Bocage shamefully; to dismiss Bute would be asking for trouble: he could always get his revenge. Ah, well, so much the worse for me; let come what may, I had no one to blame but myself . . . and as soon as Bocage came back, I told him: "You can tell Bute that we have no further use for him here."

Then I waited. What would Bocage do? What would Bute say? It was not till that evening that I heard rumors of scandal: Bute had spoken. I guessed it at first from the shrieks that I heard coming from Bocage's house; it was Alcide being beaten. Bocage is going to come see me; he is coming; I hear his old footstep on the stair, and feel my heart beating, even faster than when I was setting my traps in the woods. What an unbearable moment! All sorts of fine sentiments will be dragged out, I shall have to pretend to take him seriously. What possible explanations can I invent? Oh, God, how wretchedly I am going to play this scene—how much would I give to get out of this part! . . . Bocage comes in. I cannot understand a word that he is is saying. It's absurd: I have to make him start all over again. At the end, this is what I make out: he believes that Bute is the only one guilty. The incredible truth, that I had given Bute ten francs, simply does not register on his mind: why would I do a thing like that? He was too much a Norman to believe it. As for the ten francs, Bute stole them, there is no doubt about that. By claiming that I had given them to him he was simply adding falsehood to robbery. A foolish story to cover up his theft. He surely wasn't going to make Bocage believe a story like that! . . . There is no longer even any question of poaching. If Bocage had beaten Alcide, it was only because the boy had stayed out all night.

So then: I am saved! As far as Bocage is concerned, at least, everything is all right. What an imbecile that fellow Bute is. I must confess I have no great desire to go poaching tonight.

I thought the affair was at an end, but an hour later in comes Charles. He doesn't look in the mood for idle chatter; from the doorway, in fact, he strikes me as even more tedious than his father. And to think that last year . . .

"Well, Charles! I haven't seen you for quite some time."

"If you had wanted to see me, monsieur, you had only to come down to the farm. I don't go gallivanting about the woods in the dark of night."

"Oh, your father has told you . . ."

"My father has told me nothing because my father knows nothing. What's the use of telling him, at his age, that his master is making a fool of him?"

"Be careful, Charles. You're going too far . . ."

"Oh, all right! You're the master; you can do as you please."

"Charles, you know perfectly well that I am not making fun of anyone, and if I do as I please, it's because I am hurting no one but myself."

He shrugs his shoulders slightly. "How can you expect anyone to protect your interests when you attack them yourself? You can't protect both the keeper and the poacher at the same time."

"Why not?"

"Because . . . oh, look here, monsieur; this is all too crafty for me. It's just that I don't like to see my master joining up with a gang of criminals, and undoing the work that other people are doing for him."

Charles speaks with more and more assurance as he goes on. He is standing almost nobly. I notice that he has cut off his whiskers. Moreover, nearly everything he is saying is true; and when I make no reply (what could I have said?), he goes on: "It was you who taught me, monsieur, just last year, that one has certain duties toward his own possessions; but now it is you who seem to have forgotten it. One ought to take such duties seriously and give off playing with them . . . or else he has no right to his possessions."

Silence.

"Is that all that you have to say?"

"For this evening, yes, monsieur; but if you force me to it, the next time I come it may be to tell monsieur that my father and I are leaving La Morinière."

And he goes out, bowing very low. Scarcely taking the time to think, I shout: "Charles!" Damn it, he is right. . . . But if that's what one calls "possessions"! . . . "Charles!" I run after him, catch up with him in the dark; and all at once, as if to fix my instantaneous decision, I hear myself saying, "You can tell your father that I am putting La Morinière up for sale."

Charles bows again gravely and walks away without a word.

The whole thing is absurd.

Marceline is unable to come down to dinner that evening, and sends word to me that she is unwell. Filled with anxiety, I run upstairs to her room. She reassures me at once: "It's nothing but a cold," she says hopefully. She thinks she has caught a chill.

"Couldn't you have kept covered up?"

"But I did; I put on my shawl as soon as I felt myself shivering."

"It's before you start shivering you should put it on, not after."

She looks at me, tries to smile. . . . Oh, perhaps I was disposed to feel miserable just because the day had begun so badly. If she had said to me out loud, "Do you really care so much whether I live or not?" I could not have heard the words more clearly. Clearly, everything was falling to pieces around me; of all the things I reached for and seized, I could not hold onto one. . . . I spring toward Marceline and cover her pale temples with kisses. At that, she breaks down and falls sobbing on my shoulder.

"Oh, Marceline! Marceline! Let's get out of here! Anywhere, anywhere else I could love you as I did at Sorrento. You thought I had changed, didn't you? But once we've left this place you'll see that our love hasn't changed, it hasn't changed. . . ."

I had not yet cured her of unhappiness, but already how she snatched at this shred of hope!

It was not late in the year, but the weather was damp and cold; the last rosebuds were rotting unopened on the bushes. Our guests had long since left. Marceline was not too unwell to see to the closing up of the house, and five days later we left.

THIRD PART

I

And so I tried, once more, to hold my love tightly in my hand. What need had I, though, of peace and contentment? What Marceline gave me, what she stood for in my eyes, was like rest for a man who does not feel tired. But since I felt that she was weary, and that she needed my love, I wrapped her up in it, and pretended all the while that the need was mine. I suffered intolerably from her sufferings, and I loved her in order to cure them.

Oh, what passionate care, what tender nights I spent at her bedside! Some men try to reawaken their faith by exaggerating their devotions; I did it to stimulate my love. And Marceline, as I said, began at once to hope again. In her, there was still so much youth; in me, she thought, so much promise. We fled from Paris, as if for a second honeymoon. But on the very first day of our journey she suddenly turned much worse, and we were forced to stop at Neuchâtel.

How I loved that lake, with its pale, sea-green shores; utterly unlike a mountain lake, its waters mingle with the earth for many yards, and filter through the rushes, like those of a swamp. I was able to find a room overlooking the lake for Marceline in a very comfortable hotel. I stayed with her from morning to night.

She was so ill the next day that I sent for a doctor from Lausanne. He was quite concerned, and asked me whether I knew of any other cases of tuberculosis in my wife's family. I said yes, although in fact I knew of none; but I was not keen on telling him that *I* was her nearest stricken relative, that I had almost been given up for lost on account of the disease; that before she had had to take care of me, Marceline had never been sick a day. I blamed everything on the blood clot of the winter before, but the doctor refused to see in that anything but a contributory cause, and insisted that the basic trouble must date from further back. He strongly recommended the open air of the upper Alps, where Marceline, he assured me, would be cured; a winter at Engadine was precisely what I wanted myself, so as soon as Marceline was well enough to bear the journey, we set off.

I remember that journey so clearly—not only the events, but even the feelings, the sensations. The sky was transparent and cold; we had brought along our warmest furs. . . . At Coire, the incessant racket of the hotel kept us from sleeping almost the whole night. I could cheerfully have suffered the loss of a night's sleep without even feeling tired, but

Marceline. . . . It was not nearly so much the noise that bothered me as the fact that Marceline was unable to sleep—noise or no noise. And how much she needed the rest! The next morning we left before daybreak; we had reserved seats in the rear compartment of the Coire stagecoach; the relays were so arranged that St. Moritz could be reached in a day.

Tiefenkasten, Le Julier, Samaden . . . I remember it all, hour by hour; the strange, harsh feeling of the air; the sound of the horse-bells; my hunger; our midday stop before the inn; the raw egg that I broke in my soup, the brown bread, the chill of the bitter wine. This coarse fare did not suit Marceline. She could hardly eat anything but a few dry biscuits, which I had fortunately thought to bring along for the ride. Now I can see again the day closing in, the shadows climbing swiftly up the wooded slopes; then another halt. The air becomes more keen, more raw. When the coach stops, we plunge into the heart of darkness, into a silence that is limpid—limpid—there is no other word for it. The slightest sound achieves its perfect quality, its full sonority inside that strange transparence. We set off again, into the night. Marceline coughs . . . oh, will she never stop coughing? I am reminded of the stagecoach at Sousse. Surely I coughed better than that. She is working too hard at it . . . how weak she looks, how changed. In the shadow there I should scarcely recognize her. How her features are drawn! Could one always see so clearly those two black holes of her nostrils? . . . Oh, how dreadfully she is coughing. See where all her precautions have got her? I have an absolute horror of sympathy; it is the hiding place for every kind of contagion. One should only sympathize with the strong. . . . Oh, good heavens, surely she can't go on like this! Shall we never arrive? . . . Now what's she doing? Taking out her handkerchief; putting it to her lips; turning aside. . . . Oh my God! Is she going to spit blood too? . . . I tear the handkerchief brutally from her hands, look at it in the dim lantern light . . . nothing.

But my anxiety is clear, too clear. Marceline forces an unhappy smile and murmurs, "No. Not yet."

At last we arrive—and just in time, for she can scarcely stand. I do not like the rooms that have been reserved for us; we use them for the night, then move the next day. For me, nothing seems too fine or too expensive. And as the winter season has not yet begun, the vast hotel is almost empty and I am able to have my pick. I select two spacious rooms, bright and simply furnished; a large sitting-room adjoined them, ending in a big bow-window from which one could see both the hideous blue lake and some crude mountain or other, whose slopes were either overwooded or virtually bare. We had our meals served in the sitting-room. The suite is outrageously expensive, but what matter? I have given up my lectureship, true; but then I am selling La Morinière. And then we shall see. . . . Besides, what need have I of money? What need have I of any of this? . . . I am strong, now, healthy, able . . . a complete change of fortune, I should think, would be just as educational as a complete change of health. . . . Marceline, of course, requires this luxury; she is weak . . . oh, for her sake I shall spend so much, so very much that . . . Suddenly I was seized by both a horror and a craving for luxury. I washed in it, soaked my sensual nature to the full; then wished myself freed of it all, an unburdened wanderer down the open road.

In the meantime, Marceline was getting better; my constant attention was paying off. As she ate only with difficulty, I ordered the most delicate, the most tempting dishes to stimulate her appetite; we drank the very best of wines. I convinced myself that she had taken a great fancy to the imported vintages we sampled each day, so diverting did I find them myself: tart wines from the Rhine, Tokays so thick as to be almost syrup, heady and intoxicating. I remember especially an extraordinary Barba Grisca, of which there was only one bottle left; I was never able to find out whether its bizarre taste was typical of the wine or unique to our one bottle.

Each day we went out for a ride, in a carriage at first; later on, when the snow had fallen, in a sleigh, wrapped up in furs to our eyes. I used to come back with my face bright red, ravenously hungry, and then ready for sleep the second I had eaten. I had not given up my work entirely, however, and every day I set aside an hour or so to meditate on the things I felt I ought to be saying. History was now out of the question; I had long since lost all interest in historical research except as a means of psychological investigation. I have told you how I used to find myself falling in love with the past again whenever I thought I could see in it some dim resemblance to the present. I had had the audacity to believe that by importuning the dead I would be able to extract from them some secret information about Life. . . . Now, young Athalaric himself might have risen from the tomb to speak to me. I no longer had ears for the past, I would not have listened. Even if I had, how could antiquity have answered the question that obsessed me now: What is left for man to do? *That* was what I had to know. What has been said before—is that all there is to say? Is there nothing we do not know? Can we only repeat what has been said before, over and over? . . . And each day I felt more and more strongly the vague sense of untouched treasures, treasures covered up, hidden, smothered by culture and decency and morality.

It seemed to me then that I had been born to make strange and wonderful discoveries, unknown before. I threw myself passionately into my shadowy, mysterious work: work that demanded of the seeker, as I well knew, a complete abjuration, a total rejection of—precisely—culture, decency, and morality.

Before long, I had gone so far as to admire nothing in other men but manifestations of their most primitive selves, and to deplore anything that restricted them or held them back as nothing more than repression. I came very near to seeing in honesty itself nothing but restriction, convention, or fear. I should have liked to idolize honesty as something difficult and rare; but our system of polite manners made it into a simple contract, a mutual and commonplace formality. In Switzerland, it was just another part of one's comfort. Marceline demanded it, that I understood; but still I did not hide from her the new trend of my thoughts. As early as Neuchâtel, when she was praising this *honnêteté* that simply shines out in that region from the walls of the houses and the faces of the people, I replied: "I prefer my own. Honest people disgust me. I may have nothing to fear from them, but I have nothing to learn from them either. And besides, they have nothing to say . . . decent, honest Swiss people! So they're healthy; what good has it done them? They have no crimes, no history, no literature, no art . . . a big hardy rosebush, with neither thorns nor flowers."

I knew even before I arrived that I should be bored by this "honest" country; but at the end of two months my boredom had turned into a kind of fury, and I thought of nothing but how to get out.

We were in the middle of January. Marceline was better, much better. The constant slight fever that had been slowly sapping her strength had disappeared; fresh, healthy blood brought color back to her cheeks. She began to enjoy her walks again, for short distances, and was no longer continually tired as she had been at first. It was no great effort, then, for me to persuade her that the bracing mountain air had done her all the good we could ask of it, and that the best thing for us now would be to move south to Italy, where the genial warmth of springtime would completely restore her . . . nor had I any great difficulty in persuading myself; I was so sick and tired of those mountains. . . .

And yet now, when the hateful past comes back in full measure to haunt me in my lethargy, it is those memories out of all the rest that most obsess me. Racing along in the sleigh, the dry air so joyfully stinging, the snow spattering, a sharp appetite; stumbling uncertainly through the fog; the weird, hollow sound of one's voice; objects leaping suddenly into view; reading in the snug warmth of our rooms, the icy landscape through the glass; the tragic waiting for the snow, the outside world vanishing away, the soft, luxuriant brooding of one's private thoughts. . . . Oh, to be skating with her again, alone, just the two of us, up there on that pure, little lake, circled round with larches, lost; to come back home with her at night. . . .

Our drop down into Italy left me as dizzy as a sudden fall. The weather was fine. As we sank into the warmer, denser air, the rigid trees of the highlands—larches, stiff, orderly firs—gave way to the soft grace and ease of a richer vegetation. I felt that I had left abstraction and entered life, and although it was still winter I imagined perfumes at every breath. For much too long we had smiled at nothing but shadows. I was intoxicated from abstinence, drunk with thirst as others are drunk with wine. Oh, yes: my thrift, my self-denial had been admirable; now, on the threshold of that tolerant and promising land, all my appetites broke out at once. I was filled with an enormous reserve of love; sometimes it surged up into my head from the depths of my flesh, and stripped my thoughts of every trace of shame.

This illusion of spring lasted only a short while. The sudden change of altitude may have deceived me for a while, but as soon as we left the sheltered shores of the lakes, Bellagio, Como, where we had stopped for a few days, we moved back into winter and rain. We began to suffer from the cold—something we had not done at Engadine, where the mountain air was exhilarating and dry; here the air was sullen and damp, and Marceline's cough began again. To escape the cold, then, we kept running farther south. We left Milan for Florence, Florence for Rome, Rome for Naples, which under a winter rain is the most lugubrious town I have ever seen. I dragged along in the most indescribable ennui. We went back to Rome in the hopes of finding, if not warmth, at least a semblance of comfort. We rented an apartment on the Pincio, much too vast, but admirably situated. Already, at Florence, disgusted with hotels, we had rented an exquisite villa on the Viale dei Colli, for three months; anyone else would have been happy to stay there for a lifetime; we left after scarcely three weeks. And yet at each new stop, I made a point of arranging everything as if we were never going to leave. A demon, someone stronger than I was driving me on. . . . Add to this that we never traveled with fewer than eight trunks. There was one filled entirely with books, which I never opened once during the whole expedition.

I would not allow Marceline to have any say about our expenses, nor would I let her attempt to moderate them. I knew, of course, that they were excessive, and that we could not go on this way indefinitely. I could no longer count on any money from La Morinière; it had ceased to bring in anything, and Bocage wrote that he could not find a buyer. But all thoughts of the future only ended in making me spend that much more freely. What need should I have of so much money, I thought, once I was alone; and I watched, full of anguish and expectation, as Marceline's frail life ebbed away, more quickly even than my fortune.

Although I took care of all the arrangements, these perpetual and hurried displacements left her thoroughly fatigued; but what tired her still more (I am no longer afraid to admit it) was her fear of what I might be thinking.

"I understand," she said to me one day, "I quite understand your doctrine—for it has become a doctrine. A very fine one, perhaps—" then she added, sadly, lowering her voice, "but it does away with the weak."

"And so it should!" I answered at once, without even thinking what I was saying.

At that instant, I thought I could feel that delicate creature shiver and withdraw under the shock of my dreadful words . . . ah, perhaps you will think I did not love Marceline. I swear that I loved her passionately. Never had she been—never had she seemed to me—so beautiful. The illness had refined, etherealized her features. I hardly ever left her, I lavished on her every care, I guarded her, kept watch over her every moment of the day and night. If she slept lightly, I trained myself to sleep more lightly still; I watched her as she fell asleep, and then woke up before her in the morning. When sometimes I left her for an hour to walk by myself in the countryside or in the city streets, I was pulled quickly back to her side by a kind of loving anxiety, by the fear that she might grow weary and ill at ease in my absence. And sometimes I protested against the hold she had over me, tried to stir up my will: "Is this all you are good for, you make-believe hero?" I demanded of myself; and I would force myself, at such times, to extend my absence longer. But then I would come back with my arms full of flowers, early garden flowers or hothouse flowers. . . . Yes, I tell you: I cared for her with fondness, with great tenderness; but—how can I express this?—the more reverence I had for her, the less respect I had for myself. Who can say how many passions, how many warring dispositions can live together in a man's heart? . . .

The foul weather had long since ended; spring was on its way; suddenly the first almond trees were in bloom. It is the first of March. I go down in the morning to the Piazza di Spagna. The peasants have stripped the Campagna of its white branches, and the flower-vendors' baskets are filled with almond blossoms. I am so entranced that I buy a whole tree-full; it takes three men to carry it. I come home bringing all springtime with me. The branches catch in the doorways, petals snow upon the car-pet. I put them everywhere, in all the vases. In the moment that Marceline is out of the drawing-room, I have transformed it into a bower of white-ness. I am already imagining, relishing her pleasure . . . I hear her com-ing: here she is. She opens the door. She wavers . . . she bursts out sob-bing.

"My poor Marceline, what is it?"

I hurry to her side, cover her with kisses, caresses; then, as if to ex-cuse her tears,

"The flowers . . . the scent made me feel sick."

And it was the faintest, the most discreet scent of honey. . . . Without a word, I seize the innocent, fragile branches, break them to bits, carry them out in armloads and fling them out the door; driven by exasperation, my blood boiling, my temples throbbing: Oh, if she finds this little bit of spring too much for her! . . .

I have often thought over those tears of hers; I now believe that she already had an intimation that her end was near, that she was weeping for the loss of other springs. I also think that there are strong joys for the strong, and weak ones for the weak—those whom strong joys would in-jure. She could be surfeited with a teaspoonful, a dim ray of pleasure; one drop more, one shade brighter, and it was more than she could bear. What she called happiness I called repose, and repose was something I neither wanted nor could bear.

Four days later we left again for Sorrento. I was disappointed to find it no warmer. Everything, everyone was shivering with cold. The wind never stopped blowing, and it was all Marceline could do to stand. Our plan was to go to the hotel we had stayed at before; we were even given the same room. . . . The whole scene, we were astonished to find, had been robbed of its magic by the dismal gray sky. The place that had seemed so charming when we strolled up and down as lovers was nothing more than a dreary hotel garden.

We resolved next to sail to Palermo, whose climate we had heard praised. So we went back to Naples, where we were to embark, after a few days' stay. At Naples, at least, I was not bored; I find Naples a living city, not overshadowed by the dead hand of its past.

I spent almost every minute of the day with Marceline. At night she was tired and went to bed early. I watched over her until she went to sleep, sometimes going to bed myself. Then, when her deep, even breathing let me know she was sound asleep, I got up without a sound, dressed in the dark, and slipped outside like a thief.

Outside! Oh, I could have shouted with joy! What is it I wanted to do? I have no idea. The sky, which had been overcast all day, was swept free of clouds. I walked at random, in the light of a nearly full moon, without object, without desire, without constraint. I looked at everything with new eyes; I caught every sound with a more attentive ear; I breathed the dampness of the night, touched things with my hand. I prowled through the night.

The last night we spent at Naples I continued on my vagabond debauch until dawn. When I came back, I found Marceline in tears. She had awakened suddenly, she told me, and been frightened not to feel me there. I calmed her fears, explained my absence as best I could, and promised never to leave her again. . . . But I broke that promise on our very first night at Palermo; I went out: the first orange blossoms were out, and the slightest breath of air was filled with their scent. . . .

We stayed only five days at Palermo; then, by a long detour, made our way to Taormina, which we had both wanted to revisit. I think I have told you that the village itself is perched quite high up on the mountain-side. The station is below, at the seashore. The carriage took us up to the hotel, then had to drive me back to the station directly so that I might pick up our trunks. I stood up in the box in order to talk to the driver. He was a Sicilian boy from Catania, as beautiful as a line of Theocritus, full of brightness and odor and savor, like a fruit.

"Com'è bella la Signora!" he said, in a charming voice, watching Marceline disappear in the distance.

"Anche tu sei bello, ragazzo," I replied; and as I was leaning toward him, I could not resist: I drew him near to me and kissed him. He let me do it, laughing.

"I francesi sono tutti amanti," he said.

"Ma non tutti gli Italiani amati," I parried, laughing too. . . . I looked for him on the next few days, but never succeeded in finding him.

We left Taormina for Syracuse. Step by step we were undoing the work of our first journey, going back toward the first spring of our love. And just as week by week I had moved closer to recovery, during that first voyage, so this time, with each succeeding week's travel south, Marceline's state grew worse.

By what aberration, what obstinate blindness, what deliberate folly did I persuade myself, and above all try to persuade her, that what she needed most was more light, more heat, invoking the memory of my own convalescence at Biskra? . . . And yet the air was already growing warmer; the Bay of Palermo is genial and mild, and Marceline liked it. Right there, perhaps, she would have . . . But was I the master of my own will? Had *I* the power to determine my own desires?

We were delayed for a week at Syracuse by the roughness of the sea and the irregular boat service. Every moment that I did not spend with Marceline I passed in the old port. Ah, me . . . the little port of Syracuse! Smells of soured wine, muddy passageways, stinking little wine-stalls crawling with longshoremen and drifters and drunken sailors. To me the society of the lowest of mankind was delectable company. What need had I to understand their language when I could feel it with my whole body? Even their most brutal passions took on in my eyes the hypocritical look of health and vigor. It was in vain that I told myself that their wretched lives were nowhere near so charming to them as they seemed to me . . . no, I longed to roll under the table with them, not to wake till the first sad shiver of dawn. And in their company I only exacerbated my growing horror of luxury, of comfort, of all that I had surrounded myself with, of all those securities and safeguards that my new state of health rendered useless, of all the precautions that one takes to preserve his body from any dangerous contact with life. . . . I imagined what their life was like elsewhere; I would have liked to follow them away from the little port, to probe inside their drunkenness. . . . Then suddenly I thought of Marceline. What was she doing at that moment? Suffering, crying perhaps . . . I got up quickly and ran back to the hotel, where I imagined invisible words written over the door: No poor admitted here.

Marceline always welcomed me in the same way, without a word of reproach or of suspicion, forcing herself to smile in spite of all. We had our meals sent to the room; I made them serve her the very best food that our mediocre hotel could provide. And all through the meal I kept thinking—a piece of bread, a scrap of cheese, a stalk of fennel: that's all they would ask, that would satisfy them; it would satisfy me, too. And perhaps out there, out there under our very window, one of them is starving and has not even that wretched pittance. And here on my table is enough to stuff them for three days! I wanted to break down the walls, let the guests pour in. . . . For the thought that there were people suffering from hunger became an obsession with me, an agony. And I went back down to the old port where I flung about at random the small coins with which my pockets were filled.

Poverty makes slaves of men; in order to eat, the poor man will take on the most obnoxious and hateful work; and any work that is not joyful, I thought, is lamentable and wrong. So I paid several of them to do nothing. I told them, "Don't work if it bores you." I granted to each of these that leisure without which nothing new can flourish—neither vice nor art.

Marceline knew what I was thinking. Each time I came forth from the old port, I made no effort to conceal from her the sort of miserable sots I had been frequenting. "It's all a part of man's nature." Marceline discerned what it was I had been setting about so maniacally to uncover. I used to blame her for being too ready to credit people with virtues of her own invention; now she turned the tables on me, and said, "You, you are never satisfied until you have made people exhibit some vice, are you? Don't you understand that when you stare so at a particular feature of someone, you develop it, you exaggerate it? that you can make a person become what you think him to be?"

I would have liked to have been able to say that she was wrong, but I had to admit that the worst instinct of every human being appeared to me the most sincere. But what did I mean by sincerity?

We finally got away from Syracuse. I was obsessed by my memory of, my longing for the South. At sea, Marceline seemed better. . . . I can still see the color of that sea. It is so calm that the ship's wake seems to be carved in it permanently. I hear the sound of dripping water, liquid sounds: the swabbing of the deck, on the planks the slapping of the sailors' bare feet. I see Malta, shining white in the sun; the approach to Tunis . . . oh, how changed I am!

It is hot; it is fine; everything is glorious. Oh, if only I could distill here today in each of my words a whole summer of that sensual delight. . . . It would be foolish of me to try to give more order to my story than there has been to my life. I have been trying for so long now to explain to you how I have become what I am. Oh, if only I could rid my mind of its unbearable need for logic! . . . I feel nothing in me that is not noble.

Tunis. The light not so much strong as abundant. Even the shade is filled with it. The air seems like a luminous fluid in which everything is steeped; one dives, bathes, swims in it. A land of *volupté* that satisfies desire without stilling it; and desire is inflamed by satisfaction.

A land happily free from "works of art." I despise those who cannot recognize beauty until it has been transcribed and interpreted. The Arab people have the admirable ability to live their art, to sing it, to dissipate it from day to day: it is not frozen and embalmed in any "work." This is both the cause and the effect of their lack of great artists. . . . I have always thought that great artists were those who dared to bestow the right of beauty on natural things; so that, afterwards, when people see them, they exclaim, "How is it that I never realized until now that this too was beautiful . . . ?"

At Kairouan, which I had not seen before, and which I visited without Marceline, the night was very beautiful. As I was going back to sleep at my hotel, I remember seeing a group of Arabs lying out in the open air on mats, in front of a little café. I went and lay down to sleep beside them, and came away covered with vermin.

Marceline found the humidity and heat of the coast quite enfeebling, and I convinced her that we should make our way inland to Biskra just as quickly as we could. We were now at the beginning of April.

The journey to Biskra is a very long one. The first day we make it to Constantine without a break; the second day, Marceline is very weary and we only get as far as El Kantara. It is there that we look for (and toward evening find) shade, shade more delicious and more cool than moonlight at night. It streams around us, like some inexhaustible cooling drink. And from the bank where we are sitting, we can see the plain burning with sunset. That night Marceline is unable to sleep; she is disturbed by the strangeness of the silence, or by the tiniest noises. I am afraid that she may be feverish; I hear her tossing in her bed in the night. The next day I find her more pale. We move on. . . .

Biskra. So this is what I have been aiming for. . . . Yes, there are the public gardens, the bench . . . I recognize the bench where I used to sit during the first days of my convalescence. What was it I used to read there? . . . Homer: I haven't opened the book since. Ah, there is the tree whose bark I got up to touch. How weak I was then! . . . Look—here come some children . . . no; I recognize none of them. How serious Marceline looks. She is as changed as I am. Why is she coughing in such fine weather? Ah, here is the hotel; our rooms; our terrace. What is Marceline thinking? She hasn't said a word. As soon as she gets to her room, she lies down on the bed; she is tired and says she wants a little sleep. I go out.

I do not recognize the children, but the children recognize me. On the news of my arrival, they come running. Can they really be the same ones? What a disappointment! What has happened to them? They have all grown so—so horribly. In scarcely more than two years . . . why, it isn't possible. What weariness, what vice, what lassitude have covered with ugliness, with so much ugliness, those youthful, shining faces? What vile labors can have stunted those beautiful young bodies so soon? I feel bankrupt. . . . I question them: Bachir is washing dishes in a café; Ashour is killing himself earning a few pennies breaking stones for the roads; Hammatar has lost an eye. And who would have believed it? Sadeck has settled down; he helps his older brother selling bread in the market; he seems to have turned an idiot. Agib is working as a butcher in his father's shop; he is getting fat, ugly, rich; he refuses to speak to his one-time companions, now beneath his class. . . . What dullards, what stupid fools "honorable" careers turn people into! Good heavens, am I going to find here the same thing I despised so at home? Boukabir? Married. He is not yet fifteen. It is grotesque. —Oh, not altogether: I saw him again that evening, and he explained: the marriage was just a sham. He is utterly debauched, as far as I can tell; taken to drink, obviously, his features coarsened and gross. . . . So this is all that remains of them, is it? This is what life has made of them? I feel unbearably depressed, and realize that it was these boys, above all, that I came here to see. Menalque was right: memory is the devil's invention.

And Moktir? Ah! That little imp has just got out of jail; he is hiding somewhere. The others will have nothing more to do with him. I want to see him again. He was the handsomest of them all. Is he going to disappoint me as well? . . . Someone finds him and brings him to me. No! This one has not failed me. He is even more superb than my memory had drawn him. His strength, his beauty are flawless. . . . He smiles as he recognizes me.

"And what did you do before you went to prison?"

"Nothing."

"Did you steal?"

He protests.

"What are you doing now?"

He smiles.

"Well, Moktir, if you have nothing to do, you must come with us to Touggourt." And I am immediately seized by a great urge to go to Touggourt.

Marceline is not well; I do not know what is going on inside her. When I go back to the hotel that evening, she presses up against me without saying a word, without opening her eyes. Her wide sleeve has slipped up, and lays bare her thin, weak arm. I hold her in my arms for a long time, caressing her, rocking her like a small child one is trying to soothe into sleep. What is it that makes her tremble so? Is it love, or anguish, or fever? . . . Ah, perhaps there will still be time. . . . Shall I be able to stop myself or not? I have sought and sought for what it was that gave me my "distinction," my special value; and now I have found it. It is my strange infatuation for the worse, my stubborn persistence in evil. But how do I bring myself to tell Marceline that tomorrow we are leaving for Touggourt? . . .

Just now she is asleep in the adjoining room. The moon has been up for a long time, and is now pouring its light over the terrace. The brightness is almost terrifying. It is impossible to hide from it. The floor of my room is tiled in white, and there the light is brightest. It flows in through the wide-open window. This bright moonlight in the room, the shadow drawn by the door—I have seen these before. Two years ago the light came in still farther . . . yes, there, right there where it is moving now, it had reached to there when I got up, unable to sleep. . . . I had leaned my shoulder against that same door jamb. The stillness of the palm trees —yes, I recognize that too. What were the words I had read that night? Ah, yes: the words Christ spoke to Peter: "Now thou girdest thyself and goest where thou wouldest . . ." But where am I going? Where is it I *want* to go? . . . I have not mentioned that when I was at Naples, that last time, I went to Paestum one day by myself. Oh, I could have wept before those stones! The ancient beauty appeared so clearly, shone out from the ruins, simple, perfect, smiling—and abandoned. Art is flying from me, I feel it; but to make room for what? The harmony and contentment I once knew—they are gone too . . . I am serving some dark god whose face I cannot see, whose name I do not know. Oh, my new god! Let me live to see new races of man, undreamed of types of beauty!

The next morning at daybreak the diligence takes us away. Moktir is with us; Moktir is as happy as a king.

Chegga; Kefeldorh'; M'reyer . . . dreary stops on a still more dreary road, an interminable road. I confess I had expected these oases to be more inviting. But they are nothing more than stone and sand, than a few dwarf shrubs with weird flowers; sometimes an attempt at a palm tree or two, watered by a hidden spring. . . . Now, I prefer the desert to any oasis: the desert, this land of mortal glory and intolerable splendor. Here man's efforts look so ugly and so miserable. All other lands now simply bore me.

"You love what is inhuman," Marceline tells me. But how she stares at it herself; how greedily she looks!

The weather took a turn for the worse on the second day; a wind rose up, and the horizon was blurred with gray. Marceline is in pain. The sand in the air burns and irritates her throat; the excessive light leaves her eyes fatigued; she feels bruised and battered by this hostile country. But it is too late now to turn back. In a few hours we shall be at Touggourt.

It is that last part of the journey, though still so near in the past, that I remember least. I find it impossible to recall the landscapes we passed on that second day, or what I did when we first got to Touggourt. What I do still remember is my impatience and my haste.

It had been very cold that morning. Toward evening, a burning simoom sprang up. Marceline, exhausted by the journey, went to bed as soon as we arrived. I had hoped to find a more comfortable hotel—our room is hideous; the sand, the sun, the flies have stained, dirtied, faded everything. Having eaten almost nothing since daybreak, I order a meal to be served at once; but Marceline finds it all inedible, and I cannot persuade her to touch a thing. We have brought our own tea-things with us; I attend to that trifling business, and for dinner we content ourselves with a few dried cakes and the tea, which ends up tasting ghastly thanks to the brackish water of the region.

In the last false show of virtue, I stay with Marceline until evening. And suddenly I feel that I, too, have reached the end of my strength. Oh, the taste of ashes, the dreariness, the lassitude, the sadness of superhuman efforts! I hardly dare look at her; I know too well that my eyes, instead of seeking hers, will fix themselves horribly on the black holes of her nostrils. The expression of her suffering face is atrocious, unbearable. Nor can she look at me. I can feel her anguish as if I were touching it. She coughs a great deal; then falls asleep. From time to time, she is shaken by a sudden fit of shivering.

The night may be a bad one, and I want to know where I can go for help if I need it before it gets too late. I go out. Outside the hotel door the Touggourt square, the streets, the very atmosphere are so strange that I can hardly believe it is I who am looking at them. After a short time I go back in. Marceline is sleeping peacefully. I was wrong to be so frightened; in this peculiar country, one imagines danger everywhere. It's absurd. More or less reassured, I go out once more.

Strange nocturnal animation in the square—silent moving about; stealthy gliding of white burnouses. The wind tears off for a few instants a shred of strange music, and brings it to me from I know not where. Someone comes up to me . . . it is Moktir. He was waiting for me, he says; he knew I would be coming out again. He laughs. He knows Touggourt well, comes here often, knows where to take me. I give myself up to his lead.

We walk along in the night, come to a Moorish café and go in; it is here that the music was coming from. Arab women are dancing—if such a monotonous gliding can be called dancing. One of them takes me by the hand; I follow her; she is Moktir's mistress; he comes too. . . . We all three go into the deep, narrow room where the only piece of furniture is a bed—a very low bed on which we sit down. A white rabbit, kept locked in the room, is frightened at first, but then grows tamer and comes to eat out of Moktir's hand. Someone brings coffee. Then, while Moktir plays with the rabbit, the woman draws me to her, and I let myself go to her as one lets oneself sink into sleep. . . .

Oh, I know, I could lie to you here, I could say nothing; but why should I bother to go on telling you this story, if it ceased to be true?

I go back alone to the hotel, as Moktir is spending the night at the café. It is late. A parching sirocco is blowing; the wind is laden with sand, and torrid despite the late hour. After four steps, I am already drenched with sweat. But suddenly I feel driven to get back quickly, and I am almost running when I reach the hotel. Perhaps she has waked up; perhaps she needs me. . . . No: there is no light in her room window. I wait for a short respite in the wind before opening the door; very softly, I go into the room in the dark. —What is that noise? . . . I do not recognize her cough . . . I light the light.

Marceline is half-sitting on the bed, one of her thin arms clutching the bars to hold her upright; her sheets, her hands, her nightgown are flooded with a stream of blood; her face is all smeared with it; her eyes have grown hideously big; and no cry of agony could be more appalling to me than her silence. Her face is streaming with sweat, and I search it for some little place to put a kiss, a horrified kiss; I feel the taste of sweat on my lips. I wash her forehead, her cheeks, try to cool them, refresh them. . . . Something hard, I feel something hard under my foot near the bed; I stoop down to pick up the little rosary that she once asked for in Paris, and which she had dropped. I slip it over her open hand, but her hand falls again at once and she drops it again. . . . I don't know what to do; I want to go out and get help . . . her hand clutches at me desperately, holds me tight; good God, she's not thinking I want to leave her? She speaks.

"You can wait a little longer, can't you?" She sees that I want to speak. "Don't say anything," she adds. "Everything is all right."

I pick up the rosary again and put it back on her hand, but once again she lets it drop—this time deliberately. I kneel down at her side, and press her hand against me.

She lets herself go, half against the bolster, half against my shoulder, seems to sleep a little; but her eyes are still wide open.

An hour later she sits up again, pulls her hand away from mine; her fingers run to the neck of her nightgown, tearing at the lace. She is choking.

Toward early morning, more blood; another hemorrhage.

I have finished telling you my story. What more is there to say?

The French cemetery at Touggourt is a hideous place, half eaten away by the sand. . . . The little energy and willpower I had left I spent carrying her away from that God-forsaken hole. She lies at El Kantara, in the shade of a private garden that she liked. It all happened scarcely three months ago. Those three months feel like ten years. It all seems so long ago. . . .

Michel remained silent for a long time. We did not talk either, for each of us was overcome with a strange uneasiness. It seemed to us then, unfortunately, that by telling us his story Michel had somehow made his action more legitimate. As we had been unable, during the long, slow course of his explication, to say at what point one should object or disapprove, we felt almost like accomplices. We were now involved in it, accessories after the fact. He had finished his account without a quaver in his voice, without an inflection or a gesture to betray that he was troubled by the slightest emotion. He may have been motivated by a slightly cynical pride in *not* betraying any emotion; he may, out of a kind of reserve, have been afraid of arousing our emotions by his tears. On the other hand, he may actually have been unmoved. Even now, I cannot distinguish how much in him is pride, how much is strength, how much reserve, how much barrenness of heart.

After a minute or so he went on: "What frightens me, I admit, is that I am still very young. It seems to me sometimes that my real life has not yet begun. Please take me away from here, now, and give me some reason to live. I no longer know how to find one myself. I have freed myself; perhaps. But why, what good is it? It is a useless, purposeless freedom, and it torments me. It is not, believe me, that I am tired of my crime, if you choose to call it that; but I must prove to myself that I have not over-stepped my rights.

"When you first knew me, I had the greatest mental stability. That, I know now, is what makes real men. I no longer have it. But it is this climate that is responsible, I think. There is nothing that puts you off thinking so much as these everlasting blue skies. Satisfaction succeeds desire almost immediately here; what need is there for pursuit, for effort? Here one is surrounded by splendor and death; happiness is available, too available, on every hand, and one's surrender to it is constant and unvarying. I go to bed in the middle of the day to while away the long dreary hours and this unbearable leisure.

"Look. I have here a number of white pebbles. I let them soak in the shade, then I hold them a long time in the palm of my hand, until the soothing coolness they have acquired is exhausted. Then I start all over, changing the pebbles, putting those that have lost their coolness back in the shade. Time goes by, the evening comes. . . . Take me away from here; I can't do it myself. Some part of my will has cracked. I don't even know how I found the strength to get out of El Kantara. Sometimes I fear that the things I have suppressed will take their revenge. I should like to begin all over again. I want to get rid of what's left of my fortune; you see these walls—they're still covered with it. . . .

"I live on next to nothing here. A halfbreed innkeeper fixes me a bit of food. The boy who ran away when you came brings it to me morning and evening in exchange for a few sous and caresses. He's very shy and unsociable before strangers, but to me he is as tender and affectionate as a dog. His sister is an Ouled Naïl who goes back to Constantine each winter to sell her body to the tourists. She is very beautiful, and I sometimes let her spend the night with me during the first weeks. But one morning her brother, little Ali, surprised us in bed together. He was obviously very angry, and he refused to come back for five days. And yet he knows perfectly well how and on what his sister lives; he used to speak of her profession without the slightest embarrassment. . . . Could he be jealous?—Be that as it may, the little rascal has succeeded in his object; for, half out of boredom, half out of fear of losing Ali, I have given up the girl since that happened. She's not angry with me; but every time I meet her, she laughs and declares that I prefer the boy to her. She insists that it's he who is keeping me here. Perhaps she's not altogether wrong. . . ."

THREE   *1903—1913*

One hundred years after his birth, less than a third of Gide's biography
has been written in any detail. There are resources of the most extraordinary richness for the biographer who will one day finish the job. Many of
these resources—letters, memoirs, private papers—have already been
published, but many more have not; much will doubtless never be
known. About fifteen hundred of Gide's letters are in print, and works
now in preparation will more than double that number; but over fifteen
thousand letters to Gide are on deposit in a single Paris library, and one
cannot even guess how many more of his own may be scattered elsewhere. Scores of recollections, of brief or extended memoirs of him have
been printed, but almost none of them by members of his family or his
very closest friends. There remains, for reasons we shall see, none of
Gide's letters to his wife. Whatever secrets may be sealed in the journals
of Roger Martin du Gard, one of his most intimate, most useful, most
regular confidants, are not to be revealed until the year 2000.

All of which means that, from this point on, we are obliged to accept Gide's own account of his life more directly than heretofore, without the chance to qualify or enrich it quite so thoroughly as Jean Delay
has allowed us to qualify and enrich the account, say, of *Si le grain ne
meurt*. But the reader familiar with, forewarned of Gide's autobiographical strategies (both conscious and unconscious), the intricacies of his
legend-making, the modes of his sincerity, will know how to read his
accounts for what they are worth, and will not be greatly surprised by
any subsequent revelations.

Of Gide's testimony during the years 1903–1913, perhaps the most
difficult portion to assess, in the absence of a psychologist-biographer, are
the complaints, the cries of frustration or depression, or of moral and
mental fatigue. They are especially intense during the spring and summer of 1906; but they recur throughout the period, and at times he
seems to be insisting that the state that induced them persisted for many
years. Nor is it only in his letters and diaries that this note of tired lamen-

tation may be heard. It is the very key in which works like *Amyntas* and
Le Retour de l'Enfant prodigue seem to have been written.

(1904)   You do not have, I know, these desert stretches when
one carries his head on his shoulders like some tasteless fruit; if this
is all a preparation for something, I am certainly unaware of
it.   (Letter to Jammes, August 4)

Since October 25, 1901, the day on which I finished *L'Immoraliste,*
I have not seriously worked. . . . A dull torpor of the mind has
made me vegetate for the last three years. . . . The least sentence
costs me an effort; talking, in fact, is almost as painful as writing.   (*Journal,* November)

(1905)   Already I had accepted the inevitable, resigned to a half-
life; writing had become a chore to which my will alone forced me;
life had lost its savor.   (April) . . . I should like to take in
hand all these causes of sterility, which I discern so clearly, and
strangle them all . . . I cling to these pages as if they were
the one thing fixed among so many fleeting things.   (May)
. . . I am again losing my footing; I am letting myself roll
with this wave, carried along by the current of days. A great
drowsiness numbs me from the time I get up until evening . . .
I compare what I am to what I once was, to what I should have
liked to be. If only . . . I am aging in bits . . .   (September) . . . the succession of monotonous days, spent merely in
growing older.   (October) I have come to hate this apartment,
this furniture, this house . . . It is years now since my brain
has been warm . . . But perhaps there is still time . . . perhaps in Auteuil . . . (November)   (*Journal*)

(1906)   My head is tired, my will restless, and my personality
indecisive. . . . I sleep badly; I tremble and twitch the way wild
animals do.   (*Journal,* January 15)

For about two weeks, and for the most trivial reasons, I have been
swimming in darkness. I recall a similar prolonged period of de-

pression after the publication of *L'Immoraliste*.   (Letter to Jammes, April 6)

Impossible to go on this way; I must see a doctor. This frightful fatigue has eventually given me a sort of fear of all manifestations of life . . . I've done nothing worth while; my relaxed mind has drifted aimlessly. I *must* decide to go see a doctor. I should have made up my mind to do so three or four years ago. . . . For the last four years I have been floundering and marking time. . . . It is frightening how much I have aged recently. Certainly something is not right inside me. It is impossible to age more rapidly or to be more aware of it. . . . I experienced this hideous aging last year, at the same time of year. . . . Strange drowsiness of the mind and flesh. Lethargy . . . Prolonged insomnia. Keen suffering in my pride; this would lead to madness if daylight did not come soon enough . . .   (*Journal,* May)

I have been very ill for three months. Perpetual insomnia wore me down to such a point that I had to stop all work, all correspond-ence, even reading . . . Since spring I have been going through a frightful crisis of which I could not speak to anyone, not even to you. I felt like the dying Sinbad, struggling to drag himself toward the air hole in the suffocating City of the Dead.   (Letter to Jammes, August)

I have spent a miserable summer, my brain so fatigued (from what?) that I could neither read nor write.   (Letter to Christian Beck, October 11)

(1907)   Suddenly one morning, spells of giddiness seized me again, and for fear of falling back into last year's sorry state of cerebral fatigue, I interrupted almost all work. Then a flood of chores carried me to June 15 like a half-drowned man who, to save his breath, is satisfied to float.   (*Journal,* June 16)

For *almost two years* I have been sick with this weariness . . . I knew it often, as a child.   (Letter to Beck, July 2)

Again my mind is disjointed, upset; my flesh weak, restless, wildly listless.   (*Journal,* December 12)

I am trying to hold on to the bit of warmth left in my anemic brain for a job it has lost all hope of completing.   (Letter to Beck, December 17)

(1908)   What can I do against insomnia, or that nameless nervousness that stands in my way? Do I know in what mood I shall awake tomorrow? Can I presume to sit down to work after a night of anguish with the same heart I would have had if I were rested?   (*Journal,* January 27)

I suffer from nothing but my nerves; you can't call that a serious illness, I know, but it certainly makes one quite miserable—utterly powerless by day and driven to distraction by my spasms at night.   (Letter to Beck, October 12)

(1912)   Constant *vagabondance* of desire—one of the chief causes of the deteriorating of the personality. Urgent necessity to recover possession of oneself. But can one still make resolutions when one is over forty? . . . Even my insomnia struck me last night as a form of perplexity, a kind of difficulty in making up my mind to sleep.   (*Journal,* January)

Nothing can express the weariness of my mind . . . To my low physical condition is now added a constant headache and a great intellectual fatigue. I feel desperately far from myself.   (February)[1]

Two qualifying explanations should be entered at once against this desolate account: first, they have been selected from out of materials far more varied than this sample, far more even in their balance of pleasure and pain; and second, as Gide frequently tries to remind us, one tends in a *journal intime* to record far more commonly the dark days than the bright ones, in the hope that the very act of recording will help to alleviate the gloom. The private, therapeutic, self-equilibrating function of this journal virtually requires that it be, as a public document, incomplete or distorted.

All this granted, all necessary discounts made, the evidence of

1903–1913 is still exceptionally dark, more so than that of any other
decade of Gide's life. What are we to make of this?

His remark to Christian Beck, "I knew it [this sick fatigue] often, as
a child," gives us one clue. A great deal of Gide's distress during these
years—the headaches, insomnia, the twitches, the indecisiveness, the fits
of "anarchy" or embarrassment—is related to the basic nervous temperament we discussed in explaining his childhood illnesses. No doubt particular emotional pressures during these years affected this temperament,
one way or another. But the reverse is true as well—Gide's emotions,
opinions, his whole moral outlook were very often determined, temporarily, by the state of his nerves. One of the treasured benefits of a lucidity
such as his was that he realized this better than anyone else.

> This, however, checks my restlessness a bit: the memory of having
> gone through such periods . . . before. It is probably connected
> with a physiological state.   (1912)

> My moral state is strong when I am in good health. My anxieties,
> my depressions are the result of sleepless nights and of the intellec-
> tual fatigue that follows them. All at once I begin to question
> everything . . .   (1907)

> Everything I write this evening will strike me as silly in a short
> while. Already I feel better . . .   (1912)

> When I am well again, I shall blush at these confessions.
>   (1906)[2]

Of what is generally thought of as the "private life," the published
materials do not reveal a great deal for these years: they contain almost
no references to Madeleine, for example. But there appear to have been no
dramatic personal crises comparable to those of 1893 or 1918, and outside witnesses continue to attest to the remarkable harmony and tranquillity that appeared to reign in this *"mariage blanc."* Gide's own activities,
however, what we know of them, between his long "rest cures" at Cuverville, offer a vivid reflection of the state of inner disquiet we have already
noted.

It was during this period, for one example, that his compulsive traveling became fixed in its permanent pattern. His wife had no doubt realized well before 1903 that this near-manic wanderlust was simply a fact
of André's temperament, something they were both going to have to live

with. In that year she allowed herself to be talked into accompanying
him on his trip to North Africa and Italy, or at least the second half of it
(this was the *Amyntas* trip)—but it was for the last time. After that she
simply stayed at home and allowed André to travel without her as far
and as often as his private demons demanded. (Not, of course, without a
certain remorse of conscience on his part—as witness his pitiable journal
entry of November 1904. He knew very well what he was going in quest
of, and had not quite resigned himself to his divided and deceptive life.)

Superimposing the evidence of the *Journal,* the memoirs of acquaintances, and eleven different correspondences, I still find it difficult to
keep track of all of Gide's displacements during this decade. There were
at least nineteen trips outside France—two to England (and one to Jer-
sey), two to Switzerland, two to Belgium, two to Germany, one to Austria, two to Spain, and *seven* to Italy (twice extended into Algeria),
Gide's favorite escape-land before World War I. His months in France
were not always particularly still, either. In addition to visits to the Midi,
to the Pontigny *décades* of 1911 and 1912 in Burgundy, to the Basque
or Breton coasts, there were constant train trips between Paris and Cuverville; and even within Paris, between 1905 and 1908, he was traveling
back and forth, indulging in a favorite diversion of the unsettled rich, the
building and furnishing of an extraordinary new house—a house in
which, of course, he was to remain just as unsettled as ever, and which he
abandoned in 1928.

(This mad "villa," one of a circle of private homes built on the
grounds of an estate just west of Paris, has challenged the descriptive
powers of many of its visitors; two of the more amusing attempts are
Roger Martin du Gard's, again, and Léon Pierre-Quint's:

> I was invited, twelve days ago, a Sunday, to lunch at the Gides'. A
> strange Anglo-Egyptian fortress, avenue des "Sycamores" (!) at the
> end of the Villa Montmorency at Auteuil. A weird house, con-
> ceived entirely in the bizarre brain of a very "original" architect, for
> which Gide has had to pay, and in which he is forced to acclimatize
> himself as well as he can. . . . You enter into a huge lighthouse
> of a room with white walls, from which ascend Pompeian-red
> wooden staircases which intersect one another up to the rafters, like
> the little Japanese bridges on lacquer boxes. It's the most important
> part of the house, and used for nothing but hanging up your over-
> coat. All the rest is made out of strange corridors lined with
> benches and radiators and of wooden staircases, as on a ship. It

would appear that Gide has several studies, all fitted out by this
giddy architect. But he can work only in a corner of the corridor, on
a little folding table, against a radiator. And his presence there condemns the whole house to an absolute dead silence.

> (R. Martin du Gard, letter to Marcel
> Coppet of January 4, 1914.)[3]

The doorbell rings. Gide puts on his hat, that little soft felt tourist's
hat, his thick traveling coat, and sets off on expedition to open the
door . . . in place of a fixture, a bare bulb. Trunks piled against
the wall . . . He goes upstairs not by the freezing main staircase,
but by a little interior one. Everyone here has resigned himself to
discomfort.

The telephone rings from whatever inconvenient niche it may
be in . . .

> (Léon Pierre-Quint, *André Gide*)

Gide fought with his architect Bonnier during all three years of the
house's evolution. In it were housed the Bonnard nude he bought impul-
sively at an auction, a Gauguin, a Sisley, a Vuillard, two commissioned
sculptures by Maillol, and a ceiling fresco that Degas came to inspect
when he was probably too blind to see it. Mme Gide, not surprisingly,
was never quite at home in this expensive, unlivable error, and her terms
as hostess at the villa were to grow shorter and fewer, until in the 1920's
Gide was virtually "camping out" in it between trips with a few of his
male friends.)

References to his homosexual adventures during this decade are infrequent and, as is usual with Gide, most often oblique. But there can be
no doubt of their importance and intensity, and one may speculate on the
role they may have played in his *inquiétude.* The writing of *L'Immoraliste* was, as we have seen, a vitally liberating step; but Gide was still
keeping secret a very large domain of his life, at the price of what he
could only regard as culpable hypocrisy; and toward the end of this period both his pederast's ardors and his need to confess or defend them
seem to have mounted, in a kind of crescendo that was not to climax (in
his love for Marc Allégret and his writing of *Si le grain ne meurt*) until
the next period of his life.

He actually began the writing of what was to become *Si le grain,*
however ("wrote almost without stopping all afternoon [recollections
of Em-Barka, Mohammed of Algiers, and the little fellow in Sousse]"),

as early as June 1910—in spite of the fact that in April of that year he
was writing, "My most recent adventures have left me an inexpressible
disgust"; and by 1911 he had privately printed (an edition of twenty-
two copies) the first half of *Corydon,* his Socratic dialogues in defense of
male homosexuality. Certain of his trips abroad were at least partly in
search of sexual companions; his three years' adoption (1905–1908) of
his young cousin Paul, the "Gérard" of the *Journal*—who was to die in
the trenches of Artois in 1915—reveals at least an intimate emotional
involvement by the elder man in the younger man's life and affairs, the
first of several such involvements. The correspondences or memoirs that
might tell us most in this regard are those of Marcel Drouin, Gide's
brother-in-law, to whom he confessed his adventures most freely; and
Henri Ghéon (V. L. Vangeon), with whom he shared many of them,
both in Paris and abroad, before Ghéon's conversion to Catholicism in
1918. But neither has yet been published, although Ghéon did quite
vividly describe their nocturnal ambles about the less savory districts of
Paris in an interview of 1927.*

At quite the other extreme is the apparently religious nature of certain of
Gide's inner debates during these years. Works like *La Porte étroite* and
Le Retour de l'Enfant prodigue, nostalgic references to his early faith in
letters to Jammes and Claudel, and a few hints that he could well have
used, at times, the security of a church, the solace of a confessional, have
led readers so disposed to see in all the disquiet and anxiety of these years
nothing but the divine harassments of the Hound of Heaven. When
Gide first confessed his miserable state of 1906 to Francis Jammes, for
example, the latter (a convert of one year's standing) replied:

> . . . it is very difficult for me to explain what is wrong with you in
> one short letter. But there is only one remedy for it. . . . You are
> in the singular state of a man whose "soul needs some way to
> *breathe"* (Claudel) in order to aspire toward God [4] . . .

and he promised to write an article on Gide in which he would explain
all this at greater length. Whatever his private problems, Gide was
somewhat dismayed at the prospect, and wrote back at once.

> Please don't misunderstand me: the "anxiety" you claim to sense in
> me is something you attribute to me poetically, the way you attrib-

---

* Léon Pierre-Quint, *André Gide* (Paris, 1952), p. 416.

ute breath or a sense of smell to flowers.* I may well be at the gates of Paradise, but not at the door you're thinking of. It takes a bruised and wounded heart to go in the way you did;† and I make a profession of happiness. Don't take this as a sign of pride: for me happiness and inner strength are the same thing. And if my serenity has been somewhat troubled in recent weeks, since the publication of *Amyntas*, it is due to a weakening of this inner strength.[5]

Is that the whole story? Clearly not: none of Gide's anguishes of spirit is ever to be explained so easily; and his letters to Catholic friends worried about the state of his soul are often a devious mixture of diplomatic pliancy with an excess of self-defense. If one chooses to see the hand of God in his distresses, one is certainly free to do so. But was Gide as consciously resistant to the appeal of faith, either his family's Protestantism or his country's Catholicism, as he here pretends?

Books have been written on the subject;‡ particularly by French Catholic intellectuals, for whom the question has always been a very serious one. The events of greatest note in Gide's adult religious life belong to a later period: his rupture with Claudel of 1914, his apparently serious consideration of a return to religious faith between 1914 and 1916. The documents that record them, the exchange of letters with Claudel, entries from the special green notebook in which Gide kept his "religious diary," will be found in their proper place. But—even supposing that Francis Jammes had misapprehended the sources of Gide's disquiet—how much of this was building up in the years before the war? What can one posit with any assurance of Gide's religious attitudes during this troubled ten years?

First, that he indulged from time to time in an understandable nostalgia for the faith of his fathers, particularly for that luminous period of puritan mysticism he had shared with his cousin about his sixteenth year. The writing of *La Porte étroite* was obviously an effort to recollect this stage and its spirit, and its pathetic appeal depends very centrally on his ability to evoke, in all their purity and fervor, his own religious feelings

---

* " 'You seem to me as anxious as a cork in water,' he tells me," Gide wrote in his *Journal* that same day. "I am 'anxious' when I cannot work as much as I would like to."
† Jammes's conversion had followed hard upon a crushing disappointment in love.
‡ Among them two American studies, Catharine Savage, *André Gide, l'évolution de sa pensée religieuse* (Paris, 1962) and Harold March, *André Gide and the Hound of Heaven* (Philadelphia, 1957); very useful is Pierre-Henri Simon, "Le christianisme d'André Gide," *Revue Générale Belge*, 1951.

of the time. (Its intellectual appeal depends, one might say, on his simultaneous ability to see through them; its artistic success on the coexistence of the two.) But nostalgia for a past emotion *presupposes* that the emotion itself no longer exists: and much of the great dragging, three-years' strain Gide felt the writing of *La Porte étroite* to be was caused precisely by the fact that the religious emotions with which he was trying to imbue it were so very distant from, so very alien to his present self. This was what his Christian friends, alert for any evidence of the lost sheep's returning home, misunderstood. And Claudel may be forgiven for reading too much into certain remarks in Gide's letters of the time, further evidences of this nostalgia at forty for the lost faith of fifteen.

> What am I to say about the end of your letter?* It touches all that is deepest in me; but I can remember enough of the burning piety of my adolescence to understand the felicity which you describe to me today.[6]

Second, that he did, during moments of great mental and moral disorder, cry out for the fatherly discipline, for the consoling relief of a confessor. "How easy it would be for me to throw myself into a confessional! How difficult it is to be for oneself, at one and the same time, both he who commands and he who obeys!" "If I had a confessor, I should go to him and say: Impose on me the most arbitrary of disciplines and today I shall say it is wisdom." [7] Such cries may well have aroused hopes in the breasts of his would-be converters; but they are precisely the expressions he most immediately retracts, and attributes to a passing "bad day," a momentary weakness of the will.

Third, that the issue is probably seriously distorted by his published correspondences with two aggressively devout Catholics, Paul Claudel and Francis Jammes. Distorted first because, in the absence of the hundreds of unpublished letters he was writing at the same time to much closer, non-Catholic friends, they give an unnatural prominence to Gide's relatively infrequent reflections on religion during these years; and distorted second by the very strain of corresponding civilly with two such difficult men. He admired their poetry, and to some degree their "spirit"; as he relished friendships, he tried very hard not to offend them; and though he made every effort to stay within the legal bonds of truth, he perhaps did enjoy teasing them (particularly Claudel) by means of a few carefully turned ambiguities. I think it is fair to say that neither ever

---

* A reference Claudel had made to the joys he anticipated from a Christmas season Communion.

understood him. In fact, it sometimes seems incredible that he ever made them his friends.

> I should like never to have known Claudel. His friendship weighs on my thought, and obligates it, and embarrasses it. . . . I can still not get myself to hurt him, but as my thought asserts itself, it gives offense to his. How can I explain myself to him? I should willingly leave the whole field to him, give up everything. . . . But I cannot say something different from what I have to say, which cannot be said by anyone else.[8]

And fourth, that the most complete and balanced description of Gide's moral crisis of this period, religious or not, is probably that contained within his version of the parable of the Prodigal Son (pp. 379–393). In an important although perhaps somewhat facile letter to Christian Beck of 1907, he explained just how *Le Retour de l'Enfant prodigue* was related to his unfortunate dealings with Jammes and Claudel.

> Perhaps you were unaware that Claudel, after having found Jammes to be a willing lamb to lead to the Lord, set out after me next in turn. This is, I understand, what is called "converting." No doubt he realized that, with my heredity and my Protestant education, he was going to have his work cut out: but nothing daunted, he stuck with it, encouraged more than he should have been by the very lively appreciation I had shown for his work, and by the immense credit that this lent to his words. We went rather far, both in letters and in conversation. In the meantime I learned from Jammes that an article by him, a dithyrambic "study," was to celebrate my conversion. I realized that a serious misunderstanding was developing, and resolved that I wanted no praise from Jammes that was based on a moral compromise—involuntary, perhaps, but tacitly consented to nonetheless—so I wrote him a long letter of explanation, which led to a sudden freeze on his part. He felt that I had "slipped away."
>
> All the same, understanding in the very marrow of my bones both the INTEREST of the step both Claudel and he wished to see me take, and why I would not take it—and how, if I had taken it, it could only have been in the same way *my* Prodigal Son returned to his "Father's House," to help the younger son to escape it—I wrote this little "circumstantial" work, into which I put my whole heart, but also my whole reason. I dedicated it to Arthur Fontaine, a

friend both of Jammes's and of mine, terribly interested in the "religious question"—to whom Jammes had just dedicated his *Pensée des Jardins* before his return to the Church—as a kind of counterweight to that.[9]

The key here is not, I think, in the concept of *l'Enfant prodigue* as an indirect "answer" or message to his overenthusiastic Catholic friends, but in the admission that it was a work "into which I put my whole heart, but also my whole reason." It tells us, I think, a great deal.

One must first realize that the Prodigal Son of the story is not, of course, André Gide, in any simple way. Nor is he the "I" who says:

> My God, like a child I kneel before you today, my face streaming with tears. If I recall and transcribe here your compelling parable, it is because I know what your prodigal son was like; it is because I see myself in him . . .[10]

any more than he is the "I" of any of his other stories. ("For me the first-person singular is the summit of objectivity.") One should realize also that the little fable is a work of very conscious craft and balance, and, insofar as it is successful, a thing unto itself, detached and autonomous.

Still, I find it moving only when read in the full light of all we know of Gide; when read consciously and carefully, word by chosen word, as Gide's artful, strategic, and subtle parable of his own state in the years after 1902: which is why I include it here. Many have suggested "keys" (i.e., the Father is God, his House is the Church, the Elder Brother represents the priests, the Jammeses and Claudels; the Mother perhaps Madeleine or the spirit of his mother, *"le côté Cuverville"*; the Younger Brother the "Nathaniel" of *Nourritures terrestres,* the succeeding generation); but I think none is needed. Applied too closely, they only reduce and rigidify a narrative which, in its balance of formality and pathos, of logic and feeling, approximates very closely, I think, the fluidity, pain, and ambiguity of Gide's spirit at the time it was written.

Having said all this, I have still not mentioned what I regard as the most important part of Gide's life during these years, his active work as a man of letters. In his writing career, first of all—for we have perhaps not yet adequately explained the dominant gloom of this decade—are to be found two of his most important causes of frustration and complaint: his frequent sense of despair, first, at not *doing* anything, not achieving anything creative ("What have I produced up to now compared with what I should have produced?"), which he blames by turns on age, nerves, fatigue, indecision, apathy, or a simple decline of powers; and his disappointment at not being properly recognized and rewarded for what he *had* done. (If this seems contradictory, there are probably very few writers in whom the identical contradiction cannot be found.)

As to the first, the sense of creative impotence or sterility, it is an entirely natural sequel to that harrowing act of liberation, the writing of *L'Immoraliste.* His need to write dropped suddenly as a consequence of that act, and he could only interpret this drop as a lessening of his natural force. The effect of this "release" of 1902, this drop to a new energy level as in quantum mechanics, was to leave him, although "cured" of his demons to some degree, with a sense of lessened powers, of an energy less ardent, of *inquiétude*—at least until the tensions and complications had mounted to the point at which a new leap was necessary, in the confessional documents of the 1920's. Both the end of *Amyntas* and the *Enfant prodigue* describe this (to him) inexplicable sense of aging, of being "burned out"; this *goût de cendres,* taste of ashes. With peace had come apathy, and a kind of bitterness. The most highly charged period of his life was over, and he was never again to know a time of such freshness and psychological density, of such *chutes* and *élans* as 1893–1902. For one so conscientiously devoted to *making* his life and his work, such a release, such freedom was distressing. (The hard thing, as Michel says, is not freeing oneself; it is knowing what to do with one's freedom.) To *himself*—and we, of course, need not agree—he seemed to be drifting, wandering, marking time in affairs of slight moment, moving into middle age without either fame or the achievements that would merit it. Works like *Amyntas, La Porte étroite* ("an anachronism amidst everything we are thinking, feeling, wanting today," Gide himself called it), and even *l'Enfant prodigue* are, whatever their virtues, essentially past-looking works, nostalgic, resigned, or bitter, composed for the most part out of stilled, recollected emotions. Each of them served its particular purpose, each of them bears its authentic mark of private pain. But none of them has the fatal (or vital) necessity of *L'Immoraliste,* none of them could be called a book "the author has just managed to survive." *Isabelle,* a short novel of 1911, was even less personally important, less essential to Gide. He was right to feel the decline of his creative fire; wrong only to see in it the decline of his value as a writer.

As to his second source of literary grief, the "conspiracy of silence" he felt to surround his works, Gide's attitudes may once more seem contradictory. But once more the contradiction is one to which every honest writer would probably have to confess. There is certainly nothing exceptional or difficult to understand in an artist's at once disdaining and longing for the attention and acclaim of critics and their public. The full story (and it is a fascinating one) of Gide and his critics, the effect they had on one another, has not yet been written; but two things must be admitted: that serious critical recognition was uncommonly slow in coming to him (even by the standards of a less publicity-conscious time), and that Gide's sense of self-esteem suffered considerably from this fact.* If later on he was to become, or seem to become harder-shelled, he may be said to have grown that shell in self-defense during these painful years of demi-obscurity, to have adopted a face-saving strategy of appearing to *invite* the silence that was afforded him.†

But there can be no doubt that it wounded him and that his writings and his career were shaped as a result. "For a writer, talking to a large audience is not at all the same thing as talking to a wall," Jean Schlumberger is reported as having said of Gide in this regard.[12]

> I am beginning to be tired *of not being;* as soon as a great enthusiasm does not sustain me, I am lost. Wounded vanity has never produced anything that matters, but at times my pride suffers from a real despair. And I live certain days as if in the nightmare of the man who was walled up alive in his tomb. . . .

* He was clearly reflecting on his own case when he heard Rodin describe how his own serious public career began when he left Brussels for Paris. " 'How old were you then?' 'FORTY-FIVE.' This dominated my day." (*Journal,* May 22, 1907. Rodin was then sixty-seven, Gide thirty-seven.)

† See his letter to Jammes of October 18, 1904. "I know very well that if I had smiled at the praises people made me at first, I would probably have received others; if I had answered my letters, people would have written me more of them; if I had thanked people for the books they sent me, they would have found mine better; I know very well that if the newspapers do not publicize me, neither do I advertise in them; that if the critics never speak of my writings, I never send them to them; that if interviewers . . . etc., I simply send them packing, etc. I know that all the wounds from which my pride suffers on my weary days have been created by that self-same pride. If indeed I do have a rotten character [as Jammes had told him reputation had it], it turns against myself rather than others. It is part of my nature to slander myself: allow me the joy of suffering from it as much as I like . . ."

Or, perhaps even more honestly, his "Advice to the Young Man of Letters" of 1911: "With regard to praise or blame I cannot recommend to you an indifference I have never known myself and, moreover, have been inclined to envy. It is good to be moved to emotion, to vibrate under caresses and even more so under bites. No doubt there is something to be gained from not protesting immediately against them, but . . . the important thing is not to let oneself be poisoned . . ."[11] Jacques Copeau has referred to Gide's *"secrète nostalgie du grand public."*

I think of Keats. I tell myself that two or three passionate admirations like mine would have kept him alive. Useless efforts. I feel
at times utterly enervated by the silence.   (October 24, 1907)

I go to Marcel Drouin's, and he helps me read the German clippings until dinner. Yesterday, January 20, I received my *hundred
and fifty-third* clipping. (*Candaule* was played on the 9th)—*every
one* of them insulting, dishonest, stupid, unspeakable . . .   (January 21, 1908)

There were not very many to notice that I had never written anything more nearly perfect than *Amyntas* . . . But to whom could
the secret value of the book speak? To a few rare souls.   (November 14, 1910)

I prefer the friendship, esteem, and admiration of one gentleman to
that of a hundred journalists. But as each journalist, all alone,
makes more noise than a hundred gentlemen, you must not be
astonished if my books are surrounded by a little silence or much
unkind noise.   (1911)

I find in Gaston Deschamps's latest article: "I should be very glad
to find some masterpieces among the innumerable novels that
French publishers put on the world market every day. I welcome
new names and young talents . . ."
    And yet he has never mentioned Paul Valéry, or Paul Claudel,
or André Suarès, or Francis Jammes, or me.   (October 7, 1905)

Despite Gide's professed refusal to court critical praise, he heartily
thanked any friend who undertook to write kindly of him—some of his
closest friendships, in fact, began with his letter of gratitude for some
unknown critic's attention. Nor was he above soliciting their help, if at
second hand.

What you tell me about T. de W. [Téodor de Wyzewa] interests
me very much. I received a delightful letter from him a few days
ago, which I shall answer directly. If he really feels about my writing the way he says he does, he might show it a bit in *Le Temps* or
the *Débats;* for if he doesn't say anything, they may very well continue to ignore me until the day they print my obituary. You might

mention this to him; as for myself, I never go searching after articles.*

(Letter to Christian Beck, March 24, 1911)[13]

The moderate success of *La Porte étroite* in 1909—an edition of a
thousand copies was sold out in a week, probably because it was misread
as religious sentimentality—came as a happy shock to Gide, who until
then had had to pay the printing costs of each of his own books, which
usually sold at most two or three hundred copies. But by 1914, at the age
of forty-four, although he had written many of the works on which his
reputation now rests, Gide was still far from what anyone could call
famous. For that he had to wait another ten years.

But by whatever standards one is judging, I think it must be agreed
that the most important event in Gide's life during this decade—important for us, important for him—was the founding of *La Nouvelle Revue
Française* in January 1909, after an abortive first attempt late in 1908.
At the time, it cannot have seemed all that important, although its
founders, of course—Gide and his younger friends—took it with desperate seriousness, and no one more than he. "He was ready to write addresses, to lick stamps; he would have hand-carried the copies to sub-
scribers himself," wrote Schlumberger. "Typographical errors, omissions,
misprints, unfortunate mistakes made him positively sick." [14] Gide's lamentations do soften a bit after 1909, and surely all his activity on behalf
of the new magazine (as well as the good sale of *La Porte étroite* and the
critical attention of Edmund Gosse in England) had much to do with
pulling him out of his slough of inactivity and ennui. Suddenly in 1909,
he has stopped floundering, found his next stage; his letters are the business letters of an editor and little more, coaxing out contributions
("What's become of your work? Your play? I need not tell you, no
doubt, what a great pleasure the *N.R.F.* would have in publishing it"),[15]
worrying over deadlines and type faces and permission costs: he and
Claudel took months, took letter after letter to settle on the style of a
capital letter U; and he broke with Francis Jammes over a rejected contribution. (In 1912, he was to make one of the spectacular editorial mistakes of all time by turning down Marcel Proust's new novel. He later

---

* The two papers Gide mentions were the most influential of their day in Paris. Paul
Souday, the powerful critic of *Le Temps* (the predecessor of today's *Le Monde*), did in fact
take his first public notice of Gide just four months after this letter was written, when Gide
was nearly forty-two.

apologized abjectly, of course—see his letter on page 504—and won Proust back to the *N.R.F.*) "Thanks to my friends from the theater* and the review, I never feel alone. The Vieux-Colombier and the *N.R.F.* are still the meeting-point of so many friendships, so much devotion, so much fervor," he wrote to Edmund Gosse in 1914.[16]

And yet as late as 1912, fewer than eight hundred copies of each number were distributed, and a third of them were given away free. What Gide and his friends were doing *was,* seen in retrospect, monumentally important; but they could hardly have realized that fully. Not only was Gide, by his editorial and journalistic "busy-work," preparing himself for the public role he was to play in the 20's and 30's, the agitator rather than the actor, reformer of the mind of France, the man who gave a new kind of moral strength to European intellectual history, but their little review—"perhaps the most important literary periodical in the world," Albert Guérard has called it[17]—was serving as a kind of island of integrity, lucidity, and quality on which were nurtured and promoted the leading ideas, styles, and writers of modern France; nurtured and promoted and fostered and encouraged during these years of confusion and obscurity, when they had, a determined coterie, to keep assuring one another that they were right and the others were wrong. It took ten or fifteen more years before they emerged into the light as the acknowledged victors in the long battle against a decayed traditionalism, and the acknowledged leaders of the postwar generation.

Later on, all this was to be brilliantly clear. Reading today through the contents of a library's fat bound volumes of the first five years of the *N.R.F.* (to say nothing of all 252 issues), one cannot but be properly respectful: here, all before 1914, are the first printings of *La Porte étroite* and *Les Caves du Vatican;* of Alain-Fournier's *Le Grand Meaulnes,* of long excerpts from Proust's *A la recherche du temps perdu* and Martin du Gard's *Jean Barois;* of Claudel's *L'Otage* and *L'Annonce fait à Marie,* Valery Larbaud's *Barnabooth,* unpublished poems of Rimbaud, and Saint-John Perse's *Eloges;* here are the essays and reviews that established a new set of literary standards—even if no one seemed to be reading them. Specious reputations were scrutinized, as if for the first time; the newer classics were soundly affirmed; future masters were discovered, assessed, given their proper due. English, German, American

---

* Jacques Copeau's Théâtre du Vieux-Colombier (1913–1914, 1919–1924, "the living conscience of the French stage") was a kind of stage-extension of the *N.R.F.* In a similar way, Editions de la *N.R.F.* (later Editions Gallimard, today the leading French publisher) was to be its extension into book publishing after 1911.

writers were introduced, reviewed, translated; here the new music and art found some of their best critics.

The *"N.R.F. ethic"*—the real source, ultimately, of its importance— has rarely been spelled out, though a few attempts have been made to define it. This is only to be expected, because one of its tenets is a *resistance* to creeds and commitments, to parties literary or political. ("Parties, schools scarcely interested it at all; only individuals had any existence in its eyes." [18]) As all of its collaborators have admitted, it was in many respects a kind of "emanation" from Gide's own unique combination of qualities:

First, an exceptional (sometimes, indeed, freakish) degree of personal integrity—clearly something of Gide's early puritanism, secularized and reformed—which kept them ever on guard against any hint of public corruptness or self-indulgence or *complaisance*. This was visible in the *Revue* as a kind of fierce independence, a refusal to curry favors or join cabals, to write for friends or write to order, to incline from the upright in search of good sales or good reviews. All these virtues (or better, resistance to vices) may seem obviously desirable: but, as Pierre-Quint points out, they were virtually unique at the *N.R.F.* in 1909. They are not exactly widespread in the press today.

Second (a further extension of Gide's "secular puritanism"), the most rigorous standards of intellectual and artistic integrity: a disdain for solecism and softness, for the cheap and over-easy, for the misuse or abuse of language. They tried to keep their review clear of both self-displaying cleverness and fulsome praise, of both doctrinal prejudice and *salon* wit, of all the common stock-in-trade of literary journalism. Which meant, as Schlumberger records, that they often ended up doing all the reviews themselves: outsiders "never had the tone which struck us as appropriate: they were either too fulsome, or too diffuse, or too lyrical. And then one had to treat them with kid gloves to get them to change a word." [19] Which was not the case with the *équipe,* the first team (Gide, Schlumberger, Copeau, Ruyters, Ghéon, Drouin, later Gallimard and Rivière); as part of their communal, near-monastic self-discipline— later attacked as "Protestant" or at least un-French—each submitted his work to the criticism of the group; they would not print reviews of their own books, and left many contributions unsigned. "One may smile at this purism, but it was nonetheless the key to whatever it was that gave the *N.R.F.* its special character." [20]

"The *N.R.F.* may sometimes have appeared a bit grammarian or pedantic. It was only trying to keep to its program, which was to see clearly on one precise point and to re-establish a certain order there." [21] How much this program depended on André Gide was attested by Valery Larbaud and Saint-John Perse, "We always wrote partly for him," said Larbaud, "who remained our critic and judge . . . a subtle, reflective mind untouched by fashions, which never let itself be misled or taken by surprise . . ." [22] And Saint-John Perse summed up more eloquently than anyone else—the eloquence suffers some in translation—the qualities that made André Gide the perfect man for the job he had undertaken in 1909:

> —a sense of values which has never yet failed; an innate sense of the sources, of the very essence, as it were, of French genius; a taste for the human element in the written work, and for the universal in the individual work; a perception of the quality, the urgency, and the veracity of any thing.
>
> —an intellectual sensibility no less than an intelligence of the senses; a sureness of instinct and judgment; a delicacy as intuitive as it was analytic. Above all, the pre-eminence of taste, tact, *mésure;* an aristocracy of means refined to the point of invisibility, and a harmonious sense of all things sustained by the breathing liaison of style in the balance of creative forces.
>
> —Lucidity, sobriety, subtlety. [23]

Third of the Gidean qualities that passed into the *N.R.F.* ethic was his *disponibilité,* his openness, receptiveness, noncommitment: the moral use he made of a nervous temper. The review no more had a common style than a common attitude or creed. It is difficult to explain the co-existence of this quality with the second, of this openness with that rigor: what it meant was that theirs was not simply an eclectic search for the New, but one for the authentic and substantial New, destined to last. It was this quality that opened the review to Claudel and Jammes as easily as to Proust and Valéry; and later led French nationalists and *bien-pensants* to regard their very impartiality as a conspiracy, a direct provocation.

Beyond these three qualities, the review embodied Gide's particular faith that the aesthetic point of view comprehended and contained all others, as he so often insisted of his own work. ("The aesthetic point of view is the only one from which I wish to be judged." [24]) By this he meant that fine art is not something detached from and irrelevant to moral, social, and political life, but the truest index of it;* that something was in fact a lie if ill expressed, and that language and style could be, ultimately, the only test of truth. It is not a question of this artist being an optimist and that a pessimist, this affirming and that degrading man, but of one being a better artist than the other, and hence telling more of the truth. It is a view that dominated, briefly, during the two postwar periods, although always under fire from those committed to this truth or that—to nationalism or communism, Catholicism or anti-clericalism, the existing order or a particular kind of social reform. It falls into disfavor during ages of faith, when militancy, commitment, or the right belief come to seem—to artists and intellectuals as well as to politicians and populace—more important than anything else.

This is the whole fine point of Gide's clever "Letter to M. Edouard Ducoté" of 1905 (pp. 375–378), his first public use of the imaginary interview, which was to become one of his favorite rhetorical devices. Art *includes* politics, not politics art; the work of art cannot be asked to "serve" a civilization, since it is in fact the end product of a civilization; it is by its works of art, unforced, naturally produced, that a civilization will be judged. "What are morals, then?" "An appendage of aesthetics." Though the tone is flippant, Gide could not have been more serious. He is defending his fundamental ethic *and* aesthetic—and incidentally, that of the early *N.R.F.* as well.

And yet neither then, nor perhaps even at the end of his life could Gide have realized the full importance of this undertaking. To him, it still seemed a kind of marking time. He *would,* one day, he promised, settle down like his friend Roger Martin du Gard and write his great work, putting aside all this useful but distracting journalism. (How many writers have felt thus, at the very time they were *doing* their "great work"?)

> If I were to disappear right now, no one could suspect, on the basis of what I have written, the better things I still have to write.
> (February 7, 1912)

> . . . everything I have written up to now has been nothing but barking and outside show before the *real* show begins . . .
> (September 25, 1913)

---

* See his remarks (*Journal,* May 21, 1907) on Strauss's *Salome:* ". . . art like this *is* the real enemy."

And yet he could not and never would settle down to the "great work":
he had not the temperament, the kind of self-discipline, not the patience,
the quiet nerves, the slow heaviness of spirit of the author of *Les Thibault,* of any author who can isolate himself with his imagination for
several years—although he envied all of Roger's qualities and swore he
would acquire them. As it turned out, Gide's "great work" was to be
written in day-by-day pieces. Both as the keeper of a journal and as an
editor of and contributor to the periodical press, he was to be a journalist
above all else, one of the century's most important, for the rest of his
life.

from

THE JOURNAL

1903–1913

1903   *August, 4 o'clock in the morning*

In the train; this side of Rouen . . .

Even at the moment of leaving her, you were unable to hide your joy from her. Why were you almost annoyed that she could not hide her tears?

In the train, after Metz

Miserable sky! Landscape bathed in horror! Above the low hill where you can see the shale through the grass, a heavy downpour drags on. Everything that is not green is the color of coal. Everything is dripping.

Yesterday, from the emotion of leaving . . . I could have sobbed like a child. It was as if I were traveling for the first time. I was constantly wondering: Am I following the rules, am I in step with my fate? . . . Is it my turn yet? I used not to be this way; my violent desires gave me rights over everything, everybody. I embraced everything within reach. Today I feel like the child who is acting "like a grown-up."

Weimar

Kant's dove. Still better: the kite that thinks it could climb higher without the string . . . Those children flying kites . . . Am I amused by them, or are they amused by me? They were seated under this tree, just where I am now writing. Right now they are far away. If only I had dared to sit down beside them! . . . They are coming back. I pretend to be interested in what I am writing; but I am concerned only with them. . . .

Blond hair; pure blue eyes like a *Vergiss-mein-nicht.* Though Mme För-ster-Nietzsche was expecting me at five o'clock for tea, I tarried with the child, and a still younger child came to join him. We climbed up on a haystack; I hoisted them up onto the top and my clothes were soon full of bits of straw.

Mme Förster-Nietzsche, getting tired meanwhile of waiting for me, had started out to look for me in a carriage. In turn I started with the child to look for her. He accompanied me in the streets; he gave me his hand and talked constantly, in a full and transparent voice, although I understood but very little. When I went into Count Kessler's to pack my luggage (I was to leave that evening), the little boy stationed himself, with two little comrades, on the steps of the house opposite; he was waiting; occasionally, from the window, I would wave to him, and he would reply laughing. He refused to believe in my departure, and when I spoke of it, he said: *"Es ist nicht wahr!"* Finally Mme Förster-Nietzsche's big landau came to get me; I went down. Mme Förster-Nietzsche was in the carriage. I came very near to making the children get in. They were dazzled by the tall footman covered with braid who helped me into my coat; I was aware that they took me for a prince; and when I turned around for a last farewell, I saw my little friend weeping.

Sunday, back in Paris.

[*from* AMYNTAS (*1903; published 1906*)]

> I was of an age when life begins to have a more
> dubious taste on the lips; when one feels that
> already each moment drops from a slightly lesser
> height into the past.

Obsessed by the yearning for this country, which rose up in me every year toward the autumn, and wishing to be cured for good and all—*pro remedio animæ meæ*—I planned to write a book on Africa.

I worked all summer from my recollections. Hazy recollections, lacking vividness; I could get nowhere with them; I worked in vain. I recalled nothing of the country but its delights, which were precisely what drew me to it again . . . so I decided to go back one last time, under the pretext of recording exactly each particular flavor. . . .

Algiers, Friday morning [*October 16*]

. . . My room, at a corner of the hotel, opens onto a high terrace, which faces the town and looks down on the port. Above the sea, on the skyline, the sunrise is hidden by a thick bank of haze and steam; it is like solidified heat.

The sirocco is blowing. It is suffocating. On the terrace, barefooted;

the stones are hot. Everything is tarnished, the most delicate whites look blighted. One feels that as soon as the sun has cleared the wall of mist, the heat will be staggering. And with one leap the sun clears it.

Saturday

A hundred and two degrees in the shade. It has not rained for six months.

The strange and exhausting fact is that it is hotter by night than by day. For if there is sun during the day, there is also shade, cooled from time to time by a breeze. But after six o'clock in the evening, the wind drops; an even, dull heat settles down. Everything thirsts. One dreams of bathing, of drinking. One says to himself, "I won't be able to sleep to-night," and begins to prowl. Even the sky looks impure. With no hope, no anticipation of a storm, everything is tarnished with heat, and reminds one that, beyond the favored Sahel, an enormous continent lies out there all ablaze.

. . . I think of the parched oases . . . there I will go! Obscure and leaden nights above their palms.

I have not yet been able to discover whence this smell of sandalwood rises or falls; it floats beneath the branches in the square, it envelops and fills you.

Fort National, . . . Monday

After dinner, yesterday, I went out too late; the Arab town seemed already dead. The four or five French cafés, all too brightly lit, glared shamelessly into the night. I climbed the suspicious-looking steps which, behind the cafés, lead to the high quarter of the town. The Jewish shops are shut; everything is dark; at the top of the steps only one meager gas-lamp; I sit down on a seat made of planks. And I am no sooner seated than I hear at the turn of the street the scratching of an Arab guitar. A Moorish café . . . I notice now its feeble glow in the night, which divides the darkness scarcely more than the low sound of the guzla casts back the silence.—Shall I go and look? To see what? No doubt a miserable hovel, a dozen Arabs lying about, a musician, most probably ugly . . . Better stay here, let the night enter into you, insinuate itself with the music . . . An Arab leaves the café, comes toward me, thinks me drunk; and indeed I am.

Bou-Saada, Thursday, October 22

. . . Suddenly, round a rocky bend, an oasis—not of palms, but of fig trees, tamarisks, almonds, and oleanders. Then, giant apricots, a windmill, some flocks, some Arabs. On and on the oasis stretches, following the *oued,* now insinuating itself between narrow banks, now, because of the extreme aridity of the soil, so strangled that it seems almost no more than a green thread to the bird that flies above; then, again, widening, spreading, lifting, so that one thinks; a little sun, and these shadows would be filled with charm.

> . . . *Between Bou-Saada and M'Silah, Monday*

Impossible to write this morning; the air is icy. From five until eight, cocooned in my blankets, I struggle to make them airtight. The sky, impeccable yesterday, is overcast, and immediately after sunset takes on the hideous color of a gray ointment.

This morning I am full of hate for this country, and make frantic efforts to escape it. I listen to myself recalling the Third Symphony of Schumann. I go over, too, the Sonata to the Grand Duke Rudolf, in C minor; but here and there the violin part eludes me. When, at last, the temperature allows me to put my hands out, I take Virgil from my bag and reread the Epilogue to Pollio.

Nothing of all this satisfies me; this morning I would like to go to the Louvre, and reread La Fontaine. . . .

After a stage of giddiness, the huge plain seems to distort itself before one's eyes. One would think it liquid, crossed with eddies, flowing; then, in stretches, swollen; the swirling soil is full of currents and waves, and the suffering eye grieves at being unable to establish a perspective anywhere.

> . . . *Algiers . . . Thursday night . . .*

Up there, in a not very secret street, but in a secret loop of the street, a tiny café. I see it. At the back of that café, on a lower level, a second room; narrow, it seemed, and receiving its light from the café; from where I was, I could not see the whole of it; it extended into a recess. At times an Arab stepped into it, an Arab who had come straight from the street; I did not see him reappear. At the far end of this retreat, I suppose, a secret staircase led to other profundities. . . .

Each day I waited, hoping to see something more. I went back there every day. I went back in the evening; I went back at night. I lay half stretched out on a mat. Without moving, I waited and watched the slow disintegration of the hours; there remained at the close of the day a cinder, an ash of time, subtle, bitter to the taste, soft to the touch, rather like the cinder in that hearth between the tiny pillars, over there near the mysterious lower regions on the left—where, at moments, moving aside the ashes, the café-keeper revives a dying ember, beneath the pile of ashes. . . .

From time to time, accompanying himself on the *guembra,* one of the Arabs chants a song, slow as the hours. The hashish pipe goes round. Obstinately, despite myself, I watch the thick darkness over in the corner, the wall-mat of the retreat into which I had seen that suspect descend. . . .

One night, I was offered the pipe, with a gesture so friendly . . . Ah, the deep mouthful I inhaled! It is better to smoke hashish fasting, it would appear; I had eaten . . . I felt at once as if a great fist had struck me on the nape of the neck; everything turned, spiraled, somersaulted; I shut my eyes, then felt my feet rise above my head, then the ground fall away, flee from beneath me. . . .

A few seconds later, I was in a sweat, a cold sweat; but already nothing remained of the nausea, so abominable at first; nothing but the dizziness—dare I say pleasant?—of one who, weightless, is no longer quite sure where he is, and floats; floats. . . .

Blida

In the street of the Ouled, each woman before her door, like a statue in her niche; she laughs and offers herself to the passer-by.

But the loveliest thing I saw that night (in a passing, fleeting glance, while a woman calls to me) was through that open door; in one bound, my desire enters a dark, deep, and narrow garden (and there my desire wanders) which I can scarcely see; a cypress trunk I do see plunges into water I imagine; and, farther off, lit from the other side, luminous, hiding a mysterious threshold, a white curtain. . . .

Algiers, Monday

I should like . . . to know, when the heavy black door in front of that Arab opens, what will greet him, beyond. . . .

I should like to be that Arab; I should like what awaits him to be awaiting me. . . .

Algiers, Wednesday

In that crowded restaurant, where one eats worse than anywhere else, which is saying not a little for Algiers, two Italian mandolinists pinch and scratch throughout the meal. The air is filled with merriment and mediocrity.

Restaurant de l'Oasis, Friday

At the center of the sideboard, in parsley, on a plate, crouches an extraordinary crustaceous monster.

"I have traveled a great deal," says the maître d'hôtel; "but I've never seen anything like that except in Algiers. In Saigon, for instance, where there were crayfish as big as . . . (in vain he searches the dining-room for a suitable comparison), these are unknown. And even here they're quite unusual. In three years this is only the second one I've seen. Sea-grasshopper, monsieur . . . because of the shape of the head; there, just look at the profile. One would swear it was a grasshopper's head . . . Oh, but of course, monsieur: excellent; something like that of a crayfish, but much more delicate. Tonight we're going to cook her. If monsieur comes to luncheon tomorrow, we could offer him a taste."

The sea-beast, with six people around her and talking of her, holds her tongue. She is grave, immobile, ungainly, the color of dross, expressionless; she looks like a muddied rock.

"What? Not alive! ?" With a thrust of his thumb the maître d'hôtel drives in one on her eyes; the grasshopper, with a sudden start, lashes out fearfully with her tail and sends the parsley flying from the plate; then settles down again.

Throughout the meal I stare at her.

November 27

Three weeks ago I could have left Algiers more easily; already I have formed my habits here, my little roots . . . a few days more and I would no longer be able to tear myself away.

And every year, for so many years now, I have resolved never to return. . . .

But the longing for this garden, at night—for this midnight garden, where I used to return every night . . . Oh, how shall I endure it?

El Guerrah, Sunday, November 29 . . .

. . . Everything contributed to it: the newness of the environment and of my own self, where all that I discovered enchanted me; the most subtle, sinuous means could not have provided such a multitude of virgin delights for my enjoyment as did my puritan education. And then, in that very place, I had the good fortune to fall ill, very seriously it is true, but of an illness that did not kill me—one, on the contrary, that merely weakened me for a while; and the clearest result of it was to give me a taste for the preciousness of life. It would seem that, for the absorption of sensations, a feeble, febrile organism is more porous, transparent, sensitive, more perfectly receptive. Despite my illness, if not because of it, I was all receptiveness, all joy. Perhaps my recollection of that time is a little confused here and there, for I have a bad memory; but from the bouquet of sensations which I brought back from that first voyage, so keen a perfume still escapes that at times it keeps me from enjoying the present moment. I refrain from comparisons, however; but I do worse: six times I return to the country, demanding the past in the present and exhausting my emotion, requiring of it each time that freshness which it owed in the past to its novelty, and finding year by year ever less lively compensations for my aging desires. . . . Nothing ever equals the first touch.

Biskra, November 30

I re-enter the heart of my youth. I set my steps in my steps. Here are the banks, the charming banks of the path I trod that first day when, still weak, just escaped from the horror of death, I sobbed, intoxicated with the sheer astonishment of *being,* the enchantment of existing. Oh, how soothing were the palm-shadows to my still tired eyes! Softness of the light shadows, whisper of the gardens, perfumes, I recognize *everything,* trees, objects . . . the only unrecognizable thing is myself. . . .

They have re-channeled the river from this charming spot; flowing out of the mill, it ran past the foot of that gum tree; now, deprived of water, it withers. . . . Its shade was perfect. . . . What demon leads me back here? . . .

Saturday . . .

Misery! Desolation!—I sit down, sheltered from the wind by a mound of fallen clay, sand, and stones, beside the ruined bank of a leaden lake where the water stagnates under thick reeds. If only, while grazing his skinny goats, a little shepherd-musician would come and sit here . . . I am alone. I search within myself, contemplating so much desolation, for a lift of vitality to re-awaken delight, to feed into so much death a single tremor of emotion.—I remain here. The wind tosses the reeds. An uncertain sun tries to smile at the desert, a silvery gleam lies on the crumbling salt crust, like paint on a corpse. . . .

Sunday

In a secluded café sheltered from the noises of the street, the same Arab I listened to last year reads Antar. By the entrance, a few benches; on the café floor, mats. Inside, a whole attentive, white-wrapped audience is re-clining. Amidst so much soothing whiteness nothing shines, everything melts and mingles; the somnolent light envelops everything evenly; it has the softness of water, flowing slowly, without reflections, without a rent.

The reader of Antar is very handsome; his voice has a sonorous, tri-umphal ring. Sometimes, lowering the candle-lit book, he explains and comments on a verse. When he reads, he scans the lines with one hand; the other hand, close up to the candle, holds the book. Sometimes laughter shakes the crowd, like the laughter, I imagine, that shook the table of the gods on Olympus; some witticism of Antar's, a striking feat of arms by some Arab. Subjected, fallen, the listeners find solace, respite, and some element of splendor to sustain them in the account of their ancient prow-ess. . . . The reader's words fall faster, his voice rolls like a drum; one can hear nothing of the verses but their heroically resounding rhythms. How splendid they must have been, these people, in victory! . . .

Hot Springs

What do I come to seek here again?—Perhaps, just as a body on fire finds joy in diving naked into cold water, my spirit, stripped of everything, drenches its fervor in the ice-cold desert. . . .

Little flute with four holes, by which the ennui of the desert tells its tale, I compare you to this country, and sit listening as you scatter your flute-notes in the night. Ah, of how few elements here are composed our sounds and our silence! The smallest change tells—water, sky, earth, and palms . . . and I am in admiration, slender instrument, of all the subtle diver-sity I relish in your monotony, according to the emphasis he imparts in hurrying his measure or in lulling it beneath his charming breath, the child-musician with nimble fingers. . . .

Sunday . . . [December 27]

We have decided to leave tomorrow morning. Shall I be able to? Some-times, quite suddenly, some leftover bit of sensual pleasure awakes in me an aftertaste so secret that at once I feel myself without the courage to tear myself away. . . .

1904   *Cuverville, end of September*

. . . In the autumn of Normandy I dream of spring in the desert.

Palm trees whispering in the wind! Almond trees rustling with bees! Warm winds! Sugar-sweet air! . . .

A squall out of the north beats against my window. It has been raining for three days. —Oh, how beautiful the caravans were, at Touggourt, when at dusk the sun sank into the salt.

[*from* THE JOURNAL]

November

Since October 25, 1901, the day on which I finished *L'Immoraliste,* I have not seriously worked. My article on Wilde, my lecture in Germany, this recent one in Brussels (which I did not enjoy, and which I gave very badly) cannot be counted. A dull torpor of the mind has made me vegetate for the last three years. Perhaps, overly occupied with my garden, in contact with the plants, I have taken on their habits. The least sentence costs me an effort; talking, in fact, is almost as painful as writing. And I must admit too that I was becoming difficult: at the least suspicion of a thought, some cantankerous critic, always hiding deep in my mind, would rise up to ask: "Are you sure that it's worth the trouble to . . . ?" And, as the trouble was enormous, the thought immediately withdrew.

The trip to Germany last summer shook off my apathy somewhat; but as soon as I got back here, it took a deeper hold on me. I accused the weather (it rained incessantly that year); I accused the air of Cuverville (and I still fear that it exerts a soporific influence over me); I accused my routine (indeed, it was very bad; I never left the garden, where, for hours on end, I would *contemplate* the plants one after another); I indicted my morals (but how could such an utterly stagnant mind have triumphed over my body?). The fact is that I was becoming stultified; no enthusiasm, no joy. Eventually, seriously worried, intent on shaking off that torpor to which was added an unhealthy restlessness, I convinced myself and convinced Em. that nothing but the diversion of travel could save me from myself. To tell the truth, I did not convince Em.; I was well aware of this, but what could I do? Go ahead all the same. I therefore resolved to go. I almost killed myself in explanations to justify my conduct; it was not enough for me to go; in addition, Em. had to approve of my going. I hurled myself against a disheartening wall of indifference. No, no: I did not "hurl" myself; I sank in; I lost my footing; I was engulfed. I know well enough today and already suspected then the lamentable misunderstanding caused by Em.'s voluntary (and yet almost unconscious) . . . abnegation (I can think of no other word for it). It contributed not a little to demoralizing me. Nothing more painful than the exaggeration of my restlessness, of my feelings, etc., all to overcome that indifference. Fortunately, the memory of all that is fading now. . . . But if I had to relive my life, I could not see that period approach without anguish. . . .

1905   *Hendaye*

Were I less exhausted, I should doubtless have devoted several pages every day simply to praising this landscape. Yet I was not in love there with anything or anyone; but the azure-tinted light, that indefinable wild scent amidst the thick lushness of spring. . . .

Monday

. . . At twenty my youth, my long hair, my sentimental manner, and a frock-coat that my tailor had turned out beautifully made me acceptable in the drawing-rooms of Mme Beulé and the Countess de Janzé. If I had continued to frequent them, I should be writing today for the *Revue des deux mondes;* but I should not have written the *Nourritures.* I escaped early from that world, in which, to appear proper, I had to watch myself too closely.

Wednesday

Luxembourg Gardens. Nine in the morning. Splendid weather. I wish I had bought a Ronsard. Stendhal seems less good to me than in the rain.

Cuverville

All morning in the garden. I couldn't get myself to go in and write. I come to lunch intoxicated and Em. says that I "look like a madman." What have I done to look that way? Merely hunted insects on my rose-bushes.

May 14, in the train returning from Cuverville

I should have liked to speak of Hofmannsthal. It is rather odd that after
two hours' conversation with him, I should find nothing to set down. . . .

And yet I liked him very much. But there didn't seem to be any great
element of *shadow,* of mystery in him, nor did it seem to hide any particular divine spark. I talk with him all the more willingly, because he talks
almost all the time. I should take great pleasure in seeing him again.

Monday

I should like to take in hand all these causes of sterility which I discern so
clearly, and strangle them all. I have conscientiously cultivated every internal negation. Just now I am struggling against them. Each one taken
alone is easy enough to subdue; but they are so densely interrelated, so
skillfully tied to each other. They form a network, a web from which I
cannot get free. What good is this journal? I cling to these pages as if they
were the one thing fixed among so many fleeting things. I force myself to
write in them anything at all, just so long as I do it regularly every day.
. . . Even here I seek for my words, I grope, and I set down your name,
Loxias!

Thursday

The first really hot evening, after a stifling and radiant day. If I had some
book under way, I should write its most beautiful pages this evening. My
brain is lucid, not too gay, my flesh is at rest, my spirit staunch. This evening I should be a wonderful lover, and I cannot think of Gérard without
pity. I should like not to have met M. before yesterday and not to have
spoken to him until today. . . .

If I threw myself from my balcony tonight, I should do so saying:
"It's simpler."

Wednesday

The weather is so hot, so beautiful, that I go out again after dinner,
though already dead tired. Yet no restlessness drives me out this evening;
I go out "in order not to have a bad conscience later on"; Em. makes this
terrible remark, as she herself urges me to go out.

Four years ago on such an evening I should have prowled all night
long.

First in the Champs-Elysées, marvelous in the neighborhood of the
café-concerts; I push on as far as the Rond-Point, and return by way of the

Elysée; the crowd is in a holiday mood, more and more numerous and excited up to the rue Royale; the route that the King of Spain will follow on his way back from the Elysée is marked by luminous festoons above the Faubourg Saint-Honoré and the rue Royale, forming delightful triumphal arches. Unable to bear seeing it without Em., I return home in haste to get her; but as soon as I sit down in the apartment, I am seized with such exhaustion that we put off our excursion until tomorrow.

Tuesday, right after lunch, Em. and I go to the Champs-Elysées, where the King of Spain is to pass. Certainly, if the King had been less young and less handsome, I should not have found myself choked with sobs when I saw him salute the crowd as he passed. His face was drawn; he saluted with a stiff little military smile.

When, two hours later, we saw him return from the Elysée, his smile was very different; his features, now amused rather than contracted, expressed only an amazed and yet almost childish joy. Between the two regal parades we went to see the two Salons. Nothing so demoralizing as those exhibitions.

In the evening we drive out in a carriage to see the illuminations on the boulevards and the squares. Em. returns home; I go back alone toward the Champs-Elysées, then to the Opéra. No particularly noteworthy encounter. The air is dusty and full of flames. On the avenue de l'Opéra (which the King is to descend on his way back to the Palace of Foreign Affairs after the gala performance) the crowd packs in thicker and thicker. Finally, in considerable anxiety, I get away, and by a circuitous route reach the Place du Théâtre-Français. Here the crowd is not so thick. It is almost midnight. People come out of the Théâtre-Français. The procession should be almost here. I climb up on one of the columns of the theater portico and wait among a group of children. From that spot I heard the bomb very clearly; it made less noise than people said. Several persons near me insisted that it was a firecracker. I thought it was a revolver-shot. Again I noticed in me that disinclination to *take the event seriously*. I was highly amused, and even fear of the crowd, which hardly left me a minute, kept all my senses keyed up and made my heart beat joyfully. The next day the papers spoke of an "indescribable tumult" following the report. On the contrary, I was struck by the complete immobility that followed the detonation. For about four minutes the crowd remained as if rooted to the spot with stupor. Then an extraordinary wave was stirred up by a movement of the police. A little later a charge of the mounted police filled me with fear, horror, and a sort of wild enthusiasm. Yet I was completely master of myself, merely embarrassed by the tears that rose to my eyes. But still impossible to *take seriously* what I saw; it didn't seem to be real life. As soon as the act was over, the actors would come back and take a bow.

Saturday

I long for solitude and decide to start tomorrow without waiting for Em. I shall sleep Monday at Etretat and Tuesday can receive her at Cuverville.

The air is dark with heat.

Sunday

Back home, I wear myself out putting papers in order and packing my trunk. It is like my books, like the least of my sentences, like my whole life: I try to put too much into it.

Cuverville

It is raining pitchforks. Closed up in the greenhouse with Goethe's poems, surrounded by golden calceolarias, without fever, without anxieties, without desires, I enjoy a PERFECT FELICITY.

June

Today, the 13th of June, on the first day of good weather, I am writing outside, rather uncomfortably seated, and considerably bothered by my dog. Since we have been here, the almost incessant rain has been ruining the garden, but helping my work. Every day I have been able to add a few lines to my *Porte étroite*. I prefer such regular, disciplined work today to the finest inspiration in the world.

Between sessions of work I read German and Italian (*Werther* and the *Vita Nuova*). This morning the manuscript of the translation of *Paludes* arrived.

[July]

Today I found out what waiting is; not the impatient waiting that makes the horse froth at his bit, but that horrible anguished waiting in which the heart labors from one beat to another, as if it had to push aside a blood clot. On the road, right there, on the embankment, under the burning sun,

I wait: I wait for X.'s wagon to pass by. It doesn't come. It must have taken the other road. . . .

July 31

I have gone back to work with a certain regularity, but I make incredibly slow progress. I spend hours on a group of sentences that I shall completely rearrange the next day. The scene in Geneviève's room, in particular, when he finds her kneeling, gave me extraordinary pains. But I admire now all the things I succeeded *in not saying,* in KEEPING BACK. (I think for some time of the virtue that "reserve" can become in a writer. But who would understand that these days?) I try to consider patience as my greatest quality; in any case it is the one I must above all encourage in myself. I write "patience"; I ought to say "obstinacy"; but what is really needed is a *supple obstinacy.*

Paris, August 8

Copeau was amazed to find that I was still in the midst of Stendhal's *Journal.* There are certain writers that I read as slowly as possible. It seems to me that I am conversing with them, that they talk to me, and I should be sorry not to be able to keep them with me longer.

August 24

Nothing is consistent, nothing is fixed or certain, in my life. By turns I resemble and differ; there is no living creature so foreign to me that I cannot swear I will not resemble him one day. I do not yet know, at the age of thirty-six, whether I am miserly or prodigal, temperate or greedy . . . or rather, being suddenly carried from one to the other extreme, in this very balancing I feel that my fate is being achieved. Why should I attempt to form, by artificially imitating myself, the artificial unity of my life? I can find my equilibrium only in movement.

My heredity, which interbreeds in me two very different systems of life, can be explained by this complexity and these contradictions from which I suffer.

August 25

You cannot imagine an author so great that his most banal qualities are not the first to be appreciated. The crowd always enters by way of the "commons"—and most often never gets beyond them.

I am again losing my footing; I am letting myself roll with this monotonous wave, carried along on the current of days. A great drowsiness numbs
me from the time I get up until evening; games occasionally shake it off,
but I am gradually losing the habit of effort. I compare what I am to what
I once was, to what I should have liked to be. If only . . . but no, everything becomes soft in such an easy existence. Sensual pleasure permeates
everything; my finest virtues are dissipated and even the expression of my
despair is blunted.

How can I call absurd a rule of conduct that would have protected me
against this? At one and the same time my reason condemns it and
calls out for it: calls out for it in vain. If I had a confessor, I should go to
him and say: Impose upon me the most arbitrary of disciplines and today
I shall say it is wisdom; if I cling to some belief that my reason mocks, it
is because I hope to find in it some power against myself.

As soon as a healthy day comes along, I shall blush at having written
this.

. . . and my will which complains of growing old. If the wear were only
constant and regular, if it attacked at the same time, and equally, body and
soul; but no, it proceeds by leaps and bounds; I am aging in bits, which
become an object of amazement and sorrow for the parts not yet touched.

[Nîmes] Saturday

Mme de R. congratulates me on *L'Immoraliste,* "This book in which there
are such beautiful thoughts." Obviously she thinks they are sprinkled on
afterwards, like nasturtium blossoms on a salad. How uncultivated these
southern women are, and how paradoxical you seem to them when you
don't disguise yourself considerably!

Minutes of such excruciating joy that you think they might break the
thread of life; then, between two such, the succession of monotonous days,
spent merely in growing older.

Cuverville, October 2

Time flies. The cloudy sky is already filling with winter. My dog is sleeping at my feet. Full of anguish, I sit helpless in front of the white sheet of

paper, where one would like to be able to write everything—but on which I shall never be able to write more than *something*.

Gourmont does not understand that not all intelligence is on the side of free thought, not all stupidity on the side of religion; that the artist needs leisure for his work and that nothing keeps the mind so busy as free inquiry and doubt. Skepticism is perhaps sometimes the beginning of wisdom, but it is often the end of art.

What a child I remained for a long time, always looking for, even going out of my way to invent, sympathetic points of contact—*no matter whom I happened to be with!* It did help me, to be sure, to a more subtle understanding of others, but it also encumbered my life with pseudo-friendships that I have trouble getting out of today. Indulgence toward others is hardly less ruinous than indulgence toward oneself.

It is years now since my head has been warm. I think of that happy fever which, all the time that I was writing *Paludes,* kept my book awake.

The reading of Rimbaud and of the Sixth *Chant de Maldoror* has made me ashamed of my works and disgusted with everything that is merely the result of culture. It seems to me that I was born for something different.

But perhaps there is still time . . . perhaps in Auteuil . . . Oh! how I long . . .

At Fontaine's. Paul Claudel, whom I have not seen in more than three years, is there. As a young man he looked like a nail; now he looks like a sledge hammer. A forehead not very high, but rather wide; face without subtlety, as if carved with a knife; bull neck that runs right into his head, through which one can feel the passion rushing to flood the brain. Yes, I think this is the dominating impression: the head is of one piece with the body. I shall study him more fully next Tuesday (when he comes to lunch with us); I was a bit too concerned with defending myself, and only half responded to his advances. He gives me the impression of a solidified cyclone. When he talks, it is as if something were released within him; he proceeds by sudden affirmations and maintains a hostile tone even when you share his opinion. . . .

Claudel is wearing a little jacket that is too short and that makes him look even more thickset and lumpish. One's eyes are constantly drawn to and shocked by his necktie, a four-in-hand the color of a locust-bean.

December 2

From Russia the most alarming news, which makes a sort of figured bass to all my thoughts throughout all the day's occupations.

December 5

Paul Claudel came to lunch. Too short a jacket, aniline-colored necktie; his face still more square than the day before yesterday; his speech both precise and full of images; his voice staccato, clipped, and authoritative.

His conversation, very rich and alive, improvises nothing, one feels. He recites truths that he has patiently worked out. Yet he knows how to joke and, if he only let himself go a bit more on the spur of the moment, would not be without a certain charm. I try to discover what is lacking in that voice . . . a little human warmth? . . . No, not even that; he has something much better. It is, I believe, the most *gripping* voice I have ever heard. No, he doesn't charm; he does not want to charm; he convinces— or imposes. I didn't even try to protect myself from him; and when, after the meal, speaking of God, of Catholicism, of his faith, of his happiness, he added (as I said that I understood him): "But, Gide, then why don't you become converted . . . ?" (this without any brutality, without even a smile). I let him see, I showed him how much his words had upset me. . . .

"For a long time, for two years," he went on, "I went without writing; I thought I must sacrifice art to religion. My art! God alone could know the value of this sacrifice. I was saved when I understood that art and religion must not be set in antagonism within us. That they must not be confused either. That they must remain, so to speak, perpendicular to each other; and that their very struggle nourishes our life. One must recall here the words of Christ: 'Not peace, but a sword.' That's what Christ means. We must seek happiness not in peace, but in conflict. The life of a saint is a struggle from one end to the other; the greatest saint is the one who at the end is the most vanquished."

He speaks during the lunch of a certain "frontal sense" that allows us, without reading it, to recognize in advance a good or a bad book, and which had always warned him against Auguste Comte. I should be more amused to hear him execute Bernardin if he did not at the same time demolish Rousseau. But how many others he demolishes! Beating about him with a monstrance, he devastates our literature. . . .

He speaks with the greatest respect of Thomas Hardy and Joseph Conrad, and with the greatest scorn of English writers in general "who have never learned that the rule of 'nothing unessential' is the first condition of art."

He talks a great deal; you are aware of the pressure of ideas and images within him. When, apropos of I don't remember what or whom, I spoke of the weakening of the memory, he immediately exclaimed: "Memory doesn't weaken. None of man's faculties weakens with age. That is a gross error. All man's faculties develop continuously from birth to death."

He talks endlessly; someone else's thought does not stop his for an instant; even a cannon could not divert him. In talking with him, in trying to talk with him, one is forced to interrupt him. He waits politely until you have finished your sentence, then resumes where he had stopped, at the very word, as if you had said nothing.

He shocked Francis Jammes some time ago (in 1900) when he replied to Jammes's anguish with "*I have my God.*"

(The greatest advantage of religious faith for the artist is that it permits him a *limitless* pride.)

Upon leaving me, he gives me the address of his confessor.

Christmas Day

Natanson reports to me these sentences of Maillol: "A model! A model; what the hell would I do with a model? When I need to verify something, I go and find my wife in the kitchen; I lift up her chemise; and I have the marble." All this said with a strong southern accent.

1906   *January 5*

Yesterday, late afternoon at the Mathurins. Georgette Leblanc in *La Mort de Tintagiles.* Small theater entirely filled. Maeterlinck gives me a seat in his box. Opposite us, Mary Garden; to the right, Duse (wonderful face of an *old* woman; not a single inexpressive wrinkle). *Utter lack of interest* of Maeterlinck's face; materiality of his features; a very positive, very practical man of the North, in whom mysticism is a sort of psychic exoticism.

I expected to find Georgette Leblanc terrible, and was annoyed with myself for not being more annoyed with her; but no, the lights were dim enough so that we were spared the coarseness of her features and the indiscreet aspect of her whole body. Indeed, I am willing to admit that she set herself off rather well.

Succession of living tableaux in the Burne-Jones or Walter Crane manner. Continual music slowing down the diction and suggesting great depths behind every sentence. This interferes with the action considerably; every word tends to suggest that the action is taking place anywhere except on the stage.

January 15

Again three days of rain. My head is tired, my will restless, and my personality indecisive. Numerous chores make all real work impossible, and that is the only thing that would rest me. I dare not go back to my novel for fear of blunting my emotion and zeal. I have begun studying the piano again for the good of my health, but not methodically. My handwriting is becoming uglier. I sleep badly; I tremble and twitch the way wild animals do. . . .

Friday, at Charmoy's, a strange evening. In the studio, cluttered with huge statues fantastically lighted by a score of candles most ingeniously disposed, stuck here and there on the corner of benches, in the folds of the robes of his angels, those enormous angels supporting the monument of Beethoven—in that studio, overheated by a little cast-iron stove, we wait, José, his wife, and I wait for the Princesse de Broglie and Miss Barney.

Around ten o'clock we hear the Princesse's automobile; soon after she appears, framed by the door opening against the night. The Princesse is enveloped in an ermine wrap, which she drops into Charmoy's hands. A gown of black velvet which only comes up to her waist sets off a vast expanse of lustrous skin; the drooping bodice is suspended from jet straps. Her face is small and tired; her coiffure, almost virginal, strives unsuccessfully to make her look younger. No wrinkles, however, but her features are painfully tight.

As soon as she comes in, she stares at me through her lorgnette; a lorgnette whose gold handle is linked by a small chain to a delicate bracelet of rubies.

Flagrant preoccupation with bewitching one.

On the back of a wicker chair, which she considers "not very inviting," a fur is stretched; on the floor a foot-warmer for her little feet, which she also wraps in a shawl. Near her, behind her, Miss Barney takes refuge in an eloquent silence and lets the Princesse pose and preen.

Tuesday morning

Impossible to find the key to the glass-fronted *armoire*. Em. insists that she put it in her basket, on top of four dozen eggs. Naturally, the eggs having moved, the key—heavier than they—must have slipped to the bottom. We burrow with great care for fear of breaking the eggs. We bring up a pair of gloves, a veil, a pair of scissors, a handkerchief, what else? and ten boxes of matches! But no key. We decide to take the eggs out, one by one. Each egg is wrapped in tissue paper, which we remove. The egg is cool in one's hand, clean, and dull off-white in color. In Eugène Rouart's cloisonné bowl, so blue, so green, they make a marvelous still-life. Now it is one o'clock in the morning; the basket is empty, the bowl full; we admire the effect. But no key.

Tuesday

At the Salon des Indépendants we discover in the crowd Garnier, Mourey, Guérin, Rouart; and Retté, utterly drunk, staggering about supported by a very young man, shouting my name from one end to the other of a gallery, who says: "I am a bit drunk," and belches in your face. Verlaine drunk was *tremendous*. Drunk, Retté seems more insignificant than ever; he is merely revolting; no one pays any attention to him.

Saw nothing but very ordinary things. But how can one concentrate, caught in that ignorant throng? How can one loyally give one's attention to anything? Vauxcelles's article that was being sold at the entrance is idiotic.

March 21

Certainly the *secret aim* of mythology was to prevent the development of science.

March 29

I reread my old letters to Em. which I have brought from Cuverville. In vain I seek in them some material for my novel. But in doing so I lay bare all my intellectual flaws. There is not one of them that fails to annoy me.

April 5

Wasted two hours at the Auteuil races for ten minutes of adulterated emotion. I'm not used to such mediocre pleasures. My demoralization came especially from having paced the public enclosure over and over without meeting a single person with whom I wanted to talk or go to bed.

April 9

I reread a few pages of Anatole France. . . .

I should like France more wholeheartedly if certain rash people did not try to make of him a writer of importance. That sets me wondering. I fear that perhaps I have not been fair. I reopen *La Vie littéraire* and especially *Le Jardin d'Epicure,* in which his thought is most directly accessible. I read this sentence which I applaud: "One thing above all gives charm to men's thoughts, and that is unrest. A mind that is not uneasy irritates and bores me." . . .

He is fluent, subtle, elegant. He is the triumph of the euphemism. But there is no restlessness in *him;* one drains him at the first draft. I am not inclined to believe in the survival of those upon whom everyone agrees right away. I doubt very much if our grandchildren, opening his books, will find more to read in them than we are finding. I know that, as far as I am concerned, I have never felt him to be ahead of my thought. At most he explains it. And this is what his readers like in him. France flatters them. Each one of them is free to think: "How well put that is! After all, I wasn't so stupid either; that's just what *I* was thinking *too.*"

April 27

Since yesterday we have adopted a poor black poodle that was starving to death and prowling around our door for three days. His coat is all thick and matted from the plaster debris on which he has been sleeping in the house that is being built next door. At two a.m., Em. makes me go down to see if he isn't barking in the cellar, where we locked him up. I don't think he is intelligent, but he is affectionate.

I have bathed, I have soaped my poor dog in my tub. I hoped that cleanliness would give some luster to his coat! But now he looks more than ever like a blind man's dog. And I who wanted a pedigreed dog, I've got what was coming to me! No matter; it is time to learn once more to prefer the events that choose me to those I should have chosen myself.

Monday

Yesterday at about six there came back to see me that preposterous little fop named R.L., whose intrigue finally succeeded in slipping a rather long essay into *L'Ermitage.* Yet he is not stupid or unpolished; but I consider it impertinent that at the age of nineteen he should make me read his sixty pages without having read a single one of mine. He comes to me not because he wants to see me, but simply to push himself and because he has understood that I could get him into *L'Ermitage.* I shall explain my position to him a bit more directly if he tries again.

May 2

Jammes writes me on sky-blue paper a typical parish priest's letter, in which he reminds me of Pourceaugnac's doctors trying to persuade him that he is ill. Perhaps I am about to enter paradise, but not through the door he thinks. "You seem to me restless," he says, "like a cork bobbing on the water." I am restless when I can't work as much as I want. . . .

Yesterday went out at about two. Went to Albert's.

His wife opens the door, shouts from the bottom of the stairs leading to the studio: "Papa! it's André," then goes upstairs with me and settles down in our conversation, in our intimacy, which she hinders, which she makes impossible. And all during the two hours I stay, she doesn't budge once. It's this way *every time* I go to see Albert. With her there, we talk about almost everything that we would talk about without her . . . but not in the same way.

And I feel that Albert is fed up with this. Timidly, giving some excuse or other, he accompanies me into the hall, then onto the landing, and whispers as he leans toward me: "I can never be alone any more," and I see two giant old man's tears, which he hastens to rub away.

When both of them came to Auteuil, Em. took charge of his wife, and I was able to remain alone with him for some time. Then it was that he repeated the heartbreaking sentence with which his father's will ended: "My dear children, above all have no ambition." And Albert added lugubriously: "He knew that we were not up to it."

And I wonder what a come-down Albert's father had made too, when, toward the end of his life, he used to weep silently in the evening, with his back turned to the lamp, while his wife, beside him, read the newspaper or embroidered and Albert, out of respect for his father, pretended not to see.

Sunday

Impossible to go on this way; I must see a doctor. This frightful fatigue has eventually given me a sort of fear of all manifestations of life. This evening, after dining at my Aunt Charles's, I come home at nine o'clock my head heavy with fatigue; not worth anything. Am going to bed.

May 10

I chose this very small notebook in order to be able to put it into my pocket. I like having it on me, busying myself with it wherever I am, just as abruptly as I am doing today while waiting my turn at the barber's. The other one, too large, permitted too much affectation.

. . . I've done nothing worth while; my relaxed mind has drifted aimlessly. I *must* decide to go and see a doctor. I should have made up my mind to do so three or four years ago. I have resigned myself too long to being tired and to getting along on a reduced vigor. Absurd! What do I care about the severity of a regime if it allows me to work more! What have I produced up to now compared with what I should have produced? For the last four years I have been floundering and marking time.

Sunday

Reached Cuverville yesterday. The weather is so beautiful that this day is related to the happiest days of my childhood. I am writing this in the big room above the kitchen, between the two open windows through which the sun's warm joy surges in. Nothing but my own tired reflection in the mirror hanging above my table is an obstacle to the fullest development of my happiness. (I need to learn all over again, and methodically, how to be happy. It's a form of gymnastics, like exercise with dumbbells; it can be *achieved*.) I stretch out my feet in the sunlight, in green and blue list slippers. The warmth enters into me, rises inside me like sap. To be utterly happy, nothing more is needed but to refrain from comparing this moment with other moments of the past—which I often did not fully enjoy because I was comparing them with other moments of the future. This moment is no less full of delight than any other moment of the future or of the past. The grass of the lawn is deep, like the grass in a churchyard. The apple trees in the farmyard are nothing but thick tufts of blossom. The whitewashed trunks prolong their whiteness right down to the ground. Every breath of air brings me some perfume, especially that of the wisteria, on the left there, against the house, so overloaded with blossoms that one can hear its bees from here. A bee has come into this room and doesn't want to leave. The light anoints each object as with honey.

Yesterday before sunset I had just time to visit the garden thoroughly. The big apple tree leaning toward the tennis court, smiling and rustling in the last rays of the sun, was becoming pink. A frightful shower, a few hours before, had submerged the countryside and purged the sky of all clouds. Every bit of foliage was brimming as with tears, particularly that of the two big copper beeches, not yet copper-colored, but transparent and blond, which fell about me like soft hair. When, going out by the little gate in the bottom of the garden, I saw the sun again and the luminous cliff in front of it formed by the grove of beeches, everything struck me as so affectionately beautiful, so new, that I could have wept with joy. With me tears are not the exclusive privilege of sorrow, but also of admiration, of emotion, of a sudden and violent sympathy, of excessive joy. I cannot remember ever having wept, since childhood, for a personal sorrow, and yet I weep so easily, so willingly; in the theater the mere name of Agamemnon is enough: I weep torrents. From that physical accompaniment my emotion derives the guarantee of its authenticity.

The violence of this emotion had all but overwhelmed me. On going in I had a rather sharp headache, and immediately after dinner, heavy with sleep, went to bed.

. . . Tuesday

. . . I live with all the incoherence of a lyric poet, but two or three ideas, crosswise in my brain and rigid like parallel bars, crucify every joy; everything that would like to try its wings at random runs into them. . . .

It is frightening how much I have aged recently. Certainly something is not right inside me. It is impossible to age more rapidly or to be more aware of it. I cannot yet take this seriously, believing it a passing fatigue. Already I experienced this hideous aging last year, at the same time of year.

Wednesday

Strange drowsiness of the mind and of the flesh. Lethargy. After a great (and unsuccessful) effort this morning to wind up my first chapter, I plunge into reading (Dostoevsky's *From the Notes of an Unknown Man*).

Excellent reading of Darwin (aloud). The moments spent with Em. (particularly in the garden) are extraordinarily pleasant. Her affection, her charm, her poetry make a kind of glow around her in which I warm myself, in which my fretful mood melts.

After having labored over it for several hours, I find my work sud-

denly deciding to progress toward evening, and I make up my mind to
remain here one day more.

Thursday

No; Albert's health worries me too much. I leave, in a hurry to see him
again. . . .

The weather is cold and rainy; I should leave Cuverville without
regret if I were not leaving Em. there, and some roses ready to open.

Although I have been rather sickly, these three days spent with her
were close enough to happiness.

Friday, 18

Returned to Paris last night.

Finished the Dostoevsky in the train.

Saturday

Prolonged insomnia. Keen suffering in my pride; this would lead to madness if daylight did not come soon enough. Yes, that position was easy
enough to take; it is cruelly painful to maintain.

Ægri somnia.

Artisan of my own suffering!

When I am *well* again, I shall blush at these confessions. Let's get to
work.

May 25

Anguish—bewilderment.

I interrupt this journal; dreadful fatigue.

Leaving for Geneva. I am going to get the advice of Dr. Andréæ.

October 4

Sudden departure from Cuverville for La Poissonnière, in answer to a sad
letter from Albert that Em. brought back from Criquetot yesterday evening. Walk last night, together, in the garden full of moonlight and
shadow, late, after the others had gone up to bed. It is so warm that we are
not even wearing coats. My heart is tender and ready to melt. I hope so
much that Albert does not die in despair.

I arrive. Albert is there in bed, waiting for me.

"Oh, why did you come?" he exclaims, smiling. I sense that he is almost embarrassed not to be more seriously ill. I embrace him.

"But your letter frightened me, old man. I have come to reassure myself."

He takes my hand, presses it gently.

"I should have done the same."

Tired out from trying to sleep, he gets up; he wanders along the deserted corridors. In vain he seeks the sleep that would save him. His thought flutters within him like the sail abandoned by every propitious wind. And while the night wanes, he listens to his strength ebbing slowly within him.

November 23

It hurts me to write Jammes so flatly. But what else can I do? . . . His nose is no longer susceptible to anything but incense.

1907   *January 1*

First Jeanne, then Gérard, tell me of Arthur Fontaine's application to Briand to get me a decoration. M., Briand's chief private secretary, came to tell them on Saturday. Since M. knows nothing of Fontaine's friendship for me (which, moreover, would seem inexplicable to him), M. will certainly think that I have been putting myself out for this silly business, and yet, to speak truly, I knew nothing about it. This is profoundly distasteful to me. . . .

M. does not like me; he doesn't hide his scorn and aversion for everything I write. . . .

M. is not exactly a hypocrite; but all the same he plays an underhand game. He is small. I am suspicious of small men. For a long time I have been telling Gérard he must be afraid of M. Some day I shall try to sketch this small character, held upright by moral principles so as not to lose an inch of his height. He shows himself full of affection, of sensibility; but one always feels that he hasn't much to expend. Perfect type of climber. He succeeds by means of patience, of minute economy, of hygiene. He succeeds in everything. Forever up to his best, he considers his constancy as wisdom and calls virtue the lack of turbulence of his desires. But enough about him.

I have wasted my morning in writing him. . . .

Thursday

Barrès's formal reception into the Academy. For the first time in my life I enter the small enclosure. Paul-A. Laurens, at whose house we had lunched and who is with us, withdraws before the mob.

Why speak here of what all the newspapers will be full of? We leave before Vogüé's speech.

Barrès wears the frightful uniform as elegantly as one can. Of all of us he has changed the least. How I like his thin face, his flattened-down hair, even his common accent! What a flat speech he made! And how I suffered from the touches of cowardice, the flatteries, the concessions to the opinion of his audience, which are perhaps natural to him (I mean for which he probably did not have to distort his thought, but which met a too easy applause here); and also his thrust at Zola!

I was not the only one to notice the care with which, praising the family of Heredia, he said nothing of the sons-in-law.*

Will no one bring out with what strange and crafty cleverness this master sophist enrolled in his camp, in order to praise them, those two "uprooted" masters: Leconte de Lisle and Heredia? (And Chénier! and Moréas!)

Left the Academy quite demoralized with fatigue and melancholy. Another day like this and I shall be ready for religion.

Em. wonders whether she would like to see me (and whether I can see myself) pronouncing a speech in my turn in the Academy.

"I certainly am not heading in that direction, my dear. I am less and less attracted to gatherings in which I am not allowed to snort as much as I want."

That remark of Barrès's against Zola, as I reread it, makes me even more angry. There is some spiritual baseness in never exaggerating anything but profitable opinions.

February 6

Have forsaken this notebook the last few days, but for the sake of work. I am composing an *Enfant prodigue,* in which I am trying to put into a dialogue all the reticences and impulses of my spirit.

This morning, a letter from Claudel; a letter full of a sacred wrath,

* Barrès was elected to fill the chair of José-Maria de Heredia, one of whose sons-in-law was Pierre Louÿs.

against the epoch, against Gourmont, Rousseau, Kant, Renan. . . . Holy wrath no doubt, but wrath all the same and just as painful to my mind as the barking of a dog is to my ear. I cannot endure it, and cover my ears at once. But I hear it nevertheless and then have trouble getting back to work.

February 9

Valéry will never know how much friendship it costs me to listen to his conversation without exploding. I go away black and blue all over. Yesterday I spent almost three hours with him. Afterward nothing was left standing in my mind.

Going out with me, he accompanied me to the Bois de Boulogne. I had taken my skates, which had been lying in a packing-case for the last ten years, and, to my surprise, I didn't find them too rusty on the ice. Valéry did not leave me an instant; I suffered to see him waiting for me, so that I hardly skated at all. Leaving there with him, I abandoned him in front of the Charles Gides', where I went up to get news of Gérard.

And, of course, impossible to work this evening. After such a "conversation," everything in my head is in a state of havoc.

Valéry's conversation throws me into this *frightful* alternative: either consider everything he says absurd or else consider absurd everything I am doing. If he suppressed *in reality* everything he suppresses in conversation, I should no longer have any reason for existing. Moreover I never argue with him; he merely strangles me and I struggle back.

February 12

Yesterday went to see some paintings with Rouart. Very beautiful Gauguins, Van Goghs, Cézannes. But I was rather tired by my irritating day yesterday. I had to go to see *Notre-Dame de Paris,* as a tribute to De Max (in the role of Claude Frollo). I had made an appointment with Jean Schlumberger to help me endure the play. But he hadn't been able to come.

During the first half hour the artifice and absurdity of the play give me a desire to slap my neighbors; I think I can put up with only an act of it. But De Max is only on stage between the ninth and tenth tableaux. Good, moreover; giving a semblance of existence to that odious, declamatory puppet. I leave immediately afterwards, unable to endure any more.

Last night Strauss's *Salome*. Ghéon repeats to us the remark of Mme Strauss (as reported by Viélé-Griffin), when she found that the Parisian audience did not sufficiently applaud her husband's work: "Well, it's about time that we came back here with bayonets." Perhaps apocryphal. . . .

Abominable romantic music, with enough orchestral rhetoric to make one like Bellini. Only the parts filled with comic (the priests) or morbid relief, Salome's hesitations when Herod wants her to dance for him—almost the entire role of Herod, show a remarkable *savoir faire*. Lasserre notes the same excellence of comic truculence in Hugo—likewise in the *Meistersinger*—the same causes. Same causes for the shortcomings, too: indiscretion of means and monotony of effects, tiresome insistency, flagrant insincerity; uninterrupted mobilization of all the possible resources. Likewise Hugo, likewise Wagner; when metaphors come into his head to express an idea, he will not choose, will not spare us a single one. Fundamental inartistry in all this. Systematic amplification, etc. . . . A flaw that it is not even interesting to examine. One might better condemn the work as a whole and wait for the bayonets, because art like this *is* the real enemy.

Lunched at the Tour d'Argent with the Van Rysselberghes, Count Kessler, and Rodin. We talk to the last of his artistic "debut." For a long time, to earn his living, he makes "Carrier-Belleuses" of terracotta.* It is one of these poor insipid things that Druet recently exhibited in his window.

With *The Age of Bronze* he arouses a protest; he barely avoids a trial with great difficulty (he is accused of having exhibited a mere cast of a man). But at that moment some friends gather round to defend him. That is when he leaves Brussels for Paris.

"How old were you then?"

"Forty-Five."

This dominated my day.

. . . Vast disgust with almost all the literary production of today and with the "public's" satisfaction with it. I am ever more convinced that to obtain a success *beside* one of these successes could not satisfy me. It is

---

* Decorative statuettes named for a popular French sculptor.

better to withdraw. Know how to wait; even if I have to wait until after death. To long for lack of recognition is the secret of the noblest patience. In the beginning, with such remarks, I used to feed my pride with words. But not any more. The height of one's pride can be measured by the depth of one's scorn.

Dined *quattro giorni fa* at R.N.'s on my way back from a visit to Maillol at Marly. Very pleasant dinner, like all the dinners at the charming R.N.'s house; with a fat idiot whom I had already met through Rouart and who is named—no one knows why—Victor. His outthrust jaw, prolonged by a sort of goatee, makes him look as if he had just come down from the Ægina pediment. He grits his teeth and clenches his fists as he talks; he impresses himself as a wild man and cannot emit the most banal aphorisms without frenzy. He says: "Art? It's a vice." Emits a whistle: "I, for instance, the day before yesterday I bought all at once forty Valtats: it's a vice!" He also says: "Catholicism has made of this world a vast hollow top." He has his own ideas on religion and, after dinner, enlightens me on metaphysics, or rather on theology. He says: "The Greeks! The Greeks!" and that is enough. At table could be heard already (but since he was speaking to the ladies, there was a shade of irony in his voice): "The nature of religion . . . yes! . . . or the religion of nature . . . one or the other . . . or perhaps a bit of both. . . . Don't you think so, Madame Gide?" And my wife pretended not to hear.

And this pig is a painter. He paints on wood because his frantic brush-strokes would go right through the canvas. With this detail I leave him.

I let him believe that I am very much like him. (He says: "The Church," then adds, so that you will be sure of understanding: *"Ecclesia!"* He says: "What we need today is a cult—*cultus,* rites . . ." then, doubtless failing to find the Latin word or the Greek word, he contents himself with repeating it, rolling the *r* a bit more: *"Rrites."*)

I am merely a little boy having a good time—coupled with a Protestant pastor who annoys him.

October 18

I am writing on Anna Shackleton's little table, which was in my room at rue de Commailles. This is where I used to work; I liked it because in the double mirror of the dressing-table, above the shelf on which I was writing, I could see myself writing; after every sentence I would look at myself; my image spoke to me, listened to me, kept me company, kept me in a state of fervor. I had never since written at this table. These last few evenings I have been recapturing my childhood sensations.

October 24

. . . I am beginning to be tired of *not being;* as soon as a great enthusiasm does not sustain me, I am lost. Wounded vanity has never produced anything that matters, but at times my pride suffers from a real despair. And I live certain days as if in the nightmare of the man who was walled up alive in his tomb. Frightful state, which it is good to know, to have known. I shall write about it later when I have got out of it. . . .

I think of Keats. I tell myself that two or three passionate admirations like mine would have kept him alive. Useless efforts; I feel at times utterly enervated by the silence.

November 19

. . . After many reservations I launch into the reading of *La Porte étroite.* Very imperfect reading at first, since the first two chapters are still pastily amorphous in spots; rather dull reading altogether. . . . What causes me so much trouble in writing this book is the same thing that causes them (I am thinking chiefly of Ghéon) so much trouble in listening to it: it remains an anachronism amidst everything that we are thinking, feeling, wanting today. But no matter: I cannot not write it; and from this somewhat crushing trial I emerge, after all, less depressed than reaffirmed.

1908   *January 25*

Inquiry conducted by the *Berliner Tageblatt.*

On the occasion of the twenty-fifth anniversary of Wagner's death, they are interested in sounding out "the leading artistic and intellectual figures of all Europe as to their opinion of the influence of Wagnerism, especially in France."

I reply: "I hold the person and the work of Wagner in horror; my passionate aversion has grown steadily since my childhood. This amazing genius does not exalt so much as he *crushes.* He permitted a large number of snobs, of literary people, and of fools to think that they loved music, and a few artists to think that genius can be acquired. Germany has perhaps never produced anything at once so great and so barbarous."

Radiant weather; a blue sky we had forgotten during the last three months. My spirits full of gaiety, I go to return the Signoret proofs to the *Mercure;* get tickets at the Odéon for tomorrow's lecture (Moréas on *Electra*); I walk back with Henry Davray to his new apartment on the rue Servandoni. Go to take his ticket to Eugène Rouart, at the Ministry. It is too late to return home—besides, it is too beautiful. I go to lunch alone (for one franc seventy-five, tip included) in the little restaurant on the place Sainte-Clotilde where Ghéon and I lunched a month ago. Then obliged to drop in at the Ecole Alsacienne (a matter of straightening out an old bill), I go up the part of the boulevard Raspail that has been recently cut through, jumping over fences and wallowing somewhat in the vacant lots dug up by the construction gangs, but amused to the point of rapture by the odd aspect of those gutted houses on which the laughing sun sparkles. Old gardens, a well; caged trees, drooping and blackened; ancient courtyards, entrance steps of tumbledown private houses; all this dazzled and looking like a night bird that someone has suddenly plunged into the light. What a beautiful day!

Went to ring at Jean Schlumberger's, and he accompanied me for a moment to the Luxembourg while waiting for the school to open.—Old school; courtyard I hadn't entered in twenty years! I hardly recognized myself there—or old Papa Braünig, who spoke to me.

Back by *métro*—and work (Dostoevsky for *La Grande Revue*).

Trip to Italy—came back March 20.

Wrote to Em. every day.

Article on Dostoevsky (for *La Grande Revue*).

No more interest in keeping this journal.

Lunched yesterday at Albert Mockel's with Stefan George, Albert Saint-Paul, and a rather pleasant young man whom they called Olivier (I never could make out whether it was merely his first name). Wonderful head of

Stefan George, whom I have long wanted to know and whose work I admire each time I manage to understand it. Bluish-white complexion, skin dull and more drawn than wrinkled, sharply defined bone structure; impeccably shaved; abundant, thick mane of hair, still more black than gray and all thrown straight back. Hands of a convalescent, very delicate, bloodless, very expressive. He speaks little, but in a deep voice that forces attention. A sort of clergyman's Prince Albert with two clasps toward the top, which opens for a cravat or scarf of black velvet, above and overflowing the collar. The simple gold slide on a ribbon leading to a watch or monocle gives a discreet accent to all this black. Shoes (elastic-sided, I fancy!) of a single piece of leather tightly gripping the foot, which I didn't like, perhaps because I had seen similar ones on Charmoy.

He expresses himself in our language without a single mistake, though yet a bit cautiously, it seems, and shows a surprising knowledge and understanding of our authors, particularly our poets; and all this without self-satisfaction, but with an evident awareness of his evident superiority.

May 16

A Bonnard is put up at auction,* rather badly put together, but racy; it represents a naked woman dressing and I have already seen it somewhere or other. It climbs rather painfully to 450, 55, 60. Suddenly I hear a voice shout: "600!"—And I am dazed, for the one who has just shouted is I. With my eyes I implore a higher bid from those around me—for I have no desire to own the painting—but none is forthcoming. I feel myself turning crimson and begin to sweat in great drops. "It's stifling in here," I say to Lebey. We leave.

Absurd, such impulses. Already a similar experience had occurred to me before at the Drouot, as I recall. And the most stupid thing of all is to be cross with myself afterwards; generally speaking, it is only with difficulty that I can end up *on my own side.* (The oddest fact is that the bidding was still this side of 500 francs, so that in rounding out the sum they counted my bid as only 500 francs, as the bill showed the next day; and yet, I am certain, it was 600 francs that I shouted.)

July 28

Speaking of Valery Larbaud, Philippe said to Ruyters: "It is always a pleasure to meet someone next to whom Gide seems poor."

* At the Kessler sale, Hôtel Drouot.

October 18

I returned from Paris, where I had spent a week. Atrocious fatigue, which continues even after the Laurenses have left. Yet I finish *La Porte étroite* on the 15th—and on the 16th shave off my moustache. Shocked by the lack of expression of my upper lip (as if something that has never yet spoken could suddenly become eloquent). How old I seem! "My poor André!" Em. exclaims on seeing me. "You must see your mistake." (I do not see it so readily as all that.)

1909   *Monday, April 25 or 26*

Preview of the Nadelman exhibit at Druet's. (Elie Nadelman is the young Polish-Jewish sculptor to whose lair Alexandre Natanson took me, as I related last winter.) . . .

Nadelman went through six years of dire poverty; closed up in his den, he seemed to live on plaster; Balzac might have invented him. I find him yesterday, in a little blue suit he is doubtless wearing for the first time, talking with a very vulgar and very ugly woman whom he introduces: it is Mme X. She says, pointing to the rhomboidal back of one of the statues: "That, at least, is living! It's not like their Venus de Milo! What do I care whether she's beautiful or not? That, at least, is a real woman! It's living!" And there is precisely no epithet less applicable to Nadelman's art— which is still only a technique, and rudimentary at that. Most likely Stein likes it because it can be grasped without effort. Stein is the American collector, a great buyer of Matisses. Nadelman's exhibit has hardly opened, but he has already bought two-thirds or three-fourths of the drawings; at what price? This I don't know; but in the office of the gallery I witness this little *genre* scene: Druet takes out from under a table a plaster head, or at least the outline of a head, without eyes, nose, or mouth; in short, about as well formed as a baby chick on the third day the hen has been setting.

"How much do you want for it?"

"What! You are exhibiting it?" (I can understand the surprise; even in our era that unformed thing is not exhibitable.)

"No," says Druet; "I am keeping it in reserve; I don't want to be caught short."

"Well, I don't know . . ."

"Make up your mind. I'll act as auctioneer. . . . Come on, now: one! two! three! . . ."

"Two hundred francs!"

"Oh, it's too much! it's too much!" says Druet, taken aback that the other has entered so well into the spirit of his role.

And Nadelman in turn: "Well then, set a figure yourself. Come on: one! two! . . ."

"A hundred francs! That's enough."

And Druet leaves with the head.

July 4

Going through Paris for the review copies of *La Porte étroite,* I stop at the Valérys' to get news of Jeannie Valéry, on whom there was some question of operating. Degas is with her and has been wearing her out for more than an hour, for he is very hard of hearing and she has a weak voice. I find Degas aged, but always the same; just a bit more obstinate, more set in his opinion, exaggerating his crustiness, always scratching the same spot in his brain where the itching is becoming more and more localized. He says: "Ah, those who work from nature! What impudent humbugs! The landscapists! When I meet one of them in the countryside, I always have a great desire to start shooting. Bang! Bang!" (He raises his cane, closes an eye, and aims at the drawing-room furniture.) "There ought to be a police force to take charge of that." Etc., etc. And again: "Art criticism! What nonsense! I am accustomed to saying" (and in fact I remember hearing him say exactly the same things three or four years ago) "that the Muses never talk among themselves; each one works in her domain; and when they aren't working, they dance." And twice more he repeats: "When they aren't working, they dance." And again: "The day when people began to write *Intelligence* with a capital *I,* everything was shot. There is no such thing as Intelligence; one has intelligence of this or of that. One must have intelligence only for what one is doing."

[*The Death of Charles-Louis Philippe*]

No! no, it wasn't the same thing. . . . This time, he who disappears is a *real* man. We were counting on him; we depended on him; we loved him. And suddenly he is no longer there.

On the way to Cérilly

I am writing this in the train that carries me away—where I am still chatting with him. Already my recollections are confused. If I did not fix them today—today, when I am already utterly crushed—tomorrow I should get them all mixed up.

Saturday evening a note from Marguerite Audoux tells me that Philippe is ill.

Sunday morning I rush to his place, on the quai Bourbon; his concierge sends me to the Dubois hospital; no one has heard of him there. I learn that three persons who came to ask for him the day before went away as uninformed as I. Mme Audoux's card bears no indication. . . . What shall I do? . . . Doubtless Francis Jourdain can give me some news; I write him. The telegram I receive from him on Tuesday morning already deprives me of all hope; I rush to the address he gives me.

At the end of the corridor in the Velpeau hospital a room door remains open. Philippe is there. Ah, what does it matter now that the long windows of that room open directly into a big bright garden! It would have been good for his convalescence; but already he has lost consciousness; he is still struggling, but has already left us.

I approach the bed where he is already on the verge of death; there are his mother, a friend whom I don't know, and Mme Audoux, who recognizes and welcomes me. I lead her out to the parlor for a minute.

Philippe has been here a week. At first the typhoid fever seemed very mild and, in the beginning, of so ill defined a character that it was treated as a simple grippe. Then, for several days, Philippe was treated as typhoid cases are treated today; but the regime of cold baths was very impractical in his little lodging on the quai Bourbon. Tuesday evening he was carried to the Velpeau hospital; nothing alarming until Sunday; then suddenly meningitis sets in; his heart beats wildly; he is lost. Dr. Elie Faure, his friend, who, against all hope, insists on affording him every possible care right up to the end, from time to time risks an injection of sparteine or of camphorated oil; but already the organism has ceased to react.

We return to the bedside. Yet how many struggles are still to come; and how difficult this poor suffering body finds it to resign itself to dying! He is breathing very fast and very hard—very badly, like someone who has forgotten how.

The muscles of his neck and of the lower part of his face tremble; one eye is half open, the other closed. I rush to the post office to send some telegrams; almost none of Philippe's friends has been informed.

At the Velpeau hospital again. Dr. Elie Faure takes the invalid's pulse. The poor mother asks: "How is the fever developing?" Through her suffering she is careful to speak correctly; she is a mere peasant, but she knows who her son is. And during these melancholy days, instead of tears, she sheds floods of words; they flow evenly, monotonously, without accent or melody, in a somewhat hoarse tone, which surprises at first, as if it were not interpreting her suffering properly; and her eyes remain dry.

After lunch I come back again; I cannot make this loss seem real. I find Philippe only slightly weaker, his face convulsed, shaken; struggling with slightly less energy against death.

Wednesday morning

Chanvin was waiting for me in the parlor. We are led, on the right side of the courtyard, to a little secret room, with an oblique entrance, hiding as if ashamed. The rest of the establishment does not know of its existence, for this is a *maison de santé,* a "house of health," which you enter only to be cured—and this is the chamber of the dead. The new guest is led into this room at night, when the rest of the house is asleep; on the bare wall a notice specifies: Not before 9 p.m. or after 7 a.m. And the guest will leave here only by way of that low door, the bolted door I see over there at the end of the room, opening directly on the other street. . . .

There he is: very small on a large shroud; wearing a brownish suit; very erect, very rigid, as if at attention for roll call. Hardly changed, moreover; his nostrils somewhat pinched; his little fists very white; his feet lost in big white socks rising up like two cotton nightcaps.

A few friends are in the room, weeping silently. The mother comes toward us, unable to weep, but moaning. To each new arrival she begins a new verse of her lament, like a professional mourner of antiquity. She is speaking not to us but to her son. She calls him; she leans over him, kisses him: "Good little boy!" she says to him. . . . "I knew all your little habits. . . . Ah, they'll close you up now! close you up forever. . . ."

At first this sorrow surprises one, so eloquent it is; no expression in the intonation, but an extraordinary invention in the terms of endearment . . . then, turning toward a friend, without changing her tone, she gives an exact indication as to the funeral charges or the time of departure. She wants to take her son away as quickly as possible, take him away from everybody, have him to herself, down in their country: "I'll go and see you every day, every day." She caresses his forehead. Then turning toward us again: "Oh, have pity on me, gentlemen! . . ."

Marguerite Audoux tells us that the last half hour was horrible. Several times everyone thought it was all over, the frightful breathing stopped; the mother would then throw herself onto the bed: "Stay with us a bit more, my dear! Breathe a bit more; once more! just once more!" And as if "the good little boy" heard her, in an enormous effort all his muscles could be seen to tighten, his chest to rise very high, very hard, and then fall back. . . . And Dr. Elie Faure, seized with despair, would exclaim sobbing: "But I did everything I could. . . ."

At nine o'clock in the evening he died.

At the *Mercure de France,* where the edition of the works of Lucien Jean, for which he was to write the preface, is being held up: while I talk with Vallette, Chanvin is writing some letters of mourning. The mother wants to take the body away this very night; at eight o'clock a brief farewell ceremony will gather together a few friends, either at the hospital or at the station. I shall not go, but want to see Philippe once more. We go back there. Léautaud accompanies us.

Here we are again in the mortuary room. Bourdelle has come to take the death mask; the floor is littered with splashes of plaster. Yes indeed, we shall be happy to have this exact testimony; but those who know him only through it will never imagine the full expression of this sturdy little fellow, whose whole body had such a special significance. Yes, Toulouse-Lautrec was just as short as he, but deformed; Philippe was upright; he had small hands, small feet, short legs; his forehead well formed. Beside him, after a short time, one became ashamed of being too tall.

In the courtyard a group of friends. In the room, the mother, Marguerite Audoux (oh, how beautiful the quality of her grief seems to me!), Fargue; Léautaud, very pale against his very black beard, is swallowing his emotion. The mother is still moaning; Fargue and Werth are examining a timetable; it is agreed that we shall meet tomorrow morning at the quai d'Orsay station for the eight-fifteen train.

Thursday, 8 o'clock

Quai d'Orsay station, where Chanvin and I arrive, fortunately well ahead of time, for there we discover that the eight-fifteen train leaves from the Gare de Lyon. Alas, how many friends, ill-informed as we were, will not have time to get to the other station as we do at once! We don't see one in the train as it takes us off. Yet several had promised to come.

All night long it rained and there was a strong wind; now the air, somewhat calmed, is warm; the countryside is drenched; the sky is desolate throughout.

We have taken tickets to Moulins. From the timetable that I buy in Nevers, I discover that to reach Cérilly still takes three or four hours from Moulins in a little dawdling train, plus a long ride in the stagecoach; and that the little train will have left when we arrive. Can we make that leg of the trip in a carriage?

In Moulins we meet with refusals from three coachmen; the distance is too great: we shall need an automobile. And here it is! We light out into the country. The air is not cold; the hour is beautiful. In a moment the wind wipes away our fatigue, even our melancholy, and speaking of Philippe we say: If you are watching us from some part of heaven, how amused you must be to see us racing after you like this along the road!

Beautiful country ravaged by winter and the storm; how delicate are the greens of the pastures on the violet edge of the sky!

Bourbon-l'Archambault. This is where your twin sister and your brother-in-law, the pastry-cook, live. Ah! here is the hearse coming back from Cérilly. . . . Evening is falling. We enter the little village just before nightfall. The auto is put in the coachhouse of the hotel where we have left our bags. Here we are on the village square. We are moving about in one of Philippe's books. We are told the way to his house. It is there on the road halfway up the hill, past the church, almost opposite the house of *Père Perdrix.** On the ground floor, the shutters of the only window are closed like the eyelids of someone plunged in meditation; but the door is ajar. Yes, this is the right place: someone opens the door as he leaves, and in the narrow room opposite the entrance, between two lighted candles, we see the coffin draped with black cloth and covered with wreaths. The mother rushes toward us, is amazed to see us; the ones her child loved so much! She introduces us to some village people who are there: friends come from Paris on purpose; she is proud of it. A woman is sobbing in a corner; it is his sister. Oh, how much she is like him! Her face explains our friend's, which was slightly deformed by a scar on the left side of the jaw which the beard did not quite hide. The brother-in-law comes up to us cordially and asks if we would like to see Charles-Louis's room before more people come.

The whole house is built on his scale; because it was very small, he came out of it very small. Beside the bed-sitting-room, which is the one you enter, the bright empty room where the maker of sabots, his father, used to work; it gets its light from a little court, as does Philippe's room

* A novel by Charles-Louis Philippe.

on the second floor. Small, unornamented room; on the right of the window, a little table for writing; above the table, some shelves with a few books and the high pile of all his school notebooks. The view one might have from the window is cut short by two or three firs that have grown right against the wall of the courtyard. That is all; and that was enough. Philippe was comfortable here.

The mother does the honors of the place: "Look carefully, gentlemen; this is all important if you are going to talk about him."

In the front of the house, the best parlor, in which is collected the little luxury of this humble dwelling: decorated mantel, framed portraits, draperies; this is the room that is never used.

"Even though we are poor people, you see that we are not in dire poverty."

She intends that at the hotel where we are staying we should consider ourselves as her guests as long as we remain in Cérilly.

"Do you want to see Papa Partridge's house?" the brother-in-law asks; "it should interest you."

And we go with him to the next-to-last house in the village; but the room in which we are received has been redone. As we are leaving, the brother-in-law leans toward us: "The man you see over there is Jean Morantin; you know, 'the lord of the village.' When Louis spoke of him in his book, people wanted to get him worked up. He said: No, no, I know little Philippe! He's a good boy; he certainly didn't intend to say anything bad about me."

We return to the hotel, where we find Valery Larbaud, just arrived from Vichy, and we spent the evening with him.

The funeral takes place Friday morning at ten o'clock. No other friend has come; yes, Guillaumin, the author of *La Vie d'un simple;* he lives on a farm thirteen kilometers from here. We still "hope" for a quarter of an hour more; Cérilly lies between several railroad lines and can be reached from several different directions. Finally the short procession starts moving.

Small gray-and-brown Romanesque church, filled with shadow and good counsel. The deacon comes toward us as we remain grouped around the coffin: "This way, gentlemen! Come this way, where we have a big fire."

And we approach a brazier near the apse. Twice during the cere-

mony the brother-in-law comes toward us; the first time to tell us that
Marcel Ray has just arrived from Montpellier with his wife; then, the
second time, leaning toward us: "You should visit the Chapel of the
Saints; my brother-in-law spoke of that too in his books."

The ceremony comes to an end; we make our way toward the cemetery.
The sky is overcast. Occasionally a low-moving cloud befogs the distant
landscape. Here we are before the open grave. On the other side of the
grave, opposite me, I watch his sister; she is sobbing, someone is supporting her. Is it really Philippe that we are burying? What lugubrious comedy are we playing here? —A village friend, decorated with a violet ribbon, a shopkeeper or functionary of Cérilly, steps forward with some
manuscript pages in his hand and begins his speech. He speaks of Philippe's shortness, of his unimpressive appearance, which prevented him
from attaining honors, of his successive failures in the posts he would have
liked to hold: "You were perhaps not a great writer," he concludes, "but
. . ." Nothing could be more stirring than this naïve reflection of the
modesty Philippe always showed in speaking of himself, by which this
excellent man was doubtless taken in. But some of us feel our hearts
wrung; I heard someone whisper near me: "He's making a failure out of
him!" And I consider for a moment stepping up before the grave myself
and saying that only Cérilly could speak so humbly of Philippe; that, seen
from Paris, Philippe's stature seems to us very great. . . . But, alas,
wouldn't Philippe suffer from the distance thus established between him
and those of his little village, from which his heart never wandered?

Moreover, Guillaumin follows the other speaker; his speech is brief,
full of measure and tact, very moving. He speaks of another child of
Cérilly who went away like Philippe and died at thirty-five like him, just a
century ago: the naturalist Perron. A little monument on the square im-
mortalizes him. I shall copy straightaway the pious and touching inscrip-
tion:

PERRON

DRIED UP LIKE

A YOUNG TREE

THAT SUCCUMBS

UNDER THE WEIGHT

OF ITS OWN FRUIT

Another side of the monument bears a bronze relief showing François Perron seated under a mangrove with cockatoos perched on the branches, in an Australian landscape inhabited by friendly kangaroos.

An automobile stops at the gate of the cemetery; it is Fargue, arriving just as the speeches are ending.

I am happy to see him here; his grief is very great, like that of all who are here; but it seems, besides, that Fargue represents a whole group of absent friends—the very best of friends, in fact—and that he comes to bring their homage.

We return to the hotel, where Mme Philippe invites us to dinner; her son-in-law, M. Tournayre, represents her. I am seated beside him; he tells me certain details of his brother-in-law's early childhood: "Already at the age of five or six," he said, "little Louis used to play 'going to school'; he had made up little notebooks, which he would put under his arm and then say: 'Good-bye, *maman;* I am going to school.'

"Then he would sit down in a corner of the other room, on a stool, turning his back to everything. . . . Finally, a quarter of an hour later, the imaginary class being over, he would *come home: 'Maman,* school is over.'

"But one fine day, without saying a word to anyone, slipping out of the house, he really went to school; he was only six; the teacher sent him home. Little Louis came back again. Then the teacher asked: 'What have you come here for?' 'Why—to learn.'

"He is sent home again; he is too young. The child insists so much that he gets a dispensation. And thus he begins his patient education."

O "good little boy"! I understand now what made you like so much, later on, *Jude the Obscure.* Even more than your gifts as a writer, than your sensitivity, than your intelligence, how much I admire that wondering application which was but one form of your love!

We leave.

And during the whole trip I think of that article which I had promised him to write, was getting ready to write, on the appearance of his book, which Fasquelle is to publish any moment now—that article which he was waiting for. I fix the various points in my mind.

Philippe's death cannot make me exaggerate my praise in any regard; at most, by bringing me more sadly closer to that moving figure and by allowing me to study him better (in the papers he left behind), it will strengthen my admiration by sharpening the contours.

Some people only half knew him because they saw only his pity, his affection, and the exquisite qualities of his heart; with that alone he could not have become the wonderful writer that he was. A great writer meets more than one requirement, answers more than one doubt, satisfies various appetites. I have only the most limited admiration for those who cannot be seen from all sides, who appear deformed when looked at from an angle. Philippe could be examined from all directions; to each of his friends, each of his readers, he seemed very much whole and complete; yet no two of them saw the same Philippe. And the various praises addressed to him may well be equally justified, but each one taken alone does not suffice. He has in him what is needed to disorient and surprise—what is needed, that is to say, to endure.

1910   *January 16*

Copeau asks me to go with him to the Bibescos'; he is to be introduced to Chaumeix. I overcome my apprehension of the frightful drudgery that a society dinner is for me and get out of the closet the dress suit I bought for my marriage, which I have not worn a dozen times. At Copeau's, on the rue Montaigne, where I go to pick him up, we notice that my trousers are terribly eaten by moths! Laughter and anguish; impossible to show myself this way! The white of my underpants appears in odd patterns; we light on the black felt ribbon of a panama hat; and here we are sewing little squares and stripes onto my underpants opposite the holes.

January 20

Ghéon is with me and in a moment will go with me to the Countess de Noailles's. It's a question of getting from her the review of *La Mère et l'enfant** that she has consented to do for *La Nouvelle Revue Française*.

Mme de Noailles is at the hotel (Princess Hotel) on the rue de Presbourg; the windows of her room look out on the Arc de Triomphe. She was expecting us, and this is rather apparent: she is lying on a chaise-longue made up of two armchairs and a stool that all fit together, sinuously draped in a sort of Romanian or Greek robe of black tussah silk with a broad band of whitish-gray, of that soft white one finds in China

* A book by Charles-Louis Philippe.

paper and certain Japanese felts; the chemise floats amply around her bare arms loaded with Venetian bracelets. A scarf wanders around her, the color of the yolk of a hard-boiled, or rather a soft-boiled egg; the color of dried apricots. Like a mermaid, her body ends mysteriously under a Tunisian cloth. Her hair is undone, abandoned, and jet-black; cut in bangs on her forehead, but falling as if wet onto her shoulders. She introduces us to the Princess de Caraman-Chimay (?), who trains on me a lorgnette that she doesn't put down during the entire visit.

Impossible to set down anything from the conversation. Mme de Noailles talks with an amazing volubility; the sentences rush to her lips, crush themselves, become confused; she says three or four at a time. This makes a very tasty compote of ideas, sensations, images, a tutti-frutti accompanied by gestures of the hands and arms, of the eyes especially, which she turns skyward in a swoon that is not too artificial but rather too encouraged.

Speaking of Montfort in passing, she compares him to a tench with great goggle eyes, and imitates the fish when it comes up against the glass of the aquarium. This striking, very apt image makes us laugh, and as later on we allude to it, she becomes quite worried: "Now don't go repeating that. Oh, I beg of you, don't say that I said it! You would make me an enemy of him. And I am always promising myself never to say anything bad about anyone!"

Ghéon, very much a wondering yokel just off the train at the Gare d'Orsay with great muddy boots, but, as always, very much at ease, is much more interested, fascinated, than he expected. One would have to hold oneself very much in check not to succumb to the charm of this extraordinary poetess with the boiling brain and the cold blood.

April 24

My most recent adventures have left me an inexpressible disgust.

June 17

. . . Oh, if only man, instead of so often contributing to the spreading of the vulgar, instead of systematically pursuing with his hatred or his cupidity the natural ornament of the earth, the most colorful butterfly, the most charming bird, the largest flower; if he brought his ingenuity to bear on protecting, not on destroying but on favoring—as I like to think that people do in Japan, for instance, because it is so very far from France! . . .

Were a miracle to produce in our woods some astounding orchid, a thousand hands would stretch out to tear it up, to destroy it. If the bluebird happens to fly past, every gun is sighted; and then people are amazed that it is rare!

Van de Velde sends me, in a supplement to the *Berliner Tageblatt,* an article on Nietzsche (by Karl-Georg Wendriner) of August 22, in which I read: "Thus Nietzsche entered eternity as a corrupter of youth."
    This is perhaps the most tempting path.

NOVEL

He will say: "The taste for sensual pleasure has always been deplorably keen in me—to the point where it often dominated all others. But often a sort of curiosity preceded and even commanded my desire.
    "The fortuitous invitation of pleasure at times made me miss a whole trip."

The young men I have known who were most crazy about automobile-driving were, to begin with, the least interested in traveling. The pleasure is no longer that of seeing the country or even of quickly reaching a certain place, where nothing really attracts them; but simply that of going fast. And though one enjoys thereby sensations just as deeply inartistic or anti-artistic as those of mountain-climbing, it must be admitted that they are intense and indomitable. The period that has known them will suffer the consequences; it is the period of impressionism, of the rapid and superficial vision; one can guess what gods and altars it will choose; through lack of respect, consideration, and consistency, it will sacrifice even more on those altars, but in an unconscious or unavowed manner.

At St.-Gilles, the rue Emile-Zola, as is fitting, leads to the church. On the pediment of which, above the sculptured portico, a municipality with the purest taste has had painted in enormous letters:

REPUBLIQUE FRANÇAISE
LIBERTE—EGALITE—FRATERNITE

Edge of the Garonne, August 18

Feel voluptuously that it is more natural to go to bed naked than in a nightshirt. My window was wide open and the moon shone directly on my bed. I remembered with anguish the beautiful night of the Ramier; but I felt no desire, either in my heart or in my mind any more than in my flesh. With what stiflings would I have heard last year Armand's flute, this evening, calling me doubtfully in the darkness. O stammering melody, how I loved you on the edge of the desert! . . . But this was not even a regret; I was calm.

Bourg-Madame, the gate of Spain, owes whatever favor it enjoys entirely to the proximity of Puigcerdá. Baedeker tells us that Puigcerdá is frequented by Spanish high society. At the hour when we arrive—that is, at the end of the day—the high society is wildly deserting the town; sumptuous autos are whizzing down the slope we are climbing. Where are they going? We shall find out an hour later when, going back down to Bourg-Madame, we find them all parked along the single short street. Between five and seven o'clock, the autos of Puigcerdá go down to fill up with gasoline, which costs less in France. How rich they are! For a horn, some of them sport a dragon of gilded copper which seems to have flown over from Brazil. Nothing to do, nothing to see, nothing to drink at Bourg-Madame. For a distance of twenty yards a row of wooden benches lines the houses; there sit the señoras and señoritas of the high society, of which each Spanish auto unloads on the pavement of Bourg-Madame eight to twelve representatives. Other señoras and most of the men remain standing without saying a word, apparently without thinking of anything. All of them, of both sexes, very ugly, very vulgar, insolently rich, and immensely stupid. What do they do the rest of the day? Now that their autos have drunk, what are they waiting for? . . . On the other side of the street, the chauffeurs are taking on the airs of Spanish grandees.

At seven we sit down to dinner; all the autos are still there. At a quarter past seven, when I get up to see what has become of them, all the autos have disappeared.

October 17

I fear I shall soon have to struggle against a false image of me that is being drawn, a monster to which my name is given, which is being set up in my place, and which is terrifyingly ugly and stupid.

November 14

Finished my novel* the night before last—with too great ease, and this makes me fear that I did not put into the last pages all that I was *charged* to put in.

There were not very many to notice that I had never written anything more nearly perfect than *Amyntas.* People looked for descriptions, for the picturesque, for information about the country and its customs. There is hardly anything in the book that I could not just as well have written elsewhere, in France, anywhere. But to whom could the secret value of the book speak? To a few rare souls; the rest were disappointed.

1911   *May 8*

At the studio of R.B., a painter and engraver, perhaps a Jew, certainly a Russian—who wants to do a portrait of me. This kind of flattery will always get me. This portrait (dry-point) is to figure in an album together with a very few others: Rodin, Bartholomé, both sculptors; two painters, Besnard and Renoir; two musicians, Debussy and Bruneau; two philosophers, Bergson and Poincaré, etc. . . . Finally Verhaeren, who introduced him to my *Porte étroite* and has sent him to me.

It is in Montmartre, rue V. . . . You ring at the third-floor apartment but have to go down an inside staircase to reach the studio, on the level of the second floor or even between the first and second, for I fancy that the house has two studios for every three floors. A universal man, B. indulges—with the same genius and no shame whatever—in sculpture, engraving, and oil painting. Right now he would like to make stage sets for R. Like many today, he proves to himself that he is a colorist by using only the wildest colors; he has a cruel eye. He intends to achieve mystery by ignoring the problems of design. You can recognize in a large ceramic woman, half-naked, the same model as in a big portrait reproducing the harmonies of a wild parrot (buttercup background, aspidistra-green dress, tomato-colored book in her hand): his wife.

Considerable time is spent in seeking the pose I am to take. As soon a I am settled, I like the long silence of this study; for me, usually so easily distracted by some muscular impatience, this forced immobility invites my thought to roam; but B. wants to talk. I foresee even worse: twice, smiling

* *Isabelle.*

at the sheet of metal he is cutting into, he said: "There is someone upstairs who is burning to meet you." Suddenly, starting at a little sound from the upper floor—which must be a signal: "Véra! Véra! You know that Monsieur Gide is here. We are waiting for you!"

The woman of the portrait comes down the steps smiling at my reflection in a large mirror in front of which I am posing.

Mme B. was born on Réunion Island, whence the sparkle of her lips and the languor in her eyes. Uncorseted, the points of her well-formed breasts can be seen through the thin tussah silk of her blouse; voluptuous face and body; auburn-red hair arranged in a turban around her head. A little more familiarity with the fair sex would have warned me that *la belle Véra* wrote, and that she planned to take advantage of my pose in order to inflict a reading on me. The conversation (to which, moreover, I contributed as little as possible, for fear of breaking my pose) had no other purpose than to lead up to that reading. But the subject had to be approached from a distance. B. told me his desire to add two women to his album. "Probably Madame Curie on the one hand . . . and Madame de Noailles." But this first attempt not having started anything, the conversation was falling off when, at some turning or other, after we had talked of the husband's universal gifts, quite innocently I asked: "And you, madame, what do you do?"

"I? Oh, nothing," she replied in haste.

A silence during which B., leaning over his sheet of metal, smiles with a knowing air, then, cupping his hand as if to keep his voice from anyone but me: "She writes."

Whereupon Véra: "Will you be quiet! How absurd he is! Monsieur Gide, don't listen to him. . . . Can it be called 'writing' when all you do is set down on paper a few poems that you can't keep to yourself? . . . When I read them to Verhaeren, he wouldn't believe that I was not accustomed to writing. . . . But why should I write? This is what I ask myself every day in front of my sheet of paper: Who would be interested in this?" (And repeating her sentence with an accent on each syllable): "Who would be in-ter-est-ed-in-this?—Who *could* be interested in it? . . ." (Obviously she is waiting for me to reply: "Why—perhaps I would," but as I remain silent, she becomes more precise): "Come, Monsieur Gide, I ask you."

Then B., coming to her aid: "When the emotion is sincere . . ."

And she: "Oh, as for the sincerity! . . . In fact it's very odd: I begin without knowing what I shall write; when I reread, it's always lines of poetry; I write in meter despite myself; yes, I can't do anything about it, everything I write is in meter. Monsieur Gide, I wish you would tell me: Do you think it's possible to achieve anything by work and pruning? . . ."

Here, somewhat stupidly, I try to establish a distinction between the two words, suggesting that *"work* does not necessarily imply *pruning."* But I am not understood and it is better to skip it. The conversation starts off again on a new track.

"Do you know Verhaeren very well? What a charming conversationalist! Have you heard him tell stories? Ah! the other day at St.-Cloud we spent the whole day telling each other stories. . . . Indeed, that is one of the things that has encouraged me to write. 'It would be criminal not to write up these recollections!' he told me. That was after I had just told him about my grandfather's death. . . . Just imagine, two coffins had been ordered! Yes, two coffins; the maid had made a mistake. . . . That morning two dealers arrived, each one with his coffin; of course a heated dialogue followed; you can guess that, despite the circumstances, each one could hardly keep from laughing. One was pointing out the quality of the wood, the other the comfort of his cushions. Finally I remember that my uncle managed to get rid of one of them, who said to him as he left: 'I'll take the coffin away, but I see that you will be needing it soon.' Do you agree that I ought to write this one up? . . . Verhaeren claims that in Brittany he saw this sign in a shop window: 'Hygienic coffins. . . .' But X." (I don't remember what important name she used), "who was with us, exclaimed, 'With poets you never know where reality ends. . . .' It's like this other memory he liked so much. . . . Just imagine that I had got into the habit of buying a bouquet of flowers every morning from a little Paris urchin of about fourteen who was always in the same spot. According to the season it was violets or mimosa. . . . This went on for two years. Finally one day I was unable to go out, but a friend of mine who knew the urchin gave him my address so that he could take the bouquet to me. I see the urchin arrive and, as soon as the door is open, he throws the bouquet at me across the room, shouting: 'Ah, you think urchins don't feel anything! Yes, every day for the past two years, when you pass you look at me and you don't see that I am also looking at you. . . . Ah! you think that Paris urchins don't feel anything, because they haven't the right to say anything? . . .' And, slamming the door, he dashes away. I never saw him again. . . ."

I: "He killed himself."

She, dreamily: "Perhaps . . . Oh, I have many recollections of that kind!"

I: "And that is what you write?"

She: "No. But it comes to the same thing; what I write is, after all, made up of memories. For instance, I read Verhaeren a poem he liked very much—that is, he thought the form wasn't perfect, but the feeling was there all right."

He: "That's the important thing!"

Etc. . . . etc. . . .

"My hair is coming down," she said, stepping in front of the mirror; "I must go up and fix it."

She disappears, and reappears a moment later.

"Let's see, Monsieur Gide, if you have any Sherlock Holmes in you. Guess what I have in my right hand?" (She is holding her hands behind her back.)

It is her poems, unimaginably dull, and decidedly I have to endure the reading of them.

Then, in the vast silence that immediately follows, she plays her last trump, in desperation: "And suppose I told you that now I am writing a play!"

I: "Ahem!!!" (I take out my watch.) "Why, it's much later than I thought. Will it take you much longer?"

He: "Twenty minutes."

I, resigned: "All right! And what is your play about?"

She: "No, I don't want to talk about it. I haven't yet told it to anyone," etc.

Yet, since I don't ask any questions, she makes up her mind:

She: "Well, here it is! I start out from the observation that in contemporary literature no one ever shows anything but ordinary women characters, even shameful ones. I want to show a woman who feels maternal love gradually taking the place of her conjugal love. Do you understand?"

I: "Not at all."

She: "Yes, she has married someone rather ordinary, and little by little she feels developing for him a sort of . . . maternal love. To begin with, she raises him to her level; she gives him wings, and he, eventually, rises above her. . . . Tell me what you think of it." Etc.

Between oneself and the world raise a barrier of simplicity.

Nothing so baffles them as naturalness.

NOVEL

The man who begins to drink. Very harmonious family; eight children.

The wife dies. The father unable to take care of the children. Collapse and complete abandon. The old boarder (with spectacles) rapes one of the daughters, whom the father is obliged to leave at home while he goes to work. He suspected him, however, but didn't dare accuse him before. Sudden outbursts of rage. He struggles. He ends up by drinking with the old man. Moral decay.

Cuverville, July 3

X. (*I* later on) was accustomed to say that age had not forced him to give up a single pleasure of which he did not just happen to be on the point of getting tired.

After *Robinson Crusoe* I read *Tom Jones,* and in the intervals *Olalla* and *The Bottle Imp* by Stevenson, numerous essays by Lamb, then aloud with Mlle Siller *The Mayor of Casterbridge,* and *The End of the Tether* by Conrad; some Milton (*Samson Agonistes*), Thomson (*Evolution of Sex* —the first four or five chapters); Stevenson, *Weir of Hermiston.*

Les Sources, October 15

A Friday the 13th, I couldn't have missed it.

Traveled beside a bespectacled little tart who kept the whole compartment awake until one-thirty a.m. to read *Baiser de femme,* which she began when we were still in the Paris station and devoured at one sitting. Too annoyed with her to be able to go to sleep afterwards; and especially annoyed not to have dared say something cutting to her because of the corpulent protector who was snoozing opposite her.

Worked on *Les Caves.* Probably Lafcadio had already met Protos before his adventure in the train.

Rain outside. But when I changed trains at Avignon, the exquisite quality of the air refreshed me.

I was no sooner settled in my new compartment than there entered, badly propped up by his wife, a corpse. She is in deep mourning—one might almost think it was already for him—her face somewhat swollen, somewhat yellow, somewhat shiny; rather insignificant, effacing herself before him. Very tall; one might rather say: very long; a face that must have been rather handsome (he can hardly be more than forty-five), but which has lost every expression save that of suffering and anguish; not the waxlike color of dead men, but an ashen, leaden hue. . . . His gestures are broad and lacking in co-ordination, and while his wife says to him: "Don't be afraid: the conductor promised me not to do the coupling until you were settled" (she repeats this several times), he tumbles into the corner chair (we are in first class) and throws one leg up much higher than he needs to in order to cross it over the other. Occasionally he moans weakly. His wife says, as if speaking to someone offstage, or by way of sympathy: "From Nancy to Dijon it was all right, but it was from Dijon on that *I* began to be so tired. And yet we had been promised that we would have to change only once. . . ."

Then he, very quickly, as if fearing to run out of breath, and in an irritated voice: "I told you we hadn't taken the right train. It's that agent in Dijon who made a mistake. . . . Ouf! Ouf!"

At this moment a conductor goes down the passageway (the train hasn't started yet). The wife asks once more if this is the right train for Amélie-les-Bains. What diseases is that little hole supposed to cure? I haven't yet succeeded in discovering what is the matter with *him*.

I look at my timetable. It is barely eight o'clock. The train does not reach Amélie-les-Bains until four o'clock; *he* will never make it!

His nose is constantly running, and, as he wipes it once more: "Take out your other handkerchief," his wife says. "You can see that you already used this one when you had your chocolate."

And indeed the handkerchief is repulsive; but he doesn't give a damn. His cap slips onto one side; his wife straightens it; she spreads a little Scotch plaid over his pointed knees; then helps him slip on a pair of black cotton gloves; very painful; his extraordinarily thin, long hand is dislocated; his middle fingers fall backward like a doll's fingers. What is his disease? . . . Suppose I should catch it! But I cannot take my eyes off him. (The only other traveler in the compartment, in the corner opposite me, is resolutely hiding behind *Les Pirates de l'Opéra*—and doesn't raise his eyes during the whole trip.) The invalid says: "It's the jolts that have shaken up my insides like this."

He tries to cough, but chokes, while his wife reassures him: "You know it always does you good to sneeze."

She calls that "sneezing"! On my word, he is beginning the death rattle; he can't catch his breath; she herself becomes a bit worried and in a rather loud voice, as much, I think, for us as for him: "There's nothing to worry about; everyone knows that it's nervous."

Finally, having caught his breath, he says: "Ah! I am not at all well. . . ."

And then she begins to lament not having taken advantage of the stop at Avignon to give him an injection. (She gives him one at Tarascon, shortly afterwards.)

"That's right! It completely slipped my mind. Do you want a little piece of sugar? Do you. . . ? How do you feel?"

He says nothing. I see a thread of liquid dripping onto his vest; I think he is crying; but no, it comes out of the corner of his mouth.

We are coming to Nîmes. She says to him: "Nîmes: the Tour Magne!"

Oh, the hell with it! . . . But this is where I get off.

S H O R T N O V E L

Avignon.

The smell of the pines, the scent of the lavender.

Behind the arches of the bridges, those great swells that the water slowly carries away.

I grieve to think that, later on, my weakened memory will be unable to offer me my sensation of today, however lively; losing all sharpness of outline, all accent, it will merely seem to me like one of those medals of which the effigy has been effaced, now blurred, alas, like any other medal; only by the luster of the worn metal can one tell that it was once precious.

Later on, taking this perfumed memory in my hand, pressing it tenderly to my lips, I shall think: What was it? I no longer see it very clearly. The name of that child? Shall I confuse him, alas, with so many others? The day was delightfully radiant; the water in the *séghias,* I remember, charming. I should like to define the line of his body, and again find it adorable.

In the jury box I look again at my colleagues.* I imagine these same faces on the opposite bench; badly outfitted, unshaved, unwashed, their hair uncombed, with soiled linen or with none at all, and that fearful hunted look in the eyes that comes from a combination of worry and fatigue.

* André Gide was a member of the jury of the Assize Court of Rouen for 1912, on which he wrote a book of reflections.

What would they look like? What would I look like myself? Would the judge himself recognize the "respectable man" under that frightful disguise? He would have to be very clever to distinguish the criminal from the member of the jury!

1912   *Zurich, Wednesday*

I should like never to have known Claudel. His friendship weighs on my thought, and obligates it, and embarrasses it. . . . I can still not get myself to hurt him, but as my thought asserts itself, it gives offense to his. How can I explain myself to him? I should willingly leave the whole field to him, give up everything. . . . But I cannot say something different from what I have to say, which cannot be said by anyone else.

How much more sensuality invites to art than does sentimentality—this is what I repeat to myself as I walk about Zurich. To tell the truth, I don't understand anything here; I feel more foreign to these people, and they to me, than I should be among Zulus or Caribs.

Thursday

When I hear myself in a conversation, I long to become a Trappist. And all the disgust and exasperation I feel does not correct anything in me. The indulgence others must have to have, at times, to put up with me! . . . There are certain shortcomings of my mind that I know and loathe but cannot overcome. If at least I could be unaware of them!

Andermatt, January 27

Here I am again in this land "that God created to be horrible" (Montesquieu). The admiration of mountains is an invention of Protestantism. Strange confusion between the lofty and the beautiful on the part of brains incapable of art. Switzerland: a wonderful reservoir of energy; one has to go down how far? to find abandon and grace, laziness and voluptuousness again, without which neither art nor wine is possible. If of the tree the mountains make a fir, you can imagine what they can do with man. Aesthetics and ethics of conifers.

The fir and the palm tree: those two extremes.

Wednesday, February 7

If I were to disappear right now, no one could suspect, on the basis of what I have written, the better things I still have to write. By what temerity, what assumption of a long life, have I always kept the most important for last? Or, on the contrary, what shyness, what respect for my subject and fear of not yet being worthy of it! . . . Thus I put off *La Porte étroite* from year to year. Whom could I persuade that that book is the twin of *L'Immoraliste,* and that the two subjects grew up concurrently in my mind, the excess of one finding a secret permission in the excess of the other, and the two together establishing a balance?

Thursday

Nothing can express the weariness of my mind.

Saturday, Midnight

Catholicism is inadmissible. Protestantism is intolerable. And I feel profoundly Christian.

Sunday

Having gone out for a moment yesterday, I let myself be carried away by curiosity, following the crowd to the stadium of the Parc des Princes, which I had never before entered. For almost an hour I watched a football game, of which I understood almost nothing. Aesthetics of the grouping, of the mass, tending to take the place of the aesthetics of the individual. Hideous crowd of spectators.

Saturday, February 17

Took Ghéon to dinner. He drags me off to spend the evening at the Théâtre des Arts, where the first performance of *Mrs. Warren's Profession* is being given. I arrived bristling, predisposed against it by the author's unbearable immodesty. And the first scenes were worse than I expected; you cannot imagine anything harsher, drier, or more abstract. But during the second act I let myself be captivated without thinking of resisting (it is only fair to say that the actress who played Mrs. Warren was excellent). I recovered myself toward the end of the third act. It is annoying that the fourth should be so bad. What a grimacing art and what creaking thoughts!

Unable to go to sleep before dawn.

Friday

Yesterday morning received Einstein, a little round German who wants to found a new review to do battle on behalf of modern tendencies, which he reproaches for something or other. Likable, but still in the pasty state; like all Germans.

Saturday, March 2

I leave this evening for Marseilles—and Monday sail for Tunis.

May 7

Got back ten days ago (the Sunday before last in the evening); I should have gone back to this journal immediately. The very day after my return I went back to work; that is to say, I began to polish the pages of *Les Caves* that I had not gone over. Impatient to show them to Copeau. He came last Friday to spend three days at the Villa. Excellent reading, but it gives me a glimpse of how far I still am from where I ought to be. My characters, whom I saw in the beginning only as puppets, are gradually filling with real blood, and I am not doing my duty by them as easily as I had hoped. They demand more and more, force me to take them more and more seriously, and my original fable reveals itself to be less sufficient. Necessity for a great deal of work.

Cuverville, June 7

"Fine heads of cabbage, waving their hairy leaves, like the ears of great oxen."

This is what I read in *Trois Villes saintes,** which I received yesterday.

The *"hairy* leaves" of cabbage!! Ah! dear M. Baumann, the Virgin must not have had much trouble in appearing to you.

GOSPELS

I consider detestable all moral teachings that are not dictated by the love of humanity—but I tell you that these counsels are dictated by the love of humanity and that, through the apparent and resolute severity of that voice, I feel stirring a great suffering love, that only the dryness of your hearts, O skeptics and rationalists, prevents you from recognizing.

* A novel by the Catholic writer Emile Baumann.

Went to see Paul Claudel yesterday at his sister's. He receives me with great cordiality. I enter right away the little room he is occupying, which is dominated by a crucifix above the bed.

Paul Claudel is more massive, wider than ever; he looks as if he were seen in a distorting mirror; no neck, no forehead; he looks like a power-hammer. The conversation immediately starts on the subject of Rimbaud, whose complete works in one volume prefaced by Claudel, which the *Mercure* has just published, are on the table. He has recently had an opportunity to talk with some employee or business representative who, for some period of time, had frequented Rimbaud at Dakar or Aden; who depicted him as an absolutely insignificant creature, spending all his days in smoking, sitting on his haunches in the Oriental manner, telling silly gossip when he had a visitor, and occasionally putting his hand in front of his mouth as he laughed the sort of private laugh of an idiot. At Aden he used to go out bareheaded under the hot sun at hours when the sun on one's head is like a blow from a club. At Dakar he lived with a native woman, by whom he had had a child, or at least a miscarriage, "which is enough to wipe out" (says Claudel) "the imputations of perversion still occasionally attached to his name; for if he had had such tastes (and, it seems, nothing is more difficult to cure), it goes without saying that he would have kept them in that country where they are accepted and facilitated to such an extent that all the officers, without exception, live openly with their boy."

As I chide him for having, in his study, glossed over the ferocious side of Rimbaud's character, he says he wanted to depict only the Rimbaud of the *Saison en enfer,* in whom the author of *Les Illuminations* was to *result.* Led, for a moment, to speak of his relations with Verlaine, Claudel, with an absent look, touches the rosary in a bowl on the mantel.

He talks of painting with excess and stupidity. His speech is a continual flow that no objection, no interrogation even, can stop. Any other opinion than his own has no justification and almost no excuse in his eyes.

The conversation, by a natural slope, reaches matters of religion; he rises up violently against the group of Catholic politicians of the Action Française, then against Sorel and Péguy, whose "motives he begins to understand better."

In too great a hurry to get back to my book, I cannot note here all the turns of our conversation.

November 22

A few letters this morning painfully remind me that today I am entering my forty-fourth year.

1913   *Cuverville, June 24*

Finished *Les Caves* yesterday. Doubtless there will still be much to change after I have given it to Copeau to read, and in the proofs. Curious book; but I am beginning to be fed up with it, heartily sick of it. I cannot yet convince myself that it is finished, and can't stop myself from thinking of it. More than one passage in the first and second books seem to me weak or forced . . . but I think the hardest parts are also the most successful.

June 26

It seems to me at times that I have not yet written anything serious; that I have always presented my thought in an ironic manner, and that, were I to disappear today, I should leave an image of myself from which even my guardian angel could not recognize me.

(The belief in angels is so disagreeable to me that I hasten to add that this is only a manner of speaking—but one that expresses my thought rather well.)

June 29

Every day I read a chapter of *Marius the Epicurean* (with the greatest delight); aloud, for an hour, *The Merry Men;** I spend from three to five hours (and more often five than three) in piano-practice (exclusively Bach and Chopin). When one adds Ransome's book on Wilde, some Milton, some Keats, some Byron, etc., plus the correspondence, which every day takes one or two hours more, there is hardly any time left for personal work. I am putting it off until I travel again, when I shall have neither the piano nor any reading to finish.

July 3

Yesterday evening, after dinner, my eyes tired, I was sitting on the bench in front of the house watching the cats play, when Mius's voice rang out: "Ah, what a game! Ah, what fun we are going to have!"

However gloomy and old-appearing, Mius, at moments, recovers all

---

* The first by Walter Pater, the second by Robert Louis Stevenson.

his youth; quivering with joy, he lays his rat-trap on the steps: he has caught a big female and seven little ones. You can imagine what that family walk must have been, at twilight, with this catastrophe as its conclusion. The little ones are charming and don't seem very frightened, but the mother, who knows something about life, is furious; she makes great bounds against the wires, hurting her snout; she leaps, not to get away, but aggressively to throw herself on us. At each leap she utters an odd little war-cry. Em., whose heart is wrung at the thought of the carnage about to ensue, runs away as is her wont. The dogs are wildly excited; they are making such a rumpus that eventually they have to be locked up. Jeanne and the two maids have come running; Mius, they, and I gather around the cage, like the gods leaning over human misery.

"Well, how are we going to kill them?" Mius finally asks.

Marthe suggests pouring boiling water on them.

"No," says Mius, "I'm going to get my knife."

"You must try to keep them from suffering too much," says P., ordinarily so foolish, but who seems enlightened in this circumstance.

"Too bad for them! It serves them right," exclaims Juliette, the gardener's wife, two of whose rabbits the rats have eaten. "All they had to do was not be so wicked."

"But they don't know that what they do is harmful," says P.

I hold myself in check to keep from upsetting the trap full of little prisoners, as if by accident; and choosing the least evil, I suggest dropping the cage into a bucket of water.

The little ones did not resist for long. But the mother's suffering went on longer than I would have believed. She leaped about frightfully; occasionally you could see a new air bubble rise to the surface. Finally her lungs were filled; altogether it lasted three minutes.

from

LETTER TO

M. EDOUARD DUCOTE

(*First Imaginary Interview*)

1905

". . . Do you really mean that you consider politics and the rest, I mean, social and economic questions, matters of no serious interest and not worth the attention of a cultivated mind. . . ?"

"I will consent to answer you on that point, monsieur, since this is our first interview; but let us not bring it up again, do you agree? It would be to no purpose. Furthermore, I should not be able to say anything here but the commonplaces everybody repeats over and over. Politics, monsieur? How could you *not* pay attention to it? It has its eyes on us everywhere, forcing itself on our attention. Whether we want to or not, whether we know it or not, we are engaging in politics. Your very thoughts, according to the form they take, spontaneously assume a red or white tinge; you can't escape it; everyone is forced to sit on the side of the whites or of the reds. And you can't stay standing up, or everybody and everything starts reproaching you for it. So at first you sit down rather hesitantly. Once you are seated, the trouble begins. It's not long before your seat begins to dictate your opinions, instead of your opinions determining your seat. Soon after that you are judging other people's ideas, and even your own, by their political color. You say, when confronted with a work of art: It is red, therefore it must be bad; it is white, therefore it must be good; or the other way around. That may be serving a party, but it's also distorting the judgment."

"Yet that is the very question that has come up of late: Once you have recognized that your party is an excellent one, isn't it worth serving, even with distorted judgments?"

"If that is so, how can one tell that the original judgment, by which the party was found excellent, was not distorted, too? Let me repeat, you don't *choose* your party; you sit down where the color of your thoughts forces you to sit."

"By the way, may I ask an indiscreet question: Have you taken a seat?"

"I don't think so. I hope not. Once I was seated, I wouldn't feel at ease; however comfortable the chair, I should be worried. I never feel quite alive except when I'm moving."

"That's what your enemies, even your friends, will be quick to call hesitation, indecision. . . . Can it be that you are a dilettante, monsieur?"

"Shame on you!"

"By your wavering and indecision you do nobody any good. Since no party can claim you, you are no use to any party."

"That's where I think you are wrong, monsieur. Disinterested thought, I believe, is really more useful than the kind one can always guess in advance, the kind one knows to have been dictated by a party. Moreover, I don't care. The important thing for me is to give my thoughts free rein."

"But didn't you say a minute ago that our thoughts, by their natural color, force us to take sides with those of a matching shade? Do you mean to imply, perhaps, that you have only colorless thoughts?"

"Colorless thoughts are sickly things. I like to feel that mine have plenty of color. But . . . I have some of every color."

"That must be a nuisance."

"Thank you; but not always. In front of others, in an argument, yes; that's why I'm not very fond of arguments. At the very first turning of the discourse, I find myself abandoning my own side; whether the other fellow is red or white, suddenly there I am serving him up his color. But, as soon as I'm alone again, my dear fellow, I start in arguing with myself; there is no stopping it: quite naturally, a dialogue commences. And just as naturally, it takes the shape of a novel, of a play. . . . Isn't that the way it should be?"

"The way it should be! . . . But why? What's the use of all that?"

"Pardon me . . . I'm afraid I don't understand the question."

"I can hardly put it more clearly: What is the use, in your opinion, of the novel, or of drama—of literature, in a word?"

"Do you mean from the individualist point of view?"

"Certainly not; but from the point of view of the majority, the people, the country, of civilization."

"It's somewhat as if you were asking me what use to a tree is the fruit it bears. I find it very difficult to think of a work of art as anything but an end-product. It seems to me, furthermore, that the critic should consider it in that light. It is by its fruits that you judge the tree."

"The 'master faculty' of a critic should be, then, in your opinion . . . ?"

"Taste."

"I must admit, monsieur, that I find your ideas bewildering. I am afraid that, in our day, they will meet with little response."

"So am I; but what can be done about it? For the same principle applies here, too: should I, each time I speak, be concerned about the echo my voice will raise?"

"And if you were to be concerned about it? . . ."

"Nothing is so sure to distort the sound of one's words, nor more sure to compromise freedom of thought. 'In order to think freely,' Renan wrote somewhere, 'one must be sure that what one writes will have no serious consequences.'"

"Do you admire that remark?"

"Profoundly."

"I see nothing in it but a paradox myself. Renan knew very well, knew better than anyone else, that what he wrote would have 'serious consequences.'"

"But it wasn't *for the sake of the consequences* that he conceived it. That's the whole point."

"You will grant me at least, that the work of art—and more precisely the written work—can have repercussions . . ."

"The most prolonged, the most universally affecting, the most serious; I will even grant that the artist may be able to foresee them; but for him to bend or distort his thought for their sake—that is the great sin against the Spirit which can never be forgiven."

"In short, you refuse to consider a work of art as anything but a product, a result?"

"Like a fruit, and from which the future must be born. Enough for today, monsieur. Such introductory considerations are, I daresay, indispensable, but should really be taken for granted. It seems a shame to have to spell them out. But you are the one who is forcing me to it. For today people want to impose upon one an Apollo made in *your* image, all receptive and pitying, domesticated and even cringing. But Apollo is the proudest of the gods—that is why he gives light. Adieu, monsieur; I shall speak to you of more . . . current affairs another time. Today, I have done no more than to establish my point of view, to tell the truth."

The gentleman rises; on his way out, he suddenly turns around. "I saw," he said, "and very much enjoyed the exhibition of Maurice Denis; weren't you the one who wrote the preface to the catalogue?"

"Yes."

"At the end of it, you speak of the 'moral qualities' of a work of art or of an artist. Can it be, after what you have just been telling me, that such qualities exist for you? Do moral questions interest you?"

"Why not? That's what our books are made of!"

"But what are morals, in your view?"

"*An appendage of aesthetics.* I look forward to our next visit, monsieur."

LE RETOURDE
L'ENFANT PRODIGUE
(The Return of the Prodigal Son)
1907

I have painted here, for my secret pleasure, as they used to do in the old triptychs, the parable told us by Our Lord Jesus Christ. I have left scattered and intermingled throughout it traces of the double inspiration that led me to it. I am not seeking to prove any god's victory over me, nor my own victory over any god. And yet perhaps, if the reader demands from me some expression of piety, he will not look for it in vain in my painting; here, like a donor in the corner of his picture, I may be found kneeling, a pendant to the prodigal son, smiling, just as he is, through a face streaming with tears.

THE PRODIGAL SON

When, after a long absence, tired of his fancies and as if fallen out of love with himself, the prodigal son, from the depths of a destitution he had sought, thinks of his father's face; of that spacious room where his mother used to bend over his bed; of that garden watered by a running stream, but enclosed, from which he had always wished to escape; of his parsimonious older brother, whom he had never loved, but who still holds in trust for him that portion of his goods the prodigal was unable to squander—then the boy admits to himself that he has *not* found happiness, nor even managed to prolong for very long that intoxication he had sought in happiness's place. "Oh," he thinks, "if my father, after first being angry with me, thought me to be dead—then perhaps he would rejoice to see me again, in spite of my sins; what if I were to return to him, very humbly, my head bowed and covered with ashes, bend down before him and say, 'My Father, I have sinned against heaven and against you' . . . what shall I do if he raises me up with his hand and says to me, 'Come into the house, my son' . . . ?" And already the boy is reverently making his way home.

When, from the brow of the hill, he spies at last the smoking roofs of the house, it is evening; but he waits for the shadows of night in order to hide as best he can his wretched state. He hears from a distance his father's voice; his knees give way; he falls and covers his face with his hands, for he is ashamed of his shame, and yet he knows that he is the lawful son. He is hungry; he has nothing but a handful of sweet acorns in a fold of his tattered cloak, those acorns with which he fed himself as well as the swine he used to keep. He sees the preparations for supper under way. He recognizes his mother, coming out on the step . . . he can hold back no longer, he runs down the hill, goes into the courtyard, barked at by his own dog, who does not know him. He tries to speak to the servants, but they are suspicious and move away in order to warn the master: here he is.

No doubt he was expecting the prodigal son, for he recognizes him at once. His arms open wide; the boy then kneels before him, and hiding his forehead with one arm, he cries out, lifting up his right hand for forgiveness: "My father, my father: I have gravely sinned against heaven and against you; I am not worthy that you should call me son; but at least let me live in a corner of your house, like one of your servants, like the least of your servants. . . ."

The father raises him up and embraces him.

"My son! Blessed be this day, which returned you to me!"—and his joy overflows his heart and he weeps; he kisses his son's brow, then raises his head and turns toward the servants.

"Bring forth the finest robe; put shoes on his feet, and a precious ring on his finger. Find the fattest calf in our stables, and kill it; prepare a feast of rejoicing, for the son I thought dead is alive."

And as the news is already spreading, he hurries on: he does not want another to be the first one to say, "Mother, the son we wept for is returned to us."

The joy of the whole household mounts up like a hymn; this troubles the elder son. He sits at the common table because the father invites him to, urges him; obliges him. Alone among the guests (for even the least servant is invited), he shows an angry brow: Why more honor to the repentant sinner than to himself, who has never sinned? To him order is more valuable than affection. If he agrees to appear at the feast, it is because by giving credit to his brother he can lend him joy for one evening; it is also because his father and mother have promised to admonish the prodigal tomorrow, and because he himself is preparing to lecture him severely.

The torches send their smoke up toward heaven. The meal is over. The servants have cleared the table. Now, in the night when not a breath is stirring, soul after soul in the weary house falls asleep. But yet, in the room next to that of the prodigal, I know a boy, his younger brother, who all night through, until dawn, will try in vain to sleep.

THE FATHER'S REPRIMAND

O my God, like a child I kneel before You today, my face streaming with tears. If I recall and transcribe here Your compelling parable, it is because I know what Your prodigal son was like; it is because I see myself in him, because I hear in myself, sometimes, and repeat in secret, those words you made him cry, from the depths of his great distress: "How many hirelings of my father have bread enough and to spare, and I perish with hunger!"

I imagine the Father's embrace; in the warmth of such a love my heart melts. I imagine an earlier distress, and even—oh, I imagine all sorts of things! This I believe: that I am the very one whose heart beats when, from the brow of the hill, he sees the blue roofs of the home he has abandoned. What then holds *me* back from rushing down toward that haven, from going in?—They are waiting for me. Already I can see the fatted calf they are preparing . . . Stop! Do not set out the feast too quickly!— Oh, prodigal son, I am thinking of you; tell me first what the Father said to you the next day, the day after the welcoming feast. Oh, Father, although I know it is the elder son who prompts You, let me hear Your *own* voice, at times, through his words!

"My son, why did you leave me?"

"Did I really leave you? Father, are you not everywhere? Never did I stop loving you."

"Let us not cavil. I had a house which closed you in. It was built for you. Generations have labored so that your soul might find in it shelter, a luxury suited to its dignity, comfort, employment. You, the heir, the son— why did you escape from the House?"

"Because the House closed me in. The House is not You, Father."

"It is I who built it, and for you."

"Oh, it is not you who say that; it is my brother. You, why you built the whole world, both the House and what is not the House. The House was built by others; in your name, I know: but by others."

"Man has need of a roof under which to lay his head. Proud boy! Do you think you can sleep out in the wind and air?"

"Does that take so much pride? Poorer men than I have done it."

"They are poor men. You are not. No one can abdicate wealth. I had made you rich above all men."

"Father, you know that when I left, I carried away all of my fortune that I could. What do I care about the goods one cannot carry with him?"

"All that fortune you took away you have spent foolishly."

"I changed your gold into pleasures, your precepts into fantasy, my chastity into poetry, my austerity into desires."

"Was it for this that your parents were so saving, that they strove to instill into you so much virtue?"

"So that I might burn with a brighter flame, perhaps, when I was kindled by a new fervor."

"Think on that pure flame that Moses saw on the sacred bush: it burns but it does not consume."

"I have known a love that consumes."

"The love I want to teach you refreshes. After so short a time, my prodigal son, what have you left?"

"The memory of those pleasures."

"And the destitution that comes after."

"In that destitution, I felt closer to you, Father."

"Did it take poverty, then, to impel you to return?"

"I don't know; I don't know. It was in the dryness of the desert that I most loved my thirst."

"Your poverty made you appreciate better the value of wealth."

"No, that was not it. Don't you understand me, Father? My heart was drained of everything, and then it filled with love. At the cost of all my belongings, I had purchased fervor."

"Were you happy, then, far from me?"

"I never felt far from you."

"Then what made you come back? Tell me."

"I don't know. Idleness, laziness, perhaps."

"Idleness, my son! What? It was not love?"

"Father, I told you: I never loved you more than in the desert. But I was tired, each morning, of having to hunt out my own subsistence. In the House, at least, we are well fed."

"Yes, the servants see to that. So then: it was hunger that brought you back."

"And cowardice, perhaps, and sickness. . . . by the end these chance meals had left me weak; for I fed on wild fruits, on locusts and honey. I grew less and less able to bear the discomfort which had so kindled my fervor in the beginning. At night, when I was cold, I thought how warm and snug my bed was at my Father's house. When I went hungry, I remembered how the abundance of food served at my Father's house was always more than I could eat. I wavered; I felt I had not enough courage, enough strength to fight much longer, and yet . . ."

"So yesterday's fatted calf seemed good to you?"

The prodigal son casts himself down, sobbing, his face against the ground: "Oh Father, Father! In spite of everything, the wild savor of sweet acorns is still in my mouth. Nothing can ever cancel that taste!"

"My poor boy," the Father replies as he raises him up. "Perhaps I spoke too harshly to you. Your brother wanted me to. It is he who makes the laws here. It is he who charged me to tell you, 'Outside the House there is no salvation for you.' But listen to me: I am the one who made you; I know what lies within you. I know what it is that drove you out onto the roads. I was waiting for you at the end. You should have called me . . . I was there."

"My Father! Then I could have found you without coming back . . . ?"

"If you felt weak, you did well to come back. Go now; go back to the room I had prepared for you. Enough for today. Rest. Tomorrow you will be able to speak to your brother."

THE REPRIMAND
OF THE ELDER BROTHER

The prodigal son starts off by trying to adopt a superior tone.

"We aren't very much alike, you know, my big brother," he begins. "We aren't alike at all."

The elder brother: "That's your fault."

"Why mine?"

"Because I live according to the rules, according to order. Whatever opposes them is the fruit or seed of pride."

"Then any distinctive qualities I have about me must be faults?"

"Your only 'qualities' worth admitting are those that bring you back to order; as for the rest, you must cut them back."

"It is that very mutilation that I fear. What you want to suppress comes from the Father too."

"Not suppress: I said cut *back*."

"I understand. All the same, that's how I managed to cut back my own virtues."

"And that is precisely why I recognize them in you now. You must *exaggerate* them. Understand me: it is not a reduction, but an exaltation of yourself that I am proposing, in which the most diverse, the most insubordinate elements of your flesh and your spirit must join together, as in a symphony; wherein the worst of you must feed the best, wherein the best must submit to . . ."

"It was an exaltation *I* was looking for, too, and I found it in the desert—perhaps not very different from the one you are proposing."

"To tell the truth, I should like to force it on you."

"Our Father did not speak so harshly."

"I know what the Father said to you. It was vague. He does not express himself very clearly any more: one can make him out as saying whatever one wants to hear. But I understand his thinking well enough. Among the servants I stand as the sole interpreter, and anyone who wants to understand the Father must listen to me."

"I understand him readily enough without you."

"So you thought; but you understood incorrectly. He is not to be understood in a variety of ways; he is not to be listened to in a variety of ways. He is not to be loved in a variety of ways: it cannot be so, if we are to be united in his love."

"In his House."

"To which his love brings one back; as you see yourself, for you have come back. Tell me now: what is it that drove you to leave?"

"I had too strong a sense that this House and the universe were not the same thing. The boy you wanted me to be—there is more to me than that. I could not keep myself from imagining other races, other lands, and the roads that lead to them, roads unmarked on our maps. I imagined in myself a new creature, running down those roads. I ran away."

"Think what would have happened if I had deserted the Father's House as you did. The servants and bandits would have pillaged all our goods."

"That would not have mattered to me then; I had my eye fixed on other goods . . ."

"Which your pride overrated. My brother, the time of indiscipline is over. You will learn, if you don't know it yet, out of what chaos man has emerged. Nor has he emerged completely; he falls back into it with all his uneducated weight as soon as the Spirit no longer bears him up. Do not learn this at your own cost: the well-ordered elements that compose you are only waiting for some acquiescence, some relaxing hold on your part to fall back into anarchy. . . . But what you will never know is the length of time it took man to bring himself to this finished and ordered state. Now that we have the model, let us keep to it. 'Hold that fast which thou hast,' says the Spirit to the Angel of the Church, and he adds: 'that no man take thy crown.' *That which thou hast,* that is your crown; it is the sovereignty you possess over others and over yourself. The Usurper lies in wait for it, for your crown; he is everywhere; he prowls round about you, within you. *Hold fast,* my brother! Hold fast."

"I let go my hold too long ago; I can no longer fix my grasp over my own possessions."

"Ah yes, you can; I will help you. I have watched over them while you were away."

"What's more, I know those words of the Spirit too; you didn't quote the whole saying."

"You are right. It goes on: 'Him that overcometh will I make a pillar in the temple of my God, and he shall go no more out.' "

" 'And he shall go no more out.' That is precisely what terrifies me."

"If it is for his own happiness?"

"Oh, I know what he means. But I was there, in that temple . . ."

"And you found you were wrong to have left it, for you desired to come back."

"I know, I know. Here I am back now; I agree."

"What good can you look for elsewhere, which you do not find here in abundance? More to the point: it is *here alone* that your riches lie."

"You have kept them for me; I know."

"That portion of them which you have not squandered—which is to say that portion which we all hold in common: the property, the land."

"Then I own nothing else, on my own?"

"Yes. That special allotment of gifts which our Father may still consent to give you."

"That is all I want; I am willing to own nothing but that."

"How proud you are! You will not be consulted. That is a questionable bargain, if you ask my advice: you would do better to give up that portion. It was that very allotment of personal possessions which brought you to grief once already. Those were the gifts you wasted straightaway."

"I couldn't take the others with me."

"Which is why you will find them intact now. Enough for today. Come and rest in the House."

"With pleasure; for I am tired."

"Then blessed be your tiredness. Sleep now. Tomorrow your mother will speak to you."

THE MOTHER

Prodigal son, you whose mind is still resisting the words of your brother, now let your heart speak. How sweet it is to feel your mother's caressing hand bow your stubborn neck, as you recline at the foot of her chair and bury your face in her lap.

"Why did you leave me for such a long time?" And as you answer only with tears: "Why cry now, my son? You have been given back to me. I shed all my tears waiting for you."

"Were you still waiting for me?"

"Never did I give up hoping for you. Before going to sleep each night I used to think: If he comes back tonight, will he be able to unlock the door? And it took me a long time to fall asleep. Each morning, before I was completely awake, I used to think: Is not today the day he is coming back? Then I prayed. I prayed so much that you had to come back."

"Your prayers forced me back."

"Don't smile at me, my child."

"Oh, Mother, it is a very humble boy that comes back to you. See how I lay my head below your heart! Not one of my thoughts of yesterday does not seem to me empty today. When I am with you, I scarcely understand how I could ever have left the House."

"You will not leave it again?"

"I cannot leave it again."

"What is it, then, that attracted you out there?"

"I don't want to think of it any more: Nothing . . . Myself."

"Did you think you would be happy away from us?"

"I was not looking for happiness."

"What were you looking for?"

"I was looking for . . . who I was."

"Why, the son of your parents, and a brother to your brothers."

"I was not like my brothers. Please, let's not talk about it any more. I have come back now."

"Yes: let us talk about it. You mustn't believe that your brothers are so different from you."

"From now on my only concern will be to be like all the rest of you."

"You say that as if with resignation."

"Nothing is more exhausting than to realize one's difference. These wanderings have ended by wearing me out."

"You have certainly aged."

"I have suffered."

"My poor child! I expect your bed was not made for you every night, nor the table set for all your meals?"

"I ate whatever I could find, often nothing but green or rotten fruits which my hunger turned into food."

"But did you suffer from anything other than hunger?"

"The midday sun, the cold wind in the heart of the night, the shifting sand of the desert, the thorns that tore my feet; none of that could stop me, but—I didn't tell my brother this—I had to serve . . ."

"Why did you conceal it?"

". . . to serve evil masters who mistreated me physically, who exasperated my pride, who gave me barely enough to eat. Then it was that I thought: 'Oh, to serve for the sake of serving!' . . . In a dream I saw the House again, and I came home."

The prodigal son lowers his forehead again and his mother caresses it tenderly.

"What are you going to do now?"

"I told you: do my best to be like my older brother; take care of our property; choose a wife, as he has done . . ."

"No doubt you have someone in mind, as you say that?"

"No, anyone will do, anyone you choose will suit me. Do for me as you did for my brother."

"I would have liked to choose someone according to your own heart."

"What does that matter? My heart chose for me once already. I renounce the pride that has taken me away from you. Guide my choice. I submit, I tell you, and my children shall submit too. That way my adventure will no longer seem to have been wholly in vain."

"Listen to me; right now there is already one child you might concern yourself with."

"What do you mean? Who are you speaking of?"

"Your younger brother. He wasn't yet ten when you left. You scarcely recognized him, but nevertheless . . ."

"Go on, Mother. What is it that worries you now?"

". . . nevertheless you might well have recognized him—and yourself in him; he is exactly like what you were when you left."

"Like me?"

"Like what you were, I said; not yet, alas, like what you have become."

"And what he will become."

"What he must be made to become: at once. Talk to him; I have no doubt he will listen to you, you the prodigal. Explain to him the disappointments of your travels; spare him . . ."

"But what is it that worries you so about my brother? It may be nothing more than a resemblance of features."

"No, no: the resemblance between you two goes deeper than that. What troubles me now in him is precisely what did not trouble me enough about you, at the start: he reads too much. And not always the best books."

"Nothing more than that?"

"He often perches in the highest spot of the garden, from where you can see the countryside over the walls—as you will remember."

"I remember. Is that all?"

"He spends far more time at the farm than he does here with us."

"Aha! Doing what?"

"Oh, nothing wrong. But it isn't even the farmers he spends his time with: it's the lowest sort of men, men as unlike us as possible; why, they aren't even from this country. There is one, in particular, one who comes from far away, who tells him stories."

"Ah yes: the swineherd."

"Yes. Did you know him? . . . In order to listen to him, your brother follows him each evening into the pigsties; he comes back only for dinner, but with no appetite, and his clothes reeking. Remonstrances have no effect; he stiffens under constraint. Some mornings, at dawn, before any of us are up, he runs off to accompany that swineherd to the gate, when he is leading his herd off to graze."

"But he knows that he must not leave."

"You knew it too! One day he will escape me, I am sure of it. One day he will leave . . ."

"No. I shall speak to him, Mother. Don't be upset."

"I know he will listen to a great deal from you. Did you notice how he looked at you that first evening? With what prestige your rags were covered—and then the purple robe your father placed on your shoulders! I was afraid that in his mind he would confuse the two; and that what appealed to him more were the rags. Oh, but now this idea seems ridiculous; for after all, if you, my child, if you had been able to foresee so much misery, you would not have left us, would you?"

"I don't know how I was able to leave you: you, my own mother. I no longer know."

"Well, then: tell him all that."

"All that I shall tell him tomorrow evening. Now kiss me on the forehead as you used to do when I was a little boy and you watched me falling asleep. I am sleepy."

"Go to bed. I am going to pray for you all."

DIALOGUE WITH
THE YOUNGER BROTHER

Alongside the prodigal's room there is another, not too small, with bare walls. A lamp in his hand, the prodigal comes close to the bed where his younger brother is lying, his face turned toward the wall. He begins in a low voice, so as not to disturb the boy if he is sleeping. "I would like to talk to you, brother."

"What is stopping you?"

"I thought you were asleep."

"You don't have to sleep to have dreams."

"You were dreaming? Of what?"

"What do you care? If I can't understand my own dreams, I can't imagine you explaining them to me."

"Are they that subtle, then? If you told them to me, I would try."

"Do you pick your own dreams? Mine are what they want to be; they are freer than I am. . . . What did you come here for? Why are you bothering me when I'm sleeping?"

"You aren't sleeping, and I've come to speak to you—gently."

"What can you have to say to me?"

"Nothing, if you're going to take that tone."

"Then good-bye."

The prodigal goes toward the door, then puts the lamp on the floor so that the room is only very dimly lit; then he returns, sits on the edge of the bed, and, in the darkness, strokes his brother's forehead—the boy is still turned away—for a long time.

"You answer me more harshly than I ever did your brother. And yet I too fought against him."

The stubborn lad suddenly sat up. "Tell me: it was my brother who sent you?"

"No, my boy. Not he. It was our mother."

"Ah! You wouldn't have come on your own."

"But I come as a friend nonetheless."

Half sitting up in his bed, the boy looks the prodigal straight in the eye. "How could one of my own family possibly be my friend?"

"You are wrong about our brother . . ."

"Don't talk to me about him! I hate him . . . I have given up on him completely. He's the reason I answer you the way I do."

"Why is that?"

"You wouldn't understand."

"Tell me anyway . . ."

The prodigal cradles his brother in his arms; already the youth is beginning to yield: "The night you came back, I couldn't sleep. All night long I kept thinking: I had another brother, and I didn't know it . . . This is why I could feel my heart beating so strongly when I saw you come into the courtyard of the house, covered with glory."

"Glory? I was covered with rags."

"I know, I saw you: to me you were glorious. And I saw what our father did: he put a ring on your finger, a ring such as our brother has never had. I did not want to question anyone about you; all I knew was that you had come back from far away, and that your eyes, during the meal . . ."

"Were you at the feast?"

"Oh, I know very well you didn't see me; during the whole meal you were looking far off, and seeing nothing. And I didn't mind, on the second evening, when you went to speak to our father; but on the third . . ."

"Go on . . ."

"Oh, couldn't you have spoken then one word to me, one word of love?"

"Then you were waiting for me?"

"Oh, how I was waiting! Do you think I should be hating our brother so if you had not gone to converse with him that evening—and for so long? Whatever could you have to say to each other? You know very well, if you are like me, that you can have nothing in common with him."

"I had acted very badly toward him."

"Is that possible?"

"Well, at least toward our mother and father. You know that I ran away from home."

"Yes, I know. A long time ago, wasn't it?"

"When I was about your age."

"Ah! . . . and is that what you call acting badly?"

"Yes. It was wrong. It was my sin."

"When you left, did you feel you were doing wrong?"

"No: I felt a kind of inner obligation; I had to go."

"So what has happened since to change that first truth into a mistake?"

"I suffered."

"And is that what makes you say: I was wrong?"

"No, not exactly: that is what made me reflect."

"You hadn't reflected before, then?"

"Yes, but my feeble reason let itself be overcome by my desires."

"And then later by your sufferings. So that today you come back . . . conquered."

"No, not exactly; resigned."

"But the point is, you have given up being what you wanted to be."

"What my pride persuaded me to be."

The boy remains silent a moment, then suddenly cries out sobbing: "My brother! I am the boy you were when you left! Oh, tell me: did you find nothing but disappointments in your travels? All that I imagine outside of, different from this place—is it all a mirage? Tell me, what did you meet on your way that seemed so tragic? Oh, what *is it* that made you come back?"

"I lost the freedom I was looking for. I was a captive; I had to serve."

"I am a captive here."

"Yes, but I was serving wicked masters; here those you serve are your own family."

"Oh, to serve for the sake of serving! Have we not at least the right to choose our own bondage?"

"I had hoped so. I walked as far as my feet would carry me in pursuit of my desire, like Saul in search of his she-asses. But he found a kingdom: I found only wretchedness. And yet . . ."

"Perhaps you took the wrong road?"

"I walked straight ahead."

"Are you sure? And yet there are still other kingdoms to discover, and lands without kings."

"Who told you that?"

"I know it, I feel it. Already I can feel myself ruling over them."

"Proud boy!"

"Aha! That's what our brother said to you, isn't it? Why do you say it to me, now? Why didn't you hold on to that pride yourself? Then you would not have come back."

"And would never have known you."

"Yes, yes, out there I would have joined you, and you would have recognized me as your brother; it still seems that it is to find you that I am leaving."

"That you are leaving?"

"Have you not understood? Are you not yourself encouraging me to leave?"

"I wanted to spare you the coming back—but by sparing you the going away."

"No, no, don't say that; you don't mean it. You, you left like a conqueror, didn't you?"

"And that is what made servitude seem all the harder to bear."

"Then why did you give in? Were you already so tired?"

"No, not then; but I had doubts."

"Doubts about what?"

"Doubts about everything, about myself; at last I wanted to stop, to root myself somewhere; the comfort I had been promised by this master tempted me . . . Yes, I feel it clearly enough now. I wasn't up to it. I failed."

The prodigal bows his head and hides his face in his hands.

"But at first?"

"I had walked for a long time across a wide, untamed land."

"The desert?"

"It wasn't always the desert."

"What were you looking for there?"

"I no longer understand myself."

"Get up from my bed. Look, there on the night-stand, alongside that torn book."

"I see an opened pomegranate."

"The swineherd brought it to me the other evening, after he had been gone for three days."

"Yes, it's a wild pomegranate."

"I know; it's bitter, almost unbearably bitter; and yet I feel that if I were thirsty enough I would bite it."

"Ah. So now I can tell you. That was the thirst I was looking for in the desert."

"The kind of thirst that only sour fruits like this can quench . . ."

"No; the kind of thirst that they can make you love."

"Do you know where to find them?"

"In a little abandoned orchard; you can reach it before dark. There's no longer any wall separating it from the desert. A stream flows through it; a few half-ripe fruits hang from the branches."

"What sort of fruit?"

"The same that grows in our garden; but wild. It had been very hot all day."

"Listen; do you know why I was expecting you this evening? I am leaving before the night is over. Tonight, this very night, as soon as the first light comes . . . I have made myself ready: I have kept my sandals on tonight."

"So: what I could not do—you will do it? . . ."

"You opened the way for me; the thought of you will sustain me."

"It's now my turn to admire you—and yours to forget me. What are you taking with you?"

"You know that as the youngest, I have no share in the estate. I am taking nothing."

"It's better that way."

"What are you looking at through the window?"

"The garden where our dead ancestors lie."

"Brother . . . my brother"—and the boy, who had risen from his bed, puts an arm around the prodigal's neck—an arm now as tender as his voice. "Come with me."

"Leave me! Leave me alone! I must stay to console our mother. You will be braver without me. Look, it is time now: the sky is turning pale. Go quietly. Come! Kiss me, my young brother: you are taking with you all my hopes. Be strong; forget us; forget me. May you never return . . . Go down softly. I'll hold the lamp . . ."

"Hold my hand as far as the door. Please."

"Be careful of the steps leading down from the porch . . ."

from

LA PORTE ETROITE

(Strait is the Gate)

1909

EDITOR'S NOTE

Although the fragment printed here is celebrated in its own right—Gide once wrote that "the first two parts are there to explain Alissa's journal, which is, I believe, the best thing I have written" (Letter to Claudel, February 24, 1909)—it represents only about a fifth of the whole *récit,* and is impossible to understand, let alone appreciate, without a clear comprehension of "the other side of the story."

The short novel is told by Jérôme for the first eight chapters, and the story—essentially the story of his life-long romance with Alissa— appears to be complete when his narration ends. At this point, he learns that he has inherited certain of Alissa's papers, including her diary—a diary which casts a radically different light on everything he has related until then.

I. Jérôme describes his childhood as that of a lonely, delicate, oversensitive boy raised entirely by women—a childhood brightened almost exclusively by holidays spent in Normandy with his Bucolin cousins: Alissa, Juliette, and Robert. When he is fourteen, he learns by accident of a terrible family secret—the infidelity of his Aunt Bucolin. He is so overcome by the thought of his cousin Alissa's wretchedness that he vows to God from that moment "to shelter this child [she was two years his senior] from fear, from evil, from life." Shortly after this vow, in church with Alissa, Jérôme hears a sermon preached on the text "Strive to enter in at the strait gate"—*Efforcez-vous d'entrer par la porte étroite* —and he translates the pastor's words into a vision of puritan felicity. "We advanced together, clothed in those white robes of which the Apocalypse speaks, holding each other by the hand, looking forward to the same goal." After the service, he flees—"thinking that I should deserve her best by keeping away."

II. Jérôme describes his developing "love" for Alissa as something almost unutterably pure, and expressed primarily in acts of self-abnegation. ("Nothing that I experienced later seems to me worthier of that name—and moreover, when I became old enough to suffer from the more definite disturbances of the flesh, my feeling did not greatly change. I never sought more directly to possess the one whom, as a child, I had sought only to deserve.") Whether Alissa reciprocated his holy ardor he was never entirely sure—she seemed to regard any excessive mutual dependence as a possible hindrance to salvation.

But he dreamed of marrying her nonetheless, and felt sure he had received his mother's consent shortly before her death the following year. Although he said nothing of it to Alissa, he regarded their engagement as fixed. The next summer at Fongueusemare (the Bucolins' estate in Normandy) he told Juliette endlessly of his love for her sister, feeling too constrained to speak to Alissa directly. Just before he is to return to Paris for school, Juliette presses him: What are his plans? Why will he not declare his love to Alissa, make public their engagement? "But why should we get engaged? Isn't it enough for us to know that we do and we shall belong to each other, without announcing it to the world? . . . Oh, Juliette! Life with her seems so beautiful that I dare not—do you understand?—I dare not speak to her about it. . . . I am afraid that the immense happiness that I foresee may frighten her."

Fearful that Alissa may have overheard and misunderstood this conversation, Jérôme tries to declare himself the next day, just before going; but she begs him not to mention the subject. "Why change?" she asks. "Are we not happy enough as we are?" And they part on this uncertain note.

III. Directly on his arrival in Paris, Jérôme receives a chilling letter from Alissa, begging him to defer any plans for an engagement. Spurred on by his impetuous friend Abel Vautier, he rushes back to Fongueusemare to force the issue. Alissa only repeats her previous plea that they leave well enough alone; and in the idyllic peace of her presence, Jérôme's protestations seem to melt. "If you prefer it so, we will not be engaged. . . . I love you enough to wait for you all my life." His friend Abel, meanwhile, who had accompanied him to Normandy, has fallen madly in love with Juliette, and is puzzled and impatient at Jérôme's apparent inability to act.

IV. Jérôme's next visit to the Bucolins is at the Christmas holiday. Suddenly, out of the confusion, a new clarity begins to emerge. Alissa confesses to her aunt that she does not want to marry before her younger

sister Juliette; but to Jérôme she seems pained and distraught, and says
little. Juliette, feverish, almost furious, confronts him alone in the con-
servatory:

> "Has Alissa spoken to you?" she asked at once.
> "Barely two words. I came back very late."
> "You know she wants me to marry before she does?"
> "Yes."
> She looked at me fixedly. "And do you know who she wants
> me to marry?"
> I was silent.
> "You!" she cried.
> "But that's madness!"
> "Yes, isn't it?" she replied, in a voice ringing with both tri-
> umph and despair.

Whereupon Abel breaks the whole story, which he himself has just
pieced together: it is *Jérôme* that Juliette has loved all along; Alissa,
having discovered her sister's secret, has been sacrificing herself for Juliette. Not to be outdone, Juliette outbids her sister's sacrifice: on learning
that her love is hopeless, she accepts the proposal of a vulgar Provençal
vintner she does not love—and promptly collapses in nervous exhaustion.

V. Her sister is now seriously ill, and Alissa sends a note begging
Jérôme to stay away. There follows an absence of two years, as Jérôme
completes his schooling, travels in Italy, and does his military service.
The only link between the "lovers" is their correspondence, and a great
part of this chapter is composed of excerpts from Alissa's letters during
the period. She writes of Juliette's illness and recovery, of her determination to go through with her marriage to the vintner, and then of the
disconcerting ease with which her sister seems to find happiness in her
new role as wife and, later, mother. (To Jérôme she asks Alissa to write
"that I am cured.")

Of herself, Alissa betrays little more than an increasingly troubled
spirituality. She admits to her aunt (in a letter sent on to Jérôme) that
she has taken as her motto the Scripture text "Cursed be the man that
trusteth in man," and several times reveals a rigorous puritanism, a longing for religious retreat. But at the same time she grows rapturous over
the scents and sounds of warm summer evenings, and troubled by the
pagan quality of Provence: she longs to see Italy with Jérôme. And

although she several times begs him *not* to visit—and although each time he acquiesces—she confesses, in her letters, a greater and greater yearning for his presence.

> Sometimes I look for you involuntarily; I stop in the middle of what I am reading, I turn my head quickly . . . it seems as though you were there!

> And suddenly I wanted you there, I felt you there, close to me—with such a violence that perhaps you felt it.

> The fear of troubling you keeps me from telling you how anxiously I await you. . . . Each day I must get through before I see you again weighs on me, oppresses me. Two months more! It seems longer to me than all these months we have already spent apart. Everything I take up in the effort to while away the time seems nothing but a meaningless stopgap; I cannot apply myself to anything. My books are without quality, without appeal, my walks have lost their attraction; all Nature is without glamour, the garden deprived of color and scent . . .

And as the time grows closer to their meeting after this long absence, she confesses to the most dreadful anxiety.

VI. The meeting is a pitiful failure. They are terrified of being left alone, and find themselves with nothing to say; their hands fall apart; both are left nearly sick. In a letter she sends after Jérôme's departure, Alissa writes, "My friend, what a melancholy meeting! . . . Oh, I beg of you, don't let us see each other again! Why this awkwardness, this feeling of being in a false position, this paralysis, this dumbness, when we have everything in the world to say to each other?" She confesses that she had waited for him to come back, even gone out after him, had tried to write a letter telling him that "our correspondence was nothing but a vast mirage, that each of us, alas, was only writing to himself"; that her agitation in his presence only proved the intensity of her love, but that "when you were away, I loved you more." His love, she suspects, "was above all intellectual, the beautiful tenacity of a tender, faithful mind." They break off this frustrating correspondence, and agree not to meet until the following Easter.

VII. At the agreed-upon day, Alissa, dressed all in white, receives Jérôme with open arms in her garden. His very first remark is a promise to leave at once the minute she should wish it. The days pass silently and placidly enough, until he half-ventures to return to the subject of marriage: she grows pale, and he leaves off. We were not born for happiness, she declares, but for Holiness. And, at her request, he leaves once again.

Again she writes after him, protesting that she wished he had disobeyed her and stayed. She had felt in his presence a contentment so complete that now she is ashamed: "We were born for a happiness other than that."

> "Good-bye, my friend. *Hic incipit amor Dei.*
> Ah, will you ever know how much I love you? . . .
> Until the end, I will be your
>
> > Alissa."

"Against the snare of virtue I was defenseless," declares Jérôme. Their letters dwindle into a dry promise to meet again in the fall.

This second-to-last meeting is the strangest of all. Jérôme discovers an Alissa utterly transformed. She has willfully made herself plain, devoted herself to menial chores that leave her little time for conversation, and abandoned her music and her poetry for devotional tracts he finds disgusting. But he can find no answer to her new selfless, unworldly, Jansenist spirit. To his protest that she has changed herself, she replies that he only loves her less because she has aged—and that she loves him still.

Perhaps, he admits to himself, she *was* an illusion, the Alissa of his dreams. He flees to a teaching job abroad as to an escape.

VIII. Three years later, Jérôme comes unannounced to Fongueusemare, to find Alissa expecting him—she had been there expecting him for three days. Pale and thin now, she leans against him, but it is his turn to be cold and curt. She tries to give him a little amethyst cross, to pass on to the daughter he may one day have, in memory of their love; but he protests wildly that he could never marry, never love anyone but her, and crushes her in his arms—for the first and last time. She begs for pity, for release, insists it is too late: God has provided, she must believe, "some better thing." She bids him farewell in a look full of love, and shuts the narrow garden door—"*la porte étroite.*" For a long while Jérôme leans sobbing against the door, and dreams of forcing it open—but he cannot.

A month later, he learns in a letter from Juliette that Alissa is dead. She had fled all alone to Paris and entered a small nursing home, where she put her affairs in order and died. Among her legacies was a sealed packet of papers for Jérôme, including the diary that follows.

ALISSA'S JOURNAL

Aigues-Vives

Left Le Havre the day before yesterday; yesterday, arrived at Nîmes; my first trip away from home! With no housekeeping to do and no cooking to look after, and consequently with a slight feeling of idleness, today, May 23rd, 188–, my twenty-fifth birthday, I begin this journal—without much pleasure, to keep me company really; for, perhaps for the first time in my life, I feel lonely—in a different, almost a foreign land, one with which I have not yet made acquaintance. What it has to say to me is no doubt the same thing the land said at Normandy—the same message I listen to so untiringly at Fongueusemare—for God is nowhere different from Himself—but this southern land speaks a language I have not yet learned, and to which I listen with amazement.

May 24

Juliette is asleep on a chaise-longue nearby—in the open gallery that is the great charm of this Italian-style house; the gallery opens onto the graveled courtyard that is a continuation of the garden. Without leaving her chaise, Juliette can see the lawn sloping down to the pond, where a family of multi-colored ducks is frolicking about and two swans sail. A stream which never runs dry, so they say, no matter how hot the summer, feeds into it and then flows through the garden, which becomes a grove of ever-increasing wildness, more and more shut in between the dried *garrigue* and the vineyards, until it finally is strangled altogether.

. . . Yesterday Edouard Teissières showed my father the garden, the farm, the cellars, and the vineyards, while I stayed behind with Juliette—so that this morning, while it was still very early, I was able to make my first voyage of discovery in the park by myself. A great many plants and strange trees, whose names I should have liked to know. I pick a twig of each of them so that someone can tell me what they are at lunchtime. In some of them I recognize the evergreen oaks which Jérôme admired in the gardens of the Villa Borghese or Doria-Pamphili—so distantly related to our northern trees, of such a different character! Near the far end of the park they shelter a narrow, mysterious glade, bending over a carpet of grass so soft to the feet that it seems an invitation to the choir of nymphs. I astonish, almost frighten myself by my feeling for nature here; at Fongueusemare my response is so profoundly Christian; but here, almost in spite of myself, it is becoming half pagan. And yet the sort of fear which oppressed me more and more was religious, too. I whispered the words: *hic nemus.* The air was crystalline; there was a strange silence. I was thinking of Orpheus, of Armida, when all at once there rose a solitary bird's song, so near me, so pathetic, so pure, that it seemed suddenly as though all nature had been awaiting it. My heart began to beat strongly; I stayed for a moment leaning against a tree, and then came in before anyone else was up.

May 26

Still no news from Jérôme. If he had written to me at Le Havre, his letter would have been forwarded. . . . I can confide my anxiety only to this notebook; for the last three days I have not been distracted from it for an instant, neither by our excursion yesterday to Les Baux, nor by prayer. Today I can write of nothing else; the curious melancholy from which I have been suffering ever since I arrived at Aigues-Vives has, perhaps, no other cause—and yet I feel it at such a depth within me that it seems to me now as if it had been there for a long time past, and as if the joy on which I prided myself did no more than cover it over.

May 27

Why should I lie to myself? It is by an effort of mind that I rejoice in Juliette's happiness. That happiness which I longed for so much, to the extent of offering up my own happiness in sacrifice for it; it is painful to me, now that I see that she has obtained it without trouble, and that it is so different from what she and I imagined. How complicated it all is! Yes . . . I see clearly that, through a horrible revival of egoism, I am offended at her having found her happiness elsewhere than in my sacrifice —at her not having needed my sacrifice in order to be happy.

So that now I wonder, feeling myself made so uneasy by Jérôme's silence: was that sacrifice really consummated in my heart? I am, as it were, humiliated to feel that God no longer demands it of me. Can it be that I was not equal to it?

May 28

How dangerous is this analysis of my sadness! I am already growing attached to this notebook. Is my personal vanity, which I thought I had mastered, reasserting its rights here? No; I must never let this journal become a mere flattering mirror, before which my soul dresses itself. It is not out of idleness, as I thought at first, but out of sadness that I write. Sadness is a *state of sin,* which I had rid myself of, which I hate, from whose *complications* I wish to free my soul. This book must help me to find my happiness in myself once more.

Sadness is a complication. I never used to analyze my happiness.

At Fongueusemare I was alone too, still more alone than here—why did I not feel it then? And when Jérôme wrote to me from Italy, I was willing that he should see things without me, that he should live without me; I followed him in thought, and out of his joy made my own. And now, in spite of myself, I want him; without him every new thing I see is only bothersome to me. . . .

June 10

Long interruption of this journal, which I had scarcely begun; birth of little Lise; long hours of watching with Juliette; I take no pleasure in writing anything here that I can write to Jérôme. I should like to keep myself from the intolerable fault common to so many women—that of writing too much. Let me consider this notebook as a means of perfection.

There followed several pages of notes taken in the course of her reading, extracts, etc. Then, dated from Fongueusemare once more:

July 16

Juliette is happy; she says so, seems so; I have no right, no reason to doubt it. . . . Whence comes this feeling of dissatisfaction, of discomfort, which I have now when I am with her? Perhaps from feeling that such felicity is so practical, so easily obtained, so perfectly "made to measure" that it seems to cramp the soul and stifle it. . . .

And I ask myself now whether it is really happiness that I desire so much as the progress toward happiness. Oh, Lord! preserve me from any happiness I might too easily attain! Teach me to put off my happiness into the future, to place it as far away as Thy throne.

Several pages here had been torn out; they referred, no doubt, to our painful meeting at Le Havre. The journal did not begin again till the following year; the pages were not dated, but had certainly been written at the time of my stay at Fongueusemare.

───────

Sometimes as I listen to him talking, I seem to be watching myself think. He explains me, discovers me to myself. Should I even exist without him? I *am* only when I am with him. . . .

Sometimes I wonder whether what I feel for him is really what most people call love—the picture that is generally drawn of love is so different from the one I should be able to draw. I should like nothing to be said about it at all, to love him without knowing that I love him. I should like, above all, to love him without his knowing it.

I no longer get any joy out of that part of life which I must live without him. All my virtue exists only to please him—and yet, when I am with him, I feel my virtue weakening.

I used to like learning the piano, because it seemed to me that I was able to make some progress in it every day. That too may be the secret of the pleasure I take in reading a book in a foreign language. It is not, assuredly, that I prefer any other language whatever to our own; or that those of our writers whom I admire appear to me in any way inferior to those of other countries—but the slight difficulty that lies in the pursuit of their meaning and feeling, perhaps the unconscious pride in overcoming this difficulty, and of overcoming it each time more and more successfully, adds to my intellectual pleasure a certain spiritual contentment, which it seems to me I cannot do without.

However blessed it might be, I cannot desire a state without progress. In fact I imagine the joy of Heaven not as a simple union of the spirit with God, but as an infinite, a perpetual approach to Him . . . and if I were not afraid of playing upon words, I should say that I do not care for any joy that is not *progressive*.

This morning we were sitting on the bench in the avenue; we were not talking and did not feel any need to talk. . . . Suddenly he asked me if I believed in a future life.

"Oh! Jérôme!" I cried at once, "it is more for me than a hope; I am *sure* of it. . . ."

And it seemed to me, suddenly, as if my whole faith had been poured into that exclamation.

"I should like to know . . ." he added. He stopped a few moments; then: "Would you act differently without your faith?"

"How can I tell?" I answered; and I added: "And you yourself, my dear, in spite of yourself, you act as if you were inspired by the liveliest faith; you can no longer act in any other way. And I should not love you if you were different."

No, Jérôme, no, it is not toward some future recompense that our virtue is striving; it is not reward that our love is seeking. A noble soul is hurt by the very idea of being rewarded for its efforts. Nor does it consider virtue an adornment; no, virtue is the very form of its beauty.

Papa is not so well again; nothing serious, I hope, but he has been obliged to go back to his milk diet for the last three days.

Yesterday evening, Jérôme had just gone up to his room; Papa, who was sitting up with me for a little, left me alone for a few minutes. I was sitting on the sofa, or rather—a thing I hardly ever do—I was lying down, I don't know why. The lampshade was shading my eyes and the upper part of my body from the light; I was mechanically looking at the tips of my feet, which showed a little below my dress in the light thrown upon them by the lamp. When Papa came back, he stood for a few moments at the door, staring at me oddly, half smiling, half sad. I got up with a vague feeling of shyness; then he gestured: "Come and sit beside me," he said; and, though it was already late, he began to talk to me about my mother, something he had never done since their separation. He told me how he had married her, how much he had loved her, and how much she had at first been to him.

"Papa," I said to him at last, "please . . . please say why are you telling me this this evening—what makes you tell me this just this particular evening?"

"Because, just now, when I came into the drawing-room and saw you lying on the sofa, I thought for a moment it was your mother."

The reason I asked this so insistently was that that very evening Jérôme had been reading over my shoulder, standing behind my chair and leaning over me. I could not see him, but I felt his breath and, as it were, the warmth and pulsation of his body. I pretended to go on reading, but I could understand nothing; I could not even distinguish the lines; I was seized by a perturbation so strange that I was obliged to get up from my chair at once, while I still could; I managed to leave the room for a few minutes, luckily without his noticing anything. But a little later, when I was alone in the drawing-room, lying down on the sofa, where Papa found me and thought I looked like my mother—at that very moment I was thinking of her.

I slept very badly last night; I was disturbed, oppressed, miserable, haunted by the recollection of the past, which came over me like a wave of remorse.

Lord, teach me to be horrified by anything that has even the appearance of evil.

Poor Jérôme! If he only knew that sometimes he would have to make but a single sign, and that sometimes I am waiting for him to make it. . . .

When I was a child, even then it was for his sake that I wanted to be beautiful. It seems to me now that I have never "striven for perfection," except for him. And that this perfection can only be attained without him, my God! is of all Thy teachings, the one most disconcerting to my soul.

How happy must that soul be for whom virtue is one with love! Sometimes I doubt whether there is any other virtue than to love, to love as much as possible and always more and more deeply. . . . But on other days, alas! virtue appears to me to be nothing more than resistance to love. What then? shall I dare to name "virtue" the most natural inclination of my heart? Oh, tempting sophism, specious invitation, insidious mirage of happiness!

This morning I read in La Bruyère:

"In the course of this life one sometimes meets with pleasures so dear, engagements so tender, which are yet forbidden us, that it is natural to desire at least that they might be permitted: charms so great can be surpassed only when virtue teaches us to renounce them."

But why then did I pretend that there was anything "forbidden" in my case? Can it be that I am secretly attracted by a charm still more powerful, more sweet than that of love? Oh! that it were possible to carry our two souls forward together, by force of love, but *beyond* love!

Alas! I understand now only too well: between God and him there is no other obstacle but myself. If perhaps, as he says, his love for me at first inclined him to God, now that very love hinders him; he lingers with me, prefers me, and I have become the idol that holds him back, keeps him from making further progress in virtue. One of us two must attain it; and as I despair of overcoming the love in my coward heart, grant me, my God, vouchsafe me strength to teach him to love me no longer, so that at the cost of my merits I may bring Thee his, which are so infinitely preferable . . . and if today my soul sobs with grief at losing him, do I not lose him to find him again hereafter in Thee?

Tell me, oh, my God! what soul ever deserved Thee more? Was he not born for something better than to love me? And would I love him so much if he were to stop short at myself? How much all that might become heroic shrinks in the sight of happiness!

Sunday

"God having provided some better thing for us."

Monday, May 3

To think that happiness is here, close by, offering itself, and that one has only to put out one's hand to grasp it. . . .

This morning, as I was talking to him, I consummated the sacrifice.

Monday evening

He leaves tomorrow. . . .

Dear Jérôme, I still love you with infinite tenderness; but nevermore shall I be able to tell you so. The interdiction which I lay upon my eyes, upon my lips, upon my soul, is so hard that to leave you is a relief and a bitter satisfaction.

I strive to act according to reason, but at the moment of action the reasons which made me act escape me, or appear foolish; I no longer believe in them.

The reasons which make me run from him? I no longer believe in them. . . . And yet I do run from him, sadly and without understanding why I run.

Lord! that we might advance toward Thee, Jérôme and I together, each beside the other, each helping the other; that we might walk along the way of life like two pilgrims, of whom one says to the other at times:

"Lean on me, brother, if you are weary," and to whom the other replies:
"It is enough to feel you near me . . ." But no! The way Thou teachest,
Lord, is a narrow way—so narrow that two souls cannot walk in it side by
side.

More than six weeks have gone by without my opening this notebook.
Last month, as I was rereading some of its pages, I became aware of a
foolish, wicked anxiety to write well . . . which I owe to *him*. . . .

As though in this book, which I began only so as to help myself to do
without *him,* I was continuing to write to *him*.

I have torn up all the pages that seemed to me to be *well written.* (I
know what I mean by this.) I should have torn up all those in which there
was any question of him. I should have torn them all up . . . I could
not.

And already, because I tore out those few pages, I had a little feeling
of pride . . . a pride that I should laugh at if my heart were not so sick.

It really seemed as though I had done something meritorious, and as
though what I had destroyed had been of some importance!

July 6

I have been obliged to banish from my bookshelves . . .

I fly from him in one book only to find him in another. I hear his
voice reading me even those pages which I discover without him. I care
only for what interests him, and my mind has taken the form of his to such
an extent that I can distinguish one from the other no better than I did at
the time when I took pleasure in feeling they were one.

Sometimes I force myself to write badly in order to escape from the
rhythm of his phrases; but even to struggle against him is still to be concerned with him. I have made a resolution to read nothing but the Bible
(perhaps the *Imitation* too), and to write nothing more in this book, except, every day, the chief text of my reading.

*There followed a kind of "daily bread," a spiritual diary in which the date
of each day, starting with July 1, was accompanied by a scriptural text. I
transcribe only those which are accompanied by some commentary.*

"Sell all that thou hast and give it to the poor."

I understand that I ought to give to the poor this heart of mine which belongs only to Jérôme. And by so doing should I not teach him at the same time to do likewise? . . . Lord, grant me this courage.

I have stopped reading the *Interior Consolation*. The old-fashioned language greatly charmed me, but it was distracting, and the almost pagan joy it gives me is far removed from the edification which I had intended to get from it.

I have taken up the *Imitation* again, and not even in the Latin text, which I was too vain of understanding. I am glad that the translation I am reading is not even signed. It is true that it is Protestant, but "adapted to the use of all Christian communities," the title says.

"Oh, if thou wert sensible, how much peace thou wouldest procure for thyself and joy for others, by rightly ordering thyself, methinks thou wouldest be more solicitous for thy spiritual progress."

If I were to cry to Thee, my God, with the impulsive faith of a child and with the heavenly tongues of angels . . .

All this comes to me, I know, not from Jérôme, but from Thee.

But why, then, between Thee and me, dost Thou everywhere set his image?

Only two months more in which to complete my work. . . . Oh, Lord, grant me Thy help!

I feel—I feel by my *unhappiness* that the sacrifice is not consummated in my heart. My God, grant that henceforth I owe to none but Thee the joy that he alone used to give me.

How mediocre, how miserable is the virtue to which I attain! Do I then demand too much from myself? . . . Oh, to suffer no more.

What cowardice makes me continually implore God for His strength? My prayers now are nothing but complainings.

August 29

"Consider the lilies of the field . . ."

This simple saying plunged me this morning into a sadness from which nothing could distract me. I went out into the country and these words, which I kept repeating to myself continually, involuntarily, filled my heart and eyes with tears. I contemplated the vast, empty plain where the laborer was toiling, bent over his plow. . . . "The lilies of the field . . ." But, Lord, where are they? . . .

September 16, 10 o'clock at night

I have seen him again. He is here, under this roof. I see the light from his window shining on the grass. He is still up as I write these lines; perhaps he is thinking of me. He has not changed. He says so, and I feel it. Shall I be able to show myself to him such as I have resolved to be, so that his love may disown me?

September 24

Oh, torturing conversation in which I succeeded in feigning indifference —coldness, when my heart was fainting within me! Up till now I had contented myself with avoiding him. This morning I was able to believe that God would give me strength to be victorious, and that to turn my back on the combat forever was to prove myself a coward. Was I victorious? Does Jérôme love me a little less? . . . Alas! I hope it and I fear it at the same time. I have never loved him more.

And if it is Thy will, Lord, that to save him from me I must myself be lost, then Thy will be done.

"Enter into my heart and into my soul in order to bear in them my sufferings and to continue to endure in me what remains to Thee to suffer of Thy Passion."

We spoke of Pascal. . . . What did I say? What shameful, foolish words? If I suffered even as I uttered them, tonight I repent them as a blasphemy. I turned again to the heavy volume of the *Pensées,* which opened of itself at this passage in the letters to Mademoiselle de Roannez: "We do not feel our bonds as long as we follow willingly him who leads;

but as soon as we begin to resist and to draw away, then indeed do we suffer."

These words affected me so personally that I did not have the strength to go on reading; but opening the book in another place I came across an admirable passage which I had not known, and which I have just copied out.

The first volume of the Journal came to an end here. No doubt the next had been destroyed, for in the papers that Alissa left behind, the Journal did not begin again till three years later—still at Fongueusemare—in September—a short time, that is to say, before our last meeting.

The last volume begins with the sentences that follow.

September 17

My God, Thou knowest I have need of him to love Thee.

September 20

My God, give him to me so that I may give Thee my heart.

My God, let me see him only once more.

My God, I vow to give Thee my heart. Grant me what my love beseeches. Then I will give what remains to me of life to Thee alone.

My God, forgive me this despicable prayer, but I cannot keep his name from my lips nor forget the anguish of my heart.

My God, I cry to Thee. Do not forsake me in my distress.

September 21

"Whatever ye shall ask the Father in my name . . ."

Lord, in Thy name, I dare not.

But though I no longer formulate my prayer, wilt Thou be the less aware of the delirious longing of my heart?

September 27

Ever since the morning, a great calm. Spent nearly the whole night in meditation, in prayer. Suddenly I was conscious of a kind of luminous peace, like the image I had as a child of the Holy Ghost; it seemed to wrap me round, to descend into me. I went to bed at once, fearing that I owed my joy only to nervous exaltation. I went to sleep fairly quickly, without this felicity leaving me. It is still here this morning in all its completeness. I have the certainty now that he will come.

Jérôme, my friend! you whom I still call brother, but whom I love infinitely more than a brother . . . How many times I have cried out your name in the beech wood. Every evening toward dusk I go out by the little gate of the kitchen-garden and walk down the avenue where it is already dark. . . . If you were suddenly to answer me, if you were to appear there from behind the stony bank around which I so eagerly seek you, or if I were to see you in the distance, seated on the bench waiting for me, my heart would not leap . . . no, on the contrary: I am astonished at *not* seeing you.

Nothing yet. The sun has set in a sky of incomparable purity. I am waiting. I know that soon I shall be sitting with him on this very bench. . . . I hear his voice already. I love so much to hear him say my name. He will be here! I shall put my hand in his hand. I shall let my head lean on his shoulder. I shall breathe beside him. Yesterday I brought out some of his letters with me to reread, but I did not look at them—I was too much taken up with the thought of him. I took with me, too, the amethyst cross he used to like, and which I used to wear every evening one summer, as long as I did not want him to go.

I should like to give him this cross. For a long time past I have had a dream—that he was married and I godmother to his first daughter, a little Alissa, to whom I gave this ornament. . . . Why have I never dared tell him?

My soul today is as light and joyful as a bird would be that had made its nest in the sky. For today he must come; I feel it; I know it; I should like to proclaim it aloud to the world. I must write it here. I cannot hide my joy any longer. Even Robert, who is usually so inattentive and indifferent to what concerns me, noticed it. His questions embarrassed me, and I did not know what to answer. How shall I be able to wait till this evening? . . .

Some kind of strange transparent bandage over my eyes seems to show me his image everywhere—his image magnified; and to concentrate all love's rays on a single burning spot in my heart.

Oh! how this waiting tires me!

Lord, unclose for me for one moment the wide gateways of gladness.

October 3

All is finished. He has slipped out of my arms like a shadow. He was here! He was here! I feel him still. I call him. My hands, my lips seek him in vain in the night. . . .

I can neither pray nor sleep. I went out again into the dark garden. I was afraid—in my room—everywhere in the house—I was afraid. My anguish brought me once more to the door behind which I had left him. I reopened it with a mad hope—that he might have come back! I called. I groped in the darkness. I have come in again to write to him. I cannot accept my grief.

What has happened? What did I say to him? What did I do? Why do I always need to exaggerate my virtue to him? What can be the worth of a virtue which my whole heart denies? I was secretly false to the words which God put on my lips. In spite of all that my heart was bursting with, I could bring nothing out. Jérôme! Jérôme, my unhappy friend in whose presence my heart bleeds, in whose absence I perish, believe nothing of all I said to you just now, but the words spoken by my love.

Tore up my letter, then wrote again. . . . Here is the dawn, gray, wet with tears, as sad as my thoughts. I hear the first sounds of the farm, and everything that was sleeping reawakens to life. . . . "Arise, now. The hour is at hand. . . ."

I shall not send my letter.

October 5

Oh, jealous God, Thou hast dispossessed me of everything else, take possession now of my heart. All warmth henceforth has forsaken it; nothing will touch it any more. Help me to win out over the melancholy remnant of myself. This house, this garden encourage my love intolerably. I must fly to some place where I shall see none but Thee.

Thou wilt help me to bestow upon Thy poor what fortune I possessed; let me leave Fongueusemare, which I cannot dispose of easily, to Robert. I have made my will, it is true, but I am ignorant of the necessary formalities, and yesterday I could not talk to the lawyer properly because I was afraid he might suspect the decision I had taken and warn Juliette and Robert. I will finish this business in Paris.

October 10

Arrived here so tired that I was obliged to stay in bed the first two days. The doctor, who was sent for against my wishes, speaks of an operation that he considers necessary. What point is there in protesting? But I easily made him believe that I was frightened at the idea of an operation, and preferred waiting till I had "regained my strength a little."

I have managed to conceal my name and address. I have deposited enough money with the management of the house for them to make no difficulty about taking me in and keeping me for as long as God shall continue to think it necessary.

I like this room. The walls need no other decoration than their perfect whiteness. I was quite astonished to feel almost joyful, since I expect nothing more from life—I must be content now with God, and His love is sweet only if it fills us completely and utterly. . . .

I have brought with me no other book but the Bible; but today there resounded in me, louder than any of the words I read there, this wild, desolate cry of Pascal's:

"Whatever is not God cannot satisfy my longing."

Oh! too human joy, that my imprudent heart desired . . . Was it to wring this cry from me, Lord, that Thou hast brought me into this valley of despair?

October 12

Thy Kingdom come. May it come in me; so that Thou alone mayest reign over me and reign over the whole of me. I will no longer grudge Thee my heart.

Though I am as tired as if I were very old, my soul keeps a strange childishness. I am still the little girl who could not go to sleep before everything in her room was tidy and the clothes she had taken off neatly folded beside her bed. . . .

That is how I should like to get ready for death.

October 13

Reread my journal before destroying it. "It is unworthy of noble natures to spread round them the disturbance they feel." It is Clotilde de Vaux, I think, who says this so finely.

Just as I was going to throw this journal into the fire, I felt a kind of warning voice holding me back. I felt that it no longer belonged to me; that I had no right to deprive Jérôme of it; that I had never written it except for him. My anxieties, my doubts, seem to me now so foolish that I can no longer attach any importance to them, or believe that they will disturb Jérôme. My God, grant that he may at times catch in these lines the unskilled accent of a heart passionately desirous of urging him to those heights of virtue which she herself despaired of reaching.

"My God, lead me to the rock that is higher than I."

October 15

"Joy, joy, tears of joy . . ."

Exceeding human joy and beyond all pain, yes, I foresee this radiant joy. The rock I cannot surmount, I know it has a name: happiness. I understand that my whole life will have been in vain if it does not end in happiness. . . . Ah! yet you promise it, Lord, to the soul that renounces and is pure. "Blessed *from henceforth*" said Thy holy word, "Blessed from henceforth are those who die in the Lord." Must I wait until I die? This is the point where my faith wavers, Lord! I cry unto Thee with all my strength. I am in darkness; I am waiting for the dawn. I cry out to Thee until I die. Come and slake the thirst of my heart. I thirst for that happiness, now, at this moment. . . . Or must I persuade myself that I *have* it? And like the impatient bird whose crowing before daybreak calls rather than heralds the dawn, should I not wait for the night to turn pale before I sing?

October 16

Jérôme, I wish I could teach you perfect joy.

This morning, a fit of vomiting shook me terribly. And once it was over, I felt so weak that for a moment I almost hoped for death. But no; first a great calm came over my whole being; then an anguish pierced me, a shudder of the flesh and the spirit; it was like a sudden and disenchanting *illumination* of my whole life. It seemed to me that for the first time I saw the hideously bare walls of my room. I grew frightened. Even now I am writing to reassure myself, to calm myself. Oh Lord! let me reach the end without blasphemy!

I could still get up. I went down on my knees like a child. . . .

I should like to die now, quickly, before realizing again that I am alone.

[Jérôme's narrative: last section]

I saw Juliette again last year. More than ten years had gone by since her last letter, the one that told me of Alissa's death. A journey to Provence gave me the opportunity of stopping over at Nîmes. The Teissières occupy a rather imposing house on the avenue de Feuchères, in the noisy center of town. Although I had written to announce my arrival, it was with considerable emotion that I crossed the threshold.

A maidservant showed me up to the drawing-room, where Juliette joined me in a few minutes. I could have sworn I was looking at Aunt Plantier—the same gait, the same stoutness, the same breathless hospitality. She immediately began plying me with questions (without waiting for my answers) on my career, my manner of living in Paris, my occupations, my acquaintances; what was my business in the South? Why wasn't I going on to Aigues-Vives, where Edouard would be so happy to see me? . . . Then she gave me news of all the family, talked of her husband, her children, her brother, of last year's vintage, of the poor market. . . . I learned that Robert had sold Fongueusemare in order to live at Aigues-Vives; that he was now Edouard's partner, which left her husband free to travel and to look more specifically after the commercial side of the business, while Robert stayed on the land, improving and increasing the plantations.

In the meantime I was looking around uneasily for anything that might recall the past. I recognized, indeed, among the otherwise new furniture of the drawing-room, certain pieces that came from Fongueusemare; but Juliette now seemed to be oblivious of the past that was still quivering within me, or else to be making a great effort to distract our thoughts from it.

Two boys of twelve and thirteen were playing on the stairs; she called them in to introduce them to me. Lise, the eldest of her children, had gone with her father to Aigues-Vives. Another boy of ten was expected in from his walk; this was the one Juliette told me she was expecting when she sent me news of our bereavement. There had been some trouble over his last confinement; Juliette had suffered from its effects for a long time; then last year, as if on second thought, she had given birth to a little girl; to hear her talk, she preferred this new infant to all her other children. "My room, where she sleeps, is next door," she said. "Come and see her." And as I was following her: "Jérôme, I didn't dare write to you . . . would you consent to be the baby's godfather?"

"But of course, I accept with pleasure, if you would like me to," said I, slightly surprised, as I bent over the cradle. "What is my god-daughter's name?"

"Alissa . . ." replied Juliette, in a whisper. "She is a little like her, don't you think so?"

I pressed Juliette's hand, without answering. Little Alissa, whom her mother lifted, opened her eyes; I took her in my arms.

"What a good father you would make!" said Juliette, trying to laugh. "What are you waiting for to marry?"

"To have forgotten a great many things," I replied, and watched her blush.

"Which you are hoping to forget soon?"

"Which I hope never to forget."

"Come in here," she said suddenly, leading the way into a smaller room, which was already dark; one of its doors led into her bedroom, another into the drawing-room. "This is where I take refuge when I have a moment to myself; it is the quietest room in the house; I feel as if I were almost sheltered from life here."

The window of this small sitting-room did not look onto the town with its noises, like those of the other rooms, but rather to a sort of courtyard planted with trees.

"Let us sit down," said she, dropping into an armchair. "If I understand you rightly, it is to Alissa's memory that you mean to remain faithful."

I stayed a moment without answering. "Rather, perhaps, to her image of me. No, don't give me any credit for it. I don't think I could do anything else. If I married another woman, I could only pretend to love her."

"Ah!" she said, as though indifferently; then, turning her face away from me, she bent it toward the ground as if looking for something she had lost. "Then you think that one can keep a hopeless love in one's heart for as long as that?"

"Yes, Juliette."

"And that life can breathe upon it every day, without extinguishing it?" . . .

The evening came slowly up like a gray tide, reaching and then drowning each object, which seemed, in the gloom, to come back to life again and repeat in a whisper the story of its past. Once more I saw Alissa's room; Juliette had collected all its furniture together in this one place. And then she turned her face toward me again, but it was too dark for me to distinguish her features, so that I did not know whether her eyes were open or closed. She seemed to be very beautiful. And we both now sat still without speaking.

"Come!" said she at last. "We must wake up."

I saw her rise, take a step forward, drop again as though she had no strength, into the nearest chair; she put her hands up to her face and I thought I saw that she was crying.

A maid came in, bringing the lamp.

 FOUR   *1914—1919*

INTRODUCTION

It was part of the nature of André Gide, as of most men of letters of his generation, to regard politics, current history, what most people think of as "news" as matters of no great importance unless directly related to literature. After a dinner party in May 1906, he wrote of his disgust for a fellow guest who dismissed the May Day strike of that year, the San Francisco earthquake of the month before, as " 'unimportant little events' . . . this failing belongs to three-fourths of the literary men and intellectuals of today." But it was a failing from which he himself was not entirely exempt. This detachment from daily events, in part a legacy from Mallarmé and the Symbolists, in part the reflection of a kind of international literary withdrawal between 1890 and 1914, was accentuated in Gide's case by his constitutional reluctance to regard the world of events as altogether real. "I have never managed to take this life quite seriously . . . Indefinable impression of being 'on tour' and of playing, in makeshift sets, with cardboard daggers" (*Journal,* 1929). When confronted very nearly face to face with a "historic event" typical of the period—the assassination attempt on the King of Spain during his visit to Paris in 1905—"Again I noticed in me that disinclination," he wrote, "to *take the event seriously* . . . it didn't seem to be real life. As soon as the act was over, the actors would come back and take a bow."

So until history was suddenly forced upon his (and his generation's) attention in 1914, one can make out only a dim imprint of outside events in Gide's writings. For years he *thought* he had watched the Prussian army marching into Rouen in 1870 (when he was one year old), and was greatly chagrinned when his mother pointed out that this was impossible. One can detect a faint trace of the clashes of 1879–1880 between Royalists and Republicans, between Catholics and anticlericals in a little boy's curious questions (and his mother's more curious answers) about what atheists were, and how he was to describe his political affiliation. To the Dreyfus Case, the great polarizing issue of Third Republic France, there is almost no reference in Gide's writings of the time. Some have thought to see a kind of *dreyfusard* parable in his *Philoctète*

of 1899, which is a bit unlikely; on the affair, he wrote to Francis
Jammes in April 1898, "I have convictions, if you like, but no opinion. I
am not so fond of men—even of Frenchmen—that I can approve the
unjust oppression of one of them under the pretext of protecting them
all."

A line in Gide's *Journal* for December 1905 evokes the *Potemkin*
revolt; he attended the Meg Steinhel trial—a notorious Parisian murder
trial—in 1909; and he makes note of a long conversation on the Chinese
Revolution of 1912. But this represents about the limit to which outside
news events intrude into his written accounts before 1914. Of the Boer
War, the Russo-Japanese War, the Boxer Rebellion, the Mexican Revolution, of Moroccan massacres or Irish rioting or Balkan uprisings, of the
deaths of Victoria and McKinley and Leo XIII, of the years of rancorous
warfare between Church and State in France, of the great strikes, of the
Wright brothers' flight or the theft of the *Mona Lisa* or the sinking of
the *Titanic* there is not a word: which is of course not unusual; one does
not look to private and literary records for the headlines of an era. I point
it out only as a reminder that one of the more abrupt effects the outbreak
of World War I had on active European thinkers—like André Gide—
was that of redirecting their attention to the social and political forces
around them.

Until 1914, Gide could be called willfully apolitical, or even anti-
political. He was distressed no less by the liberal partisanship of old
friends like Léon Blum than by the traditionalist bias of his Catholic-
convert associates. He despised nothing so much as "tendentious" literature, art deformed in the interests of a cause, to the point that his obtuse,
conservative "imaginary interviewer" (in the "Letter to Ducoté" of
1905) is led to ask him, "Do you really mean that you consider politics
and the rest, I mean social and economic questions, matters of no serious
interest and not worth the attention of a cultivated mind?"

Yet Gide's activity before 1914, in the pages of the *N.R.F.* and
elsewhere, was not, as we have seen, without its implications in the political arena. The single most important issue of the time in France (of
which the Dreyfus Case was both the symbol and the climactic episode)
was the war between the entrenched forces of order—the existing order
(Church, army, monarchists)—and the advocates of political and social
liberalization (trade unionists, republicans, anticlericals). Gide cannot,
of course (as he properly insists), be said to have "taken a seat" on either
side. But his critical essays, written in the pure, non-partisan defense of
reason, most often found their targets (Barrès, Maurras, Lemaître, Pro-

fessor Faguet—all Academicians—Clouard, Senator Bérenger) on what one would have to call the Right. And what he is most determinedly *resisting* in such men are their attempts to turn patriotism into nationalism, to establish and enforce a French "orthodoxy," to brand any influences, authors, or ideas they do not like as subversive, corrupting, and "un-French" (in the same sense that the term "un-American" came to be used in the 1950's).

There could hardly have been—or so it must have seemed—a set of attitudes less appropriate, less useful than Gide's, for the new cultural conditions of wartime France, a temperament less prepared to respond to the sudden call to arms. His prized ahistorical disengagement, his individualist superiority to nationalism and politics were, overnight, rendered irrelevant, worse than useless. "We were plunging into a world in which our competence and our values had become worthless," wrote Jean Schlumberger, "in which individual destinies were to be dominated by exterior forces . . . each of us was going to have to start all over again, and try to insert himself into this new order . . ." [1]

That Gide felt this sudden discomfiture is painfully obvious. There are few spectacles more poignant than that of the dedicated (but conscientious and generous) artist trying to know what he should *do* in time of war. (Except perhaps that of the warrior in time of peace: "Othello's occupation's gone.") All Gide's carefully nurtured self-assurance could be melted into shame by the heat of inflamed public opinion—shame of his privileges, of his impotence to help, of his very individualism, his difference from others. "I cannot keep convincing myself that my role is to retreat . . . I should like to be used in some more direct fashion; offer myself to some active service." [2] "You would have to look a long way in France nowadays to find the man of letters who has not written 'on the war,'" he wrote Edmund Gosse in 1916; "in point of fact, *I* think they do it as an excuse for not being at the front." [3]

Gide's responses to the war are not to be explained or understood simply. They were, like so many of his other responses, complex and even contradictory. Of the actual events, strategy, and direction of the war, he knew very little, and he was ill-equipped to interpret what he learned. His reaction to "events," whether he saw them himself or imagined them from press reports or soldiers' and refugees' tales, is often disconcertingly like that of any excitable, ill-informed, unthinking French bourgeois. In the first weeks of the war in particular, writing every day in his *Journal,* he is snatching at rumors, reading six newspapers a day, second-guessing generals, worrying about invasions, scribbling enthusias-

tic top-of-the-head patriotism about the holy war and the new era, and
running about looking for places to serve. None of which should surprise
us: it is of the nature of such earthquakes to level everyone to a common
state, to a common helplessness, a common emotional susceptibility.
Moreover, after learning how easily the enemy had rolled over the
Somme, Gide *did* have reason to believe that his home and family at
Cuverville might be in the path of a German advance on Le Havre. He
sent most of the household to safety on the coast, then, as he wrote later
to friends, "lived through ten days of frightful anxiety, expecting the
worst," waiting at home with his wife (who would not leave), "three
maids, and two young country girls, rapable at will [*violable à
merci*] . . ." "When the communiqués gave us reason to believe that
the flood no longer threatened Normandy"—the German march had deflected southeast—"they showed it to be so close to Paris that our anxiety
merely changed form . . . Then came the victory [the Battle of the
Marne, September 6–11, which halted the German advance and froze
the Western Front], and we were able to breathe once more." [4]

Some have, out of selected quotations, made a case for Gide the
super-patriot, the *jusqu'au-boutiste* (a proponent of war "to the bitter
end")—a position which will seem as disreputable to many today as that
of pacifist or conciliator did during the war. Of course he was neither. He
was seized, as we have seen, by a rush of nationalist spirit during the first
weeks of German invasion; between 1916 and 1918, he occasionally
succumbed to the lure of Charles Maurras's proto-fascist *Action Française* ("proto-fascist," of course, is a label one applies in retrospect).
Disgusted as he was at its lies, its distortions, its regimentation of opinion, at times he thought it the only serious organ of resistance.* Moreover, he does seem to have been shaken by the specter of socialism, of the
Russian Revolution. "During the war," he wrote in 1934, "I was unable
to put up any resistance (I am sufficiently ashamed of it today) to the
mindless enthusiasms of the friends who surrounded me at that time
. . . My Uncle Charles, who had in no way given up *his* freedom of
thought, was amazed by our excessive chauvinism (I say *our,* because I
let myself be dragged into it) . . ." [5]

---

* In *Les Faux-Monnayeurs* (1927), Gide's young hero Bernard ritualistically rejects the
positions of the *Action Française*.

> "Do you think I ought to sign?"
> "Yes," said the angel, "certainly—if you have doubts of yourself."
> "I have no longer," said Bernard . . .
>
> (Part Three, Chapter XIV)

But when Gide did think independently and originally on the war
—and his journal entries, at least, are far more often independent than
"patriotic"—his thoughts ran almost naturally in what must have
seemed a subversive direction. After all, the ideas and attitudes he had
been fighting so ardently were now more dominant than ever: the
Church (which gained an immense propaganda victory of its own from
the bombing of Rheims Cathedral, virtually identifying its cause with
that of France), the chauvinistic bigotry of Maurras, the purple-prose
heroics of Barrès. Over and over again, Gide records his revulsion at the
"patriotic" lies, the partisan silences and exaggerations of the ubiquitous
anti-German, pro-French propaganda. Perversely, almost in defiance of
the propaganda, he persists in seeing French faults and German virtues
—as he was to do during the next war as well. He even wonders whether
a German victory might be a good thing for so decayed, so morally
rotten a country as France—a speculation one could no more safely express in 1914 than in 1944. Very pointedly, he reads Nietzsche, defends
Goethe, and concludes that "we have everything to learn from the Germans," that the genius of each country needs that of the other.

On the whole, it would seem that Gide tried to ignore the war. If
his imagination occasionally wandered to the trenches, he was by nature
disinclined to force a tension, to whip up a constant internal frenzy over
what were still, after all, for him "mere" historic events—be they tanks,
poison gas, zeppelin bombs, or the nine million dead, let alone the
battles or political crises of a day ("to tell the truth, political questions
do not much interest me"). The *N.R.F.* was shut down, of course—there
was no place for such a journal now—its staff in uniform and dispersed.
Gide abandoned himself as long as he could stand it (about a year and a
half) to the mind-drugging work of finding homes and food and funds
for refugees at the Foyer Franco-Belge: at first "devoured by sympathy"
for the waves of homeless families who filed past his desk, he found
himself eventually growing apathetic, demoralized, his mind numb from
disuse, his spirit sluggish and depressed from the contemplation of this
constant progression of other people's miseries. So he slipped, half-
guiltily, back to his own timeless, extra-bellum concerns: his garden, his
piano, and what a benign fellow-philanthropist called his "little literary
recreations." "Were it not for *opinion*," he wrote, "I feel that even under
the enemy fire I should enjoy one of Horace's odes." [6] All this against
the moral will (at least the expressed moral will) of a nation insisting
on militancy and nothing else: *"La guerre, rien que la guerre, jusqu'à la
victoire"*—War, nothing but war, until we win: the slogan of Clemen-

ceau. He wrote nothing new for publication during the war but a couple
of prefaces and an essay on his refugee center: what literary work he did,
once escaped from the Foyer, was confined to translating Shakespeare
and Conrad and, in particular, to writing his memoirs.

> If anyone is surprised that I can enjoy this work while the echo of
> cannon is still shaking the earth, I shall explain that it is just be-
> cause any work of imagination is impossible for me, and any intel-
> lectual work. Within and without me I feel an immense upset, and
> if I am writing these memoirs today, it is also true that I cling des-
> perately to them.   (*Journal,* June 15, 1916)

Reading in its original context Gide's little essay on "Refugees," his
contribution to a rather grand philanthropic enterprise called *The Book
of France,* I find it particularly reflective of his unique position among
the writers of the day. His spare, understated, uninflated description of
the Foyer Franco-Belge, of a typical refugee case could almost be taken
directly from the *Journal* or one of his letters. For Gide, the essay is
neither exceptional nor distinguished. But in this volume (a bilingual
gift book sponsored by an eminent honorary committee, the proceeds to
go to refugee organizations) it looks jarringly naked, surrounded as it is
by all the pompous and sentimental encrustations of 1915 rhetoric.

Here are all the dead fictions and figures of self-indulgent imagination, long out of touch with the real—a rhetoric as surely a victim of the
war as the nine million men. Here are the (to us) appalling sentimental-
ities of plucky little amputees, moonlight sparkling on the shattered
stained glass of Rheims, the matchless honor of shedding one's blood for
la patrie on the field of honor.

> No fate, surely, is so worthy of our envy as the glorious death of
> those who in a joyful sacrifice redeem their country and their race,
> achieving, not only victory, but the downfall of a tyrant and the
> triumph of human right and freedom.   (Mary Duclaux)[7]

Here are the sacred bloody flags of a chivalrous land, pacifists only "a bit
of offal from a decaying nation," the angelic cozy-pastel diaries of noble
ladies playing nurse, apocalyptic visions of the end of all civilization,
aristocratic-pastoral images of France (as opposed to horrid, vulgar, in-
dustrial Germany), Manichaean cartoons of the enemy as barbarians,
brutes, savages, and worse.

> . . . Oh to think of the gross and dastardly and brainless brutality
> of hurling those canisters of scrap-iron in volleys against the fret-

work, delicate as lace, which for centuries has reared itself proudly
and confidently in air, and which so many battles, invasions, and
whirlwinds had never dared to touch! . . . The truth is that the
barbarians had premeditated and prepared this sacrilege long beforehand. . . . It was some superstitious idea which drove them to
it, not merely their natural instinct as savages . . . [the pave-
ment] has been lately blackened and defiled by contact with the
charred flesh of human beings . . .

(Pierre Loti, *"La Basilique-Fantôme,"*
translated by Sir Sidney Colvin.)[8]

Of the distinguished contributors and their distinguished translators—Maurice Barrès, Anatole France, Thomas Hardy, Henry James, H.
G. Wells, Rudyard Kipling, Pierre Loti, Rémy de Gourmont, Rosny
ainé, three duchesses and the Comtesse de Noailles—a few do venture
home-truths about France, Germany, and war: but *all*—with the exception of Gide—are trapped in the old, decaying, no longer relevant forms
of their respective languages. And as language is the surest, most com-
prehensive index of a culture, I cannot but see in this musty anthology an
explanation both for Gide's intellectual discomfort, his "placelessness"
during the war, and for his quick rise to intellectual dominance once it
was over.

On the whole, from whatever angle viewed, the image of Gide in
wartime—as of so many Frenchmen of this century—is not a pleasant
thing to contemplate. It does change, from that of the patriot of '14 to
that of the pacifist of '17, but he was simply not the man to rise above
and to dominate external events of such magnitude and such horror.
There is a defensive, uncertain, more than usually inconsistent tone about
much of his writing in response to *"La Grande Guerre."*
    And yet a case could be made that the First World War was the
determining event in Gide's public career: that it "made" him, as we say;
that he was one of the very few authors or thinkers to have won, or won
from, the war, as Sartre and Camus and Malraux can be said to have
"won" from the next.
    As the war dragged on, through fifty-two unbelievable months,
more and more people came to realize that this was *not* to be just another
war, one of the wars old Europe had known so often: that the very nature of this ghastly war was revealing, more and more nakedly, the bank-

ruptcy of the *ancien régime*—not only of Gide's special opponents and targets, the super-patriots, the purple proseurs, but of all that, under their guidance, had passed for "civilization" until then. "Everything that represents tradition is doomed to be upset," he wrote in 1919; but he had predicted as much in 1914 or before. The World War brought millions of people by sheer main force to the same state of stark, stripped, lonely self-dependence Gide had *elected* and promulgated long before. They were ready for him now, as he was for them.

Those who wonder at Gide's belated coming to fame miss, I think, this crucial point. Without the war, or at an earlier time, his "rebellion" would very likely have remained a literary one, Joycean at best, his battles with believers grown more dated and irrelevant, his lassitude turned to rot. He was, instead, plunged into meaningful moral action, elevated to his exemplary role precisely *by* 1914–1918. In a sense, all was apprenticeship, all was simply in attendance, in abeyance, before the war, before the world caught fire and Gide's lucidity and moral freedom —the whole arsenal of moral weapons he had been forging *in vacuo*— met their test. The European world suddenly thought that its gods were all tumbling; for Gide, they had tumbled years before, and he was ready, unshocked and unflustered, to tell people how to react and behave.

In a way, it was precisely for having remained silent (and essentially unduped, uncommitted), for having been unable to speak out throughout the four years of the war—a war that did in the end reveal both sides, and the institutions behind them, to have been almost equally corrupt—it was this very silence that permitted Gide, and the *N.R.F.* writers generally, to emerge as pure and trustworthy spokesmen after the war. "I would say that at such a conjuncture," Charles Du Bos wrote in 1921, "the only proper attitude for the writer or thinking man is that adopted by Gide when the two of us founded, in October 1914, our center for refugees, and he said to me, 'The duty of a writer during the war is not to write': thus it was that, perhaps alone among writers, he found himself just as pure, just as intact after the events as before." [9] Having long proposed a way to lead the moral life in a moral desert, he suddenly became very important to a great many people who found themselves in one. For having, against all the outer and inner pressures, held to the unpopular belief that language ought only to be used with purity and accuracy, he became a rock for all those tired to death of the inflations and the lies of wartime words—inflations and lies that had come so naturally to the pens of the pre-modern breed of writers, the

Academicians, the patriots, his co-contributors to *The Book of France,* discredited so quickly after 1919.

> France is ruined through rhetoric; an oratorical nation accustomed to take words at face value, adept in taking words for things, and prompt in setting formulas above reality.[10]

The cultural distance between the two authors is immense, but Gide's protest recalls the famous "embarrassment" of Hemingway's lieutenant at "the words sacred, glorious, and sacrifice and the expression in vain." Hemingway's service to an English language debased by wartime rhetoric is, I think, distinctly comparable to Gide's service to the French.

And so out of the experience of a war in which he must sometimes have felt the most useless, dated, alien, and ill-equipped of Europeans, without even the moral assurance of a pacifist or pro-German, André Gide emerged in 1919 as one of the few relevant and trustworthy moral leaders for the generation of survivors.

As I mentioned in the last chapter, it was during this period that Gide seems to have come closest to a return to religious faith. But as I suggested as well, it is possible we overemphasize that return, for several reasons. His abiding nostalgia for a Protestant childhood (kept alive in part as an act of resistance to the Catholics on his trail), his attendant fascination with the Bible and with Christian imagery, must not be read too quickly as evidences of faith. Very often he reinterpreted and secularized this legacy, cored it of its center of dogma or faith in such a way that he could stay a freethinker without having to scuttle dear memories. The almost incredible—one is tempted to say miraculous—incidence of conversion among his closest friends led to troubled and intense interrogations: *why* had they all done it? To one unaware of this circumstance, he may sound suspiciously obsessed by, and overdefensive *against* the attractions of faith. And finally, as I noted, the particular interests of many people who have written about Gide force attention to the aspects of his thought that matter most to them.

The basic documents of this apparent near-return are his correspondence with Paul Claudel and the green, or twenty-fourth, notebook of his journals, entitled *Numquid et tu . . . ?,* in which he confided certain prayers and religious speculations of 1916. He later added two more pages, and published it in an anonymous edition of seventy copies in 1922; then printed it publicly, with the preface included here, in 1926. As I have chosen to include only small samplings of each of these documents, let me venture a brief analysis, based on the whole texts and certain other materials, of Gide's "religious activity" during the years of the First World War.

1. By his own admission he was conditioned for (if not pushed into) his "impulse toward God" in 1916 by three things: the general desolation of the wartime air, and the particular desolation of his work at the Foyer; the conversion at the front of Henri Ghéon, one of his most intimate friends from the *N.R.F.;* and particularly the wearying burden of his particular "sin," the "solitary vice" of his childhood and adolescence, into which he had refallen with the desperation of an addict. The war, the gloom, his nerves, inactivity and self-disgust lead him into manic masturbation—which for him, now, is almost more a symbol than an act, a sign of waste and introversion, a proof of the drying up of all other sources of pleasure and agitation, all other signs of life. Deprived of other people, outside interests, creative activity, a worn, listless man of forty-six seeks momentary self-release on an iron bed in a gray landscape in the second year of war, and finds himself becoming as *dependent* on this means of agitation and escape as an addict on his drugs. Because it is, of itself, so wretchedly depressing, he cannot simply "accept," yield to it in the dark of war and wait for light and life to return. He is left more ashamed and dissatisfied than ever. His friends are all turning to God; all France seems to be turning to God; he knows the way, the ritual; he is despairing of his own resources to save him from this tiresome, hopeless morass; he feels, momentarily, crushed. And so he prays, he turns to God, to *outside support:*

. . . hold out a hand to me, then. Lead me yourself to that place, near you, which I am unable to reach.*

. . . What does it matter that it is to escape yielding to sin that I yield to the Church! I yield. Oh, take off the ropes that restrain me. Deliver me from the frightful weight of this body.

O Lord, if you are to help me, what are you waiting for? I cannot do anything, all alone. I cannot.[11]

---

* The prayer is very nearly the same as one he wrote for Alissa in *La Porte étroite,* seven years before.

"Je ne puis pas, tout seul. Je ne peux pas."

2. Having made the decision, he sets about his project of yielding to divine grace, of creating in himself a state of spiritual receptivity, with remarkable system and self-discipline, as one would undertake a serious diet or a budget. He reads Bossuet until he finds it frosting his purpose, then switches to the more genial Pascal; later to readings in Fénelon, Wilfred Hale White, and always of course the Bible. Half-hour meditations on God, morning and night. A visit to a church at dusk. He is not so much actively praying as waiting, or at most praying to be able to pray; *trying very hard* to realize God, to put himself into the posture of one willing to listen, to submit to His grace. He is already so inert, so morally confused, and hence so self-disgusted that humility seems a natural posture. If his prayers seem spineless, childish, soft, mere manual-of-piety exercises, that is their intent: he is seeking to become depersonalized, unoriginal, non-resistant.

3. With little success. His "lucidity" will not be darkened, he *sees* what he is doing, and again and again his mind rebels—or what Catholics would call his pride. It rebels against Bossuet, against Claudel, against Saint Paul, against the institutional Church and its members.

> No. I cannot enter through *that* gate . . . I can affect stupidity . . . but not for long, and I soon revolt against that impious comedy I am trying to play on myself . . . I can give up my reason but I cannot distort it . . .[12]

Finally, it rebels against the whole venture, against his willed miming of memorized pious exercises, his pretended hatred of his "sins." He feels it is simply a farce, and his conscience will not let him keep it up.

> Gave up my readings and those pious exercises which my heart, utterly dry and listless, no longer approved. See nothing in it but a comedy, and a dishonest comedy, in which I convinced myself that I recognized the hand of the demon . . . (May 12, 1916)

> Forgive me, Lord! Yes, I know that I am lying. The truth is that this flesh which I hate, I still love it more than You Yourself . . . (October 3, 1916)

By March 1, 1917, he is writing, "It strikes me that I was foolish and guilty to bend my mind artificially so as to make it better understand

the Catholic teaching. That is where the real impiety lies." On March 23,
"A most touching letter from Ghéon. But, despite a few rare, stray impulses, my soul remains inattentive and closed—too enamored of its sin
to consent to follow the path that would take it away from that." By
October of the following year, trying to make use of his own religious
sentiments of 1916 in order to write *La Symphonie pastorale,* he admits,
"I have the greatest difficulty getting interested again in the state of mind
of my pastor, and I fear that the end of the book may suffer from this."
Once his decision is finally made to abandon the effort, he tries to shut
and double-lock the door, to do a kind of special penance for his own so-
long-indulged temptation to conversion by turning more determinedly,
more angrily anti-Catholic (recalling old griefs against Claudel, forever
lamenting or insulting Ghéon) than he ever had been before.

4. But already this formulation is too neat, implying as it does a
chronological progress—from fatigue to acquiescence to resistance. Actually the "truest" Gide in *Numquid et tu. . . ?* is at no moment either the
humble suppliant or the anti-Christian reasoner, but a master rhetorician
steering his devious, private course between the two. The course is shifting
and intricate, sometimes difficult to follow or to understand (and particularly resistant to analysis); but it seems absolutely necessary to Gide, more
necessary than either dependence on or independence from God. By
means of it, he is guarding some inner quality, some freedom or
equilibrium absolutely essential to him, the very quality by which one
recognizes André Gide.

This self-correcting mechanism, this compulsive "steering between"
is most evident in Gide's adoption of extra voices and characters, splitting
his conscience—or a fictionalized version of his conscience—into self and
other-self, self and God, or, especially, self and devil (a favorite device).*
Once he has done that, *he* has escaped. Our attention is fixed on the dialectic of the divided self—a dialectic or debate which the "real" Gide is now
conducting from outside. He carefully adjusts the two parts so that both
grow gradually more independent, more fictional, until finally in neither
—in nothing but the vacillating, invisible, unlocatable energy of the rep-
artee itself—can he himself be definitely traced.

It is a dazzling performance, similar to that by which his admitted
fictions were created. But it should give us pause (even granting 1, 2, and

---

* See Carrier, W., "The Demoniacal in Gide," *Renascence,* Fall, 1951; Klossowski, P.,
"Gide, Du Bos, et le Démon," Les Temps modernes, Sept. 1950; Du Bos, C., *Le Dialogue
avec André Gide* (Paris, 1947), 279–82; Watson, G. D., "Gide and The Devil," *Australian
Journal of French Studies,* Jan.–Apr., 1967.

3 above) before assigning *any* fixed opinion or belief to Gide, at any time.

He cites the strongest arguments he knows, in his surest rational voice, against his "religious" aspirations—but then hedges his bet, keeps on his private course, by calling them (possibly) the arguments of the devil. He excoriates his "sin," then immediately half-apologizes for using the very word—thus leaving himself a loophole to escape through in case he should choose to re-embrace it later on.

The cry I quoted above—"hold out a hand to me . . . I yield . . . Deliver me . . ." of October 15, 1916—was itself, I should make clear, part of a carefully dramatized dialogue with God, ever so slightly suspect in its histrionic tone. But two days later its rhetorical intricacy was trebled, was cubed by a subsequent entry:

> A happy equilibrium almost immediately followed my lapse and my distress. I should like to see in it a reply to my appeal, but at the moment that I was uttering that cry, how well I know it, the best part of my distress was over. . . .
>
> I write this without any irreverence, but because I believe both that the act of piety is not necessarily the result (the successful outcome) of the distress and that it is unseemly to seek to interest God in physical lapses that can be just as well cured by a better-ordered life.

If one can follow the private diplomacy of that remark, so exquisitely careful not to take sides, not to close any doors, he will be in closer touch, I think, with Gide's moral temper than would those who study only his prayers or only his protestations, and not this invisible "alternating current" between. One more example—I must confess I am fascinated by these examples of rhetorical ingenuity (fully the equal of Hume's or of Swift's, although aimed at an audience of one) in the service of self-preservation; but I do think their implications go far beyond the so-called religious crisis of 1916.

> Gave up my readings and those pious exercises which my heart, utterly dry, had ceased to approve. See nothing in it but a comedy, and a dishonest comedy, in which I convinced myself that I recognized the hand of the demon. This is what the demon whispers to my heart.
>
> O Lord! Oh, do not leave him the last word. I do not wish for any other prayer today.

I trace in this short, devious entry (quoted in part earlier) at least three, possibly four "about-faces," all held in dubious suspension. It is no wonder Gide found the "Evil One" so useful a fiction. In a world, like his, bare of absolute rules, there are no absolute means for testing one's acts for their "virtue." One never knows, for sure. Any act that begins in self-denial (or seems to) is likely to end in self-indulgence; and neither is a sure proof of virtue in any case. The "devil"—the symbol of *complaisance,* of yielding to the easy rather than the right answer, the voice in which one fools oneself about one's motives—is a necessary creature of this world of moral self-dependence. In so vividly dramatizing his existence, Gide dramatizes —and to some degree escapes, or at least manages to enjoy and exploit— his own dilemma, and frees himself from any obligation to choose.

5. In the end, what one makes of Gide's dialogues with God and the devil, his interpretations of Scripture and speculations on eternity will depend on the nature of one's own faith. Most of the published Green Notebook (he edited out a great deal) is composed of nothing more "religious" than a perversely Gidean exegesis of scriptural texts, and anyone who took it as a token of approaching conversion was simply not reading very carefully. Gide's peculiar and halfhearted theology—the God-to-come, created-by-us business, first put together in these years—has always struck me as the barren (and unsuccessful) attempt of a humanist-optimist to graft the word "God," out of some lingering affection for the concept, onto a philosophy which has no need of or place for it. To the believer, this "crisis" will all appear an authentic episode from the Drama of Grace—*Gide and the Hound of Heaven,* Harold March has titled it—in which all of Gide's anguish and ennui are simply trials sent by God in the hope of turning the prodigal homeward. To the believer, his rejection of the call to faith will seem not the result of a return to health and active work, of a fresh love and a new psychic equilibrium, but rather the result of pride—unbending, overweening, sinful pride; and the pitiable enchainment by his own lusts. "The truth is that this flesh which I hate, I still love it more than You Yourself."

To the non-believer (depending on the degree of his intransigence about "superstitions") this will appear either (a) a childish weakness, an unthinkably retrograde falling back on fairy tales; or (b) something to be explained entirely by psychology and the accidents of biographical background. The man trained as a Christian but now an agnostic will, in his moments of greatest strain, when he feels his own resources unable to cope, turn back to the outside resources he knows best, and knows best how to invoke. It was in this latter fashion that Gide himself, of course, tended to explain his religious fit once it had passed.

To have talked of the war and of God is still to have overlooked the events of these years that many people (prompted by Gide's own highly dramatic rendering of them, and the naturally greater *emotional* attention we pay to private than to public adventures) regard as the crucial episode of the time, if not of Gide's life: his falling in love with young Marc Allégret, and his subsequent estrangement from Madeleine Gide. In view of all that Gide has done and meant, of his literary achievement and moral influence, I tend to see this sexual-domestic crisis as less than centrally important, despite Gide's own insistences to the contrary. He seems to me to have been already established in the direction he was to follow, the role he was to play, and though I do not doubt his accounts of either the ecstatic joy or the profound wretchedness that this chain of events was to cause him, I must confess I cannot envision the essential pattern of the next thirty years of his life as falling out much differently than it did— even had he never taken up with young Marc, even had his wife never burned his precious letters. So many things were fixed by 1917–1918: at that point, Gide seems to me to be rolling irresistibly down his natural and necessary slope; these particular, so very dramatic incidents in his private life may at most have determined the manner, the momentary angle, but not, I think, the direction or ultimate goal of his descent.

Gide has expressed himself eloquently, if not completely, on both of these intersecting dramas. Let me only fill in some missing details, sketch the stories of Marc and Madeleine through to their conclusion, and leave the reader to make his own moral judgments.

Marc Allégret was born in December 1900, the fourth of five sons of the Protestant pastor and missionary Elie Allégret, an old and close friend of the Rondeaux-Gides. Pastor Allégret helped prepare young André for his first Communion in 1886; stood as his best man in 1895; and later entrusted his sons, and especially Marc, to Gide's tutorial care. During the war, Gide was a frequent visitor at the Allégrets' home in Paris, and led the boys into the shelters during air-raid alerts.

In May 1917, he fell in love with young Marc. As if by magic, three years of anguished *Journal* records—records of headaches and insomnia, of frustration and obsession to the point of madness, of "abominable" desires, "abominable" imaginings, "abominable" relapses into masturbation (and the desperate attempts to resist them)—as if by magic all that stops: so do the prayers, the waiting on God. In August, he journeyed to Switzerland to bring the boy home from camp, and the holiday they spent together Gide records with lyric and sensual delight. The word he chooses, over and over in the months ahead, to describe his new complex of emotion is *joy, joie,* the mystic's term for a luminous, inexpressible rapture. His most common image for it is that of the sun, a radiant, warm, "pagan" sun in a clear internal sky, dispelling the old clouds of frustration, obsession, and guilt.

> How beautiful it is! The sky so pure . . . Never have I felt younger and happier than I did last month . . . (September 21)

> Today glorious weather. My inner sky is even more radiant; a vast joy softens and exalts me.   (October 1)

> I have lived all these recent weeks (and, altogether, since May 5) in a giddy dream of happiness; whence the long empty space in this notebook. It reflects only my clouds.   (October 22)

> M. loves me . . . Never have I enjoyed life more, nor has the savor of life seemed more delicious to me.   (October 25)

> Joy; equilibrium and lucidity.   (October 28)

> Never have I aspired less toward rest . . . Age cannot manage to drain sensual pleasure of its power of attraction, nor the whole world of its charm.   (October 30)

> I received from M. yesterday a letter full of exquisite fancy and grace that lighted up all my thoughts.   (November 1)

> Immense delirium of happiness. My joy has something untamed, wild, incompatible with all decency, all propriety, all law . . .
> Everything in me blossoms forth; is amazed; my heart beats wildly; an overabundance of life rises to my throat like a sob. (November 30)

> I was filled with a vast, singing joy the whole time.   (December 8)

> The thought of M. keeps me in a constant state of lyricism I had not known since my *Nourritures.* I no longer feel my age, or the horror of our time, or the season . . .   (December 15)

In so passionate a relationship, all is not joy: there are other enchanted trips, but there are also days of agonizing waiting, compulsive rushes back to Paris, moments of murderous jealousy. (To Jean Cocteau, who seemed at one time a rival for the boy's affections, Gide admitted years later, "I could have killed you.")

How early and how much of this affair were known to his wife, how seriously it affected her now seems relatively clear. A letter from Henri Ghéon to her husband, which she innocently if inopportunely opened in the summer of 1916, confirmed whatever suspicions, or reinforced whatever assurance she may have had about André's sexual needs. (Ghéon, at the moment of his battlefront conversion, had apparently used the letter to renounce very specifically the sins he and Gide had shared in the past.) In the judgment of Gide's biographers, this is the "dreadful crisis" Gide alludes to in his *Journal* for September 15 of that year. Shortly after that— October 7, October 21: the time is coincident with that of his bleakest sensual anguish, his gestures toward God—we find the first explicit references of a twenty-one-years' marriage to any serious disharmony between himself and Madeleine. In the summer of 1917, she appears to have known very well what Gide's pretended solicitude for the Allégret family implied (he was not particularly discreet) and was deeply distressed at both the public impropriety and the deceit and dishonor André was visiting on the pastor and his wife, two close and respected friends of hers. A tiny warning was slipped into one of her letters from Cuverville to Paris in June 1917. "I wouldn't frequent the Allégrets too excessively if I were you: I believe there is a certain danger in it." [13]

In May 1918 he is writing to Valéry, "I just spent several charming days in the company of little Allégret, a classmate of Claude's [Valéry's son] . . . whose parents have left him in my charge. I was supposed to take him to England shortly, where they think it would be wise for him to finish his studies. I was enchanted at this excuse for a trip." He had, in fact, been dreaming of such a "honeymoon" for almost a year: he imagined "the little English cottage where we were going, to live together, alone, for the first time. It was so beautiful, so unhoped-for . . ." But the German bombing frightened the Allégrets into the country, temporarily, and the trip was deferred. On May 4, he writes (to himself): "the prolonged silence of S. A. [Suzanne Allégret, Marc's mother] worries me to the point of anguish. Getting along without M. has already ceased to seem possible to me."

But in June the prospects cleared. To his friends in Paris he announced that he feared for the safety of his wife and household during the great German offensive then in progress, bade them all affectionate farewells, and left—supposedly for Cuverville. To Edmund Gosse, in London,

he wrote on June 10: "A great longing to see England again, to hear some
English, to see *you* again has been tormenting me for a long time. I can't
bear it any longer. I take advantage of the pretext of escorting a young
nephew to Cambridge, and I am hoping to be able to embrace you early
next week," and asked Gosse's help in arranging for the necessary wartime
travel clearance. (The fiction of *"M. le neveu,"* as Arnold Bennett cynically called Marc, is maintained in the 1966 *Who's Who in France*.) To
Madeleine—after a certain time of unhealthy dissimulation ("It is hateful
to me to have to hide from her")—he confessed. The scene was vividly
recreated by Roger Martin du Gard, who wrote down this account of the
story as Gide told it to him in December 1920.

". . . The day before I left Cuverville, in the evening after dinner—
I can still see the way my poor darling came up to me—I was still
sitting down—the way she bent over me and looked deep into my
eyes, and said:
    " 'You're not going alone, are you?'
    "I stammered out 'No . . .'
    " 'You're going with X.?'
    " 'Yes . . .'
"I can still see what happened next to that poor face, the face
that had been for me the beauty, the purest love of my life. Oh, how
I was suffering! I wanted to speak. But she stopped me, with a horrible remark: 'Don't say anything. Never say anything to me again. I
prefer your silence to your dissembling.'
"I went back to my room, shattered. All night long, I walked
up and down, sitting down every so often at my desk, trying to write
her a letter. I was out of my mind. I was to leave the next morning,
at dawn. Everything was ready. And all at once I asked myself if I
ought to leave, if I had really the *desire* to make this trip. . . .
"My real act of madness was to write her that letter, and to give
it to her next day, as I was leaving . . . I thought I had done it well
enough, but I was worn out, broken with emotion, insomnia: I was
no longer in possession of my senses. I wrote her that I could no
longer stay with her in Normandy, *that I was rotting here*—I remember that awful word, *pourrissait;* that all my vital forces were
turning soft, that I would die if I stayed here, and that I wanted to, I
was going to live—by which I meant escape from this place, travel,
meet people, love people, create!
"And so I left—oh, I can't even think of it without breaking

into tears, forgive me, it's so horrible . . . so I left, leaving her
there, in the most utter moral solitude, with the abominable certitude
that I was not leaving alone. And at the last minute, dreaming that I
was somehow making amends for my sin and softening her despair, I
plunged that knife in the wound: I gave her that letter, written
straight off, as brutal as a scream, in which I let her know that,
alongside her, I was *rotting*. Afterwards, much later, I realized that it
was the gesture of a criminal. Yes, I think I almost killed her that
day, that she will never return to life again!" *

In his diary for that day, two lines: "I am leaving France in a state of
inexpressible anguish. It seems to me that I am saying farewell to my
whole past." Madeleine replied to his letter in one of her own—a letter I
have already quoted once: †

André dear,
You are mistaken. I have no doubts of your affection. And even if I
had, I should have nothing to complain of. My portion has been a
handsome one: I have had the best of your soul, the tenderness of
your childhood and your youth. And I know that, living or dead, I
shall have the soul of your last years.

I have always understood, moreover, your need to move from
place to place, your need for freedom. How many times in your fits of
nervous anguish—the price you pay for your genius—have these
words been on the tip of my tongue: "But my dear, leave, go, you are
free, there is no door on the cage, nothing is keeping you here." (I
did not say it, for fear of wounding you by giving in so easily to your
absence.)

What pains me—and you know it without my saying so—is
the road down which you are traveling, and which is going to lead
you and others to perdition. Again, please believe that I am not
saying this with any feeling of condemnation. I pity you as much as
I love you. This is a terrible temptation which has risen up before
you, one armed with every seduction. Resist it.

                                Adieu, au revoir,
                                Your Madeleine[14]

And the next month, to André still in England:

---

* Cited in Jean Schlumberger, *Madeleine et André Gide* (1956, pp. 189–90).
† There is some question of the dating of this letter, but Jean Schlumberger persuasively
argues that it belongs here.

Don't complicate your days by writing to me often. At the moment, the sight of your handwriting does me more harm than good.[15]

Meanwhile, in England, Gide's idyll with Marc seems to have been unrolling just as he had dreamed. As he says, he could hardly have turned back: "An irresistible fatality urged me on and I should have sacrificed everything to meet M.—without even being aware that I was sacrificing anything." The pretexts of having Marc study at Cambridge and take his military training away from the Western Front were both satisfied (though the war ended before he could see service), and the two settled very comfortably in or near Cambridge. From June to September, Gide boated and swam in the River Cam, read Marlowe and Herrick, attended dinner parties and premières with the Arnold Bennetts, and enjoyed being in love. He was introduced to Housman and Huxley and Lady Ottoline Merrill, and cycled out each morning for English lessons with Dorothy Bussy, the sister of Lytton Strachey, in later years his translator and intimate friend.

Back at Cuverville, Madeleine Gide felt herself abandoned, "without a single person on whom I could lean, no longer knowing what to do, what would become of me . . . At first I thought that my heart had stopped beating, that I was dying. I had suffered so much . . . I burned your letters in order to have something to do. Before I destroyed them I read them all over, one by one . . ." (Gide's relating of her words).[16]

The rest of this particular episode is told as fully as we shall ever know it in the pages from the *Journal intime* I have inserted at their proper dates (with their footnotes from 1939), although Gide allowed them to be published openly only after his death. The supplementary accounts in *Madeleine et André Gide,* the reports by his three closest friends —Roger Martin du Gard, Maria van Rysselberghe, and Jean Schlumberger—of Gide's impulsive, sobbing confessions to *them* of the whole episode—vary slightly from, but add little to that of the *Journal intime* and its footnotes.

To sum up quickly many years in the private lives of three people: Gide *was* severely broken by the overt rupture with his wife and cousin, that first and last rip in the closed texture of legend he had woven about his life and hers. He had built half of his life on this fiction, this conjugal myth of sexless, tranquil, brotherly love. "Cuverville" had been one of the two poles of his necessary tension, and in forcing the truth, Madeleine had torn that illusion. After that one time, nothing more was said, "no explanations were made, no discussions held. Everything was kept inside." [17] But he had been forced, like the Pastor in his *Symphonie pastorale,* to realize how much his illusions had wounded another, to admit that his contradictory lives, his opposing seats of satisfaction *were* in contradiction.

As for the lost letters (how many? two thousand? He claimed to have written her *every day* he was not with her, for thirty years), we have only Gide's word, to accept or to doubt, for their quality and content, and for the degree to which their loss has falsified his image. "An incomplete, inexact, caricatured, grimacing image is now all that will endure of me. My authentic reflection has been wiped out, forever . . . All that was purest, noblest in my life, all that could best have survived, and shone, and spread warmth and beauty, all is destroyed. And no effort of mine will ever be able to replace it." [18]

One may be sufficiently dubious of Gide's lyric lamentation, and sufficiently impressed with the surviving remnants not to be so utterly cast down by the loss as he professed to be. Still, it is one of the more pathetic episodes in literary history, and for a man so conscious of his image, so completely devoted to "making a life" out of written materials, such a loss may well have seemed capital and irreparable.

Thus estranged from his wife—though the visible surface of their days together changed little, and few who were not told ever suspected it—Gide came to spend more time in Paris and abroad, and, later, to depend more on substitute families like the Bussys and Van Rysselberghes. It may be held, finally, that as his "discovery" of young Marc helped to arouse him from a debilitating state of torpor, so this rupture with his wife had its therapeutic side as well. He had been, as he confesses, morally suffocating under the hypocrisies to which he was forced in 1917–1918. Now at least he was living the truth, or something nearer it, and no doubt felt encouraged to finish the job through the great public confessions of the 20's.

As for Marc Allégret, his *amitié particulière* with André Gide seems to have lasted about ten years, from 1917 to 1927, though they remained close friends until the latter's death. The *Journal* and published correspondences are silent, for the most part, from 1919 to 1921, during which time they are known to have made a return trip to Britain. In 1922, Marc's mistress Bronja appears on the scene, and there are vulgar evenings *à trois* on the town in Paris. Gide worries, in 1924, that he may be losing Marc to "cheaper pleasures." All the while he *is* watching him, helping him grow—Gide's ideal of such a relationship was closer to Socrates's than to Cocteau's. Marc has his own room, his own friends at the

villa in Auteuil, later at rue Vaneau, accompanies Gide on his travels
about France and other European countries, to Tunis, finally on the important Congo trip of 1926–1927, out of which his own career as a film-
maker developed. Gide admitted, in 1928, that he traveled largely for
the pleasure of Marc's company, and that *Les Faux-Monnayeurs* had been
written for him. But as the younger man's own creative life developed,
he began to detach himself from Gide: at first, there are a few signs of
bitterness, but in 1928 Gide is giving up plans for a trip to New Guinea
in order to force Marc to get on with his own career. In 1930, he observes himself traveling without Marc, to whom he had always "left all
initiative" for such projects, for the first time in years; and it is a new
group of young men which accompanies him to the Soviet Union in
1936. Meanwhile Marc Allégret—who has never published any of his
own reflections on André Gide—married and divorced, and continued
his successful career as a film-maker, with which Gide was from time to
time engaged. He is today, at seventy, administrator of the Cinémathèque
Française, and the author of more than fifty films, the best known
outside France probably being *Fanny, Lac aux dames, L'Amant de Lady
Chatterley* (with Simone Simon—his brother's wife at one time—and
Leo Genn), *Sois Belle et tais toi* (with Alain Delon and Jean-Paul Bel-
mondo), and *Drôle de dimanche.*

Madeleine Gide took the unfortunate episode of June 1918 as her
pretext for a determined retreat from public life—even more determined
than heretofore. According to Gide's account to Mme van Rysselberghe,
she had told him, "If I were a Catholic, I'd go into a convent." [19] Although
she continued to worry about André's influence and his enemies, she never
read another of his books or sought to know more of his life than he
chose to show her: many think she never learned of the illegitimate
daughter born to him and Elisabeth van Rysselberghe in 1923. Disapproving, in any case, of the Van Rysselberghe *ménage* next door, she
never set foot in the apartment at 1 *bis* rue Vaneau in Paris which André
bought in 1928; in fact she never even left Cuverville after he sold the
Auteuil villa in the summer of that year.

from

THE JOURNAL

1914–1919

1914   *[Returning from trip to Turkey]*

The very educative value that I derive from this trip is in proportion to my disgust with the country. I am glad not to like it more. When I feel the need of the desert air, of wild and strong perfumes, I shall go seek them again in the Sahara. In that woebegone Anatolia, humanity is not so much undeveloped as it is permanently spoiled.

Should I have gone farther? To the Euphrates? To Baghdad? No, and now I don't want to. The obsession of that country that had tormented me so long is now overcome: that maddening curiosity. What a relief it is to have enlarged on the map the space one no longer wants to go and see! For too long I believed (out of love of exoticism, distrust of chauvinistic self-satisfaction, perhaps out of modesty), for too long I thought that there was more than one civilization, more than one culture that could rightfully claim our love and deserve our enthusiasm. . . . Now I know that our Western (I was about to say French) civilization is not only the most beautiful; I believe, I know that it is the *only one*—yes, the very civilization of Greece, of which we are the only heirs.

On the Adriatic, May 29

Voluptuous calm of the flesh, as tranquil as this unruffled sea. Perfect equilibrium of the mind. Supple, even, bold, and voluptuous, like the flight of these gulls through the dazzling blue—such is the free play of my mind.

June 19

Yesterday Cuverville went to sleep in a cloud, which this morning is still chilling the surrounding country. Perhaps this numbing climate is partly responsible for the contraction, the strangling of almost all my books, which we discussed with Copeau last evening. I had to finish almost every one of them in Cuverville, contracted myself, striving to recapture or maintain a fervor that in a dry climate (in Florence, for example) came easily and naturally. I am inclined to believe that, with a little help from the climate, my production would have been easier and, hence, more abundant.

To say nothing of the physiological equilibrium that I can find only with such difficulty and danger here.

June 22

I found in the driveway yesterday morning a little starling that had fallen from the nest but was almost ready to fly. While I am writing now, he is right here beside me on the table, or more exactly between the fingers of my left hand, which are holding this notebook in place; that is the spot he most likes. He pulls in his legs, puffs up like a little ball; you can tell he is comfortable. I had tried to put him into a cage, but he beat against it; I had to leave him free in the room, where he soils everything. Every ten minutes he lets fall anywhere and everywhere a little liquid, corrosive dropping. I give him bread soaked in milk to eat, mixed with the yolk of a hard-boiled egg; or little earthworms, which he is very fond of. He just flew from the table to my shoulder as soon as he saw me come in. After he has sat for some time on my hand, I feel an odd little itch moving over the back of my hand; tiny parasites moving from him to me. Another dropping.

June 23

My starling amuses me as much as he bothers me; besides the fact that I never get tired of observing him, he is never satisfied unless he is perched on my shoulder, where I should be glad to leave him if he did not dirty me. Twenty times I picked him up to put him back on the table, until finally I was the one who got tired; I went to get a towel and wrapped the upper part of my body in it; but now he is no longer interested in perching on me.

He throws himself so greedily on the earthworms that I haven't time to chop them up; he snaps them up all at once, then a moment later strangles and gurgles as if he were stifling once and for all. He follows me when I walk up and down in the hall, trotting along behind me, and when I stop, climbs fluttering up my leg.

June 24

I do so hope that in a few days, when he can fly and get out the linen-room window, which I shall leave open, I do so hope that he will get into the habit of coming back to peck the worms that I shall always keep in reserve for him on the table.

June 28

This evening before dinner I gave my starling his liberty. In the morning I had taken him out in the hothouse garden, but he stayed perched on the branch of a plum tree; I thought he would be too easy a prey for my cat and took him back into his cage; but later in the day he began to fly so well that I thought I could let him go.

I carried him beyond the gate leading to the tennis court; and this time, as soon as I opened my hand, he flew off, almost above my head, and settled on the branch of an apple tree, where he remained. I had to leave him to go to dinner; after dinner he was still there, and I imagine that is where he spent the night.

June 29

This afternoon Copeau asked me to help him in his translation of Whitman—that is, to act as his secretary.

We had sat down on the bench behind the house, in the shade of a hazel tree; soon after, we left the bench and stretched out on the lawn beside the path. We were about to leave our work and go in for tea when there came toward us, hopping through the grass in great haste, my little starling. He came of his own accord right up next to my hand and made no effort to get away when I tried to catch him. In my hand he didn't struggle at all; he seemed perfectly happy to be there. I ran into the kitchen to ask for some bread and milk and, for fear of the cats, I carried the bird into the aviary. He ate quite willingly, but without throwing himself on the food with frantic eagerness; so it was apparently not mere hunger that brought him back. I could have shouted with joy. I prepared his mush with a hard-boiled egg, changed the water in his tub, and stayed with him for some time. Very sorry to have to leave tomorrow. As soon as I get back from Paris I shall give him his liberty.

July 6

. . . All my work up to now has been merely negative; I have shown nothing but the back side of my heart and my mind.

July 12

Les Caves du Vatican had dwelt in my mind for more than fifteen years, just as I had borne *La Porte étroite* for more than fifteen years; and scarcely less *L'Immoraliste*, the first to come out.

All these subjects developed concurrently, in parallel—and if I wrote one book before another, it was because the subject seemed to me more "at hand," as the English say. If I had been able to, I should have written them *together*. I could not have written *L'Immoraliste* if I had not known that I was one day to write also *La Porte étroite,* and I needed to have written both of them to be able to allow myself the *Caves.*

July 19

This morning my poor starling let himself be torn to pieces by the cats. They threw themselves on that poor defenseless little thing that didn't know fear; I was at the piano, but suddenly I recognized his call. At the same moment Em., who saw the scene from the steps, ran to them with a little fish in the hope of making them let go. The bird had eventually escaped, only to fall exhausted a little farther away. He was still stirring; I took him in my hand; I did not immediately lose all hope of reviving him, for at first nothing but an insignificant wound could be seen, or so it seemed to me; I tried to get him to drink a little water, but he couldn't swallow it and soon dropped back dead.

July 20

I didn't think it was possible to miss a bird so much. When I went out, I would look for him; even without seeing him, I would feel him, alive, in the foliage. I used to like to feel that little winged thing on my shoulder or see him flutter around me; then suddenly fly off toward a very high branch; then finally return.

July 26

Since Austria's ultimatum to Serbia, which yesterday morning's papers published, everyone is so nervous that when they heard the fire-alarm many people took it for the call to arms.

This morning the refusal of the delay requested by Russia crowns the general nervousness; one no longer talks of anything else, and J.-E. Blanche has given way to the blackest misgivings. . . .

July 27

A certain easing of the strain this morning. People are relieved and at the same time disappointed to hear that Serbia is giving in. The wind has fallen too; a thick fine rain has followed the squall. . . .

Three titled and rich ladies came this afternoon; one of them (Countess de C.?) I liked; great traveler with a free and easy manner

. . . but it was the other one who especially talked with me, leading me off on the subject of *La Porte étroite,* which she had "read almost ten years ago, but which was an event in her life." * She takes me aside to a corner of the room, and at each compliment she pays me, I feel like sticking out my tongue at her or shouting: Shit! "You know so well how to depict spiritual solitude. It's an entirely different thing from Bourget's *Mensonges* or *La Dame devant le miroir;* you have discovered a new psychological law that no one had ever enunciated before. The wall! Monsieur! The horrible wall! And we ourselves built it. . . ."

I: "And without windows! Madame, without windows!"

She: "No possibility of communication. When you sense it between two others you would like to knock it down."

I: "But the others would be angry at you for doing so," etc. . . .

And it goes on and on. . . . It was time to write the *Caves.*

July 28

The auto took me to Dieppe, where I expected to get on board at noon. Already I had sent a telegram to Valery Larbaud announcing my arrival at Newhaven in the thought that he could come from Hastings to meet me. A half hour later I sent him another telegram saying that I was delaying my departure. . . . Impossible to go away carrying this terrible worry. . . . Everyone expects the worst.

July 29

Yesterday, from the time we got up to the time we went to bed, no one talked of anything else. One cannot get one's mind off *it.* In addition to the papers, Mme Mühlfeld's telephone calls twice a day keep us informed.

. . . Despite everything there is some comfort in seeing private interests, dissensions, and discords disappear before this appalling common danger; in France, emulation quickly becomes a sort of fury, urging every citizen on to heroic self-sacrifice. . . .

And, all morning long, I imagined myself having to announce to Juliette the death of her son. Into what horrors shall we soon have to plunge!

July 30

The papers have no very sensational news this morning. Georges, who has just got back from Le Havre, tells us of the endless queues and the police-

* The story had first been published five years before.

men outside the banks, where everyone has gone to get money. In the restaurants, before serving, the waiters warn the customers that banknotes will not be accepted.

July 31

We are getting ready to enter a long tunnel full of blood and darkness. . . .

Very stormy weather; a gray film floats between sky and earth. The day before yesterday was divinely fair; one of those skies under which you can imagine only happiness. . . .

I answered rather brutally yesterday when Em. interrupted me in my reading; this grieved me all evening long.

I have had a heavy heart for the last few days, and especially this evening.

August 1

A day of agonizing waiting. Why don't we mobilize? Every moment we delay is that much more advantage for Germany. On the other hand, perhaps we owe it to the Socialist Party to let ourselves be attacked. This morning's paper tells about the absurd assassination of Jaurès. . . .

At about three o'clock the alarm-bell began to toll. Nevertheless J. insisted at first, in order not to miss a chance to contradict, that it was the same funeral bell that had been tolling all morning. I ran to find Mius in the garden, to warn him; and as I returned, having met no one but Edmond, I saw Em. on the flower path, looking very distraught; barely holding back her sobs: she told us, "Yes, it's the alarm; Hérouard has just come from Criquetot; the order to mobilize has been posted."

The children had set out for Etretat by bicycle. Feeling the need to busy myself somehow, I wanted to go to Criquetot to mail two letters and to get the registered envelope that I knew had arrived. The bell was silent now; after the great alarm sent out over the whole countryside, there was nothing now but an oppressive silence. A fine rain was falling intermittently.

In the fields, a few fellows all ready to leave were going on with their plowing; on the road I met our farmer, Louis Freger, called up on the third day, and his mother, who is going to see her two children go away. I was unable to do anything but shake their hands without a word.

On the way back I meet no one. Anticipating the mobilization, the baker's, shoemaker's, and saddler's apprentices were already sent off today at five o'clock. In the place of my heart I feel nothing but a wet rag in my breast; the obsessing thought of war stands like a terrible bar between my eyes, and all my thoughts stumble against it.

August 2

I am writing in the train carrying me to Paris, the last one, it is said, to be left open to civilians. I was tormented at the thought of being cut off at Cuverville. . . . T. left with me.

In Paris we shall make out somehow and shall look for something we can do. Before leaving Em. this morning, I knelt down beside her (something I hadn't done since . . .) and asked her to recite the Lord's Prayer. I did this for her sake, and my pride yielded to love without difficulty; what is more, my whole heart participated in her prayer.

. . . The air is full of a loathsome anguish. Fantastic appearance of Paris, its streets empty of vehicles and full of strange people, calm but hypertense; some are waiting with their trunks on the sidewalk; a few noisy fellows at the entrance to cabarets are bawling the *Marseillaise*. Occasionally an auto loaded down with luggage passes at great speed.

August 3

If I do not find any possible work through Arthur Fontaine, I shall sign up with the Red Cross, where Ghéon has already offered himself as a doctor.

On returning to the rue du Dragon, I witness the looting of a Maggi dairy store. I get there a bit late; the shop is already empty; two big fellows, with a sort of tacit approval on the part of the police, are just finishing breaking the shop windows with a kind of wooden rake. One of them has climbed onto the showcase; he is holding up a big, brown, earthenware coffeepot, which he exhibits to the crowd and then throws onto the sidewalk, where it crashes noisily. There is much applause.

August 4

The enthusiasm, calm, and determination of the mass of the people are wonderful. If England joins in, the chances are definitely on our side; but *will* England join in? Parliament has proposed a vote of more than a billion in military subsidies.

August 5

Yesterday, invasion of Belgium. Schoen* has left.

Germany declares war on Belgium, and England on Germany.

August 6

The idea of a possible collapse of Germany gains strength little by little; one guards oneself against it, but one cannot wholly persuade himself that it is impossible. The wonderful behavior of the government, of everyone, and of all France, as well as of all the neighboring nations, leaves room for every hope.

One foresees the beginning of a new era: the United States of Europe bound by a treaty limiting their armaments; Germany subjugated or dissolved; Trieste given back to the Italians, Schleswig to Denmark; and especially Alsace to France. Everyone talks of this remaking of the map, as if it were the next number of a serial.

August 7

Went yesterday morning to the Théos';† lunched in a *bistro* near the rue François 1ᵉʳ, where I worked all afternoon making out lists of stretcher-bearers.

Dinner at Arthur Fontaine's with Copeau.

This morning at the Red Cross. I have a sore throat and a headache.

Monday, August 10

This morning, at last, a long, exquisite, and comforting letter from Em. Everything seems to be going all right at Cuverville. . . .

I had lunched with Ghéon and Copeau; Ghéon was leaving soon after for Nouvion. Dullin came for a moment to the Café de Flore, where we were. He has just arrived from Spain, where, he tells us, the wildest rumors, originating in dispatches from Berlin, are circulating: "Poincaré assassinated. Paris in the hands of revolutionary mob. France invaded by the German army." It wasn't until he had crossed the frontier that he realized what was really going on.

---

* The German ambassador to France.
† M. and Mme Théo van Rysselberghe, with whom Gide lived in Paris in 1914.

Dinner at the Ruyters' with the Schlumbergers. André Ruyters, in a ferocious mood, declares himself ready to kill anything German he meets,
women and children as well as soldiers. Before dinner he told me that my
conversation the first day had shocked him considerably, for he can't
understand how anyone can talk of anything but the war. This made me
most uncomfortable, and I immediately ceased to be natural in his presence. I was aware that he was judging everything I said, and consequently
from then on I couldn't say anything sensible.

12, 13, 14

Spent the evening before last with Elie Allégret after having dinner with
Marcel. This good Elie, to whom I had expressed my desire to find something to do, has found a place for me: I am going to be commissioned by
the mayor's office of the 16th arrondissement to register all the boys between twelve and eighteen who show up and to think up ways of keeping
them busy! . . . I told him that I didn't think I was quite the right man
for the job.

August 14

Twelfth day since the mobilization.

The terrible battle that has been announced and expected for the
last week has not yet taken place.

"I believe that my heart will not be strong enough for the great joy
or the great trial," Em. writes me.

I reproach myself for every thought that is unrelated to this anguished waiting; but nothing is less natural to me than anything that upsets my mental equilibrium. Were it not for *opinion,* I feel that even
under the enemy fire I should enjoy one of Horace's odes. . . .

I did not go this afternoon, any more than I did yesterday afternoon,
to the Red Cross, where I merely make a pretense of being useful, although in fact I serve no purpose. There is no instance in which privilege
takes on an uglier taste. But hypocrisy is even uglier, and the farce that one
is tempted to practice on oneself for fear of falling behind the others is
absurd.

The weather is wonderful; the sky is full of an excess of warmth and
beauty. The nights are calm, one might almost say pacific. One thinks of
the camps, of sleeping in the open air, and of all those for whom this
beautiful night is the last.

August 15

Now a new rubber stamp is being created, a new conventional psychology of the patriot, without which it is impossible to be "respectable." The tone used by the journalists to speak of Germany is enough to turn the stomach. They are all falling into the ranks and showing their colors. Each one is afraid of lagging behind, of seeming a less "good Frenchman" than the others. . . .

The sky clouded over during the night, and in the early morning a big storm broke east of Paris.

The first rolling of the thunder at about four o'clock seemed enough like the explosion of bombs to make one think a flight of zeppelins had raided Paris. And in my half-sleep I imagined for a long time that Paris was being bombarded and that it was even the end of the world. From my lack of emotion I realized that I was ready for anything and everything; but that was in my dream. After all, do I have any idea how I might react when faced with real danger? Of what simple stuff are they made, the people who can guarantee their reactions at any hour of the day or night! How many soldiers anxiously wait for the event to find out whether or not they are brave? And he who doesn't react as *he would like to*—whose will alone is brave! . . .

The despair of the man who thinks he is a coward because he yielded to a momentary weakness—when he hoped he was courageous (*Lord Jim*).

Copeau came to dinner at the rue Laugier; I walked part of the way home with him and told him of my visit to poor old La Pérouse. Yes, yesterday afternoon I thought I could do nothing better than call on him. Mme de La Pérouse opened the door and immediately buttonholed me, bursting forth in recriminations against her husband, who, she claims, does whatever he can to be disagreeable to her and has now thought up the idea of letting himself die of hunger. For several days, ever since the declaration of war, I believe, he has been refusing almost all nourishment. After a few affected courtesies, she got up to "announce" me. And since she warned me that "Monsieur de La Pérouse" was in bed, I spoke of going into his bedroom.

"Oh! sir, you could hardly get in; Monsieur de La Pérouse is so finicky that no one is allowed to clean up his room. . . ."

But when she returns, she announces to me that M. de La Pérouse is expecting me.

The room I now enter for the first time is rather dark because the shutters are only half open. The open, uncurtained window looks out on a court, and the position of the shutters keeps people across the way from seeing into the room.

Old La Pérouse is not in bed. Up against the bed he lies deep in a mahogany armchair covered in threadbare claret velvet that reveals the stuffing. I sit down in another armchair just like it. He hardly makes a gesture when I come in; he lets me grasp his inert left hand; he is leaning on the right against a square table, and his elbow is resting on two little cushions in the shape of a tea cozy; on a lower level of the same table, two metal bowls are lying one in the other. I hold his hand in mine and put my arm behind him without saying a word. He doesn't say anything either. I observe his face, mottled with red and yellow, deathly pale in spots, which seems made of such a strange material that if one scratched the skin anything but blood would run from the scratch. I look at the room's odd disorder: on the right, a pile of hatboxes rising almost to the ceiling; then a bureau, one half of which is covered with a pile of unbound books; on the other half, a bottle of cider standing in a saucepan, a dirty glass, a small hot-plate, and several spirit-lamps, one of which is burning almost imperceptibly. On the left, in front of the fireplace, a low table holds a collection of mysterious pots, all of the same size and each with a cover on it. In the middle of the room, another table with toilet articles on it and, under the table, a wastebasket filled with old shoes.

Eventually the poor old man raises his head a bit and murmurs: "I am very weak."

I try then to persuade him to accept a little nourishment. Finally he confesses that, in addition to a lack of appetite, he has decided not to eat any more, to end it all. Then turning toward me: "Be good; give me a drink. Just a little cider." And with a flabby hand he points at the bottle.

I refuse to give him more than a quarter of a glass.

"Ah! I could drink the sea itself!" he sighs.

However, while talking, I lead him gradually to the idea of accepting a milk-and-flour gruel that Mme de La Pérouse is going to prepare for him. And while the soup is heating, he returns to old complaints: particularly his wife's jealousy toward all those who show him the least esteem and affection: "She has all the faults," he says; then, correcting himself, he adds: *"All the petty ones."*

For the first time I inquire about his reasons for marrying Mme de La Pérouse. As one could well imagine, those reasons were altogether sentimental: he loved her. And going back into the past, he tells me about his brother, that brother he loved most tenderly and passionately and who died at the age of seventeen. La Pérouse himself was hardly more than twenty-one at the time. A few months later he got married. In a little trunk to which he kept the key, he had locked up his brother's letters, which he did not *dare* read for several years. Then one day (most likely after his first conjugal disappointments), he locked himself in a room where he knew he would not be disturbed, opened the little trunk, and reread that correspondence. From that day on, he got into the habit of seeking consolation and support in that reading; these were hours when he could be almost sure of not being watched by his wife. But he soon became convinced that she was spying on him and suspected his little trunk; for some time already she had been rummaging in his drawers among his other papers. The day finally came when, opening his trunk, La Pérouse found his brother's letters in disorder. "It was," he told me, "just as if someone had put them back in a hurry, someone who had been surprised while reading them and hadn't had time to put them in order." He had no words with Mme de La Pérouse, but he burned those papers at once. . . .

He talks with extreme slowness, without turning toward me, his eyes staring into space; occasionally I hear an odd sound in his mouth as if he were chewing his teeth. But then he becomes lively; once more I succeed in reassuring him, in consoling him; probably the soup he ate ("with pleasure," as he confesses) is doing him good; now, surprised at it himself, he asks me to help him get up; he looks for his hat; he wants to go out. We go downstairs together and, after I have said good-bye to him in the street, I feel his eyes following me for a long time, and when I turn around again, he waves to me. . . .

August 17

Japan's declaration of war on Germany.

The wounded who have been transported to Vichy all repeat that the Germans shoot the wounded and the stretcher-bearers. The newspapers are full of horrible tales.

Every evening, under the gas flame in the Théos' little dining-room, all four of us gathered around the oak table, the Théos, Jean Schlumberger, and I, plunge into the evening papers. For the fourth or fifth time we dig the marrow out of the same stories, the same news reports. . . . Last night, fed up, irritated by this militarization of my mind, I took out of Elisabeth's library *Sesame and Lilies,** of which I read almost the whole preface (new edition); I felt as if I were plunging into a lake of clear water and that all the dust and sunburn of too long a walk on an arid road were being washed off.

Doubtless for those who are mobilized the wearing of the uniform authorizes a greater freedom of thought. But with those of us who cannot put on the uniform, it is the mind that is mobilized.

Jean Cocteau had arranged to meet me in an "English tearoom" on the corner of the rue de Ponthieu and the avenue d'Antin. I had no pleasure in seeing him again, despite his extreme kindness; he is incapable of seriousness, and all his thoughts, his witticisms, his sensations, all the extraordinary brilliance of his customary conversation shocked me like some luxury article on display in a period of famine and mourning. He is dressed almost like a soldier, and the excitement of current events has only made him look healthier. He denies himself nothing, simply gives a martial air to his usual cheek. When speaking of the slaughter of Mulhouse, he uses amusing adjectives and mimicry; he imitates the bugle call and the whistling of the shrapnel. Then, changing subjects when he sees that he is not amusing me, he claims to be sad; he wants to be sad with the same kind of sadness as you, and suddenly he adopts your mood and explains it to you. Then he talks of Blanche, mimics Mme R., and talks of the lady at the Red Cross who shouted on the stairway: "I was promised fifty wounded men for this morning; I want my fifty wounded men." Meanwhile he is crushing a piece of fruitcake in his plate and nibbling at it; his voice rises suddenly and has odd twists; he laughs, leans forward, bends toward you and touches you. The odd thing is that I think he would make a good soldier. He insists that he would, and that he would be brave too. He has the carefree attitude of the street urchin; it is in his company that I feel the most awkward, the most heavy, the most gloomy.

* By John Ruskin.

21

There begin to be seen walking the streets, hugging the walls, odd luciferous creatures such as the tide uncovers when the water withdraws.

25

The day of the 25th was most gloomy. From the height of what mad hope have we fallen! The papers had done their job so well that people began to imagine that our army had only to appear to put the entire German army to rout. And then, because we had fallen back on those positions which a week before had seemed so good, people were predicting at once the imminent siege of Paris. Everyone was seeking a word of encouragement and hope, for they were not yet completely crushed—more precisely, everyone was awakening from a dream—and people looked almost with stupor at the idiotic picture postcards representing "famine in Berlin": a big Prusco, seated in front of a toilet and fishing up, with a long fork plunged through the seat, suspicious sausages that he swallowed at once; or another German blubbering with fear at the sight of a bayonet; others running for their lives; never before, I am sure, have the silliness, the filth, and the hideousness of vulgar stupidity been revealed in a more compromising and shameful manner.

August 26

The French, who were playing fair, were indignant at the fact that in war the Germans did not observe the rules of the game.

As for the latter, it seemed as if they were aiming to discredit war forever; and as if to prove that war was an evil thing—if it is true that in war the aim is to conquer—they won by the worst means.

On the 25th and 26th, the people fleeing burning villages began to rush into Paris. An old man (Mme Ruyters's uncle) arrived almost mad, and spread terror among those around him. "We are not up to it!" he kept repeating. "We are not up to it! Those people respect nothing." On foot he had covered a tremendous distance, crawling, hiding, crossing the lines, seeing villages and farms burning all around him. Taken by surprise a few kilometers away from the village of which he was mayor, he had been unable to get back to his post, separated from his family and duty by a sudden wall of fire.

Those who came from Valenciennes were camped in the Cirque d'Eté; some children were taken in at the rue Vaneau. Mme Edwards asserted that many of these children had their hands cut off, that she had seen them. Others had their eyes put out and others abominable wounds.

This could never be verified.

With her two children she covered thirty kilometers on foot to flee the burning village.

Her neighbor, pregnant, maltreated, gave birth in a ditch.

September 4

No defeat, no victory will change the qualities and defects of these two nations. Even though German commerce may be stifled, French commerce will be unable to take its place: even without a rival, it would have yielded all along the line.

The Belgian lady was annoyed by those five thousand francs promised to the first soldier to bring back an enemy flag. "To win a flag they would be willing to lose a battle. Oh, the others are well aware of that! It's just like the Mulhouse business. Any other nation would have avoided such a thing. Three-quarters of the mistakes made in France are due to their love of the word, the gesture, the sentiment. Oh, if you think that such motives mean anything to *them!* They are practical; you are romantic. Ah, you certainly deserve your Rostand! The white plume, champagne, whatever suits that incurable triviality which makes you joke under a rain of bullets and never admit that the others are prepared. Besides, you count too much on chance. Self-confidence is a good thing; but especially when there is some reason for it."

September 7

I do not recall ever having seen in this region such a long succession of uniformly beautiful days. One's heart is overwhelmed by the sky's serenity.

September 16

The impossibility of keeping oneself in a state of tension (which is after all artificial) as soon as nothing in the *immediate surroundings* motivates it. X. goes back to reading, to playing Bach, and even to preferring the fugues with a joyful rhythm from *The Well-Tempered Clavichord,* which he can forbid himself only with great reluctance.

How easily life takes shape again, closes up. Too easy healing of wounds. Surrender to that paltry comfort which is the greatest enemy of real happiness.

Friday, October 2

Sixtieth day since the mobilization.

The days pass in a monotonous expectation. At moments I long to be in Paris. But, once there, wouldn't I regret having left Cuverville?

Wednesday, the whole household having gone out for a walk, I remained alone with Em. stringing beans on the bench in front of the house. The sky was marvelously pure. We hardly exchanged a word or two from time to time, for we could talk of nothing but *that;* and yet the great silence around us, inside us, filled us with happiness despite ourselves. . . . Then I joined Valentine and the children in the woods above the valley and we did not come back until after dark.

October 7

Horrible nights. Headaches as frequent as during my childhood, and, insofar as I can remember, of exactly the same nature. They had not come back since I was eighteen.

October 8

Françoise, Nicole, and Jacques set out to meet the Copeaus, who are coming on the three o'clock train. This is the next-to-last day that I spend here in peace; while out there, the country is plunged into mourning, devastation, and horror. . . .

We have frightful faults that defeat did not correct and victory will not correct. Those we mourn today paid for them with their lives.

October 10

The remark of the lady who was experiencing difficulties, at the station: "And besides, you know, I am beginning to have enough of your war!"

My letters to Em. have taken the place of this journal.

Luce Ruyters writes to her mother: "I am so bored that I am working for the poor." A remark that I think her father would like.

Almost complete insomnia every night.

Night of October 29

Frightful starts lately. I have just enough intelligence left to certify that I am going crazy.

November 10

At Cuverville for two days. Rest. During the last week, moreover, I have regained a bit of assurance. My horrible fatigue came, I think, from being exposed to sympathy all day long. At the Foyer Franco-Belge, not a moment of solitude in which to reassume one's own personality and relax. I felt myself *absorbed* by others. Busy morning and afternoon caring for those refugees, whom we lodge, clothe, and feed, and for whom we seek work, I would return at lunch and at night to Ghéon's vibrant gaiety, and to the excessive energy of my friends and hosts.

November 15

Visit to the Louvre—desolation.
  The end of a civilization?

The work of the Foyer Franco-Belge.
  He gave to it, as he said in the few letters he still bothered to write, "all his heart and all his time"; that meager formula allowed him to skimp his correspondence.
  How and why that work, in the beginning altogether charitable, gradually became mere administration.

> *Well then; this is our one big chance,*
> *Now that the old, still-twanging instrument is broken,*
> *Let us boldly seize hold of this advantage,*
> *And not bother bending down to pick up the pieces.*
>
> *Since our library shelves, too, were full,*
> *And our brains, so that we had no more room to put things;*
> *Since everything had been said—at least in the old-fashioned way,*
> *Everything known, everything lived, at least in the ancient mode;*
>
> *Since our old cloak of ethics was worn threadbare*
> *And it is not yet permitted to go naked;*
> *Since everything that was stifling in us cried out for mercy*
> *Without ever once having obtained any;*

Since, in our heart of hearts, we longed for the cataclysm,
The great gust of wind that sweeps away all impurity,
Praise God! if, rather than coming from outside,
It rises from the very depths of humanity!

This war is not like other wars;
It is not only a question of protecting a territory,
Patrimony, a tradition. . . . No! a whole future is struggling to be
    born,
An enormous future, whose feet are bloody with the effort to come
    free.

Oh! what a kick you are giving
To leap forth, new world!
With love and with the hope
Of a longer-lived beauty,
May the soil you crush forgive you!

Poor uncertain soul, you cannot fall in love
With both the past and the future.
It remains to be seen whether you choose to stay here, weeping over
    the ashes;
Whether there is nothing left for you but to sink toward the tomb;
Or whether you still feel yourself young enough to spring forward
    into the unknown.

1915   *October 1*

I almost left for England. I was already leaving the Théos' with my bag
and steamer rug; I had an appointment to meet Mrs. Wharton tomorrow
morning at the Gare du Nord. Henry James and Arnold Bennett were
expecting me. Yesterday I had written to Raverat to announce my arrival,
and had taken leave of the Foyer. Fortunately I encounter insurmountable
difficulties at the prefecture. Before getting my passport, I have to go to
the Invalides to regularize my military status, or at least have somebody
certify that it is regular; then to the local police station with two witnesses
and my photograph; then to the British Embassy; then to the Ministry of
Foreign Affairs. . . . And, because there was not enough time for all
these formalities, I suddenly found myself extraordinarily relieved to give
up the project altogether. If I got some pleasure from the idea of going

away, my pleasure at the idea of staying was certainly much greater, and I enjoy this late afternoon, here, like someone who has just had a narrow escape.

I rushed to Mrs. Wharton's, for she was to get my ticket. Yet it would have amused me to travel with her. But this was not the moment.

October 8

This evening I finish *The Autobiography of Mark Rutherford*. Wonderful integrity of the book. I do not know any literary work that is more specifically Protestant. How is it that this book is not better known? How grateful I am to Bennett for having told me about it. The exquisite qualities of Hale White's style (that is the author's real name) are the very ones that I should like to have.

October 9

. . . For eleven months at the Foyer I lived completely devoured by sympathy. I cannot yet say or even know what that period did to me. On certain days I came to believe that I should never pull myself out of it.

October 11

Abominable numbness. I dream with a sort of anguish of the life that Cuverville holds in store for me, and from which I don't see how I can escape except by breaking bonds and loosing myself from the most venerated and cherished obligations. It is not freedom I am looking for, but rather being able to work in good healthy conditions, which I have never yet managed to achieve. It often seems to me that in more favorable conditions I should have been able to produce much more; and that thought tortures me like remorse. But I am always timid when there are decisions to be taken. It is not toward the more attractive that my temperament drives me, but rather toward the least costly. I am quite amazed to have been able at times to travel. Far from yielding to an impulse, I had to force myself to leave each time.

October 12

Back to Paris.

October 16

Having resumed my life as a philanthropist and parasite, I no longer have a moment to write in this notebook. At the Foyer morning and afternoon; I am caught again by the extreme interest of certain cases, by the atmosphere of affection and confusion that pervades that place, and the danger-ous intoxication that self-sacrifice brings. Em. is to come to town Monday.

Frantically busy from morning to evening. We have had, these past days, an avalanche of pathetic cases. Unable to note anything.

Hardly a day goes by that one does not read in the papers, despite the censor, enough to make one wonder whether or not we really deserve to win. To tell the truth, neither of the two countries deserves to crush the other, and Germany, by obliging us to oppose her, committed a frightful mistake.

One cannot expect a very prolific people to show the same regard for human life and the same respect for the individual as a nation that is on the wane. To this consideration must be added the *idée fixe,* which domi-nates the German people, of the superiority of their race. They work ac-cording to the principles of the horticulturist, who teaches that a serious selection consists not only in preference and choice, but also in the system-atic suppression of all that is not chosen.

Confess that, if you were inhabited by the *idée fixe* of a possible amelioration of that human race, a practical and almost immediate amelio-ration, you wouldn't strive so enthusiastically to prolong the life of the deformed, the degenerate, the undesirable, etc., or to encourage, or even merely to permit, their reproduction! To permit this, sacrifice that. Noth-ing is more logical. Again, it is a question of knowing what deserves to win out.

How many times at the Foyer, caring for, consoling, supporting those poor human rags capable only of moaning, infirm, without a smile, without an ideal, without beauty, I felt rising within me the frightful ques-tion: Do they deserve to be saved? The idea of replacing them with other, more thriving examples of humanity is certainly a part of the Germanic *philanthropy.* It is logical and, consequently, monstrous.

Detestable torpor. At times it seems to me that I have already finished with living and that I am moving about in a sort of posthumous dream, a sort of supplement to life, without importance or meaning. This state of apathy is probably the natural result of the emotional strain of the Foyer.

Yesterday, at the Prisoner of War Organization where I had gone to get some information, M. C. de W., who is the head, I believe, asked me if I had been able to resume my "little literary relaxations."

From November 22 to 26, an automobile trip with Mrs. Wharton.

Hyères, November 26

I have made the acquaintance of Paul Bourget. He received me most cordially at Costebelle, at his estate named Le P., to which Mrs. Wharton had taken me. Great need to captivate someone he knows to represent another generation, another camp, another point of view. The introduction took place in the garden.

"To enter here, Monsieur Gide," he said to begin with, "you have no need to go through *the strait gate.*"

This didn't exactly mean anything but a way of showing his kindly attitude. And shortly thereafter he found a way of alluding to my *Immoraliste;* then, returning to the subject, after Mrs. Wharton had left us for a few moments to go and see Mme Bourget, who was kept in her room by a slight indisposition: "Now that we are alone, tell me, Monsieur Gide, whether or not your immoralist is a pederast."

And, as I seem somewhat stunned, he insists: "I mean: a practicing pederast?"

"He is probably more likely an unconscious homosexual," I replied as if I myself hardly knew; and I added: "I believe there are many such."

At first I thought that he had taken this way of showing me that he had read my book; but he was especially eager to develop his theories: "There are," he began, "two categories of perversion: those that fall under the head of sadism, and those that belong to masochism. To achieve sexual pleasure, both the sadist and the masochist turn to cruelty; but one, etc. . . . while the other, etc. . . ."

"Do you class homosexuals under one or the other of these perversions?" I asked, just to have something to say.

"Of course," he replied; "for, as Régis points out . . ."

But at that moment Mrs. Wharton returned and I never learned whether, according to him, the homosexual fell under the head of sadism or of masochism. I was sorry that he turned the conversation into another channel; it would have amused me to know Mrs. Wharton's opinion, if she had one.

Paul Bourget still seems extremely hardy for his age, as if gnarled and hewn out of chestnut. His least remarks are redolent of literature; he splatters you with literary allusions like the spaniel that shook off precious stones. "You are welcome to—what is anything but Elsinore," he said as we left the garden to enter the house. In less than a half hour he managed to speak of Régnier (Mathurin), Shakespeare, Molière, Racine (whom he confesses not to be very fond of), Baudelaire, Boileau, Zola, Balzac, Charles-Louis Philippe, etc., all this with an extraordinary lack of real literary taste, I mean a singular incomprehension of poetry, art, and style. It is this that allows him to admire such paltry productions as those of Psichari, for instance, for which he has just written a preface. He reads us a few pages from the proofs of the *Voyage du Centurion;* his voice catches as if he were on the point of weeping. Out of the corner of our eyes, Mrs. Wharton and I glance at each other, not knowing which deserves more wonder, Paul Bourget's emotion or the mediocrity of those pages. He insists on our reading the whole book, of which he gives us the proofs. And a little later, as I am walking with him down the corridor of the Costebelle hotel, where he has taken us after tea and a short walk and then a new conversation in Mrs. Wharton's room, in which we talked of Pascal and of the *Mystère de Jésus* . . . he takes me familiarly by the arm and, leaning toward me: "So you will promise me to read the *Voyage du Centurion?*" And, in a whisper of solemn secrecy, he adds: "Believe me: it is worth the *Mystère de Jésus.*"

On that odd declaration we parted.

December 8

My wonder as a child on seeing the first eucalyptus tree in blossom. We had just reached Hyères. I ran quickly to the hotel and was not satisfied until I had led my mother out to look at those wonderful flowers with me. I shall have to relate also the trips I made at that time to the islands; perhaps the most enchanted memory of my childhood is that of the moments, the hours, that I spent on Sainte-Marguerite (or Saint-Honorat), leaning over the rocks on the edge of the water, watching the fairyland formed, at that time, by the natural aquaria among the rocks. Sea anemones, starfish, sea urchins sprinkled the rock walls down to depths where the eye could no longer make them out clearly; everything was throbbing to the rhythm of the waves, but there were shelters untouched by even the gentlest undulation of the sea; there creatures and flowers breathed indolently; by keeping still and quiet for a long time, one could see strange, almost frightening animals issuing out of their dark lairs. I would stay there without stirring, lost in a contemplation—or rather an adoration—that nothing could interrupt until Marie's call, toward evening, in time to catch the return boat.

I am very much afraid that the shores of those islands, so charming in my childhood, have been as lamentably spoiled as the immediate surroundings of Cannes itself; as was also the coast of England, of which Edmund Gosse speaks so eloquently in *Father and Son;* as are all the most charming spots on this earth as soon as man begins to sprawl on them.

1916   *January 16*

My conversation with Copeau did me a great deal of good, the day before yesterday. My attention constantly brought back to ruins, in my life at the Foyer, it was hard for me to imagine that anyone could still be trying to build something. I am aware that the atmosphere in which I have lived for more than a year is the most depressing possible. Faced with that uninterrupted parade of misfortunes constantly tearing my heart, I became ashamed of any superiority and repeated to myself the words of Montesquieu's Eucrates: "For one man to be elevated above humanity costs all the others too much."

January 17

Ghéon writes me that he has "taken the jump." It sounds like a schoolboy who has just taken a crack at the brothel. . . . But he is really talking of the communion table.

January 18

While writing to Ghéon, I reread the beginning of the fifteenth chapter of the Gospel according to St. John and these words are suddenly illuminated for me with a frightful light: "If a man abide not in me, he is cast forth as a branch, and is withered; and men gather them, and cast them into the fire, and they are burned."

Truly was I not "cast into the fire" and already a prey to the flame of the most abominable desires? . . .

January 19

Everything in me needs to be recovered, revised, re-educated. What I have most trouble struggling against is my sensual curiosity. The drunkard's glass of absinthe is not more attractive than, for me, certain faces I meet by chance—I would give up everything to follow them. . . . What am I saying? This involves such an imperious impulse, such a secret insidious counsel, so inveterate a habit that I often wonder if I can escape it, without outside aid.

Sunday, 23

Yesterday evening I yielded, as one yields to an obstinate child—"to have peace." Lugubrious peace; darkening of the whole sky. . . .

On my return to the Foyer, I had to preside over a meeting in which nothing was going the way I wanted it. My irritation was so great that I was afraid to let it out, and forced myself to keep silent.

I no longer have any reason to stay at the Foyer and I don't like it there. For more than a year it was kept alive and throbbing by charity; now it is becoming a philanthropic undertaking in which I have neither intellectual nor emotional interest.

24

Yesterday an indescribably odd and beautiful sunset: sky filled with pink- and orange-tinted mists; I admired it especially, as I was going over the Pont de Grenelle, reflected by the Seine heavy with barges; everything melted into a warm and tender harmony. In the Saint-Sulpice tram, from which I was watching this sight with wonder in my eyes, I noticed that no one, absolutely no one, was aware of it. There was not a single face that didn't look preoccupied with cares. . . . Yet, I thought, some people travel to a great distance to find nothing more beautiful. But most often man does not recognize beauty unless he buys it, and that is why God's offer is so often disdained.

25

Very bad night. I again fall as low as ever.

This morning, up before seven, I go out a moment and hear a blackbird's song, odd, so precociously springlike, so pathetic and pure that it makes me feel all the more bitterly the withering-up of my heart.

For several days now I have been striving to free myself from the Foyer, to give up my interest in it. I have great difficulty in doing so, and the time I spend trying to interest myself in something else (not to say in myself) is put to poor use, almost lost. And since Saturday I have been assailed once again by abominable imaginings, against which I am defenseless; I find no refuge anywhere. At certain moments, sometimes for hours, I wonder if I am not going mad; everything in me yields to my mania. Yet I strive to organize the battle. . . . What patience and what deception it would take!

This evening, however, an excellent letter from Ghéon brings me a little comfort.

27

Good! Once more I have managed to recover my balance. Ghéon's letter helped me. Last night a calm meditation prepared the way for a restful night. I was able to get up early. At work at six-thirty, filled with a strange inner peace. I did not try to pray, but my entire soul opened up to divine counsel, like a body warming itself in the sun. Every hour of this day has followed the impulse of that first hour. Moreover, if a temptation had arisen, I don't believe that I should have resisted; but none arose and I reached the evening in peace.

Sunday, 30

If I had to formulate a credo, I should say: God is not behind us. He is to come. He must be sought, not at the beginning, but at the end of the evolution. He is terminal and not initial. He is the supreme and final point toward which all nature tends in time. And since time does not exist for Him, it is a matter of indifference to Him whether the evolution which He crowns follows or precedes Him, and whether He determines it by propulsion or attraction.

It is through man that God is molded. This is what I feel and believe, and what I understand in the words: "Let man be created in Our image." What can all the doctrines of evolution do against that thought?

This is the gate through which I enter into the holy place, this is the series of thoughts that leads me back to God, to the Gospels, etc. . . .

Will I one day succeed in setting this forth clearly?

For a long time already I have believed this without knowing it, and now little by little it is becoming clear to me through a series of successive illuminations. The reasoning comes after.

Monday, 31

I am continuing the reading of Bossuet's *Elévations*. He proves the existence of God by the sentiment of perfection that every man carries in his heart: "What is error if it is not a privation of truth . . . and what is ignorance if it is not a privation of perfect power? . . ." Then, passing to God's prescience, he proves it by reference to prophecy.

And this is lamentable and dishonest. I can give up my reason, but I cannot distort it. Read last night in the *Revue hebdomadaire* the third or fourth part of Francis Jammes's *Rosaire*. It is to real piety what smut is to love.

February 1

I give up the reading of Bossuet's *Elévations* before my disgust overflows and carries away with it what I should like to keep. I have gone as far as I could, but no reading is more likely to hurl me into the opposition, and I am stopping out of precaution.

I am trying to put aside a half hour every evening and every morning for meditation, self-analysis, relaxation, expectation. . . . "Remain simply attentive to that presence of God, exposed to His divine observation, thus continuing that devout attention or *exposition* . . . at peace under the rays of the divine sun of justice."

I long ardently to write that book of meditations or elevations which will balance the *Nourritures*. . . .

February 4

At lunch, as I am telling Em. how much I am stimulated by anything that upsets my habits, she replies: "That is because *you* are strong"—and immediately I hear again the bell that tolls throughout the *Immoraliste*.

February 8

Dined at Darius Milhaud's. He asks my advice about the "cantata" he wants to make of my *Retour de l'Enfant prodigue*.

February 9

I have resumed the reading of Pascal, of much greater advantage to me than Bossuet. I am beginning to feel the benefit of the daily meditation that I impose on myself every morning and evening. I am still lacking in strength, but calm; I do not pray, but I listen and wait and, for the moment at least, I do not wish for any other form of prayer.

Monday, February 14

Yesterday several visits for the Foyer (at 87 rue Boileau) in the huge "low-priced housing project." But it does me no good. Too much sensuality is constantly insinuating itself into my charity. My heart, my whole being go out unreservedly and I come away from these visits completely undone. Or else I remain utterly and painfully dry and would quite willingly suggest putting an end to the suffering by liquidating the individual who is complaining.

Who can understand that destitution can be as attractive as luxury? and huddling together in distress as attractive as the exaltation of love?

This is the point at which the highest heaven touches hell.

February 16

The day before yesterday, relapse.

One seems to fall as low as ever, and all the effort of these last days seems lost.

But one's balance returns a bit more rapidly; the surrender is not so complete.

Hell would consist in continuing to sin despite oneself, without deriving any pleasure from it. It is natural that the soul given over to the Evil One should become, without any pleasure for itself, a docile instrument of damnation for others.

I am consciously using here, as I did earlier, a vocabulary and images that imply a mythology in which it is not absolutely essential that I should believe. Suffice it that it is the most eloquent I know to explain an interior drama. And psychology could explain it just as well, just as meteorology has done for certain Greek myths . . . what does that matter to me! The deepest explanation can only be finality.

I have realized the profound truth of the words: "Whosoever shall seek to save his life shall lose it." To be sure, it is in perfect abnegation that individualism triumphs, and self-renunciation is the summit of self-assertion.

It is through self-preference, on the other hand, that the Evil One enlists and enslaves us. Who would dare to call this liberation? From what laws? As if vice were not more imperious than any duty!

Friday

Finished the evening at the home of Marcel Proust (whom I had not seen since '92). I had promised myself to relate that visit at length; but I no longer have the interest to do so this morning.

———————

During these periods of restlessness I ought deliberately to give up all reading, set nothing in front of me but blank paper. But I flee from work, begin six books at a time, not knowing where to hide from the demands I shall all too soon have to answer. . . .

Saturday

Continued with the writing of my childhood recollections. But, in connection with the walks in the Luxembourg Gardens with my father, I fall back into hesitations, erasures, and new starts, which kill all spontaneity. I must above all cure myself of this. I returned to the same passage more than six times and had to go to bed before having succeeded in getting it right.

Friday

. . . went in to say hello to old Mme Freger. Her face against the white pillow seems even redder; she coughs, spits, and gasps, but no longer complains of her dead eye, which is now quite white, colorless, and hideous to see. Old Mother Michel, who is taking care of her, has only one eye likewise. When she was first suggested to Mme Freger, the latter refused: "Mother Michel! who watches over the dead! . . . Don't want her." And yet she had to give in, for no one else could be found to take care of her.

March 22

One struggles effectively so long as one thinks it a duty to struggle; but as soon as the struggle appears vain, and one ceases to hate the enemy . . . Yet I am still resisting, though less from conviction than from defiance.

March 31

. . . I keep pushing on in the writing of my memoirs, often with many hesitations, backward glances, and fresh starts; but I refuse to reread what I have written, even to write out a clean copy, for fear of being disgusted with what I am writing and then losing the courage to go on.

It is not so much doubt and lack of self-confidence that hold me up as a sort of disgust, a nameless hatred and scorn for everything I am writing, for everything I was, everything I am. Truly, in going ahead with the writing of these memoirs, I am performing a labor of mortification.

May 3

I read in a letter from my mother to my father: "André would be very nice if he didn't have a mania for standing a long time absolutely still at the foot of a tree watching snails."

The letter must date from '73 (the year of Isabelle Widmer's marriage, which it mentions a little earlier). I was therefore four years old.

June 15

I tore out about twenty pages of this notebook; this broke the thread, and I have been unable to write anything in it for more than a month. I have given all my time to the Memoirs. If anyone is surprised that I can enjoy this work while the echo of cannon is still shaking the earth, I shall say that it is precisely because any work of imagination is impossible for me, any effort of thought. Without and within me I feel an immense disarray, and if I am writing these Memoirs today, it is also because I am clinging to them desperately.

The pages I tore up seemed like pages written by a madman.

16

Yesterday, at the request of the government, all clocks were set forward an hour. You could not imagine the number of stupid remarks to which that decision gave rise. People managed to talk about it for hours on end.

Cuverville, September 15

I resume this journal, abandoned last June, in a new notebook. I had torn out the last pages; they reflected a dreadful crisis in which Em. was involved; or, more exactly, of which Em. was the cause. I had written them in a sort of despair; to tell the truth, since those pages were addressed to her, I tore them up at her request as soon as she had read them. Or rather, even though she discreetly refrained from asking it of me, at least I was too keenly aware of the relief it would be for her not to suggest it to her at once. And probably she was grateful to me for it; but nonetheless, to speak frankly, I regret having done it; not so much because I think I have never written any pages so fine, so pathetic, nor because they might have helped me to get out of an unhealthy state of mind of which they were the sincere reflection (and into which I am only too inclined to fall again); but because that suppression halted my journal abruptly; deprived of that support, I have ever since been stumbling about in a terrifying intellectual disorder. I have made useless efforts in the other notebook. I forsake it half filled. In this one, at least, I shall not be aware of the torn-out pages.

Sunday

Yes, I remember those conversations with her and Ghéon, in Asia Minor (one at Smyrna, particularly), about the slow decomposition of France, about the unused or squandered virtues, about the imminence of war—in which Mme Mayrisch refused to believe and which, several months before the declaration, Ghéon and I foresaw, predicted, almost longed for, because it seemed to us that war itself was a lesser evil than the abominable decay into which our country was gradually falling—and from which war alone could perhaps still save us. . . .

September 19

Yesterday, an abominable relapse. The storm raged all night long. This morning it is hailing abundantly. I get up, my head and heart at once empty and heavy, full of all the weight of hell. . . . I am the drowning man who is losing heart, and who now struggles only weakly. The three calls have the same sound: It is time. It is high time. It is no longer time. So that you do not distinguish one from the other, and already the third one is sounding while you still think you are at the first.

If at least I could relate this drama; depict Satan, after he has taken possession of a creature, using him, acting through him upon others. This seems an empty image. Even I have only recently come to understand this: you are not only a prisoner; active evil demands of you a reverse activity; you must start fighting for the other side.

The great error is to form a romantic image of the devil. This is what made me take so long to recognize him. He is no more romantic or classic than the man he is talking to. He is as diverse as man himself; more so, because he adds to his diversity. He made himself classical with me, when it was necessary to catch me, because he knew that I would never willingly associate with evil a certain happy equilibrium. I did not understand that a certain equilibrium could be maintained, for a time at least, in the very worst. I regarded everything that was regulated as good. Through proper measure and proportion I thought to dominate evil; and it is through that very *mesure,* on the contrary, that it took possession of me.

A disgust, a frightful hatred of myself, sours all my thoughts the moment I wake up. The minute hostility with which I keep watch over every impulse of my being contorts it. Neither faults nor virtues—nothing about me is natural any longer. Everything I remember about myself horrifies me.

Sunday

Empty day; lost. I drag myself through the hours and long for nothing but sleep.

Monday

But don't you see that you are speaking to a dead man?

October 3

. . . I am lost if I do not manage to catch hold of myself before winter. Those summer months were hateful, with no work accomplished, months of utter dissolution. I do not think I have ever been farther from happiness. With always the vague hope that, from the depths of the abyss, will arise that cry of distress that, no, I have forgotten how to utter. . . . No matter how low you are, you can still look up toward the sky. But no: however low I was, I always looked still lower. I gave up heaven. I ceased defending myself against hell. Obsessions and all the symptoms of madness. Truly. I frightened myself; incapable in my own case of the advice I should so easily have given to someone else.

Already talking about it all so easily—does this indicate that I am already so sure of being cured?

Thursday, October 5

Rainy day. After lunch, Jeanne, Valentine, and the children set out for Etretat in a carriage. Delightfully calm afternoon with Em. I read her the first thirty letters of Dupouey, of which I had received the copy this very morning. The silence, the calm of the empty house, brought tranquillity back to my heart. This morning I opened the green notebook again (*Numquid et tu . . . ?*) and wrote a few lines in it, but still heavy with unrest, with doubt, with melancholy. My nerves are so weak, so vibrant, that I believe they never relax in the least except in silence; yes, I have already noted how the slightest noise upsets me. In silence, I feel better at once.

A few words from Em. plunge me back into a sort of despair. At last I make up my mind to speak to her of that plan of spending the winter at Saint-Clair.

"I certainly owe you that," she said with an effort of her whole nature, which at once made her face so sad, so grave, that immediately I think only of giving up this plan like so many others, because it costs her so much, and because I should have to buy my happiness at the expense of hers—so that it could therefore no longer be my happiness.

The passion slowly subsides. Yesterday, abominable relapse, which leaves my body and mind in a state bordering on despair, on suicide, on madness. . . . It is the rock of Sisyphus, which falls back to the very bottom of the mountain he was trying to climb, which falls back with him, rolling over him, dragging him along under its mortal weight, and plunging him back into the mud. What? Am I going to have to repeat this lamentable effort, once again, to the bitter end? I dream of the time when, in the flat, level ground, without the least thought of rising higher, I used to smile at every new hour, indolently seated on this rock that there was no question of raising. Alas! you took pity on me despite myself, O Lord. . . . But hold out a hand to me, then. Lead me yourself to that place, near you, which I am unable to reach.

"Poor soul, intending to raise your sin up to my level. . . ."

"O Lord! you know that I give up justifying myself against anyone. What does it matter that it is to escape yielding to sin that I yield to the Church! I yield. Oh, take off the ropes that restrain me. Deliver me from the frightful weight of this body. Oh, let me live a bit! let me breathe! Tear me away from evil. Do not let me suffocate."

Age is coming without my hoping to know anything more about my body. A happy equilibrium almost immediately followed my lapse and my distress. I should like to see in it a reply to my appeal, but at the moment that I was uttering that cry, how well I know it, the best part of my distress was over. I was like the man who feels his fever falling at the moment of swallowing his quinine; but who swallows it just the same because, all the time that his fever lasted, he kept thinking: Oh, if only I had taken some!

I write this without any irreverence, but because I believe both that the act of piety is not necessarily the result (the successful outcome) of the distress, and that it is unseemly to seek to interest God in physical lapses that can just as well be cured by a better-ordered life.

October 21

That morning, more specifically, he had waited for her—one could say "desperately"—in her room, where he had gone down as early as he could, rushing his dressing and putting off both work and prayer. It must be said that the day before she had promised to be there, and he ran as to some secret rendezvous, with a new and joyful soul; it would give a spring to his whole day.

When he had entered, the room was empty; he had found, placed on the table, D.'s letter, which the day before she had promised to read to him. She had placed it there opened, as if to say: "Read it without me," which he did not do, for he found no pleasure in it. He sat down in the windowseat, opened a book he had brought with him; but he could not fix his attention on it. He kept thinking: Where is she? what is she doing? what shall I say to her when she eventually returns? Obviously she is not inactive; I am willing to admit that some urgent problem may have called her, as is constantly occurring, all day long, every day. He made an effort not to be vexed and planned to say to her simply, sweetly: I was beginning to believe you had forgotten me; or: you had forgotten for a while that I was waiting for you. . . .

At that moment he heard her step in the vestibule; but she still was not coming upstairs; she was going back and forth; she was busying herself about something or other; there were now but a very few minutes before the bell that was to gather the household for breakfast. . . . Then it was that he heard her beginning to wind the clock. It was the big grandfather clock at the foot of the stairs; obviously, as she was going by she had seen the clock stopped and, on the point of joining him, had decided to set it. He heard it strike twice, then the half-hour, then three times. . . . The worst of it is that the clock, an old-fashioned one, struck double. It was after eight o'clock; he calculated that he still had to hear it strike fifty-four times; and each of those tones unbearably spaced out. . . . He couldn't stand it any longer, and went out into the hall.

"I had left the letter on the table so that you could read it," she said as if it were the simplest thing in the world. "You see that I had things to do. When this clock is not on time, the whole house is late."

"Yes, I noticed that; it is now twenty minutes that I have been waiting for you."

But she made no excuses; she remained so calm, and he so upset, that he began to think he had been wrong to wait for her and she right not to have come. He said nothing, but thought: "My poor dear, you will always find clocks to set, along your way, whenever it is a question of meeting me."

October 25

At the rate at which we are going, there will soon be formed a Germanophile party in France, which will be recruited not among anarchists and internationalists, but among those who will find themselves obliged to recognize the constant superiority of Germany. They will judge, and rightly, that it is good, that it is natural, for superiority to govern. And perhaps they will reflect that something in France remains superior to that very superiority; but alas! that divine something is powerless and mute. Would Germany be able to recognize that something? Would she strive to stifle it? Or would she not perhaps consent to exploit it? . . . Exploit that in which the enemy excels! What a fantasy! And indeed would that something permit itself to be exploited by the enemy?

October 26

Lapse the day before yesterday and yesterday. The best thing is not to be too upset about it. It is not good to keep rubbing one's nose in one's mistake.

October 29

The newspapers exasperate me; their contemptible and out-of-date optimism seems always to believe that victory consists in refusing to notice the blows one is receiving. It strikes me that they flatter and encourage one of the failings of the French mind most dangerous in time of war, for it is inevitably accompanied by unpreparedness. These are the same papers that denied the German peril before the war; today they seem to serve us up in detail, from day to day, the small change of that inept and ruinous self-confidence. No defeat will correct them. . . .

Saturday [*December 23*]

With a very great emotion, finished reading to Em. the first four chapters of my Memoirs; gave her the beginning of the fifth to read. My work has stopped precisely at the story of my furtive visit to the rue de Lecat. . . . To tell the truth, the impression from this reading is not bad, is even of such a nature as to encourage me greatly. But, to my taste, it is all overwritten, in too precious, too conscious a style. . . . I always write better and more easily what I have not carried too long in my head; as soon as my thought precedes my pen, it checks my hand.

Yesterday, late in the day, great fatigue and depression, enough to make me think I shall have to stop everything. But this morning, after an almost sleepless night, I get up in fairly good fettle.

[*from* NUMQUID ET TU . . . ? *(1916)*]

[*From the Foreword of 1926*]

. . . If it happened to me to be "converted," I could not bear to have that conversion made public. Perhaps some sign of it would appear in my conduct; but only a few intimate friends and a priest would know it. And should it come to be bruited about, that would be against my will, offending and wounding my modesty. I regard this as no matter for diversion or amazement. It is entirely a matter between God and me. This at least is my own feeling; and I have no intention, through these words, to throw blame on certain very well-publicized conversions.

. . . I am neither a Protestant nor a Catholic; I am simply a Christian. And as a matter of fact, I do not want anyone to make a mistake as to the testimonial value of these pages. No doubt I should still sign them today with all my heart. But, written during the war, they retain a certain reflection of the anguish and confusion of that period; and if, in all probability, I should still sign them, I should perhaps not still write them.

I do not claim that the state that followed this one is superior to it; it is enough for me that it is not quite the same.

*   *   *

It is because Christ is the Son of God, they have said, that we must believe in his words. And then came others who ceased to pay any attention to his words because they would not admit that Jesus was the Son of God.

O Lord, it is not because I have been told that you were the Son of God that I listen to your word; but your word is beautiful beyond any human word, and that is how I recognize that you are the Son of God.

---

* *"Numquid et tu Galilæus? . . ."* "Art Thou also of Galilee?" (John 7:52)

The Gospels are a very simple little book, which must be read very simply. There is no question of explaining them, but merely of accepting them. They need no commentary, and every human effort to throw light upon them only dims them. They are not addressed to learned men; learning only prevents one from understanding anything in them. They can be attained only through poverty of spirit.

Oh, to be born again! To forget what other men have written, have painted, have thought, and what one has thought oneself. To be born anew.

February 15

That Christ should have cried out: *Now is my soul troubled,* this is what constitutes his greatness. This is the point of debate between the man and the God.

And when he goes on: *Father, save me from this hour,* this is still the human speaking. When he finishes: *But for this cause came I unto this hour,* the God prevails.

The words that precede throw light on these: *Except a corn of wheat fall into the ground and die* . . . and again: *He that loveth his life shall lose it.* Here Christ renounces man; here truly he becomes God.

February 18

Et nunc . . .

It is *in eternity* that we must live, from this moment on. And it is *from this moment* that we must live in eternity.

What is the good of eternal life, if we are not conscious of its duration at every instant?

Just as Jesus said: *I AM the way, the truth,* he says: *I am the resurrection and the life.*

Eternal life is not only to come. It is right now wholly present within us; we live it from the moment that we consent to die to ourselves, to obtain from ourselves the renunciation that makes possible resurrection in eternity. *He that hateth his life in this world shall keep it unto eternal life* (John, 12:25).

Once more, there is here neither prescription nor command. It is simply the secret of the higher felicity that Christ is revealing to us, as he does everywhere in the Gospels.

If ye know these things, happy are ye, says Christ later (John, 13:

17). Not: *Ye shall be happy*—but: *happy ARE ye.* It is right now and immediately that we can share in felicity.

What tranquillity! Here truly time stops. Here breathes the Eternal. We enter into the Kingdom of God.

March 4

This is the mysterious center of Christian ethics, the divine secret of happiness: the individual triumphs in the renunciation of the individual.

Quicumque quæsierit animam suam salvam facere, perdet illam: et quicumque perdiderit illam, vivificabit eam (Luke, 17:33). . . .*

Qui amat animam suam, perdet eam: et qui odit animam suam in hoc mundo, in vitam æternam custodit eam (John, 12:25).†

He who loves his life, his soul—who protects his personality, who is particular about the figure he cuts in this world—will lose it; but he who gives it up will make it really live, will assure it eternal life; not eternal life in the future, but now: already, right now, he will make it live in eternity.

Amen, amen, dico vobis, nisi granum frumenti cadens in terram, mortuum fuerit, ipsum solum manet: si autem mortuum fuerit, multum fructum effert (John, 12:24).‡ Resurrection in total life. Forgetfulness of all particular happiness. Oh, perfect reintegration!

This is also the lesson to Nicodemus: *Amen, amen, dico tibi, nisi quis renatus fuerit denuo, non potest videre regnum Dei* (John, 3:3).§

April 20

Amen, amen, dico vobis: quia omnis qui facit peccatum, servus est peccati (John, 8:34). ‖

Sin is what one does not do freely.

Deliver me from that captivity, O Lord!

Si ergo vos Filius liberaverit, vere liberi eritis.

If the Son therefore shall make you free, ye shall be free indeed.

---

* "Whosoever shall seek to save his life shall lose it; and whosoever shall lose his life shall preserve it."

† "He that loveth his life shall lose it; and he that hateth his life in this world shall keep it unto life eternal."

‡ "Verily, verily, I say unto you, Except a grain of wheat fall into the ground and die, it abideth alone; but if it die, it bringeth forth much fruit."

§ "Verily, verily, I say unto thee, Except a man be born again, he cannot see the kingdom of God." Gide is here purposefully using the Latin Vulgate text, to avoid certain difficulties with the various vernacular translations—which he also consulted. The English translations here are those of the King James Version.

‖ "Verily, verily, I say unto you, Whosoever committeth sin is the servant of sin."

And the Evil One whispers to my heart: What good is that liberty to you if you cannot use it?

It is with these words in his heart that the Prodigal Son ran away.

May 12

Written nothing further in this notebook for the last fortnight. Gave up my readings and those pious exercises which my heart, utterly dry and listless, no longer approved. See nothing in it but a comedy, and a dishonest comedy, in which I convinced myself that I recognized the hand of the demon. This is what the demon whispers to my heart.

O Lord! Oh, do not leave him the last word. I do not wish any other prayer today.

June 2

Period of indifference, of dryness and unworthiness, my mind wholly concerned with ridiculous anxieties that wear it out and darken it.

This morning I read in Saint Paul (I did not go back to my Bible until yesterday): *And if any man think that he knoweth any thing, he knoweth nothing yet as he ought to know.*

But if any man love God, the same is known of Him (I Corinthians, 8:2–3).

June 16

I am no longer able either to pray or even to listen to God. If He perhaps speaks to me, I do not hear. Here I am again become completely indifferent to His voice. And yet I have nothing but scorn for my *own* wisdom, and, for lack of the joy He gives me, all other joy is taken from me.

O Lord, if you are to help me, what are you waiting for? I cannot do anything, all alone. I cannot.

All the reflections of You that I felt within me are growing dim. It is time for You to come.

Ah, do not let the Evil One in my heart take Your place! Do not let Yourself be dispossessed, Lord! If You withdraw completely, he settles in. Ah, do not confuse me completely with him! I do not love him that much, I assure You. Remember that I was capable of loving You.

What! Do I feel then today as if I had never loved Him?

June 22

Gratuitousness of the gift. Gift beyond question.

Abandonment of all mortal concerns.

Oh, paradisaical fruition of every instant!

To share in that immensity of happiness, yes, I feel that You invite me, Lord! And sometimes I remain on the watch, trembling at the immediate promise of so much joy.

If therefore I do not respond better to Your voice, O Lord, force me, do me violence. Seize this heart which I am incapable of giving You freely.

May the lightning of Your love consume or vitrify all the opacity of my flesh, everything mortal that I drag after me!

I am bored with everything in which I do not feel Your presence, and recognize no life that is not inspired by Your love.

June 23

Don't be surprised to feel so sad—and sad on my account. The felicity I offer you excludes forever what you used to take for happiness.

June 26

I was happy; You have ruined my happiness. Jealous God, You have poisoned with bitterness all the springs at which I used to quench my thirst, so that I have no thirst but for the water that You offered to the Samaritan woman.

"Can it be therefore that you do not believe in his miracles?"

"Do not drive my reason into a corner. You know very well that I have put it aside. If it were proved to me today that Christ did not perform his miracles, my confidence in his voice would not be shaken; I should believe in his teaching just the same."

"In short, you do not believe in his miracles."

"What! it is his miracles that make you consider him divine? What! you too—to believe in him you need a miracle? Like the 'evil and adulterous crowd' that said: 'master, we should like to see a sign from you.'"

"In short, you do not believe. . . ."

"I leave you the last word."

October 3

. . . His hand forever stretched out, which pride refuses to take.

"Do you then prefer to sink forever, slowly, forever more deeply into the abyss? Do you think that this rotten flesh will fall away from you by itself? No; not if *you* refuse to tear yourself away from it."

"Lord! without Your intervention it will first rot on me utterly. No, this is not pride; You know it! But to take Your hand, I should like to be less unworthy. My filth will soil it before its light will whiten me. . . ."

"You know well . . ."

"Forgive me, Lord! Yes, I know that I am lying. The truth is that this flesh that I hate, I still love it more than You Yourself. I am dying because I have not exhausted all its appeal. I ask You to help me, but I do it without any true renunciation. . . .

"Miserable man: you hope to marry heaven and hell in yourself. One cannot give oneself to God except wholly."

Are you really surprised if, after having left God for so long, you do not attain, as soon as you turn to Him again, to felicity, to communion, to ecstasy? . . .

November 7

My Lord, let me not be one of those who cut a fine figure in the world.

Let me not be among those who succeed.

Let me not count among the fortunate, the satisfied, the satiated; among those who are applauded, who are congratulated, and who are envied.

[*from* THE JOURNAL]

[*Detached Pages*]

> *"He believes neither in God
> nor in the devil."*
> (Popular saying)

Until then I had never realized that it was not necessary to believe in God in order to believe in the devil. To tell the truth, the devil had never yet appeared before my imagination; my conception of the devil remained entirely negative; I condemned him by default; I limited his outline by God's; and because I extended God everywhere, I did not let the *Other* begin anywhere. In any case, I admitted him only as a metaphysical entity, and merely smiled at first that autumn evening when suddenly Jacques Raverat introduced me to him.

But I was full of scruples, and before I surrendered, the demon who took me in hand had to convince me that what was asked of me was permitted, and that what was permitted was also necessary. Sometimes the Evil One reversed the propositions, began with the necessary; he would reason thus —for the Evil One is the Reasoner: "How could it be that what is necessary to you should not be permitted you? Just consent to call necessary what you can't do without. You cannot do without that for which you thirst the most. Agree not to call 'sin' what you cannot do without. You would acquire great strength," he would add, "if instead of wearing yourself out fighting thus against yourself, you fought only against the external obstacle. No obstacle can hold back the man who has learned to fight. Go, learn to triumph over yourself at last and over your own sense of decency. Haven't I taught you to see nothing but an inherited habit in your uprightness, the merest prolongation of an impulse; in your modesty, nothing but shyness and embarrassment; in your virtue, not so much decision, as mere unconcern. . . ?"

In short, he drew argument and advantage from the fact that it cost me more to yield to my desire than to continue curbing it. To be sure, the first steps I took on the downward path required, in order to risk them, a certain courage and even a certain resolve.

It goes without saying that I did not understand until much later the diabolic element in that exhortation. At that time I thought I was the only one to speak and that I was carrying on this specious dialogue with myself.

I had heard talk of the Evil One, but I had not made his acquaintance. He was already dwelling in me at a time when I could not yet distinguish him. He had made me his conquest; I thought myself victorious, of course; victorious over myself—because I was surrendering to him. Because he had convinced [*convaincu*] me, I did not feel myself to be conquered [*vaincu*]. I had invited him to take up his residence in me, as a challenge and because I did not believe in him, like the man in the legend who sells his soul to him in return for some exquisite advantage—and who continues to disbelieve in him despite having received the advantage from him!

I did not yet understand that evil is a positive, active, enterprising principle; I thought at that time that evil was caused simply by the absence of good, as darkness is by the absence of light, and I was inclined to assign all kinds of activity to light. So when, in 1910, my friend Raverat spoke to me of him for the first time, I merely smiled. But his words entered my heart no less deeply. "I began," he explained to me, "by believing in the devil. . . ." (We were in the study at Cuverville, and a reading together of Milton in the afternoon had brought our conversation around to the subject of Satan.) "And it is believing in him, *whom I actually felt,* that led me to believe in God, whom I did not yet feel." To my amazement was added a great deal of irony, and I feared that he himself was not being altogether serious. But he went on soberly, as if in reply, "Satan's great strength comes from the fact that he is never what you think he is. You have already accomplished a good deal against him before you are convinced that he is there. To recognize him properly, it is better never to let him out of your sight."

It took all my great friendship for Jacques Raverat to make me pay attention to his words. From then on I bore them within me, but like those seeds which germinate only after a long stratification; to tell the truth, they did not sprout until that first year of the war, when, having given myself completely to a relief organization, I was able to see the face of the Evil One more clearly against that background of philanthropy.

The great mistake, which allows him to slip incognito into our lives, is that, ordinarily, people are willing to recognize his voice only at the moment of the temptation itself; but he rarely risks an offensive without having prepared it. He is much more intelligent than we are, and he hides most often in the mask of reason; if we were more humble we should recognize him in the *Cogito ergo sum.* That *ergo* is the cloven hoof [*l'ergot du diable*]. He knows that there are certain souls that he cannot conquer in open battle, souls that he must persuade.

I know that to many minds it might seem absurd, as it would still have seemed to mine the day before yesterday, to go out of one's way to postulate this existence, this presence of the demon in order to explain by some apparition what one has given up trying to explain through logic; a less lazy or more subtle psychology would succeed in putting this phantom out of countenance once again, so they say. These are the same minds that think that the evolutionary explanation has succeeded in supplanting God. What shall I reply except that I had no sooner *assumed* the demon than the whole story of my life was at once made clear: that I suddenly understood what had been most obscure to me, to such a point that this assumption took on the exact shape of my interrogation and my precedent wonder.

What is more glorious than a soul when it frees itself? And what is more tragic than a soul that imprisons itself just when it *thinks* it is freeing itself?

It is actually of no importance to me whether or not the name "demon" is the right name for what I mean, and I acknowledge that I call it that out of convenience. If someone should come along later and show me that he lives not in hell but in my blood, my loins, or my insomnia, does he believe that he is going to suppress him thus? When I say *the Evil One*, I know what that expression designates, just as clearly as I know what is designated by the word *God.* I draw his outline by the deficiency of each virtue.

And because he is more intelligent than I am, everything that he invented to plunge me toward evil was infinitely more precious, more specious, more convincing, more beautiful, more clever than any argument I could have brought up to persevere in honor. I should never have stumbled upon such arguments by myself. *Cogito ergo Satanas.*

Now, this is how he proceeds: "To begin with, thank you for having brought me into being! Yes, you are well aware that it is your kindness that creates me. You are well aware that I didn't exist, but you probably needed to take off from me to believe in God—a God that might help you to fight me."

"Good Lord, how complicated all this is! I believe in God. The existence of God alone matters to me, and not yours; but the proof that you exist is that you want to make me doubt it."

"Come, come! You are not so stupid as all that! You created me in order to pile on my back all your doubts, your dejections, your fits of boredom. Everything that bothers you, that is I, everything that holds you back. If your pride protests against the bent of your mind, it is I. It is I if your blood boils, if your spirit starts wandering. When your reason balks, it is I. When your flesh revolts, it is I. Your hunger, your thirst, your fatigue are all I. Your inclination is I. In short, you give me such a wonderful role that I wonder if sometimes you do not confuse me with God. The amusing thing, I tell you, is that henceforth you cannot believe in One without the Other. Just listen to the fable of the gardener. . . ."

"By heaven, I knew it: you too; you know how to talk in parables."

"Oh, I'm not limited to any one form of expression."

"That is because you speak in turn to the mind, to the heart, to the senses; while protecting myself on one side, I am always uncovering myself on the other; so you, who keep moving around me, always address yourself to the unguarded side."

"How well we know each other! You know, if you wanted to—"

"What?"

"What good friends we should be! . . ."

1917   *January 11*

For several days I have been trying to find a title to give to these Memoirs; for neither *Mémoires,* nor *Souvenirs,* nor *Confessions* is exactly what I want. And the awkward thing about any other title is that it allows of a meaning. I am hesitating between: *Et Ego* . . . but that restricts the sense; and *Si le grain ne meurt* . . . but that slants it, while enlarging it. I believe, however, that I shall settle for the latter.

Cuverville, February 27

Yesterday back from Paris, where I had gone to spend a week. A telegram from Jeanne had called me urgently: the freezing water had burst a water-pipe in the Villa, flooded the cellar, the back stairs, etc. Great mental fatigue as I left here, dizzy spells, etc. The distraction of Paris rather rested me. Certainly it was good to interrupt for a while my work and that mental hypertension it involved. I had pushed my Memoirs as far as the end of chapter four, that is to say, nearly a hundred and eighty manuscript pages of large oblong format. Finished the translation of *Typhoon* (only a few pages are still lacking) and learned by heart a number of fugues and preludes (*Well-Tempered Clavichord; Inventions; Suites*).

My principle was that nothing rests one better from fatigue than a different fatigue; but perhaps in this case the effort I demanded of my memory was too close to that of translating (which also calls upon the memory).

March 1

Extreme difficulty in getting back to work. Everything I have written of my recollections seems to me, when I think it over, deplorably *profane* and superficial. That vacillation, that pendulum movement to which my mind yields, despite all resolutions, would plunge me back into extreme license if only outside circumstances and my physical state permitted greater exaltation. It strikes me that I was foolish and guilty to bend my mind artificially so as to put it in a better position to understand Catholic teaching. That is where the real impiety lies. I see in it that *tendency toward veneration,* which was doubtless a fortunate attitude in my youth, but which is quite out of place today; in this I am now able to see only weakness, deplorable modesty, inept confidence in the superiority of others, doubt of myself, surrender of my own thought simply because it is mine, repudiation.

It is not a question of humility before God, but rather of that humility before men which has always been my secret malady. . . .

March 7

Passing through another desert region. Atrocious, idle days, devoted to nothing but growing older. Outside, icy wind, rain. War.

March 10

Yesterday, after a somewhat better day, during which I at least succeeded in working a little, a strange dizziness overcame me in the evening, just as I was about to go upstairs to bed—yet without nausea and, if I may say so, without discomfort, but so violent that I wondered whether I should be able to get out of the armchair in which I was seated.

This morning here I am quite unable to stand up on my legs; when I tried to, everything began whirling around me; I first thought I was going to fall on the floor, and barely had time to drop back on my bed—where I am writing this, more for the sake of filling up the time than out of a need to write. I am like a man who has been bled white.

Monday

Night haunted, devastated, ravaged by the almost palpable phantom of X., with whom I walk for two hours or in whose arms I roll on the very steps of hell. And this morning I get up with my head empty, my mind scattered, my nerves aching, offering a ready access to evil. Yet last night I did not yield completely to pleasure; but this morning, not even benefiting from that repulsion which follows pleasure, I wonder if that semblance of resistance may not have been worse. One is always very wrong to engage the devil in conversation; for, however he goes about it, he always insists upon having the last word.

March 23

Heavy fall of snow last night. Anguish at the thought of our soldiers without shelter as a result of that German retreat, which, the more one considers it, seems ever more . . . But I had promised myself to stop talking of the war here. This morning the sky is radiant. I leave Cuverville at four o'clock without knowing exactly where I am going—and leave this notebook here.

A most touching letter from Ghéon. But, despite a few rare, stray impulses, my soul remains inattentive and closed—too enamored of its sin to consent to follow the path that would take it away from it.

April 21

I plunge into the translation of *Antony and Cleopatra* with rapture. Made the last changes on the typescript of *Typhoon* (first part).

April 25

The pleasure of corrupting is one of those which we have least examined; this is similarly true of everything we are at first too busy stigmatizing.

May 3

All the brilliance of the sky does not clear away the shadow that hangs over these days. The upset of the recent offensive, disguised in vain by the press, weighs frightfully on the whole nation. . . .

I have come to believe less and less that the decision can be won by arms. Since the Russian Revolution it seems clear to me that this enormous war is itself going to be swallowed up by social questions. I no longer despair of seeing Germany as a republic.

"Well then, England too?"

"All the states of Europe as a republic; the war will not end otherwise. For neither will Germany triumph over us nor shall we triumph over her; and even if we do triumph, we shall be unable to keep ourselves from being even more stricken by our victory than she by her defeat. The question today is: How much longer shall men keep dying because we are unwilling to admit this?"

There enters into a nation's resistance a great deal of virtue, and certainly of the most admirable kind, but also obstinacy and even a little stupidity. It is beautiful to be willing to perish, and to prefer perishing in order not to surrender one's virtue. But it is absurd not to understand that one is dying. This is just why many souls are fleeing these days into mysticism, souls whom reason leaves defenseless, and who know no other means of escaping it.

19

I refrain from speaking of the single preoccupation of mind and flesh. . . .

Ghéon has taken on a resemblance to the good vicar of Cuverville. That resemblance strikes both Em. and me separately. The same intonations; the same absentminded and benevolent attention; the same provisional agreement followed by the same withdrawal; even the same indefinable absence.

That day we did not touch on any of the problems that have arisen between us.

But yesterday, on the other hand, for more than an hour, I applied to our friendship all the motions of artificial respiration, all the rhythmical tractions that are customarily practiced upon drowned people in an effort to bring them back to life. And at one and the same time I tried to convince him and to convince myself that we still thought the same, and yet to yield nothing that I should later have to retract.

After that conversation I see it a bit more clearly, it seems to me: that is, that the saints are always *against* the Church to begin with. But the only way to be against the Church is to be wrong; you must make up your mind to this in advance and give in to being conquered. The Church recognizes as holy only those who have surrendered. This goes without saying.

This is monstrous, like Germania, and organized in an equally impregnable way. All this out of precaution and a need to protect material interests. Catholicism condemns society, and at the same time comes to terms with it. . . .

I stop . . . *ab irato.*

I stiffen myself against grief, but it seems to me at times that Ghéon is more lost to me than if he were dead. He is neither changed nor absent; he is confiscated.

June 1 [from *Journal intime*]

It is hateful to me to have to hide from her. But what else can I do? . . . Her disapproval is unbearable to me; and I cannot ask her to approve what I feel nevertheless that I must do.

"I loathe indiscretion," she told me. And *I* loathe falsehood even more. It is to be able finally one day to speak out that I have restrained myself all life long.

August 6

. . . the Chanivaz camp closes five days earlier than I had been told, and I am jealously counting the hours that separate me from M. I should have left Paris three days earlier if I had known.

Overcast, gray sky; rain. It is almost cold.

From Geneva to Engelberg

Although he is too taciturn, I like traveling with Fabrice.* He says, and I believe him, that at forty-eight he feels infinitely younger than he was at twenty. He enjoys that rare faculty of starting off anew at each turning-point in his life, and of remaining faithful to himself by never resembling anything less than he does himself.

---

* During this first Swiss interlude with Marc Allégret, Gide sometimes refers to himself in the third person as "Fabrice," and to Marc as "Michel."

He confessed to me that upon meeting Michel at Chanivaz, he had first experienced a strange disappointment. He hardly recognized him any more. How could this be, after an absence of scarcely a month? The fear of seeing the adolescent grow up too quickly constantly tormented Fabrice, and precipitated his love. He loved nothing so much in Michel as the childlike qualities he still preserved in his tone of voice, his high spirits, his coaxing little ways—all of which he recaptured soon afterwards, flushed with joy, when the two of them stretched out beside each other on the edge of the lake. Michel, who lived most of the time with his collar wide open, had squeezed himself that day into some kind of stiff collar that had altered even his bearing; and this is why Fabrice did not recognize him at first. Furthermore, it must be confessed that Michel had already let himself be deeply marked by Switzerland. And Fabrice began to detest that raw and starched quality that Helvetia adds to every gesture and every thought. Were it not for this, one might have thought oneself at Oxford, or in Arcadia.

August 9

Michel was at the age when one is still ignorant of almost everything about oneself. His appetite was barely awakening, and had not yet measured itself against reality. His curiosity seemed turned only in the direction of barriers; that is the disadvantage of a puritan upbringing, as soon as it is applied to someone who cannot bear to be hemmed in.

Michel's soul offered Fabrice rapturous perspectives, which were still clouded, it seemed to him, by the morning mists. What was needed to dissipate them were the rays of a first love. It was of this, not of the love itself, that Fabrice felt he might be jealous. He would have liked himself to be enough for Michel; he tried to convince himself that he could be enough; he was miserable to think that he would not be.

August 21

On certain days that child took on a surprising beauty; he seemed clothed in grace and, as Signoret would have said, "with the pollen of the gods." A sort of blond glow emanated from his face and from all his skin. The skin of his neck, of his chest, of his face and hands, of his whole body, was equally warm and gilded. He was wearing that day, with his rough homespun shorts (very short, moreover, and wide open above the knees), only a silk shirt of a sharp, purplish red, billowing out over his leather belt and open at the neck, where he wore a chain of amber beads. He was barefoot and barelegged. A scout's cap held back his hair, which otherwise would have fallen tangled on his forehead, and, as if in defiance of his childlike appearance, he held in his teeth the brier pipe with an amber tip that Fabrice had just given him, although he had never yet smoked it. Nothing could describe the languor, the grace, the sensuality of his eyes. For long moments as he contemplated him, Fabrice lost all sense of the hour, of the place, of good and evil, of the proprieties, and of himself. He doubted whether any work of art had ever represented anything so beautiful. He doubted whether the mystical vocation of the man who used to accompany and precede him in his pleasures,* and his virtuous resolve, would have held firm before so flagrant an invitation, or whether, to adore such an idol, that other man would not have declared himself a pagan again.

September 20

What good is it for me to resume this journal if I dare not be sincere in it, and if I hide my heart's secret occupation?

September 21

How beautiful it is! The sky is pure. My mind soars and floats in the calm air. I think of death, and at the same time cannot convince myself that I have only a limited number of summers to live. Oh, how little my desires have diminished, and how hard it would be for me to reduce them! I cannot consent to put my happiness in the past. And why should I? Never have I felt younger and happier than I did last month—to such a point that I was unable to write anything about it. I could only have stammered.

23

The joyful state in which I lived more than a month doubtless strengthened me and gave me confidence again. I should have liked to plunge back into work immediately afterward. Since my return, I have barely been able to write anything but letters, letters, letters. With each day's mail I am mortgaged anew. English translation of *Prométhée* (to go over), Spanish translation of *La Porte étroite*. Rights for my translation of *Antony and Cleopatra* to be discussed; the project of a translation of Locke to be examined, as well as the new translators who are offering themselves for the Conrad.—This year will have seen appear my edition of *Les Fleurs du mal,* my reprintings of *L'Immoraliste* and *Les Nourritures.* Is the little success this represents worth all the bother it costs me?

* A reference, apparently, to Henri Ghéon.

I began again to suffer severely from my nerves all day today. This evening I made up my mind to read to Em. the pages of Memoirs written in Paris at the beginning of the summer. Rather satisfied with certain passages; but the word often calls too much attention to itself, and makes too apparent my desire to write well.

October 22

Returned to Cuverville yesterday.

I have lived all these recent weeks (and, altogether, since May 5) in a giddy dream of happiness; whence the long empty space in this notebook. It reflects only my clouds.

October 30

Never have I aspired less toward rest. Never have I felt more exalted by that excess of passions which Bossuet considers the attribute of youth, in his wonderful *Panégyrique de Saint Bernard,* which I was rereading this morning. Age cannot manage to drain sensual pleasure of its power of attraction, or the whole world of its charm. On the contrary, I was more easily disgusted at twenty, less satisfied with life. I embraced less boldly; I breathed less deeply; and I felt myself to be less loved. It may also be that I longed to be melancholy; I had not yet understood the superior beauty of happiness.

November 12

I contemplated at great length this morning a bumblebee's struggle with a snapdragon that did not want to give up its honey. The insect besieged the whole circumference of the corolla, stabbed it frequently, bit it, and then tore it with a rage at first impotent, then eventually triumphant. . . .

For more than a week I have been waiting for a letter from M., with the most agonizing impatience.

November 18

. . . Em. went this morning to Cuverville to attend the funeral service for Georges's deputy mayor, old Crochemore. As people were getting ready to leave the church, an old woman began to shout in a high-pitched voice: "Look! There's God! There's God!"

Em., who is afraid of crazy people, ran out terrified, while her neighbor reassured her: "Don' be afraid, Mam Gille! She's taken like that every time."

And for some time we amuse ourselves by imagining the panic caused by the arrival of God in the church.

November 23

In the train—*going to Paris.*

What to do? I can kill myself more easily than stop my life—I mean: than limit it, reduce it. . . .

I shall die by bursting, as Mme Théo used to say.

Cuverville, November 30

The day before leaving, the 22nd, I had finished my translation of *Cleopatra*—of which I gave a reading to Ida Rubinstein at Bakst's.

Immense delirium of happiness.

My joy has something untamed, wild, incompatible with all decency, all propriety, all law. Through it I return to the stammering of childhood, for it offers my mind nothing but novelty. I need to invent everything, words and gestures; nothing of the past satisfies my love any longer. Everything in me blossoms forth; is amazed; my heart beats wildly; an overabundance of life rises to my throat like a sob. I no longer know anything; it is a vehemence without memories and without wrinkles. . . .

Cuverville, December 8

Yesterday evening back from Paris, for which I had left on the 1st. I was filled with a vast, singing joy the whole time; nevertheless, the day before yesterday, and for the first time in my life, I knew the torment of jealousy. In vain I tried to defend myself against it. M. did not come in till ten p.m. I knew he was at C.'s.* I was in absolute misery. I felt capable of the maddest things, and from my anguish I measured the depth of my love.

December 13

I am slowly putting together that preface for the letters of Dupouey. Good practice of **Granados**.

* M., of course, is Marc. C. is probably Jean Cocteau.

We are reading aloud *Under Western Eyes,* in which we admire such prophetic reflections about the Russian soul.

Why should I note all this? . . . But what else could I note down in this book, if I forbid myself to speak of political events or of the war—and at the same time of the one thing that nourishes my ardor?

December 15

Ride to Criquetot. The sky was overcast, very dark, heavy with showers; a great sea wind swept the clouds. The thought of M. keeps me in a constant state of lyricism I had not known since my *Nourritures.* I no longer feel my age, or the horror of our time, or the season, unless to draw from it a new source of exaltation; were I a soldier, with such a heart, I should go to my death joyfully.

December 18

. . . It is true that for some time, and well before the war, I was obsessed by the abominable idea that our country was dying. Everything revealed to me her exhaustion, her decadence; I saw them everywhere; it seemed to me that one would have to be blind not to see them. If something can save us, I thought, it would have to be a tremendous crisis, such as our history has already witnessed, a great danger, war. . . . And at the beginning of this war, I let myself be invaded almost joyously with hope. Our France seemed to catch hold of herself once again. We would have all given our blood to save her. Then this war made us feel at close hand all our insufficiencies, all our disorders, paid for by a tremendous outpouring of virtues. . . .

Today we accuse the war; but the sickness came from long before.

1918   *Monday, [January] 14*

I wanted to harness myself to the Memoirs again, but I have no further taste for them; the few passages that I read aloud in the presence of Mathilde Roberty disappointed me; and the comparison I made between them and the pages of Proust's marvelous book, which I was rereading at the same time, finished the job: I was crushed.

For the last four days I have been plunged into that story of *L'Aveugle**
which has been inhabiting me for so many years, and which I was giving
up hope of writing. I am forcing myself to write it without a rough draft,
and have already written some twenty pages straight off. I should like not
to reread and polish it until I work on the typed copy.

March 1

I read to Em. last night the first forty-five pages of *L'Aveugle*. Oh, how I
should like to be done with it! . . .

March 3

Lucien Maury, with whom I had lunch the other day in Paris, is greatly
worried about the wave of socialism he feels rising, which he foresees as
submerging our old world after we think the war is over. He believes
revolution inevitable and sees no way one can oppose it. When I speak to
him of the resistance organization that *L'Action Française* is working to
form, he becomes indignant. Maurras exasperates him and Léon Daudet
makes his blood boil.

"I can understand," I told him, "that they should not satisfy you. But
you will be forced to join up with them if you are anxious to resist. There
will be no third choice. It will be like the Dreyfus affair: you will have to
be *for* or *against,* willy-nilly. You don't like the *Action Française* group?
It isn't that I consider it the best, either—*but it is the only one."*

After a good (or at least somewhat better) night, today I feel quite refreshed. I write this so as to be able to read it in my hours of distress and
anguish: never have I felt as if I had a more active, more lucid mind, a
more supple body, a warmer heart. Never have I felt happier. Never has
the air filled my breast more voluptuously. Never has the suffering or the
joy of a friend—what am I saying? of the first person who comes across
my path—found greater responsiveness in me—nor the nation's anxiety a
greater echo. Never have I felt greater strength in me, nor more desire to
embrace, nor more breath to inspire.

March 4

Insomnia again; anguish, exasperation, and finally surrender . . . not so
much through excess of desire as to be done with it and be able to go back

* *The Blind Girl*: to become *La Symphonie pastorale.*

to sleep. . . . But sleep cares nothing for that paltry satisfaction, without the least subsequent relaxation. I awake feeling dulled and stupid (for nonetheless, toward morning, I had finally gone to sleep). Oh! I cry for that health, that happy equilibrium, which I enjoy in M.'s presence, and which makes even chastity easy for me when I am with him, and my flesh is smilingly at ease.

March 8

Recalled to Paris again. . . .

Em. can never know how my heart is torn at the thought of leaving her, and in order to find happiness far from her.

April 28

Period of dissolution; haunted by the memory and the need of M. Need of the beyond, of driving my demon to the very end and exhausting my desire. I ought to be annihilated and on the contrary, this evening, my mind is clear, fresh, fit—to such a point that I go up after dinner (a thing I haven't done for a long time) in order to get back to work.

May 14

If I could be sure of living twenty-five years more, it seems to me that then I should have enough; but that I shall not be satisfied with less.

June 1

I sometimes think, with horror, that the victory all our hearts wish France to have is that of the past over the future.

In Paris I read (in part) Douglas's abominable book, *Oscar Wilde and Myself.* Hypocrisy can go no further, nor falsehood be more impudent. It is a monstrous travesty of the truth which filled me with disgust. Merely from the tone of his writing it seems to me that I should be aware he is lying, even if I had not been a direct witness of the acts of his life against which he is protesting, and which he is attempting to whitewash. But even that is not enough for him. He claims that he was ignorant of Wilde's habits! and that he upheld him at first only because he thought him innocent! Whom will he convince? I do not know; but I hope not to die before having unmasked him. This book is a vile sham.

June 2

The Germans are at Château-Thierry. Days of waiting, of unbearable anxiety. The fine weather has not ceased to favor them, nor the wind to blow against us. At times it seems as if there were something impious and desperate in our resistance, and this above all breaks my heart. Oh, I am not speaking mystically! I mean that that *Liberty* we claim to represent and defend is most often nothing but the right to have our own way, to please ourselves, and would be better named insubordination. All around us I see nothing but disorder, disorganization, negligence, and waste of the most radiant virtues—nothing but falsehood, politics, absurdity. Nothing is put in its place, nothing is properly employed, and the rarest elements, those most worthy of triumphing become suspect, harmful, and ruinous through misuse.

June 8

Busy these last few days perfecting *Corydon*. Most likely I shall still have many slight changes to make in the proofs and numerous additions to the appendix—but as it is, I could hand it over to the printer. I should have liked to have thirteen copies printed—not one more—and should have taken care of this at once if Gouchtenaere (Méral) were still in Paris and if his printer had not been upset by the bombardment.

I should likewise like to bring out before the end of this year:
A new edition of *Les Nourritures;*
The big edition of *Typhoon;*
The letters of Dupouey;
A third volume of *Prétextes;*
And an edition of three hundred copies of *Le Prométhée.*

Perhaps also my translation of *Antony and Cleopatra.* And finally I hope very much to have finished my *Symphonie pastorale.*

June 18

I am leaving France in a state of inexpressible anguish. It seems to me that I am saying farewell to my whole past. . . .

Cambridge, September 2

I have been living at Merton House for a fortnight. Never in my life have I been better housed, except of course at Cuverville and at the Villa. Norton, who is offering me this hospitality, is not here.

Cuverville, October 10

Back in harbor for several days now. I don't know whether or not I shall recover the constancy to keep this journal unbroken—as I did before my trip to England? . . .

October 16

Today I have the greatest difficulty getting interested again in the state of mind of my pastor, and I fear that the end of the book may suffer from this. In an effort to give life to his thoughts again, I have gone back to the Gospel and Pascal. I long to recapture a state of fervor, but at the same time I do not want to let myself be taken in by it; I pull on the reins and wield the whip at the same time; and this produces nothing worthwhile.

Reopened the piano and played some fugues from the *Well-Tempered Clavichord* with the greatest contentment.

I have not read M. V. de Pallarès's book against Nietzsche; but, in *La Coopération des idées,* on the subject of this book, a few pages by M. G. Deherme, who approves of it while wondering, to begin with, whether Nietzsche is important enough to make it worth the trouble of speaking of him:

". . . Impulsive, unstable, obsessed, neurasthenic, a drug-addict, he was a weak man and an abulic type. This is why he speaks exclusively of what he most lacks: strength and will."

This is the accusation that was hurled at the Crucified One: "If thou art the Christ, save thyself!" I recognize it. I am not trying to compare Christ with Nietzsche—even though M. Binet-Sanglé showed us some time ago that the Nazarene too was simply a sick man and a madman!—I am merely comparing that absurd accusation which is thrown up against them and which proceeds from an identical miscomprehension. It is customary in our epoch to seek a physiological cause for an intellectual impulse; and I am not saying that this is wrong; what I am saying is that it is wrong to try to invalidate thereby the intrinsic value of the thought.

It is *natural* that any great moral reform, what Nietzsche would call any transmutation of values, should be the result of a physiological *lack of balance.* In a state of well-being, thought is at rest, and as long as the order of things satisfies it, thought cannot propose changing it. . . . At the origin of a reform there is always a *malaise,* a discomfort; the discomfort from which the reformer suffers is that of an inner lack of balance. . . . I am not saying, of course, that it is enough to be unbalanced to become a reformer—but rather that every reformer is, to begin with, unbalanced.

I do not know that there can be found a single one, among those who have offered humanity new systems of value, in whom these Messrs. Binet-Sanglé cannot discover, and quite rightly, what they would perhaps call a defect—what I should like to call simply a provocation. Socrates, Mahomet, Saint Paul, Rousseau, Dostoevsky, Luther—M. Binet-Sanglé has only to enumerate them, to suggest still others; there is not one of them that I should not recognize as abnormal.

And, naturally it is possible *afterwards* to think as these men did without being unbalanced oneself; but in the beginning it was an unbalanced state that brought these thoughts to our aid, thoughts which the reformer needed in order to re-establish the broken equilibrium in himself. In fact one man had first to be sick, in order to make possible the health of many later on. Rousseau without his madness would have been nothing but an indigestible Cicero; and it is precisely in Nietzsche's madness that I see the certificate of his authentic greatness.

You would like to know what to believe in regard to my political opinions. It seemed to you that too often I took one step forward (to the right or the left) only to take two backward immediately after, so that nothing was less trustworthy than any declarations I might have made. This is exactly why I did not make any, knowing full well the indecision of my mind, but nevertheless believing that indecision preferable to inconstancy.

To tell the truth, political questions do not much interest me; I have trouble convincing myself that any one regime is preferable in itself; and if I get to the point of wishing France a king, even if he were a despot, it is because everything proves to me, unfortunately, that of all the people I know, the Frenchman is the one who has the least natural feeling for the public good, the least sense of that common solidarity without which a republic only turns to the greatest injury to all.

Yes, political questions interest me less, and I believe them less important, than social questions; and social questions less important than moral questions. For after all I hold it a fact that the "bad organization," of which people are constantly complaining here, can be most often imputed to the negligence or lack of conscience of the employees, from the most modest to the highest, in the exercise of their functions. It is not so much the system as man himself that must be reformed, and Paul Valéry seems to me on the right track when he protested, the other day, that the most important of the ministries is that of Education.

I am well aware that if the very stuff of the mind is bad, nothing good can be embroidered on it; but it has not in fact been proved that the stuff is bad. It seems to me that here, as so often in France, it is not so much the scarcity that is to be deplored as the bad utilization of what we have.

I consider liberty as a fearful and disastrous thing that one must try to reduce or suppress in oneself first—and even, if one can, in others. The horrible thing is a slavery imposed without consent; the excellent thing is *self*-imposed slavery; and for lack of something better: the slavery to which one submits. . . .

I like to serve; I do not at all like to be a slave; slave to my past, slave to my future plans, slave to my faith, to my doubt, to my hatred, or to my love.

You meditate for months; in you an idea becomes flesh; it palpitates, it lives, you caress it; you adopt it intimately; you know its contours, its limits, its deficiencies, its reliefs, its recesses; at once its genealogy and its descendants (?). As soon as you present in public some exposé of this prolonged meditation, immediately a critic rises up to declare peremptorily that you know nothing about it; and he does so in the name of common sense, that is to say of the most general opinion, that is to say the most conventional—which it was the entire point of our effort to get away from.

Had Socrates and Plato not loved young men, what a pity for Greece, what a pity for the whole world!

Had Socrates and Plato not loved young men and aimed to please them, each one of us would be a little less sensible.

*   *   *

I call a *pederast* the man who, as the word indicates, falls in love with young boys. I call a *sodomite* ("The word is *sodomite*, monsieur," Verlaine said to the judge who asked him if it were true that he was a *sodom-ist*) the man whose desire is addressed to mature men.

I call an *invert* the man who, in the comedy of love, assumes the role of a woman and desires to be possessed. . . .

The pederasts, of whom I am one (why cannot I say this quite simply, without your immediately claiming to see a brag in my confession?), are much rarer, and the sodomites much more numerous, than I first thought . . . As to the inverts, whom I have hardly frequented at all, it has always seemed to me that they alone deserved the reproach of moral or intellectual deformation, and merited some of the accusations that are commonly addressed to all homosexuals.

It is the same as with religion. The kindest thing those who have it can do for those who don't is to pity them.

"But we are not to be pitied. We are not unhappy."

"All the more unhappy since you don't know that you are. We shall cease to pity you, then. We shall detest you."

We are accepted if we are plaintive; but if we cease to be pitiable we are at once accused of arrogance. No, not at all, I assure you. We are merely what we are; we simply admit what we are, without priding ourselves on it, but without grieving about it either.

That such loves can be born, that such relationships can be formed, it is not enough for me to say that this is natural; I maintain that it is good; each of the two finds exaltation, protection, a challenge; and I wonder whether it is the younger or the elder man that they benefit more.

*   *   *

There is no more fatal error today, either for nations or for individuals, than to believe that they can get along without one another. Everything that sets the interests of France and Germany in opposition to one another is injurious to both countries at once; beneficial, everything that tends to bring those interests closer together.

It is properly the dispute between the colossal and the individual, it has been said. Everything French tends to individualize itself; everything German, to dominate or to submit.

[*from* JOURNAL INTIME] *

November 21, 1918

Madeleine has destroyed all my letters. She has just confessed this to me, and I am crushed. She did it, she told me, just after I left for England. Oh, I know very well that she suffered atrociously from my going away with Marc; but did she have to take revenge on the past? . . . It is the best of me that disappears; and it will no longer counterbalance the worst. For more than thirty years I had given her (and I still gave her) the best of me, day after day, from the very moment I was away for even the shortest time. I feel suddenly ruined. I no longer have heart for anything. I could have killed myself effortlessly.

If this loss were even due to some accident, invasion, fire . . . But that *she* should have done that! . . .

                                                                                22

Did she realize that, in doing this, she was suppressing the only ark in which my memory could hope to find refuge later on? All the best of me I had entrusted to those letters—my heart, my joy, the changes of my mood, the way I spent my days. . . . I am suffering as if she had killed our child.

Oh, I will not endure anyone's accusing her. That is the sharpest stab of all. All night long I felt it piercing deep into my heart.

                                                                                24

Took aspirin to try to sleep. But the pain wakes me in the middle of the night and then I feel as if I am going mad.

"They were the most precious thing I owned in the world," she told me.

"After you left, when I found myself all alone again in the big house that you were abandoning, without a single person on whom I could lean, no longer knowing what to do, what would become of me . . . At first I thought there was nothing left for me but to die. Yes, truly, I thought that my heart had stopped beating, that I was dying. I had suffered so much. . . . I burned your letters in order to have something to do. Before I destroyed them I read them all over, one by one. . . ."

* In the edition I brought out, my *Journal* stops at the end of October 1918, not to resume until May 1919; again it stops almost at once for a new silence of almost a year. It is there that the following pages, which explain that long silence, should be inserted [A. G.].

Then it was that she added: "They were the most precious thing I owned in the world."

If the sacrifice had to be repeated, she would do it again, I am convinced. Even independently of any grievance, modesty alone drove her to it. She could not endure attracting attention or glances, and was constantly keeping in the background. She would like her name never to be uttered anywhere, except by a few friends' mouths and by those of the poor peasants she looks after and who call her "Madame Gille"; and above all she would like to erase every trace of her presence from my writings. . . .*

I have always respected her modesty, to such a degree that I very rarely had occasion to speak of her in my notebooks and that, even now, I stop. Never again will anyone now know what she was for me, what I was for her.

They were not exactly love-letters; effusiveness disgusts me, and she would never have endured being praised, so that I most often kept hidden from her the emotion with which my heart was overflowing. But in them the pattern of my life was woven before her eyes, little by little and day by day.†

---

* . . . I tell myself today that, out of love, she would most willingly and joyfully have agreed to appear at my side and to be associated with my fate (let us say: with my fame) in the minds of men, if the notoriety she saw me acquire had not seemed to her of such a sinister nature. In the lines I then wrote, I left out what now seems to me the most important: with all her heart and all her soul she disapproved of my conduct and the direction of my thoughts. That above all is what urged her to withdraw from my life. She suffered unspeakably at the thought of having to figure and assume a role, even a secondary one or that of a victim (and she still loved me too much not to suffer doubly in that case), in a drama that she found utterly reprehensible, in which she would have wished not to be involved at all, and especially not as an accuser—I return to what I wrote then, and, for my shame, give it without changing anything. (Luxor, February '39) [A. G.]

† . . . the despair in which I thought I was drowning came especially, no doubt, from the feeling of failure; I compared myself to Oedipus when he suddenly discovers the lie on which his happiness is built; I suddenly became conscious of the distress in which my personal happiness kept the one whom, in spite of all, I loved more than myself; but also, more surreptitiously, I suffered at knowing that she had reduced to nothing that part of me that seemed most of all to merit preservation. That correspondence, kept up since our childhood, probably belonged to both of us at once; it seemed to me born of her as well as of me; it was the fruit of my love for her . . . and for a week straight I wept without stopping, unable to exhaust the bitterness of *our* loss.

It took place at Cuverville; it was a day like all the other days. I had needed to look up a date for the Memoirs I was then writing, and hoped to find a reference in my correspondence with her. I had asked her for the key to the secretary in her room, where my letters were put away. (She never refused me that key, ordinarily; but I had not yet asked her for it since my return from England.) Suddenly I saw her become very pale. In an effort that made her lips tremble, she told me that the drawer was now empty, and that my letters had ceased to exist. . . .

For a full week I wept; I wept from morning to evening, seated beside the fireplace in the living-room where our common life was concentrated, and even more at night, after

After the conversations I have just had with her, these last three days, conversations broken by dreadful silences and sobs, but serious and without a word of accusation or reproach on either side, it seemed to me that never again could I try to live, or that I could live at best only a life of repentance and contrition. I felt finished, ruined, undone. One of her tears weighs more, I told myself, than the ocean of my happiness. Or at least— for what is the good of exaggerating?—I no longer saw that I had any right to buy my happiness at the expense of hers.

But why am I speaking of happiness? It is my life, my very existence that wounds her—what I can suppress but not change. And it is not only the sunlight but the very air that is refused me.

December 19

. . . Whatever might make *my* heart beat again could be for her only a cause of suffering and horror. I can assert nothing of myself without wounding her, and it is only by suppressing myself that I could ensure her happiness.

[*from* THE JOURNAL]

1919   *July 26. On arriving at Dudelange*

Not a day passes but what I say to myself: All the same, old man, take care, for tomorrow you might wake up mad, idiotic, or not wake up at all. That marvel which you call your body, that even more astonishing

---

having retired to my room, where I continued to hope that one evening she would come to me; I wept unceasingly, without trying to communicate anything to her but my tears, and always expecting a word, a gesture from her . . . but she continued to be busy with her trifling household duties, as if nothing had happened, frequently passing near me, indifferent, and seeming not to see me. Vainly I hoped that the persistence of my grief would overcome that apparent insensitivity, but it did not; and probably she hoped that the despair into which she saw me sinking would bring me back to God; for she would admit of no other outcome. That, I believe, is what made her refuse me even the consolation of her pity, of her affection. But for her, it was as if the tears I poured out had never happened, so long as they remained profane; what she expected from me, I suppose, was a cry of repentance and devotion. And the more I wept, the more we became strangers to each other; I felt this bitterly; and soon it was no longer for the destruction of my letters I was weeping, but for us, for her, for our love. I felt that I had lost her. Everything I had in me was collapsing, the past, the present, our future.

In the years to come, I never again really regained my zest for life; or at least not until much later, when I realized that I had recovered her esteem; but even then, I never really got back into the dance, living only with that indefinable feeling of moving about among appearances—among those appearances one calls reality. (Luxor, February '39) [A. G.]

marvel, your mind—just think what a little accident would suffice to put their machine out of order! Already I am full of admiration when, without holding onto the bannister, you go down the stairs; you might stumble, bash your head in, and that would be the end. . . . The idea of death follows my thought as the shadow follows my body; and the greater the joy, the light, the blacker the shadow.

Cuverville, October 8 [from *Journal intime*]

(Anniversary of my marriage.) I do not know which is more painful: not to be loved any longer, or to see the person you love, and who still loves you, cease to believe in your love. I cannot bring myself to love her any less, and I remain close to her, my heart bleeding, but without speaking. Ah, shall I ever again be able to talk with her? . . . What is the good of protesting that I love her more than anything in the world? She would not believe me. Alas, I can do nothing today but make her suffer more.

November 21

Worked tolerably all these recent days; but an abominable sorrow submerges me: I have caused the unhappiness of the one I love most in the world. And she no longer believes in my love.

January 1914

My dear Proust,
I have been living with your book now for several days. I have reveled in
it, saturated myself in it, with the greatest delight. Why must it be so
painful for me to love it so much? . . .

The rejection of this book will always remain the most serious mistake of the *N.R.F.*—and (since it is my shame to have been in great part
responsible for it) one of the great regrets, one of the most bitter remorses
of my life. I can only see this act as the doing of some implacable fate,
because it is certainly not a sufficient explanation of my mistake to say that
I had created a certain image of you in my mind out of our few chance
meetings in "Society," meetings which went back almost twenty years. For
me, you were still just that young man who frequented Madame X's and
Madame Z's, who wrote for the *Figaro.* I thought you—shall I confess
it?—*"du côté de chez Verdurin,"* one of the Verdurin sort; a snob, a society amateur—the most regrettable of all possible things for our magazine.
And your gesture, which I can understand so well today, your offer to
underwrite the publication of your book—and which I would have found
charming *then* if I had tried to understand it properly—this gesture, unfortunately, only served to confirm my original error. I only troubled myself so far as to open one of the notebooks of your manuscripts; I opened it
at random, and, as ill luck would have it, my attention soon plunged into
the cup of camomile tea on page 62—then tripped, at page 64, on the
phrase (the only one in the book that I still do not completely understand,
for I am not waiting for you to write before I finish the reading)—where
you speak of the "visible vertebra of a forehead."

And now, it is not enough for me to *like* the book; I feel myself
falling in *love* with it—and with you, developing for both a kind of affection, of admiration, a singular predilection.

I cannot go on . . . I am too full of regret, too full of pain—and
above all when I think that some word of my absurd refusal may have
reached you—that it may have wounded you—and that now I deserve to

be judged by you unjustly, as I have judged you. I do not excuse myself—it is only to alleviate my own pain a little that I am confessing thus to you this morning—begging you to be more indulgent with me than I can be myself.

My dear Proust,

I write you again, having just heard that there is no contract binding you exclusively to Grasset, nothing forcing you to give him the two remaining volumes of *A la recherche du temps perdu.* —Could it indeed be possible?

The *N.R.F.* is prepared to assume all the costs of publication, and to perform the impossible in order to secure the first volume to join its successors in our collection as soon as the present edition is exhausted. This is what the directors of the *N.R.F.* decided at their meeting yesterday (I came back from Florence to attend), unanimously and enthusiastically: I have been asked to inform you—and it is in the name of eight fervent admirers of your work that I write. Is it too late? . . . ah, in that case, let a single quick word of yours cut short my hopes.

> Your devoted
> A.G.

from

LES CAVES

DU VATICAN

(Lafcadio's Adventures)

1914

EDITOR'S NOTE

This novel has been published in English under three different titles—
The Vatican Cellars, The Vatican Swindle, and *Lafcadio's Adventures.*
The first two titles refer to that portion of the story *not* related in the
episodes that follow: a comically elaborate intrigue concerning false
popes, false miracles, and a giant hoax (modeled after a real hoax of
1892) designed to extract money from pious and reactionary Catholics.
The third title, that given to the current American edition, refers to the
almost entirely autonomous story of Lafcadio Wluiki ("pronounced
Luki; the 'W' and the first 'i' are virtually silent") told in the intervening
chapters. It is his story that the extracts here comprise. (Gide once performed a similar piece of surgery on this novel, reprinting the Lafcadio
chapters separately for an edition entitled *Episodes des Caves du Vatican,
choisis par l'auteur.**)

The two plots do converge from time to time; in fact, the fantastic
intricacy of the web of interconnection in this novel, its everlasting chain
of "coincidental" connections is one of its major sources of imaginative
energy. Although Lafcadio himself is not involved in the Vatican plot,
his victim Fleurissoire is one of its principal dupes, and his tormentor
Protos (a mysterious master-crook, once a classmate of Lafcadio's) a
prime mover of the great swindle. Lafcadio is the bastard son of the
Count Juste-Agénor de Baraglioul—one of many aristocratic "uncles"
his erring mother provided him with—and the count's deathbed
largesse has permitted Lafcadio to make a fresh start in life. The count's
legitimate son, the writer Julius de Baraglioul, was disconcerted by this
appearance of an unexpected half-brother, but he has taken Lafcadio into
his employ as a kind of secretary. The latter is dumbfounded to find
references to his noble half-brother in the pockets of his anonymous and
undistinguished victim; but in fact Amédée Fleurissoire and Julius de
Baraglioul had married two pious sisters, and through this connection
both of their families are implicated in the tangled "popish plot." Carola

* [Stock, Paris, 1924.]

is a former mistress of Lafcadio's (and of Protos's); he had left her the cuff-links referred to here as a parting gift.

BOOK V: LAFCADIO

> *"There is only one remedy! One thing*
> *alone can cure us from being our-*
> *selves! . . ." "Yes; strictly speaking,*
> *the question is not how to get cured,*
> *but how to live."*
>
> —JOSEPH CONRAD
> *Lord Jim*

I

After Lafcadio, with the assistance of the attorney and through the intervention of Julius, had come into the forty thousand francs a year left him by the late Count Juste-Agénor de Baraglioul, his chief concern was to let no signs of it appear.

"Off gold plate perhaps," he had said to himself at the time, "but you'll be eating the same meals."

What he had not considered—or perhaps had not yet learned—was that from then on his meals were going to have a different taste. Or rather, since he had discovered as much pleasure in struggling against his appetites as in indulging them, his resistance—now that he was no longer pressed by need—began to relax. To speak plainly, thanks to a naturally aristocratic disposition he had never allowed necessity to force him into committing a single one of those actions which he might very well commit now out of malice, out of sport, or simply for the fun of putting his pleasure before his interest.

In obedience to the count's wishes he had not gone into mourning. A mortifying disappointment awaited him when he went to replenish his wardrobe in the shops which had been patronized by his last uncle, the Marquis de Gesvres. On his mentioning that gentleman's name as a recommendation, the tailor pulled out a number of bills which the marquis had neglected to pay. Lafcadio had a fastidious dislike of swindling; he at once pretended that he had come precisely to settle the account, and paid ready money for his new clothes. The same misadventure awaited him at the bootmaker's. When it came to the shirtmaker, Lafcadio thought it more prudent to choose another.

"Oh, Uncle de Gesvres, if only I knew your address! It would be a pleasure to send him his receipted bills," thought Lafcadio. "He would only despise me for it. But I'm a Baraglioul and, from this day forward, you rascal of a marquis, I dismiss you from my heart."

There was nothing to keep him in Paris—or elsewhere; crossing Italy by short stages, he was making his way to Brindisi, where he meant to embark on some liner bound for Java.

Sitting all alone in a compartment of the train which was carrying him away from Rome, he was contemplating with some satisfaction his hands in their gray doeskin gloves, as they lay on the rich fawn-colored plaid, which, in spite of the heat, he had spread negligently over his knees. Through the soft woolen material of his traveling-suit he breathed ease and comfort at every pore; his neck was unconfined in a collar which, without being low, was only lightly starched, and from beneath which the narrow line of a bronze silk necktie ran, slender as a grass snake, over his pleated shirt. He was at ease in his skin, at ease in his clothes, at ease in his shoes—soft moccasins cut out of the same suede as his gloves; his foot in its elastic prison could stretch, could bend, could feel itself alive. His beaver hat was pulled down over his eyes and kept out the landscape; he was smoking a little pipeful of dried juniper and letting his thoughts wander at their will. He thought:

"The old woman with the little white cloud above her head, who pointed to it and said to me: 'Rain! Ha—it won't rain today!' . . . that old woman whose sack I carried on my shoulders" (for a whim, he had traveled on foot for four days across the Apennines between Bologna and Florence and had slept a night at Covigliajo), "and whom I kissed when we got to the top of the hill . . . that was one of those things the curé of Covigliajo would have called 'good deeds.' I could just as easily have strangled her, with a steady hand—when I felt her dirty wrinkled skin beneath my finger. . . . Ah! how caressingly she stroked my coat collar to brush off the dust, and said *'Figlio mio! carino!'* . . . Afterwards, still sweating, I lay down on the moss in the shade of a big chestnut tree, not smoking though—whatever could it have been that made me feel so happy? I felt as though I could have embraced the whole of mankind—or strangled it, for that matter. Human life! What a trivial thing! And I'd risk mine in a minute if only some attractive occasion would turn up— some handsome feat to be done, just a bit daring and rash . . . All the same, I can't turn pilot or mountain climber. . . . I wonder what that old stuffed-shirt Julius would advise. . . . It's a pity he's such an oaf! I should have liked to have a brother.

"Poor Julius! So many people writing, so few people reading! It's a fact. People read less and less nowadays . . . to judge by myself, as they say. It'll end by some catastrophe—some stupendous catastrophe, reeking with horror. Printing will be chucked overboard altogether; and it'll be a miracle if the best doesn't sink to the bottom with the worst.

"But the curious thing would be to know what the old woman would have said if I had begun to squeeze. One imagines *what would happen if,* but there's always a little gap through which the unexpected can creep in. Nothing ever happens exactly as one thinks it's going to. . . . That's what makes me want to act. . . . One does so little! . . . 'Let all that can be, be!', that's the way I explain the Creation. . . . In love with what might be. If I were the State, I should have myself locked up.

"Nothing very spellbinding about M. Gaspard Flamand's letters, which I claimed as mine at General Delivery in Bologna. Nothing that would have been worth the trouble of returning to him.

"Heavens! how few people one meets whose traveling-case one would care to ransack! . . . And yet how few there are from whom one wouldn't get some queer reaction if one knew the right word—the right gesture! . . . A fine lot of puppets; but, my word, their strings are so obvious. One meets no one in the streets nowadays but asses and dolts. Is it possible for a decent person—I ask you, Lafcadio—to take this farce seriously? No, no! Let's get off while there's still time! Off to a new world! Print your foot upon Europe's soil and take a flying leap. If in Borneo, in the depths of the forests, there still remains some belated anthropopithex, then let's go there and reckon the chances of a future race of men. . . .

"I should have liked to see Protos again. No doubt he's set sail for America. He used to insist that the barbarians of Chicago were the only people he esteemed. . . . Not voluptuous enough for my taste—a pack of wolves! I'm feline by nature. . . . Well, enough of that!

"The curé of Covigliajo, so meek and smiling, didn't look in the least inclined to deprave the little boy he was talking to. He was certainly in his charge. I should have liked to make friends with him—not with the priest, good heavens no!—with the little boy. . . . What beautiful eyes he lifted to mine! He was as anxious about meeting my glance as I was his—but I looked away at once. He was no more than five years younger than I. Yes, fourteen or sixteen, no more than that . . . What was I like at that age? A greedy little *stripling,* whom I should like to meet now; I think I should be quite pleased with myself, actually. . . . Faby was quite abashed at first to feel that he had fallen in love with me; it was a good thing he confessed it to my mother; he felt more light-hearted after that. But how annoyed I was by his self-restraint! Later on, in the Aurès, when I told him about it under the tent, we had a good laugh together. . . . I should like to see him today; too bad he's dead. Enough of that! *

"The truth is, I hoped the curé would dislike me. I kept trying to think of disagreeable things to say to him, but I came up with nothing that wasn't charming. . . . What an effort I find it not to seem fascinating. Yet I really can't stain my face with walnut juice, as Carola recommended, or start eating garlic. . . . Ah! don't let me think of that poor creature any more. It's to her I owe the most mediocre of my pleasures. . . . Oh my God! What on earth can that strange old man have come out of?"

The sliding door into the corridor had just let in Amédée Fleurissoire.

Fleurissoire had traveled in an empty compartment as far as Frosinone. At that station, a middle-aged Italian had got into his carriage and had begun to glower at him so darkly that Fleurissoire had made haste to take himself off.

In the next compartment, Lafcadio's youthful grace, on the contrary, attracted him.

"Dear me! What a charming boy!" thought he; "hardly more than a child! On his vacation, no doubt. How beautifully dressed he is! His eyes look so candid! Oh, what a relief it will be to drop my suspicions! If only he knew French, I should so like to talk to him."

He sat down opposite to him in the corner next to the door. Lafcadio turned up the brim of his hat and began to consider him with a lifeless and apparently indifferent eye.

"What is there in common between me and that squalid little ape?" he reflected. "He seems to think himself quite the rogue. What is he smiling at me like that for? Does he imagine I'm going to embrace him? Is it possible that there exist women who fondle old men? . . . No doubt he'd be quite surprised to know that I can read writing or print with perfect fluency, upside down, in reverse, in a mirror, on a blotter—a matter of three months' training and two years' practice, all for the love of art. Cadio, my dear boy, the problem is this: to leave a mark on that fellow's fate. But how? . . . Oh! I'll offer him a cachou. Whether he accepts or not, I shall at any rate hear in what language."

"Grazio! Grazio!" said Fleurissoire as he refused.

"Nothing doing with the old goat. Let's go to sleep," Lafcadio went on

* This was the paragraph that aroused Claudel's suspicions and objections; see his letter of March 2, 1914, p. 527.

to himself, and pulling the brim of his hat down over his eyes, he tried to spin a dream out of one of the memories of his childhood. . . .

Lafcadio, though his eyes were shut, was not asleep; he could not sleep.

"The old boy over there believes I am asleep," he thought; "if I were to open my eyes halfway, I should see him looking at me. Protos used to insist that it was particularly difficult to pretend to be asleep while one was really watching; he claimed that he could always spot pretended sleep by just that slight quiver of the eyelids . . . I'm repressing it now. Protos himself would be taken in. . . ."

The sun meanwhile had set, and Fleurissoire, in a sentimental mood, was gazing at the last gleams of its splendor as they gradually faded from the sky. Suddenly, in the curved ceiling of the carriage, the electric light leaped on with a vividness that contrasted much too brutally with the soft twilight. Fleurissoire was afraid, too, that it might disturb his neighbor's slumbers, and turned the switch; the result was not total darkness, but merely a shifting of the current from the center lamp to a dark blue night-light. To Fleurissoire's taste, this was still too bright; he turned the switch again; the night-light went out, but two side brackets were immediately turned on, whose glare was even more disagreeable than the center light's; another turn, and the night-light came on again; he gave up.

"Will he never have done fiddling with the light?" Lafcadio thought impatiently. "What's he up to now? (No! I will *not* raise my eyelids.) He is standing up. Could he be attracted by my valise? Bravo! He has noticed that it isn't locked. It was a bright idea of mine to have a complicated lock fitted to it at Milan and then lose the key straightaway, so that I had to have it picked at Bologna! A padlock, at least, is easy to replace. . . . God damn it! Is he taking off his coat? Oh! what the hell, let's have a look!"

With no eyes for Lafcadio's bag, Fleurissoire was struggling with his new collar and had taken off his coat so as to be able to put the stud in more easily; but the starched linen was as hard as cardboard and resisted all his efforts.

"He doesn't look happy," Lafcadio went on to himself. "He must be suffering from a fistula, or some such unpleasant complaint that I can't see. Shall I go help him? He'll never manage it by himself. . . ."

Yes, though! At last the collar yielded to the stud. Fleurissoire then took up his tie, which he had placed on the seat beside his hat, his coat, and his cuffs, and going up to the door of the carriage, looked at himself in the windowpane, endeavoring, like Narcissus in the water, to distinguish his reflection from the landscape.

"He can't see well enough."

Lafcadio turned the light back on. The train was running alongside a bank, which could be seen through the window, illuminated by the light cast upon it from one after another of the compartments of the train; this formed a succession of bright squares which danced along beside the rails; they were bent out of shape, each one in its turn, according to the accidents of the terrain. In the middle of one of these squares could be made out the ludicrous dancing shadow of Fleurissoire; the others were empty.

"Who would see?" thought Lafcadio. "There, right next to my hand, under my hand, this double fastening, which I can easily undo; the door would suddenly give way and he would topple forward; the slightest push would do it; he would fall into the night like a stone; you wouldn't even hear a scream. . . . And tomorrow, off for the Indies! . . . Who would know?"

The tie—a little ready-made sailor knot—was put on, and now Fleurissoire had taken up one of the cuffs and was arranging it upon his right wrist, examining, as he did so, the photograph above his seat (one of four that adorned the compartment), which represented some palace by the sea.

"A crime without a motive," Lafcadio went on: "what a nuisance for the police! As to that, however, while we're going along this blessed bank, anyone looking out of the next compartment might notice the open door, and see the old coot's shadow tumble out. At least the corridor curtains are drawn. . . . It's not so much the events that I'm curious about, as myself. A man thinks he's capable of anything, then pulls back when it comes to the act. . . . There's such a great gap between imagining something and doing it! . . . And no more right to take back your move than at chess. Bah! If you could foresee all the risks, there'd be no interest in the game! . . . Between the imagination of a deed and . . . I say! the bank's come to an end. We're on a bridge, I think; a river. . . ."

On the lower part of the window, which had now turned black, reflections appeared more distinctly. Fleurissoire leaned forward to straighten his tie.

"Here, under my hand, the double lock—now that he's looking away in the distance and not paying attention—my word, it's easier to undo than I thought. If I can count up to twelve, without hurrying, before I see some light in the countryside, the old goat is saved. Here goes! One; two;

three; four (slowly! slowly!); five; six; seven; eight; nine . . . ten, a light! . . ."

II

Fleurissoire did not utter a single cry. When he felt Lafcadio's push, and saw himself facing the gulf which suddenly opened in front of him, he made a great sweep of his arm to hold himself back; his left hand clutched at the smooth, slippery door jamb, while, half turning around, he flung his right well behind him and over Lafcadio's head, sending his second cuff (which he had just been putting on) spinning to the other end of the carriage, where it rolled underneath the seat.

Lafcadio felt a horrible claw alight upon the back of his neck, lowered his head, and gave another push, more impatient than the first; nails scraped his neck; nothing was left for Fleurissoire to catch hold of but the beaver hat, which he snatched at despairingly and carried away with him in his fall.

"Now then, let's keep cool," Lafcadio said to himself. "I mustn't slam the door; they might hear it in the next carriage."

He drew the door toward him in the teeth of the wind, and then shut it quietly.

"He has left me his frightful flat hat; in another minute I should have kicked it after him, but he has taken mine along with him, and that's enough. That was an excellent precaution of mine—cutting out my initials. . . . But there's the hatter's name in the crown, and people don't order a beaver felt of that kind every day of the week. . . . Oh, forget about it: it's all in the game. . . . Perhaps they'll think it an accident. . . . No, not now that I've shut the door. . . . Shall I stop the train? . . . Come, come, Cadio! no touching up! This is the way you wanted it, is it not?

"Proof that I'm perfectly self-possessed: I shall begin, quite calmly, by seeing what that photograph is the old chap was examining just now . . . . *Miramar!* No desire at all to go see that. . . . It's stifling in here."

He opened the window.

"That animal has scratched me . . . I'm bleeding . . . It hurts terribly! A little water would help; the toilet is at the end of the corridor, on the left. Let's take another handkerchief."

He reached down his traveling-bag from the rack above him and opened it on the seat, in the place where he had been sitting.

"If you meet anyone in the corridor, be calm. . . . No, my heart's not beating as it was. Let's go! . . . Ah! his coat! I can easily hide it under mine. Papers in the pocket! Something to while away the time for the rest of the journey."

The coat was a poor threadbare affair of a dingy licorice color, made of some rough, thin, and obviously cheap material; Lafcadio thought it slightly repulsive; he hung it up on a hook in the small lavatory into which he locked himself; then, bending over the basin, he began to examine himself in the glass.

There were two ugly gashes on his neck; one, a thin red streak, started from the back of his neck, turned leftward and came to an end just below the ear; the other, shorter one was a deep scratch just an inch above the first; it went straight up toward the ear, the lobe of which it had reached and slightly torn. It was bleeding, but less than one might have expected; on the other hand, the pain, which he had not felt at all at first, was beginning to be quite sharp. He dipped his handkerchief into the basin, staunched the blood, and then washed the handkerchief.

"Not enough to stain my collar," he thought, as he straightened his clothes. "So far, so good."

He was on the point of going out; just then the engine whistled; a row of lights passed behind the frosted windowpane of the toilet. Capua. The station was so close to the scene of the accident . . . to jump out, run back in the dark and get his beaver hat . . . the thought flashed across his brain. He regretted the loss, that hat so soft and light and silky, at once so warm and so cool, so uncrushable, so discreetly elegant. But it was never his way to let his desires go unchallenged; he did not like to give in—even to himself. But above all else, he had a horror of indecision, and for many years he had kept on him, like a fetish, one of a pair of backgammon dice which Baldi had given him in days gone by; he always carried it with him; it was there, in his waistcoat pocket.

"If I throw six," he said to himself as he took it out, "I'll get off."

He threw five.

"I shall get off all the same. Quick, the victim's coat! . . . Now for my case. . . ."

He rushed to his compartment.

Ah! how futile seem exclamations when confronted with the extravagance of fact! The more surprising the event, the more simple shall be my manner of relating it. I will therefore say in plain words, that when Lafcadio went back to his compartment to get his traveling-case—it was gone.

He thought at first that he had made a mistake, and went out again into the corridor. . . . But no! It was the right place. There was the view of Miramar. . . . but then? He sprang to the window and thought he was dreaming. There, on the station platform, and not very far from his carriage, his valise was calmly proceeding on its way in company of a strapping fellow who was carrying it off at a leisurely pace.

Lafcadio's first instinct was to leap after him; as he put out his hand to open the door, the licorice coat dropped at his feet.

"Whoa, there! in another minute I should have put my foot in it. . . . All the same, that rascal would go a little quicker if he thought there was a chance I might run after him. Could he have seen . . . ?"

At that moment, as he stood there leaning his head out the window, a drop of blood trickled down his cheek.

"Well! Good-bye to my case! It can't be helped. The dice did say I wasn't to get out here."

He shut the door and sat down again.

"There were no papers in my case and my linen isn't marked. What am I risking? . . . Never mind; I'd better sail as soon as possible; it'll be a little less fun perhaps, but a good deal wiser."

In the meantime the train started again.

"It's not so much my valise that I miss as my beaver, which I really should have liked to retrieve. Well! let's think no more about it."

He filled another pipe, lit it, and then, plunging his hand into the inside pocket of Fleurissoire's coat, pulled out all at once a letter from Arnica, a Cook's ticket, and a large manila envelope, which he opened.

"Three, four, five, six thousand-franc notes! Of no interest to honest folk!"

He returned the notes to the envelope and the envelope to the coat pocket.

But when, a moment later, he examined the Cook's ticket, Lafcadio felt his brain spinning. On the first page was written the name: *Julius de Baraglioul.*

"Am I going mad?" he asked himself. "What can he have had to do with Julius? . . . A stolen ticket? . . . No, impossible! . . . a borrowed ticket, that must be it. Oh, my God: perhaps I've made a mess of it. These old gentlemen are sometimes better connected than one thinks. . . ."

Then, trembling with anticipation, he opened Arnica's letter. The whole business seemed too strange; he found it difficult to fix his attention; he failed, no doubt, to make out the exact relationship that existed between Julius and the old gentleman; but, at any rate, he managed to grasp this: that Julius was in Rome. His mind was made up at once; an urgent desire to see his brother possessed him—an unbridled curiosity to observe the repercussions of this affair in that calm and logical mind.

"That's settled, then. I shall sleep tonight at Naples, get out my trunk, and tomorrow morning return by the first train to Rome. It will certainly be a good deal less wise, but perhaps ever so slightly more amusing."

I I I

At Naples, Lafcadio went to a hotel near the station; he made a point of taking his trunk with him, because travelers without luggage are looked at suspiciously, and because he was anxious not to attract attention; then he went out to buy a few necessary toilet articles and another hat instead of the odious straw (which was too tight besides) that Fleurissoire had left him. He wanted to buy a revolver as well, but had to put this purchase off till the next day, as the shops were already closing.

The train he wanted to take the next day started early and arrived in Rome in time for lunch. . . .

His intention was not to approach Julius until after the newspapers had appeared with an account of the "crime." The *crime!* The word seemed to him rather odd; and "criminal," as applied to himself, totally inappropriate. He preferred "adventurer"—a word as pliable as his beaver hat, and as easily adjusted to his taste.

The morning papers did not yet mention the "adventure." He waited patiently for the evening ones, for he was eager to see Julius and to feel his game getting under way; like a child playing hide-and-seek, who certainly doesn't want to be found, but still wants to be sure he is being looked for, he grew restive with waiting. It was a particularly vague state he had never experienced before; and the people he elbowed in the street seemed to him uncommonly common, disagreeable and hideous.

When evening came he bought the *Corriere* from a newspaper-vendor in the Corso; then he went into a restaurant, but he laid the paper all folded on the table beside him and forced himself to finish his dinner without looking at it—out of a kind of bravado, and as though to put an edge on his desire; then he went out, and once in the Corso again, he stopped in the light of a shop window, unfolded the paper, and on the second page, under Local News, saw the following headline:

CRIME, SUICIDE . . . OR ACCIDENT?

He then read the next few paragraphs, which I translate:

In the railway station at Naples, employees of the Company found a man's coat in the rack of a first-class carriage of the train from Rome. In the inside pocket of this coat, which is of a dark brown color, was an unfastened manila envelope containing six thousand-franc notes. There were no other papers by which to identify the missing owner. If a crime had taken place, it is difficult to account for the fact that such a considerable sum of money should have been left in the victim's coat; this seems to indicate, at any rate, that the motive for a crime was not robbery.

There were no traces of a struggle to be seen in the compartment; but under one of the seats a man's shirt-cuff was discovered with the link attached; this article was in the shape of two cats' heads, linked together by a small silver-gilt chain, and carved out of a semitransparent quartz, known as opalescent feldspar, and commonly called moonstone by jewelers.

A thorough investigation of the railway line is being made.

Lafcadio crumpled up the paper.

"What! Carola's cuff-links now! The old boy is a regular public intersection!"

He turned the page and saw in the last-minute news:

RECENTISSIME

DEAD BODY FOUND ON RAILWAY LINE

This afternoon, in the course of a thorough investigation of the railway line between Rome and Naples, the police discovered the body of a man lying in the dry bed of the Volturno, about five kilometers from Capua—no doubt the owner of the coat that was found last night in a railway carriage. The body is that of a man of average appearance, about fifty years of age. (He looked older than he was.) *No papers were on him which could give any clue to his identity.* (Good thing! That'll give me time to breathe.) *He had apparently been flung out of the railway carriage with sufficient violence to clear the parapet of the bridge, which is being repaired at this point and has been replaced by a wooden railing.* (What style!) *The height of the bridge above the river is about fifteen meters. Death must have been the result of the fall, as the body bears no trace of other wounds. The man was in his shirt-sleeves; on his right wrist was a cuff similar to the one picked up in the railway carriage, but with the cuff-link missing. . . .*

Lafcadio had not been able to suppress a start, for the idea flashed upon him that the cuff-link had been removed *after* the crime.—

His left hand was found still clutching a soft felt hat . . .

"Soft felt indeed! The barbarians!" Lafcadio murmured. . . .

. . . soft felt hat much too large for his head and which presumably belongs to the aggressor; the maker's name has been carefully removed from the lining, out of which a piece of leather had been cut of the size and shape of a laurel leaf . . .

There could no longer be any doubt about it; his crime had been tampered with; someone else had touched it up; had cut the piece out of the lining—the unknown person, no doubt, who had carried off his valise. . . .

. . . which seems to prove the crime was premeditated. . . . As soon as the police had made the necessary notes, the body was removed to Naples for the purposes of identification. . . .

V

Lafcadio . . . was reluctant to admit to himself the new sensation which had lately taken possession of his soul, for there was nothing he was more ashamed of than ennui—that secret malady from which he had hitherto been preserved by the fine carelessness of his youthful appetites, then by the harshness of necessity. He left his train compartment with a heart empty of hope and joy, and roamed from one end of the corridor to the other, harassed by a kind of ill-defined curiosity and vaguely seeking some new and absurd enterprise in which to engage. Nothing seemed adequate to his desire. He no longer dreamed of setting out for the East, and reluctantly acknowledged that Borneo did not in the least attract him, nor the rest of Italy either. He could not even interest himself in the consequences of his adventure; it appeared to him, in his present mood, compromising and ridiculous. He felt resentment against Fleurissoire for not having defended himself better; he felt himself protesting against that pitiful creature; he would have liked to wipe him from his mind.

On the other hand, he would have liked very much to meet that chap who had carried off his traveling-bag—a fine rascal he was! And at the Capua station, he leaned out of the window and raked the deserted platform with his eyes, as though hoping to discover him. But would he have even recognized him? He had seen no more than the man's back, already far away and disappearing into the darkness. In his mind's eye he followed him through the night, saw him reach the river bed, find the hideous corpse, rifle it and, almost as a challenge, cut out of the hat—Lafcadio's own hat—that little bit of leather which, as the newspapers had elegantly phrased it, was "of the size and shape of a laurel leaf." With his hatter's address inscribed on it, it was a neat little bit of evidence, and after all Lafcadio was extremely grateful to his bag-snatcher for having got to it before the police. It was, no doubt, very much to the interest of this plunderer of corpses not to attract attention to himself; but if, nevertheless, he saw fit to make use of his little cut-out, why, my word—it might be rather droll to come to terms with him.

Night by this time was drawing in. A dining-car waiter made his way through the length of the train to announce to the first- and second-class passengers that dinner was ready. With no appetite, but at any rate saved from his own sullen idleness for an hour, Lafcadio followed the procession, keeping some way behind it. The dining-car was at the head of the train. The carriages through which Lafcadio passed were empty; here and there various objects, such as shawls, pillows, books, papers, were disposed on the seats so as to mark and reserve the diners' places. A lawyer's briefcase caught his eye. Sure of being last, he stopped in front of the compartment, then went in. In reality he was not attracted by the bag; it was simply as a matter of conscience that he searched it. On the inner side of the flap, in unobtrusive gilt letters, was written the name

DEFOUQUEBLIZE
Faculty of Law—Bordeaux

The bag contained two pamphlets on criminal law and six numbers of *La Gazette des Tribunaux*.

"More merchandise for the lawyers' convention. Foo!" thought Lafcadio. He put everything back in its place, then hastened to join the little file of passengers on their way to the restaurant.

A delicate-looking little girl and her mother brought up the rear, both in deep mourning. Immediately in front of them was a gentleman in a frock coat and top hat, with long straight hair and gray whiskers—Monsieur Defouqueblize, no doubt, the owner of the briefcase. Their advance was slow and unsteady because of the jolting of the train. At the last turn of the corridor, just as the professor was going to make a dash into the kind of accordion which connects one carriage with another, an exceptionally violent bump toppled him over. He made a sudden gesture in order to regain his balance, which sent his pince-nez flying, its ribbon torn loose, into the corner of the narrow vestibule left by the corridor in front of the lavatory door. As he bent down in search of his eyesight, the lady and little girl passed in front of him. Lafcadio diverted himself for a moment or two watching the learned gentleman's efforts; pitiably at a loss, he was groping vaguely and anxiously over the floor with both hands; it was as though he were swimming abstractly, out of water; or performing the waddling dance of a plantigrade; or, in a reversion to his childhood, playing a game of "Hunt the Slipper." . . . Come, come, Lafcadio, one good deed! Listen to your heart, which is not yet corrupted. Go to the poor man's rescue! Hand him back the indispensable glasses; he will never find them by himself. His back is turned to them; in another minute he will step on them. Just then a violent jerk flung the unhappy man head foremost against the door of the toilet; the shock was broken by his top hat, which was now half-caved in and jammed tightly down over his ears. Monsieur Defouqueblize moaned; rose to his feet; took off his hat. Lafcadio, meanwhile, having judged that this farce had lasted long enough, picked up the pince-nez, dropped it like an alms into the hat, and then fled so as to escape being thanked.

Dinner had begun. Lafcadio seated himself at a table for two, next to the glass door on the right-hand side of the passageway; the place opposite him was empty. On the left side of the passage, in the same row as himself, the widow and her daughter were sitting at a table for four, two seats of which were unoccupied.

"What dullness reigns in places like this!" Lafcadio said to himself as his listless glance slipped from one to another of the diners, without finding a single face on which to light. "Herds of cattle going through life as if it were some monotonous drudgery, instead of the entertainment which it is—if you take it in the right spirit. How badly dressed they are! Ah, but naked they would be even uglier. I shall certainly expire before dessert if I don't order some champagne."

Enter the professor. He had apparently just been washing his hands, which had been dirtied by his hunt, and was examining his nails. A waiter motioned him to sit down opposite Lafcadio. The wine-waiter was passing from table to table. Lafcadio, without saying a word, pointed out a Montebello Grand Crémant at twenty francs, while Monsieur Defouqueblize ordered a bottle of St. Galmier water. He was holding his pince-nez between two fingers, breathing gently on the lenses and then polishing them on one corner of his napkin. Lafcadio watched him closely, amazed at his mole's eyes blinking under thick red eyelids.

"Fortunately he doesn't know that I'm the one who just gave him back his eyesight. If he begins to thank me, I shall clear out on the spot."

The waiter came back with the St. Galmier and the champagne; he first uncorked the latter and put it down between the two diners. The bottle was no sooner on the table than Defouqueblize seized hold of it without noticing which one it was, poured out a glassful and swallowed it at one gulp. The waiter was going to interfere, but Lafcadio stopped him with a laugh.

"Oh! what *is* this I'm drinking?" cried Defouqueblize with a frightful grimace.

"This gentleman's Montebello," replied the waiter with dignity. *"This* is your St. Galmier water! Here!"

He put down the second bottle.

"I'm extremely sorry, monsieur. . . . My eyesight is so bad. . . . Really, I'm overcome with . . ."

"You would greatly oblige me, monsieur," interrupted Lafcadio, "by not apologizing; and even by accepting another glass, if the first was to your taste."

"Alas! dear monsieur, I must confess that I found it abominable, and I cannot understand how I came to be so absentminded as to swallow a whole glassful; I was so thirsty. . . . Tell me, monseiur, I beg you: is this a particularly strong wine? . . . because I must confess that . . . I never drink anything but water. . . . The slightest drop of alcohol invariably goes to my head. . . . Good heavens! Good heavens! What is to become of me? Perhaps I ought to go back at once to my compartment? I expect the best thing would be for me to lie down."

He made as though to get up.

"No, no! Stay, my dear man," said Lafcadio, who was beginning to be amused. "Quite the contrary, you'd best eat your dinner and not trouble about the glass of wine. I will take you back myself later on, if you're in need of help; but don't be alarmed; you haven't taken enough to turn the head of a baby."

"I'll take your word for it. But really, I don't know how to . . . May I offer you a little St. Galmier water?"

"Thank you very much—will you excuse me if I say I prefer my champagne?"

"Ah! really! So it was champagne, was it? And . . . you are going to drink all that?"

"Just to reassure you."

"You are much too kind; but in your place I should . . ."

"Suppose you were to eat your dinner," interrupted Lafcadio, who was himself eating and had had enough of Defouqueblize. For the moment his attention was attracted by the widow.

An Italian certainly. An officer's widow, no doubt. What modesty in her bearing! What tenderness in her eyes! How pure a brow! What intelligent hands! How elegantly dressed, and yet how simply! . . . Lafcadio, when your heart fails to respond to such a concert of harmonies, may that heart have ceased to beat. Her daughter is like her, and what nobility—half-serious, half-sad even—tempers the child's excessive grace! With what solicitude her mother bends toward her! Ah! the devil himself would give way before such beings as these; to such beings as these, Lafcadio, who can doubt that you would offer your heart's devotion? . . .

At that moment the waiter came by to change the plates. Lafcadio let his own be taken away half-full, for at that moment he was staring at a sight that held him suddenly transfixed: the widow, the exquisitely refined widow, had bent down toward the side nearest the passageway, and deftly raising her skirt, with the most natural movement in the world, had uncovered a scarlet stocking and a neatly turned calf.

So incongruous was this fiery note, bursting into the solemnity of the concert . . . could he be dreaming? In the meantime the waiter was handing round another dish. Lafcadio was on the point of helping himself; his eyes fell upon his plate, and what he saw there was the final straw:

There, right in front of him, in plain view, in the very middle of his plate, fallen from God knows where, frightful and unmistakable among a thousand—there can be no doubt about it, Lafcadio: it's Carola's cuff-link! The cuff-link which had been missing from Fleurissoire's second cuff. The whole thing was turning into a nightmare. . . . But the waiter is bending over him with the dish. With a sweep of his hand, Lafcadio wipes his plate and brushes the horrid trinket onto the tablecloth; he puts his plate back onto the top of it, helps himself abundantly, fills his glass with champagne, empties it at once and fills it again. For if a man is to have drunken visions on an empty stomach . . . But no: it was not a hallucination; he hears the squeak of the link against his plate; he raises his plate, snatches the link, slips it into his waistcoat pocket beside his watch, feels it again, makes certain: yes, there it is, safe and sound. But who can say how it came on his plate? Who put it there? . . . Lafcadio looks at Defouqueblize: the learned gentleman is innocently eating, his nose in his plate. Lafcadio tries to think of something else; he looks once more at the widow; but everything about her demeanor and her attire has become proper again and commonplace; he doesn't think her as pretty as before; he tries to imagine afresh the provocative gesture, the red stocking; but he cannot do it. He tries to imagine again the cuff-link on his plate, and if he did not actually feel it in his pocket, he would certainly disbelieve his senses. . . . But in fact, why did he take it—a cuff-link that doesn't belong to him? What a confession is implied by this instinctive, this idiotic action—what a recognition! How he has given himself away to whoever may be observing him, keeping an eye on him—the police, perhaps! Like a fool, he has walked straight into their booby trap. He feels himself turn pale. He turns around sharply; there, behind the glass door leading into the corridor . . . No! no one . . . But just now there may have been someone there, someone who saw him! He forces himself to go on eating, but his teeth clench with vexation. Unhappy young man! it is not his abominable crime that he regrets, but this inopportune impulse. . . . What has come over the professor now? Why is he smiling at him?

Defouqueblize had finished eating. He wiped his lips; then with both elbows on the table, fiddling nervously with his napkin, he began to look at Lafcadio; his lips jerked in an odd sort of nervous smile; at last, as though unable to contain himself any longer:

"Dare I ask, monsieur, for just a little more?"

He pushed his glass timidly toward the almost empty bottle.

Lafcadio, surprised out of his uneasiness and delighted at the diversion, poured him out the last drops.

"I'm terribly sorry I can't offer you more. . . . But would you like me to order another bottle?"

"Oh, I'm sure a half bottle will do."

Defouqueblize was obviously already tipsy, and had lost all sense of decorum. Lafcadio, who had no fears of dry champagne and who was amused at his companion's naïveté, ordered the waiter to uncork another bottle of Montebello.

"No, no, don't pour me too much," said Defouqueblize, as he lifted the quavering glass which Lafcadio had succeeded in filling to the brim. "It's curious—I thought it so nasty at first. One makes such a great fuss about things, until one gets to know them—don't you agree? The fact is, I thought I was drinking St. Galmier water, and you see I thought that for St. Galmier water it had a very queer taste. It's as if someone had poured *you* St. Galmier water, when you thought you were drinking champagne: now wouldn't you say: 'For champagne, it has a very queer taste'? . . ."

He laughed at his own words, then bending across the table to Lafcadio, who was laughing too, he went on in a low voice: "I don't know what I'm laughing at so; it must be the fault of your wine. I suspect, all the same, that it's a bit more strong than you make out. Eh? Eh? What do you say? But you'll take me back to my carriage, that's agreed, is it not? We shall be alone, and if I behave indecently, you'll know why."

"When one's traveling," Lafcadio risked, "there's no fear of consequences."

"Ah, monsieur," replied the other at once, "the things one would do in this life if only one could be certain that there were no fear of consequences, as you so justly remark! If one could only be sure that it wouldn't lead to anything! . . . Why, merely what I'm saying to you just now, nothing more than this—which, after all, is nothing but a very natural reflection—do you think I should dare to utter it so directly, if we were in Bordeaux, now? I say Bordeaux, because Bordeaux is where I live. I'm known there, respected. Not married, but well-to-do in a quiet little way; I'm in an honorable walk of life—Professor of Law at the University of Bordeaux—yes, comparative criminology, a new chair. . . . You will understand that when I'm there, I'm not allowed, actually not *allowed,* to get tipsy—not even once in a while, by accident. My life must be respectable. Only imagine: supposing one of my pupils were to meet me in the street drunk! . . . Respectable, yes: and it mustn't look as if it were forced; there's the rub; one mustn't allow people to think: 'Monsieur Defouqueblize' (my name, sir) 'has a good job of it to keep himself under control.' . . . It's not enough simply never to *do* anything out of the ordinary; one must persuade other people that one *couldn't* do anything out of the ordinary, even with all the opportunities in the world—that there's nothing whatever out of the ordinary *in* one, begging to be let out. There wouldn't be just a touch of wine left? Only a drop or two, my dear accomplice, only a drop or two. . . . Such an opportunity doesn't come twice in a lifetime. Tomorrow, at the convention in Rome, I shall meet a number of my colleagues—grave, sober fellows, as tame, as disciplined, as self-restrained as I shall become myself, once I get back into harness. People who are in society, like you and me, owe it to ourselves to play a part."

In the meantime the meal was drawing to a close; a waiter went round adding up the checks and pocketing the tips.

As the dining car emptied, Defouqueblize's voice became deeper and louder; at moments its bursts of sonority made Lafcadio feel almost uncomfortable. He went on: "And when there is no society to restrain us, that little group of relations and friends whom we can't bear to displease would suffice. They confront our uncivil sincerity with an image of ourselves for which we are only half responsible—an image which has very little resemblance to us, but whose contours, I tell you, it is indecent not to match. At this moment—it's a fact—I have escaped from my own shape, taken flight from myself. . . . Oh, what a dizzying adventure! What dangerous rapture! . . . But I'm boring you to death?"

"Not at all: you interest me very much."

"I talk, I talk . . . can't be helped, it can't be helped! Once a professor, always a professor—even when one's drunk; and it's a subject I have at heart. . . . But if you've finished eating, perhaps you'll be so kind as to give me your arm back to my carriage while I can still stand on my legs. I'm afraid if I wait any longer, I'll be in no state to lift myself up."

At these words Defouqueblize made a kind of bound as though in an effort to get out of his chair, but collapsed again immediately in a half sprawl over the table—fortunately already cleared; he lifted up his head toward Lafcadio, and he went on in a lower, semiconfidential voice: "This is my thesis: do you know what is needed to turn an honest man into a rogue? A change of scene—a moment's forgetfulness: that's enough. Yes, monsieur, one little hole in the memory and sincerity comes out into the light of day! . . . a cessation of continuity; a simple interruption of the current. Naturally, I don't say this in my lectures . . . but, between ourselves, what an advantage for the bastard! Just think: a being whose very existence is the result of a sudden whim, of a bend in the straight line! . . ."

The professor's voice had again grown very loud; the eyes he now fixed on Lafcadio were bizarre; their glance, at times vague, at times piercing, began to alarm him. Lafcadio wondered now whether the man's shortsightedness were not feigned, and that look began to seem to him almost familiar. At last, more embarrassed than he cared to own, he got up and said abruptly: "Come, Monsieur Defouqueblize, take my arm. Get up. Enough talk!"

Defouqueblize got up out of his chair with a lumbering effort. Together they tottered down the corridor toward the compartment where the professor had left his briefcase. Defouqueblize went in first. Lafcadio settled him in his corner, then took his leave. He had already turned his back to go out, when a great hand fell heavily on his shoulder. He spun around at once. Defouqueblize had sprung to his feet—but was it still Defouqueblize?—this creature who, in a voice at once mocking, commanding, and jubilant, exclaimed: "You mustn't desert an old friend so quickly, Mr. Lafcadio What-the-deuceki. . . . Now, Now! Would you really have run out on me like this?"

Of the grotesque, inebriate old professor of a moment before there remained not a trace in this great strapping stalwart fellow whom Lafcadio no longer hesitated to recognize. It was Protos: grown, enlarged, magnified, a new Protos who carried an impression of formidable power.

[Paul Claudel to André Gide]   *Hamburg, March 2, 1914*

In the name of heaven, Gide, how could you write the passage which I find on page 478* of the last issue of the N.R.F.? Don't you know that after Saul *and* L'Immoraliste, *you cannot commit any further imprudence? Must I quite make up my mind, as I have never wished to do, that you are yourself a participant in these hideous practices? Answer me; you owe it to me. If you remain silent, or if you don't make yourself absolutely clear, I shall know where I stand. If you are not a pederast, why have you so strange a predilection for this sort of subject? And if you are one, cure yourself, you unhappy man, and do not make a show of these abominations. Consult Madame Gide; consult the better part of your own heart. Don't you see that you will be lost—you yourself and all those who are nearest to you? Don't you realize the effect which your books may have upon some unfortunate young people? It pains me to say these things, but I feel obliged to do so.*

> *Your distressed friend,*
> *P. Claudel*

[To Paul Claudel]   *Florence, March 7, 1914*

What right have you to issue this summons? In what name do you put these questions? If it is in the name of friendship, can you suppose for an instant that I should evade them?

It pains me very much that there should be any misapprehension between us; but your letter has already done much to create a new one— for, no matter how I take it, and whether I answer or whether I don't, I foresee that you are going to misjudge me. I therefore beg you only to consider this: that I love my wife more than life itself, and I could not forgive any word or action on your part which might endanger her happiness. Now that has been said, I can tell you that for months, for years, I

* See page 510.

have longed to talk to you—although the tone of your letter makes me despair of receiving any advice from you today.

I am speaking now to a friend, as I should speak to a priest, whose binding duty it is to keep my secret before God. I have never felt any desire in the presence of a woman; and the great sadness of my life is that the most constant, the most enduring, and the keenest of my loves has never been accompanied by any of the things which normally precede love. It seemed, on the contrary, that in my case love prevented me from desiring.

If, after that avowal, you prefer to break with me, you will, I suppose, find it seemly that I should ask you, in the name of those whom you love, to take no pretext whatever—the impropriety of my book, for instance—to bring forward in any way what I have revealed to you here. Alone, I should care nothing for the world's contempt; but I am married.

As for the evil which, you say, is done by my books, I can't believe in it, for I know how many others are stifled, as I am, by lying conventions. And do not infer from this that I commend any particular habits, or even any particular desires; but I loathe hypocrisy, and I know that some hypocrisies can kill. I cannot believe that religion leaves aside all those who are like myself; I cannot believe that it excludes even one of them. By what cowardice, since God calls me to speak, should I evade this question in my books? I did not choose to be so. I can fight against my desires; I can triumph over them, but I can neither choose the object of those desires nor invent other objects, either to order or in imitation.

Is it really possible that you should despise me, repulse me, after reading this letter? . . . I have always thought that one day I could speak to you as I have spoken here—even were you not to understand—and that I owed you this confession. Doubtless it is not necessary to understand in order to advise. Yet I do not ask for your advice today. I expect only your anger.

I feel that my letter gives you very poor answers to your questions; but at least you will feel I have not been reticent—except insofar as it is difficult to answer in a few phrases where a whole volume of explanations and the story of my life might not perhaps be enough.

Au revoir. Now it is for you to stretch out your hand to me—if, that is to say, you still consent to extend it.

A. Gide

[To Paul Claudel] *   *Florence, March 8, 1914*

All the same, Claudel, I can't believe that you would make use of my letter
and turn it against me. I am almost ashamed to conceive such an idea, so
deeply does it seem to me to injure you. . . . But I can't rid myself of the
hideous idea that the interrogations in your letter were prompted by somebody else who is waiting for you to hand on my answers; so that it would
now be difficult, almost impossible, for you not to betray me; for even if
you kept silent on the point, that silence would itself be revealing—just as
would have been, as you were saying, my own silence.

Since I wrote to you, two years ago, from these same banks of the
Arno, I have formed the habit of considering you a little as a priest, and I
sometimes let myself be persuaded that God was using you to speak to me.
Today I shall know if this is so, or if you are just a man, like the others.
Sometimes I come to wish that you would betray me, for then I should be
delivered from this esteem I have for you, and for all that you represent in
my eyes, which so often arrests and embarrasses me.

The extent to which you can misunderstand me—that is what distresses me. Why can I not speak to you instead of writing! All the same, I
ask you, whom I have always defended, to remember that I have written
La Porte étroite. . . . And perhaps, after all, this letter of yours, and my
answer, will mark an important point in my life. . . . When I asked you
once to give me the name of someone to whom I could talk, it was of this
that I wanted to speak—for truthfully I tell you that *I do not see how I
can resolve this problem* which God has inscribed in my flesh. Do you
understand me? You don't, do you? And that's why I gave up writing to
you two years ago. I realized that I had gone with you as far as was possible; yet I felt that everything remained to be said—how, I didn't know.

Adieu. Now you can do me great harm, and I am at your mercy.

André Gide

[Paul Claudel to André Gide] *   *Hamburg, March 9, 1914*

*. . . You claim to be the victim of a physiological idiosyncrasy. That
would be an attenuating circumstance, but it would not constitute a permit
or a license. You are the victim of two things above all: your Protestant
heredity, which has accustomed you to look only to yourself for your rules
of conduct, and the fascination of aesthetics, which lends luster and inter-*

---

* Gide dispatched this second letter to Paul Claudel without waiting for an answer to his
letter of March 7, 1914.

est to the least excusable of actions. In spite of all the doctors, I absolutely refuse to believe in physiological determinism. If you have abnormal instincts, the natural uprightness of your nature, allied to your reason, your education, and the fear of God, should have given you the means of resistance. Medicine is meant to cure, not to excuse. Alas! In your case you would have needed a confessor as well.

You ask for my advice. I advise you first of all to do what lies within your power. What lies within your power is to suppress at once that horrible passage in the N.R.F. *I entreat you to do it for . . . your own personal interest:*

I tell you again: you will be lost. *You will lose all position, you will become an outcast among other outcasts, rejected by humanity. Parisian opinion is more discreet, but it is also more pitiless than that of London. You will no longer matter—and you know it. You ask me to keep your letter secret, you beg me not to let your wife suspect a thing. Wretched man! And at the same time you make public, you display on every wall in Paris, a passage which everybody will interpret as a definitive and official confession. Have no illusions on that subject. At the very least, promise me that the passage will not appear when your novel is published in book form. I beg you, if you set any value on my friendship.—Little by little people will forget.*

Yes, I shall keep an absolute silence—but it is you who talk, you who make a public show of yourself! Such a thing has never been seen since pagan times. No writer, not even Wilde, has done it.

I shall not hide from you the fact that when I wrote to you I also wrote to two people: Jammes (a word only), and poor Rivière, to whom you could do so much harm. Poor boy—he trusted you! As I did. But what have I told them more terrible that what they have already learned from page 478? . . .

I wrote to a third person, too; but he is a priest. It was the Abbé Fontaine. Now you can go and seek him out. You will not astonish him—be sure of that.

And shall I say that I almost take relief in the removal of that great load of doubt which has hitherto embarrassed me in our relationship?

Poor Gide, how much you are to be pitied, and how tragic is your life!

> *I grasp your hand,*
> *P. Claudel*

I can't now contribute to your Whitman. *It's impossible.*

[*To Paul Claudel*] *March 16, 1914*

My dear Claudel,

What will you think of my silence? . . . I wrote you a very long letter, but I can't make up my mind to send it to you. "Harsh," your letter? No; it would only have been harsh, to me, if I had felt that you were withdrawing your friendship. But how can I answer you without seeming to defend myself (where, in my last two letters, could you find anything resembling an apologia or even an excuse? I simply told you *how things stand*), or without committing myself more deeply than I feel frankly able to do?

Send me the Abbé F.'s address. I am grateful to you for writing to him and making it easy for me to call on him. But persuade yourself, I beg you, not to hold it against me if my conversation with him does not lead to the results for which, no doubt, you are hoping. I shall listen respectfully, piously even, to what the Abbé tells me. But if the most ardent and constant of loves has never coaxed any response from my flesh, I leave it to you to imagine the effect of his exhortations, his counsels, and his reprimands. (And what, pray, do you mean me to *understand* by the phrase: "In spite of all the doctors, I absolutely refuse to believe in physiological determinism"?)

I thank you for the sentiments which lead you to ask me (as prudence would likewise do) to suppress a passage from my book; but I cannot consent to do so. Shall I admit to you that your words of reassurance, "Little by little people will forget," seem to me shameful? No; do not ask me either to whitewash or to compromise; or it will be I who will think less of you.

I can't make out why you felt you had to write to Rivière. I prefer to think that you gave way to an unthinking impulse. I like Rivière, I respect him, and I have the liveliest *reverence* for him. Has there ever been anything in my conversation or my actions that could disquiet him? No, nothing at all, it would seem, since you say that he refused to believe anything against me. What absurd or monstrous fancies is he going to entertain now? Couldn't you understand that you were compelling me from that moment to spell it all out for him, to embarrass him with confidences that I should have liked to spare him?

Au revoir. Be assured that I have never been more

Your friend,
A. Gide

LA SYMPHONIE

PASTORALE

(The Pastoral Symphony)

1919

FIRST NOTEBOOK

February 10, 189–

The snow has not stopped falling for three days, and all the roads are blocked. I have been unable to go to R., where it has been my custom to hold services twice a month for the last fifteen years. This morning only thirty of the flock were gathered together in the chapel of La Brévine.

I shall take advantage of the leisure this enforced confinement affords me to go back over the past, and to tell how I came to involve myself with Gertrude. I propose to write here everything that concerns the formation and development of this pious soul; it seems to me that I have led her out of the night for no other purpose but adoration and love. Blessed be the Lord for having entrusted me with this task.

Two years and six months ago, as I was going back up the hill from Chaux-de-Fond, a little girl I had never seen before came running up to get me, to lead me to a place seven kilometers away where a poor old woman lay dying. I had not yet unfastened the horse, so I made the child climb up in the carriage; but first I provided myself with a lantern, as I did not think it possible I should be back before dark.

I had thought myself entirely familiar with all of the lands surrounding my parish; but after we had passed the La Saudraie farm, the child bade me take a road I had never ventured on before. About two kilometers farther on, though, I recognized on our left a mysterious little lake where I had sometimes gone to skate as a young man. I had not seen it for fifteen years, as my pastoral duties never call me in this direction. I could no longer have told you where it was; by this time I had not thought of it for years. When I suddenly recognized it, in the rose and gold enchantment of evening, I felt I had seen it before only in a dream.

The road ran alongside a stream that steals out of this lake, cut through the farthest part of the forest, then skirted a peat-bog. I had certainly never come this way before.

The sun was setting, and we had been driving for a long time in the shade, when finally my young guide pointed out to me a cottage on the hillside which one would have thought uninhabited, had it not been for a thin ribbon of smoke that slipped out, turning blue in the shadow, then to blond in the gold of the sky. I tied the horse to a nearby apple tree, then rejoined the child in the dark room where the old woman had just died.

I was chilled by the gravity of the landscape, by the silence and solemnity of the hour. A woman still young was on her knees beside the bed. The child, whom I had taken for the granddaughter of the deceased but who was actually nothing but her servant, lit a smoky candle, then stood motionless at the foot of the bed. During the long drive I had tried to engage her in conversation, but had not been able to draw two words out of her.

The kneeling woman stood up. She was not a relation, as I had at first supposed, but only a neighbor, a friend, whom the servant girl had brought in when she saw her mistress failing, and who had agreed to keep watch over the body. The old woman, she told me, had passed away without pain. We agreed together on the arrangements for the funeral service and the burial. As it so often happened in this out-of-the-way country, I had to decide everything myself. I was a bit uneasy, I confess, at leaving this house, however wretched it may have looked, in the sole charge of this neighbor and the little servant girl. Yet it seemed hardly likely that there could be any treasure hidden away in a corner of this miserable dwelling. . . . And what could I have done about it? Nonetheless, I asked whether the old woman had left any heir.

At this the neighbor picked up the candle and lighted up a corner of the hearth, where I was able to make out an indistinct creature, crouching by the fireplace, who seemed to be asleep. A thick mass of hair covered its face almost completely.

"That blind girl—she's a niece, the servant says. It seems she's all that's left of the family. She'll have to be sent to the asylum. Otherwise I don't know what will become of her."

I was shocked to hear the poor thing's fate decided thus in her presence, and concerned for the pain these brutal words might cause her.

"Don't wake her up," I said softly, as a suggestion to the woman that she might lower her voice.

"Oh, I don't think she's asleep. But she's an idiot. She doesn't talk, and she can't understand anything you say. I've been in this room since morning, and she's not so much as budged the whole time. At first I thought she was deaf; but the servant says No. She says it's the old woman who was deaf, that she never uttered a word to her, or to anyone else either; that the old woman hadn't opened her mouth for years, except to eat and drink."

"How old is the girl?"

·   "About fifteen, I suppose. But I really know no more about it than you do."

It did not occur to me right away to take charge of the poor abandoned thing myself; but after I had prayed—or, to be more precise, *while* I was praying, on my knees at the bedside, between the neighbor woman and the little servant, both of them kneeling too—it suddenly appeared to me that God had placed a kind of moral obligation in my path which I could not get away from, short of cowardice. When I rose, I had decided to take the child away with me that very evening, even though I had not asked myself frankly what I would do with her after that, or to whom I could entrust her. I stayed a few moments longer gazing at the old woman's sleeping face; its puckered mouth looked like a miser's purse with the strings pulled tight, well trained to let nothing escape. Then, turning back to the question of the blind girl, I told the neighbor woman of my intention.

"It will be better for her not to be here tomorrow, when they come to pick up the body," she said. And that was all.

Many things would be easily done, were it not for the imaginary objections men sometimes take pleasure in inventing. From childhood on, how many times have we been stopped from doing this or that, something we would have liked to do, simply because we hear people around us saying over and over, "He won't be able to do it."

The blind girl let herself be taken away like a mindless lump. The features of her face were regular, rather fine in fact, but utterly without expression. I took a blanket off the pallet where she must have usually slept, in a corner of the room under a staircase that led to the attic.

The obliging neighbor woman helped me to wrap her up carefully, for the bright, clear night was cold. After having lighted the carriage lamp, I set out again; taking with me now this soulless package of flesh, this thing I could feel huddled against my side, in which the only sign of life was a mysterious warmth. I thought about her the whole way home: Is she asleep? And what can her dark sleep be like? . . . And how are her waking hours different from her sleep? Surely a soul lives inside this thick, dark body, a soul locked up, waiting for one ray of Thy grace to come at last and touch it, O Lord! Wilt Thou allow it to be my love, perhaps, that dispels this dreadful darkness? . . .

I have too much regard for the truth to pass over in silence the unpleasant welcome I had to endure on my return home. My wife is a garden of virtues: and even in the difficult stages we have sometimes had to cross, I have never doubted for an instant the real quality of her heart. But it is not a good idea to take her natural charity by surprise. She is an orderly person, careful neither to go beyond nor to fall short of her duty. Even her charity is measured, as though love were not an inexhaustible treasure. This is the only point on which we differ. . . .

Her first thought, when she saw me return that evening with the girl, escaped from her in a shout: "What have you saddled yourself with now?"

As always when we have to come to an understanding, I began by telling the children—who were standing there with their mouths wide open, full of questions and surprise—to leave the room. Ah, how different was that reception from what I might have wished! Only my dear little Charlotte began to dance and clap her hands when she understood that something new, something alive, was about to come out of the carriage. But the others, who are already well trained by their mother, quickly chilled her enthusiasm and made her fall into step.

There was a moment of great confusion. And as neither my wife nor the children knew yet that the girl was blind, they could not account for the great care that I took to guide her steps. I was myself quite disconcerted by the odd moans the poor invalid began to emit as soon as I let go her hand, which I had held throughout the drive. Her cries were like nothing human; one might have thought them the plaintive whimpering of a puppy. She had been torn away for the first time in her life from the narrow round of expected sensations which had formed her whole universe, and now her knees began to give way; but when I pushed a chair toward her, she let herself collapse on the floor, like someone who had never learned how to sit down. Then I led her up to the hearth, where as soon as she was able to crouch down, propped up against the mantelpiece, in the same position in which I had first seen her beside the old woman's hearth, she regained a bit of calm. In the carriage, earlier, she had slipped down off the seat, and had spent the whole journey huddled against my feet. My wife, however, came to my aid. Her instinctive impulses are always her best; but her reason is always fighting against these impulses of the heart—and too often it wins.

"What do you intend to do with *that?*" she went on, once the girl was settled.

My soul froze at her impersonal "that," and I could scarcely control a gesture of indignation. But as I was still imbued with my long and peaceful meditation, I was able to contain myself; and turning toward them all, standing once again around in a circle, I laid my hand on the blind girl's head and said, with all the solemnity I could muster, "I have brought back the sheep that was lost."

But my Amélie will not admit that there could be anything unreasonable (or beyond reason) in the teachings of the Gospel. I saw that she was going to protest, and so I made a sign to Jacques and Sarah (who are accustomed to our little conjugal differences, and who have, moreover, little natural curiosity—often *too* little, for my taste) to take the two younger children out of the room. Then, as my wife still remained speechless, and a bit exasperated, it seemed, by the intruder's presence, I added: "You can speak in front of her. The poor child doesn't understand."

Upon which Amélie began to protest that she had absolutely nothing to say to me—which is the usual prelude to her longest harangues—and that there was nothing for her to do but give in, as she always did, to whatever impractical nonsense I was going to invent, totally opposed to all manners and common sense. As I wrote above, I had not yet in the least made up my mind what I was going to do with this child. It had not yet occurred to me, or only in the vaguest way, that there was any possibility of adopting her into our *own* home, and I can almost say that it was Amélie herself who first planted the idea when she asked whether I didn't think there were "enough of us in the house already." Then she declared that I was forever dashing on ahead without ever worrying about those who couldn't keep up; that, for her part, she considered five children quite enough; that since the birth of Claude (who, precisely at that moment, as if he had heard his name, set up a howl from his cradle) she had had her fill of them; and that she was quite at the end of her rope.

At the first words of her tirade, some of the words of Christ rose from my heart to my lips; but I held them back, for I have always thought it unbecoming to justify my own behavior on the authority of the Holy Book. But when she mentioned her fatigue, I felt abashed, for I must admit that I have more than once burdened my wife with the consequences of my impulsive and inconsiderate zeal. These recriminations, however, had instructed me as to my own duty; I begged Amélie, therefore, most gently, to consider whether she would not have acted exactly the same in my place, whether she could possibly have abandoned in such distress a creature who obviously had no one left to rely on; I added that I was entirely aware of the new weight of fatigue which the care of this new inmate would add to the burden of her household chores, and that I regretted not being able to help her with them more often. In this way I pacified her as best I could, pleading with her at the same time not to direct her resentment against the innocent girl, who had done nothing to deserve it. Then I pointed out that Sarah was now old enough to be of more help, and Jacques to take care of himself. In short, God put into my mouth the words needed to help her accept what I am sure she would have willingly undertaken, had the circumstances given her time to reflect, and had I not thus anticipated her good will by my surprise.

I thought the battle almost won, and that my dearest Amélie was even now approaching Gertrude with benevolent intention; but suddenly her irritation exploded worse than ever, when, on taking up the lamp to examine the child more closely, she became aware of her state of unspeakable filth.

"Why, she's filthy!" she cried. "Go brush yourself; brush yourself quickly. No, not here! Go shake yourself off outside. Oh! Good heavens, the children are going to be covered with them. There's nothing in the world I dread so much as bugs."

It cannot be denied that the poor thing was crawling with them: and I could not hold back a shiver of disgust in thinking how long I had kept her tucked up against me in the carriage.

When I came back a few minutes later, having washed myself as best I could, I found my wife collapsed in an armchair, her head in her hands, giving way to a great fit of sobbing.

"I had no intention of putting your patience to such a test," I said to her tenderly. "In any case, it's too late to do anything tonight; we can't even see. I'll stay up to keep the fire going, and the child can sleep alongside it. Tomorrow we will cut her hair and wash her properly. You needn't start caring for her yourself until you can get over your . . . disgust." And I begged her to say not a word of all this to the children.

It was supper time. My protégée, at whom our old Rosalie threw many a scowling glance as she served us the meal, greedily devoured the bowl of soup that I handed her. The meal was a silent one. I would have liked to relate my adventure, to talk to the children, to touch their hearts by making them understand and feel the strangeness of so total a state of deprivation, to arouse their pity, their sympathy for this little guest whom God had asked us to welcome into our hearts. But I was afraid of reawakening Amélie's irritation. It was as if a secret order had been given to take no notice of what had happened, to forget it completely—though surely not one of us could have been thinking of anything else.

I was extremely touched, then, when more than an hour after everyone had gone to bed, and Amélie had left me alone in the room, I saw my little Charlotte half-open the door, and slip through gently in her nightgown and bare feet. She then threw her arms around my neck and hugged me fiercely. "I didn't say good-night to you nicely," she whispered.

Then, very softly, pointing her little finger at the blind girl who was now slumbering peacefully, and whom she had been curious to see again before going to sleep, she asked, "Why didn't I kiss her, too?"

"You shall kiss her tomorrow," I said, as I led her back to the door. "We must leave her alone now. She's asleep."

Then I went back to my chair and worked until morning, reading and preparing my next sermon.

"Certainly," I remember thinking, "Charlotte seems much more affectionate now than the older children. But then didn't each one of them know how to get round me at that age? Why even Jacques himself, nowadays so distant, so reserved . . . You think them all so tender-hearted, but all the time they're really only coaxing and wheedling, trying to get something out of you."

February 27

The snow fell heavily again last night. The children are delighted, because they say we shall soon have to go out by the windows. The door is blocked, in fact, this morning, and the only way out is through the washhouse. I made sure yesterday that the village was sufficiently provisioned, for we shall doubtless have to remain isolated from the rest of the world for some time to come. This is not the first winter we have been snowbound, but I cannot remember having seen snowdrifts so deep before. I take advantage of it to go on with the tale I began yesterday.

As I said, when I first brought home this poor invalid, I had not at all settled in my mind what place she was going to occupy in our household. I knew the limits of my wife's powers of endurance; I knew how little room we had and how scant our resources were. I had acted, as I always do, as much on natural impulse as on principle, without in the least stopping to calculate into what expenses my sudden gesture might lead me, for I have always thought that contrary to Gospel teaching. But it is one thing to trust one's cares to God, and quite another to load them on other people. I soon realized that I had laid a heavy burden upon Amélie's shoulders—so heavy that at first I was quite distressed.

I helped her as best I could to cut the girl's hair; even that, I could see, she only did with disgust. But when it came to washing and cleaning her, I was obliged to leave that chore to my wife; and I realized that I was avoiding the heaviest and most disagreeable tasks.

In other respects, Amélie, from then on, never made the least objection. She seemed to have thought things over during the night, and to have resigned herself to her new charge. She even seemed to take some pleasure in it, and I saw her smile when she had managed to get Gertrude washed and dressed. A white bonnet covered the head that I had shaved and rubbed with pomade; some of Sarah's old clothes and some clean linen took the place of the foul rags that Amélie had just thrown in the fire. The name Gertrude was chosen by Charlotte and accepted at once by us all, in our ignorance of her real name; the orphan herself had no notion what it was, and I had no way to find out. She must have been a bit younger than Sarah, whose last year's clothes fitted her well.

I must confess here the profound disappointment into which I felt myself sinking during those first few days. There is no doubt that I had built up an elaborate fiction for myself on the subject of Gertrude's education, and harsh reality forced me to pull it all down. The indifference, the obtuseness of her facial expression, or rather her utter *lack* of expression, froze my good intentions at their very source. She stayed all day long by the fireside, always on the defensive; as soon as she heard our voices, even more when one of us came near her, her features turned to stone; the only expression they ever showed was one of hostility. If anyone made the least effort to attract her attention, she began to groan and grunt like an animal. This sullenness only left her at meals, which I served her myself, and into which she threw herself with a bestial craving most distressing to observe. And, just as love responds to love, I felt a strong sentiment of aversion growing in me at the obstinate refusal of this soul. Yes truly, I confess that at the end of the first ten days I had begun to despair of her, even to lose interest in her to the point where I regretted my first impulse and wished I had never brought her home. And the absurd thing was that Amélie, in the face of these feelings (which I could not very well hide from her), began to relax in her triumph and to lavish her attentions on the girl all the more warmly, now that she saw I was beginning to find Gertrude a burden, now that I felt her presence among us as a mortification.

Things were at this stage when I received a visit from my friend Dr. Martins, of Val Travers, in the course of one of his professional rounds. He was very interested in what I told him of Gertrude's condition, and was at first quite astonished that she should be so retarded, considering that there was nothing wrong with her but her blindness. But I explained to him that in addition she had had to suffer from the deafness of the old woman, who until then had been her only guardian, and who had never spoken to her, so that the poor child had been left in a state of total neglect. He persuaded me that, in that case, I was wrong to despair; I had simply not set about it correctly.

"You are trying to build," he told me, "before making sure of your foundations. You must remember that her whole mind is in a state of chaos, that even the first rudiments have not yet taken shape. The first thing to do is to get her to connect together a few sensations of touch and taste and to attach some word, some sound to them, to serve as a label; some word you will repeat to her over and over, till you can't stand it any more; and then try to get her to say it after you.

"Above all, don't try to go too quickly; take charge of her at regular hours, and never for very long at a time. . . . This method," he added, after having explained it to me in detail, "has nothing particularly magical about it. It's not my invention—other people have already applied it. Don't you remember the time when we were seniors in high school, when our teachers entertained us with a case analogous to this one, apropos of Condillac and his animated statue . . . unless," he corrected himself, "I read that later on in a psychological review. . . . But no matter; I was struck by the story and I still remember the name of the poor girl, who was even more destitute than Gertrude, since she was deaf and dumb as well as blind. A doctor from some English county took her in, toward the middle of the last century. Her name was Laura Bridgeman. This doctor kept a journal, as you should do, of the child's progress—or at least, at the start, of his efforts to teach her. For days and weeks he kept at it, first making her touch and feel alternatively two little objects, a pin and a pen, and then putting her fingers on the two words *pin* and *pen* printed in raised Braille letters. For weeks and weeks there was no result. Her body seemed virtually uninhabited. He did not lose confidence, however. 'I felt like someone,' he recounts, 'leaning over the edge of a deep, black well and desperately dangling a rope in the hope that a hand would catch hold of it at last.' For he never doubted for one moment that there *was* someone there, at the bottom of the pit, and that a time would come he would feel a pull on the rope. And finally, one day, he saw Laura's impassible face light up with a sort of smile. I can well believe that tears of gratitude and love sprang at once to his eyes, and that he fell to his knees to give thanks to the Lord. Laura had come to understand what it was the doctor wanted; she was saved! From that day on, she paid close attention; her progress was rapid; she was soon able to teach herself, and eventually she became the head of an institution for the blind—unless I'm confusing her with someone else . . . because there have been other cases lately that the newspapers and magazines have made so much of, each trying to outdo the other in their astonishment (a bit foolish, if you ask me) that such creatures could be happy. Because it's a fact, you know: each one of these walled-up creatures *was* happy, and as soon as they were able to express themselves, it was their *happiness* they spoke of. Naturally the journalists went into ecstasies pointing out the moral for people who 'enjoy' all five of their senses and still have the audacity to complain. . . ."

Here an argument arose between Martins and myself, for I objected to his pessimism and refused to accept the idea he seemed to be proposing —that our senses only serve to make us miserable.

"That is not what I meant at all," he protested. "I merely mean that the unaided mind can more easily and more willingly conceive of beauty, comfort, and harmony than of disorder and sin, which everywhere tarnish, stain, degrade this world. Not only do our five senses reveal this state to us, but they also *contribute* to it. So much so, in fact, that I could willingly add to Virgil's *'Fortunatos nimium'* the words *'si sua mala nescient,'* instead of the *'si sua bona norint'* that we are taught: How happy men would be if they knew nothing of evil!"

Then he told me of a story by Dickens, which he believes to have been directly inspired by the case of Laura Bridgeman, and which he promised to send me directly. Indeed, four days later I received *The Cricket on the Hearth,* which I read with the greatest pleasure. It is the lengthy but at times very touching tale of a little blind girl maintained by her father, a poor toymaker, in an illusory world of comfort, wealth, and happiness. Dickens strives with all his art to disguise this deception as an act of piety, but I, thank God, shall need to avail myself of no such ruses with Gertrude.

The day after Martins's visit, I began to put his method into practice with all the application in my power. I am sorry now that I did not take notes, as he advised me to, of Gertrude's first steps along this twilight path, where I myself was at first only feeling my way. I had need of more patience during those first weeks than I would ever have believed, not only because of the time that such a primary education demands, but also because of the reproaches I was forced to incur. It is painful for me to have to say that these reproaches came from Amélie; but I can mention it here now because I have not kept the slightest trace of animosity or bitterness —I declare this most solemnly, in case she should ever read these pages later on. (Does not Christ teach us to forgive all injuries—immediately after the parable of the lost sheep?) I will go further: at the very moment when I was suffering most from her reproaches, I could not be angry with her for disapproving of the long hours that I dedicated to Gertrude. What I took exception to, rather, was that she refused to believe that my efforts could possibly be successful. Yes, it was this lack of faith that wounded me—without, however, discouraging me. How often I was to hear her repeat, "If only some good were to come of it all! . . ." She remained stubbornly convinced that all my efforts were in vain, so that naturally it seemed to her most improper that I should devote to this task all the hours that she always insisted would have been better spent elsewhere. Each time that I was occupied with Gertrude, she managed to work out that I was needed just then for someone or something else, and that I was wasting on her the time that I owed to others. In fact, I think she felt a kind of maternal jealousy, for more than once she said to me, "You never took so much trouble with any of your *own* children." Which was true; for though I love my children very much, I never felt the need to take such pains with any of them.

I have often found it to be true that the parable of the lost sheep remains one of the most difficult for certain good people to accept, people who consider themselves nevertheless to be devout Christians. That each sheep of the flock, taken by itself, should be in the eyes of the Shepherd a being more precious in his turn than the whole rest of the flock—this they cannot bring themselves to understand. And the words, "If a man have a hundred sheep and one of them be gone astray, doth he not leave the ninety and nine and goeth into the mountains and seeketh that which is gone astray?"—these words, shining with charity, such persons would, if they cared to speak frankly, declare to be abominably unjust.

Gertrude's first smile consoled me for everything and repaid me for my pains a hundredfold. For that lost sheep, "if it so be that he find it, verily I say unto you, he rejoiceth more of that sheep than of the ninety and nine which went not astray." Yes, verily indeed, none of my own children's smiles had ever flooded my heart with so seraphic a joy as did that which I saw dawn on her marble face, that morning when she suddenly seemed to begin to understand and to care about what I had been striving to teach her for so many days.

March 5—I noted this date as if a baby had just been born. It was not so much a smile as a transfiguration. All at once her features *came to life;* it was a sudden illumination, like the ruby glow which comes before dawn in the high Alps, the glow that elects one snow-covered summit to pull out of the darkness and makes it shiver with life—one could almost call it a mystical color. And I thought too of the pool of Bethesda at the moment the angel descends to awaken the slumbering water. I felt a sort of ecstasy before the angelic expression that suddenly came over Gertrude's face, for it was clear to me that what had come into her at this instant was not so much intelligence as love. Such a transport of thanksgiving then uplifted me that I felt it was to God I was offering the gentle kiss which I laid on her forehead.

The progress she made soon after that was as rapid as the first steps had been slow. It is only with an effort today that I can recall the paths we followed; sometimes it seemed that Gertrude advanced by leaps and bounds, as if in defiance of all method. I remember that at first I dwelt more on the qualities of objects than their variety—hot, cold, tepid, sweet, bitter, rough, soft, light—and then on actions: to put aside, to bring together, to pick up, to cross, to lay down, to tie in a knot, to scatter and reassemble, and so on. And soon, abandoning all method, I began to chat with her freely without troubling too much whether her mind was always able to follow; but I went slowly, inviting, provoking her to question me as she felt inclined. Obviously her mind still was working during the time I left her to herself; for each time I came back to her, I found with fresh surprise that the wall of darkness between us had grown less thick. After all, I said to myself, it is just in this way that the warmth of the air and the insistence of spring gradually win out over winter. How many times have I not marveled at the way the snow melts: its white coat seems to wear out from underneath, while to all appearances nothing has changed. And each winter Amélie lets herself be tricked. "The snow hasn't gone down at all," she declares. And just as you think it as thick as ever, it is already giving way; suddenly; in patches here and there, life begins to reappear.

Fearing that Gertrude might grow pale and enfeebled if she did nothing but sit beside the fire like an old woman, I had begun to make her go outside. But she refused to go walking unless I held her hand. I realized from her surprise and her fear when she first left the house—even before she knew how to tell me—that she had never before ventured out of doors. In the cottage where I had found her, no one had bothered any more than to give her food, and help her not to die—for I can hardly say they helped her to live. Her dark universe was bounded by the walls of that one room which she had never left; she scarcely ventured, on summer days, as far as the threshold, when the door stood open to the great universe of light. She told me later on that when she heard the birds singing, she used to suppose it was simply the effect of light, like the warmth she felt caressing her cheeks and her hands. It seemed to her quite natural that warm air should begin to sing, just as water placed on the fire begins to boil. The truth is that she had never worried about anything, had paid attention to nothing; she had lived in a state of suspended animation until the day when I took her in hand. I remember her inexhaustible delight when I told her that these little voices came out of living creatures, whose sole function seemed to be to feel and express the joy that is spread through all nature. (From that day, she adopted the habit of saying, "I am as merry as a bird.") And yet at first she was made very melancholy by the idea that these songs proclaimed the splendor of a spectacle which she could never see.

"Is the world really as beautiful as the birds say?" she used to ask. "Why don't people tell us so more often? Why do you never tell me so? Are you afraid it will hurt me because I can't see it? That would be wrong. I listen so carefully to the birds, I think I understand everything they say."

"People who can see them do not hear them as well as you do, my Gertrude," I said, hoping to console her.

"Why don't the other animals sing?" she asked. Sometimes her questions surprised me and left me perplexed for a moment, since they forced me to reflect on things I had always taken for granted. It was thus that I came to consider, for the first time, that the more attached an animal is to the earth, and the heavier he is, the more dismal he is likely to be. This is what I tried to make her understand; and I told her of the squirrel and his games.

Next she asked me if birds were the only animals that flew.

"There are butterflies too," I told her.

"And do they sing?"

"They have another way of expressing their joy," I replied. "It is written in color on their wings . . ." And I described for her the rainbow colors of the butterfly.

February 28

Now let me turn back a little; for yesterday I let myself get carried away.

In order to teach Gertrude, I had to learn the Braille alphabet myself; but she was soon able to read much more easily than I could. I had considerable difficulty in deciphering the writing, and found myself following it much more readily with my eyes than with my fingers. For that matter, I was not the only one to give her lessons. At first I was glad to have help with the work, as I have a good deal to do in the parish, the houses being so widely scattered that my visits to the poor and sick sometimes oblige me to go far afield. Jacques had managed to break his arm skating during Christmas vacation, which he had come to spend with us— for between terms he returned to Lausanne, where he had already done his preparatory work, and was a student at the Theological School. The fracture was not serious, and Martins, whom I had called at once, was easily able to set it without the help of a surgeon; but he advised Jacques to stay indoors for a while. He suddenly began to take an interest in Gertrude, whom he had scarcely even noticed up till then, and set to work helping me teach her to read. His collaboration lasted only as long as his convalescence, about three weeks; but during that time Gertrude made noticeable progress, as if stimulated by the most extraordinary zeal. Her intellect, only yesterday numb and torpid, at its very first steps, scarcely able to walk, now seemed ready to start running. I marveled at how little difficulty she found in formulating her thoughts, at how promptly she learned to express herself—not in the least like a child, but already with precision, finding images for her ideas in the most delightful and unexpected ways, in the very objects we had just taught her to recognize, or from the things we had just been speaking of or describing to her when we could not put them directly within her reach. For we always used things we could touch or feel in order to explain what was beyond her reach, like a surveyor with his transit.

But I consider it unnecessary to note here all the early steps of her education, which could doubtless be found in the education of all blind people. I suppose, too, that in every case their teachers must have been plunged into a similar dilemma by the question of colors. (And this problem led me to the reflection that there is nowhere any consideration of color in the Gospels.) I do not know how the others set about it; for my part I began by naming for her the colors of the rainbow in order; but then a confusion was set up in her mind between color and brightness; and I realized that her imagination was unable to make any distinction between the quality of a hue and what I believe painters call its "value." She had the greatest difficulty in comprehending that each color in its turn might be more or less dark, and that there could be an infinite number of mixtures among them. Nothing puzzled her more, and she kept coming back to the subject again and again.

Meanwhile I had the opportunity to take her to Neuchâtel, where I was able to let her hear a concert. The role of each instrument in the symphony allowed me to come back to the question of colors. I made her observe the different sonorities of the brasses, the strings, and the wood-winds, and how each one of them was able, in its own way, to produce the whole scale of notes, from the lowest to the highest, with varying intensity. I told her to try to imagine the colors of nature in the same way—the reds and oranges analogous to the sounds of the horns and the trombones, the yellows and greens to those of the violins, cellos, and basses; the violets and blues represented here by the flutes, the clarinets, the oboes. A sort of inner rapture now came to fill the place of her doubts:

"How beautiful it must be!" she repeated over and over. Then suddenly: "But what about the white? I can't understand what the white could be like."

And I saw at once how precarious my comparison had been.

"The white," I nonetheless tried to explain, "is the extreme upper limit, where all the tones are blended into one—just as black is the low or bass limit." But this did not satisfy me any more than it did her; and she pointed out that the woodwinds, brasses, and strings each kept their distinct tones in the treble range as well as in the bass. How many times have I had to stand silent, as I did at that moment, perplexed, searching for some comparison to which I could make appeal.

"Well," I said at last, "imagine white as something absolutely pure, something where no other color exists, but only light; and imagine black, on the other hand, as something so full of color that it has become completely dark. . . ."

I cite this fragment of dialogue here as an example of the difficulties I ran up against only too often. One good thing about Gertrude—she never pretended to have understood when she had not, as people so often do, filling their minds with inaccurate or false information which then proceeds to vitiate all their subsequent reasonings. As long as she could not form a clear idea of any notion, it remained for her a cause of anxiety and discomfort.

As for what I just wrote above, the difficulty was augmented by the fact that the notions of light and of heat had been from the first closely linked in her mind, and I had the greatest difficulty afterwards in dissociating them.

Thus it was that, thanks to her, I was made to realize over and over how much the visual world differs from the world of sounds, and how lame must be any comparison that one tries to draw between one and the other.

I have been so busy with my comparisons that I have not yet said what immense pleasure the concert at Neuchâtel gave to Gertrude. What they played, in fact, was the "Pastoral" Symphony. I say "in fact" because, as one could easily imagine, there is no single work I could have wished more for her to hear. Long after we had left the concert hall, Gertrude remained silent, as though lost in ecstasy.

"Is what you see really as beautiful as that?" she finally asked.

"As beautiful as what, my dear?"

"As that 'Scene on the Bank of a Stream'?"

I did not answer her at once, for I was reflecting that these ineffable harmonies painted the world not as it was, but rather as it might have been, as it would be without evil and without sin. And I had never yet dared to speak to Gertrude of evil, of sin, of death.

"People who have eyes," I said at last, "do not know their own happiness."

"But I who have none," she cried at once—"*I* know the happiness of listening."

She pressed herself against me as she walked, and hung on my arm the way little children do.

"Pastor, do you feel how happy I am? No, no, I don't say so just to please you. Look at me: doesn't it show on people's faces, when they aren't telling the truth? Why, I can always tell by their voices. Do you remember the day when you told me that you weren't crying, after my aunt [this is what she called my wife] had scolded you for doing nothing to help her? I cried out, 'Pastor, you're not telling the truth!' Oh, I knew at once from your voice that you weren't telling me the truth; I didn't need to touch your cheeks to know that you had been crying." And she repeated, very loudly, "No, there was no need for me to touch your cheeks—" which made me blush, for we were still in the center of town, and passers-by were turning around.

She went on, all the same: "You must not try to impose on me, you see. It would be very mean, first of all, to try to deceive a blind person—and what's more it wouldn't work," she added laughing. "Tell me, Pastor. You aren't unhappy, are you?"

I put her hand to my lips, as though to make her feel, without my having to confess it, that a part of my happiness came from her. At the same time I answered, "No, Gertrude, no, I am not unhappy. How should I be unhappy?"

"You cry sometimes, though?"

"I have cried sometimes."

"Not since the time I mentioned?"

"No, I have not cried since then."

"And you haven't wanted to cry since?"

"No, Gertrude."

"And tell me—have you, since that time, wanted to lie to me?"

"No, dear child."

"Can you promise that you will *never* try to deceive me?"

"I promise."

"Well then, tell me quickly: Am I pretty?"

Her abrupt question dumbfounded me, all the more because I had until that day studiously avoided taking any notice of Gertrude's undeniable beauty; I considered it perfectly useless, moreover, that she should be made aware of it.

"Why should you want to know?" I asked.

"I—I'm concerned," she replied. "I should like to know whether I do not—how can I say it?—whether I am not too out of tune in the symphony. Whom else should I ask, Pastor?"

"It is not a pastor's business to trouble himself with the beauty of people's faces," I said, defending myself as best I could.

"Why not?"

"Because the beauty of their souls is enough for him."

"Then you would rather let me think that I am ugly," she replied with a charming pout.

So that I gave up and exclaimed: "Gertrude, you know very well that you are pretty."

She was silent, and her face took on a very grave expression, which did not leave it until after our return home.

As soon as we returned, Amélie managed to let me feel that she disapproved of the way I had spent the day. She might have told me so before; but she had let us go, Gertrude and me, without saying a word, according to her habit of letting people do things and then reserving to herself the right to blame them afterwards. For that matter, she did not actually reproach me; but her very silence was accusing. For would it not have been natural for her to have inquired what we had heard, since she knew that I had taken Gertrude to the concert? Would not the child's joy have been multiplied had she felt someone taking the least show of interest in her pleasure? Yet Amélie did not remain entirely silent; she rather seemed to make a great show of talking only of the most trivial matters; and it was not until that evening, after the little ones had gone to bed, that I took her aside and asked her with some severity: "Are you vexed with me for having taken Gertrude to the concert?"

I received as my answer: "You do things for her you would never have done for one of your own children."

So it was still the same grievance, the same refusal to understand that one feasts the child who returns, not those who have stayed at home, as the parable instructs us. It pained me also to see her take no account of Gertrude's infirmity—the poor child could hope for no other holiday than this. And if, providentially, I happened to find myself free that day—I who am usually so much in demand—Amélie's reproach was all the more unfair, since she knew perfectly well that each one of my own children had some chore or some business to detain him, and that she herself had no taste at all for music, so that even if she had had all the time in the world, it would never have entered her head to go to a concert, not even if it were given at our door.

What distressed me still more was that Amélie had dared to say this in front of Gertrude; for although I had taken my wife aside, she had raised her voice so much that Gertrude heard her. I felt not so much sad as indignant, and a few moments later, when Amélie had left us, I went up to Gertrude, took her frail little hand and lifted it up to my face. "You see? This time I didn't cry."

"No," she answered, trying to smile. "This time it was my turn." And as she lifted her beautiful face, I suddenly saw that it was flooded with tears.

March 8

The only pleasure I can give to Amélie is to try not to do the things she dislikes. These very negative signs of affection are the only ones she permits me. She cannot realize the degree to which she has already narrowed my life. Oh, would to God she would demand of me some difficult act! With what joy would I perform for her the most audacious, the most perilous tasks! But she seems to be disgusted by anything out of the ordinary: so much so that her idea of progress in life is simply the addition of identical days to identical days. She does not desire, she will not even accept in me any new virtues, or even any increase in the old ones. She views with suspicion, if not with disapproval, any effort of the soul to find in Christianity something more than a domestication of our instincts.

I must confess that I completely forgot, that afternoon at Neuchâtel, to go and pay our dry goods' bill, as Amélie had asked me to, and to bring her back some spools of thread. But I was much more annoyed with myself for this afterwards than she could have been; especially in that I had promised myself not to forget, knowing well that "he who is faithful in little things will be faithful also in the great"—and fearing the conclusions that she might draw from my lapse. I should even have been pleased had she made me some reproach, for on this point I certainly deserved it. But as often happens, the imaginary grievance outweighed the precise and justified charge. Ah, how beautiful would life be, how much more bearable our miseries, if we would but content ourselves with *real* evils and close our ears to the phantoms and monsters of our mind! . . . but I am straying here into notations that would do better as the subject of a sermon (Matthew 12:29: "Neither be ye of doubtful mind"). It is the history of Gertrude's intellectual and moral development that I set out to trace here. Let me get back to it.

I had hoped to be able to follow that development step by step, and started out by recounting it in detail. But I no longer have the time to describe so minutely all its phases, and I find it extremely difficult, moreover, to recall their exact succession. Carried away by my story, I set down at first some reflections and conversations of Gertrude's that actually took place quite recently. Anyone who might chance to read these pages would no doubt be astonished to hear her express herself so justly, to reason so judiciously in such a short time. But her progress was in fact disconcertingly rapid. I was often amazed at the promptness with which her mind seized on the intellectual nutriment I brought her, and indeed on everything it could get hold of, all of which she made her own through a constant process of assimilation and maturation. Anticipating, even overtaking my own thought, she was a constant surprise, and often from one lesson to the next I ceased to recognize my own pupil.

At the end of a few months there remained not the least indication that her intelligence had been dormant for so long. She already showed more common sense than the majority of girls, distracted as the latter are by the outside world, their best attentions absorbed by a multitude of frivolous preoccupations. Moreover, she was a good deal older, I think, than she appeared to us at first. It seemed as if she were determined to profit from her blindness, so that I came to wonder whether this infirmity had not become for her in many ways an advantage. In spite of myself I compared her with my Charlotte; and sometimes, when I went over my daughter's lessons with her and saw her distracted by the least fly in the room, I found myself thinking, "Dear me, how much better she would listen if only she couldn't see!"

Needless to say, Gertrude was a very avid reader; but, as I wished to follow the development of her thought as closely as possible, I preferred her not to read too much—or at any rate not without me—and especially not the Bible, which may appear very strange for a Protestant. I shall explain myself in a moment; but before touching on so important a question, I wish to relate a small incident that is connected with music, and which should be placed, as far as I can recall, shortly after the concert at Neuchâtel.

Yes, the concert took place, I think, three weeks before the summer vacation, which brought Jacques back home. In the meantime I had more than once taken Gertrude to sit before the little harmonium of our chapel, which usually is played by Mlle de La M., the woman with whom Gertrude is presently staying. Louise de La M. had at this time not yet begun Gertrude's music lessons; notwithstanding my love for music, I do not know much about it; so I scarcely felt myself capable of teaching her anything myself when I sat beside her at the keyboard.

"No, no, let me do it," she said, after my first fumbling attempts. "I'd rather try by myself."

And I had left her all the more willingly in that the chapel did not seem to me a proper place in which to be shut up alone with her, as much out of respect for the holy place as for fear of gossip. As a rule I endeavor to disregard gossip entirely, but in this case, it would have concerned her as well as me. So when a round of parish visits called me in that direction, I would take her along to the church and leave her there, often for long hours together, and then go to fetch her on my return. In this way she spent her time patiently hunting out harmonies, and I would discover her toward evening pondering some new concord of sounds which had plunged her into long-lasting ecstasy.

On one of the first days of August, scarcely more than six months ago, it happened that I had gone to visit a poor widow in need of consolation and had not found her in. I returned to fetch Gertrude at the church where I had left her. She was not expecting me so soon, and I was extremely surprised to find Jacques seated by her side. Neither of them heard me come in, since the little noise I made was covered by the sounds of the organ. Now it is not in my nature to spy; but everything that concerns Gertrude touches my heart: so stepping as softly as I could, I slipped up the few steps that lead to the gallery—an excellent post of observation. I must say that during the whole time I was there I did not hear a word that either of them might not have said before me. But he did sit very close to her, and several times I saw him take her hand to guide her fingers over the keys. Was it not in itself strange that she should accept from him the very instructions and guidance she had previously told me she preferred to do without? I was more astonished, more pained than I liked to admit, and was just on the point of intervening when I saw Jacques suddenly take out his watch.

"I must leave you now," he said. "My father will be coming back soon."

I watched him next lift her unresisting hand to his lips; then he left. A few moments later. I went noiselessly down the stairs and opened the door of the church in such a way that she would hear me and think that I had just come in.

"Well, Gertrude! Are you ready to go home? How is the organ getting on?"

"Very well," she answered in her most natural voice. "I have really made some progress today."

A great sadness filled my heart, but neither of us has ever made any allusion to the episode I have just described.

I was most anxious to talk to Jacques alone. My wife, Gertrude, and the children used as a rule to go to bed quite soon after supper, leaving us two to sit up late over our studies. I was waiting for this moment. But before speaking to him, I felt my heart bursting with such a torrent of feelings, that I could not, I *dared* not broach the subject that was tormenting me. And so it was he who abruptly broke the silence, by announcing his intention to spend the rest of his vacation with us. Now, a few days before, he had informed us of a climbing-trip he wanted to make in the Alps—a plan of which my wife and I heartily approved; I knew that his friend T., whom he had chosen for his traveling companion, was expecting him. Thus it was quite obvious to me that this sudden change of plans was not unrelated to the scene I had just happened upon. At first I was stirred by a violent indignation, but was afraid to give in to it lest I should lose my son's confidence altogether. I also wanted to avoid any overly harsh words that I should afterwards regret. So, making a great effort to control myself, I said to him as naturally as I could: "I thought that T. was counting on you."

"Oh," he answered, "we hadn't settled it definitely. And besides, he will have no trouble finding someone else. I can rest just as well here as in the Oberland, and I really think I can use my time better than running around mountains."

"In fact," I said, "you have found something to occupy you at home?"

He noticed some irony in the tone of my voice, and looked at me; but, as he could not yet tell the reason for it, he went on casually: "You know I have always liked reading better than climbing."

"Yes, my dear boy," I said, returning his glance with one as searching, "but do you not find lessons in organ-accompaniment even more attractive than reading?"

No doubt he felt himself blush, for he put his hand to his forehead as if to shade his eyes from the light of the lamp. But he recovered himself almost at once, and replied in a voice I could have wished a bit less assured: "Don't blame me too much, Father. I had no intention of keeping anything from you. I was getting ready to tell you, and you simply brought it out in the open a bit sooner."

He spoke deliberately, as if he were reading a book, rounding off his phrases with as much calm, it seemed, as if it were a matter in which he had no concern. I was finally exasperated beyond control by his extraordinary show of self-possession. Sensing that I was about to interrupt, he raised his hand, as much as to say, "No, you can speak afterwards; let me finish first." But I seized his arm and shook it.

"Oh!" I cried impetuously. "I would rather never see you again than have you trouble the purity of Gertrude's soul. I don't need your confessions! To abuse infirmity, innocence, candor—what abominable cowardice! I would never have thought you capable of it. And then to speak to me of it with this detestable coolness! . . . Listen to me: it is I who have charge of Gertrude, and I will not permit you to speak to her, to touch her, or to see her one single day more."

"But Father," he went on, in that same maddeningly tranquil tone, "believe me: I respect Gertrude as much as you do. You are making a very strange mistake if you think there is the slightest thing reprehensible, I don't say only in my conduct, but even in my intentions, in my innermost secrets. I love Gertrude, and I respect her, I tell you, as much as I love her. The idea of troubling her, of abusing her innocence and her blindness, appears as abominable to me as it does to you." Then he protested that what he wanted to be for her was a support, a friend, a husband; that he had thought it wrong to speak to me about it until he had made up his mind to marry her; that Gertrude herself did not know of his intention; and that it was to me he wanted to speak of it first.

"There is the confession I had to make to you," he concluded, "and I have nothing else to confess. Believe me."

I was stupefied by his words. As I listened to them, I could feel my temples throbbing. I had prepared nothing but reproaches, and as he took away my grounds for indignation, I felt myself more and more at a loss, so that at the end of his speech I found I had nothing more to say.

"Let us go to bed," I said at last, after a rather long silence. I got up and put my hand on his shoulder. "Tomorrow I will tell you what I think of all this."

"At least let me know that you aren't still angry with me."

"I must have the night to think it over."

When I saw Jacques again the next morning, I honestly felt as if I were looking at him for the first time. I suddenly realized that my son was no longer a child, but a young man; as long as I thought of him as a child, this love of his I had discovered might well appear monstrous. I had spent the whole night convincing myself that it was, on the contrary, quite natural and normal. How then did it happen that my dissatisfaction became all the more passionate? This did not become clear for me until a bit later on. In the meantime I had to speak to Jacques and let him know my decision. And an instinct as sure as the voice of conscience warned me that this marriage must be prevented at all costs.

I had taken Jacques down to the end of the garden. There I began by asking him, "Have you said anything to Gertrude?"

"No," he replied. "Perhaps she senses something of my love, but I have told her nothing about it."

"Good. Now you must promise me not to speak to her of it for a while."

"Father, I have promised myself to obey you; but may I not know your reasons?"

I hesitated to give them, uncertain whether those that came first to my mind were the wisest to put forward first. To tell the truth, it was conscience rather than reason that dictated my conduct.

"Gertrude is too young," I said at last. "Keep in mind that she has not yet made her first Communion. You know that she is not like other children, unfortunately, and that her development has been greatly retarded. Trustful as she is, she would no doubt be only too easily moved by the first words of love she should hear; this is precisely why it is so important not to say them. To gain control of one who cannot defend herself is cowardly, and I know you are not a coward. Your feelings, you say, are in no way reprehensible. But I *do* regard them as culpable, because they are premature. It is our duty to be prudent for Gertrude's sake until she is able to be prudent for herself. It is a matter of conscience."

One excellent thing about Jacques is that all I need do to restrain him is repeat the simple words I often used when he was a boy—"I appeal to your conscience." Meanwhile, as I looked at him, I thought that if Gertrude *could* see him there she could not help but admire this tall slender body, so straight and yet so supple, the smooth handsome forehead, the frankness in the eyes, the face still that of a child, but shadowed, as it were, by a sudden gravity. He was bareheaded, and his ash-blond hair, which he wore rather long at that time, curled a little at the temples and half hid his ears.

"There is one more thing I want to ask you," I went on, rising from the bench where we had been sitting. "You had intended, you said, to go away the day after tomorrow; I beg you not to put off your departure. You were to stay away a whole month; I beg you not to shorten your trip by a single day. Is that understood?"

"Very well, Father. I will obey you."

He seemed to turn extremely pale, so pale that even his lips lost their color. But I persuaded myself that so prompt a submission argued no very great love, and I felt an indescribable relief. Besides, I was touched by his docility.

"There's the son that I love," I said gently, and drawing him to me, I touched my lips to his forehead. I felt him recoil slightly, but refused to let myself be offended by it.

March 10

Our house is so small that we are obliged to live more or less on top of one another, which is sometimes very inconvenient for my work, although I keep a little room for myself upstairs where I can receive my visitors in private; but it is especially inconvenient when I wish to speak to one of my family in private without giving the interview the air of solemnity it would have if it took place in this little parlor the children jokingly call my "inner sanctum," and which they are forbidden to enter. But on that particular morning Jacques had gone to Neuchâtel, where he had to buy his climbing boots, and since it was such a fine day, the children had gone out after lunch with Gertrude, who looks after them while they are looking after her. (I am pleased to note that Charlotte has become especially attentive.) Thus, quite naturally, I found myself alone with Amélie at tea, which we always take in the living-room. This was just what I had wished, for I was most anxious to speak to her. But I find myself so rarely talking with her privately any more that I felt almost shy; and the seriousness of what I had to say, moreover, disturbed me as much as if it were a business of some confession of my own, and not simply this of Jacques's. Before I began to speak, I was touched by the thought of how much two people who love each other, who lead virtually the same life, can still remain (or become) total mysteries one to the other, as if each lived locked in his own private cell. Words, in this case, no matter which one is speaking, begin to sound like hesitant, hollow knocks designed to test the thickness and resistance of the separating wall—a wall which, if we do not take care, will only go on growing thicker and thicker.

"Jacques spoke to me last night, and again this morning," I began as she poured the tea; my voice was as unsteady as Jacques's had been assured the night before. "He told me that he is in love with Gertrude."

"It was right of him to tell you," said she without looking at me, going right on with her pouring, as if I had announced the most natural thing in the world—or rather as if I were telling her nothing new.

"He told me he wanted to marry her; he is resolved to . . ."

"It was to be expected," she murmured with a slight shrug of her shoulders.

"Then you suspected it?" I asked, somewhat irritably.

"Oh, you could see it coming for a long time. But it's the sort of thing men never notice."

It would have been of no use to protest, and besides there was perhaps some truth in her rejoinder, so "In that case," I objected, "you might have warned me."

She gave me the little crooked smile with which she sometimes accompanies and covers over her mental reservations, and said, with a sideways nod of her head, "Ah, if I had to warn you of everything you can't see for yourself . . . !"

What was this insinuation supposed to mean? I did not know nor care to know, so I ignored it and went on: "Well, I want to hear what you think about it."

She sighed, then said, "You know, my dear, that I never approved of that child's staying with us."

With some difficulty I controlled my irritation at her everlasting raking up of the past.

"The child's staying with us is not what we are discussing," I replied.

But Amélie was already going on: "I have always thought we would live to regret it."

With a strong desire to be conciliatory, I caught at her words: "Ah then, you think such a marriage would be regrettable? Good: that is just what I wanted to hear you say. I am happy that we are of the same opinion." Then I added that Jacques had submitted quietly to the reasons I had given him, so that there was no longer anything for her to worry about; that it had been agreed that he would leave the next day for this trip, which would last a whole month.

"As I would be no more pleased than you, were he to find Gertrude here when he returned," I concluded, "I thought that the best thing would be to entrust her to Mlle de La M., at whose house I could continue to see her; for it cannot be denied that by this time I have contracted genuine obligations to her. I have just now been to sound out her new guardian, and she asks nothing but to be of service. So you will soon be freed from this presence, which has been so painful to you. Louise de La M. will take care of Gertrude—she seems delighted with the arrangement. See how pleased she is already, giving her music lessons."

Amélie seemed determined to remain silent, so I went on: "As we must keep Jacques from going down there to see Gertrude without us, I think it would be a good idea to warn Mlle de La M. of the . . . situation, don't you think?"

I put the question in the hope of getting some word out of Amélie; but she kept her lips tightly shut, as if she had vowed not to speak. I went on, not because I had anything more to say, but because I could not endure her silence: "For that matter, Jacques may have got over his love by the time he comes back. At his age, how many boys really know what they want?"

"Oh, even later on, some don't know," she said at last, rather oddly.

Her enigmatic, sententious tone irritated me, for I am myself too outspoken by nature to put up easily with mysteries. Turning toward her, I begged her to explain what that was meant to imply.

"Nothing, my dear," she answered sadly. "I was only thinking that a moment ago you wished someone would warn you of the things you don't notice yourself."

"And?"

"And I've been thinking that it isn't always easy to warn people."

As I said, I detest mysteries, and I object on principle to double meanings. "When you want me to understand you, you will try to express yourself more clearly," I replied a bit brutally, perhaps, and I was sorry as soon as I had said it, for I saw her lips tremble momentarily. She turned her head aside, then got up and took a few hesitating, unsteady steps about the room.

"But Amélie," I cried, "why do you go on being miserable now that everything is all right?" I sensed that she was upset by my looking at her, and so it was with my back turned, my elbows on the table, my head resting in my hands that I said to her: "I spoke to you harshly a moment ago. I'm sorry."

At that I heard her come up behind me; then I felt her fingers touch gently on my forehead, as she said tenderly, in a voice full of tears,

"My poor dear!"

Then she left the room at once.

Amélie's words, which seemed at the time so mysterious, became clear to me soon after; I have written them down as they appeared to me at first. All I knew that day was that the time had come for Gertrude to leave.

March 12

I had set for myself the task of devoting a little time each day to Gertrude —a few hours or a few minutes, depending on the necessary occupations of the day. The day after this conversation with Amélie, I had some free time, and as the weather was inviting, I led Gertrude through the forest to that break in the Jura, where, through a curtain of branches, beyond a vast stretch of countryside below, one can see on clear days the wonder of the white Alps rising out of a light mist. The sun was already declining on our left when we reached the place where we usually sat. A meadow of thick, close-cropped grass sloped downward at our feet; farther off, a few cows were grazing. Each one of them, in these mountain herds, wears a bell around its neck.

"They're sketching the landscape for me," Gertrude said, listening to the tinkling.

She asked me, as she did on each of our walks, to describe the place where we had stopped.

"But you know it already," I told her. "It's the edge of the forest, where one can see the Alps."

"Can you see them clearly today?"

"In all their splendor."

"You told me they were a little different every day."

"What shall I compare them to today? To the thirst of a midsummer's day. Before evening they will end by melting in the air."

"I should like you to tell me if there are any lilies in the great meadow in front of us."

"No, Gertrude; lilies don't grow at this altitude—or only a few rare species."

"Not even the ones they call lilies of the field?"

"There are no lilies in the fields."

"Not even in the fields around Neuchâtel?"

"No. There *are* no lilies of the field."

"Then why did Our Lord say, 'Consider the lilies of the field'?"

"There were some in His time, no doubt, or He wouldn't have said so. But we have plowed up the fields, and now they are gone."

"You have often told me, I remember, that what this world needs most is trustfulness and love. Don't you think that if men had a little more faith they might begin to see the lilies again? Believe me, when I hear His word, *I* can see them. I will describe them for you, shall I? They are like bells of flame, great sky-blue bells filled with the perfume of love, swinging in the evening breeze. Why do you tell me there aren't any, there in front of us? I feel them! I see the meadow filled with them!"

"They are no more beautiful than you see them to be, my Gertrude."

"Say that they are no less beautiful."

"They are just as beautiful as you see them."

" 'And yet I say unto you that even Solomon in all his glory was not arrayed like one of these,' " she said, quoting the words of Christ; and as I heard her melodious voice, it seemed as if I heard these words for the first time. " 'In all his glory,' " she repeated, pensively.

Then she was silent for a time, and I said: "I have told you before, Gertrude: it is those who have eyes who know not how to see." And I felt this prayer arise from the bottom of my heart: "I thank Thee, O God, for revealing to the humble what Thou hidest from the wise."

"If you knew," she exclaimed in a rapture of delight, "if only you could know how easily I imagine it all! Wait! Would you like me to describe the landscape to you? . . . Behind us, above us, and around us are the great fir trees with their odor of resin and their garnet trunks, with their long, dark, horizontal branches which groan when the wind tries to bend them. At our feet, like an open book resting on the sloping desk of the mountain, the broad green meadow sprinkled with colors, turning blue in the shade, golden in the sun, with flowers for the words—blue

gentians, pasqueflowers, ranunculus, and the beautiful lilies of Solomon—
which the cows come and spell out with their bells, where the angels come
to read; for you say that the eyes of men are closed. Below the book I see a
great, smoky, misty river of milk, which covers a mysterious abyss, an
immense river with no other shore but the beautiful, dazzling Alps, far,
far away in the distance. . . . That's where Jacques is going. Tell me, is
it true that he's going tomorrow?"

"He is to leave tomorrow. Did he tell you?"

"He didn't tell me. I guessed it. Will he be away a long time?"

"A month . . . Gertrude, I want to ask you . . . Why didn't you
tell me that he used to meet you in the church?"

"He came to see me twice. Oh, I didn't want to hide anything from
you; but I was afraid of hurting you."

"You hurt me by not telling me."

Her hand sought mine. "He was sorry to go."

"Tell me, Gertrude . . . did he tell you he loved you?"

"He didn't tell me, but I feel it. I knew it without his telling. He
doesn't love me as much as you do."

"And you, Gertrude, does it hurt you to see him go?"

"I think it is better he should go. I couldn't love him back."

"But tell me: Does it hurt you to see him go?"

"You know well that it's *you* I love, Pastor . . . Oh! Why do you
take away your hand? I wouldn't say that to you if you weren't married.
But no one marries a blind girl. So why shouldn't we love each other? Tell
me, Pastor: do you think that it's wrong?"

"Love in itself is never wrong."

"I feel nothing but good in my heart. I don't want to make Jacques
suffer. I don't want to make anyone suffer . . . I only want to give happiness."

"Jacques was thinking of asking for your hand."

"Will you let me talk to him before he goes? I should like to make
him understand that he must give up loving me. Pastor, you understand,
don't you, that I can't marry anyone? You will let me speak to him, won't
you?"

"This evening."

"No, tomorrow; just before he leaves . . ."

The sun was setting in majestic splendor. The air was still warm. We
got up and, talking as we went, turned back along the dark road home.

SECOND NOTEBOOK

April 25

I have had to put this notebook aside for some time.

The snow melted at last, and as soon as the roads were opened, I had to fulfill a great number of obligations that had been put off during the long weeks that our village was isolated by the snow. Only yesterday did I find myself again with a few moments of leisure.

Last night I read over everything I had written. . . .

Now that I dare call by its true name the feeling that I refused for so long to acknowledge in my heart, I can scarcely understand how I could have mistaken it until today; how certain words of Amélie's which I recorded here could ever have seemed "mysterious" to me; how, even after Gertrude's naïve declarations, I could still have wondered whether I loved her or not. The problem was that I refused to recognize at that time any lawful love outside of marriage; but refused also, at the same time, to believe that there could be anything unlawful in the inclination that drew me so passionately toward Gertrude.

The innocence of her confessions, their very frankness, reassured me. I told myself: this is a child. Real love could not be expressed without confusion and blushes. And for my part I persuaded myself that I only loved her as one loves a sick child. I cared for her, after all, as one cares for a sick person—and so I translated this passionate attachment into a duty, a moral obligation. Yes, in fact, on the very evening she spoke to me the words I have recounted—even later, when I was transcribing our conversation—I felt so full of joy, so lighthearted, that I *still* misread my true feelings. For I would have thought such a love reprehensible, and I believed that anything reprehensible would weigh heavily on the soul; since I felt no such weight on my soul, I had no suspicion of any love.

I set down these conversations exactly as they occurred; but also while I was in the same frame of mind as when they took place. To tell the truth, it was only in rereading them last night that I finally understood . . .

Soon after Jacques's departure, our life returned to its tranquil course. (I had allowed Gertrude to speak to him before he left, and when he returned for the last few days of his vacation, he went out of his way either to avoid Gertrude altogether or to speak to her only in my presence.)

Gertrude, as we had planned, went to stay with Mlle Louise, where I visited her each day. But, still very much afraid of my love, I made a point of talking with her of nothing that might arouse us. I spoke to her only as her pastor, and most often with Louise present in the room, concentrating on her religious instruction and preparing her for her first Communion, which she made just this Easter.

I too took Communion on Easter Sunday. That was just two weeks ago. To my surprise, Jacques, who was spending a week's holiday with us, did not accompany me to the Communion table. And I greatly regret having to say that Amélie also abstained, for the first time since our marriage. It seemed as though the two of them had come to some understanding, and had resolved by their defection from this solemn celebration to cast a shadow over my joy. Once again I congratulated myself that Gertrude could not see, and that I was left to bear the weight of that shadow alone. I know Amélie too well to have missed the indirect reproach she intended her action to convey. She never goes so far as to disapprove of me openly, but makes a point of showing her disdain by abandoning me in a sort of isolation.

I was profoundly distressed that a grievance of this order—a grievance so base, I mean, that I am loath even to contemplate it—could have so twisted Amélie's soul as to turn it aside from higher concerns. When we came home, I prayed for her in all the sincerity of my heart.

As for Jacques's abstention, it was due to quite other motives, as a conversation I had with him a little later will make clear.

May 3

Gertrude's religious instruction has led me to reread the Gospels with new eyes. It seems to me more and more that many of the notions which constitute our Christian faith originate not in the words of Christ, but in the commentaries of Saint Paul.

This was, in fact, the subject of an argument I have just had with Jacques. He is a bit arid by temperament—his mind is not sufficiently nourished by his heart; he is becoming traditionalist and dogmatic. He reproaches me with choosing "what pleases me" out of the Christian doctrine. But I do not pick and choose among the words of Christ. It is simply that, between Christ and Saint Paul, I choose Christ. For fear of having to set them in opposition, Jacques refuses to dissociate them, refuses to feel any difference in inspiration between them. He protests when I say that in the words of one I hear a man, while in the other I hear God. The more he argues, the more convinced I am that he simply cannot hear the uniquely divine accent that is present in the least of Christ's words.

I search through the Gospels, I search in vain for commandments, threats, prohibitions . . . They all of them come from Saint Paul. And it is precisely because he cannot find such things in the words of Christ that Jacques is upset. People like him think themselves lost the minute they can no longer reach out and touch their props, their guard-rails and bannisters. They cannot bear to see in others a liberty that they have given up, and they wish to obtain by compulsion the very things that would readily be granted them out of love.

"But Father," he said, "I too desire the soul's happiness."

"No, my friend; you desire its submission."

"It is in submission that happiness lies."

I let him have the last word, because I dislike such wrangling; but I know that happiness is endangered when we seek to obtain it by means of what should, on the contrary, be only its ultimate *effect;* and if it is true that the loving soul rejoices in willing submission, it is also true that nothing is further from happiness than submission that is granted without love.

In all other respects Jacques reasons well, and if I were not pained to see so much doctrinal harshness in so youthful a mind, I should no doubt admire the quality of his arguments and the consistency of his logic. It often seems to me that I am younger than he is, younger today than I was yesterday; and I repeat to myself the words, "Except ye become as little children, ye shall not enter the kingdom of heaven."

Do I betray Christ, do I reduce, do I profane the Gospels when I see in them above all a *method for attaining the blessed life?* The state of joy, which is obstructed only by our doubts, by the hardness of our hearts, it is required that every Christian should attain it. Every living creature is more or less capable of joy. Every creature should *aspire* to joy. Gertrude's smile alone teaches me more in this respect than all my lessons teach her.

And these words of Christ stood out brilliantly before me: "If ye were blind ye should have no sin." Sin is what darkens the soul—what obstructs its joy. Gertrude's perfect happiness, which shines out from her whole being, comes from the fact that she knows nothing of sin. There is nothing in her but light and love.

I have put into her vigilant hands the four Gospels, the Psalms, the Apocalypse, and the three Epistles of St. John, where she may read: "God is the light, and in him is no darkness at all," as she has already heard the

Saviour say in John's Gospel: "I am the light of the world: he that followeth me shall not walk in darkness." I will not give her the Epistles of Saint Paul; for if, being blind, she knows nothing of sin, what is the use of upsetting her by letting her read "that sin by the commandment might become exceeding sinful" (Romans 7:13), and the rest of the dialectic that follows, admirable though it be?

May 8

Dr. Martins came over yesterday from Chaux-de-Fonds. He examined Gertrude's eyes for a long time with the ophthalmoscope. He told me he had spoken about Gertrude to Dr. Roux, the Lausanne specialist, and is to report his observations to him. They both think that Gertrude might be cured by an operation. But we have agreed to say nothing about it to her until we can be more certain. Martins is to come and let me know after their consultation. What good would it do to awaken in Gertrude a hope that one might have to extinguish almost at once? And besides, is she not happy as she is? . . .

May 10

At Easter, Jacques and Gertrude saw each other again, in my presence—at least Jacques saw Gertrude and talked to her, but only of insignificant things. He seemed less affected than I had feared; and I persuade myself anew that if his love had truly been ardent, he would not have got over it so easily—even though Gertrude had told him before he went away last year that it was hopeless. I noticed that he uses *"vous"* instead of *"tu"* with Gertrude now, which is certainly preferable; moreover, as I had not asked him to do this, I am especially pleased that he thought of it himself. There is unquestionably a great deal of good in the lad.

I suspect, nevertheless, that this submission of Jacques's was not achieved without arguments and struggles. The unfortunate thing is that the constraint he was forced to impose on his heart now seems to him a good thing in itself; he would like to see it imposed on everyone. I felt this in the discussion I had with him recently, which I recorded a few pages back. Is it not La Rochefoucauld who says that the mind is often duped by the heart? Needless to say, I dared not mention this to Jacques then and there, understanding his mood; I see him as one of those people who are only confirmed in their obstinacy by contradiction. But that very evening I found a means of answering him—and in St. Paul, of all places (I can only beat him with his own weapons); and I took care to leave a little note in his room, on which he could read: "Let not him which eateth not, judge him that eateth; for God hath received him" (Romans 14:3).

I could just as well have copied out what follows: "I know, and am persuaded by the Lord Jesus, that there is nothing unclean of itself; but to him that esteemeth any thing to be unclean, to him it is unclean." But I dared not, fearing that Jacques might then go on to imagine some insulting misconstruction of my words with regard to Gertrude and myself—an idea that must not so much as skim the surface of his mind. I know, this passage is explicitly dealing with food; but in how many other passages of Scripture are we not called to find double, nay triple meanings ("If thine eye . . ."; the multiplication of the loaves; the miracle at Cana; etc.)? This is not simply quibbling. The meaning of this text is broad and profound; any restriction should be dictated not by law, but by love; and St. Paul exclaims directly afterwards: "But if thy brother be grieved with *thy* meat, now walkest thou not charitably." Where love fails, there the Evil One attacks. Lord, remove from my heart all that does not belong to love . . . For I was wrong to provoke Jacques: the next morning I found on my desk the same note on which I had written out the text. On the back of the sheet, Jacques had simply transcribed another verse from the same chapter: "Destroy not him with thy meat for whom Christ died" (Romans 14:15).

I reread once more the whole chapter. It is the starting-point for endless discussion. And am I to torment with these perplexities, darken with these clouds Gertrude's bright, shining sky? Am I not nearer to Christ, and do I not keep her nearer to Him, when I teach her, when I let her believe that the only *sin* is that which tries to harm the happiness of others, or endangers our own?

Alas, there are certain good souls who remain particularly ill-suited for happiness; clumsy in its presence, resistant to its appeal . . . I am thinking of my poor Amélie. I have never given off inviting her, urging her, to be happy—I would force her to be if I knew how. Yes, I would like to lift everyone up to God. But she will have none of it; she curls up tight like those flowers that no amount of sun can force open. Everything she sees disturbs her, afflicts her.

"What's the use, my dear?" she answered me the other day. "I'm sorry, but we can't all be blind."

Oh, how her irony grieves me, and what fortitude I require not to let it upset me! Moreover she should realize, it seems to me, that such an allusion to Gertrude's infirmity I find particularly distressing. She makes me aware, in fact, that what I admire most of all in Gertrude is her infinite mildness; I have never heard her express the slightest resentment against anyone. It is true that I keep her from knowing anything that might hurt her.

And as the happy soul spreads happiness by the radiation of love, so everything around Amélie becomes gloomy and morose. Amiel would write that "her soul gives off black rays." When, after a day of struggles— of visits to the poor, to the sick, to the afflicted—I return at nightfall, sometimes totally exhausted, my heart longing for repose, for affection, for warmth, what I find most often at my fireside is only cares, recriminations, vexations to which I should a thousand times prefer the cold wind and the rain outside. Oh, I know well enough that our old Rosalie insists on having things always her own way; but she is not always in the wrong, nor is Amélie always in the right when she tries to make her give in. I know that Gaspard and Charlotte misbehave atrociously; but might not Amélie get better results if she yelled at them less loudly and less constantly? So much nagging, so many orders, so many reprimands; until finally all lose their sharpness, like pebbles on the beach; alas, the children are far less upset by them than I am. I know that little Claude is teething (at least that is what his mother insists every time he starts howling); but does it not simply encourage him to howl when either she or Sarah runs to pick him up and coddle him the minute he makes a sound? I am convinced that he would scream less if just once or twice he were left to cry to his heart's content, sometime when I am not there. But I know that the women rush about more to keep him still then than at any other time.

Sarah is just like her mother, and for that reason I should have liked to send her away to school. She is not, unfortunately, like Amélie at her age, Amélie when we were first engaged; but rather like what the cares of daily life have made her—I was about to say the *cultivation* of the cares of life, for Amélie certainly does cultivate them. Indeed I can scarcely recognize in her today the angel who used to smile encouragement, not so very long ago, on each noble impulse of my heart; she who I dreamed would share freely and equally in all of my concerns, who seemed to lead me and guide me toward the light—or was I only deluded by love? . . . For I see in Sarah now none but the most mundane preoccupations. Following her mother's model, she allows herself to be entirely taken up by narrow, paltry tasks. The very features of her face, spiritualized by no interior flame, look dull and almost hard. No taste for poetry, none for reading at all; I have never overheard any conversation between her and her mother in which I had the least inclination to take part; and I feel my isolation even more pitifully when I am with them than when I retire to my study, as it is becoming my custom to do more and more often.

I have also fallen into the habit this autumn, encouraged by the early dusk, of taking my tea at Mlle de La M.'s whenever my pastoral rounds permit it—that is, whenever I can get back in time. I have not yet mentioned that since last November Louise de La M. has sheltered along with Gertrude three little blind girls, entrusted to her care by Martins. Gertrude, in her turn, is teaching them to read and to work at sundry little tasks, at which the little girls already seem quite skillful.

What a rest, what a comfort it is for me, each time I re-enter the warm atmosphere of the Grange, and how much I miss it if I am obliged to let two or three days go by without stopping in. Mlle de La M. is in a position, needless to say, to care for Gertrude and her three little boarders without putting herself out in the least: three maidservants help her with the greatest devotion and spare her all fatigue. But were ever fortune and leisure better deserved? Louise de La M. has always interested herself in the poor; she is a deeply religious soul, she seems hardly to belong to this world or to live for anything but love. Although her hair, which she wears framed in a lace cap, has almost all turned silver now, there could be nothing more childlike than her smile—nothing more graceful than her gestures, more musical than her voice. Gertrude has caught her manners, her way of speaking, the intonation not only of her voice but also of her mind, one might say, of her whole being—a resemblance upon which I tease them both, but which neither of them will admit. How sweet it is, when I have the time to linger a while in their company, for me to see them sitting beside one another, Gertrude either leaning her head on her friend's shoulder or letting her clasp her hand tightly as I read them some lines out of Lamartine or Hugo; how sweet to behold such poetry reflected in the clear, limpid innocence of their souls! Even Gertrude's three tiny charges are touched by it. These children are developing extraordinarily, making remarkable progress in that atmosphere of peace and love. I smiled at first when Mlle Louise spoke of teaching them to dance, for their health's sake as much as for their amusement; but today I am amazed at the rhythmic grace of the movements they have learned, though they themselves, alas, are unable to appreciate it. And yet Louise de La M. has persuaded me that though they cannot see, they can feel through their limbs the harmony of these motions. Gertrude takes part in the dances with the most charming grace and good nature, and moreover seems to enjoy herself immensely. Or sometimes Louise de La M. joins in the children's game herself, while Gertrude takes her place at the piano. Her progress in music has been astonishing; she plays the organ in chapel now every Sunday, and preludes short improvisations to the singing of the hymns.

She still comes to our house for Sunday dinner. My children are delighted to see her, despite the fact that their tastes and hers are diverging more and more. Amélie seems less irritable than usual on these occasions, and we get through the meal without strain. After dinner, the whole family goes back with Gertrude to the Grange for tea. It is a great treat for my children, for Louise enjoys spoiling them and loading them with delicacies. Amélie, who cannot fail to be touched by such attentions, cheers up at last, and looks quite the young woman again. I believe she would find it difficult now to do without this break in the wearisome round of her daily life.

May 18

Now that the fine weather has returned, I have been able to go out again with Gertrude—something I had not done for a long time (for there have been fresh snowfalls lately, and the roads were in a terrible state until just a few days ago). Nor have I been able to be alone with her for a long time either.

We walked quickly; the sharp air brought color to her cheeks and kept blowing her fair hair across her face. As we passed alongside a peat-bog, I picked a handful of flowering rushes and slipped the stems under her beret; then I braided them into her hair to hold them in place.

We had scarcely spoken to each other in the wonder of finding ourselves alone again together, when Gertrude turned her sightless face toward me and asked abruptly: "Do you think Jacques still loves me?"

"He has made up his mind to give you up," I replied at once.

"But do you think he knows you love me?" she continued.

Since the conversation of last summer which I related above, more than six months had gone by without (strange as it may seem) the slightest word of love having passed between us. We were never alone, as I said, and it was of course best that it was so. Now Gertrude's question made my heart beat so fast that I was obliged to slow down our pace.

"But everyone knows I love you, Gertrude," I exclaimed.

She was not to be put off. "No, no. You are not answering my question." And after a moment's silence she went on, her head lowered: "Aunt Amélie knows it; and I know it makes her sad."

"She would be sad anyway," I protested in a less than confident voice. "It is her nature to be sad."

"Oh, you are always trying to reassure me," she answered with some impatience. "But I don't want to be reassured. I know very well there are a great many things you don't tell me about for fear of disturbing me or hurting me; a great many things that I don't know, so that sometimes . . ." Her voice dropped lower and lower; she stopped as if for want of breath.

And when, taking up her last words, I asked, "So that sometimes . . . ?"

"So that sometimes," she continued sadly, "I feel that all the happiness I owe to you is based on ignorance."

"But, Gertrude—"

"No, let me say this: I don't want a happiness of that kind. You must understand that I . . . that I don't care about being happy. I would rather know. There are many things—sad things, I have no doubt—that I cannot see, but you have no right to keep them from me. I have thought about this a long time during these winter months. I am afraid, you see, that the whole world is not as beautiful as you have made me believe, Pastor—and in fact that it is very far from it."

"It is true that man has often disfigured it," I argued fearfully, for the rush of her thoughts had frightened me and I was trying to turn it aside, without much hope of success. She seemed to be waiting for these words, for she seized on them at once as though they were the missing link which closed the chain.

"Exactly!" she cried. "And I want to be sure I don't add to the evil."

For a long time we walked on very quickly in silence. Everything I might have said was checked in advance by everything I felt she was thinking. I was afraid of provoking some sentence on which both of our fates would depend. And as I thought of what Martins had told me of the possibility of her regaining her sight, a dreadful anxiety gripped my heart.

She finally spoke up: "I wanted to ask you . . . but I don't know how to say it . . ."

She had clearly summoned all her courage to speak, as I had summoned all of mine to hear what she had to say. But I could never have foreseen the question that was tormenting her: "Are the children of a blind woman always born blind?"

I don't know which one of us was suffering most from this conversation, but there was no way out now.

"No, Gertrude," I said, "except in very special cases. There is in fact no reason why they should be."

She seemed extremely reassured. I should have liked to ask in my turn the reason for her question; but I hadn't the courage, and went on clumsily: "But Gertrude, one must be married to have children."

"Don't say that, Pastor. I know it isn't true."

"I have told you what it was proper for me to tell you," I protested. "But you are right; the laws of nature do permit what the laws of man and of God forbid."

"You have often told me that the laws of God were the laws of love."

"The love that you are talking about is not the same thing as the one we call 'charity.'"

"Do you love me out of 'charity'?"

"No, Gertrude. You know that very well."

"But then you admit that our love is outside the laws of God?"

"What do you mean?"

"Oh, you know very well. I shouldn't have to be the one to speak of it."

In vain I sought to evade the issue; the beating of my heart set all my arguments flying in confusion. In distraction I cried out: "Gertrude . . . do you think your love is sinful?"

She corrected me: *"Our* love . . . I tell myself I should think so."

"And then . . . ?"

I caught, with surprise, what sounded like a note of supplication in my voice; but she went on without a breath: "But that I cannot stop loving you."

All this happened yesterday. At first I hesitated to write it down. . . . I have no idea how our walk came to an end. We ran along as if we were fleeing from something, and I held her arm pressed tightly against me. By that point my soul had quit my body—I felt that the least pebble on the road would send us both rolling to the ground.

May 19

Martins came back this morning. An operation is in order, and may well succeed. Roux is certain of it, and asks to have her under his care for a time. I cannot refuse, and yet I am such a coward that I asked for time to reflect. I asked for time to prepare her gently. . . . My heart should leap for joy, but instead I feel it weighing heavily inside me, burdened with an inexpressible grief. At the thought of having to announce to Gertrude that her sight may be restored, my heart fails altogether.

May 19, night

I have seen Gertrude again and I have not told her. At the Grange this evening there was no one in the drawing-room, so I went upstairs to her room. We were alone.

I held her for a long time pressed to my heart. She made no movement to resist, and as she lifted her face to mine our lips met . . .

May 21

Is it for us, O Lord, that Thou hast made the night so deep and so beautiful? Is it for me? The air is warm, and at my open window the moon enters and I listen to the vast silence of the skies. At the mingled adoration of the whole creation my heart melts into an ecstasy beyond words. I can only pray recklessly now, desperately. If love knows any limitation, it is set by man, O my God, not by Thee. However guilty my love may appear in the eyes of men, oh tell me, Lord, tell me that in Thine it is sacred!

I strain to lift myself above the idea of sin; but sin seems to me intolerable, and I will not, I cannot abandon Christ. No, I will not admit that I sin in loving Gertrude. I cannot tear this love out of my heart except by tearing my heart out with it, and for what? If I did not love her already, it would be my duty to love her out of pity; to stop loving her would be to betray her; she needs my love. . . .

Lord, I know not . . . I know nothing now but Thee. Be Thou my guide. Sometimes I feel that I am sinking into darkness, and that my sight is being taken away so that hers may be returned.

Gertrude went into the clinic at Lausanne yesterday and is not to come out for three weeks. I am expecting her return with extreme apprehension. Martins is to bring her back. She made me promise not to try to see her before then.

May 22

A letter from Martins: the operation was a success. Thanks be to God!

May 24

The idea that she who has loved me until now without seeing me must now see me—this idea causes me unbearable distress. Will she recognize me? For the first time in my life, I stare anxiously, questioningly into mirrors. If I feel her eyes to be less indulgent than her heart, less loving, what shall become of me? O Lord, I sometimes think that I cannot love Thee without her love!

May 27

An unusual amount of work has enabled me to get through these last days without too much impatience. Every occupation that can pull me out of myself is a blessing; but all day long, through everything I do, her image follows me.

She is coming back tomorrow. During this past week, Amélie has shown only the best side of her nature, and seems to have set for herself the task of distracting my thoughts from our absent friend; she is preparing a little festivity with the children to celebrate her return.

May 28

Gaspard and Charlotte have picked what flowers they could find in the woods and fields. Old Rosalie has made a monumental cake, which Sarah is decorating with all sorts of gilt-paper ornaments. She is expected at noon.

I am writing to fill up this wait. It is eleven o'clock. Every minute I lift my head and look out toward the road where Martins's carriage will be coming. I hold myself back from going to meet them: it is better, especially for Amélie's sake, that I should not welcome her apart from the others. My heart is bounding . . . ah! here they are!

May 28, evening

In what abominable darkness I am sunk.

Pity, my Lord, have pity! I give up loving her; only do not let her die!

How right I was to be afraid! What has she done? What is it she wanted to do? Amélie and Sarah tell me they went with her as far as the door of the Grange, where Mlle de La M. was expecting her. Apparently she wanted to go out again. . . . What has happened?

I am trying to put my thoughts into some sort of order. The accounts that they give me are incomprehensible or contradictory. Everything is mixed up in my head . . . Mlle de La M.'s gardener has just brought her back unconscious to the Grange; he said he saw her walking along the river; then she crossed the garden bridge, then leaned over—and disappeared. But as he did not at first realize that she had fallen, he did not run to her as he should have; he found her again at the little sluice-gate, where the river current had carried her. When I saw her soon afterwards, she had not regained consciousness; or had rather lost it again, for she came to for a moment, thanks to the prompt and prodigious efforts made to revive her. Martins, who, thank God, had not yet left, cannot understand the kind of stupor and lassitude in which she is now sunk. He has questioned her in vain; she seems either to hear nothing, or to have determined not to speak. Her breathing is still very labored and Martins is afraid of pneumonia; he has ordered mustard plasters and cupping, and promises to come again tomorrow. The mistake was leaving her too long in her wet clothes while they were busy at first trying to revive her; the water in the river is ice-cold. Mlle de La M., the only person who has succeeded in getting a few words from her, maintains that she wanted to pick some of the forget-me-nots that grow so thickly on this side of the river. Still unused to measuring distances, or mistaking for solid ground the floating carpet of flowers, she suddenly lost her footing . . . If only I could believe it! If only I could convince myself that it *was* an accident, what a fearsome weight would be lifted from my soul! During the whole welcoming feast, despite all its gaiety, I was made uneasy by the strange smile that never left her face—a strained smile I had never seen before, but which I tried to make myself believe was the smile of her newly opened eyes; a smile that seemed to stream like tears, from her eyes onto her face; alongside it the vulgar mirth of the others was simply offensive. She did not join in the general mirth. She seemed to have discovered some secret, which she would surely have confided to me if we had been alone. She said almost nothing. But no one was surprised at that, because she is often silent when she is with others, and all the more so as they become the more exuberant.

Lord, I beseech Thee, let me speak to her. I must know: else how can I go on living? . . . And yet, if she wanted so much to end her life, is it in fact because she *knew?* Knew what? My dearest, what horrible thing have you learned? What was the deadly thing I kept hidden from you, which you were suddenly able to see?

I have spent two hours at her bedside, never taking my eyes from her forehead, her pale cheeks, her delicate eyelids shut tight on some unspeakable grief, her hair still wet, like seaweed, spread about her on the pillow —listening for her strained and irregular breathing.

May 29

Mlle Louise sent for me this morning just as I was starting for the Grange. After a fairly quiet night, Gertrude has at last emerged from her torpor. She smiled when I came into the room and signaled me to come sit by her bedside. I did not dare to question her, and she was no doubt dreading questions; for she said to me at once, as if to forestall anything personal: "What do you call those little blue flowers that I was trying to pick by the riverside? Flowers the color of the sky. You're more careful than I am—would you make me a bouquet of them? I would like it there, next to my bed . . ."

The forced sprightliness of her voice was making me ill, as she clearly understood; for she added then more gravely: "I can't speak to you this morning; I am too tired. But do go pick the flowers for me, won't you? You can come back very soon."

And when I came back an hour later carrying her bouquet of forget-me-nots, Mlle Louise told me that Gertrude was resting again and would not be able to see me before evening.

I did see her again this evening. Pillows had been piled up on her bed to support her, almost in a sitting position. Her blond hair was now gathered up and plaited about her forehead, wound about the blue flowers I had brought her.

She was obviously very feverish and drew her breath with great difficulty. She held in her burning hand the hand that I offered her; I remained standing alongside her bed.

"I must make you a confession, Pastor," she said, "because this evening I am frightened of dying. I lied to you this morning. It wasn't to pick flowers . . . Can you forgive me if I tell you that I wanted to kill myself?"

I fell on my knees beside her bed, still keeping her frail hand in mine; but she pulled it away and began to stroke my forehead, while I buried my face in the sheets so as to hide my tears and to stifle my sobs.

"Do you think that so very wicked?" she then tenderly asked; and, as I answered nothing, "My friend, my friend," she said, "you must see that I take up too much place in your heart and your life. When I came back to you, that was what struck me at once; or at any rate that the place that I took belonged to another and that it made her unhappy. My crime is that I did not feel it sooner; or rather—for I knew it all along—that I let you go on loving me all the same. But when I suddenly saw her face, when I saw so much unhappiness on her poor face, I could not bear the thought that such unhappiness was my doing. . . . No, no, blame yourself for nothing; but let me go; let her have back her joy."

The hand stopped stroking my forehead; I seized it and covered it with kisses and tears. But she pulled it away impatiently, as some new anguish began to disquiet her.

"That is not what I meant, no, it's not that I want to say," she said over and over; and I saw the sweat break out on her forehead. Then she let her eyelids fall and kept her eyes closed for some time, as if she wanted to concentrate her thoughts, or to reach again her former state of blindness. And in a voice at first trailing and mournful, but which grew louder as soon as she reopened her eyes, which animated at last even to vehemence, "When you gave me my sight," she said, "my eyes opened on a world more beautiful than I ever dreamed it could be; yes truly, I had never imagined the daylight so bright, the air so sparkling, the sky so vast. But neither had I imagined men's faces so full of care. And when I went into your house, do you know what it was that struck me first? . . . Oh, I still must tell you: what I saw first was our fault, our sin. No, no, don't protest: 'If ye were blind ye should have no sin.' But now I can see . . . Do get up, Pastor, please. Sit down there, next to me. Listen to me now and don't interrupt. During the time I spent at the clinic, I read, or rather I had read to me some passages from the Bible which I had not known before, which you had never read me. I remember one verse from Saint Paul which I said over and over to myself through one whole day: 'For I was alive without the law once; but when the commandment came, sin revived, and I died.' "

She was speaking in a state of extreme excitement, in a very loud voice, almost shouting these last words, to the point that I was afraid someone might hear her outside. Then she closed her eyes and repeated these words in a whisper, as though for herself alone: " 'Sin revived—and I died.' "

I shivered, my heart frozen in a kind of terror. I had to distract her train of thought.

"Who read you these verses?" I asked.

"Jacques," she said, opening her eyes and staring at me. "You knew he'd become a Catholic?"

It was too much. I was going to implore her to be silent, but she was already going on: "My friend, I am going to cause you a great deal of pain; but there must be no falsehood between us. When I saw Jacques, I realized at once it was not you that I loved. It was he. He had exactly your face—I mean the face I imagined you had . . . Ah! Why did you make me refuse him? I might have married him. . . ."

"But Gertrude, you still can," I cried in despair.

"He's going to become a priest!" she said impetuously. Then, shaken by sobs, "Oh, I wish I could confess to him," she moaned in a kind of ecstasy. "You can see for yourself there's nothing left for me to do but die. I'm thirsty. Please call someone. I can't breathe. Leave me alone. Ah, I thought talking to you like this would have brought me more relief. Please go away. We must say good-bye. I cannot bear to see you any more."

I left her. I called Mlle de La M. to take my place at her bedside. Her extreme agitation made me fear the worst, but I could not help seeing that my presence only aggravated her condition. I begged them to send for me if she grew any worse.

May 30

Alas, I was never again to see her awake. She died this morning at day-break after a night of delirium and exhaustion. Gertrude's last request was for Jacques, and, telegraphed for by Mlle de La M., he arrived a few hours after the end. He reproached me cruelly for not having called in a priest while there was still time. But how could I have done so when I was still unaware that, during her stay at Lausanne, and evidently urged on by him, she had abjured the Protestant faith? He told me at one blow of his own conversion and of Gertrude's. And so they both left me at the same time; it was as if, separated by me during their lifetime, they planned to escape from me and unite themselves in God. But I tell myself that there is more of reasoning than of love in Jacques's conversion.

"Father," he told me, "it is not fitting for me to accuse you; but it was the example of your error that guided me."

After Jacques had gone away again, I knelt down beside Amélie and asked her to pray for me, as I was in need of help. She simply recited the Lord's Prayer; but she left long silences after each sentence, which were filled with our private supplications.

I would have liked to cry, but I felt my heart more dry than the desert.

 1920—1932

INTRODUCTION

By far the most important change in André Gide's life in the 1920's was his coming into a considerable degree of fame. "The dominating fact of his life . . ." (Jean Schlumberger, 1930) "is certainly the belated arrival of fame. Until he was fifty years old, he was an author almost completely unknown. With success, things change . . . The greatest event in Gide's life, at least in his *external* life, yes, I say it again, it is his success." [1]

Fame, of course, means different things to different people. When Gide died in 1951, one of the mass-circulation Paris dailies headlined its obituary: "Gide, the Nobel Prize Winner Who Became a Popular Author Thanks to Michele Morgan"—a reference to the star of the movie version of *La Symphonie pastorale,* who did indeed help sell many copies of the novel.

But such fame as most serious writers dream of did come to Gide early in the 20's; it crested about 1930, and then continued until the outbreak of world war. I have already mentioned the very human mixture of frustration and disdain with which Gide bore thirty years of obscurity. The compound of emotions with which he responded to his years of celebrity, when they finally came, is just as confused, and just as revealing.

Before 1920, almost none of his books had sold more than a few hundred copies. The case of *Les Nourritures terrestres* is notorious: of an original edition of 1,650 copies, scarcely more than 200 were sold in the first two years, 500 in the first ten. To some degree—a small degree—this lack of success was contrived. "I had an embarrassing number of copies of my first book printed," Gide wrote; "for the future, I would print only just enough—even a bit less than enough." "Why do I limit *L'Immoraliste* to three hundred copies? . . . to hide from myself as much as possible the bad sale." [2] His books were not advertised, and sometimes he made it a point of perverse honor not to send out reviewers' copies. When the leading Paris reviewer, Paul Souday, finally deigned to notice Gide in 1911, he remarked on this apparently willful reticence.

> The edition [of *Cahiers d'André Walter*] has long been out of print: nor has the book ever been reprinted. The literature of M. Gide is eminently esoteric, a coterie-literature. This writer seems to put as much effort into fleeing publicity as others put into seeking it out. He is writing, I shall be told, for himself, or at most, like Stendhal, for a hundred readers. . . . He is the man of the missing volume [*Il est l'homme du volume introuvable*] . . . he is one of those . . . whom a horror of the mob and a passion for contemplative solitude reserve for a posthumous fame.[3]

M. Souday's explanation notwithstanding, the repeated complaints in Gide's journals and correspondence during these years make it obvious that he would have liked, that he in fact hungered for a larger audience, for more appreciative critics, for a greater share of fame.

Not a great deal need be said of his critical reception, his public image before this period. As Gide so often protested, there was almost none to speak of. For the thirty years after 1890, an incomplete but generally representative bibliography of Gide's critical reception in France* lists 149 items, or an average of five a year. He could usually depend on a review, though rarely an intelligent or a friendly one, from the influential *Mercure de France,* whose editor he knew. Friends like Francis Jammes and Henri Ghéon (while they were still friends) wrote sympathetic studies of his works for lesser-known periodicals. The first mention in a major daily was Souday's of 1911, followed by another three years later and a third in 1920; the rest of the *grande presse* continued not to know him. Albert Thibaudet, the French critic of the period most highly respected today, reviewed *La Symphonie pastorale* favorably in 1920— but then he was reviewing it in the *N.R.F.* Gide was overjoyed at a generous review-essay of *La Porte étroite* that Edmund Gosse published in London in 1909. But out of this entire period, during which Gide published over twenty books—at least seven of them of the first importance —one is unlikely to find any review or critical essay sufficiently penetrating to be of much use today, except perhaps one written by Jacques Rivière, Gide's "disciple" (later editor of the *N.R.F.*), in 1911.

It is difficult to say what image his name may have evoked for the

---

* "Essai d'une Bibliographie chronologique," in *André Gide et l'Opinion en France de 1890 à 1950,* an unpublished Sorbonne thesis of 1953 by Pierre Lafille.

tiny number of Frenchmen who may have heard of the author of *L'Im-moraliste* or *La Porte étroite* or *Nourritures terrestres* before 1920. Though a few critics made efforts to take him seriously, most fell back, as reviewers always do, on a stock of easy labels, and it may be presumed that their readers did the same.

Catholic reviewers (which is to say most French reviewers) made easy fun of what they imagined to be his Protestantism, and often explained or dismissed his aberrations as the result of this un-French peculiarity. A few of the more militant among them were already beginning to find Gide subversive. "[In] these pages of virulent satire . . . M. Gide's Protestant frenzy disfigures and soils our faith with a contentious perversity that makes that of M. [Anatole] France seem innocence itself." ". . . under the gracious nonchalance of M. André Gide there lurks an irreducible hostility to everything that is Catholic and French." [4]

But most critics had not yet learned how wicked Gide was. (Most critics had not yet learned that he existed.) What they *did* know—those who noticed him—was that he was difficult, ingenious, unstable, super-subtle, egoistic, and cold. *"Cet froid jongleur,"* this frigid juggler—such was their image. Being French, they admired his style; being well-seated gentlemen who knew their own mind, they could smile at his "feminine" fragility, his nervous instability, his inability to walk a straight line. Clearly, this was a terribly clever, but rather un-French (and certainly not very important) child of the *symbolistes,* the "grand pontiff of a little group of *littérateurs* who live on the fringes of society, [who] teaches in his cellar the rules for the esoteric art of tomorrow";[5] one whose work, to cite again Paul Souday, the critic of *Le Temps,* was itself "eminently esoteric, a coterie-literature."

But his turn was to come. By the end of the 1920's, most of his books were back in print, many in foreign translations, and *Nourritures terrestres* was selling in the tens of thousands. The Lafille listings rise up to 19 critical mentions for 1920; 37 for 1923, 41 for 1927, 49 for 1929: the total for the two decades, 1920–1939, is 657, including 38 books devoted entirely to Gide.* Nor were these critics only his friends, or second-string reviewers of little magazines. Suddenly every serious reviewer was commenting on his books as they came off the press. Older Academicians like André Chaumieux and Henri de Regnier stooped to acknowledge him; Academicians-to-be studied his style and his "influence." Julian Benda, Jacques Maritain, François Mauriac, André Mau-

---

* This is, as I say, a selected list, confining itself to the more important notices, primarily in the serious Parisian press. The actual total is probably in the thousands.

rois, Jean Cocteau, Alain Fournier, André Breton—few important French writers of the 20's and 30's did *not* pause to comment on *le phénomène Gide*. Outside of France, Thomas Mann, Cyril Connolly, Arnold Bennett, Ilya Ehrenburg and others accorded his work the attention due an international master's. In 1927, E. M. Forster cited *Les Faux-Monnayeurs* as a signal instance of the New in his *Aspects of the Novel*, and by 1932 Edmund Wilson was already growing a bit tired of "the recent apotheosis of André Gide." [6] He was the subject of panel discussions, public opinion polls, and special issues of magazines. His correspondence was immense, and the solicitations of the curious had become a considerable nuisance. He thought of applying for the Academy himself in 1922,* was elected an Honorary Fellow of the Royal Society of Literature in 1923, and had a special volume of tributes in his honor published in 1928. His much-debated influence at this time on the youth, and especially the young writers, of France may well have been greater than that of any of his contemporaries. "It would be impossible to imagine the life of European youth in the third and fourth decades of this century without Gide," wrote a respondent to one survey of 1931.[7] Another critic of that year typified him as "the contested, but veritable, master of contemporary letters, the writer who has exerted the deepest influence during the past twelve years, one of those rare spirits of whom it can be said that after them literature and thought are not what they were before." [8]

In the 1930's his political activity, at least, if not his literary work, guaranteed him a continuance of notoriety. The controversy over his anti-Stalinist *Rétour de l'U.R.S.S.* in 1936 helped gain him more press notices (according to the Lafille bibliography) than for any other year of his life. An expensive fifteen-volume set of his works was published between 1932 and 1939; he made the French Encyclopedia in 1936. Nor did his fame end with the 30's: in fact, two of the most momentous tributes this world can pay to an author—the Nobel Prize for Literature and the condemnation of his entire work to the Roman Catholic Index of Forbidden Books—were accorded him in 1947 and 1952, respectively. But (as is customary) these distinctions came after the period of his greatest influence and reputation had passed.

For in the 1940's the war, first, and then a new generation of writers, a new order of priorities, displaced him from center stage. He was by this time leading what he himself called his "posthumous" life. He had

---

* From this folly, as from others, he was kept by his wise and necessary friend Roger Martin du Gard, who argued eloquently against the step in a letter of January 22, 1922.

become, as we say, a living legend, a writer who had outlasted the expected span of a literary career: a subject of theses and dissertations, an entry in literary histories, a man hunted out by disciples and interviewers and curiosity-seekers, but one probably regarded by many as already dead.

Today, after a few postwar years of reaction to the excesses of his earlier fame, he has the dubious place of a "modern classic," a place so academic and assured that his returned spirit might well long for the days of violent denunciations and more violent defenses, the days when he was thought a dangerous, diabolic "corrupter of youth," or else the greatest living French writer, the essential *contemporain capital*. He might, now, regard with mixed emotions all the manifestations of established, institutionalized literary Fame in Our Day: Sorbonne theses, Columbia seminars, the Delay biography, the Pléiade volumes, the ten *Livre de Poche* paperbacks, quotations from his works on *baccalauréat* exams, special postage stamps and exhibitions and symposia for the centennial in 1969, and his share in the great waves of American scholarly articles.

The history of a writer's reputation is obviously not the story of his life, or a reliable index to the worth of his work. In fact, it is more likely to be a picture of his contemporaries and followers, a revealing delineation of the taste and temper of the generations that have surrounded him (and sometimes of little more than their most vulgar elements: the advertisers and scandalmongers and sensation-seekers, the petty journalists and polemicists).

But this river of tribute and abuse, however artificial, however shallow, does not simply run its course unnoticed by its subject. Even a recluse like Faulkner, an arch-skeptic like Valéry cannot but be aware of, and somehow changed by the public image that wears his name. And Gide was no recluse, no scorner of reputation. In fact, he could hardly have been *less* indifferent. He was not simply aware of his popularity, his fame-created image. He lived with it, observed it closely, cultivated and manipulated it, helped to shape it and keep it alive. The noise he generated, to adopt a physical metaphor, came back to superimpose itself on, and radically to alter, his original signal.

I have said that the First World War had a great deal to do with preparing Gide's audience. "For the tormented or revolutionary spirit of the postwar years, in search of sincerity and of purity, Gide was the inevi-

table reference" (Claude Martin).⁹ But can we identify precisely the
beginning of this long-delayed fame, the fame that Jean Schlumberger
thought "the dominating fact of his life"?

Albert Guérard suggests that "Octave Mirbeau's belated mention of
L'Immoraliste and the unexpected success of *La Porte étroite* were perhaps the first notable steps toward a less private reputation" ¹⁰ for Gide;
but surely this is to start too far back. The essays by Ghéon and Rivière,
the attention of Edmund Gosse and Paul Souday may have helped
slightly. *La Symphonie pastorale* in 1920 was given greater notice in the
grande presse than any of its predecessors.

But all of Gide's commentators concur on the starting-point of his
popular reputation: the campaign of attack against his pernicious moral
influence begun by Henri Massis, a spokesman for traditional Catholic
France (now a member of the Academy) in November 1921, which
was followed in 1922 by a second campaign of attack, noisier but less
serious, by Henri Béraud. These two violent anti-Gidians soon drew
others into their wake. Partisans and defenders rushed into print. There
was talk of a duel, and soon the French press was bubbling into one of its
seasonal literary battles. In a series of literary interviews conducted by a
Paris weekly in 1923, the Gide–Béraud affair was discussed more than
any other subject. Then, in November of that year, thousands of readers
"discovered" the twenty-six-year-old *Nourritures terrestres* for the first
time when they saw it quoted, saw its power and influence fictionally
demonstrated in the latest volume of Roger Martin du Gard's novel, *Les
Thibault.* By the time the two original campaigns had played out, about
1924, Gide was famous.

"These attacks have made me more famous in three months than my
books had done in thirty years," Gide wrote in his journal; and it pleased
him to discover, some years later, a remark of Verdi's: "We artists reach
celebrity only through calumny." Nor was he entirely ungrateful to his
sponsors. "Béraud's attack astonished me by the sudden importance it
gave to my name . . . I had the peculiar fate (perhaps unique) to be
magnified by attack before I had been by praise." "Under their blows, by
the violence of their attacks, I am becoming aware of my own tough-
ness." ¹¹

[The Gide–Massis quarrel] served, at least, to reveal to Gide the
ultimate implications of his own system of thought, forced him to
take on a greater consistency and clarity—and he thanked Massis

for it: "I see reassembled there for the first time," he wrote apropos of the latter's first volume of *Jugements* on January 25, 1924, "the scattered features of my own countenance. Thanks to you, and since your study, I am clearly aware of my existence." (Claude Martin, *André Gide par lui-même*)

Massis had written, with the intention of discrediting Gide, that "what he is questioning is the very notion of *man* on which we live." Remarks such as this impressed on many people, for the first time, a sense of Gide's radical, revolutionary, and possibly exemplary role—and one of the people impressed was Gide.

> . . . for a long time I regarded myself simply as an artist; it was only by reason of these attacks that I came to realize that my primary role was to be that of an innovator . . . to tell you the truth, it was these attacks that revealed my own value to me.[12]

Educated to his own new importance, he even asked Massis if he could borrow the quotation as an epigraph for his next book.

But if the attacks of two minor antagonists (Massis is little known today except as Gide's adversary, Béraud not at all) set off Gide's explosion into public controversy, he certainly did what he could to foster it himself in the years that followed. One could cite (as Massis did) "subversive" passages from the 1921 *Morceaux choisis* or the 1923 lectures on Dostoevsky, or many earlier works; but Gide's major contribution to his own notoriety began in 1924, when he published *Corydon,* a detailed defense of his particular kind of homosexuality. In 1925, preparing to leave for the Congo, he sold at auction most of the autographed copies he had been given of other people's books—a minor scandal, compared to *Corydon,* but a scandal nonetheless ("No book of mine has ever caused so much ink to flow"[13]). In 1926 one could read, in *Si le grain ne meurt,* an unashamed confession of certain early instances of his own aberrant sexual behavior, the like of which had never been seen before in public print. In the central relationship of *Les Faux-Monnayeurs* (1926 also) many saw yet another confession and defense of "unspeakable practices, unnatural acts"; and in the novel as a whole a dramatization of the very "corruption of modern youth" of which Gide stood accused. His *Voyage au Congo,* published on his return from Africa in 1927, included an angry description of the abuses of French colonial rule, and led to another round of attacks and counterattacks. When he published his profession of faith in Soviet communism in 1932, it could only have seemed to many the latest in a decade-long series of intentional and public outrages.

The attacks made on Gide during this period range from petty and forgotten fabrications to objections so serious and fundamental that they retain their force today. Many—the cool reception given *Les Faux-Monnayeurs,* Martin du Gard's strictures on all Gide's later fictions— were primarily literary; but of greater interest to us are the moral attacks.

The journalistic war of Henri Béraud was really directed against the whole *N.R.F.* team, which he wildly imagined as some sort of conspiracy of Malvolios, a "literary trust" of joyless Protestant snobs. The worst he could find to say of Gide was that he was its leader, that his books were boring, and that he wrote bad French. He attributed the *N.R.F.* authors' reputation abroad to chicanery in high places, certain that such tiresome clots as Gide, Claudel, Romains, and Suarès—he steered clear of Proust and Valéry—could never make it on their own merits. The whole affair was mindless and silly, but Béraud's artful self-publicizing did make it the literary gossip of 1923: he proudly cites some 150 references to his campaign in the French and foreign press.

Far more serious was Massis's campaign, and it is important to understand it if one is to appreciate Gide's many references to it in his *Journal.* Massis was representative of many of Gide's traditionalist critics, and certain of his theories have dominated Gide criticism for years. (It should be understood that Gide was not his only target: he was also fighting, through Gide, against Nietzsche, Dostoevsky, and Freud, against Luther, Rousseau, and Schopenhauer, Renan, France, and Barrès; against—in a later footnote—Sartre and Camus; against, it would appear, Rimbaud and Baudelaire: against all he imagines to be enemies of his Tradition.)

Part of his quarrel is simply that of Catholic vs. anti-Catholic (Gide's own position against the Church hardened considerably under pressure of these attacks): disgust at his "blasphemies," his private readings of Scripture, his slippery agnosticism, his insults against Catholics. This may seem today an intramural affair of no great interest to outsiders, but in France of the 1920's, the Church was still the most powerful and visible defender of traditional values, and hence Gide's most formidable adversary.

The heart of his attack was directed against what Massis and others

saw—and what Gide himself came to see—as his refutation of traditional Western ethics, the very notion of Natural Law, of fixed standards,
ideal values, and transcendental ends.

> . . . his criticism impairs the unity of the human individual, the
> very organization of our spiritual being; . . . in order to *justify*
> *himself*—he feels the need to overturn the laws of nature, to put
> other laws in their place, a new *evaluation,* and to "disarrange the
> conditions of life." . . .
>
>   . . . under the cover of psychology, Gide's object is secretly
> metaphysical: for him it is a matter of breaking the unity that intelli-
> gence and will have introduced into the complexity of the senses,
> and to establish nothingness in its place, by demonstrating that in
> their intervention lies a principle of discord and trouble. . . .
>
>   What he is questioning is the very notion of *man* on which we
> live, and he is doing this in the name of a doctrine which tends
> secretly to destroy it. Under the pretext of a psychological enrich-
> ment, of "unexploited regions" to be conquered, Gide wants nothing
> more than to unchain the interior tumult, to allow "the individual
> person to unfold . . . with no other goal but self-satisfaction," *
> in a word to rip up the unity of the universal being. . . .
>
>   When we speak of "the notion of man on which we live" (on
> which we try to live), we mean that immutable and transcendant
> reality whose ruling power we acknowledge to be sovereign. By this
> essential reality is everything set in order . . . the scale of human
> and spiritual values does not depend on our individual *self,* but on
> the nature of what *is. This* is what . . . is being questioned.[14]

Gide has set up, in its place, "a morality that does not judge, that tran-
scends good and evil, that has no room for the notion of honor, and that
suppresses the idea of sin . . . a vision of the universe which is in revolt
against 'all evidence,' against equilibrium, order, satisfaction, improve-
ment, which exalts the unconditioned, unexpected, ever-irrational ca-
price, where one laughs at all the human virtues, where intelligence and
will are excluded, where law is abolished, where there is no more honor,
no more sin, where crime itself is no shame, where the final gospel doctrine is nothing more than to live 'without care.' "[15]

        For all the partisan polemic, the gratuitous insults, the quotations
out of context of Massis's essays (Gide can always be made to appear
more diabolic by giving him lines from Ménalque or Michel or Lafca-

---

* The quotation is from Charles Maurras, not Gide.

dio), it is remarkable how accurately and honestly he has described Gide's intentions, or at least his effect. He remarks on Gide's manner of stirring up tranquil young souls, making them aware of their own latent disorders and contradictions, and then leaving them to fight out the problems of reorganization themselves: it is a perfect description of Gide's practice.

Much of Massis's attack—and of all the subsequent attacks—on Gide focused on his influence on the young: his first "too well-known" article was entitled "The Influence of André Gide." In Massis, this fear of Gide's corrupting influence remains general, and logical—he does not want to see the younger generation of France lose its soul by falling into the snares of Gide's new ethic. Even when he goes so far as to call "demoniac" Gide's clear-headed, artful attempts to disturb, to "pervert" ("There is only one word to describe such a man . . ."), he is working within the strict logic of his Faith.

But others were less discreet in their accusations. To "corrupt" and "pervert" young men implies to most people something other (and something worse) than persuading them to redefine their metaphysics. When one critic speaks of Gide's "poison" or "infection," another of "the most flagrantly unpunished . . . scandal of the century," [16] when Massis himself refers to young disciples of Gide's "lost body and soul," it seems clear that it is sexual perversion to which they are alluding.

It is no easier today than it was in 1927 to explain why most people respond as they do to the idea of homosexuality.* Paul Claudel, in 1914, spoke of "abominations" and "hideous practices," of "abnormal instincts" that are "neither permitted, nor excusable, nor admissible." [17] The Vatican newspaper, *L'Osservatore Romano,* lamented in 1952 that "Thanks to Gide, things which until now would have been whispered in the ear among adults have become something to boast of—to boast of indecently—among adolescents." [18] There is no question that Gide's public defense and confession of pederasty, in 1924 and 1926 respectively, alienated a great part of his sympathetic public and entrenched his antagonists in opposition. For Paul Souday, who could smile at Massis's belief in devils, this was going too far; Thibaudet drew back in some disgust; many simply said nothing. Charles Du Bos, one of Gide's more difficult convert friends, dedicated a hundred pages of his *Dialogue avec André Gide* (1929) to proving that since all sex is tragic, and homosexuality a frustrating, deviant, unnatural form of it, then it follows that the latter cannot possibly be the joyous business Gide pretended it was.

* Ramon Fernandez tried to, in Gide's case, in his *André Gide* (1931), pp. 172 ff.

It was Du Bos who first used the phrase "generalized inversion" with reference to Gide: what he meant was something like Massis's account of Gide's "overturn[ing] the laws of nature," turning "good" (restraint, obedience, submission) into "evil" (something to be fought against). He specifically insisted that his usage of the word "inversion" had nothing to do with Gide's sexual nature ("this kind of inversion exists, in my opinion, on an entirely *spiritual* plane, and any of us could be susceptible to it" [19]). But the phrase has since been commonly used in another and subtler point of attack against Gide, by which his entire ethic is reduced to nothing more than a function of his sexual aberration —and then studied or dismissed as something pathological at best.*

A great many of the attacks of this period were little more than vulgar, malicious gossip about Gide's character and habits. He notes a few instances in his journals—newspaper fictions of his avarice or hardheartedness, folklore about men who beat their wives on Gide's instructions, boys driven to suicide by his books. The usual innuendo, of course, behind the "corrupter of youth" label was that the fifty- to sixty-year-old Gide was seducing young lads into sexual perversions.

> "Perverting young people! . . . Oh, I know very well what they mean by that, these 'normal' people! What they always imagine!
> . . . They, when they chase after a woman, it's for one thing—to possess her: consequently, if someone seeks the love of a boy, it's obviously in order to abuse him. That's how far their imagination goes! 'Perverting young people': it's very clear what they mean— *to make young inverts out of them,* to take advantage of their desire to please, of their passivity . . . How am I to defend myself, how am I to convince them that in my own case—and I am not an exception—nothing could be more false? They would laugh in my face if I swore to them that never, never . . ."
>
> (Roger Martin du Gard, *Notes sur André Gide*)

Which brings us to the more important point. Not what case this or that literary journalist or defender of the faith may have made against Gide forty years ago, but what these accusations did to *him:* how he responded to them, how they changed him.

---

* My own reply to this mode of attack would be Gide's: "It is customary in our epoch to seek a physiological cause for an intellectual impulse; and I am not saying that this is wrong; what I am saying is that it is wrong to try to invalidate thereby the intrinsic value of the thought" (*Journal,* 1918).

That he was affected by these critiques and attacks, the above quotation bears witness. Few authors, in fact, could have paid quite such constant and devoted attention to their "press" as did André Gide. He subscribed to "clipping services" most of his life, and left tens of thousands of press notices on himself among his files when he died. His *Journal* for these years is filled with references to all of the attacks I have mentioned; some of them he keeps "answering" for years. An unidentified *they*—i.e., his critics taken *en masse*—becomes the subject of innumerable entries. It is true that "they" did mount against him a campaign of exceptional intensity; but still the attention he paid them betrays a sensitivity to attack almost unique, even among the *genus irritabile vatum.*

On more than one occasion he asserted that he was untroubled by all this abuse—"I shall let my books patiently choose their readers"; after all, they said the same things of Baudelaire. "The insults come to him only from people he despises," François Mauriac wrote on his behalf (in the 1928 *Hommage*). One would like to think this was so, but the evidence suggests that Gide's indifference was about as firm as Edouard's:

> Edouard has never made the slightest attempt to attract the good graces of the critics. If they choose to turn him a cold shoulder, he is completely indifferent. But as he reads their glowing articles on his rival's book, he has to keep reminding himself just how indifferent he is.   (*Les Faux-Monnayeurs*)

"I have become much less sensitive to blame," he wrote in 1924. "The launching of the attacks of the last few months has toughened my skin." [20] Well, perhaps. We have noted his expressions of "thanks" to certain critics. But such displays of poise are outmatched by hundreds of instances of an almost physical pain, of a wincing, a need to hit back. "Oh, if only you were invulnerable," his wife wrote early in 1922, "I should not tremble. But you are vulnerable, and you know it." [21]

And he did, finally. "I do not want to pretend to be stronger or more self-assured than I am, and some of these misjudgments are extremely painful to me." His immediate response, frequently, was a self-justifying entry in his journal, often followed by a counter-insult impugning his critic's motives. Jean de Gourmont was just "a little simpleton who is dominated by his late brother"; [22] André Breton was angling to win away Gide's young disciples; and as for Marcel Arland, "if he had plagiarized me less in the past, he would disavow me less vigorously today." [23] Gide was clearly hurt, and his responses often do him little honor. They

are bad enough in the *Journal;* but on occasion he stooped to answer
back immediately in the public prints. "After having been unknown,
misunderstood, for more than thirty years, and after having borne it with
a fine resigned and silent pride [wrote Martin du Gard in 1928], he
cannot resist the temptation to take his revenge at last. He has taken to
filling up the over-resonant corridors of the little world of letters with
the noise of his protests, his petty polemics. Oh, how I wish he could be
more detached, more indifferent." [24] The newly-famous Gide of the 20's
did seem to take a kind of pleasure in these low quarrels, and lays himself
open to Edouard's remark on his rival Passavant: "If he felt that his
work was going to last, he would leave it to defend itself, and would not
be constantly seeking to justify it." [25]

Part of the reason for Gide's sensitivity to criticism was, of course,
temperamental; part the result of his individualist ethic, which demanded constant rejustification. The reason he most often gave for his
annoyance, though, is the "falsification of my image" that these attacks
produced—and his "image" was becoming an increasingly important object of concern to André Gide.

> . . . the legend is gaining credit little by little. The public knows
> nothing of me but the caricature. . . . Even if some people have
> the curiosity to read me, they do so with such a mass of prejudices
> that the real meaning of my writings eludes them. They will end up
> by seeing in them what they have been told is there, and not see
> anything else. My sincerity is taken for a grimace, and for affecta-
> tion everything that contradicts the monster they have been per-
> suaded I am.[26]

It was this very "falsification of his image," Gide often claimed, that
impelled him to publish the confessions of *Si le grain ne meurt* (and, to
a lesser degree, the implied confessions of *Corydon*). If this is true, then
it is one of the most considerable literary events imputed to hostile reviewers since Byron blamed them for killing John Keats. I think it,
frankly, too simple an explanation, and Gide himself admitted (most
notably in letters to Edmund Gosse and André Rouveyre) that there
were other reasons, private and public, behind his daring and decisive
act: the stifling private moral pain of pretense, of living a lie ("it is not
the fact of *being* a uranist that matters, but of having established one's
life, at the start, as if one were not" [27]); and a public sense of mission, of
a salutary deed only he could perform:

> I wrote this book to "create a precedent," to set an example of
> candor; to enlighten some persons, hearten others, and compel
> public opinion to reckon with something of which it is oblivious, or
> pretends to be . . .[28]

Other reasons have been instanced, with greater or less sympathy, for the
publication of *Si le grain ne meurt*: exhibitionism; a will to martyrdom;
a perverted notion of sincerity; an answer to the priests; an answer to
Marcel Proust. (Proust's *Sodome et Gommorhe*—*Cities of the Plain,* in
English—had been published six years before, and Gide regarded it as a
harmful misrepresentation of the homosexual case.) I tend to think the
first, the private reason—the increasing difficulty Gide felt, as his public
image grew, of living a private lie—to have been the most exigent. It is
clearly linked to his "emancipation" during the previous decade, the result, as I have described it, of two interrelated events—his partial break
with Mme Gide, and his open acceptance and enjoyment of his own
sexual nature during his years with Marc Allégret. Now that more
people were looking at him, his peculiarly demanding conscience insisted
on a total revelation, a total emancipation, a total end to the public pretense of being a normal French husband—and to the public whispers
that he was something unspeakably worse. "He felt himself struck, not
because he thought himself guilty, but because he was masking his true
identity" (Pierre-Quint). But if the lies, the whispers, the questions, the
distortions were in some part responsible for pushing Gide's memoirs
into the light of day, then we may be grateful to his critics in proportion
to our admiration for *Si le grain ne meurt.*

This, then, is how Gide responded to his critics in the years of his first
fame. In what ways, now, can either critics or fame be said to have
changed either Gide or his works, for the last thirty years of his life?
  The first place to look, as so often, is the *Journal.* There the change
is considerable, and not entirely for the better. What had been an instrument of private therapy, often dramatic, vacillating, appealingly unsure,
becomes more and more a weapon, an instrument of public polemic in
defense of the works and person of André Gide. More and more, the
privacy of the journal seems a ruse, a device used to get even with enemies he cannot (or dare not) attack in public. There is even a mild hint
of paranoia, of battles mounted from a writing desk against imagined
enemies who are not present and cannot reply. This is all an impression:

much of what Gide was writing may have been justified by the campaigns of attack. But read today *in vacuo,* as it were, out of context, it creates an unfortunate effect. All those angry letters of self-defense—"which, naturally, I do not send"—but which he does publish.

Which leads into a very important (and perhaps unanswerable) question: Just when did Gide first begin to nourish the idea of publishing his journals? and how did this idea alter their nature?

As early as 1893, he was tearing out from his journal pages he didn't like, pages "which take for granted a future fame or celebrity that will render them interesting. And that is utterly base." In 1909–1910, he contributed regularly a "Journal sans Dates" to the *N.R.F.,* pages of public, literary reflections often taken direct from his private journal. The first hint I find (after 1893) that he may be thinking of his journals as books in print, read by others—whether during his lifetime or after—is in February 1916: "If these notebooks should come to light, later on, how many will they repel, even then!" His desolation, in November of that year, over the loss of his letters to Madeleine, proves that he foresaw at least the posthumous publication of his private papers. "If my journal is published later on," he wrote in February 1924—how *much* later on?—"I fear that it will give a rather false idea of me." A journal written in the shadow of such an idea is perhaps already on its way to becoming "false" itself.

Travel journals—which don't quite count—Gide had been publishing ever since 1891, including the relatively intimate *Amyntas* of 1906. But with *Voyage au Congo,* which began appearing in installments in the *N.R.F.* in November 1926, he was naming names, and citing his own private daily behavior more explicitly than he had ever done in public print before. Roger Martin du Gard, on watch as ever, saw fit to warn Gide of the dangers involved. But a precedent had already been set: in the *Journal des Faux-Monnayeurs,* printed in the *N.R.F.* for August–September 1926, Gide had interspersed paragraphs of technical reflections with accounts of his dreams and conversations.

It is in mid-1926, then, that Gide clearly came to some decision about publishing at least parts of his *Journal intime* (thereby ending its status as a *journal intime*). He is sending important pages from his journals-in-progress—sometimes within weeks after writing them—to the *N.R.F.* from June 1932 on, and he begins to print it substantially (although leaving out many names) in Volume III of his *Œuvres complètes,* which came out in March of 1933. (The fifteenth volume, of 1939, brings his *Journal* up to 1932; he had already printed pages from

1932–1935 in 1936, however, and finally brought out the whole, 1889–1939, in the one-volume Pléiade edition of the latter year.)

We are interested here, though, in the period 1920–1932: toward the end of this period, Gide is admitting that a change has taken place. "By now [October 1930] . . . I am too well aware that I am being observed . . ." "Some time ago [March 1932] this notebook ceased to be what it ought to be: an intimate confidant. The perspective of even a partial publication of my journal, as an appendix to the volumes of my *Œuvres complètes,* has distorted its meaning." Already in 1929, Paul Valéry was complaining, "I want to talk to you, but I see at once the hand of the writer, the page of your *Journal,* and the *Nrf* with its pink wrapper." [29]

> The *Journal,* in its last twenty years, became less and less the essential work that it had been at the beginning. . . . [Gide became aware,] about 1926–1927, that everything he entered in his *Journal* would be, in ever shorter lapses of time, delivered up to the public—whence its half-confessed character of a "speech for the defense."
>
> > (Claude Martin,
> > *André Gide par lui-même*)

But all this falls short of explaining the really radical changes that I think fame (and to a degree age, and the release from certain private tensions) brought to André Gide. In the same two letters in which Valéry complained to Gide about his indiscreet publishing of their private conversations, he tried to explain the peculiar things that notoriety had done to his own sense of self, and why he clung so tenaciously to what was left him of privacy.

> As for myself, I no longer *see* myself . . .
>
> The base has not changed; you know how simple that is. But between *Me* and *me,* things and people have set up a ring of coral. I am an Atoll.
>
> Between *You* and *Me* is built up the fact that we are both public objects . . .
>
> . . . it is annoying to live as a third party among strangers . . .
>
> This sensibility has become more extreme the more I became a public man. Between my name and my *self,* I make an abysmal distinction . . .[30]

I think the gap, for Gide, between his "name" and his "self" was equally wide; but I am not sure he was as aware of this as his friend was. In December 1924 he vowed not to write anything he would not have written *without* the complications of fame; "The essential thing . . . is to go on being what one is, just as simply as if this weren't being questioned." And perhaps he did. But there is a revealing admission in a letter he wrote to Roger on February 1, 1931: "When I find myself called on to play the star, I do it without conviction, timidly; or else swaggering about and posing. I am playing a role that I would have liked not to have assumed until after my death."

What *does* happen to a man, a man with the temperament we have seen, when he suddenly realizes that a great number of people are watching him?

I think one must begin by admitting that age and "emancipation" had already changed Gide considerably by the mid-20's. Many have remarked on the new "serenity" that he seemed to respire after his return from the Congo. He himself noted, with some distaste, the wrinkles, the torpor, the waning of physical desire: "acceptance; confidence; serenity: virtues of an old man. The age of struggling with the angel is over." "For a long time I have not experienced anything intense, not even self-disgust or boredom." [31] He is nearing sixty, and he begins to complain about the immaturity and haste of the younger generation of writers. He even rudely disclaims, in the guise of his *Œdipe,* the young men he was so notoriously supposed to be "influencing": "From my example they have taken only what they find comforting—the justifications and the license—overlooking the constraint; overlooking the difficult and the best." [32]

His own writing, he confesses (except for the *Journal*) is becoming mechanical, the dull duty of a professional man of letters. He had said, in *Si le grain ne meurt* and *Corydon,* the "great thing" he had to say, he had freed himself from the anguish that made writing necessary. "Certainly I am no longer tormented by an imperious desire to write." [33] With no exhilarating new enterprises like the *N.R.F.,* with no surrounding crises like the world war, with no great private despair and no great private joy, he was freed . . . to do what?

To a considerable degree, to do what Marcel Proust did: spend the last third of his life staring at, studying, analyzing, and writing about the first two-thirds.

And here the various pieces of this chapter fall together—the 70,000 press clippings; the wrangling with critics; the thanks to Massis for letting him see "what he is"; the private journal sent off to the publishers; the concern over a "falsified" image; Valéry's notion of a *Moi* forever separated from a *moi*. Gide was freed, yes: freed to contemplate his *œuvre,* to curry his image, to mull over his "profound significance," the "significance" his antagonists had taught him all too well, the significance of an André Gide who no longer was, an André Gide who had died when his public image was born. He turned into a kind of master scholar or curator of the works of André Gide, reading and judging theses and studies on himself, defending his subject against all comers, devotedly tending his own shrine and rearranging his own image for posterity. It is a very strange thing to observe.

This is not the whole story of these years, of course. The birth of his daughter Catherine, his relations with Marc and Madeleine, his extraordinary trip to Central Africa, other friends, other travels, his reading, his writing—particularly of *Les Faux-Monnayeurs*—these are all part of 1920–1932. The wise reflections of his *Journal,* the genial and various self of his letters would qualify and brighten the image I have drawn of André Gide confronting his Fame. But this confrontation, I am convinced, is the single most important fact of Gide's life in the 1920's.

from

THE JOURNAL

1 9 2 0 – 1 9 2 5

1920   *October 5*

The 6th, day of my departure for Cuverville, Roger Martin du Gard comes to the Villa at nine-thirty. He brings back *Si le grain ne meurt,* of which I had taken him a copy the day before yesterday. He informs me of his deep disappointment: I have sidestepped my subject; from fear, modesty, anxiety about the public, I have dared to say nothing really intimate and only succeeded in arousing questions. . . .

Since I have been here, received from him a long, excellent letter in which he goes over all the points our conversation had touched upon. And yet I honestly feel that I have related of my childhood everything of which I have kept any recollection and as indiscreetly as possible. It would be artificial to put more shadow, more secrecy, more deviousness into it. Perhaps, however, Jacques Raverat is right when he tells me (he came yesterday from Montivilliers) that often my account, in an effort to be clear, simplifies my acts a bit too much, or at least my motives—and that it is true here as it is of all my books, each one of which taken by itself falsifies my figure. "In order to have a portrait of you more or less lifelike," he told me very justly, "one would have to be able to read them all at the same time. As soon as one knows you well, one understands that all of the states which, in the interests of art, you depict as successive can be simultaneous in you; and this is just what the accounts in your Memoirs do not make one feel."

October 28

Yesterday evening I took out all my youthful "journals." I cannot reread them without exasperation—and were it not for the salutary *humiliation* I find in reading them, I should tear up everything.

Each step forward in the art of writing is bought only by the yielding up of some self-satisfaction. At that time I had more than my share, and hung over the blank page as one does a mirror.

Before my departure, went to see *Parade*—of which I don't know what to admire the more: the pretension or the poverty. Cocteau is walking up and down in the wings, where I go to see him; aged, contracted, painful. He knows that the sets and costumes are by Picasso, that the music is by Satie, but he wonders if Picasso and Satie are not by him.

January 3 [from *Journal intime*]

Oh, if only I could believe that my presence here was pleasing to her. . . . But even that joy is denied me; and all day long I can think only that she is merely tolerating me. Nothing of me interests her any more or matters to her; and, as it always takes love to understand what differs from you, I feel nothing in her toward me but incomprehension, misjudgment, or, what is worse, indifference.

And yet, at times, I wonder if I am not mistaken as well. Ah, if only we could talk it over! But the least words issue so painfully from my heart that I no longer know how to talk to her.*

If only I were permitted the hope of bringing her a little happiness. . . .

January 6 [from *Journal intime*]

It is with despair that now he realizes that it was only out of love for him that she interested herself in those things (art, music, poetry) which for him remain the supreme occupation of his life. She ceased to take pleasure in them and to believe in them at the same time that she lost her love for him.

January 12

When the path your mind begins to take saddens unto death creatures who are infinitely dear to you, you can, at one and the same time, believe that it is the path you must follow and yet advance in it trembling; remain with a divided heart; know hesitations and backward steps . . .

---

* That was indeed the most tragic part of it: that frightful silence during those long days, those long successions of days which we lived in each other's company. And this is also, often at the limit of my endurance and feeling my love agonizing in that silence, what made me entrust at least to my *Journal*, in these pages I am transcribing, what I could not manage to tell her. (1947) [A. G.]

January 26 [from *Journal intime*]

I no longer savor here even the joy of making her happy; that is to say, I no longer have that illusion; and the thought of that failure haunts my nights. I have even come to the point of thinking my love a burden to her; and at times I reproach myself with that love as a weakness, a madness, and try to argue myself into giving it up and ending this suffering. . . . I cannot reconcile myself to the divorce of our thoughts. She is the only one I love in the world, and I really cannot love anyone but her. I cannot live without her love. I am willing to have the whole world against me, but not her. And I have to hide all this from her. I must act out with her a comedy of happiness such as she is acting out with me.

May 14

Spent an hour of yesterday evening with Proust. For the last four days he has been sending a car to pick me up every evening, but each time it missed me. . . . Yesterday, as I had in fact just told him that I did not expect to be free, he was getting ready to go out, having made a rendezvous in town. He says that he has not been out of bed for a long time. Although it is stifling in the room in which he receives me, he is shivering; he has just left another, much hotter room, where he was drenched in perspiration; he complains that his life is nothing but a slow agony, and although he had begun, as soon as I arrived, to talk of homosexuality, he interrupted himself to ask me if I could enlighten him somewhat as to the teaching of the Gospels; someone or other has told him that I talk particularly well on the subject. He hopes to find there some support and relief for his sufferings, which he describes at great length as atrocious. He is fat, or rather puffy; he reminds me somewhat of Jean Lorrain. I am bringing him *Corydon;* he promises to speak to no one about it; and when I say a word or two about my Memoirs:

"You can tell everything," he exclaims; "on the condition that you never say *I.*" Which will certainly not suit me.

Far from denying or hiding his homosexuality, he displays it, one might almost say boasts of it. He claims never to have loved women except spiritually, and never to have known love except with men. His conversation, everlastingly cut across by relative clauses, runs on with no sense of order. He tells me his conviction that Baudelaire was homosexual: "The way in which he speaks of Lesbos, in fact the mere need of speaking of it, would be enough to convince me," and when I protest:

"In any case, if he was homosexual, it was almost without his knowing it; and you can't believe that he ever practiced. . . ."

"What!" he exclaims. "Why, I am sure of the contrary; how can you doubt that he practiced? He, Baudelaire!"

And in the tone of his voice it is implied that by doubting I am insulting Baudelaire. But I am willing to believe that he is right; and that homosexuals are even a bit more numerous than I thought at first. In any case I did not think that Proust was so exclusively so.

Wednesday

For a long time I wondered if Proust did not take advantage somewhat of his illness to protect his work (and this seemed quite legitimate to me); but yesterday, and already the other day, I could see for myself that he is really seriously ill. He says he spends hours on end without being able even to move his head; he stays in bed all day long, for day after day. At moments he traces down the side of his nose with the edge of a hand that seems dead, with its fingers oddly stiff and separated, and nothing could leave more of an impression than this eccentric, awkward gesture, which seems the gesture of an animal or a madman.

We scarcely talked, this evening again, of anything but homosexuality. He says he blames himself for that "indecision" which made him transpose into *"à l'ombre des jeunes filles"* (in order to feed the heterosexual part of his book) all the gracious, tender, and appealing memories of his homosexual experiences, so that he had nothing left for *Sodome* but the grotesque and the abject. But he is evidently quite affected when I tell him that he seems to have wanted to stigmatize homosexuality; he protests; and eventually I understand that what we consider vile, an object of laughter or disgust, does not seem so repulsive to him.

When I ask him if he is never going to present us that Eros in a young and beautiful guise, he replies that, to begin with, what attracts him is almost never beauty; he considers it to have very little to do with desire— and that, as for youth, this was what he could most easily transpose (what lent itself best to a transposition).

July 11

That felicity I had promised myself from a perfect communion with her is receding from my grasp; and now it seems that my desire for everything else is less ardent.

July 14

Finished the third chapter of the second part of *Si le grain ne meurt* . . . —That is to say, all that I intend giving to the printer now. I doubt whether I shall be able to extend the writing of these Memoirs any further than this. And yet what interest they would have!

July 20

Struggle against that itching to pour personal experiences into the novel, and particularly those which have made one suffer, in the fallacious hope of finding some consolation in the picturesque rendering one gives them.

They would not appear particularly interesting to us if we were not the ones they had happened to.

July 21

The declarations of the nationalists too often make me think of the protestations of Lear's daughters. The deepest love does not leap so easily to the lips. I hold for the silence of Cordelia.

Colpach, August 28

A blind man could imagine colors more easily than an insensitive person could imagine the mysterious attraction that emanates from the appearance of a body. How could he understand that agitation, that need of enveloping, of caressing, that commandeering of our whole being, the wandering imprecision of desire?

Cuverville, October 12 [from *Journal intime*]

I manage to protect my tranquillity, to maintain my even temper, and to preserve some interest in work, in life itself, only by turning my attention away from her, from her situation, from our relationship. If I happen to think of this at night, there can be no question of sleep, and I roll into an abyss of anguish and despair. At such times I feel that I love her as much as ever and suffer frightfully at not being able to let her know this. This attitude she imposes on me, this mask of indifference that she forces me to put on, certainly seems to her more sincere than whatever truth I might try to stammer out. She holds fast to it; and I have no right to disturb the calm it gives her. In order to maintain that calm, she needs to believe that I no longer love her, that I never loved her much; it is only thus, no doubt, that she can maintain a sort of apathy in my regard.

October 16

Leaving Cuverville this time was like dying.

October 17

I drag after me an abominable fatigue and melancholy. All humanity seems to me desperately ugly and tarnished. What bestiality, what egotism in the expression of all these faces! What an absence of joy, of real life! Is it to redeem each of these that a Christ died?

November 1

Arrived yesterday evening at Roquebrune. . . . The nearer I came to the moment of leaving her, the more painfully I felt everything that attached me to her, and I came to wonder if reason really counseled this departure. How hard I find it not to prefer the more austere course, or at least not to believe in its superiority! Instinctive distrust for everything that pleasure adorns.

November 26

Returned to Cuverville the evening of the 24th. It seems to me now that I dreamed this trip . . . Pisa, Siena, Orvieto, Rome; perfect weather, if it had not been taken from work. Immediately I plunge into it again, cursing that lecture on Dostoevsky for which Copeau, on my way through Paris, extracted the promise.

November 29

Only today have I returned to the piano. I am rereading *The Idiot,* and have again plunged with intoxication into *The Ring and the Book,* which I understand much more easily. There is nothing headier than Browning, not even Dostoevsky. Yet perhaps I should get less excited if I knew his language perfectly. The slight fog that occasionally floats between the lines lends them imaginary depths.

December 2

I have read Proust's latest pages (December issue of the *N.R.F.*) with, at first, a shock of indignation. Knowing what he thinks, what he is, it is hard for me to see in them anything but a pretense, a desire to protect himself, a camouflage of the cleverest sort, for it can be to no one's advantage to denounce him. Even more: that offense to truth will probably please everybody: heterosexuals, whose prejudices it justifies and whose repugnances it flatters; and the others, who will take advantage of the alibi and their lack of resemblance to those he portrays. In short, considering the public's cowardice, I do not know any writing that is more capable than Proust's *Sodome et Gomorrhe* of confirming the error of public opinion.

December 12 [from *Journal intime*]

What am I to do? What is to become of me? Where shall I go? I cannot stop loving her. Her face on certain days, the angelic expression of her smile, still fill my heart with ecstasy, love, and despair. Despair at being unable to tell her this. Not a single day, not a single moment, have I dared speak to her. Both of us remain walled up in our silence. And occasionally I tell myself that it is better so, and that anything I could say to her would merely bring on other sufferings.

I cannot imagine myself without her; it seems to me that without her I should never have been *anything*. Each of my thoughts came into being in relation to her. For whom else should I have felt so urgent a need to explain myself?

December 15

"M. Gide does not even incarnate a literary school, not even the review for which he writes. His work is the most flagrantly unpunished intellectual and moral scandal of the century," I read in *La Revue française* that the Argus clipping-service sends me this morning. It is signed René Johannet.

This is the two hundred and eighth clipping (I paid the bill six weeks ago). In addition to advertisements, I receive nothing but savage attacks.

December 26

Prolonged insomnia. Never have I felt my mind so active. Last night, if I had had a secretary at hand, I should have dictated a quarter of a book.

I have heard it said that I am running after my youth. This is true. And not only after my own. Even more than beauty, youth attracts me, and with an irresistible appeal. I believe that the truth lies therein; I believe that youth is always right when it takes sides against us. . . .

Very few of my contemporaries have remained faithful to their youth. They have almost all compromised. That is what they call "learning from life." They have denied the truth that was in them. The borrowed truths are the ones to which one clings most tenaciously, all the more so because they remain alien to one's intimate self. Much more care is required to deliver one's own message, much more boldness and prudence, than to sign one's name and add one's voice to a party someone else has already formed. Whence that accusation of indecision, of uncertainty that some people hurl at my head, precisely because I believed that it is above all to oneself that it is important to remain faithful.

I call "journalism" everything that will be less interesting tomorrow than today. How many great artists win their cases only on appeal!

1922   *January 3*

Em. writes : "What troubles me so much is this vicious campaign they have started against you. Of course it is the force of your thought and its authority that have set this in motion. Oh! if only you were invulnerable, I should not tremble. But you are vulnerable, and you know it; and I know it."

Vulnerable . . . I am so, I was so, only through her. Since it is of no consequence to me, I no longer fear anything. . . . What have I to lose that is still dear to me?

January 16

Charlie Du Bos sends me *The Marriage of Heaven and Hell,* which I had told him I wished to read, sure as I was of finding in it a revelation and a confirmation of certain thoughts that have been stirring within me for a long time. My meeting with Blake is an event of the greatest importance to me. Already I had glimpsed him, during the first year of the war, in a book of *Selections* from Elisabeth van Rysselberghe's library, rue Laugier, where I was then living with the Théos. Like an astronomer who postulates the existence of a star whose rays he does not yet perceive directly, I foresaw Blake, but did not yet suspect that he formed a constellation with Nietzsche, Browning, and Dostoevsky. The most brilliant star, perhaps, of this group; certainly the strangest and the most distant.

February 4

Freud. Freudianism. . . . For the last ten, fifteen years, I have been indulging in it without knowing it. . . .

"Here is something that, I fear, will bring grist to your mill," Rivière said to me.the other day, speaking of Freud's little book on sexual development. I should say!

It is high time to publish *Corydon*.

February 18

Yesterday, first lecture on Dostoevsky. Too many quotations, far too many. A certain intellectual shyness, modesty, impelled me to yield the floor to Dostoevsky as much as possible; it was also the fear of falling short of my time that made me prepare those quotations in advance, like so many safety-islands—which I had to use even after they had become useless. All together, rather dissatisfied with myself; *very* dissatisfied when I think of what it might have been. But this will be a lesson for the next one.

March 17

Relapse; fatigue and apathy. The dizzy spells have become so frequent that I no longer dare risk making plans to see anyone. I delivered my fourth lecture last Saturday in such a state of discomfort that I wondered whether or not I could get through it; the theater walls swayed before my eyes; but my thoughts were swinging back and forth even more. I began each sentence without having any idea how I should finish it; without even knowing what I could fill it up with. It goes without saying that that lecture was "the best," if I am to believe those who complimented me on the way out.

March 22

Constant vertigo; fatigue. Return of winter; we are shivering. Everything takes on a frightful taste of ashes.

I do not understand very well what they mean by "my influence." Where do they see it? I don't recognize myself anywhere. It is what differs most from me that I prefer; I have never tried to push anyone anywhere but in his own path, toward his own joy.

A good teacher is constantly preoccupied with teaching his pupils how to get along without him. But because I say to Nathaniel, at the end of my book: "And now throw away this book; leave me," they get angry.

For me, sadness is almost never anything but a form of fatigue. But I must confess that there have been moments, these last few days, when I have felt mortally sad.

March 28

Gave, last Saturday, my last lecture on Dostoevsky. In view of my great fatigue, and fearing that I might lack presence of mind, I had written down almost all of it.

July 14

This morning, I finish translating the first act of *Hamlet* and decide to go no further. I have spent three weeks on these few pages, at the rate of four to six hours a day. The result does not satisfy me. The difficulty is never completely overcome, and in order to write good French, one has to leave Shakespeare too far behind. (It seems to me that this is peculiar to *Hamlet,* that the text of *Antony and Cleopatra* was much less thorny and allowed one to follow it better. And though the very subject of *Hamlet* is stranger, richer, more subtle, and touches us more deeply right now, I did not for a moment experience those trances of rapture that shook me all through the reading of *Othello*.) Marcel Schwob's translation, exact though it be, is obscure, almost incomprehensible in spots, amorphous, arhythmical; it seems to be unbreathable. Is it really this text that we heard at Sarah Bernhardt's?—without changes, without cuts? What a cumbersome strain it must have been for the actors! Certain of Shakespeare's sentences are diabolically twisted, full of redundancies . . . I should like an Englishman to explain their beauty to me. Faced with Schwob's sentences, which strive to sacrifice neither a repetition nor a turning, you think: It must be very beautiful in English. But *Hamlet* has been a sacred text so long we admire it without questioning.

Carry-le-Rouet, August 4

It is not a fear of being mistaken, it is a need of sympathy that makes me seek with passionate anxiety the call or the recall of my own thought in others; . . . that made me translate Blake and present my own ethic under the shelter of Dostoevsky's. . . . —Nothing is so absurd as that accusation of *influence* (in which certain critics excel every time they note a resemblance).—How many things, on the contrary, I *have not said* because I later discovered them in others! Nietzsche's influence on me? . . . I was already writing *L'Immoraliste* when I discovered him. Who could say how much he got in my way . . . ?

August 5

However tedious that work may have been (the translation of *Hamlet*), now I miss it. My idle mind slips toward melancholy despite my effort to brake it on the slope. . . .

Carry-le Rouet, August 7 [from *Journal intime*]

A letter from her. A simple little sentence announcing that she has given to her godchild Sabine Schlumberger the gold necklace and little emerald cross she used to wear; it cuts me like a knife in the heart. That cross, which I lent to Alissa in the novel—I cannot bear the idea that anyone else should wear that cross. . . . What can I write in reply? She no longer believes in my love and does not want to know the least thing about my heart. In order to detach herself from me more completely, she needs to believe in my indifference. I think I have never loved her more; I hate myself for having made her suffer, for making her suffer still. I no longer cling to anything; I often feel so detached from everything at this point that it seems to me I am already dead and was living only through her.

Colpach, September 10 [from *Journal intime*]

. . . I feel forsaken by her. Everything good, generous, pure that she aroused in my being relapses, and that abominable ebbing draws me down toward hell. Often I wonder, as I did at Llanberis, whether she is not secretly and mystically warned, by some exquisite intuition, of all I do at a distance from her, or at least of whatever might wound her the most.* Did she not give away her necklace the very day when, on the beach at Hyères, Elisabeth came to join me (16 July)? † . . .

* Gide visited Llanberis (Wales) with Marc Allégret in August 1920.
† Elisabeth van Rysselberghe gave birth to Gide's daughter Catherine in April 1923. According to Jean Lambert, who married Catherine Gide in 1946, Gide first asked Elisabeth (who was almost thirty years his junior) if she would bear his child in a note slipped to her on a train as they were returning from a friend's funeral in December 1916. (Jean Lambert, *Gide familier* [Paris, 1958], p. 91). Claude Martin discreetly suggests, on the evidence of a passage in Gide's novel *Geneviève,* that the adventure referred to in this *Journal* entry may have been a loveless experiment that Gide undertook simply to verify his procreative power. "For I was elsewhere able to prove that I was not incapable of the impulse (I am speaking of the procreative impulse), but only providing that there was no admixture of the intellectual or the sentimental" (*Et nunc manet in te,* in *Journal* 1939–1949 [Pléiade ed.], p. 1130). See also C. Martin, *André Gide par lui-même* (Paris, 1967), pp. 134–5; A. Gide, *Geneviève,* in *Romans* (Pléiade ed.), pp. 140–6.

Sunday, November 12 (?)

Leaving for Paris tomorrow, where I am going to spend a week. Altogether, worked rather well of late. Wrote the first thirty pages, more or less, of *Les Faux-Monnayeurs*. Went over *Corydon* and wrote the *Préface*. Learned by heart the three odes of Keats (*To a Nightingale, To Psyche, To Autumn*). Reread *Les Provinciales, La Double Méprise,* and aloud *La Maison Nucingen* and *Les Secrets de la Princesse de Cadignan.*

I am reading rapidly, but with a rather lively interest, *Les Mystères de Paris* and, with the most complete and firm adherence, Sainte-Beuve's *Port-Royal* (but I turned at once to the third volume to accompany my reading of *Les Provinciales*).*

December 21

In Christianity, and each time that I plunge into it again, it is always she that I am pursuing. She feels this, perhaps; but what she feels above all is that I do so in order to tear her away from it.

Wednesday

Stopped at the Terminus. With M. and his mistress, B., spent one of the dullest evenings, at the Casino de Paris, where everything seemed to me frightful. Silliness, vulgarity, lack of taste, idiotic and hideous spectacle of the costumes.

1923   *January 11*

I say a few words to Em. of the "drama" that calls me to the side of E.†

I have no reason to hope, or even to wish, that Em. should ever be able to consider what she glimpses and imagines of that story otherwise than as a most lamentable catastrophe. And yet it is with the greatest difficulty that I keep from protesting when she concludes, from the little I dare tell her: "I have always thought it was unfortunate that El. was brought up without religion."

---

* *Les Provinciales* by Pascal; *La Double Méprise* by Mérimée; *La Maison Nucingen* and *Les Secrets de la Princesse de Cadignan* by Balzac; *Les Mystères de Paris* by Eugène Sue.
† Elisabeth van Rysselberghe. The "drama," of course, is that of Elisabeth's pregnancy. It is presumed that Gide's "few words" did not include a revelation of his own role. Catherine was born at Annecy in April.

Leaving for Roquebrune, for Genoa, for the unknown.—I never leave Cuverville without a sort of heartbreak.

A week at Annecy with E. Charming little Savoie hotel, of which, thanks to the season, we are the only guests. Read aloud Shakespeare's *Merry Wives* and *The Vicar of Wakefield,* which delights us. I finish at Annecy Keats's wonderful *Endymion,* which I did not yet know and which kept me in a state of drunkenness for days on end.

The air is light; the warmth gentle; the sky radiant. Casablanca, where I was expecting only shapeless warehouses, delights me. I don't regret in the least that it does not have a more "African" character.

The triumph of objectivity is allowing the novelist to borrow the "I" of other people. I have misled my readers by succeeding too well in this; some have taken my books for a series of successive confessions. That abnegation, that poetic depersonalization that makes me feel the joys and sorrows of others more keenly than my own—no one has described it so well as Keats (*Letters*).

The good writing I admire is that which, without drawing too much attention to itself, makes the reader stop and pause, and forces his thought to advance slowly. I want his attention to sink at every step into a soil rich and deeply broken. But what the reader generally looks for is a kind of endless belt that will carry him along.

It seems to them that one has ceased to advance as soon as one no longer advances in their direction.

Nothing irritates certain Catholics more than to see us attain naturally to a renunciation that they, with all their religion, have such difficulty achieving. If they could, they would accuse you of cheating; virtue must remain their monopoly, and whatever you achieve without saying your beads doesn't count. Likewise, they do not forgive us our happiness; it is impious; they alone have the right to be happy. It is, moreover, a right they rarely indulge.

Saint-Martin-Vésubie, July 11 [from *Journal intime*]

I have never wanted anything but *her* love, *her* approval, *her* esteem. And since she has withdrawn all that from me, I have lived in a sort of infamy in which good has lost its reward and evil its ugliness, even pain its sting. A kind of numbness of my soul is matched by a deadening of all things, and nothing sharp ever penetrates me any more; indeed, *nothing* really penetrates me.

July 18

Finished rereading for the third time from cover to cover the collection of Shakespeare's *Sonnets.* And I read each sonnet twice in succession. Many among them are exasperating; but there are many whose suavity appears only on rereading. To be sure, I admire them; but I also admire myself considerably for having got to the point of admiring them. . . .

July 21

Spent the night at Nice; arrived at Hyères-Plage yesterday. Swim yesterday; swim today, after which an extraordinary sense of well-being. I breathe better than at Saint-Martin; here I find the air lighter and the temperature less overwhelming. The sea is indescribably beautiful. And no flies!

At Nice spent the morning playing with a wonderful child of four, brown as a mushroom, laughing and brazen; and talking with his eighteen-year-old sister, as tanned as he was, gay and apparently naked under a floating black dress. She lets me take the little fellow to the Galeries Lafayette, where I buy him a pistol with darts. For love of them I should have been glad to stay in Nice and almost missed my train.

Finished *The Tempest.*

August 3

I am taking Elisabeth van Rysselberghe and André Allégret to Corsica. We embark this morning for Ajaccio.

Vizzavone, August 5

Wonderful Monte d'Oro; one of the most beautiful peaks I have seen. Long walk this morning; reached the crest opposite the mountain, then came back down through the narrow valley inhabited by pines of an unknown variety that look like cedars and give a Chinese look to the landscape. Bathed twice in deep basins while following the bed of the torrent. Ah, how much less young I felt at twenty!

August 11

Back to Nice on the 9th. Yesterday traveled by night. Stop at Carnoules from three a.m. to six. We sleep on a bench. Splendid night. Behind the station, to the left, a tremendous forest fire lights up the sky; to the right, high in the sky, a thin crescent moon.

October 10

On certain days, at certain moments, I lose completely the notion of reality. It seems to me that at the least misstep I am going to slip into the other side of the scenery.

November 21

Went to see Bernard Faÿ, who talks to me at length of his brother Emmanuel, M.'s friend. He has just died in New York. He did not kill himself, but it's the same thing: he let himself die; he made himself die. He said to his brother, one of the last days:

"One has no heart in playing, in a world where everyone cheats."

December 21

Jacques Maritain came then Friday morning, December 14, to the Villa on the stroke of ten, as it had been agreed. I had prepared a few sentences, but none of them was of any use, for I understood at once that I did not have to play a character in his presence, but on the contrary had simply to reveal myself, and that this was my best defense. His curved, bent way of carrying his head and his whole body displeased me, and a certain clerical unction in his voice and gesture; but I overlooked that, and pretense seemed unworthy of the two of us. He tackled the question at once and declared without circumlocution the purpose of his visit, which I knew and which was to beg me to suspend the publication of a certain book*

* *Corydon.*

that François Le Grix had told him must be imminent, and of which he begged me to recognize, as he did, the danger.

I told him that I had no intention of defending myself, but that he must be aware that everything he could think of saying to me about this book I had already said to myself, and that a project that resists the trials of the war, of lost friends, and of all the meditations that ensue runs the risk of being too deeply anchored in the heart and mind for an intervention like his to hope to be able to change it. I protested that, moreover, there had been no obstinacy in my case and that even after a first reading to a friend (Marcel Drouin) ten years ago of the first two chapters of this book, on the advice of that friend I had interrupted my work; that I had almost given it up, despite the profound disarray that renunciation caused me; that if, at the end of the second year of the war, I had nonetheless taken it up again and completed it, that was because it appeared clear to me that this book had to be written, that I was uniquely qualified to write it, and that I could not without a sort of moral bankruptcy release myself from what I considered my duty.

We both spoke with extreme slowness, anxious to propose nothing that might misconstrue or go beyond our thought. He conveyed to me Henri Massis's fear of having, by the provocation of his articles, hastened that publication. I begged him to leave Massis all his fears and regrets and remorse, and spoke of the wonderful letter Claudel had written me, also on the subject of my *Dostoevsky,* in which I felt at least the animation of a truly Christian mind, which I did not recognize in the least in Massis's articles. Maritain then told me that Massis might have made a mistake, and as I indicated to him certain points in those articles that obviously revealed a desire to falsify my thought: "He may not have understood it properly . . . ." I protested that he was too intelligent on other points not to force me to regard that falsification as conscious and voluntary.

"I have," I told him, "a horror of falsehood. It is perhaps here that my Protestantism has taken refuge. Catholics cannot understand that. I have known many; and indeed, with the single exception of Jean Schlumberger, I have nothing but Catholics as friends. Catholics do not like the truth."

"Catholicism teaches the love of truth," he said.

"No, do not protest, Maritain. I have too often seen, and with too many examples, what 'accommodations' were possible. And even (for I have that intellectual failing, which Ghéon used to reproach me with, of too easily putting words into my adversary's mouth and of inventing arguments for him) I see what you might reply to me: that the Protestant often confuses truth with God, that he adores Truth, not understanding that Truth is but one of the attributes of God. . . ."

"But don't you think that this particular truth, the truth your book claims to reveal, can be dangerous? . . ."

"If I thought so, I should not have written the book, or at least I should not publish it. However dangerous that truth may be, I hold that the falsehood that covers it is even more dangerous."

"And don't you think that it is dangerous for you to say it?"

"That is a question that I refuse to ask myself."

He then spoke to me of the salvation of my soul and told me that he often prayed for it, as did several of his friends who were convinced, as he was, that I had been designated by God for higher ends, which I sought in vain to evade.

"I am inclined to believe," I said to him smiling, "that you are much more concerned with the salvation of my soul than I am myself."

We spoke at length, on this subject and likewise of the Greek equilibrium and the Christian lack of equilibrium. As the hour was advancing, he made a motion as if to rise.

"I should not like to leave you before—Will you allow me to ask you something?"

"Ask whatever you like," I said with a gesture indicating that I did not guarantee a reply.

"I should like to ask a promise of you."

"? . . ."

"Promise me that when I have gone you will put yourself in a state of prayer and ask Christ to let you know, directly, whether you are right or wrong to publish this book. Can you promise me that?"

I looked at him for a long time and said: "No."

There was a long silence. I continued: "Understand me, Maritain. I have lived too long and too intimately in the thought of Christ, as you well know, to agree to call on him today as one calls someone up on the telephone. Indeed, it would seem to me unworthy to call on him without having first put myself in a state to listen to him. Oh! I do not doubt that I can succeed in doing so. I know, moreover, just how that state is achieved; I have the recipe. But on my part there would be, today, a certain amount of affectation, and I should find that repugnant. And moreover, may I tell you this: never, even at the time of my greatest fervor, even at the time when I used to pray—I do not say only every day, but at every hour, at every moment of the day—never was my prayer anything but an act of adoration, a thanksgiving, a surrender. Perhaps this is simply an indication of how much a Protestant I am. There are some who would ask Christ's advice about how to tie a pair of shoelaces; I cannot; I will not. It has always seemed to me unworthy to demand anything of God. I have always accepted everything from him, with gratitude. No, do not ask me to do that."

"I shall then be obliged to leave you disappointed?" he asked sadly as he held out his hand.

"*At first,*" I replied, putting into these words all the meaning I could, without exactly knowing just what meaning. And thereupon we separated.

I am writing this immediately upon my return to Cuverville, while my memory of it is still fresh.

1924   *January 5*

I have gone back to William James's *Psychology,* but drop it after reading two chapters (among which the one on instinct) and assuring myself of its mediocrity.

February 13

If my journal is published later on, I fear that it will give a rather false idea of me. I have never kept it during the long periods of equilibrium, health, and happiness; but instead during those periods of depression when I needed it to catch hold of myself, in which I show myself as whining, whimpering, pitiable.

As soon as the sun reappears. I lose sight of myself and am completely taken up by my work and my life. My journal reflects none of this, but only my periods of despair. I haven't known any for a long time now.

June 19

Off for Cuverville. In the compartment I read various articles in the special number of the *Disque vert* devoted to Freud.

Ah, how troublesome Freud is! And how easily it seems to me we would have discovered his America without him! It sees to me that the thing I should be most grateful to him for is having accustomed readers to hearing certain subjects treated without having to protest or blush. What he brings us above all is audacity; or, more exactly, he spares us a certain false and encumbering modesty.

But how many absurd things in that imbecile of genius!

Paris, August 6

Dined yesterday evening with Copeau. Under a driving rain he takes me to an excellent little restaurant near Montparnasse that Suarès had recommended, where we enjoy a tasty lobster and a heady Burgundy. . . . Copeau is in funds, in luck, in verve, and he catches me up in his fantasies.

Paris, August 17

"To be right" . . . Who still wants to be? . . . A few fools.

Chartres, September 6

Unadulterated awe; and not only in front of the cathedral. On this warm morning so soft and blue, I wandered in the old quarter of the lower town, on the banks of a charming, grassy, shady canal and then of a stream whose name I don't know. A bit worried at the thought that perhaps Roger Fry, who came with me, is waiting for me in the hall of the hotel. But *there is a spell upon me,** and I need solitude. I persuade myself that he does too. How young I should still feel if I did not know that I no longer am!

September 9

As if the world were an enigma to which we had to find the key!

October 26

At Cuverville the last three days. Departure for the Congo put off. Reasons: M.'s examinations; finishing of *Les Faux-Monnayeurs*. Insufficient preparation, etc. . . . Leaving in November, I thought to be back in April. Six months are too little for this trip. Leaving in July, it will probably be for a full year.

Shall I be able to finish my book between now and July? I doubt it.

November 6

Day on which we were to leave. The weather is beautiful.

* In English in the original.

November 7

"You ought to get married. Try to make another person happy . . . You would see how unhappy you can be . . . both of you; yes, both of you. But it is instructive."

December 3

New attacks by the little Gourmont in this month's *Mercure* (apropos of the reprinting of Rivière's *Etudes*). He blames my writings for being "full of tears and moonlight," to which, he adds, I owe my success among society people. Which is the more amazing? his silliness or his bad faith? If he is convinced, how stupid he is! If he is intelligent, what a liar he is!

I hope that some critic, later on, will gather together these attacks and some of the perfidious shafts that certain reviews shoot at me the first of every month. Since no friend steps up to protest any more than I do, the legend is gaining credit little by little. The public knows nothing of me but the caricature, and since it hardly invites anyone to know me better, people don't bother to go any further. What am I saying? Even if some people have the curiosity to read me, they do so with such a mass of prejudices that the real meaning of my writings eludes them. They will end up by seeing in them what they have been told was there, and not see anything else. My sincerity is taken for a grimace, and for affectation everything that contradicts the monster they have been persuaded I am.

December 13

He (the demon) creates in us a sort of reverse repentance, an abominable repentance, a regret not for having sinned, but for not having sinned more, for having let some occasion for sin slip by without committing it. . . .

1925   *January*

Everything that André Breton makes me say in his false interview is much more like him than like me. The form of ambition he ascribes to me is absolutely foreign to me; but it is the form of ambition that *he* is most disposed to understand. There is not one of the sentences he puts into my mouth that I do not disavow; I say this for simplicity's sake—for the extreme perfidy of his article comes from the fact that there is not a single one of those sentences that I can swear I never said; but it is presented in such a way as to denature its meaning absolutely. The very sound of my voice is falsified.

And in this camouflage, unfortunately, I see rather a malignant cleverness than any clumsiness. I cannot believe that Breton, so very careful about the influence he intends to exert over young minds, did not aim to discredit me, to destroy me. And it must be granted that he has succeeded in composing a very consistent and very hideous portrait.

*Beginning of January 1925** [from *Journal intime*]

I must admit that my suffering at Cuverville three years ago was much greater than any I should have upon leaving life today. Did Madeleine realize this? I do not think so. I fear she may have seen some exaggeration in my tears. . . . That is why, since then, I have never been able to talk with her.

Presuming that she did regard them as sincere, Madeleine might have believed that my sufferings then would regenerate me. But to tell the truth, it was during those dreadful days that I ceased living; it was then that I took my leave.

Since then I have lived only a sort of posthumous life; a life carried on, as it were, in the margins of real life.

"Nothing good can come from that," she frequently said to me, as if trying to persuade herself of this. But it is not true. It is on the contrary from that dreadful judgment that all the bitterness in my life has come.

Abominable.

I have not ceased to love her, even at the periods when I seemed, and when she had a right to think me, farthest from her—to love her more than myself, more than life itself; but I was no longer able to tell her this. . . .

All my work is inclined toward her.

Until *Les Faux-Monnayeurs* (the first book I wrote in an effort *not* to take her into account), I wrote everything to convince her, to win her over. It is all nothing more than a long plea for the defense; no work has been more intimately motivated than mine—and no one is seeing very deeply who fails to distinguish this.

---

* From the little notebook I took to the hospital where I was operated on for appendicitis. [A.G.]

Saturday, January 10

It is now just fourteen days since I was operated on. . . .

I believe I am sincere in saying that I clearly envisaged death. That is to say that, before the operation, I put myself in the frame of mind of one who was not to return; and I did so quite naturally. . . .

February [from *Journal intime*]

. . . I should like Agnès, then, to whom she listens, to tell her and to make her realize—if I were not to return from this voyage to the Congo—that she was the dearest thing to me in the world; and that it was because I loved her more than life itself that, after she had withdrawn from me, life seemed to me of so little value.

Marseilles

A frightful number of hours pass without bringing either profit or pleasure. I am simply "marking time," and it seems that one might just as well not have lived through it. Too tired to work, I have sought nothing but sexual pleasure since morning. Empty day. A cold that freezes up all lyricism and brings tears to one's eyes.

Wandered in the Arab quarter, which I did not know before. Sordid poverty and melancholy. Some Sicilian workmen are fighting and rolling in the gutter. Children in rags, chilled to the bone.

May 15

Yesterday evening, visit to Claudel. He had asked me to come and was waiting for me. At 80 rue de Passy, an apartment set back, not facing the street. I go through two rooms, the second of which is rather large, and find myself in a third one, larger still, which he uses as both bedroom and study. Open camp-cot in a corner; a low bookcase goes around two sides of the room; it is decorated by a number of objects brought back from the Far East.

At my ring, Claudel came to meet me and holds out his hand. He seems to have shrunk. A short, swansdown-lined jacket of coffee-colored silk makes him look still thick. He is enormous and short; he looks like Ubu. We sit down in two armchairs. He completely fills his. Mine, a sort of chaise longue, has such a low back that to be comfortable in it I should have to get too far away from Claudel. I give up and lean forward.

In the presence of Claudel I am aware only of what I lack; he dominates me; he overhangs me; he has more base and surface, more health, money, genius, power, children, faith, etc., than I. I can imagine no other course but to bow my head and obey.

Cuverville, end of May

Visit from Paul Valéry. Cleaning up and typing of five chapters of *Faux-Monnayeurs*. A deadly chore, but one that suits my apathy. I have given up counting on anything but the Congo to get me out of it. Preparations for this trip and the dream of new landscapes have disenchanted the present; I am experiencing the truth of the saying that happiness lies in the moment. Nothing strikes me as more than provisional. (The hope of eternal life excels equally in this.)

My sight has weakened considerably of late. I wear glasses to relieve this deficiency. Would that the brain could wear them too! Difficulty my mind has in "focusing" the idea it is examining; analogous to that of my eyes today. The outlines remain blurred.

June 8

Finished *Les Faux-Monnayeurs*.

July 14

Departure for the Congo.

from

VOYAGE

AU CONGO

(*Travels in the Congo*)

1925-1926

PART ONE: *To the Congo*

(*Voyage au Congo*)

I   *Voyage Out—Brazzaville*   *July 21—Third day of passage out*

Inexpressible languor. Hours without shape or content. . . .

I have plunged into this journey like Curtius into the gulf. Already I no longer feel as though I had so much willed it (though for many months past my will has been bending toward it), as had it imposed upon me by a sort of ineluctable fatality, like all the important events of my life. And I come near to forgetting that it is nothing but a project made in youth and realized in maturity; I was barely twenty when I first made up my mind to make this journey to the Congo—thirty-six years ago.

August 9, 5 p.m.

We enter the waters of the Congo. The captain's launch set us down at Banane. Every opportunity of going ashore finds us ready and eager. Returned at nightfall.

My joy is perhaps as keen; but it penetrates less deeply. Oh, if only I could forget that life is retracting its promises before me! . . . My heart beats no less strongly now than at twenty.

Nighttime. We are slowly ascending the river. On the left bank, in the distance, a few lights; a bush fire on the horizon; at our feet the terrifying thickness of the waters.

August 23

Third visit to the Congo rapids. . . .

August 24 and 25

The Sambry Trial.

The less intelligent the white man is, the more stupid he thinks the black.

An unfortunate official is being tried who was sent out to the colonies too young and placed in a remote station without sufficient instructions. He needed a strength of character and a moral and intellectual quality that he simply did not have. When these are lacking, a man tries to make the natives obey and respect him by the spasmodic, outrageous, and precarious use of brute force. He gets frightened; he loses his head; having no natural authority, he tries to reign by terror. He feels himself losing hold, and soon it becomes impossible to quell the growing discontent of the natives, often perfectly amenable by nature, but goaded to fury and revolt by injustice, violent reprisals, and cruelty.* . . .

During the third and last hearing of this melancholy trial, a very beautiful butterfly flew into the law court, of which the windows were all open. After circling about for some time, it settled most unexpectedly on the very desk at which I was sitting, and I managed to catch it without spoiling it.

II Up-River   *Monday morning, September 7*

The most magnificent spectacle on awakening. The sun was rising as we entered the pool of Bolobo. Not a wrinkle was to be seen on the immense sheet of winding water, not even the slightest shiver to blur its surface; an intact and perfect shell, holding the pure and smiling reflection of the purest sky. In the east, the sun was crimsoning a few long, trailing clouds. Toward the west, sky and lake were the same pearl-color, a delicate and tender gray; in this exquisite mother-of-pearl all the blended colors still lay sleeping, yet it was already quivering with the promise of the day's splendor. In the distance a few low-lying islands floated ethereally in a liquid haze. . . . The enchantment of this mystic scene lasted only a few seconds; soon the contours were reasserted, the outlines grew definite; we were on common earth once more.

---

* However serious the misdeeds attributed to Sambry, we were to encounter much worse, I regret to say, later on. I could not foresee that these agonizing social questions, which I had then only caught a glimpse of, questions of our dealings with the natives, would soon engage my attention so much as to become the chief interest of my journey and that I should find in studying them the *raison d'être* of my presence in the country. All that I felt when faced with them then was my own incompetence. But I was soon to learn. [A. G.]

September 8

. . . Not a single flower; not a note of any color but green, a very dark, constant green, which gives the landscape the solemn tranquillity of the monochromatic African oases, and creates an impression of dignity unapproached by our northern landscapes, with their diversity of tones and shades.

The spectacle is coming closer to what I expected it to be; it is becoming "true to life." The abundance of extremely tall trees no longer stops the eye with its impenetrable curtain; they stand a little farther apart from each other now, so that deep gulfs of green and mysterious recesses open out between them; if they are interlaced with lianas, it is in such gentle curves that their embrace looks voluptuous—an embrace less of suffocation than of love.

September 25

A beautiful half-moon, like a cup above the river, pours its light on the waters. We have moored off the side of an island; the boat's searchlight is illuminating the jungle fantastically. The whole forest is vibrating with a continuous sound of shrill creaking. The air is warm. The lights of the *Largesse* have just been put out. All is quiet.

III By Car   *September 28*

The falls of the M'Bali, if they were in Switzerland, would be surrounded by enormous hotels. Here, solitude; a hut, two huts with straw roofs, in which we are to sleep, do not spoil the wild majesty of the landscape. Fifty yards from the table where I am writing, the cascade—a great misty curtain, silvered by the light of the moon between the branches of the great trees.

October 12

The little orphan leper, cast off by everyone; the woman to whom Marc gave money for a week's manioc for him has not kept her word. . . . Never in my life have I seen a more miserable creature.

Bambari, October 13

Haunted by the memory of the little leper, by the thin and as though distant sound of his voice, all the way from Foroumbala to Alindao, where we lunched; and from there to Bambari, where we arrived only at nightfall (ten hours in a Ford). There were a good many minor accidents on the road; a number of engine breakdowns; a bridge gave way as we were crossing it and I don't know how we escaped spilling into the river.

Bambari, October 14

This morning, as soon as we were up, a dance by the Dakpas. There were twenty-eight little boy dancers from eight to thirteen years old who were completely painted white from head to foot; on their heads was a kind of helmet stuck all over with forty or so red and black spikes; on their fore-heads a fringe of little metal rings. Each of them held in his hand a whip made of rushes and plaited string. Some of them had black and red checks painted round their eyes. A short skirt made of raffia completed this fantastic get-up. They danced gravely, in Indian file, to the sound of twenty-three earthen or wooden trumpets of unequal lengths (from about one foot to four feet long) which can each make only a single note. Another band of older Dakpas (these were all black) performed their evolutions in the opposite direction to the first. Then a dozen or so women mingled in the dance. Every dancer advanced with little jerky steps which made his anklets tinkle. The trumpet players formed a circle, and in the middle an old woman beat time with a feather brush made of black horsehair. At her feet a great black demon writhed in the dust in feigned convulsions, but without ceasing to blow his trumpet. The din was deafening, for, with the single exception of the little white dancers, they never stopped singing and yelling at the top of their voices a strange tune (I noted it down) which was heard even above the bellowing of the trumpets.

IV The Great Forest Between Bangui and Nola   *October 21*

At M'Baike we visited M.B., the representative of the Compagnie Forestière. We found two missionary fathers seated on his veranda, drinking apéritifs.

How agreeable these agents of the Great Companies manage to make themselves! The government official who does not guard himself against their excessive friendliness will find it difficult later on to take sides against them. It will be almost impossible for him not to lend a hand, or at least not to shut his eyes, to the little irregularities they commit —and then to the formidable exactions.

October 28

We were so dejected by Samba N'Goto's deposition and by Garron's tales that when, in the forest, we came across a group of women who were mending the road, we had no heart even to smile at them. These poor cattle were working in the pouring rain, a number of them with babies at the breast. Every twenty yards or so there were huge pits by the side of the road, generally about ten feet deep; it was out of these that the poor wretches had dug the sandy earth with which to bank the road, and this *without proper tools.* It has happened more than once that the loose earth has given way and buried the women and children who were working at the bottom of the pit. We were told this by several persons. As they usually work too far from their village to return at night, the poor women have built themselves temporary huts in the forest, wretched shelters of branches and reeds, useless against the rain. We heard that the native soldier who is their overseer had made them work all night in order to repair the damage done by a recent storm and to enable us to pass.

October 29

The accounts of the Bambio chief confirm everything that I heard from Samba N'Goto. In particular, he gave me an account of the "ball" last market day at Boda. I here transcribe the story as I copied it from Garron's private diary.

"At Bambio, on September 8, ten rubber-gatherers (twenty, according to later information*) belonging to the Goundi gang, who work for the Compagnie Forestière—because they had not brought in any rubber the month before (but this month they brought in double, from forty to fifty kilograms)—were condemned to go round and round the factory under a fierce sun, carrying very heavy wooden beams. If they fell down, they were forced up by guards flogging them with whips.

"The 'ball' began at eight o'clock and lasted the whole day, under the eyes of Messrs. Pacha and Maudurier, the company's agent. At about eleven o'clock, a man from Bagouma, called Malingué, fell to get up no more. When M. Pacha was informed of this, he merely replied, 'What the hell do I care?' and ordered the 'ball' to go on. All this took place in the presence of the assembled inhabitants of Bambio and of all the chiefs of the neighboring villages who had come to attend the market."

---

* They were all fined a sum equal to the price of their work. Consequently they worked for two months for nothing. One of them, who tried "to argue," was besides condemned to a month's imprisonment. [A. G.]

The chief spoke to us also of the conditions reigning in the Boda prison, of the wretched plight of the natives, and of how they are fleeing to some less accursed country. . . .

My indignation against Pacha is naturally great, but the Compagnie Forestière plays a part in all this, which seems to be very much graver, though more secret. For, after all, it—its representatives, I mean—knew everything that was going on. It is the company (or its agents) that profits from this state of things. Its agents approved Pacha, encouraged him, were his partners. It was at their request that Pacha arbitrarily threw into prison the natives who had not furnished enough. . . .

When I accepted this mission, I had no idea at first what it was I was undertaking, what part I could play, how I could be useful. I understand it now, and I am beginning to think that my coming will not have been in vain.

During my stay in the colony, I have come to realize how terribly the problems which I have to solve are interwoven one with the other. Far be it from me to raise my voice on points which are not within my competence and which necessitate a prolonged study. But this is a matter of certain definite facts, completely independent of questions of a general order. . . .

October 30

Impossible to sleep. The Bambio "ball" haunted my night. I cannot content myself with saying, as so many do, that the natives were still more wretched before the French occupation. We have taken on responsibilities toward them which we have no right to evade. The painful sense of this injustice is now rooted in me permanently; I know things to which I cannot reconcile myself. What demon drove me to Africa? What did I come to find in this country? I was at peace. Now I know: I must speak.

But how can I make people listen? Until now, I have always spoken without the least concern whether anyone was listening or not; always written for tomorrow, with the single desire of lasting. Now I envy the journalist, whose voice carries at once, even if it perishes immediately after. Have I been walking until now between great painted screens of falsehood? I want to get back out through the wings, out onto the other side of the set, and learn what it is they are hiding, even if it is something horrible. It is that "horrible something," which I now suspect, that I want to see.

Spent the whole day composing my letter.

Long conversation with the two chiefs of the Bakongo village. But the one who at first was talking to us alone stopped as soon as the other came up. He would not say another word; and nothing could be more harrowing than his silence and his fear of compromising himself when we questioned him about atrocities committed in the Boda prison, where he himself has been confined. When he was again alone with us later on, he told us that he had seen ten men die in it in a single day as a result of ill-treatment. He himself bears the marks of flogging and showed us his scars. He confirmed what we had already heard, that the prisoners receive as their only food, once a day, a ball of manioc as big as (he showed us his fist).

He spoke of the fines that the Compagnie Forestière is in the habit of inflicting on (I was about to say "deducting from") the natives who fail to bring in sufficient quantities of rubber—fines of forty francs—that is to say, all that they could hope to earn in a month. He added that when the wretched man has not enough to pay the fine, he can escape being thrown into prison only by borrowing from someone better off than himself, if he can find such a person—and then he is sometimes thrown into prison "into the bargain." Terror reigns, and the surrounding villages are deserted. Later, we talked to other chiefs. When they are asked: "How many men in your village?" they count them by naming them off, and bend down a finger for each one. There are rarely more than ten.

V   From Nola to Bosoum   *November 7*

We lunched with Dr. B. and a representative of the Compagnie Wial, which trades in skins. They have both just come back from Bania. The doctor spoke at length of the Compagnie Forestière, which manages, he says, to evade the wise regulations of the medical service, eludes the visits of sanitary inspectors, and treats with contempt the system of health certificates for the natives, whom it recruits from village to village and groups in the "Bakongo" settlements; hence the propagation of sleeping sickness, which thus escapes all control. He considers that the Compagnie Forestière is ruining and devastating the country. He has sent confidential reports on the subject addressed to the Governor, but is convinced they are held up at Carnot (to which circumscription Nola is temporarily attached for want of sufficient staff), so that the Governor continues to be ignorant of the situation.

November 9

. . . The sky is low and uniformly gray; everything looks dull and dismal; one goes round and round as if in a kind of oppressive dream, a nightmare. When one goes on ahead of the rest of the party and stops, alone, as I did, lost in the immensity, the strange, disquieting songs of many jungle birds make one's heart beat faster.

November 10

. . . Every day we sink a bit deeper into strangeness. All today I lived in a state of torpor and unconsciousness,

*as though of hemlock I had drunk,**

losing all notion of time, of place, and of my own self.

The sky grew a little clearer toward evening, and as I write this, night is mounting into an admirable sky. At last we have escaped from the oppression of the forest. At times it was very beautiful, with more and more of the gigantic trees, whose trunks seem to be suffering from elephantiasis. But in the absence of any ray of sunlight, everything seemed to be sunk in sleep, and hopelessly sad.

I cannot understand why all whites, almost without exception, officials as well as traders, women as well as men, think it necessary to treat their servants roughly—in speech, at any rate—even when they show them real kindness. I know a lady, otherwise charming and gentle, who never calls her boy anything but *"tête de brute,"* though she never raises her hand against him. Such is the custom. "You will come to it too. Wait and see." We have waited ten months, with the same servants the whole time, and we did not "come to it." Were we particularly well served, by some lucky chance? Perhaps. . . . But I am inclined to think that every master has the servants he deserves; and what I say does not apply only to the Congo. What servant in our country would make a great point of remaining honest if he heard his master deny him the possession of a single virtue? If I had been Mr. X.'s boy, I should have robbed him the very same night I heard him declare that all Negroes were cheats, liars, and thieves.

"Your boy doesn't understand French?" I asked with some uneasiness.

* Quoted in English.

"He speaks it admirably. . . . Why?"

"Aren't you afraid that what he has just heard you say . . . ?"

"It'll teach him that I'm not taken in by him."

At the same dinner, I heard a guest declare that all women (and he wasn't talking of Negresses this time) care for nothing but pleasure as long as they are worthy of our attentions, and that no woman is ever really pious before the age of forty.

These gentlemen obviously know Negroes about as well as they know women. Experience rarely teaches us anything. A man uses everything he comes across to strengthen him in his own opinion and sweeps everything into his net to prove his convictions. . . . No prejudice so absurd but finds its confirmation in experience.

Negroes, who are prodigiously malleable, more often than not become what people think, or want, or fear them to be. I would not swear that our boys too might not easily have been turned into rascals. One has only to set about it in the right way; and at this, the colonials show themselves remarkably ingenious. One teaches his parrot to say: "Get out of here, you dirty nigger!" Another is angry because his boy brings vermouth and bitters after dinner when he had asked for liqueurs. "Double-dyed idiot! Don't you know yet what an apéritif is? . . ." Another time, the boy thought he was supposed to warm up the porcelain teapot before serving it (it was his first time): the poor creature, who thought he was doing the right thing, is abused before the whole company of whites, and again called a fool. Hadn't he been taught that hot water breaks glasses?

I am going on with Adoum's reading lessons. His application is touching; he is getting on steadily, and every day I am becoming more attached to him. When the white man becomes indignant at the black's stupidity, he is usually only displaying his own foolishness! Not that I think them capable of any but the slightest mental development; their brains as a rule are numb and stagnant—but how often the white man seems to make it his business to bury them in their darkness!

November 30

. . . All these villages—*kagamas* in Babouan—are very nearly deserted, as much on account of Samba's flight and for fear of the reprisals which may result from it as for the fear (only too comprehensible, alas!) that we white men, immediately followed, as we are, by the commandant, may be scouring the country in order to requisition men for the railway and seize them by any means in our power. However much kindness and consideration one shows them, they are suspicious—and no wonder.

I am writing this after dinner—the full moon is shedding its immensity of light over the village of Dahi, where we are spending the night; toward the east the heights of Bouar, which we are to climb tomorrow, can be made out through a faint blue haze. There is not a breath in the air, not a cloud in all the sky, which is not in the least black, but azure like the sea, so intense is the moonlight. Not far from us are our boys' and porters' fires; and farther off again, those of the villagers. The people here have not fled. A good hundred of them hurried up to welcome us, though we arrived after nightfall, crowding round us in cannibal-like demonstrations, so close that we were almost suffocated.

VI   From Bosoum to Fort Archambault   *Bosoum, December 9*

I picked up a minute chameleon on the road, which I brought back with me to the hut and spent nearly an hour observing. It is certainly one of the most astonishing animals in creation. . . .

December 14

Finished rereading La Fontaine's fables from end to end. Has any literature produced anything more exquisite, wiser, more perfect?

December 16

A radio message of November 19 has just been communicated to us: Valéry has been elected to the Academy.

Bossa, December 18

. . . What delayed us was our meeting, an hour after sunrise, with a troop of prisoners who were being led off by the chief of a neighboring village. There were eleven of them, with a rope round their necks—to tell the truth, it was nothing but a string—that tied them together. They looked so miserable that our hearts ached with pity at the sight of them. They were all carrying a load of manioc on their heads—a heavy one, no doubt, but not excessive for a man in good health; but these men seemed hardly capable of carrying themselves. Only one among them had no load; a little boy of about eleven or twelve, frightfully thin, and exhausted with misery, fasting, and fatigue; at moments he trembled all over and the skin of his stomach quivered spasmodically. The top of his head looked as if it had been scraped and as if his scalp had been replaced in parts by the kind of skin that forms over wounds or scalded bodies. He seemed incapable of ever smiling. And all his companions in misery were so pathetic that there was hardly a gleam of intelligence to be discovered in their eyes. While we were questioning the chief, we emptied the contents of our provision bag into the boy's hands, but, as ill luck would have it, they contained only three bits of very stale bread. As we had been certain of arriving early at our next stopping place, we had let our porters go on ahead without providing ourselves with food for the journey. The boy devoured the crusts like an animal, without a word, without even a look of gratitude. His companions, though not so weak as he, seemed no less famished. From their answers to our questions, it appeared that they had eaten nothing for five days. According to the chief, they were fugitives who had been living in the bush for the last three months—like hunted beasts, I imagine.

December 20

Quantities of insignificant little villages—if one can give that name to the groups of a few miserable huts, whose inhabitants, squatting beside a miserable fire, or on the threshold of their doors, make no sign of greeting to us—hardly turn their heads to see us pass. These huts remind one of the rough sheds our charcoal-burners build in the woods. A trifle less and they would be animals' dens. And this absence of welcome when we arrive, of smiles and greetings as we pass through, does not seem to mark hostility so much as profound apathy, the benumbed dullness of stupidity. When one goes up to them, they stir hardly more than the animals of the Galápagos; when one holds out a new penny to a child, he is terrified and cannot understand what is expected of him. The idea that he might be given anything is incomprehensible to him, and if an elder, or one of our porters, tries to explain our good intentions, he looks astonished and then holds out his two hands like a cup.

VII   Fort Archambault, Fort Lamy   *End of December*

From morning on, the splendor, the intensity of the light is dazzling. We are on the other side of hell. At Fort Archambault, on the borders of Islam, beyond the reach of barbarism, one enters into contact with another civilization, another culture. A still rudimentary culture, no doubt, but one that brings with it a refinement, a feeling for nobility and hierarchy, a disinterested spirituality, and a relish for the immaterial.

In the regions we have just been through, there are nothing but downtrodden races, not so much brutal perhaps as brutalized, enslaved, aspiring to nothing more than the grossest satisfactions; pitiable human herds without herdsmen. Here at last are to be found real homes; at last, individual possessions; at last, specializations.*

1926   *January 30*

I had been astonished at seeing so few crocodiles; now suddenly there are incredible numbers of them. I have just counted a group of thirty-seven on a little sand bank fifty yards long. They are of all sizes; some hardly longer than a walking-stick; others enormous, monstrous. Some are striped, others solidly gray. At the boat's approach, most of them drop heavily into the water, if they happen to be on a sloping sand beach. If they are a little farther from the river, you see them get to their feet and run. The way in which they slide into the water has something heavily sensual about it. Sometimes they are too sleepy or to lazy to move at all. During the last hour we have certainly seen more than a hundred.

February 1 or 2

. . . Again, the enormousness, the formlessness, the indecision, the absence of direction, of design, of organization, which troubled me so much during the first part of our journey, and which is indeed the chief characteristic of this country. But here this perplexity of nature, this wedding and interpenetration of the elements, this *blending* of sea-green and blue, of grass and water, are so strange and recall so little anything in our countries (except perhaps certain swamps in the Camargue or in the neighborhood of Aigues-Mortes) that I cannot stop gazing at it.

The turning-point is past. We have reached the farthest limit of our journey. From now on, we are on our way home. It was not without regret that I bade farewell, no doubt for the last time, to all that lies on the other side of the Chad. (This is perhaps an opportunity for saying what it is that attracts me so much about the desert.) I have never felt fitter. . . .

---

*On rereading these notes they seem to me greatly exaggerated; but when I wrote them, we had hardly shaken ourselves dry from our long plunge into limbo. [A. G.]

Incredible numbers of crocodiles on the mud banks. They lie flattened out close against the ground, mud- and bug-colored, motionless, and looking as if they had grown directly out of the slime. A rifle shot and they all disappear—dissolved in the water of the stream as if they had melted.

February 20. Morning

We left Fort Lamy in three whaleboats. We are on our way back. From now on, every day brings me nearer to Cuverville.

PART TWO: *Return from Chad*
(Le Retour du Tchad)

I *On the Logone*   *February 26 or 27*

The country is becoming more and more desolate; the desolation of fire is added to the desolation of aridity. As far as the eye reaches, there is nothing to be seen but reddish brown and black. There is a slight touch of green on one of the river banks, and on the other an edging of golden sand. The blue of the sky is almost tender, and the water—a mingled green, blue, and gold—is of an exquisitely lovely shade.

Passed a little village in the making, with no name as yet on any map. As soon as they saw us, fifty or so natives, smiling and welcoming, got up a tamtam in the full heat of the midday sun. Some of the women would not be bad-looking except for the terrible plates which distend their lips. This is one of the most disconcerting of aberrations; nothing excuses or explains it; none of the theories that have been put forward (depreciation of the women to save them from raids, for instance) holds water for a moment. These unfortunate women, with their continually streaming lips, look stupid, but not at all unhappy; they laugh, sing, and prance about, and seem to have no suspicion that they are not captivating. There is not one over fourteen or fifteen who has not been disfigured in this way.

March 3

At about eleven o'clock yesterday morning I myself was taken ill in a rather odd manner. While I was reading *Faust* in the veranda, I suddenly felt sleepy. I went back to my bed to lie down for a moment, and as soon as I was off my feet was seized with a violent dizziness; a cold sweat, nausea. Soon after came an attack of vomiting. The illness lasted till nighttime. No fever.

Marc in the meantime again went up to 104°. He is sweating profusely and has rather a bad headache.

At times I feel tottering on the verge of an abyss of horror. I think really that it was my violent anxiety for Marc that brought on my own attack . . . unless it was my swimming in the river this morning? . . .

I am writing this lying down in the whaleboat, which I got back to with some difficulty, for the slightest movement makes me sick.

II *Turning Back*

I think I am better. I still have dizzy spells, but I was able to sit at Marc's bedside and eat a little breakfast with him. Porridge and boiled rice, with some delicious stewed apricots (we have drawn upon our choicest stores), washed down with Vichy and Moët.

March 5

The people of these primitive races, I am more and more persuaded, do not have our method of reasoning; and this is why they so often seem to us stupid. Their acts are not governed by the logic which from our earliest infancy has become essential to us—and from which, by the very structure of our language, we cannot escape.

III *Second Ascent of the Logone*   *March 7*

After breakfast, I was reading under my mosquito net, when I was disturbed from *Samson Agonistes* by a strange noise like a waterfall. The whaleboat stopped. I came out from under my shimbeck. This noise of slapping water was being made by the wind in the fans of four big palm trees above our heads. Marc's whaleboat had stopped too. At that moment Adoum told me that some hippopotamuses had come into view. Marc, who had arrived a little before us, was on the lookout for them; our coming had disturbed the game for a moment, but soon their monstrous snouts reappeared downstream. There were four of them quite close to us, and the river at this place is not at all wide. We climbed up the steep bank, where the men fired at the poor beasts, who put up their snouts every five minutes to breathe. No apparent result, though some balls seemed to have hit. And then, suddenly, fifty yards away from us, upstream, a new snout, more enormous than any of the others—and just beside it the snout of a young one, which Adoum declared was on its mother's back. What monsters hunters are! Marc fired, and this time there was a great disturbance in the water. Certainly the hippopotamus had been knocked over; it was one of its feet, not its snout, that came up again next and splashed the water about. Another ball; another somersault; all our boatmen, on the bank and in the whaleboats, were dancing with excitement. Then no more. We waited.

March 8

This morning, to make up for the bad night, there was great rejoicing— the dead hippopotamus was in sight. It looked like a heap of grass, a lump of earth, and formed a little island near the steep river bank. We sent one of the whaleboats to reconnoiter. Yes, it was he! And our men leaped and yelled for joy.

We interrupted our breakfast and started on another whaleboat to go and look at the monster. It had drifted onto a shoal, from which it was dislodged with the greatest difficulty. The men pushed at it with their poles, all talking at once, but they could not succeed in co-ordinating their efforts and pushing together. These natives, who are so near nature and who, one would think, would be clever at such simple tasks, are incredibly clumsy and stupid whenever anything new has to be undertaken. While they were all pushing on one side of the animal, one of them, who was on the whaleboat, stuck his pole right across in the opposite direction and considerably thwarted their efforts. Unfortunately those of us who would have been able to direct them did not know the language. Finally, however, the hippopotamus, with a chain on its foot, got itself towed along by Zézé's whaleboat. We went into the other whaleboat and got Marc's motion-picture equipment ready. Unfortunately, the light was poor. At some distance from the shore, the hippopotamus foundered again. I saw its head for the first time, and for the first time understood the hugeness of its body. It took twenty men to roll it over, so that it showed in turn its back, its side, and then its pink belly, on which its short paws were daintily folded.

At last it got to the shore, and the work of cutting up began. Thirty-four men applied themselves to it with enthusiasm; they had three machetes and a few cutlasses—ridiculously small ones for such a task. Some of them held the limbs or pulled on the skin while the others cut. They all shouted, gesticulated, and scurried about, but there was not the slightest dispute: they all laughed and joined in the game. The cutting up, the slow, gradual dividing of the great bulk, lasted two good hours. Piece by piece, it was all finally taken away. Opening up the stomach and scraping out the tripe gave forth the most appalling smells. Luckily the wind was strong enough to carry them off. When the lungs were torn out, the coagulated blood issued from the *vena cava* like a long, purple serpent; I felt I was going to faint. Nothing was thrown away, nothing wasted. The vultures and eagles that circled above us were disappointed. Every moment they became more daring; some of them, taking a sudden, useless plunge, almost touched us with their wings. . . . I went back to my whaleboat and took a glass of brandy to steady my inside. It was heaving with disgust.

At lunch we had hippopotamus steak—very good too, believe it or not! Then we started off again in our whaleboats, which had been encased with raw meat. The smell is abominable, but it will be worse in a few days. In order to get to my bed, I have to scale a foot, and then climb a jaw and a big roll of skin thicker than any carpet. A heap of bleeding gobbets, of entrails, of unspeakably pestilential fragments, are spread out on the shimbeck to dry in the sun; and festoons of purplish strips are hung by long palm cords on the whaleboat's sides. Horror! it is raining blood through the roof of my shimbeck! And not only blood—some foul discharge as well. I gaze like King Canute at the red and yellowish drops dripping onto the floor, the canteens, my bag, the top of my mosquito net, under which I take refuge. But what is all this compared to the Saras' joy, their laughter, their gratitude?

March 11

The abominable stench makes night in the whaleboat a serious trial. . . .

Yes, however perfect a place for reading and meditation a whaleboat may be, I shall be glad to leave this one. It was all right till the hippopotamus came, but since the boatmen have hung us all round with these stinking festoons, one hardly dares breathe.

An excellent nap has completely restored my equilibrium. I had no sooner got up than the Sultan of Mala made his appearance with a numerous suite. The sultan is an enormous man: he could never fit into a coach. One shuddered at the idea of offering him a seat. Deck chair, English armchair —everything we have would surely break down under his weight. It was a great relief when we saw one of his servants step forward with a solid affair, specially designed for his use. . . .

I was anxious to see whether I could bring a smile to the sultan's lips, and made Adoum relate the shooting of the hippopotamus, then the cutting up of the beast and the appalling smell of our whaleboats, which had been turned into tanneries. The story was highly successful. The whole suite (fifteen men) joined in the sultan's laugh.

"This shows," he ordered the interpreter to say to me, "that you are a great chief. A small chief would never have borne such a thing for the sake of his men."

IV   Second Stay with the Massas   *March 16*

I sometimes feel that there is a gulf of flames separating me from M. —a Gehenna, which I despair of ever crossing.

March 17

. . . The natives here believe in the devil, in many devils—and believe only in them. No other supernatural power helps man to defend himself against them. The most one can say is that certain objects, certain actions, have the property of frightening the devil and of thwarting his evil intentions; but this beneficent property does not issue from any supreme principle. Nor is there anything that can influence the conduct of man, whose whole wisdom consists in knowing what harms and what preserves him.

In the same way, after death there is nothing. "After a man is dead—" repeated Adoum, who is a Mussulman himself and certainly expects to go to paradise—"among the people here, it's like after the wind has gone by."

I should like to know in which cases it is that their dead are not even buried, but simply thrown into the river.

V   Through the Bush. Marova. Adoum Leaves.   *March 20*

Halted after about fifteen kilometers. A few isolated trees on a baked soil (like terracotta pottery). It was about eleven o'clock. The sun was beating down. We rested in the shade of the biggest tree. The wind roasted one's skin as it passed; it was a curious skein of mixed and alternating winds; one, blowing no doubt from the river at a temperature of about 98°, seemed cool; the other blew from a furnace—a breath from hell. Every object one touched, unless it was wet, was hotter than one's hand. . . .

The second part of the day was one of the most trying so far—I really think the most exhausting of our whole trip. The sky was thick, loaded with something—we didn't know what, except that it wasn't rain.

The vast plain through which we rode on horseback was utterly without charm or grace—baked and parched; it was covered with short, dry grass of a dirty yellow color, which made one almost prefer the great stretches that have been burned black by fires.

This evening, after three hours' rest, shade, and night, I still feel as if I had not eliminated the excess of sunlight. I feel like a garden wall that remains saturated with heat long after the sun has disappeared. I was so completely dehydrated when I arrived, with no saliva in my mouth but a kind of bitter froth, that within three hours I had drunk enough liquid to drown a Brinvilliers. The strange thing is that one does not mind drinking water that is not cold—almost tepid. Fortunately the water we boiled before starting today has not got the horrible taste of crocodile, which the river water has had for the last few days.

Ginglëi, March 12

It was not too hot at first—not much more than 95°; but it is 110° now in the Ginglëi rest-house, where I am writing this. One simply collapses. And the light! the light is like a dagger in one's eyes. . . .

Water is scarce. There are wells near the villages for domestic purposes, and watering places where the cattle are led to drink. A poor old woman defended one of these precarious reservoirs all by herself against our porters' thirst.

Ginglëi; a large and hideous village—a chance conglomeration of sordid, dilapidated cabins. Here and there in the surrounding country, a few fine trees—some of them non-deciduous—emerging out of a monotonous but fairly thick undergrowth. A torrid winter.

A strange kind of *tipoye,* improvised by tying a large chaise longue onto two long poles, which four enormous porters hoisted onto their heads. I was suspended more than two yards above the ground. It was sunset before we reached the camping place.

The sultan came to meet us with music and a dozen or so men on horseback. Their custom is to charge at you full tilt with their assegais and rifles pointed as though for an attack, kicking up a terrific dust. The old sultan—a delightful old fellow—had an ox killed for our porters, which they at once cut up and roasted in front of great fires. We put up our beds in the open air, near a gigantic tree in the middle of the station compound.

Maroua

Terrible heat for the last three days. There is a curious, incomprehensible epidemic. It is not recurrent fever; the treatment recommended for the latter has no effect. People—women especially—are seized with sudden illness, fall down, and succumb almost at once. The epidemic has been going on for about a month and now seems to be diminishing; but the number of deaths has been extraordinary. I dare not give the figures.

March 25

It is hot. One can think of nothing else . . . of that, and of getting out.

In order to gain time, we have given up an expedition into the mountains, which Chadourne suggested. All our remaining faculties and powers are aimed at getting home. . . .

We sleep out of doors on the terrace. After midnight the temperature goes down a little and becomes delicious. One feels that if it went below 86°, one would catch cold. The sheets one lies down on seem as hot as if they had just been warmed. Everything one touches—clothes, towels, the cushions one sits on—everything is hot. Chadourne, who is himself feeling the heat severely, has managed to get on for some time now only by means of injections of cacodylate.

I am rereading *Heart of Darkness* for the fourth time. It is only after having seen the country it describes that I realize how excellent it is.

March 26

A sleepless night, in spite of sedobrol and soneryl. I am in great nervous anxiety and fear that I may not have the necessary endurance to get through the three weeks' furnace that lies between us and N'Gaoundéré. Yesterday I had an attack of dizziness while I was trying to pack my canteen. I was obliged to give it up and leave the job to Marc. . . .

One can think of nothing but the heat.

VI   *Léré, Binder, Bibémi*   *Mindif, March 27*

We are out of the furnace. At five o'clock this morning, the air was *suave*. I could do with two sweaters on when I first got up. Not more than 75°.

March 28

We arrived exhausted, physically and nervously, at Lara about ten o'clock in the evening. The heat is appalling, terrifying. One longs to take shelter, but one doesn't know from what. The air is so dry that it shrivels up one's eyelids and temples. We dined by moonlight, but we could think of nothing but sleep. Our beds were already set up close by, but before we were able to go off to sleep, the wind rose up so violently that our mosquito nets were in danger of being shredded. We had to go in and suffocate in the encampment.

The wind has become ferocious. I rose twice, thinking it was a whirlwind. It seems to begin on the spot and go no farther. The roof of the hut will certainly be carried off. A blast from hell. Imagine a fierce wind that is hotter than one's body. The more violent it becomes, the deeper it burns; it cracks the earth; it withers everything.

Arrived at Domourou before the hottest part of the day. From six in the morning on, one simply gasps. One wonders anxiously, almost desperately: will I be able to hold out? Life in the camp goes on in slow motion. By means of a copious watering, which turned the bed coverings into rivers and lakes . . . we managed to bring the temperature down to 104°, but we were dripping with the humidity. I went out into the furnace of the veranda to get dry. We reflect with terror that perhaps the heat has not reached its maximum. And it is no good saying you will get used to it. On the contrary; from day to day one becomes weaker and less able to bear it.

Binder, March 29

Dined by moonlight. I have a sore throat. Slept in the courtyard of the *bordj*. At last the temperature is going down. It was almost cool this morning (61°). Unspeakably delicious rest.

March 30

Arrived at nine or ten o'clock in the evening. Left at four o'clock in the morning, to try to avoid the heat. One can think of nothing else. I have hardly strength to write these few shapeless notes.

Léré, March 31

This morning, tired and incurious. Let Marc visit the village by himself.

To think that one has reached the point of thinking the air cool at 100°!

April 1

It is possible, we are told, for it to be "much hotter." A pity! We should have liked to experience the worst. But what am I saying? Am I, too, going to give way to the madness of record-breaking?—Incapable of doing anything all day long.

April 2

Left Léré toward the end of the day—much too late. But it has never been so difficult to tear ourselves loose. Marc had to do everything himself, and merely watching him exert himself made me sweat in great drops. After a too abundant luncheon with Rousseau, the big-game hunter, a walk home in the sun, and a missed siesta I felt sick and unwell—incapable of making an effort or a decision. . . .

Even Rousseau, who has been seven years in the country and is absolutely climate-proof (eighty kilometers a day shooting elephants, so he says), declares that "it is terribly hot." The sky is completely overcast, not with mist, as at Mala, but with thick clouds.

The idea of getting home has become an obsession.

In spite of the unfavorable weather, Marc has been filming the whole morning—a dance of the Moundangs in the strangest ceremonial costumes— . . .

The storm is coming nearer. It rolls over us: already the temperature begins to grow milder. Imagine what it means: *the first rain of the year!* We expected cataracts—alas! only a few parsimonious drops fell from an inky sky. A prolonged gust of wind swept up all the dust of the camp.

April 6

We urged our horses on a little and arrived at the end of the stage before sunset, having left our porters far behind. The stage was a long one, and we expected to see them come in exhausted. I had a bonfire lighted to guide them and cheer them on their way. The night had long since closed in, and we lay down on some reed mats to wait for them, as we ourselves were utterly done in. At last they arrived, invaded the enclosure, and, to our great amazement, as soon as they had put down their loads, began to dance round us a wild, extravagant dance, to loud cries of "Thank you, Government!" I pass it on.

Ah! How far from ready these excellent fellows are for laying claim to social rights!

VII   Reï-Bouba   *April 8*

We left Djoroum as early as half past four in the morning.

We had to reach Reï by nine o'clock, the hour we had appointed. It was a four hours' march to Reï, and every hour a fresh messenger arrived to renew and enlarge the sultan's greetings and express the impatience with which he was expecting us.

At a certain spot pointed out by the interpreter, we halted all our porters and dismounted, so as to wait for everything to be ready, and to arrive neither too soon nor too late for this resolutely theatrical entry; also so as to lace up our boots and put on clean coats. We felt as if we were playing hide-and-go-seek.

At last we were told that the moment had come.

And then we saw advancing toward us twenty-five horsemen, whose appearance, although bizarre, was dark and severe; it was only when they had come quite close that we saw they were dressed in burnished steel coats of mail and had on their heads helmets topped by very strange crests. The horses were sweating, prancing, kicking up the dust magnificently. Then they spun about and rode before us. Half a kilometer farther on, the curtain of horsemen divided and let through sixty admirable lancers, dressed and helmeted as for the crusades, on caparisoned horses à la Simone Martini. And almost immediately after, these parted in their turn, like the bursting of a dike, under the pressure of a wave made up of a hundred and fifty horsemen in Arab robes and turbans, each bearing a lance in his hand.

More floods of men then succeeded each other more and more rapidly, pushed forward by a thick wall of foot-soldiers—archers in serried ranks and perfect order. Behind these one could make out something at first incomprehensible—this was a long line of shields made of hippopotamus hide; they were nearly black and were held at arm's length by the performers in the rear. I myself was carried away by this extraordinary ballet, and everything seemed to melt into a glorious symphony; I lost sight of details, and behind this last curtain of men as it parted, I beheld nothing but the sultan himself—surrounded by his bodyguard and standing before the town walls, just an arrow's flight from the door through which we were to enter, at the foot of a little slope and in the shade of a clump of enormous trees. At our approach, he descended from a kind of palanquin drawn by stooping, naked men. There were two parasols over him—one, of crimson, shaded him directly; the other, much larger one, was black, shot through with silver, and was held over the first. We dismounted from our horses and, extremely careful to represent as best we could France, civilization, the white race, we advanced with dignity, slowly and majestically, toward the outstretched hand of the sultan; we were flanked on either side by our two interpreters, the one who has come with us from Binder, and the sultan's, who came to meet us yesterday.

The sultan is very tall; less so, however, than I had expected from hearsay. I was struck by the beauty of his expression. He certainly aims rather to be loved than to be feared. He spoke in a low voice, with his arm paternally, and as it were tenderly, laid on the interpreter's shoulder. After the first compliments had been exchanged, we mounted our horses again and went on in front of him into his town. Six trumpets sounded continuously (composed of a very long antelope horn, which is connected with an ivory mouthpiece by a sheath made of crocodile skin). The populace was picturesquely arranged in groups halfway up the slope, in front of the city walls. . . .

An hour later we visited the sultan, after having announced our coming beforehand. At the foot of the great surrounding wall (it is about twenty feet high and built of earth) were ranged about a hundred captives in ceremonial attire, their backs to the wall, their javelins cast down at their feet. The gateway is very wide and long. When they cross this threshold, the servants take off their clothes, as they are only permitted to enter the sultan's presence naked to the waist. The roof is supported by large pillars with false capitals, recalling the entablatures of the palace at Susa. The wooden gates are extremely massive. Three men preceded us, bent double. They advanced as though they were crawling, making their gestures on a level with the ground. We then found ourselves in an oblong enclosure sanded with coarse river-sand, opposite a little piece of rising ground, on the top of which the sultan was sitting under a large tree. He rose at our approach, came down from the terrace, pressed our hands, and renewed his speeches of welcome. We followed him into a narrow, oblong room—a sort of passage. He made us sit down on a kind of divan-sofa, and himself lay down on a lower divan, not opposite, but beside us. The two interpreters remained crouching at the door; the sultan's private interpreter remained prostrate during the whole of our visit. An important subject of conversation was the Citroën which the sultan has ordered and which was no doubt still waiting at Lagos for the rainy season, which will enable it to be sent up the Bénoué. Marc is going to write the necessary letters to get it forwarded at once.

April 9

Another visit to the sultan, to whom we present some trifling objects we thought might please him—a map of the country, a rubber hot-water bottle, a magnifying mirror, some Bengal lights, some rolls of cotton. We promised to send him a watch and a new map from Paris. We also promised to do what was necessary at Douala in order to retrieve a sewing machine that is being held up there. So much amiability on our part no doubt encouraged him, and when I took leave of him, he held out his hand to me with a smile, but without rising.

April 12

At times one feels completely done in with fatigue—at the end of one's rope; one would like to give the whole thing up, like a child who calls "Time out!" in order to get out of the game. But perhaps the finest thing about this journey is the necessity of going on, the impossibility, as a rule, of paying any attention to the state of the weather, of one's own fatigue. . . .

On account of these perpetual fires, on account of the repeated displacement of races and villages, on account of the old forest's having been replaced by more recent vegetation, the constant and dominant impression —mine, at any rate—is of a new country, *without a past,* of immediate youth, of an inexhaustible spring of life, instead of the ancestral, prehistoric, prehuman feeling which travelers in this land prefer to talk of. The most gigantic trees of the equatorial forest do not perhaps appear so old as certain French oaks or Italian olives.

April 13

Started at five o'clock this morning and arrived at the end of our stage at about one o'clock—after two brief halts of twenty minutes—in a state of physical and nervous exhaustion. I am filled with remorse as I think of our porters. Not only do Marc and I carry nothing, but we have our horses and our *tipoyes* in case of need (it is true we hardly ever use them), and cold drinks of iced tea and lemonade to refresh us en route. We know that at the end of the day's march we shall find a deck chair to sink into, a bed to nap on, a table ready served. They have got to do the whole march with a load of forty or fifty pounds on their heads. You expect to see them arrive completely exhausted? They are singing. Grumbling?—They say:

"Thank you, Governor." Not a word of recrimination, not a single complaint. Always a pleasant smile in response to the word or two of friendly greeting we give them when we pass. They are admirable people.

What an unspeakable relief—rain, an attempt at a storm! Although it was not much, all nature seemed immediately washed, refreshed, revarnished. After months of drought and waiting, the rapidity of the growth after a first shower must be amazing.

Haldou, April 15

. . . If people think that I am complaining a great deal, I reply that I see no reason why I shouldn't. Out of self-esteem? I have very little, and what I have doesn't depend on my keeping silent. The stoical silence which people admire in Vigny and which made him put one of the worst and most absurd lines in our language into the wolf's mouth:

Puis après, comme moi, souffre et meurs sans parler
(And then afterwards, suffer and die silently, like me)

(as if it were stoicism that prevents wolves from speaking any more than carp!) seems to me more ridiculous than admirable; and, as Molière would have said, "pure affectation." As for me, it is my custom, when I suffer, to heave great romantic sighs, sighs more grand than they are painful, so profound that my suffering feels slight by comparison.

. . . I went on by myself on foot and got well ahead of the others. It was intoxicating to feel oneself all alone in the midst of this strangeness, far from everyone, all contact with mankind lost; to hear no other sound but the songs of birds, etc. Great empty spaces where one hoped to surprise wild creatures. And here and there, in the monotonous forest, astonishing low palm trees with wide leaves.

VIII   N'Gaoundéré   *April 26*

Yesterday evening we were invited to have tea with the Swedish missionary. I have not enough imagination to take this simple and naïve creature for a spy. The tea party dragged a little; it was followed by an open-air sermon, as on every Sunday. The good man learned the Haussa language in *Denmark!* He admits that so far he has not made a single conversion and that no one listens to him. These lectures of his must be curiously painful. "They go on talking to each other, but they hear me all the same," he said, "and Christ's truth slowly sinks in." Marc wanted to film the scene, but a violent storm dispelled these projects. Our first real tropical storm. Diluvial rain and terrific claps of thunder.

May 2

Rose early, urged out of doors by the fine weather, which I positively *felt* before I saw the heavens—admirable in their blue serenity. An almost full moon was still queen of the sky, a sky paling into dawn. The quality of the air was extraordinary—soft, warm, caressing, light, of an incomparable suavity. . . . Around the great trees, drowned in mists which the sun was beginning to dissipate, there floated strange, unknown perfumes. Soft, flexible vegetation, rich with hidden strength. Groups of trees, so fine, so great, so noble, that one said to oneself: "This is what I have come to see!" Songs of birds. Chirping of insects. My heart was flooded with a confused sort of adoration. But is it the exotic vegetation that I admire so? . . . Is it not—above all—the spring itself?

Silence, traversed by the songs of mysterious birds. Flowers of gigantic plants; one of them, extraordinarily hairy—or, rather, bristling with spikes—was covered with bunches of orange fruit, like fat hairy grapes. Sad seeing all this without Marc. I am incapable of enjoying anything by myself.

This is the last day. Our journey is over. Perhaps I shall never see the virgin forest again. It has never been more beautiful, and we passed by like travelers in a hurry to reach their goal, when this *was* the goal. Oh! if I could see it again, even just for a moment! We are only twenty-five kilometers away from it. The car would take us back in less than an hour. . . .

May 3–6

Back to civilization. The forest which the railway passes through is marvelously beautiful. We traveled very comfortably in a baggage car with our boys and all our paraphernalia. But I have lost the urge to write things down.

Douala, May 7

What a hotel! The most primitive of jungle way-stations was better than this. And what white people! Ugly, stupid, vulgar. . . . As for me, who am always afraid of disturbing other people—other people's thoughts, other people's rest, other people's prayers—such want of consideration fills me first of all with amazement and then with indignation. But I end by saying to myself that if these people disturb us, it is unwittingly; for as they themselves neither meditate, nor read, nor pray—and sleep the sleep of brutes—they are never disturbed by anything. I should like to write a *Praise of Discretion.*

May 14

It is all over. We have looped the loop. The ship has weighed anchor and Mount Cameroon is disappearing slowly into the fog.*

* The following entry from the journal of Roger Martin du Gard may help one to understand the last stages of Gide's Congo journey:

> It was only later on that I was to learn—partly from Gide, but largely from Marc—what a horror the last part of their trip had been, after Fort Lamy. This is what happened: at about the same time, in the whaleboat, Marc fell victim to a severe fever, and Gide to dysentery. They were twelve days away from the last medical station, and twenty days away from the next. Suddenly terrified, they decided to go back. They arrived at the medical station, as it turned out, all but cured, and spent very little time there. But this misadventure caused them to lose three weeks, at a time when they had not a day to lose if they were to reach the sea before the hot season commenced.
>
> This delay forced them to spend a month on the road, in burning, desert country, in temperatures of 110°. Gide was seized with panic, and felt sure that he was not going to make it, that he would die before reaching the port; so, weak as he was, he kept extending each day's march, refusing to make the necessary stop every two or three days; for a month, therefore, they ran a veritable race, a hellish race against Death, breathing in that burning air, sweating from the anxiety as well as the heat, scarcely speaking a word, thinking of nothing but the distance covered, the distance yet to go, and calculating a hundred times an hour whether or not their strength would last out until the end. (June 24, 1926: from Gide–Martin du Gard, *Correspondance,* I, p. 679)

from

THE JOURNAL
1 9 2 6 – 1 9 3 2

1926   *July 1*

X. will say:

"The slow progress of Catholicism on her soul; it seems to me that I am watching the spreading of a gangrene.

"Every time I come back, after having left her some time, I find new regions affected, deeper, more secret regions, forever incurable. And, even if I could, would I attempt to *cure* her? The 'health' that I would offer her—might it not be mortal to her? Any effort exhausts her.

"What a convenience, what a comfort, what a minimum of effort is offered her by that carefully measured piety, that fixed-price menu for souls that cannot spend very much!

"Who could have believed it?—Could God himself have expected it? Everything that attached me to her, that vagabond mood, that fervor, that curiosity—all that did not really belong to her, then? Really? It was only out of love for me that she put it all on? All that comes undone, falls off, reveals the bare soul, unrecognizable and fleshless.

"And everything that constitutes my *raison d'être,* my life, becomes foreign and hostile to her."

August 6

Em. has informed me of J.'s fears about Jean T. and my growing power over him. She begs me to do nothing to attract Jean. She fears my "influence." I had to promise to "give him the cold shoulder." This is absurd. I am sure that I could do that child good and perhaps spare him serious mistakes. He is at the age when one has the greatest need of advice. It is thought that mine could only be bad. Just try to protest! Yet it would suffice to have a look at what became of the young men in whom I have really been able to take an interest. Those on whom I was able "to have an influence." There is not one of them that I tried to draw in my direction. Quite the contrary: my constant care has been to push them in their own direction. There is not one of them of whom I haven't the right to be proud. As for Jean T., I should like merely to warn him. He is going ahead in life like a scatterbrain and will probably acquire experience only after burning his fingers painfully. But no one pays any attention to my disinterestedness and to the respect for others that prompts my advice in every case.

August 15

The poor old woman who is called "Grandma" here is eighty-six. So humpbacked, or at least so bent double (for her back is straight) by constant gardening that she cannot straighten up and walks with her rear higher than her head, in little steps, leaning on a cane. She has always worked, always struggled. From Hyères she went to Saint-Clair, whence Mme Théo brought her here out of pity and rather than let her enter the poorhouse. Her hands are completely deformed by rheumatism; it seems that her feet are worse. At night she suffers so that she cannot sleep. From morning to night one sees her working in the garden, for she is always afraid of being dependent and insists on earning her own living. She pulls up the weeds—and sometimes the flowers too, but with such zeal that no one dares correct her. She is told: "Grandma, take a rest. It's Sunday." But when she is not working, she is bored. She envies those who know how to read. She remains seated on the canal embankment, her eyes half-closed, turning over old memories in her mind. I approach her, for she claims that she is bored and that she enjoys chatting. But when she complains, says that she would like to die, that life is nothing but one long suffering for her, and "yet I can't kill myself . . ." and then adds: "I'd like to, though" —I don't know what to say.

It is for such creatures, to help them endure their suffering, to put up with life, that rosaries exist, and prayers, and belief in a better life, in the reward for one's labors. Skepticism, incredulity, are all right for the rich, the happy, the favored, those who don't need hope and for whom the present is enough. And that is just the saddest part of it: poor Grandma does not believe in God, or that anything beyond death will make up for her sorry life.

She says: "Do you want me to tell you? If there is a God, well, he's an idiot—or else a bad one. . . . He takes away Madame Flé, so young, who wanted nothing better than to go on living and whom everyone liked. And I want nothing better than to die, but he drags me on. . . ." All this said with the accent of the Midi.

October 16

Paris again. Tumult. I feel myself becoming unsociable. No desire to talk to people any more. Even more absolutely: no desires. Conversation with Adrienne Monnier, who does not like *Les Faux-Monnayeurs.* In general what is happening with this latest book is exactly what has already taken place so many times with the preceding ones. The most recent work is liked only by those who haven't yet liked the others, and all the readers who had been won over by the earlier books declare they like "this one much less." I am accustomed to it and know that it is enough to wait.

Adrienne Monnier talks to me for some time and rather eloquently of the coldness and fundamental *malice* this book reveals, which must be my basic nature. I don't know what to say, what to think. Whatever criticism is made of me, I always acquiesce. But I know that Stendhal likewise was long accused of insensibility and coldness. . . .

1927   *Saint-Clair,* February 8*

Everything I might write to explain, exonerate, or defend myself—I must deny myself all of it. I often imagine such a preface for *L'Immoraliste,* for *Les Faux-Monnayeurs,* for *La Symphonie pastorale*—one, above all that would set forth what I mean by fictional objectivity, that would establish two sorts of novels, or at least two ways of looking at and depicting life, which in certain novels (*Wuthering Heights,* Dostoevsky's novels) are joined. The first, exterior and commonly called objective, which begins by visualizing others' acts and events and then interprets them. The second, which begins by paying attention to emotions and thoughts and runs the risk of being powerless to depict anything that the author himself has not felt first. The resources of the author, his complexity, the antagonism of his excessive and varied possibilities, will permit the greatest variety in his creations. But it is from him that it all derives. He is the only guarantee of the truth he is revealing, the only judge. All the heaven and hell of his characters is in him. It is not himself that he paints, but what he paints he could have become if he had not become *all* that he is. It was in order to be able to write *Hamlet* that Shakespeare did not let himself become Othello.

. . . Yes, I could set forth all this. But haven't I already said it, or let it be sufficiently understood, when I spoke of Dostoevsky? What is the good of saying it again? It is better to say to the reader: Read me more carefully, reread me; and go on to something else.

* The Van Rysselberghes' country house in the South of France.

February 12

Call on L., who offers me 24,000 francs to bring out a new edition of a thousand copies of *Si le grain ne meurt*. . . . No other reason to let him do it but "the profit motive." I resist. He will tell himself that he did not offer me enough. He will never know that it was above all his son who killed the deal, a fat fellow of about thirty who talks in a cynical manner and regrets not having a sister "who could give him money. . . ."

February 13

"The approbation of a single mere *respectable man*," she told me, "is the only thing that matters to me, and that your book will not get." But whoever approves my book ceases to appear respectable in her eyes.

Likewise, before some of the most important acts of my life she would write me: "Nothing good can come of it," and consequently would refuse to recognize as good anything that might ensue.—These are judgments which one cannot appeal.

February 26

Exasperated by the life I am leading and by all those who make me waste my time. Exasperated against myself for not knowing how to defend myself better. I no longer take any pleasure in conversations, even when I shine in them.—Paul Valéry writes me a heartbreaking letter. Will it be like this until death, and shall we never again know leisure? "O fruitful idleness!"—People trespass frightfully on one another.

On the train to Cuverville, March 5

They insist on seeing *Les Faux-Monnayeurs* as a failure. They said the same thing of Flaubert's *Education sentimentale* and of Dostoevsky's *The Possessed*. (I remember that what made me read *The Possessed* and *The Brothers Karamazov* was the retreat of that great ninny Melchior before these "apocalyptical and sinister" books.) Before twenty years are up, it will be recognized that what people now hold against my book is precisely its qualities. I am sure of this.*

Zurich, May 5

Some people rot and others ossify; all get old. Nothing but a great intellectual fervor can overcome the fatigue and the withering of the body.

* In 1950, *Les Faux-Monnayeurs* was named one of the "twelve best [French] novels of the half-century" by a jury of critics.

With M. my whole youth left me; I doze while awaiting his return and waste my time as if I still had a great deal to waste. I sleep too much, smoke too much, digest badly, and am hardly aware of the spring. The creature gives in when he has no one to think of but himself; it is only through love that I still make an effort; that is to say, when it is for someone else.

> *Ah! que revienne*
> *Le temps où l'on s'éprenne!* *

May 7

Even the masks of central Africa, the native sculptures, are the product of a religious sentiment. Primitive mentality is more religious than ours and, in this regard, the Negro is more than a match for us.

"How can they *believe* in that?" you wonder, you who believe. My sorry amazement in regard to your faith is of the same nature as your amazement before theirs.

The palace of faith. . . . You find consolation there, assurance and comfort. Everything in it is arranged to protect your laziness and guarantee your mind against effort.

May 8

No, no, it is not my doctrine that is wrong. The principles were good, but I have not followed them.

I remember having heard Wilde say: "It is not through excessive individualism that I have sinned. My great mistake, the error I cannot forgive myself, is having, one day, ceased to persist in my individualism, ceased to believe in it in order to listen to others, ceased to believe that I was right to live as I did, doubted myself."

You blame my ethic; I accuse my inconsistency. Where I was wrong was when I thought that perhaps you were right.

What I admire most in Valéry is perhaps indeed his constancy. Incapable of real sympathy, he never let his line of conduct be broken, never let himself be distracted from himself by anyone.

---

* Ah! that it would return—
  The time when one could burn!

Heidelberg, May 12

The game is lost, which I could have won only with her. Lack of confidence on her part, and presumption on mine. Recriminations are of no use, nor even regrets. What is not is what could not be. Whoever starts out toward the unknown must consent to venture alone. Creusa, Eurydice, Ariadne—there is always a woman lagging behind, worrying, afraid to let go and to see break the thread that ties her to her past. She pulls Theseus back, makes Orpheus look around. She is afraid.

. . . Acceptance; confidence; serenity: the virtues of an old man. The age of struggling with the angel is over.

Cuverville, June

Youth attracts me, and even more than beauty. A certain freshness, an innocence one would like to recapture. . . .

July 3

Good God, how complicated everything is becoming! Lines in all directions; and no guidance. No way of knowing what to believe, what to think! . . .

Cuverville

Unhealthy torpor. The constrictions and pains in the esophagus (?) are becoming almost continuous and unbearable. I take refuge in sleep like a sulky child withdrawing from the game.

October 5

How to get into a novel that impression felt as I entered the D.s' the other evening? . . .

When, after dinner, I enter their little living-room, he is smoking his pipe beside a gramophone that he is playing probably not so much for his sake as to amuse his young wife and his sister-in-law; she lives with them to help in the housekeeping; the three of them are there in that little room to which he returns after the day's work. This is the only time he has to himself. And even this time, when he could catch hold of himself, is completely taken up by the family. In order to live on the same level as "his own people," he comes down from himself, sets himself on that modest plane. Could he, with greater financial resources, spend more time by himself? I don't think so. I don't think he would try to. He owes these evening hours to his young wife, whom he has not seen all day. He feels mediocrity taking him over; but what can he do about it? He doesn't fight it; he sacrifices himself, burying deep within him his ambitions, his dreams, his hopes, everything that would compromise that domestic felicity.—The chapter would be entitled:

CONJUGAL HAPPINESS
*Et tibi magna satis . . .**

And no possible way out; no escape that does not appear cowardly, egotistical, impious . . . to the weak person.

October 20

My grandmother Rondeaux had saved up for the end the best of what she had to say, the last instructions and recommendations she wished to leave with her children. When she felt that the solemn hour was approaching, she gathered them all round her, but at that moment was seized with a paralysis of the tongue and, instead of a sublime speech, could utter only a tremendous scream. Such a loud scream, Albert told me as he related this recollection, that it was heard all the way to the end of the garden. This took place at La Mivoie.

That is perhaps what lies in store for me if I wait too long.

October 23

All the thoughts that desire once nourished, all the anxieties it provoked, ah, how difficult it becomes to understand them when the source of lust dries up! And how then can one be surprised by the intransigence of those who have never been led by desire? . . . It seems, with the coming of age, that one had somewhat exaggerated its demands, and one is astonished to see younger men who still let themselves be tormented by it. The waves subside when the wind drops; the whole ocean falls asleep and reflects only the sky. Knowing how to wish for the inevitable—this is the summit of wisdom. For the old.

November 4

Daniel Simond, from Lausanne, whom I met the day before yesterday on the boulevards and invited to lunch this noon, tells me that his professor has suggested to him as a thesis subject: the influence of Nietzsche on my work. It is flattering, but to what can it lead? To seeking out, in my *Im-*

* "And large enough for you . . ." (Virgil).

moraliste for example, everything that might recall Zarathustra, and paying no attention to what life itself taught me. . . .

I have reflected considerably about this question of "influences," and believe that very gross errors are committed concerning it. The only thing that is worth anything in literature is what life teaches us. Everything we learn only from books remains abstract, a dead letter. Had I not encountered Dostoevsky, Nietzsche, Blake, or Browning, I cannot believe that my work would have been any different. At the most they helped me to disentangle my thoughts. And even then, I took pleasure in saluting those in whom I recognized my own ideas. But the ideas were mine, and it is not to these men that I owe them. Otherwise they would be worthless. The one great influence, perhaps, to which I have really *submitted* is that of Goethe, and even then I am not sure whether or not my admiration for Greek literature and Hellenism would not have sufficed to counterbalance my early Christian education.

Furthermore, I feel rich enough never to have tried to pass off as mine the thoughts that belonged to someone else.

Alibert told me that he wondered if one ought not to see precaution, prudence on the part of Racine's wife, rather than the indifference that is generally imputed to her, in her refusal to read or see any play by her husband. Shouldn't one see in it respect for the work and a need to give such an assurance of tact and discretion with regard to a domain that fell outside her competence? * . . . Perhaps Alibert outlined that thesis to me only because he was thinking more of Cuverville and of me than of Racine, and perhaps he was attempting, under this pretext, to show me discreetly how capable he was of understanding the modesty and secret wisdom of such a feminine reserve. In Racine's household it went hand in hand with Racine's renunciation and the near disavowal of his whole past life.

November 6

Those who claim to act according to rules of life (however beautiful those rules may be) strike me as idiots, or at least blunderers incapable of taking advantage of life—I mean: of learning from life. In any case, unbearable people.

* I believe today that one must see in it a most Christian horror of what belongs to the demon, and that Mme Racine had much to do with her husband's silence. (Added in 1929.) [A. G.]

November 11

A poor woman comes to tell Eugène MacCown her troubles, the sorry life that her lover, a young writer by the name of M. (I believe), makes her lead. He beats her. This is because he is influenced by me. "He goes to see Gide every day," this woman tells Eugène, "tells him that he has beaten me, and Gide says to him: 'Bravo; that was well done!'" Moreover, she is not taken in, and even before he confesses it, she can tell by his look: "You have just been to see André Gide."

With a few bits of malicious gossip of this sort, my reputation is well established.

November 24

B. sends me a series of American newspaper and magazine articles on the translation of *Les Faux-Monnayeurs*.

Sad to note that there is not one of them that is not better than the best of the articles that appeared in France.

With one or two exceptions, when a French critic wants to write an article about me, he strives not to explain or understand me, but to take up and maintain a position against me.

November 25

To observe the progressive decay of age requires a form of sincerity that is most difficult to obtain from oneself. A journal that kept track of it would be vastly interesting. Moreover I do not believe that that decay is unavoidable, and were it not for a slight weakening of my senses (sight especially), I should barely feel touched by age; if I did not see it in the mirror, and if I did not constantly repeat it to myself, nothing in me would remind me that three days ago I entered my fifty-ninth year. But perhaps one of the privileges of age is that it is not too conscious itself of what is a glaring fact to everyone else.

Cuverville, November 30

I spend two mornings replying to the study (if one can use this word) of my work by a certain Victor Poucel that appeared in *"Etudes*—a Catholic review of general interest." And finally I do not send my letter. What is the good? We are so infinitely far apart. There is not one of my features that, voluntarily or involuntarily, is not distorted. But, after all, he is right, they are right to look upon me as the enemy. The amusing thing is that I am considered likewise as *the enemy* by their adversaries. It is essential not to let oneself be crushed, or saddened, or exasperated, or conceited, but on the other hand to find a certain equilibrium of the heart and mind in the balancing of these hatreds. And to keep *oneself* from hating.

1928   *Cuverville, January 2*

. . . went a long way out the next day to the Malendins' to see the three little orphans who had spoken to me so nicely on the road as I was coming back from the Déhaises' and to whom I wanted to take something to help them celebrate New Year's Day a bit more gaily. Immensity of human misery. In contrast to which the indifference of certain rich people or their egotism is becoming more and more incomprehensible to me. Preoccupation with oneself, one's comfort, one's ease, one's salvation, denotes an absence of charity that is becoming more and more disgusting to me.

Each one of these young writers who goes about indulging his suffering from the *"mal du siècle,"* or from mystic aspirations, or from *inquiétude,* or from boredom, would be cured instantly if he strove to cure or to relieve the *real* sufferings of those around him. We who have been favored have no right to complain. If, with all we have, we still don't know how to be happy, it is because we have a false idea of happiness. When we understand that the secret of happiness lies not in possessing but in giving, by making others happy we shall be happier ourselves.—Why and how have not those who call themselves Christians better understood this initial truth of the Gospel?

Cuverville, January 3

Despite every resolution of optimism, melancholy occasionally wins out; man has decidedly botched up the planet.

Tuesday, February 28

No longer aiming toward consonance and harmony, toward what is music heading? Toward a sort of barbarism. Sound itself, so gradually and exquisitely liberated from noise, is returning to it. At first only the lords, the nobles, are allowed to appear on the stage; then the bourgeoisie; then the masses. Once the stage is overrun, there is no way to tell it from the street. But what can be done about it? What madness it is to strive to oppose that inevitable progress! In modern music the consonant intervals of the past seem to us like fossils of the *ancien régime.*

March 10

No, there is absolutely no need of being mean to hurt someone else. And this is the most tragic thing about it: that good people who love each other can torment and grieve each other with the best will in the world.

Cuverville, March 30

T.V. would like love; I can only give her friendship. However great this may be, the expectation I sense in her of a more affectionate state falsifies all my acts and leads me to the edge of insincerity. I explain myself this evening in a letter, which will perhaps hurt her and which it is hard for me to write; but the fear of causing pain is one of the forms of cowardice, and my whole being revolts against it.

June 9

Lassitude and calculation of death.

For a long time now, no further enjoyment in writing in this notebook. Aged considerably. Kept myself busy, but didn't really work.

After a trip to Belgium (lecture and showing of the film in Brussels) and to Holland (The Hague and Amsterdam) to prepare our trip to New Guinea, we give up the project.

When I think that I am only now beginning to shake off the Congo (I am still involved in correcting proofs for the big edition), I am somewhat terrified by the possible results of this new trip, even more than by the trip itself. Since our return Marc has done almost nothing; or at least has not really worked. I fear that, *for greater facility,* he may give up the best that is in him.

I fear, if I take him to New Guinea, that I may be doing him a disservice and getting him definitely out of the habit of work. It is the pleasure, the happiness of being with him, that leads me there, even more than any curiosity for distant places. That felicity, to which I surrender, seriously falsifies my thought. It was for him, to win his attention, his esteem, that I wrote *Les Faux-Monnayeurs,* just as I wrote all my preceding books under the influence of Em., or in the vain hope of convincing her. Urgent need to be alone, to get hold of myself. It is no longer a matter of charming someone else—which can never be done without concessions and a certain self-deception. I must accept the fact that my path takes me away from those toward whom my heart inclines; and even recognize that it *is* my path because of that very fact: that it isolates me. . . .

Marseilles, July 1

In Paris I at least can fall back on blaming others for making me waste my time. Here I can only hold it against myself. And I don't know when that pursuit is more degrading and more empty—when one encounters pleasure or when one seeks it without finding it? I am writing this now that I am getting old, and this evening when I feel tired. And tomorrow I shall begin again.

Paris, 22

Not only does M. not know what it is to love—but he does not even know that he doesn't know it. He knows affection and desire—not love.

October 20

I have been aging, for some time now, in a frightful way.

Roquebrune,* October 22

. . . I force myself to rest and keep constantly saying to myself: No, poor old boy, this is not laziness; you are really very tired.

Whoever would note down simply, from day to day, the cracks, the crumbling of his person, the gradual effect of age . . .

At one time, to accompany that sudden sensation of falling off to sleep, I used to dream that I was falling into an abyss; now, simply that I am missing a step.

That lack of curiosity of the flesh which precedes by far impotence and even the dying-out of desires, which makes the latter compromise and finally ease their dominion, no, it is not apathy; but, the mind resuming the upper hand, it leaves the way open for moralizing.

1929   *Algiers, January 13, 6:30 a.m.*

The moment when I feel most violently like leaving a town is when I have just arrived there. What squalor! What poverty! What approximations! What piddling "promises of happiness"! or rather: how few promises, and of what piddling happiness!

* The site of "La Souco," Simon and Dorothy Bussy's villa near Nice.

15

Wisdom begins where the fear of God ends. There is not a single progress of thought that did not seem at first harmful and impious.

16

Slept, since yesterday, an unbelievable number of hours. Is it old age, an accumulation of fatigue, or an unhealthy disposition? Veritable orgy of nothingness to which the cold and ugliness of the weather, my utter lack of curiosity with regard to Algiers, and a complete absence of all desires invited me. . . .

I search my memory whether ever such empty, such dull hours . . . I search in vain.

17

When I think of all that is spared me: toothaches, stomachaches, heartaches, money troubles, I wonder that there are not more people to jump into the river, and judge that humanity, all in all, shows remarkable guts. It is perhaps also because humanity lacks that little bit of courage that is necessary to end it all.

January 21

What I call "fatigue" is old age, and nothing can rest one from it but death.

Of all this "bad because contrary to nature," which is the worse? To refuse oneself pleasures as a young man or, as an old man, still to seek them?

March 5

I would not swear that at a certain period of my life I was not very close to being converted. Thank God, a few converts among my friends took care of that, however. Neither Jammes, nor Claudel, nor Ghéon, nor Charlie Du Bos will ever know how instructive his example was for me. I repeat this to myself as I read in that monument of immodesty and unconscious self-indulgence, Charlie's journal. Throughout, it breathes an astonishing need for self-admiration, doubled by a naïveté such that it provokes and disarms laughter at the same time.

I am by nature little inclined to egotism; by the end of my early childhood, my love for my cousin took me outside of myself; but in the beginning of my life my eyes were always on myself, as were those of my parents, of whom I was the only child.

[August]

That original Christian upbringing, irremediably, *detached* me from the
world, inculcating in me, doubtless, not so much a disgust for this earth as
disbelief in its reality. . . . I have never managed to take this life quite
seriously; by no means because I have ever been able to believe (insofar as
I remember) in eternal life (I mean in an afterlife), but rather in another
facet of this life which escapes our senses and of which we can have but a
very imperfect knowledge. . . . Indefinable impression of being "on
tour" and of playing, in makeshift sets, with cardboard daggers.

Met Valéry on the eve of my departure for Le Tertre;* that is, Saturday,
the last day of July (?). In the back of the *N.R.F.* shop he was autographing some copies of the new printing of *Teste.* He took me by the arm and
accompanied me to the corner of the rue de Bellechasse and the boulevard
Saint-Germain. Then we walked up and down in front of the Ministry of
War until the twelve-thirty bell reminded him that he was expected for
lunch. More intelligent, more charming, more affectionate than ever. Yet
I leave that conversation considerably depressed, as I do almost all my
meetings with Valéry. But this time it is not so much in feeling an intelligence so incomparably superior to mine attach no value to the provisions I
can supply, accept as authentic only the currency in which I am most poor;
no, it was not that frightful feeling of bankruptcy (which used to drive
me to despair), but a much more subtle feeling, closely related to the one I
tried to describe yesterday. Valéry, unlike me, is closely attached to life.
He relates to me his conversations with Marshals Foch and Pétain; he
always says exactly what is appropriate to say, which is always a bit more
and a bit different from what one expects. He tells of Barthou's petty in-
trigues to take away from him the speech of welcome for Pétain, which
Valéry is scheduled to give, but which Barthou would be glad to give in
his place "if it just happened that it bored you or that you felt tired." He is
playing his life like a game of chess that it is important to win, and as he

* The Martin du Gards' estate in Normandy.

writes his poems, placing just the right word, as one moves up a pawn, in just the right place. He has managed his life so well that mine, in comparison, seems to me nothing but a sorry succession of blunders. I remember that, still quite young, Valéry said to me: "If I wanted to be rich, it would be in order to be able, always and in any society or circumstance whatever, to wear the appropriate costume. . . ."

I show him the letter I have just written to Poincaré in gratitude for his very kind letter thanking me for my *Voyage au Congo.* I was at that moment on my way to take the letter to the hospital in rue de la Chaise, where Poincaré has just been operated on; so I take it out of my pocket to show it to Valéry. He finds almost nothing in it that does not need to be changed, to be rewritten; almost nothing that is appropriate. And he is right. His remarks, his suggestions are excellent. As soon as I get home, rewriting my letter, I take them into account, very glad to have met him, but plunged into the deepest consternation by the *inappropriateness* of my being and all of its manifestations. . . .

Le Tertre, August 11

That year the two B. brothers were at Pontigny. One night (I had talked with the two of them at length, during the evening) I had a frightful nightmare: I dreamed that there were three of them. (The third was an equestrienne in a ballet skirt.) I woke up in a sweat.

Cuverville, August 14

The rather narrow wish for a comfortable victory of "good" over "evil" has lamentably retarded the progress of humanity.

September 27

The ugliness, the vulgarity of the people in the *métro* depresses me terribly. Oh, to go back among the Negroes! . . .

Paris, October 3

Certain days (today, for instance) life has such a bad taste that one would like to be able to spit it out.

October 7

Utterly destroyed by a very bad night. The fate of X. and of Y., which is at stake, torments me so that I cannot sleep for more than four hours. I have with one, then with the other very serious conversations; have no idea what to fear, what to hope for. . . .

I cannot write in this notebook anything of what is most dear to me; thus it is that not a trace will be found here of the Constantinople adventure, which, during the last three months, has so filled my mind and which I am not yet willing to believe closed. I think of it every day, and never pass in front of the concierge's door without looking anxiously to see if perhaps at last a letter . . . I cannot believe that Emile D. will allow anyone to forbid him to write to me. . . . It is better to say nothing of it than to say too little.

Cuverville, October 8

. . . In my childhood I was subject to frequent nightmares, which left me terrorized; I used to wake up screaming or in tears and would be afraid to go back to sleep. At a certain age, around sixteen, I don't know just what happened . . . the anguish left me. Sometimes it happened that I dreamed the same things; yes, the very ones that a short time before would have filled me with terror; but interest and curiosity took the place of the fear, horror, or distress of the past. . . .

How can it be that I am not more disturbed by little Emile D.'s sudden silence, even though not an hour of the day passes without my thinking of it? . . .

I should nevertheless like to be sure that the little fellow did not kill himself. In the state of exaltation he had reached, he was capable of doing so if he suddenly met a blind, absurd opposition from his parents; if he were to kill himself after being driven to despair by them, they would certainly consider me responsible for that death . . . just as they already considered me responsible for everything that upset them, for everything they did not understand in their child, for everything in him that escaped them and in which they could no longer recognize themselves. They were terrified to see their son "become too fond of me." Even if he were, as the mother wrote me, "on the road to damnation," who was more capable of understanding him, of holding out a hand, of saving him . . . than I?

October 12

What is he doing? Where is he? Is he thinking of me? Is he telling himself that I am forgetting him? . . . This constant interrogation plays a muffled accompaniment to all my thoughts.

October 13

. . . Everything tires and bores me. When that boy went away, I lost all the youth that was left me.

October 17

As I pass the concierge's door he gives me a letter from Emile. At last! I cannot read it at once, but keep on fingering it in my pocket until the very moment I feel its dagger's thrust in my heart. Certainly he had no idea how cruel his letter would be to me. The abominable calumnies he has been told about me have affected him, and as he believes what he has been told—that I am a two-faced, heartless person—he has no fear of making me suffer. He is in Paris; was going by near the rue Vaneau a few days ago, almost came up to see me; congratulates himself on not having done so; tells me at one and the same time that he still loves me and has made up his mind not to love me any more. He talks as if all the feeling were on his side. Finally he asks me to make no attempt to reach him, to forget him as he is going to forget me; and, to be sure of my silence, refuses to give me his address.

To pull myself together I read Massis's two scathing articles in the *Revue universelle.* They are entitled "The Bankruptcy of André Gide," and are dedicated to the book by Du Bos, who has so masterfully and pertinently distinguished and exposed in his former friend a case of "generalized inversion." Etc., etc.

It seems to me that in the whole affair of little Emile I let myself be taken in most absurdly. This is precisely because I was unwilling to look upon it as a game (which is the surest means of all of letting oneself be taken in)—and this is why it is all so painful to me today. We should be half cured of an infatuation if we could convince ourself that the person with whom we are in love is, after all, but a rather ordinary creature. The strength of the attachment comes from the gnawing conviction that there is in the beloved something exceptional, unique, irreplaceable, which we shall never again find.

October 21

In the evening read a few pages of La Bruyère, which washed me clean of all the agitations, the torments, the petty and vain contortions of this day.

The love of truth is not the same thing as the need for certainty, and it is very unwise to confuse one with the other.

October 28

Yesterday, visit from Valéry. He tells me once again that, for many years
now, he has written only on order and when pressed by a need for money.

"That is to say that, for some time, you have written nothing for your
own pleasure?"

"For my own pleasure?!" he continues. "But my pleasure consists
precisely in writing *nothing*. I should certainly have done something other
than write, if it had been a question of my own pleasure. No, no; I have
never written anything, and I never write anything, save under compulsion, forced to, and cursing against it."

November 4

. . . I bump into this: "Man by nature is, Mr. Gide feels, good." I reflect,
look into my mind. No, I do not believe, like Rousseau, that the natural
man is always good, or that all the evil is the result of deformations and
deviations brought about later by civilization, society, etc., etc. . . . I
consider it awkward, unprofitable, uninstructive to stand (solely) on the
plane of *good* and *evil* in order to judge human actions, or, more exactly,
in order to appreciate their value. That idea of humanity's *progress* which
now dominates my life (and of which, as I have said elsewhere, the "progress" Flaubert laughed at is but the caricature) leads us to see that the idea
of *the good* (comfortable, reassuring, and such as the middle classes cherish) invites to stagnation, to sleep. I believe that often *evil* (a certain evil
that is not the result of a *deficiency,* but rather a manifestation of energy)
has a greater educative and initiatory value than what you call *good.* Yes, I
believe this firmly, and more and more all the time.

. . . today we rate humanity much too high; man is not interesting,
important, worthy to be adored, for his own sake; what invites humanity
to progress is precisely to consider itself (and its comfort and the satisfaction of its desires) not as an end, but rather as a means through which to
achieve and realize something. This is what made me say, through the
person of my Prometheus: "I do not love man; I love what devours him,"
and made me put my wisdom in this: knowing how to prefer to man the
eagle that feeds upon him.

December 2

Radiant morning. Managed to devote from four to five hours to the piano
all these recent days; perfected (and really succeeded in bringing to perfection) several *Etudes* and *Préludes.*

Marseilles, December 27

I wander in the streets of Marseilles, striving to warm up old desires. I encounter nothing but poverty, ugliness, sorrow . . . nothing that does not incline one more to pity than to desire. Can it be that, younger and more full of desire, all this would have seemed different to me?

La Souco–Roquebrune, December 30

Splendid weather. Oh, to set sail, and for no matter where! Why, how did I allow myself to be held back so long, during my youth? At present I feel more desires in me than can be satisfied in the time that I have left to live. Why did I not meet, at twenty, someone who would have taken me off—someone I should have accompanied to the very ends of the earth! But at that time no one spoke of traveling; and it was already quite an achievement to have got as far as Algeria. What would my *Nourritures* have been like, had I known enough to drag my hunger off to the very tropics? But the strength of the bonds to be broken constitutes the beauty of the liberation, and my first care was to forge the bonds. I should like to regret nothing and to convince myself that, more obviously vagabond, my life would have been less significant; and that I should never have written *La Porte étroite.*

1930   *January 9*

Returned from the south on the 7th with Lacretelle; seats reserved by him in the Pullman. . . .

At the table directly opposite us was a rather attractive young couple. Probably a wedding trip, for the table is covered with flowers. The young man was reading *Les Caves du Vatican.* This is the first time I have ever happened to meet someone actually reading *me.* (The scene: "Oh! Monsieur Duhamel!!") Occasionally he turned toward me and, when I was not looking at him, I felt him staring at me. Most likely he recognized me. Lacretelle kept telling me: "Go ahead! Tell him who you are. Sign his book for him. . . ." In order to do that, I should have had to be more certain that he liked the book, in which he remained absorbed even during the meal. But suddenly I saw him take a little knife out of his pocket. . . . Lacretelle was seized with uncontrollable laughter on seeing him slash *Les Caves.* Was it out of exasperation? For a moment I thought so. But no: Carefully he cut the binding threads, took out the first few sections, and handed a whole part of the book that he had already read to his young wife, who immediately plunged into her reading.

Roquebrune, February 4

It is most likely that a "problem" that interests only one country will likewise concern only one moment of its history.

This revival of Thomism, and the writings of Maritain, and the quarrel of *L'Action Française,* etc., in which we flay each other, will soon seem only historical curiosities and I wonder if anyone but an archæologist will be able to take any interest in them.

Cuverville, March 31

. . . as I look back over my life, what saddens me rather is the thought of the little I have done, the thought of all I might have and should have done. All the books I should have written, so many countries I might have known, so much happiness I might have caused. An unaccountable diffidence, modesty, shyness, reticence, laziness, excessive understanding of the *other side,* etc., have constantly held me back, unfailingly checked me in mid-course. I have always been paralyzed by scruples and by fear of hurting the one I loved; and nothing is more ruinous when what one loves is different from oneself.

It goes without saying that it is especially at Cuverville, near to Em., that I feel all this. He whose heart is free can go far; I have never been able to keep myself from taking into account all manner of things that kept me from advancing; never been able to resign myself to going alone. I have always been more eager to lead others than to venture forth myself. Real pioneers do not care whether or not they are followed; they march straight ahead without looking back.

Berlin, May

It is not going to paradise myself, but leading you there that matters to me. What unbearable happiness if one had to enjoy it alone. . . .

And what can be said of a happiness that is achieved only at the expense of another?

Berlin, May 18

It was Barrès who made it fashionable. That need of looking for a lesson, a "message," everywhere and constantly; it is intolerable to me. Vassalage that debases the mind. Great works do not so much teach us as they plunge us into a sort of almost loving bewilderment. To me, people who are everywhere seeking out some "benefit" are like those prostitutes who, before delivering themselves, want to know: "How much are you giving?"

At once my only desire is to get away.

June 6

This will perhaps not last much longer (and I keep telling myself this), but I feel in possession of my faculties; more so, it seems to me, than I have ever been. I also believe that my memory (which was not very good) is better. But what is diminishing is that sort of inner pressure, that ardor, that tormenting need to embrace, which (as I sometimes feared) might have led me to crime or to madness. I am not yet so tempered, however, that on certain days I do not still frighten myself.

June 22

At Cuverville I had read quite a lot, and with great appetite: the latest Mauriac (in installments in the *Revue de Paris*), *Demian* by Hesse (in translation), Jouhandeau's remarkable *Parricide imaginaire;* unable to get interested in *Babbitt;* then everything concerning Delphi in the *Greek History* of Curtius (Vol. II). Reread with very lively pleasure the first book of *Dichtung und Wahrheit* in German. For the seventh or eighth time (at least), attempted *Also sprach Zarathustra*. IMPOSSIBLE. The tone of this book is unbearable to me. And all my admiration for Nietzsche cannot succeed in making me put up with it. Finally, it seems to me slightly supererogatory in his work; it would assume importance only if all the other books did not exist. I constantly feel him here to be jealous of Christ, anxious to give the world a book that can be read *as the Gospel is read*. If this book has become more famous than all the others of Nietzsche, this is because, basically, it is a *novel*. But, for this very reason, he addresses himself to the lowest class of his readers: those who still have need of myths. And what I especially like in Nietzsche is his hatred of fiction.

July 21

I have just finished the wonderful *Moby Dick*.

August 1

I go to buy some cigarettes at Criquetot.

The sight of that ordinary little village (moreover so exactly similar to many others in the region), depresses me each time I return to it. What insufficient regard for hygiene, for comfort, for well-being, for gaiety!

(Expert gradation in the choice of words.) A kind of sordid economy seems to have dictated the placing and the constriction of the dwellings, in which no one but equally sordid people could achieve a semblance of happiness, in which any aspiration toward a better state is condemned to languish miserably. Everything there is ugly, shabby, fixed. No public garden, no place except the café to gather in on Sunday; no song, no game, show, or music; no invitation to distract oneself for even a minute from one's work and one's most egoistic interests. There are few regions in which one feels less happy to be alive, despite its relative prosperity. And I reflect sadly on those new villages I saw in Germany, where everything seems attractive, both houses and people. . . .

Little François D., whom I question about what he is going to do now that he has received his school diploma, tells me that he wanted to continue studying to become a schoolteacher (his mother wanted to hire him out as a farmhand). Immense desire to help him, which immediately filled my heart and made tears come to my eyes. . . .

August 3

Yesterday went to Angerville to see Lechevallier, who used to be schoolteacher at Cuverville, to ask his advice about little François D. The best would probably be to get him, in October, into the school of Montivilliers, which takes boarders. Lechevallier is to write to the headmaster. I have promised to be responsible for all the expenses if, as he intimates, it is already too late to get a scholarship for this first year.

In the latest *Candide,* which Jacques brought us yesterday from Paris, a diverting article by Montfort (it is a long time since I had read anything by him) on Catulle Mendès. Montfort is of the opinion that people "do not do justice" to that sorry poet, so happily forgotten (happily for us and for him). It is hard to understand today the extraordinary celebrity he achieved in his lifetime. Then he spread out everywhere; he reigned supreme; he debased everything his pen touched, and it claimed to touch everything. Fortunately I encountered him only very rarely; yet the last vision I had of him remains unforgettable. It was in a theater lobby during an intermission. He had on his arm an enormous tart wearing an outrageously low-necked gown (for the epoch), who was simpering and playing with her fan; he himself, in evening dress, was strutting, thrusting out his potbelly, throwing back his head like some Christ of the brothels, above a low, wide-winged collar, from which cascaded a soft white silk tie; his long blond hair made him a kind of tarnished halo; his languishing and insipid eyes slipped about from under heavy, half-closed lids. The couple was so large, so voluminous, that it blocked the passage. Not being known to him, I was able to stand there looking at him. Both of them seemed boneless, soft, and as if covered with Vaseline. They gave off an extraordinary scent of eau de cologne or Lubin water, of toilet water, of library paste, of the bed, and of cigarette butts. Young men kept rushing up and bowing before this Moloch. It was impossible to see, even to imagine, anything more shameful.

August 4

François D., who comes to recite to us the little comedy he was learning for the commencement exercises, is bewildered and dejected by his brother Paul's opposition. The latter cannot accept the idea of François's spending so much time, by entering the Montivilliers school, without contributing to the support of their mother. It is his turn to help her (he is now twelve). In short, he has made it a matter of scruple, and the little fellow, without support, without example, without advice, frightened by his "egotism," gives up with a broken heart.

Arcachon, August 10

Mme D., when little François, her son, had confessed his ambition to her (to continue his studies in order to become a teacher) exclaimed: "But, my boy, aren't you aiming too high . . . ?"

It is she who repeats her own words to me, repeating them thrice over, following them with: "That's what I told him. . . ."

If I were to begin my career over again, it is stories like that of the D. family that I should like to write.

Narbonne, August 18

Arrived last night at Carcassonne; spent the day with Alibert. Since yesterday, after weeks of rain, marvelous weather; as pure a sky as if I were twenty. But I left Jean-Paul* so ill, with so little hope of getting well (although he prides himself on still hoping), that I find it hard to yield to joy. Spent six frightful days with him, encouraging him, helping him to suffer, lying to him, trying to hide death from him. Yet we were not afraid

---

* Jean-Paul Allégret, Marc's eldest brother. He was to die of tuberculosis later that year. See the selection from *Les Nouvelles Nourritures* (1935), pp. 818–819.

to speak of it; we were more afraid, in fact, to speak of his approaching convalescence, although it seems that his condition, already so pitiable, can only get worse soon. He is already suffering so much that one comes to hope that the end will not be too long in coming. When I told him that the doctor considered him very courageous, his eyes filled with tears. He wants to be worthy of the love that he is aware people have for him. He fears letting himself go, and forces himself, twice a day, to go down for meals. Going back up one flight exhausts him. However slowly and cautiously he goes about it, stopping every two steps to catch his breath, waiting for the rapid beating of his heart to calm down a bit, he takes considerable time getting back to normal, shaken by his cough, gasping, with the anguished look of a drowning man. He suffers everywhere: otitis, hydrarthrosis of the knee, sciatica, hepatic colics, breathlessness—nothing is spared him, and each week the illness invents some new evil. Meanwhile his mother writes him that God is sending him these trials because He sees that the preceding ones were not enough to bring him back to Him.

"Remarks like that fill my heart with blasphemy," Jean-Paul says to me.

August 20

Reached Marseilles last night. I sail at three o'clock for Bastia, where we arrive tomorrow at dawn; whence I plan to reach Calvi the same day.

August 22

Wonderful flight of the palm trees, in the night, along the quay of Calvi; wonderful outpouring of their palms. Wonderful façades of the tall houses behind them; balconies, terraces above the narrow street, already dark. On the quays a half-naked people circulate, the high society of several pleasure yachts mingling with the fishermen of the little harbor; all this breathing out insouciance and pleasure-making. The atmosphere invites one to momentary lusts, to games, to debaucheries, and remains wholly inappropriate for meditation.

Intoxicated from a day spent in the open sun, in the open air. B.'s auto took us into the mountains; then, leaving the car, we followed for a long time and at random a very steep mule path, without any other reward than a glorious fatigue.

On the way back, we bathed among the rocks.

August 25

I am letting myself be carried off by new acquaintances who propose a three-day excursion to Bonifacio by car. I shall meet them this evening at Ajaccio, where the *Ile de Beauté* will take me by sea. A silvery fog spreads over the smooth sea, veiling the coast that we are following; the vague horizon withdraws to suit my whim; from moment to moment a prolonged bellowing from the ship assures us of our reality.

August 28

Lunched at Ile Rousse. Back to Calvi. In all my life I have never seen a purer sky, a more radiant sun.

August 30

I allow myself to be led once again into a trip to Saint-Florent, which takes us the whole day, my last in Corsica.

Yesterday I had been to tea at Tristan Tzara's, who is charming; his young wife even more charming.

Short night, for I must be on board before six o'clock. I come back drunk with sun, with pleasure, my mind quite volatilized.

Noon, September 1

Col d'Allos.

I do not believe my joy has ever been deeper or keener. The air has never been softer, I have never breathed it more lovingly. My subtly active mind, beclouded by no worry, smiles at the humblest and pleasantest thought, as my flesh does at the azure, at the sun, and my heart at everything that lives. I did not feel any younger at twenty; and I know better now the value of each moment. I was more tormented then by desires, by imperious demands. To my excesses at Calvi I owe a great calm. My glances are disinterested, and the mirror of my mind is like the surface of a tranquil lake on which all the reflections of the surrounding terrain come voluptuously, but very purely, to take their place.

Doubtless some catastrophe is awaiting me in Paris, to make me pay for all this happiness.

My greatest emotion of this day, the one that will live most vividly in my memory: at the last turn in the road before going through the Col d'Allos, suddenly a tremendous flock of sheep grazing the short grass of those heights. The evening sun was casting its last rays on those slopes, and the russet-green grass, the russet-white of the sheep, spread out like a frieze, made a powerful and perfect harmony under the sky. It seemed to me that it had been a long time since I had seen anything so beautiful.

Saint-Clair, November 7

After several days of violent mistral, radiant weather. Read between Paris and Marseilles *The Virgin and the Gypsy,* which Bennett had sent me; the most recent book by D. H. Lawrence, by whom I had not yet read anything. The discovery of Lawrence, Ruyters told me, was the great event of his life. I fear that a good deal of resentment may enter into his present predilection for contemporary English literature. I think, I hope, that Lawrence's other books are better. This one struck me as so empty and so crude in its brutality that its cynicism, which I might otherwise like, becomes quite inoffensive. There are few books I have disliked so much.

Tunis, November 15

Saw last night a film by René Clair: *Sous les toits de Paris.* Surely one of the best French films; perhaps the best.

1931   *January 22*

Too many projects. Not knowing which to put first, I vacillate, and time flies. With *Œdipe* now finished, I have ahead of me those *Notes sur Chopin,* my *Geneviève,* the story of Paumier (Mulot) at La Roque, which I should like to turn into a new chapter for *Si le grain ne meurt* . . . it could be, it should be important; finally and especially the *Nouvelles Nourritures.* . . . And, in my indecision, I turn back to piano-practice, as to a drug that calms the turbulence of my thought and pacifies my restless will. Each of the last few days I have spent from four to five hours at the piano (Mozart's concertos, the Bach-Busoni *Orgelchoralvorspiele,* and Granados's *Goyescas*).

Cuverville, January 26

No more soporific atmosphere than that of this region. I suspect that it contributed greatly to the slowness and difficulty with which Flaubert worked. When he thought he was struggling against words, he was struggling against the sky; and perhaps in another climate, the dryness of the air exalting his spirits, he might have been less exigent, or have obtained the same results without so much effort.

. . . the thing I am most bitterly reproached with is having worked for the emancipation of the mind. This seems unpardonable to the group that, on the contrary, aims only toward the most complete submission to authority, to rules, to tradition, etc. That group, which is very powerful, always uses the same weapons, which it always has at hand. The best reason it can find to prove that man *must* not change is that he *can* not change. For as soon as one glimpses the possibility of a progress, how can one fail to wish to obtain it? . . .

Some people would be sufficiently tenderhearted, but they lack imagination to the point of not being able to imagine, even dimly, the sufferings of those who are not close to them. What happens far away no longer seems quite real to them, and they read descriptions of the imprisonment and torture suffered by the "suspect" or "unorthodox" professors in Poland, etc., etc., in the same spirit as accounts of horrors of past ages. It does not *touch* them. A clever novelist would be able to move them more. In that sympathy for imaginary misfortunes, there is a certain flattering self-indulgence; the knowledge of real sufferings only embarrasses. One thinks: What do you expect me to do about it? And, in the certainty of one's inability to help, each one finds permission to sit back and do nothing.

As for feeling, through their very opinions, somewhat on the side of the oppressors and torturers, this never occurs to them in the least. Obviously they feel and tell themselves that if they lived in the countries where such abominations take place, *they* would be on the right side. . . .

It is not at all that I feel more "human" today than at the time when no trace of such preoccupations could be found in my work. I simply took care to forbid them access to it, judging that they had nothing to do with art. I am no longer so sure of this, nor that anything can and must remain foreign to art; it runs the risk of becoming, it necessarily becomes artifice if what is closest to the artist's heart is banished from it.

I am getting ahead with *Clarissa*. I am now up to page 220 of the second volume; but there are five, of five hundred pages each. Rarely read a book with so much application.

February 5

The mother-in-law of Davidson (who is making a bust of me, and at whose house I lunch today), a charming old lady of eighty-four, when I—on the point of lighting a cigarette after the meal—ask her if smoking bothers her, tells us that a similar question was put to her, before 1870, by Bismarck, in a train compartment between Paris and Saint-Germain in which she happened to be alone with him. To which she replied at once: "Sir, I do not know. No one has ever yet smoked in my presence."

Bismarck immediately had the train stopped so that he could change to another compartment.

March 8

Before leaving Paris, I had gone to rue de Villejust. Saw Valéry; for the first time in months and years, *not tired,* not out of patience, in full possession of himself, fully *realized* so to speak, and filling out his character to the very limits. . . .

I cannot help regretting, oh, quite selfishly, that Valéry has never made an effort to understand me better, and that the impression he has of me remains so substantially the same, the very one that Pierre Louÿs must have had at the time of our worst disagreements. To him, to them, I represented the Protestant, the moralist, the puritan, the sacrificer of form to idea, the anti-artist, the enemy. I do not know how, despite that, there remained in Valéry's heart rather than in his mind so true a friendship for me. He has given me as many opportunities to assure myself of it as to assure myself no less of his incomprehension.

March 18

Finished *Clarissa.*

For the third time (I believe it may even be the fourth) I gather up my strength to launch into Huxley's *Point Counter Point,* for I have been told that one must get past the beginning. But what can I think of a book, when I read attentively the first seventy pages without being able to find a single line even halfway firmly drawn, a single personal thought, emotion, or sensation, the slightest enticement for the heart or mind to invite me to go on?

Went as far as page 115 with great effort. Unreadable. Yet I can usually read almost anything. I cannot even understand how there were people able to go on.

March 20

I definitely drop Huxley's book, in which I cannot get interested. Mme Théo very ingeniously compared it to Mauclair's *Couronne de clarté.* There is probably more intelligence in Huxley, but just as much rubbish.

March 22

Reread at one sitting *Eugénie Grandet,* which I had not looked at since the day when I first devoured it, at the age of sixteen, in the barn at La Roque. It is the first Balzac I ever read. It does not seem to me one of the best. . . .

Marseilles, March 31

Greatly enjoyed seeing Saint-Exupéry again at Agay, where I had gone to spend two days with P. Back in France barely a month now, he has brought back from Argentina a new book and a fiancée. Read one, saw the other. Congratulated him heartily, but primarily for the book; I hope the fiancée is as satisfactory. . . .

Tonio's stories are so strange and gripping that I should like to note them down at the moment of hearing them. He talks to us at length of his fellow-pilot Guillaumet. Guillaumet was on the air-mail route from X. to Y. (?); there had been no news of him for six days. It was said that his plane had been caught in a storm while crossing the Andes; he must have crashed in the mountains in a particularly inaccessible, unknown region, to which none of the inhabitants of the country whom the company had tried to send out searching for him had been willing to venture.

Tonio de Saint-Exupéry was dining in a grand hotel in Buenos Aires when the news began to spread: Guillaumet was alive, had been found. The emotion was so great that everyone got up; there was general embracing. Tonio saw him soon after. He plans to write the story that Guillaumet told him of his amazing adventure.

The plane had come down in the snow at an altitude of nearly ten thousand feet. The storm was so violent that he had first to wait for forty-eight hours in the shelter he had dug under the plane. If he had not been alone, he would still be there. A comrade would not have had his extraordinary resistance, and Guillaumet would not have wanted to leave him. . . . Fortunately he had on him a small pocket compass that his chief had by chance given him a few days before. No rope, no ice-axe. No experience of mountain-climbing. No hope of getting out alive. And the thing that first made him set out was the desire to leave his body clearly visible, for it occurred to him that his widow would have to wait four years before getting his insurance if there were any question of his not being dead. But as long as he was walking, he might as well go toward salvation. And once on the way . . .

Nothing with which to warm himself. Nothing to eat. . . . But, above all, the great preoccupation: not to go to sleep. To rest, he picked rocks with such a slope that he could keep himself from falling only by staying awake. Terrible temptation to let oneself go to sleep. The lure of the snow-fields; voluptuous torpor. . . . The third day, he slides to the bottom of a ravine, from which he gets out completely soaked. He has the constancy to go back, climbing a three-thousand-foot slope in order to dry himself in the first rays of the sun. And for four days, no food. He fears losing control of his thoughts, and concentrates his entire will on the *choice* of those thoughts!

Courage in this case lies not in risking one's life, but in the reverse . . .

All this is what Tonio is to relate. I ask to go over his story, for I shall never forgive him if he spoils it. What is most wanting in our literature today is heroism.*

Paris, April 10

Back in Paris two days now. Bad work at Vence, at Grasse, at Saint-Clair. . . . My idle brain manufactures gloom, disgust, boredom, and the call of spring finds no answer in my heart. Unfaithful to myself and to all my rules of life, I suffer from a limitless liberty without employment. Any occupation whatever that tied me down would be welcome; some task to accomplish. This is where religious devotions are so useful. The thinking creature who has no other end than himself suffers from an abominable void. . . .

April 30

Increasing lack of self-confidence. I shall end up by no longer daring to write anything at all.

May 2

The typing-up of my old journals, which has kept me busy since I have been at Cuverville, plunges me into an indescribable disgust for myself.

---

* The story is told in Saint-Exupéry's *Terre des hommes* (*Wind, Sand and Stars*).

Lunched the day before yesterday at Sèvres, at the Bertaux's, with J. Schlumberger, the Thomas Manns, and the Soupaults. I did not yet know Thomas Mann, who had been so kind to me on several occasions that I could not decently ignore his being in Paris. Meeting under excellent circumstances, which I am happy to owe to Bertaux. Very good lunch; most cordial atmosphere; natural, jovial conversation. It was perfect.

Thomas Mann and his wife (she in particular) speak French perfectly. Moreover their pronunciation, when they express themselves in German, is so distinct that not a word escaped me.

I liked both of them enough that I am eager to see them again. It seems to me that one can talk with him effortlessly of anything and everything.

Devout Spain* is burning her convents more ferociously than did ever the land of Voltaire. It can certainly be said that she richly deserves these excesses, and that her own ancient Inquisition prepared these long-range reprisals. And it would not even be necessary to go back so far as that. I doubt if this fury is a sign of real liberation, unfortunately. There is something spasmodic about it that might well not last.

I should like those who are shocked by such violences to explain to me how a chick is to get out of the egg without breaking the shell.

But above all I should like to live long enough to see Russia's plan succeed, and the states of Europe obliged to bow down before something they have insisted on ignoring. How could so novel a reorganization have been achieved without, first, a period of profound disorganization? Never have I stared into the future with a more passionate curiosity. My whole heart applauds that gigantic and yet entirely human undertaking.

Those who are most inclined to doubt its success are precisely the *believers* who used to profess the greatest scorn for doubt as soon as it touched their religious convictions. They do not admit a faith so different in nature from their mystical faith. And faced with this miracle to be accomplished, a quite natural and practical miracle (so that it can be called a miracle only by misuse of the term), it is now they who play the skeptics; but, here too, the first condition of the plan's success is to believe

* Gide uses the expression "Satin-slipper Spain"—a reference to Claudel's drama, *Le Soulier de satin* (1929), in which the heroine entrusts her satin slipper, as a symbol of her virtue, to a statue of the Virgin.

obstinately that it will succeed. Far from defying the intelligence, it *calls* upon it, and it is intelligence that must triumph in this case.

In Mme B.'s *salon,* which I stumbled into late in the day, a great gathering of society people. No less than three princesses. That is more than my limit.

June 1

Spent an hour yesterday evening at the Cirque Médrano. Profoundly demoralized by the public's delirious joy over a clown act, very badly performed and as stupid as possible; besides, openly filthy. Nothing to be done for, nothing to be hoped from such a public. And nothing is more saddening for some (of whom I am one) than to belong—oh, quite despite oneself—to an élite, and to be unable to bring oneself to communicate with the vast majority of humanity. I remember my childish sobs when, for the first time, I felt "not like the others."

June 14

It is no longer a matter of restoring ruins, but of building anew on a ground that must first be tested. Everything must be questioned, doubted again; nothing must be accepted but the authentic, from which all mysticism is banished. I mean by mysticism: any blind belief.

June 21

It is not in suffering, in adversity, that my optimism finds a stumbling block, but in the ugliness and maliciousness of men.

It is enough to discourage good will and make a laughing-stock of all devotion, all sacrifice.

One wonders upon seeing certain books: Who can read them?—Upon seeing certain people: What can they read?—Then eventually the two fit together.

Munich, July 1

The doctor (whom Em. had come to consult in Paris) said to her at once: "You must have had very delicate hands."

. . . She had the most exquisite hands that can be imagined. I loved them especially, not merely as a part of her, but in themselves. She convinces herself and tries to convince me that her hands lost their shape naturally; but there is more to it: she deformed them by misusing them, by making them undertake coarse duties for which they were not made, and which Em. assumed out of modesty, abnegation, mortification, and for a great pile of virtuous reasons that would have made me look with horror on the spirit of sacrifice. And it was the same with her mind, gifted with the most exquisite and rarest qualities, suited for the most delicate preoccupations. Her natural humility would not admit that she could be superior in anything, and thus she condemned herself to the most ordinary occupations, in which nevertheless her superiority was obvious. From witnessing, powerless, this progressive renunciation, which she even refused to recognize, I suffered unspeakably. Had I complained of it, she would have said that all these superiorities I saw her relinquishing existed merely in my loving imagination. She really believed that, and thereby revealed herself to be superior to those very superiorities which her virtue esteemed so little.

"Intention to destroy all religion." In a meeting of the Comité National d'Etudes (March 16, 1931), of which I am reading the report; painfully, but with all my heart on their side.

(Writing these words, how can I avoid thinking of Em.? Because of her, these words ring false. But now it is only because of her.)

The persecutions have always been (or almost), up to now, in the name of a religion. That free thought should start persecuting in its turn is what religion finds so monstrous. But can it truly be called persecution? I have always found it very difficult to accept a "truth" when it is so much in someone's interest to make us believe it. The last testimonies at this meeting completely contradict the first; and the first are but hearsay. But they call "persecution" forbidding priests the right to pulverize and knead the brains of children. . . .

What is more hollow, more stupidly sonorous, than the sentence with which Father R. de J. closes his declaration: "There exist unalterable principles on which doubt is not permitted." Humanity makes, and can make, no progress without giving these excellent souls something of a shake.

Saturday

Whole morning spent coaxing a bad headache, which I dragged about all day yesterday and which hardly let me sleep all night. Motor trip to the Starnberger See, where I am taken by the family of Thomas Mann, whom

I have the greatest pleasure in seeing again. The two youngest children, gloriously handsome, go with us, and Klaus, whom I scarcely knew at all before. All charming; Mme Mann particularly. But, the headache making my mind obdurate, I have the bad grace to maintain the contrary of her opinion—namely, that butterflies are not transformed into caterpillars, which would be too discouraging. . . .

Mann had just read, in the great hall of the university, two chapters from his *Joseph* (in composition still), which I was very happy to understand well (thanks to Mann's very clear and vibrant diction) and to admire. It even seems to me that Mann has never written anything better.

A journalist who knows his trade does not write: "They were ready to come to terms with the Soviets"; but rather: "They were ready to forget all the crimes past and present, to grasp the bloodstained hands of the Moscow torturers in a passionate embrace." The whole article in *La Gazette de Lausanne* (of July 6) is in this tone. (Signed Edm. R.) It is entitled: "America against the Soviets," and bears witness to a noble case of the jitters.

July 24

The Spanish revolution, the struggle of the Vatican against fascism, the German financial crisis, and, above all, Russia's extraordinary effort . . . all this distracts me frightfully from literature. I have just devoured in two days Knickerbocker's book on the Five-Year Plan . . .

July 27

In Paris again, but for only two days. Tomorrow, board meeting of the *N.R.F.* in the morning, and in the afternoon reading of Roger Martin du Gard.

I should like to shout out loud my sympathy for Russia; and I should like my cry to be heard, to be important. I should like to live long enough to see the success of that tremendous effort; a success which I wish with all my soul, and for which I should like to work. To see what can be produced by a state without religion, a society without the family. Religion and the family are the two worst enemies of progress.

Cuverville, July 28

These letters of Proust to Mme de Noailles discredit Proust's judgment (or sincerity) much more than they serve the glory of the poetess. Flattery cannot go further. But Proust knew Mme de N. well enough—knew her to be vain and sufficiently incapable of self-criticism—to hope that the most exaggerated praise would seem to her the most deserved, the most sincere; he played with her as he played with everyone. And I see in these shameless flatteries less hypocrisy than an obsessive need of serving up to each individual what he would most like, without any care for truth, but simply for opportunism; and especially a desire to open up the ones he breathes on most warmly, to entice them to yield.

September

Try all one's life never to make the least insincere gesture, not to write a single sentence that goes even the slightest beyond one's thought, and one can then hope to be called, at about sixty, a "play-actor" by an M.A.* This is a term he would never think of applying to all our masters in camouflage; he reserves it for me alone, accompanied by the epithet "magnificent," which excuses him for having admired me all the same, but explains why—after having seen through me—he now turns away. . . . What pride! What pettiness! If he had plagiarized me less in the past, he would disavow me less vigorously today. I do not like that way some people have of taking your fountain pen, then moving away from you in order to avoid suspicion.

Sunday, 13

Excellent crossing. But I am unable to surrender to joy without repeating to myself: you again! . . . Aren't you ashamed? Make way for others. It is time. . . .

Calvi, Monday

Arrived at Ajaccio at about ten o'clock. Wild desire to go back at once. Absurd longing, to want to begin the past over again! The town seemed to be charming. Last summer, I don't know why, I had been unable to see it. At the period of the *Nourritures* I should have wept with joy over it. The first rays of the sun were turning the houses pink along the harbor. Large seabirds were hovering over the ship. I had need of a very young companion who would have been stirred, he at least, by the discovery of what aroused me so much in the past. I merely noted (and with almost no rise in temperature) that it was quite worthy of stirring someone. . . .

---

* Marcel Arland, a former collaborator at the *N.R.F.*

September 18

In Massis's reply to an inquiry by *Candide* I read with amusement:

"Never, at the height of their fervor, did the greatest Gidians among us speak of Gide with the enthusiasm and ecstasy of these newcomers."

Decidedly you did not bury me very deep, my dear Massis! And all those "Let's get out of here; he's beginning to smell" of your declarations of my "bankruptcy" did not, after all, do me the great harm you had hoped.

But you prefer to admit that you were wrong in your prognostics about the postwar generation, and to bury it altogether in the same grave with me, rather than admit that I was perhaps not so dead as you used to say.

October 19

Marius on the screen. Wonderful acting. Raimu masterful. Excellent dialogue, uselessly (hence tiresomely) broken by views sure to put the audience's imagination to sleep. An art in which nothing is left to suggestion. Better the theater. . . .

Cuverville, late October

. . . There is one thing I lack: belief in liberty. It is most difficult for me to bring my own thought to light. The notion of liberty, as it is taught us, seems to me singularly false and pernicious. And if I approve the Soviet constraint, I must likewise approve the discipline of the Fascists. I am more and more inclined to believe that the idea of liberty is nothing but a trap. I should like to be sure that I should think the same if I were not free myself, I who cherish above all my own freedom of thought; but I also believe, more and more all the time, that man achieves nothing worthwhile without constraint, and that the people who are capable of finding that constraint in themselves are very rare. I also believe that the authentic color of an individual thought takes on its full value only when it is set against a background that is not itself multicolored. It is the uniformity of the mass that allows a few rare individuals to rise, in contrast to it. The "Render unto Cæsar the things which are Cæsar's, and unto God the things that are God's" of the Gospel seems to me more than ever a teaching full of wisdom. On God's side, freedom, that of the mind; on Cæsar's side, submission, that of acts. The single concern with the happiness of the greatest number, on the one hand; on the other, the single concern with truth.

But what I am writing of this here barely satisfies me. This remains: constraint for constraint, fascism's strikes me as a return to the past, whereas that of the Soviets seems a tremendous effort toward the future. That costly experiment is the concern of all humanity, and may liberate it from a frightful weight. The mere idea that it might be interrupted and forced to fail I find insupportable, that such a gigantic effort toward the never-yet-attempted might have been in vain. The idols that they are overthrowing out there have long seemed to me the most oppressive of the false gods.

Cuverville, November 8

Oh, how much time I am wasting! though I tell myself constantly that the night is coming and my hours are numbered. But I feel very tired; incapable of really good work, to which I should like to bring a fresh brain, washed clean of slag after a good soaking in sleep. If I were to deduct from my life the days that follow nights of insomnia . . .

I have often noted that the number of decent people (capable of heroism, abnegation, etc.) is much greater than is thought. And they are the ones who give the most advantageous and also the most real image of humanity. And this is what keeps me from being a revolutionary; or at least what allows me to be one only by going against my heart's inclination. I can wish for communism while still reproving the frightful means you propose for obtaining it. The "whoever accepts the end accepts the means"—even though it may have changed sides—still leaves my heart very ill at ease. I do not like feeling hatred, injustice, and arbitrariness fighting at my side. You tell me that we shall never achieve this without that. Alas, I fear so! But it is too frightful a moment to go through.

I am glad that in Russia at least that sorry chore is done, that at least *that* is in the past, and that there is no need to repeat it! Whoever looks back, like Lot's wife mourning over the ruin of Sodom, runs the risk of being changed into a statue of tears.

November 30

The great strength of Nietzsche. . . . How I feel constantly held back by sympathy. Constantly feeling that my thought can and must bruise those I love. . . .

. . . Occasionally and too often I resign myself to never writing again. The publication of my *Œuvres complètes,* on which I have been working considerably for a month, has the annoying effect of inviting me to silence, as if everything I had to say were said. I do not want to repeat myself, and fear works of decadence in which the slow ebbing of one's vigor can be measured. Doubtless as soon as I am rested I shall disown these sentences and the semi-resignation which prompts them today. But there is another reason for my silence: the excessively keen interest I take in events now in progress, and particularly in the Russian situation, turns my mind away from literary preoccupations.

It has often been said: The judgments we pass on our contemporaries are counterfeit. Not only are we under obligations to friendship, but also we lack the necessary perspective and, according to our humor, disparage or magnify to excess those whose work is too close to us. Some who appear important, whose reputation, thanks to the complicity of the critics, seems even in foreign eyes to bring new luster to France, will soon surprise us by their insignificance. I deserve to be forgotten if before two generations have passed the names of Curel, Bernstein, and Bataille are any more esteemed than that of Mendès is today.

I had promised myself to speak henceforth only of the dead, but it would grieve me to leave in my writing no trace of one of the most intense admirations I have ever felt for a contemporary writer; doubtless I would say *the most intense,* if Paul Valéry did not exist. Despite what I have said above, I do not think I overstate the importance of Marcel Proust; I do not think it can be overstated. It seems to me that, for many years, no writer has enriched us more.

Mme B. was telling me yesterday that she had always been near-sighted; her parents were not at first aware of it, and it was not until she was about twelve that she was made to wear glasses. "I remember so well my joy," she told me, "when for the first time, I could make out all the pebbles in the courtyard." When we read Proust, we begin suddenly to perceive detail where until then we had seen only a mass. He is, you will tell me, what is termed an analyst. Not so. The analyst separates with great effort; he explains; he takes pains. In Proust, this feeling is utterly natural. Proust is someone whose eyes are infinitely more subtle and attentive than our own, and who lends us his eyes as long as we are reading him. And as the things he looks at (so spontaneously that he never seems to be observing) are the most natural things in the world, he always seems, while we are reading him, to be permitting us to look inside ourselves. Through him all the confusion of our being emerges out of chaos and becomes conscious; and, just as the most diverse feelings exist in each man at the larval stage (unknown to him, most often), and await sometimes only an example or a designation—I was on the point of saying, an accusation—before declaring themselves, we imagine, thanks to Proust, that we have ourselves experienced this or that detail; we recognize it, adopt it, and suddenly it is our *own* past that this abundance has enriched. Proust's books act like a powerful developing solution for the half-veiled photographic plates of our memories, in which suddenly reappear a certain face, a forgotten smile, together with the emotions that had trailed into oblivion with them as they faded.

I do not know which is more to be admired—the hyperacuity of the inner glance, or the dazzling artistry that can seize the detail and offer it to us shimmering with freshness and life. Proust's style is the most *artistic* I know (to employ a word which the Goncourts had spoiled for me but which, when I think of Proust, ceases to displease me). He never feels hampered by it. If, in order to give form to the ineffable, there is no word, he turns to the image; he has at his disposition a whole treasury of analogies, equivalents, and comparisons so precise and so exquisite that sometimes you begin to wonder which lends the other more life, light, and pleasure; you wonder whether the emotion is abetted by the image, or whether this floating image was only waiting for the emotion before alighting. I look for the defect of this style, and I cannot find it. I look for its dominant qualities, and I cannot find them either; it does not have this or that quality; it has them all (but this is not perhaps altogether praise), not in turn but all at once, at the same time; his suppleness is so baffling that alongside his, every other style seems stiff, dull, imprecise, summary, inanimate. Must I admit it? Each time I plunge anew into this lake of delights, I sit for days without daring to take up my own pen again, unable to admit—as is customary during the time that we remain under the spell of a masterpiece—that there are other ways of writing well, and seeing in what is called the "purity" of my style nothing but poverty.

You have said that you often find the length of Proust's sentences exhausting. But just wait until I get back, when I can read those interminable sentences to you aloud; how everything falls into place, how the different planes stand out, what depth is given to the landscape of the mind! . . . I picture a page of *Guermantes* printed in the manner of Mallarmé's "Coup de dés"; my voice gives the proper relief to the structural words, I orchestrate in my own way the parenthetical remarks, I shade them, moderating or quickening my delivery; and I shall prove to you that there is nothing superfluous in this sentence, that every word was needed to maintain the different planes in position, to permit a total flowering of such complexity. However detailed Proust may be, I never find him prolix; although luxuriant, he is never diffuse. "Minute" but not "meticulous," Louis Martin-Chauffier has remarked very perceptively.

Proust clarifies for me in exemplary fashion what Jacques Rivière meant by the word "lump," which he used to attack the mental laziness of those who are content to take up at once whole armloads of the sentiments that custom has bound together, the bundles of feelings we are deceived into thinking homogeneous. Proust on the contrary carefully unties each sheaf, and sets straight the tangle. Indeed, he is not satisfied unless he can show us, together with the flower, not only the stem but even the delicate beard of roots. What curious books! You move into them as into an enchanted forest; from the first pages you are lost, and happy to be lost; soon you no longer remember where you came in, nor know how far you are from the edge of the forest; sometimes it seems that you walk without getting anywhere; other times that you get somewhere without walking; you watch everything along the way; you no longer know where you are, or where you are going; and then:

> Suddenly my father would stop us and ask my mother: "Where are we?" Exhausted by the walk, but proud of him, she would confess affectionately that she had not the slightest idea. He would shrug his shoulders and laugh. Then, as if he had taken it from the pocket of his coat together with the key, he would point out directly in front of us the little back door of our garden which had joined with the corner of the rue du Saint-Esprit to wait for us at the end of those unknown paths. My mother would say to him, admiringly: "You are remarkable! . . ."

You are remarkable, my dear Proust! It seems that you were speaking to us only about yourself, and yet your books are as crowded as the entire *Comédie humaine;* your narrative is not a novel: you never bother to weave and then untie plots, and yet I know of none that we follow with keener interest; you introduce your characters to us only incidentally, it might almost be said by a fluke, but we soon know them as intimately as we know Cousin Pons, Eugénie Grandet, or Vautrin. It seems that your books are not "composed" and that you scatter your wealth at random; but though I wait on your following books to judge with certainty, I suspect already that all the elements unfold according to a hidden order like the branches of a fan fastened at one end, the divergence of which is webbed by a delicate fabric whereon you display all the shifting, varied colors of your Maya. And you find the means, along the way, to talk about everything, mingling with the apparent fragmentation of memory, observations so penetrating and original that I find myself wanting an appendix to your work, a kind of lexicon which would permit us to turn readily to particular remarks on sleeping and insomnia, on sickness, music, dramatic art, the art of acting, a lexicon that would even now bulk large but in which I think it would be necessary to enter virtually all the words in our language when all the volumes you promise us will have appeared.

If I seek, finally, to define what I most admire in this work, I believe it to be its gratuitousness. I know no work that is less utilitarian, no work less bent on proving something. I am well aware that every work of art lays claim to this definition, and that each one finds its justification, ultimately, in its beauty. But—and this is its characteristic—the component parts are under tension, and although the ensemble itself may be useless, nothing appears or should appear that is not useful *to* the ensemble, and we know that, in this sense, all that is not useful is damaging. In *Recherche du temps perdu,* this subordination is so deeply-hidden that each page in turn seems to find its perfect end in itself. Hence this extreme slowness, this reluctance to quicken the pace, this continuous satisfaction. I know of no similar nonchalance but in Montaigne, and it is doubtless on that account that I can compare the pleasure I find in reading Proust only to that given me by the *Essais.* They are works of long leisure. And I do not mean merely that the author in order to produce them must have felt his mind perfectly disengaged from the rush of hours, but also that they require on the reader's part a like disengagement. They require it and obtain it, both at once; that is their real benefit. You will say that the character of art and of philosophy is precisely that of escaping the demands of time; but Proust's book is characterized by close attention to each moment; it could be said that the flight of time itself is his theme. Having broken free of life, he does not turn away from life; leaning over it, he contemplates it, or rather he contemplates within himself life's reflection. And the more disturbed the image, the steadier is the mirror, the more contemplative the gaze.

It is strange that such books come at a time when the event triumphs everywhere over the idea, when time is lacking, when action scorns thought, when contemplation seems no longer possible, no longer permissible, when, not yet recovered from the war, we esteem only what can be useful, only what can be of service. And suddenly the work of Proust, so disinterested, so gratuitous, appears to us more profitable and of greater relief than so many works whose goal is usefulness alone.

from

LA NOUVELLE

REVUE FRANÇAISE

1921

. . . When I abandon my thoughts to their natural course, they go toward the extreme left, and I bring them back toward the right only through an effort of my reason. I made such an effort during the war, because of circumstances, because of the emergency, and I still make it out of regard for certain friends whom it displeases me to displease—and who certainly have no idea what I am putting on on their behalf. I do not say that my reasoning is distorted in this process of "rectifying" my ideas; I say simply that this direction is not natural to them. And I cannot persuade myself that the natural direction of thought is not the best direction. One is easily swayed by patriotic or personal interest, by sympathy; but I can see no value in a man unless I feel that he is *not* being swayed. Which is why I said nothing during the war.

We have passed through doleful times, when all the thoughts of heart and mind were enlisted; there was no question of anything but helping France, each to the limit of his modest powers, helping France to win, to come out of it all alive. Now France has come out: victorious, but exhausted. And now we are told that this submission of the mind is more necessary than ever. Some who, during the war, heroically consigned their brains to their knapsacks are trying now to persuade us that the arrangement is a satisfactory one, that there is no point to shifting position, that, at the very least, it is *useful* to leave them there—to permit the revival, the uplifting of France. Worst of all, they believe it. The dilemma is, then, whether to run the risk of disturbing momentarily a factitious and manifestly provisional order by airing certain ideas that do not adjust to it, or to consent to compromises of the mind, to allow our judgment to be adulterated, to blunt our critical sense, and in a word, to tarnish the fair mirror that France used to hold up, a mirror wherein truth could see, better than anywhere else, her own clear face.*

The concept of *la patrie* is a most complex one. There are not only

---

* "French intelligence, in this state of permanent mobilization, will soon run the risk not only of being no longer intelligence, but also of being no longer French," your friend Thibaudet wrote in his excellent article on "The Demobilization of the Intellect" (*N.R.F.,* January 1, 1920), an article to which I can really add nothing. [A. G.]

fields and interests and cathedrals to be protected; there are also intellectual and ethical values of incalculable worth, whose progressive diminution may go unnoticed, because with them there is lost the sense of their worth; it is these that are in great danger.

I realize that such considerations are deadly; if you prefer silence from me, do tell me. But first let me read you these few lines from a letter of Michel Arnauld:*

> What frightens me is to see how separate now are the noblest activities of the mind. Everything I see, everything I read, demonstrates that taste is in no danger. Art flourishes; it takes its place among the newly rich; it leaves thought, the work of intellect, for the permanently poor. If there was ever a time when knowledge and abstract logic hampered intuitive judgment, we are well out of it, and today's problem is worse. When the assembling of information and the construction of a logical order are called for, we make decisions as though we were selecting a line or a shade of color for a painting. People insist that we think as we feel, and feeling rightly, we think falsely. In regard to our country and to social peace, the votes of a Congress of Tours are less threatening than this absence of reflection among the cultivated classes.

I hesitate to send you these pages; this letter scarcely fits the picture, I feel certain, of what you had hoped for from me. May I better repay your patience another day! But because I have kept silent for so long, the first thing I must do is get rid of this primary obstacle.

* The pseudonym of Gide's brother-in-law, Marcel Drouin, one of the co-founders of the *N.R.F.*

from

DOSTOEVSKY

[*Lecture III*]

1 9 2 3

What we have done up to now has hardly been more than a clearing of
the ground. Before turning to Dostoevsky's ideas, I should like to warn
you against a grave misconception. During the last fifteen years of his life,
Dostoevsky devoted a good deal of his time to editing a review. The articles he wrote for this periodical have been collected in what is known as
the *Journal of an Author.* In these articles Dostoevsky sets forth his ideas.
It would seem the simplest and most natural thing in the world to make
constant reference to this book; but I may as well tell you at once that it is
profoundly disappointing. In it we find an exposé of his social theories;
but they remain vague, nebulous, and are most awkwardly expressed. In it
we find political predictions: not one of them has come true. Dostoevsky
tries to foretell the future state of Europe, and is mistaken in practically
every instance.

M. Souday, who recently devoted one of his literary reviews in
Le Temps to Dostoevsky, seems to enjoy pointing out his mistakes. In
these articles of Dostoevsky's he professes to see nothing more than the
most commonplace sort of journalism, with which judgment I am quite
prepared to agree. But I do protest when he goes on to say that these same
articles are a wonderful revelation of Dostoevsky's ideas. As a matter of
fact, the problems Dostoevsky deals with in his *Journal of an Author* are
not the problems that interest him most. Political questions, it should be
recognized, seemed less important to him than social questions; and social
questions less important, far less important, than moral and individual
ones. The rarest and deepest truths that we can expect from him are psychological; and let me add that, in this province, the ideas he arouses are
most often left in the nature of a problem or an unanswered question. He
is seeking not so much a solution as an exposition—an exposition of those
very questions which, *because* they are so very complex, so mingled and
interinvolved, are as a rule left obscure and ill defined. In a word, Dostoevsky is not, properly speaking, a thinker; he is a novelist. His most valuable, most subtle, most original ideas must be sought in the speeches of his
characters, and not always in those of his leading characters either: it of-

ten happens that his most important and daring ideas are accorded to subordinate members of the cast. Dostoevsky is awkwardness itself when expressing himself under his own name. One might well apply to him the sentence he puts into Versilov's mouth in *A Raw Youth:*

> "Explain?" he said. "No, it's better not to; besides, I've a passion for talking without explanations. That's really it. And there's another strange thing; if it happens that I try to explain an idea I believe in, it almost always happens that I cease to believe what I have explained."

One could even say that it is exceptional for Dostoevsky *not* to turn against his own idea as soon as he has expressed it. It seems as if for him it immediately breathed an odor of decay, like that which emanated from Father Zossima's dead body—the very body everyone had expected to work miracles—and which made the deathwatch so painful for his disciple, Alyosha Karamazov.

It is evident that for a philosopher this feature would be something of a drawback. His ideas are practically never absolute; almost always, they remain relative to the characters who express them. I shall press the point even further, and say that they are relative not merely to these characters, but to a precise moment in the lives of these characters. The ideas are, as it were, the product of a particular and momentary state of the character expressing them, and relative they remain, subservient to and conditioned by the particular fact or action which determines them or which they determine. As soon as Dostoevsky begins to theorize, he disappoints us. Thus even in his article "Of the Nature of Lying," despite his prodigious skill in dramatizing every possible kind of liar (and how different his are from Corneille's), and making us realize by this means what drives the liar to lie, as soon as he tries to explain all this to us, as soon as he attempts to theorize on the basis of his examples, he becomes stale, of virtually no interest whatever.

This *Journal* makes very clear to what degree Dostoevsky's genius is that of a novelist; for although, in the theoretical or critical articles he never rises above mediocrity, he becomes excellent as soon as some character appears on the scene. It is in this *Journal* that we come across the handsome tale of *The Peasant Krotchkaya,* one of Dostoevsky's most powerful works, a kind of novel that is really only one long monologue, like the *Notes from Underground,* written at about the same period.

Better still, or rather, more revealing, are the two instances in this *Journal* when Dostoevsky allows us to watch the almost involuntary, almost subconscious activity of his mind engaged in the construction of a narrative.

After he tells us his delight in watching people walking in the streets, and occasionally in following them, we see him suddenly attach himself to a chance passer-by:

I notice a workman passing; he has no wife leaning on his arm, but he has a child with him, a little boy. Both have the sad face of lonely people. The man is about thirty years of age: his face is faded and unhealthy-looking. He is wearing his Sunday best, a topcoat, rubbed at the seams, the buttons worn bare of cloth. The coat collar is very soiled, the trousers are cleaner, but look as if they had just come from the secondhand-clothes man. His tall hat is very shabby. I have the idea he is a printer. His expression is hard, gloomy, almost mean. He holds the boy by the hand; the youngster lags behind a little. The child is two, or not much more, very pale and undernourished, neatly dressed in a jacket, little boots with red leggings, and a hat decorated with a peacock's feather. He is tired. The father says something to him, perhaps teasing him for his tiny little legs. The youngster makes no reply, and a few paces farther on, his father bends down, lifts him up in his arms, and carries him. The child seems pleased, and throws his arms around his father's neck. He catches sight of me, and from his perch stares down at me in astonishment and curiosity. I give him a little nod, but he frowns and clings closer still to his father's neck. They must be great little friends, these two.

In the streets I love to watch the passers-by, gaze into their unknown features, guess who they might be, imagine how they exist and what can be their interest in life. Today I have eyes for none but this father and child. I imagine that the wife and mother died not long since, that the widower is busy working the whole week in the shop while the child is left to the care of some elderly woman. They probably live in a basement where the father rents or even only shares a little room, and, today being Sunday, the father is taking the boy to see some relative, the mother's sister probably. I like to think of this aunt (whom they don't go to see very often) as married to a non-commissioned officer and living in the basement of the barracks, but in a separate apartment. She mourned her sister's death, but not for long. The widower does not show much grief either, during this visit anyway. He remains preoccupied the whole time, has little to say for himself, and replies only to personal questions. Soon he falls silent altogether. Then the samovar is brought in and they all have tea. The boy is left sitting on a bench in the corner, first pouting, then frowning, and finally dropping off to sleep. The aunt and her husband take scant notice of him, except for passing him a piece of bread and a cup of milk. The husband, dumb at first, comes out suddenly with a coarse barrack-room joke directed at the little boy, whom his father begins to scold. The child wants to leave at once, and the father carries him home from Vyborg to Liteinyi.

Tomorrow the father will be back at his workshop, and the youngster left once more with the old woman.

In another passage of the same book, we read the account of his meeting with a woman a hundred years old. As he passes along the street, he sees her sitting on a bench. He speaks to her, then goes on his way. But in the evening, "after the day's work was done," the old woman comes back to his mind. He imagines her homecoming and her family's remarks to her. He describes her death: "It pleases me to imagine the end of the story. Besides, I am a novelist, and I love telling stories."

Yet, Dostoevsky never invents by chance. In one of the articles in the same *Journal,* apropos of the widow Kornilov's trial, he reconstitutes and rebuilds the story in his own way; after the judicial inquiry has thrown full light on every aspect of the crime, he is able to write: "I divined almost everything," and then adds, "Chance enabled me to go and see Madame Kornilova. I was astonished to see that my suppositions were almost identical with the true facts. I had, I admit, made a few errors of detail: for instance, Kornilov, though a peasant, wore European dress, etc.," and he concludes: "All in all, my errors have been slight; the basis of my suppositions remains true."

If to such a genius for observation, story-telling, and the reconstruction of reality one adds the quality of sensibility, one can make a Gogol or a Dickens (and perhaps you remember the beginning of the *Old Curiosity Shop* where Dickens, too, is busy following the passers-by, observing them, and after he has left them, going on to imagine their lives?). But such gifts, remarkable as they are, would not be enough to account for a Balzac, a Thomas Hardy, a Dostoevsky. They would certainly not be enough to make Nietzsche write: "The discovery of Dostoevsky was for me even more important than that of Stendhal; he is the only one who ever taught me anything of psychology."

Long ago I copied from Nietzsche a page I should like to read to you. When he wrote it, had Nietzsche not in view what constitutes the essential value of the great Russian novelist, what sets him in opposition to many of our modern novelists, to the Goncourts, for example, whom Nietzsche seems to indicate in these lines?

> A Moral for Psychologists: do not go in for notebook psychology. Never observe for the sake of observing! Such things lead to a false point of view, to a squint, to something forced and exaggerated. To experience things *intentionally*—this will never do. In the midst of an experience, a man should not turn his eyes upon himself; in such cases, every glance becomes that of an "evil eye." A born psychologist instinctively avoids looking just for the sake of seeing. And the same holds true of the born painter. Such a man never works "from Nature"—he leaves it to his instinct, to his own camera obscura to sift and to define the "case," the "nature," the "thing experienced." The general idea, the conclusion, the result is the only thing that reaches his consciousness. He knows nothing of that willful process of deducing from particular cases. What is the result when a man sets about the matter differently?—When, for instance, after the manner of Parisian novelists, he goes in for notebook psychology on a grand scale? Such a man is constantly spying on reality, and every evening he bears home a handful of fresh curios. But look at the result. . . .

Dostoevsky never observes for the sake of observation. His work is not born out of observations of reality; or at least, not of that alone. Nor is it the fruit of a preconceived idea, and that is why it is never mere theorizing, but remains steeped in reality. It is born of the intercourse between fact and idea, a *con-fusion,* a blending, in the proper English sense of the word, of the one with the other, so perfect that it can never be said that one element outweighs the other. Hence the most realistic scenes in his novels are also those most charged with psychological and moral significance. To be precise, each work of Dostoevsky's is produced by the fertilization of fact by idea. "The idea of this novel has been in me for the last three years," he wrote in 1870, referring to *The Brothers Karamazov*—which he did not write until nine years later. In another letter he says: "The principal question to be dealt with through all the parts of this book is the very one which has tormented me, consciously or unconsciously, all my life: the question of the existence of God."

But the idea is left floating about in his brain until it comes into contact with some fact from real life (in this instance, a criminal court case, a *cause célèbre*) which can fecundate it. Then—and not until then—can we speak of the work as conceived. "I am writing with a purpose," he says in the same letter, speaking of *The Possessed,* which reached fruition about the same period as *The Karamazovs*—another novel with a purpose. Certainly nothing could be less gratuitous, in the modern sense of the term, than Dostoevsky's work. Each of his novels is in its way a demonstration, I might even say a speech for the defense; or better still, a sermon. And if I dared to find something to reproach in this magnificent artist, it could be that he sought to *prove* only too well.

Let me not be misunderstood: Dostoevsky never tries to sway our opinion. He seeks only to bring light, to make plain certain hidden truths, which appear to him—and will soon appear to us—dazzlingly clear and of paramount importance; the most important, no doubt, to which the mind of man can attain: not truths of an abstract nature, not truths beyond human reach, but truths secret and intimately personal. On the other hand, and this is what saves his work from the disfigurements inseparable ·from all writing with a purpose, these truths, these ideas of Dostoevsky's are always subordinated to fact and deeply infused with reality. Toward these realities of human experience, his attitude is ever humble and submissive; he never applies pressure, never slants an event toward his own advantage. It would seem that even to his very thought he applied the Gospel precept: *"For whosoever will save his life shall lose it; but whosoever will lose his life for My sake, the same shall save it."*

Before attempting to trace some of Dostoevsky's ideas through his books, I should like to speak of his method of working. Strakhov tells us that Dostoevsky worked almost exclusively at night: "About midnight," he writes, "when everything was entering into repose, there was Fyodor Mikhailovich Dostoevsky left alone with his samovar; and he used to go on working till five or six in the morning, sipping cold, weak tea the whole time. He rose about two or three in the afternoon, spent the rest of the day receiving guests, walking, or paying visits to friends." Dostoevsky was not always able to content himself with cold, weak tea; during the last years of his life, he let himself go, we are told, and drank a great quantity of alcohol. One day, so the story runs, Dostoevsky came out of his study, where he was busy writing *The Possessed* in a state of remarkable mental exhilaration, obtained in some degree by artificial stimulus. It was Madame Dostoevsky's day for receiving. Fyodor Mikhailovich burst wild-eyed into the drawing-room where several ladies were sitting; one of them, cordiality itself, hastened forward to him with a cup of tea in her hand. "The devil take you and all your dishwater!" he shouted. . . .

Do you remember the Abbé de Saint-Réal's little phrase?—and well might it appear stupid had not Stendhal made use of it as a cover for his own aesthetic principles: "A novel is a mirror that one carries along the road." In France and in England, of course, there are numerous novels that fit this formula: the works of Lesage, Voltaire, Fielding, Smollett . . . But nothing could be more remote from this description than a novel of Dostoevsky's. Between his novels and those of the authors mentioned above, aye, and Tolstoy's too, and Stendhal's, there is all the difference possible between a picture and a panorama. Dostoevsky composes a picture, a painting, in which the most important consideration is the apportionment of light. The light proceeds from a single fire. In one of Stendhal's novels, or Tolstoy's, the light is constant, steady, and well diffused. Every object is illuminated in the same way, and can be seen from all sides; there are no shadows. But in a book of Dostoevsky's, as in a painting of Rembrandt's, what matters above all else is the shadows. Dostoevsky groups his characters and events, then projects an intense light upon them, in such a way that it strikes them on only one side. Each of his characters is bathed in shadow. We notice in Dostoevsky a strange impulse to group, concentrate, centralize: to create among the varied elements of a novel as many cross-connections as possible. Events, with him, instead of pursuing their slow and measured course, as with Stendhal or Tolstoy, come together at some place and drown themselves in a kind of vortex; the elements of the story—moral, psychological, and external—sink and rise again in the whirlpool. We find no attempt to simplify things, to purify the line in Dostoevsky; he is happiest in complexity; he encourages and fosters it. Feelings, thoughts, and passions are never presented in the pure state. He never isolates them.

And now I come to a consideration of Dostoevsky's draftsmanship— his manner of drawing his characters. But first of all let me read these very pertinent remarks of Jacques Rivière's:

> Once the idea of a character has taken shape in his mind, a novelist has two ways of materializing it: he can either insist on its complexity, or emphasize its coherence; in this soul he is about to engender, he can deliberately reproduce all of its darkness and obscurity, or he

can dispel it all, for the reader's sake, in the very process of describing it; he will either keep hidden the depths of the soul or lay them open.

You see what Rivière's notion is: the French school explores the depths, the caverns of the soul, whereas certain foreign novelists, and Dostoevsky in particular, respect and cherish their gloom.

> In any case [Rivière continues], it is these abysses that interest Dostoevsky most, and his whole effort is directed toward suggesting how utterly unreachable they are. . . . We, on the other hand, faced with a soul's complexity, and insofar as we want to portray it, instinctively we seek to organize our material.

This is already serious enough; but there is more to come:

> At need, we force things a trifle; we suppress a few small divergent traits and interpret certain obscure details in the sense most favorable toward establishing a psychological unity. . . . The complete closing up of every gulf—that is the ideal we are striving toward.*

I am not absolutely certain at this point that one cannot find some "abysses," some dark gulfs in Balzac, inexplicable and abrupt; nor am I sure either that Dostoevsky's are always as unfathomed as at first would be imagined. Shall I give you an example of one of these abysses of Balzac's? I find it in *La Recherche de l'absolu.* Balthazar Claès is seeking the philosopher's stone: he has completely forgotten, to all appearances, the religious training of his childhood. He is absorbed by his quest. He neglects his wife, the pious Josephine, who is horror-stricken at her husband's unbelief. One day she enters the laboratory without warning. The draft of the opening door sets off an explosion, and Madame Claès falls fainting. . . . What is the cry that escapes Balthazar's lips? A cry in which suddenly reappears all his childhood belief, so long overlaid by the deposits of his atheism. "Thank God you're still alive! The Saints have preserved you from death!" Balzac does not press the incident any further, and no doubt nineteen out of every twenty readers will never even detect the fault. The abyss of which it gives a glimpse remains without explanation—perhaps no explanation is possible. As a matter of fact, that was of no interest to Balzac. His one concern was to produce characters consistent with themselves, in which he was in perfect accord with the spirit of the French people; for what we French require most of all is logic.

---

* *La Nouvelle Revue Française,* February 1, 1922, pp. 176–7.

Moreover, I can say with respect not only to the *Comédie humaine,* but also to the comedy of everyday life as we live it, that the characters— which is to say all Frenchmen, every one of us—take shape according to the Balzacian ideal. The contradictions of our nature, should such exist, seem to us awkward and ridiculous. We deny them. We try to ignore them, to play them down. Each of us is conscious of his unity, his continuity even, and whenever we detect one of these repressed and unconscious anomalies (like the religious sentiment that suddenly reasserts itself in Claès), we try to suppress it completely; failing that, we refuse to consider it of any importance. We consistently behave as we judge the character we are—or believe we are—ought to behave. The greater part of our actions are dictated, not by the pleasure we take in doing them, but by the need of imitating ourselves and projecting our past into the future. We sacrifice truth (that is to say, sincerity) to continuity, and purity of the line.

And in face of all this, what does Dostoevsky offer us? Characters who, without any thought for consistency, yield complacently to all the contradictions and negations, of which their particular constitution is capable. This seems to be what interests Dostoevsky above all else: *incon- sistency.* Far from concealing it, he emphasizes and illuminates it over and over.

There is admittedly much that he fails to explain. I do not think there is much that *could* not be explained, however, were we to admit, as Dostoevsky invites us to do, that man can be the dwelling-place of contra- dictory feelings. Such cohabitation seems often in Dostoevsky all the more paradoxical in that his characters' feelings are forced to their extreme and exaggerated to the point of absurdity.

I believe it right to insist on this point, for you may be thinking that this is an old story, nothing more than the conflict between passion and duty as we see it in Corneille. But it's not that at all. The French hero, as Corneille depicts him, throws before himself the image of an ideal: the image is still of himself, but himself as he would like to be, as he strives to be; not as he naturally is, or as he would be if he yielded to his nature. The inward struggle Corneille depicts is the fight between the ideal being, to which the hero tries to conform, and the natural being, which he seeks to deny. In short, we are not so far removed in this instance, it seems to me, from what M. Jules de Gaultier terms *bovarysme*—a name he has given, after Flaubert's heroine, to the tendency of certain human beings to double their own lives by means of imaginary lives, in which they cease to be what they are and become what they *think* they are or would like to be.

Every hero, every man who is not content merely to drift, but struggles toward some ideal and tries to match it, offers us an example of this double-life, this *bovarysme.*

But the examples of dual existence we find proposed in the novels of Dostoevsky are quite different things. They have no connection (or at most very little) with those frequently observed pathological states in which a second personality is grafted upon the original, the one alternating with the other: two groups of sensations and associations of ideas are then formed, the one unknown to the other; so that soon we have two distinct personalities, rival tenants of the same flesh. They changed places, the one succeeding the other in turn, all the time ignorant of its neighbor (of which Stevenson gives us an extraordinary illustration in his fine fantastic tale, *The Strange Case of Dr. Jekyll and Mr. Hyde*).

But what is disconcerting in Dostoevsky is the simultaneity of all this, and the fact that each character remains perfectly conscious of his inconsistency, of his dual personality.

It happens that one of his heroes, in great stress of feeling, is uncertain whether it is love or hate that moves him, for these opposing emotions are mingled and confounded within him.

> And suddenly a strange surprising sensation of a sort of bitter hatred for Sonia passed through his [Raskolnikov's] heart. As it were wondering and frightened of this sensation, he raised his head and looked intently at her; but he met her uneasy and painfully anxious eyes fixed on him: there was love in them; his hatred vanished like a phantom. It was not the real feeling—he has taken the one feeling for the other.*

One could find similar examples of this misinterpretation of emotion by the person who is feeling it in Marivaux, or in Racine.

Sometimes one of these feelings will exhaust itself by its very exaggeration. It seems as if the expression of the feeling disconcerts the character expressing it. This is not yet quite the same thing as genuine duality of feeling; but here is something more definite. Let us hear Versilov, the father of the *Raw Youth:*

> "If only I were a weak-willed nonentity and suffered from the consciousness of it! But you see that's not so. I know I am exceedingly strong, and in what way do you suppose? Why, just in that spontaneous power of accommodating myself to anything whatever, so characteristic of all intelligent Russians of our generation. There's no

* *Crime and Punishment.*

crushing me, no destroying me, no surprising me. I've as many lives as a cat. I can with perfect convenience experience two opposite feelings at one and the same time, and not, of course, through my own will."

"I do not undertake to account for this co-existence of conflicting feelings," says the narrator in *The Possessed* deliberately; and Versilov goes on:

". . . my heart is full of words which I don't know how to utter; do you know I feel as if I were split in two?"—He looked round at us all with a terribly serious face and with perfectly genuine candor.— "Yes, I am really split in two mentally, and I'm horribly afraid of it. It's just as though one's second self were standing beside one; one is sensible and rational oneself, but the other self is impelled to do something perfectly senseless, and sometimes very funny; and suddenly you notice that you are longing to do that amusing thing, goodness knows why; that is, you want to, as it were, against your will; though you fight against it with all your might, you want to. I once knew a doctor who suddenly began whistling in church, at his father's funeral. I really was afraid to come to the funeral today, because, for some reason, I was possessed by a firm conviction that I should begin to laugh or whistle in church, like that unfortunate doctor, who came to a rather bad end. . . ."

from

LES FAUX-

MONNAYEURS

(*The Counterfeiters*)

1926

EDITOR'S NOTE

There is no immediately obvious justification for my selections here from
Les Faux-Monnayeurs, as there was for those from *La Porte étroite* and
Les Caves du Vatican. There was not room to include the whole of this,
Gide's most elaborate and extended fiction, so I simply chose the chapters
I thought best in their own right, and was pleased to find that they recomposed into a narrative fragment of at least as much coherence as the
original. Each chapter may seem to be the beginning of a new novel, but
this effect of discontinuity was a part of Gide's design, and is as apparent
in the full text as in this condensation. In general, the characters introduced here are followed through to the end of their careers in the novel,
and there is, I think, no particular need for a prefatory gloss.

    The only source of confusion may be Boris's "talisman," the appari-
tion of which causes him such dismay. This was a bit of paper inscribed
with five apparently meaningless words, which Boris had long kept
sewed up in a little cloth like a scapular around his neck, and which he
identified in some way with the "magic" of masturbation he had enjoyed
with a childhood friend. Frustrated by maternal edicts against his habit,
he lapsed into a severe nervous debility. The uncovering of his talisman
and its significance played a major part in his "cure" at the hands of Mme
Sophroniska, a Polish psychologist. But, unfortunately for Boris, she
gave the "magic" paper to one Strouvilhou—a reappearing Dostoevskian
creature of almost unqualified corruptness.

P A R T   O N E :   I I
The Profitendieus

> *There is no trace in Poussin's letters of*
> *any feeling of obligation toward his*
> *parents.*
> *He never in later days showed any regret*
> *at having left them. Transplanted to*
> *Rome of his own free will, he lost all*
> *desire to return to his home—and even,*
> *it would seem, all recollection of it.*
>   PAUL DES JARDINS (Poussin)

Monsieur Profitendieu was in a hurry to get home and wished that his colleague Molinier, who was keeping him company up the boulevard Saint-Germain, would walk a little faster. Albéric Profitendieu had just had an unusually heavy day at the law courts; an uncomfortable sensation in his right side was causing him some uneasiness; fatigue in his case usually went to his liver, which was his weak point. He was thinking of the bath he was going to take; nothing rested him better from the cares of the day than a good bath—with an eye to which he had taken no tea that afternoon, esteeming it imprudent to get into any sort of water—even warm— except with an empty stomach. Merely a prejudice, perhaps; but prejudices are the very props of civilization.

Oscar Molinier walked as quickly as he could and made every effort to keep up with his companion; but he was much shorter than Profitendieu and of slighter crural development; besides which his heart was comfortably padded with fat, and he easily became shortwinded. Profitendieu, still sound at fifty-five, trim of build and brisk of step, would have gladly given him the slip; but he was very particular as to the proprieties; his colleague was older than he and higher up in the profession; he owed him a certain respect. And besides, since the death of his wife's parents, Profitendieu had a very considerable fortune to be forgiven him, whereas Monsieur Molinier had for his sole wealth nothing but his salary as *président de chambre*—a derisory salary, completely out of proportion to the high situation he occupied with a dignity all the more imposing because of the mediocrity it cloaked. Profitendieu concealed his impatience; he turned to Molinier and watched him mopping himself; for that matter, he was exceedingly interested by what Molinier was saying; but their point of view was not the same, and the discussion was beginning to get warm.

"Have the house watched, by all means," said Molinier. "Get the reports of the concierge and the sham maidservant—all this is very well! But be careful: if you push the inquiry a bit too far, the affair will get out of your hands. . . . I mean there's a risk of your being led on much further than you bargained for."

"Such considerations have nothing to do with justice."

"Oh, come, come, my dear sir; you and I know very well what justice ought to be and what it is. We act for the best, of course, that's understood, but however well we act, we never get more than an approximation. The case before you now is a particularly delicate one. Out of the fifteen accused persons—or persons who at a word from you will be accused tomorrow—nine are minors. And some of these boys, as you know, come from very honorable families. In such circumstances, I consider that to issue any warrant at all would be the most terrible blunder. The enemy press would get hold of the affair, and you open the door to every sort of blackmail and calumny. Oh, you'd have your work cut out: in spite of all your efforts, you'll not prevent names from coming out. . . . It's no business of mine to give you advice—on the contrary, you know very well how much happier I am to receive yours, how much I have always praised your high-mindedness, your lucidity, and your integrity. . . . But if I were you, this is what I should do: I should try to put an end to this abominable scandal by laying hold of the four or five instigators. . . . Oh yes, I know they're difficult to catch; but what the deuce, that's part of our trade. I should have the apartment—the scene of these orgies—closed, and I should take steps for the brazen young rascals' parents to be informed of the affair—quietly and secretly; and merely in order to avoid any repetition of the scandal. As to the women, go after *them* by all means! I'm entirely with you there. We seem to be confronted with a set of creatures of unfathomable perversity, and society should be cleansed of them at all costs. But, let me repeat, leave the boys alone; content yourself with giving them a fright, and then cover the matter over with some label like 'youthful indiscretion.' Their astonishment at having got off so cheaply will last them for a long time to come. Remember that three of them are not fourteen years old, and that their parents no doubt consider them to be angels of purity and innocence. But really, my dear fellow, between ourselves, come now: did *we* think of women when we were that age?"

He came to a stop, out of breath from his own eloquence rather than from walking, and forced Profitendieu, whose sleeve he was holding, to stop too.

"Or if we thought of them," he went on, "it was ideally—mystically

—religiously, if I may say so. The boys of today, don't you agree, have no ideals whatever. . . . Which reminds me, how are your boys? Of course, I'm not alluding to them when I speak of such things. I know that with your careful bringing-up—with the education you've given them, there's no fear of any such reprehensible follies."

And indeed, up to that time, Profitendieu had had every reason to be proud of his sons. But he had no illusions—the best education in the world was of no avail against bad instincts. God be praised, *his* children had no bad instincts—nor Molinier's either, no doubt; they were their own best protection against bad companions and bad books. For of what use is it to forbid what one cannot prevent? The very books you forbid children, they read on the sly. His own system was perfectly simple—he didn't forbid bad books, but he managed things so that his children had no desire to read them. As for the matter in question, he would think it over again, and he promised Molinier, in any case, to do nothing without consulting him. He would simply give orders for a discreet watch to be kept, and as the evil thing had been going on for three months already, it might just as well go on for another few days or weeks. Besides, the summer holidays were upon them and would necessarily disperse the delinquents.

"Au revoir!"

At last Profitendieu was able to walk a bit more quickly.

As soon as he got in, he hurried to his dressing-room and turned on the water for his bath. Antoine had been looking out for his master's return and managed to come across him in the passage.

This faithful manservant had been in the family for the last fifteen years; he had seen the children grow up. He had seen a great many things —and suspected a great many more; but he pretended not to see anything which he noticed the family obviously trying to hide.

Bernard was not without affection for Antoine. He had not wanted to leave the house without telling him good-bye. Perhaps it was out of irritation against his family that he made a point of confiding to a servant that he was going away, when none of his own people knew it; but, in excuse for Bernard, it must be pointed out that none of his own people was in the house at that time. And besides, Bernard could not have bidden them farewell without their trying to stop him: he dreaded being asked to explain. Whereas to Antoine, he could simply say: "I'm going away." But as he said it, he put out his hand with such a solemn air that the old servant was astonished.

"Monsieur Bernard will not be back to dine?"

"Nor to sleep, Antoine." And as Antoine hesitated, not knowing what he was expected to understand or whether he ought to ask any further questions, Bernard repeated still more meaningfully: "I'm going away"; then he added: "I've left a letter for . . ." He couldn't bring himself to say "Papa," so he corrected his sentence to "on the desk in the study. Good-bye."

As he squeezed Antoine's hand, he felt as moved as if he were then and there saying good-bye to all his past life. He repeated "good-bye" very quickly and then hurried off before the sob that was rising in his throat burst from him.

Antoine wondered whether it were not a heavy responsibility to let him go in this way—but how could he have stopped him?

That this departure of Bernard's would be for the whole family an unexpected, a monstrous event Antoine was well aware; but his role as a perfect servant was to pretend not to be surprised in the least. He had no business knowing what Monsieur Profitendieu did not know. No doubt, he might simply have said to him: "Does monsieur know that Master Bernard has gone away?" But by saying that, he would lose his advantage, and that was highly undesirable. If he awaited his master so impatiently, it was in order to let slip, in a noncommittal, deferential tone, as if it were a simple message Bernard had left him to deliver, this sentence (which he had carefully prepared in advance): "Before going away, sir, Master Bernard left a letter for you in the study"—a sentence so simple that it ran the risk of passing unperceived; he had sought in vain for something which would be more striking, but had found nothing which would be natural at the same time. But as it happened that Bernard never left home, Monsieur Profitendieu, whom Antoine was observing out of the corner of his eye, could not repress a start.

"What! Before going . . ."

He pulled himself up at once; it was not for him to show his astonishment before a subordinate; the consciousness of his superiority was one that never left him. He continued in a tone of perfect calm, of absolute mastery.

"Very good." And as he went toward his study: "Where did you say the letter was?"

"On the writing table, sir."

And in fact, as Profitendieu entered the room, he saw an envelope placed conspicuously opposite the chair in which he usually sat when writing; but Antoine had no intention of letting go so easily, and Monsieur Profitendieu had not read two lines of the letter, when he heard a knock at the door.

"I forgot to tell you, sir, that there are two persons waiting to see you in the small salon."

"What 'persons'?"

"I don't know."

"Are they together?"

"They don't seem to be."

"What do they want?"

"I don't know. They want to see you, sir."

Profitendieu felt his patience giving way.

"I have already said and repeated that I don't want to be disturbed when I'm at home—especially at this time of day; I receive people at posted times at the law courts. Why did you let them in?"

"They both said they had something very urgent to say to you, sir."

"Have they been here long?"

"Nearly an hour."

Profitendieu took a few steps up and down the room, and passed one hand over his forehead; with the other he held Bernard's letter. Antoine stood at the door, dignified and impassive. At last, he had the joy of seeing the judge lose his temper and of hearing him, for the first time in his life, stamp his foot and roar angrily: "Oh, shut up and leave me alone! Can't you leave me alone? Tell them I'm busy. Tell them to come another day."

Antoine had no sooner left the room than Profitendieu ran to the door.

"Antoine! Antoine! . . . And then go and turn off my bath."

Much inclined for a bath now! He went up to the window and read:

Monsieur,

Owing to an accidental discovery I happened to make this afternoon, I have become aware that I can no longer regard you as my father, which is, I must say, an immense relief to me. Realizing as I do how little affection I feel for you, I have for a long time thought myself to be an unnatural son; I prefer knowing I am not your son at all. You will perhaps judge that I ought to be grateful to you for having treated me as one of your own children; but, in the first place, I have always felt the difference between your behavior to them and to me, and secondly, I know you well enough to feel certain that you acted as you did because you were afraid of the scandal, and to conceal a situation which did you no great honor—and, finally, because you could not have acted otherwise. I prefer to leave without seeing my mother again, because I am afraid that the emotion of bidding her a final good-bye might affect me too much, and also because she might feel herself in a false position in my presence—which would be disagreeable to me. I doubt whether she has any very particular affection for me; as I was almost always away at school, she scarcely had time to come to know me, and as the sight of me must have continually reminded her of an episode in her life which she would have liked to efface, I think that she will see me go with relief and a certain pleasure. Tell her, if you have the courage to, that I bear her no grudge for having made me a bastard; on the contrary, I prefer that to knowing I was born your son. (Pray excuse me for writing in this way; it is not my object to insult you; but my words will give you an excuse to despise me, and that should relieve you.)

If you wish me to keep silent as to the secret reasons which have induced me to leave your roof, I must beg you not to attempt to make me return to it. The decision I have taken to leave you is irrevocable. I do not know how much you may have spent on supporting me up till now; I could accept living at your expense as long as I was ignorant of the truth, but it is needless to say that I prefer to receive nothing from you for the future. The idea of owing you anything at all I find intolerable and I would rather die of hunger than sit at your table again. Fortunately I seem to remember having heard that my mother was richer than you when she married you. I am free to think, therefore, that the burden of supporting me fell only on her. I thank her, consider her absolved of any further obligations, and beg her to forget me. You will easily find a way of explaining my departure to those it may surprise. I give you free leave to blame me (not that I think you will have awaited my permission to do so).

I sign this letter with that ridiculous name of yours, which I should like to throw back at you, and which I am looking forward soon to dishonor.

Bernard Profitendieu

P.S. I am leaving all my things behind me. They belong more legitimately to Caloub—at any rate I hope so, for your sake.

Monsieur Profitendieu tottered to an armchair. He would have liked to reflect, but ideas were spinning round confusedly in his head. Moreover he felt a little stabbing pain in his right side, there, just below his ribs. There could be no question about it: it was a liver attack. Would there be any Vichy water in the house? If only his wife had come back! How was he to break the news of Bernard's flight to her? Ought he to show her the letter? It is unjust, this letter, abominably unjust. He ought to be angry, indignant. But it is not anger he feels—he wishes it were—it is sorrow. He breathes deeply and at each breath exhales an "Oh my God!" as swift and low as a sigh. The pain in his side begins to mingle with his other pain, to verify and localize it. He feels as if his grief were in his liver. He drops into an armchair and rereads Bernard's letter. He shrugs his shoulders sadly. Yes, for him it is cruel, this letter—but there is spite in it, defiance, bravado. Not one of his other children—his real children— would have been capable of writing it, any more than he himself would have been. He knows this well, for there is nothing in them which he does not recognize as well in himself. He always thought it his duty, of course, to censure Bernard for his rawness, his roughness, his insubordination; but he can think it no longer, as he realizes that it is for those very qualities that he loved him as he had never loved the others.

For some moments now he had been hearing Cécile in the next room. She had come in from her concert, had begun to practice the piano, and was obstinately going over and over again the same phrase in a barcarole. At last Albéric Profitendieu could bear it no longer. He opened the drawing-room door a little way and in a plaintive, half-supplicating voice —for his liver was beginning to hurt him cruelly (and besides he had always been a little frightened of her): "Cécile, my dear," he said, "would you mind seeing whether there's any Vichy water in the house, and if there isn't, sending out to get some? and it would be very nice of you to stop playing for a little."

"Are you ill?"

"No, no, not at all. I've just got something that needs thinking over a little before dinner, and your music disturbs me."

And then out of kindliness—for suffering tended to soften him—he added: "That's a very pretty thing you're playing. What is it?"

But he went away without waiting for the answer. For that matter, his daughter, who was aware that he knew nothing whatever about music and could not distinguish between "Viens, poupoule" and the march from *Tannhäuser* (at least, so she used to say), had no intention of answering. But here he is at the door again!

"Has your mother come in?"

"No, not yet."

Absurd! She would be coming in so late that he would have no time to speak to her before dinner. What could he invent to explain Bernard's absence in the meantime? He really couldn't tell the truth—let the children into the secret of their mother's temporary lapse. Ah! all had been forgotten, forgiven, made up. The birth of their last son had sealed their reconciliation. And now, suddenly this avenging specter had re-risen from the past, this corpse had been washed up by the tide . . .

What's this? Someone else? As the study door noiselessly opens, he slips the letter into the inside pocket of his coat; the portière is gently raised. Caloub.

"Oh, Papa, please, this Latin sentence—can you tell me what it means? I can't make it out at all. . . ."

"I've already told you not to come in here without knocking. And then you mustn't come disturbing me like this for anything and everything. You are getting too much into the habit of relying on other people instead of making an effort yourself. Yesterday it was your geometry problem, and now today it's . . . who's the Latin sentence by?"

Caloub holds out his notebook.

"He didn't tell us; but just look at it; *you'll* recognize it, I'm sure you will. He dictated it to us, but perhaps I took it down wrong. I'd at least like to know if it's correct. . . ."

Monsieur Profitendieu took the notebook, but he was in too much pain. He gently pushed the child away.

"Later on. It's just time for dinner. Has Charles come in?"

"He went down to his office." (Charles, an attorney, receives his clients downstairs.)

"Go and tell him I want to speak to him. Quick!"

A ring at the door bell! Madame Profitendieu at last! She apologizes for being late. She had a great many visits to pay. She is sorry to see her husband so poorly. What can be done for him? He certainly looks very unwell. He won't be able to eat a thing. They must sit down without him, but after dinner, will she come to his study with the children?—Bernard? —Oh, yes; his friend . . . you know—the one he's been studying mathematics with—came and took him out to dinner.

Profitendieu felt better. At first he had been afraid he would be too ill to speak. And yet it was essential that he give some explanation of Bernard's disappearance. He knew now what he must say—however painful it might be. He felt firm and determined. His only fear was that his wife might interrupt him by crying, by a shriek, that she might faint. . . .

An hour later she comes into the room with the three children. He makes her sit down beside him, close against his armchair.

"Try to control yourself," he whispers, but in a tone of command, "and don't speak a word, do you hear? We will talk together afterwards."

And all the time he is speaking, he holds one of her hands in both of his.

"Come, my children, sit down. It upsets me to see you there in front of me, standing as if I were some kind of examiner. I have something very sad to say to you. Bernard has left us and we shall not see him again . . . for some time to come. I am obliged to tell you now what I concealed from you at first, so anxious was I that you should love Bernard like a brother; because your mother and I loved him like our own child. But he was not our child . . . and one of his uncles—a brother of his real mother, who confided him to us on her deathbed—came this evening to take him away."

A painful silence follows these words. Caloub can be heard sniffling. Everyone waits, expecting him to go on. But he waves his hand and says: "You can go now, my dears. I must speak to your mother."

After they have left the room, Monsieur Profitendieu remains silent for a long time. The hand which Madame Profitendieu had left in his seems like a dead thing; with the other she presses a handkerchief to her eyes. Leaning on the big table, she turns away to weep. Through the sobs which shake her, Monsieur Profitendieu hears her murmur: "Oh, how cruel you are! . . . Oh! You have sent him away. . . ."

A moment before, he had resolved not to show her Bernard's letter; but at this unjust accusation, he holds it out: "Here: Read this."

"I can't."

"You must read it."

He has forgotten his pain. He follows her with his eyes all through the letter, line by line. Just now when he was speaking, he could hardly keep back his tears; but now all emotion has left him; he watches his wife. What is she thinking? In the same plaintive voice, broken by the same sobs, she murmurs again: "Oh! why did you tell him? . . . You shouldn't have told him."

"But you can see for yourself that I never told him anything. Read his letter more carefully."

"I did read it. . . . But then how did he find out? Who told him?"

So *that* is what she is thinking! *Those* are the accents of her grief! This loss should have brought them together, but, alas! Profitendieu feels obscurely that their thoughts are traveling in divergent directions. And while she laments and accuses and recriminates, he endeavors to bend her unruly spirit and to bring her to a more pious frame of mind.

"This is the expiation," he says.

He has risen, from an instinctive need to dominate; he stands there before her upright—forgetful or regardless of his physical pain—and lays his hand gravely, tenderly, authoritatively on Marguerite's shoulder. He is well aware that her repentance for what he chooses to consider a passing weakness has never been more than half-hearted; he would like to tell her now that this sorrow, this trial may serve to redeem her; but he can find no expression that quite satisfies him, none that he can hope she will listen to. Marguerite's shoulder resists the gentle pressure of his hand. She knows so well that from the most trivial event of life he invariably, intolerably extracts, as with a forceps, some moral teaching; that he interprets and translates all to suit his own dogma. He bends over her. This is what he would like to say: "You see, my poor darling, no good thing can be born of sin. It was no use trying to cover up your transgression. Alas, I did what I could for the child. I treated him as my very own. God is showing us now that it was an error to pretend. . . ."

But at the first sentence he stops.

And no doubt she understands these words, so teeming with meaning; no doubt they have struck home to her heart, for though she had stopped crying some moments before, her sobs break out afresh, even more violently than at first: then she bows herself, as though she were going to kneel before him, but he stoops over her and holds her up. What is it she is saying through her tears? He stoops his ear almost to her. He hears: "You see . . . You see . . . Oh! why did you forgive me? Oh, I shouldn't have come back!"

He is almost obliged to guess at her words. Then she stops. She too is now lost for words. How can she tell him that she feels imprisoned in this virtue which he exacts from her . . . that she is stifling . . . that it is not so much her fault that she regrets now as having repented of it? Profitendieu raises himself.

"My poor Marguerite," he says with dignity and severity, "I am afraid you are a little obstinate tonight. It is late. We had better go to bed."

He helps her up, leads her to her room, puts his lips to her forehead, then returns to his study and flings himself into an armchair. A curious thing: his liver attack has subsided; but he feels shattered. He sits with his head in his hands, too sad to cry. . . . He does not hear a knock at the door, but at the noise the door makes in opening, he raises his head—his son Charles.

"I came to say good-night."

He comes near. He has understood everything, and he wants his father to know this. He would like to show his pity, his tenderness, his devotion, but—who would believe it of an attorney?—he is extraordinarily awkward at expressing himself; or perhaps he becomes awkward precisely from the time his feelings are sincere. He embraces his father. The insistent way in which he lays his head upon his father's shoulder and leans and lingers there convinces Profitendieu that his son has understood. He has understood so thoroughly that, raising his head a little, he asks in his usual clumsy fashion—but his heart is so anxious that he cannot refrain from asking: "And Caloub?"

The question is absurd, for Caloub's looks are as strikingly like his family's as Bernard's are different.

Profitendieu pats Charles on the shoulder: "No, no; don't worry. Only Bernard."

Then Charles begins pompously: "God has driven the intruder away . . ."

But Profitendieu stops him. What need has he of such words? "Hush!"

Father and son have no more to say to each other. Let us leave them. It is nearly eleven o'clock. Let us leave Madame Profitendieu in her room, seated on a small, straight, uncomfortable chair. She is not crying; she is not thinking. She too would like to run away. But she will not. When she was with her lover, Bernard's father (we need not concern ourselves with him), she said to herself: "No, no, you're wasting your time; try as you may, you shall never be anything but an honest woman." She was afraid of liberty, of crime, of ease—so that after ten days, she returned repentant to her home. Her parents were right when they used to say to her: "You never know *what* you want." Let us leave her. Cécile is already asleep. Caloub is gazing in despair at his candle; it will never last long enough for him to finish the storybook with which he is distracting himself from thoughts of Bernard. I should be curious to know what Antoine can have told his good friend the cook. But it is impossible to listen to everything. This is the hour when Bernard was to go meet Olivier. I am not sure where he dined that evening or even whether he dined at all. He has passed the concierge's room without hindrance; he climbs stealthily up the stairs. . . .

PART ONE: IV

Vincent and the Comte de Passavant

> *My father was a dolt, but my mother*
> *had spirit; she was a quietist; she was a*
> *sweet little woman who said to me often,*
> *"My son, you will be damned." But this*
> *never seemed to bother her.*
>
> FONTENELLE

No, it was not to see his mistress that Vincent Molinier went out every evening. Quickly as he walks, let us follow him. He goes along the rue Notre-Dame-des-Champs, at the further end of which he lives, until he reaches the rue Placide, which it runs into; then down the rue du Bac, where a few belated passers-by still wander. In the rue de Babylone, he stops in front of a porte-cochère; it opens: the residence of the Comte de Passavant. If Vincent were not in the habit of coming often, he would enter this sumptuous mansion with a less confident air. The footman who comes to the door knows well enough how much timidity this feigned assurance hides. Vincent, with a touch of affectation, does not hand him his hat, but tosses it onto an armchair some yards away. It is only recently that Vincent has taken to coming here, however. Robert de Passavant, who now calls himself his friend, is the friend of a great many people. I am not exactly sure how he and Vincent became acquainted. At the lycée, I expect—though Robert de Passavant is perceptibly older than Vincent; they had lost sight of each other for several years and then, quite lately, had met again one evening when, by some unusual chance, Olivier had gone with his brother to the theater; during the entr'acte, Passavant had offered them both an ice; he had learned that Vincent had just finished his medical examinations and was undecided as to whether he should take an internship; the natural sciences, to tell the truth, attracted him more than medicine, but the necessity of earning his living . . . in short, Vincent accepted with pleasure the very remunerative proposition Robert de Passavant had made him a little later of coming every evening to attend his old father, who had lately been left quite shaken by a very serious operation; it was a matter of bandages to remake, of injections, of delicate soundings—in fact, of all the usual ministrations that demand an expert hand.

But, added to this, the vicomte had secret reasons for wishing a nearer acquaintance with Vincent; and Vincent had still others for consenting. Robert's secret reason we shall try to discover later on. As for

Vincent's—it was this: he was urgently in need of money. When your heart is in the right place, and a wholesome education has early inculcated a decent sense of your responsibilities, you don't get a woman with child without feeling yourself more or less indebted on her account—especially when the woman has left her husband to follow you.

Until then, Vincent had lived virtuously, by and large. His adventure with Laura appeared to him alternately, according to the hour of the day, as either monstrous or perfectly natural. If you add together a quantity of little facts—little facts which, taken separately, are very simple and very natural—you may very often arrive at a sum which is monstrous. He said all this to himself over and over again as he walked along, but it didn't get him out of his difficulties. No doubt, he had never thought of taking this woman permanently under his protection—of marrying her after a divorce, or of living with her without marrying; he was obliged to confess to himself that he had no great passion for her; but he knew that she was in Paris without resources; he was the cause of her distress; at the very least, he owed her that first precarious aid which he felt himself less and less able to assure her—today less than yesterday, yesterday less than the week before. For last week he still possessed the five thousand frances which his mother had patiently and laboriously set aside to give him a start in his profession; those five thousand francs would have sufficed, no doubt, to pay for his mistress's confinement, for her stay in a nursing home, for the child's first needs. To what demon's advice, then, had he listened? That sum, which he had as good as given to Laura, which he had laid by for her, pledged to her—what demon had whispered to him, one evening, that it would probably be insufficient? No, it was not Robert de Passavant; Robert had never said anything of the kind; but his proposal to take Vincent with him to a gambling club had occurred precisely the same evening. And Vincent had accepted.

The gambling den in question had this particularly vicious quality, that all its habitués were people in society; all "the best of friends." Robert introduced his friend Vincent to one and another of them. Vincent, who was taken unawares, was not able to play high that first evening. He had hardly anything on him, and refused the few notes which the vicomte offered to advance him. But, as he was winning, he regretted not being able to stake more, and promised to go back the next night.

"Everybody knows you now; there's no need for me to come with you again," Robert told him.

These meetings took place at Pierre de Brouville's, commonly known as Pedro. After this first evening Robert de Passavant had put his

car at his new friend's disposal. Vincent used to look in about eleven
o'clock, chat with Robert for a quarter-hour or so, smoke a cigarette, then
go on upstairs, lingering with the old count for a period of time commen-
surate with the latter's mood, his patience, or his needs; after that, the car
would take him to Pedro's in the rue St. Florentin, whence about an hour
later the car took him back—not actually to his own door, for he was
afraid of attracting attention, but to the nearest corner.

Two nights earlier, Laura Douviers, seated on the steps which led to
the Moliniers' apartment, had waited for Vincent till three o'clock in the
morning; it was not until then that he had come in. As a matter of fact,
Vincent had not gone to Pedro's that night. For two days now he had not
had a penny left of the five thousand francs. He had informed Laura of
this; he had written that he could do nothing more for her; that he advised her to go back to her husband or her father—to confess everything.
But at this point confession seemed impossible to Laura, and she could not
even envisage it with any sort of calm. Her lover's objurgations aroused in
her nothing but indignation, an indignation which only subsided to abandon her to despair. That was the state in which Vincent had found her.
She had tried to hold him; he had torn himself from her grasp. Doubtless,
he had to steel himself to do it, for he had a tender heart; but, more of a
pleasure-seeker than a lover, he had easily persuaded himself that it was
his duty to be firm. He had answered nothing to all her entreaties and
lamentations, and as Olivier, who had heard them, told Bernard afterwards, when Vincent shut his door against her, she had sunk down on the
steps and remained for a long time sobbing in the dark.

More than forty hours had gone by since that night. The day before,
Vincent had not gone to Robert de Passavant's, whose father seemed to be
recovering; but that evening a telegram had summoned him. Robert
wished to see him. When Vincent entered the room in which Robert usually sat—a room which he used as his study and smoking-room and which
he had been at some pains to decorate and furnish in his own fashion—
Robert carelessly held out his hand to him over his shoulder, without rising.

Robert is writing. He is sitting at a desk littered with books. In front
of him, the French window giving onto the garden stands wide open in
the moonlight. He speaks without turning round.

"Do you know what I am writing? But you won't mention it, will
you? You promise, eh?—a manifesto for the opening number of Dhur-
mer's review. I shan't sign it, of course—especially as I'm praising myself

in it. . . . And then as it will certainly come out in the long run that I'm financing the review, I don't want it known too soon that I'm writing for it. So mum's the word! But it's just occurred to me—didn't you say that young brother of yours wrote? What's his name again?"

"Olivier," says Vincent.

"Olivier. Yes; I had forgotten. Don't stand there like that! Take a chair. You're not cold? Shall I shut the window? . . . It's poetry he writes, isn't it? He ought to bring me something to see. Of course, I don't promise to take it . . . but, all the same, I should be surprised if it were bad. He looks very intelligent, your brother. And then he's obviously *au courant*. I should like to talk to him. Tell him to come and see me, eh? Mind, I count on it. A cigarette?" And he holds out his silver cigarette-case.

"With pleasure."

"Now then, Vincent, listen to me. I must speak to you very seriously. You behaved like a child the other evening . . . so did I, for that matter. I don't say it was wrong of me to take you to Pedro's, but I feel responsible, a little, for the money you've lost. I don't know if that's what's meant by remorse, but, upon my word, it's beginning to disturb my sleep and my digestion. And then, when I think of that unhappy woman you told me about . . . But that's another department; we won't speak of that; sacred affair. What I want to say is this—that I wish—yes, I'm absolutely determined to put at your disposal a sum of money equivalent to what you've lost. It was five thousand francs, wasn't it? And you're to risk it again. Once more, I repeat, I consider myself the cause of your losing this money; I owe it to you; so there's no need to thank me. You'll pay me back if you win. If not—worse luck! We shall be quits. Go back to Pedro's this evening as if nothing had happened. The car will take you there, then come back here to fetch me for Lady Griffith's, where I'll ask you to join me later on. I count upon it, now. I'll send the car to pick you up at Pedro's."

He opens a drawer and takes out five notes which he hands to Vincent. "Off with you, now."

"But your father?"

"Ah! I forgot to tell you: he died about . . ." He pulls out his watch and exclaims: "Good gracious! how late it is! Nearly midnight. . . . You must go quickly. Yes, about four hours ago."

All this said without the least precipitation—on the contrary with a kind of nonchalance.

"And aren't you going to stay to . . ."

"To watch by the body?" interrupts Robert. "No, that's my young brother's business. He is up there with his old nurse, who was on better terms with the deceased than I was."

Then, as Vincent does not budge, he goes on: "Look here, my dear fellow, I don't want to appear cynical, but I have a horror of ready-made sentiments. In my early days I cut out in my heart a filial love for my father according to the pattern; but I soon saw that my measurements had been too ample, and I was obliged to take it in. The old man never in his life occasioned me anything but trouble and vexation and constraint. If he had any tenderness left in his heart, he certainly never showed it to me. My first impulses toward him, in the days before I knew how to behave, brought me nothing but rebuffs—and I quickly learned my lesson. You must have seen for yourself, when you were attending him. . . . Did he ever thank you? Did you ever get the slightest look from him, the least fleeting smile? He always thought everything his due. Oh, he was what people call a *character!* I think he must have made my mother suffer very greatly, and yet he loved her—that is, if he ever really loved anyone. I think he made everyone around him suffer—his servants, his dogs, his horses, his mistresses; his friends, no; he had no friends. His death will raise a general sigh of relief. He was, I believe, a man of great distinction in 'his line,' as people say; but I have never been able to discover what it was. He was very intelligent, I am quite sure. At heart, I had, I still have, a certain admiration for him. But as for fiddling with a handkerchief . . . as for wringing out tears . . . no, I'm no longer infant enough for that. Be off with you now! And join me in an hour's time at Lilian's —What's that? You're worried about not being properly dressed? Don't be a fool! What does it matter? We'll be the only ones there. Hold on: I promise I'll not dress either. All right? Now, light a cigar before you go. And send the car back quickly—it'll fetch you again later on."

He watched Vincent go out, shrugged his shoulders, then went into his dressing-room to change into his evening clothes, which were laid out for him on a sofa.

In a room on the first floor, the old count is lying on his deathbed. Someone has placed a crucifix on his breast, but has omitted to join his hands over it. A beard of some days' growth softens the stubborn angle of his chin. Beneath his gray hair, which is brushed up *en brosse,* the transversal wrinkles that line his forehead seem less deeply graven, as though they were relaxed. His eye has sunk back in under the deep arcade of a brow exaggerated with bristly hairs. I know that we shall never see him again, and that is the reason I am looking at him so closely. Beside the head of the bed is an armchair, in which is seated the old nurse Séraphine. But she has risen. She goes up to a table where an old-fashioned oil lamp is dimly lighting the room; it needs turning up. A lampshade casts the light onto the book young Gontran is reading. . . .

"You're tired, Master Gontran. You had better go to bed."

The glance that Gontran raises from his book to rest upon Séraphine is very gentle. His fair hair, which he pushes back from his forehead, falls over his temples. He is fifteen years old; his gentle, almost feminine face expresses nothing as yet but tenderness and love.

"Ah, but what about you?" he says. "It is you who ought to go to bed, my poor old Fine. Last night, you were on your feet nearly the whole time."

"Oh, me, I'm used to sitting up. And besides I slept during the day-time—but you . . ."

"No, I'm all right. I don't feel tired; and it does me good to stay here thinking and reading. I knew Papa so little; I think I should forget him altogether if I didn't take a good look at him now. I'll stay with him until daylight. How long has it been, Fine, that you've been with us now?"

"I came the year before you were born; and you're nearly sixteen."

"Do you remember *maman* very well?"

"Do I remember your *maman?* What a question! You might as well ask me if I remember my own name. But of course, I remember your *maman.*"

"I remember her too, a little, but not very well. . . . I was only five when she died. Tell me—did Papa talk to her very much?"

"It depended on his mood. He was never one to talk much, your papa, and he didn't care to be spoken to first. Still, he was a little more talkative in those days than he has been of late. . . . But there now! It's better not to stir up the past; just let the dear Lord be the judge of all that."

"Do you really think the Lord cares about such things, dear Fine?"

"Why, if He doesn't, who should then?"

Gontran puts his lips on Séraphine's red, roughened hand. "You know what you ought to do now? Go to bed. I promise to wake you as soon as it is light; and then it'll be my turn for sleep. Please!"

As soon as Séraphine has left him alone, Gontran falls upon his knees at the foot of the bed; he buries his head in the sheets, but he cannot bring himself to weep. No emotion stirs his heart; his eyes remain despairingly dry. Then he gets up. He looks at that impassive face. He would like, at this solemn moment, to feel something rare, sublime, indescribable, to hear a message from the world beyond, to send his thought sailing into ethereal, suprasensible regions; but it remains obstinately attached to the earth. He looks at the dead man's bloodless hands and wonders for how much longer the nails will go on growing. The sight of the unclasped hands shocks him. He would like to bring them together, join them, make them hold the crucifix. That's a good idea. He thinks of Séraphine's astonishment when she sees the dead hands folded together; the thought of this amuses him; and, almost at once, he despises himself for being amused. Nevertheless he leans over the bed. He seizes the dead man's arm farthest from him. The arm is already stiff and refuses to bend. Gontran tries to force it, but only makes the whole body move. He seizes the other arm, which seems a little more supple. He almost succeeds in putting the hand in the proper place; he takes the crucifix and tries to slip it between the fingers and the thumb, but the contact of the cold flesh makes him sick. He thinks he is going to faint. He has half a mind to call Séraphine back. He lets it all go—the crucifix falls at an angle on the wrinkled sheet, the arm drops lifelessly back into its first position; then, through the depths of the funereal silence, he suddenly hears a brutal "God damn!" which fills him with terror, as if someone else . . . He turns around; but no: he is alone. It was from his own lips, from his own heart, that that resounding curse had broken forth—he who until today has never uttered an oath! Then he sits down and plunges back into his reading. . . .

PART ONE: VII

Lilian and Vincent

.   .   .

She settled down on the rug beside the bed, crouching between Vincent's legs like an Egyptian statue, with her chin resting on her knees. When she had finished her meal, she began:

"I was on the *Bourgogne,* you know, on the day it went down. I was seventeen, so now you know how old I am. I was an excellent swimmer, and to show you that I'm not hard-hearted, I'll tell you that if my first thought was to save myself, my second was to save someone else. I'm not entirely sure, in fact, whether it wasn't my first. Or rather, I believe I thought of nothing at all; but nothing disgusts me so much in such moments as the people who think only of themselves—yes: all those women who scream. There was a first lifeboat, filled mainly with women and children; and some of them were yelling so loud it was enough to make anyone lose his head. The boat was so badly handled that instead of dropping down onto the sea straight, it dived down nose first, and everyone in it was flung out before it even had time to fill with water. The whole scene took place by the light of torches and lanterns and searchlights. You can't imagine how ghastly it was. The waves were very big, and everything that was not in the light was lost in darkness on the other side of the hill of water.

"I have never lived more intensely; but I was as incapable of reflection as a Newfoundland dog, I suppose, when he jumps into the water. I can't even understand now what happened; I only know that I had noticed a little girl in the boat, a darling thing of about five or six; and when I saw the boat overturn, I immediately made up my mind that it was her I would save. She was with her mother at first, but the poor woman was a bad swimmer; and as usual in such cases, she was hampered by her skirts. As for me, I must have undressed almost mechanically; someone called me to take my place in the next lifeboat. I must have got in; and then obviously I jumped straight into the sea out of the boat; all I can remember is swimming about for a long time with the child clinging to my neck. It was terrified and squeezed my neck so tight that I couldn't breathe. Luckily the people in the boat saw us, and either waited for us or rowed toward us. But that's not why I'm telling you this story. The memory which has remained the most vivid, which nothing will ever efface from my brain and my heart is this: there were about forty or so of us in the boat, all crowded together, for a number of desperate swimmers had been picked up, like me. The water was almost on a level with the edge of the boat. I was in the stern and I was holding the little girl I had just saved tightly pressed against me to warm her and to prevent her from seeing what I couldn't help seeing myself: two sailors, one armed with a hatchet and the other with a kitchen knife; and do you know what they were doing? . . . They were hacking off the fingers and hands of the swimmers who were trying to pull themselves into our boat by the ropes. One of these two sailors (the other was a Negro) turned to me, as I sat there, my teeth chattering with cold and fright and horror, and said, 'If one more gets in we shall be bloody well done for. The boat's full.' He said that it was a thing they had to do in all shipwrecks; but that naturally no one talked about it.

"I think I fainted then; at any rate, I can't remember anything more, just as one remains deaf for a long time after too violent a noise. And when I came to, on board the ship that picked us up, I realized that I was no longer the same, that I never could again be the same sentimental girl I had been before; I realized that I had let a part of myself go down with the *Bourgogne;* that from then on there would be a whole heap of delicate feelings whose fingers and hands I should hack away to keep them from climbing into my heart and pushing it under."

She looked at Vincent out of the corner of her eye and, twisting her torso backwards, said: "It's a habit one must get into."

. . .

PART TWO: III
Theory of the Novel

. . .

Tea-time found them as a rule all assembled in the big sitting-room; it often happened that, at their invitation, Mme Sophroniska joined them, generally on the days when Boris and Bronja were out walking. She left them very free, in spite of their youth; she had perfect confidence in Bronja and knew that she was very prudent, especially with Boris, who always did exactly what she said. The countryside was safe; for of course there was no question of their venturing into the mountains, or even of climbing the rocks near the hotel. One day when the two children had obtained leave to go to the foot of the glacier on condition they did not leave the road, Mme Sophroniska, who had been invited to tea, was em-boldened, with Bernard's and Laura's encouragement, to beg Edouard to tell them about his next novel—that is, if he had no objection.

"None at all; but I can't tell you the plot."

And yet he seemed almost to lose his temper when Laura asked him (evidently a tactless question) what the book would be like?

"Nothing!" he exclaimed; then immediately, and as if he had only been waiting for this provocation: "What is the use of doing all over again what other people have done already, or what I myself have already done, or what other people might do?"

Edouard had no sooner uttered these words than he felt how im-proper, how outrageous and absurd they were; at any rate they seemed to *him* improper and absurd; or at least he was afraid that was how they would seem to Bernard.

Edouard was very sensitive. As soon as people began talking of his work, and especially when they made him talk of it, he seemed to lose his head.

He had the most perfect contempt for the usual fatuity of authors; he smothered his own as well as he could; but he was willing to let his modesty depend on other people's consideration; if that consideration failed him, modesty immediately went by the board. He attached particular importance to Bernard's estimation. Was it in order to win Bernard over that, whenever he was in the boy's company, he set his Pegasus prancing? It was, of course, the best way to lose him, as Edouard well knew; he told himself so over and over again; but in spite of all his resolutions, as soon as he was with Bernard, he behaved quite differently from what he wished, and spoke in a manner which he immediately judged absurd (and which indeed was so). By which one might almost suppose that he loved Bernard? . . . No; I don't think so. But a little vanity is quite as effectual in making us pose as a great deal of love.

"Is it because the novel, of all literary genres, is the freest, the most *lawless*," Edouard held forth, ". . . is it for that very reason, for fear of that very liberty (for the artists who are always sighing after liberty are often the most bewildered when they get it), that the novel has always clung to reality so timidly? And I am not speaking only of the French novel. It is the same with the English novel; and the Russian novel, for all its throwing off of constraints, is every bit as much a slave to resemblance. The only progress it imagines is to get still closer to nature. The novel has never known that 'formidable erosion of contours,' as Nietzsche calls it; that deliberate distancing from life, which gave style to the works of the Greek dramatists, for instance, or to the tragedies of the French seventeenth century. Do you know of anything more perfect and more profoundly human than those works? But that's just it—they are human only in their depths; they don't pride themselves on appearing so—or, at any rate, on appearing real. They remain works of art."

Edouard had got up, and, for fear of seeming to give a lecture, he began to pour the tea as he spoke; then he moved up and down, then squeezed a lemon into his cup; but all the same he kept on talking:

"Because Balzac was a genius, and because every genius seems to bring to his art a definitive and exclusive solution, it has been decreed that the proper function of the novel is to rival our birth and marriage and death certificates, our tax and military records, our *états-civil*. Balzac built his own work, yes; but he never claimed to be codifying the novel; his article on Stendhal proves that. Rival the *état-civil!* As if there weren't enough baboons and boors in the world as it is! What have I to do with the *état-civil? L'état c'est moi!* I, the artist; civil or not, my work doesn't pretend to rival anything."

Edouard, who was getting excited—a little factiously, perhaps—sat down. He affected not to look at Bernard; but it was for him that he was speaking. If he had been alone with him, he would not have been able to say a word; he was grateful to the two women for setting him on.

"Sometimes it seems to me there is nothing in all literature I admire so much as, for instance, the discussion between Mithridates and his sons in Racine; we know perfectly well that no father and his sons could ever have spoken in that way, and yet (I ought to say: for that very reason) it's a scene in which all fathers and all sons can recognize themselves. By localizing and specifying, one restricts. It is true that there is no psychological truth unless it be particular; but there is no art unless it be general. The whole problem is right there: to express the general by the particular; to make the particular express the general. May I light my pipe?"

"Do, do," said Sophroniska.

"Well, I should like a novel which should be at the same time as true and as removed from reality, as particular and at the same time as general, as human and as fictitious as *Athalie* or *Tartuffe* or *Cinna.*"

"And . . . . the subject of this novel?"

"It hasn't got one," Edouard replied brusquely, "and perhaps that's the most astonishing thing about it. My novel hasn't got a subject. Yes, I know, it sounds stupid. Let's say if you prefer that it hasn't got *one* subject . . . 'A slice of life,' the naturalist school said. The great defect of that school is that it always cuts its slice in the same direction; in time, lengthwise. Why not in breadth? Or in depth? As for me, I should like not to cut at all. Please understand; I should like to put everything into my novel. I don't want any cut of the scissors to limit its substance here, or there, or anywhere. For more than a year now that I have been working at it, nothing happens to me that I don't put into it—everything I see, everything I know, everything that other people's lives and my own teach me. . . ."

"And all this stylized, I suppose?" Sophroniska asked, feigning the liveliest attention, but no doubt a little ironically. Laura could not suppress a smile. Edouard shrugged his shoulders slightly and went on:

"And even that isn't what I want to do. What I want is, on the one hand, to represent reality, and on the other to represent that very effort to stylize it of which I have just been speaking."

"My poor dear friend, you will make your readers die of boredom," Laura said; as she could no longer hide her smile, she had made up her mind to laugh outright.

"Not at all. In order to achieve this effect—do you follow me?—I invent the character of a novelist, whom I make my central figure; and the subject of the book, if you must have one, is precisely that struggle between what reality offers him and what he himself intends to make of it."

"Yes, yes; I'm beginning to see," said Sophroniska politely, though Laura's laugh was very near to conquering her too. "But you know it's always dangerous to represent intellectuals in novels. The public is bored by them; one only manages to make them say absurdities, and they give an air of abstraction to everything they touch."

"And then I see exactly what's going to happen," Laura cried; "in describing this novelist of yours, you won't be able to help painting yourself!"

She had lately adopted in talking to Edouard a jeering tone by which she astonished herself, and upset Edouard all the more in that he saw a reflection of it in Bernard's malicious glance. Edouard protested:

"No, no. I shall take care to make him very disagreeable."

"That's just it," Laura interrupted. "Everybody will recognize you!" And she burst into such hearty laughter that the others were caught by its infection.

"And is the plot of the book worked out?" Sophroniska asked, trying to regain her composure.

"Of course not."

"What do you mean, 'Of course not'?"

"You must understand that it's essentially out of the question for a book of this kind to have a plot. Everything would be falsified if I were to decide anything in advance. I wait for reality to dictate to me."

"But I thought you wanted to get away from reality."

"My novelist wants to get away from it; but I shall continually bring him back to it. In fact that will be the subject; the struggle between the facts presented by reality and the ideal reality."

The illogical nature of his remarks was flagrant, painfully obvious to everyone. It was clear that Edouard lodged under his hat two irreconcilable demands, and that he was wearing himself out in the effort to bring them together.

"Have you got on very far with it?" Sophroniska asked politely.

"It depends on what you mean by far. To tell the truth, not a line of the actual book has been written. But I have worked at it a great deal. I think of it every day, incessantly. I work at it in a very odd manner, as I shall explain: day by day in a notebook, I note the state of the novel in my mind; yes, it's a kind of diary that I keep as one might keep that of a child. . . . That is to say, that instead of contenting myself with resolving each difficulty as it presents itself (and every work of art is only the sum or the product of the solutions of a great number of small difficulties), I set forth each of these difficulties and then study it. My notebook contains, as it were, a running criticism of my novel—or rather of the novel in general. Just think how interesting such a notebook kept by Dickens or Balzac would be; if we had the diary of the *Education sentimentale* or of *The Brothers Karamazov*!—the story of the work, of its gestation! How thrilling it would be . . . more interesting than the work itself. . . ."

Edouard vaguely hoped that someone would ask him to read these notes. But not one of the three showed the slightest curiosity. Instead:

"My poor friend," said Laura, with a touch of sadness, "I see quite clearly that you'll never write this novel of yours."

"Well, let me tell *you* something," Edouard cried impetuously. "I couldn't care less. Yes, if I don't succeed in writing the book, it'll be because the history of the book will have interested me more than the book itself—have taken the book's place; and it'll be a very good thing."

"Aren't you afraid, when you abandon reality in this way, of losing yourself in regions of deadly abstraction and of making a novel about ideas instead of about human beings?" Sophroniska asked timidly.

"And even so!" Edouard cried with redoubled energy. "Must we condemn the novel of ideas because of the incompetents who have stumbled through it before now? Until now we have been given nothing but execrable *romans à thèse,* novels with a purpose parading as novels of ideas. But that's not it at all, as you may imagine. Ideas . . . ideas, I must confess, interest me more than men—interest me more than anything. They live; they fight; they perish like men. Of course one may say that our only knowledge of them is through men, just as our only knowledge of the wind is through the reeds that it bends; but all the same the wind is of more importance than the reeds."

"The wind exists independently of the reed," Bernard ventured. His intervention made Edouard, who had long been waiting for it, start afresh with renewed spirit:

"Yes, I know; ideas exist only because of men; but that's what's so pathetic about it; they live at their expense."

Bernard had listened to all this with great attention; he was full of skepticism and very near to taking Edouard for a mere dreamer; but during the last few moments he had been touched by his eloquence, and had felt his mind bend with its drift. "But," Bernard thought, "the reed lifts it own head again once the wind has passed." He remembered what he had been taught at school—that man is swayed by his passions and not by ideas. In the meantime Edouard was going on:

"What I should like to do, you see, is something that would be like *The Art of the Fugue.* And I don't see why what was possible in music should not be possible in literature. . . ."

To which Sophroniska rejoined that music is a mathematical art, and moreover that Bach, by dealing only with figures and by banishing all pathos and all humanity, had achieved an abstract masterpiece of boredom, a kind of astronomical temple, to be entered only by the few rare initiates. Edouard at once protested that, for his part, he found the temple admirable, and considered it the apex and crowning point of all Bach's career.

"After which," Laura added, "people were cured of the fugue for a long time to come. Human emotion, finding it no longer habitable, went to look for somewhere else to live."

The discussion trailed off into useless arguments. Bernard, who until then had kept silent, was beginning to fidget in his chair, and at last could bear it no longer. With extreme, even exaggerated deference, as was his habit whenever he spoke to Edouard, but with a kind of playfulness which seemed to make a jest of his deference:

"Forgive me, monsieur," he said, "for knowing the title of your book, since I do so thanks to an indiscretion—which I believe, however, you have been kind enough to excuse. But the title seemed to me to announce a story."

"Oh, tell us what the title is!" said Laura.

"If you wish it, my dear. . . . But I warn you that I may possibly change it. I am afraid it's rather deceptive. . . . Well, tell them, Bernard."

"May I? . . . *The Counterfeiters,*" said Bernard. "But now *you* tell us—who are these Counterfeiters?"

"Oh my! I have no idea," said Edouard.

Bernard and Laura looked at each other, then looked at Sophroniska. Someone emitted a long sigh; I think it was Laura.

In reality, it was of certain of his fellow novelists that Edouard had at first been thinking when he hit upon the title of *The Counterfeiters;* and in particular of the Vicomte de Passavant. But the attribution had been considerably widened since; according as the wind of the spirit blew from Rome or from elsewhere, his heroes became in turn either priests or freemasons. If he allowed his mind to follow its bent, it soon tumbled headlong into abstractions, where it was as comfortable as a fish in water. Ideas

of exchange, of depreciation, of inflation, etc., gradually invaded his book
(like the theory of clothes in Carlyle's *Sartor Resartus*) and usurped the
place of the characters. As it was impossible for Edouard to speak of this,
he kept silent in the most awkward manner, and his silence, which seemed
like an admission of poverty, began to make the other three very uncomfortable.

"Have you ever had the opportunity to hold a counterfeit coin in
your hands?" he asked at last.

"Yes," said Bernard; but the two women's "No" drowned out his
voice.

"Well, imagine a ten-franc gold piece that's counterfeit. In reality it's
not worth two sous. But it will be worth ten francs as long as no one
recognizes that it's false. So if I start from the idea that . . ."

"But why start from an idea?" Bernard interrupted impatiently. "If
you were to start from a fact, and describe it well, the idea would come of
its own accord to inhabit it. If I were writing *The Counterfeiters,* I should
begin by showing the counterfeit coin, the little ten-franc piece you were
speaking of just now . . . and here it is."

So saying, he pulled out of his pocket a small ten-franc piece, which
he flung onto the table.

"Just hear how true it rings. Almost the same sound as the real one.
One would swear it was gold. I was taken in by it this morning, just as the
grocer who passed it on to me had been taken in himself, he told me. It
isn't quite the same weight, I think; but it has the brightness and the sound
of a real piece; it is coated with gold, so that, all the same, it is worth a
little more than two sous; but it's made of glass. As it wears, it'll turn
transparent. No; don't rub it; you'll spoil it. You can almost see through
it already."

Edouard had seized it and was considering it with the utmost curiosity.

"But where did the grocer get it from?"

"He didn't know. He thinks he has had it in his drawer some days.
He amused himself by passing it off on me to see whether I should be
taken in. I swear, I was just going to accept it! But he's an honest man, and
he told me the truth; then he let me have it for five francs. He wanted to
keep it to show to what he calls 'amateurs.' I thought there couldn't be a
better one than the author of *The Counterfeiters;* and it was to show you
that I took it. But now that you have examined it, give it back to me! I'm
sorry that the reality doesn't interest you."

"Yes, it does," Edouard said; "but it upsets me."

"That's too bad," Bernard replied.

. . .

PART THREE: XVII
"The Strong Men"

Boris only learned of Bronja's death from a visit of Madame Sophroniska's to the boarding school a month later. Since his friend's last sad
letter, Boris had been without news. He saw Madame Sophroniska enter
Madame Vedel's drawing-room one day when he was sitting there, as was
his habit during recess, and as she was in deep mourning, he understood
everything before she even said a word. They were alone in the room.
Sophroniska took Boris in her arms and they cried together. She could
only repeat: "My poor little thing. . . . My poor little thing . . ." as if
Boris was the person to be pitied, and as though she had forgotten her own
maternal grief in the presence of the immense grief of the little boy.

Madame Vedel, who had been told of Madame Sophroniska's arrival, came in, and Boris, still convulsed with sobs, drew aside to let the
two ladies talk. He would have liked them not to speak of Bronja. Madame Vedel, who had not known her, spoke of her as she would of any
ordinary child. Even the questions which she asked seemed to Boris tactless in their banality. He would have liked Sophroniska not to answer
them, and it hurt him to see her exhibiting her grief. He folded his away
and hid it like a treasure.

It was certainly of him that Bronja had been thinking when, a few
days before her death, she had said to her mother:

"*Maman*, I would like so much to know—what exactly is it that
people mean when they say 'idyll'?"

These words pierced Boris's heart, and he would have liked to be the
only one to hear them.

Madame Vedel offered tea. There was some for Boris, too, which he
swallowed quickly, as recess was almost over; then he said good-bye to
Sophroniska, who was leaving next day for Poland on business.

The whole world seemed a desert to him. His mother was too far
away, and always absent; his grandfather was too old; even Bernard, with
whom he was beginning to feel at home, had gone away. . . . A tender
soul like his has need of someone to whom it can bring its nobility and its
purity, as an offering. He had not pride enough to be pleased with himself.

He had loved Bronja much too much to be able to hope that he would ever again find that reason for loving that he had lost when he lost her. The angels that he longed to see—from now on, without her, how could he believe in them? Heaven itself was now empty.

Boris went back to the schoolroom as one might plunge oneself into hell. No doubt he might have made a friend of Gontran de Passavant; Gontran is a good, kind boy, and they are both exactly the same age; but nothing distracts him from his work. There is not much harm in Philippe Adamanti either; he would be quite willing to be Boris's friend; but he lets himself be led so by Ghéridanisol that he does not dare have a single feeling of his own; he marches in step, and Ghéridanisol is always quickening the pace; and Ghéridanisol cannot endure Boris. His musical voice, his grace, his girlish look—everything about Boris irritates, exasperates him. The very sight of Boris seems to inspire him with that instinctive aversion which, in a herd, makes the strong ruthlessly fall upon the weak. It may be that he has listened to his cousin's teaching and that his hatred is somewhat theoretical, for in his mind it assumes the shape of reprobation. He finds reasons for being proud of his hatred. He fully realizes how sensitive Boris is to the contempt he shows him; he laughs at it, and pretends to be plotting with Georges Molinier and Phil Adamanti, merely to see Boris's eyes grow wide with a kind of anxious interrogation.

"Oh, how inquisitive the fellow is!" says Georges then. "Shall we tell him?"

"Not worthwhile. He wouldn't understand."

"He wouldn't understand." "He wouldn't dare." "He wouldn't know how." They are constantly casting these phrases in his face. He suffers horribly from being kept out. He cannot even understand the humiliating nickname they give him: "Doesn't-have-one" [*n'en a pas*]; and is mortified when he understands. What would not he give to be able to prove that he is not the wretched coward that they think!

"I cannot endure Boris," Ghéridanisol said one day to Strouvilhou. "Why did you tell me to let him alone? He doesn't want to be let alone as much as all that. He is always looking in my direction. . . . The other day he made us all split with laughter because he thought that a woman '*à poil*' * meant a bearded woman! Georges laughed at him, and when at last Boris figured it out I thought he was going to burst into tears."

Then Ghéridanisol plied his cousin with questions, until finally Strouvilhou gave him Boris's talisman and explained its use.

* The French slang expression means "naked."

A few days later, when Boris went into the schoolroom, he saw this paper, which he had almost forgotten, lying on his desk. He had put it out of his mind along with everything else that related to the "magic" of his early childhood, of which he was now ashamed. He did not at first recognize it, for Ghéridanisol had taken pains to frame the words of the incantation

"GAS . . . TELEPHONE . . . ONE HUNDRED THOUSAND RUBLES."

with a large red and black border adorned with obscene little imps, who, it must be owned, were not at all badly drawn. This decoration gave the paper a fantastic, an "infernal" appearance, thought Ghéridanisol, which he calculated as the most likely to upset Boris.

Perhaps it was done in play, but it succeeded beyond all expectation. Boris blushed crimson, said nothing, looked right and left, and failed to see Ghéridanisol, who was watching him from behind the door. Boris had no reason to suspect him, and could not understand how the talisman came to be there; it was as though it had fallen from heaven—or rather, risen up from hell. Boris was old enough to shrug his shoulders, no doubt, at these schoolboy pranks; but they stirred up a troubled past. He took the talisman and slipped it into his jacket. All the rest of the day, the recollection of his "magic" practices obsessed him. He struggled until evening with unholy solicitations and then, as there was no longer anything to support him in his struggle, he gave in as soon as he was alone in his room.

He felt that he was going to hell, sinking farther and farther away from heaven; but he took pleasure in so falling—found in his very fall itself the stuff of his enjoyment.

And yet, in spite of his misery, in the depths of his distress, he kept such stores of tenderness, his companions' contempt caused him suffering so keen, that he would have dared anything, however dangerous, however absurd, for the sake of a little consideration.

An opportunity soon offered.

After they had been obliged to give up their traffic in counterfeit coins, Ghéridanisol, Georges, and Phil had not remained unoccupied for long. The ridiculous pranks with which they amused themselves for the first few days were nothing but ways to kill time. Ghéridanisol's imagination soon invented something a little more substantial.

At first, the only *raison d'être* of the Brotherhood of Strong Men consisted in the pleasure of keeping Boris out of it. But it soon occurred to Ghéridanisol that it would be far more perversely effective to let him in; that could be the way to force him into certain promises by means of which he might gradually be led on to some horrible deed. From that moment, Ghéridanisol was possessed by this idea; and as often happens in all kinds of enterprises, he thought much less of the object itself than of how to bring it about; this may seem trifling, but it is perhaps the explanation for a good number of crimes. For that matter, Ghéridanisol was ferocious; but he thought it wise to hide his ferocity, at least from Phil. There was nothing cruel about Philippe; he was convinced up to the last minute that the whole thing was nothing but a joke.

Every brotherhood must have its motto. Ghéridanisol, who had his idea, proposed: *"The strong man cares nothing for life."* The motto was adopted and attributed to Cicero. Georges proposed that, as a sign of fellowship, they should tattoo it on their right arms; but Phil, who was afraid of being hurt, declared that good tattooers could only be found in seaports. Besides which, Ghéridanisol objected that tattooing would leave an indelible mark which might be inconvenient later on. After all, the sign of fellowship was not an absolute necessity; the members would content themselves with taking a solemn vow.

At the time they were starting their traffic in counterfeit coins, there had been some talk of pledges, and it was on that occasion that Georges had produced his father's letters. But this idea had been dropped. These children, thank heavens, are not particularly consistent. As a matter of fact, they settled practically nothing, either as to "conditions of membership" or as to "necessary qualifications." What was the use, since it had been understood all along that the three of them were "in it," and that Boris was "out of it"? On the other hand, they decreed that "anyone who flinched should be considered as a traitor, and forever excluded from the brotherhood." Ghéridanisol, who had determined to make Boris come in, laid great stress upon this point.

It had to be admitted that, without Boris, the game would have been dull, and the whole point of the brotherhood would have been lost. Georges was better qualified to get round him than Ghéridanisol, who risked arousing his suspicions; as for Phil, he was not sufficiently sly, and preferred not to compromise himself.

And in all this abominable story, what perhaps seems to me the most monstrous is the comedy of friendship which Georges agreed to play. He pretended to be seized with a sudden affection for Boris; until then, he had seemed never so much as to set eyes on him. And I even wonder whether he was not taken in by his own game, and whether the feelings he pretended were not on the point of becoming sincere—whether they did not *actually* become sincere as soon as Boris responded to them. Georges drew near him with an appearance of tenderness; in obedience to Ghéridanisol, he began to talk to him. . . . And, at the first words, Boris, who was panting for a little esteem and love, was conquered.

Then Ghéridanisol elaborated his plan, and disclosed it to Phil and Georges. His idea was to invent a "test" to which the member on whom the lot fell should be submitted; and in order to set Phil at ease, he let it be understood that things would be arranged in such a manner that the lot could fall only on Boris. The object of the test would be to put his courage to the proof.

Ghéridanisol did not at once divulge the exact nature of the test. He was afraid that Phil would offer some resistance.

And, in fact, when Ghéridanisol a little later began to insinuate that old La Pérouse's pistol might come in handy, Phil flatly declared, "No. I won't agree to that."

"What an ass you are! It's only a joke," retorted Georges, who was already persuaded.

"And then, you know," Ghéri added, "if you want to play the fool, you have only got to say so. We don't need you."

Ghéridanisol knew that this argument always worked with Adamanti; and as he had prepared the paper on which each member of the brotherhood was to sign his name, he went on: "Only you must say so at once; because once you've signed, it'll be too late."

"All right. Don't get so excited," said Phil. "Hand me the paper." And he signed.

"As for me, old fellow, I'd be delighted," said Georges, his arm fondly round Boris's neck. "It's Ghéridanisol who won't have you."

"Why not?"

"Because he doesn't trust you. He says you'll flinch."

"What does he know about it?"

"That you'll wriggle out of it at the first test."

"He'll see."

"Would you really dare to draw lots?"

"What do you think?"

"But do you know what you're letting yourself in for?"

Boris did not know, but he wanted to. Then Georges explained. "The strong man cares nothing for life." It remained to be seen.

Boris felt a great swimming in his head; but he nerved himself and, hiding his agitation, asked "Is it true you've signed?"

"Here, look." And Georges held out the paper so that Boris could read the three names.

"Have you . . ." he began timidly.

"Have we what? . . ." Georges interrupted so brutally that Boris did not dare go on. What he wanted to ask, as Georges perfectly understood, was whether the others had bound themselves likewise, and whether one could be sure that they wouldn't flinch either.

"No, nothing," he said; but from that moment he began to doubt them; he began to suspect they were saving themselves and not playing fair. "Well, so what?" he thought then; "what do I care if they back down? I'll show them that I've got more nerve than they have!" Then, looking Georges straight in the eyes: "Tell Ghéri he can count on me."

"Then you'll sign?"

Oh, there was no need now—he had given his word. He said simply: "Why not?" And, underneath the signatures of the three "Strong Men," he inscribed his name on the accursed paper in a large, painstaking hand.

Georges took the paper back in triumph to the two others. They agreed that Boris had behaved very well. Then they took counsel together.

"Of course, we won't load the pistol! For that matter we don't have any cartridges." Phil was still afraid, because he had heard it said that sometimes a too violent emotion is enough all by itself to kill someone. His father, he declared, knew of a case when a pretended execution . . . But Georges shut him up:

"Your father's a dago!"

No, Ghéridanisol would not load the pistol. There was no need to. The cartridge which La Pérouse had one day put into it, La Pérouse had not taken out. That was what Ghéridanisol had made sure of, though he took good care not to tell the others.

They put the names in a hat; four little pieces of paper all alike, all folded in the same manner. Ghéridanisol, who was "to draw," had taken care to write Boris's name a second time on a fifth, which he kept in his hand; and, as though by chance, his was the name to come out. Boris suspected that they were cheating, but he said nothing. What was the use of protesting?

He knew that he was lost. He would not have lifted a finger to defend himself; and even if the lot had fallen on one of the others, he would have offered to take his place, so great was his despair.

"Poor old Boris! Your luck's bad today," Georges thought it his duty to say. The tone of his voice rang so false that Boris looked at him sadly.

"It was bound to happen," he said.

After that, it was agreed there should be a rehearsal. But as there was a risk of being caught, they agreed not to make use of the pistol at first. Only at the last minute, when they were "playing for keeps," would they take it out of its case. Nothing must give their game away.

On that day, therefore, they contented themselves with fixing the hour and the place, which they marked on the floor with a piece of chalk. It was in the classroom, to the right of the teacher's desk, in a little recess formed by a closed-off door which used to open onto the entrance hall. As for the time, it was to be during study hour. It was to take place under the eyes of all the other boys; that would wake them up a bit.

They went through the rehearsal when the room was empty, with the three conspirators as the only witnesses. But in reality there was not much point in this rehearsal. They simply established the fact that, from Boris's seat to the spot marked with chalk, there were exactly twelve paces.

"If you aren't in a panic, you won't take one more," Georges said.

"I won't be in a panic," Boris said, outraged by this incessant doubt. The little boy's firmness began to impress the other three. Phil wondered if they shouldn't stop where they were. But Ghéridanisol was determined to play the joke out to the very end.

"Well! tomorrow," he said, with a peculiar smile, which just curled the corner of his lip.

"Suppose we kissed him!" Phil cried enthusiastically. He was thinking of the accolade of the *preux chevaliers,* the knights of old; and he suddenly flung his arms around Boris. It was all that Boris could do to keep back his tears when Phil planted two fat, childish kisses on his cheeks. Neither Georges nor Ghéri followed Phil's example; Georges thought the whole business rather undignified. As for Ghéri, what the devil did he care! . . .

PART THREE: XVIII

Boris

The next afternoon, the bell had assembled all the boys of the school.

Boris, Ghéridanisol, Georges, and Philippe were seated on the same bench. Ghéridanisol pulled out his watch and put it down between Boris and him. It showed five-thirty-five. Study hour began at five o'clock and lasted until six. Five minutes to six was the moment fixed upon for Boris to put an end to himself, just before the boys were let out; it was better that way; it would be easier to escape immediately after. And soon Ghéridanisol said to Boris, in a half whisper, and without looking at him, which gave his words, he considered, a more fatal ring:

"You've only got a quarter of an hour more, my friend."

Boris remembered a storybook he had read long ago, in which, when the bandits were on the point of putting a woman to death, they told her to say her prayers so as to convince her she must get ready to die. Like a foreigner who gets his papers ready as he arrives at the border of the country he is leaving, Boris searched his heart and head for prayers, and could find none; but he was at once so tired and so overstrung, that he did not worry much about it. He made an effort to think, but could not. The pistol weighed in his pocket; he had no need to put his hand on it to feel it there.

"Only ten minutes more."

Georges, sitting on Ghéridanisol's left, watched the scene out of the corner of his eye, but pretended not to see. He was working feverishly. The class had never been so quiet. La Pérouse hardly knew his young rascals, and for the first time was able to breathe. Philippe, however, was not at ease; Ghéridanisol frightened him; he was not entirely assured that the game wouldn't turn out badly; his bursting heart hurt him, and every now and then he heard himself heave a deep sigh. At last, he could bear it no longer, and tearing a half sheet out of his history notebook (he was preparing for an examination, but the lines danced before his eyes, and the facts and dates in his head), the bottom of a page, scribbled on it very quickly: "Are you quite sure the pistol isn't loaded?"; then gave the note to Georges, who passed it to Ghéri. But Ghéri, after he had read it, shrugged his shoulders, without even glancing at Phil; then, screwing the note up into a ball, sent it rolling with a flick of his finger till it landed on the very spot which had been marked with chalk. After which, satisfied with the excellence of his aim, he smiled. This smile, which began by being deliberate, remained fixed until the end of the scene; it seemed to have been imprinted on his features.

"Five minutes more."

He said it almost aloud. Even Philippe heard. He was overwhelmed by intolerable anxiety, and though the hour was just coming to an end, he feigned an urgent need to leave the room—or was perhaps seized with a perfectly genuine colic. He raised his hand and snapped his fingers, as boys do when they want to ask permission from the teacher; then, without waiting for La Pérouse to answer, he darted from his bench. In order to reach the door he had to pass in front of the teacher's desk; he almost ran, tottering as he did so.

Almost immediately after Philippe had left the room, Boris rose in his turn. Young Passavant, who was working diligently behind him, lifted his eyes. He told Séraphine afterwards that Boris was "frightfully pale"; but that is what people always say on these occasions. As a matter of fact, he stopped looking almost at once and plunged again into his work. He reproached himself for it bitterly later. If he had understood what was going on, he would certainly have been able to prevent it; so he said afterwards, weeping. But he suspected nothing.

So Boris stepped forward to the appointed place; he walked slowly, like an automaton, his eyes fixed before him—or rather like someone walking in his sleep. His right hand had grasped the pistol but still kept it in the pocket of his coat; he took it out only at the last moment. The fatal place was, as I have said, in the recess made by a disused door on the right of the teacher's desk, so that the teacher could only see it by leaning forward.

La Pérouse leaned forward. And at first he did not understand what his grandson was doing, though the strange solemnity of the boy's actions was of a nature to alarm him. Speaking as loudly as he could, in a voice he tried to make authoritative, he began:

"Master Boris, kindly return at once to your . . ."

But suddenly he recognized the pistol: Boris had just raised it to his temple. La Pérouse understood and immediately felt an icy cold, as if the blood were freezing in his veins. He tried to get up and run toward Boris, stop him, call to him. . . . A kind of hoarse rattle came from his lips; he remained rooted to the spot, paralyzed, shaken by a violent trembling.

The shot went off. Boris did not drop at once. The body stayed upright for a moment, as though caught in the corner of the recess; then the head, falling onto the shoulder, bore it down; it all collapsed.

When the police made their inquiry a little later, they were astonished not to find the pistol near Boris's body—near the place, I mean, where he fell, for the little corpse was carried away almost immediately and laid upon a bed. In the confusion which followed, while Ghéridanisol had remained in his place, Georges had leaped over his bench and succeeded in making away with the weapon without anyone's noticing him; while the others were bending over Boris, he had first of all pushed it backwards with a kick of his foot, seized it with a rapid movement, hidden it under his coat, and then surreptitiously passed it to Ghéridanisol. Everyone's attention being fixed on a single point, no one noticed Ghéridanisol either, and he was able to run unperceived to La Pérouse's room and put the pistol back in the place from which he had taken it. When, in the course of a later investigation, the police discovered the pistol in its case, it might have seemed doubtful whether it had ever left it, or whether Boris had used it, had Ghéridanisol only remembered to remove the empty cartridge. He certainly lost his head a little—a passing weakness, for which, I regret to say, he reproached himself far more than for the crime itself. And yet it was that weakness that saved him. For when he came back down and mixed with the others, at the sight of Boris's dead body, which they were carrying away, he was seized with a fit of trembling, which was obvious to everyone—a kind of nervous attack—which Madame Vedel and Rachel, who had hurried to the spot, mistook for a sign of excessive emotion. One prefers to suppose anything rather than the inhumanity of so young a creature; and when Ghéridanisol protested his innocence, he was believed. Phil's little note, which Georges had passed him and which he had flicked away with his finger, was found later under a bench and this crumpled little note also contributed to help him. True, he remained guilty, as did Georges and Phil, of having lent himself to a cruel game; but he would not have done so, he insisted, if he had thought the weapon was loaded. Georges Molinier was the only one who remained convinced of his entire responsibility.

Georges was not so corrupted but that his admiration for Ghéridanisol yielded at last to horror. When he reached home that evening, he flung himself into his mother's arms; and Pauline had a burst of gratitude to God, Who by means of this dreadful tragedy had brought her son back to her.

Edouard's Journal

Without exactly pretending to explain anything, I should not like to put forward any fact without a sufficient motive. That is why I shall not use little Boris's suicide for my *Counterfeiters;* I have too much difficulty in understanding it. And then, I dislike *"faits divers,"* police-court items. There is something peremptory, irrefutable, brutal, outrageously real about them. . . . I accept reality when it comes as a proof in support of my thought, but not when it precedes it. I do not like being surprised. Boris's suicide seems to me *indecent* because I was not expecting it.

A little cowardice enters into every suicide, notwithstanding La Pérouse, who no doubt thinks his grandson was more courageous than he. If the child could have foreseen the disaster which his dreadful deed has brought upon the Vedels, there would be no excuse for him. Azaïs has been obliged to break up the school—for the time being, he says; but Rachel is afraid of ruin. Four families have already removed their children. I have not been able to dissuade Pauline from keeping Georges at her side; especially as the boy has been profoundly shaken by his school-fellow's death, and seems inclined to mend his ways. What repercussions that calamity has had! Even Olivier is touched by it. Armand, notwithstanding his cynical airs, feels such anxiety at the ruin which is threatening his family that he has offered to devote the time that Passavant leaves him to working in the school; for old La Pérouse has become manifestly incapable of doing what is required of him.

I dreaded seeing him again. It was in his little bedroom on the second floor of the pension that he received me. He took me by the arm at once, and with a mysterious, almost a smiling air, which surprised me greatly, for I was expecting tears:

"That noise," he said, "you know . . . the noise I told you about the other day . . ."

"Well?"

"It has stopped. It's gone. I don't hear it any more. I've listened very hard."

As one humors a child, I said, "I bet that now you miss it."

"Oh! no; no. . . . It's such a rest. I have so much need of silence. Do you know what I've been thinking? That in this life we can't know what real silence is. Even our blood makes a kind of continual noise; we don't notice it, because we have been used to it ever since our childhood. . . . But I think there are things in life which we can't succeed in hearing—harmonies . . . because this noise drowns them. Yes, I think it's only after our death that we shall really be able to hear."

"You told me you didn't believe . . ."

"In the immortality of the soul? Did I tell you that? . . . Yes; I suppose I did. But I don't believe the contrary either, you know."

And as I was silent, he went on, nodding his head and with a sententious air:

"Have you noticed that, in this world, God always keeps silent? It's only the devil who speaks. Or at least, at least . . ." He went on, ". . .

however carefully we listen, it's only the devil we can succeed in hearing. We have not the ears to hear the voice of God. The word of God! Have you ever wondered what it could be like? . . . Oh, I don't mean the word that has been cast into human language. . . . You remember the first words of the Gospel: 'In the beginning was the Word.' I have often thought that the word of God was the whole of creation. But the devil got hold of it. And now his noise drowns out the voice of God. Tell me, tell me: don't you think that all the same it's God Who will end by having the last word? . . . And if, after death, time no longer exists, if we enter at once into Eternity, do you think we shall be able to hear God then . . . directly?"

A kind of transport began to shake him, as if he were going to fall down in convulsions, and he was suddenly seized by a fit of sobbing.

"No, no!" he cried, in confusion. "The devil and God are one and the same; they work together. We try to believe that everything bad on earth comes from the devil, but it's because, if we didn't, we should never find the strength to forgive God. He plays with us, like a cat with a mouse it's tormenting. . . . And then afterwards He wants us to be grateful to Him as well. Grateful for what? for what?"

Then, leaning toward me:

"Do you know the most horrible thing He's done? . . . Sacrificed His own son to save us. His son! His son! . . . Cruelty! that's the principal attribute of God."

He flung himself on his bed and turned his face to the wall. For a few moments a spasmodic shudder ran through him; then, as he seemed to have fallen asleep, I left him.

He had not said a word to me about Boris; but I thought that in this mystical despair was to be seen the indirect expression of a grief too blinding to be looked at head on.

I hear from Olivier that Bernard has gone back to his father's; and, indeed, it was the best thing he could do. When he learned, from a chance meeting with Caloub, that the old judge was not well, Bernard followed the impulse of his heart. We are to meet tomorrow evening, for Profitendieu has invited me to dinner with Molinier, Pauline, and the two boys. I am very curious to know Caloub.

Paris, April 17, 1928

Cher Monsieur:

I read your letter with the most attentive interest but am sorely embarrassed as to what to reply.

You may be sure that in matters of psychology there are nothing but individual cases and that, in a case like yours, over-hasty generalizations may lead to the most serious mistakes.

With this reservation, allow me to consider as most unwise a matrimonial experiment which, if it fails, will surely compromise a woman's happiness and very probably yours as well, if your heart is what it should be. But let me repeat that all cases are individual, and in order to advise you pertinently, it would not be enough for me to know you better; I should also have to know her to whom you would be attaching yourself.

The question of a confession is extraordinarily perplexing. I am tempted to tell you: If you do not make one immediately (I mean before the marriage), never make it. But in that case arrange things so as never to have to make one—and you will surely need to make one sooner or later if you are not capable of acting as a husband.

As a general rule, it is better to sacrifice oneself than to sacrifice another for oneself. But all this is theoretical; in practice it happens that one becomes aware of the sacrifice only long after it is accomplished.

Adieu, monsieur. To this semblance of advice I add my best wishes and beg you to believe them most sincere.

André Gide

from

AN ESSAY

ON MONTAIGNE

1929

"A worthy reader often discovers in the writings of another man perfections different from those the author put and perceived there, and lends to them a sense and an aspect more rich," writes Montaigne. To the "worthy reader" of today, will Montaigne himself be "worthy," sufficient? and will he know how to respond to the new questions that we have to ask him?

No doubt an author's importance resides not only in his own proper value, but also, and even more, in the timeliness of his message . . .

"Were a man equal to him born at this hour," he wrote of Socrates, "few men would recognize him"; and we may say the same of him. In this postwar era, it is the constructive spirits who are in particular favor; any author who does not propose some new system is held in very low esteem. Montaigne, of course, brings us no system, and one is perhaps best off insisting on his skepticism—even to the point of seeing in his *"Que scais-je?"*—"What do I know?"—the last word of his wisdom and his teaching. But I daresay that this skepticism is *not* the thing that I like about the *Essais,* or the lesson that I draw from them. If I do in fact take them to heart, it is to draw out something far better than doubts and interrogations.

It seems to me that, faced with Pilate's dreadful question, the echo of which has sounded across the ages—"What is truth?"—Montaigne took for his own answer the divine reply of Christ: *"I* am the truth"—although in a quite human fashion, in a manner decidedly profane and in a sense very different from Christ's. By this I mean that he judged himself *truly* unable to know anything other than himself. Hence that extraordinary defiance, as soon as he sets out to reason; hence that confidence, that assurance, as soon as he abandons himself . . . to himself; as soon as he makes himself the end of all his designs. It is this that leads him to talk so much of himself; for at once self-knowledge comes to seem more important than any other. "One must take the mask off things as well as persons," he writes. If he paints himself, it is in order to take off his mask, convinced as he is that "the real self is the beginning of all great virtue." I would like to inscribe these admirable words as a headnote to his *Essais*. . . .

He begins, in the Third Book of the *Essais* . . . to see clearly this profound truth: that the portrait of himself he is presenting may well be of greater general interest the more unique and particular it is to him; for "each man bears in himself the whole model of the human state." While all his other certitudes are collapsing, this one at least is left him: that on the subject of himself, he is "the most knowledgeable man alive"; and this encourages him, since "no man will ever attain clearly and precisely the end that he had proposed for his labors," therefore the only virtue that he demands is "fidelity." And at once he thinks himself justified in adding, "This I have: the sincerest, the purest one could find."

And what interests me, as his reader, is certainly not the knowledge, for example, that he could "hold his water for ten hours," but rather the indiscreet *need* that he felt to tell me this. I see here something more valuable than mere frankness: rather a kind of protest against decorum; whatever is ordinarily kept silent, kept hidden, is the thing he takes greatest pleasure in telling, in displaying. Despite his most cynical efforts, he is always considering it possible to go further still: "I speak truly—not as much as I would like to, but as much as I dare; and I dare a bit more the older I get." . . .

"There is no description as difficult to make as the description of ourselves —nor, certainly, as useful," we read in the *Essais;* for Montaigne, a man in whom we are too often pleased to see nothing but an egoist, is concerned with the public good. Two passages, otherwise perfectly irreconcilable (even though separated by no more than a few lines), in the first chapter of the Third Book, help us nevertheless to understand just how little Montaigne was made for the direction of public affairs. Moreover, they will help us to understand how, when he resigned his functions as magistrate, and then later quit his position as mayor of Bordeaux in order to devote his attention exclusively to himself, he could judge quite soundly that in revising and extending his *Essais* he would be rendering the greatest possible service to the State:

In truth—and I am not the least ashamed to admit it—I can easily light two candles, as the need may be: one for Saint Michael, the other for his devil.

To keep oneself irresolute and hybrid, to keep one's affections motionless and without any inclination to the troubles of his country in a time of public division, I hold this to be neither handsome nor honest: one must take sides. . . .

What I enjoy considering with Montaigne is this "real self," this naïve, sincere, uncounterfeited being which he thinks it so important to extract, since it is on this that he wants to build; soon he will tolerate no other support, no other foundation for the building of virtue and morality, in despite of (or in defiance of) all custom and convention: "There is no one who cannot discover in himself, if he would but listen, his own form, his master-form, which does battle against both the mis-education and the storm of passions which oppose it." . . . It pleases me to match this text with several others, in which he clarifies and strengthens this thought: "Wherever I wish to let go, I am forced to break some barrier of custom, so carefully does custom rein in all of our releases." (Custom, institution; it matters little which.) Was individualism ever expressed in more explicit or stronger terms? "All general judgments are loose, slovenly, imperfect, . . . and there is no way of life so foolish or enfeebled as that which is led by strict rule and discipline." Let us hasten to add that here, as always in Montaigne, reason intervenes and balances all his declarations; a constant love of order, of *mésure,* an almost aesthetic horror of the prevalence of his private interest over the interest of all: ". . . and will make us feel, as is reasonable, that the private convenience must yield to public." On the other hand, the rectitude of his private judgment is always for him the most important thing: ". . . better to break the neck of affairs than to twist my faith in their service." This man, so little the mystic, remains on this one point inflexible: "What matter that we twist our arms out of shape, provided we do not do it to our thoughts?" And, a bit further on, these tragic words: "The public welfare demands that we betray, that we lie" (later he was to add, "and that we massacre"); "let us resign the commission to men more obedient and more supple." Clearly, Montaigne was not a man for the political life. I remember having heard Barrès say, when he was asked the greatest pain one had to bear in the Chamber of Deputies: "To vote with one's party." . . .

La Boétie, in one of the fragments of Latin verse that he addressed to Montaigne, said to him, "You have more things to fight against, dear friend; you whom we know to be susceptible to both the vices and the virtues of fame." But once La Boétie was gone, Montaigne bothered less and less about such internal warfare. A personality—a *non*-personality, I should say—artificially, laboriously, contentiously put together, built according to the rules of morality, decency, custom, and prejudice—to Montaigne there is nothing more repugnant. One could say that the genuine self, the self that all this hinders, hides, or falsifies, retains for him a sort of mystical value, and that he expects from it heaven knows what revelation. Of course, I know how easy it is to play with words, to refuse to see anything in this teaching of Montaigne's but the advice to abandon oneself to one's nature, to follow one's instincts blindly—even to give preference to the vilest, which always appear the most sincere, that is to say the most natural: those which, by their very density, their heaviness, will always be found faithfully at the bottom of the vessel even after it has been shaken up by the divinest of transports. . . . But I think this would be seriously to misunderstand Montaigne, who, although he makes a very generous allowance (perhaps too generous) for those instincts that we have in common with the animals, knows how to keep a jump ahead of them, and never consents to be their victim or their slave. It is the particularity of each countenance (his own, to begin with) that is important to him; and I think him not so much a materialist, a cynic, an epicurean, as an individualist—a "particularist," if I may use the word—looking for a sort of instruction in each living creature, so long as he be authentic: "I shall willingly correct my accidental errors; I am full of them . . . but the imperfections which are usual and constant in me, it would be treason to cut them out." He is willing to call them "imperfections"; but, deep down in his heart, he is not really convinced that the things considered such in his time might not, in another land, another time, hold some value unknown and hidden to him. The most important thing in him, he feels and knows, is that which is unique. . . .

. . . Each time that Montaigne speaks of Christianity, it is with the strangest (one might almost say sometimes with the most malicious) impertinence. He often speaks of religion; never of Christ. Not once does he refer to his words. It leads one to wonder whether he ever read the Gospels; or, rather, to be quite certain that he never read them well. As for the reverence that he shows with regard to Catholicism, there is no question

that it is partly inspired by a certain amount of prudence. The example of
Erasmus put him on his guard; it is clear, besides, that the prospect of
being forced to write a set of *Retractions* held little appeal for him. I
know, of course, that Erasmus never had to write his either; but at the last
he had to promise to write them, and before long this promise became
galling. Far better to temporize. Montaigne left his security when he wrote
(a passage added in the edition of 1588): "The imagination of those who
seek after solitude through devotion, filling their hearts with the certitude
of the divine promises of another life, is far more judiciously stocked"
[than the imagination of those who hope to assure themselves an earthly
immortality by writing]: "They set for themselves an object infinite both
in goodness and in power—God. Here the soul may find what it needs to
satisfy its desires in complete liberty." How well thought that is, how well
said! And better still that which follows: "It is honestly worth giving up
the conveniences and sweets of this life of ours for the one single goal of
another life, happy and immortal . . ." Ah yes, one is forced to admit it,
here are thoughts which could only have issued from a truly religious soul.
But if we read on, certain suspicious epithets quite soon after these force us
to be on our guard: ". . . and he who can enkindle his heart with the
ardor of this living faith and hope, genuinely and constantly, he builds for
himself in his solitude a life *voluptuous and delicate,* far away from every
other form of life." Evidently the ardor of this living faith and hope never
inflamed the soul of Montaigne, or else he would have chosen other words
to depict it, and would not for an instant have dreamed of annexing this
same longing for eternal life to his own voluptuous epicureanism. . . .

The closing pages of the *Essais* are without doubt the fullest and densest
that Montaigne ever wrote; but also, to put it bluntly, the shrewdest and
most ambiguous; for he makes it impossible for us to see how far he is
exposing himself in putting aside the precepts of religion. He prudently
(and suddenly) rules out of his audience the "truly religious," whom he
quickly places in a region infinitely superior to that where he has just put
himself and us, and where it pleases him to stay. "I do not here touch
upon, or mix into this rabble of brats that we are, this vanity of lusts and
cogitations which distracts us, those venerable souls, exalted by the ardor
of devotion and religion to a constant and conscientious meditation upon
divine things"; but he quickly adds, "That is a privileged study." And
then, sensing that he is not quite clear of the matter, and realizing that he
has (perhaps) dispatched Christian preoccupations a bit too quickly and

cavalierly, he strains himself to eulogize these souls, "who, anticipating, by dint of keen and vehement hope, the enjoyment of eternal food, the final goal and last resting place of Christian desires, the only pleasure constant [but he esteems only inconstancy] and incorruptible [but which scarcely excites *him*], scorn to give their attention to our beggarly comforts [according to him, the only ones both righteous and sensually pleasing], so fluid and so ambiguous [so like him], and readily resign to the body the concern and enjoyment of sensual and temporal fodder." But he returns, a few lines further on, to his original text: "They want to get out of themselves and escape from the man. This is madness; instead of changing themselves into angels, they change themselves into beasts; instead of raising themselves, they lower themselves." And then he adds further, "These transcendental humors frighten me, like lofty and inaccessible places; and nothing is harder for me to stomach in the life of Socrates than his ecstasies and demonic possessions." Then he concludes: "It is an absolute, near-divine perfection to know honestly how to enjoy one's own being." . . .

Nothing can better help us to understand Montaigne truly than to trace through the *Essais* (and the successive editions of the *Essais*) the slow modification of his attitude in face of the idea of death: ". . . there is nothing with which I have more occupied my mind than with images of death: even in the most licentious season of my life," he writes almost at the beginning of the *Essais,* in the chapter which he entitles "That to Philosophize Is to Learn to Die." And he adds, speaking of the "sting of such images," that, "by handling them, going over them, in the long run we unquestionably tame them." This is what he strove to do for so long. But in the last edition that he gives us of the *Essais,* he adds, ". . . thank God, I can quit this place whenever He wants, without regretting anything at all—except perhaps life, should its loss come to weigh heavily on me. I have disentangled myself from everything, I have already half-taken my leave of everyone—except myself. No man ever prepared himself to quit this world more cleanly and thoroughly, nor disengaged himself more universally than I expect to do." ". . . the unexpected arrival of death will teach me nothing new." He forces himself to love this death, as a natural thing. He praises Socrates for having shown himself "courageous in death, not because his soul is immortal, but because he is mortal." It pleases him to reflect that "the failing of one life is the passage to a thousand others." In speaking of this "failing," he finds the most delicate words: "that [death] which surprises us, to which old age conducts us, is of all the most gentle and not the least sweet"; but also, the most solemn words, the most grave: "I plunge stupefied into death, my head bowed, neither recognizing nor examining it, as into a deep, dark, silent pit which suddenly devours me and overwhelms me in an instant with a powerful sleep full of insipidity and indolence." I know of no more admirable sentence in all of the *Essais.*

Montaigne, we are told, enjoyed a most Christian deathbed. Let us remember that he can scarcely be said to have aimed for it. It is true that his wife and his daughter were present at his last moments; and they doubtless urged him (out of sympathy, as so often happens) to die not that death "gathered into myself, tranquil and alone, completely my own, a death suitable to my retired and private life" with which he would have been "happy"; but more piously, I am sure, than he would have done had he been alone. Was it the presentiment of that which led him to write, "If it were in any way up to me to choose [my death], it would be, I think, rather on horseback than in bed, out of my house and far from my family."

Montaigne never felt a particularly keen tenderness for his family; or if he did, his writings, at least, scarcely show any trace of it. He seems to have married without any great enthusiasm; had he been a good husband all the same, he would not have let himself write, toward the end of his life, "It is probably easier to do without the female sex altogether than to keep oneself faithful on every point in the company of one's wife"; which hardly indicates that he did. There is nothing comparable here with his friendship for La Boétie, on which he dwells at such length in the *Essais,* and of which the memory pricks him even long after the death of his only friend. Montaigne loved women, but of course; a little more than melons, no doubt, but he *esteems* them not much higher. He takes his pleasure with them, and beyond that, he confines them to household affairs. I have picked out from the *Essais* the passages where Montaigne speaks of women: there is not one that is not insulting. He goes so far as to say, "It is dangerous to leave to their judgment the dispensation of our succession, according to the preference they will make among [our] children" (and he includes in the word "children" productions of the mind, as a passage that I shall quote further on will show)—"a preference that is at every turn iniquitous and fantastic. For the disordered appetite and sick taste that they have at the time of their pregnancies, they have these in their hearts at all times."

As for the children that he had, "I lost them all before they were weaned," he informs us summarily, and these successive bereavements do not appear to have affected him much. Does he not write in the same chapter ("Of the Affection of Fathers for Children"), "Loving our children and calling them our second selves because we have begotten them leads us, I think, to consider another sort of procreation whose offspring should no less recommend itself to our love. The works our soul engenders, the issue of our understanding, heart, and abilities, spring from nobler parts than our body, and are more truly our own. We are both father and mother in this act of generation. They cost us a great deal more; and if they have any good in them, bring us more honor. For the worth that lies in the children of our body is much more theirs than ours . . . these [the "children of our mind"] represent and resemble us much more vividly than mere human children." In the Third Book of the *Essais,* he will write even more distinctly: "I have never thought that to be childless was a deficiency that should render one's life less complete or less content. The sterile vocation surely has its advantages too. Children, I would hold, are among the number of dispensable things."

Montaigne, however, was in no wise incapable of sympathy, particularly with regard to the lower orders. "I devote myself gladly to the cares of the poor and humble, either because there is more glory in it, or out of natural compassion, which has limitless power over me." But it is important to the equilibrium of his mind that he regain control of himself directly: ". . . I sympathize most tenderly with the afflictions of others, and would readily weep out of fellowship, whatever the occasion should be, if I knew how to weep." La Rochefoucauld will later say (anticipating Nietzsche's "Let us be hard"), "I am little sensible to pity; I should like not to be at all." But such declarations move me more particularly coming from a Nietzsche or a Montaigne, men who were tender-hearted by nature.

Should I be accused of having sharpened to excess the ideas of Montaigne, I would answer that numbers of his commentators have already busied themselves enough in blunting his point. I have done nothing but unwrap them, pull them out of the hay that somewhat muffles and clogs the *Essais* and often keeps the thrusts from hitting home. Faced with impudent authors, who have nevertheless become classics, the great occupation of the pedagogues is to render them inoffensive; I am amazed at how many years' work has already been quite naturally devoted to this task. At the end of a short time, it seems that the edge of all new thought is dulled; correspondingly, a sort of familiarity allows us to handle it without the fear of hurting ourselves any longer.

Montaigne, during his trip to Italy, was astonished to find the highest monuments of ancient Rome often half-buried under the rubble. We are marching, he wrote, on the roofs of houses. The ground rises bit by bit; and if, in our time, some spire seems to us less lofty, that is also because we are contemplating it from higher ground.

 SIX

1932–1938

INTRODUCTION

There is a good deal one could say in the way of analysis about Gide's great interest in and attachment to the Communist cause; but there seems to be very little one can add factually to what he has written and published himself. Almost everyone who has commented on his Communist "flirtation" (or "honeymoon," "temptation," "conversion," "deception" —the choice of word usually depends on one's own politics) has said the same things, varying only their order and emphasis; and what they have had to say, in almost every case, Gide himself said first. If his attachment to the Soviet adventure was something emotional, unexamined, and unorthodox, pseudo-Christian and anti-Catholic, a matter of old sympathies and biases rather than new convictions; if it was, above all else, something one hundred per cent personal, something uniquely his own—he knew it. He knew it very well, both before and after his trip to Russia in 1936.

The first public shock came in the summer of 1932, when Gide published in the *Nouvelle Revue Française* certain pages from his journal which we have already read:

> . . . above all I should like to live long enough to see Russia's plan succeed . . . My whole heart applauds that gigantic and yet entirely human undertaking.
>
> (May 13, 1931, first published June 1932)

> I should like to shout out loud my sympathy for Russia; and I should like my cry to be heard, to be important. I should like to live long enough to see the success of that tremendous effort; a success which I wish with all my soul, and for which I should like to work.
>
> (July 27, 1931, first published September 1932)

Not that there was anything exceptional about a Western writer's declaring his sympathy for the Soviet cause in 1932. In France, Henri Barbusse, Romain Rolland, and Louis Aragon had already made "declarations" far more outspoken than Gide's. In the United States, the same month that Gide made public his "sympathy for Russia," six American writers—Sherwood Anderson, Clifton Fadiman, Waldo Frank, Michael Gold, Granville Hicks, and Edmund Wilson—explained in *The New Masses* why they had turned toward Marx, Russia, and the Left. In Germany, Arthur Koestler felt the stirrings of a widespread impulse. Looking back (in *The God that Failed*) he wrote:

> I joined the Party . . . in 1931, at the beginning of that short-lived period of optimism, of that abortive spiritual renaissance . . . The stars of that treacherous dawn were Barbusse, Romain Rolland, Gide, and Malraux in France; Piscator, Becher, Renn, Brecht, Eisler, and Säghers in Germany; Auden, Isherwood, Spender in England; Dos Passos, Upton Sinclair, Steinbeck in the United States. . . . It looked indeed as if the Western world, convulsed by the aftermath of war, scourged by inflation, depression, unemployment, and the absence of a faith to live for, was at last going to
>
> *Clear from the head the masses of impressive rubbish;*
> *Rally the lost and trembling forces of the will,*
> *Gather them up and let them loose upon the earth,*
> *Till they construct at last a human justice.*   (Auden)[1]

And yet anyone who has followed the life and writings of André Gide this far will understand, and perhaps share, the surprise and shock generated by his gesture of pro-Soviet sympathy in the summer of 1932. It comes virtually out of the blue, considering his almost absolute silence on the subject of the Soviet Union during the first fifteen years of its existence. It comes from a man who is, as we have seen during World War I, resolutely and constitutionally unpolitical—in some respects even conservative and élitist. He kept insisting on this, in fact, *during* the next two years: I am "utterly unfit for politics"; "I know nothing of politics"; "by mood and by temperament, I could not be less revolutionary." Most surprisingly of all, this gesture of sympathy comes from a man who up till now has played the role of the Western world's most determined individualist. That he should declare his support for *any* cause, this arch-distruster of causes, is surprising in itself: but that he should declare it for a communizing, leveling, de-individualizing political cause struck many as incredible.

Nor was it only a matter of declarations of sympathy in a semi-private journal. André Gide also "served the cause," as the pages ahead will demonstrate—at least between 1932 and 1936—as actively as any

French intellectual of similar stature. (One could cite four other important French writers *more* actively engaged; but Rolland and Barbusse had not quite Gide's Olympian distinction, and the full reputations of Aragon and Malraux were yet to be made.) The man whose writings bear no trace of the political anguish that surrounded his first forty-five years; who could find no more suitable means of "engaging" in the Great War than sixteen months of anonymous philanthropy; who insisted again and again that *moral* questions were antecedent to social ones— this man's political activity between 1932 and 1937 is only sketched in the outline that follows.*

July 1932: In reply to a letter from Félicien Challaye, Gide declared his adherence to the declaration of the Amsterdam Conference against War—"against war," in Rolland's phrase, "whatever it be, wherever it comes from, whomever it threatens."

Summer 1932: He published pages from his *Journal* declaring his support for the Soviet Union.

December 1932: Specially appealed to by Henri Barbusse—"We attach, my dear Gide, a great importance to your adherence"—he wrote to the Association of Revolutionary Writers and Artists, the *A.E.A.R.* (p. 803), that though he did not feel it wise to join them officially, he assured them of his sympathy for the U.S.S.R. (He did, subsequently, attend many of their meetings, sometimes even speaking or presiding.)

March 6, 1933: Five weeks after Hitler took over as Chancellor of the Reich, one week after the Reichstag fire and Hitler's subsequent reprisals, he wrote a letter to *L'Humanité,* the French Communist daily, protesting the savage oppressions and persecutions in Germany (". . . only a class war, I mean that of each country against its own imperialism, can ward off the new conflict that is being prepared—a conflict that, this time, will be mortal" [2]).

March 21, 1933: Gide made his first public political speech at a meeting of the *A.E.A.R.* In it, he insisted on the distinction between the "necessary," future-oriented repressions of Russia—"certain painful abuses of force were no doubt necessary [there]"—and the cruel, reactionary repressions taking place in Hitler's Germany. Later he claimed to have been "tricked into" giving the speech, a job for which he felt singularly unfit. "Gide is so upset by the idea that he

* For a fuller account, see George Brachfeld, *André Gide and the Communist Temptation* (1959), and particularly Yvonne Davet's notes to Gide's *Littérature engagée* (1950).

cannot eat," wrote a friend who visited him shortly before he gave
the speech. "I don't think I've ever seen him this way." After reading of his friend's performance, Roger Martin du Gard wrote an
impassioned letter warning Gide that he was being *used,* a letter for
which Madeleine Gide thanked Roger "with all my heart."

March 31, 1933: He wrote a "Letter to the Young People of the
U.S.S.R.": "We look to you with . . . envy for your very sufferings, for your heroic courage . . . You have broken the chains of
the past."[3]

April 1933: He attended a public meeting to discuss an offer of asylum
to Albert Einstein, banished from Germany.

May 1933: At a meeting of the Friends of the Soviet Union in Paris,
organized by Barbusse and Rolland, Gide was seated on the platform alongside Maxim Gorki.

June 1933: Despite his pleas to have his name left off the program,
Gide found himself listed as one of the directors of a mass meeting
of the European Workers' Anti-Fascist Association at the Salle
Pleyel in Paris. Although he did not attend, he did not insist that
his name be removed, and once again wrote a note expressing his
sympathy with the aims of the rally.

July 1933: Gide's name was listed, along with those of Barbusse, Rolland, and Paul Vaillant-Couturier (the editor of *L'Humanité*) as
one of the directors of a new leftist review, *Commune,* edited by
Aragon.

September 1933: Once again he pleaded to be left out—"I beg you,
don't announce me . . . I am not made for public meetings"—
but once again yielded and allowed himself to be named one of the
Honorary Presidents of a World Youth Conference against Fascism
and War, held in Paris. Again he did not attend: again he contributed a fulsome, pro-Soviet note of support: "The example of the
October days has awakened the masses from the prostration in
which capitalist oppression had maintained them . . ."[4]

October 1933: He joined his name to a telegram of congratulations sent
by Barbusse and Rolland to Georgi Dimitrov, the Bulgarian Communist leader who had just made an eloquent self-defense in Leipzig against the charges that he and his comrades had been responsible for the Reichstag fire.

November 1933: He presided at a "non-partisan" protest rally in Paris
against Dimitrov's continued imprisonment, and was named co-

president (with André Malraux and the physicist Paul Langevin) of a French "Free Dimitrov" Committee.

January 1934: In this role, he traveled with Malraux to Berlin, with the intention of pleading with Joseph Goebbels for Dimitrov's release; Goebbels was out of town, but they left a polite letter of protest (p. 807) with his ministry.

(Unable to attend a second "Free Dimitrov" rally that same month, Gide sent to the meeting a very emotional "Address to Dimitrov's Mother.")

April 1934: Following the Fascist riots and subsequent general strike in Paris in February 1934, Gide signed his name to the Communist-inspired "Call to the Workers"—despite his private insistence the year before that "I systematically refuse to countersign any declaration whatever of which I myself have not written the text." [5] But then 1,200 other intellectuals (including Martin du Gard) signed the text as well; the right-wing riots of February 6 had helped to propel many lukewarm liberals to the Communist cause. (A sidenote: Ramon Fernandez has told of a construction worker who declared, a week after the riots, "We ought to have rifles and go down to the rich quarters . . . then we need a man to march at our head, a leader . . . a fellow of Gide's type." [6] His popular image had definitely changed in two years.)

May 1934: With Dimitrov freed, Gide transferred his interest in the Reichstag fire defendants to Ernst Thaelmann, leader of the German Communist Party, who was still in prison, although he had never actually been charged with complicity; he attended a protest meeting in Thaelmann's behalf in May.

August 1934: He sent a message to the first Soviet Writers' Conference (p. 808), in which he first publicly proposed his unorthodox ideal of a "Communist individualism." *

October 23, 1934: Gide gave his second public speech on communism (entitled "Literature and Revolution," p. 809), this time before 4,500 people at the Palais de la Mutualité in Paris who had gathered to hear the French delegates' report on the Moscow Writers' Conference. Again he stressed the artist's need for independence within the Communist society: "Literature must not place itself at

---

* Although recent "Marxist humanists" like Herbert Marcuse and Eric Fromm have professed to see a similar ideal in the early writings of Karl Marx (first published in 1959), it was still clearly unorthodox in 1934.

the service of the Revolution." On the platform with Gide were
Ilya Ehrenburg, Fernand Léger, and André Malraux (who had
been one of the delegates).

November 1934: His signature was among those on a note of protest
sent to the President of Spain regarding Franco's brutal repression
of the Asturias insurrectionists.

December 1934: He wired (on request) a message of congratulations
for the fifteenth anniversary of the Soviet cinema.

January 26, 1935: André Gide was the subject of (and a participant
in) a panel discussion held under the auspices of the Union pour la
Verité. It was devoted primarily to an interrogation of Gide by his
supporters and his adversaries (most notably, among the latter, the
Catholic writers Gabriel Marcel, Jacques Maritain, and François
Mauriac, and his old enemy Henri Massis) on the subject of his
Communist adherence. In it Gide delivered—spontaneously—
what is probably the most honest and thorough exposition of his
position; portions of the edited transcript are printed here, pp. 809–
815.

February 1935: A ten days' visit investigating working conditions in
the Belgian mines.

March 1935: His name appears on a message of congratulations and
support sent to Ernst Thaelmann, still in jail, on the occasion of his
fiftieth birthday.

May 1935: He attended a Writers' Conference at Hossegor, near Biar-
ritz: This was the locus of the amusing "I am India" story (p.
788).

June 21–25, 1935: Gide presided over a great International Writers'
Conference for the Defense of Culture—perhaps his most visible
moment of "service" to the cause (the gathering, like so many
other of these "non-partisan" congresses, was essentially engineered
by the French Communist Party). As on other occasions, Gide protested that he hated the job: "Another thing that worries me
greatly is the *role* I am going to be called on to play, FORCED to
play, on the occasion of this International Writers' Conference that
is about to take place," he wrote Martin du Gard. "It is very nearly
impossible, and it would be quite clearly improper—and a bit cowardly—for me to back out now." [7] The conference was attended by
230 delegates from 38 countries, including E. M. Forster and Al-
dous Huxley from England (both of whom spoke), Ehrenburg,
Pasternak, and Alexei Tolstoy from Russia, Brecht and Heinrich

Mann from Germany, Mike Gold and Waldo Frank from the
United States. Many of the delegates have written describing Gide's
welcoming speech, his major address on the second day (translated
into many languages), and his intervention from the chair on the
closing day to stop a serious row between pro-Soviet and Trotskyist
delegates. "In a case like this," he reminded the dissidents, "our
confidence is the greatest proof of love we can give [the U.S.S.R.]." [8]
(The row was occasioned by the case of Victor Serge, a Belgian-
born anarchist writer living in Russia, who had been persecuted
and finally deported for his "Trotskyist" opinions. Gide, who was
deeply depressed by this division in the party, wrote to the Soviet
ambassador the next day to appeal on Serge's behalf.)

June 29, 1935: He presided at the dedication of the rue Maxim Gorki
in Villejuif, a town south of Paris.

October 1935: He signed a protest against Mussolini's invasion of
Abyssinia.

November 1935: Gide presided at a second meeting of the International Association of Writers for the Defense of Culture, and gave a
brief opening speech in homage to Henri Barbusse, who had just
died.

December 1935: *L'Humanité* reprinted a message of congratulations
Gide had telephoned to Moscow (on request) for the eighteenth
anniversary of the Revolution.
In that same month, Gide made another speech recalling the
Dimitrov affair—"Two Years after the Leipzig Trial"—at a meet-
ing called on behalf of the still-imprisoned Thaelmann.

January 6, 1936: He led a group in protest against the imprisonment by
the Greek government of two writers as political prisoners; they
were later freed.

January 31, 1936: He presided at a meeting in honor of Romain Rolland, praising the Communist writer as "one of those who incarnate
the honor and glory of France and of all humanity." [9]

February 1936: He published reports sent to him clandestinely of the
tortures of political prisoners in Yugoslav jails.

Summer 1936: Gide was for ten weeks the guest of the Soviet government and the Association of Soviet Writers in a triumphant tour of
the U.S.S.R.—a tour he had put off more than once, undertaken
with four young friends. He gave three major speeches—including
the address of eulogy at Gorki's funeral, when he appeared on the
reviewing platform of Red Square in Moscow alongside Stalin and

Molotov, a speech broadcast over loudspeakers throughout the city. At each stop in his progress, he was greeted with flowers and fêtes and banners, banners his companions jokingly insisted must have been packed into the car ahead and unrolled anew at each stop. His photograph and biography appeared in the papers each day, and thousands of copies of his works were sold in Russian translations.

On his return, he wrote a report of his visit, *Retour de l'U.R.S.S.* (*Return from the U.S.S.R.,* pp. 825–832), more critical than his hosts or his French comrades had anticipated. It elicited the most outraged response from Communist circles, was called "mediocre, poor, superficial, puerile, and contradictory" by Romain Rolland,[10] and a "stab in the back to Republican Spain" by others. It sold over a hundred thousand copies (far more than any of Gide's other works), and had been translated into fifteen languages by the end of 1937. It was banned in several Communist countries. Despite a few more gestures of social protest, the book—"my liberation," Gide called it—may be taken, for our purposes, as the End of the Affair.

Just as liberal intellectuals by the hundreds were acclaiming Russia's role in the Spanish Civil War, Gide was detaching himself completely: had he retained any heart at all for politics, he might have continued to serve as a kind of French Orwell, an early (and unregarded) anti-Stalinist. But he had had enough. Late in 1937, he is back defending the gratuitous, non-utilitarian work of art, and writing of "the *illusion* that a better social state can ever overcome poverty" (my italics). In April 1938, he writes Martin du Gard of "this immense advantage of having 'desolidarized' myself with all *parties.* I am more and more convinced that our ideas have no value unless they are not bundled together with other people's; and I feel myself more and more incapable of 'giving my whole support' to *any* collective manifestation." [11] And in 1949 he will let the story of his disaffection be used—along with Silone's, Spender's, Koestler's, Richard Wright's, and Louis Fischer's—as one of six celebrated object lessons about a "God that Failed."

Several remarks may be made that will qualify somewhat this record of five years' activity on behalf of the Communist cause. Some of it was merely honorary; some of it was over protest; some of it entailed no more than a signature—although the signature of an André Gide is no small thing. Much of it is not so much pro-Communist as anti-war, or anti-Hitler, or simply anti-injustice. It coincides, this activity, with the years between Hitler's assumption of power and the Hitler–Stalin pact, when many in the intellectual world thought that the only viable way to vote against Nazi Germany was to vote for communism and Russia—an illusion that a threatened Russia fostered in every possible way.

But still, and again, the puzzling point is not that some leading intellectual did all this, but that André Gide did. How are we to reconcile this enlistment and activity with the first sixty-two years of his life? People who knew him best—Roger Martin du Gard, Jean Schlumberger, Dorothy Bussy, his wife—were frankly appalled.

And yet many observers have taken Gide's claims at face value ("I have always been a Communist"; "I have not changed direction"), and insisted that his Communist period is no more than a natural and predictable stage. The moment of truth, the birth of Gide's social conscience is usually assumed by these observers to have taken place during his Congo voyage in 1926–1927, with his discovery of the brutality inherent in colonialist exploitation. An entry in his travel diary provides a perfect "proof" of this sudden and unsought commitment:

> The painful sense of this injustice is now rooted in me permanently: I know things to which I cannot reconcile myself. What demon drove me to Africa? What did I come to find in this country? I was at peace. Now I know: I must speak. (October 30, 1925)

But Gide himself resented, and quite naturally, the implication that he had lived devoid of social awareness and sympathy before 1926. He was just as aware of the abuses of colonialism, he wrote Jean Schlumberger, in Algiers in 1894, but simply judged it out of his competence, and chose to say nothing. Justin O'Brien traces the 1932 declaration back to his overwhelming sense of sympathy, and then traces *that* back to his fourth or fifth year.

Genealogies of social sympathy, though, seem inadequate to explain something so *different* in Gide's life as the political affiliation and activity of these five years. He does acknowledge, in his journals and letters, that these are, for him, "new preoccupations," preoccupations that began in the spring of 1931. Later on, he even withdrew his claims of unwavering continuity, and admitted that "It would be false to say that my opinions have not changed." [12]

If one is willing to grant (as I think one must) that a serious change did occur, how is the change to be explained? In his angry argument against Gide's commitment (the letter of April 3, 1933), Martin du Gard berated his friend for his "desire to proselytize, into which there enters a great deal of generosity, a little bit of childishness, and a certain amount of pride"—which probably takes the right approach, at least, by suggesting that there were *several* motivations. At times Gide does speak of his horror of capitalism, his pain at the thought of the suffering and oppressed, his disgust with the corruption of a rotting world; and at times, perhaps, he felt all three. But I have a difficult time convincing myself that they were of even one-tenth the importance to Gide that they are, for example, to Jean-Paul Sartre. Others have written, perhaps unjustly, of his need for a faith, a goal, a place to join, a secular substitute for religion. "I long to sign . . . something," he wrote Roger in February 1932. ". . . to aim toward something . . . what an indescribable satisfaction!" His age may have had something to do with it, his age and his quasi-mystical optimism, his ideal of this-worldly progress: there is a growing sense that his classical values may be rapidly going out of date, which is perhaps related to a willingness to risk more and move faster, so as not to miss the Future-bound wave. (And there is, of course, the pleasure of *camaraderie de combat* with all those enthusiastic young men.) Gide offered one other partial explanation that cannot be ignored: that the drying-up of his own creative powers left a void that politics came opportunely to fill, left him far more willing to dispense with fine art, if need be, in the interests of revolution. ("The same thing happened to Tolstoy . . .")

But I would propose two reasons in particular for his sudden change of direction: first, a growing realization (through the Congo experience, no doubt, and the spread of world depression) that not only his creature-comforts, but his very art and ideas were in some respects the fruits of his privileged social class—the eternal dilemma of the non-starving artist; and secondly, a reaction *against* the opinions of his traditional enemies, who hated godless Russia even more than they hated André Gide. During the Congo journey, and later back home in 1928, one finds the first hints of a certain growing sense of uneasiness about his wealth—something he had given little thought to all his life, perhaps because he had indulged himself so little, had so ill-developed a "sense of property."

> I feel today seriously, painfully, that *inferiority*—of never having had to earn my bread, of never having had to work out of absolute need.

> This state of things has become unbearable to me, all the more
> unbearable because I am profiting from it, because my brother is
> suffering from it and I am not.[13]

Through that opening wedge, all sorts of radically disturbing thoughts
begin to enter (hurried along, no doubt, by the theories of certain Communist friends):

—Do I (he is in effect asking himself) possess my comforts and
my freedom *because* of the bondage and sufferings of others?

—Are my treasured freedom of thought, my scruples, my very critical spirit, my moral *raison d'être* not perhaps luxuries dependent on a
vicious capitalist system, with its oppressions and inequities?

—How many of my ruling ideas were determined by my class, and
its attendant comforts?

—Does all art, perhaps, demand social inequity as its precondition?
Is it, "in times like these," a criminal self-indulgence?

Léon Pierre-Quint refers to such questions as "an intellectual's sentimen-
talities"; others—Sartre and Camus, notably—have taken them in
deadly earnest, taken them in fact much further than Gide did. But I do
think they were for him—at least for a few years—quite living concerns,
and if he ultimately decided that it was too late for him to change, that
he really did care more about art and truth than about suffering humanity, he at least gave to these questions some very thoughtful and valuable
attention during the years he allowed them to trouble him.

This inescapable squirrel-cage of questioning might have led him
only to silence or despair. What led him into the arena, I am sure, "sput-
tering on platforms and writing 'We' to *L'Humanité*" (as Dorothy
Bussy wrote[14]), was above all else the chance to take sides again against
the enemies of a lifetime. This may seem to be treating Gide's social
activism as something personal and rather cheap: but I *do* think it was
something personal and rather cheap. I see it in great part as a negative
affair, an extension of his hardening stance of almost doctrinaire anti-
Catholicism. The enemy of my enemy is my friend.

> I should like . . . to see what can be produced by a state without
> religion, a society without the family. Religion and the family are
> the two worst enemies of progress.

> It is against religion that I am protesting, against the Church,
> dogma, faith, etc.

Only atheism can pacify the world today . . .

It is also, it is in great part, the stupidity and dishonesty of the attacks on the U.S.S.R. that today make us defend her with a certain obstinacy.[15]

Almost every analysis of Soviet policy in his *Journal* is written in the form of an answer to traditionalist, Catholic, anti-Soviet critics—a kind of conditioned reflex, perhaps, imprinted by all those self-defenses in the 20's; but the suggestion is that he is more interested in them, the French critics (he still calls them "You"), than in the U.S.S.R. In speech after speech, he insists that the Soviet experiment must succeed—else how will we ever rid mankind, for once and all, of its "false gods," its "ancient idols," its "enemies of progress"? In light of these quotations, Gide's *rapprochement* to the Soviet Union seems to me to be really a form of battle in his war against the Church. He thinks he has found, at last, a comrade-in-arms strong enough to finish the job he (and Nietzsche) began. Sometimes he expressly admits—as in the third quotation above—that it is in order to fight them, the wretched asses who are opposing communism (or at least to distinguish oneself from them), that one ought to join the Communist cause. The same argument, interestingly enough, was used in 1928 by Henry de Montherlant, as a justification for defending André Gide: "Whatever reservations one may have about his character, his art, or his moral code, when one sees the kind of people who attack him one can do nothing but join his side." [16]

What I find disheartening, ultimately, about Gide's whole Communist affair is the false premise of so much of it, the wrong-headedness: Gide's misconception and abuse of the idea of communism in the first place; his specious adherence, and then his specious disavowal; the apparent involvement of a great thinker with a great movement, when in fact they never really met. He seems to have had, through it all, no idea what institutional communism was or was all about. He never thought through the implications of the social problems with which he was dealing, never analyzed either communism *or* capitalism with the seriousness they demand. Gide's mental and emotional equipment was such that it simply could not comprehend political matters—as he so often admitted.

He made mechanical protests, imitated anti-Fascist anger, parroted slogans he didn't really believe. He contrived queer Gidean compromises between a cause to which he was sentimentally attached and biases and preferences rooted deep in his nature—compromises, "reconciliations" that must have puzzled his readers and auditors, and by which he made of "communism" something as exclusively his own as he earlier had made of "Christianity."

Throughout he was, from the Communist point of view, unorthodox, inconsistent, intractable—as he well knew. More than once, he hinted to Martin du Gard: You really needn't worry; I'm not in this as deeply as you may think. I cannot help but approve Martin du Gard's judgment, "that he ventured off into communism with generosity, oh beyond a doubt, but with an unforgivable levity; that his adherence, and his present withdrawal [he was writing in 1937] have about them exactly the same quality of incompetence, of naïveté." [17] Moreover, as with his earlier venture into religion, I cannot help feeling that he left himself loopholes of escape scattered throughout his *Journal,* kept his exit-route cleared and protected—as if he knew, or at least half-knew, knew at some level of consciousness, that it was to be no more than a few years' fling, a few years' vacation from the arduous moral job of being André Gide.

All this said, Gide's detour into communism still has a certain interest, even a certain value, above and beyond its necessary place in the story of his life:

—He may have helped, in his way, to correct a few misconceptions about Stalin and the Soviet Union in his little book of 1936.

—The experience helped him to straighten out his own head, to clear it of certain cant and inconsistency, certain false compromises and self-delusions, to understand better (as Massis's attacks had once done) who he was and where he stood, the real hierarchy of his values.

—Some of his reflections may help sounder political thinkers to realize things that he could not, and to carry his own analyses—of the place of art in a socialist society, for example, or of the "luxury" of freethought—to more complex and fruitful levels.

—And his story may be read with profit, I think, for three reasons, by students of cultural history. First, he does typify, in his way, an experience shared by many intellectuals of the time. Second, he did add his ounce's weight to the current polemics. And third, he provides a remarkable case-study of the way in which a celebrity, intellectual or not, perceptive or not, can be made use of by a political movement.

Of the strategic "usefulness" of Gide's adherence to the Communist cause there can be no question, however wrong-headed or ill-informed or delusive or superficial we may think that adherence today. "The ostentatious display of prestige names . . . became [under Maurice Thorez, after 1930] a regular feature of Party propaganda," writes David Caute in *Communism and the French Intellectuals* (1964). "The brandishing of names was clearly taken to be of cardinal importance in the struggle, with the result that other considerations tended to be swept under the carpet."

And yet, as a leading French Communist deputy wrote in 1937— the year of Gide's disaffection—"for our Party an intellectual can . . . become the worst of things if he comes . . . without the spirit of discipline, of total devotion." [18] Which perhaps explains why the hatred of those who once supposed themselves his masters—the hatred that followed his "recantation"—was so violent and so long-lasting. It even followed him into the grave:

M. ANDRÉ GIDE IS DEAD

M. André Gide died yesterday, at 10:40 P.M., in Paris.

Born in Paris on November 22, 1869, he spent his whole life exalting false individualism, sterile introspection, and the gratuitous act—to say nothing of more questionable sentiments.

For youthful intellectuals, he was a maker of myths and a Master in Discouragement; for the bourgeosie, a clever servant and a king in the arts of diversion.

His *Return from the U.S.S.R.* won him the pardon and the gratitude of those who had been mistakenly disturbed by his pretended adherence to communism. The book also earned him the scorn of all honest people, which he was further to justify by his attitude during the Occupation, a time when he declared that he "could live happily even in a cage."

In these last few years, M. Gide had become one of the glories of the proprietary class. In 1947, he was awarded the Nobel Prize for Literature, and recently a great fuss was made about his stage version of *Les Caves du Vatican*, played at the Comédie Française.

But youth was turning its back more all the time on the Counterfeiters of culture; and when all is said and done, the man who has just died was already a corpse.

M. Gide once said: "The thinking creature who has no other end but himself suffers from an abominable void." M. Gide must have suffered a great deal. Peace to his ashes.

(*L'Humanité*, February 20, 1951)

January 11

Most often one attributes to others only the feelings of which one is capable oneself . . . but that is the way one blunders. Among the refugees whom we aided at the Foyer Franco-Belge, there were very few who did not attribute the most interested motives to our charitable activity; in the eyes of all, we were paid employees who, besides, took a little graft on the side, at their expense. What would have been the good of speaking of disinterestedness, of love of duty, of the need of serving in our own way and of reducing suffering? They would have laughed in our faces.

January 21

. . . I am going to try to arrange my life differently. This necessity of going out for my meals (and there is no restaurant near) wears me out. My mornings are completely devoured by correspondence, telephone calls, etc. I must not make myself accessible until after noon and ask the concierge not to bring up the morning mail. *Curiosity* is my greatest enemy. It sometimes happens that I close my door to everyone, and then run nevertheless at the first ring of the bell. . . . Discipline indispensable. And stop telling myself, as I did recently in such cowardly fashion, that henceforth I shall write nothing worthwhile and that my work is finished.

January 25

These young people who send or bring you a manuscript and ask your advice do not know how much they put you out. That is their excuse. It takes me hours to get to know a book properly; when it is not so bad that I can judge it from the first pages and drop it at once, when I give myself to it, I do so wholly. And my work, once interrupted, does not allow itself to be picked up immediately afterwards. My mind keeps drifting round, like a whirlpool. . . . And then afterwards, I have to write to the author, or let him come up and talk. I have there, on a shelf in my library, fourteen begging manuscripts, which, if my glance happens to fall on them, make me long to be dead.

At two-thirty I get up staggering with fatigue and dress. Impossible to get to sleep, in spite of the double dose of sleeping potion. And it has been this way every night for a week. What can I do? Whether I go to bed late or early, whether I eat little or much at dinner, drink wine, beer, or water, it is all the same. And spasms, twitchings, discomforts. . . . Before dressing I got up ten times, to wash, to close the window, to open it again, to remake my bed, to drink some milk, to urinate, to write a letter. . . . It is exasperating, exhausting. In a moment I am going to stretch out on my bed fully dressed. . . . I give up leaving tomorrow for Cuverville, where insomnia is accompanied by even more painful tortures. I feel my nerves as taut as the string of a bow. Sleep comes in the early morning, and when I have to get up at about eight, I do so with an inexpressible lassitude and feeling of age. While I am writing these lines, merely to occupy my mind, I have trouble clearly making out the letters I am forming—and I got stronger lenses just three months ago. Under such conditions, what becomes of work?

Cuverville, January 28

Alarming rumors are going about; country people are getting worried; tradesmen cannot get payment. . . .

"Is it true what they say, that we are going to have war again?"

Three times in the last four days this question has been asked of Em., who hastens to reassure as best she can.

"No country is in a state to make war today," she replies.

"But then why have matches gone up two sous?"

January 29

Hatred of mysticism . . . yes, no doubt. And yet my anguish is almost mystical in nature. That so much suffering should remain vain, this idea is intolerable to me; it keeps me awake at night; wakes me up. . . . I cannot, I will not admit it.

February 9

. . . since it appears to me that individualism itself, properly understood, must serve the community, it is essential to me to preserve its rights, and I consider it wrong to oppose it to communism. I see nothing obligatory, nothing essential in such an opposition, and I am not willing to admit it. I say: "Individualism . . . properly understood." I am applying myself to understanding it better.

February 14

To try to build up the future in imitation of the past—what reprehensible folly! . . .

My poor Uncle Charles is leaving life step by step. At eighty-four, his first illness will also be his last. He preserves all his memory and his lucidity, all his intelligence.

February 21

Answering a telephone call, I go to see Paul Valéry at about four o'clock and stay more than two hours talking with him. Those who have never known him cannot imagine the charming graciousness of his eyes, his smile, his voice, his kindliness, the abundant resources of his intelligence, the amusement of his sallies, the sharpness of his views—through so rapid an elocution, often so confused and mumbled that I have to make him repeat many sentences.

A bad cold confines him to his room; he says he is worn out, and looks it; his handsome face is lined with care; harassed by the obligations of his fame, tormented by money questions, exasperated by the correspondence that cuts holes in his time (he shows me a letter from a general offering him a 250,000-franc diamond, "an excellent bargain"), much troubled by the general situation and convinced that the miserable work of political men is leading us to the abyss and all Europe with us. He reads me a declaration by Einstein, distinctly individualistic, to which he subscribes more willingly than to the Soviets. Impossible to build up a unified front to stand up against the ruinous demands of the nationalists. He convinces me of this, and I leave our conversation deeply grieved, for I cannot doubt that he is right. The catastrophe strikes me as almost inevitable. I have come to wish most heartily for the overthrow of capitalism and of everything that lurks in its shadows—abuses, injustices, lies, and monstrosities. And I cannot convince myself that the Soviets must fatally and necessarily lead to the strangling of everything we live for. A well-understood communism must favor valuable individuals, to take advantage of all the individual's values, to get the best return from each one. And individualism, well understood, has no reason to oppose a system that would put everything in its proper place, make the most of everything.

Cuverville, February 25

I read with the greatest interest Stalin's new speech, which exactly answers my objections and fears . . . (speech of June 23, 1931); I subscribe to it with all my heart.

As long as I glimpsed only miserable palliatives to a ruinous state of things, to lying credos, to cowardly intellectual compromises, I could still remain undecided, although all those things seemed to me more and more deplorable. And more and more clearly it appeared to me against *what* my heart and mind were rebelling, were so willing to fight; but I could not be satisfied with mere protest. . . . Now that I know not only *against* what but also *for* what—I am voting. And I wonder at the fact that all those who used to reproach me for my "indecision" are all on the other side. They used to throw back at me that letter from Charles-Louis Philippe (which I had quoted myself), that sentence which ended the letter: "Be a man: choose," as if they were unwilling to admit that one could make any other "choice" than theirs.

I know in their camp people of such great heart and such good will that, even when I was convinced that they were wrong, it was indescribably painful for me to have to declare myself against them. But how can one not declare oneself, when one's silence is taken for acquiescence? Indifference, tolerance are out of place as soon as the enemy takes advantage of them and one sees prospering what one decidedly considers to be bad.

February 26

That the ideas of Lenin and Stalin might overcome the resistance the states of Europe are trying to bring against them—this is beginning to appear possible to those states; and this fills them with terror. But that it might be desirable for those ideas to win out, this is something they refuse to envisage. There is a great deal of stupidity, a great deal of ignorance, a great deal of stubbornness in their refusal; and also a certain deficiency of imagination that keeps them from believing that humanity can change, that a society can be built up on different foundations from those they have always known (even though they deplore them), that the future can be anything but a repetition and reproduction of the past.

February 27

No longer simply to walk on ahead, but to aim toward something . . . what an indescribable satisfaction! But was I not won over to the Party even before it was formed and had formulated its doctrines? And if my

wishes too often remained vague, was not that in part because their realization seemed to me too distant? Emotionally, temperamentally, intellec-
tually, I have always been a Communist. . . .

To find an *end* for one's pursuit, one's quest, the agitation of one's spirit;
i.e., *to make an end.* "To devote oneself to a noble cause." To make up
one's mind. To choose. To have found. . . .

Have I not let myself be somewhat influenced by their urgings, their
advice? And, through wanting to *serve,* do I not run the risk of forsaking
my real usefulness? I feel, I know, that by insisting on taking sides I have
everything to lose; and the others, even those I should like to serve, little
to gain.

For some time this notebook has ceased to be what it ought to be: an
intimate confidant.

The perspective of even a partial publication of my journal, as an
appendix to the volumes of my *Œuvres complètes,* has distorted its meaning; and also fatigue or laziness, and the dislocation of my life, fear of
losing what I ought to have put into books or articles which, through
some lack of confidence or other, I lost hope of ever bringing off satisfac-
torily. I am writing even these lines without assurance. To be sure, I have
known long periods of diminished fervor before, and I know that I got
over them; but at that time I was young. I wonder: Is there enough room
left ahead of me, from now on, to make a new leap forward? For all the
impetus acquired in the past seems to me of no use for what I want to write
now. And that above all is the reason for my silence. I have come to this
clinic to rest, to take care of myself, to find out what I am still worth and
whether or not I can still dare.

I am recovering a bit of assurance. It is through the loss of all self-
confidence that my fatigue becomes apparent at once; that humble, crest-
fallen, submissive, hunted appearance I take on in such cases. . . .

This too, this above all, withholds my pen: the thought, of which I
keep reminding myself, that many things still dear to us will have neither
value nor significance for those whom I feel coming, and whom my heart

beckons. It is to them that I should like to speak, for them that I should like to write; but they will not listen to me. And besides they will do right, having no need, for their part, to hear what I, for my part, would have to tell them. My sympathy means nothing to them; what do they care that it is toward them that I turn? It would be madness to let this depress me.

April 23

. . . In the state of nature, and without man's intervention, any creature incapable of taking care of itself is eliminated; and especially the least resistant. The protection of the puny and sickly, the artificial prolongation of their existence, is all man's doing; which allows us to say that man, far from having decreased suffering on this earth, has everywhere introduced and supported it, even with the help of pity.

That *state of devotion* in which feelings and thoughts, in which the whole being is oriented and subordinated—I now recognize it again as in the time of my youth. Moreover, is not my present conviction comparable to *faith?* For a very long time I systematically "deconvinced" myself of any credo that could not hold up under free inquiry. But it is from that very inquiry that my credo of today is born. There is nothing "mystical" in it (in the sense in which this word is commonly understood), so that this state cannot find recourse, or this fervor release, in prayer. My whole being, quite simply, is reaching out toward a desire, an aim. All my thoughts keep coming back to it, whether I will them or not. In the abominable distress of the present world, Russia's new plan now seems to me salvation. There is nothing that does not persuade me of this! The miserable arguments of its enemies, far from convincing me, simply exasperate me. And if my life were necessary to ensure the success of the U.S.S.R., I should give it at once . . . as so many others have done, will do, and without distinguishing myself from them.

I write this without passion and in all sincerity, because of the great need to leave at least this testimony in case death should come before it is possible for me to declare myself better.

June 13

Indeed I do not insist that the tower in which I take refuge should be an ivory tower! But I am no good if I leave it. Glass tower; observatory in which I welcome every ray, every wave; fragile tower in which I feel badly sheltered; do not want to be; vulnerable on all sides; but confident in spite of everything, and my eyes fixed on the east. My desperate waiting, despite everything, takes on the color of hope.

That enrolling of Christ is, of all the frauds, the most shameful; of all hypocrisies, perhaps the most abominable. "Not peace, but the sword," Christ himself said. That is what they retain of his gospel of peace. They have so effectively linked the idea of religion to the idea of country that it is in the name of God that they arm and mobilize. . . .

That will toward atheism on the part of the Soviets, however, is what most arouses against them certain genuinely devout minds. A world without God can only go toward ruin, they think; only toward perdition a humanity without rituals, without devotions, without prayers. . . . Why do not these pious souls convince themselves that one can never suppress any but false gods? The need of adoring lives at the center of man's heart.

But religion, our religion, the only one, is a *revealed* religion, they say, those pious souls. Man can know the truth only through the revelation of which we are the guardians. Any felicity, any harmony achieved without the aid of God seems to them criminal; they refuse to consider it real; they deny it and oppose it with all their piety. They prefer humanity unhappy to seeing it happy without God, without their god.

I have always been a Communist, in heart as well as in mind, even while remaining a Christian; which is why I had such trouble separating them from each other, and even more trouble opposing them to each other. I should never have reached this point all alone. It required people and events to educate me. Do not speak of "conversion" in this case; I have not changed directions; I have always walked forward; I am continuing to do so; the great difference is that for a long time I saw nothing in front of me but space and the projection of my own fervor; at present I am going forward orienting myself toward something; I know that somewhere my vague desires are being organized and that my dream is on the way to becoming reality.

All the same, utterly unfit for politics. So do not ask me to belong to a party.

July 19

If social questions occupy my thought today, it is partly because the creative demon is withdrawing from it. These questions take over the field only when the other has already given it up. Why try to overrate oneself? to refuse to admit in myself (what appears clear to me in Tolstoy): an undeniable diminution? . . .

When I had begun this new notebook, however, I had promised myself not to deal with such questions here. The result was simply that I spent several weeks without writing anything. These questions preoccupy me almost exclusively; I constantly return to them and cannot turn my thought away from them. Yes, truly, I think of almost nothing else. Everything I see, everything I read brings me back to them, or else it does not interest me. The war was less obsessing: forced to accept everything passively, one tried to think of it as little as possible; one repressed one's indignations and revolts; duty consisted, we then thought, in keeping silent. But did they not take considerable advantage of this: that they knew us to be *men who would do our duty?* Which is precisely why, on the contrary, we feel today that our duty, today, is to speak out. If we kept silent we know very well that you would make us, by our very silence, your accomplices. Just as, in the Congo, if I had kept silent about the abuses I denounced, I should, by my silence, have become an accomplice of those abuses.

Cuverville, July 29

Nothing to note. Dreadful confusion after reading the Trotskyite manifestoes that Pierre Naville lent me. But, however well founded certain criticisms may seem to me, it strikes me that nothing can be more prejudicial than divisions within the party.

Cuverville, Tuesday, December 27

That art and literature have nothing to do with social questions and can only, if they venture into them, go astray—of this I remain almost convinced. And that is partly why I have been silent since such questions have become uppermost in my mind.

We are just now beginning to emerge from the mystical stage; but I am ready to believe that the "fine arts" belong to it and that they need that climate to prosper. I prefer not to write anything rather than to bend my art to utilitarian ends. To convince myself that they must be uppermost today is tantamount to condemning myself to silence.

Montherlant is probably right when he says (and he says it magnificently) that youth rejects the idea of a peace that would offer no nourishment for its appetite for glory and its need of enthusiasm. But what
communism proposes to us today is a way of fighting against war, which
demands more courage and permits more heroism than war itself. In
truth, war would call for nothing but a blind submission.

That future war which we are being forced to imagine, abject in every
way, will no longer have a place for heroism; so that that last allurement,
that prestige it still holds for the noblest among our young men, will be
taken away from it.

New titles of nobility, new forms of sanctity, of devotion, of heroism
(and not at all as you say: merely new facilities); that is what we need.
People are unaware of this only because of an absurd misunderstanding, a
profound misapprehension of human nature and its mysterious appetites.
It is you on the contrary who offer it stagnation in the inherited comfort
that all your efforts are bent on preserving.

Paris, January 6

The truth is that I can neither resign myself to being separated from
Em., nor dissociate my brain from my heart. . . . This is the secret of all
my indecisions; my very reticences are the most passionate thing about me.
But no, there is nothing to be done about it, nothing to be tried; "No man
can serve two masters"—and "The man whose heart is divided is incon-
stant in all his ways. . . ."

Every time I see her again I feel afresh that I have never really loved
anyone but her; and even, at times, it seems to me that I love her more
than ever. And it is because it takes me away from her that every step
forward is so painful to me. I can no longer think without cruelty. A "state
of anxiety" sufficient to explain many sleepless nights. . . .

Probably it is because I feel her suffer from it that each attack on
Christ still wounds me so painfully. Sometimes I even wonder if it is not
also because, without wanting to admit it to myself, without even knowing it or being exactly aware of it, I never completely gave up believing in
him myself. Yes, believing in him, in his immanent omnipresence, in
the aggravation of his sufferings through our faults, etc. . . .

February 8

The sky over Europe and the entire world is so heavy with storm; hearts are so full of hatred—that at times one comes to think that nothing but a conflict of classes could forestall today the mortal conflict of nations.

I am making a great effort to sober my thought with a little wisdom; but what an error it is to believe that wisdom is always on the side of moderation! And those who say, "Rather war than revolution"—how can they not understand that the revolution would inevitably follow the war, and that, by trying to avoid one, we should have them both?

March 14

Those who (René Schwob in particular) see my writings encumbered with sexual obsession seem to me as absurd as those who used to claim that those same writings were frigid. Sensuality remains, in their mind as in their flesh, so closely linked to the object that awakens it that when the object is changed, they can no longer recognize it. Then, taking their clue from me, they saw it everywhere, that sensuality, after having seen it nowhere. It influenced my will, they said, distorted my thought, rotted my prose; each of my books was impregnated with it. . . . How many stupidities they wrote on this subject!

April 5

What would be Barrès's attitude in regard to Hitler? He would approve him, I believe. For, after all, Hitlerism is simply a Boulangism that succeeds.* What made it prove abortive in France? Circumstances or men? Would the French people have let themselves be led into such excesses? Doubtless Hitlerism was favored by unemployment, poverty, and that constant irritation which France, alas, seems to have taken it upon herself to provide.

April 7

Since Germany seems bent upon getting rid of her brains, could not France offer to take in that "gray matter" which our neighbors seem to scorn?

Could not the French government, above and beyond all political questions, offer Einstein, forced into exile by Germany, a chair in the Col-

---

* General Boulanger, named Minister of War by Clemenceau in 1886, later became a Royalist and threatened the Republic in 1888–1889 as a popular demagogue who might have seized power. Barrès was among his many admirers.

lège de France, as was done in the past for Mickiewicz? A laboratory and the means of continuing his research. . . . In order to create a sort of foreign annex to this Collège, which would perpetuate an ancient tradition of receptivity of which France would have reason to be proud, it would probably not be hard to gather together the necessary funds. Shall we have enough sense to make this gesture before another country does it first? And this time, what a fine reason we should have for "being glad to be French"!

I speak of this to Malraux, who promises to speak of it to Monzie.

Roquebrune, April 10

. . . I have the greatest difficulty, nowadays, getting interested in fiction. Yet I have reread from beginning to end *La Condition humaine.** This book, which in serial form seemed to me excessively involved, disheartening because of its richness, and almost incomprehensible because of its complexity . . . seems to me, as I reread it all together, perfectly clear, ordered in its confusion, admirably intelligent, and, despite that (I mean: despite the intelligence), deeply embedded in life, involved, and panting with a sometimes unbearable anguish.

Unhappy that I do not feel up to writing about this book, and to contribute to its success, the article it deserves.

April 11

This evening *L'Eclaireur de Nice* informs us that Einstein accepts the chair that Spain has just offered him at Madrid. The event is announced in large capitals; *L'Eclaireur* grasps its importance, then.

I cannot admit that those qualified to make him a similar offer in the name of France did not think of it. . . . What reasons did they have for not doing so? . . . I am seeking, and for myself too, excuses. . . .

As soon as the news of Einstein's exile appeared, I should have put forth the suggestion in *Marianne* or the *N.R.F.* Still better: instead of barking with the others at that public meeting, have that suggestion to the French government voted by acclamation by that very large audience. How I blame myself for not having thought of this then!

Every good Frenchman should be inconsolable that France did not have the sense to make this fine gesture, which would have been so natural to her, and in which we should all have recognized ourselves.

* Malraux's novel, called in English *Man's Fate.*

April 14

. . . That wretched creature in a doorway on the corner of the boulevard Saint-Germain and the boulevard Raspail. His coat pinned together with a safety-pin to hide the lack of shirt. A vacant stare. . . . I saw him again, two hours later, as I left the *Nouvelle Revue Française,* in the same place, in exactly the same pose, an image of utter despair. I tried to speak to him, but he seemed not to understand anything; he almost dropped the bill I slipped into his hand. Back at the rue Vaneau, I could think of nothing else. . . .

Cuverville, May 20

Excellent speech by Hitler in the Reichstag. If Hitlerism had never made itself known except by such speeches, it would be more than merely acceptable. But it remains to be seen where the real face ends and the grimace begins.

May 25

I receive a visit from a young Communist of twenty-six, who looks only twenty; he is bringing me an article in which, to hear him tell it, he has forever shut up Benda; the latter, recognizing that he would be unable to answer it, has supposedly opposed the inclusion of this article in the *Nouvelle Revue Française.* The abovementioned young man is counting on me to go over his head. It is to the interest of the Party that this article be accepted. It is not he (whose name I have forgotten) who is involved, but the cause, and I am betraying the Party if I do not force Paulhan's hand. When I tell him that I have never wanted to exert any authority at the *N.R.F.,* that I have always left Paulhan complete freedom of choice, that, in short, I refuse to intervene, he declares, raising his voice, that he is "stupefied," profoundly disappointed, that after my declarations he had a right to expect me to support him and, since that's the way it is, he is ready to announce my falling away, my desertion as loud as he can. I tell him that this is blackmail; he at once exclaims: "So it is, but legitimate blackmail. . . ." He talks louder and louder, gets excited, seizes me by the arm; eventually I put a chair between us. . . . "Is that really your last word?" he asks in his most threatening tone. And when I reply that I have nothing to add: "Too bad. I'm sorry for you, but you've asked for it. You will live to regret this."

This conversation amused me too much for me not to push it beyond reasonable limits, so that, toward the end, we simply repeated the same things without getting anywhere. I especially enjoyed the identification that X. insisted on maintaining between the fate of his article and the success of the cause; besides, he seemed quite sincerely convinced and thus rather sympathetic in spite of everything. (Several times he protested "that it was not a question of his article," to which I replied "that on the contrary it was a question solely of his article.")—Somewhat concentrated, the dialogue might be excellent. Young X. played rather well his role of zealot—which is, after all, rather an easy role to play, like all the roles of stock characters.

Cuverville, June 2

The day before I left for Cuverville, I endured a sermon by Father Gillet at Saint-Louis des Invalides. . . . "In the name of Christ, let us arm France until we make her incapable of being attacked": that might be a résumé of his panegyric, characteristic of that noble French Hitlerism which is going to lead us nobly to war.

Cuverville, June 6

I have received, since the Hitler crisis has been raging in Germany, a dozen solicitations from different groups whose objects, it would seem from their declarations, are the same, so that one might properly wish to see them get together and not let their efforts be scattered. Having the possibility of declaring myself when I want to and in the way that seems suitable to me, I systematically refuse to countersign any declaration whatever of which I myself have not written the text. There is in this no desire whatever to set myself apart; and I very well understand how important it is, in any occasion of this sort, to group together, to unite; but I do not believe I have yet encountered a single proclamation of this type which I can agree with completely, which did not distort my thought on some point.

All interested opinions are suspect to me. I like to be able to think freely and begin to fear being taken in as soon as some advantage comes to me from the opinion I am professing. It is as if I were accepting a bribe.

By mood and by temperament, I could not be less revolutionary. Furthermore, I personally have every reason to be pleased with the state of things. But, you see, what bothers me is precisely that: being in a position to be pleased with it; telling myself that if you were not born on the right side, you would perhaps not think the same way; having to think: if you are a conservative, it is your advantages that you want to conserve and hand on.

Vittel, June

Lamentable hideousness of this petit-bourgeois crowd. Not a single creature whose existence one would want to prolong. Cannot manage to convince myself that I am suffering from anything that people come to treat here.

I have already said so: I know nothing about politics. If they interest me, they do so as a Balzac novel does, with their passions, their pettinesses, their lies, their compromises. Everything is debased, even the noblest causes, as soon as politics gets mixed up with them and takes them in hand. . . .

I have a tendency to underestimate my merits. This is, it seems, so rare a mania that it appears suspect. People see in it pretense, hypocrisy, affectation.

The result perhaps merely of low blood-pressure.

Vittel, July 4

. . . if only I were not bothered by: . . . *feeling on the right side.*

It is easy for me to endure the scorn of the rich; but the look of an outcast enters my heart more deeply than . . .

This state of things has become unbearable to me, all the more unbearable because I am profiting from it, because my brother is suffering from it and I am not. Unbearable this thought: what is today will be, and nothing can change anything.

August 14

It seems to me that the World Congress in preparation must pay quite special attention to honoring the young people who refuse to take part in the game of war. English or American students, French schoolteachers, "conscientious objectors" of all countries; to clearing them of that perfidious accusation of cowardice by which people try to discredit them and disqualify their conduct. It is important to let them know, in reply to such calumnies, that we give them our esteem, often even our admiration,

* A popular spa.

knowing full well that it requires more real courage to set oneself, in isolation, against a collective enthusiasm than to fall into line, even if the ranks are marching to face death; knowing all the initiative that this personal courage involves, and that it leads, not only to material sanctions, but also to those of public opinion—for some people all the more fearful.

"Put everything at stake, risk one's life, give it on purpose for a revolution, so that a step forward may be taken—what is greater? But for these mad wars in which men are sacrificed, not even for illusions, not even, perhaps, intentionally, for special interests . . . but for a sclerotic, inhuman, soulless system that is turning in the same groove, that is taking a tailspin, leading the world to some unimaginable slaughter, to some haggard and empty rage—for such wars, who will convince me that I am a madman or a coward if I say: No?"

I do not hide from myself the fact that, faced with the Hitlerian threat, such declarations may seem to some particularly inopportune; I, on the contrary, believe them more useful than ever at the moment when the nationalist fury of certain countries is becoming particularly provocative, and may run the risk of dragging neighboring countries into a similar madness through fear or emulation.

August 29

Those last lines scarcely satisfy me, and I am quite aware of all that remains to be said. The question is rather: Does all that the conservatives are protecting deserve to be saved?

It seems to me quite useless to reply that the best will always survive the shipwreck; for nothing seems less certain to me; and that confidence implies a mysticism that I guard myself against elsewhere. I fear quite the contrary: that in this case the good may be swept away with the worst. . . .

It seems to me that no one has pointed out a thing that seems strange to say the least: that "mysticism" today is on the side of those who profess atheism and irreligion. For it is as a religion that the Communist doctrine exalts and nourishes the enthusiasm of the young people of today. Their very action implies a belief; and if they transfer their ideal from heaven to earth, as I do with them, it is nonetheless in the name of an ideal that they are struggling and will, if need be, sacrifice themselves. And this is what frightens me: even that Communist religion, even it, involves a dogma, an orthodoxy, texts to which one refers, an abdication of the critical spirit. . . . This is too much. I very well understand the need of appealing to an authority and of rallying the masses around it. But at this point I quit; or at least, if I remain with them, it is because my very heart and reason advise me to do so, and not because *"it is written . . ."* Whether the text invoked be by Marx or Lenin, I cannot abide by it unless my heart and my reason approve it. If I have escaped from the authority of Aristotle or the Apostle Paul, it was not in order to fall under theirs. Yet I recognize the necessity of a credo, to bundle together individual wills; but my adhesion to that credo has no value unless it is freely consented to. I add that, in the immense majority of cases, so-called freedom of thought remains utterly illusory. And I understand as well that desire to unify thought which is today tempting Hitler, in imitation of Mussolini, but which can be achieved only at the price of what a frightful impoverishment of thought! The specific and individual value yields to some collective value or other, which then ceases to have any intellectual value at all.

September 2

. . . since when has the experience of history been of any use? And to whom? What is the meaning of an "experiment"* that cannot be verified and repeated, of which the elements elude our precise knowledge and in which, when the omelette has turned out badly, one can never really know whether it is the fault of the cook, of the frying-pan, of the butter, or of the eggs?

How wise is everything Valéry says about history! And how weak the arguments that Madelin opposed to him yesterday in *L'Echo de Paris*! To neglect the teaching of history, he says in substance, amounts to refusing the advice of a guide who, already knowing the road, would warn, etc. . . . As if one could ever know in advance what the new dangers would be! As if the road were ever the same, and the same he who enters upon it! As if the future ever reproduced the past! As if the difficulty did not come precisely from this: that one is constantly playing a game ever new, with cards whose value has not yet been tested!

Cuverville, October 27

I have loved Racine's lines above all other literary productions. I admire Shakespeare tremendously, but with Racine I feel an emotion that Shakespeare never gives me: that of perfection. Jean S., in a very interesting

* The French word *expérience* means both "experience" and "experiment."

discussion, reproaches Racine's characters for not going on living once the curtain has fallen, whereas those of Shakespeare, he says, and very justly, appear for a moment before the footlights, but we feel that they do not end there and that we could find them again, beyond the stage. But it is precisely that exact limitation that I like, that non-protruding from the frame, that sharpness of outline. Shakespeare, no doubt, is more human; but something quite different is involved here: it is the triumph of a sublime fitness, an enchanting harmony in which everything enters in and contributes, which fully satisfies at one and the same time the intelligence, the heart, and the senses. Man and nature, in his windswept plays, all poetry laughs, cries, vibrates in Shakespeare; Racine is at the summit of art.

December 5

"Besides, it's very simple," said that excellent lady, at that excellent luncheon yesterday. . . . "Besides, it's very simple; if I didn't have servants I couldn't knit any more for the poor."

December 14

You were told: The fear of God is the beginning of wisdom; then, with God missing, the fear remained. Understand today that wisdom begins where fear ends, that it begins with the revolt of Prometheus.

You were told, you let yourself be told, that the first important thing is to believe. The first important thing is to doubt.

There is not one of these conversions in which I do not discover some inadmissible secret motivation: fatigue, fear, blighted hope, sickness, impotence sexual or sentimental.

Today people call "constructive spirits" the prudent restorers of ruins.

For too long now I have dared think only in a whisper; and this is a way of lying.

1934 *Manosque, March 30*

It has already occurred to me two or three times in my life to envisage the possibility of suicide; but never, I believe, with so much force and clarity as that evening during the little time between the Champs-Elysées and the rue Vaneau in the taxi that dropped me at my door.

What does this gentleman want, who is approaching me while I am paying the driver?

"Monsieur Gide?"

I reply with a grunt, but he insists: "You are Monsieur André Gide, aren't you?"

At this hour of the night in the now deserted street, what can he want of me?

"It is just that," he says to me, "the rumor of your suicide has been all over Paris this evening; I am a reporter on *Le Petit Journal* and, like many of my colleagues, I had come to get the details. . . ."

July 14

That Russian lady thinks she has conquered me by telling me the tremendous pleasure she has got from my . . . *Symphonie inachevée!** But the book of mine she prefers is my *Faux-Monnayeurs,* which she has reread so often that she almost knows it by heart. Yet from what she says of it, it appears that she is thinking of my *Caves du Vatican.* Fame very rarely offers an unwrinkled bed for our vanity to stretch out on in comfort.

July 25

. . . For a long time it can no longer be a question of works of art. In order to listen to new, indistinct chords one would have to be able to ignore all the wailing and lamentation. There is almost nothing left in me that does not sympathize. Wherever I turn my eyes, I see nothing around me but distress. Anyone who remains a contemplative today gives evidence of either an inhuman philosophy, or a monstrous blindness.

How cleverly my laziness puts forward all these fine sentiments! A flattering shelter that would be overturned at once by a new burst of health.

---

* "Unfinished Symphony."

It is not becoming to lay on the back of virtue the weariness of old age. The table of successive renunciations would not be without eloquence, if one could get oneself to make such admissions without self-indulgence.

July 26

That we are to go beyond communism may well be. But first of all we must reach it. The "beyond" will come later. . . .

July 31

I wrote, in the past: "It is a duty to be happy." I may still think it; but that duty is becoming more difficult for me each day.

August 1

The young Czech Communist who comes to see me congratulates me on certain pages of *Prétextes* (*Nationalisme et littérature,* concerning Ricardo's theories) which, he says, "are impregnated with a pure Marxist spirit."—So much the better! So be it! But, I beg of you, if I am a Marxist, let me be so without knowing it.

Prague, August 5

Very strange city; made somewhat ugly by non-indigenous contributions, a sort of American or Soviet modernism: signs, advertisements. After the elegance and luxury of the Karlsbad shops, the ugliness and poverty of the shop windows here surprise; but what a large number of bookshops, and so well supplied! Wonderful look of the city, the first day, in the rain. Glorious, painful, tragic city; widely spread out in time and space; a sort of mystical vehemence keeps it in motion and stirs it up.

Despite the bad weather, the animation of the boulevard where our hotel is, at night. Mute gathering of a crowd around an unfortunate newsdealer who is crying, in a recess of a wall, turning his back to life, his face hidden in his upraised arm, an image of the deepest despair. . . . That other one who lifts a metal grille to recover a still-lighted cigarette butt that a passer-by has just thrown away.

August 11

I launch, with Stoisy, into *Die Raüber.** Absurdity in pathos, uncontrol, lack of moderation could not possibly be pushed further; and this without even the excuse of verse. But how representative it is! It is probably natural to Hitler's people to feel at home in the frantic.

* Schiller's play *The Robbers.*

August 15

The wound one must not allow to heal over, but which must always remain painful and bleeding, that wound inflicted by contact with frightful reality.

August 19

When the nationalists in our country work to make France hateful to (because hating) the people of other nations, it is as a Frenchman that I suffer. I should like a noble, likable, generous France, and am unconvinced that a politics inspired by noble sentiments would necessarily be that of a dupe. Less bitter, less vindictive, the Treaty of Versailles would have been more clever, and all Europe would suffer less from it today. Each state is now bound to the selfish interests that then prevailed, and the cruel consequence of an initial mistake, once committed, was our having to stick to it. It is in the name of honor (of false honor) that one gives oneself away. No one ever gives himself away so thoroughly as he who makes it a point of honor to give himself away.

1935   *March 8*

I feel today, seriously, painfully, that *inferiority*—of never having had to earn my bread, of never having had to work out of absolute need. But I have always had such a great love of work that that would probably not have spoiled my happiness in it. Besides, that is not what I mean. But a time will come when this will be looked upon as a deficiency. There is something in it for which the richest imagination cannot provide a substitute, a certain kind of profound education that nothing, later on, can ever replace. A time is coming when the bourgeois will feel in a state of inferiority compared with the mere workman. This time has already come for some.

March 28

. . . Fine function to assume: that of *disseminator of unrest.*

With this so imperfect world, which could be so beautiful, shame on him who is satisfied! The *so be it,* as soon as it favors carelessness or neglect, is impious.

Wherever I go and whatever I do, it is always out of season. But I like it that way. Sole guest of a gloomy grand hotel (gloomy simply because it is empty) which will not begin to fill up before July. I shall be gone well before. I should like this country if only I could find someone to fall in love with; but I search the countryside in vain. . . .

At this Writers' Congress so many delegates from so many countries would still like to speak, ought to speak. But what can be done when faced with the eloquence of certain orators who go on at length (only to call for, it so happens, to insist on, everyone's right to speak)? The oratorical excess of a few reduces the others to silence. I am thinking in particular of that woman who represents Greece and who has been pointed out to me. I am told that she is waiting her turn, waiting in vain. She made the long trip, I am told, in fourth class—a painful trip, painfully paid for by a group of workers, her comrades. . . . It is most likely she that I see at a distance, on the platform, in the second row, wearing a saffron-colored peplum, seated alone. At once I approach her and, putting into my voice all the sympathy I can: "It is fortunate, comrade, that Greece is represented here."

Then she, turning her beautiful face toward me, and in an undertone: "I am India."

What sensitive souls do not like is red. They have a horror of the shedding of blood, of shots. Let a few men suddenly be killed in a fray, and they are shocked and all at once what a row in the papers! They can bear more easily the fact that thousands of starving people should perish, but little by little, without a sound, and not too close to them. And, moreover, "the statistics are most likely exaggerated"; and *their* paper says nothing of it.

It is good that the voice of the indigent, too long stifled, should manage to make itself heard. But I cannot consent to listen to nothing but that voice. Man does not cease to interest me when he ceases to be miserable; quite the contrary. That it is important to aid him in the beginning goes without saying, like the plant it is essential to water at first; but this is in order to get it to flower, and that is what interests me.

August 4

Oh, if only, when they stopped suffering, they knew how to become men! Alas, how many of them owe their dignity, their claim on our sympathy, merely to their misfortune!

On certain days boredom can suddenly swoop down upon me like a vulture, with the force of a passion almost resembling hatred. And the whole world suddenly seems to me like the gray wall of a lantern no longer lighted up from within. And I think with horror of all those for whom this condition, so fleeting with me, is constant. They are the hardest to help (for there are such), those who owe only to themselves the dreadful impossibility of being happy.

August 7   •

To all the outcasts, those bent under the yoke and heavy-laden, thirsting, sore at heart, aching—assurance of a compensatory afterlife! However chimeric it may be, would you dare rob them of that hope? Yes, if it is to tell them: even "here below." Either leave them eternal life, or give them the revolution.

Or rather: rob them of eternal life, and you will have the revolution.

August 15

I couldn't get in at the rue Vaneau; the safety-bolt kept me out and I did not want to disturb the concierge at so early an hour.

I went out again into the still-empty streets, filled with that heady feeling of superiority which comes from being out before everyone else.

Today is a holiday; everyone will get up late. . . .

I am noting all this in order to re-accustom this notebook to its role of journal, for it has long been nothing but a cemetery for stillborn articles.

September 17

. . . today I am paying for my refusals of former years, of that long time when everything I knew to be transitory and belonging to politics and history seemed to me unworthy of real attention. The influence of Mallarmé urged me in this direction. I came under his influence without being aware of it, for it merely encouraged me in my natural tendency . . .

The Refugee   *October 28*

He rings just as I was about to go out. I have an appointment with the dentist; am already late. No one to open the door and tell him: "Monsieur is not in." I come lacing up my shoes. The refugee begins an endless story to explain to me that his case ought to interest me particularly. He takes out of a leather briefcase an album containing many signatures of celebrities, urges me to add mine; this is odious to me. When he hears me sniffle, he thinks he is showing kindness by exclaiming: "Have you a cold?" He would like to move me to pity, but I haven't time to be stirred. "Come back another day; you see that today I cannot . . ." "I had already come yesterday." Now that he has me, he wants to take advantage; this is awkward of him; he only succeeds in irritating me; he feels this and wastes a little more time excusing himself. All the hope he had put in my advice, my help, my aid, is deflated. His voice trembles, he tries to find words. . . .

And all day long I carry about my remorse for that insufficient help, for my abruptness, for my impatience. If I had only taken down the poor fellow's name and address, as I generally do. But no, no way of making up. . . .

Intolerable *moral feeling* of deficiency, of indigence (I am the indigent one in this case).

October 30

No, it would be false to say that my opinions, my thoughts, have not changed, and it would be dishonest of me to claim it. But the great, the very important change is this: I had thought, until quite recently, that the important thing first was to change man, men, each man; and that this was where one had to begin. That is why I used to write that the ethical question was more important to me than the social question.

Today I am letting myself be convinced that man himself cannot change unless social conditions first urge him and help him to do so—so that it is to them we must first pay attention.

1936 *Cuverville, May 16*

The annoying habit I have recently assumed of publishing numerous pages from this journal in the *N.R.F.* (partly from impatience and because I was no longer writing anything else) has gradually detached me from it as from an indiscreet friend to whom one cannot trust anything without his repeating it at once. How much more abundant my confidence would have been if it could have remained posthumous! And even while writing this, I imagine it already printed, and calculate the reader's disapproval. At times I get to the point of thinking that the absence of any echo to my writings, for a long time, allowed to them everything that constituted their value. It was important to assure my words a survival that would allow them to reach future readers. I am extraordinarily embarrassed by this immediate repercussion (approbation no less than blame) which will henceforth greet everything that falls from my pen. Ah, the happy time when I was not listened to! And how well one speaks as long as one speaks in the desert! To be sure, it was certainly to be heard that I spoke, but not right away. The odes of Keats, the *Fleurs du mal,* still remain as if enveloped in that silence of their contemporaries, in which their eloquence is amplified for us.

May 17

Too constantly clothed, it is odd the number of people in whom the mere idea of nakedness immediately awakens lewd echoes.

Paris, September 3*

. . . A tremendous, a dreadful confusion. Dined with Schiffrin, who is trying to cling to me and find some succor in my conversation. He speaks to me of his having been deceived, disappointed by the U.S.S.R., and Guilloux as well; relates the long conversation they had on the way back. I argue: the words "deception" and "disappointment" seem to be inexact; but I do not know just what to suggest in their place.

September 4

Yesterday I saw Malraux again. He has just arrived from Madrid, to which he returns in two days.† When I arrive at the rue du Bac, Clara takes me aside. She is a bit calmer than yesterday. Little Flo is playing near

---

* Gide's trip to Russia took place from June to August of this year; see the selections from *Return from the U.S.S.R.,* pp. 825–832.

† Malraux was fighting for the Loyalists in Spain as an aviator.

us, as she did yesterday. (She is given the biggest dahlia of a bouquet, which she pulls apart to make a "salad.")

And, while André soaks in a bath: "Do you know what he said upon arriving? That since I had left him he had been able to *act* much more."

"Does that mean there was a scene?"

"Oh, no! But he needs to detach himself from everything. . . . Why, when he saw the child, he exclaimed: 'What! the child is here?' "

"He didn't know it?"

"No, I had taken care not to tell him. I knew it would upset him to see her again. He needs to feel his heart free."

"He is not annoyed that I should come?"

"Oh no! I had told him that you would come at half past six. And just now he asked me: 'Why doesn't Gide come?' He needs to talk. I am so grateful to you for coming! He needs to pull himself together; to resume contact with . . . something else."

She told me that, for some time now, he has been sleeping no more than four hours a night. Yet when I see him, he doesn't seem to me too tired. His face is even less marked by nervous tics than ordinarily, and his hands are not too feverish. He talks with that extraordinary volubility which often makes him so hard for me to follow. He depicts their situation, which he would consider desperate if the enemy forces were not so divided. His hope is to gather together the governmental forces; now he has power to do so. His intention, as soon as he gets back, is to organize the attack on Oviedo.

September 5

See Malraux again. Clara M. receives me alone at first. Then the three of us go to dine together (and very well!), place des Victoires, at a restaurant where he had already taken me. And for two hours I am in awe before his dazzling and staggering flow of words. . . .

Shopping at the Bon Marché, where I lunched while reading the report of the Moscow trial (which the *Journal de Moscou* of August 25 gives in detail)—with an indescribable sense of *malaise*. What to think of those sixteen men under indictment accusing themselves, and each one in almost the same terms, and singing the praises of a regime and a man for the suppression of which they once risked their lives?

. . . when social preoccupations began to encumber my head and my heart, I stopped writing anything of value. It is not fair to say that I remained insensitive to such questions; but my position in regard to them was the only one that an artist can reasonably take, the one he must strive to defend. As for Christ's "Judge not," I interpret it also from the artist's point of view.

September 6

I wander for a moment on the boulevard Montparnasse, then take a taxi to the Cinéma Edouard VII, but at the entrance the stills from the film discourage me from going in. I enter for a moment a little movie house on rue Caumartin where they show "comic" films at two or three francs a ticket, and see some painfully loony and lamentably stupid shorts. Then I wander interminably, a prey to fierce boredom, gloomy and feeling capable of the worst stupidities. Everything seems frightful. Everywhere I feel the catastrophe coming. Anxious not to spend too much (for the condition of my account at the *N.R.F.,* received yesterday, seriously alarmed me), I enter, after long hesitations, a dull little restaurant where I am writing this while finishing a table d'hôte dinner considerably worse than mediocre, which it will certainly take me an enormous time to digest.

Nice, October 2

Ceased to keep this notebook up to date all the time I was at Cuverville, entirely absorbed by writing my reflections on the U.S.S.R. I wrote them directly and rapidly, and now find a good deal that needs rewriting. . . .

1937   *Paris, May 7*

Yesterday evening I knocked about wildly from Clichy to Pigalle, then from Pigalle to Clichy, not making up my mind to dine until nine o'clock; then starting out again in pursuit of adventure, of pleasure, of surprise, and finding nothing but dullness, banality, and ugliness. Took the *métro* to get home; done in; but I was counting on fatigue to assure me a passable night; and, altogether, I succeeded.

What else did I want to say? Everything, now, seems to me a repetition. . . . And that preface to Thomas Mann's *Letter* that I promised to write!* . . . I want to cry "Time Out!" and quit the game. My worktable (if I dare use the expression) is not more encumbered than my

---

* Mann's letter in reply to the Dean of the Faculty of Philosophy of the University of Bonn, which had withdrawn his honorary degree.

brain. I should have held to my ethical system; it was good; but receptivity was a part of it; and now everything is upset to such a point, overturned and mixed up, that I haven't the heart for the task of putting everything back in place and that, and that too. We are entering a new era, that of confusion.

Went to meet Elisabeth Herbart (back from London) at the Gare Saint-Lazare. Nothing is more odious to me. With my infirmity of not recognizing anyone, I drift about, bumping into anyone whatever with both heart and head, haggard, bewildered, and naturally I missed her. Returned home exasperated, ill.

May 8

. . . I rail against the bores who besiege me, against the petty daily obligations; and, as soon as I am free of them and at liberty, do not know what to do; and would like to sleep, to sleep still more, all day long. I do not even have any eyes for spring, which is going on without me, before I have finished correcting my proofs. I have forgotten how to live. . . . I used to know so well!

Cuverville, May 13

Unfaithful; I have not been able to force myself to keep this notebook up to date. And yet I was counting on it to get me *out of my indifference.*

I have given my book to the printer; I have already received the proofs. I ought to feel liberated. I keep repeating this to myself; but all those preoccupations of yesterday still inhabit me and I take no interest in anything else. I cannot manage to disengage my mind. As soon as I am not bound by some precise occupation, I feel vague, wandering, unemployed. I should like to forget everything; live for a long time among naked Negroes, people whose language I didn't know and who didn't know who I am; and fornicate savagely, silently, at night, with anyone whatever, on the sand. . . .

I see nothing but distress, disorder, and madness everywhere; justice mocked, the right betrayed, falsehood. And I wonder what life could still bring me that would matter. What does all this mean? What is it all going to lead to, and the rest? Into what an absurd mess humanity is sinking! How and where to escape?

But how beautiful the last rays were this evening, gilding the beech grove! . . . Alas, for the first time I am not associating myself with the spring! And now, those pathetic songs of birds, in the night. . . .

May 14

I did well to write those lines, yesterday. It purged me. This evening I feel quite reconciled with the universe and with myself.

June 28

I see less well and my eyes become tired more quickly. I also hear less well. I tell myself that it is probably not a bad thing that this earth should withdraw from us progressively, this earth one would otherwise have too much trouble leaving—that one would have too much trouble leaving all at once. The wonderful thing would be, at the same time, to get progressively nearer to . . . something else.

June 30

Nothing more useless than that thirst for education which still torments me. If I could break with that habit of thinking that my time is wasted as soon as I remain unoccupied! That unrelieved recourse to the thought of others, partly through fear of being left alone with my own, is a form of laziness. I even come to congratulate myself on the weakness of my eyes, which will soon deny me these everlasting readings.

July 2

The pressure of the accumulated liquor demanded licentious images from the brain. I have great trouble today imagining anything exalting. Reality must provoke me to it; my pretense will not take the initiative.

July 12

Invited to the last rehearsal of Cocteau's play.

At the entrance, the super-elegant aspect of the audience made me flee; the smiles especially, the bows. . . . The next day I read in the papers that I arrived too late and had to leave, not having found a seat.

Sorrento, August 5

The buildings, the walls along the roads, are covered with inscriptions in huge characters; appeals to the Duce and quotations from him, perfect slogans, wonderfully chosen and likely to galvanize young people, to *en-roll* them. Out of all of them, these three words: *Believe. Obey. Fight* return most frequently, as if conscious of summing up the very spirit of the Fascist doctrine. This permits a certain clarification of ideas, and at the same time points out to me the "positions" of anti-fascism. And nothing leads to greater confusion than the adoption of this slogan by communism itself, which claims to be still anti-Fascist, but is so only politically, for it too asks the Party faithful to *believe, obey,* and *fight,* without inquiry, without criticism, with blind submission. Three-quarters of the Italian inscriptions would be just as suitable to the walls of Moscow. I am told that one can triumph over an adversary only on his own ground, only by using his own arms; that it is proper to fight sword with sword (something of which, by the way, I am in no way convinced). It is proper first and foremost to fight the spirit with the spirit, and this is what is scarcely ever done any more. Historians of the future will examine how and why, the end disappearing behind the means, the Communist spirit ceased to be opposed to the Fascist spirit, ceased even to be differentiated from it.

August 9

The need Pascal has of making man despair and of undermining his joys for the sole purpose of precipitating his conversion, that systematic depreciation of the gratuitous, of art ("what a vanity is painting . . ."), of everything that distracts man from the necessity of death—all that strikes me as much more fruitless than pleasure itself. How much wiser seems to me Hebbel's witticism: "What is the best thing the rat can do when caught in a trap?—Eat the cheese."

. . . It is odd that Catholicism, so ready to denounce as pride a man's first wanderings from the teachings of the Church, does not deign to see that same pride in resistance and refractoriness to natural laws. . . . That he [Pascal] should moan is all very fine; his moans are very beautiful; but that he should want to force us to moan; that he should go so far as to write: "I can approve only those who seek in moans and tears"—is not this enough to make us exclaim that we approve only of those who find; who find with shouts of joy?

September 3

What more would I like to express? That this superabundance of written matter, of printed matter, stifles me and that in Paris, where it all piles up, overflowing the insufficient bookshelves onto tables, chairs, the floor even and everywhere, my thought can no longer move or breathe. I am like Pompeii under the rain of ashes; and do not want to add to it by writing myself. When I happen at times to open one of these new books, it always seems to me that the tiny bit of truth and newness it brings would be improved by being said more briefly—or that it might not be said at all. So that when the desire to write seizes me, I hesitate and wonder: is it really worth saying? Have not others said it before me? Have I not already said it myself? And I keep silent.

October 12

English horticulturists send us their catalogues. Under "Sweet Peas" one reads descriptions of astounding varieties. One is named: *Venus;* another that is even better: *Venus improved.*

October 25

All these young people from whom I receive letters begging encouragement or counsel could hardly imagine (that is their excuse) the time it takes to answer them. They imagine even less that the book they are thereby keeping you from writing might answer them and many others at the same time. But each of them would like an individual reply to questions that are not in the least individual.

Cuverville, October 30

What keeps me from writing now is not lassitude, it is disgust.

December 15

"The imagination imitates. It is the critical spirit that creates," said Wilde. . . . You can imagine my astonishment, my joy, in finding this same profound and fecund truth quite unexpectedly while leafing through the *Œuvres complètes* of Diderot—and enunciated by him in almost exactly the same terms: "The imagination creates nothing, it *imitates.*" I was pleased to be able to quote this sentence alongside Wilde's "paradox" in an article on "The Abandonment of the Subject in the Plastic Arts." This morning, I open the first number of the sumptuous magazine *Verve,* in which the article appears, and my eyes fall at once on this sentence: "The imagination creates nothing, it *invents.*" A zealous proofreader (too zealous) thought he was doing the right thing to correct a text that was obviously faulty in his eyes.

It is related that Rosny, exasperated by the typographical errors that the printers made or let slip by, wrote a vengeful article entitled *"Mes Coquilles."* When he opened his newspaper the next day, he read with stupefaction, in heavy type, this odd title: "MES COUILLES." A negligent or malicious printer had let the *q* drop out. . . .*

I am writing this to console myself.

---

* *"Mes Coquilles"* means "My Misprints," whereas *"Mes Couilles"* means "My Balls."

(Summer 1937)

In Marx's writings I stifle. Something is lacking, some ozone or other that is essential to keep my mind breathing. Yet I have read four volumes of *Das Kapital* patiently, assiduously, studiously; plus, from end to end, the volume of extracts very well chosen by Paul Nizan. Of Engels, the *Anti-Dühring*. Plus a number of writings inspired by and on the subject of Marxism. I have read all this with more constancy and care than I brought to any other study; and more effort too; with no other desire than to let myself be convinced, to submit even, and to learn. And each time I came away aching with fatigue, my intelligence bruised as by instruments of torture. I went about repeating to myself: you must; knowing full well that I was not looking for pleasures, which have nothing to do with Marxism. But today I think that what especially bothers me in it is the theory itself, with everything, if not exactly irrational, at least artificial (I was about to say artful), fallacious, and inhuman that it contains.

I think that a great deal of Marx's prestige comes from the fact that he is difficult of access, so that Marxism involves an initiation and is generally known only through mediators. It is the Mass in Latin. When one does not understand, one bows down. Throughout all of Marx's writings (with perhaps the sole exception of the *Communist Manifesto*—and even there . . .), his thought remains scattered, diffuse, in a nebulous state; never does it coalesce or achieve density. Aside from the two famous slogans—"Proletarians, unite," and "It is not a question of understanding the world, but of changing it" (wonderful formula)—one cannot manage, going from page to page and from chapter to chapter, to find a sentence that stands and isolates itself from a confused magma. And the success of Marxism comes likewise from the fact that, not letting itself be gripped by any such projection, its enormous mass escapes seizure and attack, too nebulous to crumble and weather. Blows simply sink in and never seem to carry.

I care very little whether or not my writings conform to Marxism. That "fear of the Index" that I used to express in the past, the absurd fear of being found in error by the purists, bothered me greatly for a long time, to such an extent that I no longer dared write. What I am saying will seem very childish. But I don't care. I am not interested in showing myself off to advantage, and I believe that what I am most willing to expose is my weaknesses. But now I am free of that sterilizing fear. And that fear has taught me a great deal; yes, much more than Marxism itself. The discipline I imposed on myself for three years has not been profitless; but now I find greater advantage in liberating myself from it than in continuing to submit. That plunge into Marxism allowed me to see the essential thing it was lacking.

Did it require the collapse of the U.S.S.R. to lead me to think this? It is the illustration of my own disappointment. And one first tries to tell oneself: it failed through infidelity. Then one again hears ring out the sinister words: "There has not been a revolution that has not. . . ." *

Oh, how right you were to see in my coming to communism a matter of sentiment! but how wrong you were not to understand that I was right! According to you, the only communism that matters is the one that is reached through theory. You speak as theoreticians. To be sure, theory is useful. But without warmth of heart and without love it bruises the very ones it claims to save. Let us beware of those who want to apply communism coldly, of those who want, at whatever cost, to plow straight furrows on a curving earth, of those who prefer to each man the idea they have formed of humanity.

All the same, the U.S.S.R. really did something. Despite the present ebb-tide, something of it will remain. And if one can think that the revolutionary movement in Russia brought about by reaction the Fascist resistance of other countries, it is not paradoxical to say that it was Bolshevism and the great fear people had of it that determined the Fascist governments to make protective social reforms, to which they would never have consented otherwise; a way of disarming the adversary. Even the Church saw that it was in her interest to pay more attention to social questions, and that it was her neglect of her duties that had so singularly reinforced the legitimacy of her enemies' claims. It was essential to take away Bolshevism's justification; to put it out of countenance was the best way to oppose it.

It is noteworthy that certain pure theoreticians of Marxism expect, hope, demand of society, of the social state, what they utterly refuse to begin by achieving in themselves. For the Christian, the revolution takes place

* ". . . that has not, in the end, resulted in a reinforcement of the bureaucratic machine" (Lenin, 1917, cited by Gide earlier).

within himself. I should like to be able to say: within himself *first;* but most often that inner revolution is enough for him; while the outer revolution is enough for the others. I should like these two efforts, these two results, to be complementary, and I believe that they are often rather artificially opposed.

A constant need of reconciliation torments me; it is a failing of my mind, although it is perhaps a good quality of my heart. I should like to marry heaven and hell, *à la* Blake; reduce oppositions, and most often refuse to see anything but misunderstandings in the most ruinous and fatal antagonisms. "Individualism and communism . . . how can you claim to reconcile those adversaries, even in yourself?" my friend Martin du Gard said to me laughingly. "They are water and fire." From their marriage is born steam.

What a sorry need of hatred I feel everywhere today! a need of opposing all things that ought to understand one another, complete one another, fecundate one another, join together! . . .

I had felt these conflicts at work within me before meeting them on the outside. I was aware of them, and it was through personal experience that I knew how much one wears oneself down, and how uselessly, in the struggle; a struggle that I had long encouraged between the very opposed elements of my nature, until the day when I said to myself: what is the good of it? when I sought, not struggle and partial triumph, but accord; in order to see at last that the more widely separated are the elements of the agreement, the richer is the harmony. And likewise, in a state, that dream of the crushing of one party by another is a dark, a gloomy utopia; that dream of a totalitarian state in which the subjugated minorities could no longer make themselves heard; in which (and this is worse) each and every one would think the same. There can be no more question of harmony when the choir sings in unison.

1938   *Kaolak**

Pleasant house in which we are camping. Everything in it is as clean as can be, doubtless; for how can one keep from being invaded by black beetles —or cockroaches. I always confuse them, as I do porpoises with dolphins.

Agonizing night. Went to bed early, very sleepy; but great difficulty

* Senegal. Gide made semi-official trips to French West Africa in 1936 and 1938.

breathing. Stomach churning; never again take that frightful soft and sticky meat which is called "fish" in this country.

At midnight I decide to have recourse to my medication. Badly closed tubes, which open and scatter the lozenges in my valise. In the bathroom, where I go to get some distilled water (but a mistake was made: the bottle contains syrup), I surprise cockroaches in the act of copulating. I thought they were wingless; but some (probably the males), unfold enormous trembling wings without taking flight. When I am ready to go back to bed, I notice rising above the top of the wardrobe opposite my bed the erect head of a python, which soon becomes just an iron rod.

February 11

Left Kankan at 5:40 a.m., our special train scheduled twenty minutes ahead of the regular train.

Reached Mamou at 5:30 p.m. I am paid military honors. The people of the administration in dress uniform, with all medals flying; in my colored shirt and khaki trousers, lamentably untidy, I feel I am playing *The Inspector General.* Strive to make up for the undress of my costume by an excessive dignity in bearing.

The fact is that many enterprises here can prosper only with a system rather close to slavery.

Paris, March 12

. . . I went nearby to pick up Robert Levesque, whom I had not seen since my return from French West Africa; invited him to go with me to the Jardin des Plantes, where I wanted to see my chameleon again. Unable to feed him properly, I had turned him over to the vivarium, where he is stuffed with cockroaches for lack of flies, rather rare in this season. "Timothy," the only one of his species, cuts a very elegant figure beside two enormous chameleons from Madagascar, the color of cinders. He immediately decked himself in grass-green, spotted with black; this is his party dress.

I feel again that extraordinary serenity which Butler said he experienced in the contemplation of big pachyderms, which I enjoy indistinctly in this place where all human activity is devoted to the study of animals and plants. Probably the way of communing with God that most satisfies me is that of the naturalists (I do not know that of the astronomers). It seems to me that the divinity they approach is the least subject to caution.

Chatted almost an hour with Auguste Chevalier, with great profit and pleasure.

As soon as I return to that atmosphere of the natural sciences, I tell myself again: I missed my vocation; it is a naturalist that I should have liked to be, should have been.

———————————————————————————————— *

* This double ruled line, which appears without commentary in the French edition, marks the death of Mme André Gide during the spring of 1938.

LETTERS, SPEECHES, AND PANEL DISCUSSION

from LITTERATURE ENGAGEE

1932–1936

To the Officers of the Association
of Revolutionary Writers and Artists

December 13, 1932

No, dear comrades. The clearest result of such a commitment would be to prevent me, very soon, from writing anything more at all. I have declared as loudly and as directly as I could my sympathy for the U.S.S.R. and for all that she represents in our eyes, in our hearts—despite all the imperfections of which her enemies remind us. I believe, and with no reservations in my particular case, that my assistance would be of more genuine benefit to your cause—to *our* cause—if I were to give it freely, and if I am known *not* to be a member. It may be that I am wrong, that I need only the chance to talk with some of you to be persuaded; but I must admit that, up to the present time, I have not been able to comprehend the practical intent of your association. To write, from now on, according to the "principles" of a "charter" (I am using the expressions of your circular) would be to strip whatever I should write from now on of all real value; or, more precisely, it would mean—for me—sterility. I beg you not to take what I am saying as a mere desire for personal protection, for safety. You have already seen me "compromise" myself far enough. But those who read me today—and on whom I may exercise some influence (whether intentionally or otherwise), and may thus lead toward your side —they would no longer even listen to me as soon as they knew I was thinking and writing to order. . . .

Most considerately and cordially yours,
André Gide

FASCISM

(Opening address to the Association of Revolutionary Writers and Artists, Paris, March 21, 1933)

Ladies and Gentlemen,
Dear comrades,

I am happy to be here with you, and to bear witness by my presence to my sympathy for this group of writers and artists, among whom I already number many of my friends, and in all of whom I am interested.

The one thing I am least is an orator; you cannot know how unqualified I feel to preside. I should like to be permitted, after having said a few words, to leave the podium and hide myself among the ordinary listeners.

A great and common anguish has called us together, an anguish caused by recent tragic events in Germany. This recapture of control by the Nationalists (which some people are now hailing) brings with it the risk, through fear, through emulation, through our need to outbid them, of precipitating a dreadful conflict. Some people desire this; or, if they do not desire it openly, they are behaving in such a way as to render it inevitable. What unites us here, I believe, is the conviction that only an allegiance superior to that of nations, an interest common to different peoples, one that unites them instead of opposing them, can turn back this conflict. The social struggle is the same in all countries, and the men who are sent to fight for reasons they do not understand (and which they would often reject if they did understand), these men have each one the same deeper common concern, which they are only now beginning to recognize. The soldiers who died in the course of the Great War were mistaken. They had been persuaded that they were fighting "The War To End All Wars"; and by that absurd slogan, whose inanity, alas! we should have recognized, they were invited to make the sacrifice of their lives. Who can say how many of them would have agreed to that heroic sacrifice if they could have foreseen the distress in which Europe is about to find herself today? How many of them would agree to it again, if they could be brought back to life? No, comrades; we know that the only way to fight "The War To End All Wars" is to fight the war against imperialism—each of us, each people, each in his own country; because every imperialism, of necessity, gives birth to war.

You have all been struck by the extraordinary motion of the courageous students of Oxford,* which was followed directly by that of the students of Manchester. It may be that a great number of these students still treasure the illusion (which has been mine for a long time too, I must confess) that a simple abstention will suffice, that a passive resistance will do. Such a resistance, unfortunately, is likely soon to be swept aside. But, as for any other sort of resistance, I would like to say this: in order for resistance to be effective, the greatest possible union is required; a close union among all of you, a union of the whole working class, crossing all frontiers.

What has brought us together here is the fact, the very serious fact that an important part of the German population, the very people by whom we might and should have hoped to be understood, has just been muzzled, gagged, reduced to silence. They could not be suppressed entirely, despite the enormous effort made by Hitler's party to crush them; but their voice has been taken away. Their right to speak has been taken away, the very possibility of their making themselves heard; no more appeals to justice are open to them; their protests have been stifled.

"The same thing has happened in the U.S.S.R.," we shall be told. I have no doubt; but the end there was utterly different; and certain painful abuses of force were no doubt necessary to permit the establishment of a new society, and to give—at last—a voice to those who, until then, had always been the oppressed, to those who until then had never had the right to speak.

Why and how have I come to approve in the one case what I denounce in the other? Because in the German terrorism I see a repetition, a re-establishment of the most deplorable, the most detestable aspects of the past; in the establishment of the Soviet society, a boundless promise for the future.

It is monstrous to assert that those who have not spoken are those who have nothing to say, be they individuals or oppressed peoples, races, or social classes. They have been subjugated by force, brutalized, stupefied to such a degree that even their plea remains crude. The ruling class, those who have seized the platform, pretend to be "protecting" it. They have "protected" it long enough. And now that there is danger of its being taken from them, they are shouting all the louder. The history of humanity is the story of the slow, miserable coming into the light of all those who at first were kept under the yoke and under the bushel.† However it

---

* In February 1933, The Oxford Union Society passed, by a large majority, a celebrated motion that "this House will in no circumstances fight for its King and Country."

† (Not spoken at the original reading): The Christians of today who, in shameful be-

may be delayed for the moment, this march toward liberation is no less sure, no less ordained; and it is not in the power of any imperialism to stop it.

What can we do today for the oppressed party of Germany? This, no doubt, is what those more competent than I are about to tell you, and I hasten to yield them the rostrum.

It is a matter of maintaining our union with the oppressed beyond the Rhine, across national boundaries; but it is a matter first of maintaining that union among ourselves. I believe that all those who are going to speak today are aware of this; and I hope that they will dedicate themselves to put first the common and international interest that binds us, ahead of any other interest that might become an object of dissension.

To Ramon Fernandez

(June 1933?)

My dear Ramon Fernandez,

I have received the proofs of your book. Everything you say there I have already said often to myself—and a good deal less gently than you have done. While waiting, I am no longer writing anything. Rest assured.

It is curious, this—for forty years everyone reproached me for my indecision, for not knowing how to take sides. You are one of the first to have thought, and the first to have said (how grateful I am to you for it!) that the free play of my thought, so carefully preserved up till then, was precisely the best of my qualities. Now you warn me of the danger that there is in the subjection of that thought, which, enslaved, would at once lose all its value. Indeed yes—how well I know the sacrifice involved. But is the cause worth the cost? That is the question; and for me, that is all.

But remember that if, as you say, I "am doing a great deal for communism by my adherence," it is in great part because I have waited, wavering and balancing, forty years before making this decision. No sacrifice is worthwhile unless it is the highest. . . .

---

trayal of Christ, attach themselves to nationalist imperialisms, these Christians should remember that, at the start and for many years, it was *they* who were the oppressed. Should they rally today to the cause of capitalism, it would be a monstrous error, and will drag Catholicism to its ruin along with capitalism. Because . . .

To the Officers of the "World Youth Congress against War and Fascism"

Cuverville, August 31, 1933

I have already declared my sympathy (and the word "sympathy" seems to me quite weak) for the ideas that inspire you. I shall find other occasions to declare them again. But believe me, I am worth nothing at meetings, I have not the voice that is needed to speak in public, and in any case, I am wretchedly qualified to preside. The role is not made for me, it does not suit me, and I would only disappoint you in accepting it. I beg you, then, not to let my name appear on the prospectus of the Congress, if it has not been already printed, and to believe me nonetheless quite cordially on your side. Leave me peacefully alone to write that which is left to me to write; it is thus that I shall be able to help you best and most enduringly.

To Minister for Propaganda Joseph Goebbels

Thursday, January 4, 1934

Sir:

On behalf of the delegates of the Dimitrov Committee,* of which we have accepted the presidency, we have come today from Paris to ask for an audience with you. Having learned at the Ministry of the circumstances which called you to and which detain you at Munich, we ask your permission to write what we had hoped to discuss with you in person.

The Dimitrov Committee was established in several countries after the Leipzig verdict, and is based on the judgment of the imperial tribunal. We should like to make clear that we have accepted the mission of representing it before you only on the clear assurance that in doing so we would be representing neither a nation nor a political party. The great number of letters received from all nations by our committee makes clearer every day the uneasiness which your prolonged indecision has occasioned throughout all of Europe; we feel ourselves obliged, apart from all political considerations, to share with the authority best qualified to understand them the sentiments which these communications express. We would like to be able to report to those who have commissioned us an answer from you relative to the decisions of the Reich with regard to Dimitrov, Tanev, and Popov, hoping that it will be of a nature to appease their anxiety.

* See editor's introduction, p. 756.

It is in this hope that we beg you, sir, to accept the expression of our high consideration.

André Gide and André Malraux

Message to the First Soviet Writers' Conference

August 17, 1934

On that highroad of History where each country, each nation must sooner or later set forth, the Soviet Union has gloriously taken the lead. Today, she is giving us a model of that New Society of which we have dreamed, but for which we dared not hope.

In the domain of the spirit as well, it is important that the Soviet Union set the example. She owes it to herself to prove to us that the Communist ideal is not, as her enemies have been pleased to affirm, an "ideal of the anthill." Her task today is to inaugurate, in literature and in art, a *Communist individualism* (if I dare to couple these two words customarily opposed, in my opinion quite erroneously). Doubtless a period of intemperate affirmation was necessary; but the U.S.S.R. has already passed that stage, and nothing convinces me of this more than the most recent articles and speeches of Stalin.

Communism will be able to implant itself only by taking account of the particularity of each individual. A society in which each man resembles the other is scarcely desirable; I would even say that it is impossible; and such a literature more impossible still. Each artist is by necessity an individualist, however strong may be his Communist convictions and his attachment to the Party. It is only thus that he can do useful work and serve the society.

In the first lecture I ever gave, in March 1900, I expressed this same idea, an idea I continue to find profoundly true: "Every real artist (I should say, every great man) has but a single concern: to become as human as he possibly can; let us say rather, to become commonplace." I added: "And the wonderful thing is that in doing so he becomes most distinctive." I consider foolish and shameful that fear—a fear, moreover, known only to the impotent—of being reabsorbed into the mass. Communism has need of strong personalities—just as they have need of communism, in order to discover their proper purpose, their *raison d'être*.

From LITERATURE AND REVOLUTION

(*Address delivered October 23, 1934*)

. . . There exists a bourgeois conventionalism, against which I personally have always fought; there could just as easily exist a conventionalism of the other side. I consider all literature to be in great peril from the time a single writer feels himself bound to obey a password. That literature, that art can serve the Revolution goes without saying; but it must not be preoccupied with serving it. It will never serve it so well as when it is preoccupied with the truth. Literature must not place itself at the service of the Revolution. A subservient literature is a debased literature, however noble and legitimate the cause it serves. But as the cause of truth is identified in my mind, in our minds, with that of the Revolution, then art, in concerning itself exclusively with truth, necessarily serves the Revolution. It does not follow it; it does not submit to it; it does not reflect it. It enlightens it. It is thus that it is differentiated, essentially, from the Fascist, Hitlerian, imperialist productions of whatever country, those that do answer to a password, a *mot d'ordre:* for them, it is not a question of speaking the truth, but of covering it up. Apollo becomes a servant in the house of Admetus. From this can come nothing of value; that we know. It is unworthy of the Soviet Union.

. . . If the Soviet Union triumphs—and it must triumph—its art will soon disengage itself from the battle; . . . it will emancipate itself . . .

From ANDRÉ GIDE AND OUR TIME,

a panel discussion held in Paris, January 26, 1935

. . .

G. GUY-GRAND— . . . All the while adhering to the Communist ideal, you have said that the task of the U.S.S.R. is "to inaugurate, in literature and in art, a *Communist individualism.*" One might wonder whether this definition would be accepted by an orthodox Communist. It seems to prove that the value you hold most dearly is your own private liberty . . .

ANDRÉ GIDE—The value I hold most dearly is my art.

I *want* to believe that an understanding is possible between art and Communist doctrine. But I must confess that until now I have not known how to find the point of fusion and accord—in part because of long and settled habits. This is why I have produced nothing for four years. This has been a sacrifice, there is no doubt. But the question for me is this: Is the sacrifice justified? . . .

JACQUES MARITAIN—Your embracing of communism seems to me, when all is said and done, only a substitute for that evangelical, holy life that you have always sought—in all the wrong places. . . .

To my mind communism is lacking one thing—a thing that, even in the social and temporal order, only Christianity could perform. . . .

ANDRÉ GIDE—"Could?"

JACQUES MARITAIN—Shall . . .

ANDRÉ GIDE—At first you said "could"; then you corrected yourself and said "shall." I rather think it is the past tense that one must use: "did." There is an Arab society, a Buddhist society; but there is no longer a Christian society worthy of the name. This one in which we live, which calls itself Christian, is pathetic, lamentable. A Christian society may have existed in the Middle Ages. But when one thinks of the teaching of Christ, and then sees what has been made of it in the modern world, one is heartbroken . . .

In my mind Christianity is bankrupt, as a result of its compromises. I have written, and I deeply believe, that if Christianity had imposed itself, if the teachings of Christ had been accepted as they were, there would be no question today of communism. There would not even be a "social question."

I was struck by something that you said, M. Maritain, on the possibility of achieving, of realizing Christianity in time. I have been impressed, in reading the Gospel, by the words *"et nunc"*—"and now"—which are constantly repeated.

JACQUES MARITAIN—There are two sorts of *"et nunc."* There is the "now" of eternity which dominates and contains the "now" of our time.

ANDRÉ GIDE—It seemed to me that, in the Gospel, they were one and the same.

Our impatience is certainly understandable, after two thousand years. Clearly this is little enough, compared to eternity; but for us it is a long time.

I think that the belief in another life, that the hope of finding, in a future life, a sort of recompense, of compensation for the evils of this one, greatly enfeebles the force of protest in the class of the oppressed, and in doing so, plays into the hands of the class of the oppressors—who consequently find considerable advantage in declaring and proclaiming themselves Christians, even though they take so little account of the teachings and precepts of Christ.

JACQUES MARITAIN—The convenience of oppressed classes has nothing to do with metaphysical essences.

ANDRÉ GIDE—There is another point which seems to me especially grave (and by "grave" I mean "dangerous"): that the Christian religion pretends to base itself on *revelation*—just like the Jewish or the Moslem religion. Where there is belief in revelation, there is of necessity fanaticism.

I received, two years ago, in the same week, by a coincidence that some might call providential, three visits that completely dumbfounded me. One visitor was a Catholic, the second a Jew, the third a Mohammedan. The first was M. Berdyaev. Yes, I was dumbfounded by what he said; but he forced me to realize that the danger of religious convictions lies in their fanatic force. . . .

The visit of the Moslem upset me just as much. There was in this man the most profound conviction. For him, Mohammed alone was called to set the social question in order. The young Jew was equally convinced. He quoted phrases from the Talmud with a choke in his voice . . . These three successive interviews frightened me by forcing me to realize that, insofar as others possessed similar religious convictions, war was inevitable. And it was soon after that that I wrote the phrase which has so much offended certain believers: Only atheism can bring peace to the world today. . . .

JACQUES MARITAIN—Do you not see that communism is a religion as well? . . . There is no religion more intolerant than Communist atheism.

ANDRÉ GIDE—I grant that communism is a religion; but the important thing is that it is a reasonable, reasoned religion, a learned religion, not a revealed one. That is what matters. . . .

DANIEL HALÉVY—The statements of M. Gide astonish me. . . . What is it he is doing? He is simply calling up one more dogmatism, all freshly sharpened. . . . In vain I ask myself what sort of *ménage* his master

Montaigne and his master Lenin could possibly form together inside his head. . . .

ANDRÉ GIDE—There is, clearly, a conflict; a great conflict, and it results in a great sacrifice.

DANIEL HALÉVY—What is this personal sacrifice, this silence of which M. Gide tells us? . . .

ANDRÉ GIDE— . . . There is the material sacrifice, which is of no importance. We need not speak of that. But there is also an intellectual sacrifice. Montaigne is always alive inside me; but on his "soft and sweet pillow" I can no longer consent to "rest a well-made head." I used to need this cushion of ignorance and incuriosity (about social questions) in order to write. In the four years that I have been preoccupied with social questions, I have written nothing. . . .

THIERRY MAULNIER— . . . The progress of Gide's thought seems to me the reverse of that of those individualists who escape from society, and then ask what it can do for them; with Gide the question is to know what man can do for society. . . .

ANDRÉ GIDE—The last thing in the world I am is a theoretician. I find it extremely difficult to explain theoretically a position which I hold in deep sincerity. To me the important thing is that it be sincere; that it continues to be sincere. Well then, I have just been told that I have contradicted myself. If I have in fact, I will feel it keenly myself; and if I do not feel it after a certain amount of time, then this contradiction is not essential, not real.

If I have not felt any contradiction between the Communist and the individualist positions, is this not, after all, because this contradiction is in fact theoretical, factitious? For myself, I am convinced of it. Certain Catholics, moreover, have explained to me that on this point I was perfectly in accord with Aristotle and Saint Thomas, have written and proved this to me with any number of supporting texts. This has forced me to think, "There, it may well be then that I am right." But I do not insist on being right; this is not an affair of "reasoning" in my case—at least not at first. The reasonings only come afterwards, to corroborate the feeling. "Man is led by feelings, not ideas."

Similarly it was certainly not the reading of Marx that led me to communism. I did make a great effort to read him. I still do. But what drew me to the cause was certainly not the theory of Marxism. What made me come to communism, with all my heart, was the situation that I found taught me a great deal; yes, much more than Marxism itself. The discipline I imposed on myself for three years has not been profitless; but now I find greater advantage in liberating myself from it than in continuing to submit. That plunge into Marxism allowed me to see the essential thing it was lacking.

Did it require the collapse of the U.S.S.R. to lead me to think this? It is the illustration of my own disappointment. And one first tries to tell oneself: it failed through infidelity. Then one again hears ring out the sinister words: "There has not been a revolution that has not. . . ." *

Oh, how right you were to see in my coming to communism a matter of sentiment! but how wrong you were not to understand that I was right! According to you, the only communism that matters is the one that is reached through theory. You speak as theoreticians. To be sure, theory is useful. But without warmth of heart and without love it bruises the very ones it claims to save. Let us beware of those who want to apply communism coldly, of those who want, at whatever cost, to plow straight furrows on a curving earth, of those who prefer to each man the idea they have formed of humanity.

All the same, the U.S.S.R. really did something. Despite the present ebbtide, something of it will remain. And if one can think that the revolutionary movement in Russia brought about by reaction the Fascist resistance of other countries, it is not paradoxical to say that it was Bolshevism and the great fear people had of it that determined the Fascist governments to make protective social reforms, to which they would never have consented otherwise; a way of disarming the adversary. Even the Church saw that it was in her interest to pay more attention to social questions, and that it was her neglect of her duties that had so singularly reinforced the legitimacy of her enemies' claims. It was essential to take away Bolshevism's justification; to put it out of countenance was the best way to oppose it.

It is noteworthy that certain pure theoreticians of Marxism expect, hope, demand of society, of the social state, what they utterly refuse to begin by achieving in themselves. For the Christian, the revolution takes place

---

* ". . . that has not, in the end, resulted in a reinforcement of the bureaucratic machine" (Lenin, 1917, cited by Gide earlier).

within himself. I should like to be able to say: within himself *first;* but most often that inner revolution is enough for him; while the outer revolution is enough for the others. I should like these two efforts, these two results, to be complementary, and I believe that they are often rather artificially opposed.

A constant need of reconciliation torments me; it is a failing of my mind, although it is perhaps a good quality of my heart. I should like to marry heaven and hell, *à la* Blake; reduce oppositions, and most often refuse to see anything but misunderstandings in the most ruinous and fatal antagonisms. "Individualism and communism . . . how can you claim to reconcile those adversaries, even in yourself?" my friend Martin du Gard said to me laughingly. "They are water and fire." From their marriage is born steam.

What a sorry need of hatred I feel everywhere today! a need of opposing all things that ought to understand one another, complete one another, fecundate one another, join together! . . .

I had felt these conflicts at work within me before meeting them on the outside. I was aware of them, and it was through personal experience that I knew how much one wears oneself down, and how uselessly, in the struggle; a struggle that I had long encouraged between the very opposed elements of my nature, until the day when I said to myself: what is the good of it? when I sought, not struggle and partial triumph, but accord; in order to see at last that the more widely separated are the elements of the agreement, the richer is the harmony. And likewise, in a state, that dream of the crushing of one party by another is a dark, a gloomy utopia; that dream of a totalitarian state in which the subjugated minorities could no longer make themselves heard; in which (and this is worse) each and every one would think the same. There can be no more question of harmony when the choir sings in unison.

1938   *Kaolak**

Pleasant house in which we are camping. Everything in it is as clean as can be, doubtless; for how can one keep from being invaded by black beetles —or cockroaches. I always confuse them, as I do porpoises with dolphins.

Agonizing night. Went to bed early, very sleepy; but great difficulty

* Senegal. Gide made semi-official trips to French West Africa in 1936 and 1938.

breathing. Stomach churning; never again take that frightful soft and sticky meat which is called "fish" in this country.

At midnight I decide to have recourse to my medication. Badly closed tubes, which open and scatter the lozenges in my valise. In the bathroom, where I go to get some distilled water (but a mistake was made: the bottle contains syrup), I surprise cockroaches in the act of copulating. I thought they were wingless; but some (probably the males), unfold enormous trembling wings without taking flight. When I am ready to go back to bed, I notice rising above the top of the wardrobe opposite my bed the erect head of a python, which soon becomes just an iron rod.

February 11

Left Kankan at 5:40 a.m., our special train scheduled twenty minutes ahead of the regular train.

Reached Mamou at 5:30 p.m. I am paid military honors. The people of the administration in dress uniform, with all medals flying; in my colored shirt and khaki trousers, lamentably untidy, I feel I am playing *The Inspector General.* Strive to make up for the undress of my costume by an excessive dignity in bearing.

The fact is that many enterprises here can prosper only with a system rather close to slavery.

Paris, March 12

. . . I went nearby to pick up Robert Levesque, whom I had not seen since my return from French West Africa; invited him to go with me to the Jardin des Plantes, where I wanted to see my chameleon again. Unable to feed him properly, I had turned him over to the vivarium, where he is stuffed with cockroaches for lack of flies, rather rare in this season. "Timothy," the only one of his species, cuts a very elegant figure beside two enormous chameleons from Madagascar, the color of cinders. He immediately decked himself in grass-green, spotted with black; this is his party dress.

I feel again that extraordinary serenity which Butler said he experienced in the contemplation of big pachyderms, which I enjoy indistinctly in this place where all human activity is devoted to the study of animals and plants. Probably the way of communing with God that most satisfies me is that of the naturalists (I do not know that of the astronomers). It seems to me that the divinity they approach is the least subject to caution.

Chatted almost an hour with Auguste Chevalier, with great profit and pleasure.

As soon as I return to that atmosphere of the natural sciences, I tell myself again: I missed my vocation; it is a naturalist that I should have liked to be, should have been.

_____ *

* This double ruled line, which appears without commentary in the French edition, marks the death of Mme André Gide during the spring of 1938.

myself in in the world, that of one of the "chosen people." I found this intolerable. In *Les Faux-Monnayeurs,* I made reference to a direct conversation that I had had with one of the survivors of the *Bourgogne* disaster. This man told me how he found himself in a lifeboat to which a certain number of people had been admitted—people who, in the lifeboat, were able to consider themselves saved. If any more had been let in, the boat would have sunk. On both sides of the boat, individuals armed with knives and hatchets cut off the fists of those who tried to climb on board. However, the feeling of being in the boat, of being sheltered, while others around us are drowning, you must understand that this feeling could become unbearable. Oh, you will make me all sorts of rationalizations, I know. I haven't the strength to answer them all, that is clear. The only thing I insist on is this: that I can no longer accept a boat in which only certain people are afforded protection. Even if I be permitted to think that these "certain people" are, in any case, the best! What exasperates me most are those who come to me and say, "What in the world are you complaining about? You must admit that things are going quite nicely, for us in the boat." Indeed they are! And those who aren't in it think so to. . . .

You ask me, Mauriac, what prevents me from writing today. I am going to tell you quite clearly, if somewhat paradoxically. What keeps me from writing is the fear of the Index. Understand, it is not a matter of any exterior Index; no, it is a fear of stepping outside the norm. From the day when a writer realizes that it is a good thing to have a norm, a rule (for reasons one has suspected all along), the fear of acting independently, of playing the knight-errant, the *cavalier seul,* when there is no real reason to do it, can seriously disturb him. I have always declared myself enemy to every orthodoxy. That of Marxism appears to me quite as dangerous as any other—dangerous at least for the work of art. And if it be proven to me that the Marxist orthodoxy be useful, indispensable—at least provisionally—to assure the formation, the establishment of a new social order, then I will judge that it is worth the cost; yes, that to obtain this it is worth the cost of consenting to the sacrifice of a few "works of art." And perhaps it is a good thing that there be today a rule-book, a *mot d'ordre* (I mean in the Communist Party). But the work of art itself cannot follow any book of rules, answer to any *mot d'ordre.* . . .

As Malraux said very handsomely the other day: an artist, in our society, swims against the current instead of being carried along by it. Until now, I have always written without concerning myself in the least about public approbation; but if, now, I need the approbation of a party in order to write . . . I prefer, while still approving of the party, not to write at all. . . .

G. GUY-GRAND—It is all very well for you to wish not to be unorthodox; but in abstaining from writing, in not wanting to write, are you not unorthodox *in fact?*

ANDRÉ GIDE—Ah, don't say that I don't *want* to write. Quite simply, I *cannot* maintain the sincerity of my thought in the face of certain exigencies.

A MEMBER OF THE AUDIENCE—It would be dangerous for a doctrine to be unable to reconcile itself with a work of art.

ANDRÉ GIDE—We must give communism time to get seated. And sometimes it is good to have silence.

I would also like to say this: there cannot be a Soviet philosophy, any more than a mathematics or an astronomy different from philosophy, mathematics, or astronomy in France. The *cogito ergo sum* of Descartes remains just as true in the U.S.S.R. as it does here. But what applies here is not so much a *"petition de principe"* [a "begging of the question"] as what I would call a *"petition de poêle"* [an "appeal of the coal-stove"]. In order for Descartes to think clearly, the first thing he needed was a coal-stove, a source of warmth and comfort. Without the stove, no *"cogito"* at all. What I mean is that, for a time, material questions must be given priority. For a long time I was convinced that the moral question was more important than the social question. I said and I wrote, "Man is more important than men," and any number of other phrases of that sort. For forty years I believed that: today I am no longer quite so sure. It appears to me today that the social question *must* take priority, and that it must be resolved first, in order to permit man to give what he needs to give. The great mistake is to come and say to the Soviet Union, "This is monstrous! You are concerning yourself only with material questions!" No: material questions are not, precisely, the most important, but they are the first, the most important in time; that is to say that they are the decisive ones. So much so that if they are not resolved, no one will be able to do anything on or of his own; or at most, the only ones who will be able to do anything "privately" are precisely those few privileged beings of whom I am ashamed to admit myself a member. I have just been told, "You give more importance to the feet of the statue than to its head or its heart." Not at all! But before troubling ourselves over the head or the heart, we must be sure that the feet are on the pedestal; and without a solid pedestal, nothing will stand. It is in this way, and only in this way, that the pedestal or the feet might be considered the most important parts—at first. . . .

I believe that spiritual reform depends on material reform. The material question does not interest me in itself, but as an indispensable condition of intellectual liberation.

from

LES NOUVELLES

NOURRITURES

(*The New Fruits*)

1935

There are on this earth such immensities of misery, distress, poverty, and horror that the happy man cannot think of it without feeling ashamed of his happiness. And yet no one can do anything for the happiness of others if he knows not how to be happy himself. I feel an imperious obligation to be happy. But all happiness seems to me hateful that is obtained only at the expense of others and by possessions of which others are deprived. One step further and we come up against the tragic social question. All the arguments of my reason will not hold me back on the downhill slope that leads to communism. But what seems to me mistaken is to demand of the possessor that he divide up his goods among others; what folly to expect that he will willingly resign the possessions to which his whole soul is attached! As for myself, I have taken an aversion to every "private property," to every possession that is exclusive; my happiness consists in giving, and death will not rob me of any great deal. The most I shall be deprived of are those many widespread natural riches which cannot be appropriated, and which are common to all. But of those in particular I have taken my fill. As for the rest, I prefer the meal of a roadside inn to the best-served table, the public gardens to the finest wall-enclosed park, and the book I am not afraid to take out with me on a walk to the rarest edition. And if I had to be alone in order to look at some work of art, the finer it was, the more my pleasure would be outweighed by my sadness.

My happiness is to increase that of others. To be happy myself, I need the happiness of all.

It is toward sensual pleasure that all nature's efforts tend. It is pleasure that makes the blade of grass grow, the bud develop, and the flower bloom. It is pleasure that opens the corolla to the sunbeam's kisses, invites every living thing to wedlock, sends the obtuse larva to its nymphosis and makes the butterfly escape from the prison of its chrysalis. Guided by pleasure, all things aspire to greater well-being, to expanded consciousness, to progress.

. . . This is why I have found more instruction in sensual pleasure than in books; why I have found in books more darkening than light.

There was no deliberation nor method about it. It was unreflectively that I plunged into this ocean of delights, astonished to find myself swimming in it, not to feel myself swallowed up. It is in sensual pleasure that our whole being becomes conscious of itself.

All this took place without resolution; it was quite naturally that I let myself go. I had of course heard it said that human nature was bad, but I wanted to find out for myself. I felt, in fact, less curious about myself than about others—or rather the secret workings of carnal desire drove me out of myself toward an enchanting confusion.

The search for a moral code did not seem to me very wise, or even possible, so long as I had no idea who I was. When I stopped looking for myself, it was in love that I found myself again.

For some time I had to consent to the abandonment of all moral considerations and to give up resisting my desires. They alone were capable of instructing me. I yielded to them.

And yet how many times, just on the point of plucking some joy, I have suddenly turned away from it as might an ascetic.

It was not renunciation, but such a perfect foreknowledge of what that felicity could be, so complete an anticipation, that no realization could have instructed me further, and nothing remained but to pass on, with the knowledge that to guarantee ourselves some pleasure by preparing for it is to despoil it in advance; that the most exquisite delights are those that ravish our whole being by surprise. But at the very least I had succeeded in ridding myself of all reticence and modesty, the reservations of decency, the hesitations of timidity—of all that makes sensual pleasure fearful and predisposes the soul to remorse after the flagging of the flesh. All the blossoming, all the flowering I met on my way seemed merely the echo and reflection of the springtime I carried within me. I burned with such intensity that I felt I could communicate my fervor to every other creature, as one gives a light from one's cigarette only to have it glow the brighter. I shook away from me all that was ash. Love unconfined, unsubdued, laughed in my eyes. Goodness, I thought, is only the irradiation of happiness; and I gave my heart to all, by the simple situation of being happy.

*Then, later . . . No, it was not diminution of desire, nor satiety, that I
felt coming on with age; but often, as I foresaw the over-prompt draining
of my pleasure in the greediness of my lips, possession seemed to me less
precious than pursuit, and more and more I came to prefer thirst itself to
the quenching of it, the promise to the reality of pleasure, and to satisfaction the never-ending expansion of love.*

I went to see him in a village in the Valais where he was supposed to be
completing his convalescence, but where, in reality, he was making ready
to die. He was so changed by illness at that point that I hardly recognized
him.

"Well, no," he said, "I'm not well—not at all. All my organs have
been attacked, one after the other, liver, kidneys, spleen. . . . As for my
knee! Have a look at it, just for curiosity's sake."

And half-lifting the bedclothes and bringing his wasted leg into
view, he showed me a kind of enormous ball just at the joint. As he was
sweating profusely, his shirt clung to his body and accentuated its thinness.
I tried to smile so as to hide my sorrow.

"In any case, you knew your recovery would take a long time," I said.
"But you're comfortable here, aren't you? The air is good. The food—?"

"Excellent. And the saving thing is that my digestion is still good. In
the last few days I have even gained weight. I have less fever. Oh, all
things considered, I'm decidedly better."

The appearance of a smile twisted his features and I understood that
perhaps he had not lost all hope.

"Besides, spring is upon us," I added quickly, turning my face to the
window, for my eyes were full of tears which I wanted to hide. "You will
soon be able to sit in the garden."

"I go down to it already for a few minutes every day after the midday
meal. For it's only dinner I have brought up to my room. I force myself to
have lunch in the dining-room and so far I have missed only three days.
Going up the two flights again afterwards is a bit of an effort; but I take it
slowly; not more than four steps at a time, then a pause to get my breath.
In all, it takes me a good twenty minutes. But it gives me a little exercise;
and I'm so glad afterwards to get back to my bed! And then it leaves them
time to do my room. But what I'm most afraid of is giving in. . . .
You're looking at my books? . . . Yes, that's your *Nourritures terrestres.*
That little book never leaves me. You can't imagine the consolation and
encouragement I get out of it."

This touched me more than any compliment I could ever have; for I must confess that I was afraid my book could find favor only with the strong.

"Yes," he went on, "even in my state, when I am in that garden so near to flowering, I want to say, like Faust, to the passing moment: 'Stop! You are so beautiful!' Then everything seems to me so harmonious, so suave. . . . What troubles me is that I myself am, as it were, a false note in the concert, a blot on the picture. I do so wish I could have been handsome!"

He remained some time without saying any more, his eyes turned to the blue sky, which showed through the wide-open window. Then in a lower voice, and, it seemed to me, almost timidly, "I wish you would send news of me to my parents. I've reached the point where I no longer dare write to them—least of all to tell them the truth. Whenever my mother gets a letter from me, she answers at once that if I'm ill, it's for my own good; that God is blessing me with these sufferings for the sake of my salvation; that I ought to take a lesson from them and amend my life, that not until I do shall I deserve to get well. Then I invariably tell her that I am better, so as to avoid these reflections—they simply fill my heart with all sorts of blasphemies. Write to her—you."

"It shall be done this very morning," I said, taking his wet hand.

"Oh! don't squeeze too hard; you're hurting me."

He was smiling.

Our literature, and particularly our romantic literature, has praised, culti-vated, and propagated sadness; not the active, resolute sadness that makes men rush to glorious deeds, but a kind of flabbiness of soul, which was called melancholy, which gave a becoming pallor to the poet's brow and filled his eyes with yearning. There was a great deal of fashion and smug-ness about it. Happiness seemed vulgar, the sign of an excess of foolish good health; to laugh was to distort the features. Melancholy reserved to itself the privilege of spirituality, and hence of profundity.

As for me, who have always preferred Bach and Mozart to Beetho-ven, I consider Musset's greatly vaunted line

Les plus désespérés sont les chants les plus beaux

(*The most beautiful songs are those of greatest despair*)

a blasphemy, and I will not admit that men should let themselves be beaten down by the blows of adversity.

Yes, I know that this is more a matter of determination than of yield-

ing to nature. I know that Prometheus suffered, chained to his rock in the Caucasus, and that Christ died on the cross, both of them for having loved men. I know that, alone among the demigods, Hercules bears on his brow the stamp of care, for having triumphed over monsters, hydras, all the dreadful powers that were keeping mankind in subjection. I know that there are still—and perhaps will always be—dragons to conquer. . . . But in the renunciation of joy there is a confession of failure, a kind of abdication, of cowardice.

That man has hitherto risen to a state of comfort—a state in which happiness is possible—only at the expense of others, only by settling himself ruthlessly on top of his fellows—this is what we ought no longer to admit. Nor will I admit that the greater number should be compelled to renounce on this earth the happiness that springs naturally out of harmony.

But what men have made of the promised land—the granted land—is enough to make the gods blush. The child who breaks a toy, the animal that lays waste the pasture where it might eat and muddies the water it might drink, the bird that fouls its nest, are no more stupid. Oh, the squalid approaches to our towns! Ugliness, discord, stench!

Know thyself. *A maxim as pernicious as it is ugly. Any man who observes himself arrests his own development. The caterpillar that tried to "know itself" would never become a butterfly.*

I have sometimes—I have often—out of spite, spoken more ill than I thought of other people and, out of cowardice, more good than I thought of many works, books, or pictures, for fear of setting their authors against me. I have sometimes smiled at people I did not think at all funny, and pretended to think silly remarks witty. I have sometimes pretended to enjoy myself when I was being bored to death and couldn't bring myself to go away because someone had asked me to stay. I have too often allowed my reason to stop the impulse of my heart. And, on the other hand, when my heart was silent, I have too often spoken out all the same. I have sometimes done foolish things in order to meet with approval. And, on the other hand, I have not always had the courage to do the

things I thought I ought to do, because I knew they would meet with
disapproval.

Their wisdom? . . . Oh, their wisdom, don't let's make too much of it.

It consists in living as little as possible, distrusting everything, taking endless precautions.

There is always something stale in their advice, something stagnant.

They are like those mothers who drive their children silly with injunctions:

"Don't swing so hard, the rope's going to break."

"Don't stand under that tree, it's going to thunder."

"Don't walk where it's wet, you're going to slip."

"Don't sit on the grass, you're going to get dirty."

"At your age you ought to know better."

"How many times do I have to tell you—don't put your elbows on the table."

"This child is unbearable!"

Oh, madame, not nearly as much as you are!

ENCOUNTERS

I

In Bourbonnais I once knew a charming old maid

Who kept all her old medicines in a cupboard;

It was so full that there was hardly room left for anything else;

And as the old lady was then in perfectly good health,

I ventured to say that perhaps it was not very practical

To keep so many things that could no longer be of the slightest use to her.

Then the old lady got very red in the face.

And I thought she was going to cry.

She took out the bottles and the boxes and the tubes one after the other.

"This," she said, "rid me of colic, and this of a quinsy;

This ointment cured me of an abscess in the groin

Which might very well, one never knows, come on again;

And these pills were a great comfort to me

At a time when I suffered a little from constipation.

As for this object, it must, I think, have been an inhaler,
But I fear it has almost completely ceased to work. . . ."
Finally she confessed that once upon a time all these medicaments
had cost her a great deal of money,
And I understood that it was that above all that kept her from
throwing them out.

2

Then the time comes when we must leave all this.
What will this "all this" be? For some people it will be
Hoards of accumulated wealth, estates, libraries,
Divans on which to enjoy pleasure,
Or simply leisure;
For many others it will be toil and trouble;
To leave family and friends, children who are growing up;
Tasks begun, work to be done,
A dream on the point of becoming real;
Books they still wanted to read;
Perfumes they had never breathed;
Unsatisfied curiosities;
The less fortunate who were depending on your help;
The peace, the serenity they were hoping to attain—
And then suddenly *"les jeux sont faits; rien ne va plus"*; game's up,
ladies and gentlemen.
And one fine day someone says:
"You know—Gontran. I've just been to see him. I'm afraid he's
done for.
He's had one foot in the grave for a week now.
He kept saying: 'I feel, I feel I'm going.'
There was still some hope, though. But now there's none."
"What's the matter with him?"
"They think it's something to do with the endocrine glands,
But his heart was in a bad state.
A kind of insulin poisoning, the doctor said."
"That's odd, now, isn't it?"
"They say he's left a fairly large fortune,
A collection of coins and pictures.
His relations won't get a penny on account of the taxes."

"Coins! I could never understand how people could be interested in that."

You needn't pretend to be so clever. You have seen people die; there's nothing so very funny about it. You try to joke so as to hide your fear; but your voice trembles and your fake poem is frightful.

Perhaps. . . . Yes, I have seen people die. In most cases it seemed to me that just before death and once the crisis was past, the sharpness of the sting was in a way blunted. Death puts on velvet gloves to take us. He does not strangle us without first lulling us to sleep, and what he robs us of has already lost its distinctness, its presence, and, as it were, its reality. The universe becomes so colorless that it is no longer very difficult to leave it, and there is nothing left to regret.

So I say to myself that it can't be so difficult to die since, when you come down to it, everybody manages to do it. And, after all, it would perhaps be nothing but a habit to fall into if only one died more than once.

But death is dreadful to those who have not filled their lives. In their case it is only too easy for religion to say: "Never mind! It's in the other world that life begins; there you'll get your reward."

It is here and now that we must live.

Comrade, believe in nothing—accept nothing without proof. Nothing was ever proved by the blood of martyrs. There is no religion, however mad, that has not had its own, none that has failed to rouse someone to passionate conviction. It is in the name of faith that men die; and it is in the name of faith that they kill. The desire for knowledge springs from doubt. Stop believing and start learning. People never try to impose their opinions except when they cannot prove them. Do not let yourself be credulous. Do not let yourself be imposed upon.

O you for whom I write—whom in other days I called by a name that seems to me now too plaintive—Nathaniel—whom today I call comrade—rid your heart henceforth of all that is plaintive.

Learn how to obtain from yourself all that makes complaining useless. No longer beg from others what you yourself can obtain.

I have lived; it is your turn now. From now on it is in you that my youth will be prolonged. I hand you my powers. If I feel that you are taking my place, I shall resign myself more readily to dying. I pass on my hopes to you.

The knowledge that you are brave and strong enables me to leave life without regret. Take my joy. Let your happiness be to increase that of others. Work and strive and accept no evil that you might change. Keep saying to yourself: "It is up to me." It is only the coward who can resign himself to man-made evils. Stop believing, if you ever believed it, that wisdom consists in resignation; or else stop laying claim to wisdom.

Comrade, do not accept the life that men offer you. Never give off arguing yourself into believing that life might be better—your own life and others'; not a distant, future life that might console us for the present one and help us to accept its misery. Do not accept. As soon as you begin to understand that it is not God but man who is responsible for nearly all the ills of life, from that moment you will no longer resign yourself to bearing them.

Do not sacrifice to idols.

from

RETOUR DE
L'U.R.S.S.

(Return from the U.S.S.R.)

1936

FOREWORD

Three years ago I declared my admiration and my love for the U.S.S.R. An unprecedented experiment was being attempted there which filled our hearts with hope, and from which we expected an immense advance, an impetus capable of carrying the whole human race forward in its stride. It is indeed worth while living, I thought, to be present at this springtime, this renewal of the race, and worth while giving one's life in order to help it on. In our hearts and in our minds we resolutely linked the future of culture itself with the glorious destiny of the U.S.S.R. We have said so many times. We should have liked to say so again.

Already, even before we went to look for ourselves, we could not help feeling disturbed by certain recent decisions, which seemed to denote a change of orientation. . . .

Resolving, however, to maintain my confidence until I had more to go upon, and preferring to doubt my own judgment, I declared once more, four days after my arrival in Moscow, in my speech in the Red Square on the occasion of Gorki's funeral: "The fate of culture is bound up in our minds with the destiny of the Soviet Union. We will defend it." . . .

The Soviet Union is "under construction"; one cannot say it too often. And from that arises the extraordinary interest of a visit to that immense country now in labor; one feels that one is present at the parturition of the future.

Good and bad alike are to be found there; I should say, rather, the best and the worst. The best was often achieved only by an immense effort. That effort has not always and everywhere achieved what it set out to achieve. Sometimes one is able to think: not yet. Sometimes the worst accompanies and shadows the best, seems almost to be the consequence of it. And one passes from the brightest light to the darkest shade with disconcerting abruptness. . . .

Now my mind is so constructed that its severest criticisms are addressed to those whom I should like always to be able to approve. To confine oneself exclusively to praise is a bad way of proving one's devo-

, and I believe I am doing the Soviet Union itself and the cause that it presents in our eyes a greater service by speaking without dissimulation or indulgence. It is precisely because of my admiration for the Soviet Union and for the wonders it has already accomplished that I am going to criticize it; because, also, of what we still expect from it; and above all because of what it had allowed us to hope for.

Who can say what the Soviet Union has been to us? More than a chosen land—an example, a guide. What we have dreamed of, what we have hardly dared to hope, but toward which we were straining all our will and all our strength, was coming into being over there. A land existed where Utopia was in process of becoming reality. Tremendous achievements had already made us exacting. The most difficult tasks, it seemed, had already been accomplished, and we ventured joyfully and boldly into a kind of commitment to that land, contracted in the name of all suffering peoples.

Up to what point, in case of failure, should we feel ourselves likewise engaged? But the very idea of failure is inadmissible. . . .

I do not hide from myself the apparent advantage that hostile parties —those in whom "a love of order is indistinguishable from a preference for tyrants" *—will try to derive from my book. And that would have prevented me from publishing it, from writing it, even, did not my conviction remain firm and unshaken that, on the one hand, the Soviet Union will end by triumphing over the serious errors that I point out; and on the other, and this is more important, that the particular errors of one country cannot suffice to compromise the truth of a cause which is international and universal. Falsehood, even that which consists in silence, may appear opportune, as may perseverance in falsehood, but it leaves far too dangerous weapons in the hands of the enemy, and truth, however painful, wounds only in order to cure.

*   *   *

I visited several dwellings in one highly prosperous kolkhoz.† I wish I could convey the queer and depressing impression produced by each one of these "homes"—the impression of complete depersonalization. In each, the same ugly furniture, the same portrait of Stalin, and absolutely nothing else—not the smallest object, the smallest personal souvenir. Every dwelling is interchangeable with every other; so much so that the kol-

---

* Tocqueville: *Democracy in America.*
† In many others there are no such things as individual dwellings; people sleep in dormitories—"barrack-rooms." [A.G.]

khozians (who seem to be as interchangeable themselves) might move from one house to another without even noticing it.* In this way, no doubt, happiness is more easily achieved! And moreover, so I was told, the kolkhozians take all their pleasures in common. A kolkhozian's room is nothing more than a shelter to sleep in; the whole interest of his life has passed into his club, his park of culture, his various meeting-places. What more could one desire? The happiness of all can be obtained only by de-individualizing each. The happiness of all can be obtained only at the expense of each. In order to be happy, conform.

In the U.S.S.R. everybody knows beforehand, once and for all, that on any and every subject there can be only one opinion. And in fact, people's minds have been so molded that this conformity becomes easy, natural, and imperceptible, so much so that I do not think there is the least bit of hypocrisy in it. Are these really the people who made the Revolution? No; they are the people who profit by it. Every morning *Pravda* teaches them just what they should know and think and believe. And he who strays from the path had better look out! So that every time you talk to one Russian, you feel as if you were talking to them all. It is not exactly that everyone is performing to order; but that everything is so arranged that nobody can differ from anybody else. Remember that this molding of the spirit begins in earliest infancy. . . . This explains their extraordinary attitude of acceptance, which sometimes amazes you if you are a foreigner, and a certain capacity for happiness which amazes you even more.

You are sorry for those people who have to stand in line for hours; but they find it perfectly natural. Their bread and vegetables and fruit seem bad to you; but there are no others. You find the materials, the articles you are shown frightful; but there is no choice. If every point of comparison is removed, save that with a past that no one regrets, you are delighted with what is offered you. What is important here is to persuade people that they are as well off as they can be until a better time comes; and to persuade them that people elsewhere are worse off. The only way of achieving this is carefully to prevent any communication with the outside world (the world beyond the frontier, I mean). Thanks to this the Russian workman who has a standard of living equal or even noticeably infe-

---

* This impersonality of each and all leads me to suppose that the people who sleep in dormitories suffer much less from the promiscuity and the absence of privacy than if they were capable of individuality. But can this depersonalization, toward which everything in the U.S.S.R. seems to tend, be considered as progress? For my part, I cannot believe it. [A.G.]

rior to that of a French workman thinks himself well off, *is* better off, much better off, than a workman in France. Their happiness is made up of hope, confidence, and ignorance. . . .

We admire in the U.S.S.R. the extraordinary impulse toward education and toward culture; but the only things their education teaches are those which will lead the mind to congratulate itself on the present order, and to exclaim: *"Oh! U.S.S.R. . . . Ave! Spes unica!"* And their culture is shunted entirely down a single track. There is nothing disinterested about it; it merely accumulates, and (in spite of Marxism) the critical faculty is virtually bankrupt. Of course I know that they make a great to-do about what is called "self-criticism." When at a distance, I admired this, and I still think that it might have produced the most wonderful results, if only it had been seriously and sincerely applied. But I was soon made to realize that apart from denunciations and complaints ("The canteen soup is badly cooked" or "The club reading-room is badly swept"), criticism consists merely in asking oneself whether this, that, or the other is "in the right line." The line itself is never discussed. What is discussed is whether such and such a work, or gesture, or theory conforms to this sacred line. And woe to him who seeks to cross it! As much criticism as you like—up to a point. Beyond that point criticism is not allowed. There are examples of this kind of thing in history. . . .

The Soviet citizen is left in an extraordinary state of ignorance concerning foreign countries.* More than that—he has been persuaded that everything abroad, in every realm, is far less prosperous than in the U.S.S.R. This illusion is wisely maintained, for it is important that everyone, even the least satisfied, should be grateful to the regime which preserves him from greater ills. . . .

As a matter of fact, though they do take some interest in what is happening abroad, they are far more concerned about what the foreigner thinks of them. What really interests them is to know whether we admire them enough. What they are afraid of is that we should be inadequately informed as to their merits. What they want from us is not information but praise. . . .

The questions you are asked are often so staggering that I hesitate to report them. It will be thought that I have invented them. They smile skeptically when I say that Paris too has a subway. Have we even got streetcars? Buses? . . . One of them asks (and these were not children,

* Or at least he is only informed of things which will encourage him to go on thinking as he does. [A.G.]

but educated workmen) whether we had schools too in France. Another, slightly better informed, shrugged his shoulders; "Oh yes, the French have got schools; but the children are beaten in them." He has this information on the best authority. Of course all workers in our country are wretched; that goes without saying, for we have not yet "made the Revolution." For them, outside the U.S.S.R., the reign of night begins. Apart from a few shameless capitalists, the whole rest of the world is struggling in the dark. . . .

As we cannot doubt, unfortunately, that bourgeois instincts, flabby, pleasure-seeking, careless of others, slumber on in many people's hearts despite all their revolutions (for man cannot be reformed entirely from without), it disturbs me very much to observe, in the U.S.S.R. today, that these bourgeois instincts are indirectly flattered and encouraged by recent decisions that have been alarmingly approved of over here. With the restoration of the family (in its function of "social cell"), of inheritance, and of legacies, the thirst for gain, for private property, is beginning to dominate the need for comradeship, free sharing, and the common life. Not for everybody, of course; but for many. And we see the reappearance of social strata if not of classes, and of a kind of aristocracy; I am not referring here to the aristocracy of merit and of personal worth, but only to the aristocracy of respectability, of conformity—which in the next generation will become that of money.

Are my fears exaggerated? I hope so. As far as that goes, the Soviet Union has already shown us that it is capable of abrupt reversals. But I do fear that in order to cut short these bourgeois tendencies which are now being approved and favored by the rulers, a sudden revulsion will soon appear necessary, which will run the risk of becoming as brutal as that which put an end to the N.E.P. . . .

This petit-bourgeois spirit, which I greatly fear is in process of developing in Russia, is in my eyes profoundly and fundamentally counter-revolutionary.

But what is known as "counter-revolutionary" in the U.S.S.R. of today is not that at all. In fact it is very nearly the opposite.

The spirit which is today held to be counter-revolutionary is that same revolutionary spirit, that ferment which first broke through the half-rotten dam of the old tsarist world. One would like to be able to think that an overflowing love of mankind, or at least an imperious need for justice, filled every heart. But once the revolution was accomplished, triumphant, stabilized, there was no more question of such things, and the feelings which had animated the first revolutionaries began to get in the way, like cumbersome objects that have ceased to be useful. I compare them, these feelings, to the props which help to build an arch, but which are taken away when the keystone is put in place. Now that the revolution has triumphed, now that it is stabilized and tamed, now that it is beginning to come to terms, and, some will say, to grow prudent, those still animated by that revolutionary ferment, who consider all these successive concessions to be compromises—these become troublesome, these are branded and suppressed. So would it not be better, instead of playing on words, simply to acknowledge that the revolutionary spirit (or even simply the critical spirit) is no longer the correct thing, that it is not wanted any more? What is wanted now is compliance, conformity. What is desired and demanded is a vote of confidence in all that is being done in the U.S.S.R; and what they are trying to obtain is a vote of confidence that is not merely resigned, but sincere, even enthusiastic. The most astounding thing is that they have got it. On the other hand, the smallest protest, the slightest criticism, is liable to the severest penalties, and in fact is immediately stifled. And I doubt whether in any other country in the world, even in Hitler's Germany, mind and spirit are less free, more bowed down, more fearful (terrorized), more vassalized. . . .

Stalin's effigy is met with everywhere; his name is on every tongue; his praises are invariably sung in every speech. In Georgia particularly, I could not enter a single inhabited room, even the humblest, the most sordid, without remarking a portrait of Stalin hanging on the wall, in the same place no doubt where the ikon used to be. Out of adoration, love, or fear, I do not know; always and everywhere he is there. . . .

In the establishment of the first and second Five-Year Plans, Stalin has shown such wisdom, such an intelligent flexibility in the successive modifications that he has seen fit to bring to them, that one begins to wonder whether it was even possible to be more consistent; whether this gradual divergence from the first lines, this departure from Leninism, was not necessary; whether more obstinacy would not have demanded from the people a truly superhuman effort. But in either case, the pill is bitter. If not Stalin, then it is man, humanity itself, that has disappointed us. What had been attempted, what had been desired, what was thought to be on the point of achievement, after so many struggles, so much blood, so many tears—was that then "above human strength"? Must one wait still longer, relinquish one's hopes, or defer them to some distant time? That is what one asks oneself in the Soviet Union with painful anxiety. But that the question should even enter one's mind—already that is too much.

After so many months, so many years, of effort, one had the right to ask the question: Are they now, at last, going to be able to lift up their heads? Never have they been more abjectly bowed down. . . .

There is another fear—the fear of "Trotskyism" and of what is now called over there the "counter-revolutionary spirit." For there are some people who refuse to believe that all this compromising was necessary; all these "accommodations" appear to them as so many defeats. Explanations, excuses, can be found for the deviation from those first directives, it may well be; the deviation alone is the important thing in their eyes. But what is demanded today is a spirit of submission, of conformity. All those who do not declare themselves to be satisfied are to be considered "Trotskyists." So that one begins to wonder, if Lenin himself were to return to earth to-day . . . ?

We were promised the dictatorship of the proletariat. We are far from the mark. A dictatorship, yes, obviously; but the dictatorship of a man, not of the united workers, not of the Soviets. It is important not to deceive oneself, and it must be frankly acknowledged: this is not what was desired. One step more, and we should even say: this is exactly what was *not* desired.

To suppress the opposition in a state, or even merely to prevent it from declaring itself, from showing itself in the light of day, is a very serious thing; an invitation to terrorism. If all the citizens of a state thought the same way, it would without any doubt be more convenient for the rulers. But in the presence of such an impoverishment, who could still dare to speak of "culture"? Without a counterweight, what is there to keep all thought from pouring into one side? It is a proof of great wisdom, I think, to listen to one's opponents, even to nurture them if need be, while preventing them from doing harm; combat, but not suppress, them. To suppress the opposition . . . ? It is fortunate, no doubt, that Stalin should succeed so badly in his efforts to do so.

"Humanity is not simple, we must make up our minds to that; and any attempt to simplify, to unify, to reduce it from the outside will always be odious, ruinous, and disastrously grotesque. . . ." as I wrote in 1910.

. . . "You see," he went on, "an artist in our country must first of all keep in line. Otherwise even the finest gifts will be considered as *formalism*. Yes, that's our word for designating whatever we don't wish to see or hear. We want to create a new art worthy of the great people we are. Art today should be popular, or not be." . . .

In the U.S.S.R., however fine a work may be, if it is not "in line" it is scandalous. Beauty is considered a bourgeois value. However great a genius an artist may be, if he does not work in line, attention will turn away —will be turned away—from him. What is demanded of the artist, of the writer, is that he shall conform; and all the rest will be added to him. . . .

"In the days of my youth," X. said to me, "people recommended certain books and advised us against others; and naturally it was to the latter that we were drawn. The great difference today is that the young people read only what it is recommended they read, and have no desire to read anything else." . . .

If the mind is forced to answer to a password, to obey a command, it can feel, at least, that it is not free. But if it has been so manipulated beforehand that it obeys without even waiting for the command, it loses even the consciousness of its enslavement. I believe many young Soviet citizens would be greatly astonished if they were told that they had no liberty of thought, and would vehemently deny it.

And as it always happens that we come to recognize the value of certain advantages only after we have lost them, there is nothing like a stay in the U.S.S.R. (or, of course, in Germany) to help us appreciate the inappreciable liberty of thought we still enjoy in France—and sometimes abuse.

LETTERS

from LITTERATURE ENGAGEE

1936–1937

Cuverville, December 10, 1936

My dear X.,

I spent ten days last year in the Borinage, going down into the mine and mingling with the workers, especially with the unemployed. The misery of your comrades at Lille could not be any greater than theirs. Believing in the Soviet Union does not make this misery any less frightful. At any rate, you will say, this belief can lull them into hope. Then better the hope of eternal life and of compensations beyond the grave.

I insisted too much, in my book,* on the loss of "intellectual values." When a people is dying of hunger and cold, it is not those values which it seeks first to preserve. Moreover, I would have been willing to see them compromised for a long time, if the material situation of the people had thereby been better assured. But in the Soviet Union they are now on the way to losing both; and it is horrifying.

It is horrifying to see abandoned, one after the other, so many of the advantages which the Revolution took such pains to secure. It is high time that eyes were opened to this abominable failure, which threatens to sink *our* hopes as well. It is essential that we not let ourselves be dragged down. The way Russia is going, we shall very soon see restored all that we most blame in the capitalist regime. The disproportion between wages is increasing, the social classes are forming anew, bureaucracy is triumphant. Once again: I would be willing to see the mind in Russia just as restricted as it is in Germany or Italy, if the well-being of the masses was at least assured; but we are far, far from that point. I am told: accept the present state, the sickness is only transitory; it is but a landing, the step of a great staircase. But on this staircase the Soviet Union is not going up; it is going down; and very soon the October Days will have to be fought again. It is time to warn, to cry "Halt!"

* *Retour de l'U.R.S.S.*

My dear Guéhenno,

While reading the letter addressed to you from André Wurmser in *L'Humanité* of February 13, I took a few notes:

At the beginning of this letter, Wurmser quotes a sentence from your article "The Useless Death," written apropos of the latest Moscow trial: "As for us, we need be neither Stalinists nor Trotskyites; these are specifically Russian affairs." Permit me to be of a decidedly different opinion. You too, like everyone else, will be obliged sooner or later to commit yourself. But I hold that one can disavow Stalin without thereby necessarily becoming a Trotskyite.

Soon after, Wurmser quotes a passage of my own, taken from my *Retour de l'U.R.S.S.:* "The particular errors of one country cannot suffice to compromise the truth of a cause which is international and universal." I wrote that sentence, not in the least, as Wurmser tries to demonstrate, *against* the cause of the Revolution, but precisely the reverse: to safeguard its interests, now that Stalin's Russia has abandoned them—a fact that appears to me more and more obvious, that must very soon be realized by every man of good faith who will allow himself to be blinded no longer. I believe (and it is necessary to insist on this) that it is extremely dangerous today to link the cause of the Revolution to the Soviet Union, which, I repeat, is compromising it.

It is for having denounced these compromises that Trotsky is treated as a public enemy (when for him these are only the compromises of Stalin), and all of a sudden identified with the Fascists—which is really a bit too simple. He is far more an enemy of fascism than Stalin himself, and it is precisely as a revolutionary, as an anti-Fascist, that he denounces the latter's compromises. But how in the world to make a blinded people understand this?

Nor can I accept your remark, "It seems impossible to doubt the guilt of the accused and condemned men . . . these men are guilty." If this were truly proven, I should say, however horrified I might be by the executions: Stalin has done well to suppress them. But the real value of all these confessions remains for me highly questionable. . . .

The evil is so profound that we hesitate to acknowledge it. We are deluded by the sumptuous appearance of a worm-eaten fruit.

To Pierre Alessandri   *Cuverville, September 15, 1937*

. . . the small number of true Leninists, opposed to Stalin, is going to increase. I received fraternal expressions of support from every country. From France as well. The still-isolated elements are going to unite. For myself (but my "case" remains a special one), I think it wiser to withdraw from the battle for the moment. But if some unifying association should develop (if I dare to speak thus!), I shall be there. . . .

 1938–1951

INTRODUCTION

On April 17, 1938, the day his wife died, André Gide interrupted his journal and drew a dark double line across the notebook page. When he resumed it, four months later, it was with the words I have chosen to open this last chapter:

> . . . since Em. left me I have lost the taste for life . . .
> Since she has ceased to exist, I have merely pretended to live, without taking any further interest in anything outside, or in myself, without appetite, without taste, or curiosity, or desire, in a disenchanted universe; with no further hope than to leave it.

It is an assertion he repeated frequently in these last thirteen years. I am inclined to see in it, however, a certain amount of literary affectation, or at least of sentimental exaggeration. His emotional dependence on *"le côté Cuverville"* seems to me to have declined a great deal after 1918, despite a kind of unspoken reconciliation during Madeleine Gide's last years. His real family was now the Van Rysselberghe group at the rue Vaneau, backed by Simon and Dorothy Bussy on the Riviera. During her lifetime, his wife may indeed have, in some occult way, forced him to harder work and a more fruitful inner tension than he was capable of achieving now that she was dead. But by 1938—so long and so radically had they been separated—she seems to have become for him primarily a reminder of a love story out of his very distant past.

Whatever the reason, though, the last period of Gide's life does have the quality of what he called "posthumous" years, years of retirement and retreat. He kept writing, of course, in and out of his journal; he remained a great celebrity, corresponded voluminously, traveled a great deal. But I regard it nevertheless as a period of retirement, of old age and declining powers (of which Gide was for the most part perfectly aware). I have already left out of the pages ahead a great deal of material that reflects this only too clearly, and I am half-inclined to let what remains pass without commentary.

I say this in part, I must admit, because there exists so *much* secondary material on these last years of Gide's life, material which often seems
reductive, degrading, and ultimately—however accurate it may be—distorting. All the evidence seems to indicate that the septuagenarian Gide
was something of a crank; demanding, devious, difficult to live with.

> . . . He is more self-centered than ever, demanding that all his
> little quirks be attended to: he can hardly bear to be interrupted.
> . . . He pays virtually no attention to others. He finds it com-
> pletely natural that people serve him, take him about, be at his beck
> and call . . .
> . . . last autumn in Paris, I found an aged Gide, always exhausted,
> breathing with difficulty, irritated over everything, fussy and tyran-
> nical, a real invalid, with whom conversation was difficult. Always
> affectionate, and making a great effort to take an interest in what
> one is saying, but visibly fatigued by the effort, absentminded, pre-
> occupied above all else by his drops and his blankets, with not get-
> ting too hot and not getting too cold. A sick man withdrawn into
> himself, indifferent to everything else. . . .
>
> (from Roger Martin du Gard's journal for
> August 8, 1945, and April 24, 1949; in Gide–
> Martin du Gard *Correspondance,* II, pp. 547
> and 561)

For all his lamentations over diminished desires, he still had a lively
taste for young lads; he was still indiscreet, still hypersensitive, still
self-centered in the most complicated way: in addition, now, he was old,
famous, and much sought after.

Being old, he often seemed, especially to the young, to be some
grotesque kind of fossil: sitting, as James Baldwin once imagined him,
like a wrinkled old toad in the Mediterranean sun, swathed in heavy dark
cloaks and scarves and shawls, his tired eyes fixed on the sea, except for
the occasional glance at a passing village boy.

Being famous (though clearly well out of his creative prime), Gide
was to find his acts, words, gestures, and tics magnified gigantically by
the optic of public opinion and the press at a time when privacy might
have served him far more kindly. I grant that he himself continued at
least to accept, and to make use of, if not to encourage his celebrity; and I
certainly do not mean to call him senile—it is, in fact, his *mixture* of
crankiness and lucidity that is so difficult to come to terms with. I only
suggest that one can exaggerate the characteristics of a famous man's old

age ("From Marlb'rough's eyes the streams of dotage flow, / And Swift
expires a driv'ler and a show").

Being, then, much sought after, much visited, much seen, our aging
grand homme became the subject of a whole shelf of *"tel que je l'ai
connu"* books and articles, "Gide as I Knew Him," written either in
homage or in hostility or in cold objectivity by some of the swarms of
people who came to see him in these years. Each great occasion released
another flood of recollections—the publication of the *Journal* in 1939,
the Nobel Prize of 1947, his eightieth birthday in 1949, his death in
1951. And, because another intellectual style than his was then dominant, because children must resist their fathers, and because Gide in his
seventies may have appeared less ingratiating to many of these witnesses
than he had earlier to others, many of their accounts are decidedly unflat-
tering.

A matter that has always caused some difficulty to Gide's advocates is his
behavior with regard to the Second World War. In many respects it was
not unlike his behavior with regard to the First: again, one can note
     —the same radical unfitness for enlistment, for taking sides, for
nationalist combat;
     —the same confusion, the rumor-mongering of any average, ill-
informed non-combatant, far from the front;
     —the same disgust at the lies and opportunism of French propa-
ganda, the same disdain for the flaccidity of the French spirit;
     —the same converse and perverse inclination to believe the best of,
to see all that is noble on the enemy side;
     —the same brief period of working for refugees;
     —the same attempt, finally, to keep still and ignore the war as far
as possible.

And yet the same pattern of action that seems now to have been
uncommonly wise, even honorable with regard to the first war, looks to
many quite disreputable with regard to the second. The difference, of
course, lies in the fact that in our historical judgment (more particularly
in the French historical judgment) of the war nearer to us in time, there
is still a right and a wrong: the wrong is Hitler, his associates, his collaborators; the right the Allies, and, in defeated France, the Resistance.

Unfortunately, Gide's responses and opinions very often ran counter to the subsequent judgment, or at least the subsequent myth, of history. Hitler he persisted in seeing as a genius—"perfidious, cynical, oh of

course, as much as you like," but a genius; and the German forces as
superior in every way to the French, Italian, and even American.

> I once more admire Hitler's consummate cleverness and the habit-
> ual stupidity of the French . . .   (July 19, 1940)

> . . . many examples are given of the incompetence and lack of
> spirit of the American army, turning tail at the slightest threat and
> refusing to fight so long as they are not sure of being twenty to
> one . . . they are utterly inexperienced, incapable of measuring
> up to the quality of the Germans . . .   (January 3, 1943)

> Germans everywhere. Well-turned-out, in becoming uniforms,
> young, vigorous, strapping, jolly, clean-shaven, with rosy cheeks.
>   (January 8, 1943)

His heart goes out to the German soldiers in their defeat:

> The German army is finally crushed at Stalingrad on February 2,
> after a heroic and useless resistance. What must have been the
> suffering of those sacrificed soldiers . . . ?   (February 4, 1943)

> . . . what I am writing here [of the Allied liberation of Tunis]
> must not be taken as a degrading reflection on the worth of the
> German troops. They gave proof, up to the last few days, of ex-
> traordinary endurance, discipline, and courage, yielding only to su-
> perior equipment and numbers.   (May 13, 1943)

Of the French, he is never taken in by the doubletalk of "loyal
collaboration," "neither victors nor vanquished"; he despises the lies, the
reactionary "National Revolution" of Vichy (supported by so many of
his old enemies); and he is quick to "subscribe heartily" (in his journal,
at least) to General De Gaulle's declaration of resistance on the B.B.C.

But he also wonders (as did many others) if Pétain may not be a
secret Gaullist; he sees sanity and wisdom in submission to superior
force; he contributes to, and tacitly supports, the first issue of the revived
N.R.F.* to appear with the sanction of the occupying powers; and he
regards any movement of organized resistance (October 14, 1940) as
"desperate" and excessively dangerous. Worse, he sees the French people
(as did many supporters of Vichy) as incurably frivolous, lazy, vain, and
selfish, with no sense of discipline or duty and no real national spirit; and
their leaders as either stupid or corrupt. More than once, he wonders (as

---

* ". . . or the N.R.A., as it pleases certain people to call it today" [1]—i.e., the *Nouvelle
Revue Allemande*, the New German Review.

he did in 1914, as did Pétain) whether "it might be good for France to bend for a time under the yoke of an enforced discipline," * and he ventures, on July 1, 1942, this rhetorical question:

> Just when, from what moment on will you consent to admit that an adversary who constantly and in all domains reveals so flagrant a superiority deserves to win out?

Now, there are a great many things one may say in Gide's defense about such remarks.† Several of them—his judgments on Pétain, on French patriotism, on the new *N.R.F.,* on the possibility of resistance, and on the American forces—he retracted as soon as circumstances proved him wrong; certain critics have found, in his willingness to publish his errors (and confess them to be such), something honorable and disarming. Others he at least tried to explain.

> These pages of the journal that I kept (very irregularly, moreover), in the course of the dark months that followed our defeat, I cannot see that I have any right to revise them. They reveal me as no more heroic than I actually was. . . . I am no longer in the same state of mind that made me write them, a mind still drenched with defeat . . . All that goes back to the period of dejection immediately following the defeat. . . . I would like no one to accord to any of these pages—particularly the earlier ones—anything more than a relative value . . .[3]

Moreover, there is almost always a partial justice, a salutary integrity in much of Gide's "perverse" commentary on the war. For although De Gaulle and the *résistants* may have chosen the more heroic part (so much so that they could still, almost thirty years later, trade off the accumulated capital of their choice), the actual state, the actual facts and history of France, then and since, beneath the golden legend of *"Martyres de la Résistance"*—beneath, as well, the hard facts of the Resistance —were such as to lend some credence to Gide's bitter insights and

---

* Compare: "The defeat is the result of our laxity, our laziness. The spirit of pleasure destroys what the spirit of sacrifice has built. It is an intellectual and moral *redressement* that I am calling you to make first of all."   Marshal Pétain, June 25, 1946.[2]
† To begin with, one may note that the historical myth of the second war is uncommonly hard on the French. In the miserable confusion into which France was thrown in the middle of 1940, very few were the good men who could have divined the role that we now judge it proper for them to have played. Roosevelt, it should be remembered, "guessed wrong" about Vichy, and many worthy Englishmen about Hitler.

prophecies. The state of the French army and of public morality, the burning of the fleet, the retreat and rapid defeat, the quality of French governments, the actual fact of collaboration, in one form or another, on a national scale, of the abysmal state of national depression after the war—and of the nation's willing acceptance of something like the "French dictator" Gide had called for—all this indicates how much he was justified in his "insulting" and "unpatriotic" view of France and the French.

And yet, in the light of history's judgment, he will still appear, on the whole, to have been wrong: wrong over and over again. Following life-hardened directions, toiling "upward" and against public opinion, accepting the lash, denying the obvious, belying propaganda—things he had always done, responses completely natural to him—he seems grotesquely to have misconceived. Nor, however just some of his insights may have been, is the rhetoric he used likely to win him friends. The voices and deeds of the *résistants* cannot but take precedence in our imagination over those of a bitter old Cassandra-prophet disgusted with his countrymen—however "right" or "wise" he may have been (and however much their role may have been later inflated in the interests of national self-esteem). Sartre in a German prison-camp, Camus working for the underground press, Malraux an important *chef de maquis,* Raymond Aron—these men would far more easily find their place of honor after the war.

There are those who have tried to have Gide included in this band of literary *résistants* by citing certain "heroic" acts—his break with Drieu la Rochelle (the collaborationist editor of the wartime *N.R.F.*), the attacks and even threats he endured from Vichyites, the "hidden messages" they see planted, like code-words, in certain of his literary essays of the period for *Figaro,* his forced hiding-out in Tunis in the spring of 1943. Others make the defensive point of contrasting his role with that of out-and-out literary *collaborateurs* like Maurras, Drieu, and Chardonne, or his own old critics Massis and Béraud; or of German sympathizers more ardent than he, like Cocteau, Montherlant, Céline, and Giono. Both courses seem to me as futile and wrong-headed as the reverse—trying to make him out a culpable pro-Nazi traitor, as the poet and propagandist Louis Aragon was to do late in 1944.

In fact, Gide ought not to be tried in this court at all. He is not, publicly, politically, a figure of any importance in occupied, "free," or liberated France. One would have to be a very anxious partisan of Gide's to make out his role in World War II as in any sense considerable, for good or for bad: it was not. His name would probably not be mentioned in a history of the period. He was an old man whose important work was done, responding privately to a set of circumstances he saw only from afar and understood badly.

Gide's responses to the war do, however, tell us something about him. On the one hand, they remind us of things we have known all along; on the other, they reveal certain new and unmistakable signs of age.

Of the familiar characteristics of Gide's nature activated by this war, perhaps the most striking is his constitutional inability to take mere political events seriously ("In any case, it's none of my business," he wrote Roger Martin du Gard); or to take sides in any cause, however just. "For a mind made the way mine is, how painful it is to have to take a position—and to have to stick to it!" Worse still, "Recognizing the good points and virtues of the enemy has always been my weakness, and it may well make me look like a traitor to the partisans of either camp." [4]

As impressive here as in World War I is Gide's resistance to and hatred of lying propaganda—and of course his refusal to serve it. He condemns with equal force that of the Paris press, the B.B.C., the Vichy government, the German films, and—to him most despicable—the vengeful super-patriots of the brief and terrible period of "purification" after the war. ". . . It is not so much from the defeat that I am suffering as from . . . the unconscious approval of falsehood and the retreat of all integrity. Words themselves are divorced from their meanings . . . The mind stifles in this atmosphere of organized falsehood. . . . It is to vomit!" [5] Here, if you like, was his real *résistance*.

Ultimately, Gide is far more concerned about intellectual freedom —his own specialty, as it were, his private *patrie*—than about physical freedom.* This is why, disbelieving in the feasibility of an armed French resistance, he would choose the brute force of Germany over the corrupting conformism of Vichy.

> I . . . see less spiritual danger in accepting despotism than in that form of resistance [the "religious revival" identified with Vichy], because I regard any mental subordination more harmful to the interests of the spirit than a yielding to force. [6]

* It must be admitted, however, that Gide's professed willingness to forego physical freedom and comfort—and to have his countrymen forego them as well (see *Journal,* July 10, 1940) —comes a bit inopportunely from one who sought and obtained an extraordinary measure of both during a period of great general privation.

It is, after all, "the interests of the spirit" that are his concern, and he keeps assessing the chances of victory not in terms of Hitler or the allies, but in terms of those interests. It is this very specialized attention that led him (along with many *collaborateurs*) to see more to fear in the prospect of rule by a soulless America or Russia than in German domination. It is this refinement of interests that allowed him, finally, to decide that the values he really treasured were beyond the reach of mere wars, and to seek a retreat, as he wrote to Martin du Gard, "in the immaterial."

But this time his retreat was considerably further than it had been before from the concerns of his fellowmen. It is here, I think, that one can mark the effects of age.

There is, first, in Gide's writings on the second war, a new kind of "view from Olympus," a foggy view from the spiritual mountaintop to which he had ascended. Vague, unspecified visions of "the French genius" and "civilization" and "spiritual values" begin to recall the kind of rhetoric he had taken the lead in deflating one war ago.

There is, second, a particular insistence on the "old man's" values of duty, dignity, and discipline, and a crusty impatience with any of the excesses of freedom—picked flowers in a public park become a symbol of national moral anarchy. This shift in moral emphasis—"I do not believe in *Liberty* (we are dying of its idolatrous cult)" [7]—is one that seems frequently to accompany the cooler blood and harder arteries of age, the careful husbanding of one's own declining energies.

And there is, finally, the melancholy, frequently repeated confession of a sense of displacement, of hopeless perplexity, of superannuation—a sense that goes far deeper than his usual discomfort and alienation in time of war. "I remain without opinion in the face of events, wondering at times whether I shall be able to find a place and a *raison d'être* in the new universe that is confusedly taking shape . . . Is there still something left for me to say? Some work to accomplish? . . . What can I possibly be good for from now on?" "Real exile," Martin du Gard quotes Montalambert to him in 1945, "is not to be uprooted from one's country; it is to go on living there, and no longer find any of the things that once made you love it." [8]

What was he doing during these years? His literary work, of course, when he felt well enough to do it. Sometimes, the very useful secondary work of translating and editing—a translation of *Hamlet* for Jean-Louis Barrault, stage versions of Kafka's *The Trial* and of *Les Caves du Vatican,* the Pléiade *Anthologie de la poésie française,* his patronage of the review *L'Arche;* and three "posthumous" editing chores, those of his own correspondences with Claudel and Jammes and his *Journal 1889–1939,* the literary event of the year when it was published just before the war.

Much of Gide's original work during this period, though, is of a surprising mediocrity. It is not at all what one expects (or rather wants) from the old age of a great man—especially from one who had himself so assiduously cultivated the Goethean, the "Great Man" role. Roger Martin du Gard and Jean Schlumberger were both, apparently, dismayed by their friend's willful refusal to live up to his own reputation, to write "Nobel Laureate" works. Martin du Gard, in fact (who had strict notions of literary propriety), professed himself grievously disappointed by everything after *Les Faux-Monnayeurs,* by the whole last act of Gide's career. "He has made a mess of his old age"(*"Il a raté sa vieillesse"*). . . . Posterity is going to judge severely this narrowed and commonplace final act." [9]

To the dedicated student of Gide, certain of these later writings, like certain of the strange early fables, will prove attractive and informative, useful additions to the man. But given the spotlight of fame in which he lived, they are almost defiantly "minor." In some cases, he came to agree (or pretend to agree) with his critics, and declared certain works embarrassingly bad (*Geneviève,* the play *Robert,* his Oxford lecture). In other cases, the surprising triviality, the limiting of scope, the very chatty superficiality of what he wrote seem to have been quite intentional (e.g., the *Interviews imaginaires*). These may have resulted from a very "Gidean" gesture of resistance to the role assigned him, a willful refusal to put on the heavy, constricting robes of the Great Man's part; or they may have been no more than an accurate reflection of his state and spirit at seventy, which he refused artificially to darken or deepen.

This explanation leaves unexplained certain other works of these last years, works like *Œdipe* and *Thésée,* his preface to Goethe's Dramatic Works, his letter to the Nobel Committee, certain lectures and prefaces in defense of "Civilization" and "the Human Spirit," certain samples of late-Victorian optimism-become-secular religion (God is "the summation of all human effort toward the good and the beautiful") : works disappointing precisely *because* of their heavy banality, their affectations and affirmations, their Mandarin diction, because of their *"banalité de grandhomme"* (Jean Lambert), their *"ton de vieux"* (Martin du Gard).

The latter works, perhaps, represent his occasional yieldings to the temptation of his public image—Gide writing the oracular, avuncular things that demand very little hard or original reflection, things that it was only too easy for a man in his position, at his age, to write. The former, then, the word-games and light anecdotes that so disappointed Martin du Gard, may be taken as his struggles to resist that temptation by excesses of the opposite sort. By writing "perversely" light, superficial, anecdotal sketches, he was at least protecting himself from becoming something he despised—an Académie Française Man of Letters—and having fun at the same time. As for his own conscience, if he wrote in good French and told the truth, that would do. In any case, after *Les Faux-Monnayeurs,* he seems to have felt no impulse at all—for all Martin du Gard's urging—to write another "major work."

Otherwise Gide's life from 1938 to the end was primarily one of reading, resting, and moving about, usually to be a guest at grand hotels or the villas of friends. (The only vestige of his early *inquiétude,* his son-in-law wrote, was an inability to stay very long in one place.) He gave to the reading of Latin the hours he had once given to the piano, read through Boswell's Johnson and Eckermann's Goethe ("as if recognizing," observed Justin O'Brien, "the company in which he belongs" [10]), but also Sartre and Steinbeck and Dashiell Hammett and the Kinsey Report.

A log of his travels for these years is difficult to assemble, so frequent had they become. There are two relatively fixed points: the first is his rue Vaneau apartment in Paris, with his old friend Maria van Rysselberghe across the landing to share his meals when she was in. The place, by all accounts, was almost always in disorder; secretaries came and went; central heating was installed only in 1949. The spare room ("Marc's room") lodged, among others, the Denis de Rougemonts, Jean Malaquais, Gide's daughter Catherine, and Albert Camus. The second fixed locus is a triangular region of the Côte d'Azur about twenty miles wide, with angles at Nice, Cap d'Antibes, and the inland hill-village of Cabris, near Grasse. Here he lived during the first thirty months of war, here he returned again and again to enjoy the hospitality of his friends the Bussys, the Herbarts, and of rich patronesses of the arts like the American Florence (Mrs. Frank Jay) Gould at Juan-les-Pins* and the

* "To see you blissfully imprisoned in this billionaire's showpiece, piled with puerile attentions and expensive presents, crammed with candied fruits, steeped in champagne, housed, warmed, fed, washed, served, and basely flattered in the bargain—I felt something very near to shame! . . . Give up the place to other familiar parasites, who at least have the excuse of coming there to gobble up the roast chickens, drink the liqueurs, and smoke the imported

luxembourgeoise Mme Mayrisch de Saint-Hubert in her estate "La Mes-
suguière" at Cabris ("a kind of castle filled with books, Matisses, and
Dufys," Henri Thomas wrote to his friend Jean Lambert).[11]

He spent the second half of the war in North Africa, the guest first
of friends in Algiers, then of friends in Tunis; it was in Tunis that he saw
and reported the cycle of German occupation, Allied bombardment, and
finally the Liberation. His three years' voluntary exile has been variously
explained as a search for better meals and a better place to work, as an
escape from importunate mobs, and as self-protection against possible
political missteps. If they saved him from the rigors of metropolitan
France, those three years without regular work or familiar friends may
well have accelerated his decline into certain less admirable characteristics of old age.

There were long trips to Egypt in 1939 and 1946, the second by
plane (to lecture, to play tourist, to seek out young companions); a
desert journey with "La Petite Dame," Maria van Rysselberghe, in 1945;
a youth conference in Innsbruck in 1946. He accompanied his daughter
and her new husband to Lake Maggiore in the spring of 1947, then went
to England for his honorary Oxford degree; from England to Munich for
a lecture (the Herbarts "relaying" the Lamberts in looking after papa),
followed by visits at two country estates. He was at Neuchâtel, Switzerland, visiting friends and awaiting the birth of a grandchild, when he
suffered his first stroke; convalescing there in November 1947, he received the news of his Nobel Prize. His illness kept him from making
the trip to Stockholm, but neither it nor the news could keep him from
that night's weekly movie, a Fernandel. (Gide was an irrepressible
moviegoer, and had, like many members of his entourage, actively engaged in various aspects of the film business. He first became a "best-
seller" on the fiction lists, as I have mentioned, when Michele Morgan
starred in a sentimentalized version of *La Symphonie pastorale,* a Cannes
Festival prize-winner of 1947.)

With the Nobel Prize money he bought a small property for his
daughter's family, and what his son-in-law called a "sumptuous . . .
huge, deeper-than-ultramarine blue" De Soto limousine, imported with
some help from cabinet ministers. This became his mode of transport for
the last years of his life, on trips to Switzerland, Italy, and the South of
France. He longed to accept invitations to America in 1948 (a lecture at

---

cigarettes they can't afford to buy for themselves." Martin du Gard, taking issue with Gide
over Mrs. Gould's hospitality.

Johns Hopkins, a degree from Columbia, a villa in Florida), but had to decline them on doctor's orders; and was planning a trip to Marrakech with Elisabeth when he entered his final illness in 1951.

The years were marked by illness, as one might expect: an attack of nephritis in 1940, the paralyzing strokes of 1947 and early 1949, a long battle with hepatitis that he fully expected to be his last in June of the latter year: sciatica, sinusitis, insomnia; cures at mountain spas, medicines and injections, months of convalescence. He was, he had to admit, "afraid to travel alone."

Nor did he have to. André Gide's last years were eased and supported by a remarkable collection of faithful friends. In addition to his new four-generation family (the widow Maria van Rysselberghe; her daughter Elisabeth, and Elisabeth's husband Pierre Herbart; Elisabeth's —and Gide's—daughter Catherine, and Catherine's husband Jean Lambert; and the Lamberts' three little children), the Simon Bussys, the Marc Allégrets, and the Martin du Gards, there were new friends at Algiers and Tunis and Paris and Neuchâtel, a new generation of writers, and young *fils à papa* like Claude Mauriac and Gerard Maurois to talk to and write to and travel with and visit.

The limitations, the disappointments of this final chapter may almost all be traced to the simple fact that our subject has grown old. But as I noted, he himself was as aware of this as anyone; he wished people would stop asking his opinion on things he knew or cared little about.

> Oh, to go back to the time when people were very little concerned as to my opinion about individuals, works, and things, which allowed me not to have any at all. Today America or China is eager, it seems, to know what I think about the atom bomb, the latest vote in the English Parliament, etc. Good heavens! [12]

He appreciated the separate but not equal validity of youth and age, and saw no reason why he should be excited at eighty by the enthusiasms of teen-agers, nor they by what pleased him.

It is this fine awareness of his own age and aging that makes *Ainsi soit-il,* the final postscript to his journal, perhaps the most moving of his later writings, even more so than the oft-quoted conclusion to *Thésée.** I

---

* "If I compare my destiny with that of Œdipus, I am content: I have fulfilled it. Behind me I leave the city of Athens. It has been dearer to me than even my wife and my son. I have built my city. My thoughts can now live on there after me for all time. It is with a willing heart, and all alone, that I draw near to death. I have enjoyed the good things of the earth. It pleases me to think that after me, and because of me, men will recognize themselves as being happier, better, and more free. I have done my work [*j'ai fait mon œuvre*] for the good of future humanity. I have lived." [13]

know of no one else who could have painted so coolly and so calmly this very human self-portrait of a sane and honest man declining into death. His reflections on suicide, on illness, on anorexia, the death of desires, boredom, fatigue, the sense of being out of place compose a unique and exemplary self-examination. Millions of men fold into wrinkles and harden into habits, feel their bodies and minds and passions grow cold and gray. But few remain clear-headed, exigent, unafraid, even interested enough to write so quietly moving an account of the process. He is like one of those pitiless, brilliantly decaying creatures out of Beckett:

> . . . those bags under the eyes, those hollow cheeks, those ravaged features, those lackluster eyes. . . . I am enough to frighten anyone, and that leaves me terribly down. But let us carry on.[14]

For me, Gide's own story, told from within, at least balances all the many hard eyewitness accounts that have been written of this "difficult old man."

> Oh, how hard it is to age well! You would like to do a favor for others, and you feel yourself becoming a burden . . .
> I had not made arrangements to live so old.[15]

1938   *Paris, August 21*

Finding myself quite alone and with almost no work to do, I decide to begin this notebook, which, for several months, I have been carrying with me from one stop to another with the desire to write in it anything but this; but since Em. left me, I have lost the taste for life and, consequently, have given up keeping a journal that could have reflected nothing but disorder, distress, and despair. . . .

Since she ceased to exist, I have merely pretended to live, without taking any further interest in anything outside, or inside myself, without appetite, without taste, or curiosity, or desire, in a disenchanted universe; with no further hope than to leave it.

26th, in the evening

What does not seem to me quite honest, on the other hand, is holding my loss, my bereavement responsible for my languid state; it is my loss that led me to it; it is not that, above all else, which keeps me in it. And I am probably not in very good faith when I convince myself of it. I find in it too easy an excuse for my cowardice, a cover for my laziness. I was expecting this loss, I foresaw it for a long time, and yet I imagined my old age, in spite of grief, only as happy. If I cannot succeed in attaining serenity again, my philosophy is bankrupt. To be sure, I have lost that "witness of my life" who committed me not to live "negligently," as Pliny did for Montaigne, and I do not share Em.'s belief in an afterlife which would lead me to feel her eyes following me beyond death; but, just as I did not allow her love, during her life, to influence my thought in her direction, I must not, now that she is no longer, let the memory of that love weigh upon my thought more than her love itself. The last act of the comedy is no less good because I must play it alone. I must not try to get out of it.

August 27

. . . I am better; I am even as well as I can reasonably hope to be at my age. To work effectively—I mean, to give myself up to some productive work—the only thing I lack now is solitude. Em., while living at my side, knew miraculously how to surround me with a harmonious silence in which my thoughts could unwind without breaking; I have never done anything worth while without a long perseverance in effort. I let myself give too much time to conversation, to tennis, to chess. The house is almost full; it will be completely full in a few days. Everyone is in perfect accord with everyone else. I withdraw for hours at a time, interrupted by nothing, calm, without a thought for the future (I am speaking of my own), studious; and when the evening comes I am astonished to have done so little.

September 5

A succession of splendid days; a pure, radiant sky; as soon as it rises, the sun spreads an opulent felicity over the fields, even though the harvests have been gathered; it seems that everything that breathes ought to feel happy. And yet, faced with this display of beauty, my heart remains indifferent, almost hostile. Since she is no longer here, invitations to happiness are an intrusion. What serenity in the blue sky! What divine indifference to the infinite misery of man!

Free at last and with no tie left, like a kite with the string suddenly cut, I toppled over, diving soul-first toward the ground, where I crashed.

Braffy, September 13

Listened to Hitler's Nuremberg speech on the radio. The call to arms permits a facile eloquence; it is easier to lead men to combat and to stir up their passions than to temper them and urge them to the patient labors of peace. The flattery springs from this: that the affirmation of strength allows one to be stupid.

September 16

I had gone with Jean Schlumberger to Lisieux and was waiting for him in his little car, which was to take us back to Braffy and was parked on the square, where the shadow was already beginning to spread. The sky was completely pure; the air was warm. . . . And suddenly I wondered what kept me from being happy, from feeling utterly happy at this precise present moment. Nothing but phantoms, I told myself, stand in the way; my happiness is prevented only by the shadows they cast. Is it impossible for me to push them aside? To forget for a time my grief, the Spanish massacres, the anguish weighing upon Europe? . . . I could not do it. And I am well aware that I shall never again know that full, naïve joy, that first joy which . . . but to describe it one would have still to feel it.

October 7

. . . Since the 22nd of September we have lived through days of anguish . . . it seemed to me that reason (if not justice and right) was winning a victory over force; but I was not so convinced of this that I was not greatly shaken in my optimism by the admirable letter Jef Last wrote me. He is willing to see in the Munich talks nothing but a shameful defeat, which can only result in a new strengthening of Hitler and new claims; for us, nothing but new withdrawals, and with dishonor. Would Germany have yielded to a firmer attitude, or at least to firmness that did not come so late? would a war have ensured the triumph of justice? or merely that of brute force?

October 8

Anniversary, today, of my marriage. A day that I made a great point of spending with her, occasionally rushing back from a great distance. During these recent days of anguish I came to the point where I was no longer sad that she was no longer here; she could not have endured all this. . . .

I am becoming gradually accustomed to the idea of having to live without her; but without her, I am no longer interested in my life.

October 25

Yesterday at the Valérys'; exquisite and charming luncheon. I feel much more at ease with Paul since I have learned how to limit the disastrous effect of his conversation. His extraordinary intelligence gives him, more than anyone else, a right to scorn. I know, better than in the past, how to get out from under his crushing superiority. Or, more exactly, I am less affected by some of his annihilating statements, and by the fact that he recognizes no value in anything that is not quoted on his exchange. Moreover, there is a great deal in his scorn that I share; but if I had to limit my approbations to his, I should feel destitute.

I accompany him to the Radio Council and sit beside him at the green table. The name of the *Iliad* having been pronounced, Paul leans toward me and in a low voice: "Do you know anything more boring than the *Iliad?*"

Dominating a sudden protest, I find it more . . . friendly to reply: "Yes, the *Chanson de Roland,*" which makes him agree at once.

November 21

I have taken leave. However hardy I may still feel, already I look at everything from a distance; each awakening (especially after a siesta) brings me back with greater difficulty from a slightly greater distance, and I must make a greater effort to disengage myself (with ever greater pain) from a sleep in which I enjoy ever greater pleasures. I think of the time when I used to spring from bed, ready armed. . . . Today at my very rising I am seized again by anguish upon contemplating the thick cloud that is spreading so frightfully over Europe, over the whole universe. An anguish that my optimism is not sufficiently egotistical to overcome. I see nothing anywhere but a promise of death for everything that is still dear to me and for which we live. The threat seems to me so urgent that one would have to be blind not to see it and to continue hoping.

December 3

Hoping for what? Oh, merely that the spirit should win out. I am well aware (so I tell myself, at least) that it always ends up by winning out. But while brute force only exalts it by trying to master it, falsehood and compromise, by bending it, do it much greater harm. The sense of Truth is going to be lost . . . or is it merely that I am becoming ever more sensitive to the distortions that opportunistic compromises impose upon it?

Our foreign policy—how little honesty or integrity there is in it! How little there is in anything "political" . . . but I withdraw in distraction.

December 23

No, no . . . it is with her that I had begun the game. Since she has quit it, I am no longer capable; I have lost interest in the great game of life and long to quit it myself.

1939   Marseilles, January 26

Before leaving Paris, I was able to finish going over the proofs of my *Journal.* Upon rereading it, it seems to me that the systematic suppression (at least until her death) of all the passages relative to Em. have, so to speak, *blinded* it. The few allusions to the secret drama of my life become incomprehensible, due to the absence of what is needed to illuminate them; incomprehensible or inadmissible, the image of this mutilated self that I give there, which presents, in the ardent place of the heart, nothing but a hole.

Obsessed by the thought of Spain's atrocious agony.

[*from* CARNETS D'EGYPTE (*Egyptian Notebooks*) (1939)]

February 3, 4 p.m.

No, I no longer have any great desire to fornicate, at least it is no longer a need, as it was in the heyday of my youth. But I do need to know that if I wanted to I could: do you understand? I mean that a country does not please me unless numerous opportunities for fornication are available. The most beautiful monuments in the world cannot take the place of that; why should I not admit it quite frankly? This morning, finally, crossing the native quarter of Luxor, my need to know was satisfied. With my eyes I caressed ten, twelve, twenty lovely faces. It seemed to me that my glance was understood directly; I was answered by a smile about which one could not be mistaken. There are villages, there are whole countries where a glance overcharged with desire will not evoke the least echo; while there are others . . . let me give you an example: from one end of Russia to another, the slightest wink will come back to you like Noah's dove, bearing its olive branch. The laws of a country have nothing to do with this, they are simply material obstacles; the willingness is there, and a sort of happy connivance which has no need of words to express itself. . . . What annoyed me, in the native quarter at Luxor, was that if I offered the least little gratuity, I would have a whole mob at my heels. For fear of this, I had to pretend to be completely indifferent, and take no notice of them, so as not to compromise my stay here in any way. But when I was almost at the end of the native town (it was infinitely more extensive than I had thought at first), the crowd became less dense and I risked giving an answer to the playful greeting of a fine-looking lad who was passing by. Possibly no more handsome than many others, but robust, glowing with good health and good spirits; his smile revealed a perfect set of teeth. No more than fourteen, fifteen at most. He was walking in the opposite direction, but suddenly turned about in order to follow me. He was carrying an armful of greens—no doubt he had just bought them at the market and was taking them home to his family; he picked off a few choice center leaves for me, and I munched on them. A friend of his who was a bit younger had been walking along with him, and he turned about too. An ugly one, his friend—but what matter?

We were heading toward the Karnak road, but it was already quite late in the morning, and I soon indicated my intention of returning to my hotel by a side road. The whole time he walked at my side, Ali never once stopped talking; I could tell from his laughter and his mimicry that he was talking obscenities, and I smiled back my encouragement, without ever being able to make out whether he was trying to speak Arabic or English. Ali seemed to want to lead me off somewhere; but it was getting late; I could see no unlocked garden, no shady place where we could sit down. We had turned back and were heading toward Luxor again on a wide road where the coaches for Karnak drove past. The sun beat down hard. I spied some cut-down palm trees on a field below the road which could serve as benches; we sat down for a few minutes and, to my surprise, the young friend ran off without asking for a tip. When we set off again, Ali and I, he soon led me off the main road. The path that we took crossed a sordid little village, almost uninhabited. Suddenly, spying a low door in an earthen wall, Ali pulled an enormous key out of the pocket of his filthy Western-style jacket, opened the door, and bade me enter a wretched little court. He closed the door behind us, took me by the hand to lead me into a second court even smaller than the first, then into a very dark room off in a corner. At that moment someone banged so hard on the door that it shook. Ali ran out; there was a violent argument through the door (which was not very securely locked), but it only lasted a few seconds. Ali came back to me and entered into the little hovel; I followed him only with considerable misgivings, but curious to know what sort of proposals he was going to make (although resolved to accept none of them, whatever they might be). As it turned out, they were simple, direct, and unmistakable; quite the reverse of those of the Arabs of Tunisia. Ali, in the half-light of the little shed, took off his long tunic, and let fall his shorts, which revealed the lower half of a most agreeable body, and without more ado offered his backside. This was all I wanted; I had not the least desire to prolong this adventure any further—all the less, in fact, in that I was carrying on me all I had, and was running a great risk in case his companion (who had no doubt followed us at a distance) decided to return with reinforcements, as they may have agreed in advance. At first Ali put up some resistance when I tried to leave the shed; I had to argue with him, but I did so smiling, with a few gentle pats—so as to leave him in hopes of another time. I had learned what I wanted to know.

I went back down the market road, in the vague hope of finding Ali again. I wandered through the thick crowd for more than an hour without meeting a single tourist, not even a middle-class Egyptian. I cannot imagine this crowd very different from what it must have been at the time of the Pharaohs, and I was no more out of my element yesterday among the ruins of Karnak than I was here. Outside the marketplace itself, the vendors clutter up the fronts of houses, squatting before their piles of goods; they bring here all the produce of their gardens—sugarcane and vegetables, but also chickens, pigeons, a great number of turkeys, rabbits, and, farther off, kids; and things they have made as well, woven baskets and mats. Prodigious animation: was it some sort of special day? I must come back tomorrow to find out. My unwonted presence seemed to pass virtually unnoticed, in such a way that I was able to move through all this strangeness as in a dream. As I was on the point of leaving the town, I cut across to rejoin the main road to Karnak, then turned to the left to come back. But first I tried to find, in an alleyway I thought I recognized, the doorway of the little court that Ali had bade me enter. All the doorways, all the alleys looked alike. . . . But a little farther on, I came upon Ali himself. He pulled me off at once in the direction of the Nile, which we came upon after crossing through some ruined courtyards and buildings. Ali tried to persuade me that these ruins were full of all sorts of excellent hideaways; but not until we got to the banks of the river did I sit down next to him. His hideous collection of rags could not succeed in making him look ugly. He is certainly very poor, but not, I think, unhappy. I am pleased he is not a beggar. Got back (following the river bank) just in time for lunch.

February 15

Very little work; but still I managed to finish, two days ago, the editing job I set myself to do;* very indiscreet, but it could not be otherwise; I am free either not to publish it at all, or to leave it to be published only after my death. Still a few retouches to make; I need to reread these forty-three pages from a certain distance. It is much shorter than I thought it would be; but nevertheless I think I have said almost everything I had set my heart on saying.

* No doubt the pages from his *Journal intime* referring to the conjugal crisis of November 1918 (pp. 500–502), the notes to which Gide dated "Luxor, February '39." They were published after his death.

March 2

Continued my reading of Thomas Mann's *Joseph in Egypt*, with ever-growing boredom.

Saturday, March 4

Finally finished Thomas Mann's tedious novel. A very remarkable thing, assuredly, but dependent on a Wagnerian aesthetic that seems to me at the opposite end of the world from art . . .

March 11

. . . wrote to Dorothy Bussy, from whom I have just received two good letters. Also received an enormous, very heavy package containing the complete proofs of the *Journal,* with the proper names underlined in red and blue pencil for me to check against the index; unfortunately I have already sent the proofs of the index back to Schiffrin, so that now I have no means of checking it. Quite a risky enterprise, actually, leaving a book of such great importance (to me!) to be seen through to completion in my absence. Despite Schiffrin's devotion, I expect a few lamentable blunders . . .

Finally decided (gave in) to buy a fly-swatter.

[*from* THE JOURNAL]

September 10*

Yes, all that might well disappear, that cultural effort which seemed to us so wonderful (and I am not speaking merely of the French effort). At the rate at which we are going, there will soon not be many to feel the need of it, to understand it; not many left to notice that it is no longer understood.

One strives and strains one's ingenuity to shelter these relics from destruction; no shelter is safe. A bomb can do away with a museum. There is no acropolis that the flood of barbarism cannot reach, no ark that it cannot eventually submerge.

One clings to the wreckage.

* Hitler invaded Poland September 1, 1939; England and France declared war two days later.

September 11

My body is not so worn out that life with it is no longer bearable. But as for giving a reason, an aim to one's life . . . Everything hangs suspended as we wait.

The war is here. In order to escape from its obsession, I am going over and learning long passages of *Phèdre* and of *Athalie.* I am reading *The Atheist's Tragedy* of Cyril Tourneur and Eichendorff's *Taugenichts.* But the oil lamp throws a poor light; I must close the book, and my mind returns to its anguish, to its interrogation: Is this the twilight or the dawn?

October 30

No, decidedly, I shall not speak on the radio. I shall not contribute to these pumpings of oxygen into the public. The newspapers already contain enough patriotic yappings. The more French I feel, the more loath I am to let my mind be twisted. If it "signed up," if it joined the team, it would lose all its value.

It is by insisting upon the value of the particular, it is by its force of individualization, that France can and must best oppose the forced unification of Hitlerism. Today, however, it is a matter of meeting one united front with another, and, consequently, of entering the ranks and being a part of the unit. Temporarily, they say. . . . Let us hope so. Moreover, isolated voices can no longer make themselves heard today. I will store up my unseasonable thoughts in this notebook as I wait for better days.

November 1

Reading the newspapers, I am shocked and dismayed. The war warps all minds. Everyone blows in the direction of the wind. And Maurras still complains that the censorship does not allow patriots to speak frankly! . . . In short, everything calls me to frank silence.

1940   *February 7*

One must expect that after the war, even though we should win, we shall plunge into such a mess that nothing but the most resolute dictatorship will be able to get us out of it. One can see the soundest minds gradually progressing in that direction (if I am to judge from myself, as the fellow says), and many insignificant facts, one little decision after another (which, taken singly, seem each time the wisest thing in the world, and altogether unavoidable), are progressively accustoming us to that idea.

February 15

I should have been quite capable of being "converted" at the last moment —I mean at the hour of death, in order not to cause her too much suffering.

And that is what made me long rather to die far away, in some accident or other, of a sudden death, far from my family, as Montaigne also wished to do, without any witnesses ready to attach to those last moments an importance that I refused to grant them. Yes, without any other witnesses but chance and anonymous ones.

April 25

Twenty-third day in bed and on a diet. Better informed, I might have forestalled this attack of nephritis, which leaves me as if I had been wounded in the side.

Never before have I approached so close to nonexistence.

May 8

. . . "Not an inch of ground" or "until our last drop of blood" . . . empty formulas in which vanity takes refuge and which help to lift the shadow of the great ghost of defeat. No one knows to whom they are addressed, nor whom they are intended to convince. . . .

May 11

I was supposed to reach Paris yesterday (my seat was already reserved) and should have been just in time to learn the shocking news.* Shocking but not surprising, alas! The radio yesterday evening managed to talk a great deal without exactly telling us anything. They protest, they express indignation, all in a stiff, noble tone, with great bursts of historical allusion; enough to make Hitler laugh, if he didn't have something better to do than listen to our announcers.

May 25

Letters from young men at the front, letters from Belgian refugees; enough to fill one's heart with tears and horror. May tomorrow not bring still worse.

* Germany invaded the Low Countries on May 10.

May 30

The social question! . . . If I had encountered that great trap at the beginning of my career, I should never have written anything worth while.

La Tourette, June 5

We reached Saint-Genès-la-Tourette in twenty-two hours, with a single stop of two hours at Le Puy, where we had lunch (but stopped twenty times during the night for verification of our identity papers). The young Belgian and Dr. Cailleux took turns at the wheel. We had left Vence at about 7 p.m., and fear of a sudden withdrawal of driving permits and of a requisition of autos set us tearing along the road. That very morning Menton had been evacuated. The doctor (who had just learned this) had rushed in from Nice to take me away, and to allow me to take advantage of the unhoped-for chance he was offering me.

. . . Despite the moonless night, our drive across the mountains was splendid, then the daybreak in a perfectly pure sky. But the first news we got was that of the bombardment of Paris.

Vichy, June 8

At the general delivery window I find a telegram that finally quiets my fears about Domi* of whom we had had no news since May 10. Caught in the "glorious" Dunkerque retreat, he is in England, saved!

All communications with invaded Belgium have been cut off, and the unfortunate refugees can get no news of the members of their family who stayed behind.

The roads are thick with wandering families fleeing at random and without knowing where. Children have got separated from their families, and their desolate parents are looking for them. Last night, through the open window of my room giving onto the end of the park, three times I heard a heart-rending cry: "Pierre! Pierre!" and almost went down to find the poor demented man who was calling out so desperately in the night. And for a long time I could not go to sleep, unable to stop imagining that distress. . . .

This morning I speak of it to Naville. He heard the cry, of course, as well as I: but, he tells me, it was the night watchman, who shouts: *"Lumière! Lumière!"* whenever he sees a lighted window, like mine.

* His nephew, Dominique Drouin.

Vichy, June 11

This evening Naville learns that the Paris trains are not running. . . . Atrocious anguish for those at Cuverville.

June 14*

. . . From now on—even from the day before yesterday—the struggle is useless; our soldiers are getting killed in vain. We are at the mercy of Germany, who will strangle us as best she can. Despite everything, we shall shout very loudly, "Our honor is saved!" like that lackey in Marivaux who says: "I don't like people who show disrespect for me" while receiving a kick in the rear.

Doubtless there is no shame in being conquered when the enemy forces are so far superior, and I cannot feel any; but it is with an indescribable sadness that I listen to these phrases—they simply display all the shortcomings that misled and destroyed us: vague and stupid idealism, ignorance of reality, improvidence, carelessness, and an absurd belief in the value of token remarks that have long ceased to have credit except in the imagination of simpletons.

How can one deny that Hitler played the game in masterful fashion, not letting himself be bound by any scruple, by any rule of a game that, after all, has no rules; taking advantage of all our weaknesses, which he had long and skillfully favored. In the tragic light of events there suddenly appeared the profound decay of France, which Hitler knew only too well. Everywhere incoherence, lack of discipline, the invoking of imaginary rights, the disregard of all duties.

What will the high-minded young men who yesterday were so concerned with remaking France do with the miserable ruins that will remain? I am thinking of Warsaw, of Prague. . . . Will it be the same with Paris? Are the Germans going to give the best of our energies time to breathe and regain their strength? They are not going to be satisfied with our material ruin. Today we cannot yet envisage the fearful consequences of this defeat.

We should not have won the other war. That false victory deceived us. We were not able to endure it. The relaxation that followed it has brought us to our ruin. (Nietzsche, on this subject, spoke brilliantly. *Thoughts out of Season*). Yes, we were ruined by victory. But shall we let ourselves be instructed by defeat? The sickness goes so deep that it is impossible to say whether it can be cured.

---

* The German armies entered Paris.

Pétain's speech is quite simply admirable: "Since the victory, the spirit of enjoyment has won out over the spirit of sacrifice. People were asking for more than they gave. They wanted to save effort; today they are discovering their misfortune." One could not say it better, and these words console us for all the *flatus vocis* of the radio.

June 23

The armistice was signed yesterday evening. And now what is going to happen?

June 24

Yesterday evening we heard with amazement Pétain's new speech on the radio. Can it be? Did Pétain himself deliver it? Freely? One suspects some infamous trick. How can one speak of France as "intact" after handing over to the enemy more than half of the country? How is one to make these words accord with those others, so much more noble, which he pronounced three days ago? How can one fail to approve Churchill? Not subscribe with all one's heart to General De Gaulle's declaration?* Is it not enough for France to be conquered? Must she also be dishonored? This breaking of her word, this denunciation of the pact which bound her to England, is indeed the cruelest of defeats, and this triumph of Germany the most complete, for they have forced France to debase herself at the very moment she hands herself over.

June 25

Hostilities ended last night. One hardly dares rejoice, thinking of what lies ahead for us.

July 7

The blow seems to me to have been prepared with consummate skill: France and England are like two puppets in the hands of Hitler, who now amuses himself, after having conquered France, by setting up against her her ally of yesterday. . . .

I doubt that this sudden turn surprised Hitler much. He was counting on it, I would swear; perfidious, cynical, oh of course, as much as you like, but here again he acted with a sort of genius. And what I am most amazed at, perhaps, is the variety of his resources. Since the beginning of the war (what am I saying? since long before) everything has taken place exactly

---

* De Gaulle, from London, had called for continued French resistance on June 18: "Whatever happens, the flame of French resistance must not and shall not be put out."

as he had foreseen it, wanted it; without even a change of schedule; on the appointed day—the day he knows so well how to wait for, letting the machinery that he has set in motion run its silent course, the machinery that must not be allowed to explode ahead of time. There is no known historical game, nor can one imagine one, more skillfully engineered, involving so little chance. . . . Soon the very people he is crushing will be forced, at the same time they are cursing him, to admire him. He does not seem to have been mistaken in any of his calculations; he correctly evaluated the power of resistance of each country, the value of its citizens, their reactions, the advantage that could be drawn from it, taking everything into consideration. . . . We have been very nicely maneuvered, without even being aware of it, by Hitler, the sole master of the revels, whose sly and hidden smartness surpasses that of the great captains.

One awaits with breathless curiosity the next chapter of this great drama which he had so minutely and patiently elaborated.

I should like to be told which of his insults (the insults that made us call him a monster), which of his contemptuous acts has not been found, has not been proved to have been motivated. His great cynical strength consisted in his not deigning to take account of any token values, but only of realities; of acting according to the dictates of an unencumbered brain. He has never been taken in by empty words; he has only used them to take in others. One may well hate him, but he is most decidedly a formidable fellow.

July 9

Splendid morning; a radiant sky. The mountain opposite is pouring off a bright, clear blue light. The countryside with its golden wheat is bathing in peace and joy, and every bird, intoxicated with the sunlight, is telling about it. Amid so much serenity I cannot bring myself to feel very sad; and besides, I am not trying to; I believe that it is bad to force oneself, even in mourning. Effort is useless unless carried into action; in sensations or emotions it distorts everything. The speeches I heard yesterday on the radio are proof of that.

It is not given to many Frenchmen to be constantly aware of the nation's great affliction. One is much more likely to experience individual sufferings; for most people, this means the inconvenience of the restrictions, the discomfort of exile, the fear of tomorrow's famine. If the German domination were to assure us abundance, nine Frenchmen out of ten would accept it, and three or four of them with a smile. And there is no occasion to be shocked by this, any more than by what I am saying of it.

Those who are capable of being genuinely moved for intellectual reasons
are very rare; capable of suffering from non-material privations. And perhaps it is better so. Hitler's great achievement consists in having made the
youth of his country want something other than comfort. But the spirit of
conquest and domination is still a relatively easy thing to inspire.

July 10

In the eyes of obstinate partisans they will seem to be "opportunists,"
shameful and contemptible—those who, not granting in the long run
much importance to the regime or the social state, are above all horrified
by disorder and claim few other rights than the right to think and love
freely. If I were granted no more than this, I should put up with constraints willingly enough, it seems to me, and should accept a dictatorship,
which is the only thing, I fear, that might save us from decomposition. Let
me hasten to add that I am speaking here only of a *French dictatorship*.

July 13

It requires considerable imagination, and that of the rarest type: imagination within the reasoning faculty, to visualize the remote consequences of a
defeat and the way in which each may suffer from it. . . . To tell the
truth, it is through the restrictions it involves, and only thereby (or almost), that the great majority will be touched by defeat. Less sugar in
one's coffee, and less coffee in one's cup—that is what they will feel. But
since they will be told that it is the same in Germany, these privations will
seem to them the result not so much of the defeat as simply of the war;
and they will not be altogether wrong.

The whole education of children ought to tend to raise their minds
above material interests. But try to talk to the farmer of France's "intellectual patrimony," of which he will be very little inclined to recognize himself as an heir. Which one of them would not willingly accept Descartes's
or Watteau's being a German, or never having existed, if it would allow
him to sell his wheat for a few cents more?*

---

* From the Proceedings of the Provisional Consultative Assembly, Algiers, July 7, 1944:
M. Giovanni asks the Commissioner for Information:
   "Is it possible to print in Algiers remarks such as the following, which I shall read you
without superfluous comment:
      It is through the restrictions it involves, and only thereby (or almost), that the
   great majority will be touched by the defeat. Less sugar in one's coffee, and less coffee
   in one's cup—that is what they will feel. . . .
      Which one of them [the farmers] would not willingly accept Descartes's or Wat-
   teau's being a German, or never having existed, if it would allow him to sell his
   wheat for a few cents more? . . .

July 17

. . . [These letters lead me to] regret not having been more directly tried by the war. After all, I shall have known nothing of it but through its echo, shall have suffered from it only through sympathy. The "intellectual" who aims first and foremost to take shelter loses a rare opportunity to learn something. The imagination is powerless to contrive substitutes for real contact, for experience that cannot be invented. On this score at least, the real "profiteers" of the war will be those who have directly suffered from it. I am angry with myself, just now, for having stayed on the outside and for having "profited" so little.

July 25

If tomorrow, as one may well fear, freedom of thought, or at least the expression of that thought, is denied us, I shall try to convince myself that art, that thought itself, will lose less thereby than in excessive freedom.

August 28

I am rereading Kafka's *The Trial* with an even greater admiration, if that is possible, than when I first discovered that amazing book.

September 9

I have been braver in my writings than in my life, respecting many things that were probably not so respectable and giving much too much importance to the opinion of others. Oh, what a good mentor I should now be

"These remarks are by M. André Gide, and were printed in the April–May 1944 issue of the review *L'Arche*. . . .

"If Clemenceau were here, the author of these infamous writings would already be arrested, brought before the military tribunal under the law that punishes traitors with death in time of war; the managing editor of that review would be brought before the same court; the review would be suppressed and the paper that is allocated to it would be turned over to the few patriotic newspapers and reviews of Algiers.

". . . I believe that at a time when the fate of our country is at stake, a well-known writer must not publicly indulge in certain speculations tainted with narcissism and egocentricity.

"André Gide has placed himself 'above the fray'; the sounds of the battle do not reach him. He has seriously insulted the farmers and peasants of France by accusing them, in almost the same terms as the traitor Flandin once did, of 'sordid materialism.' He has insulted the patriotism of the French and has today misjudged the French peasants as much as he once did those of the U.S.S.R. In short, this adulterated writer, who has exercised such a questionable influence over young minds, is playing at defeatism in the very midst of war. His mania for originality and exoticism, his immoralism and his perversity make of him a dangerous individual.

"Today literature is an arm of war. That is why I demand prison for André Gide and public prosecution for the managing editor of *L'Arche*."

for the man I was in my youth! How well I should know how to drive myself to my limits! If I had listened to my own advice (I mean: the man I once was, listening to the one I am today), I should have gone around the world four times . . . and I should never have married. As I write these words, I shudder as at an act of impiety. This is because I have remained through it all very much in love with what most restrained me, and I cannot swear that it was not that very restraint that got the best out of me.

I believe that it is harder still to be just toward oneself than toward others.

September 29

We are entering a period in which liberalism will become the most suspect and impracticable of virtues.

October 14

To love the truth is to refuse to let oneself be depressed by it.

There can be seen cropping out everywhere and vying with one another the vices that led to our downfall, for we are not and never shall be cured of them: taking words for realities and deceiving ourselves with empty phrases. Hitler's great strength comes from the fact that he never tried to take in anyone but others with fine words. He knows what suits the French, alas, and that when they are told very forcefully and very often that their honor is intact, they eventually almost believe it. "Loyal collaboration," "neither victors nor vanquished"—so many checks without funds, and one doesn't know whether he who issues them or he who accepts them is the bigger dupe. Yet it seems to me that the wise man, today, would be the one who did not show too clearly that he knows he is a dupe, and who consequently would cease to be one though acting as if he were. It is a dangerous game, to be sure; but probably less so than a desperate resistance or, even worse, a revolt which at very least would be premature and would run the risk of involving in horrible sanctions even those who had taken no part in it.

November 23

I finish rereading *Werther* not without irritation. I had forgotten that he took so long to die. He refuses to get on with it, and one would eventually like to take him by the shoulders and push him. On four or five occasions what one hoped to be his last sigh is followed by another even more ulti-mate. . . . Frayed departures exasperate me.

Then, to rest my mind and reward me (for I read German only with effort and difficulty), I turn from German to English. Each time I plunge again into English literature I do so with delight. What diversity! What abundance. It is the literature whose disappearance would most impoverish humanity.

November 25

I ought at least to have dated these *Feuillets* taken from my *Journal*, which I have just reread with displeasure in the issue of the resuscitated *N.R.F.* I am no longer in the state of mind that made me write them, a mind still drenched with defeat. Furthermore, my reflections on the lapses and intermittences of the patriotic sentiment no longer seem to me quite fair. There is nothing like oppression to give that sentiment new vigor. I feel it reawakening everywhere in France, and especially in the occupied zone. It assures and affirms itself in resistance, like any thwarted love. And that struggle of the spirit against force, of the spirit that force cannot dominate, stands a good chance to become something admirable. Could it be that our defeat has at last reawakened our virtues? Many examples permit one to hope this, and France shows herself less fallen than I at first feared.

1941 *January 8*

A shift of which it is already impossible to be completely aware. My con-tributing to the review, the *Feuillets* that I gave to it, the very plan of resuming publication—all that goes back to the period of dejection im-mediately following the defeat. Not only was resistance not yet organized, but I did not even think it possible. To fight back against the inescapable seemed to me useless, so that all my efforts at first tried to see submission as wisdom and, from inside my distress, to straighten out at least my thoughts.

January 12

My torment is even deeper; it comes also from the fact that I cannot de-cide with assurance that right is on this side and wrong on the other. It is not with impunity that, throughout a whole lifetime, my mind has made an effort to understand *the other side.* I succeed in this so well today that the "point of view" most difficult to maintain is my own.

In this vacillating state of mine decisions are too easily made by sympathy.

Oh, I should like to be left alone, to be forgotten: free to think in my own way without its costing anything to anyone, free to express without constraint or fear of censure the wavering and oscillation of my thought. It would develop into a dialogue, as it did at the time of my *Enfant prodigue,* and would simultaneously put out branches in opposite directions. That is the only way that I might come near to satisfying myself.

"Neither victors nor vanquished!" I do not much relish that slogan. It implies on both sides a pretense so flattering for our self-esteem that I am suspicious. A "collaboration" such as is proposed to us today could not be "loyal" when it is based on such a lie. It is doubtless fine and noble and reassuring after a boxing match to see the two adversaries reach out and shake hands, but there is no question of denying that one of them has beaten the other. We are defeated. As soon as we showed any inclination to doubt this, our adversary would be able to remind us of the fact, let there be no doubt about it. And if he is helping us to get back on our feet today, this is only to allow us an effort from which he intends to keep for himself the greater part of the profit. He supposes quite rightly that our labor and the production we can supply will be better (or, to speak more directly, that our output will be greater) if we are not reduced to slavery and if we keep the illusion of working freely and for ourselves.

"It is therefore your opinion that we should refuse to play this game?"

Perhaps be a party to it at first, and, if possible, without too much bitterness; but also without illusions, in order to avoid, subsequently, too bitter a disappointment. Shall I tell you just what I think? I believe it is good for France to bend for a time under the yoke of an enforced discipline. Just as she was not capable, in the depths of moral laxity and decay into which she had fallen, of winning a real victory over an enemy much better equipped than she, a united, resolute, tenacious, and pugnacious enemy skillfully led by a man with his mind made up to override all the scruples that weaken us, all the considerations that stand in our way; so too, I do not believe France capable today of rising back up all alone, solely by her own efforts. I say "today" but as early as 1914 I wrote: "We have everything to learn [*apprendre*] from Germany; she has everything to take [*prendre*] from us." I hold by that formula.

"Do you not feel something mortifying, insulting, intolerable in what you are saying?"

The most elementary wisdom consists in taking things, people, and events as they are and not as one would like them to be, or to have been. A wisdom we have often lacked, for we have a great tendency to take words for existing things, and we are satisfied with anything so long as it is well said. One has to play with the cards one has.

"We hold excellent trumps."

But they are scattered and we don't know how to use them properly. This is what keeps me from being too upset if the conqueror, with his fine methods, takes over our hand for a while.

"Those trumps will not survive if their freedom of self-determination is taken away."

Too much liberty has ruined us.

"And then you are leaving out the fact that the conqueror will not allow us to show ourselves, in any domain whatever, as superior to him. He will manage things in such a way as to subjugate our own values and to discredit those that will not submit; both the values and the men who possess or represent them."

That may be, but what can we do about it? Besides, it occurs to me as we are talking that the only values I really respect are those that cannot be used.

"Oh, those too will be made to serve. Yes, I recall that remark of yours you are quoting. But I also recall another remark that I read in your *Journal*. It too comes from the period of the other war. 'I sometimes wonder,' you wrote, 'I wonder with horror' (and, good heavens, how right you were!) 'whether the victory we are longing for is not that of the past over the future.' Well, you must be happy now: this time the forces of the future have triumphed."

In point of fact, nothing depresses me more nowadays than seeing France looking for her salvation only in a rededication to everything in her that is oldest and most worn out. Their fine "National Revolution" gives me a pain in the neck. If our country is to be reborn (and I firmly believe that it will be), it will be in spite of that, against that. I expect our salvation to come from something that is getting ready in the shadows, something that cannot emerge into the light of day until tomorrow.

I doubt if I would use that freedom of expression which is denied us today for the primary purpose of protesting against despotism. Yes, I wonder if this constraint does not hinder me even more in the other direction, for it takes away any values from everything I might think or say just now that might seem to be in agreement with *them*. Any advantage one may derive from his ideas taints them with self-interest.

Consequently, forgetting, forcing myself to forget that constraint for a time, if I let the voice of hell speak out, this is what I hear it whisper in my brain:

"But after all, why and against what are you protesting? Have you not said yourself: 'The family and religion are the two greatest enemies of progress'? Were you not wont to look upon humanity as it still is—prostrate and sprawling—as abject? Were you not wont to scorn with all your heart the paltry interests that keep man from rising above himself? Did you not even write, at a time when your mind was bold: 'I do not love man; I love what devours him'? A paradox no doubt, but not altogether. You meant, if I understood you correctly, that nothing great or beautiful is achieved but by sacrifice, and that the loftiest representatives of this miserable human race are those in whom the sacrifice is voluntary. Have you not constantly denounced as the worst obstacle the cult of false gods? Ought you not to be grateful to me for paying no attention to what you were accustomed to call so properly 'fiduciary values'—that is, the ones that have no other reality than what we grant them? Did you not discover, when you used to indulge in gardening, that the only way of preserving, protecting, safeguarding the exquisite and the best was to suppress the less good? You are well aware that this cannot be done without apparent cruelty, but that such cruelty is prudence. . . ."

Immediately the other voice rises up, heard perhaps less by my brain than my heart: "What is this *best* you are speaking of? The work undertaken by him who aims to be the great gardener of Europe—this work is not so much superhuman as inhuman. If he were to bring it to completion, I suspect, there would remain on earth neither a voice to moan nor an ear willing to hear it; and no one left to know or to wonder whether what his force is suppressing is not of infinitely greater value than his force itself and what it claims to bring us. Your dream is great, Hitler; but for it to succeed would cost far too much. And if it fails (for it is too superhuman to succeed), what will remain on earth, after all is done, but death and devastation? That, until now, has been the most obvious result of your enterprise; and everything leads us to believe that it will be the only one."

January 16

What they are seeking for, hoping for is a restoration of the past, and that past, however pleasant it was for some, did not seem very respectable to me. It may even be said that people took pleasure in a rather shameful state of affairs. Humanity seemed to me to deserve a little slavery; and if only the slavery that threatened us, that still threatens us, had been a submission to nobler values, I am not sure that I might not have gone so far as to welcome it. The only man who seems to me worthy of liberty is one who could utilize it for some other end than himself, or who would demand of himself some exemplary development. The stagnation of the greatest possible number of representatives of a mediocre race in a mediocre, commonplace happiness is not an "ideal" to which I can lose my heart. We can and must aim toward something better.

March 30

I am reading with amazement and dismay this book of Chardonne's which I have just received. Present circumstances give it a rather considerable importance. And in the same mail I receive a letter from Drieu trying to persuade me that it would be good for me to make a public appearance in Paris. . . . He is himself in Lyon at the moment, but does not give me his address there; I notice that omission just as I want to send him this telegram:

APPRECIATE YOUR CORDIAL LETTER AND REGRET comma AFTER READING LAST PAGES OF CHARDONNE'S BOOK CLARIFYING YOUR POSITIONS comma HAVING TO ASK YOU REMOVE MY NAME FROM COVER AND ADVERTISEMENTS OUR REVIEW.

Yet I am grateful to Chardonne for having written this book, which leaves everything in doubt except himself and the position he has taken, in consultation (or at least in company) with A. de Chateaubriant and Drieu La Rochelle. This book works on me by reaction; for as I read it I feel clearly that this position is at the opposite pole from the one I must and will take; and it is important for me to declare it at once. My mind is only too inclined, by nature, toward submission; but as soon as submission becomes advantageous or profitable, I am on guard. An instinct warns me that I cannot agree to be with them on "the right side"; I am on the other.

April 17

Honor, integrity, good faith—merely to pride oneself on having them amounts to relinquishing them somewhat.

May 6

. . . Our present state of decay, which our defeat so sadly revealed, affects me far more than the defeat itself. Yes, I doubt that, alone, we shall be capable of getting back up on our feet; when the time comes that England gives back to us that "Liberty, sweet Liberty," we shall simply turn it into license. I even go so far as to think subjection to Germany preferable for a time, with its painful humiliations, less harmful for us, less degrading, than the discipline that Vichy offers us today.

June 21

The shortest night of the year.

The last four days have been more beautiful than one can say; more beautiful than I could endure. A sort of call to happiness in which all nature conspired, in a miraculous swoon, reaching a summit of love and joy in which the human being has nothing further to wish for but death. On such a night one would like to kiss the flowers, caress the tree trunks, embrace any young and ardent body whatever, or prowl in search of it till dawn. Going off to bed alone, as I must nevertheless decide to do, seems sacrilegious.

August 9

I had never before seen lizard's eggs. Someone came and brought me six. Rather like the snake's eggs I used to dig up as a child in the old sawdust at the sawmill at Val Richer.* Big enough so that I thought they could be nothing other than those very large green lizards which used to amaze me so, and which, I am told, are rather common in this region. They were ready to hatch, and, from one of them that we broke open, there emerged a small, fully formed lizard, but which still had its unresorbed nutritive sac on its side. It wiggled for a few minutes. We buried the other five in a pot full of dirt, and four days later, examining the pot, we noticed that nothing remained of three of them but empty shells. The little ones, having hatched, had got away. I hastened the hatching of one of the two remaining eggs, cutting the soft shell with a razor blade. The little lizard came out slowly, and then, having tested the weather, trotted off with astonishing agility, with as complete assurance in his movements as an adult, and as if in no wise surprised by the sudden discovery of the outer world.

* See pages 59–60.

September 11

How much I miss a piano, *my* piano! . . . On certain days that need, that longing for music, becomes a sort of almost physical pain. The other day, alone at Germaine Tailleferre's while waiting for her, I reread the delightful Sonata in B-flat major, a marvel of grace and emotion; then the slow Etude of Chopin in E-flat minor. I estimated that it would take me probably no more than half an hour to learn it by heart again. To be able to get back to the piano . . . I should enjoy moments of complete happiness. What prevents me from doing so? The physical conditions in which I am living; but above all the obsessing fear of bothering the neighbors, a fear that in my case increases with age, becoming almost pathological. As if it would ever occur to the neighbors to worry about *us!*

December 7

Abandoned this notebook since I began my articles for the *Figaro.* However good they may be, they could not take the place of what I might have said here.

I am writing in the semi-darkness of a movie theater while waiting for the showing (announced for eleven o'clock) of anti-Bolshevist "documentaries." Tickets are two francs apiece, with a special price for soldiers, students of any sort, legionnaires, etc. The result is that the place is crowded. . . .

The film was most painful; even if all the shots were honestly taken and offered us nothing that was not authentic, the camera's ability to choose and present only one aspect of reality leads it into the worst kinds of deception. It is essential to arouse public indignation against Bolshevism. Nothing is easier: here are hideous aspects of poverty, sordid hovels, ragged creatures dying of hunger. And the Red film that offered only this aspect of tsarism would be just as unfair.

The public greatly applauded the overturning of a statue of Lenin, then the recruiting of French soldiers, and Italians especially, which allowed one to figure out who the audience was made up of. Enough to disgust one out of all concern for the fate of men. The systematic belittling of the enemy merely debases the victor.

1942   *Nice, January 1*

. . . I sit still, without opinion, in the face of events, wondering at times whether I shall be able to find a place and a *raison d'être* in the new universe that is confusedly taking shape. This I believe: that it can have no relation to this farce called a "national revolution," which I cannot bring myself to take seriously. The real heartbeats of France are hidden and cannot let themselves be heard. For the moment, it is all nothing more than a temporary pageant, nothing but boasting and deceit. The soil is still too far from firm for anything to be built on it. Everything depends on . . .

January 6

Not a day goes by without my opening the morning paper with the hope of finding news of some amazing event. . . . But no, just the ordinary run of things: ships sunk, cities bombed or burned; people killed and wounded, always by the thousands . . . a monotonous daily refrain.

February 6

Last night at the movies. The French newsreels fill one's heart with tears and make one blush. It seems as if the wine of defeat has intoxicated us; never have we shown ourselves to be prouder than now that there is so little reason to be. They spread out across the screen all our claims to past glory, in the hope that some of their brilliance will spill over onto the present. People congratulate and admire themselves, go into raptures over the splendor, the fragile enormity of our "Empire." It is enough to make one weep.

And, for a conclusion, a giant fuss about the bicycle race called the "Tour de France," on which, if one is to believe them, the entire universe has its eyes fixed. "The most important in the world." Just think: a five-thousand-kilometer race! And the reproduction "by Belinogram" (that "French invention") of the winner's photo in the newspapers of the world. Oh, good grief! Germany can well afford to leave us this bauble, if that's all we want!

February 15

I have spent two hours trying to write a reply to Gillouin's accusations in the *Journal de Genève* (No. 33) of the first of February.* But Roger M.

---

* René Gillouin's article in the *Journal de Genève* was entitled: "Responsibilities of Writers and Artists." In it he wrote: "I received a few years ago, and many other writers must have received likewise, a letter in which a father related with a sorrow all the more convincing for being restrained how his son, a young man of great promise, had been perverted, dissipated, and finally led to suicide by the influence of André Gide. To just what extent was André Gide responsible for the death of that adolescent (and for the demoralization, at the very least, of many others)? God alone knows."

du G., to whom I show that article and this outline of a reply, points out something I hadn't noticed: Gillouin implies that that "young man of great promise" for whose suicide Gillouin claims me to be responsible (this is an old story served up again) had presumably killed himself not merely after having read my books, but under my direct influence; that frequenting me perverted him, and even that I directly "depraved" him.

From beginning to end that story is a pure (or impure) invention, what the English call "a forgery."

Should I cite in reply the testimony of those I have saved from despair, of those already close to suicide? . . . What's the use?

April 10

There was a time when, painfully tormented and driven by desire, I used to pray for the time when the flesh would be subjugated, would let me give myself completely to . . . but to what? To art? To "pure" thought? To God? What ignorance! What madness! This was tantamount to believing that the flame will shine brighter from a lamp that has run out of oil. Abstract, my very thought goes out; even today it is the carnal in me that feeds it, and now I pray: may I remain carnal and full of desire unto death!

The public garden vandalized. No guard. The children trample the lawns, break the branches of trees, strip flowering bushes of their buds. And not a parent to put a stop to this absurd havoc, which they don't even much enjoy. It is merely a matter of destroying and of keeping from anyone what ought to belong to all. Is this a question of the French temperament? Or merely (I should prefer it so) of education? Nation unworthy of the liberty it demands; makes one constantly and everywhere long for policemen, keepers of the peace and of order, fences, and "Keep Off" signs.

April 11

Wherever had I got the idea that it was all over, that springtime no longer interested me, would never take possession of me again? For days now, since the weather has become fine again and the air is warm, I feel that I have the soul of a migrating bird and think of nothing but setting out. I book a berth on the ship leaving Marseilles for Tunis on May 2. Ah, why am I not already there! Everything will have begun already. Once again I shall miss the Overture.

. . . Those last days in Marseilles did me in. So many hours spent chasing from office to office to get the necessary visas, indentification marks and stamps . . . all very Kafka. I keep thinking of *The Trial.* Feeling of things not yet "being in order." If one had to go through so many formalities to die. . . . Material for a wonderful tale. "You can't go away *like that."* . . .

Another great delight in Marseilles was the meeting with Jean-Louis Barrault. Marc, who was awaiting me when the train from Nice got in, had taken me to dinner with him and Madeleine Renaud the first evening in a cheap little restaurant near the station, where Barrault ate his meal in a hurry before going to the radio station where he was to read some scenes from *Le Soulier de satin.* Wonderful face alive with enthusiasm, passion, genius. In his company Madeleine Renaud, with charming modesty, remains in the background. His graciousness, his naturalness, put me at once at my ease. Neither in him nor in her do I sense any of the actor's usual unbearable deficiencies. Talented enough to remain simple.

I saw both of them again the day before I left, lunching with them at their invitation in a very good restaurant on the square where the wide avenue du Prado begins. Barrault urges me insistently to finish my translation of *Hamlet* for him; and I have such confidence in his advice that I should like to get to work at once. I am much pleased to learn that he and Sartre are very close friends. In their company, through a keen personal affection, I feel my hopes rejuvenated.

It is good to be able to direct one's admiration toward the future. It would be a matter for despair if one had to be satisfied with this made-to-order renaissance that is offered us today, this mediocrity so willingly accepted.

The packages of tobacco I owe to the generosity of American friends cause me serious troubles with the customs, from which the most obliging Tournier arrives a bit too late to save me. Lunch at the restaurant of the Tunisia-Palace. Lyric voracity. Ten varieties of hors d'oeuvre (I counted them!). Everything strikes me as good beyond all hope after the near-fast of Nice. I devour in an unbelievable way, then go and sleep for two hours.

May 10

The set is new, but it is the same act of the same play that goes on. I am no longer here. For some time now I have not existed. I am merely occupying the seat of someone who is taken for me.

May 22

X. asks me: "Don't you understand that everything that is now taking place is but one more scene of the great drama of the *class struggle?* . . ." And this in the same tone as if he had said: "Don't you see that all this is, after all, merely a 'solar myth'?" . . .

La Mersa, June 12

The time is approaching, and I feel it quite near, when I shall have to say: I am finished: I can do no more.

I do not believe in *Liberty* (we are dying of its idolatrous cult), and am ready to accept many restrictions; but I cannot bow before certain iniquitous decisions, give even a tacit consent to certain abominations.

June 22

I have given up trying to force myself to work, aware of writing nothing worth while. Is there still something left for me to say? Some work to accomplish? . . . What can I possibly be good for from now on? Whatever am I being saved for?

My thoughts escape me like spaghetti slipping off both sides of the fork.

Some Arab children have made a plaything of a little bird. They are dragging it along on a string attached to one leg and are amused by the useless efforts the bird occasionally makes to get away. I hesitate to take it away from them; but the half-dead bird cannot survive; the only point would be to finish it off as quickly as possible, sparing it a longer agony. And I wonder what a sorry "image" of the world can have been formed by this starling fallen from the nest, during this brief span of suffering and repression? . . .

"Just when, from what moment on will you consent to admit that an adversary who constantly and in all domains reveals so flagrant a superiority deserves to win out?"

"But then this is the end of freedom of thought. . . ."

"Will *you* be able to carry your liberalism to the point of permitting me to think this freely?"

"To think what?"

"That the path pointed out to us by the excellent Father X., for instance (whom I love and venerate), the path he would like to lead us on, seeking to restore in us a sense of the sacred and to obtain from us a submission of the mind, without inquiry or verification, to truths recognized in advance, truths insusceptible of argument—that that path, I insist, is as dangerous for the mind as the path of Hitlerism itself, to which it is opposed; perhaps even more dangerous. . . . Despotism can be opposed only by another despotism, to be sure, and it is an easy matter for Father X. to maintain that it is better to submit to God than to a man; but, for my part, I can see on one side as on the other nothing but an abdication of the reason. In order to escape a very obvious danger, we hurl ourselves toward another, more subtle and not yet apparent, but which will only be all the more dreadful tomorrow. And thus it is that the civilizations that appear the most solidly established come to collapse, in a way that we very quickly find incomprehensible. As for ours, a few years earlier we should not have thought it possible; and even today very, very few people recognize in this so-called recovery, this pseudo-revival of France, in this return to the past, in this 'withdrawal to one's minima,' as Barrès used to say, the most tragic result of our defeat, the true disaster: this almost involuntary, half-unconscious relinquishment, by the best, of the possessions acquired most slowly and with the greatest difficulty, the hardest to appreciate, the rarest of all. . . .

"I admire martyrs. I admire all those who are able to suffer and die, for whatever religion. But even if you were to convince me, dear Father X., that nothing can resist Hitlerism but the Faith, I should still see less spiritual danger in accepting despotism than in that form of resistance, because I regard any mental subordination more harmful to the interests of the spirit than a yielding to force, since the spirit, at least, is in no way committed or compromised by the latter.

"Yet if it is in the name of Faith, through Faith, that we succeed in driving the enemy out of France . . ."

"I should indeed applaud the remedy by which we had overcome a great sickness. But how much time and vigilance and effort should we need then in order, as Sainte-Beuve said, to 'cure us of the remedy'?"

August 8

This morning a card from Saucier to tell me that a client is offering him two hundred thousand francs for the manuscript of *Si le grain ne meurt,* which I sold to B. for forty-five thousand before leaving Nice. I make an effort to consider this very funny.

September

Still at Sidi-bou-Saïd. Thanks to the charming hosts who are putting me up, I am finding here rest, comfort, calm, and salvation. From the terrace of the villa I watch the plain as it faints away. Exhausting heat, which I am ashamed to endure so badly. And, for the first time in my life, probably, I am making the acquaintance of what is called nostalgia. I think of the mysterious inner woods at La Roque in which the child I was could not venture without trembling; of the edges of the pond thick with flowering plants; of the evening mists over the little stream. I think of the beech grove at Cuverville, of the great autumn winds carrying away the russet leaves; of the rooks' call; of the evening meditation beside the fire, in the calm house that was falling asleep. . . . Everything I owe to Em. comes to mind, and I have been thinking constantly of her for several days with regret and remorse for having so often and so greatly been in debt to her. How often I must have seemed to her harsh and insensitive! How poorly I must have corresponded with what she had a right to expect me to be! . . . For a smile from her today, I believe I should give up life, give up this world in which I could not meet and unite with her. . . .

September 16

Every night (or almost) I have been dreaming of her, for some time now. And always, in each dream, I see some obstacle, often petty and absurd, rise up between her and me to separate us; I lose her; I set out in search of her, and the whole dream is but the development of a long adventure in pursuit of her. . . .

Ah, it is better that you are not here! . . . (I am constantly telling myself this). You would have had to suffer too much from the degradation of France.

October 6

As a result of my article on *Iphigénie* in *Le Figaro* for August 30, I have received from M.K., a magistrate in Pau, a long letter from which I want to copy some passages here, for I believe them to be particularly illustrative of a state of mind that is tending to spread; these are the last sentences of the letter:

"The writer is responsible for the consequences of his writings. Your proposition* is, in my opinion, most pernicious. This is why I have taken the liberty of writing you this letter. I have fought to save my country. Why do you then take the liberty of poisoning it with such false maxims interspersed amid so accurate and so captivating a critique? You have no right to act like this at such a moment when the France of Saint Louis needs her lights in order to remain worthy of her tradition. You less than anyone else, to whom has been given the gift of writing well, which places you above all the Immortals of the moment, except the Marshal,† who is the magnificent servant of the Word."

What can I reply to that? . . . *Cedant rationes mentis vulneribus corporis.*‡

November 12

Occupation of "Free" France by Germany and of North Africa by the U.S.A. . . . Events deprive me of any desire to say anything. Always tempted to think that all this has no importance *basically* and does not interest me, even were I to lose my head from it.

November 26

Large posters cover the walls of Tunis. They inform the population that, invaded in cowardly fashion by the Anglo-Saxon pirates and incapable of defending herself, North Africa must gratefully welcome the Axis troops who have come generously to offer to defend her.

If the latter are victorious, this is the version of history that will prevail.

---

* He is talking about this sentence from my article, "which I was quite amazed to read," says M.K.: "The Christian soul refers back to and relies on God, whereas the pagan soul puts its trust and finds support only in itself." [A.G.]
† Pétain.
‡ "Let the mind's reasons yield to the body's wounds."

December 3

Heard on the radio last night, with great discomfort, the commentaries of London on the speech Mussolini has just made. Can it be that such coarse insults find an echo in the hearts of the majority; is it this majority, then, that the radio must seek to satisfy? Can they not be made to realize (and precisely by means of a victory) that one debases oneself by trying to debase a conquered enemy, and that it is essential to be superior otherwise than by force?

December 5

The fragments of Mussolini's speech given in the Germanophile paper of Tunis are such as to justify the scornful vituperations of the English radio. One cannot imagine anything more stupid, more false, more flat. Impossible that there are not, even in Italy, many people sufficiently sensible and well informed to suffer from it.

December 7

. . . Finished rereading, for the third or fourth time, the extraordinary *Cousin Pons,* after which I shall be able to move on from Balzac, for he has done nothing better.

I am rereading *Le Rouge et le noir* with indescribable rapture.

December 11

In every street of Tunis, a great number of Italian or German soldiers; the former in dirty uniforms, sluggish and unhealthy-looking, utterly without military bearing and quick to show insolence; the Germans well equipped, clean, disciplined, appearing at once smiling and resolute, no doubt ordered to show themselves agreeable and attentive toward the civilian population, to make their domination desirable, and going about it just right. Everywhere considerable munitions and armaments. . . . I fear we may be in for a long siege.

The official communiqués on both sides are most contradictory, each one announcing nothing but victories, retreats on the part of the opposition, and encircling of enemy forces. The mind stifles in this atmosphere of organized falsehood.

December 15

The Italian soldiers' sniping, the Anglo-American bombs, the anti-aircraft guns, the intermittent din of German autos, armored cars, trucks, or ambulances tearing past under our windows, and then waiting for all these noises kept anyone from sleeping last night. It is by far the heaviest bombing Tunis has suffered so far. Yesterday alone, ninety dead. Who can tell the number of victims last night? . . .

December 17

. . . The broad stars made by the flares lighted up the lake of Tunis and La Goulette, where bombs set fire to a munitions dump; the blaze shook the horizon with a spasmodic red glow. Other bombs fell on the harbor and, not far from us, on the town, their explosions shaking the walls. Showers of tracer bullets from the anti-aircraft guns streaked the sky. It would be impossible to imagine more glorious fireworks. For fear of missing any of it, I had gone to bed fully dressed, and never let myself fall more than half-asleep; each time it resumed, I would leap from my bed to the living-room window, my heart beating—not from fear (and that was how I came to realize just how little I care now for life), but from a sort of amazement and panic horror, from expectation composed of apprehension mixed with hope.

December 21

What people one meets in the streets! Emaciated, sordid, in tatters. Where were they hiding until now? Hideous outcasts who seem forever unfit for everything that constitutes human dignity, unfit likewise for happiness and having no possible contact with us but their poverty.

December 26

NOTICES in three languages (French, Arabic, and Italian) are abundantly posted on the walls of the city. They make known to the Jews that before the end of the year they will have to pay the sum of TWENTY MILLIONS as an aid to the victims of the Anglo-American bombings, for which *they are responsible,* "international Jewry" having, as it has long been well known, "wanted and prepared for the war." (The Jewish victims are naturally excluded from the number of people to be aided.) This is signed by "General Von Arnim, Commander of the Axis Forces in Tunisia."

December 31

Last day of this year of disgrace, on which I want to finish this notebook. May the one that follows reflect less somber days!

1943　　　　　　　　　　　　　　　　　　*Tunis, January 1*

. . . More bombs fell on Tunis at noon and at five o'clock; the results of
the explosions are appalling. Jean Tournier, with a team of young men,
has been busy the last few mornings extracting corpses and wounded men
from under the ruins of a block of houses in the Arab town which had
been demolished by three bombs early in the week. They counted between
three and four hundred victims. It was impossible to reach in time those
who were walled off in the cellars and calling for help. And clusters of
corpses, already rotting, continue to be brought out from under the piles of
masonry, beams, and rubble.

January 2

. . . many examples are given of the incompetence and lack of spirit of
the American army, turning tail at the slightest threat and refusing to
fight so long as they are not sure of being twenty to one. At another point
(Tebourba?) a column of tanks, attacked by enemy aviation, is said to
have been routed, the men forsaking their wonderful and costly machines
intact to flee under the olive trees; so that the German army, having seized
the tanks, brought them in triumph into town, where everyone could see
them. Their equipment (the Americans') is supposedly marvelous, excellent even in its smallest details, but the combat value of the men almost
nonexistent; in any case, they are utterly inexperienced, incapable of measuring up to the quality of the Germans, who are sending their best men to
Tunisia. I fear that there may be much truth in this; and in any case the
Allies have to deal with serious opponents, resolute, convinced men, long
prepared and disindividualized to the point where they no longer exist
except as part of a combat unit.

We are wallowing in suppositions; but one certainty is that a dozen
eggs cost a hundred and twenty francs.

January 6

Bombs fell last night on the avenue Roustan barely sixty yards from the
house of which we are occupying the fourth floor. The explosion blew in a
French door of the room in which I was sleeping and broke a large, heavy
mirror in the living-room. By an extraordinary stroke of bad luck we had
not made sure the windows were unlocked last night because of yesterday's
heavy wind. A rather large bomb-fragment cut through the wooden shut-
ter and knocked out the lower pane of one of the living-room windows.

January 8

Germans everywhere. Well-turned-out, in becoming uniforms, young, vigorous, strapping, jolly, clean-shaven, with rosy cheeks. The Italian soldiers cut a rather sorry figure in comparison. And the Arabs show themselves full of obsequious attention for the Germans.

In the streets of Tunis, where I wander aimlessly, what wretched specimens of humanity! Not one face that it is a pleasure to look at. Men and women, Italians as well as Arabs, marked with anxiety, looking withered and miserable. Toward evening many of them carry suitcases, baskets, mattresses, and blankets for the night's encampment. Sickly children. Poor cattle, fearful and hunted.

January 10

I sleep. I sleep as if to make up now for all the insomnias of my childhood. My siestas, which used to last a half hour at most, sometimes last more than two hours, without doing any harm to my long night's sleep. I had gone to bed yesterday without supper, my stomach still heavy from the lavish luncheon the Cattans had served me. What a meal! It would have seemed perfect to me if I had been able to divide it four ways. Preceded by a delicious "West Indian punch" (for Mme Cattan comes from Guadeloupe), it began with "breiks" (which are large triangles of very flaky pastry surrounding a soft-boiled egg in the midst of a succulent meat hash; one cannot imagine anything better), followed by copious hors d'oeuvres, which would alone have satisfied me until evening. Then came an extraordinary duck with orange, in a curaçao sauce thickened with minced chicken livers; it was so good that I could not resist helping myself a second time. That was unwise, for I next had to do honor to a loin of milk-fed veal with mushrooms; then to a lobster and vegetable salad *à la russe*. To finish off, to finish me off, two huge cakes, one made with almonds and the other a sort of cream tart covered with thick caramel. All this washed down with four kinds of old and perfect wines: Sauternes, Beaune, Pouilly, and one other, from their very best stock. I begged them not to uncork a last bottle of real champagne, prewar Veuve Cliquot, "such as will not be seen for a long time." Dead-drunk and overstuffed, I let myself fall on the couch the Cattans had prepared for me in a quiet room. . . .

All she expected of me and I was unable to give her—indeed, that was due her . . . there are days when I think of nothing else. . . . In what a state of blindness I have lived!

Read much of late despite my tired eyes. But my brain receives nothing any more but the most fleeting impressions; it seems that nothing else can be deeply inscribed in it. So that, all in all, I draw very little profit from all these readings. I am continuing, as a matter of duty, my reading of Boswell's *Johnson*. Boswell is considerably more intelligent and resistant than Eckermann, but Johnson is obviously less important than Goethe; one is more amused than taught by him, and Boswell is often quite right to stand up to him, and not to accept his opinions and judgments except with many reservations. Not much of a lesson to be hoped for from conformists. I am eager, as soon as the Boswell is finished, to launch into Gibbon's *Decline and Fall*.

An unhoped-for, doubtless the last, opportunity to return to France: I am offered a seat on one of the planes that are to repatriate certain officers and civilians. I pretend to myself to be perplexed while knowing full well, at heart, that I shall not accept. The game that is being played here is too captivating, and my fate is tied to that of these new friends whose life I have been sharing for more than six months. I would feel as if I were deserting. That game, of which I saw the beginning and which I have followed from day to day, I want to see through to the end. . . .

Read in succession the four *Pleasant Plays* of Shaw (in English). Amazing cleverness; but at times the dose of Sardou wins out over the dose of Ibsen. How amusing they must be to act, though! And to see them presented by good actors!

Joy at recognizing Julien Green's friendly voice in the message from America. Then, immediately thereafter, the customary display of preparations, the number of new ships launched, their tonnage, the future crushing superiority of the American fleet and arms over those of the Axis.

. . . After that the least setback will necessarily seem shameful, and victory nothing but the triumph of superior numbers and equipment. The Americans, people keep saying, will not make up their minds to fight until they are sure of being ten to one. There is nothing to boast about in that; and there are those who, while they of course wish with all their hearts for the downfall of the Axis, deplore that ostentation. The superior force is now in different hands, but it is still *force* that is called upon to win out over human values, to assert itself. It cannot be otherwise, it will be said, and what alone matters is making that force serve the spirit. . . . The spirit, in that case, will do well to be on the side of material interests. I fear that, in any case and whatever happens, it will be she, the spirit, who will remain, when all is said and done, the great loser in this whole sorry business.

February 4

The German army is finally crushed at Stalingrad on February 2, after a heroic and useless resistance. What must have been the suffering of those sacrificed soldiers, deprived now even of the hope that their death might contribute to victory? What could they have thought of Hitlerism and of Hitler during their agony? But what does Hitler think of himself?

Il descend, réveillé, l'autre côté du rêve. *

Boswell is beyond question superior to Eckermann. A pity that Johnson remains so inferior to Goethe. His wisdom is wonderfully representative of that of his time, but never rises above it. He has very racy sallies and retorts, but one listens to him without real profit, constantly aware of the limitations of his genius. Constricted, moreover, by the creed to which he constantly renews his allegiance; but one wonders whether without that curb he would have been able to venture very far. He remains a man of letters throughout everything, and one is grateful to him for that. His style is rich, full of images, consistent, rhythmical, and almost succulent; in comparison Swift's seems fleshless. Nonetheless, if Johnson seemed to dominate his time, he did so, I think, especially by his mass. He overwhelmed.

February 10

Sorry need of insulting and vilifying one's opponent, a need equally common to both sides, which causes me to listen so painfully at times to the

* "He awakes and goes down the other side of his dream." (Hugo)

radio broadcasts, those from London and America as well as those from Berlin and Paris–Vichy. What! Do you really think that all the intelligence, nobility of heart, and good faith are solely on your side? Are there nothing but base interests and stupidity among your opponents? Or perhaps you will tell me that it is good to convince the masses of this, for otherwise they would have less heart for the conflict? It is essential to persuade the soldier that those he is being urged to massacre are bandits who do not deserve to live; before killing other brave, decent fellows like himself, his gun would fall from his hands. It is a matter of activating hatred, and one blows on the passions to make them glow brightly. To fight brutes, we need brutes; so let us brutalize.

Recognizing the good points and virtues of the enemy has always been my weakness, and it may well make me look like a traitor to the partisans of either camp. Which of course is why I should keep silent today, even if I were given license to speak. Today there is no place for anything but falsehood; people will listen to nothing else. And everything I am saying about it is absurd. . . .

February 18

I finished Boswell yesterday evening. Those thirteen hundred pages can be read almost without a single moment of fatigue or boredom. How much Johnson's robust intelligence is paralyzed or held in check by his religious convictions; and his perpetual fear of going beyond them is something that Boswell himself implicitly admits (though he shares Johnson's convictions); and that through them "he had perhaps, at an early period, narrowed his mind somewhat too much, both as to religion and politics." And it is not one of the least interests of this book that it allows us to follow the voluntary restriction of that fine free mind. "He was prone to superstition, but not to credulity," as Boswell excellently says. It is in this respect that his book is most instructive, despite him: we see, by example, how a vigorous mind can remain entangled in dogma.

February 20

The American army has withdrawn, has fled in retreat, forsaking tanks, cannon, munitions; and not even pursued by Germans, but by the Italians whom the Germans sent after them. With the killed and wounded, the prisoners and the missing, twenty-five thousand men were presumably lost, says the American radio, which is not covering up the disaster. I did not hear it myself and know only what is repeated to me this morning by V. This at least will keep America from judging us too severely.

February 21

. . . the details V. gave me yesterday are still unconfirmed. The Americans' retreat is certain, but their losses seem to be monstrously exaggerated. According to Z., that figure of twenty-five thousand which V. gave me yesterday presumably includes their total losses since the beginning of the war, and on all fronts. It is when opinions are not better supported and informed that they most easily turn into "convictions." "The shadows of Faith," as Fénelon says, are what permit religious convictions.

March 3

Yesterday, shortly before noon, a more intense bombing than any of last month. . . . In front of the hospital gate was pressed a crowd of poor people, with whom I mingled for a time vainly seeking some face to look upon with pleasure. Nothing but diseased, deformed, poverty-stricken outcasts, ugly enough to discourage pity. A great anguish of loss weighed upon that sorry mass of humanity. They were waiting to be allowed to approach the victims, which could not be done until after the latter had received first aid. I saw some on stretchers as they left the ambulance, disfigured by hideous wounds, with only half a face left; others bloodless and pale, their eyes closed, perhaps already dead. . . .

Lunch at the hospital, then back into town immediately after. Learned on returning to the avenue Roustan that all the windowpanes in my room had been blown out. About thirty yards from the R.'s house, a bomb destroyed the buildings of the registry office.

No more electricity; no more gas; no more water.

. . . bombs everywhere around did frightful damage; one dug up the pavement of the avenue Jules-Ferry (the continuation of the avenue de France) in front of the big café, the largest in town, now become the "Wehrmacht Kaffee"; all the plate-glass windows of its façade are blown in. The large movie theater next door, likewise reserved for Germans, is nothing but a shapeless mass of ruins. If only the hall had been filled. . . .

The appearance of the bombed-out houses is hideous; the thin sheathing which gave the buildings a rather respectable look has flaked off, leaving visible everything people had striven to hide: a pitiable, cheap construction out of unmentionable materials. The streets are littered with fragments of glass and rubble. In the gutted apartments everything is faded, soiled, tarnished. Walking along, you raise a heavy, whitish, choking dust that brings tears to your eyes. Disgust is even greater than horror.

. . . At five a.m., alert. At the first explosions I followed Chacha and Victor to the shelter. It serves as a dormitory for many refugees, who have spread out mattresses, most of them directly on the ground. I hear someone near me say: "Some day, though, these bombings will have to come to an end!" Yes, but we might come to an end before they do. To die buried under the ruins, die by slow asphyxiation in a sordid promiscuity, amid the excrements of both soul and body. . . . No, I think I shall not again go down to the shelter.

March 7

The journal notebook (January to May 1942) that I had entrusted to Hope Boutelleau for typing fell into the hands of the Italian police at the time of the house search at Sidi-bou-Saïd; the Italian police handed it over at once to the German authorities, who, I am told, were concerned by certain passages . . .

. . . long before the war, France stank of defeat. She was already falling to pieces all on her own, to such a degree that perhaps the only thing that could save her was, *is* perhaps, this very disaster in which she can retemper her energies. Is it illusory to hope that she will emerge from this nightmare strengthened? I believe that right now she is pulling herself together.

We were barely beginning to get out of the mythological era. Germany and Russia concurrently did much to free us from it, if only by means of the incomparable prestige and value of their respective armies; but also, and principally, by transferring to this present world all the vague aspirations toward an imagined world beyond by materializing human unrest, so to speak, through the new ethical code that each imposed. If only humanity, in its artistic manifestations, can avoid being too much impoverished thereby! Contemporary Russian literature, at least, seems to reveal that this is possible, and to stand the test nobly. More and more, better and better, man is called upon to *be sufficient unto himself.*

March 15

Since yesterday we have had electricity again. Delight at being able to read until eleven! (Gibbon's wonderful *Decline and Fall.*)

March 16

I notice in one of Gibbon's notes (Guizot edition, Chapter iii; A.D. 117), *Of Hadrian* (in regard to Antinoüs): ". . . We may remark that, of the first fifteen emperors, Claudius was the only one whose taste in love was entirely *correct.*"

March 29

Nine hundred tons of explosives dropped on Berlin last Saturday, the London radio announces. The destruction must have been frightful. One can hardly imagine it, considering that less than a hundred tons at most have caused all the devastations in Tunis.

April 10

Oh heavens, yes, I know very well in what sense I could say, as Valéry says, that "events do not interest me." None of the things which really matter to me spiritually is dependent on this war, to be sure; but it is the future of France, it is our future, that is at stake. Everything to which we still devote our thoughts may disappear, sink into the past, have no significance for the men of tomorrow but that of the archaic. Other problems, undreamed of yesterday, may disturb those to come, who will not even understand what reason we had for existing. . . . (I am writing this without really thinking it.)

April 11

I have patiently reread from end to end the interminable *Vanity Fair*. I should not have time enough in France; here nothing presses me; all my time is leisure time, while I wait. (I should also like to take up a Walter Scott again.) But I wonder whether, in my youth, I had actually gone on reading the Thackeray to the end; or whether the translation I read at twenty was not considerably abridged. The number of idle reflections rather unfortunately *date* this novel, and only certain chapters remain remarkable. *Henry Esmond* seems to me much better (that is, if I can judge by my memory of it).

Rather disappointed by a rereading of *The House of the Seven Gables,* which I take up immediately afterward. Less sensitive to the poetic aura with which Hawthorne can envelop our outer world than to the often exasperatingly slow progress of his narration.

. . . But to feel useless, of no service for this great action that is about to begin; to feel one's intelligence not so much diminished perhaps as slowed down, without sudden reactions and ripostes, without retorts, still an excellent spectator, but not a participant in the struggle, and too acquiescent in the event, whatever it may be. . . .

A "nature" like mine is utterly unfit for politics. Not that I am totally devoid of the spirit of intrigue; but it is very difficult for me to convince myself that all the wrongs are on the side of the adversary; I am more inclined to dedicate my efforts to understanding than to combating them. Consequently I am worth nothing in arguments. I quit my position to follow my opponent, get thrown off the track, and soon have no idea where I am. It's pitiful.

Dazzled by *Richard II,* of which I had retained but the vaguest impression. Wonderful, the second scene of the first act—Mowbray accused by Bolingbroke (Harry Hereford, Lancaster), with a rather long series of rhymed verses. Wonderful, the profession of love for England by John of Gaunt, the King's brother, on his deathbed (Act II, Scene i)—which I ought to learn by heart. . . .

Art—called upon to disappear from the earth; progressively; completely. It was the concern of a chosen few; something impenetrable for the "common run of mortals." For them, vulgar joys. But today the chosen few themselves are battering down their privileges, unwilling to admit that anything should be *reserved* for them. By a somewhat silly magnanimity, the best people today desire: *the best for all.*

I can imagine a time coming when aristocratic art will give way to a *common* well-being; when the individual will lose its *raison d'être* and will be ashamed of itself. Already we have seen people in Russia castigated for betraying private and individual feelings; we have seen men no longer accepting anything that cannot be understood by the commonest of men; which will end up with their accepting nothing but the commonest of things. Humanity is waking up from its deep mythological sleep, and venturing forth into reality. All these children's playthings are going to be relegated among the obsolete, the worn-out things. People to come will no longer even be able to understand how we could have been amused by them for so many centuries.

As soon as I have read it, I reread *Richard II* almost entirely. One of the most imperfect, the least constructed of Shakespeare's plays, but one of the strangest, the most laden with poetry.

These days—I feel as if they were stolen from life. I have now passed eight of them in this hideaway, a gloomy enough place despite the extreme kindness of my hosts and companions in captivity. They, for their part, have been cloistered for almost six months now, not even daring to put their noses out the window, or, above all, to appear on the balcony in full view of the neighboring terraces; even less to risk themselves in the streets, where one is exposed to mass round-ups. That my own person is sought by the German authorities is not altogether proved. Arrested as a suspect? Suspected of what? No, but perhaps a lawful prize, a witness likely to talk, whom they prefer not to leave for the English. This is what I was suddenly told, and that I should do better to "hide out," as so many others were doing, without further delay. Even though I find it hard to convince myself that, if it came to that, my person or my voice could be of any importance, it was better not to run the risk of a forced voyage to and sojourn in Germany or Italy.

The only books I took into my retreat were Gibbon and Shakespeare. X. lends me *Ivanhoe,* which he has just finished. (It just happens that I had promised myself to read, or reread, a Walter Scott, but I should have preferred any other one.)

I despise this papier-mâché, Viollet-le-Duc style. I seem to recall that *The Antiquary* was less historical. . . . Worth looking into; for, whatever else, there are great qualities of narration and dialogue in it; one understands why Balzac found it fruitful.

We are living here without electricity, and consequently without any news from the radio; often without water, almost without alcohol or gas or oil, on what is left of our almost exhausted supplies, barely kept alive by meals that become less adequate every day, brought in from the outside by the diligent and devoted family of the incomparable Flory's wife.

April 24

*Parler de loin, ou bien se taire.**

These lines from La Fontaine (*L'Homme et la Couleuvre*) might serve very well as an epigraph if I happen to publish the pages of this journal in America.

May 7

Explosions and fires in every direction on the periphery of the city. I counted more than twenty fires. They are not the result of the Anglo-American planes. The Germans, hunted down, before evacuating the city are blowing up their depots. This is a way of breaking camp. Thick columns of smoke darken the sky tragically.

May 8

While I was writing these lines yesterday, the Allies were already entering the city. This is what everyone said yesterday evening. This morning, awakened at dawn by a dull, constant, indeterminate roar, which sounded like the roar of a river. I dressed in haste and soon saw the first Allied tanks approaching, cheered by people who had come down from the nearby houses. It is hard to believe that what you have been so long waiting for has taken place, that *they* are here; you don't yet dare believe it. What! Without any more resistance, more battles, more fighting? . . . It is over: they are here! The amazement increases even more when we learn from the first of these liberators to be questioned that these tanks and these soldiers belong to the Eighth Army, the very one that we thought was held in check in front of Zaghouan; that glorious army which came from the Egyptian frontier after having swept Libya, Tripolitania, conquered the Mareth Line and the Wadi Acarit Line, whose progress we had followed from day to day in southern Tunisia. How is it that they are the first? Which way did they come? There is something miraculous about it. One imagined the liberation and entry into Tunis in many ways, but not like this. Quickly I close up my bag, my suitcase, and get ready to go back to the avenue Roustan. No more reason to hide. All the hunted people of yesterday come out of the darkness today. People embrace one another, laughing and weeping with joy. This quarter near the nursery, which was said to be peopled almost exclusively with Italians, unfurls French flags at almost every window. Quickly, before leaving my retreat, I shave my four-

* Speak from a distance or else keep silent.

weeks beard and go down with my companions in captivity into the street, where they have not appeared for exactly six months. We enter the wildly rejoicing city.

Odd: in this city where every language was spoken, today nothing but French is heard. The Italians are silent, are in hiding, and one meets but a few rare Arabs.

In General Giraud's proclamation, which is posted on every wall, a threatening and inexplicit sentence fills them with fear. Their conscience is not at ease; is that vague threat aimed at them?* They are not hiding, it might be said, but are in no wise taking part in the celebration, remaining shut up in the Arab town. So that this frantic, swarming, cheering mob is made up in great part (and in certain quarters almost exclusively) of Jews. Everyone is shouting: *"Vive la France!"* As soon as one of the tanks stops, it is surrounded, besieged by a crowd; children climb in and sit down beside the conquering heroes. And, as if by the sky's approval, all yesterday's clouds have disappeared; the weather is splendid.

May 10

Yesterday the whole victorious army was drunk. Little improvised bars opened everywhere, where unscrupulous merchants unloaded their stocks of adulterated products, the Germans having previously made a clean sweep of all the decent wines, liqueurs, and other drinks. Toward evening trucks passed by, gathering up and taking back to their units all those who were incapable of standing upright. Dragging on the ground, victory soils its wings.

May 13

. . . what I am writing here must not be taken as a degrading reflection on the worth of the German troops. They gave proof, up to the last few days, of extraordinary endurance, discipline, and courage, yielding only to superior equipment and numbers. Probably also, in the last days, to the suddenness of the Allied advance, which is transforming the retreat into a rout. It is only natural that Von Arnim, seeing the game irremediably lost, wanted to avoid an inevitable and useless massacre. I am saying this only in objection to the radio's camouflage.

May 20

Great joy upon seeing Jean Denoël again; but greatly depressed by his stories. The French losses have been enormous and are due, apparently,

* "As for those who abetted the enemy in his work of misery and pain, they will be

to the stupid routine (as in 1914) of certain military leaders, to their out-dated conception of courage, of honor, of whatever false gods they have now. Some of them led their men to slaughter without advantage of any sort, and as if in answer to the call of a tradition. Mere common sense should have kept them from launching that attack without artillery prepa-ration—an attack everyone knew would be useless. Alas, these are the same men who are likely to be governing us tomorrow. It is easy to under-stand why the hearts of some are filled with indignation and revolt.

Denoël, enrolled in a "surgical unit," was called upon to attend to a great number of people, and especially of very young children mutilated, maimed, gashed by the mines with which the Germans studded every bit of ground they gave up.

I am told that they hid their explosives even in corpses, which ex-plode in your face as you go to bury them. Even more horrible: a wounded man shouted to the ambulance man approaching him: "Look out! Don't come near me: the bastards have mined me!"

Algiers

So at last I have left Tunis! On this Thursday, May 27. We left the El Aouina field at seven o'clock; the trip, which was to last but two hours, took more than twice that, with stops at Zaghouan and at Le Kef. I had not slept all night, and after a choppy trip I reach Algiers fairly knocked about. The charming welcome of the Heurgons and an excellent lunch instill new life in me.

Great joy upon finding Saint-Exupéry.

The Americans, in our Old World, make themselves liked by everyone everywhere. With such ready and cordial generosity, so smiling and natu-ral, that one is more than willing to feel obliged to them.

At the Heurgons', I yield to the intoxication of a new library, read-ing one after another a little Leopardi, then a little Dante, then a little Stendhal, then a little Virginia Woolf: wandering at random in a garden.

Algiers, June 26

I dined, then, yesterday evening with General De G. Hytier, who accom-panied me, had come to pick me up in a car at about eight. The auto took

pitilessly and promptly punished. I give you my formal assurance of this. There is no room among us for traitors" [A. G.].

us to El Biar, directly to the villa whose terrace overlooks the city and the
bay. We moved into the dining-room almost at once and took our places,
Hytier and I, on the two sides of the General. On my right sat the son (or
the nephew) of General Mangin; I did not catch the names of the other
guests, two of whom were in civilian clothes, all close associates of the
General. We were eight in all.

De Gaulle's welcome had been very cordial and very simple, almost
deferential toward me, as if the honor and pleasure of the meeting had
been his. People had told me of his "charm"; they had not exaggerated at
all. Yet one did not feel in him, as one did excessively in Lyautey, that
desire or anxiety to please which used to lead Lyautey into what his friends
laughingly called "the dance of seduction." The General remained very
dignified and even somewhat reserved, almost distant, it seemed to me.
His great simplicity, the tone of his voice, his attentive but not inquisito-
rial eyes, filled with a sort of amenity, all helped to put me at ease. And I
should have been completely so if I did not always feel, next to a man of
action, how remote the world I inhabit is from the world in which he
operates.

I had just read with very keen interest (why not say it? with admiration) many excellent pages of his writing, pages capable of making one
like the army, presenting it not as it is, unfortunately, but as it ought to be.
Reminding him of the remark he quotes to the effect that Jellicoe had all
the qualities of Nelson save that of knowing how *not* to obey, I asked him
how and when, in his opinion, an officer could and should take it upon
himself to disregard a command. He replied, very properly, that it could
happen only at the time of the most serious events, when the feeling of
duty entered into opposition with a received command. Some of the guests
then joined the conversation to compare military obedience to the obedience demanded by the Church. One could have taken it much further than
we did. The conversation soon dropped and I did not feel strong enough
or in the proper mood to start it up again.

After the meal, the General suggested to me that we take a little
walk on the terrace. This amounted to offering me the opportunity of a
private conversation, and I took advantage of it to speak to him at some
length of Maurois. In the General's writings a particular sentence had surprised and hurt me somewhat, I told him, the one in which he states that
he met Maurois only once and hopes sincerely never to see him again. I
tried to explain Maurois's attitude, which, I said (and this was going
rather far on my part), would have been very different if he had been
better informed. I added: His eyes will open soon enough when he talks

with the friends who are expecting him here any day. If Maurois is deceived, it is because he has *been* deceived. He thinks it is his duty to remain faithful to the Marshal, and thinks so all the more because the duty is so painful to him; in acting thus, he is setting all his former friends against him.

The General's features had hardened somewhat, and I am not sure that my rather vehement defense did not irritate him. (Less sure, in fact, that my arguments were all valid—or so it seemed to me after seeing Maurois again.)

We spoke next of the advisability of creating a new review to group together the intellectual and moral forces of Free France or those fighting to be free. But we did not take that very far either. He then told me how much he suffered from the lack of men.

"Those you ought to have around you," I said to him, "are unfortunately under the wooden crosses of the last war." One has to play out the game with the hand one has. There are not many trumps.

We joined the rest of the company again and all went back into the drawing-room. The desultory conversation began to languish, and I think everyone was grateful to me for breaking up the gathering shortly thereafter. I thought sadly of what that interview might have been if Valéry had been in my place, with his competence, his clairvoyance, and his extraordinary *presence of mind.*

I had spoken to the General, during our brief tête-à-tête, of the resistance in Paris and particularly of that session of the Academy in which Valéry opposed addressing congratulations to the Marshal as some Academicians proposed. The General knew all about it.

He is certainly called upon to play an important role and he seems "up to it." No bombast in him, no conceit, but a sort of profound conviction that inspires confidence. I shall find no difficulty in hanging my hopes on him.

December 25

Reread *David Copperfield* (which I remembered remarkably, anyway), but it is not my favorite among Dickens's novels. He seems to me to have outdone himself in *Great Expectations* and to be at his best in the nightmare of *Martin Chuzzlewit;* he cheapens himself in my opinion when he tries to flatter his public by a display of facile sentimentality. In the horrible he is almost the equal of Dostoevsky, and that is when I prefer him. He does not amuse me at all in *Pickwick.*

. . . Deprived of sleep, I am not good for anything. The gears of my brain get choked up; the springs of my will relax. But coming out of the Fountain of Youth that is sleep, I almost forget how old I am, and can believe myself to be still fit. The outer world recovers its savor for me and I take a new interest in life.

February 7

An order has reached me to return to Algiers at once. The telegram comes from the Ministry of the Interior: a precise and urgent summons constituting an order for an official mission, with which I must comply.

On the way to Gao, April 3

Maison-Blanche. Waited in vain for the happy accident that would have kept me from leaving. Raynaud and Morize went with me to the airfield, where we take off at seven-thirty. Very cloudy sky.

I must have dropped off for scarcely half an hour, and already we are flying over a completely different country: sand-colored, covered with strange signs, with a sort of mysterious writing, inhumanly and incomprehensibly beautiful; elementary; nothing living, nothing even merely vegetable mars its surface.

Unable to note anything during the trip. Flew over a stupefying landscape. Almost mystical beauty.

At Gao, everything is swooning with heat. After sunset the thermometer goes down only a few degrees; not below 96° except for a few hours before dawn; the only moments in the day when one can breathe. . . .

The waters of the Niger are at their low-water point, and the vast river now presents nothing but a number of minuscule and shallow arms, which the flocks ford at nightfall. Summer spreads out over the plain. Incapable of movement, of will, of thought, I let myself be annihilated before that profuse splendor.

Excellent hotel, which I leave only for the shade of the market arcades, where the natives display unknown spices, pungent-smelling aromatics, a great pile of odd things for sale. Naked children hold out their hands, offer their smiles, the trusting and naïve felicity of their eyes. Beauty of the women. Paradisal insouciance. Strangeness.

Gao

I cannot bring myself to despise the joys of the flesh (and, besides, I scarcely make any effort to). Some engine difficulty in the plane that was to take us back (a providential accident, I shall say) allowed me to enjoy one of the keenest the night before last; all my memories of Gao radiate from it.

Today, May 21, I finished *Thésée.* I still have large parts to rewrite, and particularly the beginning, for which I had not yet been able to find the proper tone. But now the entire canvas is covered. For the past month I have worked on it daily and almost constantly, in a state of joyful fervor that I had not known for a long time and thought I should never know again. It seemed to me that I had returned to the time of *Les Caves* or of my *Prométhée.* Furthermore, exalted by daily events and by the recovery of France. The friends surrounding me here have been perfect. I owe them much, and without them should never have been able to bring my work to a happy conclusion. I should like to dedicate my *Thésée* to each of them in particular (there are really only a few of them), as a sign of my gratitude.

Nothing amuses me so much as work; not even the noble game of chess, in which I get beaten every day by Jean Amrouche. Delighted to learn that Minos was already addicted to it, if we are to believe the archæologists.

The young people who come to me in the hope of hearing me utter a few memorable maxims are quite disappointed. Aphorisms are not my forte. I say nothing but banalities, nothing but platitudes to them; but, above all, I question them; and that is just what they like best: talking about themselves. I listen to them, and they go away enchanted.

June 6

ALLIED LANDING IN NORMANDY.

June 25

It was with her that I had promised myself to achieve it (to achieve happiness). For each of us two the drama began on the day when I was forced to realize (and when she realized as well) that I could accomplish myself only by turning away from her. Yet she did nothing to hold me or draw me back; she merely refused to accompany me on my impious way, or at least on what she considered to be such.

Ever ready to belittle herself, to efface herself before others. If the word "modesty" did not exist, one would have to invent it for her. Never was she heard to say: "As for me, I . . ."

July 5

I receive *Peace and War,* the official publication of the documents concerning "the foreign policy of the United States" from 1931 to 1941. That publication closes before the rescue of France. It is with amazement that the mind rehearses the various stages of that extraordinary story. Mussolini's excesses, his overweening conceit dragging the Italian people along in his ruin prefigures the fate of Hitler and the German people. They are still resisting, while the Italians are now bitterly embarrassed and cast down. What Shakespeare will one day portray the immensity of this disaster?

It is essential for the salvation of humanity that Germany should feel prostrated by the wind of defeat. At the time of the preceding war, because of our serious error of not pushing victory into the very heart of Germany, the Germans did not feel conquered. It is essential for the future that the smugness of that arrogant people should be crushed and that the oppression of force should be made known to those who, through force, claimed to dominate the spirit. *"Et debellare superbos."* *

I am reading with great interest and profit John Stuart Mill's treatise *On Liberty,* which Raymond Mortimer sent me through the offices of the very kind Gill, with Mill's *Autobiography* and *The Memoirs of a Justified Sinner* by Hogg, one of the most extraordinary books *I have ever read.* I bless Mortimer for having introduced me to it. Can it be that it has not yet been translated? And if translated, that it is so little known? I should like to get Roger, Mauriac, Breton, Green, and many others to read it. . . .

Every day, two or three hours of Latin: Sallust or Virgil.

Algiers, September 5, 6, or 7

Having nothing to do, my mind empty, my eyes tired. . . . Never yet has a wait seemed so long to me; doubtless just because events are occurring in such rapid succession. A special order to go to Rome is to reach me soon,

---

* "And to tame the proud in War." (Virgil)

sending me off to Italy, when it is in France that I should like to be, that I *could* be already . . . oh, how I long to be there! I fear I may not have enough breath at the last moment to climb that final slope, not have time left to embrace the few people whom I should still like to see again before closing my eyes forever. Six times a day I listen on the radio to the same news I had already read in the morning newspaper, as if my attentive impatience could hasten events. . . .

Yesterday, December 11, finished the complete reading of the *Æneid* (without skipping a single line) and immediately afterward I re-read at one sitting Book VI, easily, almost fluently, with delight.

1945   *January 15*

The U.S.S.R. . . . I should astonish many people by telling them that there is probably no country in the world to which I should more like to return . . .

. . . Nowhere more beautiful landscapes, nor, to inhabit them, a people with whom I felt more readily in a state of sympathy, in a state of communion (though I did not speak their language; but it seemed that that mattered little, so easily was that sympathy established through looks and gestures).

I am speaking of the people, of the "masses"; for what made me suffer there was seeing the social classes taking shape again despite the vast and bloody effort of the revolution, convention winning out over an endangered freedom of thought, and falsehood over reality. . . .

. . . I think that the fundamental justice of some of my accusations will be readily recognized, in particular the one about the oppression of thought. What I said of that remains true, and that oppression is beginning to be exercised, in the Soviet manner, here in France. Any thought that does not conform becomes suspect and is at once denounced. Terror reigns, or at least tries to reign. All truth has become expedient; that is to say that the expedient falsehood is at a premium and wins out wherever it can. Soon only the *bien-pensants,* the "right-thinking" people will have a right to express their thoughts. As for the others, let them keep silent, or else. . . . Doubtless it is only through an anti-Nazi totalitarianism that one can overcome Nazism; but tomorrow it will be essential to fight against this new conformism.

January 30

No longer tempered by light or checked by the outer world, the insomniac's thought puts out its branches at will and stretches them to the point of enormity, of monstrosity, in the night.

February 15

. . . *animosque ad sidera tollunt* *

The Germans too, to be sure; the Germans especially. And the Americans, not at all.

February 17

I had a desire to reread St. Augustine. Mystical nausea. Fit to vomit.

April 3

That veneration which you nourish for your saints I bestow on these martyrs, and should like to see their name celebrated, their story told, not in some fabulous "golden legend," but simply according to the actual evidence. It would show the effort of Faith to arrest the progress of knowledge, and belief in the dogmas of the Church setting itself in opposition to the researches of science. A Vanini (who even knows his name today?) denounced by the clergy as tainted with atheism, condemned to the stake after having his tongue torn out, on February 9, 1619. According to the terms of the sentence, he was divested of all his clothing but his shirt, a noose was put around his neck, and a sign hung on his shoulders with these words: "Atheist and blasphemer of the name of God." Called upon to retract, Pompeio (that was the name Vanini had taken, having found refuge in Toulouse after an initial condemnation concerning the *Dialogues* which he had published during his stay in Paris) refuses. And as the magistrate in charge of the case repeated to him: "The court has ordered that you ask pardon of God, of the King, and of justice!" "There is no God," exclaims Vanini. "As for the King, I have in no way offended him; and as for justice, if there were a God, I should pray him to hurl his thunderbolt at the Parliament, as wholly unjust and wicked." And with a voice "that the cold caused to tremble because he was without clothing in the midst of winter, he did not cease to deny God aloud and the divinity of Christ, proclaiming that there was no other God than nature, that Jesus was a man like him, that the soul could not survive by itself, and that death led to nothingness; that was also why, he said, it was sweet and

* "Their spirits soar to the stars" (Virgil).

welcome to the unfortunates who, like him, were tired of fearing and suffering. For them it was liberation, the end and remedy of all their ills." Such was his belief, such his doctrine. And as if he had feared that the Parliament flattered itself that his doctrine would perish with him, he added that he was sure that it would continue to live in the books he had written to disseminate it. Aware of setting an example, he exclaimed at intervals that he was dying as a philosopher. When he reached the scaffold, amidst the vociferations of the crowd, he said: "You see, a wretched Jew is the reason I am here!"

The witnesses, the story adds, did not dare report the rest.

When he was attached to the stake, the executioner, having thrust the pincers into his mouth, tore out his tongue down to the roots and threw it into the fire. At that moment Vanini uttered a cry of pain so strong and so heartrending that those present shuddered. A reverend Jesuit, relating this fact later, considers it "very amusing."

April 17

Back to Constantine yesterday evening for an expedition to the south.

By auto to El Kantara (an hour's stop to initiate Mme Théo to the charms of the oasis, and subsequently no oasis seemed to us so beautiful), then arrival at Biskra for lunch, by auto to El Oued, then Touggourt, and back to Biskra by train and likewise to Constantine.

Reread the *Æneid* all along the way, every day.

Last days of 1945

Finally at Luxor, for the last four days. At Cairo the marvelous Abbé Drioton explains the museum with reassuring competence. That museum, besides, tires me less since I have made up my mind not to try to admire everything. Faced with Egyptian art (with very few rare exceptions), I become nothing but resistance and opposition.

1946   *January*

That turn of mind (that vicious turn of mind) that people used to blame in me was what saved France. An attitude of insubordination, or revolt; or even initially and simply an attitude of inquiry.

The Academy? . . . Yes, perhaps, accept becoming a member if without solicitations, bowing and scraping, visits, etc. And immediately afterwards, for my first deed as an Immortal, a preface to *Corydon* declaring that I consider that book to be the most important and most "serviceable" (we have no word, and I don't even know if this English word expresses exactly what I mean: of greater usefulness, of greater service for the progress of humanity) of my writings. I believe this, and it would not be difficult to prove it.

Aswân, January 21

The Ponte Santa Trinità (in Florence) destroyed . . . a marvel of harmonious equilibrium, of slimness and of bold grace, which moved me as much as the most imposing architectural feats of Egypt. I like what exalts man, not what prostrates and humiliates him.

Nothing bothers me so much as the fame of a landscape . . . Before these black rocks of Aswân too many imbeciles have swooned. . . .

The letter from Mme X. that the hotel porter gives me this morning exasperates me, for it says: "I am sure that we share certain sensations, those that you must have irresistibly felt here before the black rocks on these rose-colored mornings." No, madame, faced with these black rocks, I felt nothing at all. I am a gentleman; and the emotions I might have had politely made way for yours.

January 24

I am continuing my reading of Forster's *Passage to India.* If I understood it better, I should be reading with rapture, I believe; for the book strikes me, insofar as I can judge, as a marvel of intelligence, of tact, of irony, of prudence, and of skill. But too many things escape me, and perhaps I am giving him too much credit, filling to Forster's advantage all the blanks resulting from my lack of understanding; for everything I do understand seems to me of the highest quality. I like, even more than what he says, what he suggests and insinuates, as if incidentally and without committing himself, in apparently inoffensive sentences that force the reader to a sort of complicity. How I like, for example: "There was a moment's silence, such as often follows the triumph of rationalism." (p. 205, Penguin edition)

January 31

On the Nile . . .

Landscape more extraordinary than beautiful, but startlingly strange. Almost mystical exaltation. Villages the color of the soil, of the sand, of the rock; villages that I suppose to be Coptic, inhabited by apprentice stylites. Harshness that the Nile fails to soften. . . .

What can the inhabitants of these villages live on? Around the mud houses not a blade of grass, not the slightest vegetation. It is the reign of the Holy Ghost.

. . . I shall have to take leave of this earth ill-satisfied, having known almost nothing of it. That absurd laziness which induced me to return to the same places because it cost less effort. I look with a kind of despair at a map of all the rest, waiting out there. . . . Regret for all I might have seen, should have seen, borders on remorse. Wadi Halfa, the terminus of this journey, should be a point of departure. It is from Khartoum onward that I should like to go up the Nile. . . .

Staggering, the temple of Abu Simbel; yet nothing to say of it but what has already been said.

November 22

My seventy-seventh birthday . . .

. . . Clouard was very perspicacious when he entitled an article: "Gide, or the Fear of Being Right." That was very long ago; but that has remained one of the few constant elements in my nature; and it is this that makes me worthless in politics: I understand the adversary too well (at least so long as he remains sincere and does not try to deceive me).

. . . that broadcast of yesterday evening:* it seems to me definitely indecent to bother friends with a request of that kind, which it is very hard for them to sidestep gracefully. Amrouche went about it so well that even Roger Martin du Gard, who generally refuses, thought he had to play his part (I am going to write him a note of apology), while probably wishing me in hell, along with Amrouche; for nothing is more disturbing than that sort of obligation. Which did not prevent his message from being charming; I was touched all the more, because I knew the effort he must have gone to in order to write it. I have not yet been able to find out what Malraux, Schlumberger, Paulhan, and Camus had to say. . . .

. . . The rehearsals of *Le Procès* keep me in Paris, where I run the risk of

* A radio broadcast of birthday tributes to Gide.

being wiped out with the first frosts; but Barrault's undertaking interests me too much for me to let myself be distracted from it.*

Yesterday afternoon, intolerable chore of autographing the "complimentary copies" of *Hamlet*.† Nothing more exhausting.

I am entering my seventy-eighth year in rather good shape, all things considered; with still enough curiosity to want to go on living; not too bored or disgusted with myself; not loving myself much, but finding myself easy to live with, accommodating.

The other evening Catherine and I amused ourselves by wondering in whose skin she and I might like to live; and, everything considered, concluded that we should not gain anything by changing.

It is time to go and light Mme Théo's fire.

November 23

A sumptuous armful of roses. It is Mme Voilier transferring to me some of the attentions she used to shower on Valéry. Red carnations brought by Dominique Aury. . . .

A most unexpected telephone call: it is Colette wishing me a happy birthday and expressing her desire to see me again. She was touched by what I said of her in my *Journal;* I wondered if she had known of it. I shall no doubt respond to her call, knowing too well, unfortunately, that immediately after the first effusions we shall have nothing to say to each other.

Opening by chance Rouveyre's book on Léautaud, I fall upon this:

> A.G. has confided to the *Virginia Quarterly Review* that if he were going to withdraw to a desert island, he would take along the following books: *La Chartreuse de Parme, Les Liaisons dangereuses, La Princesse de Clèves, Dominique, La Cousine Bette, Madame Bovary, Germinal, Marianne.*

I protest: I had been asked to designate my ten favorite *French novels.* If, in exile, I could take along only ten books, not one of these would be among them.

December 1

The extraordinary prestige that great actors enjoy often comes from this (in addition to their own merits): the mass of the public is not capable of

---

* The stage version of Kafka's *The Trial* by Gide and Jean-Louis Barrault was staged by Barrault with great success on October 10, 1947.
† Gide's complete translation of *Hamlet* appeared in Paris in 1946.

understanding and appreciating a masterpiece of dramatic art through mere reading; but only when it is *interpreted.*

Olivier in *King Lear.* I have no doubt that he is admirable in it, and I should have enjoyed applauding him. . . . But I renounce this with disconcerting ease: I renounce anything and everything: pleasure, travels, epicurean delights, all without effort, without regrets. I have had my fill. "Next gentleman." I withdraw. No merit in this; I am yielding to a natural tendency. . . .

December 2

Finally let myself be taken to *King Lear* last night. No effort to get there. Enid MacLeod comes to pick me up in an embassy car, which is to bring me home as well. Elisabeth, though she had already seen the play the day before yesterday, goes along. Everything is arranged in the best possible way. But as soon as I am seated in the box (directly facing the stage) or very soon after the curtain goes up, I begin to be numbed by a mortal boredom, a rather special sort of boredom that I hardly ever feel except in the theater. There are pauses, suspenses, slow moments, arrangements of effects, all unbearable. Like a child at the Châtelet, I keep waiting for the next set.

As for Olivier, he is without contest a great actor. The fact that he can, with the same success, impersonate one after the other the dashing young officer of Shaw's *Arms and the Man* and old Lear is amazing. And the whole company surrounding him is definitely above average, completely homogeneous; excellent ensemble. But shall I dare write here what I think of *King Lear?* Yesterday's production fixes me in my opinion: I am very near the point of considering the play execrable; of all Shakespeare's great tragedies the least good, and by far. I kept thinking: how Hugo must have liked it! All his own enormous faults sprawl through it: constant antitheses, devices, arbitrary motives; barely, from time to time, some glimmer of a sincere human emotion. I cannot even understand very well what is considered to be so difficult in the interpretation of the first scene: difficulty of getting the public to accept the King's naïve stupidity? For all the rest is in keeping: the entire play from one end to the other is absurd. It is only through pity that one becomes interested in the tribulations of that old dotard, victim of his own fatuousness, his senile smugness, his stupidity. He hardly moves us at all except at the rare moments of pity that he himself shows for Edgar and for his gentle fool. Parallelism of the action in the Gloucester family and in his: the bad daughters and the wicked son; good Edgar and sweet Cordelia. The white hair in the tempest; the brutality unleashed against weak innocence . . . nothing that is not intentional, arbitrary, forced; and the crudest means are employed to seize us by the guts. It is no longer human, it is *enormous;* Hugo himself never imagined anything more gigantically artificial, more false. The last act ends with a gloomy hecatomb in which good and evil are mingled in death. Olivier's company gets out of it by a sort of final apotheosis *à la* Mantegna: *tableau vivant,* very careful grouping; everything is there, even to the architecture of the arcades which frames the admirably ordered ensemble. The triumph of art. There is nothing left to do but applaud.

The enthusiastic audience gives Olivier and his company a standing ovation.

1947   *Neuchâtel, November*

A Swedish interviewer asked me if I did not regret having written any particular one of my books (I do not know whether he was thinking of *Le Retour de l'U.R.S.S.* or of *Corydon*). I replied that not only did I not disown any of my writing, but that I should certainly have bade farewell to the Nobel Prize if, in order to obtain it, it had been necessary for me to disown anything.*

Neuchâtel

I shall be able to say "So be it" to whatever happens to me, even were it ceasing to exist, disappearing after having been. But just now I am and do not know exactly what that means. I should like to try to understand.

Please, leave me alone. I need a little silence around me in order to achieve peace within me.

What a nuisance you are! . . . I need to collect my thoughts.

Oh, that my mind could let fall its dead ideas, as the tree does its withered leaves! And without too many regrets, if possible! Those for which the sap has withdrawn. But, good Lord, what beautiful colors.

---

* André Gide was in Neuchâtel in November 1947 when he learned that he had been awarded the Nobel Prize for Literature.

What rubbish all that literature is! And even were I to consider nothing but the finest writings, what business have I, when life is here at hand, with these reflections, these carbon copies of life? The only thing that matters to me is what can lead me to modify my way of seeing and acting. Merely living calls for all my courage; merely living in this atrocious world. . . .

"By speaking thus of that serenity on which you pride yourself you put it on show; by putting it on show you compromise it. It is in your features and in your deeds that one must read it, not in phrases that you do not know why or for whom you are writing. . . ."

Get along without God. . . . I mean: get along without the idea of God, without a belief in an attentive, tutelary, and remunerative Providence . . . not everyone who wants to can achieve this.

The harshness of the time is such that we find it hard to imagine (or, rather, are unwilling to admit) that there could have been an equally tragic one at any other moment in history. Better informed, we should perhaps come to realize that, on the contrary, the only exceptional time was the long period of toleration in which we lived before the unleashing of the horrors (which so decidedly feel *at home* on this earth)—so natural seemed to us that intellectual freedom, a freedom so lamentably compromised today. Now a time is returning in which all will be considered as traitors who do not think "as they should."

Some, it is true, are still resisting; and they are the only ones who count. It matters little that they are not very numerous: it is in them that the idea of God has taken refuge.

But the temptation that it is hardest to resist, for the young, is that of "committing oneself," as they say, of *"engagement."* Everything urges them to do so, both the cleverest sophistries and the apparently noblest, most urgent of motives. One would have accomplished a great deal if one could persuade young people that it is through letting themselves go, through laziness that they commit themselves; . . . if one could persuade them that it is essential—not to be this or that, but—to be.

Take things, not for what they claim to be, but for what they are.

Play the game with the hand one has.

Insist upon oneself as one is.

This does not keep one from struggling against all the lies, falsifications, etc., that men have brought to and imposed upon the natural order of things, and against which it is useless to revolt. There is the incurable, there is the modifiable. Acceptance of the modifiable is in no wise included in the *amor fati.*

This does not keep one, either, from demanding of oneself the best, after one has recognized it as such. For one does not make oneself any more *lifelike* by giving precedence to the less good.

1948   *Neuchâtel, January 5*

I have not kept a journal for more than a year. I have lost the habit. I have not exactly promised myself to resume it, but all the same I should like to try; for in the state in which I am at present, I fear that any other attempt at production would be doomed to failure. I have just reread with disgust the few pages I had written at Neuchâtel; they smell of effort, and the tone strikes me as artificial. Doubtless they were not written naturally, and they betray an anxiety to escape certain reproaches, which it is absurd to take into account. My great strength, even in the past, lay precisely in my caring very little about public opinion and not trying to construct myself consistently; writing as simply as possible and without trying to prove anything.*

January 9

I return to Sartre's book.† However just some of his most important assertions seem to me (for instance, that "it is the anti-Semite who creates the Jew"), only apparently paradoxical, it remains nonetheless true that anti-Semitism is not (or not solely) an invention made up out of whole cloth by hatred, by the need of motivating and feeding it. Psychologically and historically, it has its *raison d'être,* on which Sartre, it seems to me, is not sufficiently explicit.

When I was in Tunis in '42, I had occasion to talk with several lycée professors, "Aryans" themselves. Each of them told me, independently (and this would have to be verified), that in each class and each subject

---

* Yet it is these pages, reworked, that I wish to put into this *Journal,* just as I once brought back into my *Journal* the "green notebook" of *Numquid et tu . . . ?* [A. G.]

† *Reflections sur la question juive. (Reflections on the Jewish Question)*

the best pupils were Jews. They were constantly at the head, and over the head, of the others. Even so, this does not necessarily mean that the Jews have an intelligence superior to the "Aryans," but perhaps merely that the qualities of the latter, more profound, develop and manifest themselves more slowly; I should be rather inclined to believe the latter; I am very wary of precocity. . . . But in any case: the die is cast, and now these hearts are already sown with the seed of fierce passions, which await nothing but the opportunity to release themselves, even in violence if need be, with that sort of permission and right to injustice which theoretical anti-Semitism provides them.

From the whole of Sartre's book, often pasty and diffuse, I retain this excellent passage:

"The Jews are the mildest of men. They are passionately opposed to violence. And that obstinate mildness they preserve amidst the most atrocious persecutions, that sense of justice and reason which they set up as their sole defense against a hostile, brutal, and unjust society, is perhaps the most important message they have for us, and the true mark of their greatness." Bravo, Sartre! I could not agree with you more. But there is all the same a "Jewish question," agonizing, obsessive, and far from being settled.

We (the modern world) are stifling, and tomorrow it will be worse, in a dense forest of insoluble problems, in which, I fear, force alone—and the most willfully blind, the most monstrous and absurd, the most brutal force—will be called upon to enlighten us, to cut clearings and glades; to win out.

I am writing this while striving not to believe it . . .

January 19

However different Valéry, Proust, Suarès, Claudel, and I were from one another, if I were to seek out some way in which one might realize we were of the same age (I was about to say of the same team), I think it would be the great scorn we had for mere "news," the things of the moment. And it was in that way that we were marked by the more or less secret influence of Mallarmé. Yes, even Proust in his depiction of what we used to call "the contingencies," and Fargue, who of late has been writing for newspapers to earn a living—it was still with a very clear conviction that art operates in the eternal and debases itself in trying to serve even the noblest of causes. I wrote: "I call journalism everything that will interest people less tomorrow than it does today." Consequently nothing seems to me at once more absurd and more justified than the reproach that is directed at me today of never having been able to *commit myself.* I should say! And it is in this regard that the leaders of the new generation, who gauge a work according to its immediate efficacy, differ most from us. They also aim for immediate success, whereas we considered it quite natural to remain unknown, unappreciated, and disdained until after forty-five. We put our faith in time, and were concerned only with forming an enduring work like those we admired, on which time has but little hold, and which aspire to seem as moving and timely tomorrow as today.

Nevertheless, when there was a need to *bear witness,* I had no fear of committing myself, and Sartre admitted this with perfect good faith. But the *Souvenirs de la Cour d'Assises* have almost no connection with literature, any more than the campaign against the Great Concessionary Companies of the Congo or the *Retour de l'U.R.S.S.*

January 22

Gandhi's victory, his pacific triumph, seems to me one of the most surprising facts of history. Pierre Herbart, who has come to spend a couple of days with me, is as much moved by it as I am. We spoke of it at once, and at great length. Is it appropriate to deplore the fact that such a miracle of unanimity among a whole people cannot be achieved, or even sought for, by a Latin or Anglo-Saxon people? A subject of infinite discussion. But the extraordinary thing is that that unanimity should arise on the side of renunciation. A strange example of virtuous "totalitarianism."

January 30

Gandhi has just been murdered by a Hindu. I just learned this from Pierre's telephone call. Two days ago a bomb had already been thrown at him. It was too beautiful, not to be hoped for, that mystical victory, in which spiritual fervor forced the respect of brutal strength; my heart is filled with admiration for that superhuman figure; filled with tears. This is like a defeat for God, a step backward.

June 8

There is nothing to do but pick up again, without explanation, as if nothing had happened. The summer (after freezing days, we now have warm, glorious days . . .) helps me return to life. Yes, suddenly I caught myself enjoying life again. Last night, in a sort of joyous intoxication, a new lease on life, I could not resign myself to going to bed until after midnight, and this morning I was awake before seven o'clock. I should have worked admirably if my whole morning (it is now half past twelve) had not been eaten away by correspondence, like every day, or almost—and almost exclusively letters of refusal or excuse. That puts you in a sort of grumpy state of mind, or at least in a posture of defense from which your friends run the risk of suffering. It wrinkles both forehead and heart . . .

The worst is that it leads people to think: "Yes, since the Nobel Prize, Gide has *become distant."* After which there remains nothing but to go and drown or hang oneself. And it so happens that since the warmth has returned, I no longer have any desire to do so. But before that, on certain days, I felt already completely disengaged; this, however, held me back: the impossibility of getting anyone to understand, to accept, the real reason for a suicide; that this way, at least, I would get people to leave me alone and in peace. But go away on a trip . . . already on the steps of the train, what a relief to feel out of reach, liberated! But where to go? I think of that little hotel that Alix told me about (I noted it down) in a fishing village on the Lago di Garda. If only I were sure of finding room there. . . . Constantly called upon, I must put it off from day to day; and constantly I hear the eldest of the Fates whispering in my ear: You haven't much time left.

September 3

An extraordinary, an insatiable need to love and be loved: I believe this is what dominated my life and drove me to write; an almost mystical need, moreover, for I consented to its not being satisfied during my lifetime.

Torri del Benaco, September 7

I believe I am sincere in saying that death does not frighten me much (I am constantly thinking of it); but I am watching this summer go by with something like despair.

Never before had I seen such a long series of such beautiful, such splendid days.

Two wonderful, prodigious storms:
*Fluctibus et fremitu assurgens Benace marino.**

But since the beginning of September the air has been light; the midday heat is no longer excessive; the mornings and evenings are cool. To

---

* "You, Lake Benacus, surging up with waves and a roar like the sea" (Virgil). Benacus is the modern Lago di Garda, on the shore of which stands Torri del Benaco.

the daily splendor is added a constant feeling of death nearby which makes me keep repeating to myself that these fine days are the last for me. I write this without bitterness.

. . . I have taken leave; I am free to go; there is no need to reconsider. I even feel a sort of aesthetic disapproval of this postscript, which does not fit in with the ensemble, but remains outside as an appendix, as something extra. . . . The Catholic will claim that this overtime is a windfall granted me by God, in his infinite kindness, to allow me an exemplary conversion. . . .

Paris, December 15

Last words. . . . I do not see why one should try to pronounce them any louder than the others. At least I do not feel the need of doing so.

1949   *May 15*

. . . when I was at Cuverville, I was present at the lugubrious delivery of my sister-in-law—I mean by this that I had to help the doctor in the dreadful operation to which he consented only after making sure that the baby's heart had stopped beating (he would have had to have recourse to a cesarean, but he did not have the proper surgical instruments)—so I had to hold fast my sister-in-law's legs while he extracted what was already nothing but a corpse. . . . No, I cannot relate that; nothing more painful can be imagined. And I recall that later on, in the night, the two of us alone, face to face, beside that sleeping woman—we looked at each other. He was sweating. "We are assassins," he said. "But when the child is no longer living, one tries to save the mother." (The pains had lasted thirty hours.) Although she had not been put to sleep (it was still contrary to principles; we have made some progress since), she was lying unconscious. Near her a jumbled mass of bloody, soiled debris. . . .

When the morning came, I naïvely said, "Get rid of that thing," to the gardener's wife when she at last came to see "how everything was." Could I have imagined that that shapeless mess, to which I pointed while turning away with disgust, could I suppose that in the eyes of the Church it already represented the human and sacred creature they were getting ready to dress? O mystery of the incarnation! You can imagine my amazement, a few hours later, when I saw *it* again, which for me already had "no name in any language," cleaned up, adorned, bedecked with ribbons, lying in a little cradle in preparation for its ritual entombment. No one, fortunately, had been aware of the sacrilege I had been on the point of committing, had already committed in thought, when I had said: "Get rid of that thing." Yes, quite fortunately no one had heard that thoughtless command. And I remained a long time lost in contemplation before *it;* before that little face with the crushed forehead that someone had carefully hidden; before that innocent flesh which, if I had been alone, yielding to my first impulse, I should have thrown onto a dunghill near the afterbirth, and which now religious attentions had just saved from nothingness. . . . I told no one what I experienced then, what I am relating here. Must I think that, for a few moments, a soul had inhabited this body? It has its tomb at Cuverville, in that cemetery to which I do not want to go back.*

Half a century has passed. . . . I cannot say, to tell the truth, that I can exactly recall that little face. No, what I recall very clearly is my surprise, my sudden emotion before its extraordinary beauty. I had never before seen anything, I have not since seen anything, to compare. The faces of the dead can be beautiful. Death often brings to our features a sort of peacefulness and serenity in the renunciation of life. But that little body had not lived; its beauty remained utterly inexpressive. Some (some mothers especially) go about exclaiming over the beauty of newborn babies. As for me, I do not believe I have ever seen a single other one that did not seem to me almost hideous, I confess, shriveled, grimacing, congested. . . . This one (it was partly to this that he obviously owed his beauty) had not known the pangs of being born. And it was surely not enough that his features were beautiful (my sister-in-law was beautiful; my two other nephews and my niece were among the most beautiful children I have ever seen), but besides, completely bloodless; the substance of which he was made did not seem like human flesh, but rather some ethereal substance, some translucent and nacreous paraffin, some immaterial pulp; it seemed like the flesh of a sacred Host. A bow of blue satin (it would have been pink, the gardener's wife told me, if the baby had been a girl) on the right side of a delicate lace bonnet, as in the portrait of an infant by Sustermans (I believe), further emphasized the paleness of that face and of that uninhabited forehead. That little cranium had been emptied of the brain matter, which had indeed been

---

* Gide's body was buried there in 1951.

thrown on the manure pile with the scraps from that frightful operation, the mucus and the placenta.

This tale aims to prove what? That the soul knows not where to take refuge when its carnal support is gone? The Church provided for this when she enjoins us to believe in "the resurrection of the flesh."

As for the soul, it goes without saying that I believe in it! Why, of course I believe in the soul. I believe in it as in the glow that comes from phosphorus. But I cannot imagine that glow without the phosporus that produces it. In any case, I am not indulging in theories here. Theories and ratiocinations only annoy me. *Animus, Animum, Anima. . . .*

. . . there is probably no word of the Gospel which I took to heart earlier or more completely, subordinating my whole being to it and letting it dominate my thoughts: "My kingdom is not of this world." So much so that "this world," which, for the mass of human beings, alone exists—to tell the truth, I do not believe in it. I believe in the spiritual world, and all the rest for me is nothing. But that spiritual world, I believe that it has existence only through us, in us; that it depends on us, on that support which our body provides it. And when I write: "I believe that . . ." there is no question whatever of an act of faith. I say: "I believe" because there is no other way of expressing the affirmation of that obvious fact by my reason. What have I to do with *revelations?* I want to appeal to nothing but my reason—which is the same and has always been the same at all times and for all men.

Beneath which my constant sensuality sprawls at ease.

I believe that there are not two separate worlds, the spiritual and the material, and that it is useless to set them in opposition. They are two aspects of one and the same universe; as it is vain to oppose the soul and the body. And vain is the torment of the mind that urges them to war. It is in identifying them, one with the other, that I have found calm. And that the spiritual world prevails in sovereign importance is a notion of my mind, which depends intimately on my body; both conspire and agree in order to achieve harmony in me. I will not and cannot try to subject and subordinate one to the other, as the Christian ideal proposes to do. I know by experience (for I long strove to do so) what it costs. On whichever side, body or soul, victory inclines, the victory is artificial and temporary, and we shall one day have to pay the expenses of the conflict.

May 16

Yes, I know: all the indications are excellent (except that of the white corpuscles), so much so that I do not know how to explain the overwhelming fatigue of the last three days. In the morning I have difficulty "getting out of the sands": quicksands. I feel at the bottom of a slope, and it is not at all certain I shall be able to climb back up it. Yet I am writing these few lines in order to help me do so. . . .

May 23

Too worn out, these last few days, to have a desire to note anything. But without pain or distress. And I almost got to the point of accepting ending up thus in a sort of numb torpor. I have no idea yet whether or not I am heading toward convalescence. It is not when a limb is dead with cold that one suffers; it is when life returns to it. Today, restlessness . . . analogous to the twinges and tinglings in fingers as they reawaken.

May 27

Piling up of days in the hospital; vague mass of more than a month; hesitating between better and worse. Succession of days filled almost solely with reading. Sort of desert morass, with the daily oasis, charming beyond all hope, of the regular visits of the incomparable friend that Roger Martin du Gard has been for me during this long period of purgatory. His mere presence already tied me to life; he foresaw and alleviated all the needs of my mind and body; and however gloomy I might have been before his coming, I soon felt quite revived by his remarks and by the affectionate attention he paid to mine. I do not know whether ever in the past I could have been more aware of the ineffable benefit of friendship. And what an effacement (even to excess) of his own interests, of himself! No, no! Religion achieves nothing better, or so naturally.

The *Anthologie* so long awaited has finally appeared.* *Grosso modo,* very satisfied; and especially, perhaps, at not having made my personal taste, it seems to me, prevail unduly. I hope I have brought to light a number of exquisite little pieces that deserved to be known and that I had not seen quoted elsewhere.

May 31

At Saint-Paul at last! Shall I dare confess now that I had but a feeble hope of leaving the hospital alive? Here, what calm! Night has fallen. No other sound than the rhythmic croaking of the frogs. Then, as if in response to some mysterious signal or cue, all fall silent at once; then all start up again in chorus.

---

* Gide's *Anthologie de la poésie française.*

These insignificant lines date from June 12, 1949. Everything leads me to
think that they will be the last of this *Journal*.

André Gide
January 25, 1950

IMAGINARY

INTERVIEW I

1941

I don't like interviewers. They may be all right for those of other professions, men who are full of all sorts of wise and useful ideas, but whose job is not precisely that of putting them into words. We *littérateurs* have no need of interpreters to communicate with the public—men who, more often than not, present a sad travesty of our thoughts, even with the best intentions in the world. And yet this particular interviewer, I don't really know why, had won his way into my favor. I had already received him twice. That was a great while ago, but it created a precedent of which he availed himself for this third visit, knowing as he did that once we open the door a first time, we are bound. I scarcely recognized him, and when he began to say that I hadn't changed in the least, that I was always the same, I answered that I wasn't sure whether or not to take this polite social lie for a reproach.

"What sort of reproach could you possibly see in it?" he asked.

"Oh, the sort that is usually phrased, 'The war hasn't taught him a thing.'"

"But didn't you write long ago," he said, "that events only root each one deeper in his own predispositions?"

"I still believe it. Sometimes events open our eyes, on the other hand, to faults and vices; but they are usually those of our neighbors."

"Well, if that leads us to try to correct them . . . we do try, you know; and I should imagine you approve of the effort."

"But of course."

"And doubtless you would also agree that it is a good thing, for our redemption, to offer a common ideal to youth? That was something we lacked."

I was willing to admit that French youth, in the years between the wars, had rushed off in all directions.

"But," he said with a timid smile, while addressing me for the first time as *"cher maître"*—"but didn't you add to that confusion, by encouraging each of us to follow his own bent?"

Then, after waiting vainly for my answer: "Wouldn't you at least be willing to admit that our literature, generally speaking, had its share of responsibility for our defeat?"

Instead of giving him a direct reply, I said: "Let me repeat a fable that is told by the natives of the Congo. Perhaps you aren't familiar with the story.

"A great number of people, hoping to cross a broad river, had crowded into the ferryman's boat. Overloaded, the boat stuck fast in the mud. Certain passengers would have to get out: the question was which. The ferryman began by putting ashore a fat merchant, then a shyster lawyer, a dishonest financier, and the madam of a bawdy house. The ferry was still glued to the mud. Next to be sent ashore were the proprietor of a gambling den, a slave-dealer, and even a few respectable people. Still the boat couldn't be moved, but it was getting lighter all the time, until at last, when a missionary, thin as a nail, stepped to the bank, it began to float. 'He's the one,' shouted the natives, 'the Father of Gravity. May he be accursed!' "

"Did the others get back in the boat?"

"The fable doesn't say."

"Then the whole story is ridiculous," he said. "What good is a ferryboat if nobody can ride in it?"

"The fact remains that our own ship has to be refloated."

"Yes, I see what you mean. There are people who say that such and such passengers, mentioned by name, have prevented us from crossing the river."

"And to be sure the vessel stays afloat this time, they would like to get rid of them."

"They want to let on board only the pure," he said.

"Indeed. The whole question is one of 'purification.' Naturally we are speaking only of literature. It is being accused of many crimes: of having enervated, discouraged, and emasculated the nation."

"Let us admit that many of our prewar writers, even some of the best, were often lacking in—shall I say?—civic virtues."

"Weren't they reflecting the state of the country? Moreover, they are not the only writers under attack. We sometimes hear insults hurled at a whole period, a whole century: it was 'the stupid nineteenth century,' according to Léon Daudet; it was the eighteenth that should be thrashed, according to Abel Bonnard. The Catholics indict Diderot, Renan, even Montaigne; the freethinkers Bossuet. They take up the old refrain:

C'est la faute à Voltaire

C'est la faute à Rousseau . . .*

Claudel vomits out Michelet and Hugo."

"Lamartine fell into a rage at La Fontaine, on finding that his *Fables* taught the most pernicious lessons."

"Please don't interrupt. A recent anthology of French poetry exalts our sixteenth century only at the expense of the magnificent, soaring flight of our romantics, salvaging out of all their work only a few wing-beats, a few isolated verses. That is mere derision, not judgment; and we could smile at such vain devastations, if it weren't that the books under attack are on the way to being effectively suppressed from our bookshops."

"Do you think it is really possible that . . ."

"I think anything is possible, and nothing in the world strikes me as more naïve than the cry I heard uttered so many times by those who were fleeing in disorder before the invasion: 'Such things are unheard of!' "

" 'Unheard of': from certain points of view, I should think that would please you."

"Yes, from certain points of view, as you say. And if it weren't all so cruel, sometimes it would even seem exhilarating. But we are overwhelmed by all these novel events, these monstrous cataclysms 'without precedent in history.' The mind finds it hard to get used to them. The heart even more."

I was silent for some moments. The interviewer is one of those people who don't understand silences. He began again: "A passage from Montesquieu, in the volume that Grasset has just published, seems made to reassure us. I copied it out." (He took a little notebook from his pocket.) "Listen: 'One of the things that should be noted in France is the extreme facility with which the country has always recovered from its losses, its plagues, its depopulations, and the resourcefulness with which it has always borne or even surmounted the internal vices of its divers governments.' "

"Read what follows. If I remember rightly, it's about the diversity of our country."

" 'Perhaps this is to be explained by the very diversity of France, thanks to which no evil has ever been able to strike such deep roots that it could destroy entirely the fruit of her natural advantages.' "

---

* "It is the fault of Voltaire;
  It is the fault of Rousseau."

"The passage," I said, "was not so completely unknown that I hadn't read it before. But Grasset did well to reprint it along with the others. The words are those of a sage. Nevertheless, it is this diversity that is under attack. Today people would like to see it curtailed."

I had risen.

The interviewer: "Before leaving, might I ask if you are working?"

"Yes, I went back to work some weeks ago."

"Might we know on what?"

"First of all, on an introduction to Goethe's dramatic works, which are to be published by the *Pléiade;* in French, I am sorry to say, but the translation is a very good one. And I don't intend to reduce Goethe to my own outline, or to ferret through his work for my own favorite ideas, including those on individualism; for perhaps those ideas came from Goethe in the first place, or at least he encouraged them. Whatever the case may be, Goethe remains for us the supreme example of a serviceable individualism. Mind you, I did not say servile, but serviceable, ready to serve. He had a deep sense of duty; yes, of duty toward himself. His apparent and evident egoism always brings him back to that point, and he submits. Those who have charged him for this egoism have, I think, ill understood the austere obligations that a healthy individualism sometimes implies."

"Haven't you said all that before?"

"You remind me of a remark made by a friend of mine, also in his seventies. He has just been reproached with saying the same things over and over. 'At my age,' he replied, 'one must be willing to repeat oneself, if one wishes to keep from talking nonsense.' "

"Is your friend by any chance related to those imaginary hangers-on whom Sainte-Beuve used to pretend to quote when he wanted to pay himself compliments?"

"You're very sharp."

"Shall I see you again?"

"Could well be. Wait till I send for you."

from

AN INTRODUCTION

TO GOETHE'S

DRAMATIC WORKS

1942

III

Yes, Goethe triumphed over himself and the world, but one begins to wonder whether his triumphs weren't sometimes a little easy (even though the idea of merit is out of place in this discussion). Then one remembers what Nietzsche wrote about other victories, that they might sometimes diminish or demoralize the victor; and one is forced to admit that Goethe's demon, surrounded by all the comforts of success, was becoming somewhat middle class. Heaped with honors all during his life, with triumphs of every sort; a man of wealth, courted and coddled, he had even the good fortune to meet, toward the close of his career, a zealous Eckermann who was devoted without being obsequious, and who had just enough servility to furnish a stepladder to his glory, so that access to the genius was made simple, and so that the genius, descending ever so little, could more comfortably receive his due homage. . . . He attained a very advanced age without losing his faculties; he died without pain, surfeited with everything. . . . How then does he dare to speak of "renunciation"? Renunciation of what? Doubtless of a certain instinctive fervor that was revealed in the ebullience of his youth. Goethe, the rebel of yesterday, grows temperate—ah, blessed virtue! He renounces. And soon we see him retreating almost to the other side of the world from that high promontory, that rock on which he had once been exposed by his genius. Somewhere concealed in the word "renunciation" is there not a longing for the driven spray?—some secret regret for everything that was generous or heroic in the wildness of his youth?

Having paid Goethe our tribute, let us continue with our summing up for the prosecution.

We are a little embarrassed, or at least perplexed, by his attitude toward Napoleon, as well as by the opportunism I mentioned before; in this case it caused him to display the Legion of Honor on his breast, to the horror of his more patriotic fellow citizens, at a time when it would have seemed more fitting not to boast of his decoration and not to derive material advantages from something that wounded his country. But Goethe was still dazzled (as how could he fail to be?) by a dream that seemed on the point of being realized: the dream of a pacific and glorious unification of all Europe, one that might have cost most of the smaller states their autonomy and their reason for being, but that would have accorded at least to Weimar, at least to himself, to Goethe, an even greater importance, while preserving (so he judged) all his liberty of thought. Moreover, how could he fail to be flattered (and Goethe was extremely, almost childishly susceptible to praise) by the particular consideration he received? "You are a man, Monsieur Goethe," the Emperor said.

"In that case, you are another, Sire, as I am glad to acknowledge."

I can imagine him thinking these words, almost speaking them. And we have no reason to suppose that he would perhaps have been disenchanted by the outcome; for Napoleon had a sense of and a respect for values. This, indeed, was precisely what Goethe could glimpse in the future: that he himself would be properly appreciated.

The truth is that he felt himself very little affected by historical events; in the proper sense of the word, they did not interest him. His influence had spread far beyond the borders of the Grand Duchy of Weimar, and beyond all Germany; now that Napoleon was creating One Europe by force of arms, Goethe would lord over it by spiritual force; he would broaden his fatherland to include a continent. He had no further worries as soon as he knew that freedom of thought would remain untouched and that the invasion would not upset his little collections of natural-history specimens, of ancient art in plaster casts, of engravings and medallions: that was his life, his real life. Not once was Goethe touched, as we are today, or at least as we were not many days ago, by the fear of seeing the very soil from which he sprang and on which his genius rested tremble and disappear beneath him. In short, nothing close to his heart was threatened; quite on the contrary, he might well have thought that . . . But enough of this; let us leave him in peace.

Goethe was a naturalist; he could not have been less a historian. He expressed himself quite clearly: history was of use to him only insofar as it could provide material for the generalizations of his poems. He was concerned with the permanent, not the episodic; with what recurred necessarily, according to eternal laws; not with anything produced by a circumstantial cast of the dice, never to be repeated.

One remembers his conversation with Eckermann soon after the French revolution of 1830, which had caused no little excitement in Germany. "Well!" Goethe cried, hastening toward him. "What do you think of the news? The volcano is in eruption; everything is taking fire; this is what comes of little discussions behind locked doors."

"A frightful story," Eckermann answered, "but it was no more than you could expect with such a ministry. Considering all the circumstances, the royal family . . ."

Goethe interrupted him: "We are talking at cross-purposes, my dear friend; I wasn't speaking about those people at all. My concern was with something quite different. I was referring to the statement that Geoffroy de Saint-Hilaire has just made before the Academy of Sciences; his dispute with Cuvier is of the greatest importance. . . ."

I therefore like to imagine the extreme interest that Goethe would have shown in the recent advances of science; doubtless not so much in practical inventions, like the airplane, the telephone, the motion-picture camera, as in the discoveries capable of upsetting altogether our conception of the cosmos—that of Einstein, which sets our best-established notions of physics and geometry tottering; that of radium, touching on the very permanence of matter; and those others, most importantly, that have been made precisely in the realms to which Goethe would pay no attention, because he believed that human investigation could never reach them, or at least extract nothing profitable from them: astronomy, paleontology, the origins of the universe, of our earth, of matter, of life. Why wear out one's head with such questions? "The life of man," he said to Eckermann (October 3, 1828), "is sufficiently darkened by his passions and misfortunes, generally speaking, without his feeling the additional need of plunging into the shadows of a barbarous past. What he needs is clarity, serenity, and joy. (*Er bedarf der Klarheit und der Aufheiterung*)." And a few days later (October 7), caught up in a general conversation and urged to give his opinions on the creation of man, on the first appearance of the human species on this earth, Goethe returned to the same theme: "As for racking one's brains to learn how the thing happened, I regard that as an idle occupation, one we should leave to those who pass their time with insoluble problems because they have nothing better to do." This is a remark that he would doubtless not dare to make today, after undreamed-of researches into these "insoluble problems" have revolutionized science, and put scientists on the road to some of their most fruitful discoveries.

It is the custom to rhapsodize over his thirst for clarity; everybody admires his last words: *"Mehr Licht!"* although nobody knows whether to interpret them as a simple demand for more light or a cry of gratitude for a celestial vision. (Believers are skilled in giving a mystical interpretation to the last stammered words of the dying.) On the contrary, I beg leave to deplore this horror of darkness. I hold it to be Goethe's most serious weakness and error. It is the point at which he approaches Voltaire, and the point at which Shakespeare and Dante draw apart from him, neither fearing in the least to plunge ahead, the one among dolorous shades, the other into the black gulfs of the human soul. Goethe, on his side, has no desire to leave the sun's rays, has no eyes except for the luminous colors of the prism; and doubtless nothing would have astonished him more than to learn (but in his days who would have suspected?) that the rainbow concealed anything whatever in its dark fringes. And yet he realized that it was in the shadows beyond daylight that the "Mothers"—those mysterious matrices from which "emanates everything that has form and life"— waited and watched. Why could he not have overcome his horror of darkness, and questioned further that "Mouth of Shadow," in the hope of extorting some of its secrets?

And now we ask ourselves: however grand, however noble, however serenely beautiful may be the image of man that Goethe has left us, does it wholly satisfy us? Reasonable, of course: logical, cultured, he was that to the highest degree; but penetrating all this wisdom I hear the cry of Saint Paul: "Would to God ye could bear with me a little in my folly." * I also remember Schiller and his lesson of heroism; and I say to myself that there was nothing more admirable in Goethe's life than the friendship he bore to Schiller. Standing before his death mask, with its eyelids forever closed on so much inner serenity, I evoke the ravaged or tragic masks of Dante, of Pascal, of Beethoven, of Nietzsche, of Leopardi; their voices had deeper, less steady tones. Hölderlin, before sinking into madness, had also turned his eyes toward the radiance of Greece; and today his poetry affects us even more than Goethe's *Roman Elegies,* for all their splendor. Finally, after Goethe has gorged himself with all the good things of this earth, while talking about "renunciation," does he really expect us to believe that his arms could have held more than he embraced?—that he might have taken still more? Or, speaking more seriously, might the question not be: Did Goethe embrace the best? And what is the best for man, to which nothing else is to be preferred?

Christians alone have the right to ask this first and supreme question. That it never disturbed Goethe's serenity is precisely what concerns us here. And Goethe would cease to be Goethe if doubt or suffering had

* II Corinthians 11:1.

added the pathetic touch of a few wrinkles to the patiently acquired calm of that admirable effigy. We remain grateful to Goethe, for he gives us the finest example, at once smiling and grave, of what man can obtain by and from himself, without recourse to Grace.

from

IMAGINARY

INTERVIEW XI

1942

He— . . . I wanted to make what seems to me a serious criticism of your "Introduction to Goethe's Dramatic Works." You give your readers the impression (and I am thinking particularly of certain phrases at the end of the essay) that each man is obliged to choose between the Christian position and the one adopted by Goethe. As if there were not any number of ways to escape the domination of Christianity, without necessarily following Goethe's path.

I—And yet the examples I cited, those of Nietzsche, Leopardi, Hölderlin (and I could have mentioned many others), should leave no doubt of what I meant to say. Goethe does not teach heroism; and we have need of heroes. Christianity can lead us to heroism, one of the highest forms of which is sainthood; but every hero is not necessarily a Christian. Free thought does not always wear the indulgent smile of Renan, the sarcastic smile of Voltaire, or the flippant smile of Anatole France. Men have been led to the stake for their refusal to accept Christian dogma, for their simple probity of spirit. Theirs was a martyrdom without glory, with no hope of future recompense, and for that reason all the more admirable. Without going to their extreme, let us say that human dignity, and the sort of moral demeanor or *consistency* on which our hopes are pinned today, these can readily do without the support and comfort of Faith.

He—Perhaps. There are scattered cases. But don't you think that only a common faith can unite the energies that have certainly not ceased to exist in France, although you yourself have often complained of their disorientation? From your own writings, I could easily assemble statements to the effect that discipline, even a sort of enlistment, are not necessarily opposed to a certain individualism—"individualism rightly understood," as you once said.

I—Yes; I was speaking of communism, and since then I have had to change my tune somewhat. The Christian religion undoubtedly shows more respect for human personality than communism does.

He—Which shows no respect for it whatever, as you must have recognized.

I—I also recognize that our present task is to unite, to be united.

He—For the mind, too, there are moments and even historical periods of expansion or diastole, just as there are for the heart.

I—And we are now in a period of systole; one might say at its very crest; or better, trough.

He—Do you remember the lines you quoted from Goethe, which you translated rather freely:

> Oh, Deliverance,
> Do not delay! *

I—It was because of the rhythm; I was trying to preserve it.

> *Uns loszureissen*
> *Ist noch nicht zeitig*

simply means, as I am well aware, that the time of diastole has not yet come.

He—But you are turning a simple statement of fact into an anxious desire.

I—But the first line of the stanza: "Who will free us?" seemed to justify an impulse that came straight from my heart.

He—In these days we must learn to repress many of our impulses. . . .

---

* Much has been made of the "secret message" Gide may have intended to convey through these words in the second year of German occupation.

GOD,

SON OF MAN

(*Imaginary Interviews,*
Algiers series, II)

1943

. . .

I—I let myself be carried away ridiculously the other day; I beg you to excuse me. Immediately after your departure, reflecting on what had led to my loss of control, I thought that . . .

He—Allow me: it is you, not I, who is bringing it up. However, you promised to touch on nothing with me except literary questions.

I—But some days you feel you will suffocate, if you keep on hiding what fills up your heart.

He—You were then thinking that . . . you were saying?

I—That what upsets me, holds me back is certainly not the Gospels, which contain better advice than any other book in the world. And I was even forced to understand, very quickly, that all that I used to look for in communism (and look for in vain; where I hoped to find love, I found nothing but theory) was what Christ had always taught: he taught that, and all the rest besides.

He—Then what stops you?

I—It is that act of blind belief the Church demands: the act of Faith. Reason itself, with love, leads me to the Gospels; so why deny reason?

He—Does Faith deny it?

I—Good heavens, yes; in fact, strictly speaking, that is what "believing" is. One believes *against* all verification, all evidence. In order to *believe* you have to put out your eyes. You have to stop looking at the object of belief in order to see it. You know very well that belief in a personal God, in Providence, implies abdication of everything reasonable in us. I even prefer, very much so, the *Quia absurdum* to all the ratiocinative efforts of some people to attach to a divine plan the dangerous effects of natural forces and natural laws, or the criminal follies of mankind. It is franker and more honest, and the believer has won the game as soon as he refuses to play it. Won it for himself at least. For, as for me, to believe in the God *he* offers me would lead me very quickly into saying, with Orestes,

In no matter what direction I turn my eyes from this place,
I see nothing but misfortunes; and they all condemn his God.

I find more consolation in considering God as an invention, a creation of man, something that man composes little by little, tends to form
more and more by means of his intelligence and his virtue. It is in Him
that creation has its end and aim, and not *from* Him that it emanates. And
as time does not exist for the Eternal, for Him it amounts to the same
thing either way.

He—It seems to me Renan said almost the same thing.

I—Oh! don't interrupt me, I beg you. I have enough trouble already keeping track of my thoughts. . . . Where was I? . . . Oh, yes. Faith. And
notice that for them, the believers, nothing but that counts. A life devoted
to search for the truth is nothing, for the only truth, for them, is that
Truth that one "would not search for if one had not already found it."
And that Truth, found all ready-made, takes care of everything: why, it is
enough to cover up a whole life of dissipation and errors.

He—It is true also that belief in that Truth brings about an amendment of
life.

I—Or at least should bring it about. But what is the use of quibbling
about it? The very property of dogma is to be indisputable. So let's not
dispute it.

He—And yet you admit the teaching of the Gospels.

I—With all my heart, yes; but outside of (apart from) Faith. Now, if I
should put every teaching of Christ into practice, conform my whole life
to them, in the eyes of the believer nothing of that would count—without
Faith.

He—You are wrong. All that retains its importance. I fear you have been
misinformed. You are judging from your old memories. The Church of
today shows herself ready to recognize, even in unbelievers of good behavior and good will, every effort toward the good and the true. Deploring
only that these efforts are not offered to the Lord, the Church today is
much more disposed to pity than to condemn.

I—Why yes; I am not ignorant of the fact that the Church has very charitably and wisely withdrawn its frontal attack. It would no longer condemn Galileo, good heavens! It does not stop, nor will it stop in its
progress backwards. *L'Histoire universelle* of Bossuet makes even priests
smile today. Step by step, the Church is losing ground, beating a retreat,
yielding. . . .

He—And in this very withdrawal orthodoxy is strengthened.

I—My mind refuses to submit itself to any orthodoxy whatever.

He—And yet you recognize the excellency of the Gospel precepts. The finest life led according to them loses all significance without Faith.

I—Let us say that it takes on a different significance; and one for which I have a preference.

He—Yes; through pride.

I—I was expecting that word. Believers owe it to themselves to give a pejorative interpretation to everything great and noble and fine in independence.

He—Independence! Ah, the time has come to talk about that. Yet you recognize today how important it is to assemble, to organize, to bend in order to employ, to subject in order to make useful. . . .

I—Go on, finish it; say, to swear them in. . . . One can always find excellent motives for repudiating reason and keeping man from thinking. Unite wills, that's all very well; nothing great is accomplished without submission and discipline. But, through a forced devotion, to prevent reason from being exercised, to regulate thought by general order: you will end up with a population of sheep. *Amissa virtute pariter ac libertate,** with no one left to be aware of it, no one to suffer from it; for inactivity of the mind is like that of the body and every other form of sloth; first one accepts grumblingly, then the mind quickly takes its ease in an outwardly devotional acquiescence, and that's just where the danger lies; *Invisa primo desidia, postremo amatur.*†

He—What in the world has started you quoting so much Latin?

I—For the past few days, I have been buried in Tacitus.

He—Do you read him easily?

I—More easily than I would have thought; but not without a translation on the opposite page; and with inexpressible satisfaction. There is no question that I am delighted with the bounding manner of a Stendhal; you always seem to be surprising his ideas as they've just jumped out of bed, before they've had a chance to get properly dressed. I don't like thoughts which are made up and decked out, but those that are concentrated and compact. Tacitus's sentence is taut. It is his *Life of Agricola* that I am reading, and from the very start I was at his command. What authority!

---

* Virtue is lost at the same time as liberty.
† Idleness at first is hateful; we finally come to love it.

What gravity! What fervor! How pleased I am, more than by ease or grace, by that austere, savage asperity! I take this book with me; I read as I walk; I chew over and over, without exhausting all the bitter sap, some of the vigorous sentences by which my will is stiffened: "We should have lost our memory as well as our voice if it had been as easy to forget as to keep silent" . . . *Si tam in nostra potestate esset oblivisci quam tacere.* What precedes it is equally fine. Reread it.

He—You read a great deal?

I—I have never read so much, nor so well; with the kind of eagerness I had in my youth and which, when I think of my age, seems almost a little ridiculous; but I can't do anything about it; as for my age, I think of it as little as possible; and when I do think of it, it is to say to myself: Hurry up. But this digression is carrying us. . . .

He—Not in the least. It leads us back to God. Everything leads the attentive soul back to God. "Hurry up," you say you hear: don't you recognize that as His call? "Hurry up and give me your heart, your love."

I—I shall try to explain. Not so much to explain to you as to explain to myself the point at which my thought has arrived, slowly, almost in spite of myself:

There can be no question of two Gods. But I take care not to confuse, under this name of God, two very different things, different to the point of opposing each other. On one hand, the whole cosmos and the natural laws that govern it; matter and forces, energies; that is the role of Zeus; and that can be called God, but only if you divest the word of all personal and moral significance. On the other hand, the summation of all human efforts toward the good and the beautiful; the slow mastery of brute forces, and their utilization in order to *realize* the good and beautiful on earth; that is the role of Prometheus, and Christ's role, as well; it is the opening up, the flowering of man, and in it all the virtues have a part to play. But this God does not inhabit nature at all; he exists only in and through man; he is created by man, or, if you prefer, it is through man that he creates himself; and every effort to exteriorize him by prayer is in vain. It was with Him that Christ united himself to share punishment and reward; but it is to the *Other* One he addresses himself when, dying, he utters his despairing cry: "My God, why hast thou forsaken me? . . ."

He—In order that "all be accomplished," says the believer.

I—But I who do *not* believe see it only as a tragic misunderstanding. There can be no "forsaking" there because there was never an agreement;

because the god of natural forces has no ears and remains indifferent to human sufferings, whether in chaining Prometheus to the Caucasus or in nailing Christ to the cross.

He—Allow me: it was not natural forces that crucified Christ; it was the wickedness of man.

I—The God whom Christ represents and incarnates, the Virtue-God, must fight at the same time against Zeus *and* the wickedness of man. That last word of Christ (the only one of the seven words of the Crucified reported by two Evangelists, the simple apostles Matthew and Mark; and they report *only* that word) would keep me from confusing Christ with God, if I had not already been warned by all the rest. How can one not see, in that tragic word, not a letting go, not a treachery on God's part, but this: that Christ, believing and making others believe that he was one with God, was deceived and deceived us; that the One he called "my Father" had never recognized him for Son; that the God he represented— the God he himself was—was only, as he sometimes says, "the Son of Man." It is that God and that God only that I am able to and want to adore.

JUSTICE

OR CHARITY

1945

It is deplorably difficult, in Algiers, to get a look at the Paris newspapers. So I could not check the accuracy of what I hear: that an article of mine on "Benda's latest book" has appeared in the valiant paper *Combat* under a title not chosen by me, in which (to give it more of a current twist) the words *Justice* and *Charity* stand side by side, introduced by a quotation of Malebranche's cited by Benda and reproduced in my article. This tempts me to clarify my thinking on that delicate point.

Having been on the jury at the Assize Court, I no longer believe very much in Justice. (I am speaking of human justice; as for the divine, we shall have to wait for another life, doubtless, to meet up with it.) The disproportion between the crime and the penalty, for the crimes that one is called upon to judge today, remains so flagrant that one ends by understanding lynch law and the torture of a Brinvilliers. "An eye for an eye; a tooth for a tooth." But how many millions of eyes and teeth would Hitler need to be satisfied? . . . Without going as far as that, what relationship, what comparison can there be between the fact of having, for so many years, poisoned public opinion in the *Action Française, Je suis partout* or *Gringoire,* and imprisonment (even life imprisonment) or death?* And what is more, is it just that the poisoner should pay no more than the poisoned, and those whose sole crime will be (according to our later judgment) not to have thought "as one should"? (For the crime of "Commerce with the enemy" is often no more that, provided, at least, that no shameful profit was obtained from that commerce.)

Justice and *Charity,* it is important to realize, are often more than merely different ideas: they are antithetical. And to patch together some cloak with which one hopes to fit the two at once would simply be to travesty them both.

Strictly speaking, the question of Justice is never once brought up through all the Gospels. Christians never notice this sufficiently. A number of them would be astonished, and would protest if one were to tell

* Gide is referring to the trials then in progress of *collaborateurs* like Charles Maurras, who was condemned to life imprisonment in 1945.

them that it is by this fact especially that the Christian religion is distinguished from all others; and that for this very reason, it is vain to search (as is sometimes done) for any common ground of understanding between Christianity and other religions. At heart, they will tell you, we are all searching for the same thing, are we not? Catholic or Protestant Christians, Mohammedans, Jews, disciples of Confucius or of Buddha: love and peace among men, the limitation of selfishness, the triumph of altruism, etc. . . . But this is to misunderstand the singular distinction of Christ's teaching, never more admirable than here, wherein it differs from all others. The notion of justice remains a human notion. The teaching of Him who has told us "Judge not" goes beyond justice: it is something superhuman; believers will say it is divine. What could be more revolting, from the point of view of justice, than to pay the worker who arrives at the last hour the same as the diligent day laborer? Than the solicitude for one lost sheep taking precedence over the attention given to the rest of the flock? Than that preference of the individual to the mass? Than that disconcerting advice not to pull up the weeds, but to let them grow along with the good grain? Than that passport accorded the repentant sinner ahead of those who have practiced good works all their lives? Than that tearing of oneself away, by means of love, from all other obligations considered sacred before? . . .

Is this not what makes Christianity such an extraordinary school of individualism, through which it has made fruitful all the world? It has already been remarked how favorable for revolutions are lands first worked by Christianity, that leavening so admirably suited to lifting a thick mass. To misunderstand, to deny this particular quality, would it not be to take away from Christianity its most singular virtue, to take away from the salt its savor?

The Christian ideal defies all human prudence. And it does not appear particularly appropriate at a time when to turn the left cheek (after receiving a slap on the right), a proceeding quite contrary to military discipline and to what we call "honor," would risk bringing terrible losses to one's party, to the homeland, and to all that binds us to it. We can speak of all that tomorrow, after the victory and the peace. But it is that very problem that so torments certain Christian consciences today, in the midst of all this talk of sanctions, of purges, and of giving precedence, for what may be a long time, to the entirely human and inexact ideal of justice, over the so clearly superior, but disastrous ideal of charity.

THE RADIANCE

OF PAUL VALERY

1945

The death of Paul Valéry does not bereave France alone; from the entire world goes up the lamentation of all those whom his voice could reach. The work remains, it is true, as immortal as any human work can claim to be, and one whose radiance will continue to spread across space and time. I leave to others the task of eulogizing this imposing life's work, capable of instructing and fertilizing the most distant and the most diverse minds; that prose and verse of a severity, of a plenitude, of a beauty so perfect that they force the admiration, and can be compared only to the purest jewels of our literature. It is of the man himself I should like to speak; of what Paul Valéry was. In him I am losing my oldest friend. A friendship of more than fifty years, without lapses, without clashes, without breaks; the friendship we deserved, no doubt, different as we were from each other. Even though he hated confessions, and held the particular, the individual in considerable scorn, I am sure he would pardon me for giving expression today to my personal sense of loss. Because he considered that, in general, he had no obligation to reveal to the world anything but his ideas, many people came to misunderstand him, and see in him only a prodigious intelligence, a man who could play with all things and all people without ever committing himself, or permitting himself to be moved or touched by any. His reticence in regard to his private sentiments was extreme, as was his reserve; so much so that he himself scarcely seemed to suspect the existence of those secret vibrations which his exquisite sensibility, which the qualities of his heart had contributed even to his noblest and most elevated lines. And it was those very qualities of heart, that affectionate attention, even at times that tenderness, which made Valéry's friendship so precious to us. As for the rest, that intellectual treasure, I shall find all that again in his books; but his smile, so affectionate (as soon as he had given off being ironical), his look, certain almost caressing inflections of his voice . . . Ah well; all that is nothing more now than a memory.

At the beginning of May 1942, on the point of embarking for Tunis, I had the joy of seeing Valéry again; he had come to join me at Marseilles. He who, so often, in Paris, weighed down by cares, by duties, by obligations, betrayed such painful fatigue, appeared to me, during those two days of sun and holiday we spent together, rested, as though rejuvenated, in full possession of his worth, more alive, more loving, more expansive than in the best days of his youth. An extraordinary gaiety animated his bright profusion of remarks, and I was left quite dazzled by the resources of his intelligence, charmed by his ease and his affectionate grace.

When, after my three years' exile in North Africa, I was finally able to get back to Paris, I found Paul Valéry again, older than I had allowed myself to expect. "I've reached the end," he said to me; he had been secretly touched by the disease that was soon to become evident. Stomach ulcers, hemorrhages, tuberculosis . . . for a month in bed, penicillin and blood transfusions; the most assiduous care of those nearest to him succeeded only in prolonging the atrocious pains. The few times I was able to see him again, the suffering inscribed on his features made him almost unrecognizable. At the time of my next-to-last visit, he kept me a long time at his bedside, one of my hands held tightly between his, as though he expected from that contact a sort of mystical transfusion. He made an effort to speak to me and, for a long time, leaning over him, I made an effort to understand him; but I could not, alas! make out anything from his mouth but indistinct words. He had, nevertheless, kept his perfect presence of mind; and a few days before, he had still been taking some pleasure, some comfort at least, in reading: a huge bound volume lay on his bed; it was Voltaire's *Essay on the Spirit and Customs of Nations;* of that Voltaire of whom he said, at the Sorbonne, last December 10: "He is the intellectual *par excellence,* the most subtle of humans, the most prompt, the most alert . . . possessing, up to his last day, almost inexhaustible resources of reflex energy." Was he aware, as he wrote these words, that they could just as well be applied to him?

I still read, in that same last lecture of Valéry's, these sentences in which he paints himself in painting Voltaire: "Everything excites his desires to know, to reduce, to combat; everything is food for him and serves to feed that fire, so clear, so bright, in which a perpetual transmutation is at work . . . in which the genius of dissociation resolves every appearance of truth that drags on into the century and still imposes itself on the indolence of our minds."

O least indolent of beings! animated not only by that "genius of dissociation," but by a splendid poetic genius that never visited Voltaire at all: you fought your life through with the loyal arms of the Mind alone, for durable and pacific victories. On all sides darkness hems us in; but through you France spreads a radiance over the world; and what you bring to the world cannot be taken from us.

from

ET NUNC

MANET IN TE

(*Madeleine*)

1947, *published* 1951

... *et nunc manet in te.* *
VIRGIL (Culex)

Yesterday evening I was thinking of her; I was talking with her, as I often used to do, more easily in imagination than in her presence; when suddenly I said to myself: But she is dead. . . .

To be sure, I often came to spend long successions of days away from her; but in childhood I had got into the habit of bringing back to her the harvest of my day and of mentally associating her with my sorrows and joys. This is what I was doing yesterday evening, when suddenly I remembered that she was dead.

At once everything lost its color and luster, both these recent recollections of a time spent far from her and this very moment now when I was recalling them, for I was reliving them in thought only for her. I immediately realized that, having lost her, I had lost my *raison d'être,* and no longer knew why I was going on living.

I never liked very much the name Emmanuèle which I gave her in my writings, out of regard for her reticence. Perhaps I only liked her real name because, from my childhood on, it evoked all she represented for me of grace, sweetness, intelligence, and kindness. It seemed to me usurped when borne by someone else; she alone, it seemed to me, had a right to it. When, for my *Porte étroite,* I invented the same of Alissa, I did so not out of affectation but out of reserve. There must be only one Alissa.

But the Alissa of my book was not she. It was not her portrait that I drew. She served me merely as a starting-point for my heroine, and I do not think she recognized herself much in Alissa. She never said anything to me about my book, so that I can only guess at her reflections as she read it. Those reflections are still painful to me, like everything that resulted from that deep sorrow which I began to suspect only much later, for her extreme reserve kept her from letting it be seen and from talking of it.

Did not the drama that I imagined for my book, however beautiful it may have been, prove to her that I was still blind to the real drama? How

* . . . and now she abides in thee.

much simpler than Alissa, more normal and more *ordinary* (I mean less like a Corneille heroine, and less intense) must she have felt herself to be? For she was constantly unsure of herself, of her beauty, her merits, of everything that made up the force of her radiance and her worth. I believe that, late in life, I came to understand her much better; but at the strongest point of my love, how very much I was mistaken about her! For the whole effort of my love was bent less on bringing us close together than on bringing her close to that ideal figure I had invented. At least that is the way it strikes me today; and I do not think Dante acted differently with Beatrice. It is partly, it is especially through a need for making amends that I am trying, now that she is gone, to recover and retrace what she was. I should not like the ghost of Alissa to obscure the person she really was.

When I approached the bed where she was lying, I was surprised by the gravity of her face. It seemed as if the grace and amenity that radiated so powerfully from her goodness had lived altogether in her eyes, so that now that her eyes were closed, nothing remained in the expression of her features but austerity; so that, in addition, the last look I had at her forced me to recall not her ineffable tenderness, but the severe judgment she must have passed on my life.

What would I have been if I had not known her? I can ask myself this today; but the question was never asked then. Everywhere I discover, thanks to her, a silver thread in the weave of my thoughts. But whereas I saw nothing but brightness in hers, I had to recognize that there was a good deal of darkness in me; it was only the best of me that communed with her. However great the impulse of my love, it served only, it now seems to me, to divide my nature even more deeply, and I was soon obliged to realize that, although I intended to give myself to her completely (however much I remained a child), that religious veneration in which I held her would never succeed in suppressing all the rest.

. . . Critical articles and certain insults must have informed Madeleine sufficiently about the nature of some of my writings, even though she had not read them herself. She carefully hid from me the suffering they must have caused her. Rather recently, however, she let me know of it by a sentence in a letter that seems to contradict what I have just written: "If you could have known the sorrow that those lines would cause me, you would not have written them."

. . . No explanation took place between us. I merely passed over all that; and her love did likewise.

. . . when, today, I muse on our common past, it seems that the sufferings she endured by far surpassed her joys: some of them, indeed, so cruel that I cannot bring myself to understand how, loving her as much as I did, I was not able to shelter her from them better than I did. But that was in part because there was so much thoughtlessness and blindness mixed in with my love. . . .

I am amazed today at that aberration which led me to think that the more ethereal my love was, the more worthy it was of her—for I was so naïve that never once did I ask myself whether she would have been contented with an utterly disincarnate love. That my carnal desires should be addressed to other objects, therefore, scarcely worried me at all. And I even came to comfort myself with the conviction that it was better so. Carnal appetites, I thought, belonged to man; it reassured me not to admit that women could experience anything similar—barring, of course, women of "easy virtue."

Such, then, was my blindness, my obtuseness: however outrageous it may seem, I must confess it. I can find no explanation or excuse for it, except in that ignorance in which life had maintained me, by offering for my example only those admirable female types who watched over my childhood: first my mother, then Miss Shackleton, my aunts Claire and Lucile, all models of decorum, respectability, and reserve; to attribute the least carnal perturbation to any one of them would, it seemed to me, have been an insult. As for my other aunt, Madeleine's mother, her misconduct had at once cast her into disrepute, excluded her from the family, from our horizon, from our thoughts. Madeleine never spoke of her and, so far as I know, had never shown the least indulgence for her; not only through an instinctive protest of her own uprightness, but also in great part, I suspect, because of the sorrow felt by her father, whom she worshipped. That reprobation contributed to my blindness.

It was not until much later that I began to understand how cruelly I had managed to hurt, to wound, the one for whom I was ready to give my life—not until, through my dreadful thoughtlessness, the most intimate wounds and most painful blows had long since been dealt. To tell the truth, my private self could develop only by striking against her. I realized that somewhat; but what I did not know was that she was very vulnerable. I wanted her happiness, to be sure, but what I did not bother myself about was this: that the happiness to which I wanted to lead her, even to force her, would be unbearable to her. Since she seemed to me all soul and, as far as the body was concerned, all fragility, I did not regard it as any great deprivation to keep from her a part of me that I counted all the less important because I could not give it to her. . . . Between us no explanation was ever attempted. From her side, never a complaint; nothing but mute resignation and an unconfessed disappointment.

Doubtless I told myself—and with what remorse!—that she might have liked to be a mother, but I told myself also that we could never have agreed about the education of children, and that other sorrows, other disappointments, would have been the price she would have paid for maternity. . . . Nonetheless, those sorrows, those cares, would at least have been merely normal. I have the remorse of having twisted her destiny.
. . .

I have spoken of my extraordinary sexual ignorance at that age; but my own nature (I mean that of my desires) worried me nonetheless. Shortly before becoming engaged, I had therefore made up my mind to tell my story to a doctor, a specialist of considerable renown, whom I was rash enough to consult. He smiled as he listened to the confession, which I made as cynically complete as possible; then: "You say, however, that you are in love with a girl and that you are hesitating over marrying her, knowing your inclinations to the other side. . . . Get married. Marry without fear. And you will soon see that all the rest exists only in your imagination. You act like a starving man who has been trying until now to live on pickles." (I am quoting his words exactly; heaven knows, I remember them well enough!) "As for the natural instinct, you won't be married long before you realize what it is and return to it spontaneously." . . .

Love exalted me, to be sure, but, despite what the doctor had predicted, it in no wise brought about through marriage a normalization of my desires. At most, it got me to observe chastity, in a costly effort that served merely to split me further. Heart and senses pulled me in opposite directions.

And that she should have been misled in the beginning of our union—that goes without saying; but I now believe that that misunderstanding of hers lasted much less long than I then imagined. How could she have been expected to credit a sensuality of which I gave her so few proofs? Before she came to understand and to admit to herself that that sensuality was addressed elsewhere, she was astonished, she told me, that I could have written my *Nourritures terrestres,* a book that she said was so unlike me. Yet even as we moved on into Italy after leaving the Engadine during our wedding trip, she was likewise astonished by my animation when the carriage in which we were heading south was escorted by the *ragazzi* of the villages we were going through. Inevitably the connection must have come to her mind, however disagreeable and offensive it may have been for her, so contrary to all the admitted facts and upsetting to all the norms on which her life was supported. She felt left out of the game, as it were, pushed aside; loved, oh no doubt, but in what an incomplete way! She would not immediately admit herself beaten. Why, whatever advances feminine modesty allowed her—were they to remain useless, without echo, without reply? . . . Painfully I see again the stages of that voyage.

In Florence we visited together churches and museums; but in Rome, completely absorbed by the young models from Saraginesco who then used to come and offer themselves on the stairs of the Piazza di Spagna, I was willing (and here I cease to understand myself) to abandon her for long hours at a time, which she filled somehow or other, probably wandering bewildered through the city—while, on the pretext of photographing them, I would take the models up to the little apartment we had rented in the Piazza Barberini. She knew it; I made no secret of it, and if I had, our indiscreet landlady would have taken care to tell her. But as a crowning aberration, or else to try to give to my clandestine occupations a justification, a semblance of excuse, I would show her the "art" photographs I had taken—at least the first, altogether unsuccessful ones. I ceased showing them to her the moment they turned out better; and she was scarcely interested in seeing them, any more than she was in discussing the artistic considerations that drove me, as I told her, to take them.

Moreover, those photographs soon became nothing more than a pretext, needless to say; little Luigi, the eldest of the young models, was not at all misled by them. Any more than Madeleine herself, probably; and I am inclined to believe today that of the two of us, the blinder one, the only blind one, was I. But aside from the fact that I found it advantageous to imagine a blindness that permitted me my pleasure without too much remorse—for, after all, neither my heart nor my mind was involved—it did not seem to me that I was unfaithful to her in seeking elsewhere a satisfaction of the flesh that I did not know how to ask of her. Besides, I didn't reason. I acted like someone witless and irresponsible. A demon inhabited me. And he never had control of me more imperiously than on our return to Algiers, during the same honeymoon trip:

The Easter vacation had ended. In the train taking us from Biskra, three schoolboys, returning to their lycée, occupied the compartment next to ours, which was almost full. They were half-undressed, for the heat was tantalizing, and, alone in their compartment, were making a terrible racket. I listened to them laugh and jostle one another. At each of the frequent but brief stops the train made, by leaning out of the little side window I had lowered, my hand could just touch the arm of one of the three schoolboys, who amused himself by leaning toward me from the next window, laughingly entering into the game; and I tasted excruciating delights in feeling the downy amber flesh he offered to my caress. My hand, slipping up along his arm, rounded the shoulder. . . . At the next station, one of the two others would take his place, and the same game would begin again. Then the train would start again. I sat down, breathless and panting, and pretended to be absorbed by my reading. Madeleine, seated opposite me, said nothing, pretended not to see me, not to know me. . . .

On our arrival in Algiers, the two of us alone in the bus that was taking us to the hotel, she finally said to me, in a tone in which I felt even more sorrow than censure: "You looked like either a criminal or a madman."

. . . Let me say at once that that reconciliation *in extremis* allowed us to recapture, despite the setbacks, and before separating forever, a sort of harmonious felicity as perfect as her love deserved. I shall return to that; but first I must speak of the ordeals. . . . Mine came later, just as unbearable as hers had been, to such a degree that each of us in turn made desperate efforts to detach himself from the other: we were suffering too much. It was in religion that she sought refuge—as was natural, for she had always been very devout—and in a re-establishment of those bourgeois ideas and practices which assured her the sort of moral comfort her fragility so greatly needed. The emancipation to which I wanted to lead her had made a sorry showing, and could only appear to her as rash and inhuman; in any case it was not made for her, and succeeded only in wounding her. I tried to bring this out in my *Immoraliste,* a book that seems to me today very imperfect, very incomplete at least, for it did not take into account, indeed it scarcely provided even a glimpse of, the sharper edge of the sword.

That sword soon turned against me. For she was not to be satisfied merely with detaching herself from me; it seemed that she made every effort to separate me from her, lopping off from herself little by little everything that made me love her. Powerless, I was forced to watch that sacrilegious mutilation. I had cast away the right to intervene, to protest; she made me feel this by disregarding everything I found to say to her; without ever resisting, without deviating from her smiling amenity; simply by taking no account whatever of my admonitions. . . .

. . . The dreadful thing is that I came to believe (and she strained her ingenuity to force me to believe) that she was not capable of a more complete flowering, that the most exquisite part of all that I cherished in her existed only in my imagination; that the real person she was fell far short of my dream. . . . The truth is that she believed I had ceased to love her. Consequently what was the use of making herself attractive to please me? As for pleasing me, there was no longer any point in thinking of it. From then on, what did culture, music, poetry matter? She avoided the paths on which she might have run the risk of encountering me; she buried herself in devotion. I was free either to be jealous of God or to follow her onto that mystic ground, the only one where she would still allow me to communicate with her. She confined herself to it rigidly.

She was two years older than I; but the difference in age, from her appearance on certain days, seemed to be that between two generations. I remember a ride we took to Fécamp. I was counting on a great deal of pleasure from this little time spent alone with her; but she consented to the interruption in her trifling daily chores only on condition that we take along the two maids, "who will enjoy the ride even more than I," she said. For the happiness of others always came before her own. I was well aware, during the whole drive, that she pretended to enjoy it in order not to sadden me, and that she was no doubt sensitive to the beauty of the countryside, to the soft, full light on the opulence of the wheatfields; but also that she never once stopped thinking of all she ought to have done at Cuverville and that she was accepting that distraction only for the sake of not detracting from my joy. At Fécamp I had dropped behind to buy some cigarettes; I recall that before catching up with her, I stopped first and looked at her, some twenty yards ahead of me, walking between the two maids; and that she seemed to me so pitifully aged that I doubted it was she. "Why, is that what remains of you, my dear? That is what you have made yourself become!" And I tarried behind for fear of not being able to hide from her the anguish that filled my heart and wanted to pour forth in tears. Tears of remorse as well, for I told myself: this is my work! It was entirely up to me to keep her from forsaking life. Now it is done. It is too late, and I can no longer change anything. . . . I had not the courage to catch up with her, and I let her go back to the hotel alone. And when, a little later, I heard one of the hotel servants say to me: "Your mother is waiting for you in the carriage," I was certainly much more deeply grieved than she herself may perhaps have been to notice that I was taken for her son.

After the war, fleeing society, she never left Cuverville any more. How were her days spent? Her evenings were short, for she got up before dawn; as soon as she had made her devotions, she would go down to light the kitchen fire and prepare the work for the young maids she was training . . . who would regularly leave her, as soon as they were trained, to go and get a job in town. She hardly read any more at all, for lack of time, she said. Constantly busy, she would run about with brisk little steps from one end of the house or garden to the other; you would see her pass, smiling but elusive, and only with great difficulty could I get her to grant me an hour to read aloud to her—a reading often interrupted by one of the maids coming to ask her help or advice, by farmers, tradesmen, beggars, and all the poor of the countryside.

. . . tired of constantly watching over her, of wearing myself out in ever-useless objurgations, I had finally resolved to let her do as she wished without saying another word. Yes, I was dreadfully, mortally tired of taking care of her; I could do no more. The contest was lost; I gave up. Henceforth I would give her free rein! Besides, I no longer loved her; did not even want to; loving her made me suffer too much. As for all that I had dreamed, all that I associated with her, did it not already belong to the past, to the tomb where it would all eventually end up?

But, wonder of wonders, it was when I had finally forced myself to so artificial a detachment that she began to draw closer to me—oh, in an almost imperceptible way; without changing her manner of living in the least. I had come to believe that my presence was a burden to her, bothered her; but what bothered her, she gave me to understand, was only my remonstrances (for there had never been the slightest *explanation* between us). And slowly, from the very wreckage of our love, a new harmony, as if supernatural or superhuman, took shape. No, I had not ceased loving her.

For that matter, since nothing carnal had ever entered into my devotion for her, that devotion was not to let itself be altered by the weathering that time had brought; for that matter, I never loved Madeleine more than aged, stooped, suffering from varicose veins in her legs which she would let me bandage, almost disabled, at last surrendering to my care, sweetly and tenderly grateful.

What is our love made of, then, I used to wonder, if it persists in spite of the crumbling of all the elements that compose it? What is hidden behind the deceptive exterior that I recapture and recognize as the same through all the dilapidations? Something immaterial, harmonious, radiant, which must be called soul, but what does the word matter? She believed in immortality; and I am the one who ought to believe in it, for it is she who left me. . . .

from

AINSI SOIT-IL,

OU LES JEUX SONT FAITS

(*So Be It, or The Chips Are Down*)

1950–1951

. . . as for the game I was playing, I have won it. But I have lost any real interest in it since Em. left me. Since then it often seems to me that I do nothing but pretend to live; she was my reality. It doesn't matter if I fail to make myself understood. I myself don't entirely understand what I mean. For instance, I don't really know what I mean by reality. For her, reality was a God in whom I could not believe. . . . I have given up trying to understand anything at all.

If what I have just written were to cause any young man who might read me to stumble or to slacken his ardor, I should tear out these pages immediately. But I beg him to consider my age, and to make an effort to realize that at eighty one need not still be trying to leap ahead—unless out of oneself. Let that young man look elsewhere, in my youthful writings, for invitations to joy, to that natural exaltation in which I lived so long; he will find them in abundance. But at present I could not reassume them without affectation. . . .

No, it's quite a different state that I'm depicting now, one in which I scarcely recognize myself at all. Until close to my eightieth year, I had managed to maintain in me (and quite naturally; I mean without any artifice) a sort of curiosity, of almost frisky cheerfulness, which I portrayed as best I could in my books, and which made me spring forward toward everything that seemed to me worthy of love and admiration, despite frequent disappointments. The inhibition I feel today comes neither from the outer world nor from others, but from myself. Through sympathy I long kept myself in a state of fervor. When I travel, I do so with a young companion, and live by proxy. I take his astonishments, his joys as my own. . . . I think I should still be capable of some of them myself. But it is precisely myself that I am becoming progressively less interested in, more detached from. Yet I still remain extremely sensitive to the spectacle of adolescence. Moreover, I have taken care not to let my desires slumber, listening here to the advice of Montaigne, who is particularly wise on this score. He knew, and I know too, that wisdom does not lie in renunciation, in abstinence, and took care not to let that secret spring dry up too soon, even going so far as to encourage himself toward physical pleasure, if I understand him correctly. . . . Nonetheless, my anorexia comes partly, comes especially, from a withdrawal of the sap, I am forced to admit. Even at the age of eighty, one does not willingly admit such things. King David was probably about my age when he invited the very young Abishag to come and warm his couch. That passage, like many another in the Bible, would seriously embarrass commentators if they were not able to look for, and find, a mystical interpretation for it—which is not obvious to me at all.

Anorexia. To overcome it, at least momentarily, I needed only these few pages I have just written as fast as I could. To me idleness is unendurable. . . . Now that I have resolved to let my pen run where it will (though I do weigh the words I am writing), I again enjoy moments of perfect felicity. I am not rereading myself, and shall wait until later to find out the worth of what I have just written. This is an experiment I have never before tried, for ordinarily I carry the least project in my head for months, years. If I had my life to begin over again, I should grant myself greater license. But had I slackened the reins, I might perhaps have done nothing worth while. It took me a very long time to realize to what an extent my heredity tied me down. In other and simpler words: I was much less free than I thought I was, extraordinarily held down, held in check, held back by the feeling of *duty*. To how many invitations I now regret not having yielded! For my greater enrichment, doubtless; but perhaps also for the dissolution of my character. . . . It is futile to try to add up the two sides.

How often I have longed to write a book that would completely disregard my past, that people would try in vain to link up with what is pompously called "my work." It's no good; I fall back into the themes already gone over, which I no longer think I can still turn to account. I feel much more disposed to laughter than I was in my youth. I then took seriously many "problems" that make me smile or laugh today. I except the political, social, or economic problems that concern others in an often tragic way; I am thinking of those I used to imagine, often quite gratuitously, between man and the divinity. It seems to me now that most often it is all pure invention, and that the best thing to do is to carry on without paying too much attention to it. . . .

All the same, there would be pretense in depicting myself as more frivolous than I am. It is myself I have great trouble taking seriously, not other people. Give up one's life for another? . . . Yes, perhaps. For a cause? . . . We have too often been fooled.

Man's relations to God always seemed to me much more important and interesting than the relations of men among themselves. Moreover, it was natural enough that, born into easy circumstances, I never had much cause to be concerned with the latter. If my parents had had to work hard for their living, this would probably not have been true. My heredity and then my Protestant upbringing turned my mind almost exclusively toward moral problems. In those early years I had not yet grasped the fact that duties toward God and duties toward the self could be the same. At present I have a great tendency to take one for the other, perhaps too completely. I am still exigent: much more toward myself than toward others; but I no longer believe that there is anyone outside myself, any power superior to me, independent of me, that does the exacting. To tell the truth, I no longer keep accounts, as I once did. At night before trying to go to sleep, I no longer make what the Protestant calls his "examination of conscience"; I act as if I had passed the examination. And don't see this at once as a matter of pride. It sometimes happens, indeed quite often, that I am very little satisfied with myself: when I have let some mean impulse dictate my conduct. . . .

But as for declaring myself satisfied with the present state of affairs . . . ah, no! That's asking too much of me. Everywhere I look, I see nothing but illegitimate favors and injustices, or that sort of complacent acceptance of the iniquity by those who don't have to suffer from it personally. . . . In the notebook in which I had begun writing again, at random rather as I am doing here, and which I lost at Rapallo, I had related the horrible lynching of a very young German parachutist at the beginning of the war. It took place in a village through which we happened to pass the next day. The furious peasants had thrashed him, beaten him black and blue with shovels and rakes until he died, without being able to get anything out of that obstinate youth but a stubborn *"Heil Hitler!"* Such martyrs, and authentic martyrs they are for all that, such zealots of divergent doctrines, are most embarrassing, to be sure. One wonders at the gate of what other paradise what other Saint Peter will meet them . . .

I no longer have any great curiosity as to what life may still bring me. I have said more or less well what I thought I had to say, and I am afraid of repeating myself. But idleness is a burden to me. Yet the thing that would keep me from killing myself (although I do not at all consider suicide reprehensible) is that some people would try to see in that deed a sort of confession of failure, the obligatory conclusion to my error. Others would go so far as to assume that I was trying to escape from Grace. It would be hard to convince people that, simply, I have had my fill of days and don't know how to use the little time left me to live. Anorexia. The hideously inexpressive face of Boredom.

I am especially disheartened by the concentric character of anything I might undertake from now on. . . . Oh, how hard it is to age well! You would like to do a favor for others, and you feel yourself becoming a burden.

If I had my life to begin over again and it were permitted me to dispose of it at will, from the way I see things today I should probably give more time to work (I mean, to that of my education), but surely more time to adventure. I find it hard to console myself for not knowing Greek, for not speaking English and German fluently, and especially for having been so wary—a thing that doesn't jibe with my instinctive scorn of comfort. Dare I add in my own defense that my wife gave very little encouragement to my venturesome undertakings, which immediately struck her as fool-hardy? She foresaw dangers everywhere. I don't yet understand, even today, how and where I sometimes found the strength to override her objections, despite all my love and my fear of hurting her. Paying too much attention to her fears, I realized in time, would have meant failure. Yet she took the greatest care not to cut short my impulses, and constantly to make me understand that she had no desire to influence my will or my thought in any way. But how could I not have sensed, through her very silences, her constant desire to see me turn back? The sexual problem was eventually added to all that; but I think it was not an essential part of the issue. Nevertheless, as it could not be solved by mere submission, I believe it pushed me along the path of revolt much more rapidly and further than I should have gone by myself. Oh, let's not go back over that again.

I once wrote, I don't know now just where, that I was certainly not in-different to the fate of the world after I should cease to be here to suffer from or to enjoy it. That is true, and I have often shown myself (or more precisely pretended) to be more optimistic than I was in reality. Some days, if I let myself go, I should scream with despair. But a few glimmers of true virtue, self-sacrifice, nobility, and dignity are enough to push back into the darkness the discouraging accumulation of stupidity, gluttony, and abjection. The sparks of virtue seem to me more dazzling by contrast. And I am willing to admit that without them our sorry world would pre-sent nothing but an incoherent tissue of absurdities. But there they are, nevertheless, and I intend to count on them.

It is only too easy to spin out fine-sounding phrases on this subject. And you have only to sprinkle it with mysticism to see gather around you an angelic choir, animated with excellent intentions and ready to quote edifying verses from the Gospels, which will leave no room for doubt as to the favorable timing of your conversion. A certain number of my former friends, some of the best of them, became converts. Without having ex-actly broken off with them, I was immediately convinced that conversa-tion with them had become impossible. Any subject that was dear to me had to be cautiously avoided. It didn't seem to me that their conversions profoundly amended their characters; on the contrary, their worst short-comings drew encouragement from being henceforth consecrated to God. Copeau, Jammes, Claudel, Ghéon (I am citing only those who declared themselves openly) even buttressed their own arrogance from that mo-ment forth with a sort of conceit that quickly made them unbearable to me. Backed by the Church, they *couldn't* be wrong. I was the arrogant one for refusing to give in, to subordinate my own thought to what had been acknowledged as true, etc. . . . . later on I recognized the same collective conceit among the Communists, though on a quite different plane. Both groups taught me something, and by their own absurdity helped me ap-preciate the value of the individual.

. . . we penetrate so superficially the conscience of others, we understand them so dimly. We see and hear things, but everything inside remains a mystery. This is partly why in my *Faux-Monnayeurs* I forbade myself, as it were methodically, the current turns of phrase that novelists use: "He thought that . . ." "He could not believe that . . ." "He said to himself that . . ." What do you know about it, dear colleague? . . .

This is also why I so often adopted the form of narration that made such subterfuges impossible, relating more of my *récits* in the first person. To be sure, in the "journal" (Alissa's, the minister's in my *Symphonie pastorale,* the uncle's in my *Faux-Monnayeurs,* etc.) the sincerity can just as well be questioned, but the game is more subtle and the reader is invited to take part in it. He is "in league" with the author.

. . . oh! conversations bore me! How I fear and flee them. It is so rare that anyone tries to understand anyone else, or even to hear him! And what a waste of strength and time if you acquiesce, as I am tempted to do at the start out of kindness. I struggle against that tendency, and believe I am somewhat better able to resist than I once was. But it is so much simpler, so much less a strain to agree! The trouble is that weeks, or months, or even years later, the man you were talking to comes and reminds you: "But that's not at all what you told me in April 19—."

Oh, to go back to the time when people were very little concerned as to my opinion about individuals, works, and things, which allowed me not to have any at all. Today America or China is eager, it seems, to know what I think about the atom bomb, the latest vote in the English Parliament, etc. Good heavens! . . .

Back in Paris, where life resumes its savor, I regain my pleasure in living. What is the use of constantly reminding myself of my age? Let's leave that to infirmities. They bother me, to be sure, but none of them is unbearable. Hardly being able to walk any more keeps me more at home. I shall try to persuade myself that this is for the best.

But if only other people would leave me alone! O bliss! . . . so keen that I doubt whether I shall be able to sleep tonight, and tomorrow I may feel laid flat by my insomnia. Indeed, it is important for me not to encounter myself in a mirror: those bags under the eyes, those hollow cheeks, those ravaged features, those lackluster eyes. . . . I am enough to frighten anyone, and that leaves me terribly down. But let us carry on. . . . To obtain what I want, I am tenacious, bold, even foolhardy; I give no thought to the obstacles; but to resist what puritans call "temptation," I am worthless. I don't even try. If I believed in the devil (I sometimes pretended to believe in him; it's so convenient!), I should say that I come to terms with him at once.

In Paris I also find the familiar disorder and litter: not a table, not a shelf that is not overloaded with books. Books that I should not find time to read even if I did nothing but that . . . Every day the mail brings new ones. Some are accompanied by a letter. Other letters accompany manuscripts: the author needs to know what I think of his poems (most often it is verses that people send me). How disturbing such appeals can be! The fact that they are not aware of this is almost the only excuse one can make for those who send such things out. Most often I try to go on with my work without listening to them, without even hearing them. Then I turn back: supposing I were wrong! . . . Occasionally I have committed such gross, such unpardonable errors—with Proust, for instance, with Dorothy Bussy. . . . Would I have recognized at once the obvious value of Baudelaire, of Rimbaud? Might I not at the outset have looked upon Lautréamont as a madman? And eventually the question must be asked in the most serious way possible: Am I capable of being moved by an utterly new form of poetry that breaks with tradition in every regard? And isn't that just what would deserve praise most of all? Even though it is not enough, in order to prove one's genius, simply to break with the artificial, the conventional . . .

Were I to find myself suddenly faced with a few new burning bushes comparable to the *Illuminations,* to the *Chants de Maldoror,* and supposing that I should recognize their radiance at once, I fear that at present I might be less dazzled than embarrassed by it. At my age, and for some time now, I have had my fill of poetry. The same is true for music; and I am almost on the point of adding: and for love. The young adventurer launching out into life fills his heart very readily, though there are all sorts of things competing for a place there. And this is a good thing. Dante may subsequently meet other Beatrices, Romeo other Juliets; he will not even glance at them, for he has all he needs of love and adoration. The rapture and enthusiasm that Hugo inspired in me when I read him at sixteen may be kindled in the heart of today's adolescents by others than Hugo. Each of us retains a particular gratitude to the one who initiated him. And nothing subsequently can ever equal those first transports.

In my testamentary arrangements I left no directions regarding my funeral and I am worried about the difficult situation my executors will be in. But, however I sound myself out, I cannot get myself to make a definite

*decision. Cremation, to tell the truth, does not seem unattractive. I am
rather tempted by it, but I confess that I prefer being nibbled by worms
and absorbed by the roots of plants and trees to being sniffed haphazardly
by a lot of halitosis-ridden bastards.*

(. . . in setting down that sentence, which I originally liked, I detect in it a rather aggressive cynicism that is not at all like me.)

. . . certain recollections overlap, telescope, fuse together, creating the effect of double exposures. These are particularly powerful in dreams. If I live but a little while longer, the terrors and horrors of the two World Wars will eventually blend into one in many regards. Just as my wife's face, at times (but only in dreams), subtly, as if mystically takes the place of my mother's without really surprising me. The outlines of the faces are not sharp enough to keep me from shifting from one to the other; my emotion remains keen enough, but its cause is floating and ill defined. Indeed, the role played by both of them in my dreams is about the same: an inhibitory role. And this explains or motivates the substitution.

People insist that I should be Claudel's enemy. That he owes it to himself to be mine is not quite the same thing. I am not at all averse to his taking his stand against me. What an odd state of mind he has! On the side opposite the Church he can see nothing but insignificant twaddle. Yet not so stupid but that he realizes . . . Realizes what? That what he considers the Truth is opposed by more than just intellectual conceit. My admiration for certain bursts of his genius is just the same as it was in my youth, and his most insulting denials cannot change it in any way. . . . .

If *Les Caves* gains some success in the near future, Claudel will be furious; not so much against the book or the play as against the public, as he was at the time of the Nobel Prize. As it is proved by "the Scriptures" that I have no talent and could not have any, any attention that is granted me can only be the result of intrigue. The Faith cannot be bothered with whatever nasty tricks it is necessarily called upon to play on truth (I should say to truths, in the plural, for the Church possesses the only Truth). "A Protestant clique," Claudel said of the Nobel jury. Great analogy with the Communist cult: you can enter the house only after leaving outside, first your judgment, common sense, and critical spirit—all freedom of thought.

. . . "Nobility, dignity, grandeur" . . . I am afraid and almost ashamed
to use these expressions, so shamelessly have they been abused. Wrenched
as they are today, they seem almost obscene words—like all noble words,
moreover, beginning with the word "virtue." But it is not only the words
that have become debased, it is also what they mean: the meaning of these
words has changed, and their devaluation only makes flagrant the general
collapse of all that seemed to us sacred, of all that encouraged us to live, of
all that saved us from despair. The Christian gets along all right, as we
know; and the Moslem, and all those who are willing to close their eyes
and believe in some superhuman power, in some god concerned about
each one of us. Mere human reason prevents some from accepting that too
easy consolation. Therefore it is in themselves, in themselves alone, that
they must seek and find recourse. And should a little pride enter into this,
is it not legitimate? and the austere and noble feeling of duty worthily
accomplished, of the restoration in oneself of human potentiality, of what
allows the tortured man to look at his torturer and think: it is you who are
the victim?

Oh, of course, I am well aware that it is easy for me to talk of all this,
sitting calmly far from the fight; but do ideas deserve to be propagated
only when they are distorted and created under pressure? What I am writing freely now I want to see opposed tomorrow to whatever I may be
forced to say. For I have no idea whether or not my weak flesh is the stuff
of which martyrs are made. And, besides, they have such clever means
today to undermine the will itself and to turn the hero into an instrument,
docile and debased!

And since I have interrupted myself, I should like to make something clear. For, after all, it would not do for anyone to misunderstand
me: I continue to note down in this book everything that comes into
my head. Now, there appears here almost no trace of the dreadful events
upsetting everything round about and threatening to change the face of
the world. Is this the same thing as saying that they leave me indifferent?
It is easy for Valéry, from within his closed system, to write: "Events do
not interest me"; and I understand very well what he means by that. It is
not quite the same with me. I take an interest—I even occasionally claim
to take a part—in "what happens"; but, to tell the truth, I must confess
that I cannot really bring myself to believe in it. I don't know how to
explain this, though for a very perspicacious reader it must, I think, have
already emerged from my writings (and besides, I have at times noted it

explicitly): I cannot now, I have never been able to "fit" reality, to adapt myself to it completely. There is always someone in me who acts and someone else who observes him; but this is not, properly speaking, a case of split personality. No, it is the very one who acts, or who suffers, who doesn't take himself seriously. I even believe that at the moment of death I shall say to myself: "Look! He's dying." Hence, the misery all around us can come closer and closer and lay siege to my door; I am as moved by it as anyone can be (and sometimes even, sometimes, I think, more than if I were suffering), and become occupied and even preoccupied with it; but it doesn't take its place on my list of real things. I think this failing (for obviously it is one) must be linked to what I said above: my lack of a proper sense of *time*. Whatever happens to me, or to someone else, I immediately put it in the past. Enough to distort seriously my judgment about events destined to become historical. I bury people and things, and myself, with disconcerting ease; the only thing I keep (unintentionally, of course) is their meaning. And, judging from the way the world is going, I keep repeating to myself that these ratiocinations may well, before long, be swept away with all the rest. But I nonetheless write them, just like little Hauviette in Péguy's *Jeanne d'Arc,* who declares that if the last day were imminent, if "the angel were beginning to blow his trumpet" she would neither more nor less go on playing *boquillons* as if nothing were happening.

Today we are both witnesses of and actors in a vast tragic farce, and no one knows what will come of it. We have been surfeited with horror, and the farce is not yet near its end. Thousands of persons have been confronted with the question: Is it my duty to say yes or no? The question still looms up before them, but with the atrocious certainty that their acceptance or rejection will hardly matter at all. But what does matter is each one of them, taken individually. What is important is that each of them be able to die satisfied with himself, without having forsworn himself. If the problem should arise likewise for me, all of a sudden, I should not know how to solve it . . . and should go back to playing *boquillons* until I began to understand better.

There are two distinct worlds. I can well imagine Noah in his Ark writing the *Ethics* or the *Discourse on Method* just as if calamitous waves were not flooding the universe. People sometimes express amazement at the little impression that Napoleon's conquests made on French letters. Today the various compartments are less watertight, but I doubt if there is any reason to congratulate ourselves on that. Each of us is more or less implicated in the general anguish, and it may seem monstrously selfish to try to avoid it. The writings of the present (and I am speaking even of the best) suffer a sort of contamination which I, for one, consider degrading. The plague was ravaging Florence and every day brought fresh subjects for grief while Boccaccio was writing his *Decameron*. I don't dream of taking refuge in a delightful villa at Fiesole, so as to be able to look down with impunity on this particular plague. No indeed; if events force me, I am ready to face them. I shall try not to dishonor myself, not to tremble too much before the horror. But don't ask me to assume a false voice and introduce quavers into my writing through expediency. . . .

I would give my life that God might be. Yes, that is all right. But: I give my life to prove that God *is*—that will not do at all; that ceases to have any meaning whatever. But we are no longer on a theosophical plane today. Thousands of people are ready to give their lives to bring about a better state of things on earth: for more justice, for a more equitable distribution of material goods. I don't dare add: for more liberty, because I don't really know what is meant by that.

In any case, keeping quiet is in no wise the same thing as being indifferent. Those who approach me are well aware of this. The only question I have a right (I was about to say: a duty) to ask myself is: What good can I be? For this is where we stand: amid such universal distress (if not universal, it spares only the privileged, only the "happy few" to which one is either loath or ashamed to belong), how can one reduce that distress, even a little? That is the problem, and in face of it I know and feel that I can do almost nothing. During the First World War, I had wisely made up my mind to keep silent and to devote all my time to helping refugees; at least that kept me from thinking of anything else. American gifts poured in to us; we were simply the dispensing agency; but examining each case of need kept us so busy that we had no leisure at all. I do not think it would have been possible to be more zealously and conscientiously concerned with others than some of us were for months. Dare I speak cynically? With few exceptions, the cases of destitution we helped were not very interesting. I mean that had it not been for their need, nothing would have fixed our attention and our sympathy on the lamentable derelicts who came to us for help. What a school of misanthropy! At times, but very rarely, some faint glimmer kept us from thinking: what's the use? Almost all of those to whom we gave the means of continuing to live seemed to us lamentable dregs of humanity. Let it be added at once that almost every one of them showed himself in his least favorable aspect, in the most unattractive light. Sometimes, during my visits to their lodgings, I happened to discover, next to our applicants, more authentic sufferers who, through modesty and common decency, were reluctant to let themselves be seen; immediately we would direct all our attention to the latter. But even then, what were we in a position to know except by-products of the war, moraines eroded away from their position on the edge of a glacier? At that time there was not yet the mashing-up of whole nations, the concentration camps, the inhuman atrocities that the following war offered us. . . .

Even more imperiously there arose before me, there still constantly arises, the question: What is, what can be, my best service? . . .

So I come back to that question of the best service. It is certain that the man who wonders, as he takes up his pen: What service can be performed by what I am about to write? is not a born writer, and would do better to give up producing at once. Verse or prose, one's work is born of a sort of imperative one cannot elude. It results (I am now speaking only of the authentic writer, of prose or poetry) from an artesian gushing-forth, so to speak, almost unintentional, in which reason, critical spirit, and art intervene only as moderators. But once the page is written, he may wonder: What's the use? . . . And when I turn to myself, I think that what above all drove me to write was an urgent need of sympathetic understanding. It is that need that prompts the ratiocinations with which I am filling this notebook today, and makes me banish all overstatement from them. I hope the young man who may read me will feel on an equal footing. I have no doctrine to bring; I refuse to give advice; and in an argument, I beat a hasty retreat. But I know that today many seek their way gropingly, and don't know in whom to trust. To them I say: Believe those who are seeking the truth; doubt those who find it; doubt everything, but don't doubt yourself. There is more light in Christ's words than in any other human word. It is not enough, it seems, to be a Christian: in addition, one must *believe*. Well, I do not believe. Having said this, I am your brother.

Some remarks I wrote at the beginning of the last war, or more exactly after the disaster and at the beginning of the occupation, were bitterly held against me. It would have been very simple for me not to let them be published, and I was well aware of the moral harm I was likely to do myself in making them public. But it struck me as unseemly to cheat by hiding my weaker moments. It is certain that for a rather long time I

thought all was lost. I was alone then near Carcassonne, and nothing justified me in supposing that there was even a ghost of resistance. An organization of resistance seemed to me even more fanciful. When I resumed
contact with old friends at Nice and Cabris a little later, I began to realize
that the game was not so completely lost as I had feared and that, in any
case, some people had made up their minds to play it out to the end with
all its risks. In the beginning, for lack of information, I thought that some
of the most valiant of our young people were rushing blindly toward certain disaster. Their sacrifice ran the risk of bringing about a hecatomb of
all our best men, a total slaughter to no advantage whatsoever, and France
would find herself more impoverished, more bloodless, than she was before.

. . . The French gave proof of secret virtues of which I confess that
I should not have thought them capable except in a quite exceptional way.
Decidedly, our honor was restored. The question facing us thenceforth
was of a quite different nature: What could be, what should be our
role now in a new world? It was essential not only to resume and to
strengthen our place, but also to reconstruct, and to reconstruct on shifting
sands. . . .

I was worried to the point of anguish by the confusion of the rising
generation. It had nothing before it but the spectacle of failure, of bank-
ruptcies. Once it had slept off the first intoxication of triumph, nothing
seemed worth living for. Everywhere one could discover cheating, exploitation, corrupt practices; words themselves had lost the authentic meanings around which one might have liked to rally. Eventually I came to
realize that the only possible basis for agreement was negative: there was
that which we were obliged to accept, at least temporarily, and that which
we positively refused to agree to: falsehood. What wiles, what subterfuges, what degrading compromises! Neither toward oneself nor toward
others, whether it comes from the Left or the Right, be it Catholic or
Communist, should one put up with falsehood. What I am saying makes
you smile? Well, then, that is because I am not saying it properly.

The farther human suffering is from us, the more abstract it becomes.
I know many very charitable souls who cease to be charitable at a distance.
Whether that distance is in time or space. Of certain agonies those souls
would dare to say, if they were really sincere: "But after all . . . it's too
far away." Imagination fails when it is stretched too tight. We hear the
S.O.S. sent out from next door, but beyond the first corner the brief call
may not even reach us, and too much static gets in the way. There are also
many people who are more sensitive to the imaginary than to the real, and

who are more likely to sympathize with the sufferings of a fictional hero, as long as they are well described, than with those of their neighbors—which, to tell the truth, they don't really see.

Our potentialities for compassion are most often extraordinarily limited; sometimes they are used up almost at once. And it is such a mistake to think that a hundred misfortunes are a hundred times more moving than a single one! And when it is a question of not hundreds but thousands, one might as well give up at once. Consequently, when faced with huge catastrophes, with disasters multiplied too many times, our sentiment changes: it is no longer pity but indignation that fills the heart and the mind, a revolt against the unacceptable: something must be changed. *Then* one begins to fight. There is no further possibility of withdrawing from the game. The gods have decidedly failed, and it is up to man himself to check humanity's collapse. The oddest thing is that this apparent collapse (could it be that it is not real?) coincides with an undreamed-of development of man's power, which would probably suffice if we were willing to apply it properly. But first we need agreement, at a time when everything works for division. The threat grows, and trembling, I repeat to myself Shakespeare's line:

So foul a sky clears not without a storm.

I had not made arrangements to live so old. From a certain age onward, it seemed to me that I had given up my part. My optimism became strained, or else it ran away. I had to admit that the look of the world hardly justified it, and that I could manage to keep it up only by refusing to look around me. Desolation everywhere, and no way of escaping it except through a sort of egoism that revolted me: *"I* at least . . ." or through what the Catholics call Faith, against which my reason protested. Was I therefore somehow involved in all the world's suffering? I would have needed a kind of cynicism to distract my mind, and I lacked it dreadfully. My temperament naturally led me toward joy, to be sure; but to maintain myself in this state of joy, I should have had to be ignorant of or to forget too many things. The world was decidedly not ripe enough to be able to get along without God; it was foundering in a dismal bankruptcy.

. . . We can help one another so little, and often, unfortunately, it is in such a ridiculously inadequate and awkward way. . . . But as soon as suffering is shared, it becomes easier to endure. Often the most painful thing it has to encounter is the indifference of others. Having said that, I hasten to add that there are many sufferings which I insist are imaginary, and toward which I declare myself pitiless: few things interest me less than so-called broken hearts and sentimental affairs. Often mockery suffices to cauterize them; it is soon evident that they involve a large share of self-pity, falsehood, and pretense. One is less really in love than one imagines, and more's the pity. Whereas the man dying of hunger, seeing his children around him die of hunger—his sufferings are real. And I keep myself, it goes without saying, from shrugging my shoulders in the face of those dilemmas, so frequent today, in which man is led to endure the worst sufferings in order to protect his dignity. They are the ones, above all, which elicit my sympathy, but a sympathy that most often is not in a position to express itself; especially as these are the imponderable, the inadmissible, the incalculable sufferings, but those in which the very value of man is at stake. The lamentable thing is that his market value has fallen so low today that it often merely makes people smile. It is essential to raise it. Let us be among those who work to do so.

Now, the question arises. It constantly rises before me: What will remain of all this? Oh, I am not speaking particularly of what I have just written, which could be effaced with one stroke of the pen, but of all that is being written today, in France and elsewhere. What will remain of our culture, of France itself, of what we have lived for? . . . Let's make up our minds that everything is destined to disappear.

No, I cannot assert that with the end of this notebook everything will be closed; that all will be over. Perhaps I shall have the desire to add something. To add something or other. To add . . . Perhaps. At the last moment, to add something still . . . I am sleepy, it is true. But I don't feel like sleeping. It strikes me that I could be even more tired. It is I don't know what hour of the night or of the morning. . . . Do I still have something to say? Still something, I don't know what, to say?

My own position in the sky, in relation to the sun, must not make me find the dawn any less beautiful.*

---

* Written on February 13, 1951. Gide lapsed into unconsciousness on Saturday, February 17, and died peacefully at 10:20 p.m. two days later.

NOTES AND BIBLIOGRAPHY

NOTES

The following short titles are used for frequently cited sources:

Journal I   (André Gide, *Journal 1889–1939,* Pléiade edition, Paris, 1951)

Journal II   (André Gide, *Journal 1939–1949—Souvenirs,* Pléiade edition, Paris, 1954)

Romans   (André Gide, *Romans, Récits et Soties, Œuvres Lyriques,* Pléiade edition, Paris, 1958)

Delay   (Jean Delay, *La Jeunesse d'André Gide,* 2 vols. Paris, 1956–57)

Schlumberger (Jean Schlumberger, *Madeleine et André Gide,* Paris, 1956)

Gide-Claudel (Paul Claudel et André Gide, *Correspondance 1899–1926,* Paris, 1949)

Gide-Jammes (Francis Jammes et André Gide, *Correspondance 1893–1938,* Paris, 1948)

Gide-RMG   (André Gide—Roger Martin du Gard, *Correspondance 1913–1951,* 2 vols., Paris, 1968)

Gide-Valéry   (André Gide—Paul Valéry, *Correspondance 1890–1942,* Paris, 1955)

When practical, Gide's Journal entries are identified simply by date.

Introduction, pp. 3–18:

1 Richard Ellmann and Charles Feidelson, *The Modern Tradition* (New York, 1965), p. vi.
2 Jean-Paul Sartre, "The Living Gide," in *Situations* (New York, 1965), pp. 52–53.
3 Kevin O'Neill, "Gide Today," *AUMLA* (Journal of the Australasian Universities Language and Literature Association) 32 (November, 1969), 190.
4 G. W. Ireland, in *Entretiens sur André Gide,* ed. Marcel Arland and Jean Mouton (Paris and The Hague, 1967), pp. 129–30.
5 Justin O'Brien, Introduction to *The Journals of André Gide,* I (1889–1913) (New York, 1947), p. vii.

6 O'Neill, *op. cit.*, p. 205.

7 Jean Hytier, *André Gide* (London, 1963), p. 9.

8 Albert Guerard, *André Gide* (Cambridge, Mass., 1951), p. 184.

9 Guerard, *op. cit.*
Delay, I, p. 24.
Gide-Claudel, p. 245.
Vino Rossi, *André Gide, The Evolution of an Aesthetic* (New Brunswick, N.J., 1967), p. vi.
Gide-RMG, I, p. 179.

10 *Journal,* June 26, 1913.
Schlumberger, p. 193. From Roger Martin du Gard's account of a conversation with Gide in December, 1920.
Journal, November 29, 1921.

11 Gaëtan Picon, "Actualité d'André Gide," *Fontaine* 156, x (November, 1946), p. 619.

12 Maurice Blanchot, "Gide et la littérature d'expérience," *L'Arche* 23 (1947), pp. 90–91.

One (1869–1893), pp. 21–33:

1 Letter of Roger Martin du Gard to André Gide of October 7, 1920, in Gide-RMG, I, p. 158.

2 *Si le grain ne meurt,* in *Journal* II, pp. 492, 500–501, 547n.

3 *Ibid.,* p. 438.

4 *Ibid.,* p. 424.

5 Delay, I, p. 284.

6 *Si le grain ne meurt,* in *Journal* II, p. 410.

7 *Ibid.,* p. 608.

8 Letter of André Gide to his mother of October 8, 1893, in Delay, II, p. 275.

9 Letter of André Gide to Saint-Georges de Bouhelier of January, 1897, in Delay, II, p. 642.

10 Letter of André Gide to his mother of May 27, 1892, in Delay, II, p. 166.

11 *Si le grain ne meurt,* in *Journal* II, p. 529.

12 Letter of André Gide to Paul Valéry of December, 1891, in Gide-Valéry, p. 141.

13 Letter of André Gide to Marcel Drouin of March 18, 1893, in Delay, II, p. 215.

14 *Si le grain ne meurt,* in *Journal* II, p. 519.

15 *Ibid.,* p. 430.

16 *Les Cahiers d'André Walter* (Paris, 19th ed., 1952), pp. 79, 64, 179.

17 Journal of Madeleine Rondeaux, quoted in Delay, II, p. 30.

18 *Ibid.,* pp. 29, 27, 31.

19 Letter of Madeleine Rondeaux to André Gide of June 17, 1892, in Delay, I, p. 126.
Delay, I, p. 127.
Letter of Madeleine Rondeaux to André Gide of July 23, 1895, in Delay, II, p. 176n.

20 Letter of André Gide to Madeleine Rondeaux of October 20, 1892, in Delay, II, pp. 184–5.

Two (*1893–1902*), *pp. 101–114:*

1 Letter of André Gide to Francis Jammes of May, 1902, in Gide-Jammes, p. 189.
2 Letter of André Gide to his mother of February 2, 1895, in Delay, II, p. 460.
3 Letter of André Gide to Marcel Drouin of May 10, 1894, in Delay, II, pp. 318–20.
4 Letter of André Gide to his mother of February 2, 1895, in Delay, II, p. 459.
5 *Ibid.*
6 Letters of André Gide to his mother of March, 1895, in Delay, II, pp. 473, 474, 475.
7 Delay, II, p. 485.
8 Letter of Madeleine Rondeaux to André Gide of June 27, 1895, in Schlumberger, p. 117.
9 *Si le grain ne meurt,* in *Journal* II, p. 612.
10 Letter of Madeleine Gide to André Gide of June 1918, in Schlumberger, p. 14.
11 Letter of André Gide to Francis Jammes of October 23, 1895, in Gide-Jammes, p. 55.
12 Justin O'Brien, Introduction to *Madeleine: Et Nunc Manet in Te* (New York, 1952), pp. xvii–xix. The inset quotation is from Roger Martin du Gard, *Notes sur André Gide* (Paris, 1951), p. 66.
13 Letter of André Gide to Francis Jammes of April 1902, in Gide-Jammes, p. 184.
14 Letter of André Gide to Paul Valéry of January 24, 1896, in Gide-Valéry, p. 258.
15 Letter of Madeleine Gide to Claire Demarest (December 1900?), in Schlumberger, p. 168.
16 Letter of André Gide to Francis Jammes of April 1898, in Gide-Jammes, p. 139.
17 Letter of André Gide to Francis Jammes of April 1899, in Gide-Jammes, p. 150.

Three (*1903–1913*), *pp. 295–315:*

1 Note: The letters of André Gide to Christian Beck were printed in the *Mercure de France* for July 1 and August 1, 1949.
2 *Journal,* Monday [February 5], 1912 (*Journal* I, pp. 364–5).
  Letter of André Gide to Christian Beck of July 2, 1907, in *Mercure de France,* August 1, 1949, p. 622.
  Journal, Tuesday [January 23], 1912 (*Journal* I, p. 359).
  Journal, Saturday [May 19], 1906 (*Journal* I, p. 221).
3 In Gide-RMG, I, p. 649.
4 Letter of Francis Jammes to André Gide of April 30, 1906, in Gide-Jammes, p. 235.
5 Letter of André Gide to Francis Jammes of May 2, 1906, in Gide-Jammes, p. 236.
6 Letter of André Gide to Paul Claudel of January 7, 1911, in Gide-Claudel, p. 159.
7 *Journal,* Neuchâtel [January], 1912 (*Journal* I, p. 358).
  Journal, September 1, 1905.

8 *Journal,* Zurich, Wednesday [January 24], 1912 (*Journal* I, p. 359).

9 Letter of André Gide to Christian Beck of July 2, 1907, in *Mercure de France,* August 1, 1949, p. 621.

10 *Romans,* p. 477.

11 In *Journal* I, p. 343.

12 In Léon Pierre-Quint, *André Gide* (Paris, 1952), p. 431.

13 *Mercure de France,* August 1, 1949, p. 634.

14 Jean Schlumberger, *Eveils* (Paris, 1950), p. 205.

15 Letter of André Gide to Paul Claudel of February 15, 1910, in Gide-Claudel, p. 120.

16 Letter of André Gide to Edmund Gosse of January 8, 1914, in *Correspondence of André Gide and Edmund Gosse* (New York, 1959), p. 108.

17 Albert Guérard, *André Gide* (Cambridge, Mass., 1951), p. 16.

18 Jean Schlumberger, "Gide et les débuts de la *N.R.F.,*" in *André Gide* (Editions Capitole, Paris, 1928), p. 262.

19 Jean Schlumberger, *Eveils* (Paris, 1950), p. 209.

20 *Ibid.,* pp. 204–5.

21 Jean Schlumberger, "Gide et les débuts de la *N.R.F.,*" in *André Gide* (Editions Capitole, Paris, 1928), p. 262.

22 Quoted by Justin O'Brien in "The *N.R.F.,*" in *The French Literary Horizon* (New Brunswick, N.J., 1967), p. 179.

23 Saint-John Perse, "Face aux lettres françaises (1909)," in *Hommage à André Gide* (N.R.F., Paris, 1951), p. 76.

24 *Journal,* April 25, 1918.

Four (1914–1919), pp. 419–440:

1 Jean Schlumberger, *Eveils* (Paris, 1950), p. 249.

2 *Journal,* September 17, 1916.

3 Letter of André Gide to Edmund Gosse of July 27, 1916, in *The Correspondence of André Gide and Edmund Gosse* (New York, 1959), p. 136.

4 Letter of André Gide to Paul Valéry of October 4, 1914, in Gide-Valéry, p. 443. *Journal,* September 16, 1914.

5 *Journal,* September 13, 1934.

6 *Journal,* August 14, 1914.

7 In *The Book of France,* ed. Winifred Stephens (London and Paris, 1915), p. 118.

8 *Ibid.,* p. 75.

9 Charles Du Bos, *Journal* I (Paris, 1946), p. 23.

10 *Journal,* February 5, 1916.

11 *Journal,* October 15, 1916. *Numquid et tu* (in *Journal* I, p. 599), June 16, 1916.

12 *Journal,* January 29, 1916.

13 Letter of Madeleine Gide to André Gide of June, 1917, in Schlumberger, p. 181.

14 Letter of Madeleine Gide to André Gide of June, 1918, in Schlumberger, p. 14.

15 Letter of Madeleine Gide to André Gide of July, 1918, in Schlumberger, p. 203.

16 *Et nunc manet in te* (in *Journal* II, p. 1146), November 24, 1918.

17 *Ibid.,* p. 1127.
18 From Journal of Roger Martin du Gard for December 22, 1920, in Schlumberger, pp. 193–4.
19 From Catherine van Rysselberghe's account of a conversation with Gide in January, 1919, in Schlumberger, p. 196.

Five (1920–1932), pp. 579–596:

1 Jean Schlumberger, as quoted in Léon Pierre-Quint, *André Gide* (Paris, 1952), pp. 431–2.
2 *Si le grain ne meurt,* in *Journal* II, p. 525.
    Journal, January 8, 1902.
3 Paul Souday, in *Le Temps,* July 25, 1911.
4 Henri Massis, "La Perversité d'André Gide," in *L'Eclair,* June 23, 1914.
    Abbé Delfour, "Gide le Nietzschean," in *L'Univers,* October, 1915.
5 Jean de Pierrefeu, *L'Opinion,* November 23, 1911.
6 Edmund Wilson, *A Literary Chronicle 1920–1950* (Garden City, N.Y., 1956), p. 171. Originally published in *The New Republic,* August 9, 1933.
7 Erich Ebermeyer, "Enquête sur André Gide," *Latinité,* January, 1931, p. 46.
8 Marcel Arland, "André Gide," *N.R.F.,* February, 1931, p. 255.
9 Claude Martin, *André Gide par lui-même* (Paris, 1967), p. 137.
10 Albert Guérard, *André Gide* (Cambridge, Mass., 1951), p. 15.
11 *Journal,* December 3, 1924.
    Journal, July 5, 191.
    Letter of André Gide to André Rouveyre of October 31, 1924, in André Gide–André Rouveyre, *Correspondance 1909–1951* (Paris, 1967), p. 84.
    Journal, May 2, 1923.
12 Letter of André Gide to André Rouveyre of October 31, 1924, *op. cit.*
13 Letter of André Gide to Roger Martin du Gard of May 1, 1925, in Gide-RMG, I, p. 259.
14 Henri Massis, *D'André Gide à Marcel Proust* (Paris, 1948), pp. 47, 101, 102, 36.
15 Massis, *op. cit.,* pp. 93, 97.
16 Rene Johannet, in *La Revue française,* quoted in *Journal,* December 15, 1921.
17 Letter of Paul Claudel to André Gide of March 2, 1914, in Gide-Claudel, p. 217.
18 *L'Osservatore Romano,* June 1, 1952.
19 Charles Du Bos, *Le Dialogue avec André Gide* (Paris, 1947), p. 315n.
20 *Journal,* August 6, 1924.
21 *Journal,* January 3, 1922.
22 *Journal,* December 3, 1924.
23 *Journal,* September, 1931 (*Journal* I, p. 1072).
24 Roger Martin du Gard, *Notes sur André Gide* (Paris, 1951), p. 93.
25 *Romans,* p. 991.
26 *Journal,* December 3, 1924.
27 Letter of André Gide to André Rouveyre of November 22, 1924, in André Gide–André Rouveyre, *Correspondance 1909–1951* (Paris, 1967), pp. 89–90.
28 Letter of André Gide to Edmund Gosse of January 16, 1927, in *The Corre-*

spondance of André Gide and Edmund Gosse (New York, 1959), pp. 190–91.

29 Letter of Paul Valéry to André Gide of February 5, 1929, in Gide-Valéry, p. 510.

30 Letters of Paul Valéry to André Gide of January, 1929, and February 5, 1929, in Gide-Valéry, pp. 508, 509–10.

31 *Journal,* May 12, 1927 and May 7, 1927.

32 *Œdipe* (Paris, 1931), pp. 118–19.

33 *Journal,* October 20, 1930.

Six (1933–1938), pp. 753–757:

1 In *The God that Failed,* ed. Richard Crossman (New York, 1949), pp. 20–21.

2 Gide, *Littérature engagée,* ed. Yvonne Davet (Paris, 1950), p. 21.

3 *Ibid.,* p. 27.

4 *Ibid.,* p. 38.

5 *Journal,* June 2, 1933.

6 Quoted by Ramon Fernandez, "Littérature et Politique," *N.R.F.,* February 1, 1935, p. 286.

7 Letter of André Gide to Roger Martin du Gard of May 5, 1935, in Gide-RMG, II, p. 28.

8 Quoted in Léon Pierre-Quint, *André Gide* (Paris, 1952), p. 276.

9 *Littérature engagée,* p. 126.

10 Letter printed in *L'Humanité,* January 18, 1937.

11 *Journal,* Summer 1937 (*Journal* I, p. 1291).
   Letter of André Gide to Roger Martin du Gard of April 6, 1938, in Gide-RMG, II, 131.

12 *Journal,* 1935 (second-to-last entry).

13 *Journal,* March 8, 1935.
   Journal, July 4, 1933.

14 Letter of Dorothy Bussy to Roger Martin du Gard of November 26, 1933, in Gide-RMG, I, p. 731.

15 *Journal,* July 27, 1931; July 4, 1933; June 13, 1932; and 1935 (last entry).

16 In *André Gide* (Editions Capitole, Paris, 1928), p. 215.

17 Roger Martin du Gard, Journal for February 27, 1937, in Gide-RMG, II, p. 520.

18 Georges Cogniot, *L'Avenir de la culture* (Paris, 1937), p. 6.

Seven (1938–1951), pp. 839–851:

1 Letter of André Gide to Roger Martin du Gard of January 24, 1941, in Gide-RMG, II, p. 231.

2 Quoted in Henri Amouroux, *Quatre Ans d'Histoire de France* (Paris, 1966), pp. 47–48.

3 Foreword to *Pages de Journal* (New York and Algiers, 1944), reprinted in *Journal* II, p. 344.

4 Letters of André Gide to Roger Martin du Gard of April 19, 1940, and January 24, 1941, in Gide-RMG, II, pp. 202 and 231.

Journal, February 10, 1943.

5 *Journal,* September 24, 1942, and December 11, 1942.
Letter of André Gide to Roger Martin du Gard of May 7, 1940, in Gide-RMG, II, p. 205.

6 *Journal,* July 1, 1942.

7 *Journal,* June 12, 1942.

8 *Journal,* January 1, 1942 and June 22, 1942.
Letter of Roger Martin du Gard to André Gide of August 21, 1945, in Gide-RMG, II, p. 329.

9 From Journal of Roger Martin du Gard for February 27, 1937, in Gide-RMG, II, p. 520.

10 Introduction to *The Journals of André Gide,* IV (1939–49) (New York, 1951), p. ix.

11 Letter of Roger Martin du Gard to André Gide of April 21, 1950, in Gide-RMG, II, p. 479.
Jean Lambert, *Gide familier* (Paris, 1958), p. 124.

12 *Ainsi soit-il,* in *Journal* II, p. 1192.

13 *Romans,* p. 1453.

14 *Ainsi soit-il,* in *Journal* II, p. 1193.

15 *Ibid.,* p. 1178, p. 1237.

BIBLIOGRAPHY

The following is a list of Gide's writings published in English translation.

Afterthoughts on the U.S.S.R. (Dial, New York, 1938; Secker and Warburg, London, 1938)

Amyntas (Bodley Head, London, 1958)

Autumn Leaves (Philosophical Library, New York, 1950)

The Correspondence between Paul Claudel and André Gide (Pantheon, New York, 1952; Secker and Warburg, London, 1952; Beacon paperback)

The Correspondence of André Gide and Edmund Gosse (New York University Press, New York, 1959; Peter Owen, London, 1960)

Corydon (Farrar Straus, New York, 1950, 1961; Secker and Warburg, London, 1952; Noonday paperback)

The Counterfeiters (Knopf, New York, 1927; Cassell, London, 1927 [as *The Coiners*]; published together with *Journal of "The Counterfeiters,"* Knopf, New York, 1951; also Modern Library, Penguin paperback. Latter published separately as *Logbook of "The Coiners,"* Cassell, London, 1952)

Dostoevsky (J. M. Dent, London, 1925; Knopf, New York, 1926; Secker and Warburg, London, 1949; New Directions paperback, Penguin paperback)

The Fruits of the Earth (including *New Fruits of the Earth*) (Knopf, New York, 1949; Secker and Warburg, London, 1949)

If It Die . . . (Random House, New York, 1935; Secker and Warburg, London, 1950; Modern Library, Vintage paperback, Penguin paperback)

Imaginary Interviews (Knopf, New York, 1944)

The Immoralist (Knopf, New York, 1930, 1970; Cassell, London, 1930; Vintage paperback, Penguin paperback, Bantam paperback)

The Journals of André Gide (*1889–1949*), including *Numquid et tu . . .* (Knopf, New York, 1947–1951: 4 vols.; Secker and Warburg, London, 1947–1951: 4 vols.; abridged versions, Vintage paperback, 2 vols.; Penguin paperback)

Lafcadio's Adventures (Knopf, New York, 1925, as *The Vatican Swindle;* under present title in 1928; Cassell, London, 1925, as *The Vatican Cellars;* Vintage paperback; Penguin paperback, with *Strait Is the Gate*)

The Living Thoughts of Montaigne (Longmans Green, New York, 1939; Cassell, London, 1939)

Madeleine (*Et nunc manet in te*) (Knopf, New York, 1952; Secker and Warburg, London, 1952, as *Et nunc manet in te;* Bantam paperback)

Marshlands and *Prometheus Misbound* (New Directions, New York, 1953; Secker and Warburg, London, 1953; latter title first published in English as *Prometheus Ill-Bound,* Chatto and Windus, London, 1919)

Montaigne (Liveright, New York, 1929; Blackmore Press, London, 1929)

My Theatre (including *Philoctetes, King Candaule, Saul, Bathsheba,* and *Persephone*) (Knopf, New York, 1952)

The Notebooks of André Walter (Peter Owen, London, 1968; Philosophical Library, New York, 1968; first portion published as *The White Notebook* [Philosophical Library, New York, 1964; Peter Owen, London, 1967; Citadel paperback])

Notes on Chopin (Philosophical Library, New York, 1949)

Pretexts (Meridian, New York, 1959; Secker and Warburg, London, 1959; Delta paperback)

Recollections of the Assize Court (Hutchinson, London, 1941)

Return from the U.S.S.R. (Knopf, New York, 1937; Secker and Warburg, London, 1937; McGraw-Hill paperback)

Return of the Prodigal Son, in *French Stories,* ed. Wallace Fowlie (Bantam paperback; with *Saul,* Secker and Warburg, London, 1953)

The School for Wives (with *Robert* and *Geneviève*) (Knopf, New York, 1929, 1950; Cassell, London, 1929)

Self-Portraits, the Gide/Valéry Letters, 1890–1942 (abridged) (University of Chicago Press, Chicago, 1966)

So Be It (*or The Chips Are Down*) (Knopf, New York, 1959)

Strait Is the Gate (Knopf, New York, 1924; Secker and Warburg, London, 1924; vintage paperback; Penguin paperback, with *The Vatican Cellars*)

Travels in the Congo (Knopf, New York, 1929; Secker and Warburg, London, 1930; University of California Press paperback)

Two Legends (*Œdipus* and *Theseus*) (Knopf, New York, 1950; Secker and Warburg, London, 1950 [as *Œdipus* and *Theseus*]; Vintage paperback. *Theseus* first published separately in English in *Horizon,* London, 1946, and by New Directions, New York, 1949)

Two Symphonies (*Isabelle* and *The Pastoral Symphony*) (Knopf, New York, 1931; Cassell, London, 1931; Penguin paperback)

Urien's Voyage (Philosophical Library, New York, 1964; Peter Owen, London, 1964 [as *Urien's Travels*]; Citadel paperback)

The basic text of Gide's writings in French is often taken to be that of the fifteen-volume *Œuvres complètes* (Gallimard, Paris, 1932–1939) edited by Louis Martin-Chauffier and limited to slightly over three thousand sets. But these were not even "complete" as of 1932, and are far from being so today. Nonetheless, the *Œuvres complètes* is the only place in which many of Gide's shorter works are reprinted, and it is this text that is often cited in modern scholarly studies. An *Index détaillé* to this edition was prepared by Justin O'Brien and published at Asnières in 1954.

More useful and more practical are the compact volumes of Gide's works in the series "Bibliothèque de la Pléiade" of Editions Gallimard:

I   *Journal 1889–1939* (Paris, 1939, 1940, 1941, 1949, 1951)
     Includes *Numquid et tu . . .* (1922)*

II   *Journal 1939–1949—Souvenirs* (Paris, 1954)
     Includes *Si le grain ne meurt* (1926), *Souvenirs de la Cour d'Assises* (1914),
     Voyage au Congo (1927), *Le Retour du Tchad* (1928), *Carnets d'Egypte,
     Feuillets d'Automne* (1949), *Et nunc manet in te* (1951), and *Ainsi soit-il*
     (1952)

III *Romans, Récits et Soties, Œuvres Lyriques* (Paris, 1958)
     Includes *Le Traité du Narcisse* (1891), *Le Voyage d'Urien* (1893), *La Ten-
     tative amoureuse* (1893), *Paludes* (1895), *Les Nourritures terrestres* (1897),
     Les Nouvelles Nourritures (1935), *Le Prométhée mal enchaîné* (1899), *El
     Hadj* (1899), *L'Immoraliste* (1902), *Le Retour de l'Enfant prodigue*
     (1907), *La Porte étroite* (1909), *Isabelle* (1911), *Les Caves du Vatican*
     (1914), *La Symphonie pastorale* (1919), *Les Faux-Monnayeurs* (1926),
     L'Ecoles des femmes (1929), *Robert* (1930), *Geneviève* (1936), and
     Thésée (1946)

IV   A fourth volume in the series, *Œuvres critiques,* is scheduled for publication
     in 1971.
     It will include, among other critical works, *Prétextes* (1903), *Oscar Wilde*
     (1903), *Nouveaux Prétextes* (1911), *Dostoevsky* (1923), *Incidences*
     (1924), *Journal des Faux-Monnayeurs* (1926), *Essai sur Montaigne* (1929),
     Divers (1931), *Notes sur Chopin* (1938), *Interviews imaginaires* (1943),
     Eloges (1948), and the critical essays from *Feuillets d'Automne* (1949).

Additional French sources include:

A   *Plays*

Théâtre (including *Saül* (1903), *Le Roi Candaule* (1901), *Œdipe* (1931),
     Perséphone (1934), and *Le Treizième Arbre*) (N.R.F., Paris, 1942)
Théâtre complet (including the plays above plus *Philoctète* (1899), *Le Retour,
     Bethsabe* (1912), *Ajax, Le Retour de l'Enfant prodigue* (1907), *Proserpine,
     Robert,* the dramatic version of *Les Caves du Vatican,* Gide's translations into
     French of *Hamlet* and *Anthony and Cleopatra,* and his dramatic adaptation
     (with Jean-Louis Barrault) of Kafka's *The Trial* (1947)) (Ides et calendes,
     Neuchâtel and Paris, 1947–1949: 8 vols.)

B   *Letters* (a selected list)

"Lettres à Christian Beck," in *Mercure de France,* July 1 and August 1, 1949
Correspondance André Gide–Arnold Bennett (Droz, Geneva, and Minard, Paris,
     1964)
Paul Claudel et André Gide, *Correspondance 1899–1926* (Gallimard, Paris, 1949)

* Dates in parentheses are those of first commercial publication, when it was not that of the
particular edition cited.

Francis Jammes et André Gide, *Correspondance 1893–1938* (Gallimard, Paris, 1948)

André Gide–Roger Martin du Gard, *Correspondance 1913–1951* (Gallimard, Paris, 1968: 2 vols.)

"Lettres à François Mauriac," in *La Table Ronde,* January 1953

André Gide–André Rouveyre, *Correspondance 1909–1951* (Mercure de France, Paris, 1967)

André Gide–Paul Valéry, *Correspondance 1890–1942* (Gallimard, Paris, 1955)

C *Miscellaneous*

Amyntas (Mercure de France, Paris, 1906; N.R.F., Paris, 1926)

Anthologie de la poésie française (Gallimard, Paris, 1949)

Les Cahiers d'André Walter (Didier Perrin, Paris, 1891; with *Les Poésies d'André Walter,* G. Crès, Paris, 1930; Gallimard, Paris, 1952)

Corydon (N.R.F., Paris, 1924 [first public edition], 1929; Gallimard, Paris, 1948)

Littérature engagée, ed. Yvonne Davet (Gallimard, Paris, 1950)

La Séquestrée de Poitiers (Gallimard, Paris, 1930) and *L'Affaire Redureau* (Gallimard, Paris, 1930) have been reprinted, along with *Souvenirs de la Cour d'Assises* (N.R.F., Paris, 1914; Gallimard, Paris, 1930), under the general title of *Ne jugez pas* (Gallimard, Paris, 1969).

Many of the individual titles included in the four volumes of the "Bibliothèque de la Pléiade" series are also available separately. The following have been reprinted as *"Livre de Poche"* paperbacks: *Les Caves du Vatican, L'Ecole des femmes, Les Faux-Monnayeurs, L'Immoraliste, Isabelle, Les Nourritures terrestres, Paludes, La Porte étroite, Saül, Si le grain ne meurt,* and *La Symphonie pastorale.*

PROPERTY OF
HIGH POINT PUBLIC LIBRARY
HIGH POINT, NORTH CAROLINA

ABOUT THE AUTHOR

ANDRÉ GIDE *was born in Paris in 1869 and received a strict Protestant education there. His first literary works, published in his early twenties, established him as a member of the new Symbolist group, but in 1895, after a voyage of self-discovery in North Africa, he turned to the glorification of life and freedom in works close to the spirits of Nietzsche and Whitman. With Paris and his Normandy estate as headquarters, Gide spent much of his life restlessly traveling through Europe and Africa while devoting himself almost entirely to literary creation and to fighting for his beliefs about human relationships—personal, ethical, and political. He was awarded the Nobel Prize for Literature in 1947 and died in Paris in 1951.*

ABOUT THE EDITOR

DAVID LITTLEJOHN *was born in San Francisco in 1937.
After being graduated from the University of California, Berkeley,
he took his M.A. and Ph.D. degrees in English at Harvard University.
Since 1963, he has been on the University faculty at Berkeley, where
he is presently Associate Professor of Journalism. His published
writing includes* DR. JOHNSON: HIS LIFE IN LETTERS (1965);
BLACK ON WHITE: A CRITICAL SURVEY OF WRITING BY AMERICAN
NEGROES (1966); INTERRUPTIONS (*collected essays and notes*,
1970); *and* GIDE: A COLLECTION OF CRITICAL ESSAYS (1970).
*He serves regularly as a critic for National Educational Television,
and has been awarded a Fulbright Professorship and A.C.L.S.
Fellowship for work in France. Mr. Littlejohn, his wife, and their two
children live in Kensington, California.*

A NOTE ON THE TYPE

The text of this book was set on the Linotype in Garamond (No. 3), a modern rendering of the type first cut by Claude Garamond (1510– 1561). Garamond was a pupil of Geoffroy Troy and is believed to have based his letters on the Venetian models, although he intro- duced a number of important differences, and it is to him we owe the letter which we know as old-style. He gave to his letters a certain elegance and a feeling of movement that won for their creator an immediate reputation and the patronage of Francis I of France.

Composed, printed, and bound by H. Wolff Book Manufacturing Company, New York, N.Y. Typography and binding design by Betty Anderson.

179805

848.912 C
G453a

Gide, Andre Paul Guillaume
The Andre Gide reader.

HIGH POINT PUBLIC LIBRARY
HIGH POINT, NORTH CAROLINA

DEMCO